Skip·Beat!

Skip·Beat!

Volume 7

CONTENTS

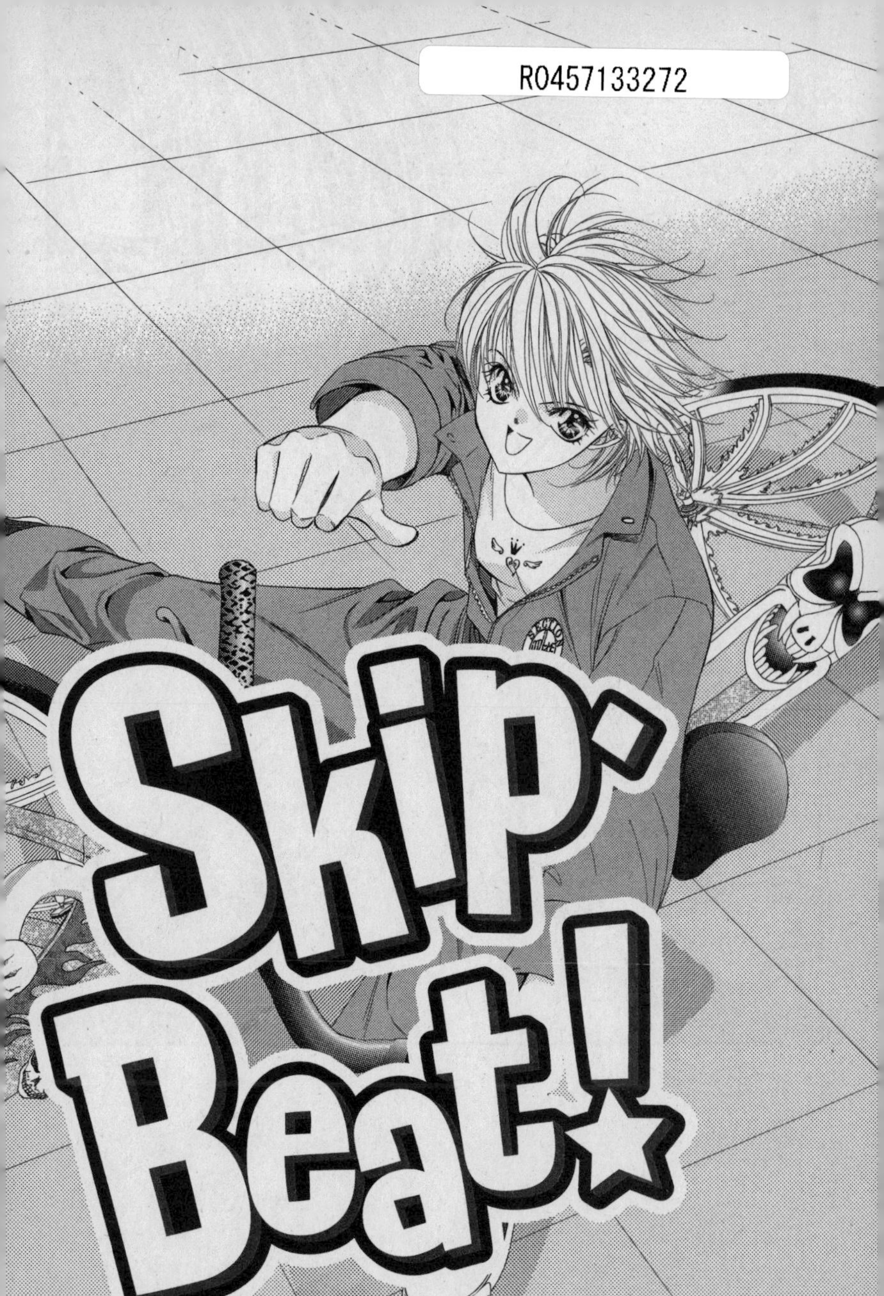
Skip Beat!

Act 36: The Road of Glamorous Success

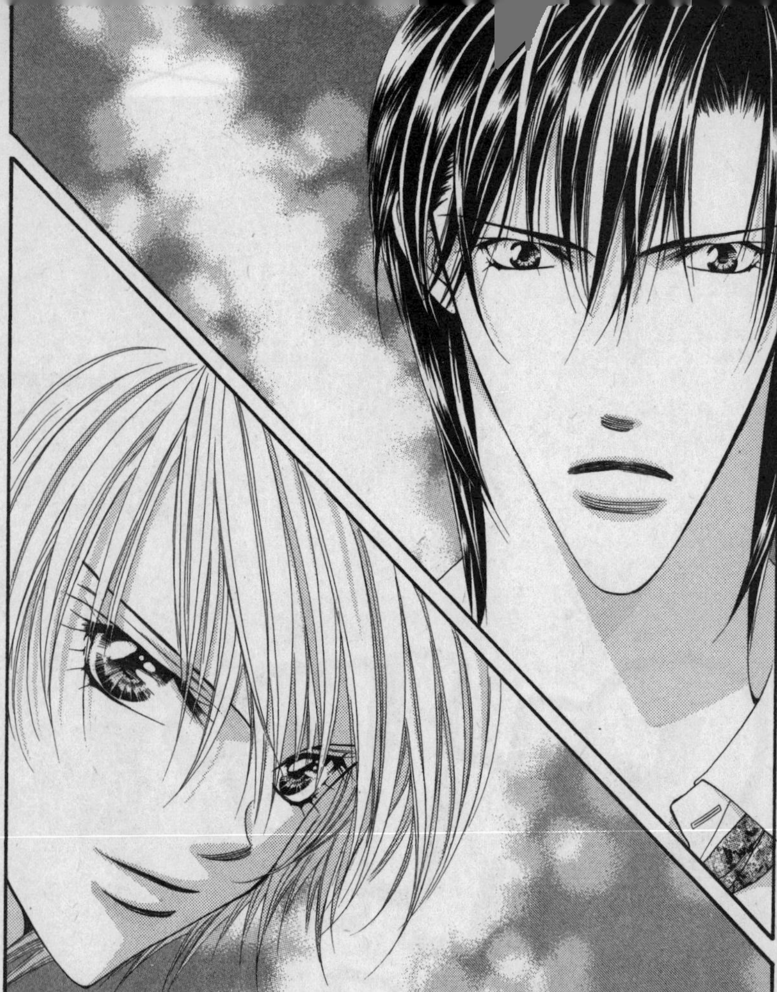

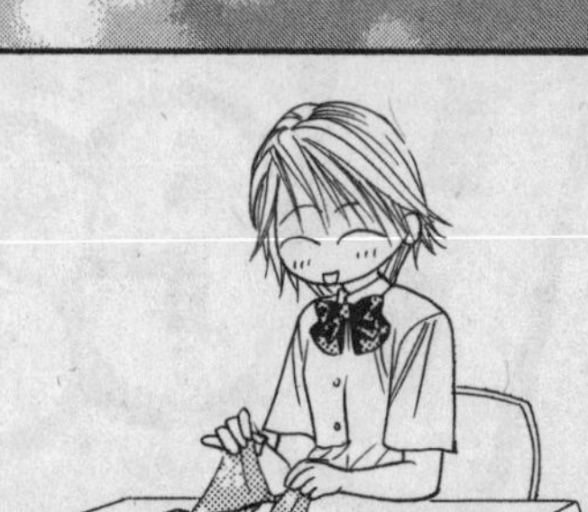

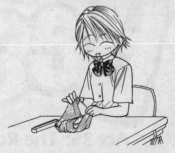

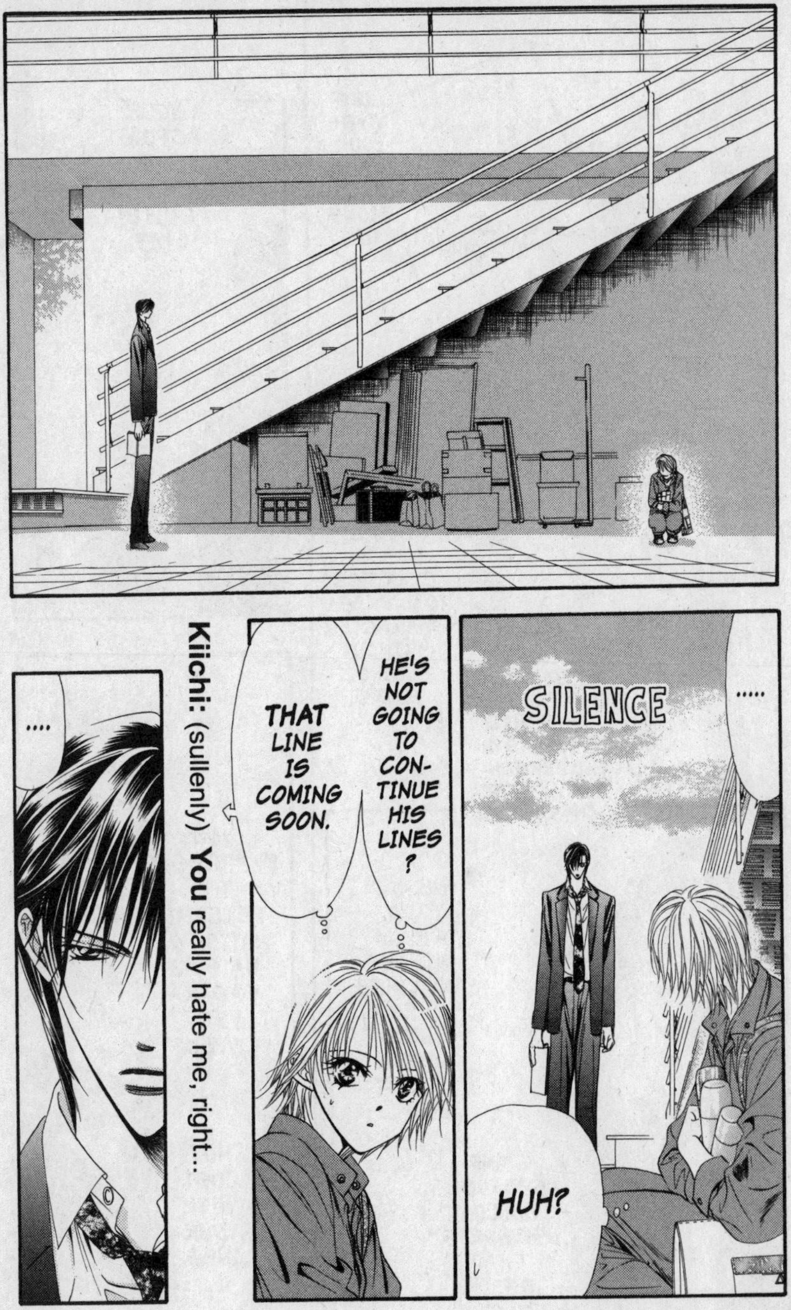
SILENCE
....
HUH?
HE'S NOT GOING TO CONTINUE HIS LINES?
THAT LINE IS COMING SOON.
....
Kiichi: (sullenly) You really hate me, right...

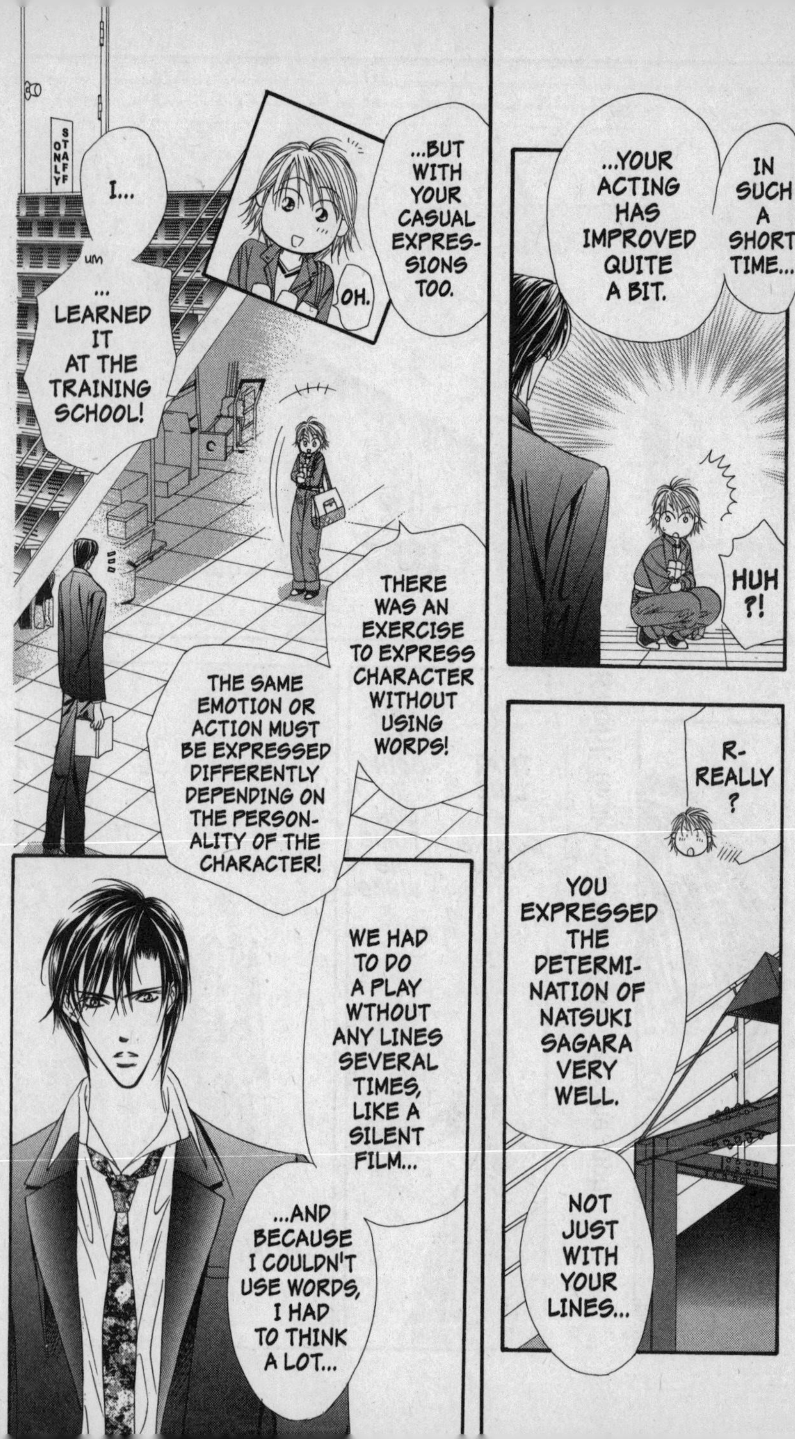

IN SUCH A SHORT TIME...
...YOUR ACTING HAS IMPROVED QUITE A BIT.
HUH?!
R-REALLY?
YOU EXPRESSED THE DETERMINATION OF NATSUKI SAGARA VERY WELL.
NOT JUST WITH YOUR LINES...
...BUT WITH YOUR CASUAL EXPRESSIONS TOO.
OH.
STAFF ONLY
I...
um
...LEARNED IT AT THE TRAINING SCHOOL!
THERE WAS AN EXERCISE TO EXPRESS CHARACTER WITHOUT USING WORDS!
THE SAME EMOTION OR ACTION MUST BE EXPRESSED DIFFERENTLY DEPENDING ON THE PERSONALITY OF THE CHARACTER!
WE HAD TO DO A PLAY WTHOUT ANY LINES SEVERAL TIMES, LIKE A SILENT FILM...
...AND BECAUSE I COULDN'T USE WORDS, I HAD TO THINK A LOT...

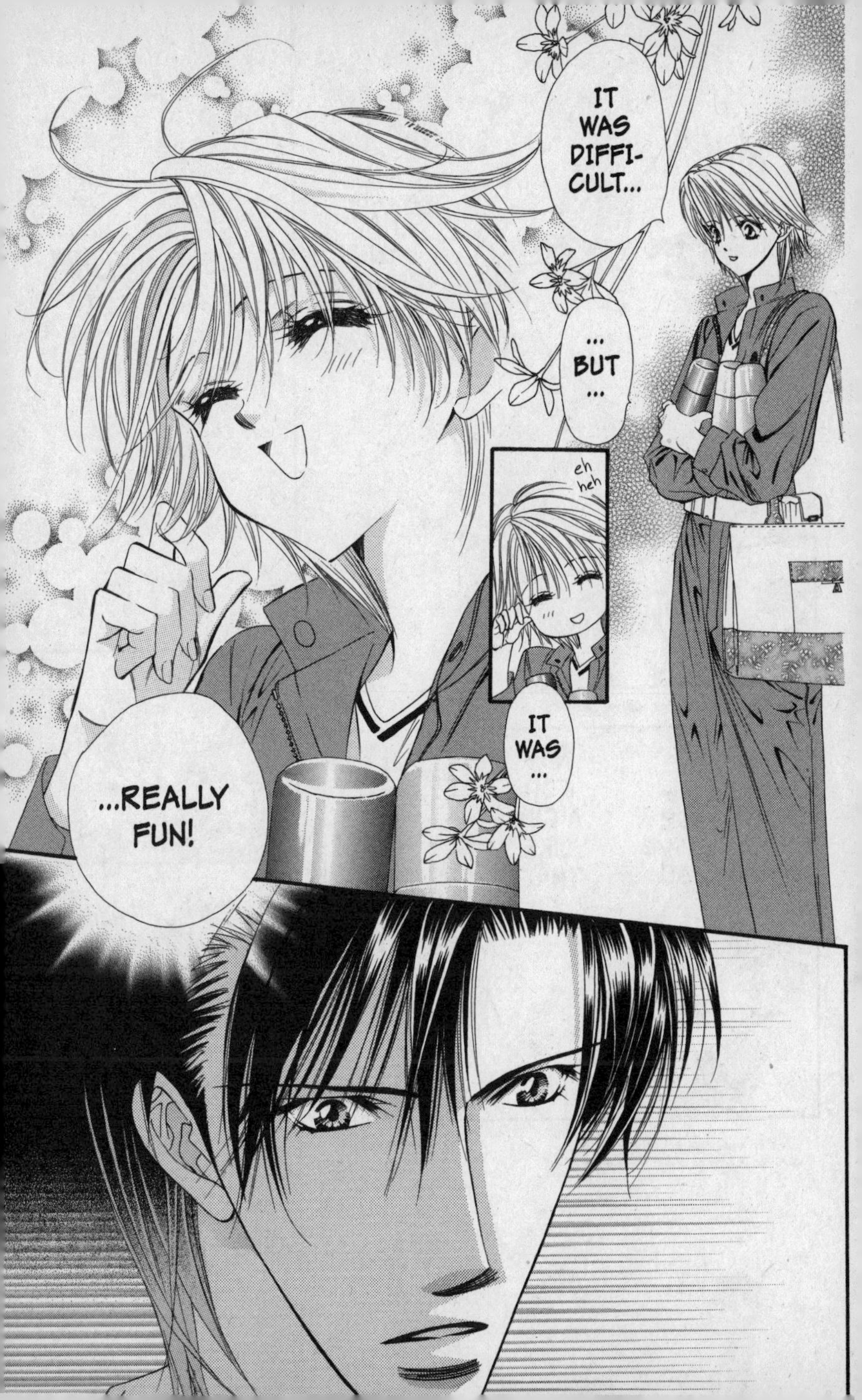
IT WAS DIFFI- CULT...
... BUT ...
eh heh
IT WAS ...
...REALLY FUN!

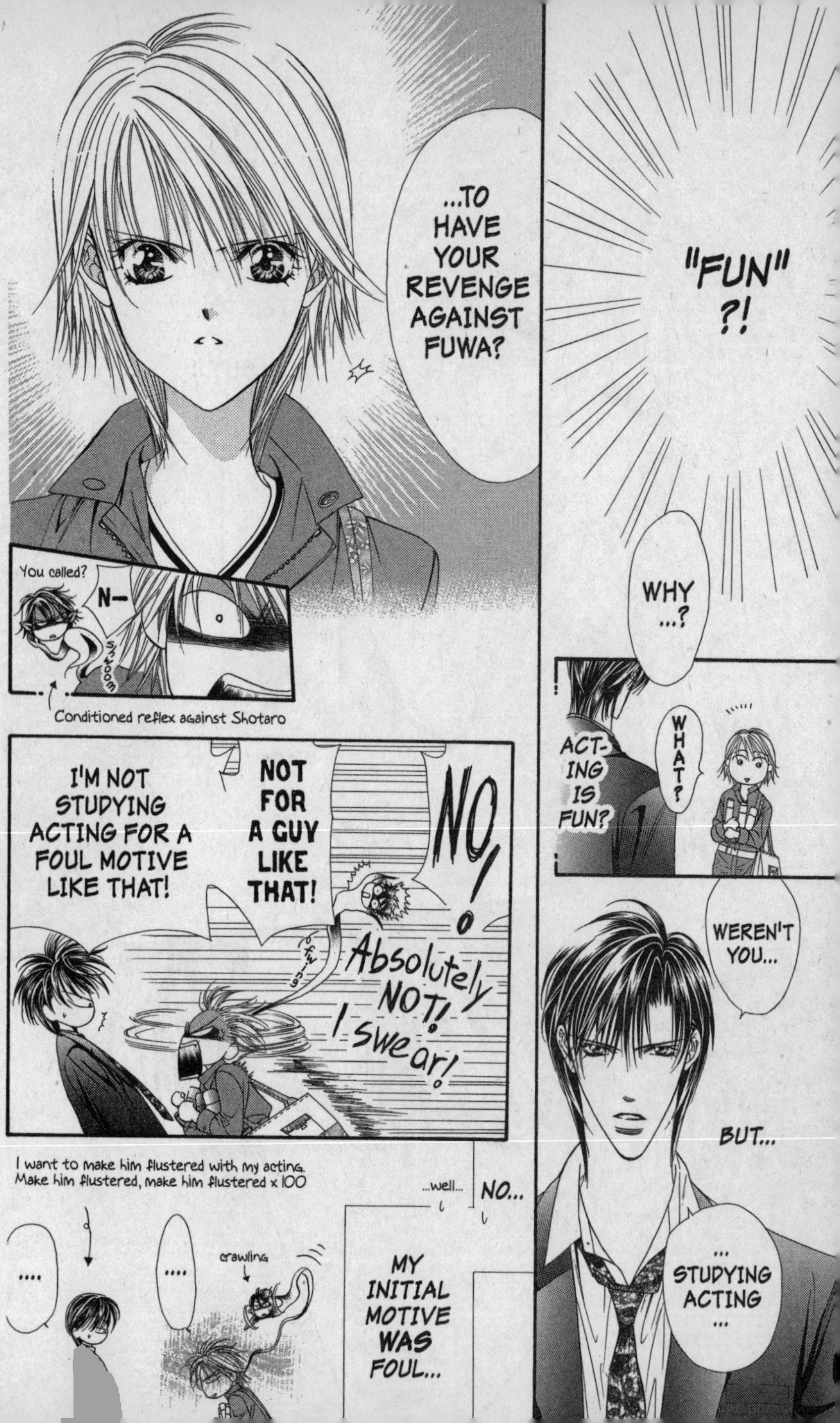
"FUN" ?!
WHY ...?
ACTING IS FUN?
WHAT?
WEREN'T YOU...
BUT...
... STUDYING ACTING ...
...TO HAVE YOUR REVENGE AGAINST FUWA?
N-
You called?
swoom
Conditioned reflex against Shotaro
NO!
NOT FOR A GUY LIKE THAT!
I'M NOT STUDYING ACTING FOR A FOUL MOTIVE LIKE THAT!
Absolutely NOT! I swear!
I want to make him flustered with my acting. Make him flustered, make him flustered x 100
NO...
...well...
MY INITIAL MOTIVE WAS FOUL...
....
....
crawling

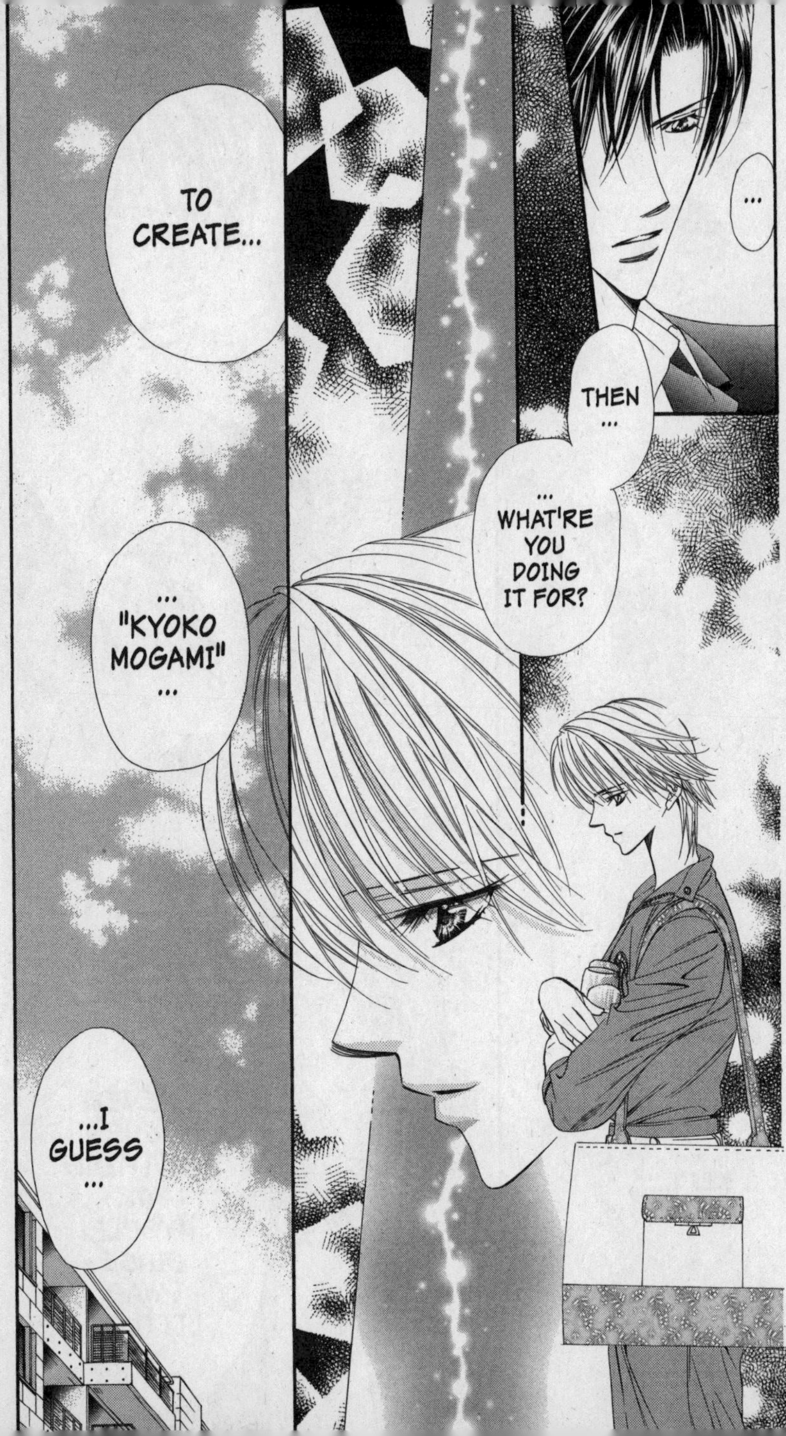
...
THEN ...
... WHAT'RE YOU DOING IT FOR?
TO CREATE...
... "KYOKO MOGAMI" ...
...I GUESS ...

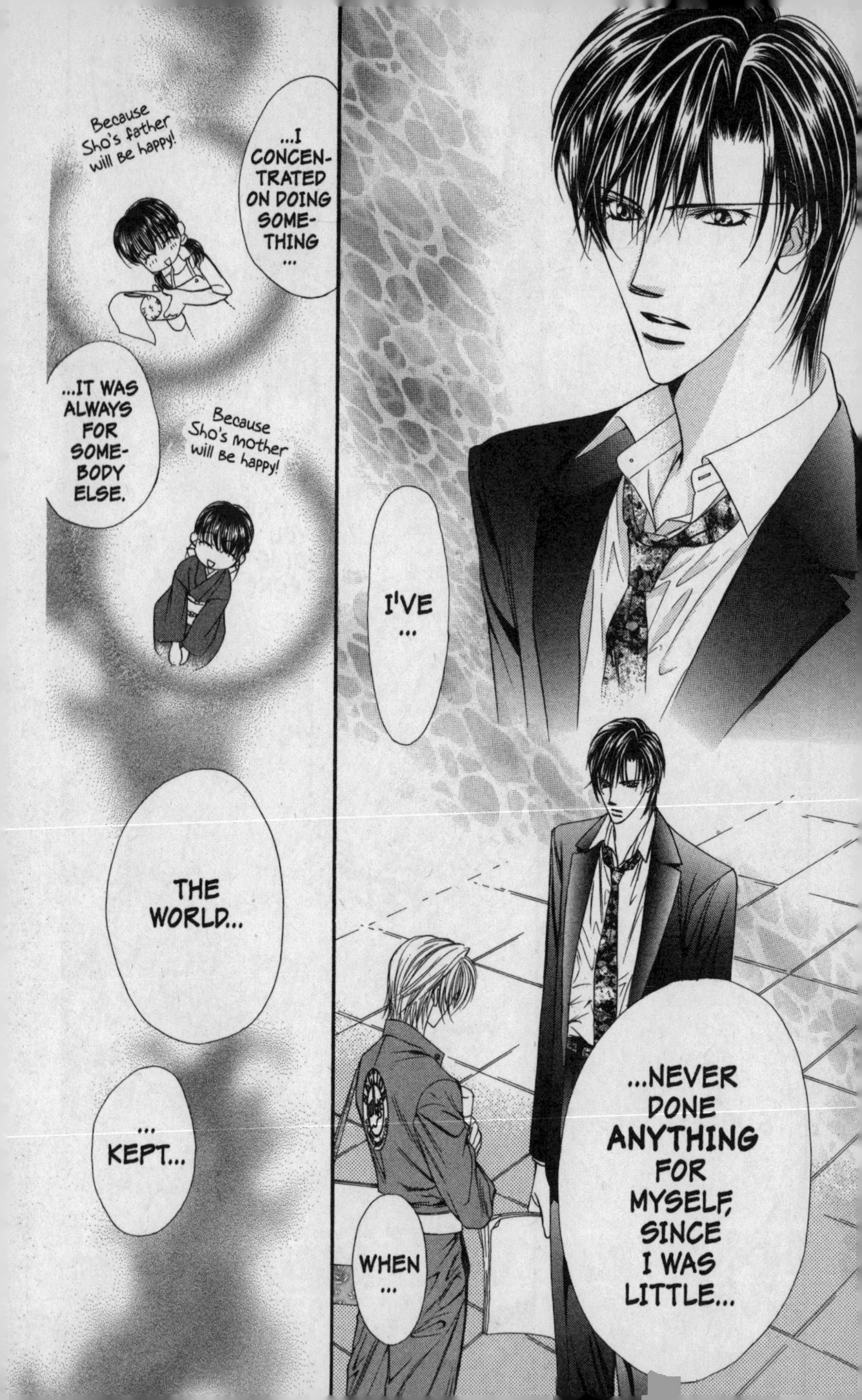
I'VE ...
...NEVER DONE ANYTHING FOR MYSELF, SINCE I WAS LITTLE...
WHEN ...
...I CONCENTRATED ON DOING SOMETHING ...
Because Sho's father will be happy!
...IT WAS ALWAYS FOR SOMEBODY ELSE.
Because Sho's mother will be happy!
THE WORLD...
... KEPT...

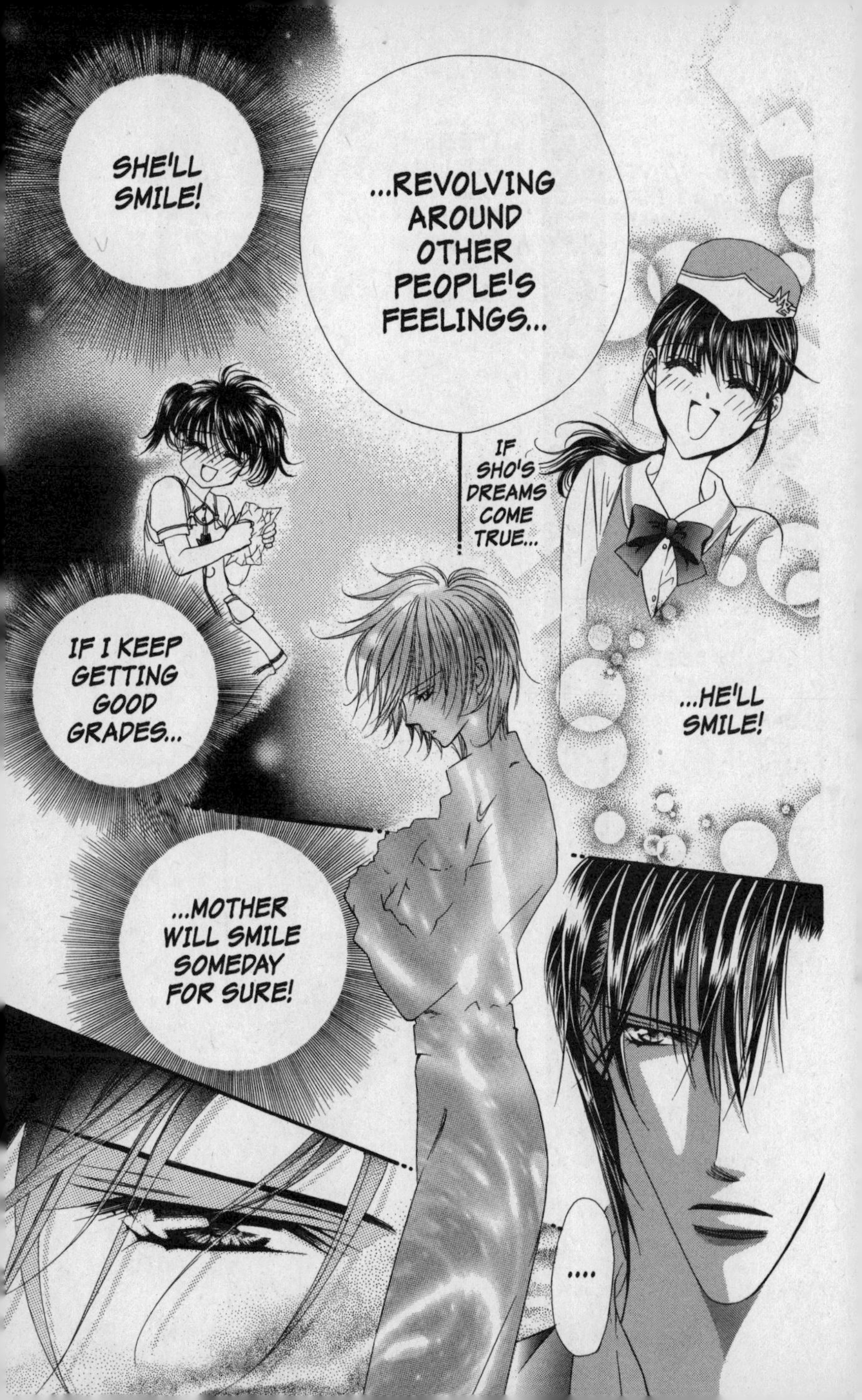
...REVOLVING AROUND OTHER PEOPLE'S FEELINGS...
IF SHO'S DREAMS COME TRUE...
...HE'LL SMILE!
SHE'LL SMILE!
IF I KEEP GETTING GOOD GRADES...
...MOTHER WILL SMILE SOMEDAY FOR SURE!
....

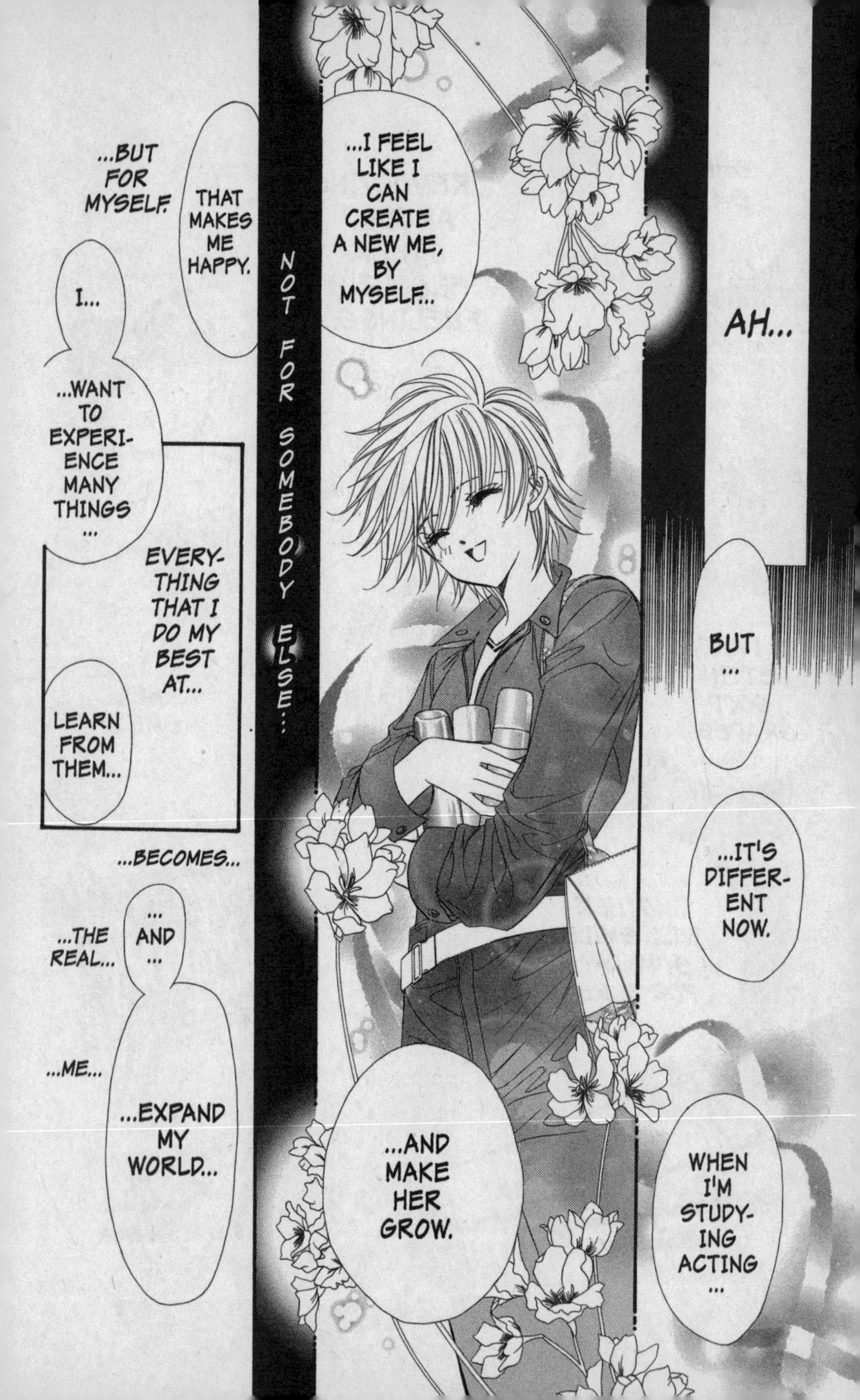
AH...
BUT...
...IT'S DIFFERENT NOW.
WHEN I'M STUDYING ACTING...
...I FEEL LIKE I CAN CREATE A NEW ME, BY MYSELF...
NOT FOR SOMEBODY ELSE...
...AND MAKE HER GROW.
THAT MAKES ME HAPPY.
...BUT FOR MYSELF.
I...
...WANT TO EXPERIENCE MANY THINGS...
EVERYTHING THAT I DO MY BEST AT...
LEARN FROM THEM...
...BECOMES...
...AND...
...THE REAL...
...ME...
...EXPAND MY WORLD...

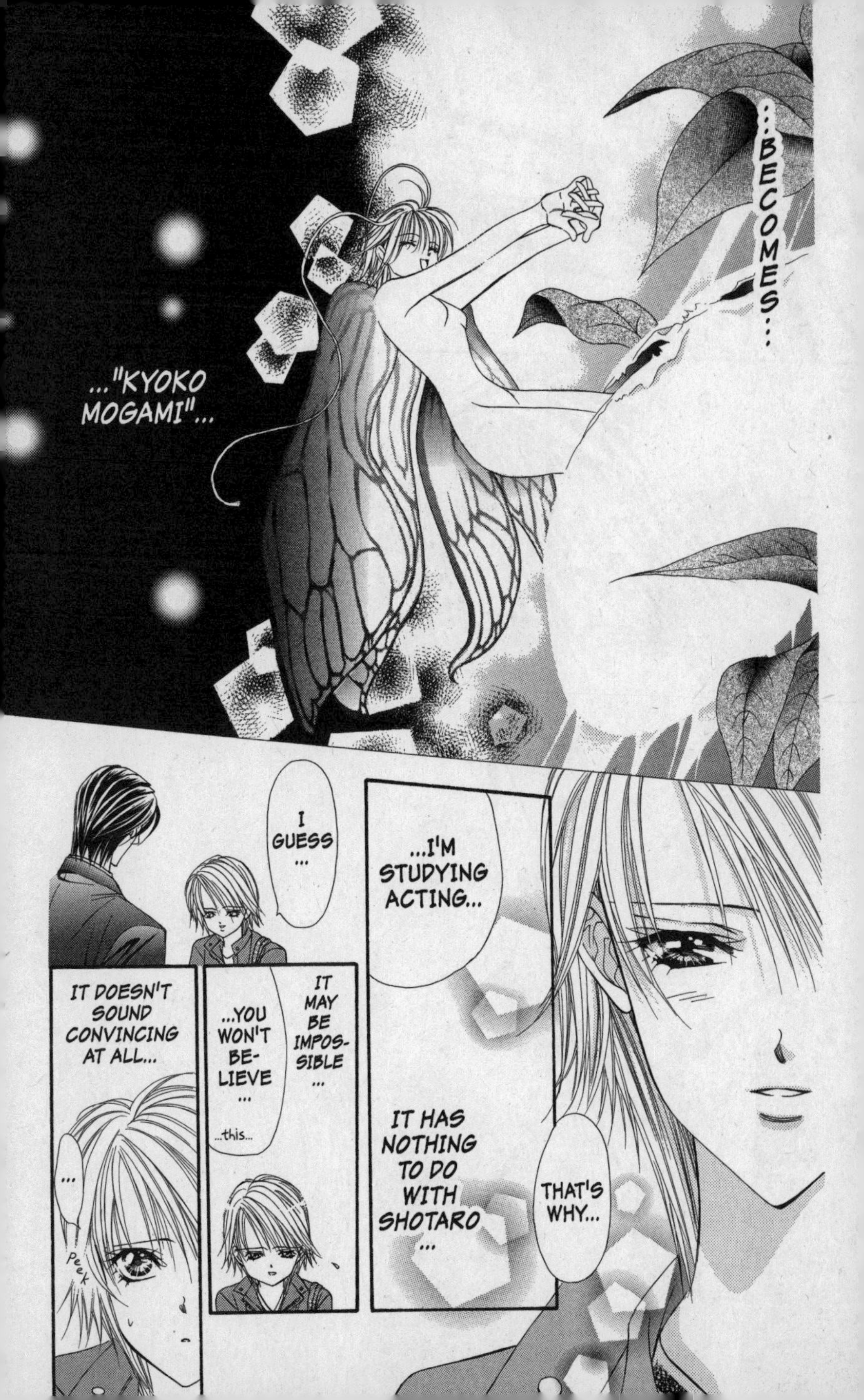
...BECOMES...
..."KYOKO MOGAMI"...
...I'M STUDYING ACTING...
IT HAS NOTHING TO DO WITH SHOTARO...
THAT'S WHY...
I GUESS...
IT MAY BE IMPOS-SIBLE...
...YOU WON'T BE-LIEVE...
...this...
IT DOESN'T SOUND CONVINCING AT ALL...
...
Peek

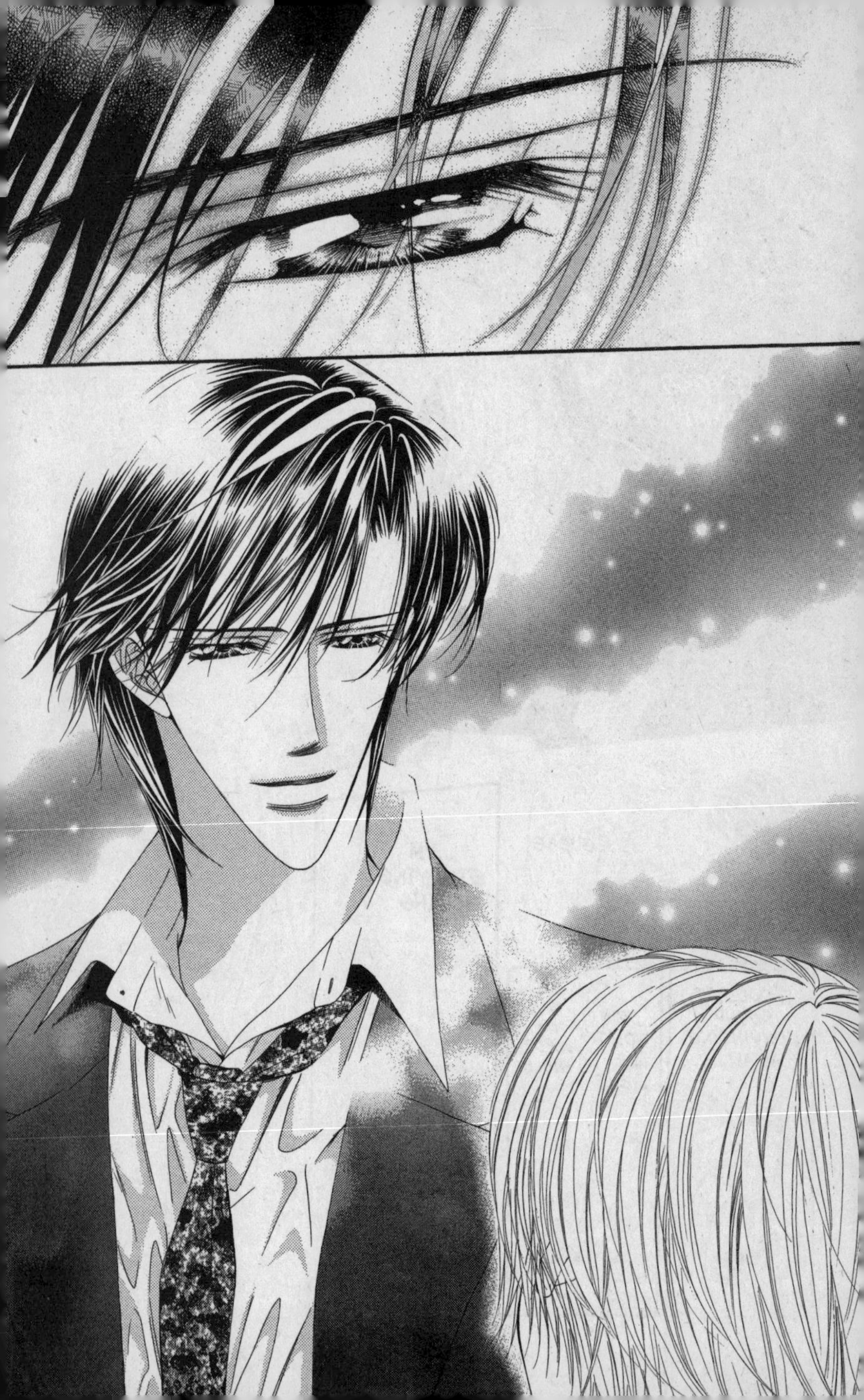

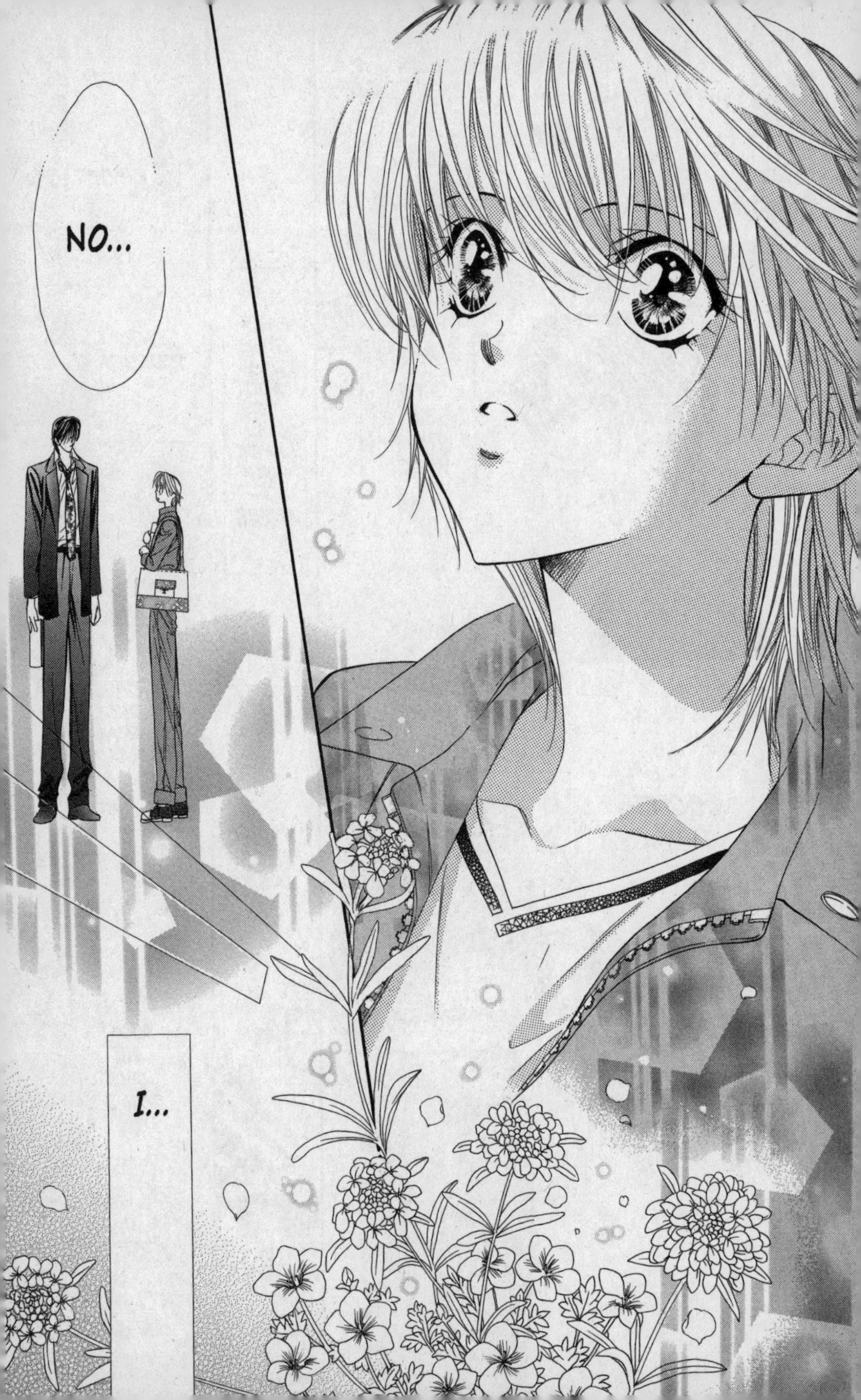
NO...
I...

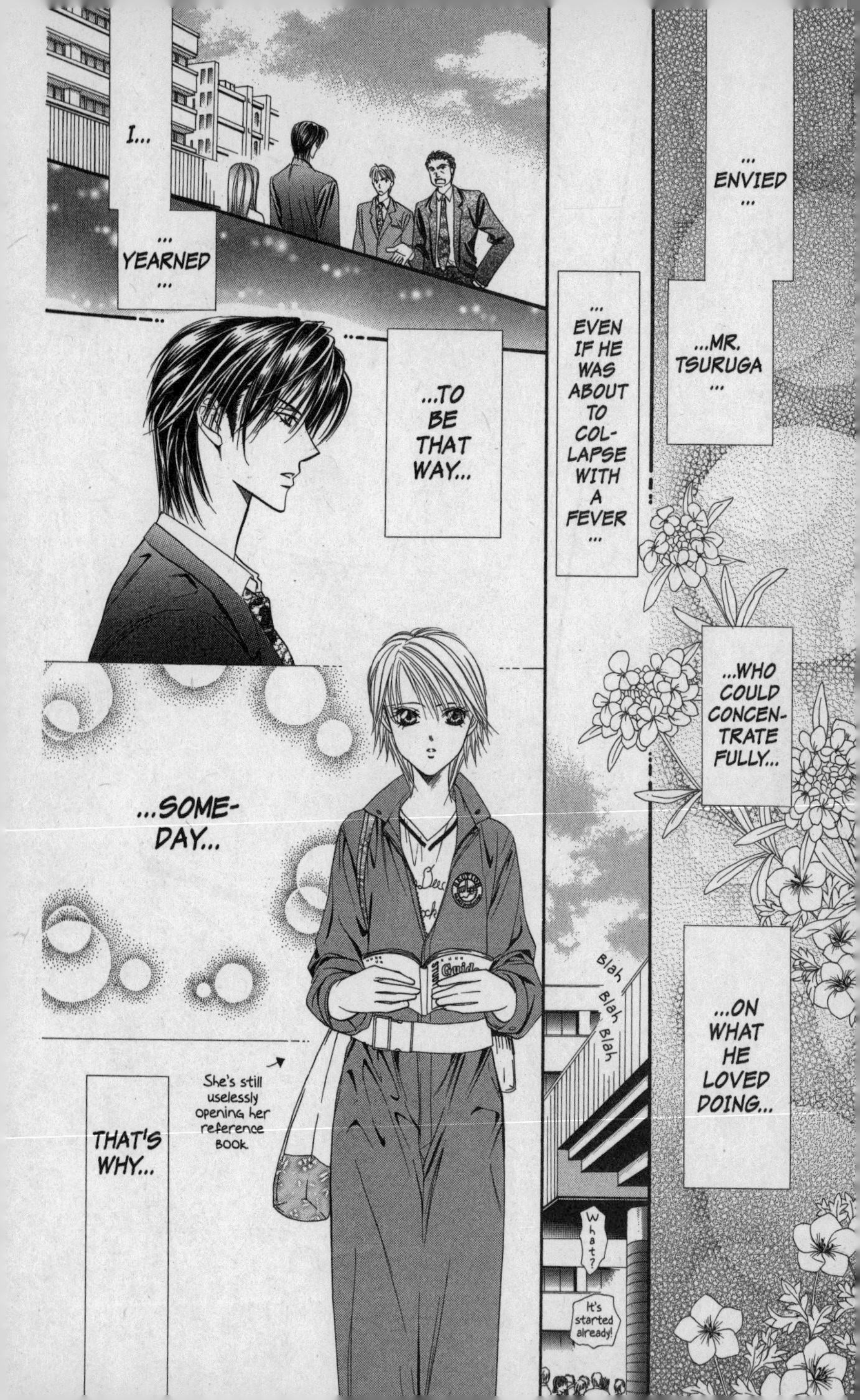
... ENVIED ...
...MR. TSURUGA ...
...WHO COULD CONCENTRATE FULLY...
...ON WHAT HE LOVED DOING...
... EVEN IF HE WAS ABOUT TO COL-LAPSE WITH A FEVER ...
Blah Blah Blah
What?
It's started already!
I...
... YEARNED ...
...TO BE THAT WAY...
...SOME-DAY...
THAT'S WHY...
She's still uselessly opening her reference book.
Guide

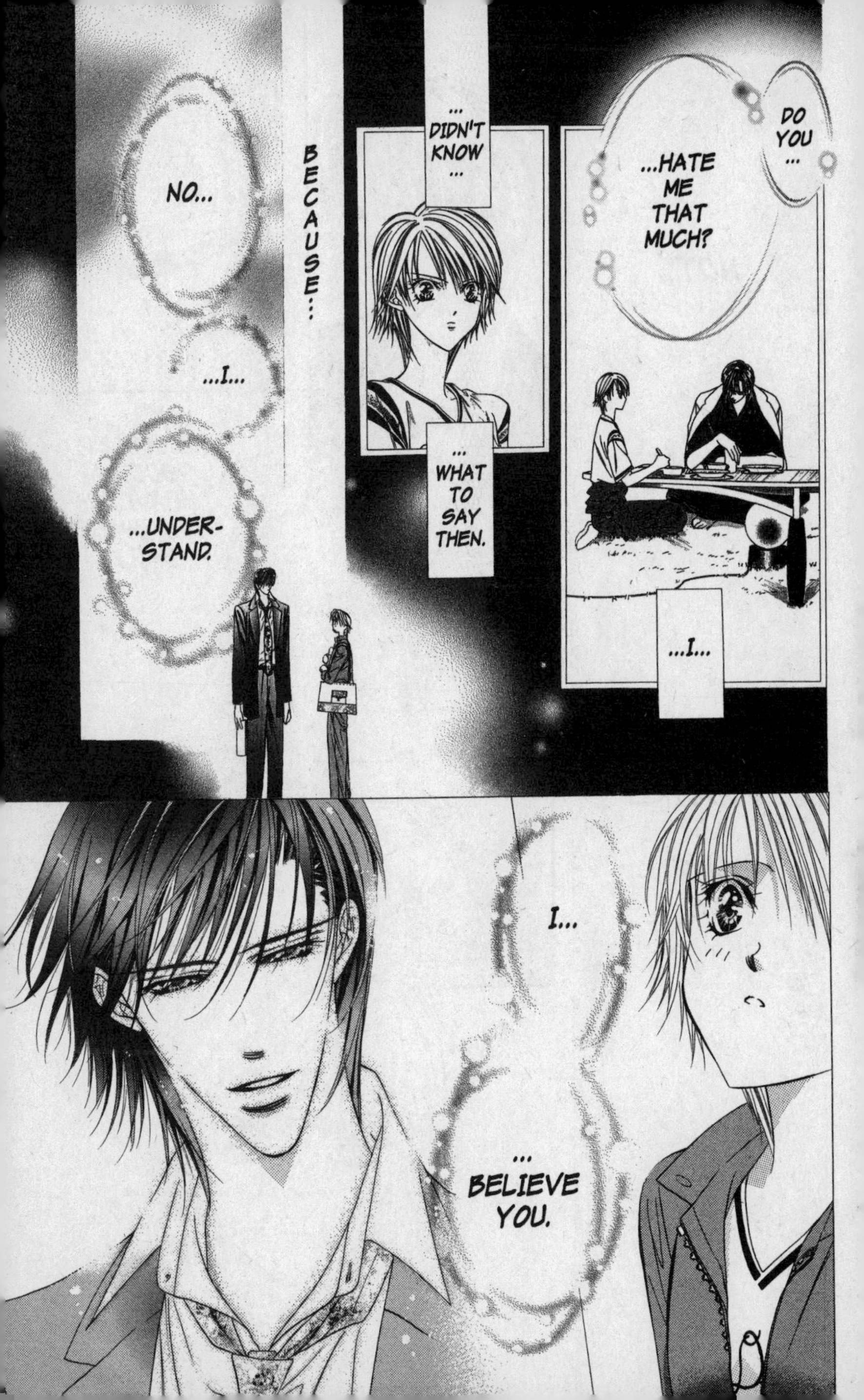
DO YOU ...
...HATE ME THAT MUCH?
...I...
...DIDN'T KNOW...
...WHAT TO SAY THEN.
BECAUSE...
NO...
...I...
...UNDER-STAND.
I...
...BELIEVE YOU.

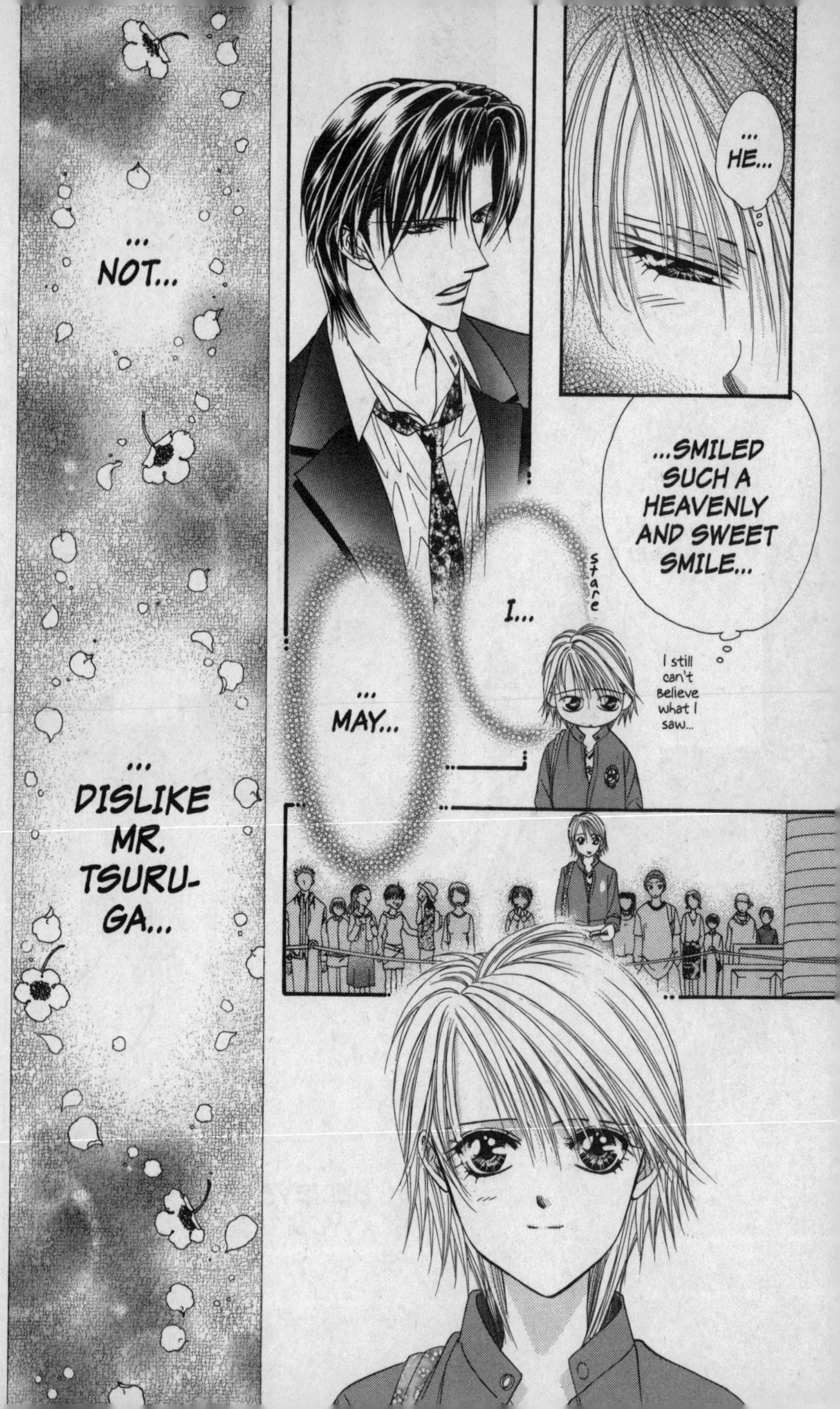
... HE...
...SMILED SUCH A HEAVENLY AND SWEET SMILE...
stare
I still can't believe what I saw...
I...
... MAY...
... NOT...
... DISLIKE MR. TSURU-GA...

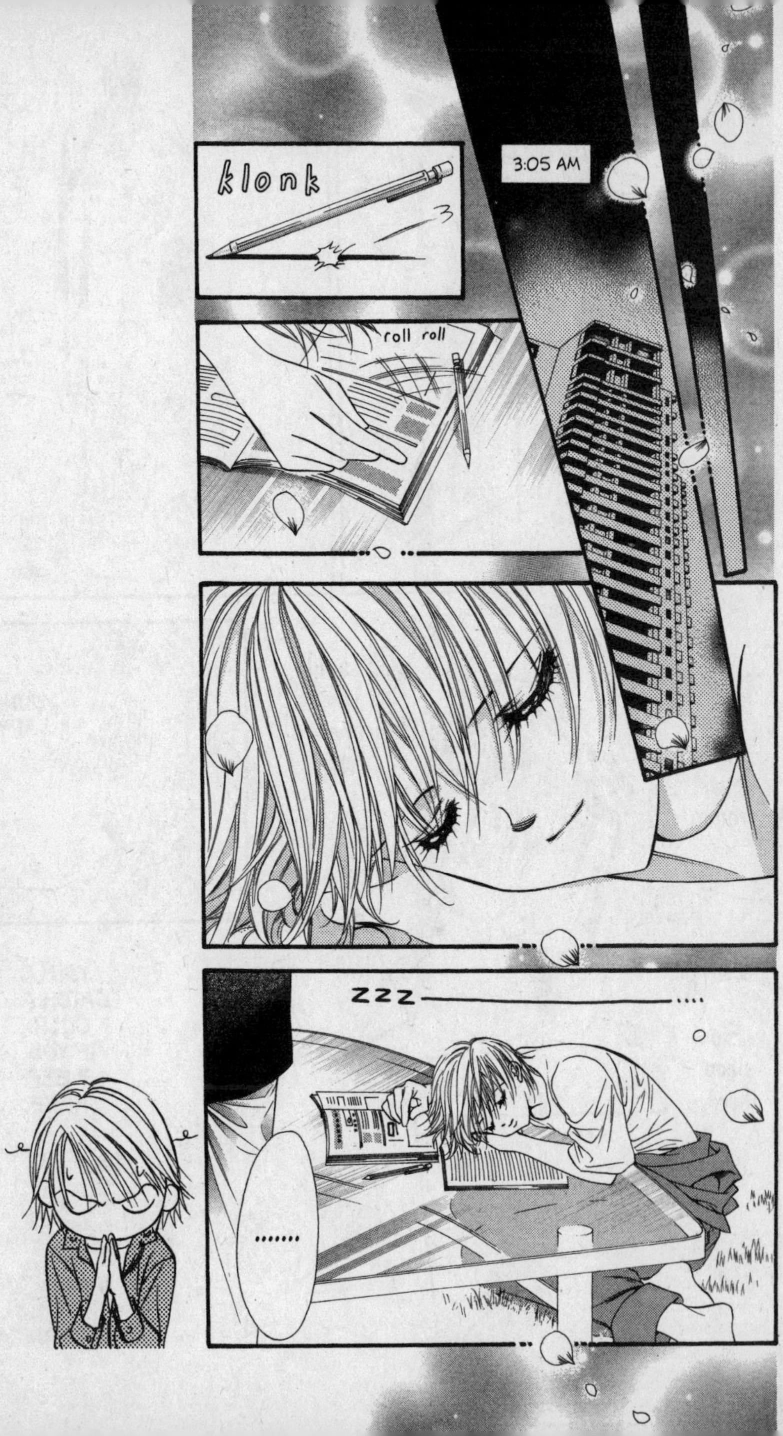
3:05 AM
klonk
roll roll
zzz.....
....

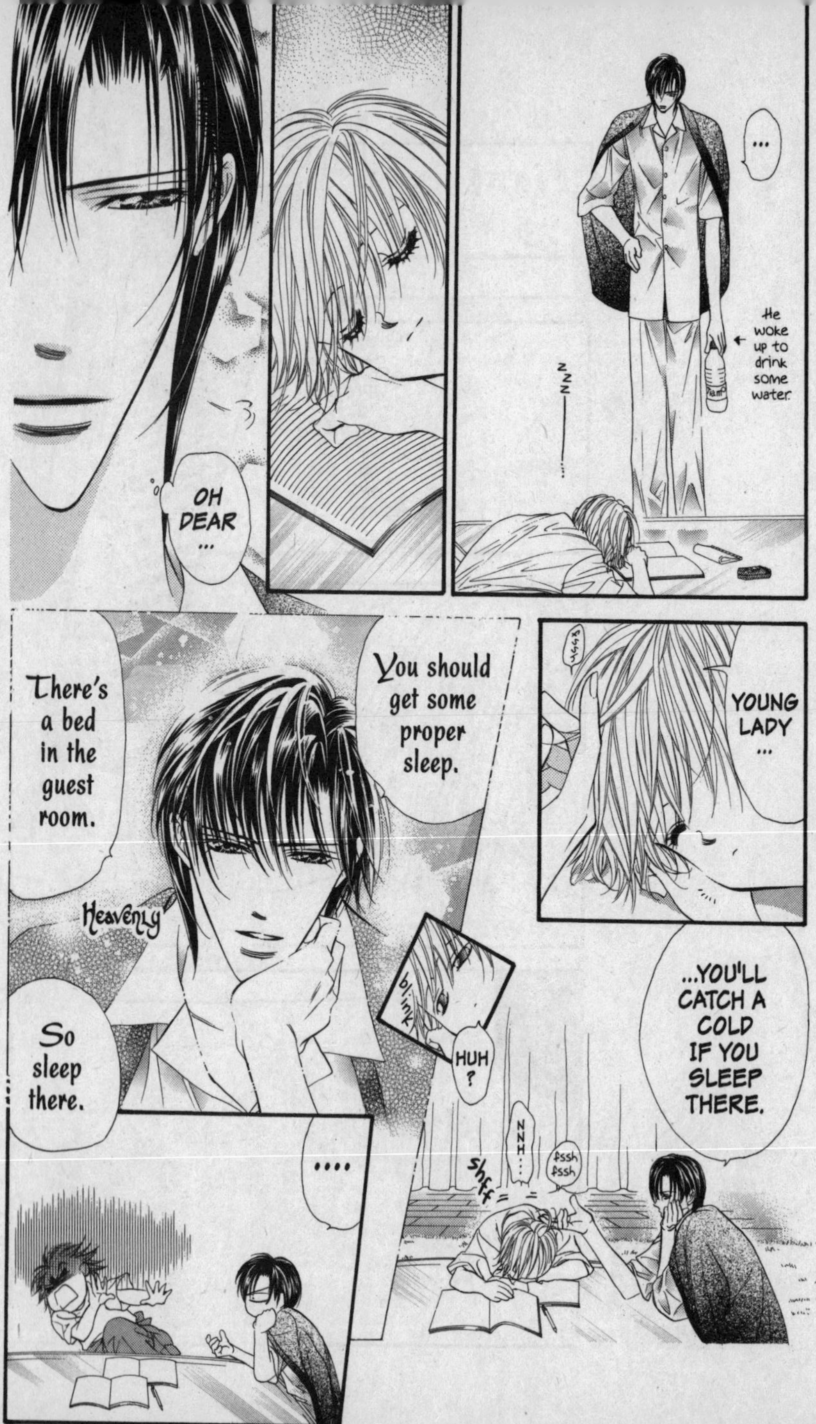
...
He woke up to drink some water.
ZZZ......
OH DEAR ...
YOUNG LADY ...
...YOU'LL CATCH A COLD IF YOU SLEEP THERE.
NNH...
fssh fssh
shff
blink
HUH?
You should get some proper sleep.
There's a bed in the guest room.
Heavenly
So sleep there.
....

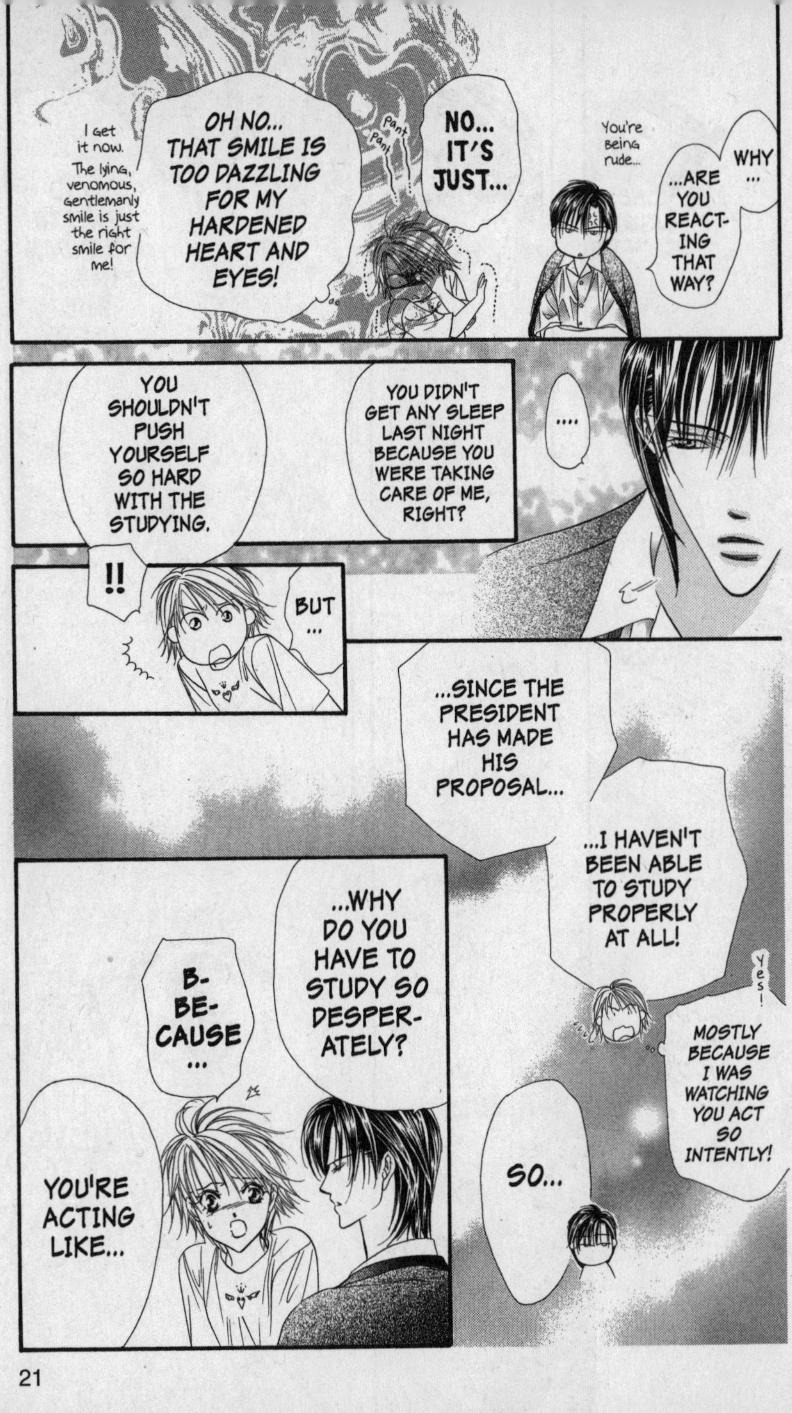
WHY... ...ARE YOU REACTING THAT WAY?
You're being rude...
NO... IT'S JUST...
Pant Pant
OH NO... THAT SMILE IS TOO DAZZLING FOR MY HARDENED HEART AND EYES!
I get it now. The lying, venomous, gentlemanly smile is just the right smile for me!
....
YOU DIDN'T GET ANY SLEEP LAST NIGHT BECAUSE YOU WERE TAKING CARE OF ME, RIGHT?
YOU SHOULDN'T PUSH YOURSELF SO HARD WITH THE STUDYING.
!!
BUT...
...SINCE THE PRESIDENT HAS MADE HIS PROPOSAL...
...I HAVEN'T BEEN ABLE TO STUDY PROPERLY AT ALL!
Yes!
MOSTLY BECAUSE I WAS WATCHING YOU ACT SO INTENTLY!
SO...
...WHY DO YOU HAVE TO STUDY SO DESPERATELY?
B-BE-CAUSE...
YOU'RE ACTING LIKE...

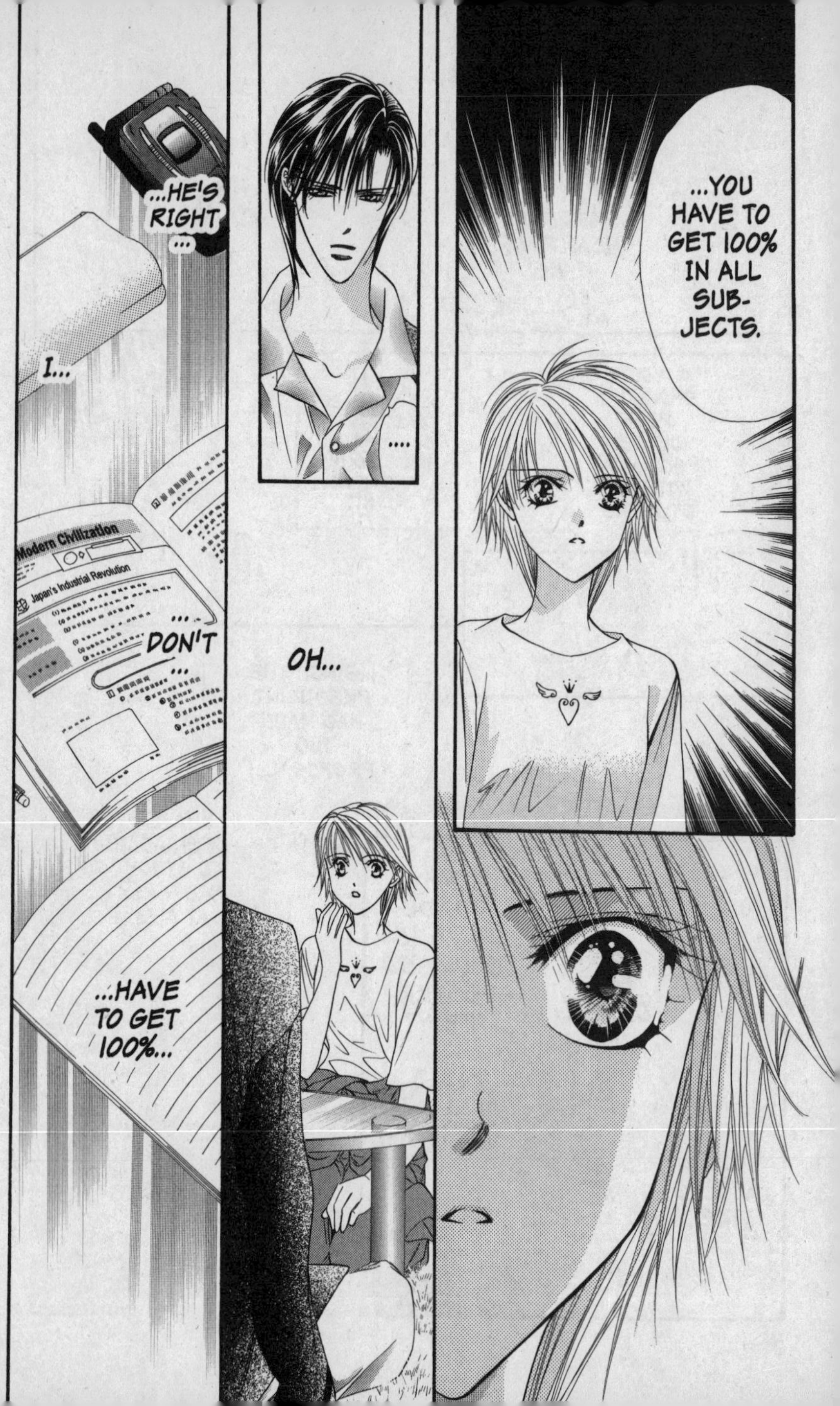
...YOU HAVE TO GET 100% IN ALL SUB-JECTS.
....
OH...
...HE'S RIGHT ...
I...
Modern Civilization
Japan's Industrial Revolution
...DON'T ...
...HAVE TO GET 100%...

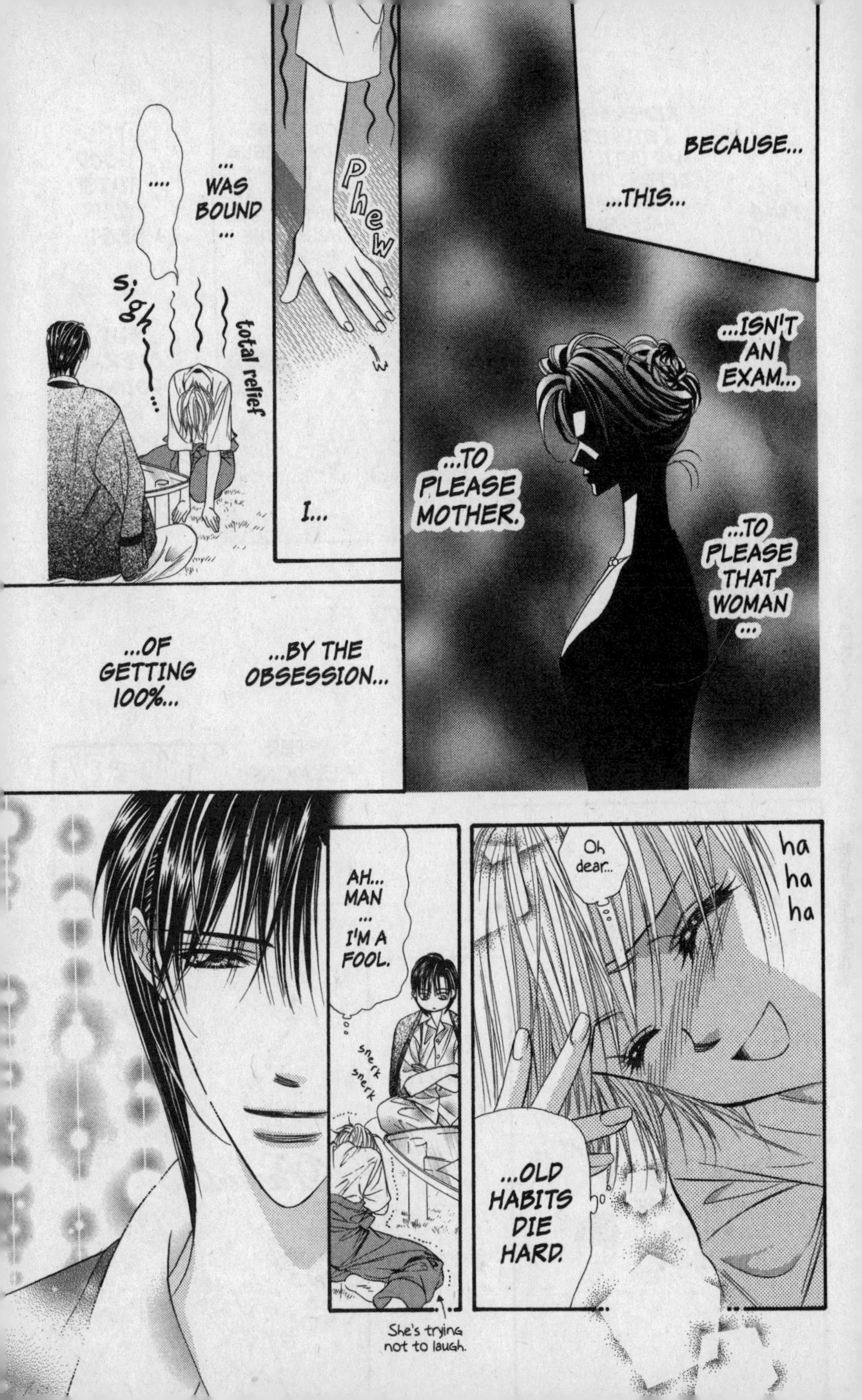
BECAUSE...
...THIS...
...ISN'T AN EXAM...
...TO PLEASE THAT WOMAN...
...TO PLEASE MOTHER.
Phew
I...
...WAS BOUND...
....
total relief
sigh~...
...BY THE OBSESSION...
...OF GETTING 100%...
ha ha ha
Oh dear...
...OLD HABITS DIE HARD.
AH... MAN ... I'M A FOOL.
snerk snerk
She's trying not to laugh.

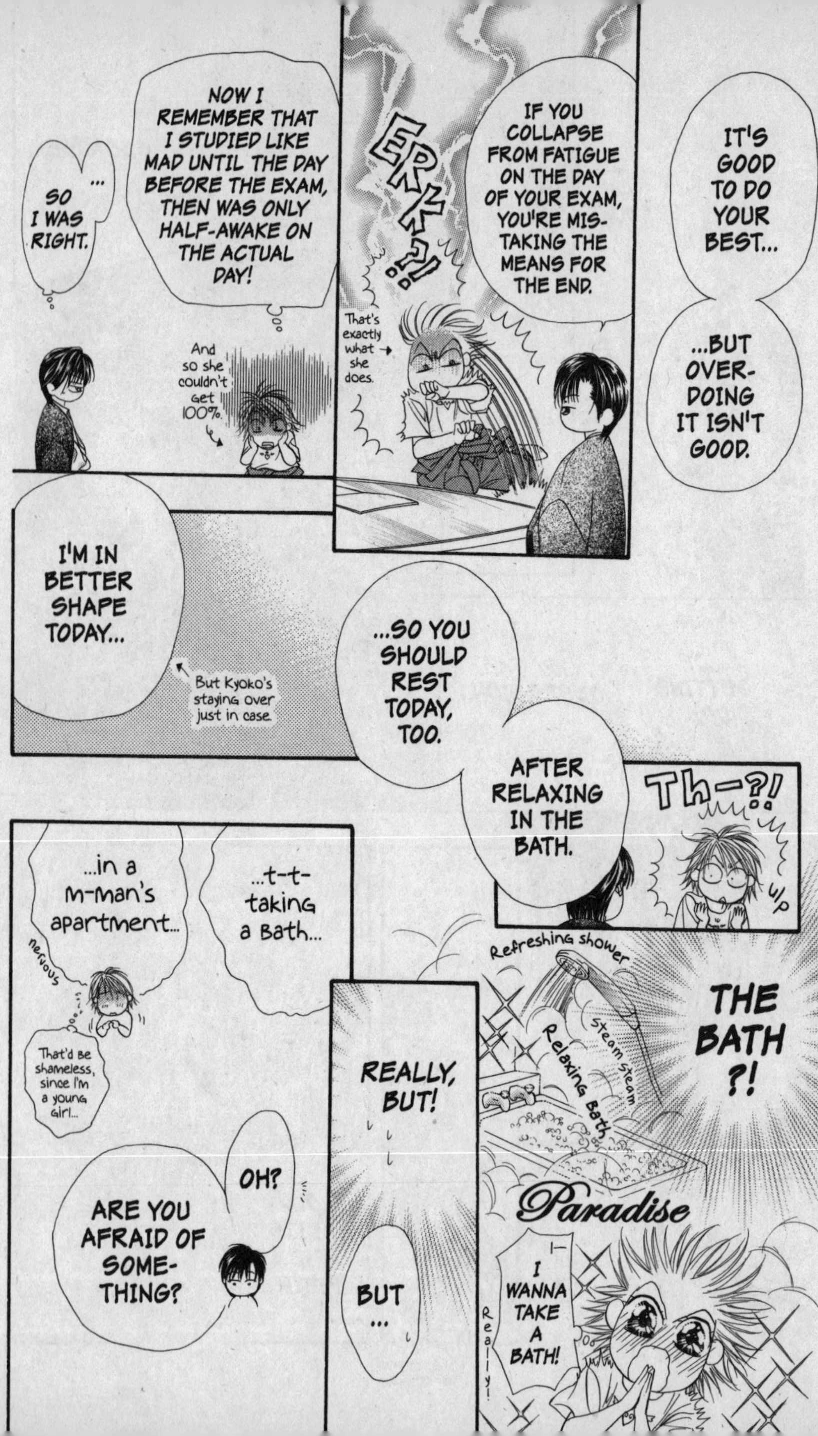
IT'S GOOD TO DO YOUR BEST...
...BUT OVER-DOING IT ISN'T GOOD.
IF YOU COLLAPSE FROM FATIGUE ON THE DAY OF YOUR EXAM, YOU'RE MIS-TAKING THE MEANS FOR THE END.
ERK?!
That's exactly what she does.
NOW I REMEMBER THAT I STUDIED LIKE MAD UNTIL THE DAY BEFORE THE EXAM, THEN WAS ONLY HALF-AWAKE ON THE ACTUAL DAY!
...
SO I WAS RIGHT.
And so she couldn't get 100%.
I'M IN BETTER SHAPE TODAY...
But Kyoko's staying over just in case.
...SO YOU SHOULD REST TODAY, TOO.
AFTER RELAXING IN THE BATH.
Th-?!
THE BATH?!
Refreshing shower
Steam steam
Relaxing Bath
Paradise
...t-t-taking a Bath...
...in a m-man's apartment...
nervous
That'd be shameless, since I'm a young girl...
OH?
ARE YOU AFRAID OF SOME-THING?
REALLY, BUT!
BUT...
I- I WANNA TAKE A BATH!
Really!

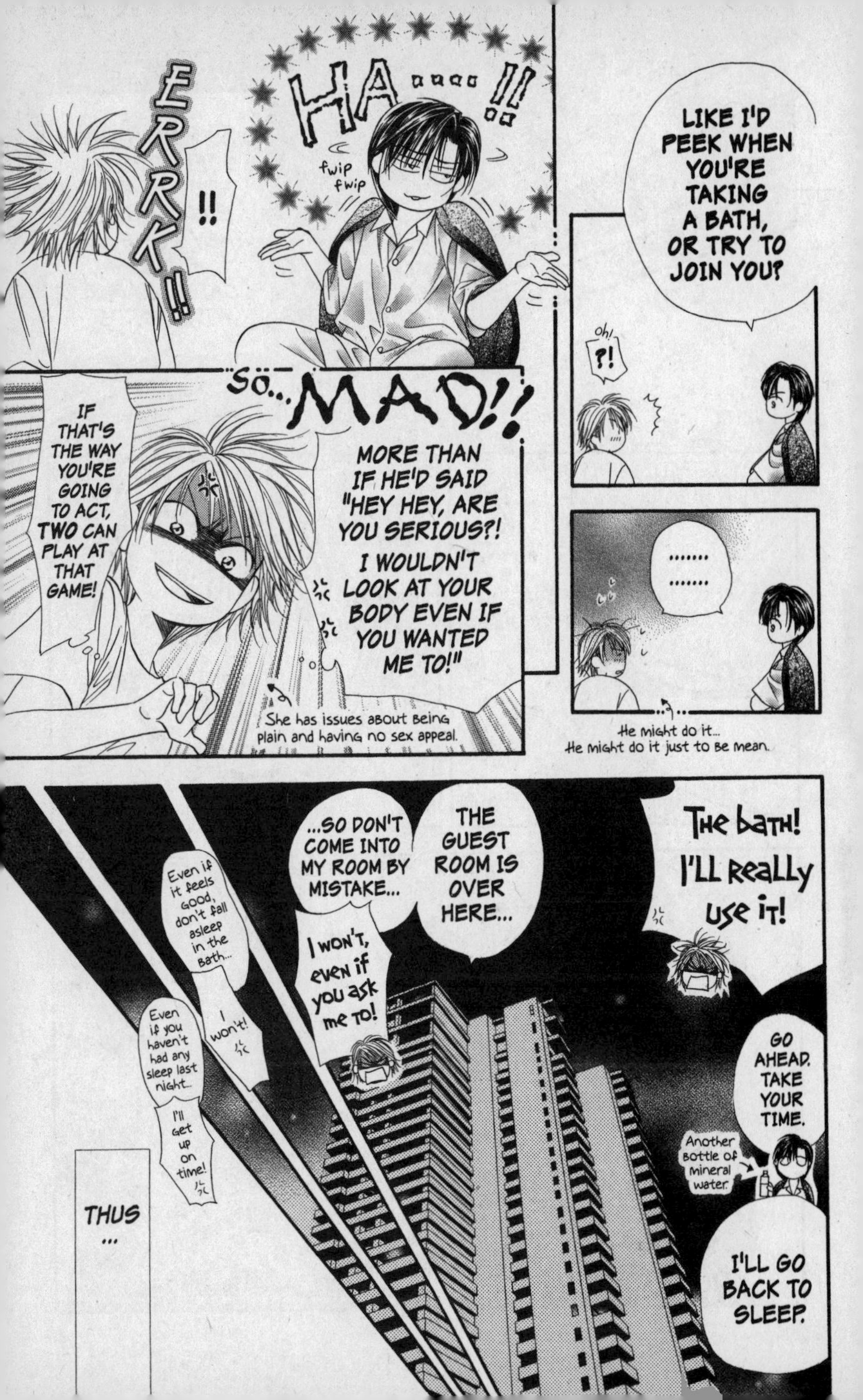

LIKE I'D PEEK WHEN YOU'RE TAKING A BATH, OR TRY TO JOIN YOU?
oh!
?!
......
......
He might do it... He might do it just to be mean.
HA....!!
fwip fwip
ERRK!!
!!
SO... MAD!!
MORE THAN IF HE'D SAID "HEY HEY, ARE YOU SERIOUS?! I WOULDN'T LOOK AT YOUR BODY EVEN IF YOU WANTED ME TO!"
IF THAT'S THE WAY YOU'RE GOING TO ACT, TWO CAN PLAY AT THAT GAME!
She has issues about being plain and having no sex appeal.
The bath! I'll really use it!
GO AHEAD. TAKE YOUR TIME.
Another bottle of mineral water.
I'LL GO BACK TO SLEEP.
THE GUEST ROOM IS OVER HERE...
...SO DON'T COME INTO MY ROOM BY MISTAKE...
I won't, even if you ask me to!
Even if it feels good, don't fall asleep in the bath...
I won't!
Even if you haven't had any sleep last night...
I'll get up on time!
THUS...

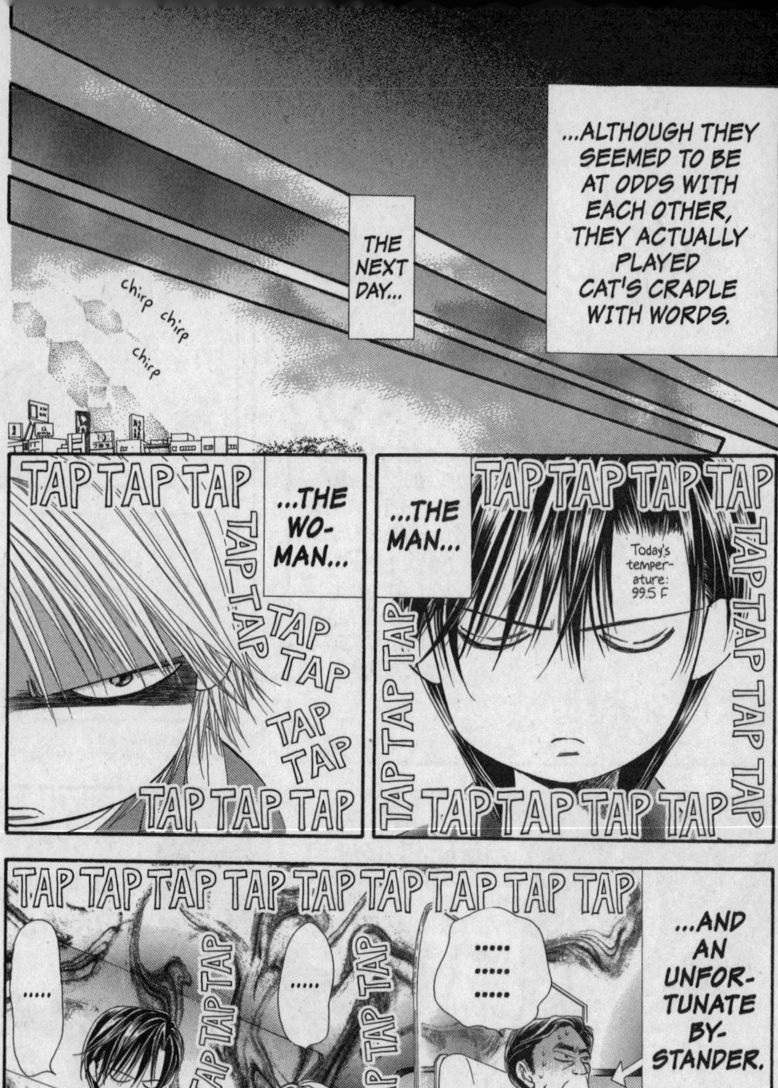
...ALTHOUGH THEY SEEMED TO BE AT ODDS WITH EACH OTHER, THEY ACTUALLY PLAYED CAT'S CRADLE WITH WORDS.
THE NEXT DAY...
chirp chirp
chirp
TAP TAP TAP TAP TAP
...THE MAN...
Today's temperature: 99.5 F
TAP TAP TAP TAP TAP TAP
TAP TAP TAP TAP
TAP TAP TAP
...THE WO-MAN...
TAP TAP TAP TAP TAP TAP TAP
TAP TAP TAP
TAP TAP TAP TAP TAP TAP TAP TAP TAP
...AND AN UNFORTUNATE BYSTANDER.
....
TAP TAP TAP TAP TAP
.....
TAP TAP TAP TAP TAP TAP
.....

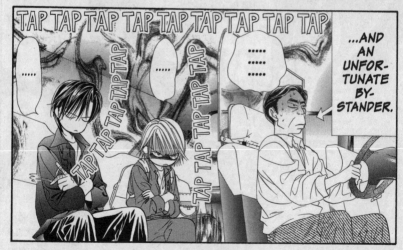

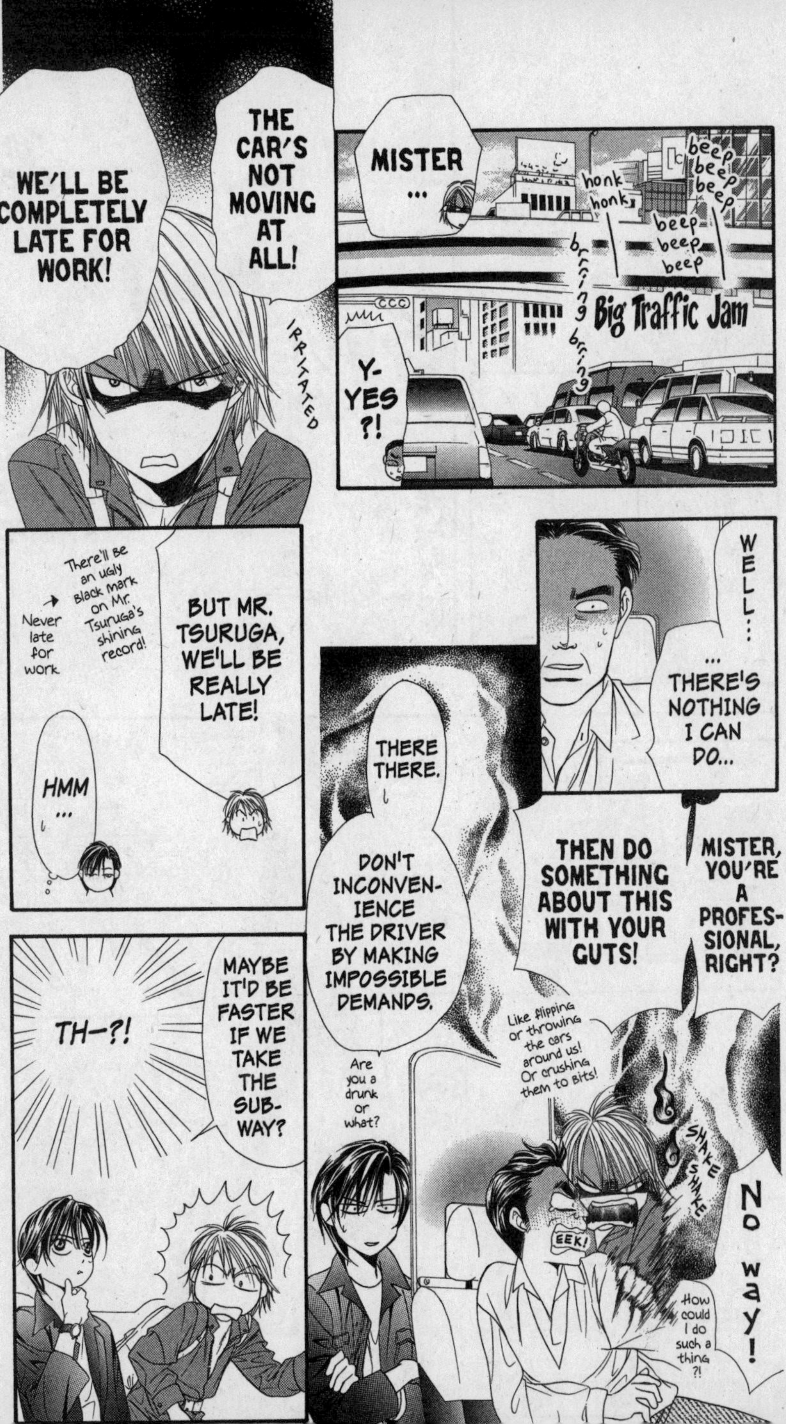
beep beep beep
honk honk
MISTER ...
beep beep beep
brring brring
Big Traffic Jam
Y-YES?!
THE CAR'S NOT MOVING AT ALL!
IRRITATED
WE'LL BE COMPLETELY LATE FOR WORK!
WELL...
... THERE'S NOTHING I CAN DO...
MISTER, YOU'RE A PROFESSIONAL, RIGHT?
THEN DO SOMETHING ABOUT THIS WITH YOUR GUTS!
Like flipping or throwing the cars around us! Or crushing them to bits!
THERE THERE.
DON'T INCONVENIENCE THE DRIVER BY MAKING IMPOSSIBLE DEMANDS.
Are you a drunk or what?
SHAKE SHAKE
EEK!
No way!
How could I do such a thing?!
BUT MR. TSURUGA, WE'LL BE REALLY LATE!
There'll be an ugly Black Mark on Mr. Tsuruga's shining record!
Never late for work
HMM ...
MAYBE IT'D BE FASTER IF WE TAKE THE SUBWAY?
TH-?!

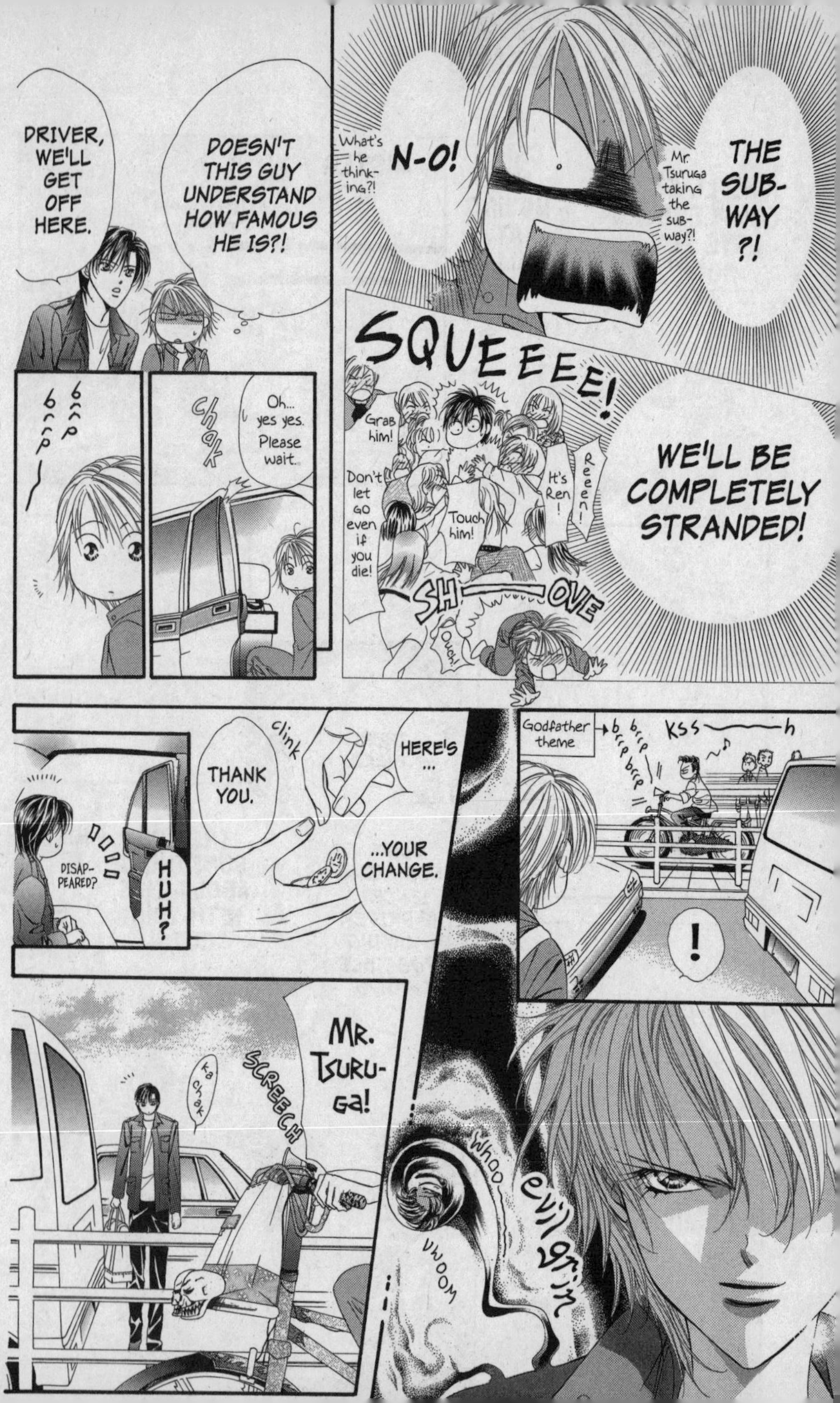
THE SUB-WAY?!
Mr. Tsuruga taking the sub-way?!
N-O!
What's he think-ing?!
DOESN'T THIS GUY UNDERSTAND HOW FAMOUS HE IS?!
DRIVER, WE'LL GET OFF HERE.
WE'LL BE COMPLETELY STRANDED!
SQUEEEEE!
Reeen!
It's Ren!
Touch him!
Grab him!
Don't let go even if you die!
SH——OVE
Ouch!
Oh... yes yes. Please wait.
chak
brrp brrp
KSS———h
brrp brrp brrp brrp
Godfather theme
!
HERE'S...
...YOUR CHANGE.
clink
THANK YOU.
HUH?
DISAPPEARED?
whoo
evil grin
vwoom
MR. TSURU-GA!
SCREECH
ka chak

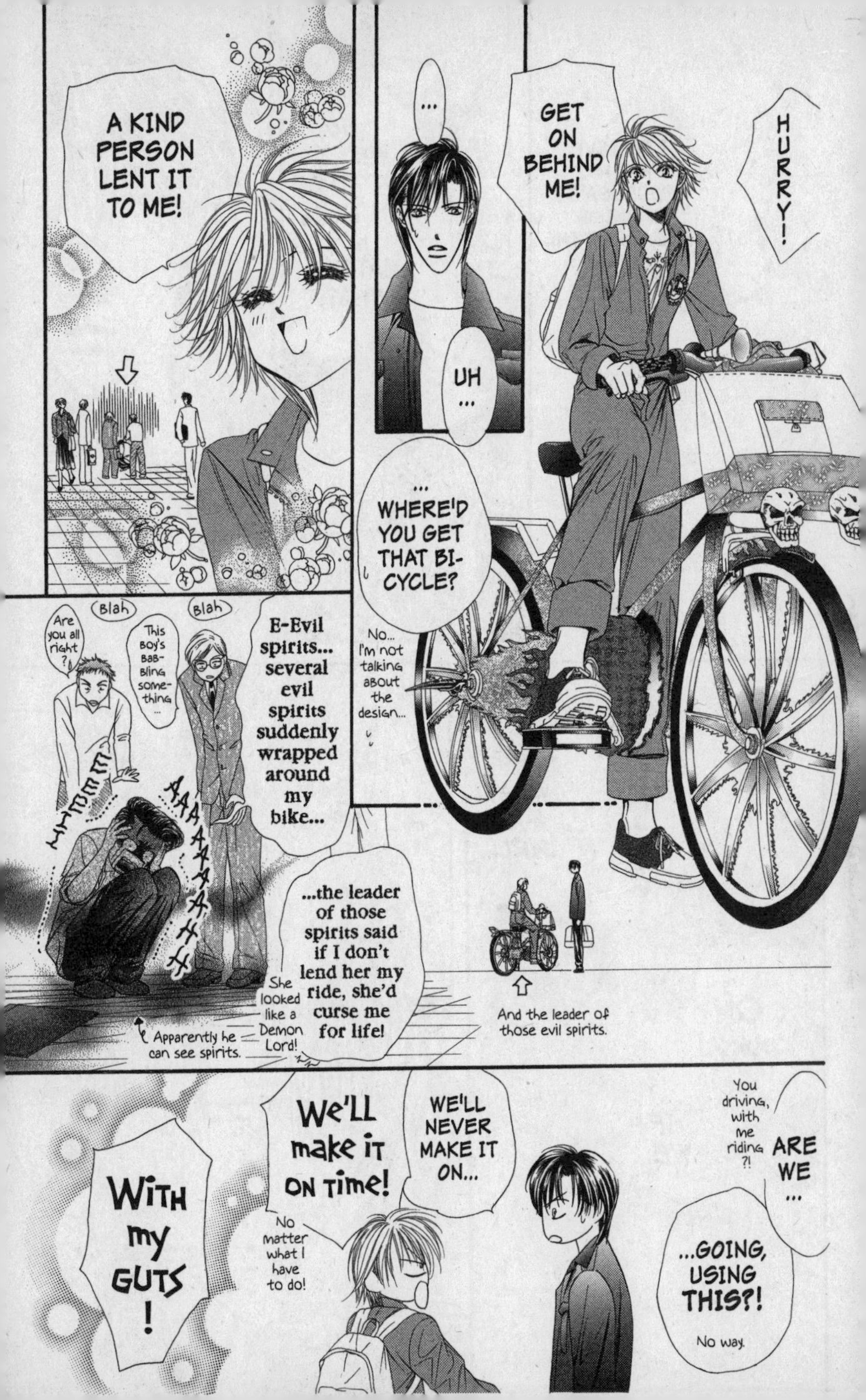
HURRY!
GET ON BEHIND ME!
...
UH...
...WHERE'D YOU GET THAT BI-CYCLE?
No... I'm not talking about the design...
A KIND PERSON LENT IT TO ME!
Blah
Blah
E-Evil spirits... several evil spirits suddenly wrapped around my bike...
This boy's bab-bling some-thing...
Are you all right?
...the leader of those spirits said if I don't lend her my ride, she'd curse me for life!
She looked like a Demon Lord!
Apparently he can see spirits.
And the leader of those evil spirits.
ARE WE...
...GOING, USING THIS?!
You driving, with me riding?!
No way.
WE'LL NEVER MAKE IT ON...
We'll make it on time!
No matter what I have to do!
With my GUTS!

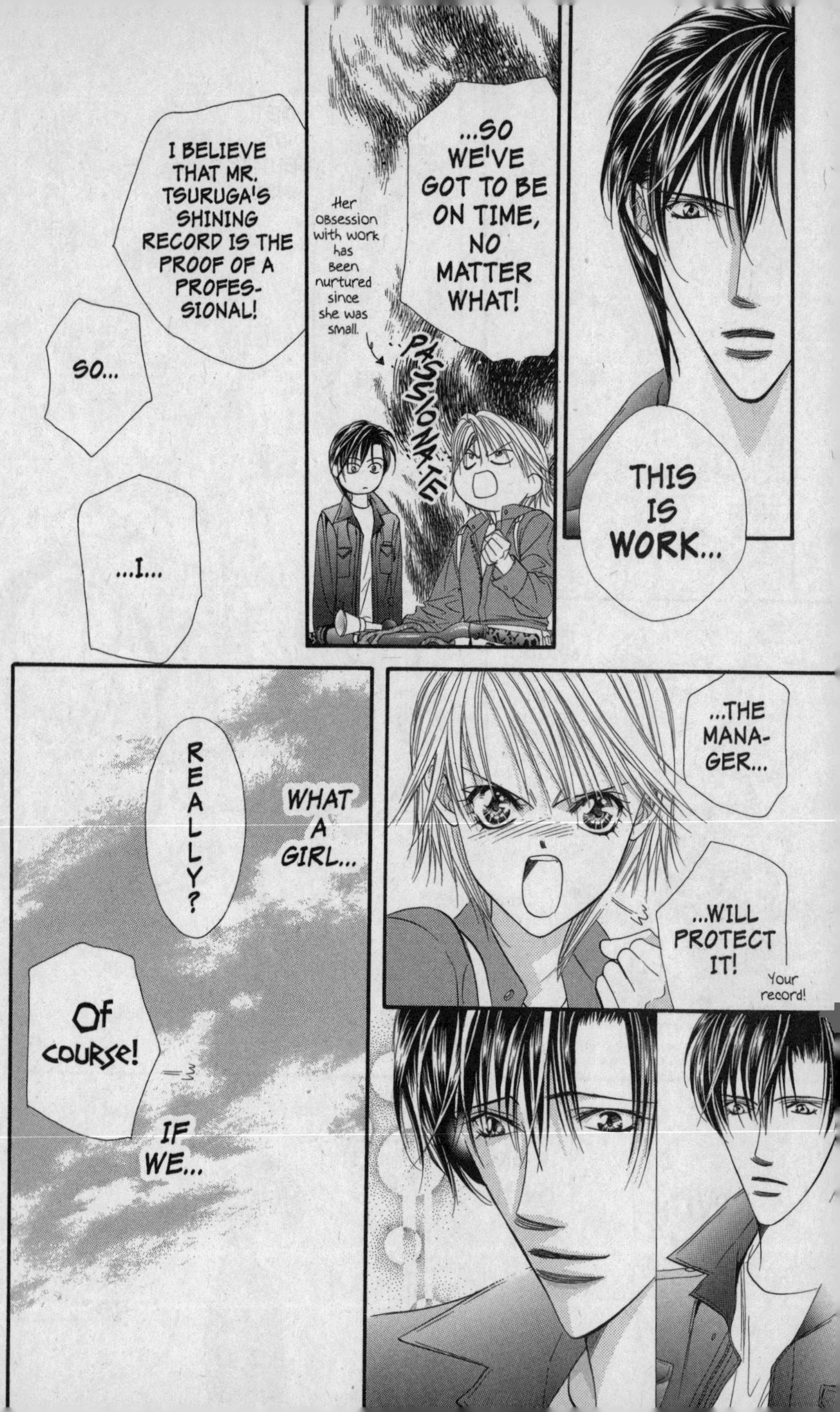

THIS IS WORK...
...SO WE'VE GOT TO BE ON TIME, NO MATTER WHAT!
Her obsession with work has been nurtured since she was small.
PASSIONATE
I BELIEVE THAT MR. TSURUGA'S SHINING RECORD IS THE PROOF OF A PROFESSIONAL!
SO...
...I...
...THE MANAGER...
...WILL PROTECT IT!
Your record!
REALLY?
WHAT A GIRL...
Of course!
IF WE...

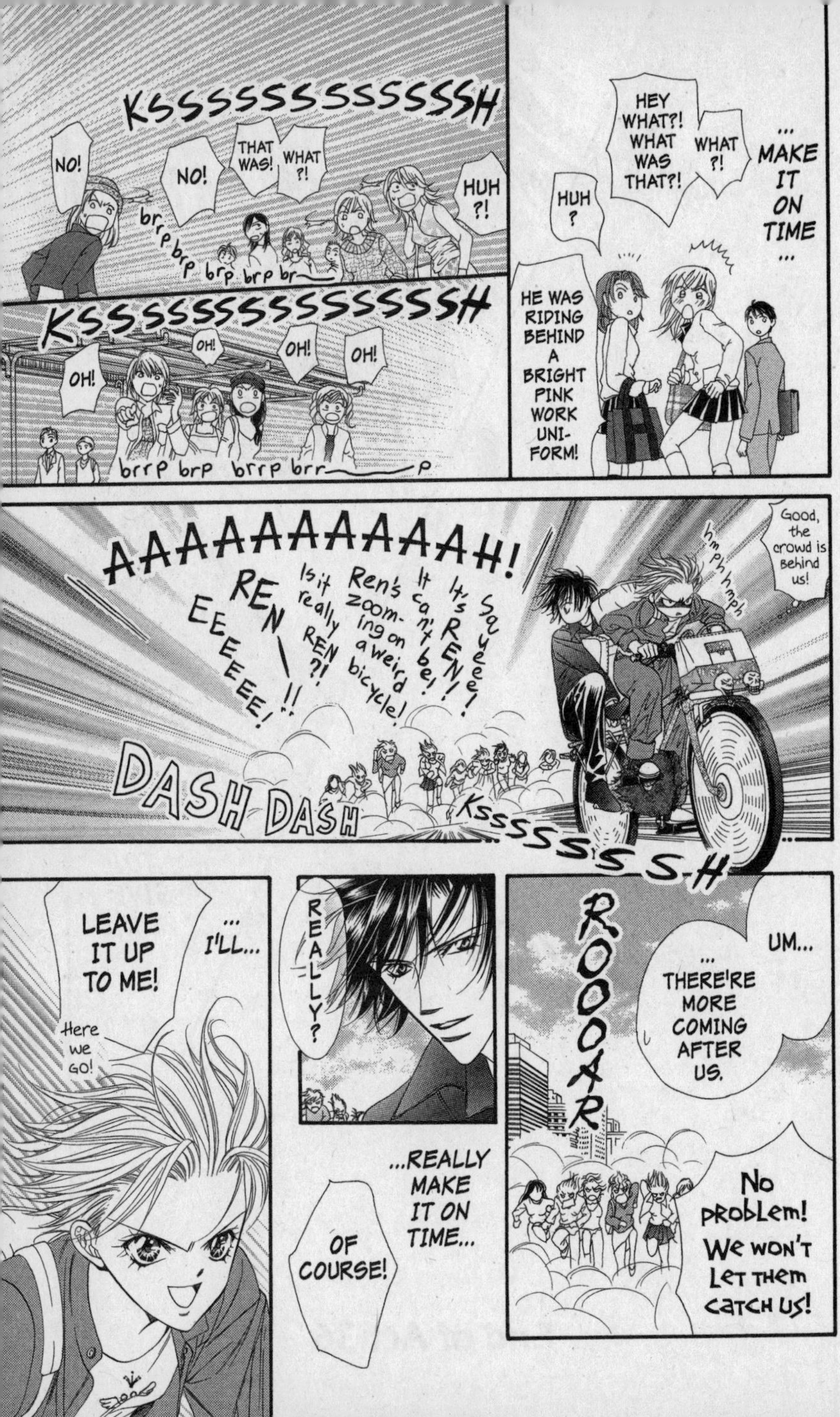
... MAKE IT ON TIME ...
WHAT ?!
HEY WHAT?! WHAT WAS THAT?!
HUH ?
HE WAS RIDING BEHIND A BRIGHT PINK WORK UNI- FORM!
KSSSSSSSSSSSSSH
HUH ?!
WHAT ?!
THAT WAS!
NO!
NO!
brrp brrp brp brp brp br——
KSSSSSSSSSSSSSSH
OH!
OH!
OH!
OH!
brrp brp brrp brr———p
Good, the crowd is behind us!
hmph hmph
AAAAAAAAAAAH!
Squeee!
It's REN!
It can't be!
Ren's zoom- ing on a weird bicycle!
Is it really REN ?!
REN!!
EEEEEEE!
DASH DASH
KSSSSSSSH
UM...
... THERE'RE MORE COMING AFTER US.
ROOOOAR
No problem! We won't let them catch us!
REALLY?
...REALLY MAKE IT ON TIME...
OF COURSE!
... I'LL...
LEAVE IT UP TO ME!
Here we GO!

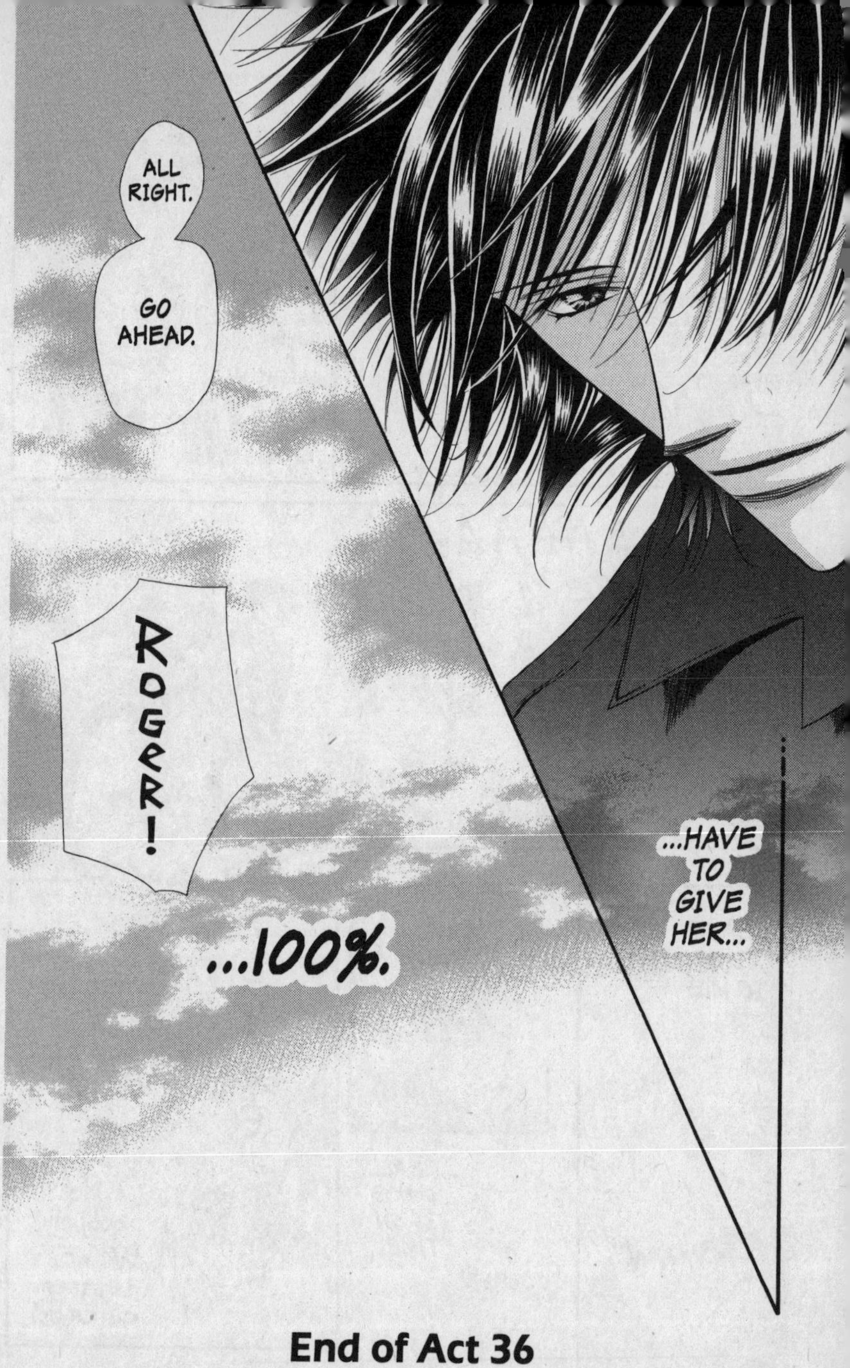
ALL RIGHT.
GO AHEAD.
ROGER!
...HAVE TO GIVE HER...
...100%.

End of Act 36

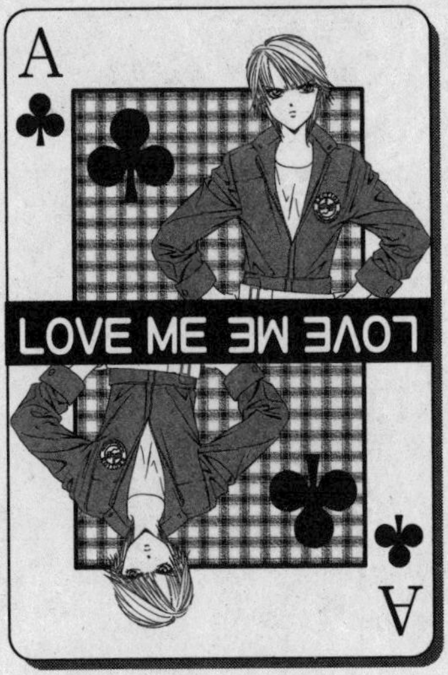
A
LOVE ME

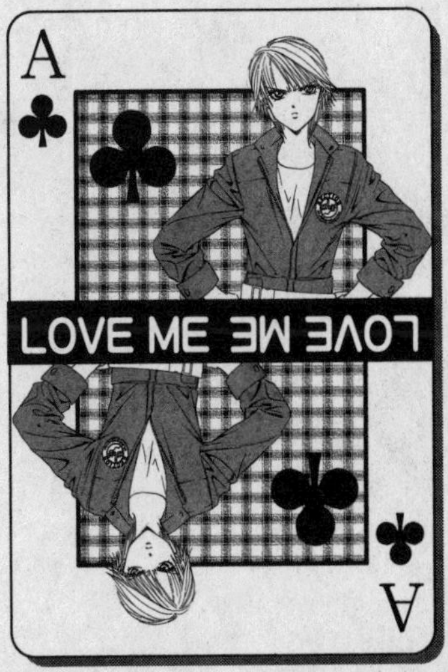
A
LOVE ME

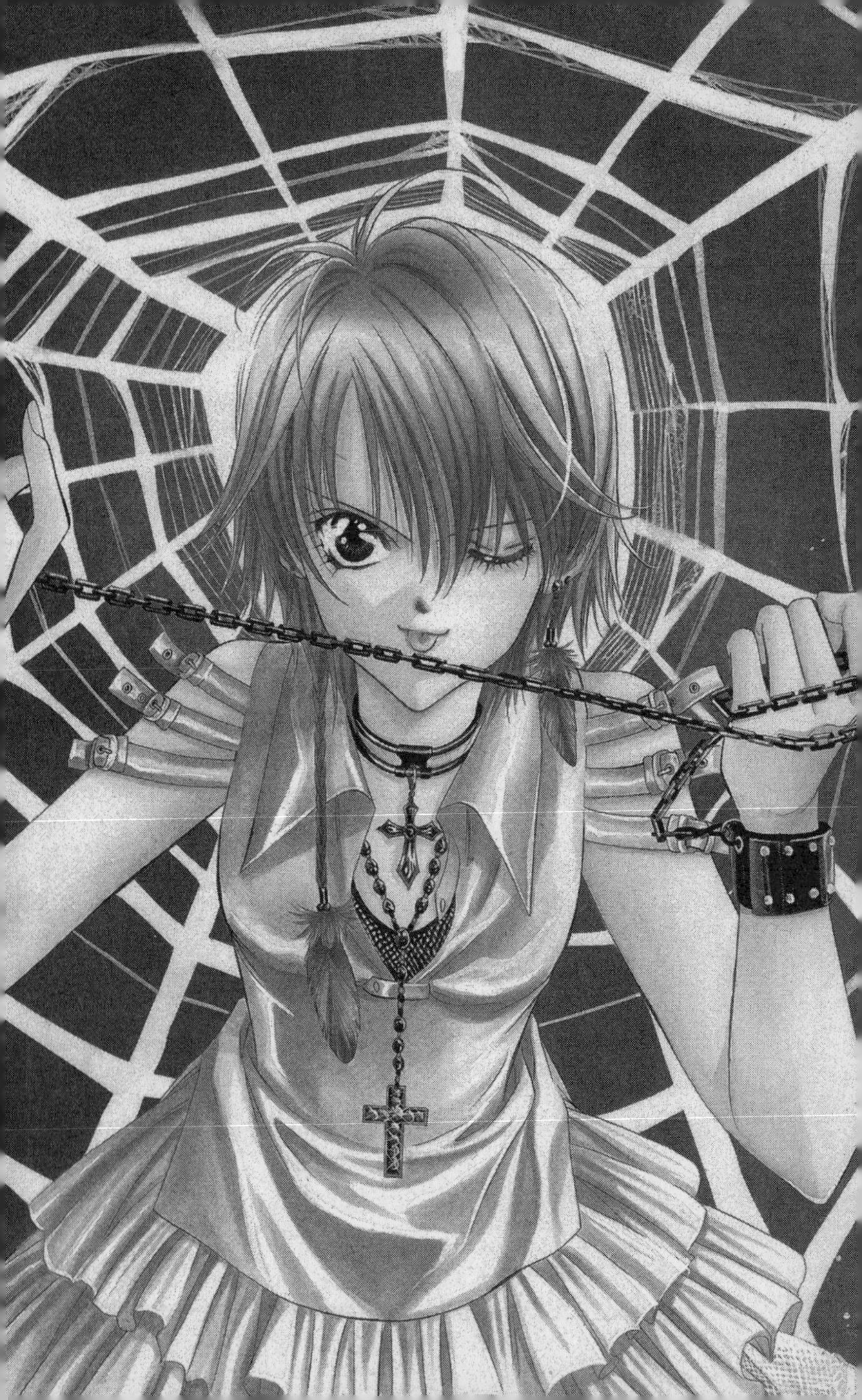

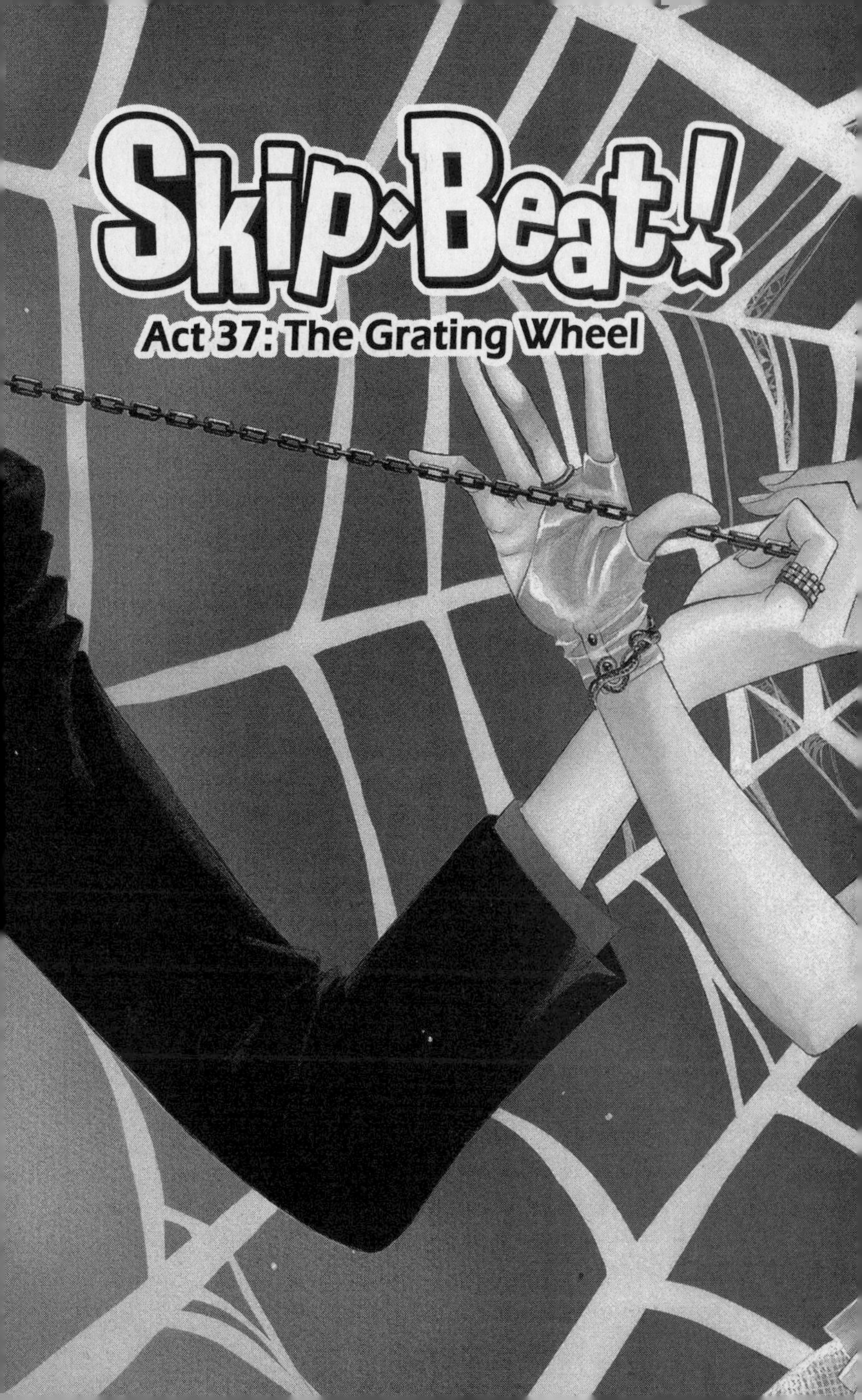
Skip·Beat!
Act 37: The Grating Wheel

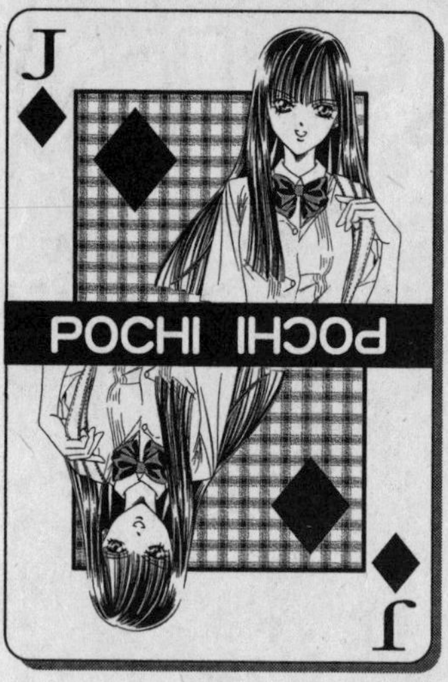
J
POCHI POCHI
J
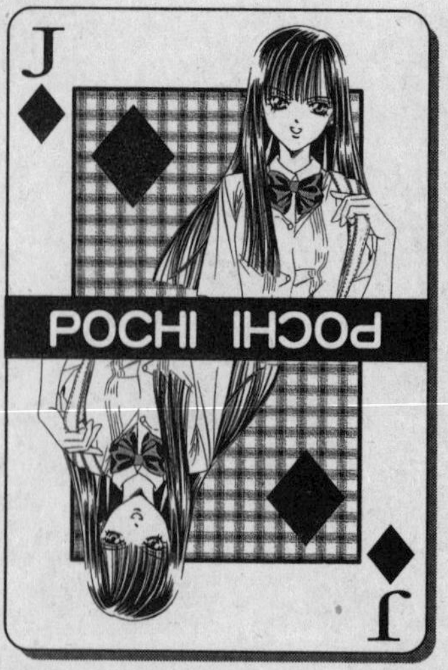
J
POCHI POCHI
J

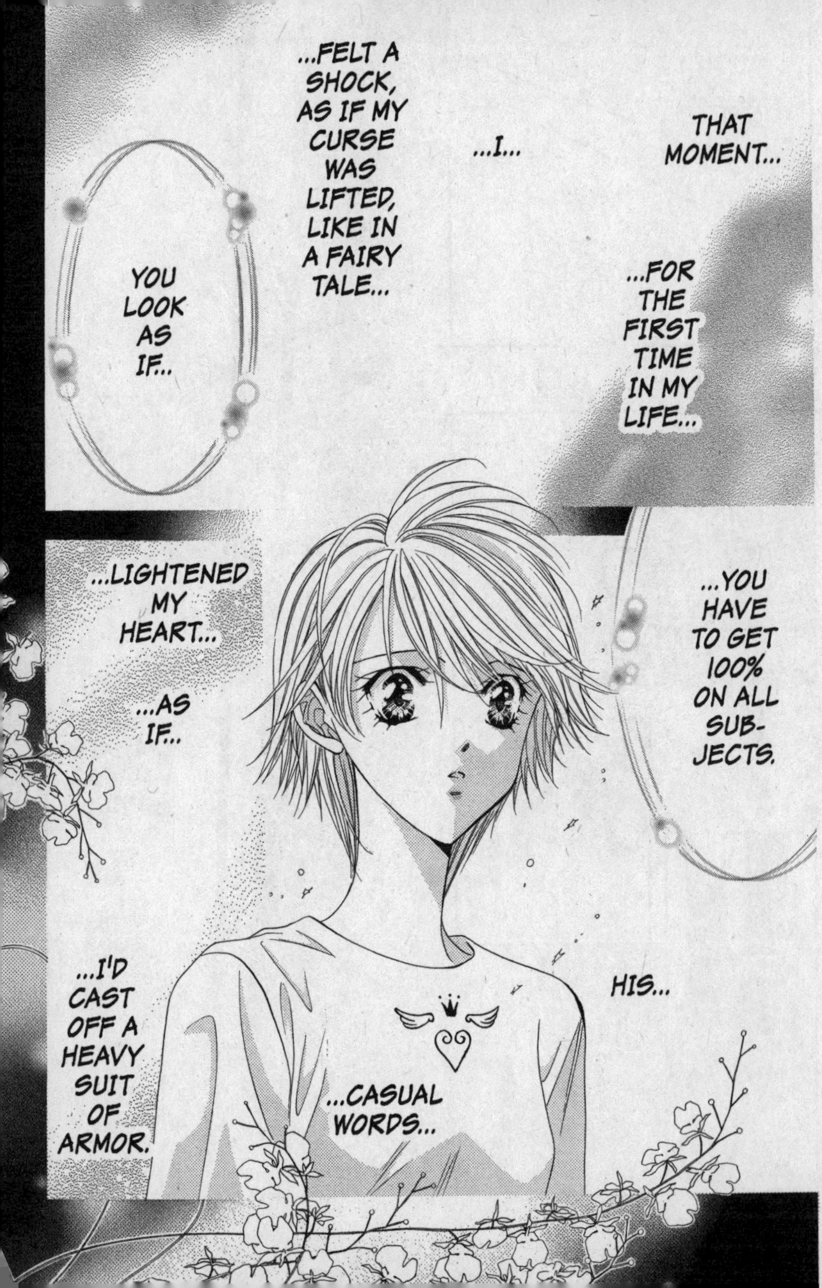
THAT MOMENT...
...I...
...FELT A SHOCK, AS IF MY CURSE WAS LIFTED, LIKE IN A FAIRY TALE...
...FOR THE FIRST TIME IN MY LIFE...
YOU LOOK AS IF...
...YOU HAVE TO GET 100% ON ALL SUB-JECTS.
HIS...
...CASUAL WORDS...
...LIGHTENED MY HEART...
...AS IF...
...I'D CAST OFF A HEAVY SUIT OF ARMOR.

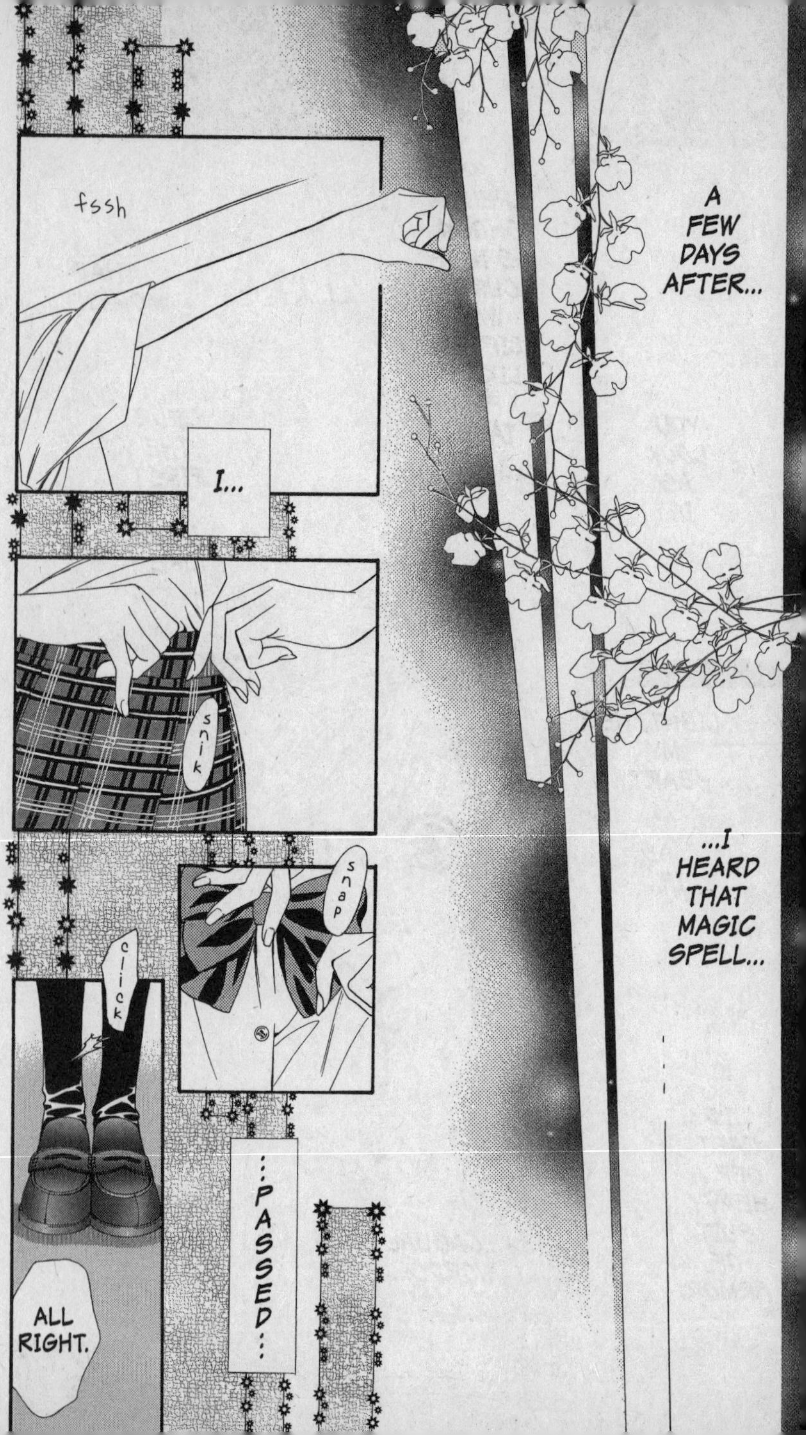
A FEW DAYS AFTER...
...I HEARD THAT MAGIC SPELL...
fssh
I...
snik
snap
click
...PASSED...
ALL RIGHT.

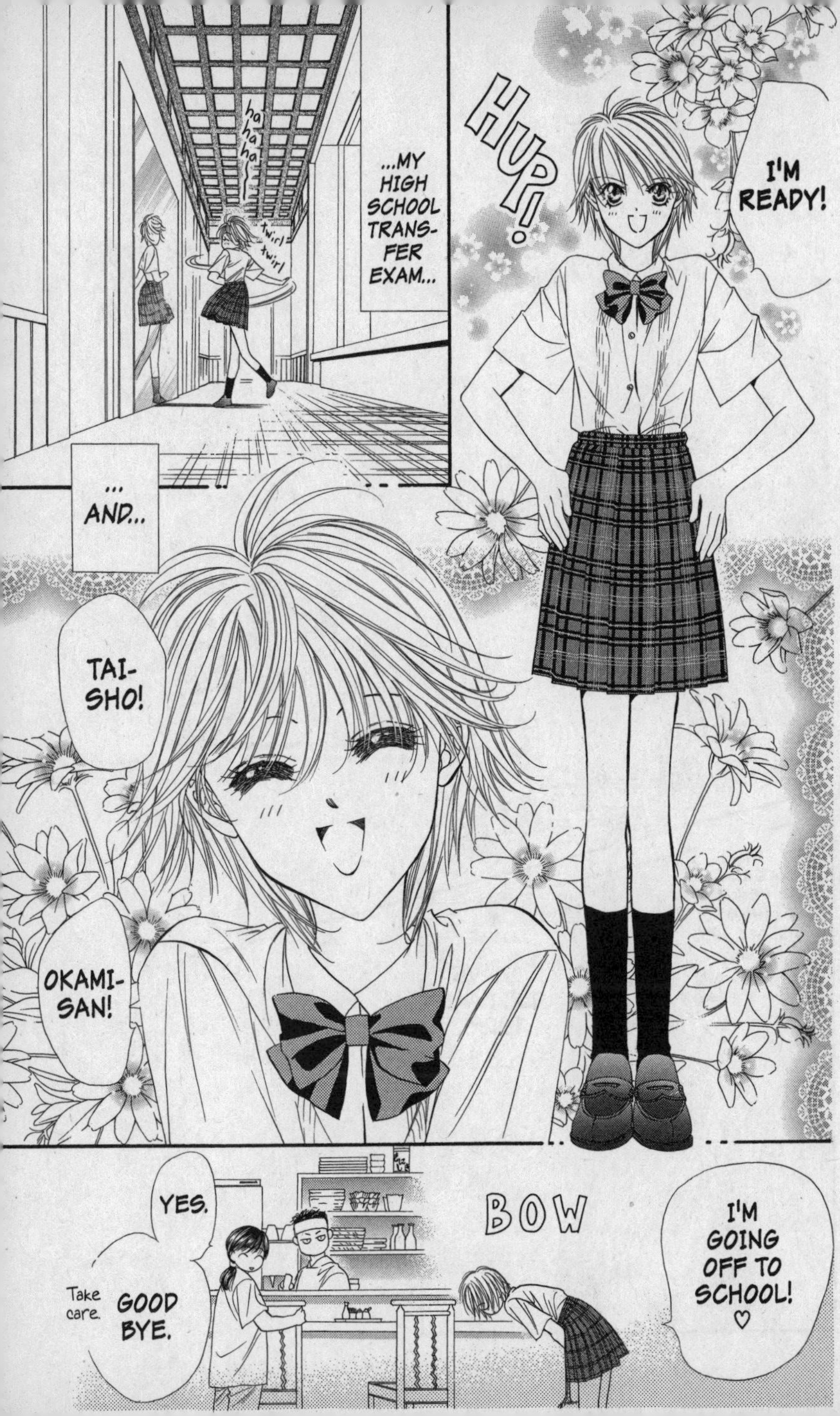
HUP!
I'M READY!
...MY HIGH SCHOOL TRANS-FER EXAM...
ha ha ha~
twirl twirl
... AND...
TAI-SHO!
OKAMI-SAN!
I'M GOING OFF TO SCHOOL! ♡
BOW
YES.
GOOD BYE.
Take care.

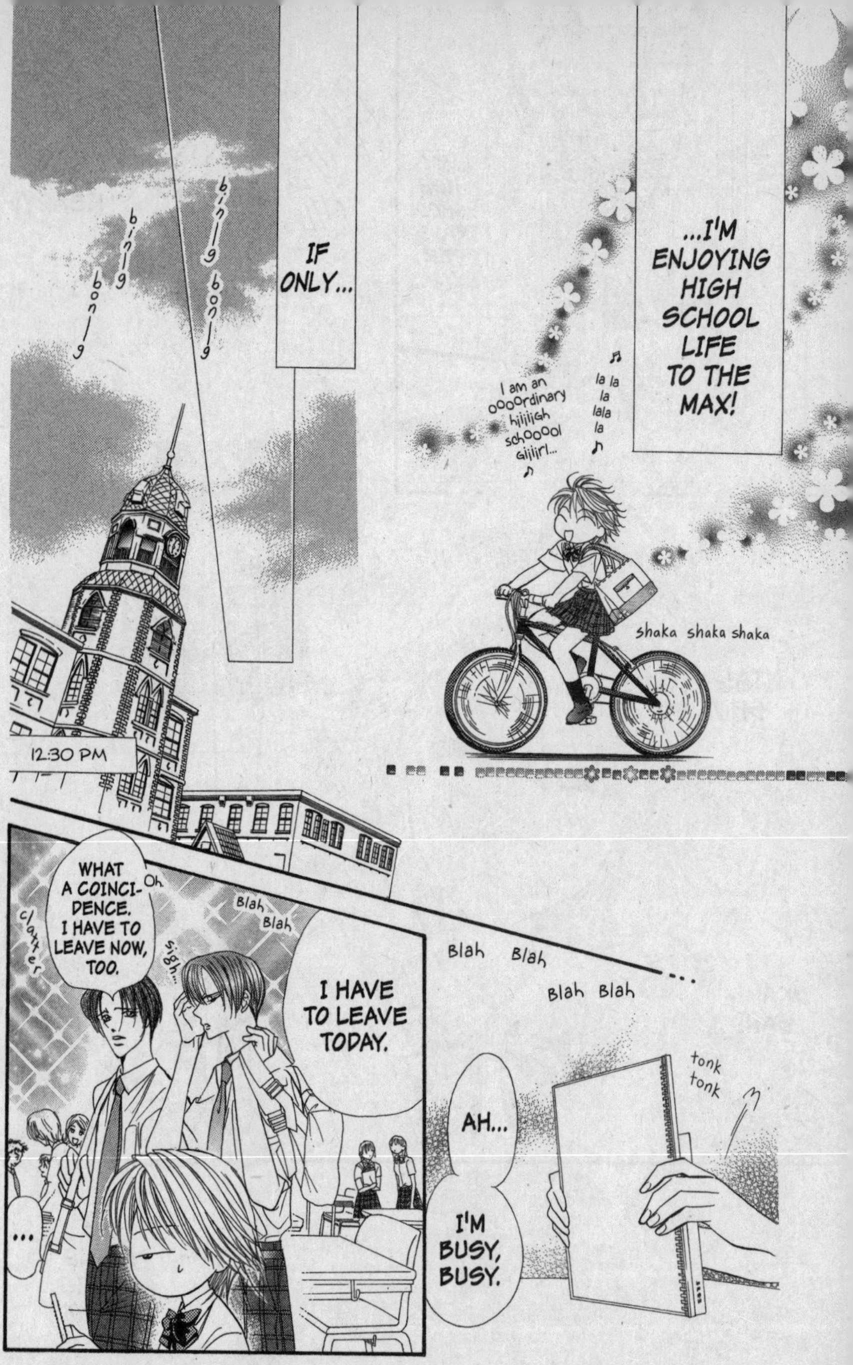
...I'M ENJOYING HIGH SCHOOL LIFE TO THE MAX!
la la la lala la
I am an ooooordinary hiiiiigh schoooool Giiiirl...
shaka shaka shaka
IF ONLY...
bing bong
bing bong
12:30 PM
Blah Blah
Blah Blah
tonk tonk
AH...
I'M BUSY, BUSY.
I HAVE TO LEAVE TODAY.
Blah Blah
Oh.
WHAT A COINCIDENCE. I HAVE TO LEAVE NOW, TOO.
sigh...
clatter
...

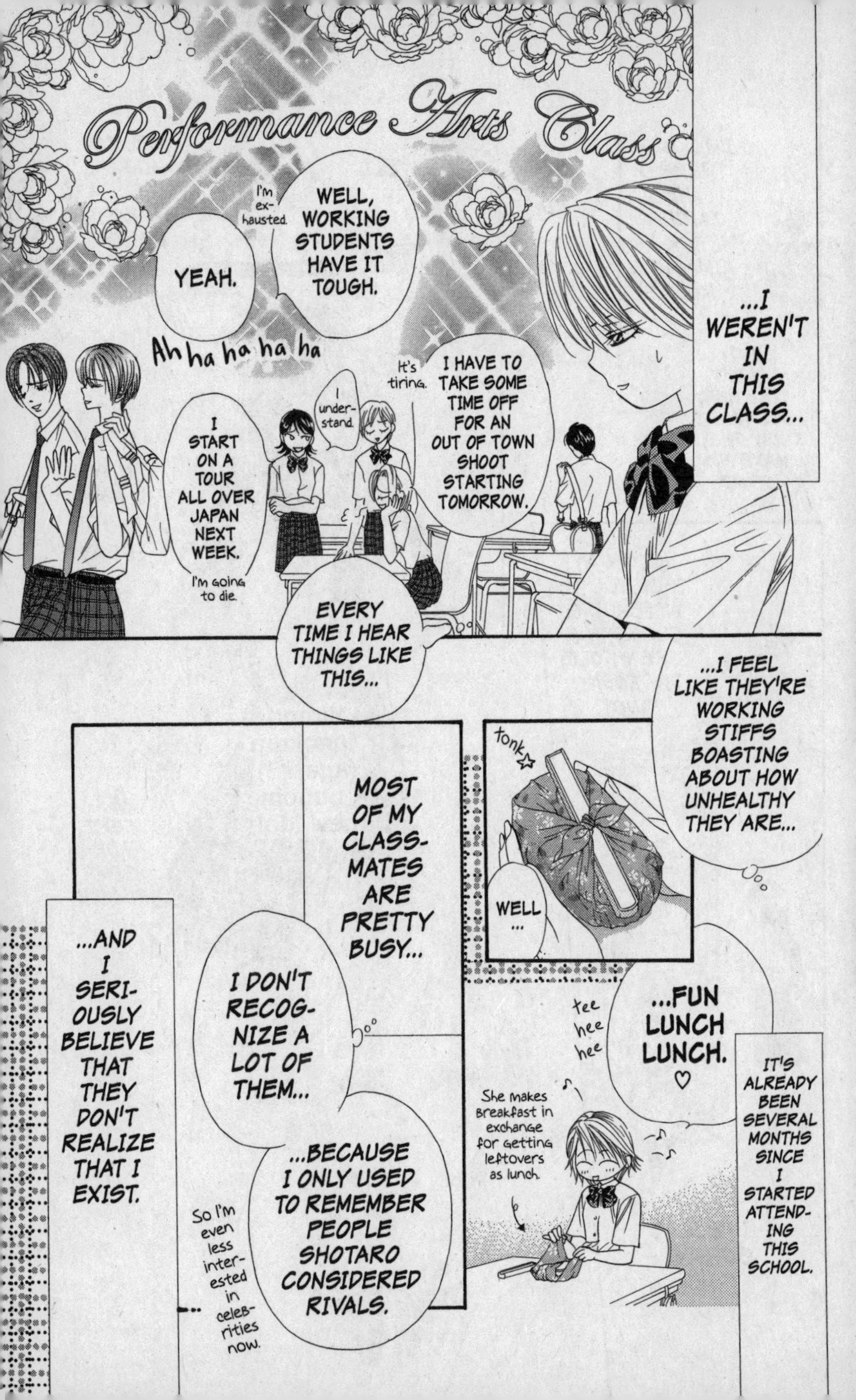
Performance Arts Class
...I WEREN'T IN THIS CLASS...
WELL, WORKING STUDENTS HAVE IT TOUGH.
I'm exhausted.
YEAH.
Ah ha ha ha ha
I HAVE TO TAKE SOME TIME OFF FOR AN OUT OF TOWN SHOOT STARTING TOMORROW.
It's tiring.
I understand.
I START ON A TOUR ALL OVER JAPAN NEXT WEEK.
I'm going to die.
EVERY TIME I HEAR THINGS LIKE THIS...
...I FEEL LIKE THEY'RE WORKING STIFFS BOASTING ABOUT HOW UNHEALTHY THEY ARE...
tonk☆
WELL...
MOST OF MY CLASSMATES ARE PRETTY BUSY...
IT'S ALREADY BEEN SEVERAL MONTHS SINCE I STARTED ATTENDING THIS SCHOOL.
...FUN LUNCH LUNCH. ♡
tee hee hee
She makes breakfast in exchange for getting leftovers as lunch.
I DON'T RECOGNIZE A LOT OF THEM...
...BECAUSE I ONLY USED TO REMEMBER PEOPLE SHOTARO CONSIDERED RIVALS.
So I'm even less interested in celebrities now.
...AND I SERIOUSLY BELIEVE THAT THEY DON'T REALIZE THAT I EXIST.

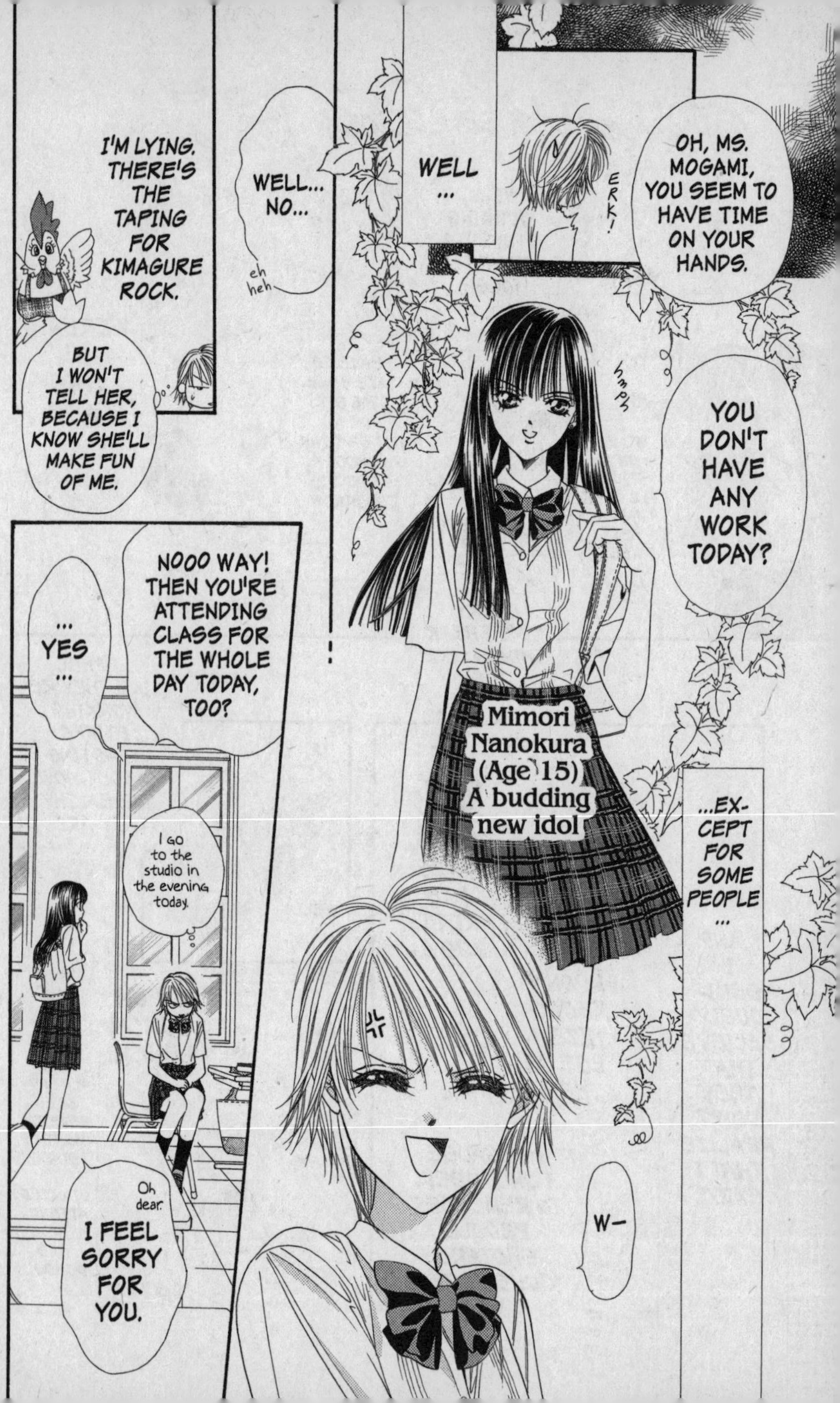
OH, MS. MOGAMI, YOU SEEM TO HAVE TIME ON YOUR HANDS.
ERK!
WELL ...
YOU DON'T HAVE ANY WORK TODAY?
hmph
Mimori Nanokura (Age 15) A budding new idol
WELL... NO...
eh heh
I'M LYING. THERE'S THE TAPING FOR KIMAGURE ROCK.
BUT I WON'T TELL HER, BECAUSE I KNOW SHE'LL MAKE FUN OF ME.
NOOO WAY! THEN YOU'RE ATTENDING CLASS FOR THE WHOLE DAY TODAY, TOO?
... YES ...
I go to the studio in the evening today.
Oh dear.
I FEEL SORRY FOR YOU.
W—
...EX-CEPT FOR SOME PEOPLE ...

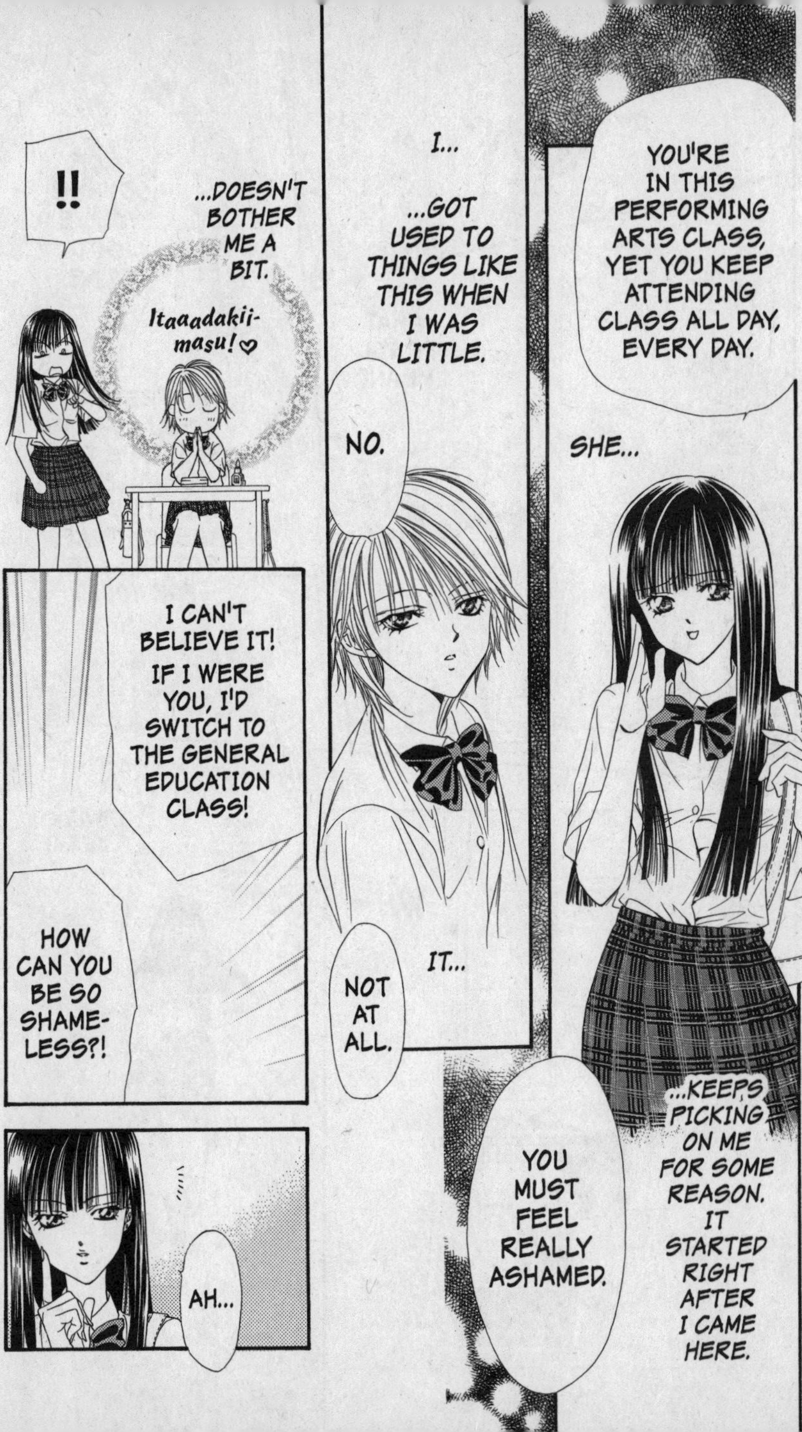
YOU'RE IN THIS PERFORMING ARTS CLASS, YET YOU KEEP ATTENDING CLASS ALL DAY, EVERY DAY.
SHE...
...KEEPS PICKING ON ME FOR SOME REASON. IT STARTED RIGHT AFTER I CAME HERE.
YOU MUST FEEL REALLY ASHAMED.
I...
...GOT USED TO THINGS LIKE THIS WHEN I WAS LITTLE.
NO.
IT...
NOT AT ALL.
...DOESN'T BOTHER ME A BIT.
!!
Itaaadakii-masu!♡
I CAN'T BELIEVE IT! IF I WERE YOU, I'D SWITCH TO THE GENERAL EDUCATION CLASS!
HOW CAN YOU BE SO SHAMELESS?!
AH...

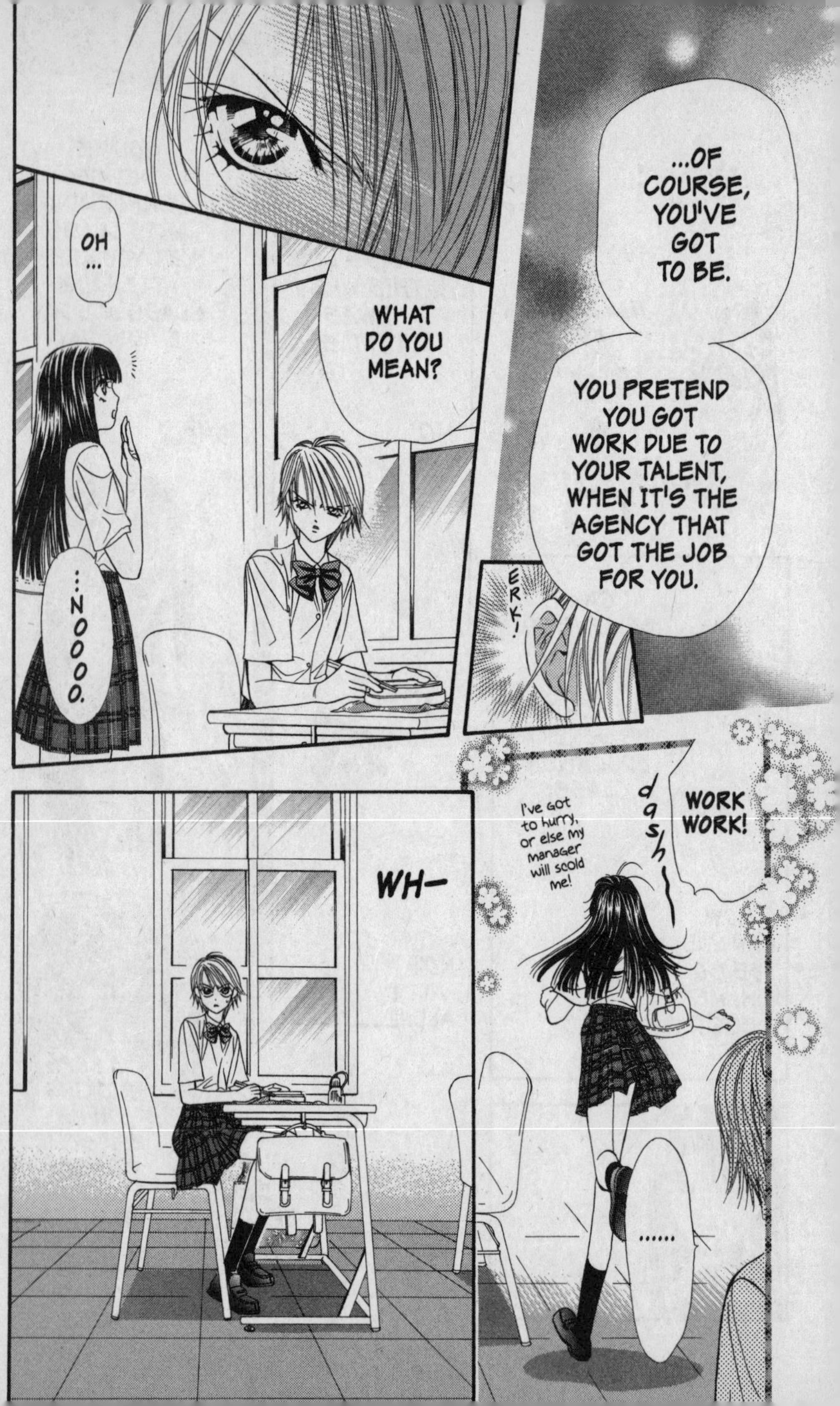
...OF COURSE, YOU'VE GOT TO BE.
YOU PRETEND YOU GOT WORK DUE TO YOUR TALENT, WHEN IT'S THE AGENCY THAT GOT THE JOB FOR YOU.
ERK!
WHAT DO YOU MEAN?
OH...
...NOOOO.
WORK WORK!
dash
I've got to hurry, or else my manager will scold me!
......
WH-

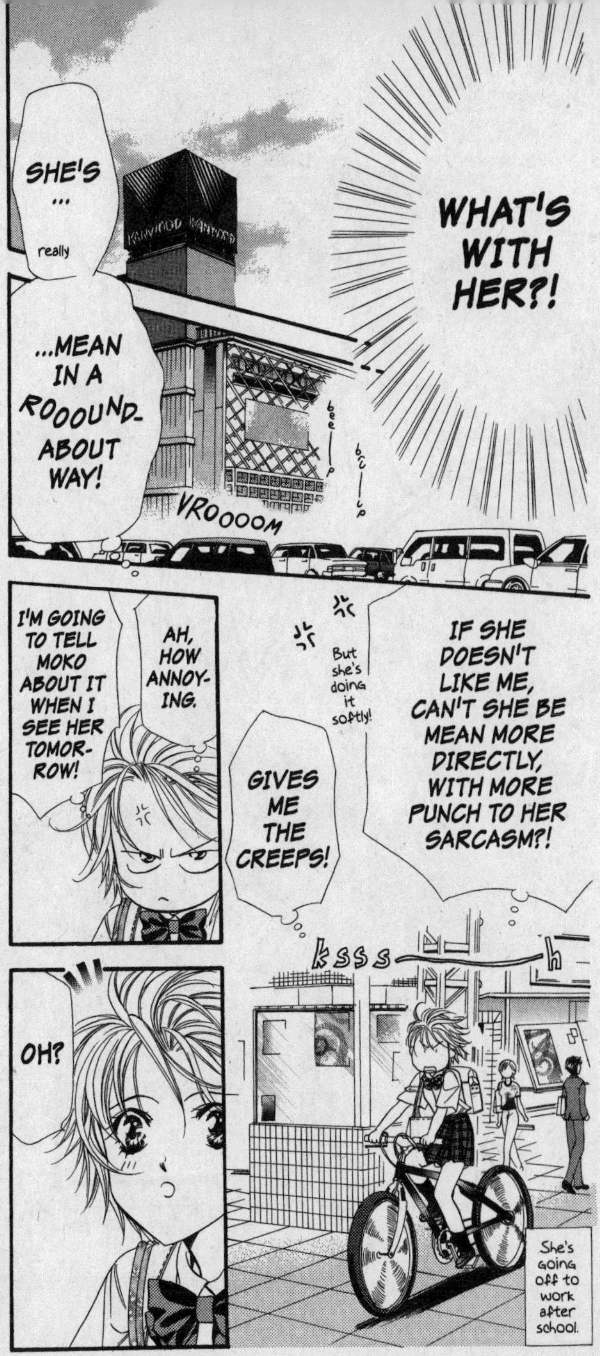
SHE'S ...
really
...MEAN IN A ROOOUND-ABOUT WAY!
WHAT'S WITH HER?!
bee—p
bee—p
VROOOOM
IF SHE DOESN'T LIKE ME, CAN'T SHE BE MEAN MORE DIRECTLY, WITH MORE PUNCH TO HER SARCASM?!
But she's doing it softly!
GIVES ME THE CREEPS!
AH, HOW ANNOY-ING.
I'M GOING TO TELL MOKO ABOUT IT WHEN I SEE HER TOMOR-ROW!
ksss——h
She's going off to work after school.
OH?
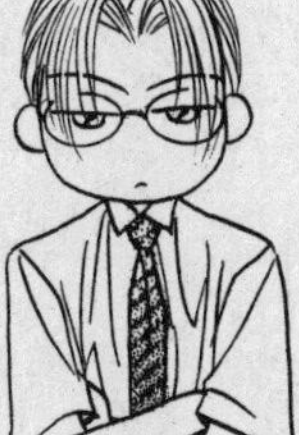

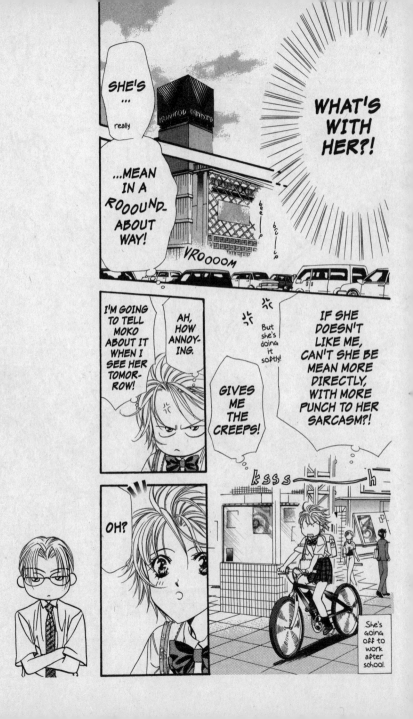

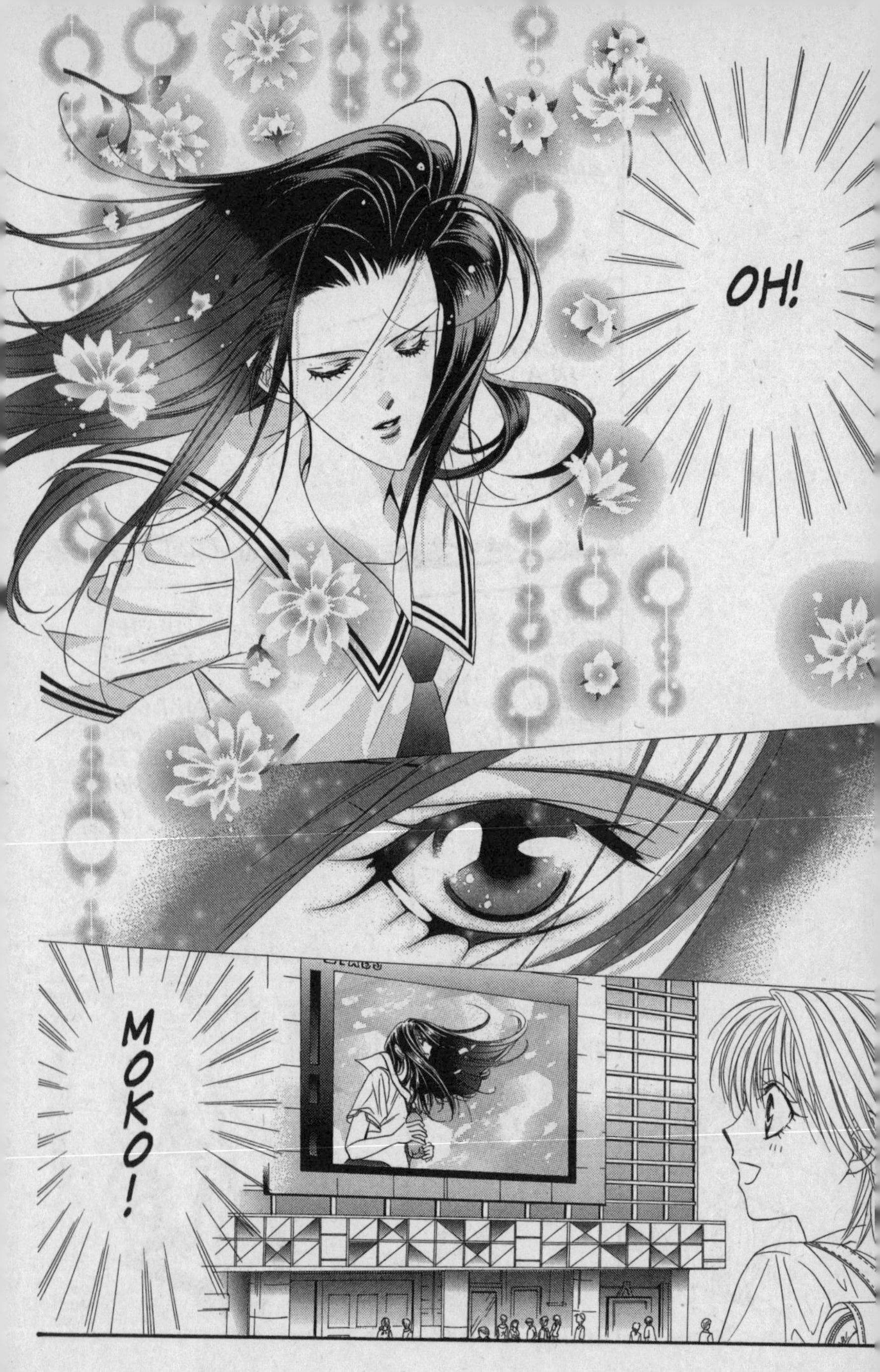
OH!
MOKO!

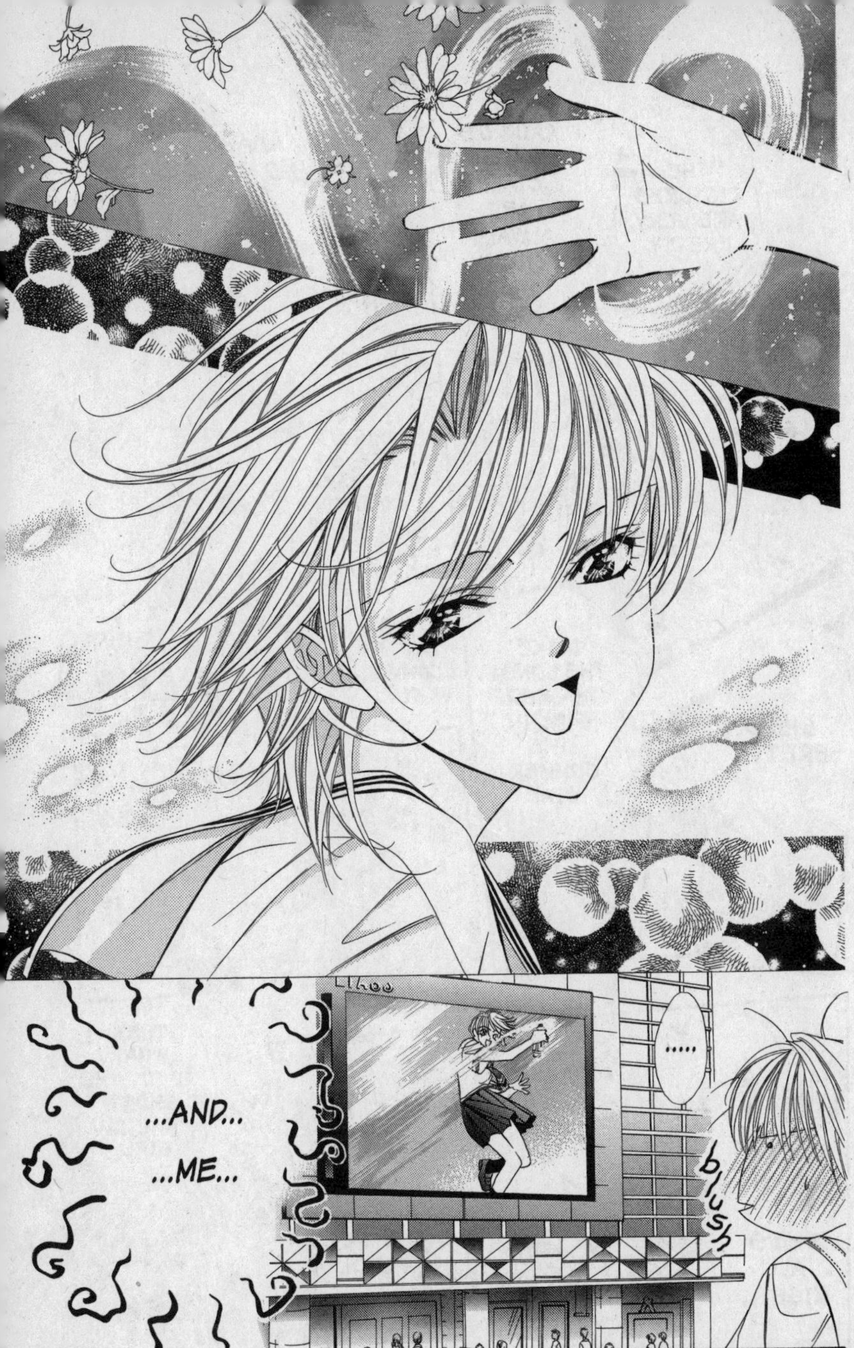
.....
blush
...AND...
...ME...

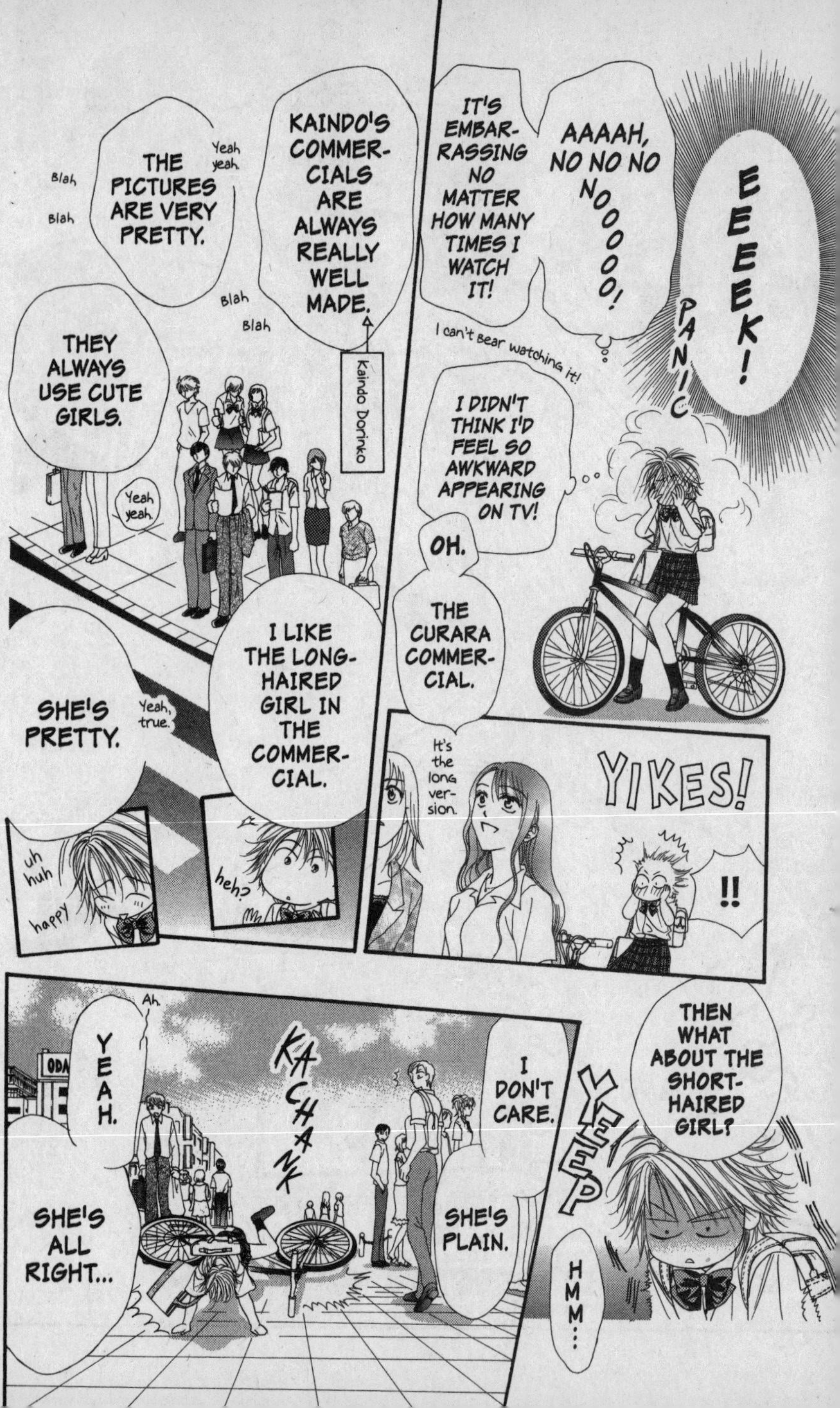
EEEEK!
PANIC
AAAAH, NO NO NO NOOOOO!
IT'S EMBARRASSING NO MATTER HOW MANY TIMES I WATCH IT!
I can't Bear watching it!
I DIDN'T THINK I'D FEEL SO AWKWARD APPEARING ON TV!
OH.
THE CURARA COMMERCIAL.
YIKES!
!!
It's the long version.
KAINDO'S COMMERCIALS ARE ALWAYS REALLY WELL MADE.
Kaindo Dorinko
Yeah yeah.
THE PICTURES ARE VERY PRETTY.
Blah
Blah
Blah
Blah
THEY ALWAYS USE CUTE GIRLS.
Yeah yeah.
I LIKE THE LONG-HAIRED GIRL IN THE COMMERCIAL.
Yeah, true.
SHE'S PRETTY.
heh?
uh huh
happy
THEN WHAT ABOUT THE SHORT-HAIRED GIRL?
YEEP
HMM...
I DON'T CARE.
SHE'S PLAIN.
KACHANK
Ah.
YEAH.
SHE'S ALL RIGHT...

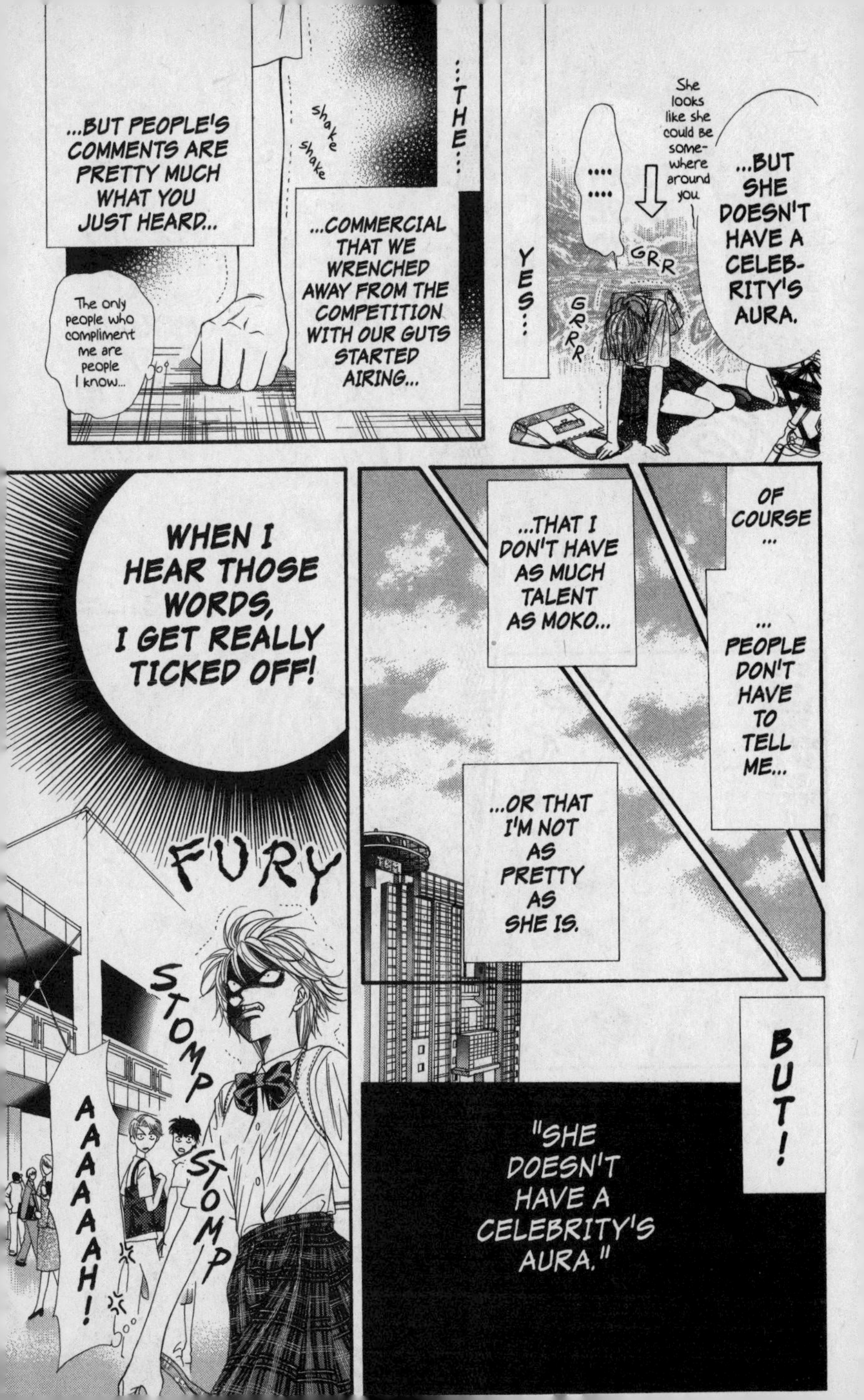

She looks like she could be somewhere around you.
...BUT SHE DOESN'T HAVE A CELEBRITY'S AURA.
....
....
GRR
GRRR
YES...
...THE...
shake shake
...COMMERCIAL THAT WE WRENCHED AWAY FROM THE COMPETITION WITH OUR GUTS STARTED AIRING...
...BUT PEOPLE'S COMMENTS ARE PRETTY MUCH WHAT YOU JUST HEARD...
The only people who compliment me are people I know...
OF COURSE...
...PEOPLE DON'T HAVE TO TELL ME...
...THAT I DON'T HAVE AS MUCH TALENT AS MOKO...
...OR THAT I'M NOT AS PRETTY AS SHE IS.
BUT!
"SHE DOESN'T HAVE A CELEBRITY'S AURA."
WHEN I HEAR THOSE WORDS, I GET REALLY TICKED OFF!
FURY
STOMP
STOMP
AAAAAAH!

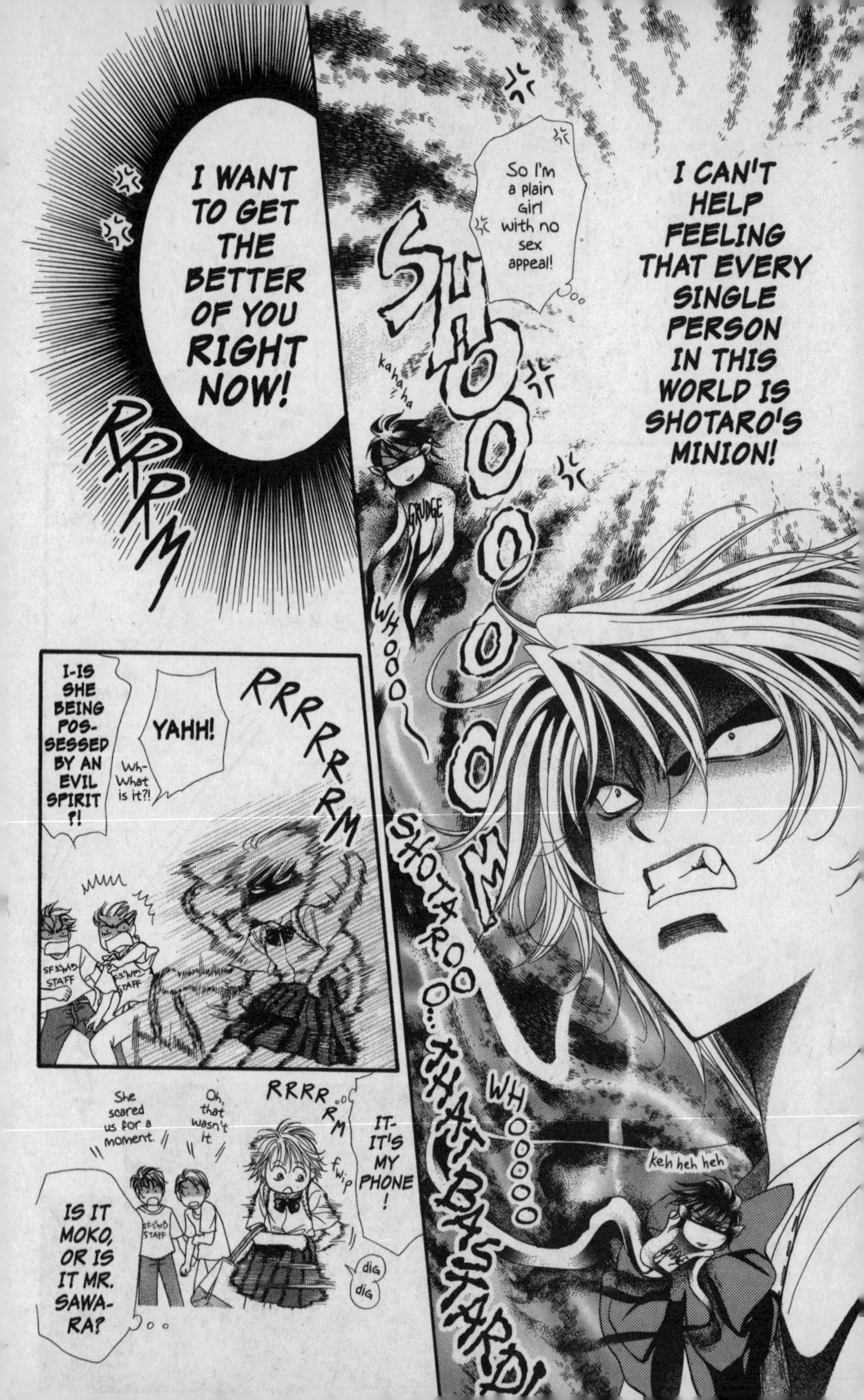
I CAN'T HELP FEELING THAT EVERY SINGLE PERSON IN THIS WORLD IS SHOTARO'S MINION!
So I'm a plain girl with no sex appeal!
SHOOOOOOM
kahaha
GRUDGE
WHOOOO
SHOTAROO... THAT BASTARD!
WHOOOOO
keh heh heh
I WANT TO GET THE BETTER OF YOU RIGHT NOW!
RRRM
RRRRRRRM
YAHH!
Wh-What is it?!
I-IS SHE BEING POS-SESSED BY AN EVIL SPIRIT?!
SF STAFF
RRRRRM
IT-IT'S MY PHONE!
fwip
dig dig
Oh, that wasn't it.
She scared us for a moment.
IS IT MOKO, OR IS IT MR. SAWARA?

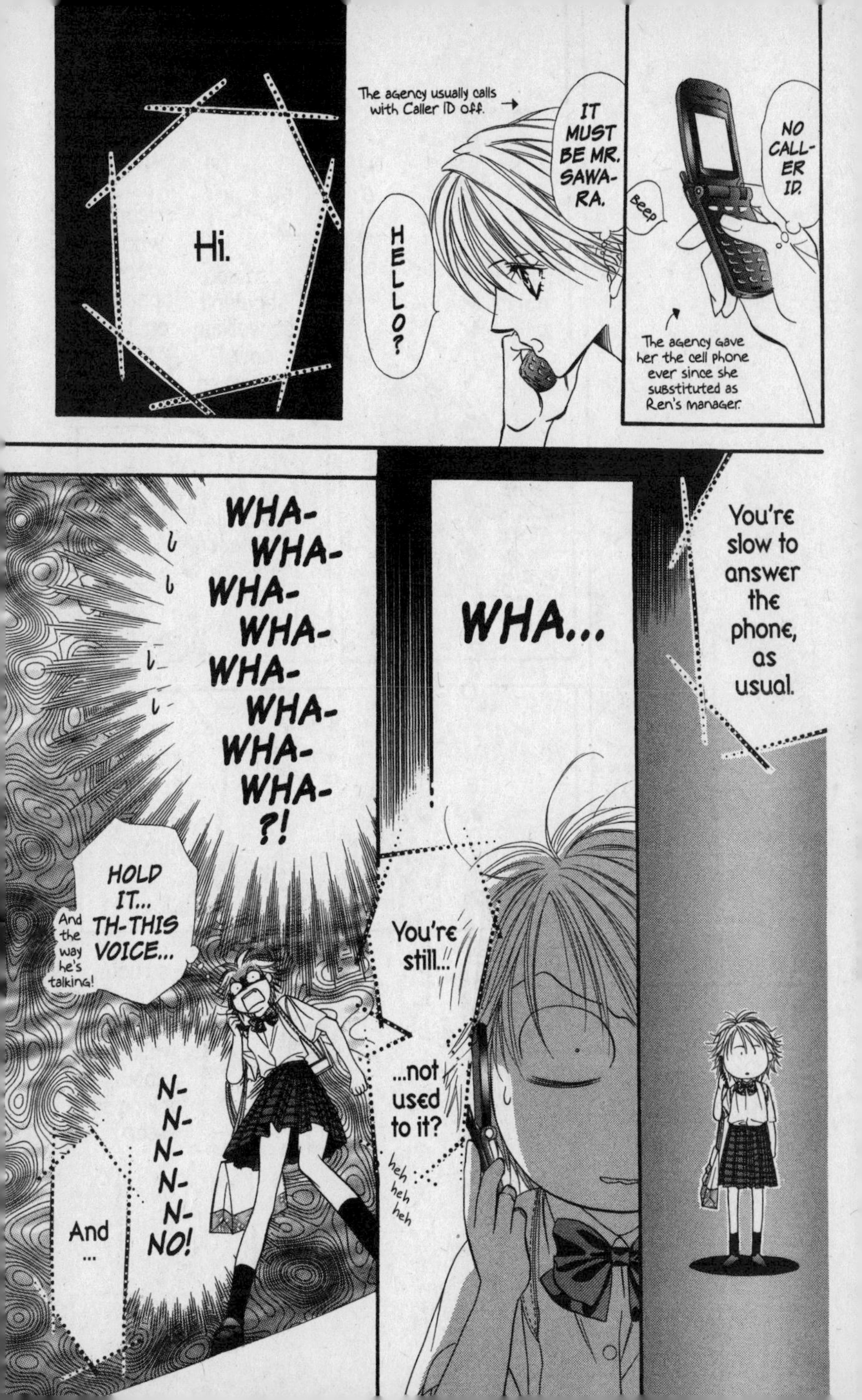
NO CALLER-ID.
Beep
The agency gave her the cell phone ever since she substituted as Ren's manager.
The agency usually calls with Caller ID off.
IT MUST BE MR. SAWARA.
HELLO?
Hi.
You're slow to answer the phone, as usual.
WHA...
You're still...
...not used to it?
heh heh heh
WHA-WHA-WHA-WHA-WHA-WHA-WHA-WHA-?!
HOLD IT... TH-THIS VOICE...
And the way he's talking!
N-N-N-N-N-NO!
And ...

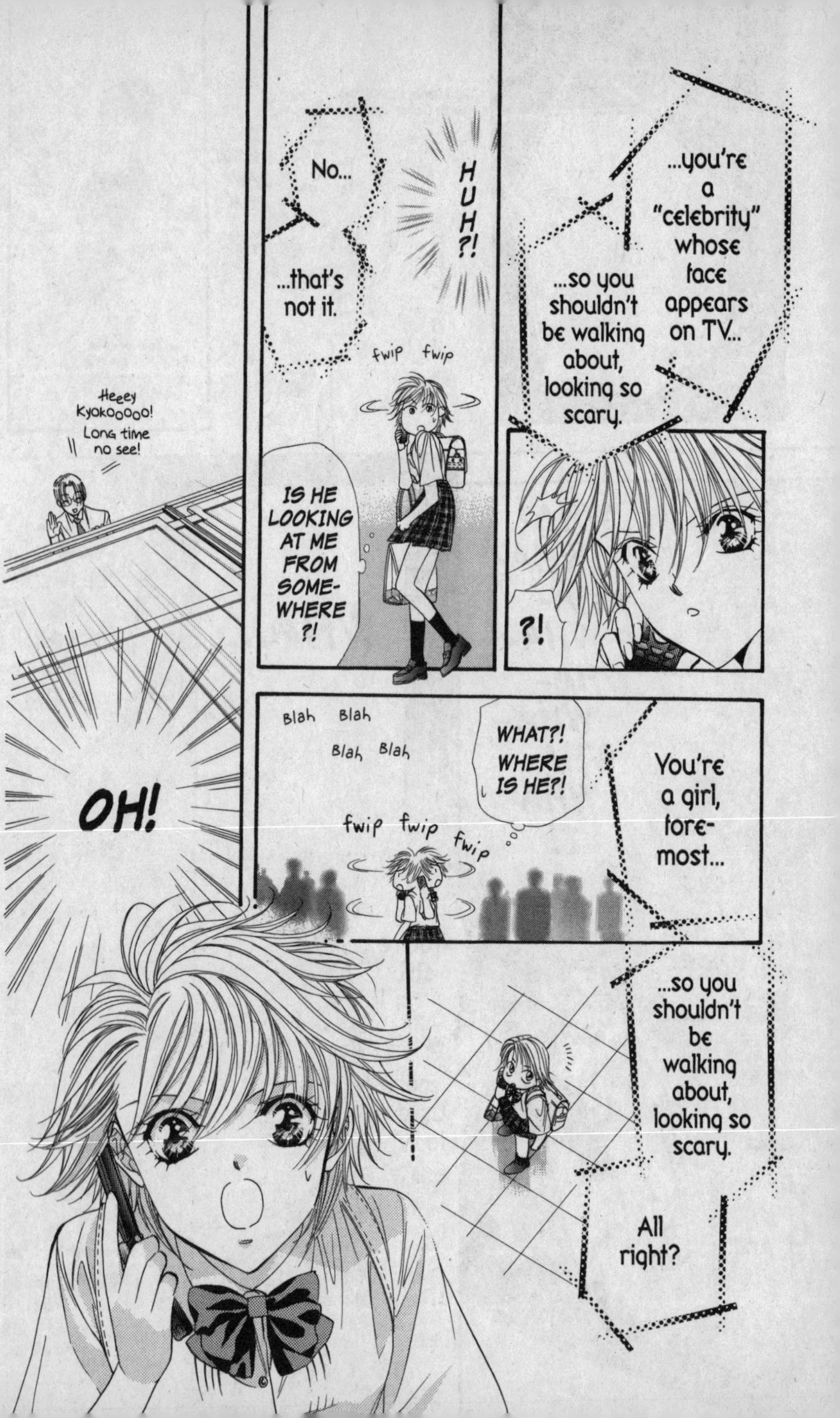

...you're a "celebrity" whose face appears on TV...
...so you shouldn't be walking about, looking so scary.
?!
No...
...that's not it.
HUH?!
fwip fwip
IS HE LOOKING AT ME FROM SOME-WHERE ?!
You're a girl, fore-most...
WHAT?! WHERE IS HE?!
Blah Blah
Blah Blah
fwip fwip fwip
...so you shouldn't be walking about, looking so scary.
All right?
Heeey Kyokoooooo! Long time no see!
OH!

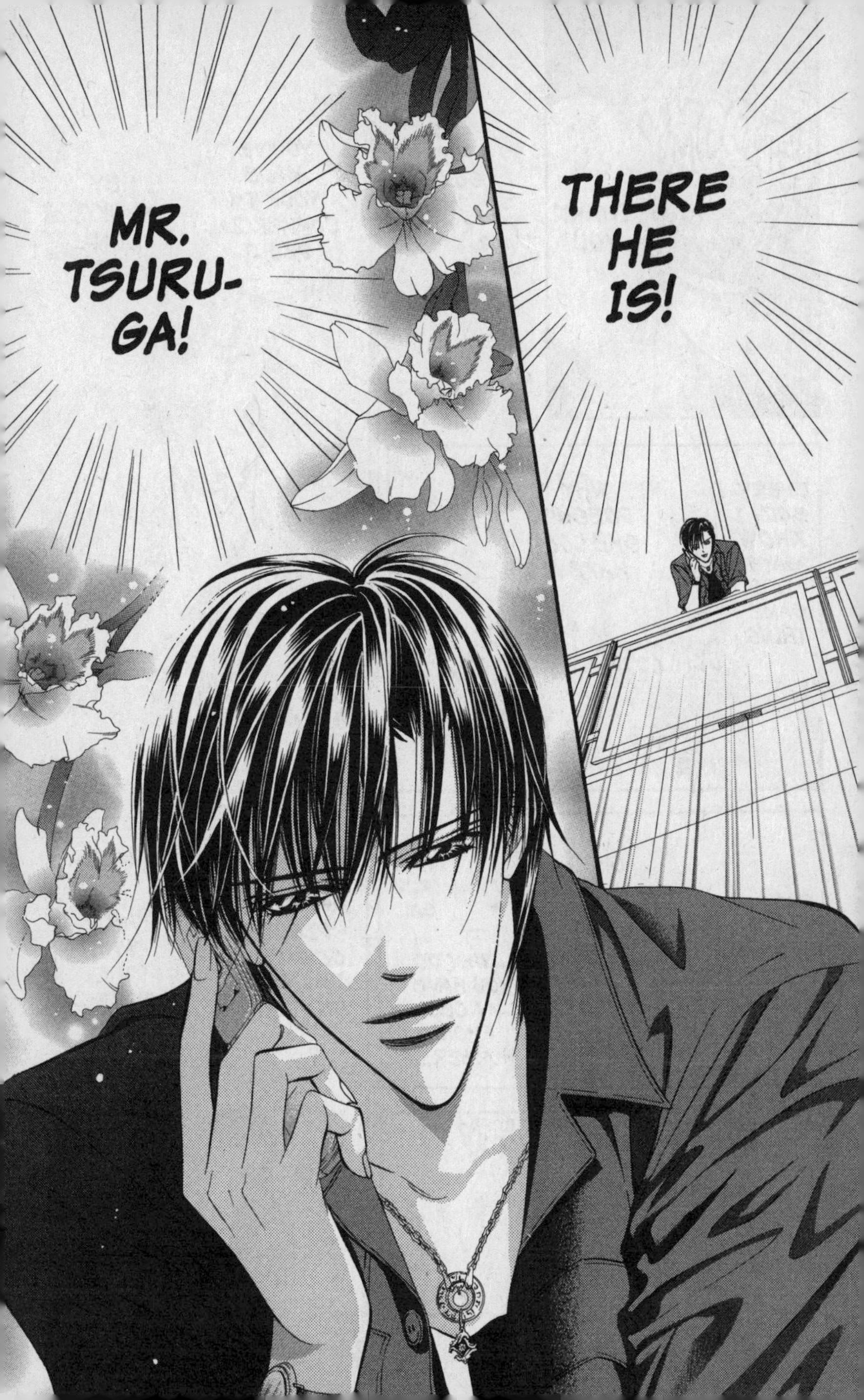
THERE HE IS!
MR. TSURU-GA!

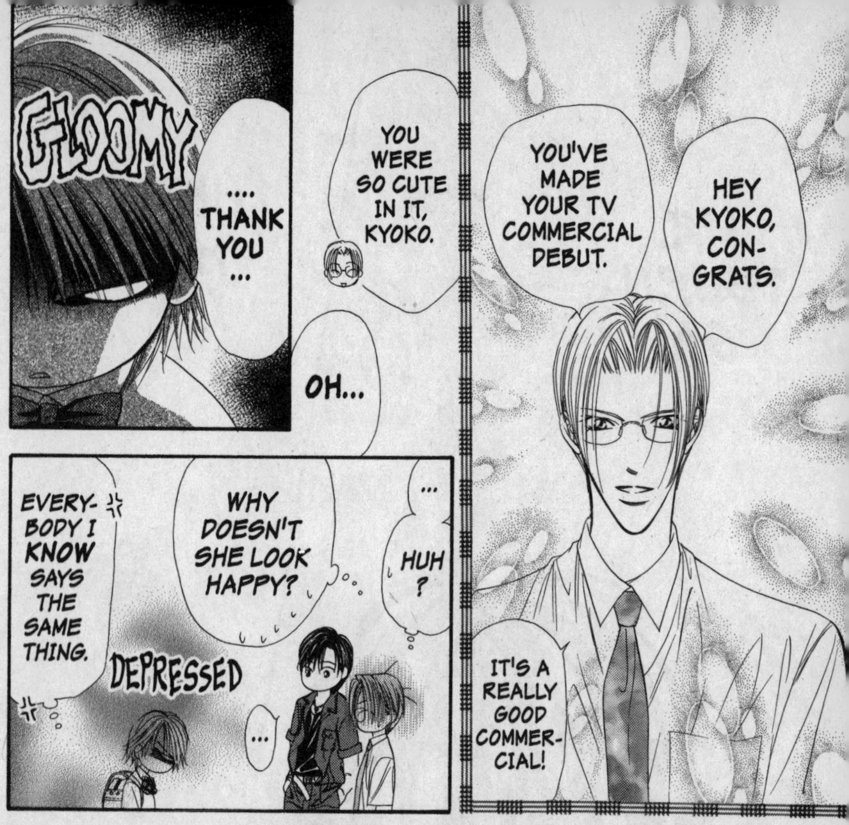
HEY KYOKO, CON-GRATS.
YOU'VE MADE YOUR TV COMMERCIAL DEBUT.
IT'S A REALLY GOOD COMMERCIAL!
YOU WERE SO CUTE IN IT, KYOKO.
OH...
.... THANK YOU ...
GLOOMY
...
HUH ?
WHY DOESN'T SHE LOOK HAPPY?
EVERY-BODY I KNOW SAYS THE SAME THING.
DEPRESSED
...
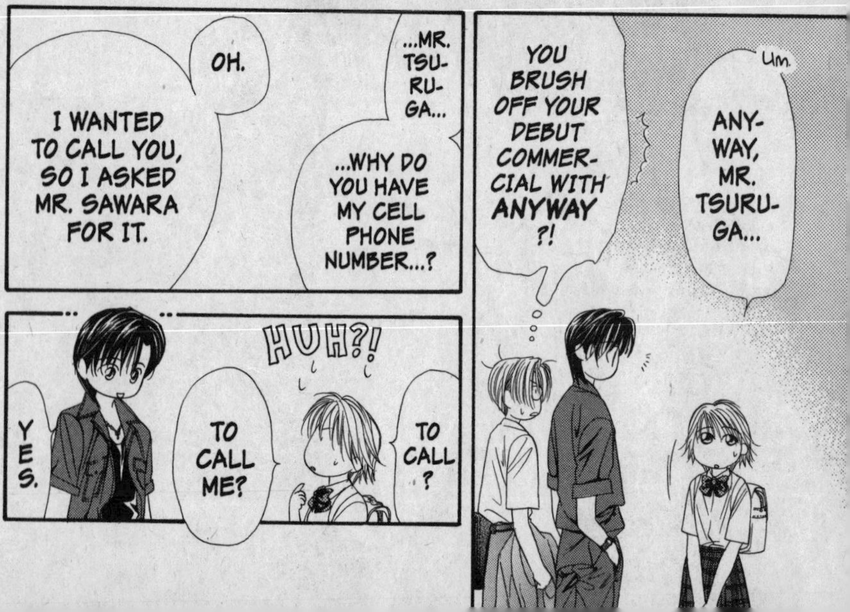
Um.
ANY-WAY, MR. TSURU-GA...
YOU BRUSH OFF YOUR DEBUT COMMER-CIAL WITH ANYWAY ?!
...MR. TSU-RU-GA...
...WHY DO YOU HAVE MY CELL PHONE NUMBER...?
OH.
I WANTED TO CALL YOU, SO I ASKED MR. SAWARA FOR IT.
TO CALL ?
HUH?!
TO CALL ME?
YES.

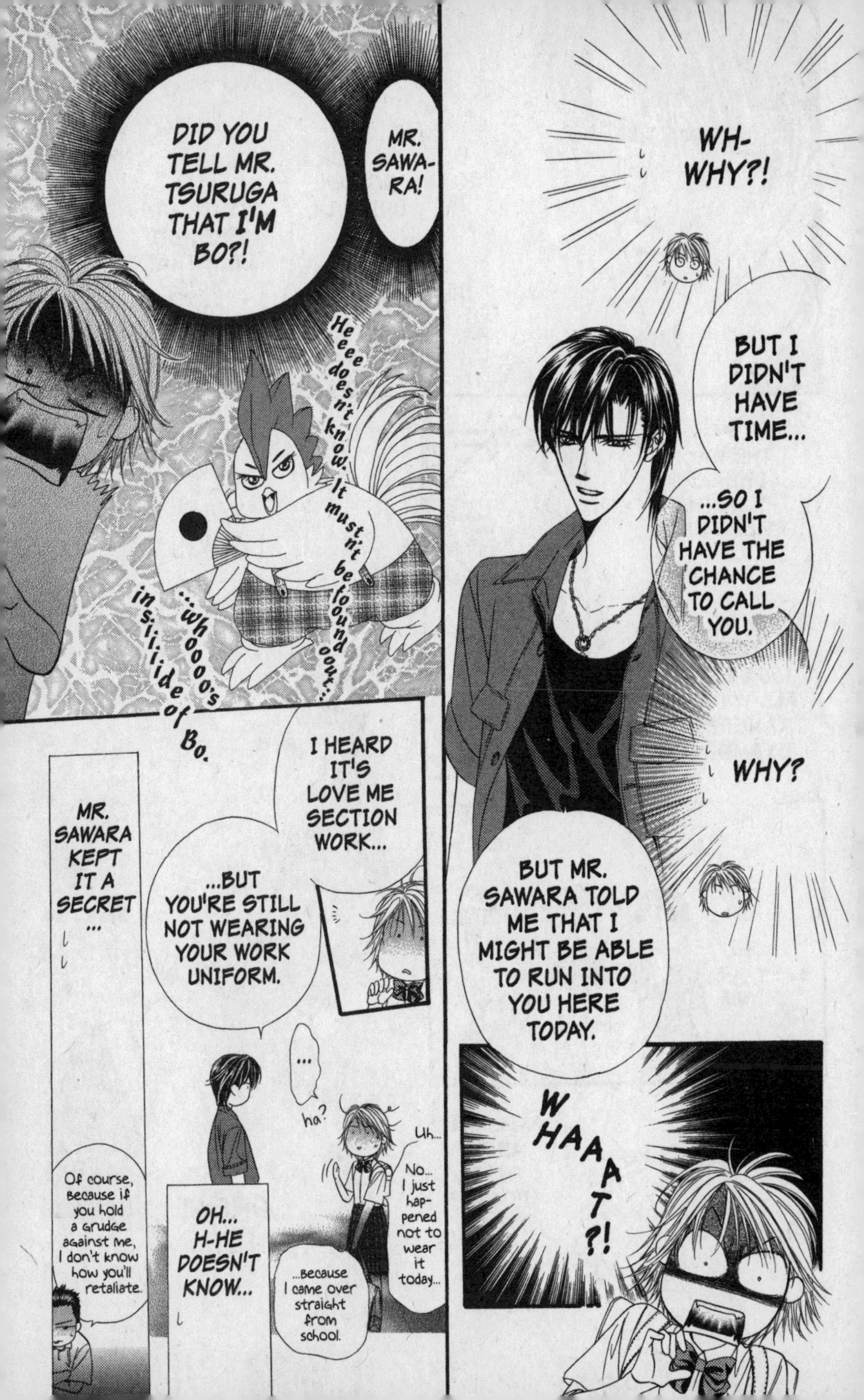
WH-WHY?!
BUT I DIDN'T HAVE TIME...
...SO I DIDN'T HAVE THE CHANCE TO CALL YOU.
WHY?
BUT MR. SAWARA TOLD ME THAT I MIGHT BE ABLE TO RUN INTO YOU HERE TODAY.
WHAAAT?!
MR. SAWARA!
DID YOU TELL MR. TSURUGA THAT I'M BO?!
Heeee doesn't know. It mustn't be found out...
...whoooo's insiiiide of Bo.
I HEARD IT'S LOVE ME SECTION WORK...
...BUT YOU'RE STILL NOT WEARING YOUR WORK UNIFORM.
MR. SAWARA KEPT IT A SECRET...
...
ha?
Uh...
No... I just happened not to wear it today...
...Because I came over straight from school.
OH... H-HE DOESN'T KNOW...
Of course, because if you hold a grudge against me, I don't know how you'll retaliate.

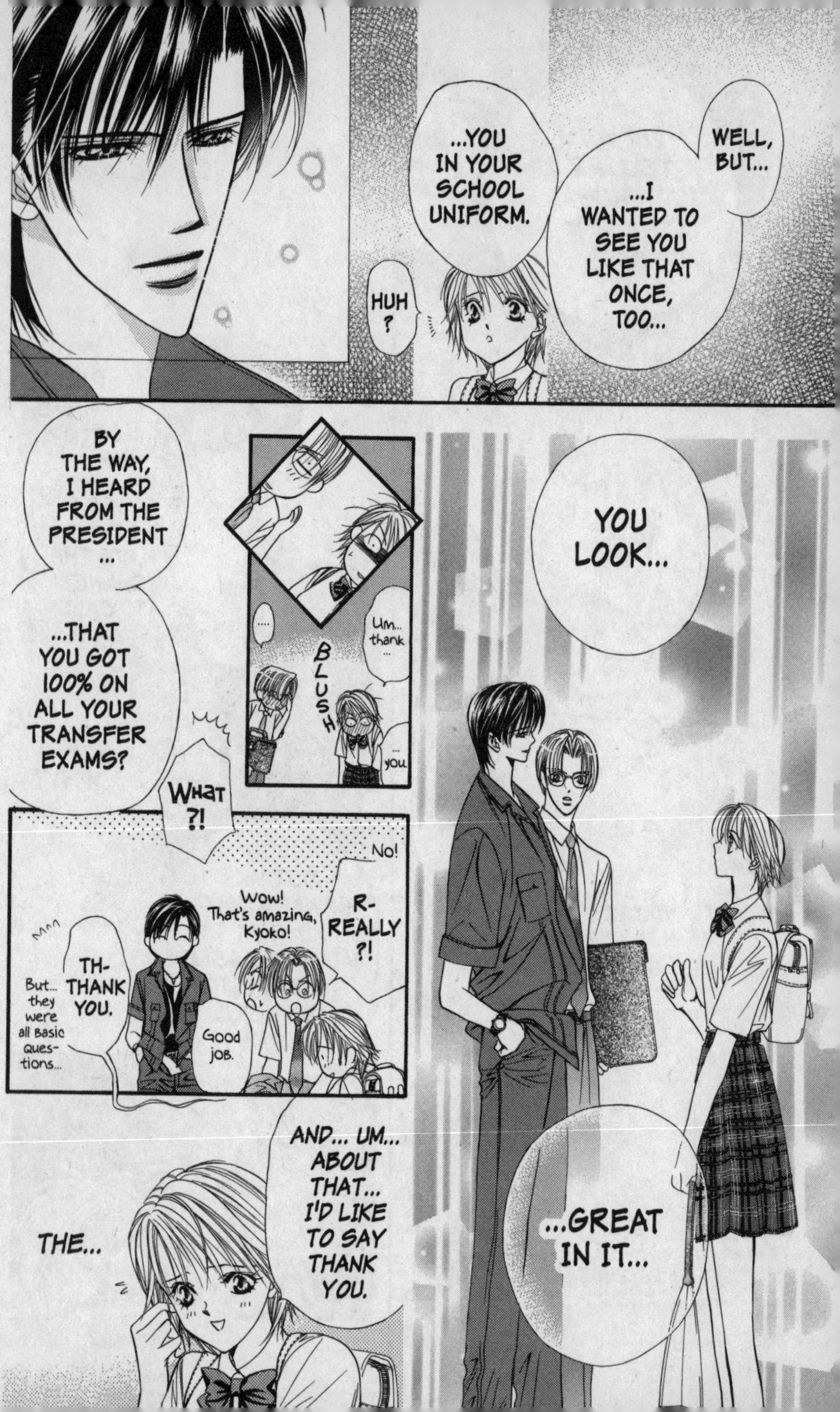
WELL, BUT...
...I WANTED TO SEE YOU LIKE THAT ONCE, TOO...
...YOU IN YOUR SCHOOL UNIFORM.
HUH?
YOU LOOK...
...GREAT IN IT...
....
Um... thank ... you.
BLUSH
BY THE WAY, I HEARD FROM THE PRESIDENT ...
...THAT YOU GOT 100% ON ALL YOUR TRANSFER EXAMS?
WHAT ?!
No!
R-REALLY ?!
Wow! That's amazing, Kyoko!
TH-THANK YOU.
Good job.
But... they were all basic questions...
AND... UM... ABOUT THAT... I'D LIKE TO SAY THANK YOU.
THE...

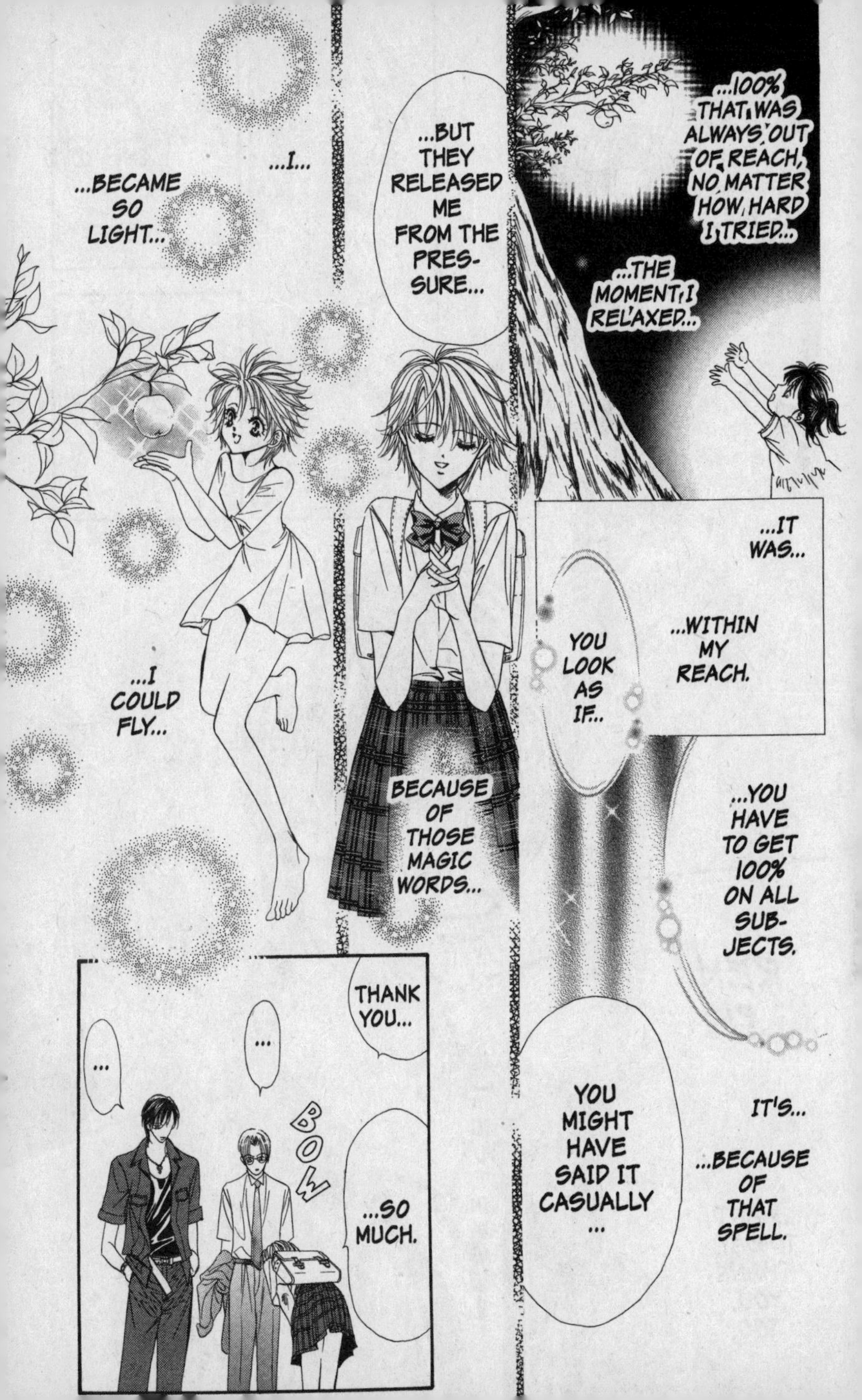
...100% THAT WAS ALWAYS OUT OF REACH, NO MATTER HOW HARD I TRIED...
...THE MOMENT I RELAXED...
...IT WAS...
...WITHIN MY REACH.
YOU LOOK AS IF...
...YOU HAVE TO GET 100% ON ALL SUB-JECTS.
YOU MIGHT HAVE SAID IT CASUALLY...
IT'S...
...BECAUSE OF THAT SPELL.
...BUT THEY RELEASED ME FROM THE PRES-SURE...
BECAUSE OF THOSE MAGIC WORDS...
...I...
...BECAME SO LIGHT...
...I COULD FLY...
THANK YOU...
...SO MUCH.
BOW
...
...

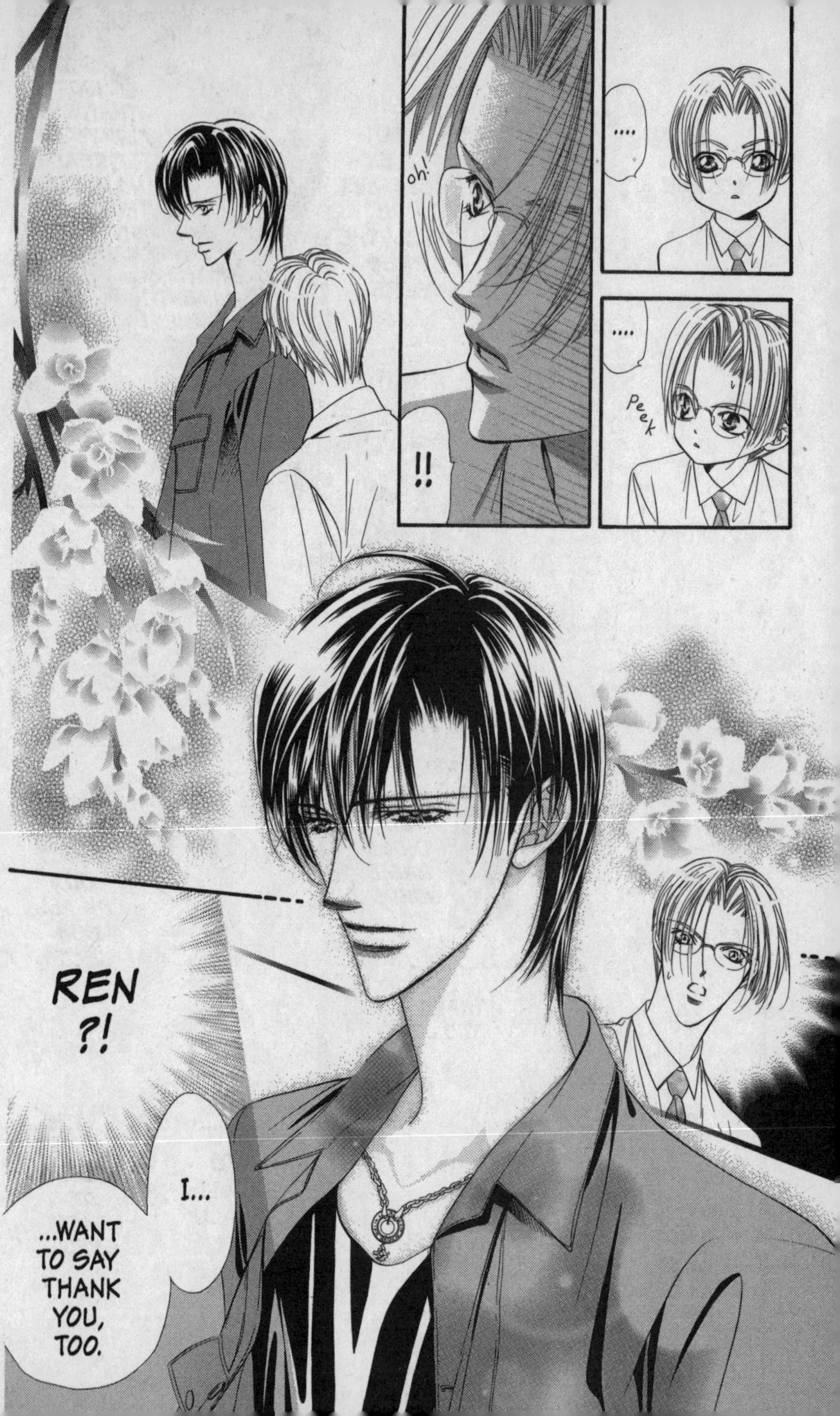
....
....
Peek
oh!
!!
REN ?!
I...
...WANT TO SAY THANK YOU, TOO.

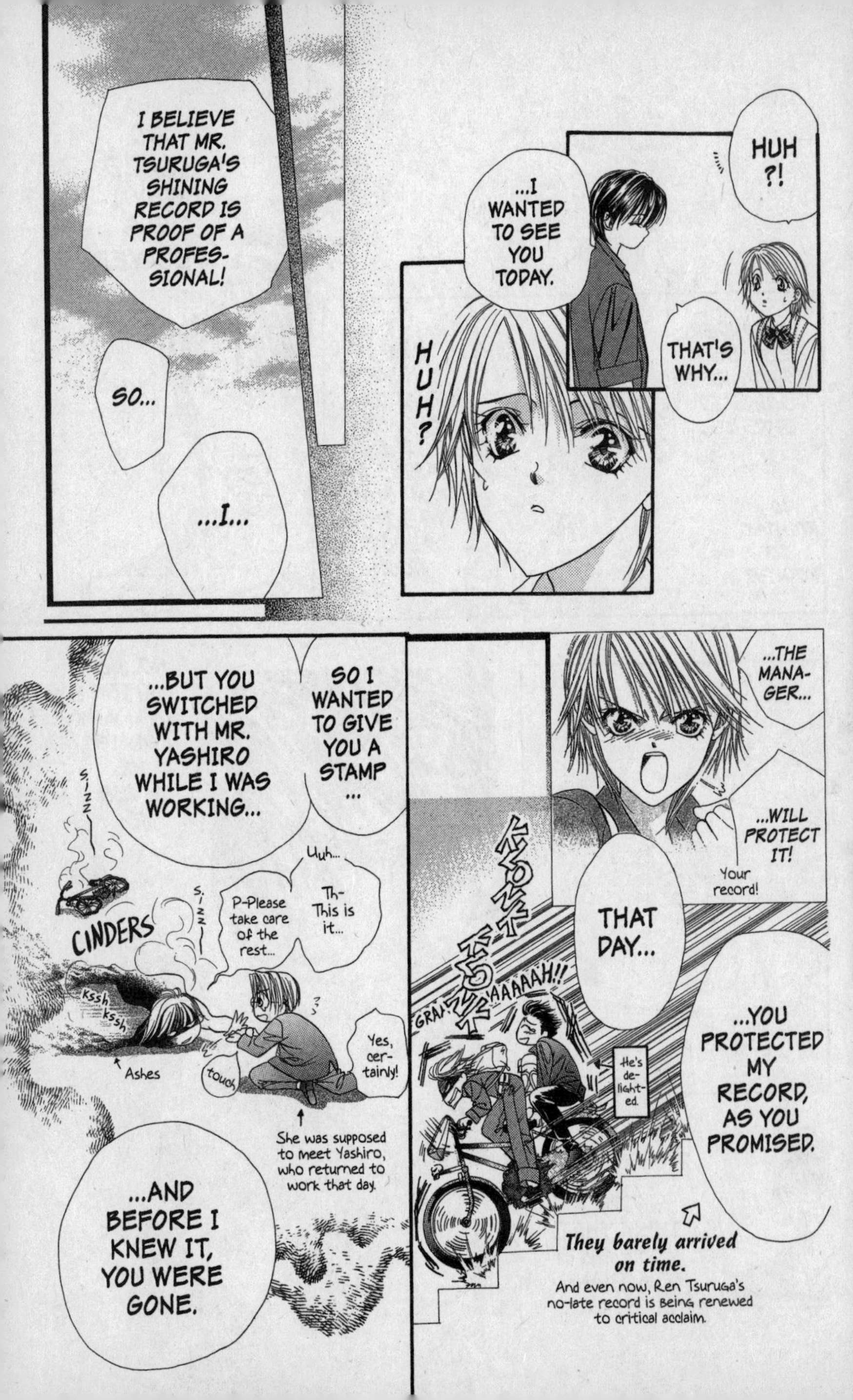
HUH ?!
...I WANTED TO SEE YOU TODAY.
THAT'S WHY...
HUH?
I BELIEVE THAT MR. TSURUGA'S SHINING RECORD IS PROOF OF A PROFES-SIONAL!
SO...
...I...
...THE MANA-GER...
...WILL PROTECT IT!
Your record!
THAT DAY...
KLONK
GRA
AAAAAH!!
He's de-light-ed.
...YOU PROTECTED MY RECORD, AS YOU PROMISED.
They barely arrived on time.
And even now, Ren Tsuruga's no-late record is being renewed to critical acclaim.
SO I WANTED TO GIVE YOU A STAMP ...
...BUT YOU SWITCHED WITH MR. YASHIRO WHILE I WAS WORKING...
Uuh...
Th-This is it...
P-Please take care of the rest...
SIZZ
SIZZ
CINDERS
kssh kssh
Ashes
touch
Yes, cer-tainly!
She was supposed to meet Yashiro, who returned to work that day.
...AND BEFORE I KNEW IT, YOU WERE GONE.

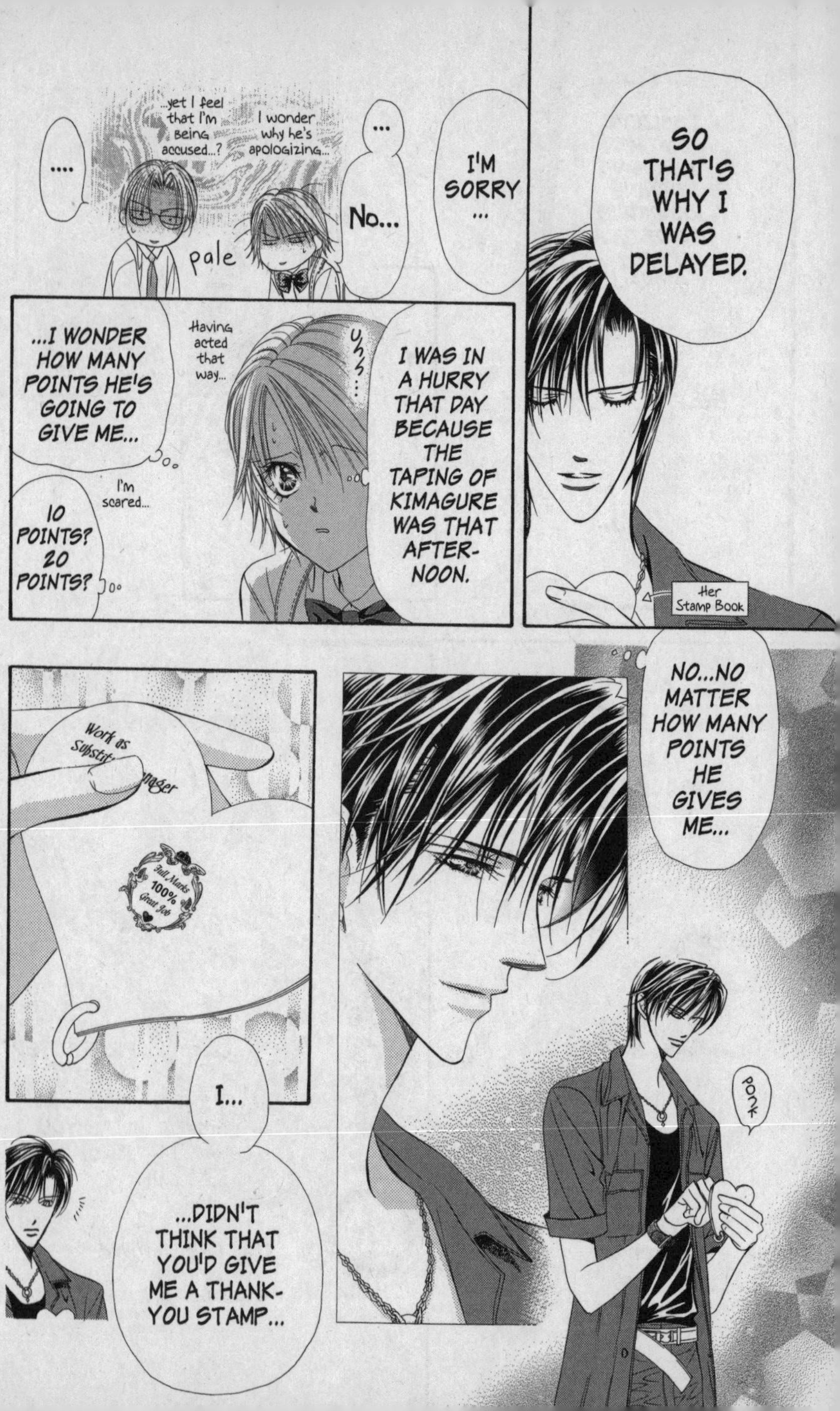
SO THAT'S WHY I WAS DELAYED.
Her Stamp Book
I'M SORRY ...
No...
...
I wonder why he's apologizing...
...yet I feel that I'm being accused...?
....
pale
I WAS IN A HURRY THAT DAY BECAUSE THE TAPING OF KIMAGURE WAS THAT AFTER-NOON.
Having acted that way...
...I WONDER HOW MANY POINTS HE'S GOING TO GIVE ME...
I'm scared...
10 POINTS? 20 POINTS?
NO...NO MATTER HOW MANY POINTS HE GIVES ME...
PONK
I...
...DIDN'T THINK THAT YOU'D GIVE ME A THANK-YOU STAMP...
Work as
Full Marks 100% Great Job

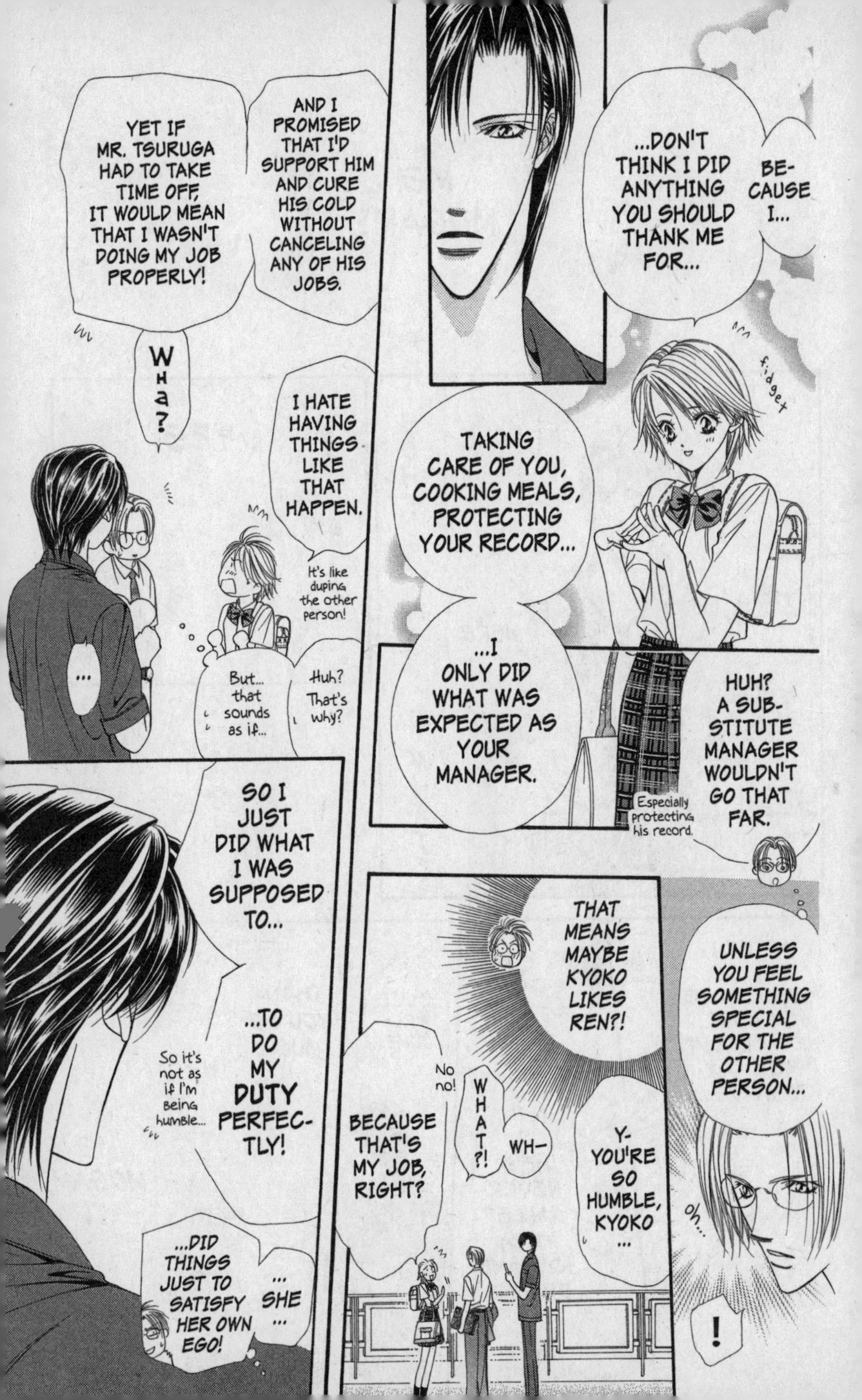
BE-CAUSE I...
...DON'T THINK I DID ANYTHING YOU SHOULD THANK ME FOR...
fidget
TAKING CARE OF YOU, COOKING MEALS, PROTECTING YOUR RECORD...
...I ONLY DID WHAT WAS EXPECTED AS YOUR MANAGER.
HUH? A SUB-STITUTE MANAGER WOULDN'T GO THAT FAR.
Especially protecting his record.
AND I PROMISED THAT I'D SUPPORT HIM AND CURE HIS COLD WITHOUT CANCELING ANY OF HIS JOBS.
YET IF MR. TSURUGA HAD TO TAKE TIME OFF, IT WOULD MEAN THAT I WASN'T DOING MY JOB PROPERLY!
Wha?
I HATE HAVING THINGS LIKE THAT HAPPEN.
It's like duping the other person!
Huh? That's why?
But... that sounds as if...
...
UNLESS YOU FEEL SOMETHING SPECIAL FOR THE OTHER PERSON...
THAT MEANS MAYBE KYOKO LIKES REN?!
oh...
!
Y-YOU'RE SO HUMBLE, KYOKO...
WH-
WHAT?!
No no!
BECAUSE THAT'S MY JOB, RIGHT?
SO I JUST DID WHAT I WAS SUPPOSED TO...
...TO DO MY DUTY PERFECTLY!
So it's not as if I'm being humble...
...SHE...
...DID THINGS JUST TO SATISFY HER OWN EGO!

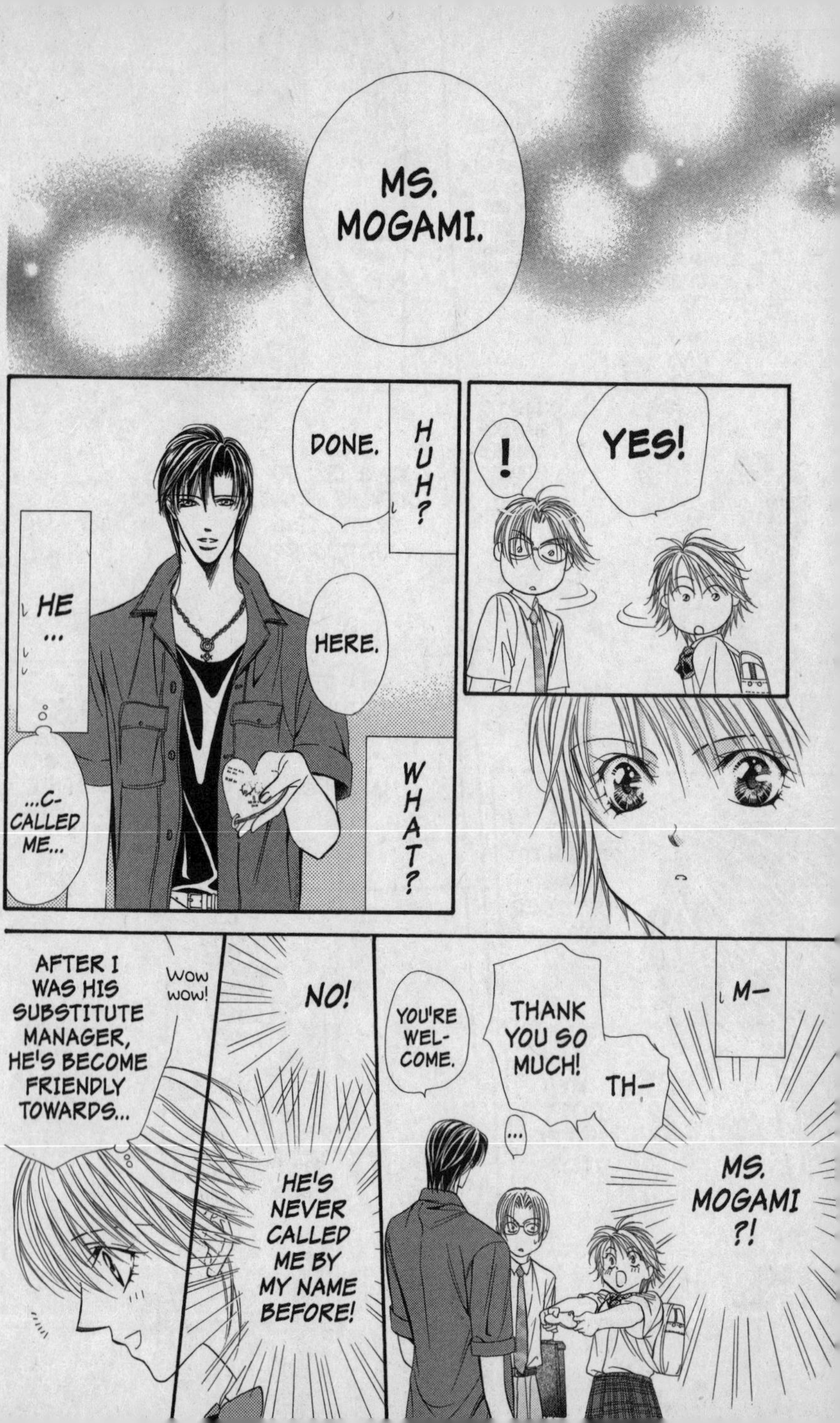
MS. MOGAMI.
YES!
!
HUH?
DONE.
HERE.
WHAT?
HE ...
...C-CALLED ME...
M-
TH-
THANK YOU SO MUCH!
YOU'RE WEL-COME.
...
MS. MOGAMI?!
NO!
WOW WOW!
AFTER I WAS HIS SUBSTITUTE MANAGER, HE'S BECOME FRIENDLY TOWARDS...
HE'S NEVER CALLED ME BY MY NAME BEFORE!

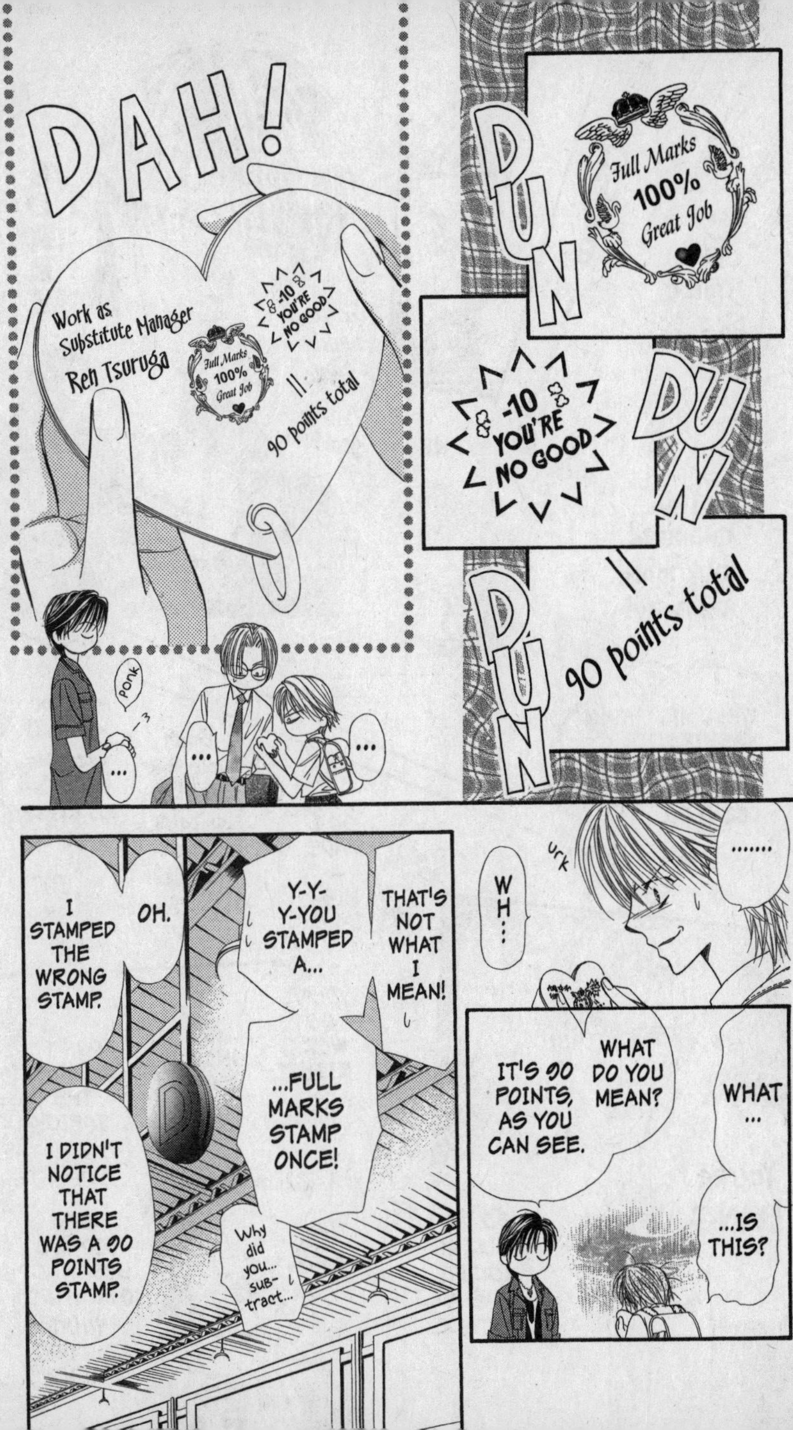
Full Marks 100% Great Job
DUN
-10 YOU'RE NO GOOD
DUN
= 90 points total
DUN
DAH!
Work as Substitute Manager Ren Tsuruga
Full Marks 100% Great Job
-10 YOU'RE NO GOOD
= 90 points total
ponk
...
...
...
....
urk
WH...
WHAT ...
...IS THIS?
WHAT DO YOU MEAN?
IT'S 90 POINTS, AS YOU CAN SEE.
THAT'S NOT WHAT I MEAN!
Y-Y-Y-YOU STAMPED A...
...FULL MARKS STAMP ONCE!
OH.
I STAMPED THE WRONG STAMP.
Why did you... sub-tract...
I DIDN'T NOTICE THAT THERE WAS A 90 POINTS STAMP.

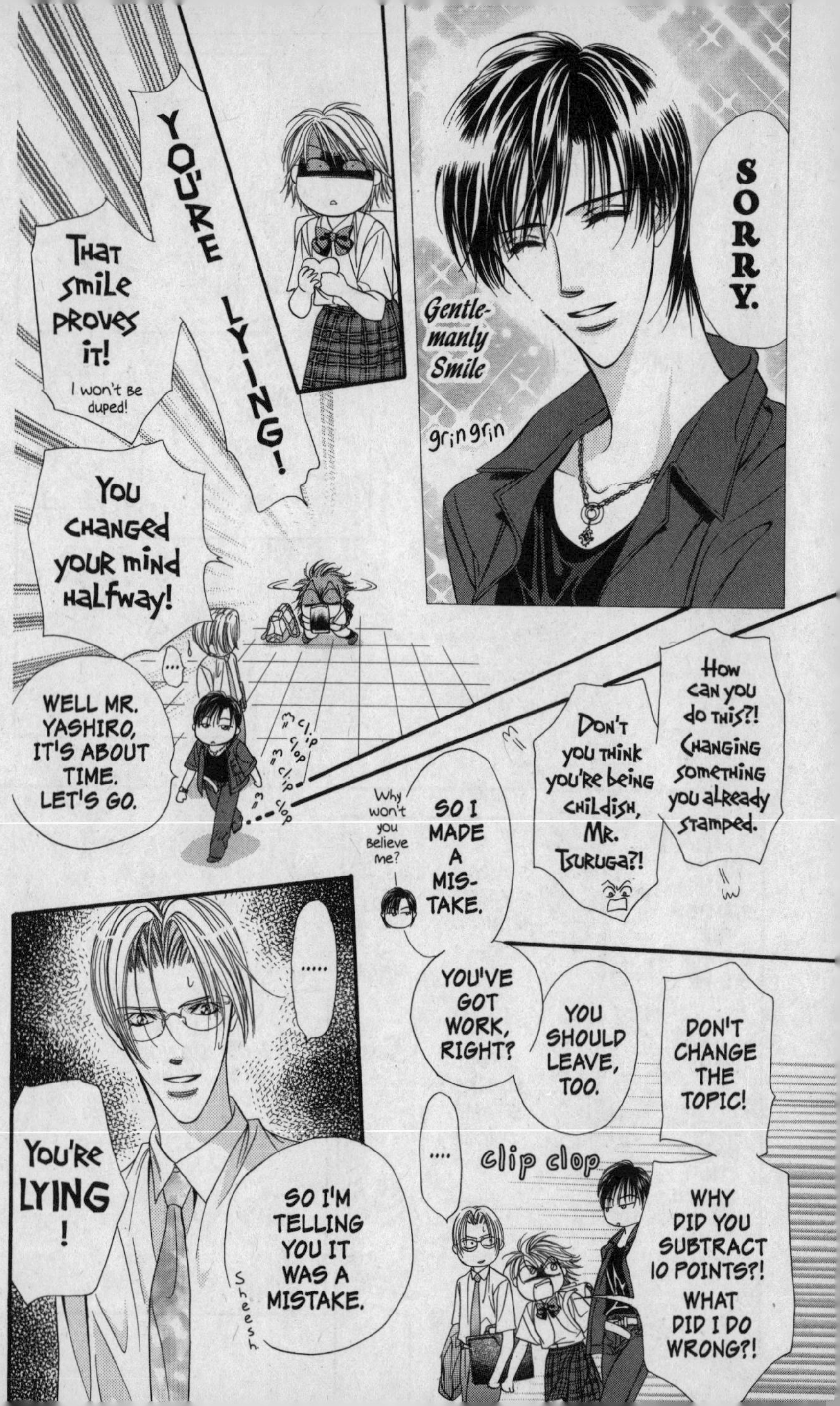
SORRY.
Gentle-manly Smile
grin grin
YOU'RE LYING!
THAT smile PROVES iT!
I won't be duped!
YOU CHANGED YOUR mind HALFWAY!
....
WELL MR. YASHIRO, IT'S ABOUT TIME. LET'S GO.
clip clop clip clop
HOW can you do THIS?! CHANGING SOMETHING you already STAMPED.
DON'T you THINK you're being CHILDISH, MR. TSURUGA?!
SO I MADE A MIS-TAKE.
Why won't you Believe me?
DON'T CHANGE THE TOPIC!
YOU SHOULD LEAVE, TOO.
YOU'VE GOT WORK, RIGHT?
WHY DID YOU SUBTRACT 10 POINTS?! WHAT DID I DO WRONG?!
clip clop
....
.....
SO I'M TELLING YOU IT WAS A MISTAKE.
Sheesh.
You're LYING!

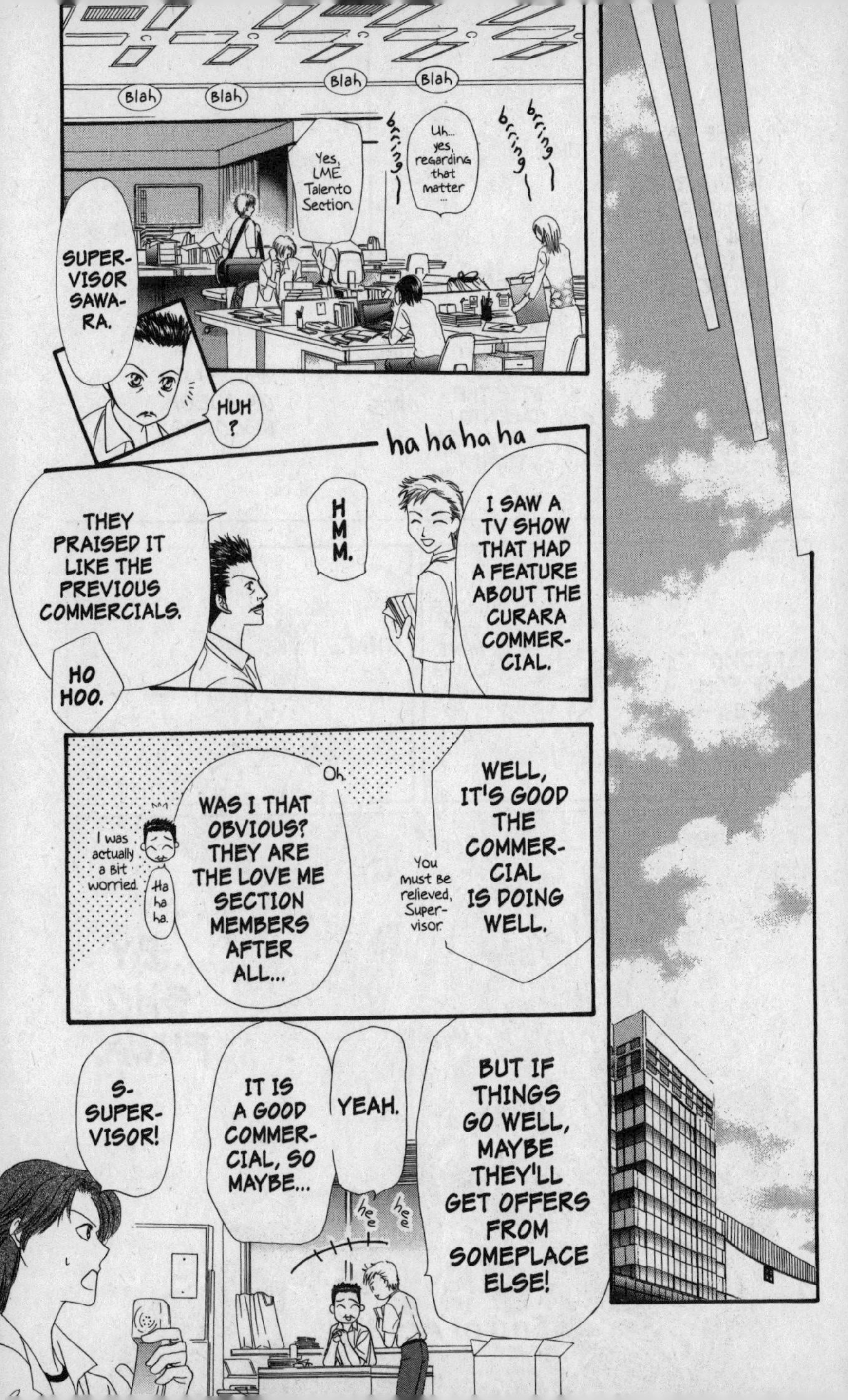
Blah
Blah
Blah
Blah
brring brring
Uh... yes, regarding that matter...
brring
Yes, LME Talento Section
SUPERVISOR SAWARA.
HUH?
ha ha ha ha
I SAW A TV SHOW THAT HAD A FEATURE ABOUT THE CURARA COMMERCIAL.
HMM.
THEY PRAISED IT LIKE THE PREVIOUS COMMERCIALS.
HO HOO.
WELL, IT'S GOOD THE COMMERCIAL IS DOING WELL.
You must be relieved, Supervisor.
Oh.
WAS I THAT OBVIOUS? THEY ARE THE LOVE ME SECTION MEMBERS AFTER ALL...
Ha ha ha.
I was actually a bit worried.
BUT IF THINGS GO WELL, MAYBE THEY'LL GET OFFERS FROM SOMEPLACE ELSE!
YEAH.
IT IS A GOOD COMMERCIAL, SO MAYBE...
hee hee
S-SUPERVISOR!

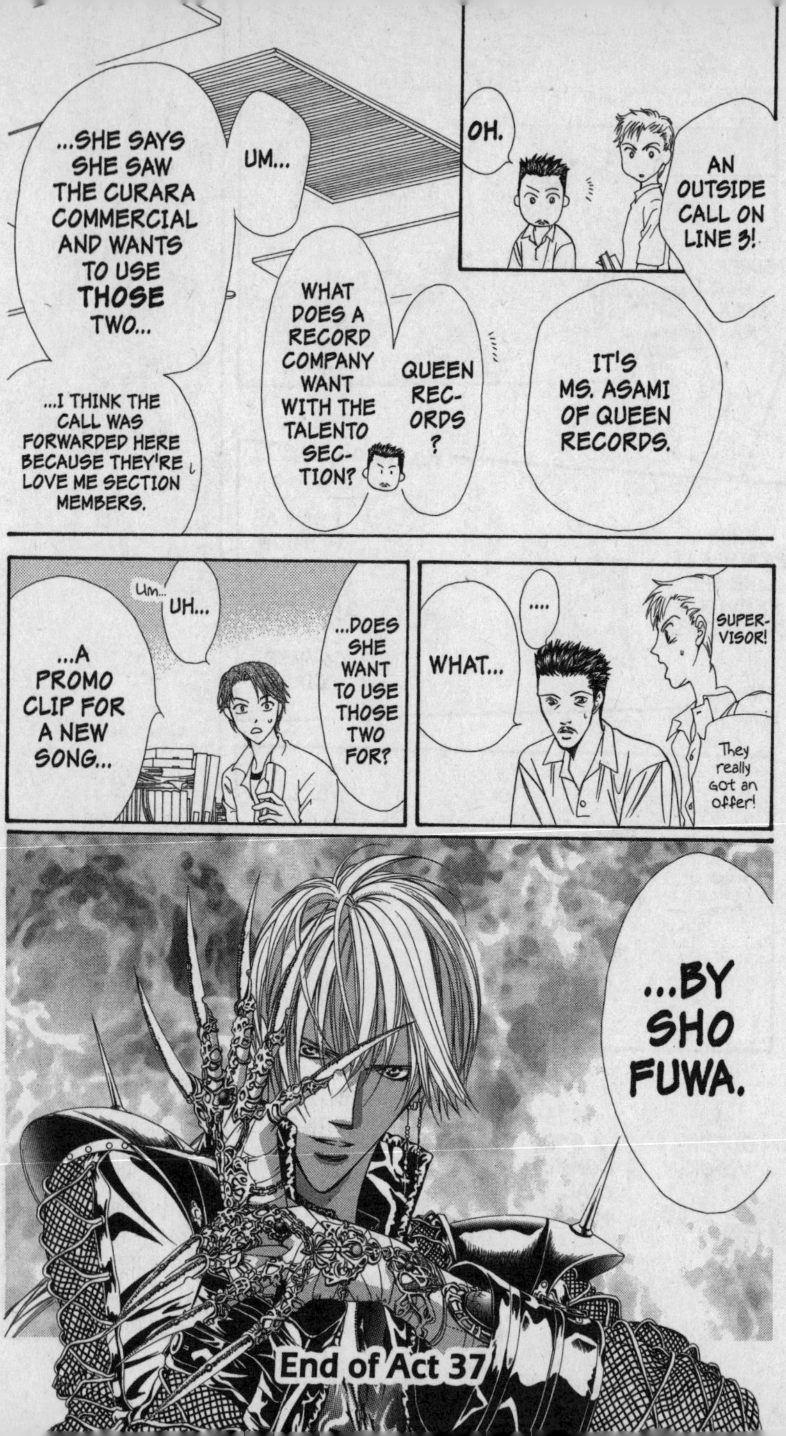
AN OUTSIDE CALL ON LINE 3!
OH.
IT'S MS. ASAMI OF QUEEN RECORDS.
QUEEN RECORDS?
WHAT DOES A RECORD COMPANY WANT WITH THE TALENTO SECTION?
UM...
...SHE SAYS SHE SAW THE CURARA COMMERCIAL AND WANTS TO USE THOSE TWO...
...I THINK THE CALL WAS FORWARDED HERE BECAUSE THEY'RE LOVE ME SECTION MEMBERS.
SUPERVISOR!
....
WHAT...
They really got an offer!
...DOES SHE WANT TO USE THOSE TWO FOR?
Um... UH...
...A PROMO CLIP FOR A NEW SONG...
...BY SHO FUWA.
End of Act 37

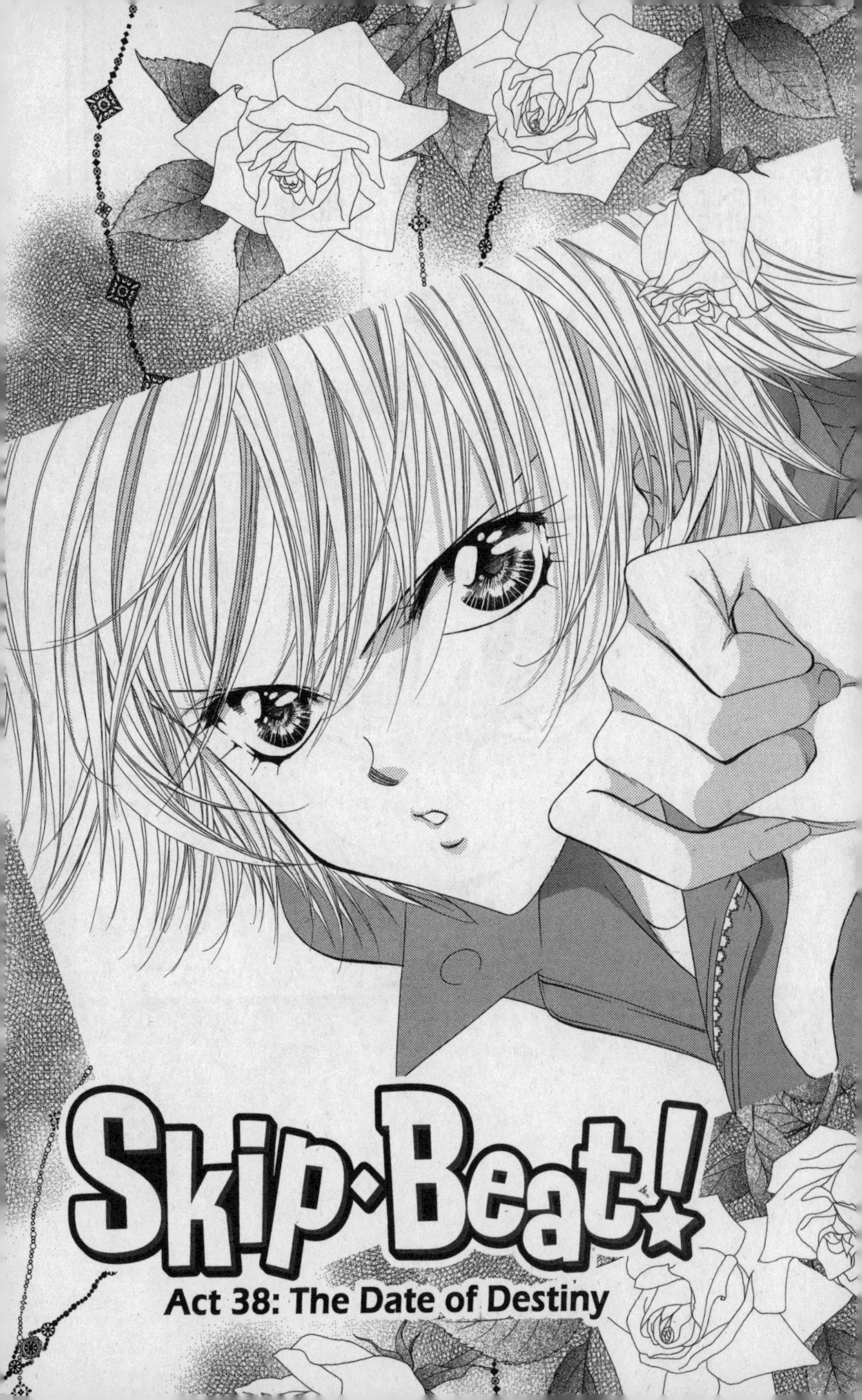
Skip·Beat!
Act 38: The Date of Destiny

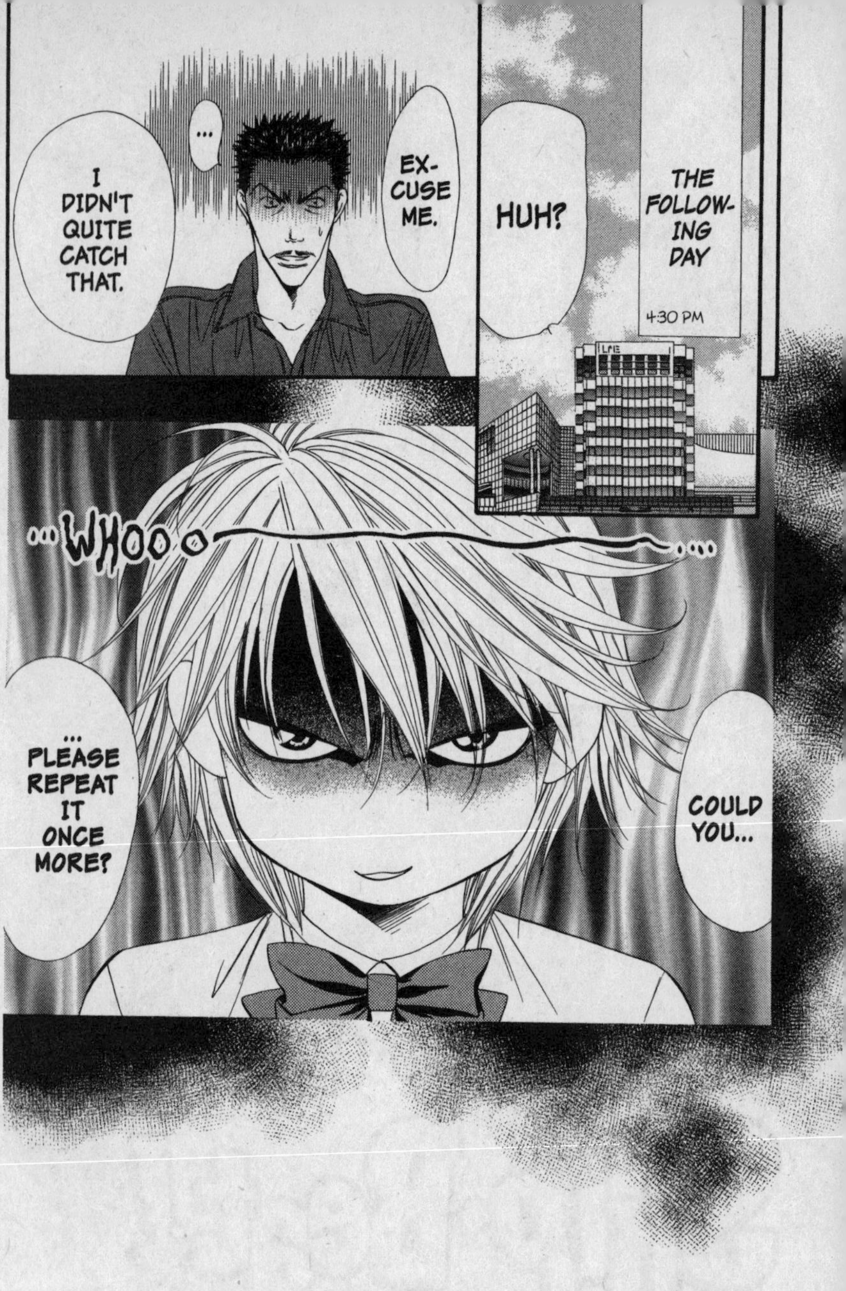
THE FOLLOWING DAY
4:30 PM
HUH?
EX-CUSE ME.
...
I DIDN'T QUITE CATCH THAT.
...WHOO......
COULD YOU...
...PLEASE REPEAT IT ONCE MORE?

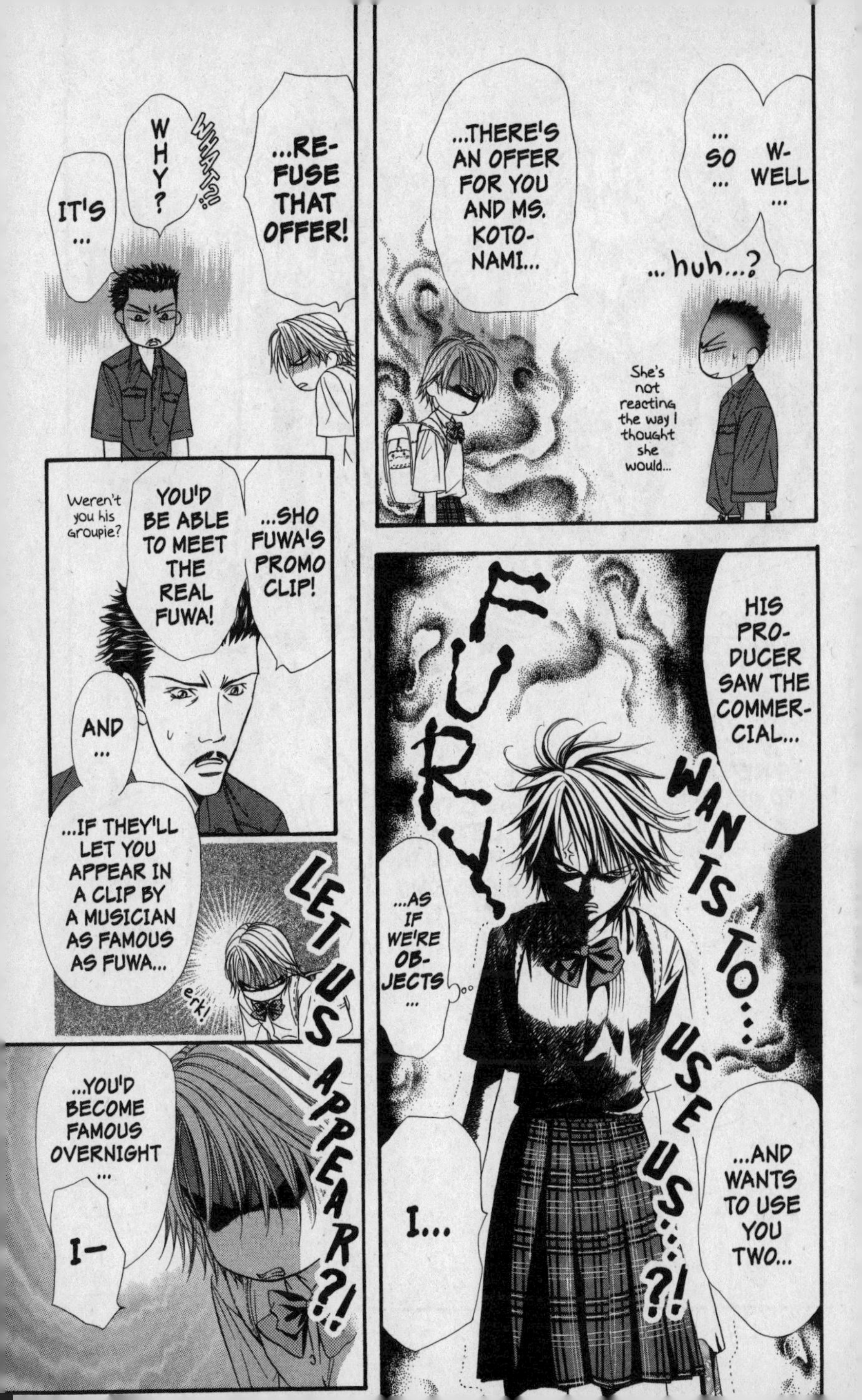

W-WELL...
...SO...
...huh...?
...THERE'S AN OFFER FOR YOU AND MS. KOTO-NAMI...
She's not reacting the way I thought she would...
HIS PRO-DUCER SAW THE COMMER-CIAL...
WANTS TO...
FURY
...AND WANTS TO USE YOU TWO...
USE US...?!
...AS IF WE'RE OB-JECTS...
I...
...RE-FUSE THAT OFFER!
WHAT?!
WHY?
IT'S...
...SHO FUWA'S PROMO CLIP!
YOU'D BE ABLE TO MEET THE REAL FUWA!
Weren't you his groupie?
AND...
...IF THEY'LL LET YOU APPEAR IN A CLIP BY A MUSICIAN AS FAMOUS AS FUWA...
LET US APPEAR?!
erk!
...YOU'D BECOME FAMOUS OVERNIGHT...
I—

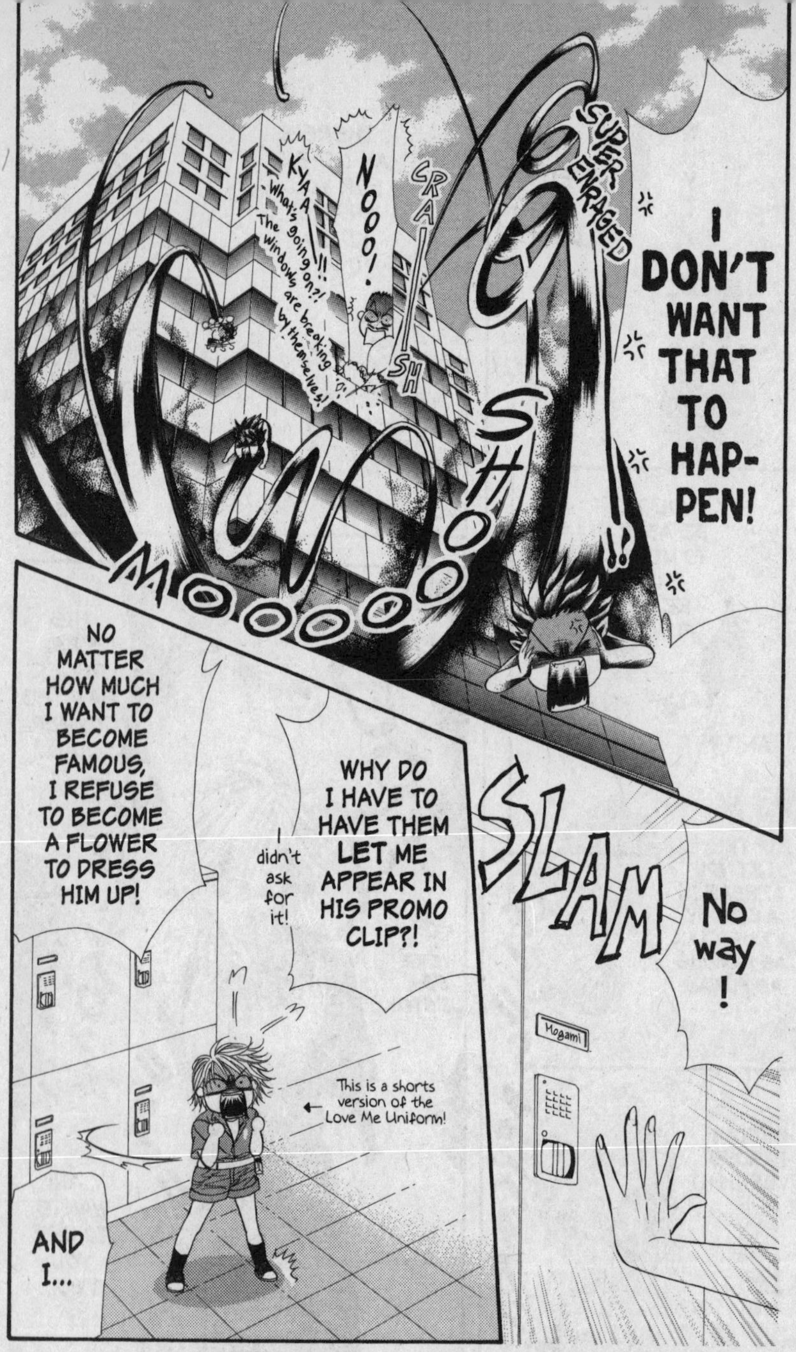
I DON'T WANT THAT TO HAPPEN!
SUPER ENRAGED
CRA-SH
NOOOO!
KYAA!! What's going on?! The windows are breaking by themselves!
SHOO!!
MOOOOO
SLAM
Mogami
No way!
WHY DO I HAVE TO HAVE THEM LET ME APPEAR IN HIS PROMO CLIP?!
I didn't ask for it!
NO MATTER HOW MUCH I WANT TO BECOME FAMOUS, I REFUSE TO BECOME A FLOWER TO DRESS HIM UP!
This is a shorts version of the Love Me Uniform!
AND I...

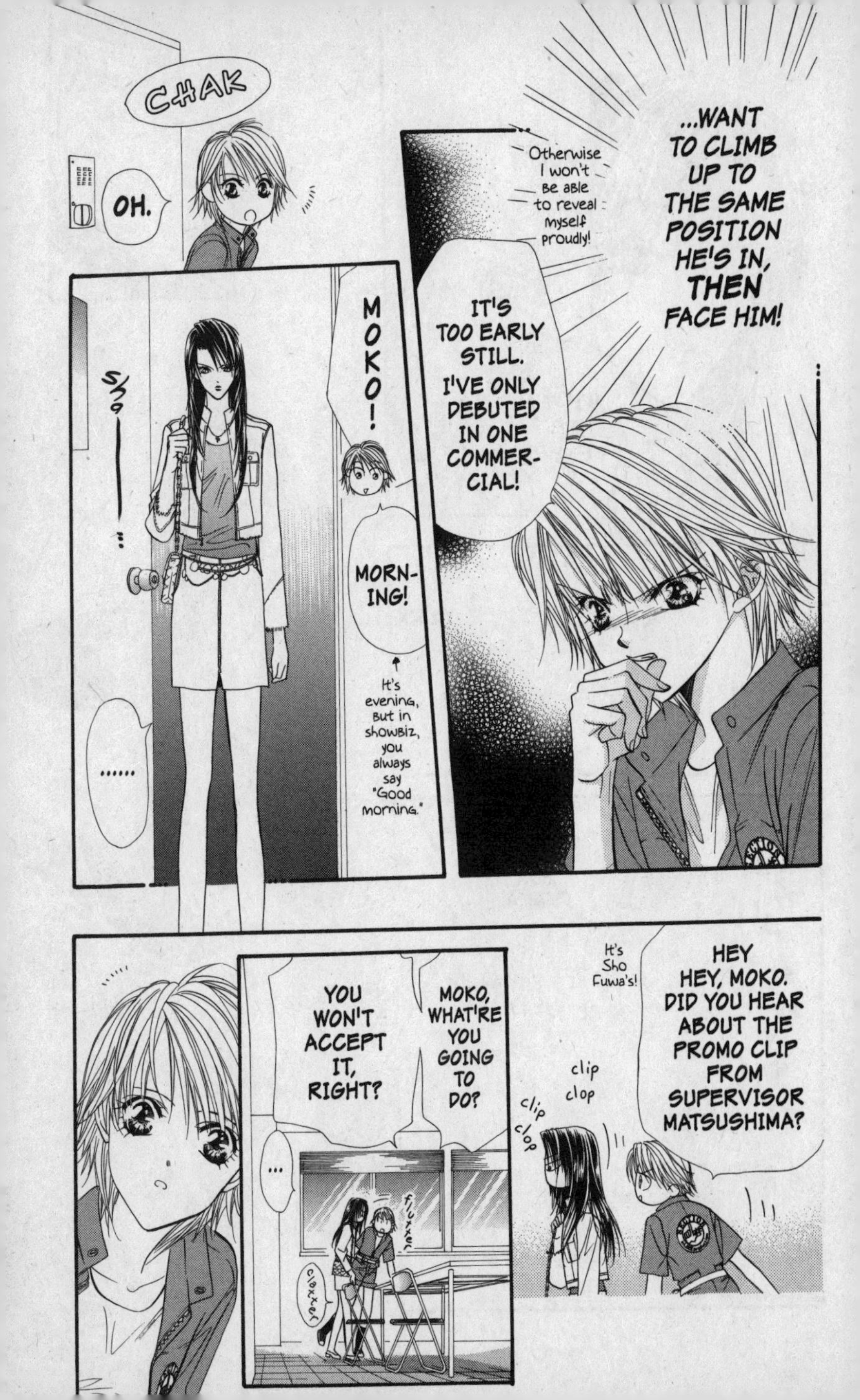
...WANT TO CLIMB UP TO THE SAME POSITION HE'S IN, THEN FACE HIM!
Otherwise I won't be able to reveal myself proudly!
IT'S TOO EARLY STILL. I'VE ONLY DEBUTED IN ONE COMMERCIAL!
CHAK
OH.
MOKO!
MORNING!
It's evening, but in showbiz, you always say "Good morning."
......
HEY HEY, MOKO. DID YOU HEAR ABOUT THE PROMO CLIP FROM SUPERVISOR MATSUSHIMA?
It's Sho Fuwa's!
clip clop
clip clop
MOKO, WHAT'RE YOU GOING TO DO?
YOU WON'T ACCEPT IT, RIGHT?
...
fluxxer
cloxxer

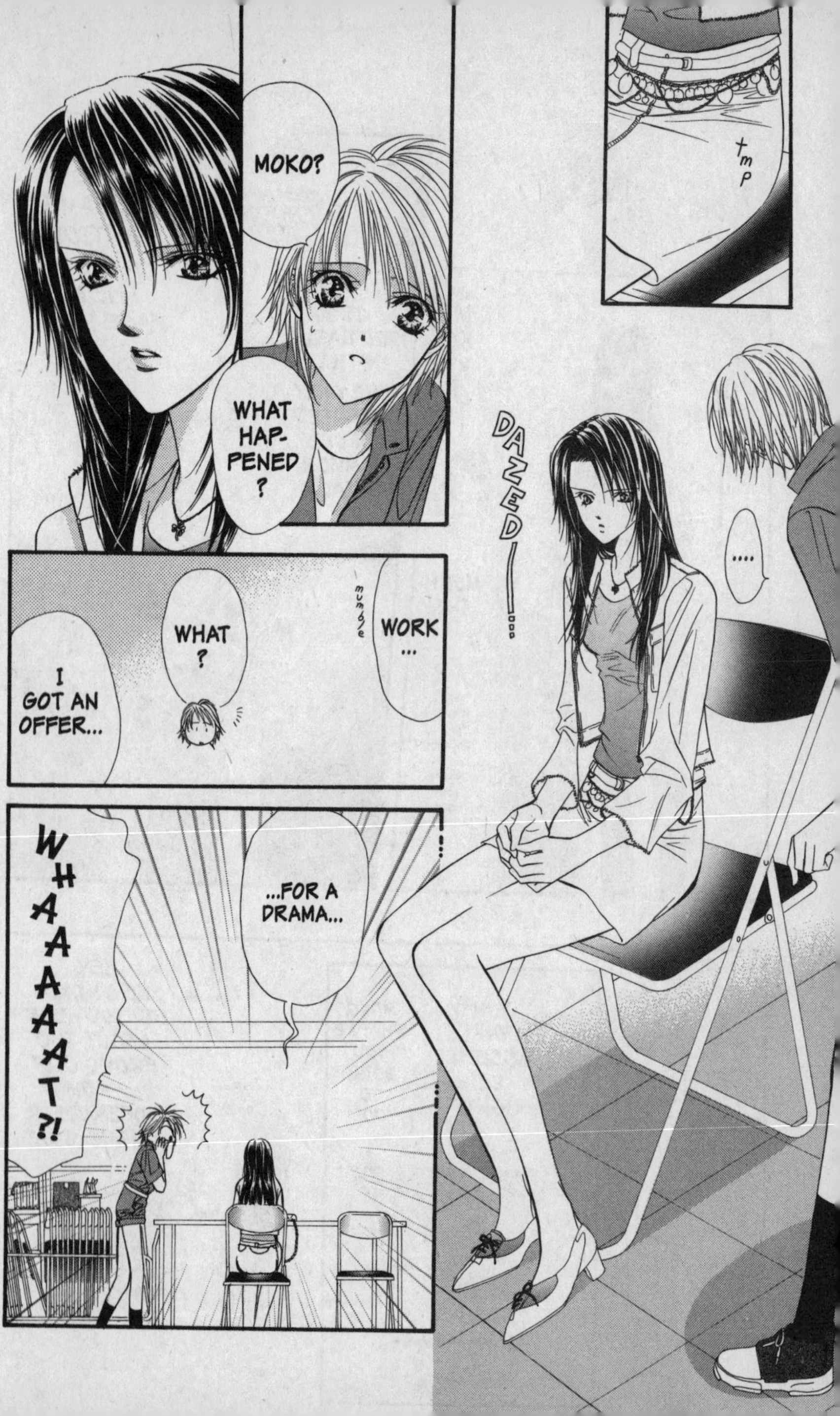
tmp
DAZED
....
MOKO?
WHAT HAP-PENED?
WORK...
mumble
WHAT?
I GOT AN OFFER...
...FOR A DRAMA...
WHAAAAAT?!

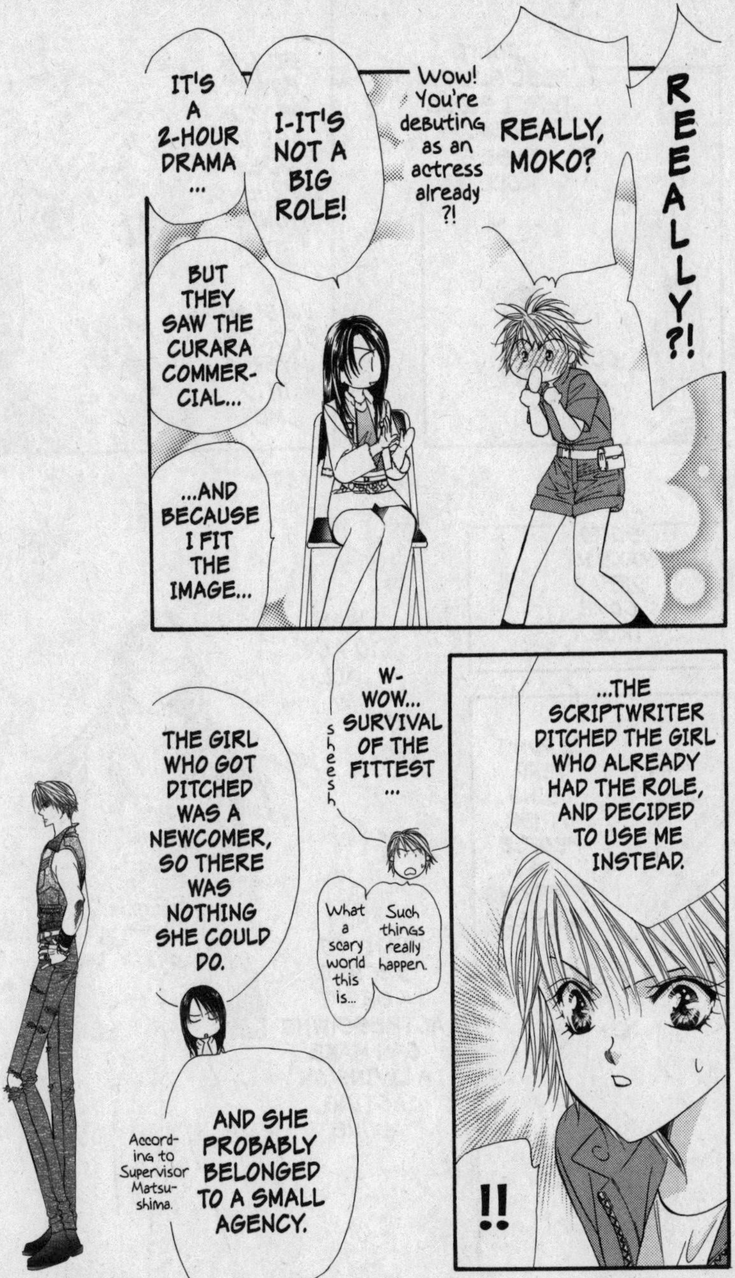
REEALLY?!
REALLY, MOKO?
Wow! You're debuting as an actress already?!
I-IT'S NOT A BIG ROLE!
IT'S A 2-HOUR DRAMA...
BUT THEY SAW THE CURARA COMMERCIAL...
...AND BECAUSE I FIT THE IMAGE...
...THE SCRIPTWRITER DITCHED THE GIRL WHO ALREADY HAD THE ROLE, AND DECIDED TO USE ME INSTEAD.
!!
W-WOW... SURVIVAL OF THE FITTEST...
sheesh
Such things really happen.
What a scary world this is...
THE GIRL WHO GOT DITCHED WAS A NEWCOMER, SO THERE WAS NOTHING SHE COULD DO.
AND SHE PROBABLY BELONGED TO A SMALL AGENCY.
According to Supervisor Matsushima.

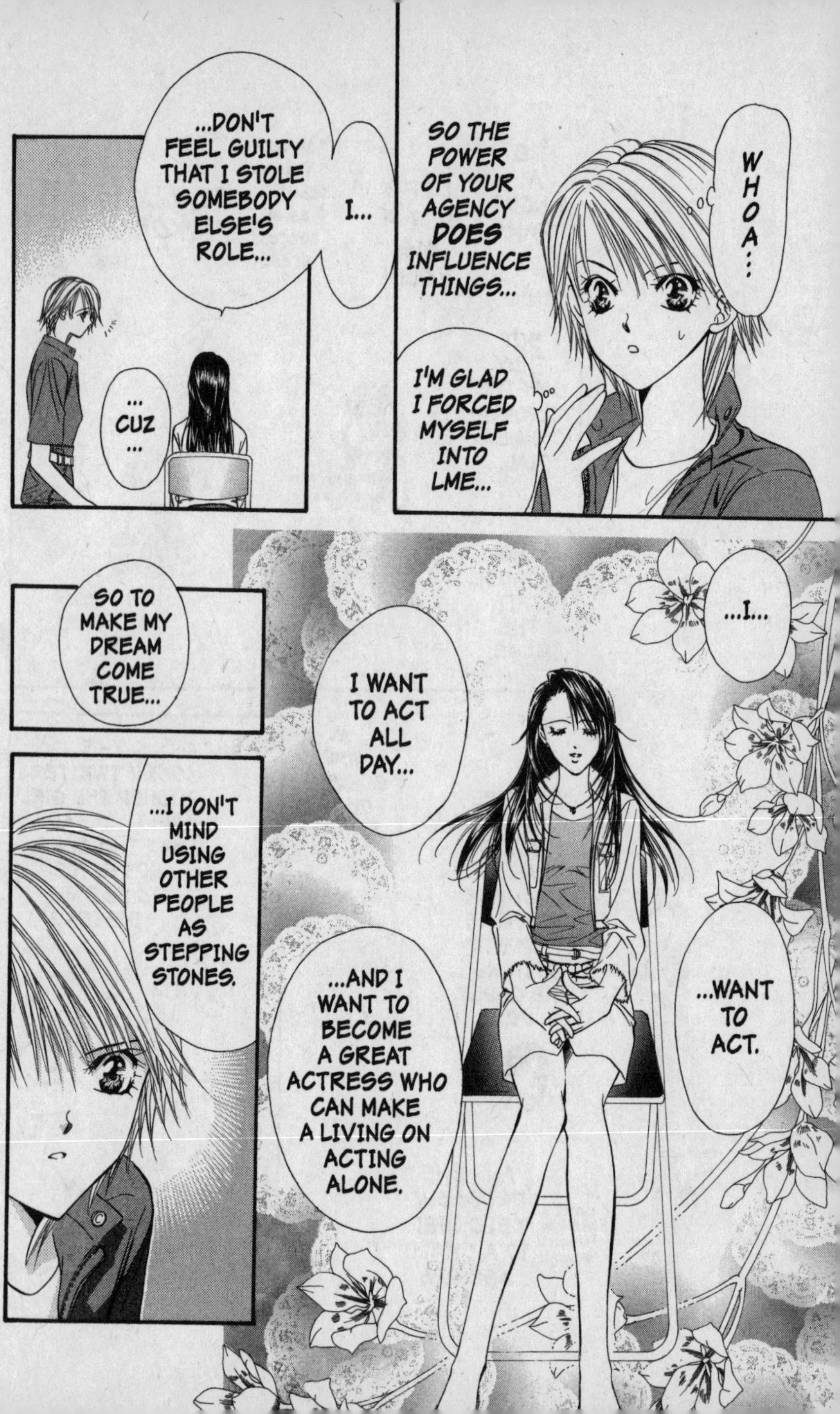
WHOA...
SO THE POWER OF YOUR AGENCY DOES INFLUENCE THINGS...
I'M GLAD I FORCED MYSELF INTO LME...
I...
...DON'T FEEL GUILTY THAT I STOLE SOMEBODY ELSE'S ROLE...
...CUZ...
...I...
...WANT TO ACT.
I WANT TO ACT ALL DAY...
...AND I WANT TO BECOME A GREAT ACTRESS WHO CAN MAKE A LIVING ON ACTING ALONE.
SO TO MAKE MY DREAM COME TRUE...
...I DON'T MIND USING OTHER PEOPLE AS STEPPING STONES.

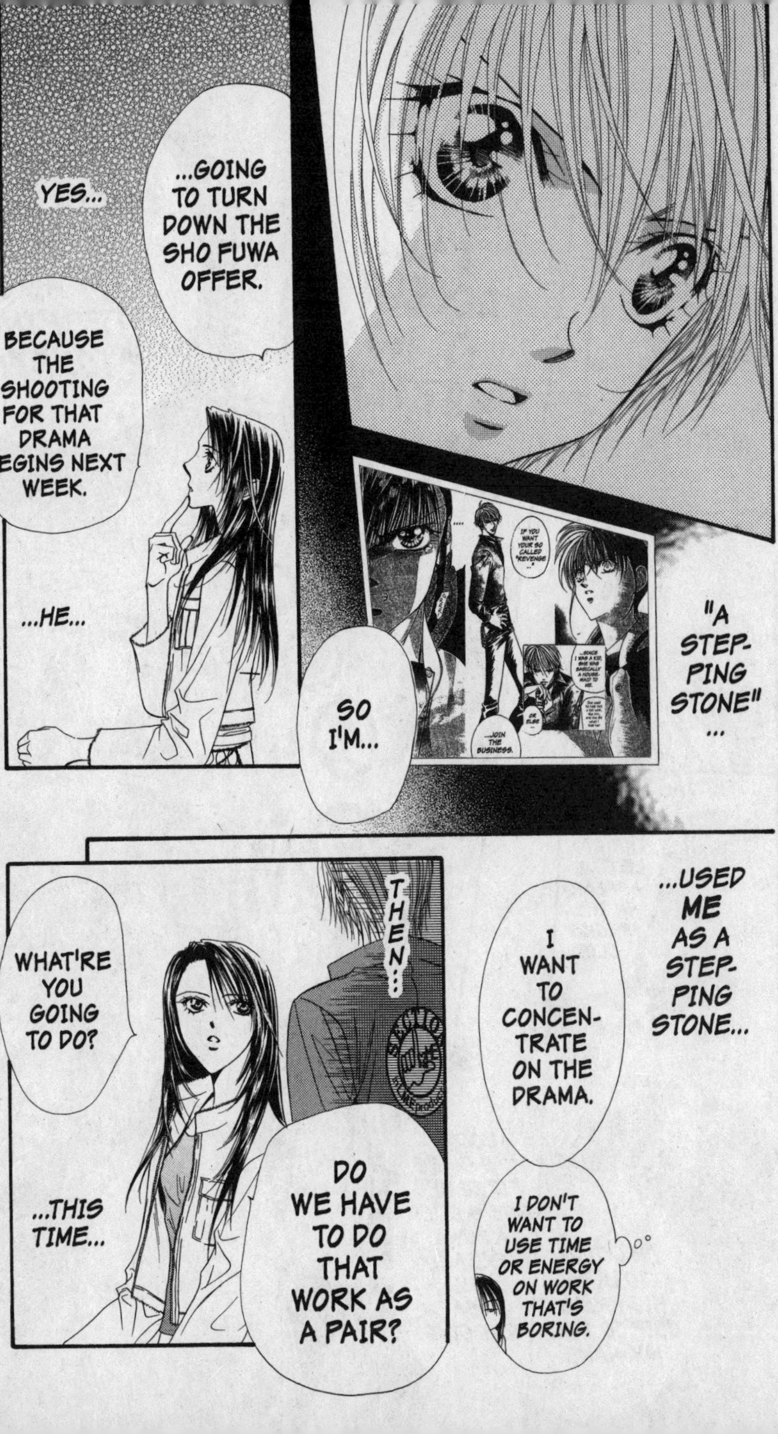

....
IF YOU WANT YOUR SO CALLED "REVENGE"...
...SINCE I WAS A KID, SHE WAS BASICALLY A HOUSE-MAID TO ME.
OR ELSE
...JOIN THE BUSINESS.
"A STEP-PING STONE"...
SO I'M...
...GOING TO TURN DOWN THE SHO FUWA OFFER.
YES...
BECAUSE THE SHOOTING FOR THAT DRAMA BEGINS NEXT WEEK.
...HE...
...USED ME AS A STEP-PING STONE...
I WANT TO CONCEN-TRATE ON THE DRAMA.
I DON'T WANT TO USE TIME OR ENERGY ON WORK THAT'S BORING.
DO WE HAVE TO DO THAT WORK AS A PAIR?
THEN...
WHAT'RE YOU GOING TO DO?
...THIS TIME...

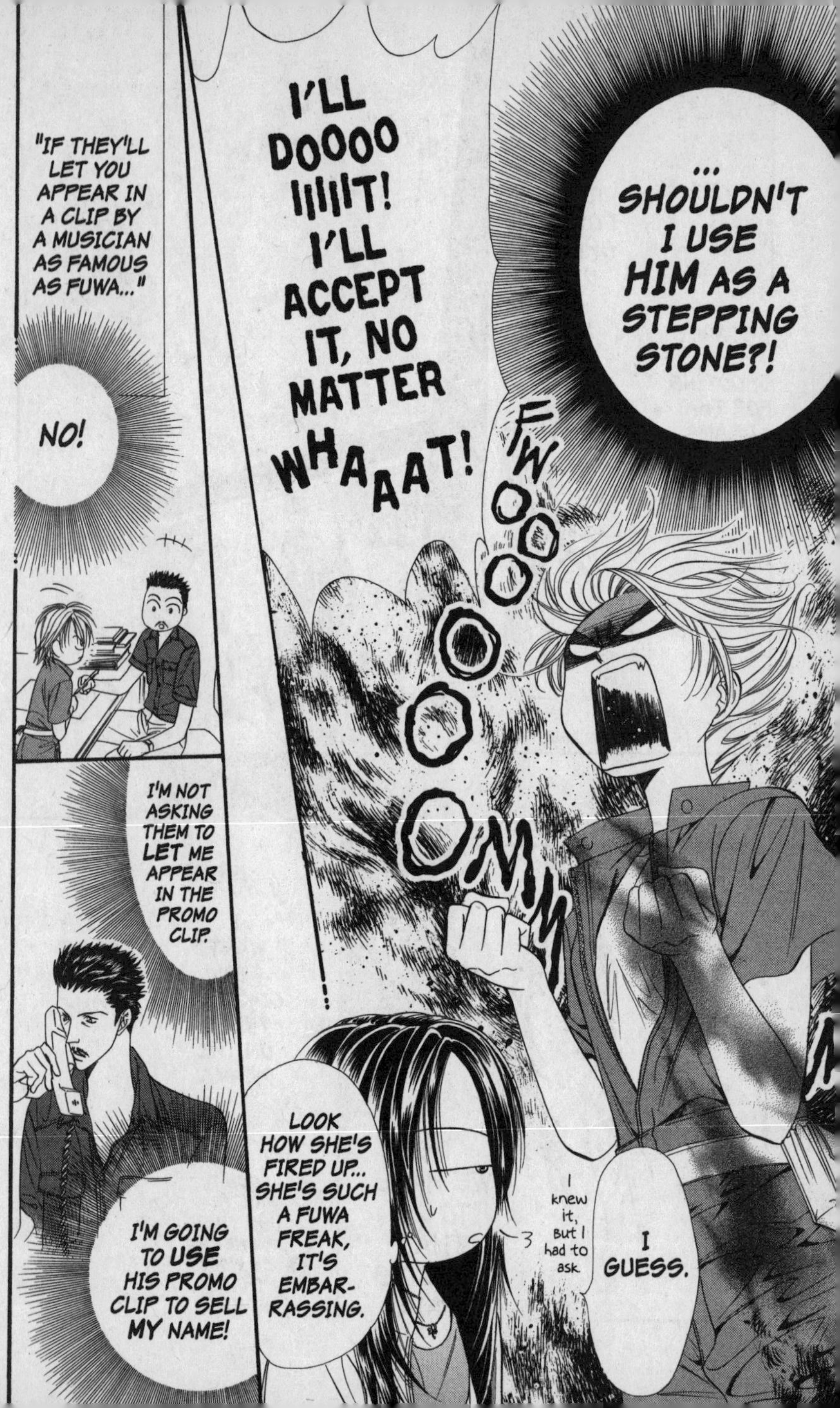

...SHOULDN'T I USE HIM AS A STEPPING STONE?!
I'LL DOOOO IIIIIT! I'LL ACCEPT IT, NO MATTER WHAAAT!
FWOOOOOOMM
I GUESS.
I knew it, but I had to ask.
LOOK HOW SHE'S FIRED UP... SHE'S SUCH A FUWA FREAK, IT'S EMBARRASSING.
"IF THEY'LL LET YOU APPEAR IN A CLIP BY A MUSICIAN AS FAMOUS AS FUWA..."
NO!
I'M NOT ASKING THEM TO LET ME APPEAR IN THE PROMO CLIP.
I'M GOING TO USE HIS PROMO CLIP TO SELL MY NAME!

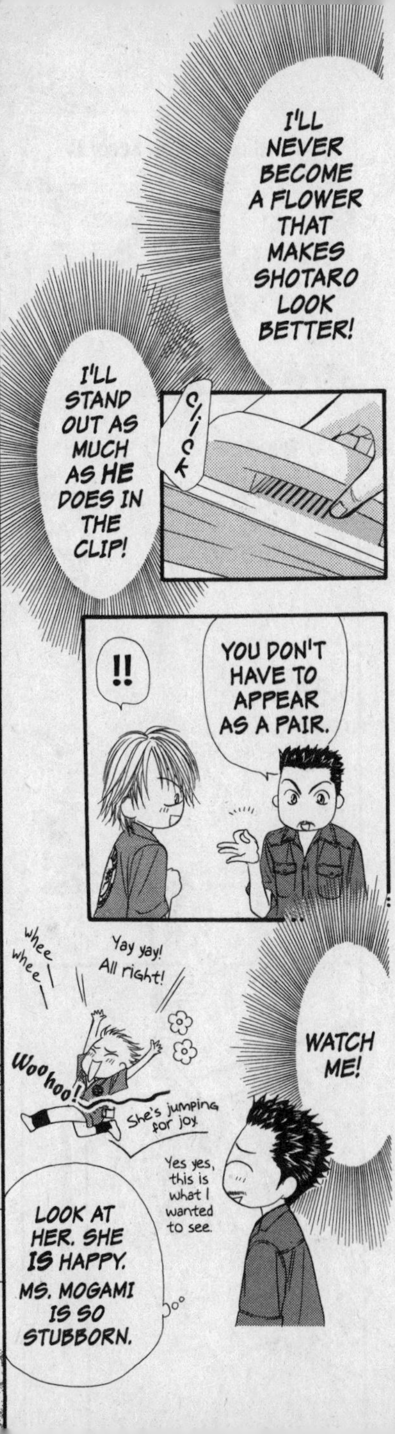
I'LL NEVER BECOME A FLOWER THAT MAKES SHOTARO LOOK BETTER!
click
I'LL STAND OUT AS MUCH AS HE DOES IN THE CLIP!
YOU DON'T HAVE TO APPEAR AS A PAIR.
!!
WATCH ME!
Yay yay! All right!
whee whee
Woohoo!
She's jumping for joy.
Yes yes, this is what I wanted to see.
LOOK AT HER. SHE IS HAPPY. MS. MOGAMI IS SO STUBBORN.

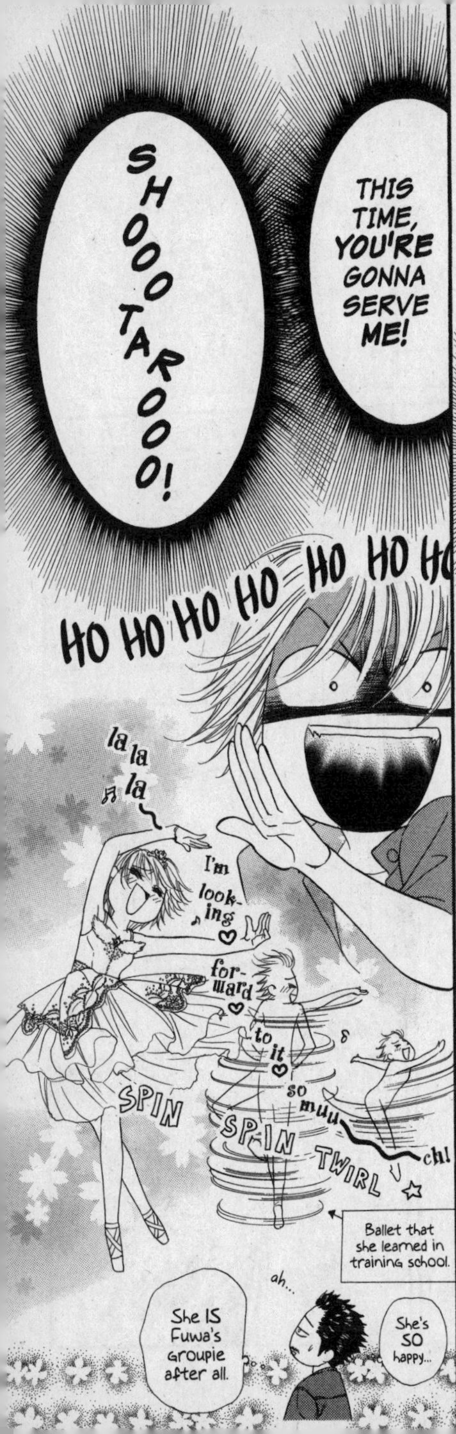
THIS TIME, YOU'RE GONNA SERVE ME!
SHOOOOTAROOOO!
HO HO HO HO HO HO HO
la la la
I'm looking forward to it so muuuch!
SPIN
SPIN
TWIRL
Ballet that she learned in training school.
She's SO happy...
ah...
She IS Fuwa's groupie after all.

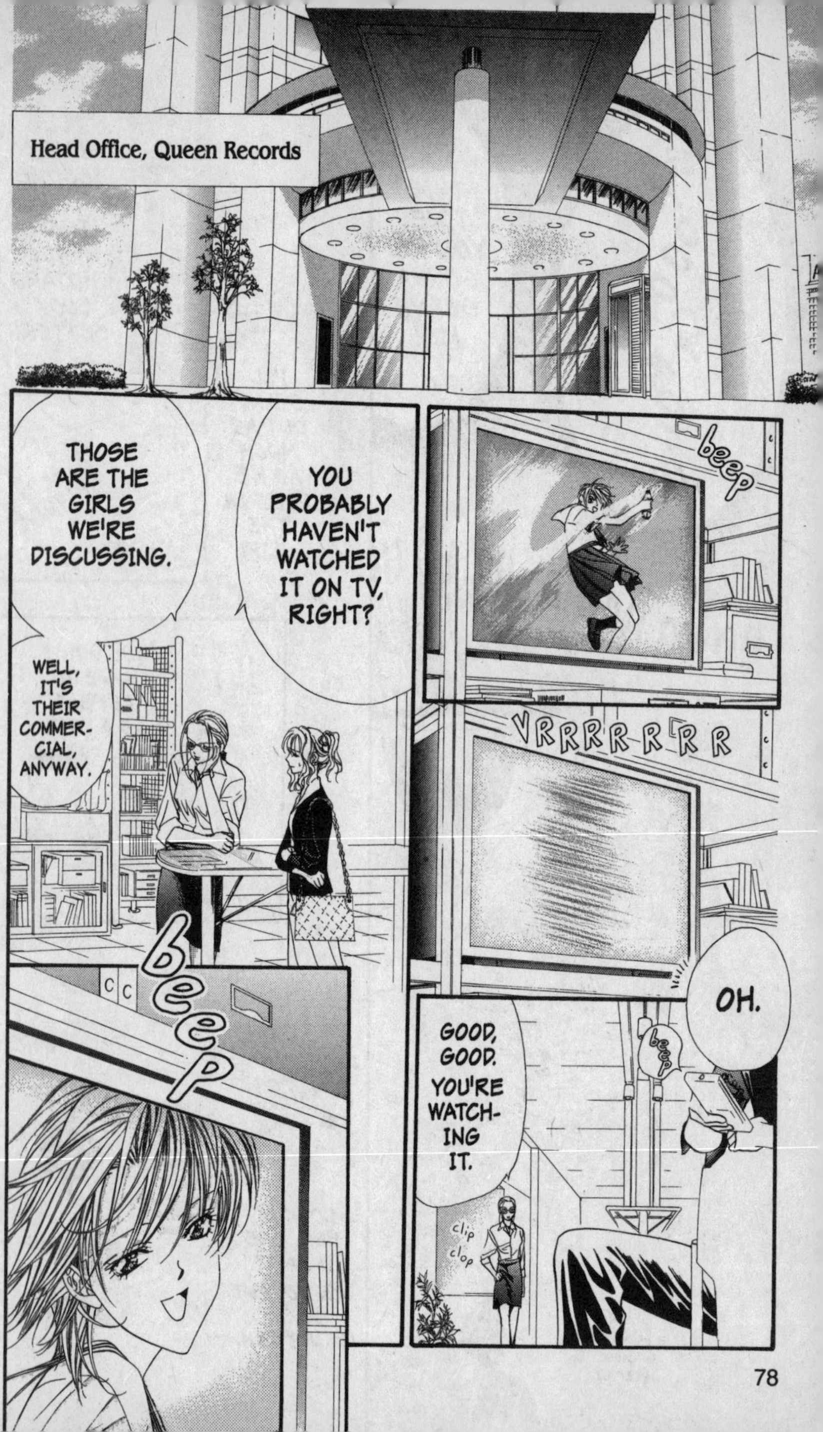
Head Office, Queen Records
beep
VRRRRRRR
OH.
beep
GOOD, GOOD. YOU'RE WATCHING IT.
clip clop
YOU PROBABLY HAVEN'T WATCHED IT ON TV, RIGHT?
THOSE ARE THE GIRLS WE'RE DISCUSSING.
WELL, IT'S THEIR COMMERCIAL, ANYWAY.
beep

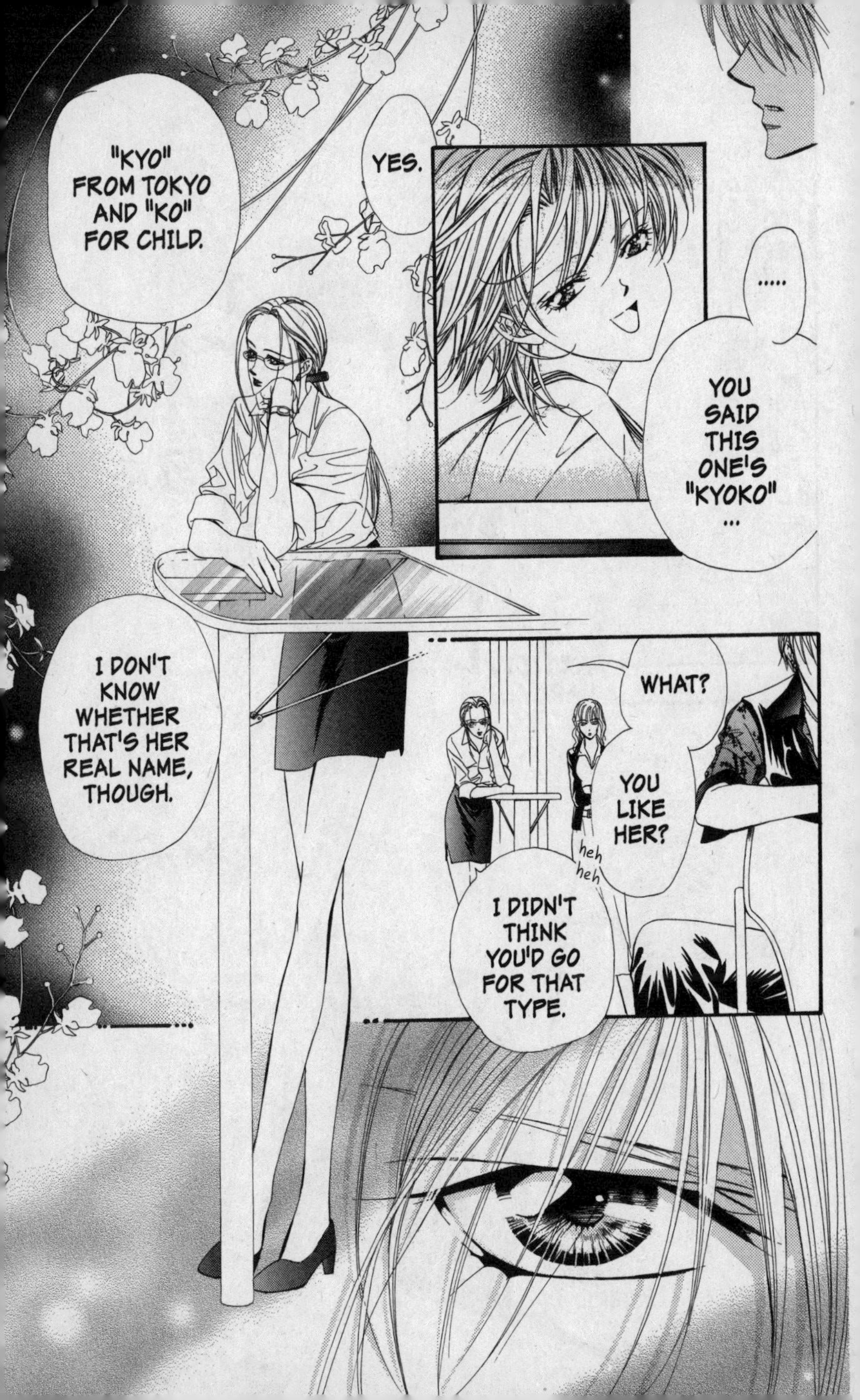
.....
YOU SAID THIS ONE'S "KYOKO" ...
YES.
"KYO" FROM TOKYO AND "KO" FOR CHILD.
I DON'T KNOW WHETHER THAT'S HER REAL NAME, THOUGH.
WHAT?
YOU LIKE HER?
heh heh
I DIDN'T THINK YOU'D GO FOR THAT TYPE.

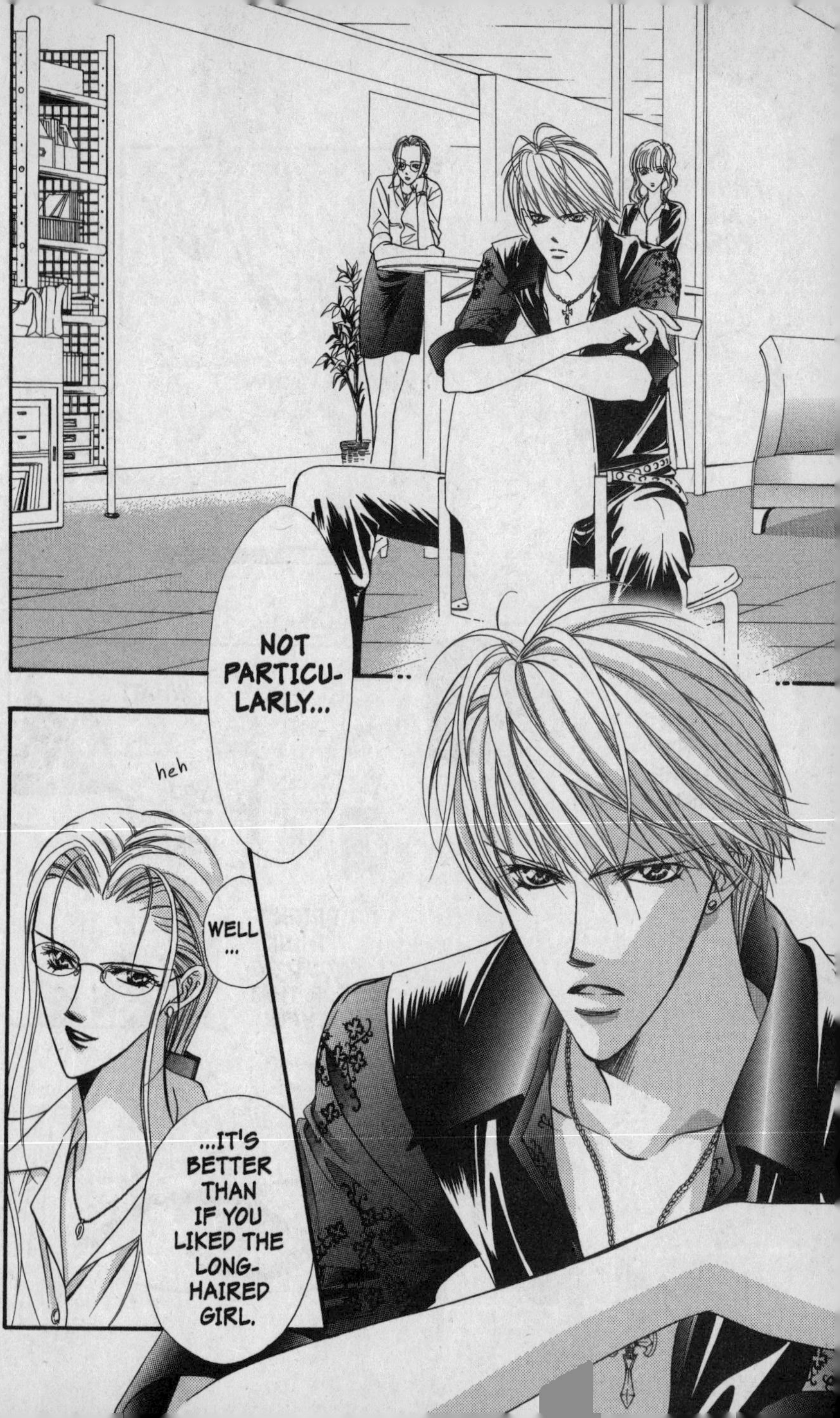
NOT PARTICU-LARLY...
heh
WELL ...
...IT'S BETTER THAN IF YOU LIKED THE LONG-HAIRED GIRL.

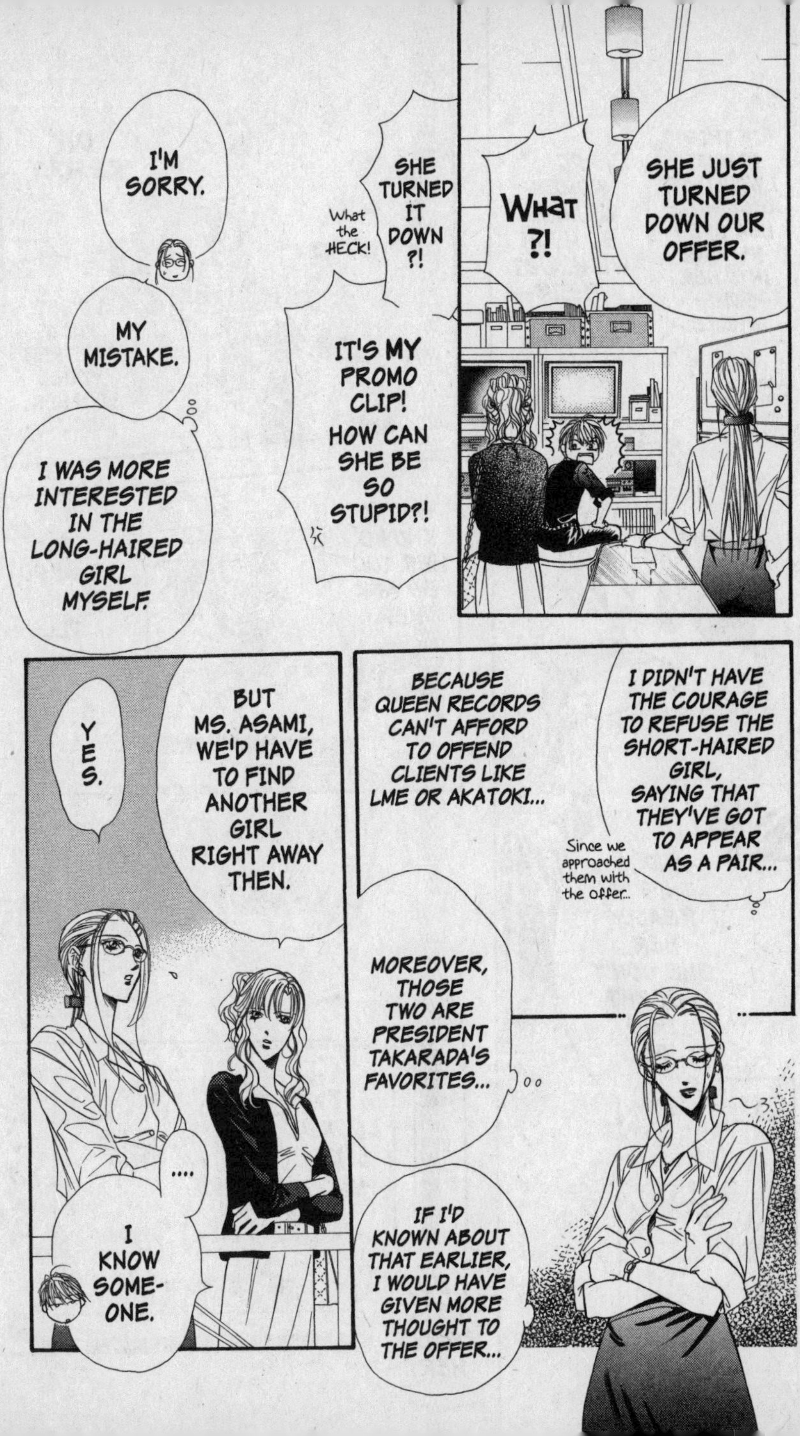
SHE JUST TURNED DOWN OUR OFFER.
WHAT?!
SHE TURNED IT DOWN?!
What the HECK!
IT'S MY PROMO CLIP! HOW CAN SHE BE SO STUPID?!
I'M SORRY.
MY MISTAKE.
I WAS MORE INTERESTED IN THE LONG-HAIRED GIRL MYSELF.
I DIDN'T HAVE THE COURAGE TO REFUSE THE SHORT-HAIRED GIRL, SAYING THAT THEY'VE GOT TO APPEAR AS A PAIR...
Since we approached them with the offer...
BECAUSE QUEEN RECORDS CAN'T AFFORD TO OFFEND CLIENTS LIKE LME OR AKATOKI...
MOREOVER, THOSE TWO ARE PRESIDENT TAKARADA'S FAVORITES...
IF I'D KNOWN ABOUT THAT EARLIER, I WOULD HAVE GIVEN MORE THOUGHT TO THE OFFER...
BUT MS. ASAMI, WE'D HAVE TO FIND ANOTHER GIRL RIGHT AWAY THEN.
YES.
....
I KNOW SOME-ONE.

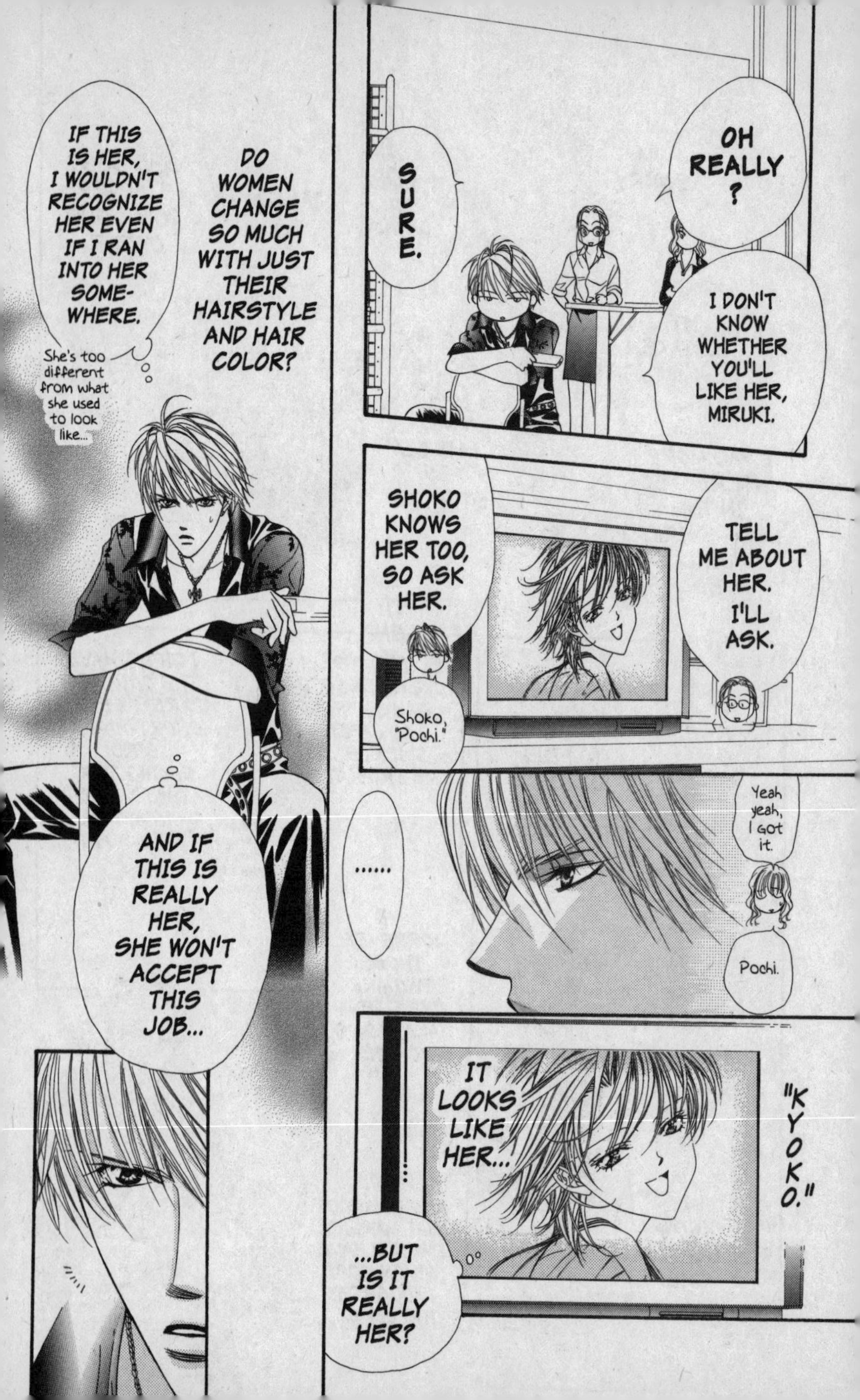
OH REALLY?
I DON'T KNOW WHETHER YOU'LL LIKE HER, MIRUKI.
SURE.
TELL ME ABOUT HER. I'LL ASK.
SHOKO KNOWS HER TOO, SO ASK HER.
Shoko, "Pochi."
Yeah yeah, I got it.
Pochi.
......
"KYOKO."
IT LOOKS LIKE HER...
...BUT IS IT REALLY HER?
IF THIS IS HER, I WOULDN'T RECOGNIZE HER EVEN IF I RAN INTO HER SOMEWHERE.
DO WOMEN CHANGE SO MUCH WITH JUST THEIR HAIRSTYLE AND HAIR COLOR?
She's too different from what she used to look like...
AND IF THIS IS REALLY HER, SHE WON'T ACCEPT THIS JOB...

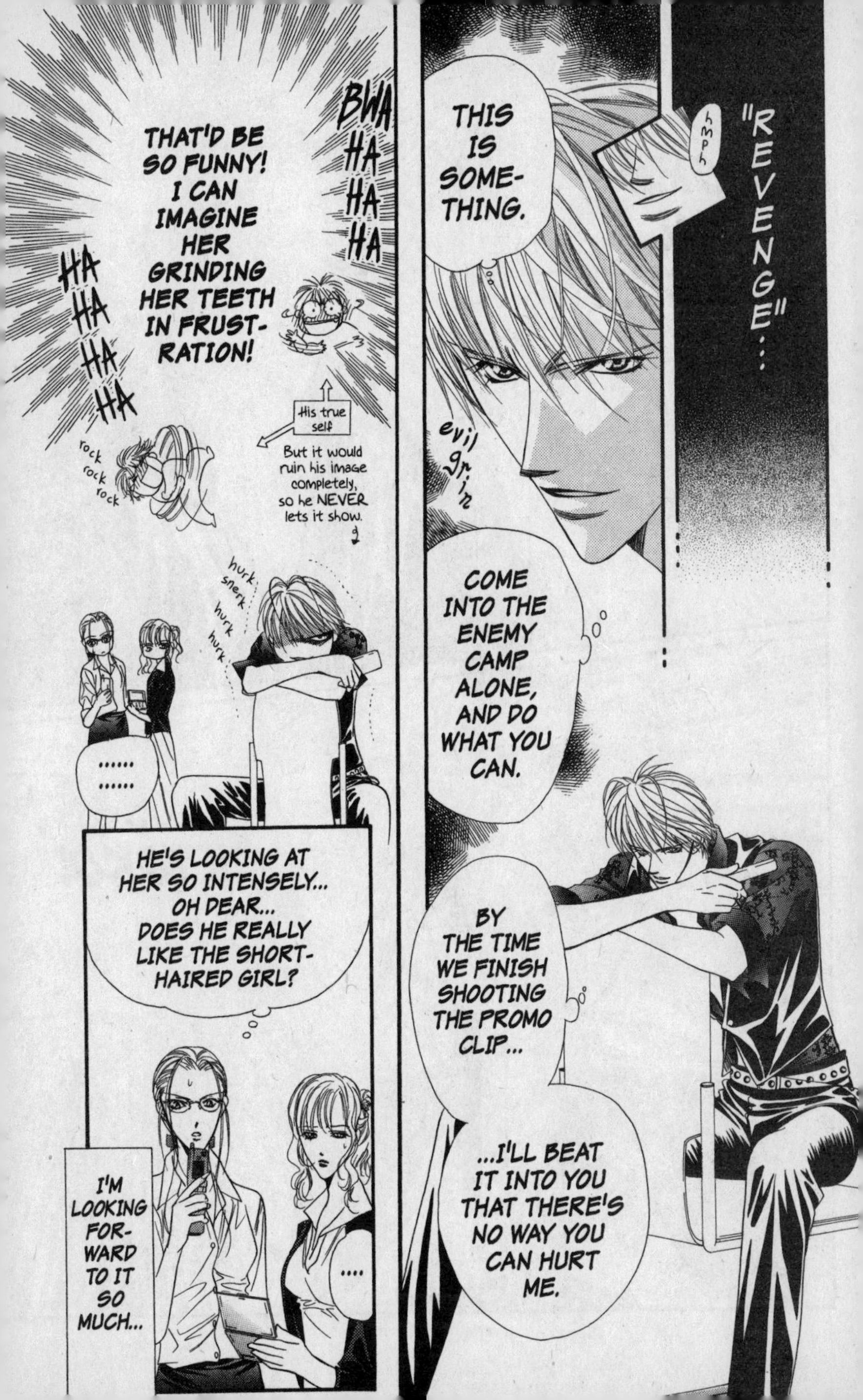
"REVENGE"...
hmph
THIS IS SOME-THING.
evil grin
COME INTO THE ENEMY CAMP ALONE, AND DO WHAT YOU CAN.
BY THE TIME WE FINISH SHOOTING THE PROMO CLIP...
...I'LL BEAT IT INTO YOU THAT THERE'S NO WAY YOU CAN HURT ME.
BWA HA HA HA HA
THAT'D BE SO FUNNY! I CAN IMAGINE HER GRINDING HER TEETH IN FRUST-RATION!
HA HA HA HA HA
His true self
But it would ruin his image completely, so he NEVER lets it show.
rock rock rock
hurk snerk hurk hurk
......
......
HE'S LOOKING AT HER SO INTENSELY... OH DEAR... DOES HE REALLY LIKE THE SHORT-HAIRED GIRL?
I'M LOOKING FOR-WARD TO IT SO MUCH...
....

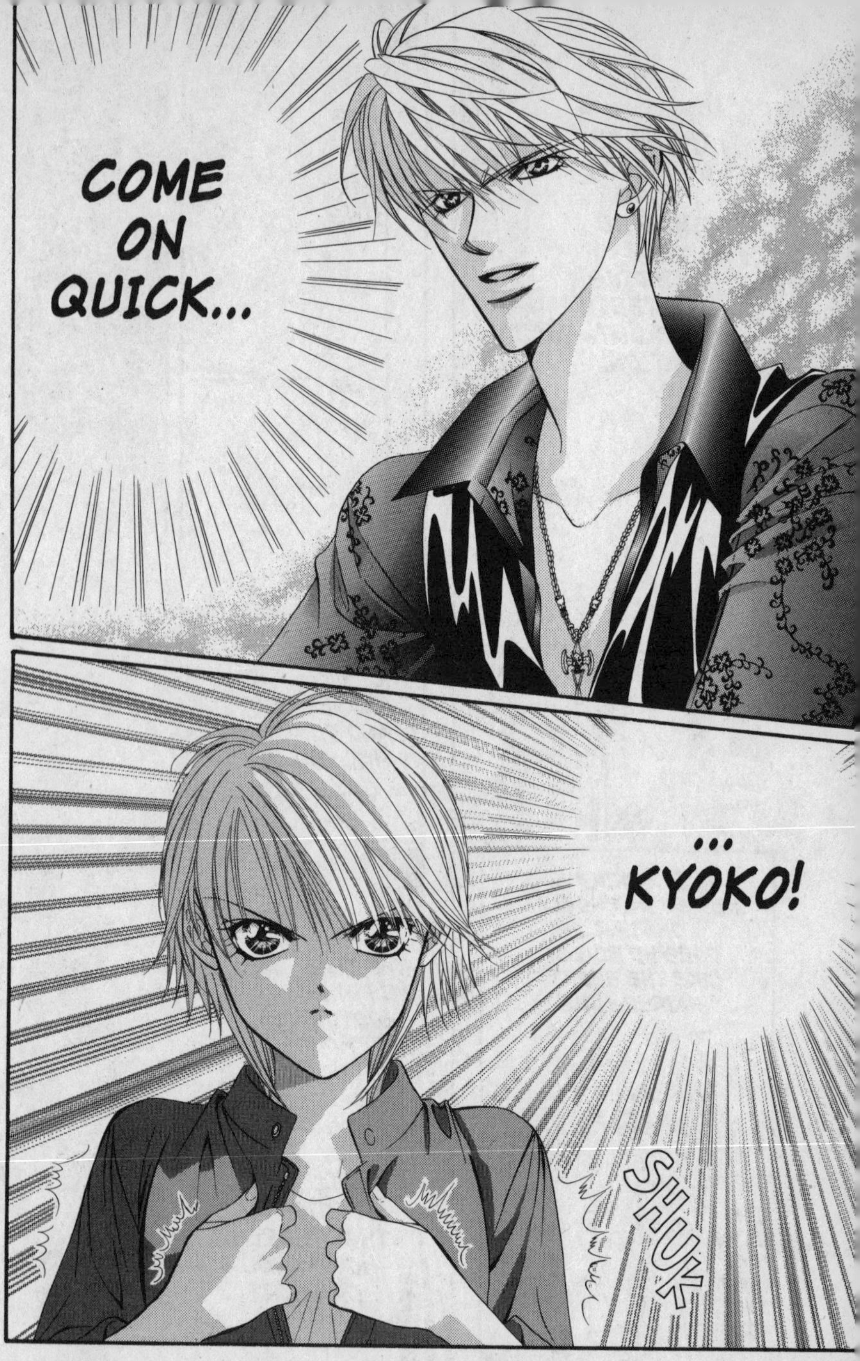
COME ON QUICK...
... KYOKO!
SHUK

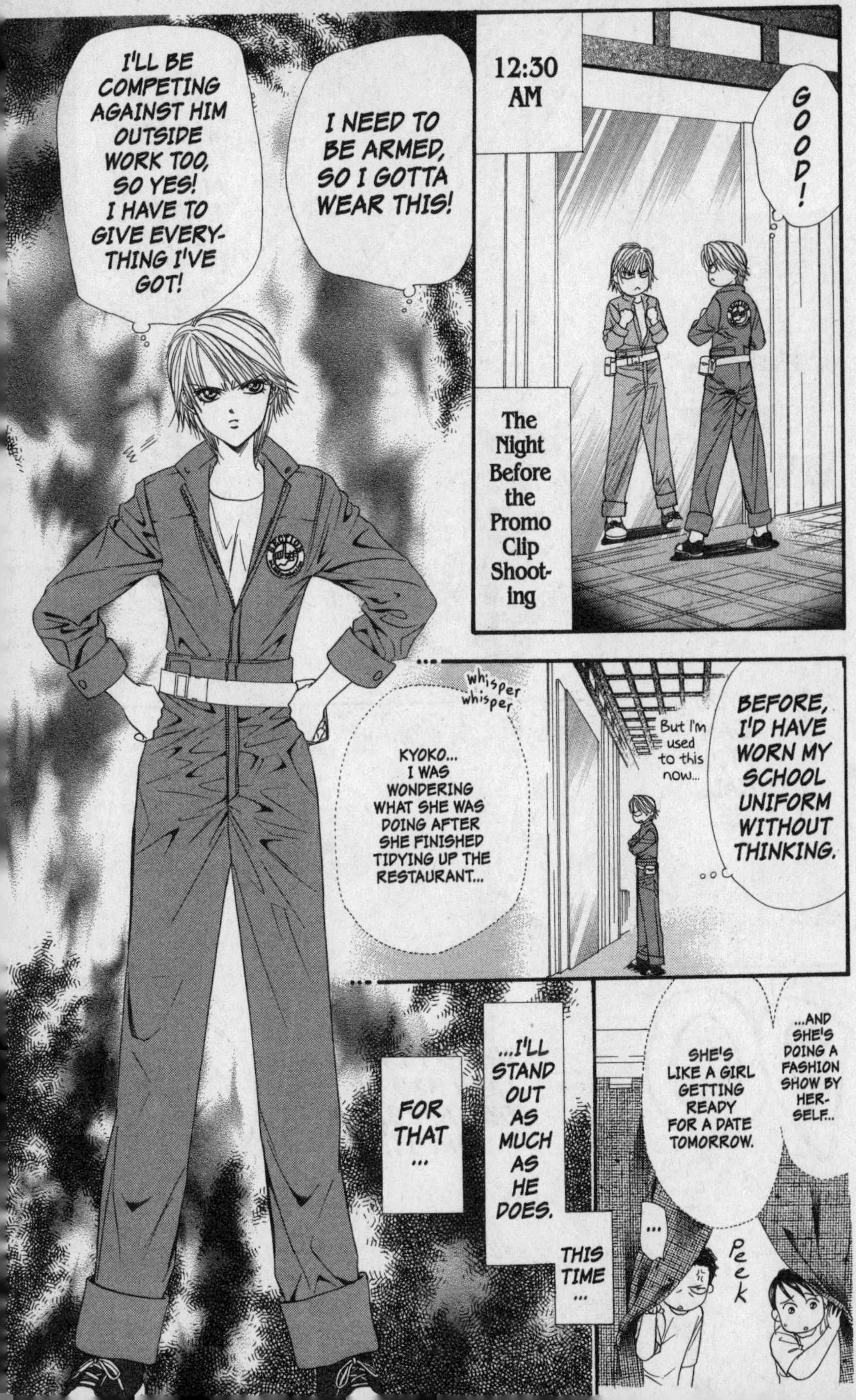
12:30 AM
The Night Before the Promo Clip Shooting
GOOD!
whisper whisper
KYOKO... I WAS WONDERING WHAT SHE WAS DOING AFTER SHE FINISHED TIDYING UP THE RESTAURANT...
BEFORE, I'D HAVE WORN MY SCHOOL UNIFORM WITHOUT THINKING.
But I'm used to this now...
...AND SHE'S DOING A FASHION SHOW BY HER-SELF...
SHE'S LIKE A GIRL GETTING READY FOR A DATE TOMORROW.
...
Peek
THIS TIME...
...I'LL STAND OUT AS MUCH AS HE DOES.
FOR THAT...
I NEED TO BE ARMED, SO I GOTTA WEAR THIS!
I'LL BE COMPETING AGAINST HIM OUTSIDE WORK TOO, SO YES! I HAVE TO GIVE EVERY-THING I'VE GOT!

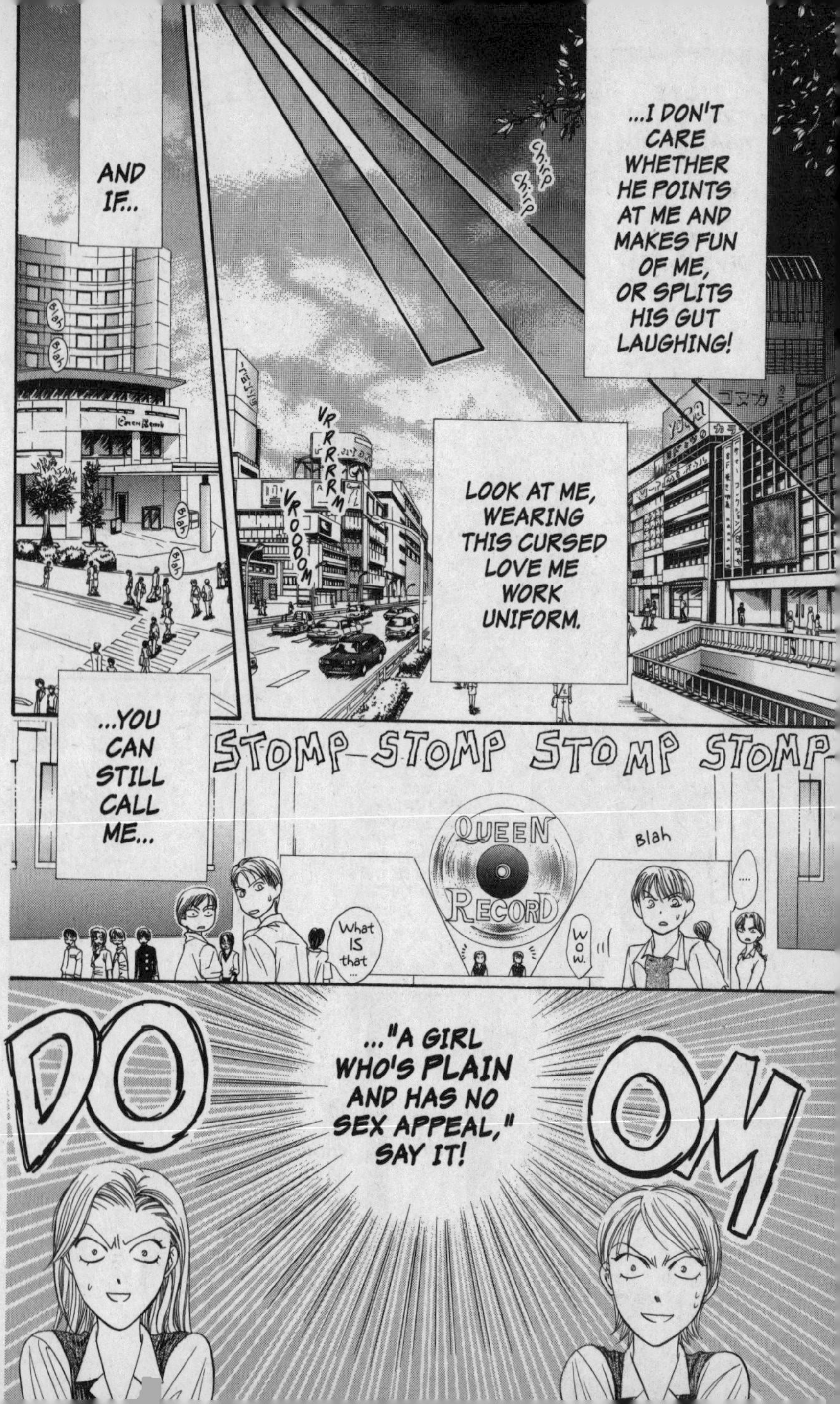
...I DON'T CARE WHETHER HE POINTS AT ME AND MAKES FUN OF ME, OR SPLITS HIS GUT LAUGHING!
chirp chirp
LOOK AT ME, WEARING THIS CURSED LOVE ME WORK UNIFORM.
VRRRRM
VROOOOOM
AND IF...
Blah Blah
Blah Blah
STOMP STOMP STOMP STOMP
Blah
....
WOW.
QUEEN RECORD
What IS that...
...YOU CAN STILL CALL ME...
DOOM
..."A GIRL WHO'S PLAIN AND HAS NO SEX APPEAL," SAY IT!

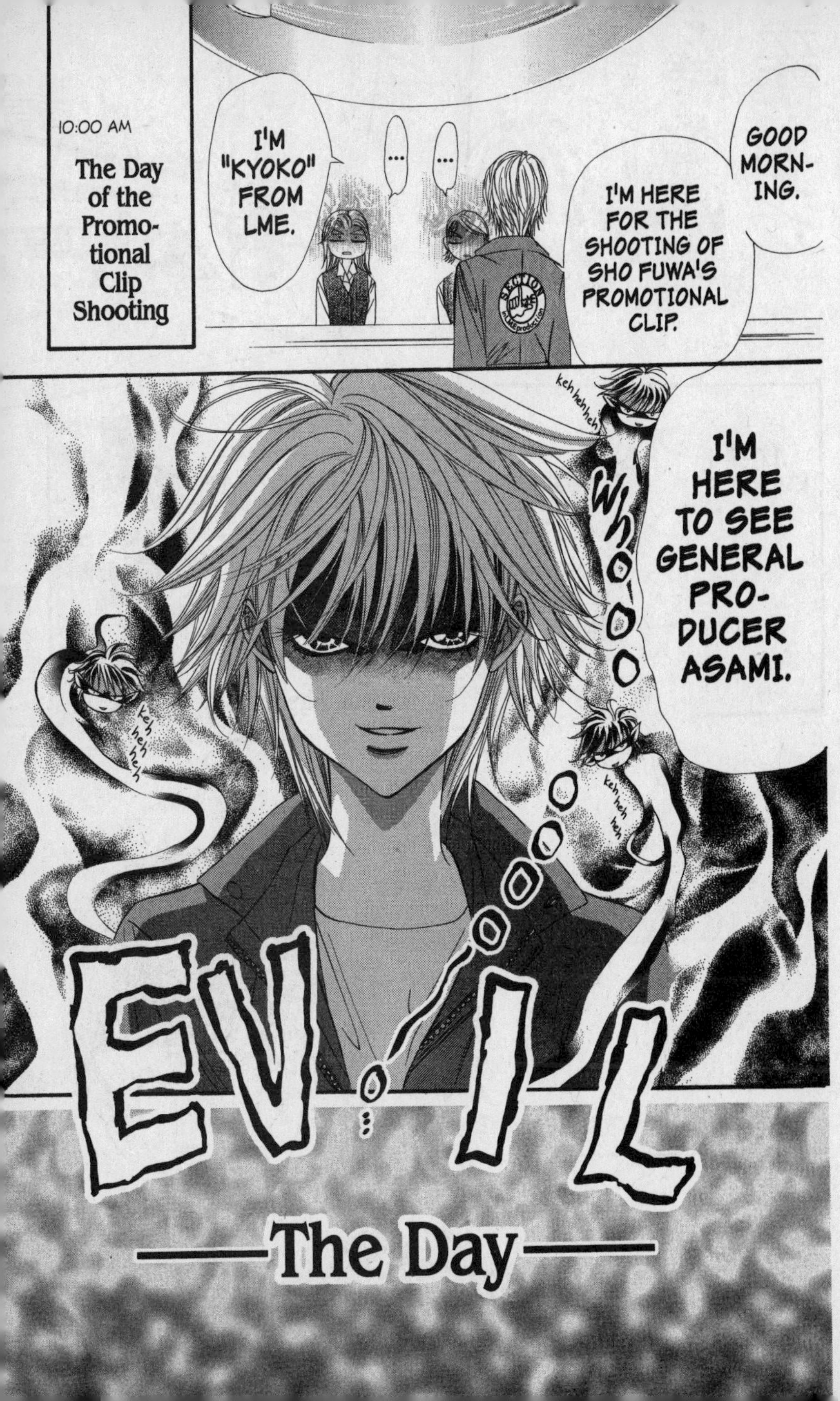
GOOD MORNING.
I'M HERE FOR THE SHOOTING OF SHO FUWA'S PROMOTIONAL CLIP.
...
...
I'M "KYOKO" FROM LME.
10:00 AM
The Day of the Promotional Clip Shooting
keh heh heh
I'M HERE TO SEE GENERAL PRODUCER ASAMI.
Whoooooooo
keh heh heh
keh heh heh
EV..I..L
—The Day—

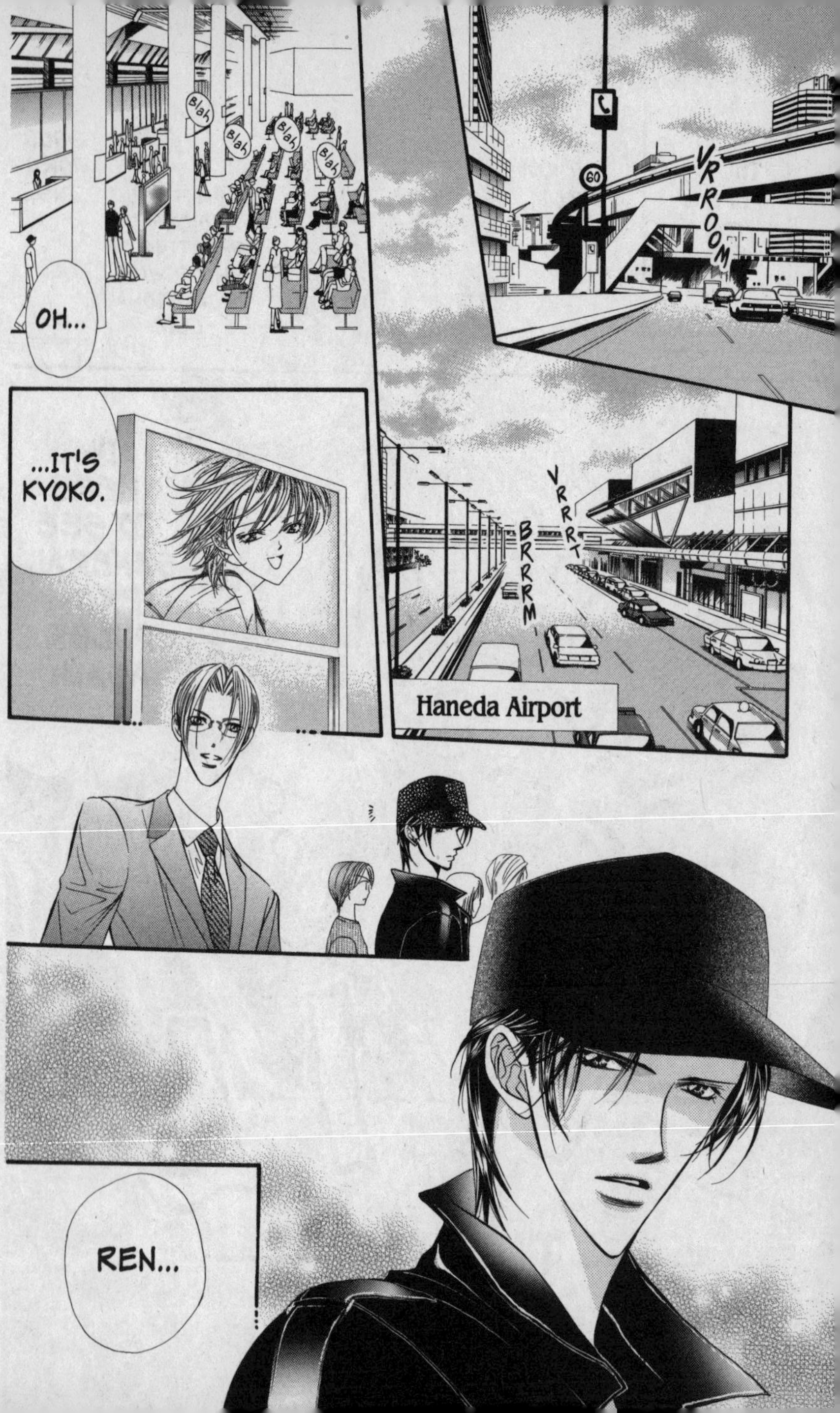
VRROOM
Blah
Blah
Blah
Blah
OH...
VRRRT
BRRRM
Haneda Airport
...IT'S KYOKO.
REN...

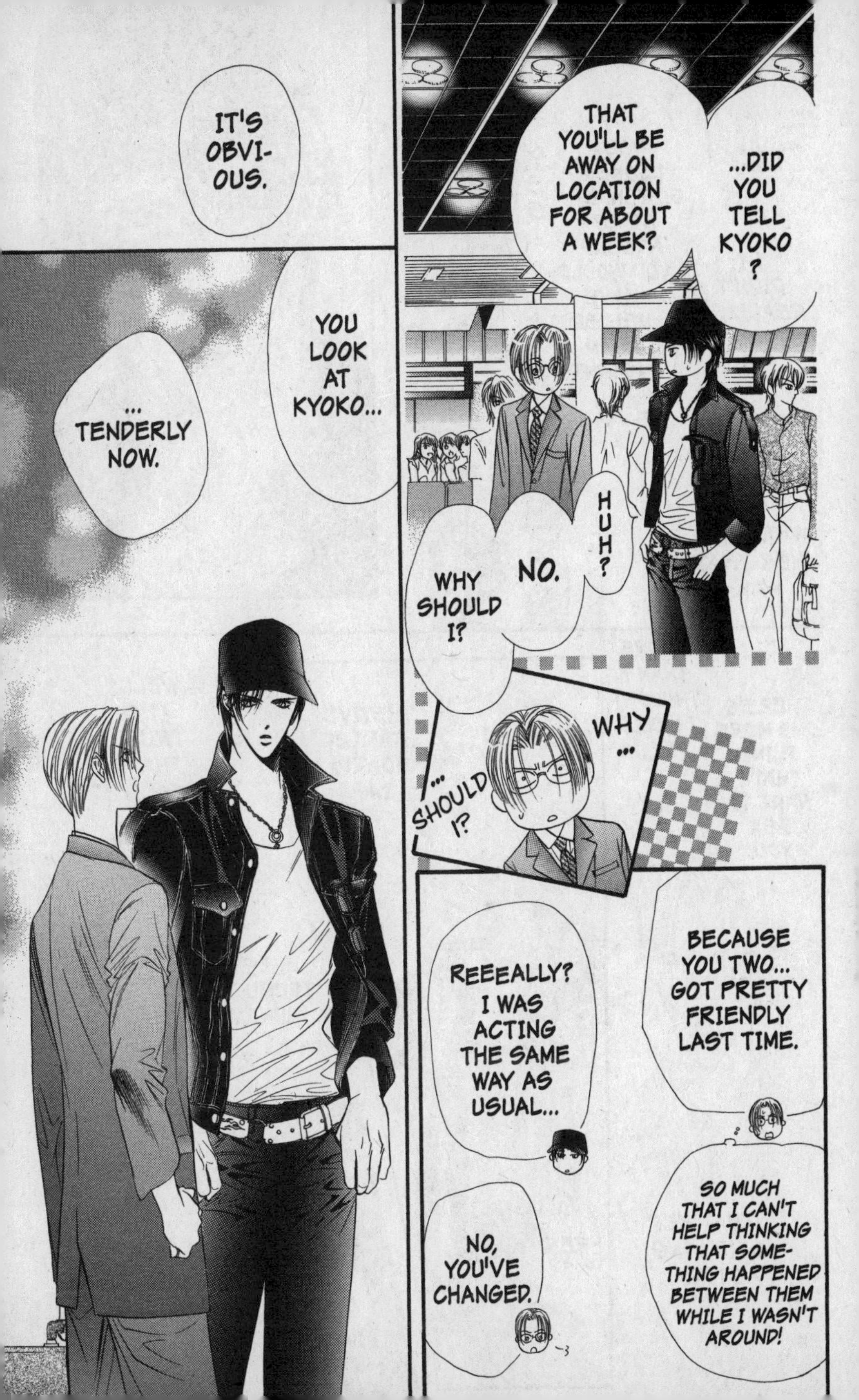
...DID YOU TELL KYOKO?
THAT YOU'LL BE AWAY ON LOCATION FOR ABOUT A WEEK?
HUH?
NO.
WHY SHOULD I?
WHY...
...SHOULD I?
BECAUSE YOU TWO... GOT PRETTY FRIENDLY LAST TIME.
REEEALLY? I WAS ACTING THE SAME WAY AS USUAL...
SO MUCH THAT I CAN'T HELP THINKING THAT SOME-THING HAPPENED BETWEEN THEM WHILE I WASN'T AROUND!
NO, YOU'VE CHANGED.
IT'S OBVI-OUS.
YOU LOOK AT KYOKO...
...TENDERLY NOW.

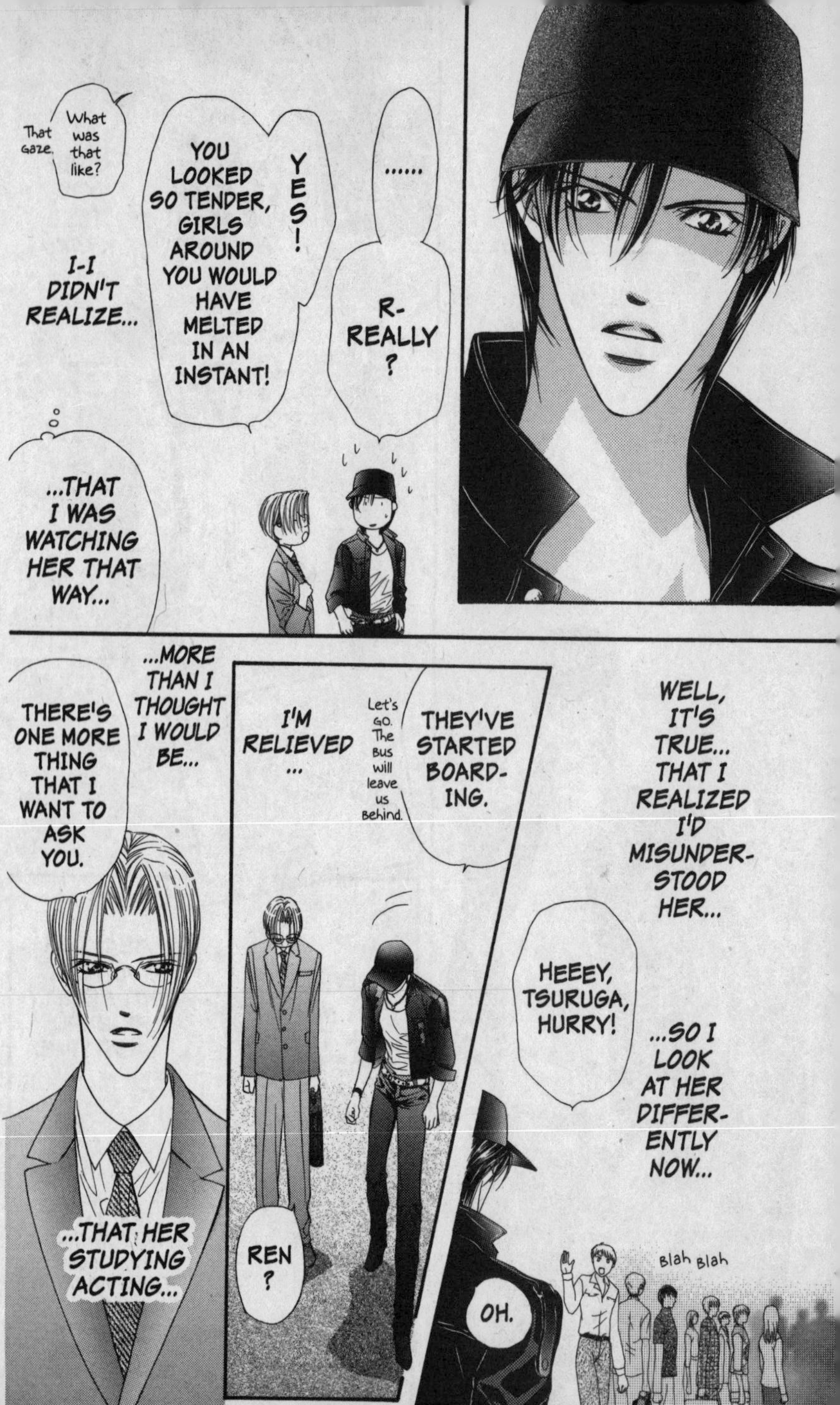

...... R-REALLY?
YES!
YOU LOOKED SO TENDER, GIRLS AROUND YOU WOULD HAVE MELTED IN AN INSTANT!
What was that like?
That Gaze.
I-I DIDN'T REALIZE...
...THAT I WAS WATCHING HER THAT WAY...
WELL, IT'S TRUE... THAT I REALIZED I'D MISUNDERSTOOD HER...
HEEEY, TSURUGA, HURRY!
...SO I LOOK AT HER DIFFERENTLY NOW...
Blah Blah
OH.
THEY'VE STARTED BOARDING.
Let's GO. The Bus will leave us Behind.
I'M RELIEVED...
REN?
...MORE THAN I THOUGHT I WOULD BE...
THERE'S ONE MORE THING THAT I WANT TO ASK YOU.
...THAT HER STUDYING ACTING...

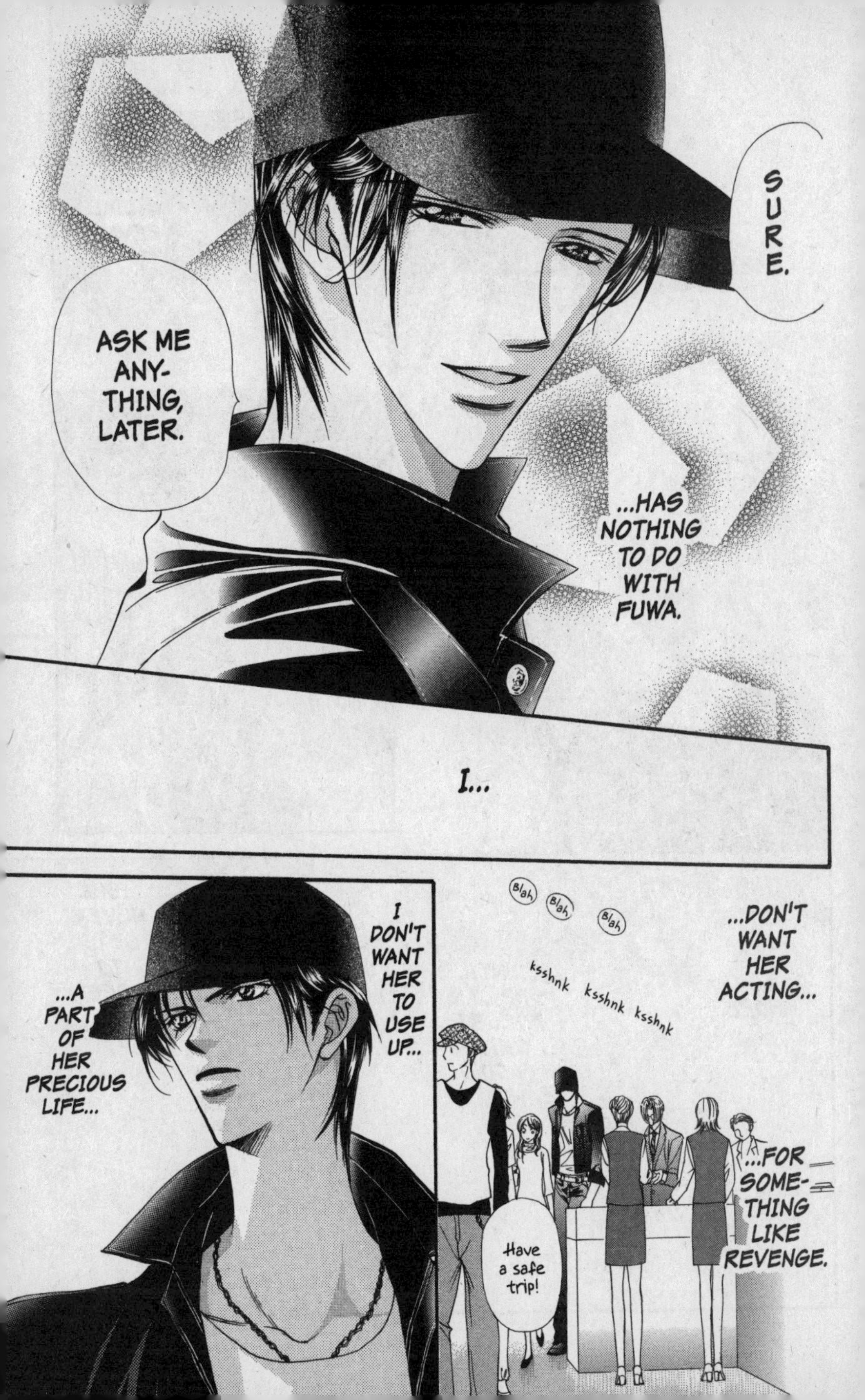
SURE.
ASK ME ANY-THING, LATER.
...HAS NOTHING TO DO WITH FUWA.
I...
Blah Blah Blah
ksshnk ksshnk ksshnk
...DON'T WANT HER ACTING...
...FOR SOME-THING LIKE REVENGE.
Have a safe trip!
I DON'T WANT HER TO USE UP...
...A PART OF HER PRECIOUS LIFE...

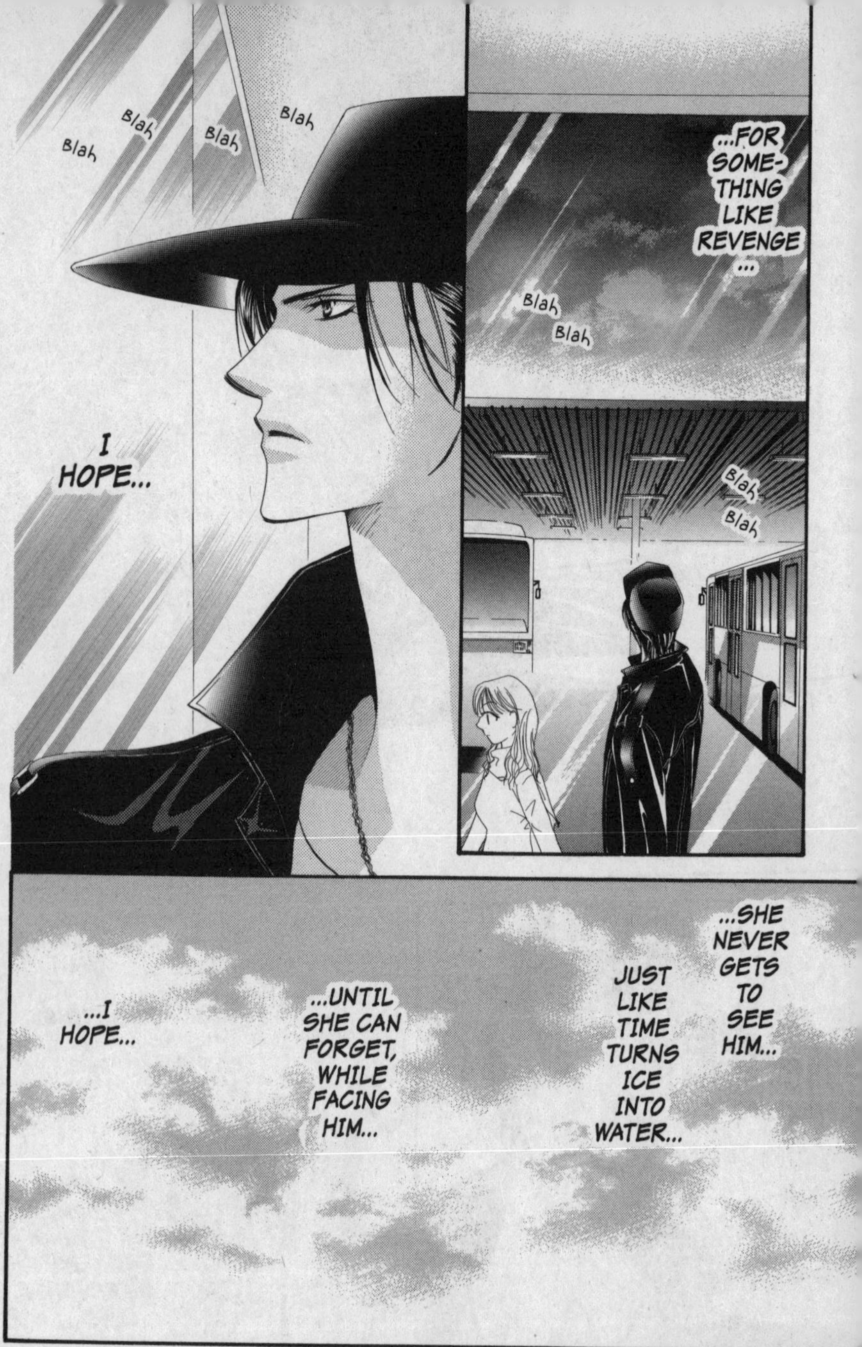
...FOR SOMETHING LIKE REVENGE...
Blah
Blah
Blah
Blah
Blah
Blah
Blah
Blah
I HOPE...
...SHE NEVER GETS TO SEE HIM...
JUST LIKE TIME TURNS ICE INTO WATER...
...UNTIL SHE CAN FORGET, WHILE FACING HIM...
...I HOPE...

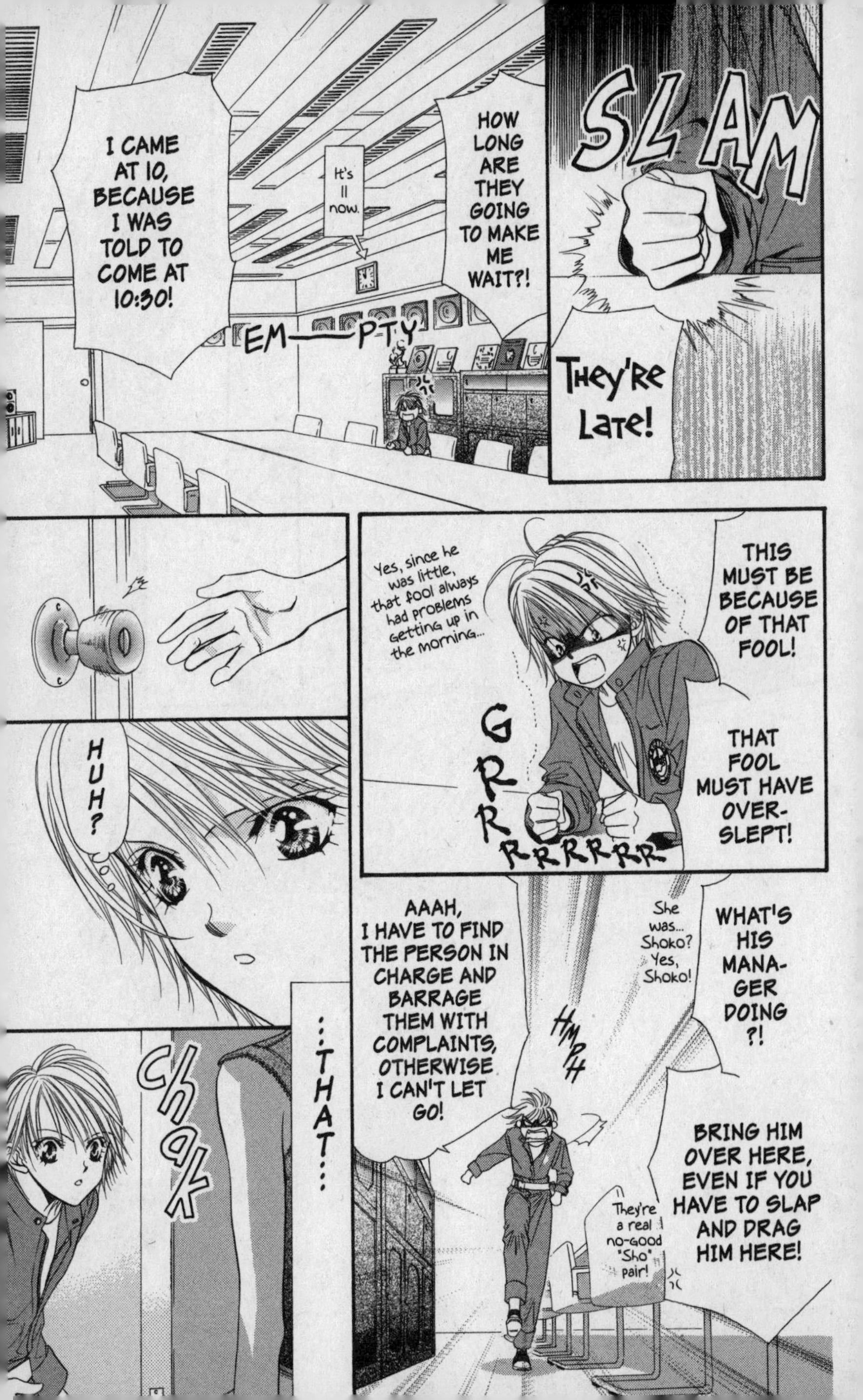

SLAM
They're Late!
HOW LONG ARE THEY GOING TO MAKE ME WAIT?!
It's 11 now.
I CAME AT 10, BECAUSE I WAS TOLD TO COME AT 10:30!
EM—PTY
THIS MUST BE BECAUSE OF THAT FOOL!
THAT FOOL MUST HAVE OVER-SLEPT!
Yes, since he was little, that fool always had problems getting up in the morning...
GRRRRRRRRR
HUH?
WHAT'S HIS MANA-GER DOING?!
She was... Shoko? Yes, Shoko!
AAAH, I HAVE TO FIND THE PERSON IN CHARGE AND BARRAGE THEM WITH COMPLAINTS, OTHERWISE I CAN'T LET GO!
HMPH
BRING HIM OVER HERE, EVEN IF YOU HAVE TO SLAP AND DRAG HIM HERE!
They're a real no-good "Sho" pair!
...THAT...
Chak

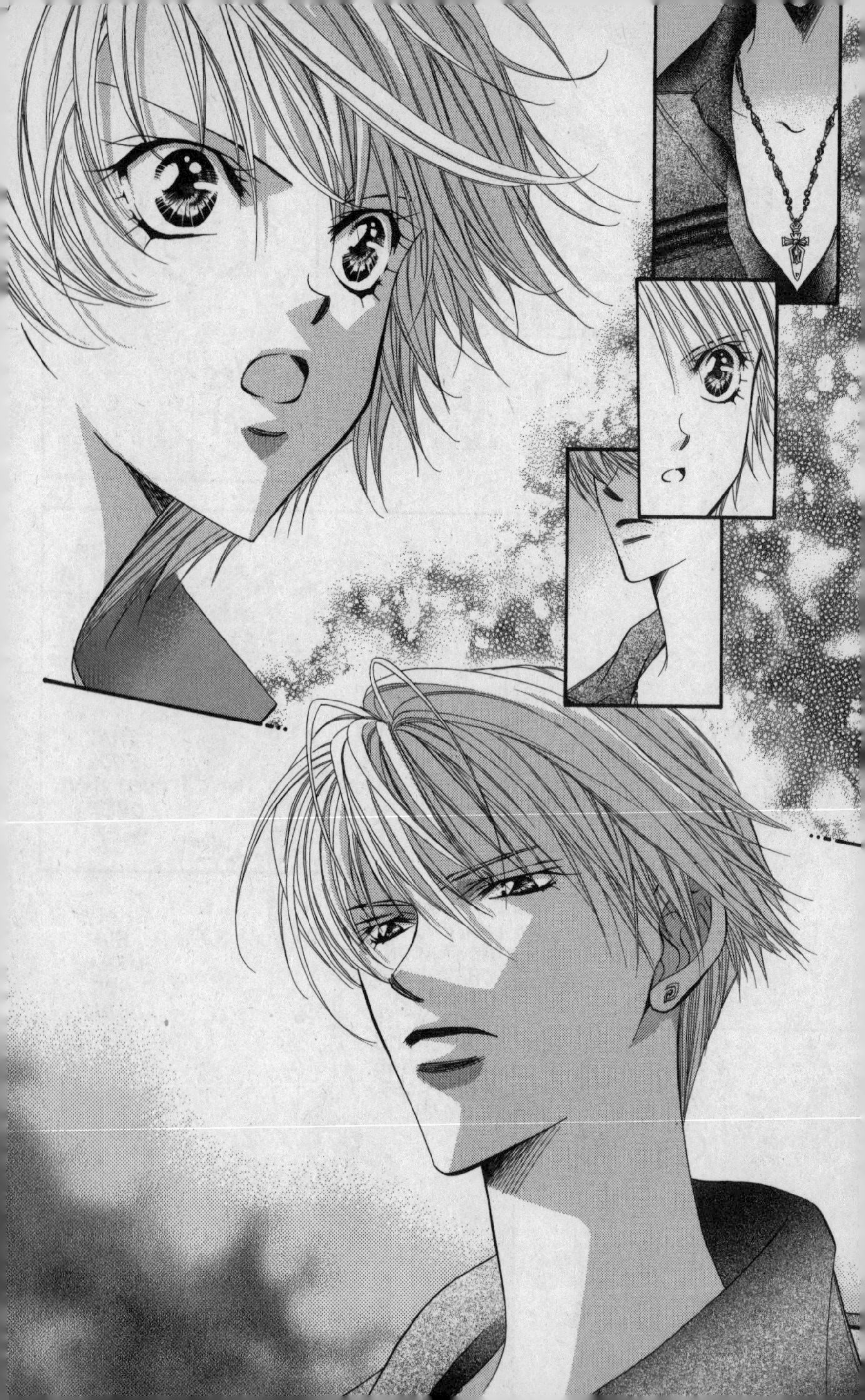

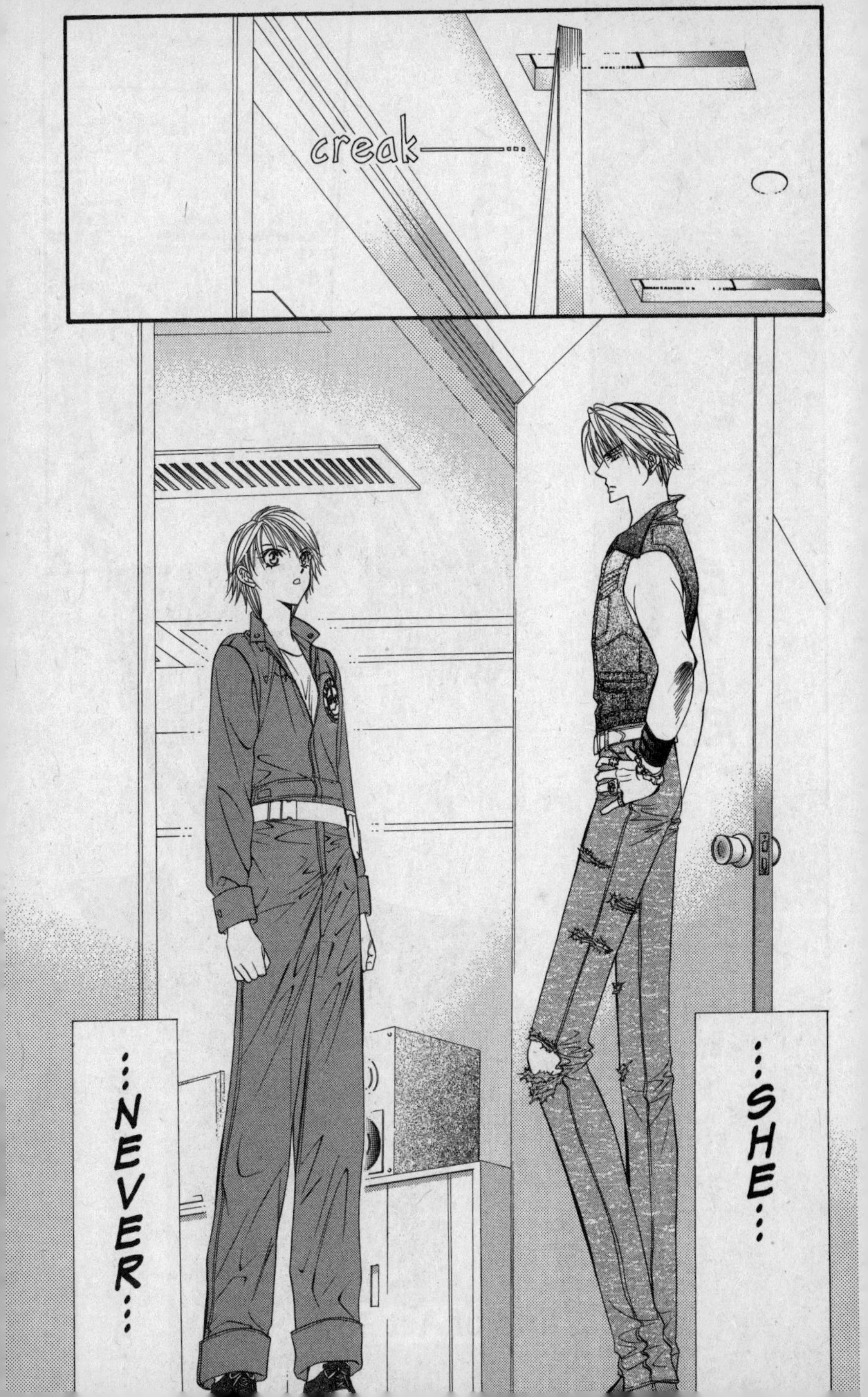
creak
...SHE...
...NEVER...

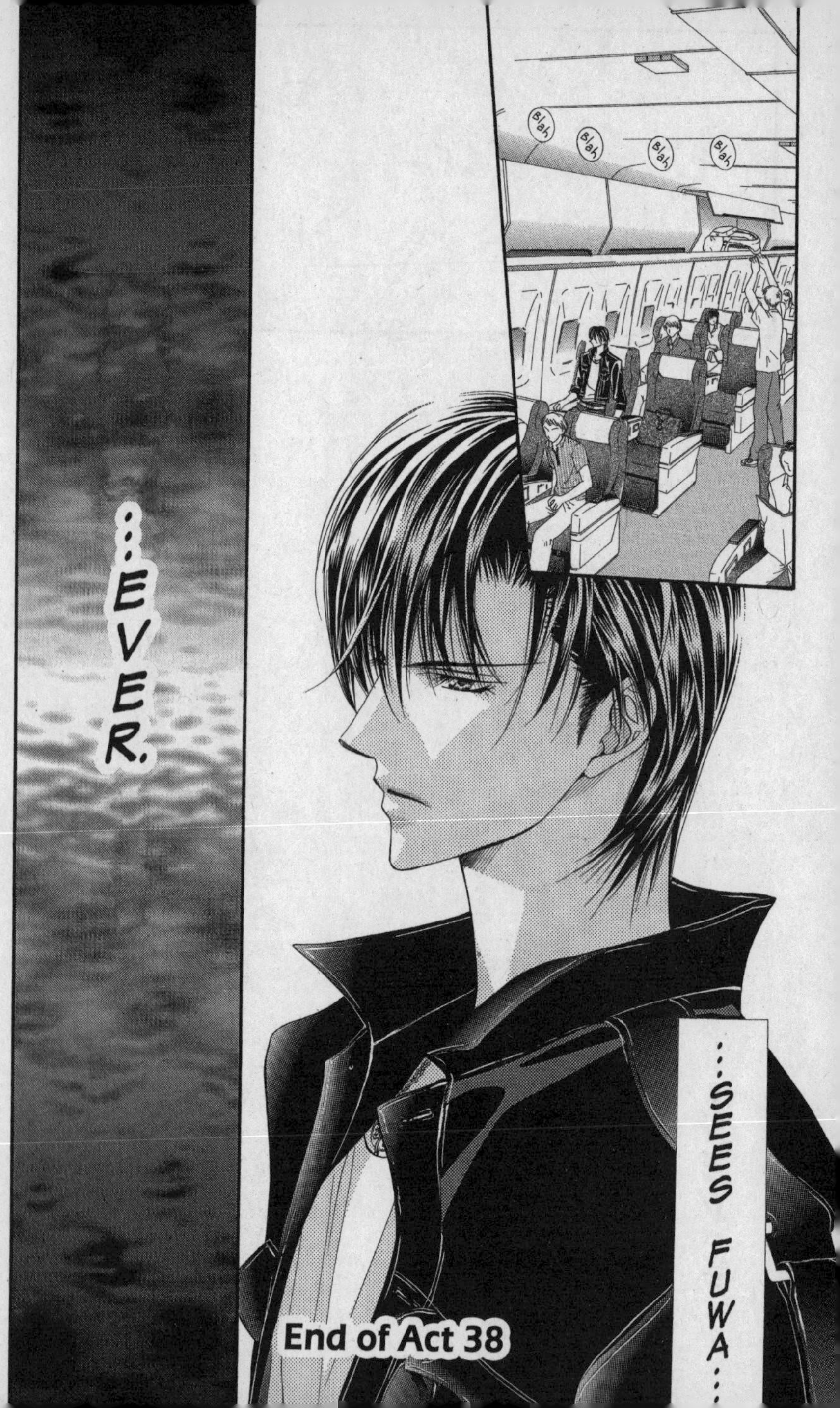
Blah
Blah
Blah
Blah
...SEES FUWA...
End of Act 38
...EVER.

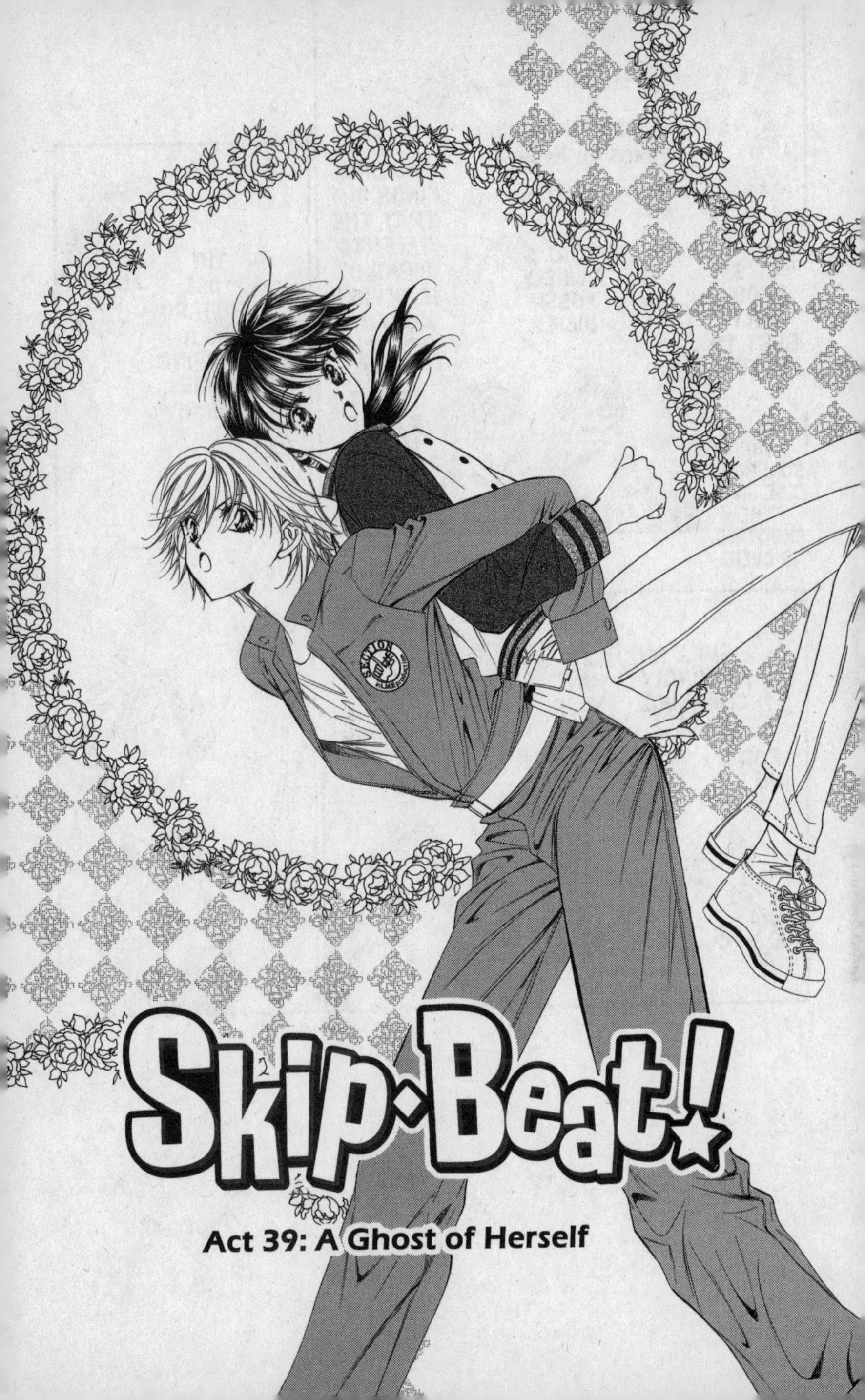
Skip·Beat!
Act 39: A Ghost of Herself

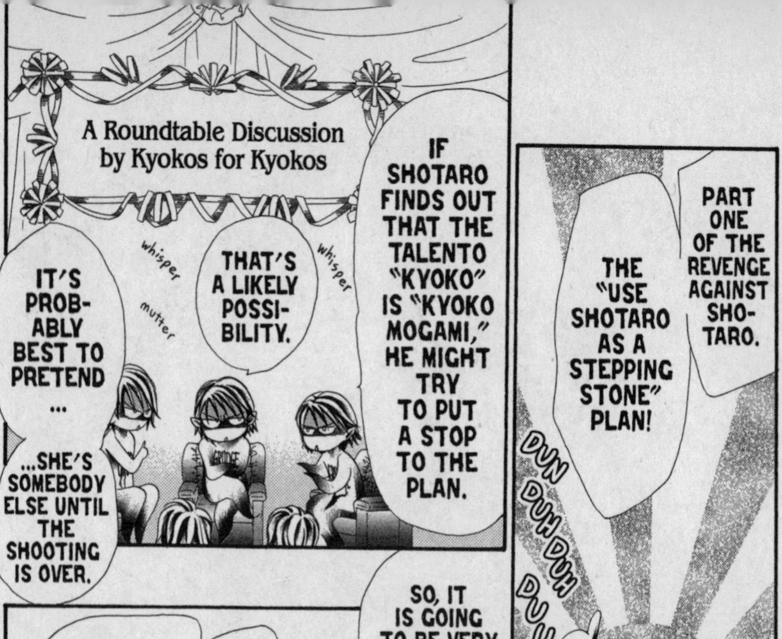
PART ONE OF THE REVENGE AGAINST SHO-TARO.
THE "USE SHOTARO AS A STEPPING STONE" PLAN!
DUN DUH DUH DUU—N
GRUDGE
A Roundtable Discussion by Kyokos for Kyokos
IF SHOTARO FINDS OUT THAT THE TALENTO "KYOKO" IS "KYOKO MOGAMI," HE MIGHT TRY TO PUT A STOP TO THE PLAN.
whisper
THAT'S A LIKELY POSSI-BILITY.
whisper
mutter
IT'S PROB-ABLY BEST TO PRETEND ...
...SHE'S SOMEBODY ELSE UNTIL THE SHOOTING IS OVER.
GRUDGE
SO, IT IS GOING TO BE VERY DIFFICULT, WITH THE TARGET RIGHT IN FRONT OF YOU...
... BUT ...
...TO HAVE YOUR RE-VENGE ...
...SMILE AN AMAZINGLY CHARMING SMILE...
...FOR HIM.
GRUDGE
GRUDGE
GRUDGE
GRUDGE
GRUDGE

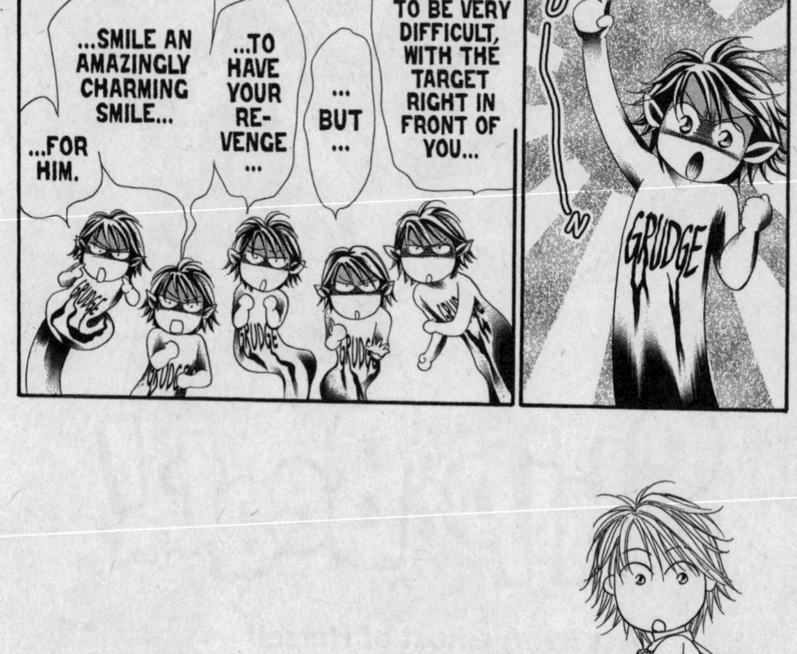

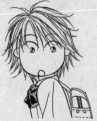

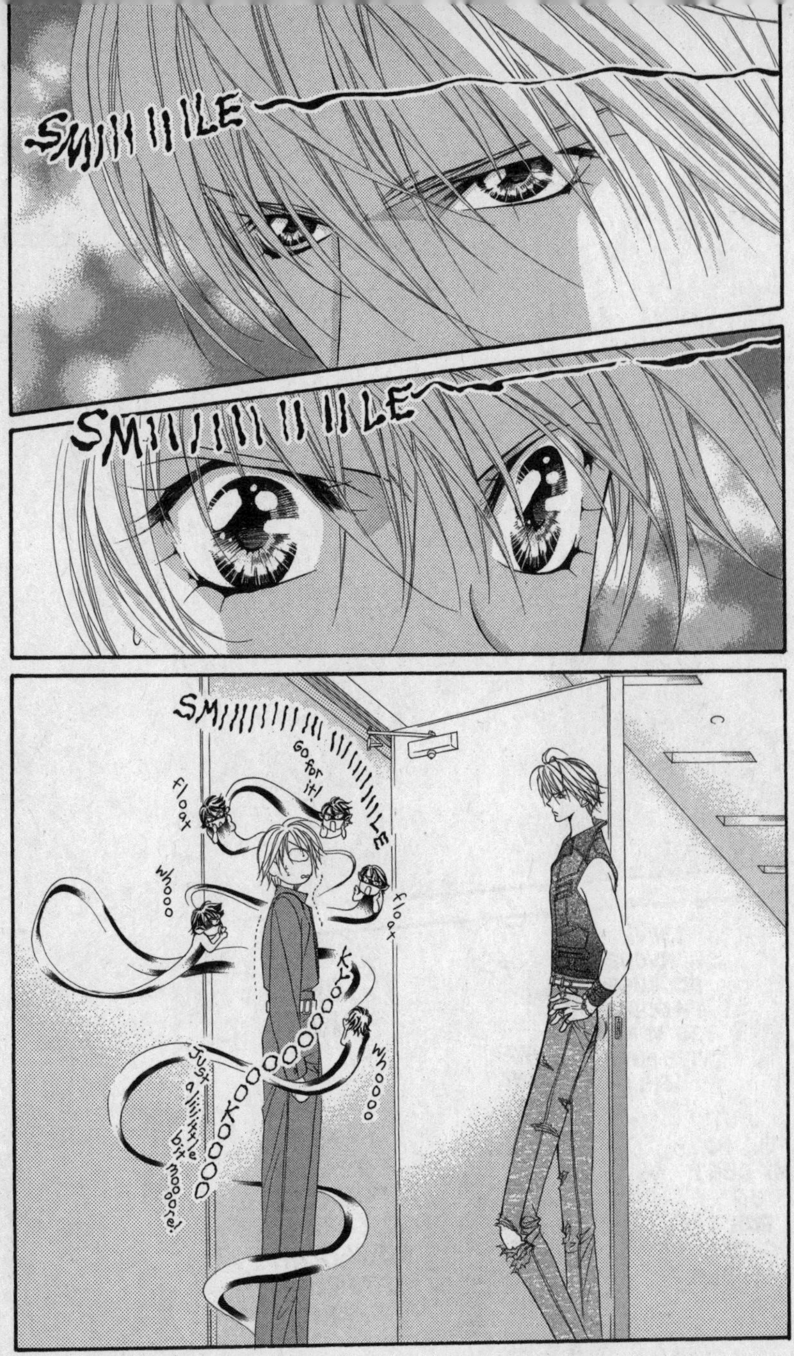
SMIIIILE
SMIIIIIIIIILE
SMIIIIIIIIIIIIIIIIILE
Go for it!
float
float
whooo
whoooooo
KYOOOOOOOOKOOOOO
Just a liiiittle bit mooooore!

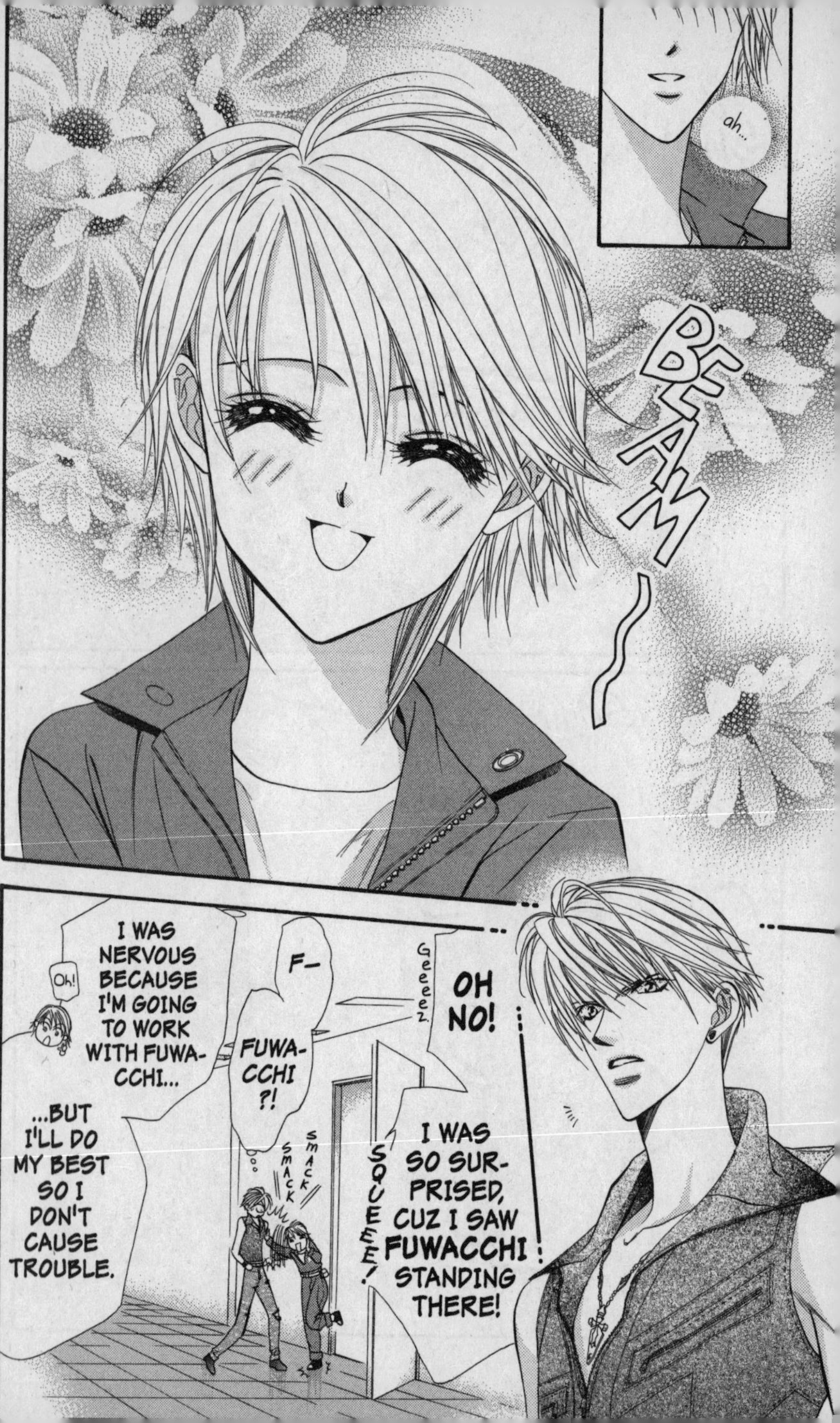
ah...
BEAM
OH NO!
Geeeez.
F—
I WAS NERVOUS BECAUSE I'M GOING TO WORK WITH FUWACCHI...
Oh!
I WAS SO SURPRISED, CUZ I SAW FUWACCHI STANDING THERE!
SQUEEEE!
FUWACCHI?!
SMACK SMACK
...BUT I'LL DO MY BEST SO I DON'T CAUSE TROUBLE.

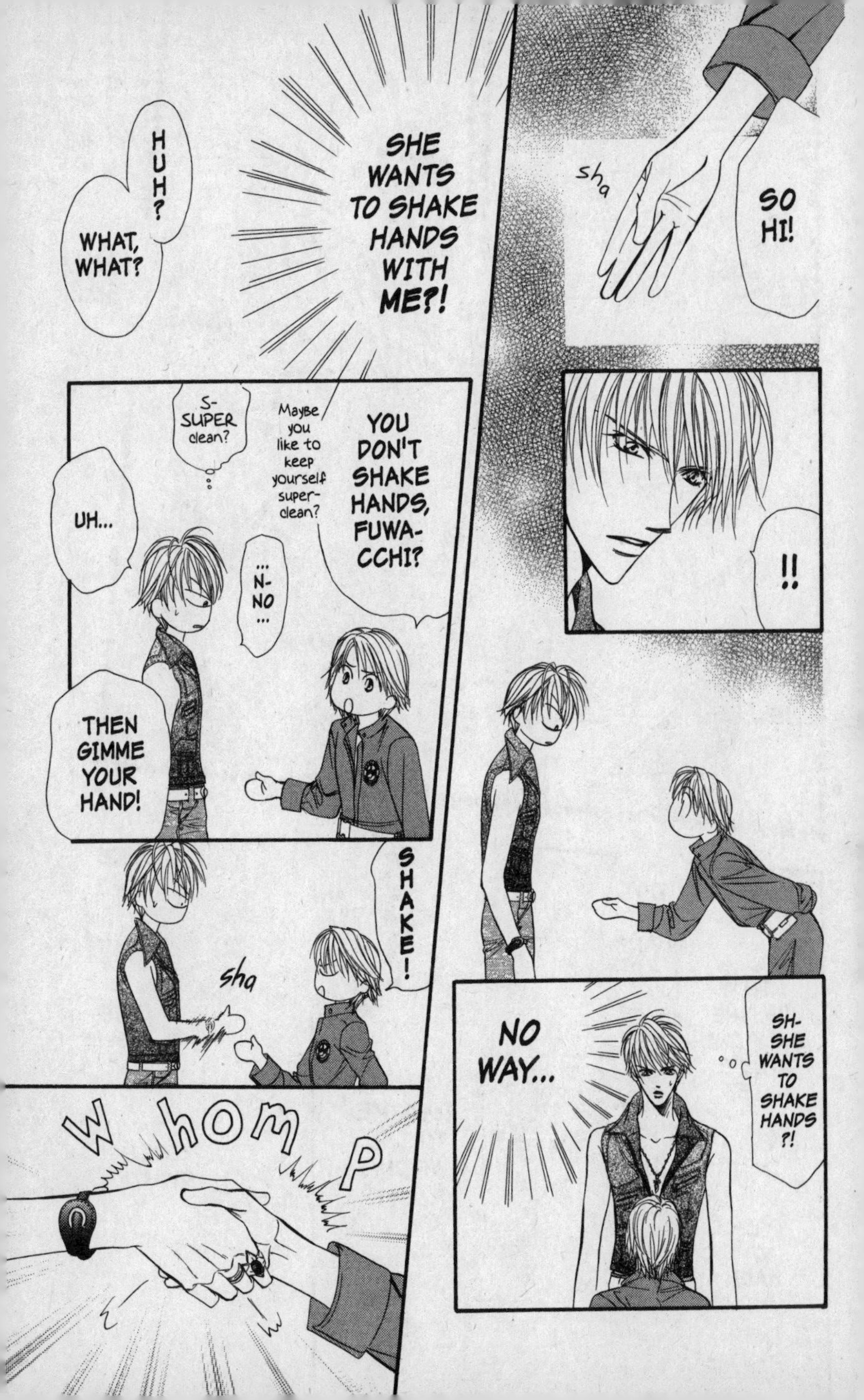
sha
SO HI!
!!
SH-SHE WANTS TO SHAKE HANDS?!
NO WAY...
SHE WANTS TO SHAKE HANDS WITH ME?!
HUH?
WHAT, WHAT?
YOU DON'T SHAKE HANDS, FUWACCHI?
Maybe you like to keep yourself super-clean?
S-SUPER clean?
...N-NO...
UH...
THEN GIMME YOUR HAND!
SHAKE!
sha
WHOMP

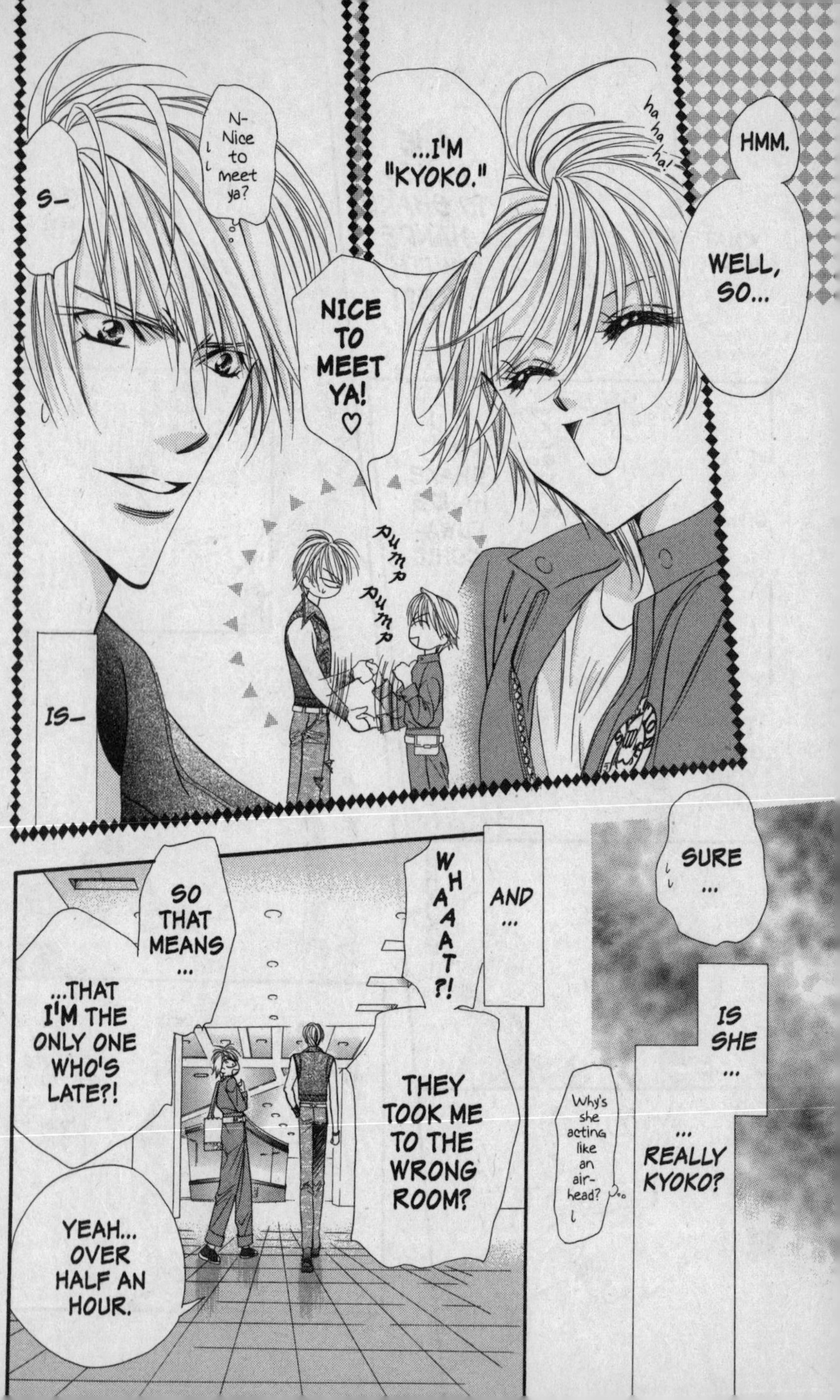
HMM.
ha ha ha!
WELL, SO...
...I'M "KYOKO."
NICE TO MEET YA! ♡
pump pump
S—
N-Nice to meet ya?
IS—
SURE...
IS SHE...
...REALLY KYOKO?
Why's she acting like an air-head?
AND...
WHAAAT?!
THEY TOOK ME TO THE WRONG ROOM?
SO THAT MEANS...
...THAT I'M THE ONLY ONE WHO'S LATE?!
YEAH... OVER HALF AN HOUR.

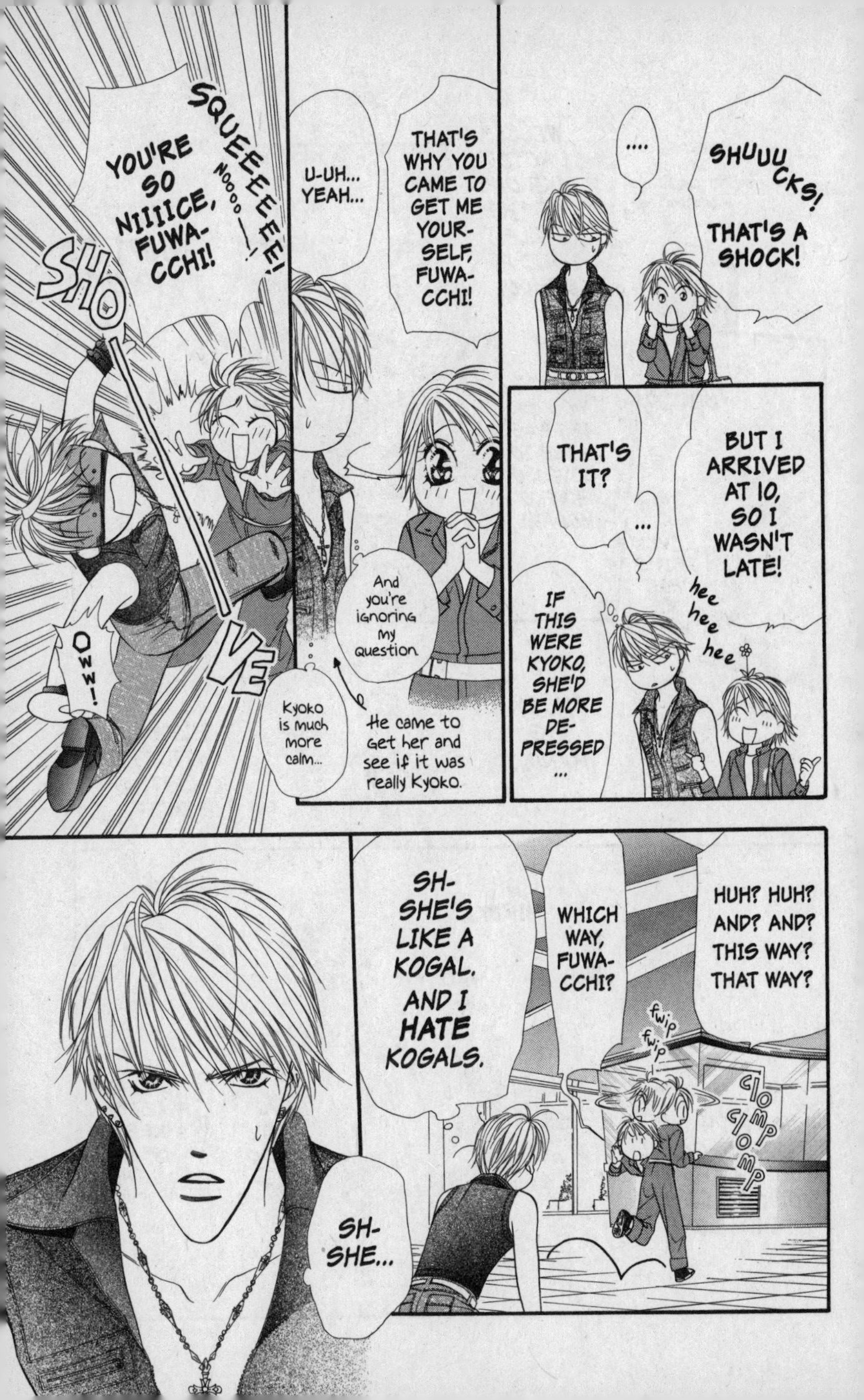
SHUUUCKS!
THAT'S A SHOCK!
....
BUT I ARRIVED AT 10, SO I WASN'T LATE!
THAT'S IT?
...
hee hee hee
IF THIS WERE KYOKO, SHE'D BE MORE DE-PRESSED ...
THAT'S WHY YOU CAME TO GET ME YOUR-SELF, FUWA-CCHI!
U-UH... YEAH...
And you're ignoring my question.
He came to get her and see if it was really Kyoko.
Kyoko is much more calm...
SQUEEEEEEE!
Noooo—!
YOU'RE SO NIIIICE, FUWA-CCHI!
SHOVE
OWW!
HUH? HUH? AND? AND? THIS WAY? THAT WAY?
WHICH WAY, FUWA-CCHI?
fwip fwip
CLOMP CLOMP CLOMP
SH-SHE'S LIKE A KOGAL. AND I HATE KOGALS.
SH-SHE...

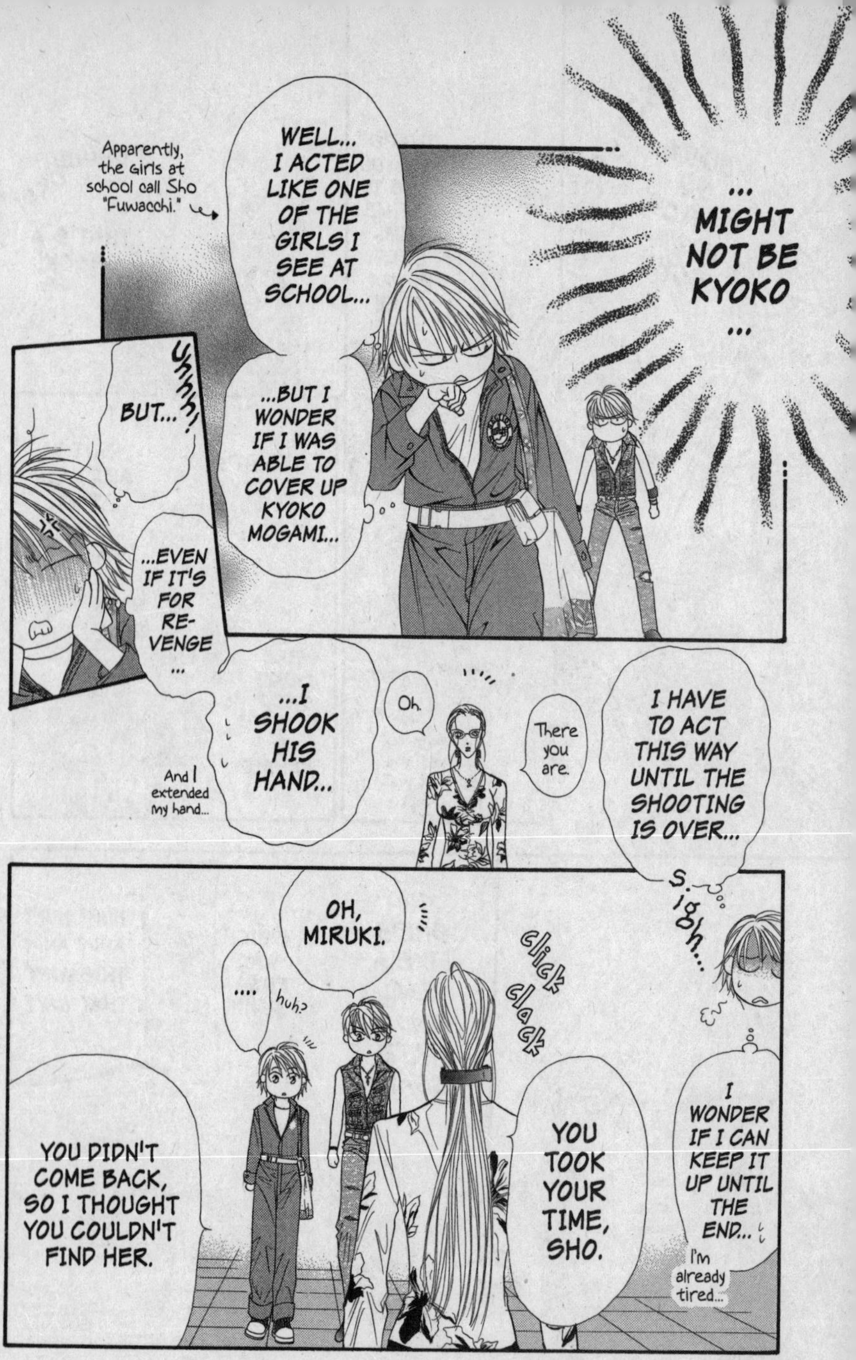

...MIGHT NOT BE KYOKO...
WELL... I ACTED LIKE ONE OF THE GIRLS I SEE AT SCHOOL...
Apparently, the girls at school call Sho "Fuwacchi."
...BUT I WONDER IF I WAS ABLE TO COVER UP KYOKO MOGAMI...
Ummm!
BUT...
...EVEN IF IT'S FOR REVENGE...
I HAVE TO ACT THIS WAY UNTIL THE SHOOTING IS OVER...
There you are.
Oh.
...I SHOOK HIS HAND...
And I extended my hand...
sigh...
I WONDER IF I CAN KEEP IT UP UNTIL THE END...
I'm already tired...
click clack
YOU TOOK YOUR TIME, SHO.
OH, MIRUKI.
huh?
....
YOU DIDN'T COME BACK, SO I THOUGHT YOU COULDN'T FIND HER.

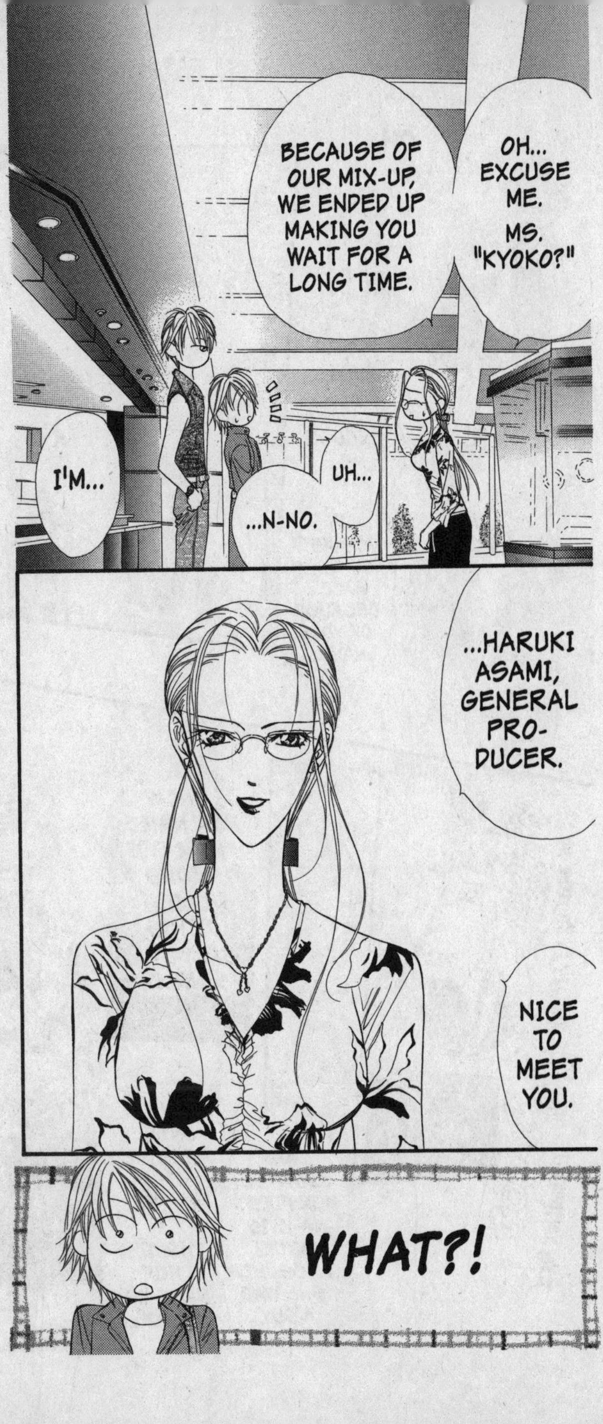
OH... EXCUSE ME. MS. "KYOKO?"
BECAUSE OF OUR MIX-UP, WE ENDED UP MAKING YOU WAIT FOR A LONG TIME.
UH...
...N-NO.
I'M...
...HARUKI ASAMI, GENERAL PRO-DUCER.
NICE TO MEET YOU.
WHAT?!
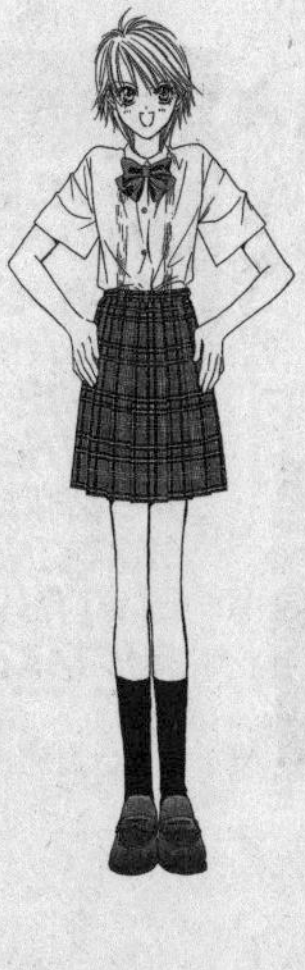

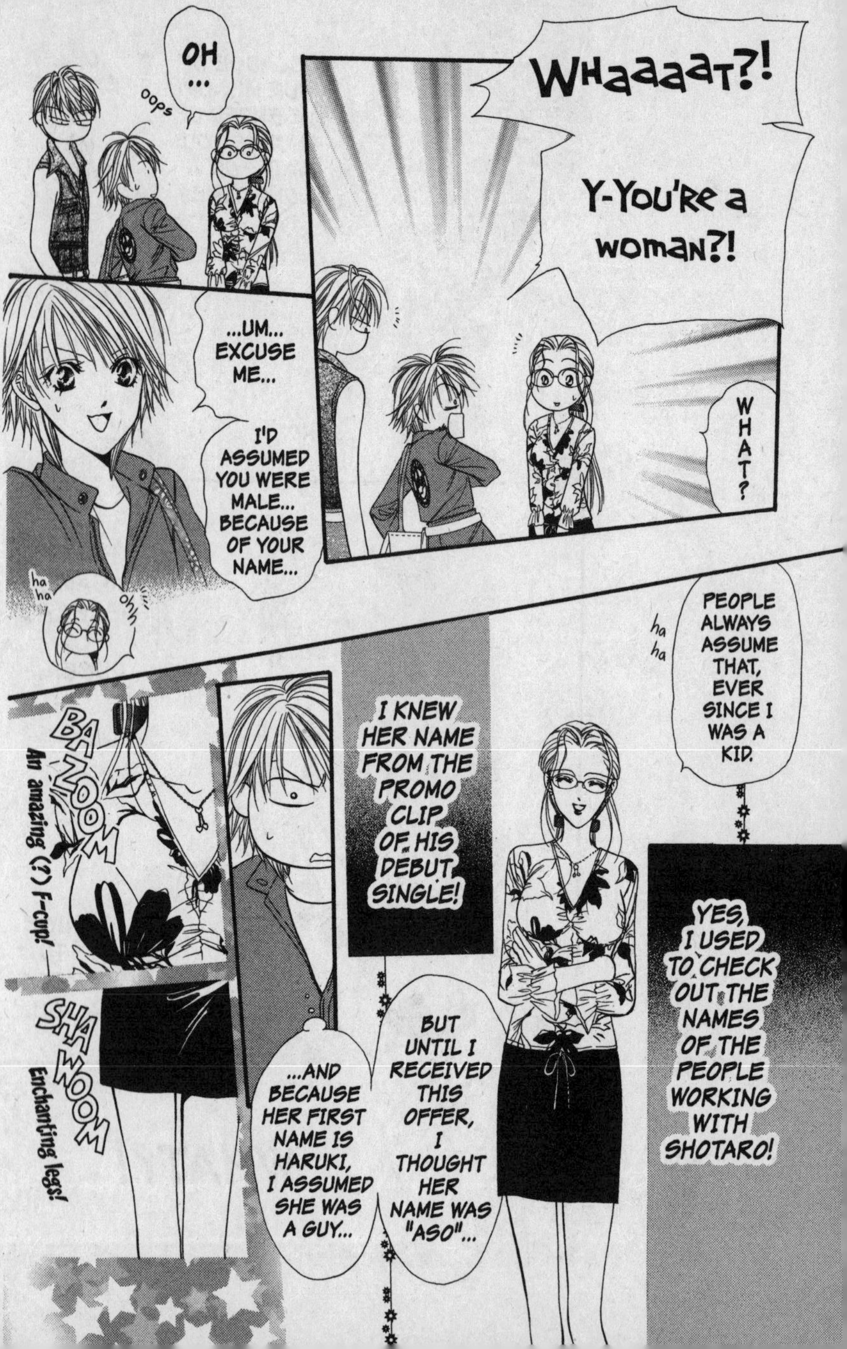
WHaaaaT?!
Y-You're a woman?!
WHAT?
OH...
oops
...UM... EXCUSE ME...
I'D ASSUMED YOU WERE MALE... BECAUSE OF YOUR NAME...
ha ha
oh h
ha ha
PEOPLE ALWAYS ASSUME THAT, EVER SINCE I WAS A KID.
YES, I USED TO CHECK OUT THE NAMES OF THE PEOPLE WORKING WITH SHOTARO!
I KNEW HER NAME FROM THE PROMO CLIP OF HIS DEBUT SINGLE!
BUT UNTIL I RECEIVED THIS OFFER, I THOUGHT HER NAME WAS "ASO"...
...AND BECAUSE HER FIRST NAME IS HARUKI, I ASSUMED SHE WAS A GUY...
BAZOOM
An amazing (?) F-cup!
SHAWOOM
Enchanting legs!

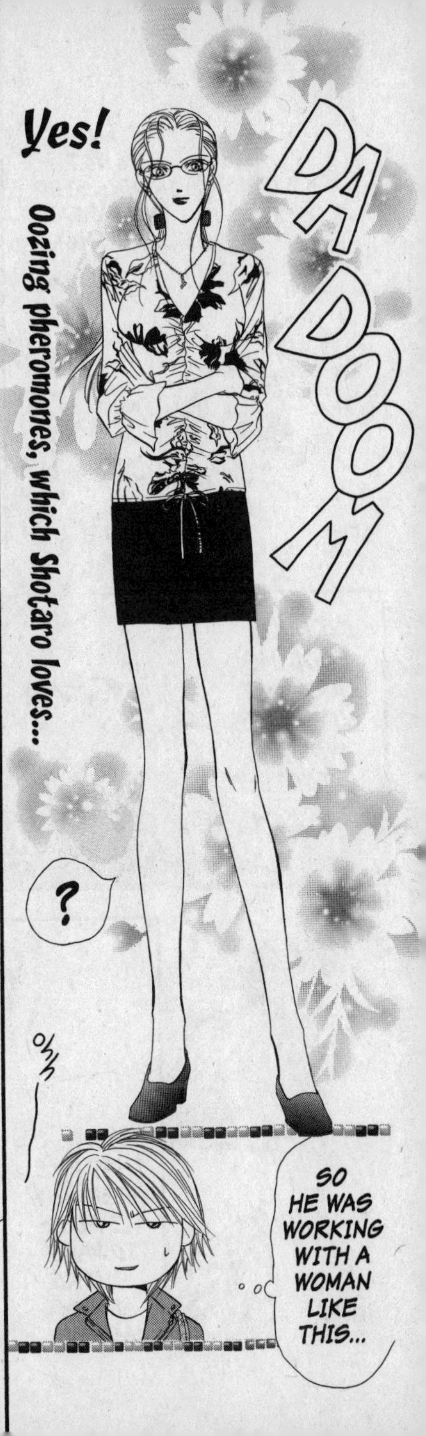
DA DOOM
Yes!
Oozing pheromones, which Shotaro loves...
?
SO HE WAS WORKING WITH A WOMAN LIKE THIS...

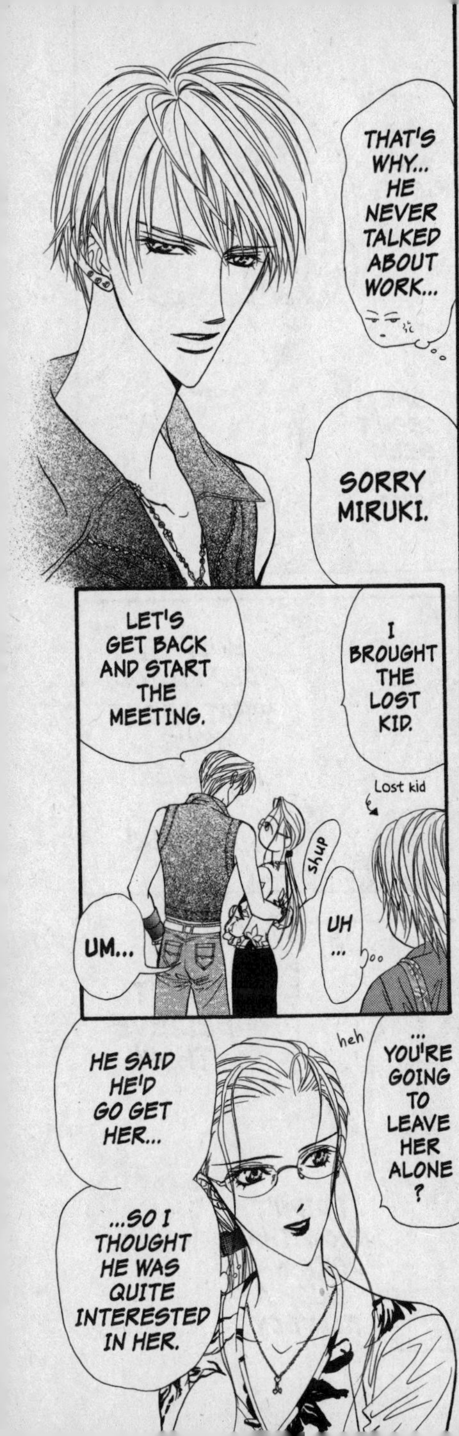
THAT'S WHY... HE NEVER TALKED ABOUT WORK...
SORRY MIRUKI.
I BROUGHT THE LOST KID.
LET'S GET BACK AND START THE MEETING.
Lost kid
shup
UH ...
UM...
... YOU'RE GOING TO LEAVE HER ALONE ?
heh
HE SAID HE'D GO GET HER...
...SO I THOUGHT HE WAS QUITE INTERESTED IN HER.

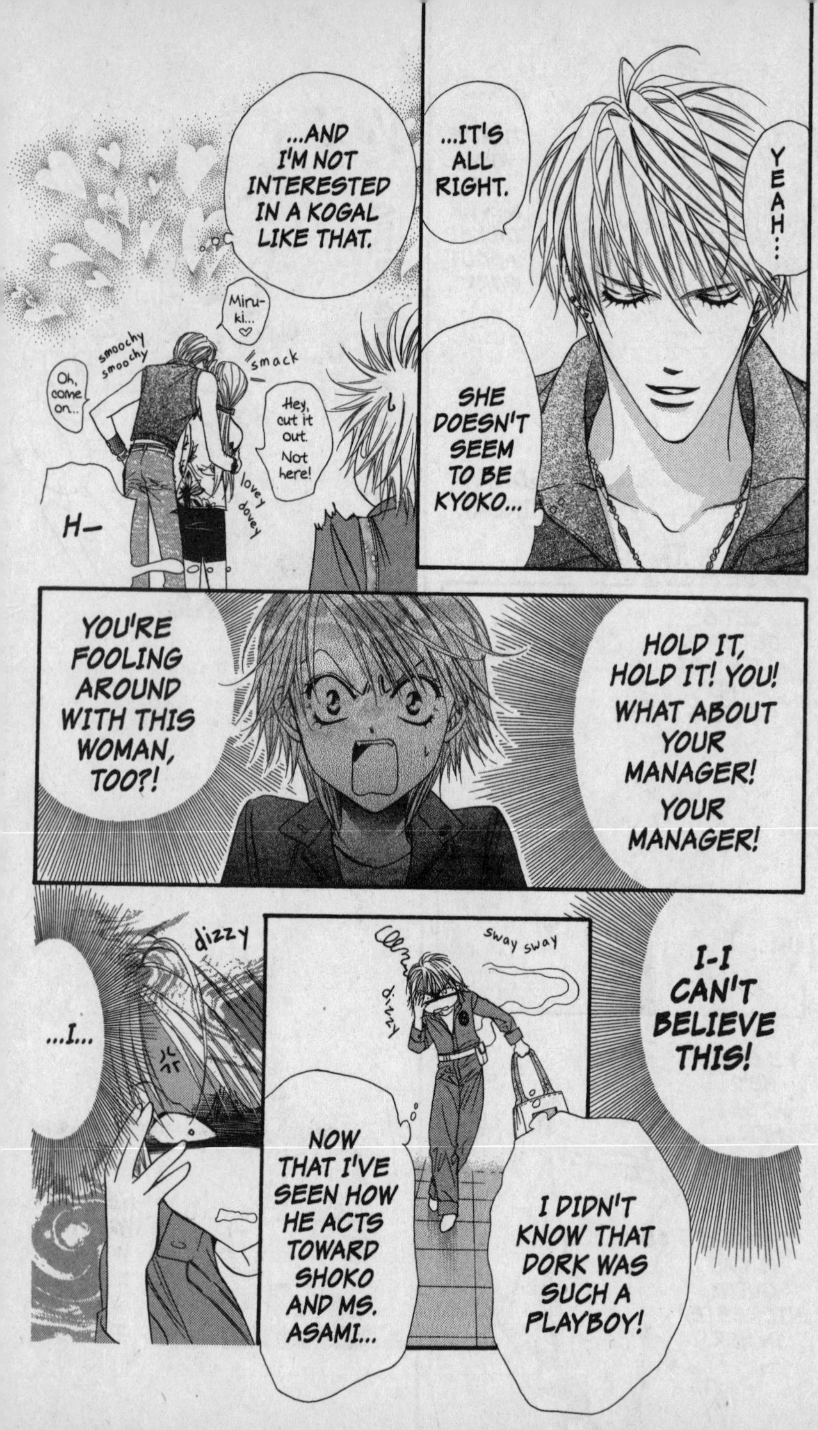
YEAH...
...IT'S ALL RIGHT.
SHE DOESN'T SEEM TO BE KYOKO...
...AND I'M NOT INTERESTED IN A KOGAL LIKE THAT.
Miru-ki... ♡
smack
Hey, cut it out. Not here!
smoochy smoochy
Oh, come on...
lovey dovey
H—
HOLD IT, HOLD IT! YOU! WHAT ABOUT YOUR MANAGER! YOUR MANAGER!
YOU'RE FOOLING AROUND WITH THIS WOMAN, TOO?!
I-I CAN'T BELIEVE THIS!
I DIDN'T KNOW THAT DORK WAS SUCH A PLAYBOY!
sway sway
dizzy
NOW THAT I'VE SEEN HOW HE ACTS TOWARD SHOKO AND MS. ASAMI...
dizzy
...I...

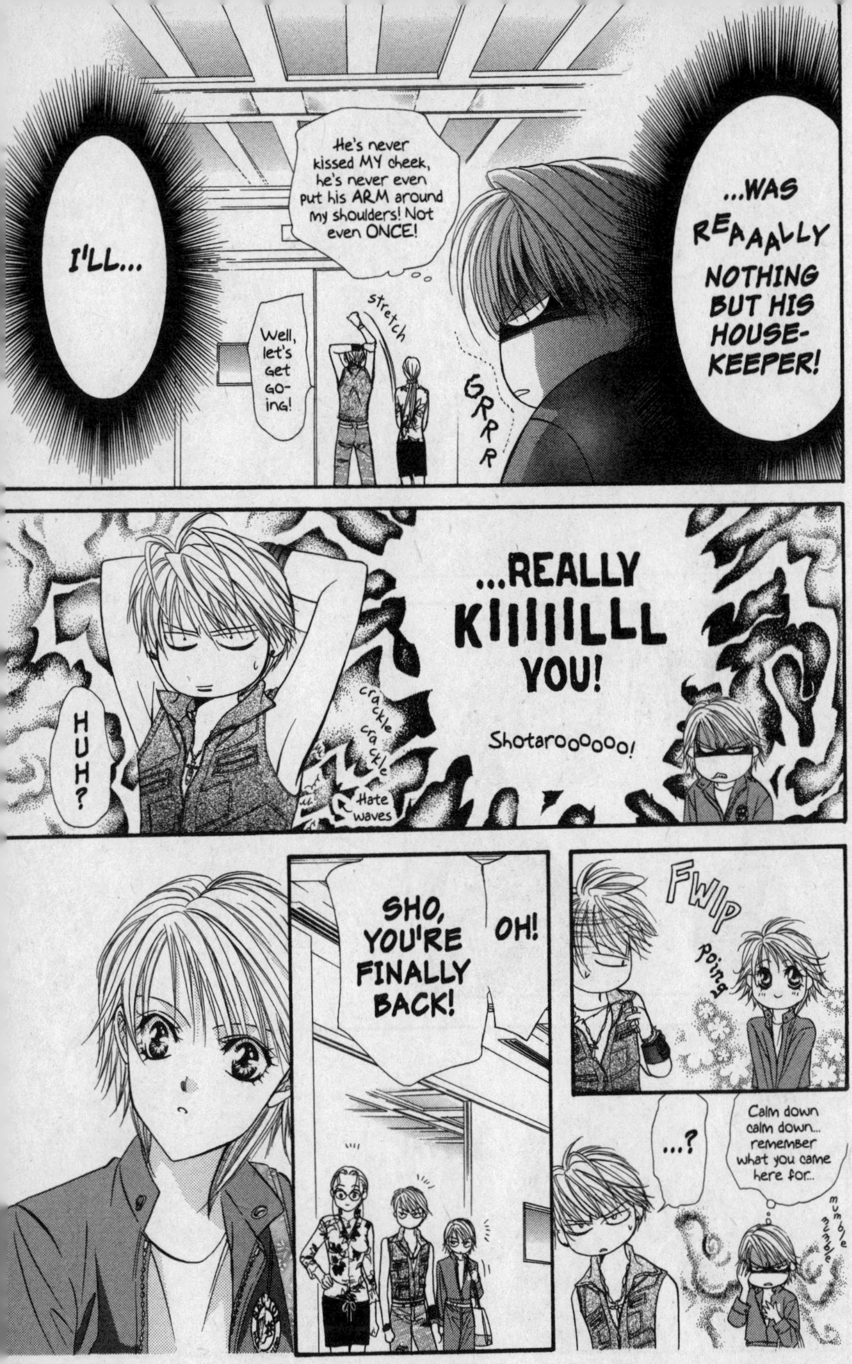

...WAS REAAAALLY NOTHING BUT HIS HOUSE-KEEPER!
He's never kissed MY cheek, he's never even put his ARM around my shoulders! Not even ONCE!
GRRR
stretch
Well, let's get go-ing!
I'LL...
...REALLY KIIIIILLL YOU!
Shotarooooooo!
crackle crackle
Hate waves
HUH?
FWIP
poing
Calm down calm down... remember what you came here for...
mumble mumble
...?
OH!
SHO, YOU'RE FINALLY BACK!

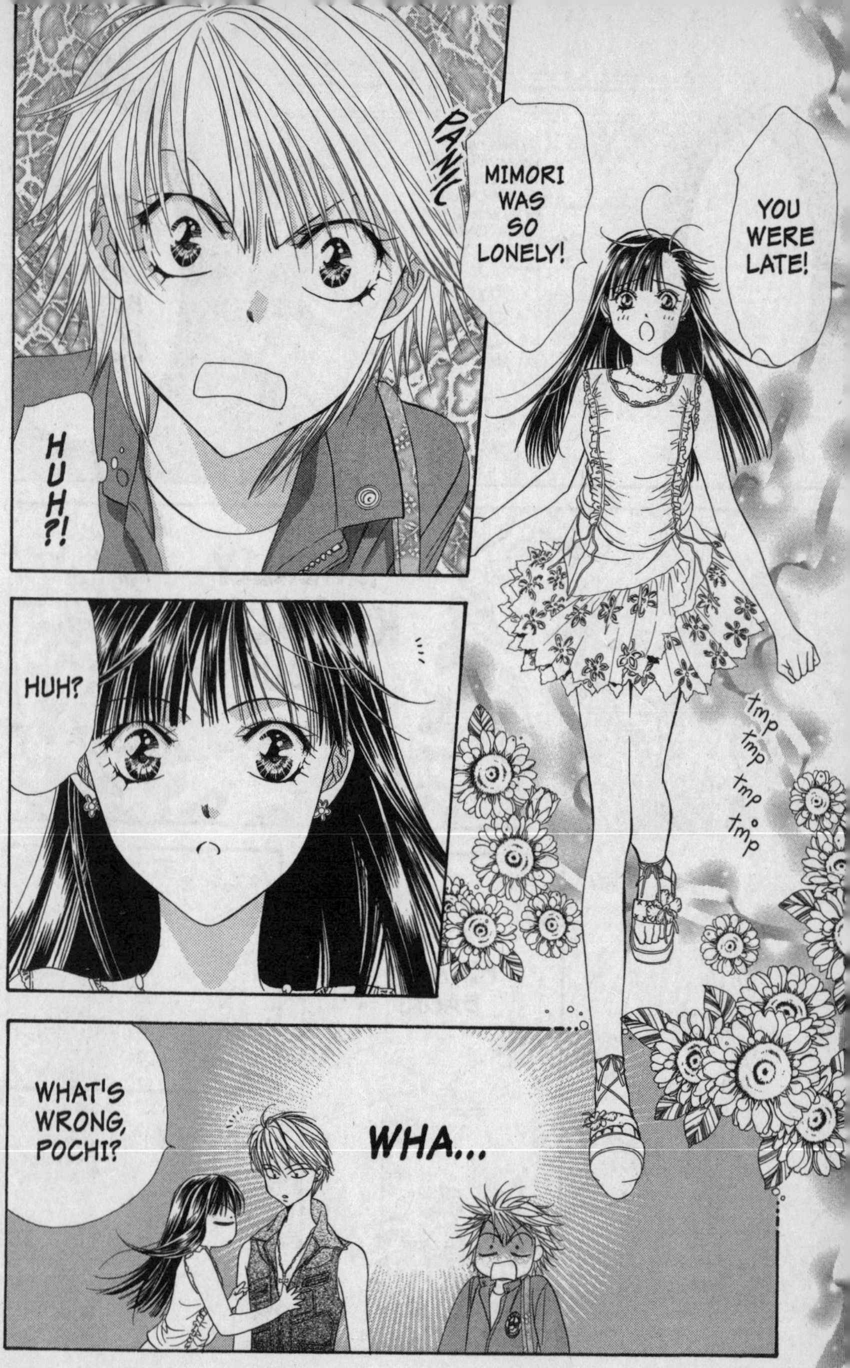
YOU WERE LATE!
MIMORI WAS SO LONELY!
tmp tmp tmp tmp
PANIC
HUH?!
HUH?
WHAT'S WRONG, POCHI?
WHA...

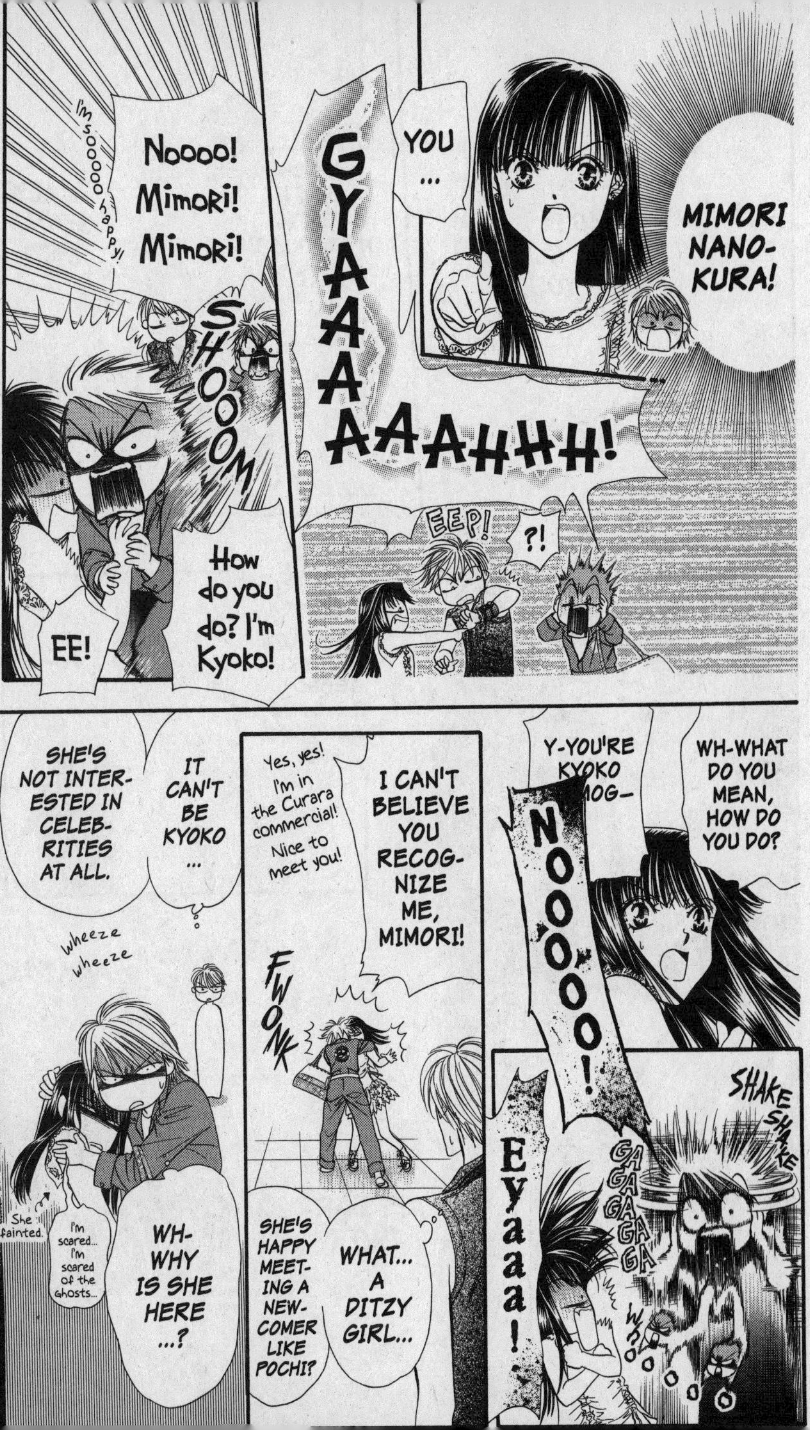
MIMORI NANO-KURA!
YOU ...
GYAAAAAAHHH!
EEP!
?!
I'm soooo happy!
Noooo! Mimori! Mimori!
SHOOOOM
How do you do? I'm Kyoko!
EE!
WH-WHAT DO YOU MEAN, HOW DO YOU DO?
Y-YOU'RE KYOKO MOG—
NOOOOOO!
SHAKE SHAKE
GAGAGAGAGA
Eyaaa!
I CAN'T BELIEVE YOU RECOGNIZE ME, MIMORI!
Yes, yes! I'm in the Curara commercial! Nice to meet you!
FWONK
WHAT... A DITZY GIRL...
SHE'S HAPPY MEETING A NEWCOMER LIKE POCHI?
IT CAN'T BE KYOKO ...
SHE'S NOT INTERESTED IN CELEBRITIES AT ALL.
wheeze wheeze
WH-WHY IS SHE HERE ...?
I'm scared... I'm scared of the ghosts...
She fainted.

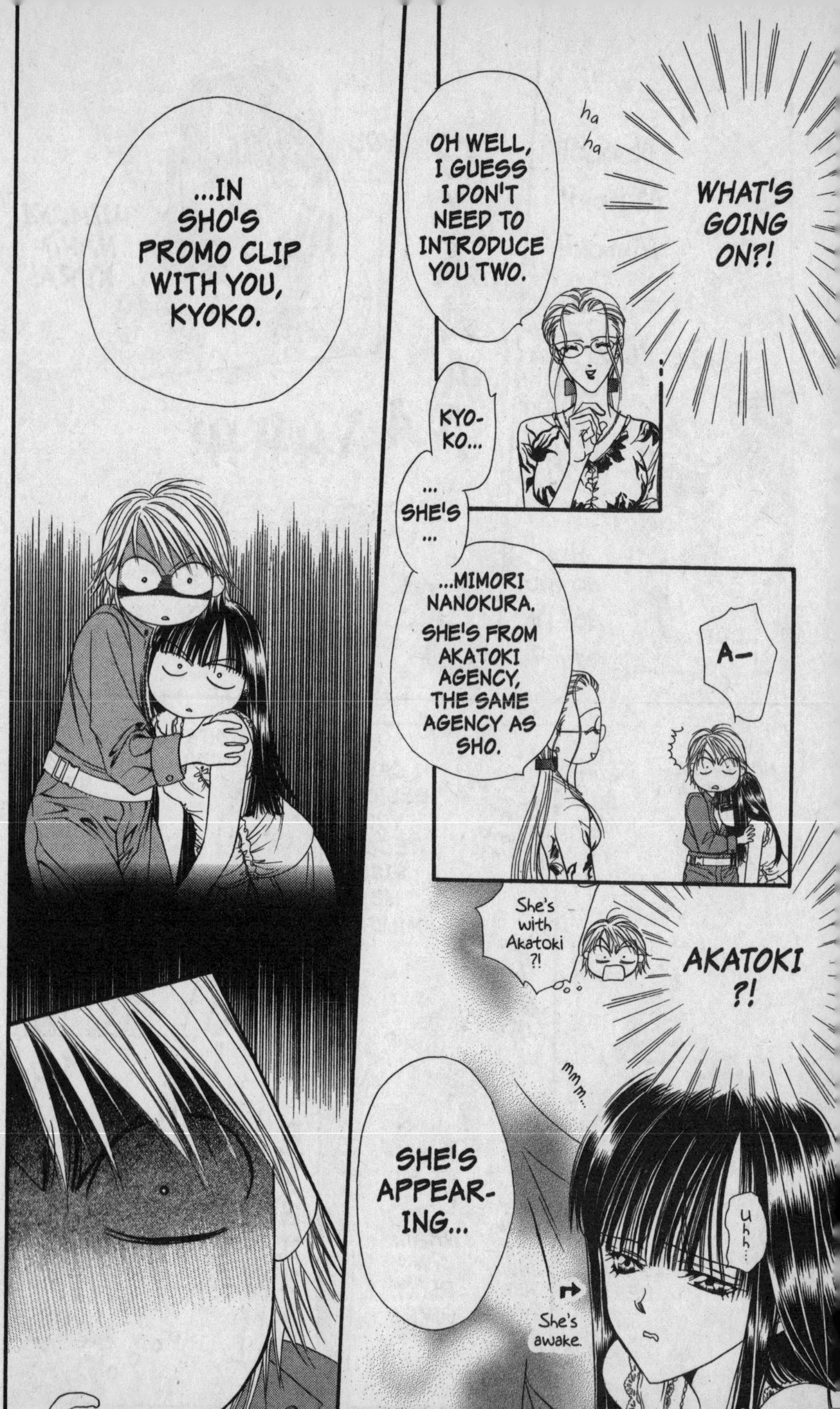
ha ha
WHAT'S GOING ON?!
OH WELL, I GUESS I DON'T NEED TO INTRODUCE YOU TWO.
KYO-KO...
... SHE'S ...
...MIMORI NANOKURA. SHE'S FROM AKATOKI AGENCY, THE SAME AGENCY AS SHO.
A-
AKATOKI ?!
She's with Akatoki ?!
mmm...
Uhh...
She's awake.
SHE'S APPEARING-ING...
...IN SHO'S PROMO CLIP WITH YOU, KYOKO.

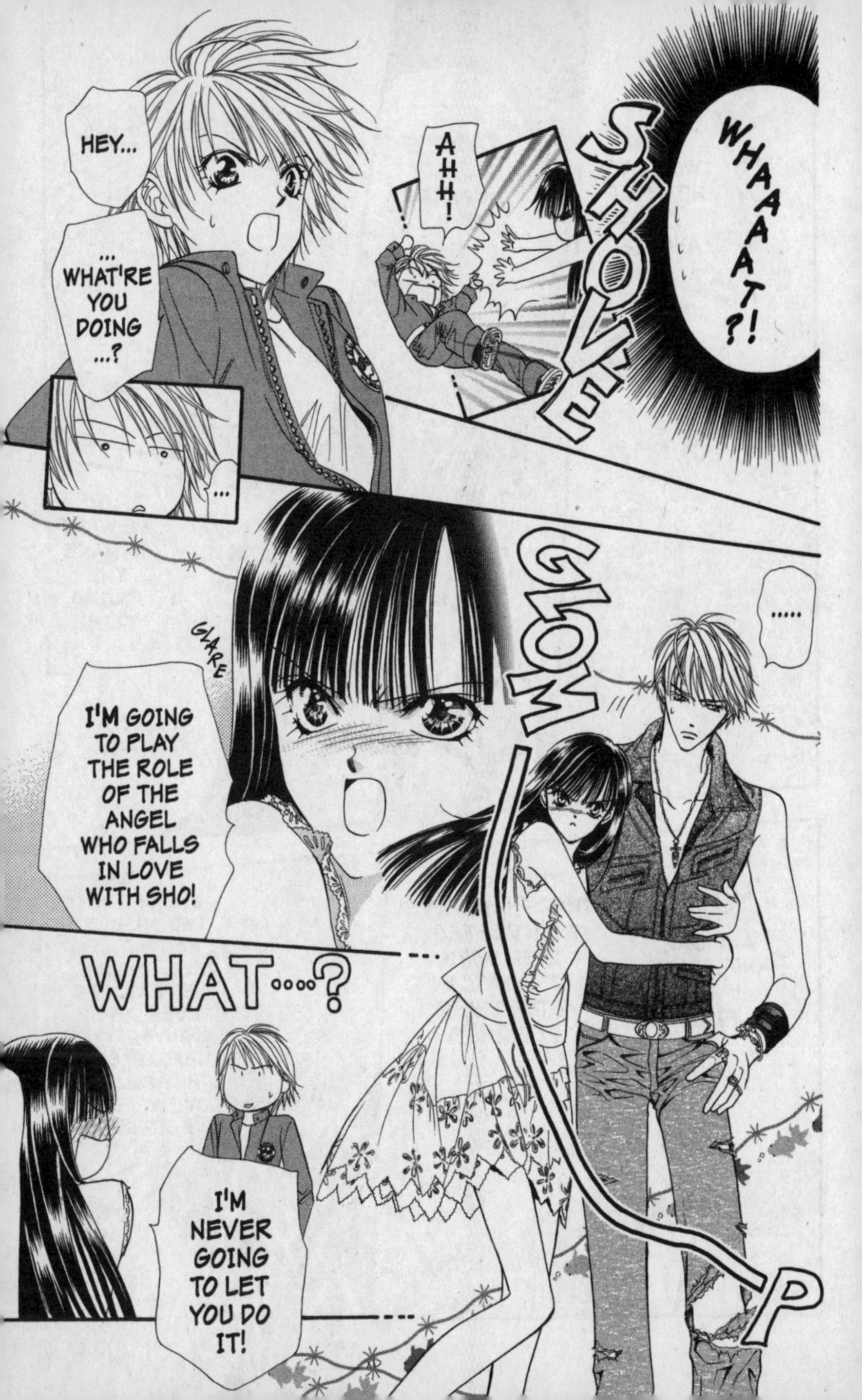
WHAAAAT?!
SHOVE
AHH!
HEY...
...WHAT'RE YOU DOING...?
...
.....
GLOW
GLARE
I'M GOING TO PLAY THE ROLE OF THE ANGEL WHO FALLS IN LOVE WITH SHO!
SNAP
WHAT....?
I'M NEVER GOING TO LET YOU DO IT!

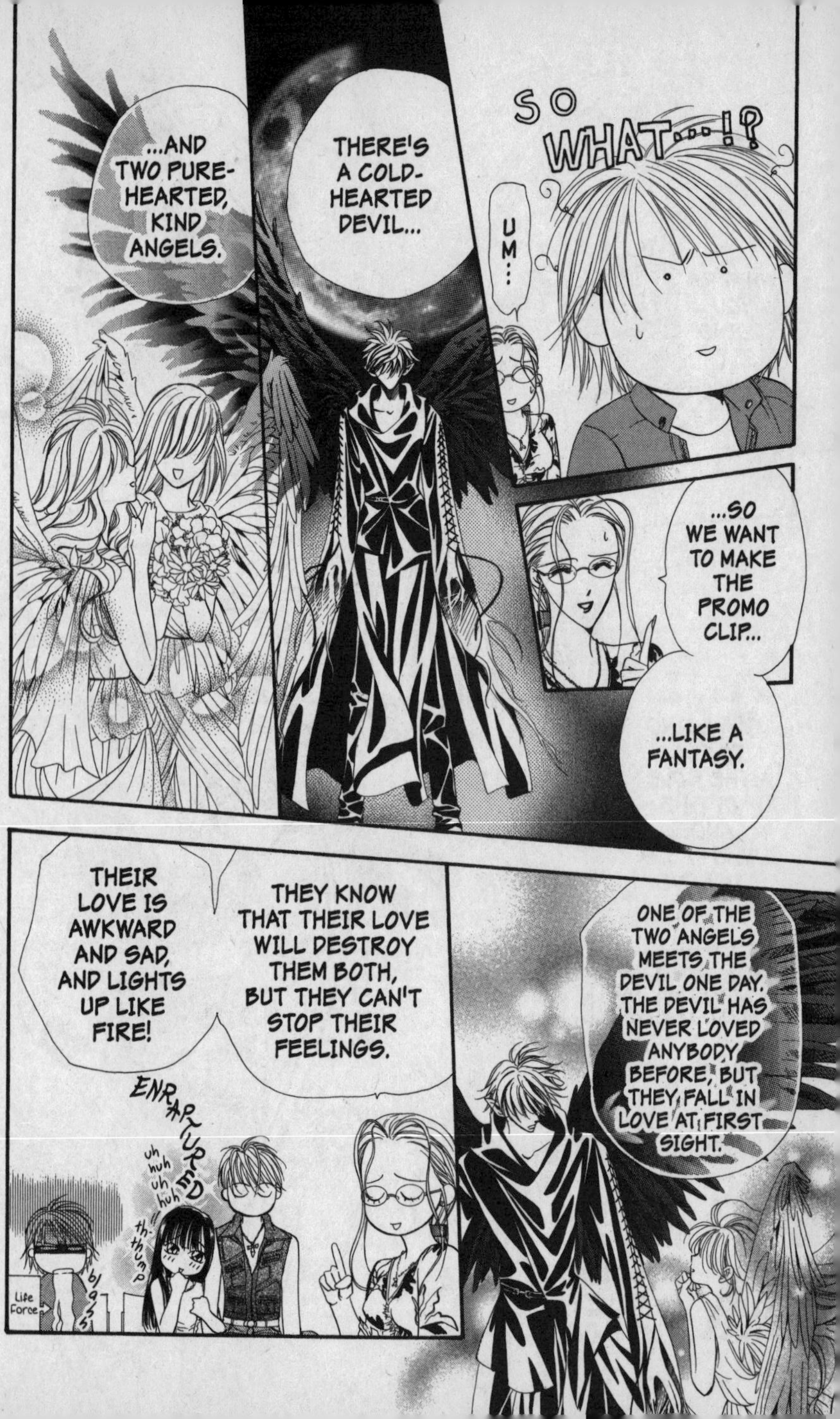
SO WHAT...!?
UM...
...SO WE WANT TO MAKE THE PROMO CLIP...
...LIKE A FANTASY.
THERE'S A COLD-HEARTED DEVIL...
...AND TWO PURE-HEARTED, KIND ANGELS.
ONE OF THE TWO ANGELS MEETS THE DEVIL ONE DAY. THE DEVIL HAS NEVER LOVED ANYBODY BEFORE, BUT THEY FALL IN LOVE AT FIRST SIGHT.
THEY KNOW THAT THEIR LOVE WILL DESTROY THEM BOTH, BUT THEY CAN'T STOP THEIR FEELINGS.
THEIR LOVE IS AWKWARD AND SAD, AND LIGHTS UP LIKE FIRE!
ENRAPTURED
uh huh uh huh
th-thump
Life Force

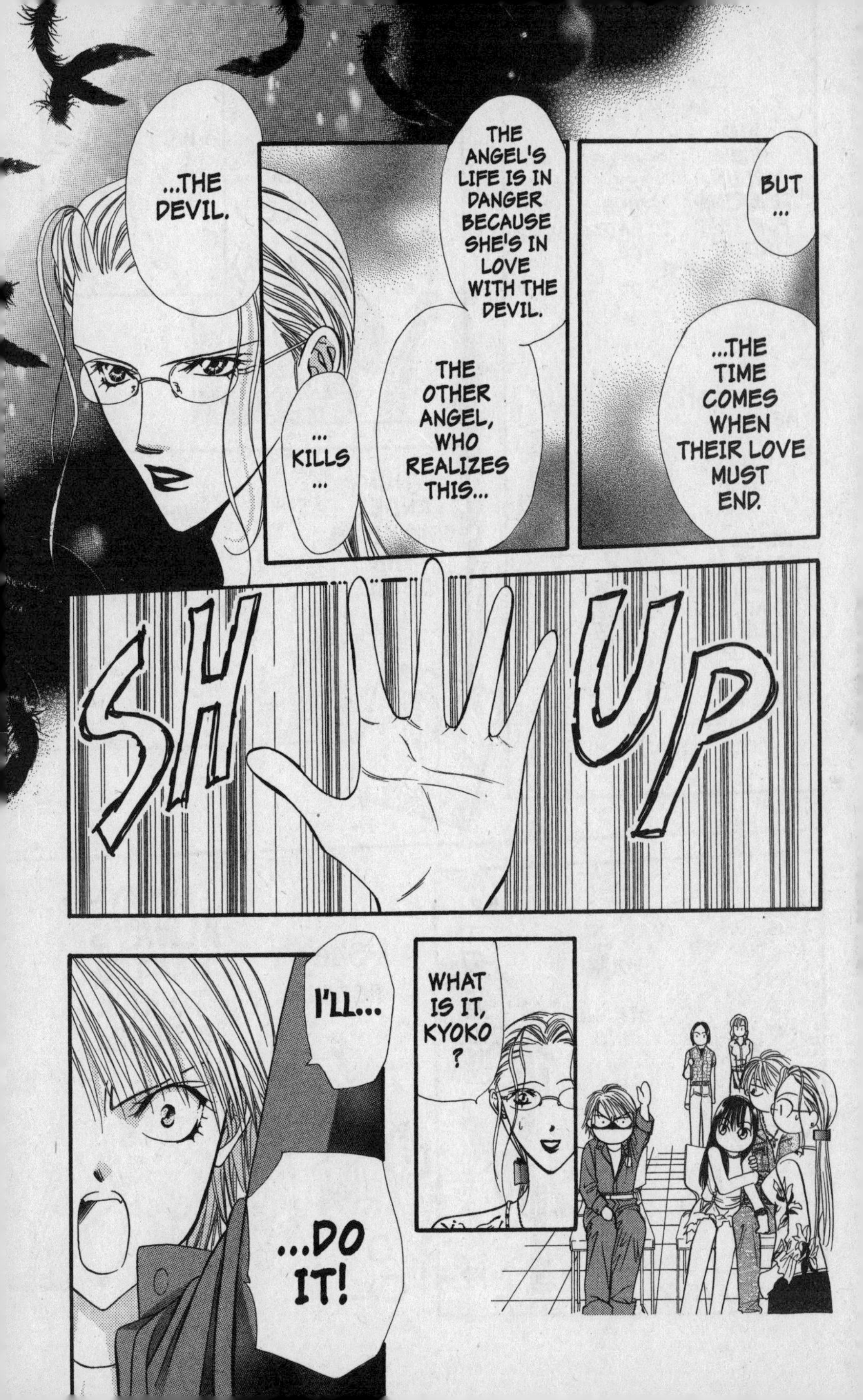
BUT...
...THE TIME COMES WHEN THEIR LOVE MUST END.
THE ANGEL'S LIFE IS IN DANGER BECAUSE SHE'S IN LOVE WITH THE DEVIL.
THE OTHER ANGEL, WHO REALIZES THIS...
...KILLS...
...THE DEVIL.
SH UP
WHAT IS IT, KYOKO?
I'LL...
...DO IT!

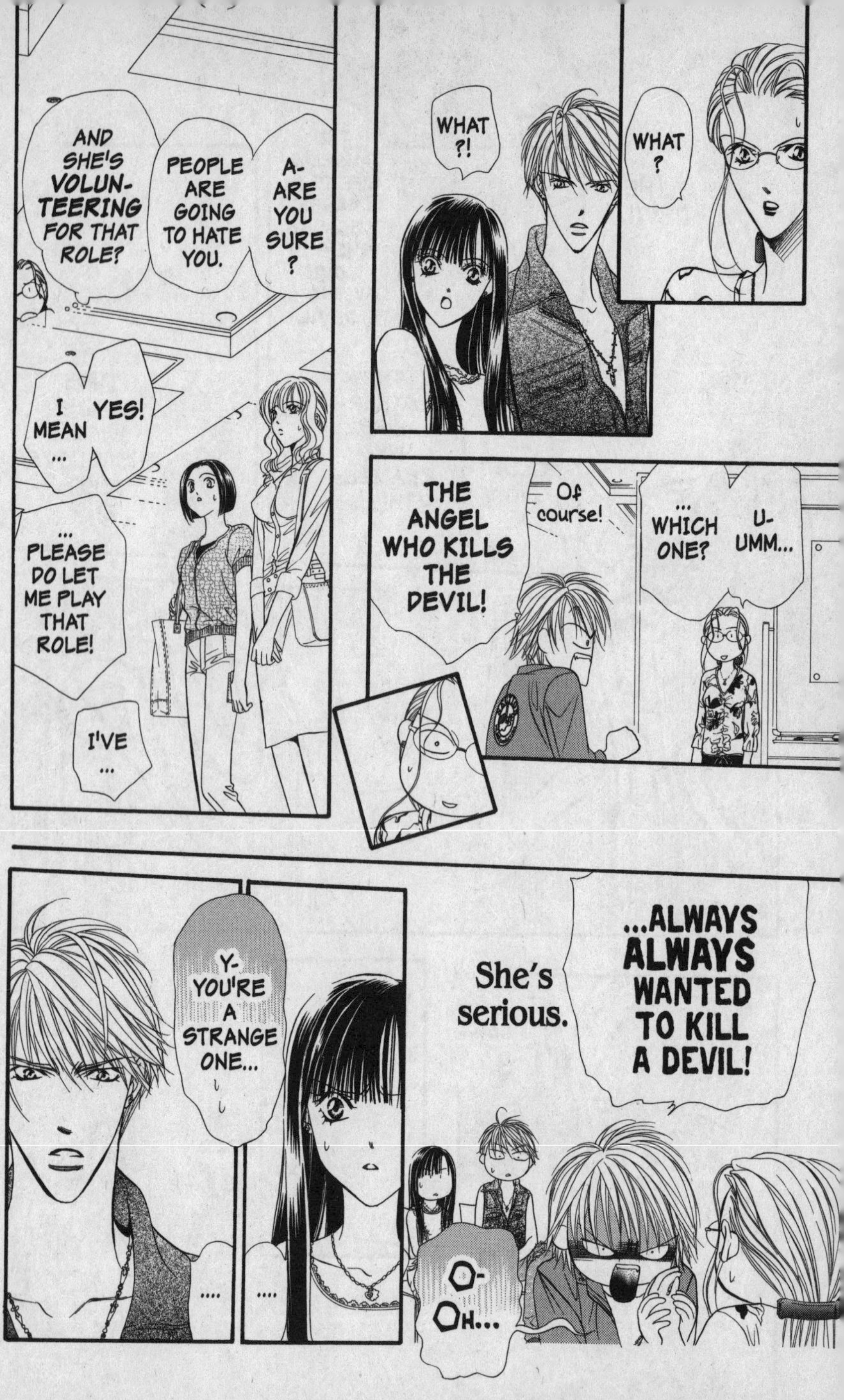
WHAT ?
WHAT ?!
U- UMM...
... WHICH ONE?
Of course!
THE ANGEL WHO KILLS THE DEVIL!
A- ARE YOU SURE ?
PEOPLE ARE GOING TO HATE YOU.
AND SHE'S VOLUN- TEERING FOR THAT ROLE?
YES!
I MEAN ...
... PLEASE DO LET ME PLAY THAT ROLE!
I'VE ...
...ALWAYS ALWAYS WANTED TO KILL A DEVIL!
She's serious.
O- OH...
Y- YOU'RE A STRANGE ONE...
....
....

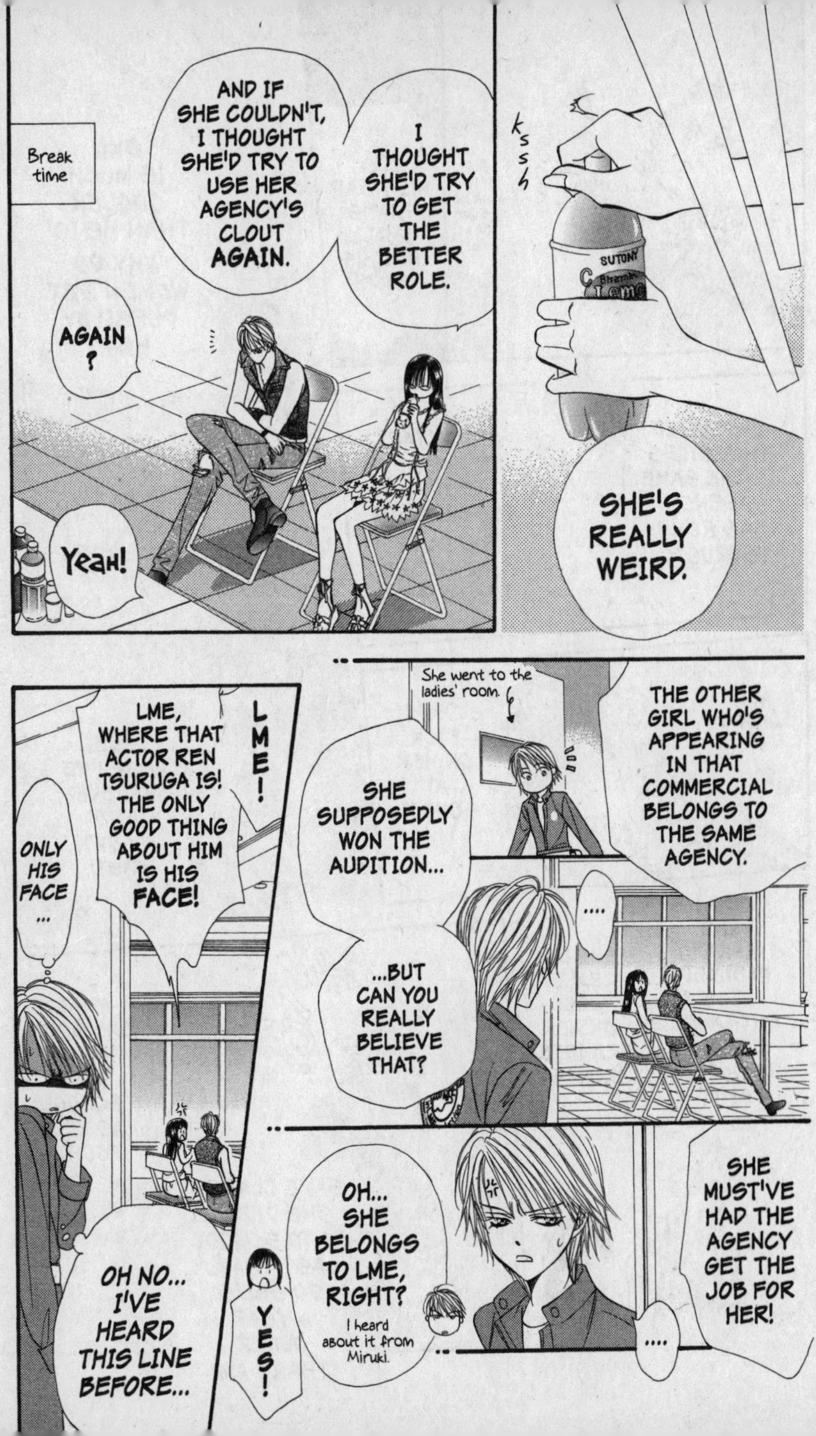

kssh
SHE'S REALLY WEIRD.
I THOUGHT SHE'D TRY TO GET THE BETTER ROLE.
AND IF SHE COULDN'T, I THOUGHT SHE'D TRY TO USE HER AGENCY'S CLOUT AGAIN.
Break time
AGAIN?
Yeah!
THE OTHER GIRL WHO'S APPEARING IN THAT COMMERCIAL BELONGS TO THE SAME AGENCY.
She went to the ladies' room.
SHE SUPPOSEDLY WON THE AUDITION...
....
...BUT CAN YOU REALLY BELIEVE THAT?
SHE MUST'VE HAD THE AGENCY GET THE JOB FOR HER!
....
OH... SHE BELONGS TO LME, RIGHT?
I heard about it from Miruki.
YES!
LME!
LME, WHERE THAT ACTOR REN TSURUGA IS! THE ONLY GOOD THING ABOUT HIM IS HIS FACE!
ONLY HIS FACE...
OH NO... I'VE HEARD THIS LINE BEFORE...

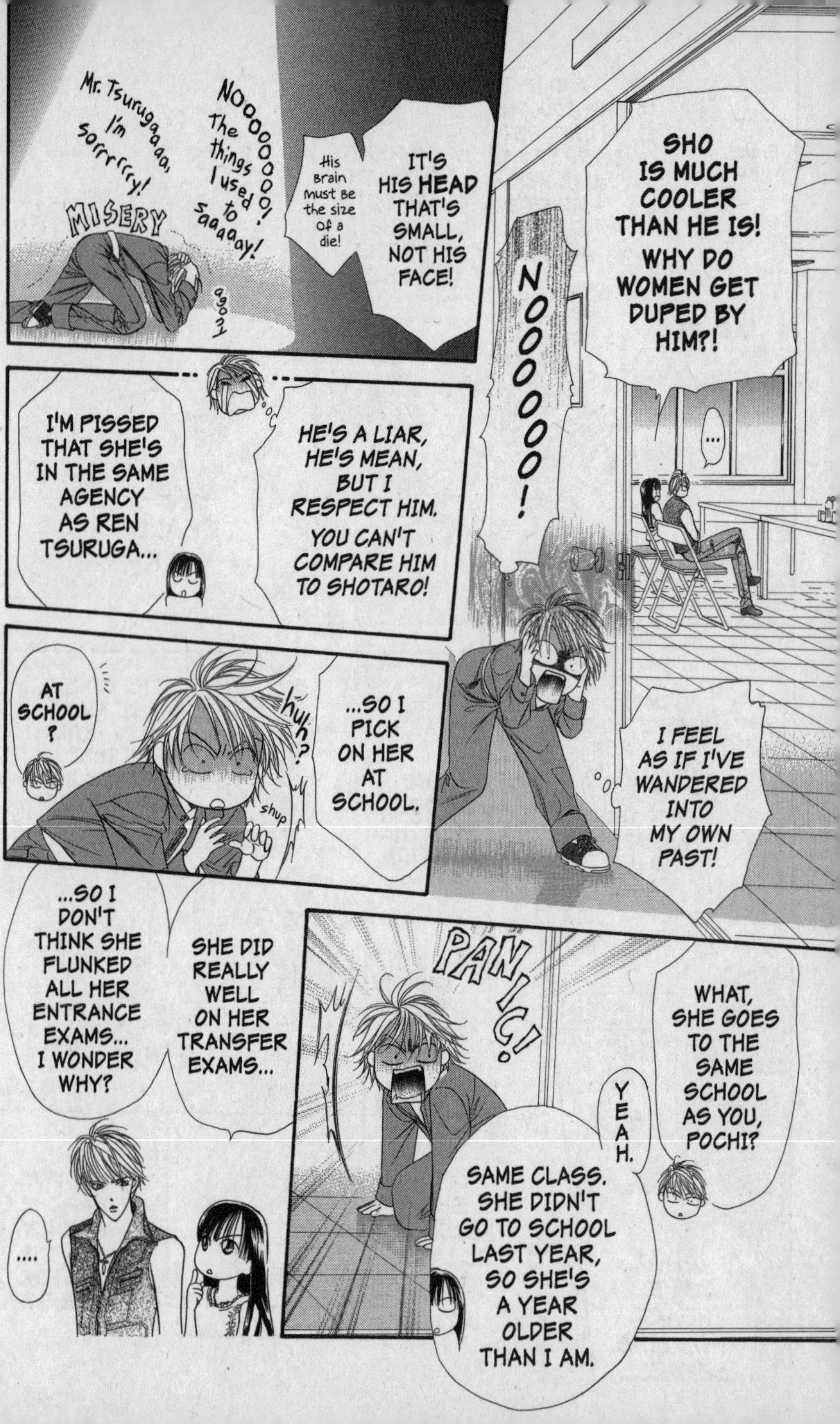
SHO IS MUCH COOLER THAN HE IS!
WHY DO WOMEN GET DUPED BY HIM?!
...
NOOOOOOO!
I FEEL AS IF I'VE WANDERED INTO MY OWN PAST!
IT'S HIS HEAD THAT'S SMALL, NOT HIS FACE!
His Brain Must Be the size Of a die!
Noooooooo! The things I used to saaaaay!
Mr. Tsurugaaaa, I'm sorrrrrry!
MISERY
agony
HE'S A LIAR, HE'S MEAN, BUT I RESPECT HIM.
YOU CAN'T COMPARE HIM TO SHOTARO!
I'M PISSED THAT SHE'S IN THE SAME AGENCY AS REN TSURUGA...
...SO I PICK ON HER AT SCHOOL.
huh?
shup
AT SCHOOL?
WHAT, SHE GOES TO THE SAME SCHOOL AS YOU, POCHI?
YEAH.
PANIC!
SAME CLASS. SHE DIDN'T GO TO SCHOOL LAST YEAR, SO SHE'S A YEAR OLDER THAN I AM.
SHE DID REALLY WELL ON HER TRANSFER EXAMS...
...SO I DON'T THINK SHE FLUNKED ALL HER ENTRANCE EXAMS... I WONDER WHY?
....

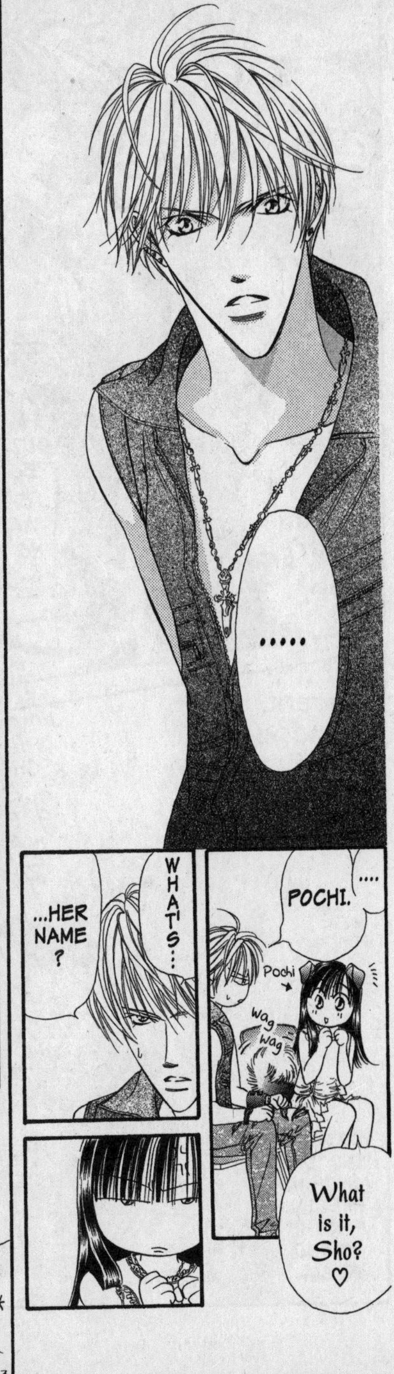
.....
....
POCHI.
Pochi
wag wag
What is it, Sho? ♡
WHAT'S...
...HER NAME?

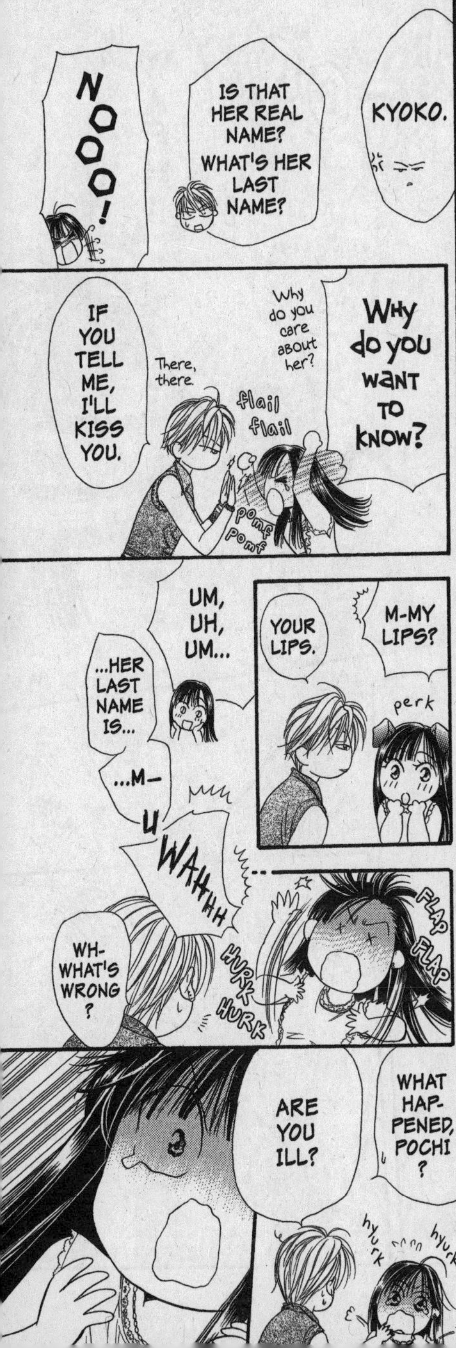
KYOKO.
IS THAT HER REAL NAME? WHAT'S HER LAST NAME?
NOOOO!
WHY do you WANT TO KNOW?
Why do you care about her?
flail flail
There, there.
IF YOU TELL ME, I'LL KISS YOU.
pomf pomf
M-MY LIPS?
YOUR LIPS.
perk
UM, UH, UM...
...HER LAST NAME IS...
...M-
UWAHHHH
FLAP FLAP
HURK HURK
WH-WHAT'S WRONG?
WHAT HAP-PENED, POCHI?
ARE YOU ILL?
hyurk hyurk

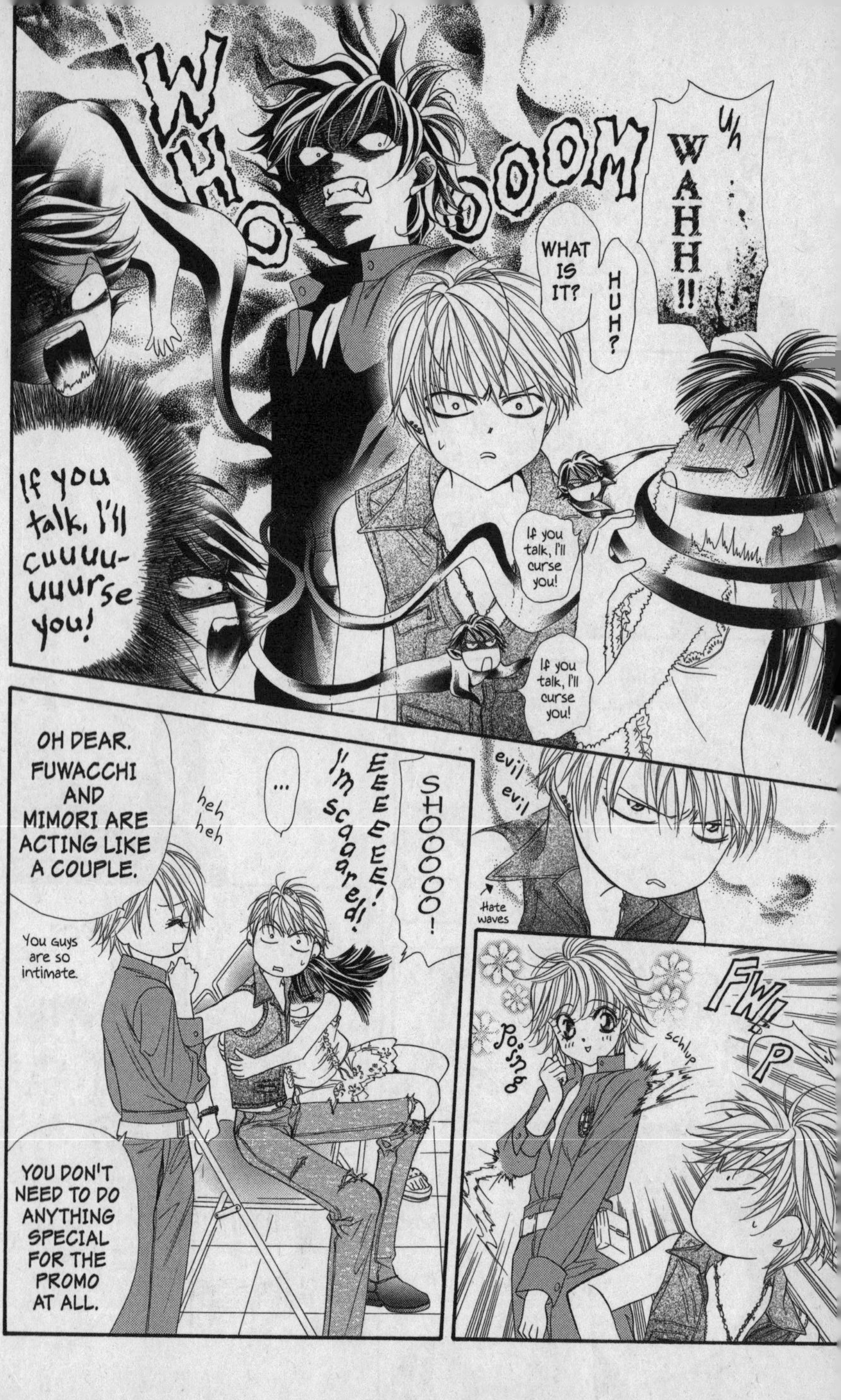
WHOOOOOM
Uh WAHH!!
WHAT IS IT?
HUH?
If you talk, I'll cuuuu-uuurse you!
If you talk, I'll curse you!
If you talk, I'll curse you!
evil evil
Hate waves
SHOOOOO!
EEEEEE! I'm scaaared!
...
OH DEAR. FUWACCHI AND MIMORI ARE ACTING LIKE A COUPLE.
heh heh
You guys are so intimate.
YOU DON'T NEED TO DO ANYTHING SPECIAL FOR THE PROMO AT ALL.
FWIP
schlup
posing

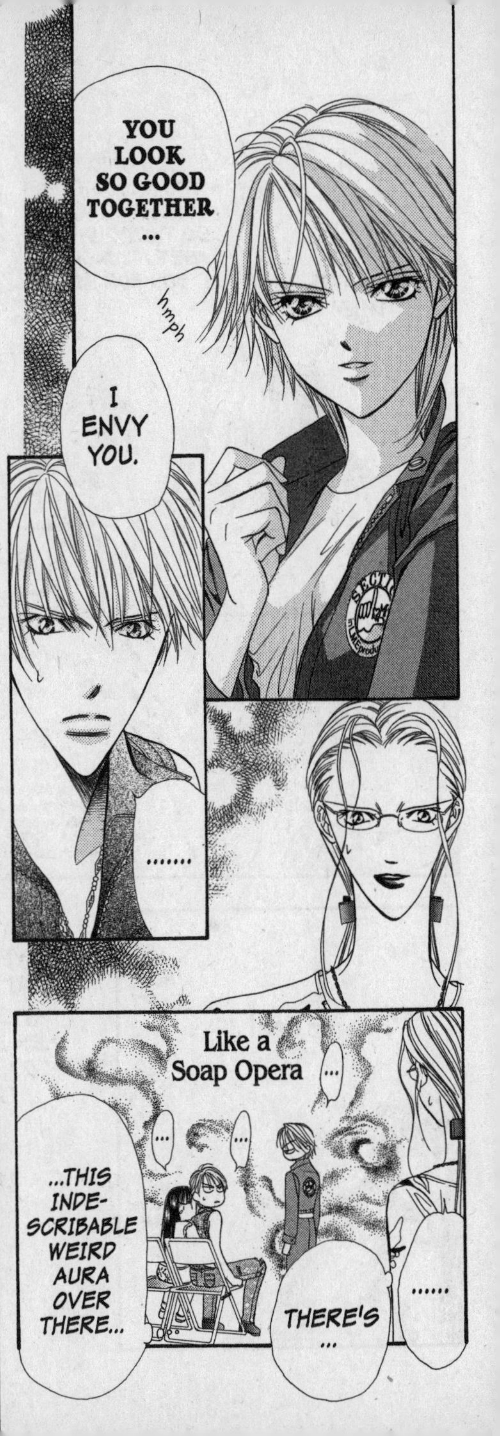
YOU LOOK SO GOOD TOGETHER ...
hmph
I ENVY YOU.
....
Like a Soap Opera
...
......
THERE'S ...
...
...
...THIS INDE-SCRIBABLE WEIRD AURA OVER THERE...
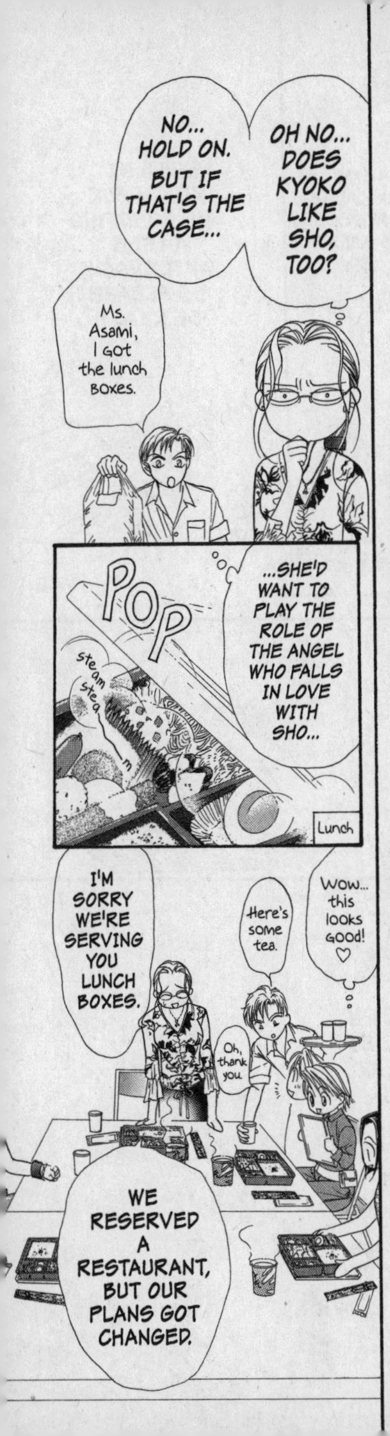
OH NO... DOES KYOKO LIKE SHO, TOO?
NO... HOLD ON. BUT IF THAT'S THE CASE...
Ms. Asami, I got the lunch boxes.
...SHE'D WANT TO PLAY THE ROLE OF THE ANGEL WHO FALLS IN LOVE WITH SHO...
POP
steam steam
Lunch
Wow... this looks good! ♡
Here's some tea.
I'M SORRY WE'RE SERVING YOU LUNCH BOXES.
Oh, thank you.
WE RESERVED A RESTAURANT, BUT OUR PLANS GOT CHANGED.

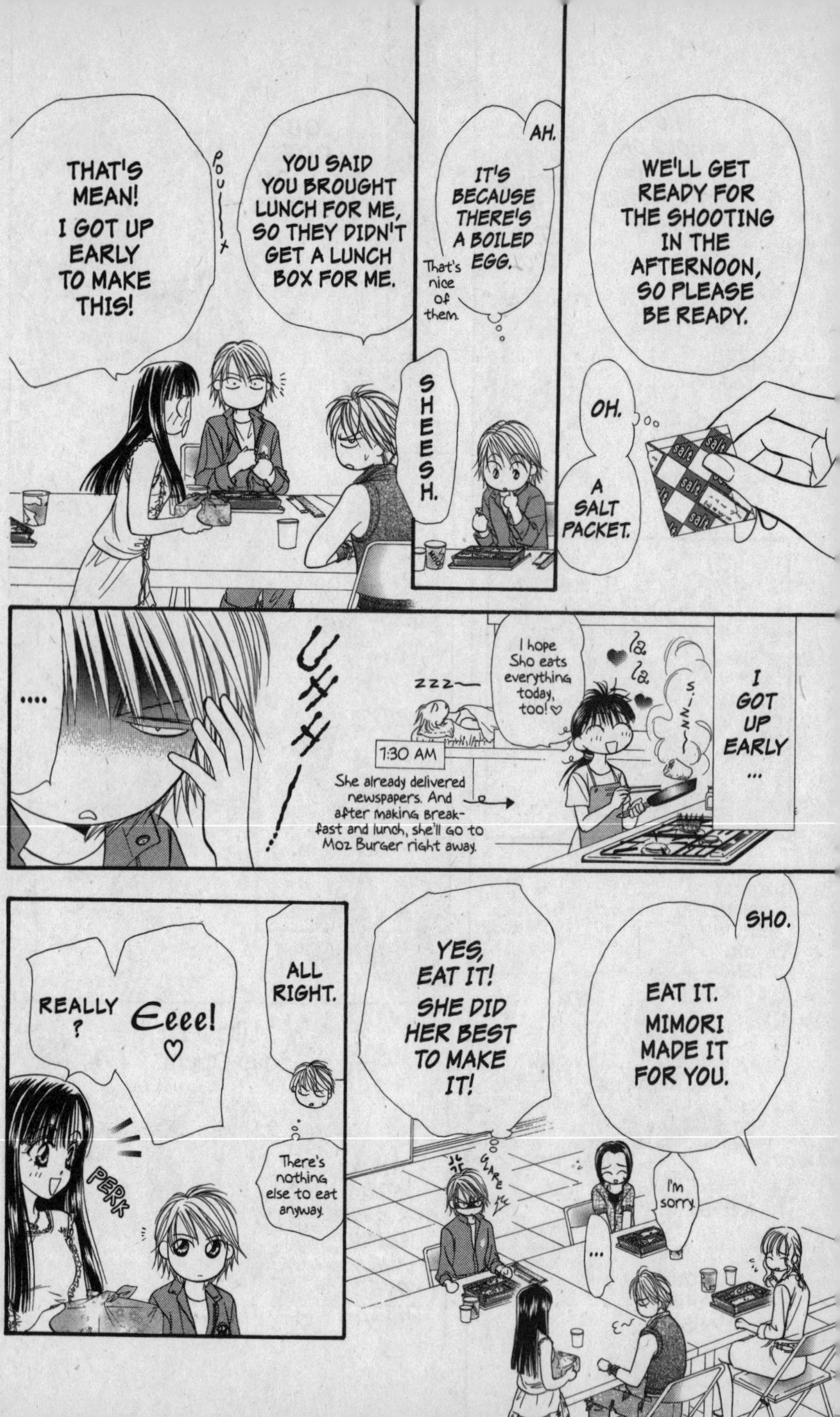
WE'LL GET READY FOR THE SHOOTING IN THE AFTERNOON, SO PLEASE BE READY.
OH.
A SALT PACKET.
salt
AH.
IT'S BECAUSE THERE'S A BOILED EGG.
That's nice of them.
SHEESH.
YOU SAID YOU BROUGHT LUNCH FOR ME, SO THEY DIDN'T GET A LUNCH BOX FOR ME.
POU~X
THAT'S MEAN! I GOT UP EARLY TO MAKE THIS!
I GOT UP EARLY...
la la
I hope Sho eats everything today, too! ♡
zzz~
1:30 AM
She already delivered newspapers. And after making breakfast and lunch, she'll go to Moz Burger right away.
UHH~...!
....
SHO.
EAT IT. MIMORI MADE IT FOR YOU.
I'm sorry.
...
YES, EAT IT! SHE DID HER BEST TO MAKE IT!
GLARE
ALL RIGHT.
There's nothing else to eat anyway.
REALLY?
Eeee! ♡
PERK

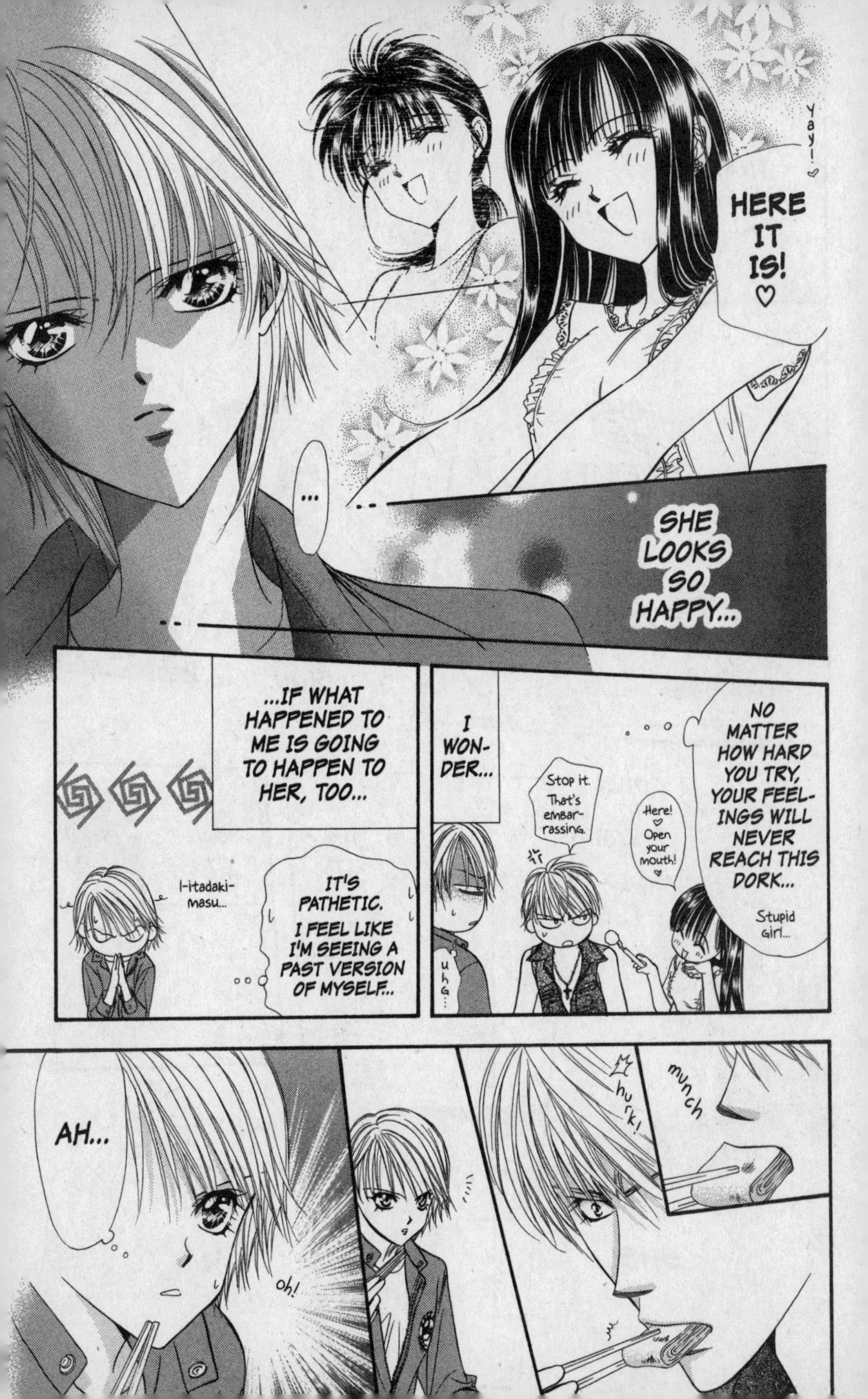
Yay! ♡
HERE IT IS! ♡
SHE LOOKS SO HAPPY...
...
NO MATTER HOW HARD YOU TRY, YOUR FEELINGS WILL NEVER REACH THIS DORK...
Stupid girl...
Here! ♡ Open your mouth! ♡
Stop it. That's embarrassing.
I WONDER...
uhg...
...IF WHAT HAPPENED TO ME IS GOING TO HAPPEN TO HER, TOO...
IT'S PATHETIC. I FEEL LIKE I'M SEEING A PAST VERSION OF MYSELF...
I-itadaki-masu...
munch
hurk!
AH...
oh!

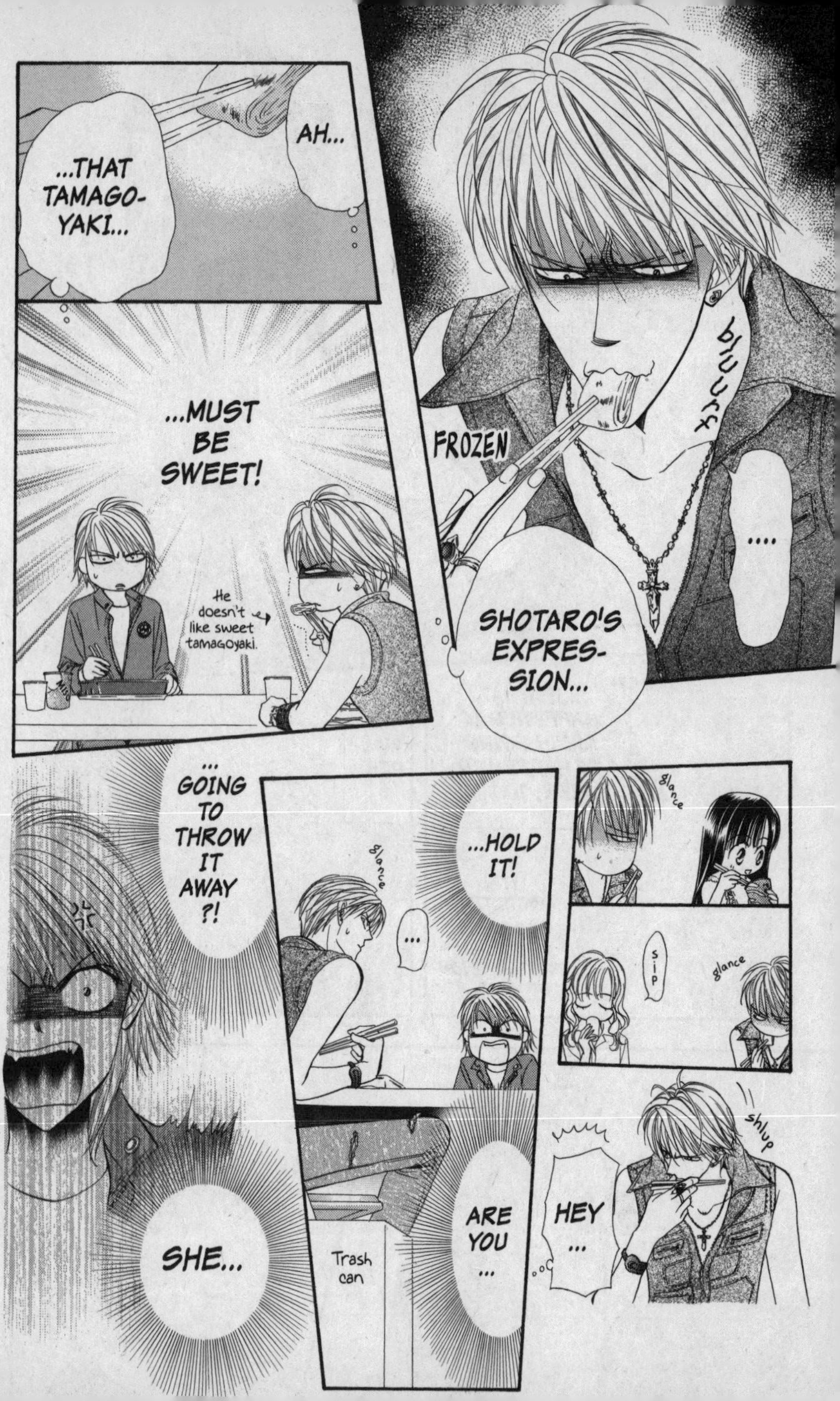
bluurf
FROZEN
....
SHOTARO'S EXPRES-SION...
AH...
...THAT TAMAGO-YAKI...
...MUST BE SWEET!
He doesn't like sweet tamagoyaki.
glance
sip
glance
shlup
HEY ...
ARE YOU ...
...HOLD IT!
glance
...
... GOING TO THROW IT AWAY ?!
Trash can
SHE...

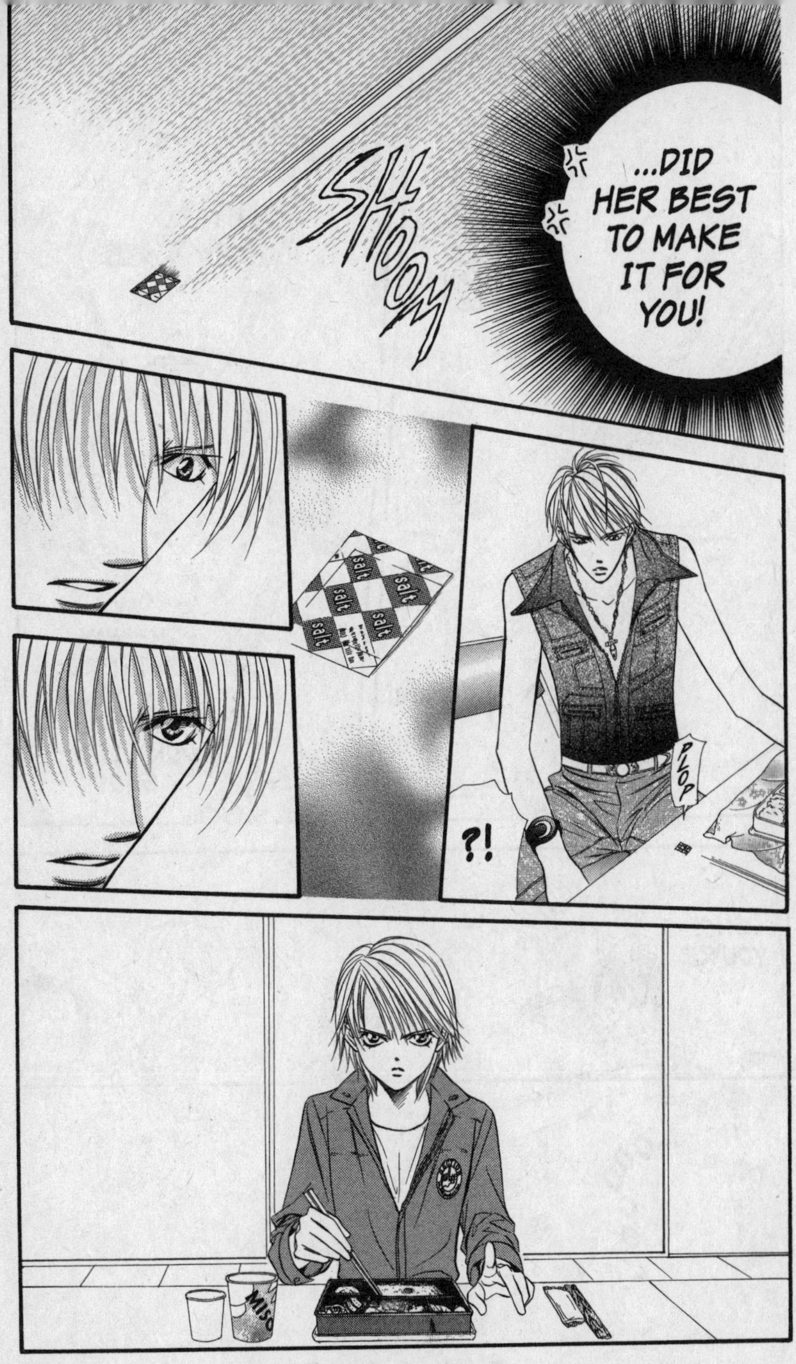
...DID HER BEST TO MAKE IT FOR YOU!
SHOOM
PLOP
?!
salt
MISO

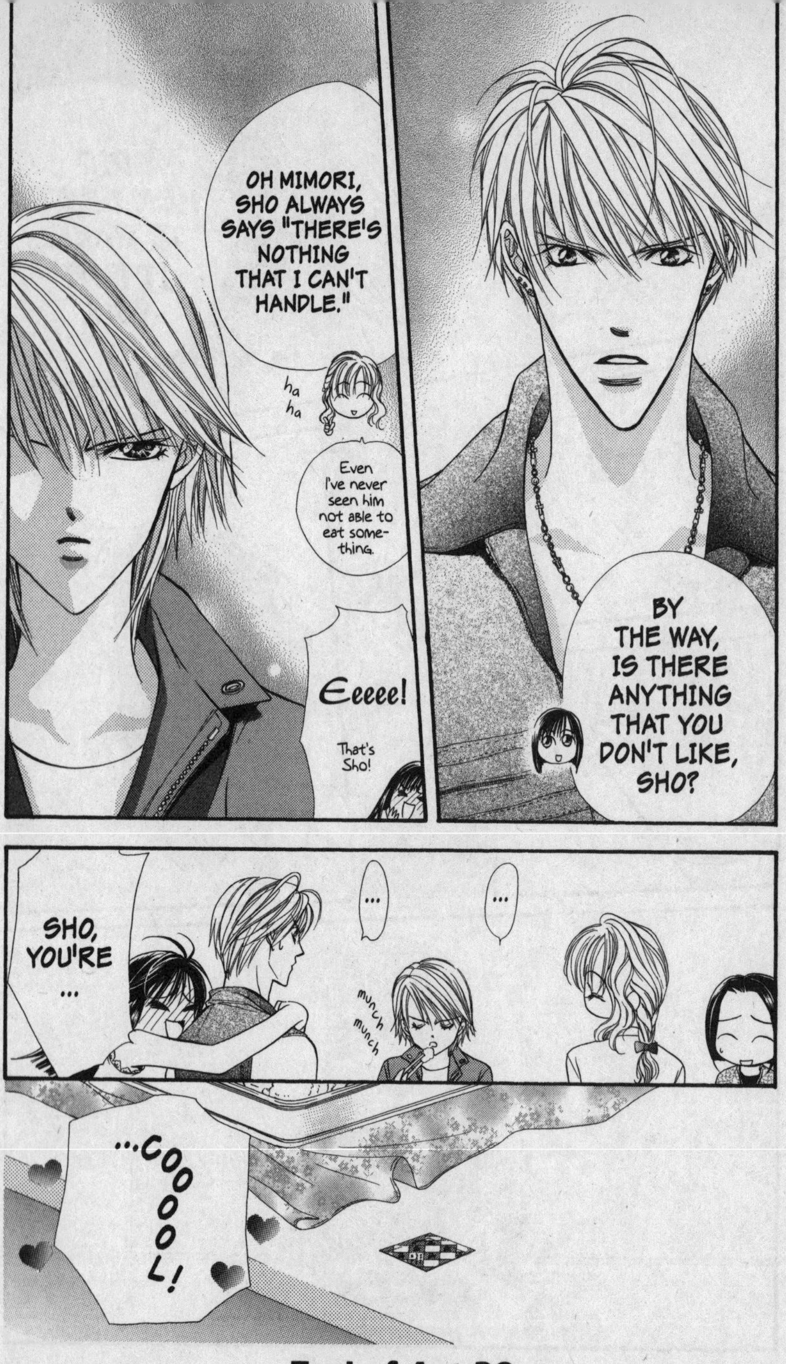
BY THE WAY, IS THERE ANYTHING THAT YOU DON'T LIKE, SHO?
OH MIMORI, SHO ALWAYS SAYS "THERE'S NOTHING THAT I CAN'T HANDLE."
ha ha
Even I've never seen him not able to eat some-thing.
Eeeee!
That's Sho!
...
...
munch munch
SHO, YOU'RE ...
...COOOOOL!

End of Act 39

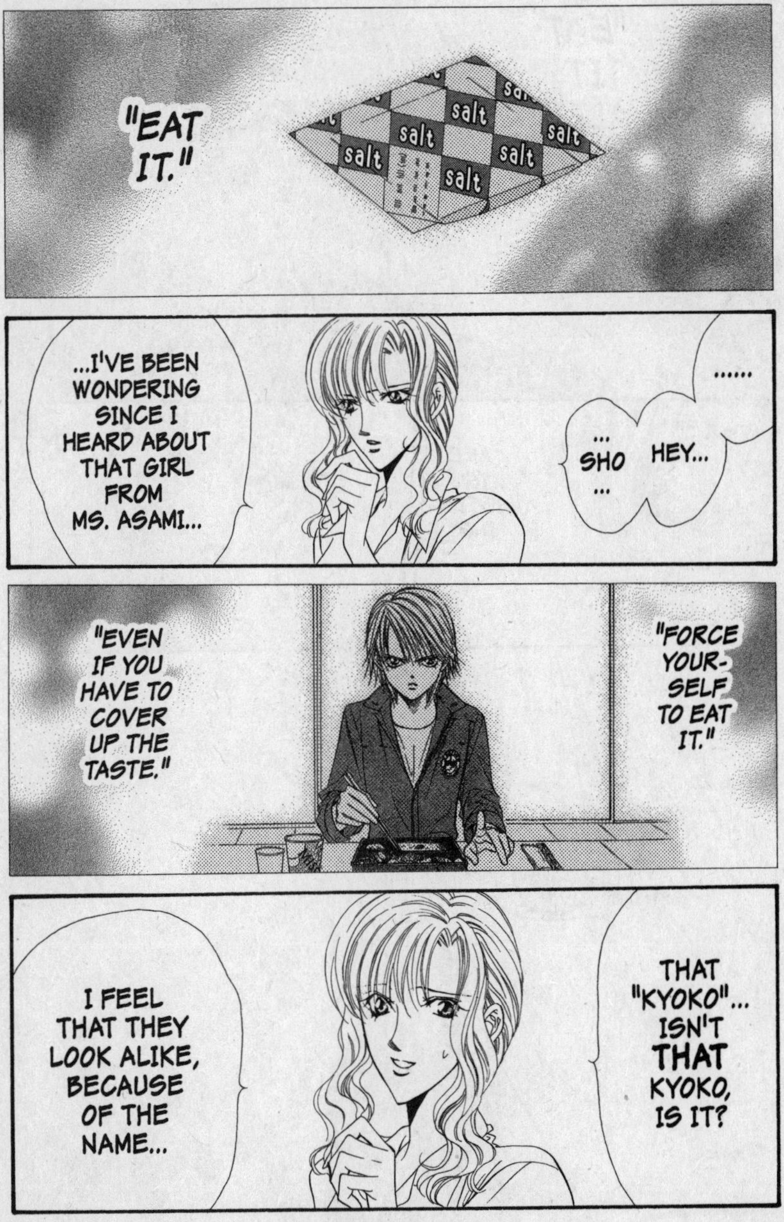
"EAT IT."
salt
salt
salt
salt
salt
salt
salt
......
HEY...
...SHO...
...I'VE BEEN WONDERING SINCE I HEARD ABOUT THAT GIRL FROM MS. ASAMI...
"FORCE YOUR-SELF TO EAT IT."
"EVEN IF YOU HAVE TO COVER UP THE TASTE."
THAT "KYOKO"... ISN'T THAT KYOKO, IS IT?
I FEEL THAT THEY LOOK ALIKE, BECAUSE OF THE NAME...

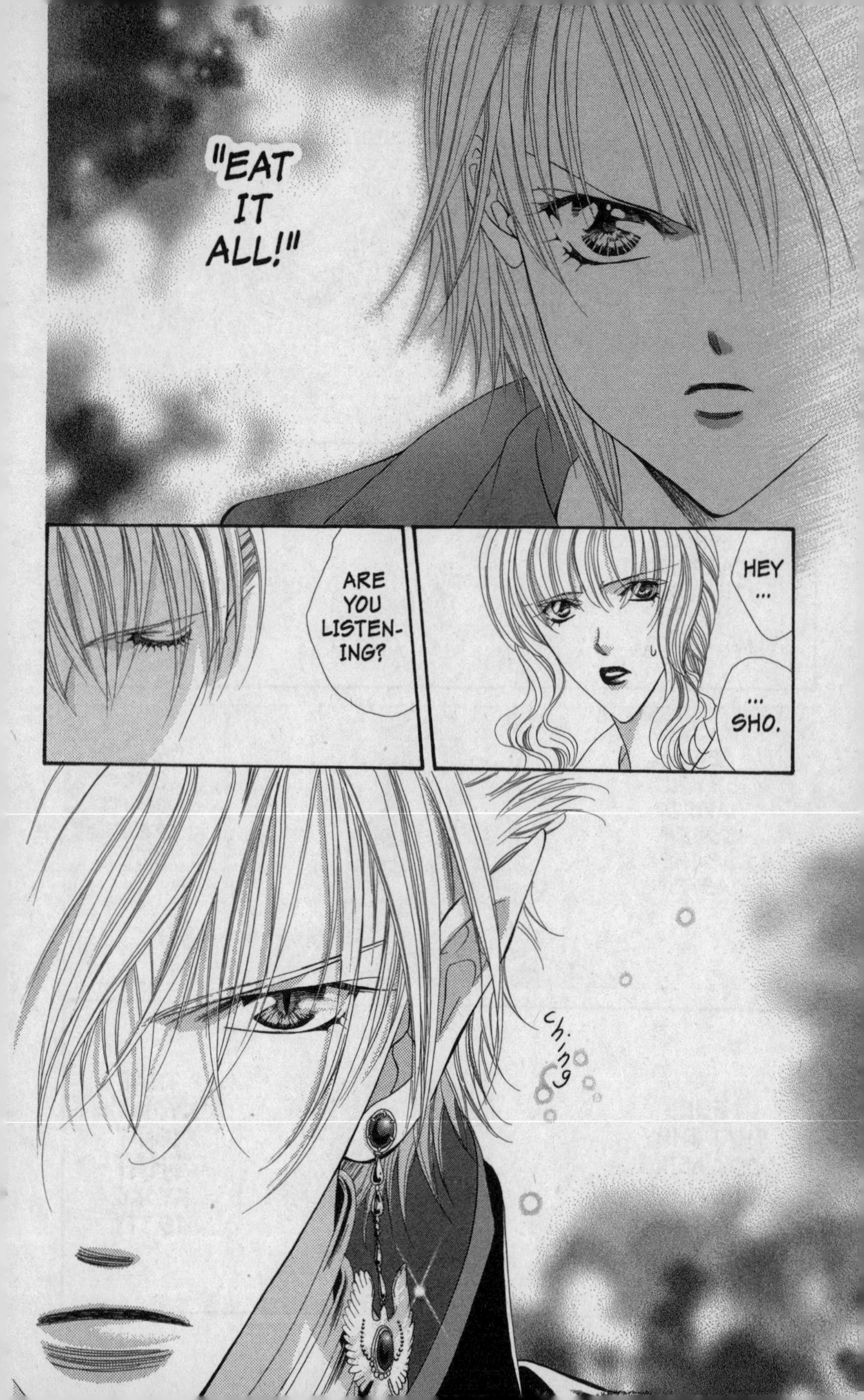
"EAT IT ALL!"
HEY ...
... SHO.
ARE YOU LISTEN-ING?
ching

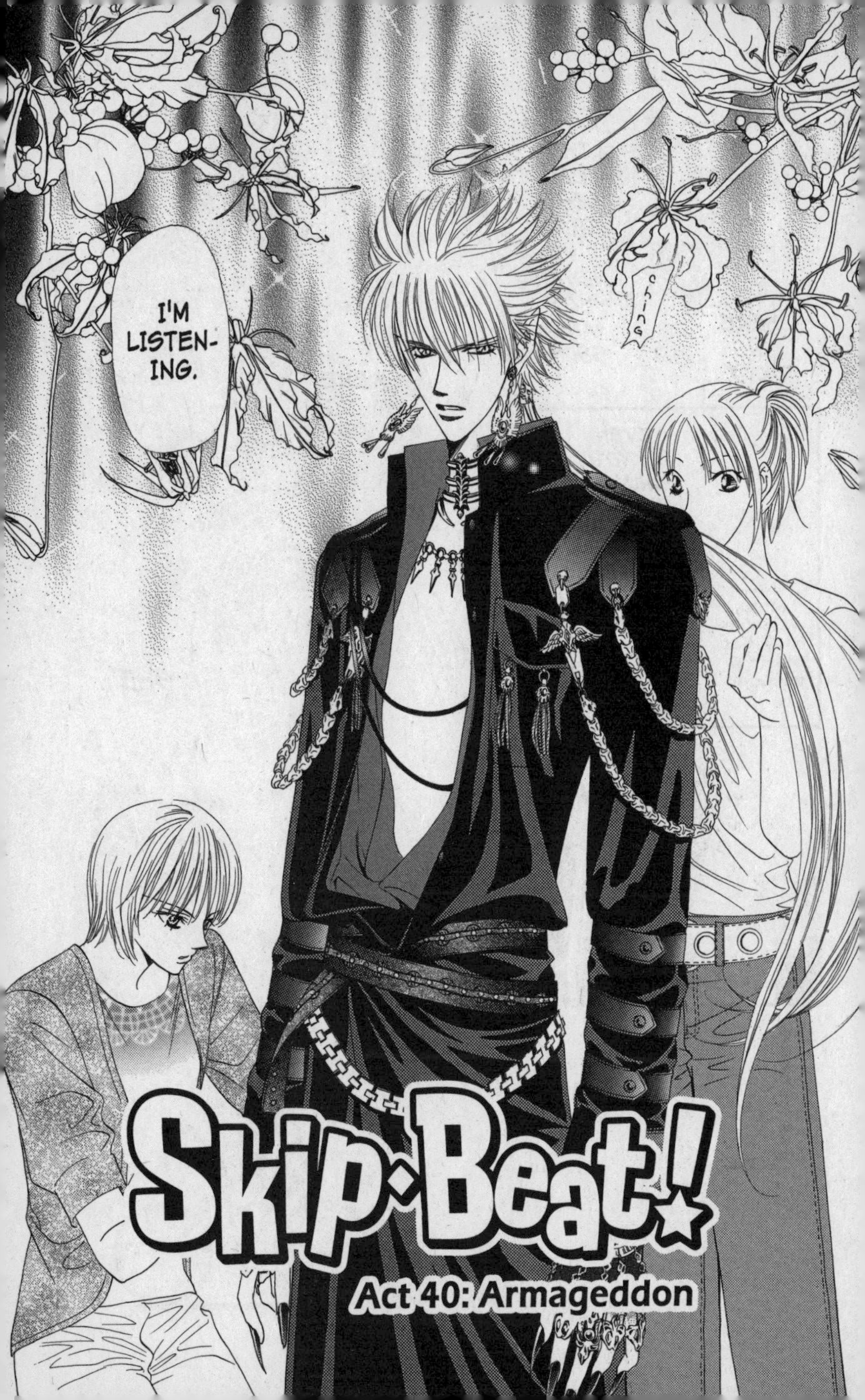
ching
I'M LISTEN-ING.
Skip·Beat!
Act 40: Armageddon

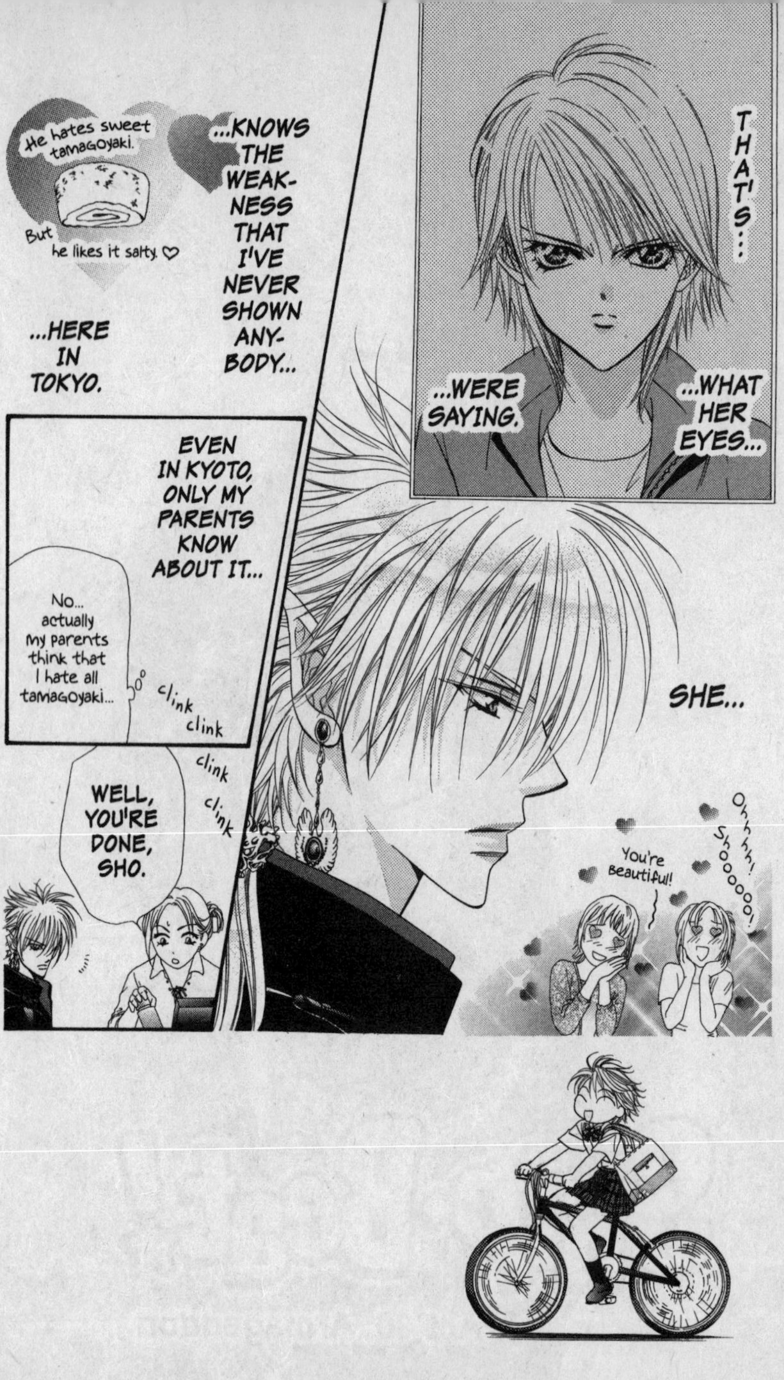
THAT'S...
...WHAT HER EYES...
...WERE SAYING.
SHE...
...KNOWS THE WEAKNESS THAT I'VE NEVER SHOWN ANYBODY...
...HERE IN TOKYO.
He hates sweet tamaGoyaki.
But he likes it salty. ♡
Ohhhh! Shoooooo!
You're Beautiful!
EVEN IN KYOTO, ONLY MY PARENTS KNOW ABOUT IT...
No... actually my parents think that I hate all tamaGoyaki...
clink clink
clink clink
WELL, YOU'RE DONE, SHO.

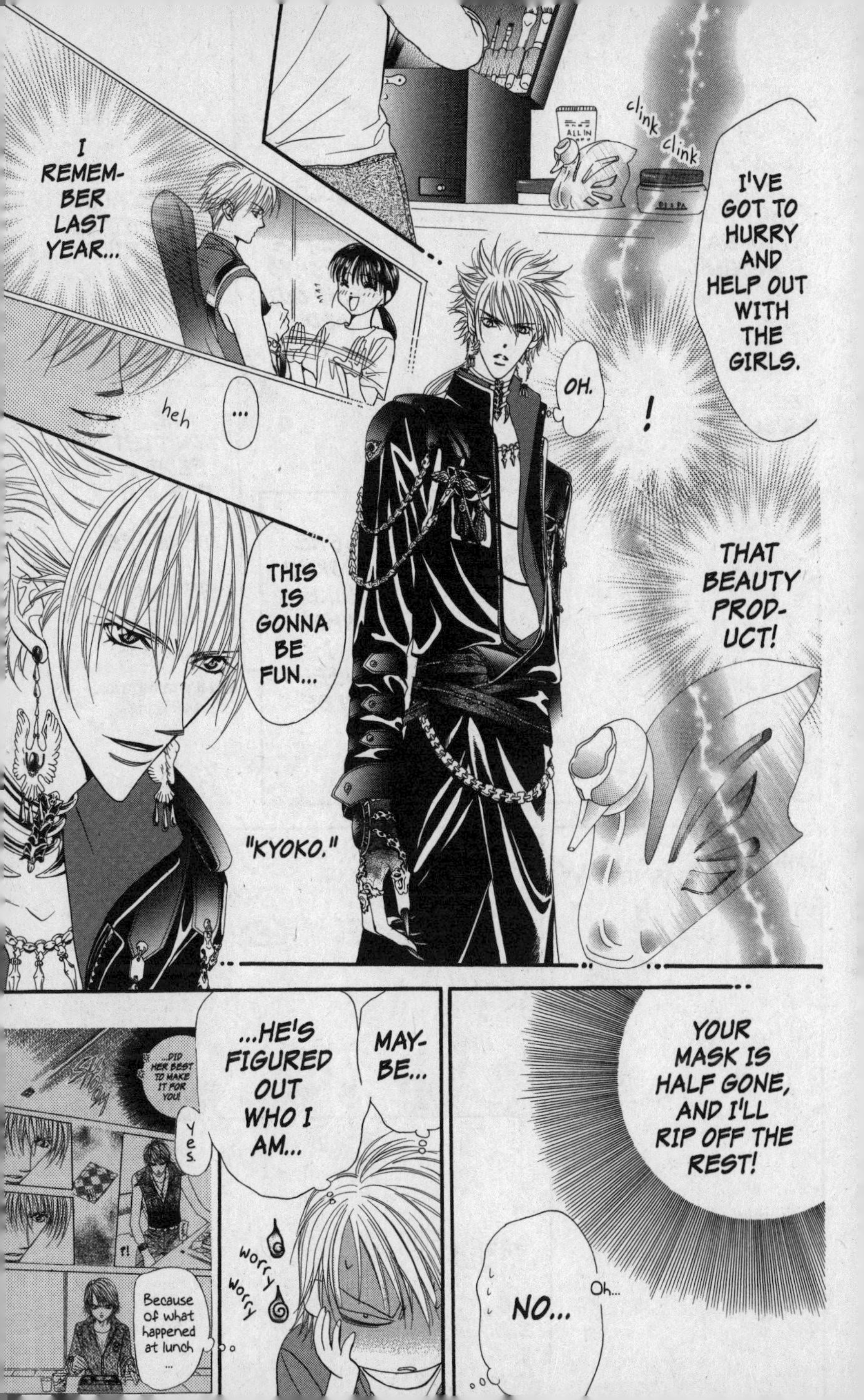
clink
clink
I'VE GOT TO HURRY AND HELP OUT WITH THE GIRLS.
!
THAT BEAUTY PROD-UCT!
OH.
I REMEM-BER LAST YEAR...
...
heh
THIS IS GONNA BE FUN...
"KYOKO."
YOUR MASK IS HALF GONE, AND I'LL RIP OFF THE REST!
Oh...
NO...
MAY-BE...
...HE'S FIGURED OUT WHO I AM...
worry worry
...DID HER BEST TO MAKE IT FOR YOU!
Yes.
?!
Because of what happened at lunch...

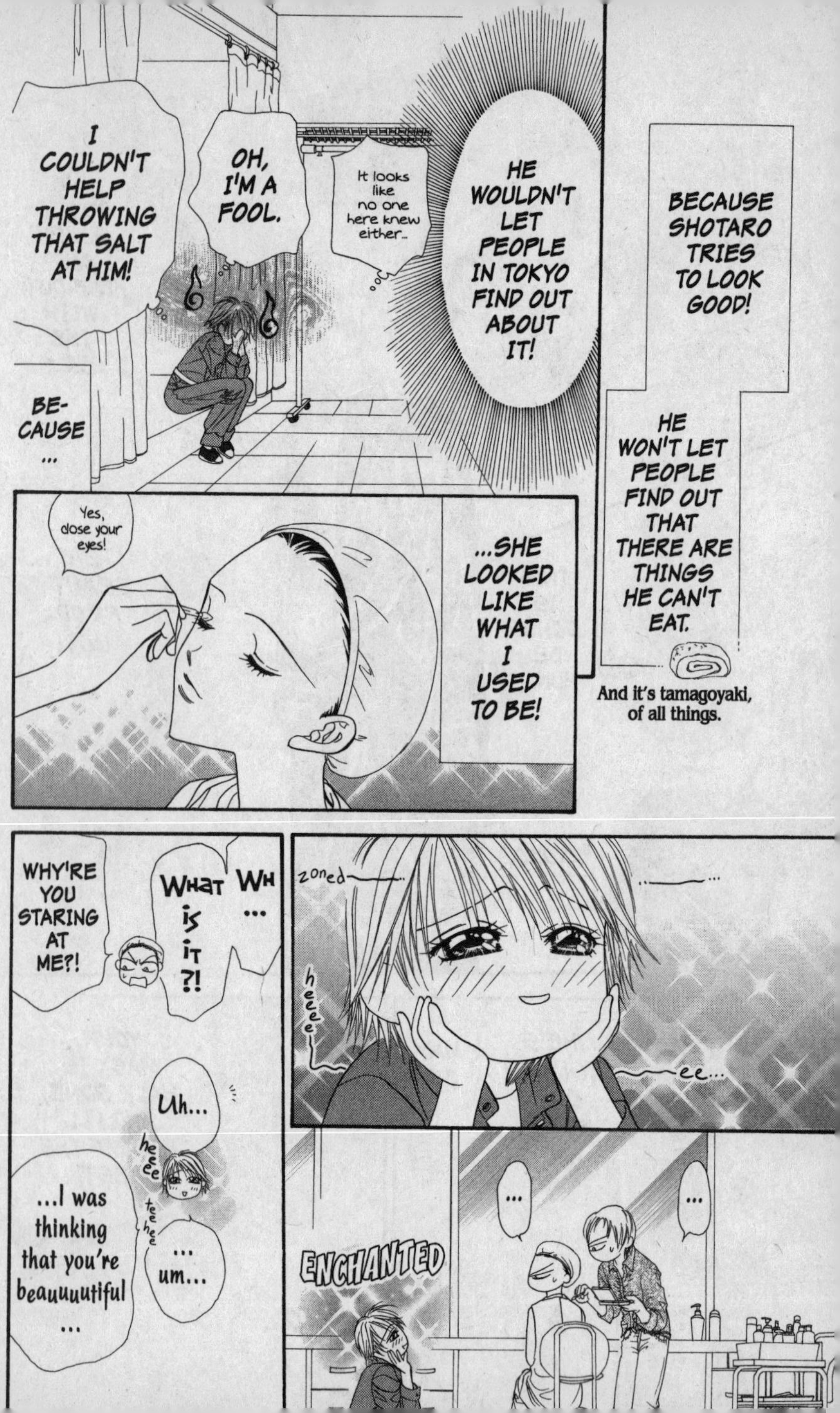
BECAUSE SHOTARO TRIES TO LOOK GOOD!
HE WON'T LET PEOPLE FIND OUT THAT THERE ARE THINGS HE CAN'T EAT.
And it's tamagoyaki, of all things.
HE WOULDN'T LET PEOPLE IN TOKYO FIND OUT ABOUT IT!
It looks like no one here knew either..
OH, I'M A FOOL.
I COULDN'T HELP THROWING THAT SALT AT HIM!
BE-CAUSE ...
...SHE LOOKED LIKE WHAT I USED TO BE!
Yes, close your eyes!
......
zoned
heeee
ee...
WH...
WHAT IS IT?!
WHY'RE YOU STARING AT ME?!
...
...
ENCHANTED
Uh...
heeee
...um...
tee hee
...I was thinking that you're beauuuutiful ...

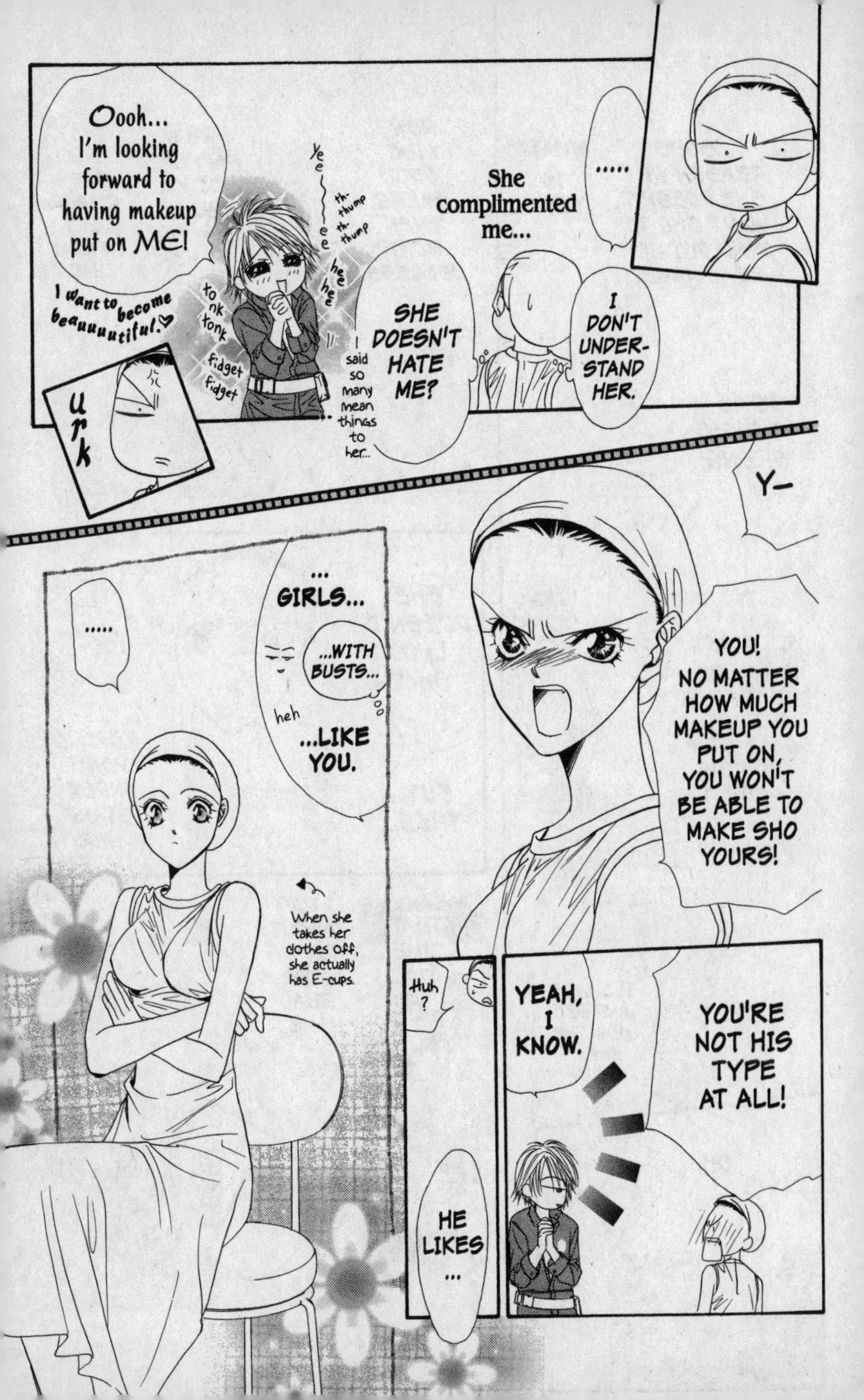
.....
She complimented me...
I DON'T UNDERSTAND HER.
SHE DOESN'T HATE ME?
I said so many mean things to her...
Yee~~ee
th-thump th-thump
hee hee
Oooh... I'm looking forward to having makeup put on ME!
I want to become beauuuutiful.♥
tonk tonk
fidget fidget
Urk
Y-
YOU! NO MATTER HOW MUCH MAKEUP YOU PUT ON, YOU WON'T BE ABLE TO MAKE SHO YOURS!
... GIRLS...
...WITH BUSTS...
heh
...LIKE YOU.
.....
When she takes her clothes off, she actually has E-cups.
YOU'RE NOT HIS TYPE AT ALL!
YEAH, I KNOW.
Huh?
HE LIKES ...

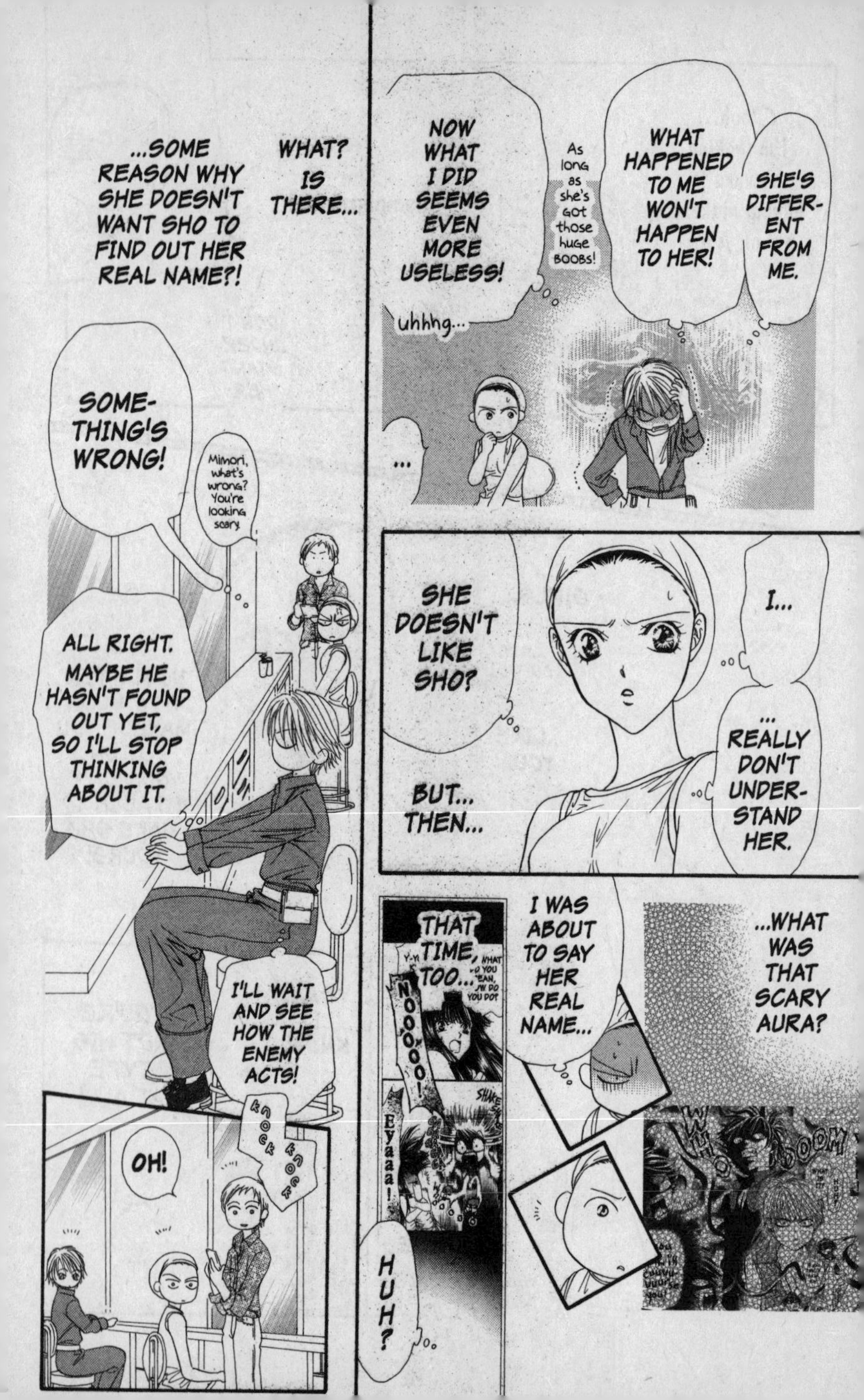
SHE'S DIFFERENT FROM ME.
WHAT HAPPENED TO ME WON'T HAPPEN TO HER!
As long as she's got those huge BOOBS!
NOW WHAT I DID SEEMS EVEN MORE USELESS!
uhhhg...
...
I...
...REALLY DON'T UNDERSTAND HER.
SHE DOESN'T LIKE SHO?
BUT... THEN...
...WHAT WAS THAT SCARY AURA?
I WAS ABOUT TO SAY HER REAL NAME...
THAT TIME, TOO...
NOOOOO!
Eyaaaa!
HUH?
WHAT? IS THERE...
...SOME REASON WHY SHE DOESN'T WANT SHO TO FIND OUT HER REAL NAME?!
SOMETHING'S WRONG!
Mimori, what's wrong? You're looking scary.
ALL RIGHT. MAYBE HE HASN'T FOUND OUT YET, SO I'LL STOP THINKING ABOUT IT.
I'LL WAIT AND SEE HOW THE ENEMY ACTS!
knock knock
OH!

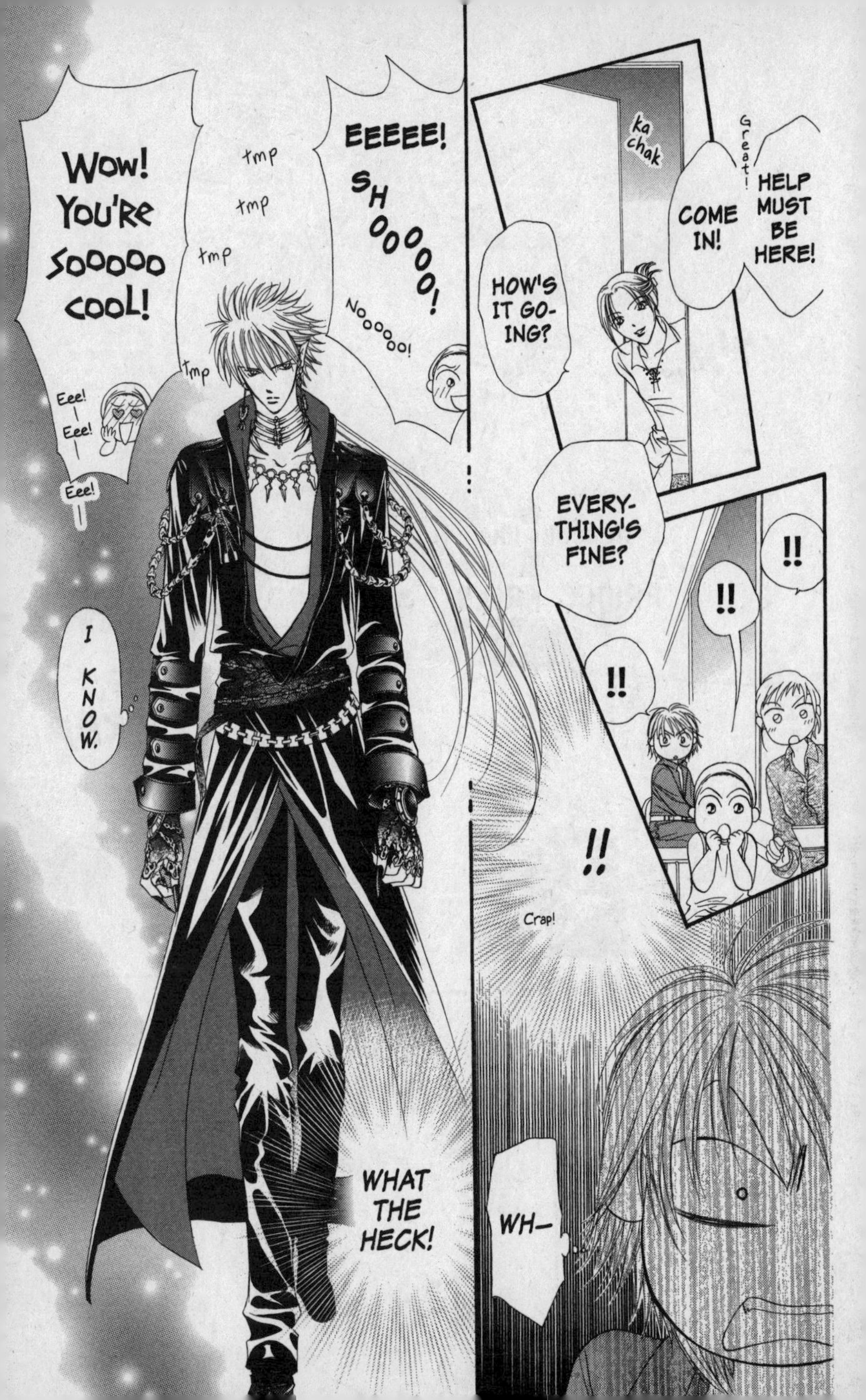

ka chak
Great!
HELP MUST BE HERE!
COME IN!
HOW'S IT GO-ING?
EVERY-THING'S FINE?
!!
!!
!!
!!
Crap!
WH—
EEEEE! SHOOOOOO!
Noooooo!
WOW! YOU'RE SOOOOO COOL!
tmp
tmp
tmp
tmp
Eee! Eee! Eee!
I KNOW.
WHAT THE HECK!

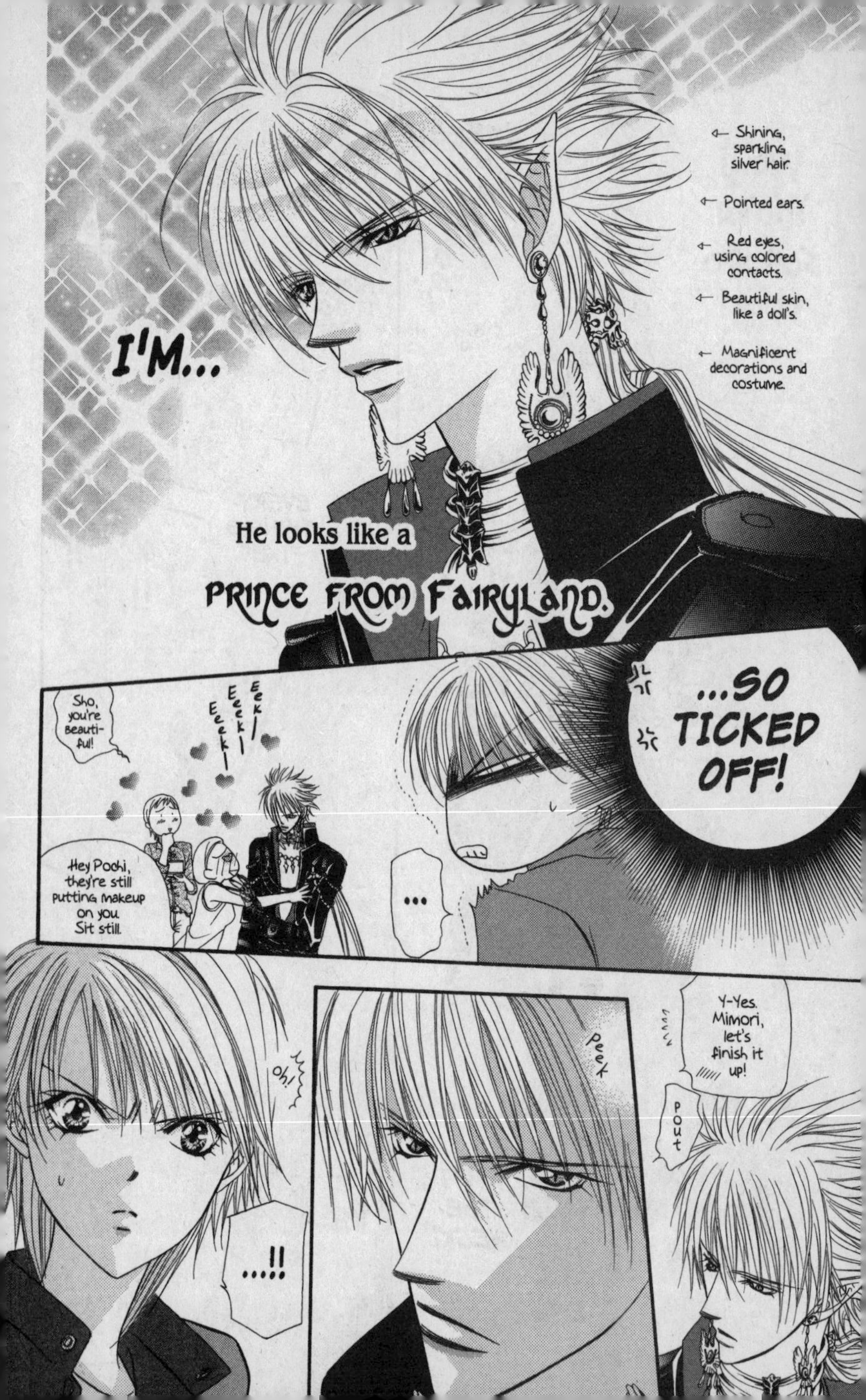
← Shining, sparkling silver hair.
← Pointed ears.
← Red eyes, using colored contacts.
← Beautiful skin, like a doll's.
← Magnificent decorations and costume.
I'M...
He looks like a
PRINCE FROM FAIRYLAND.
...SO TICKED OFF!
...
Eek! Eek! Eek!
Sho, you're beauti-ful!
Hey Pochi, they're still putting makeup on you. Sit still.
Y-Yes. Mimori, let's finish it up!
Pout
Peek
Oh!
...!!

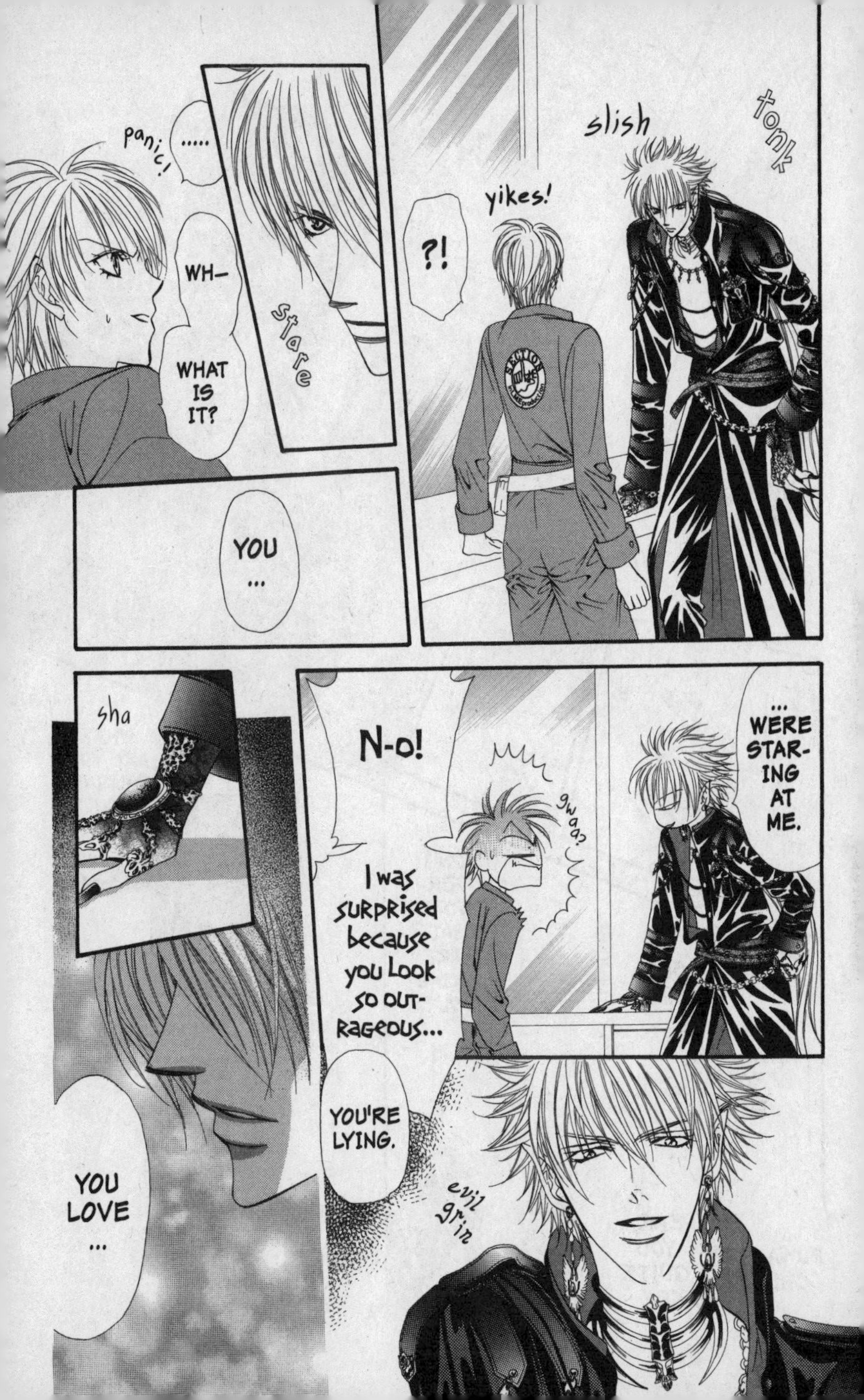
tonk
slish
yikes!
?!
stare
......
panic!
WH—
WHAT IS IT?
YOU ...
... WERE STARING AT ME.
N-O!
gwaa?
I was surprised because you look so outrageous...
sha
YOU'RE LYING.
evil grin
YOU LOVE ...

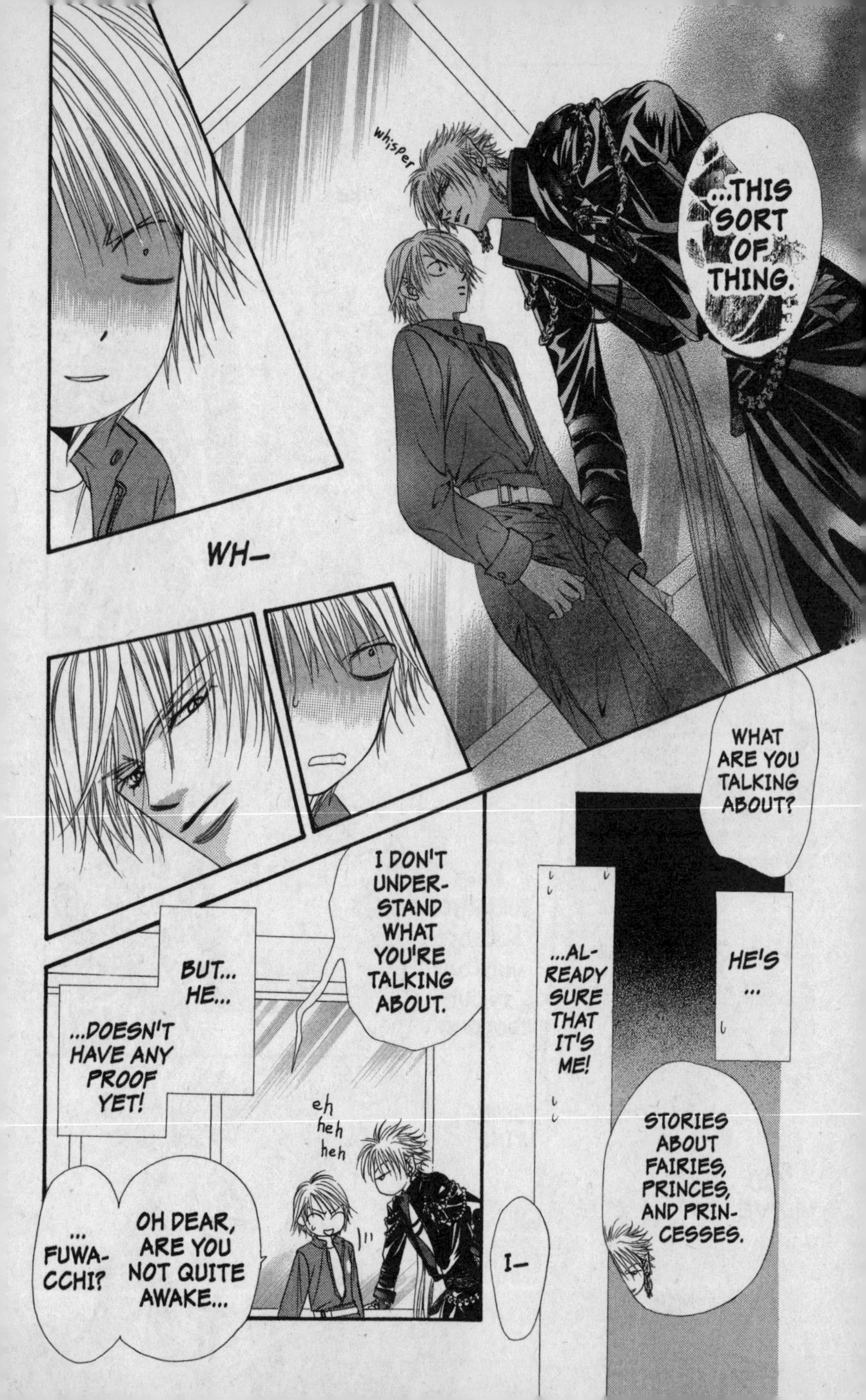
whisper
...THIS SORT OF THING.
WH—
WHAT ARE YOU TALKING ABOUT?
HE'S ...
...ALREADY SURE THAT IT'S ME!
STORIES ABOUT FAIRIES, PRINCES, AND PRINCESSES.
I—
I DON'T UNDERSTAND WHAT YOU'RE TALKING ABOUT.
BUT... HE...
...DOESN'T HAVE ANY PROOF YET!
eh heh heh
OH DEAR, ARE YOU NOT QUITE AWAKE...
... FUWACCHI?

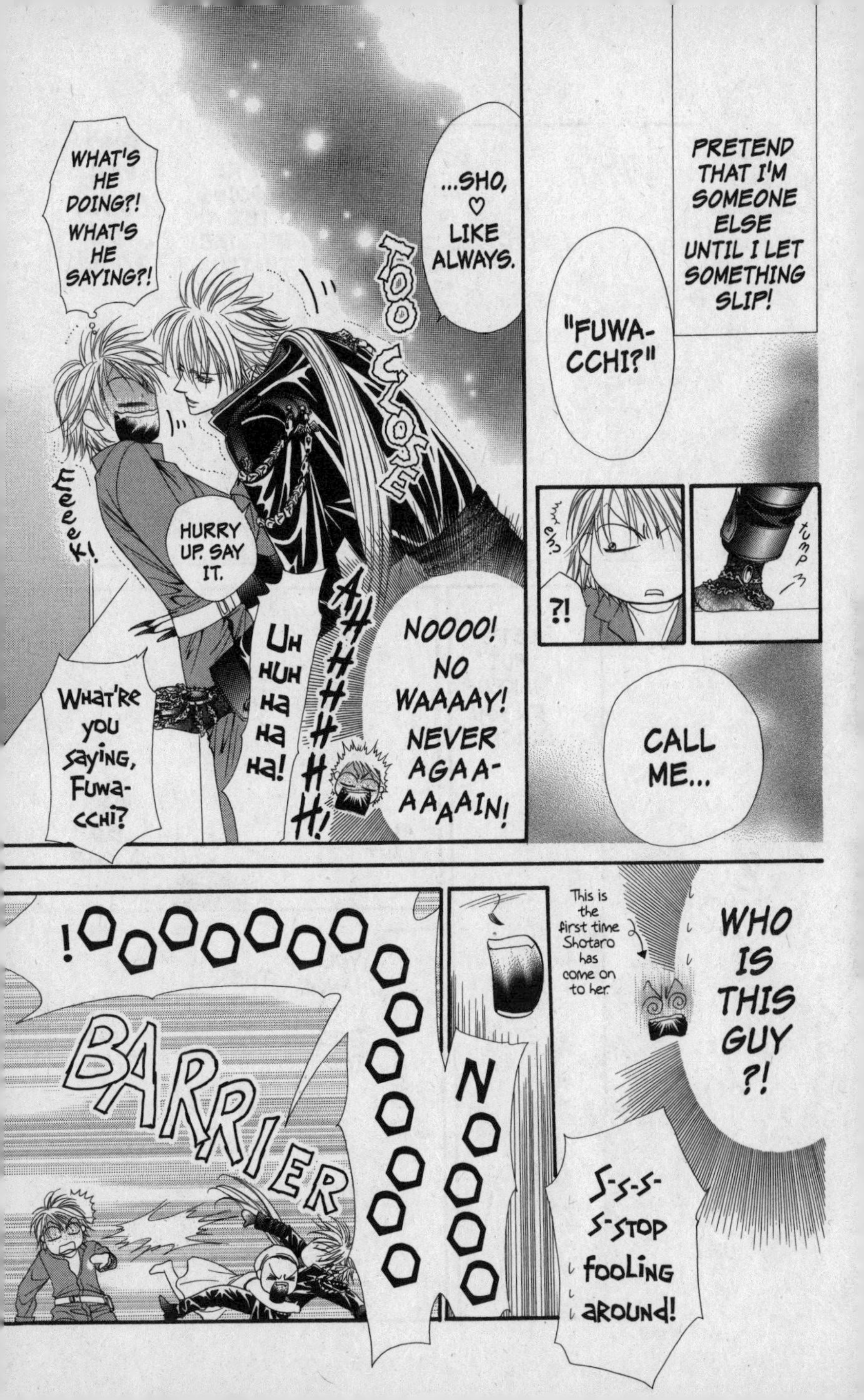
PRETEND THAT I'M SOMEONE ELSE UNTIL I LET SOMETHING SLIP!
"FUWA-CCHI?"
TUMP
eh?
?!
CALL ME...
...SHO, ♡ LIKE ALWAYS.
TOO CLOSE
WHAT'S HE DOING?! WHAT'S HE SAYING?!
Eeeek!
HURRY UP. SAY IT.
NOOOO! NO WAAAAY! NEVER AGAA-AAAAAIN!
AHHHHHHHH!
UH HUH HA HA HA!
What're you saying, Fuwa-cchi?
WHO IS THIS GUY?!
This is the first time Shotaro has come on to her.
S-S-S-S-STOP fooling around!
NOOOOO
OOOOOOOOOOOOOOOO!
BARRIER

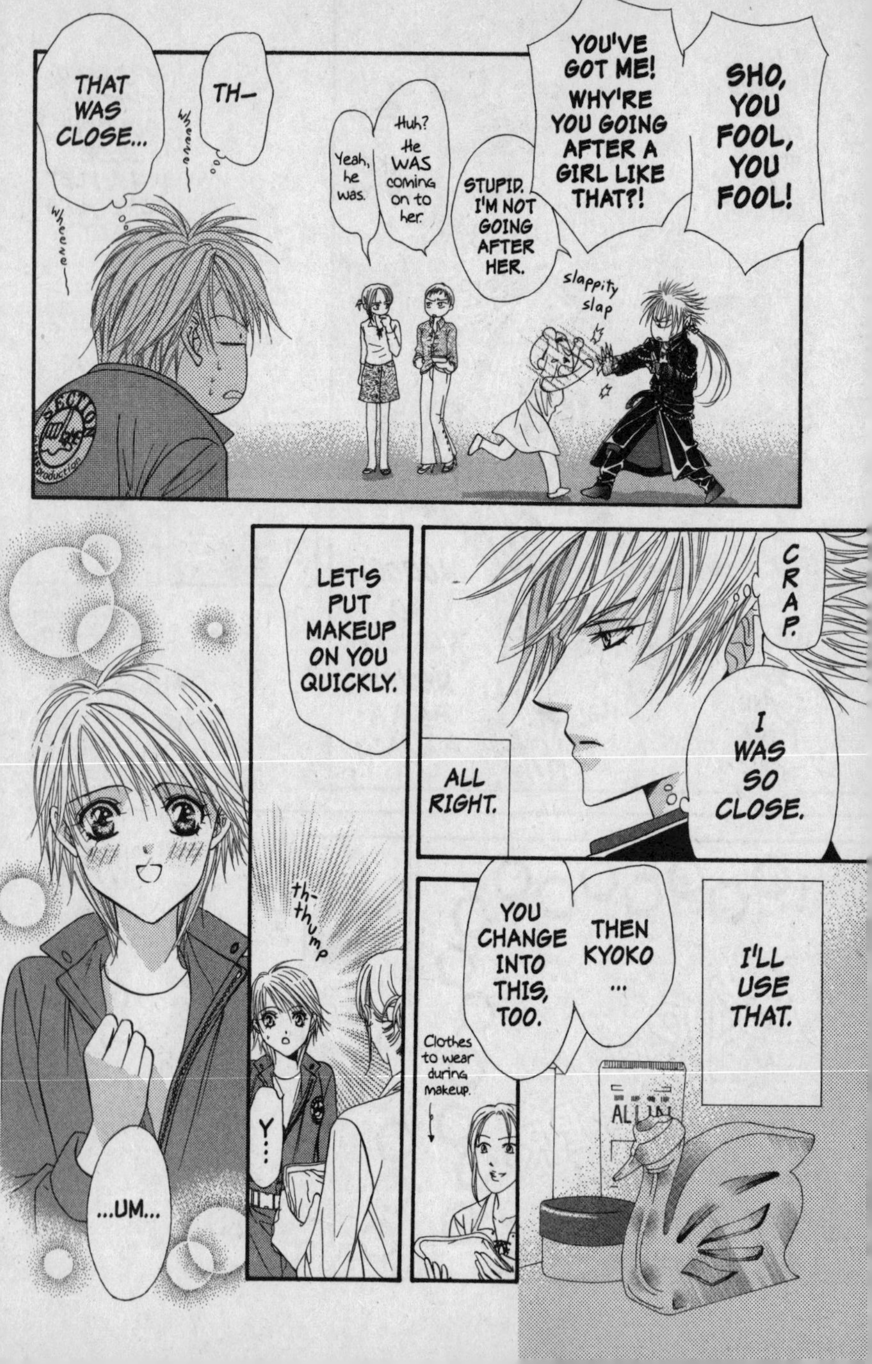
SHO, YOU FOOL, YOU FOOL!
YOU'VE GOT ME! WHY'RE YOU GOING AFTER A GIRL LIKE THAT?!
STUPID. I'M NOT GOING AFTER HER.
slappity slap
Huh? He WAS coming on to her.
Yeah, he was.
TH—
wheeze—
THAT WAS CLOSE...
wheeze—
CRAP.
I WAS SO CLOSE.
ALL RIGHT.
I'LL USE THAT.
THEN KYOKO...
YOU CHANGE INTO THIS, TOO.
Clothes to wear during makeup.
LET'S PUT MAKEUP ON YOU QUICKLY.
th-thump
Y...
...UM...

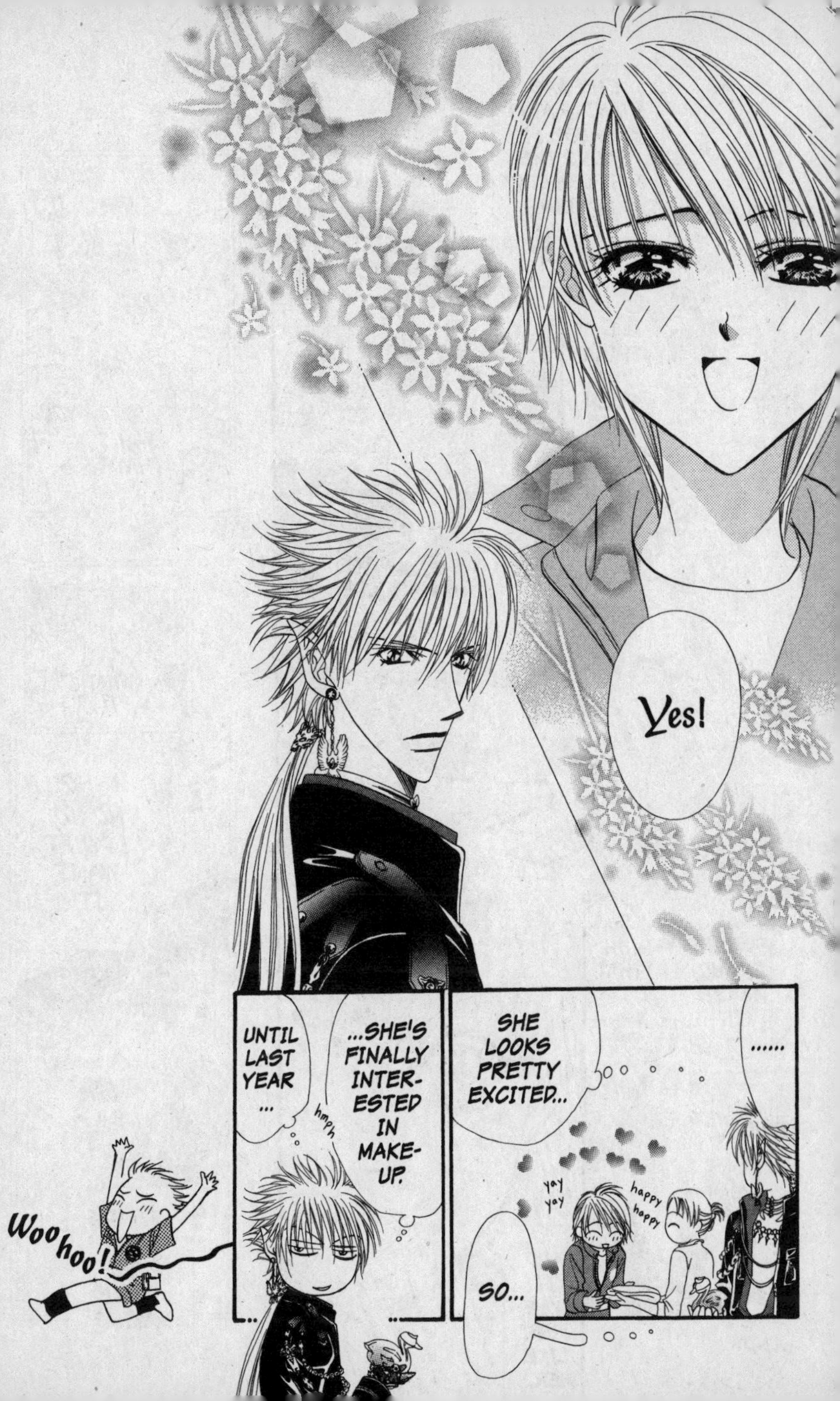
Yes!
......
SHE LOOKS PRETTY EXCITED...
happy happy
yay yay
SO...
...SHE'S FINALLY INTERESTED IN MAKE-UP.
hmph
UNTIL LAST YEAR...
Woohoo!

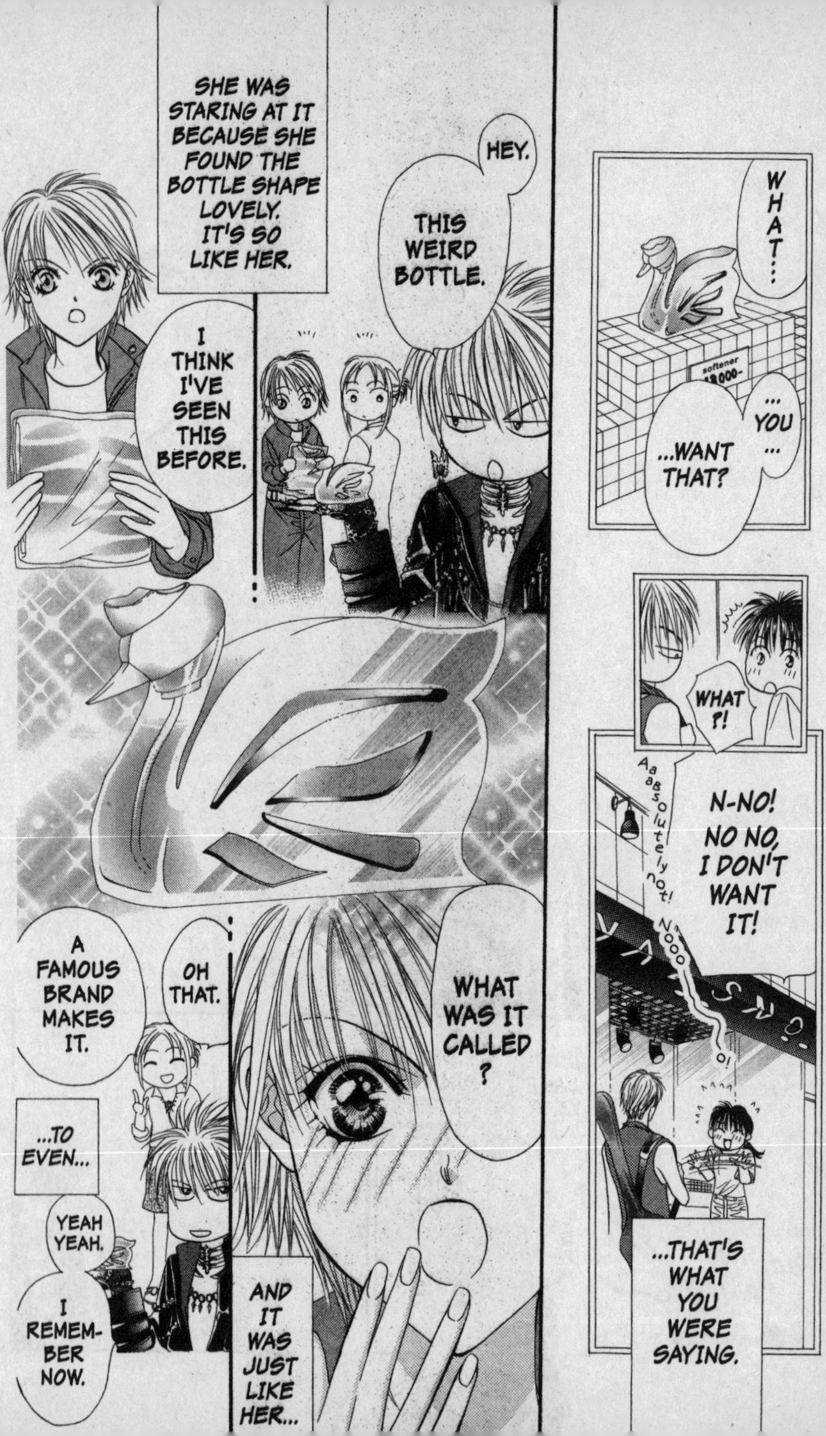
WHAT...
softener
...YOU...
...WANT THAT?
WHAT?!
N-NO! NO NO, I DON'T WANT IT!
Aa absolutely not!
Nooo...o!
...THAT'S WHAT YOU WERE SAYING.
HEY.
THIS WEIRD BOTTLE.
SHE WAS STARING AT IT BECAUSE SHE FOUND THE BOTTLE SHAPE LOVELY. IT'S SO LIKE HER.
I THINK I'VE SEEN THIS BEFORE.
WHAT WAS IT CALLED?
AND IT WAS JUST LIKE HER...
OH THAT.
A FAMOUS BRAND MAKES IT.
...TO EVEN...
YEAH YEAH.
I REMEM-BER NOW.

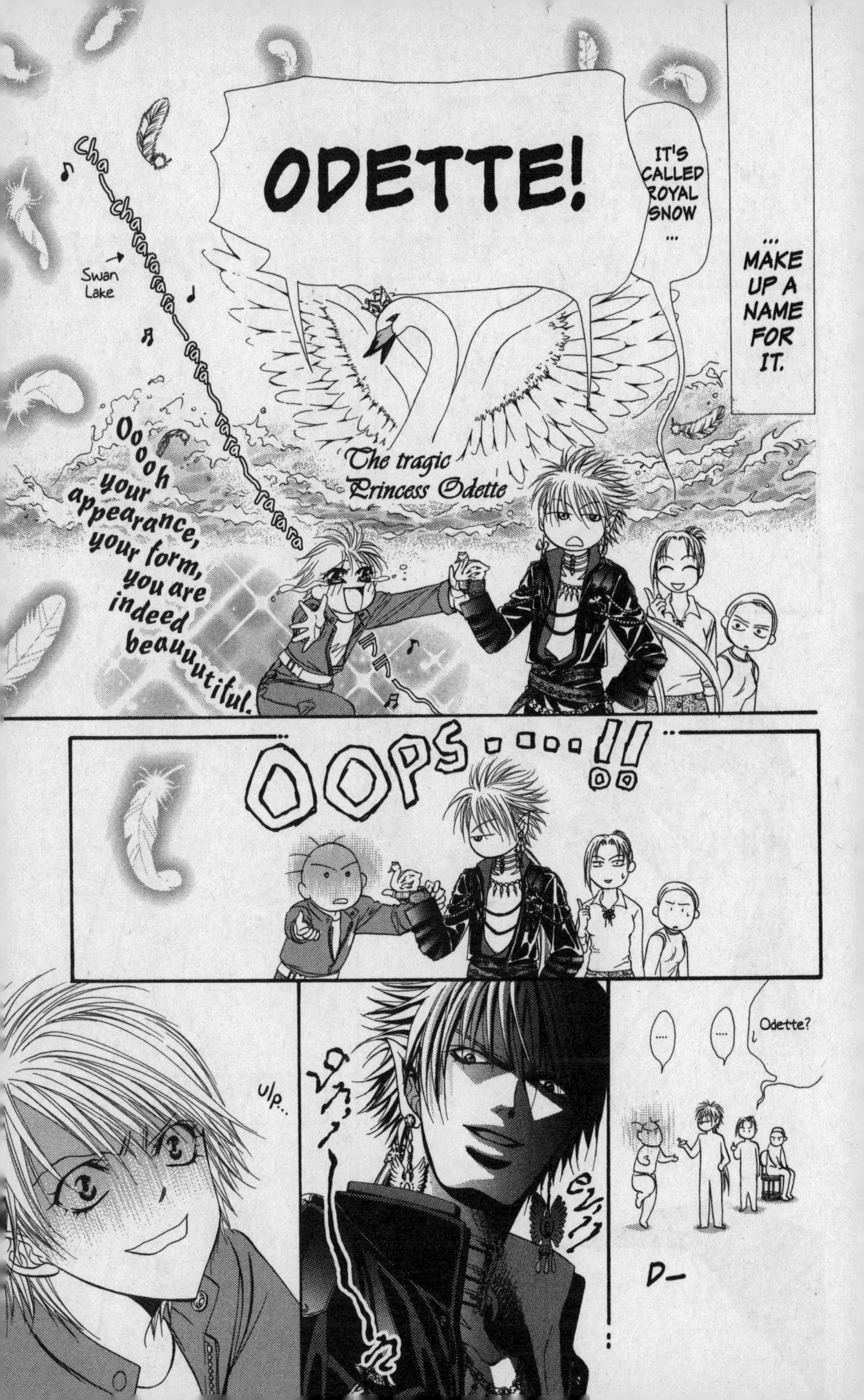

... MAKE UP A NAME FOR IT.
IT'S CALLED ROYAL SNOW ...
ODETTE!
Cha—chararara—rara—rara—rarara
Swan Lake
The tragic Princess Odette
Ooooh your appearance, your form, you are indeed beauuutiful.
OOPS.....!!
....
....
Odette?
D—
evil!!
ulp...

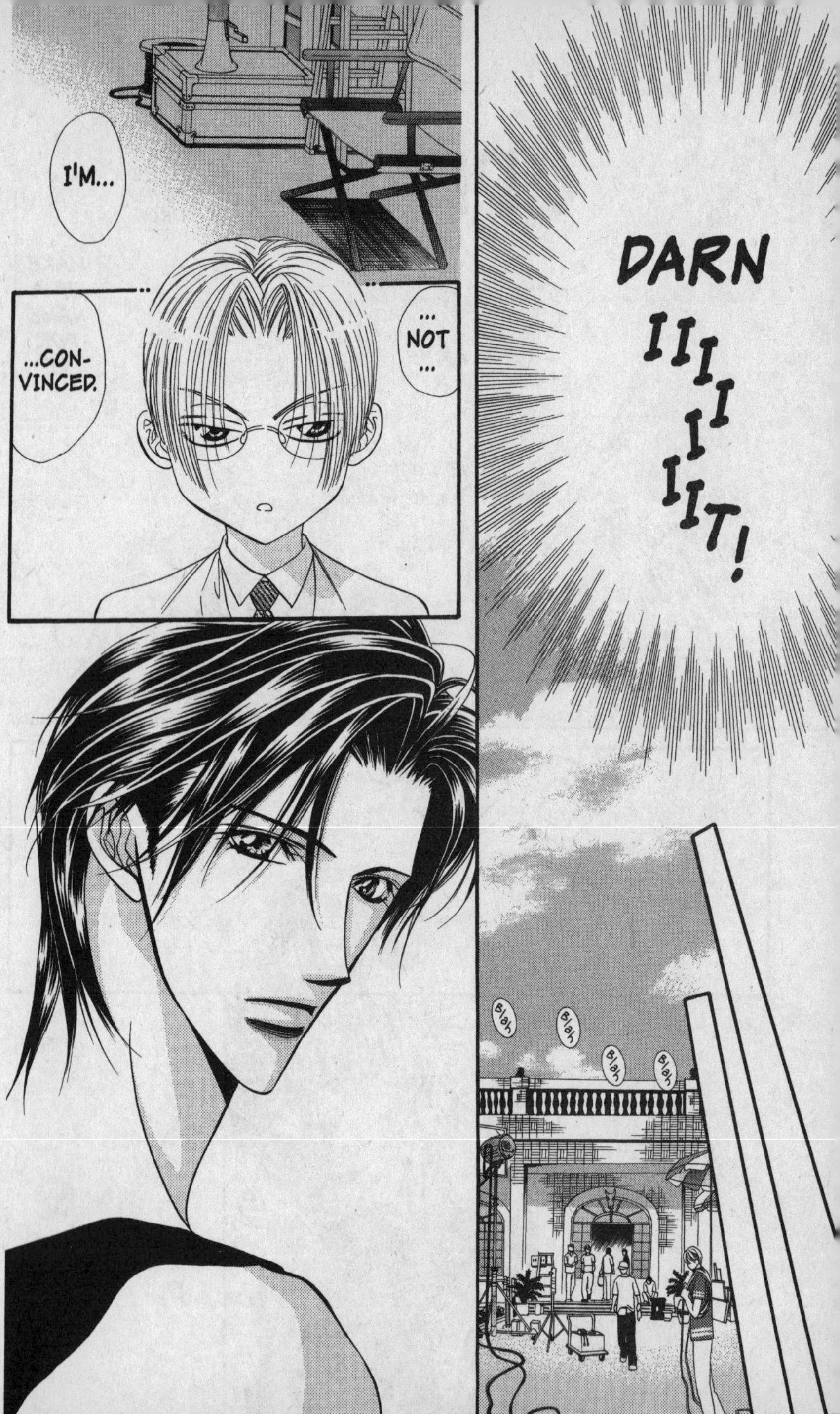
DARN IIIIIIT!
Blah
Blah
Blah
Blah
I'M...
... NOT ...
...CON-VINCED.

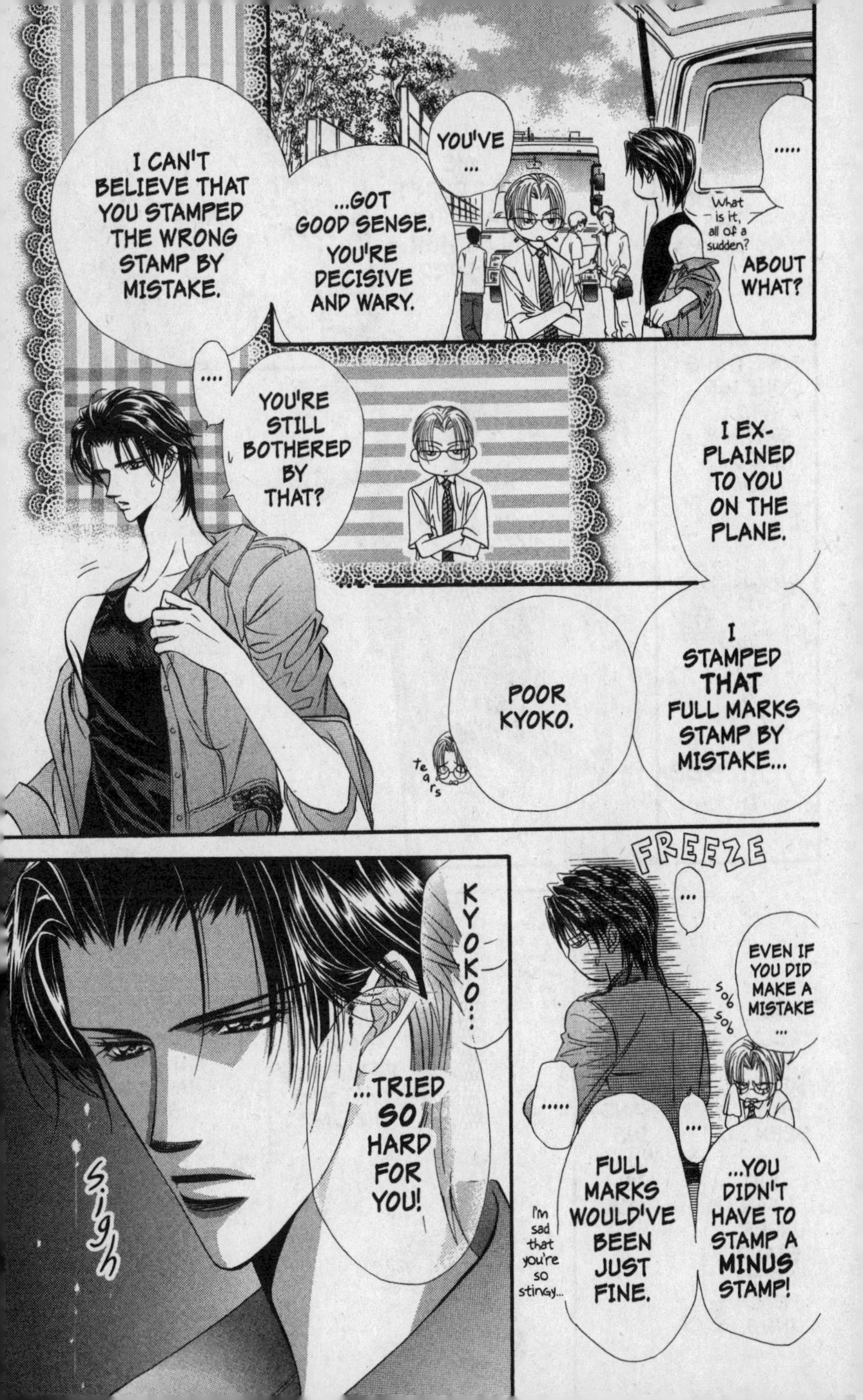

.....
What is it, all of a sudden?
ABOUT WHAT?
YOU'VE ...
...GOT GOOD SENSE. YOU'RE DECISIVE AND WARY.
I CAN'T BELIEVE THAT YOU STAMPED THE WRONG STAMP BY MISTAKE.
....
YOU'RE STILL BOTHERED BY THAT?
I EX-PLAINED TO YOU ON THE PLANE.
I STAMPED THAT FULL MARKS STAMP BY MISTAKE...
POOR KYOKO.
tears
FREEZE
...
EVEN IF YOU DID MAKE A MISTAKE ...
sob sob
...
...YOU DIDN'T HAVE TO STAMP A MINUS STAMP!
.....
FULL MARKS WOULD'VE BEEN JUST FINE.
I'm sad that you're so stingy...
KYOKO...
...TRIED SO HARD FOR YOU!
Sigh

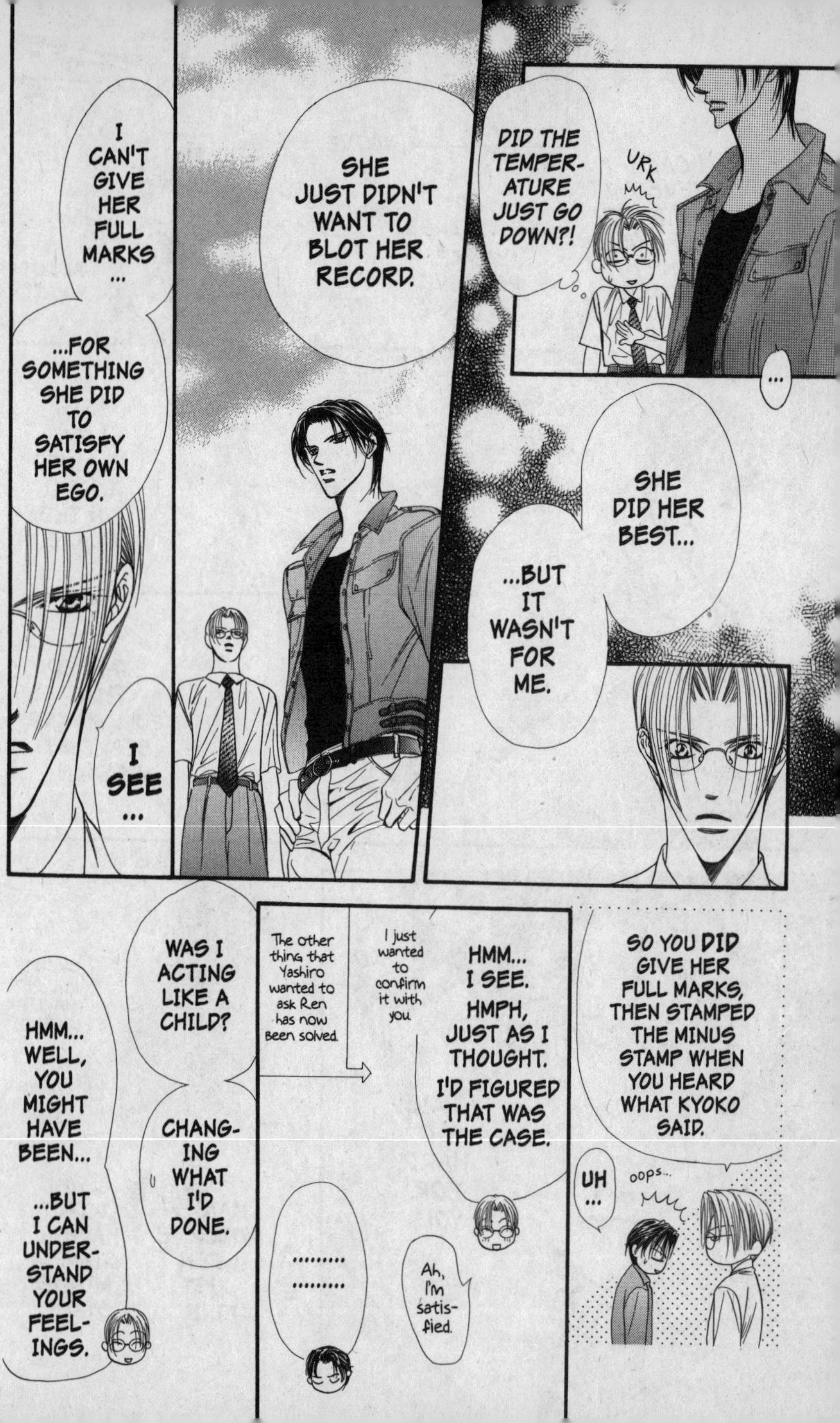
DID THE TEMPERATURE JUST GO DOWN?!
URK
...
SHE DID HER BEST...
...BUT IT WASN'T FOR ME.
SHE JUST DIDN'T WANT TO BLOT HER RECORD.
I CAN'T GIVE HER FULL MARKS...
...FOR SOMETHING SHE DID TO SATISFY HER OWN EGO.
I SEE...
SO YOU DID GIVE HER FULL MARKS, THEN STAMPED THE MINUS STAMP WHEN YOU HEARD WHAT KYOKO SAID.
UH...
oops...
HMM... I SEE. HMPH, JUST AS I THOUGHT. I'D FIGURED THAT WAS THE CASE.
I just wanted to confirm it with you.
The other thing that Yashiro wanted to ask Ren has now been solved.
Ah, I'm satisfied.
....
....
WAS I ACTING LIKE A CHILD?
CHANGING WHAT I'D DONE.
HMM... WELL, YOU MIGHT HAVE BEEN...
...BUT I CAN UNDERSTAND YOUR FEELINGS.

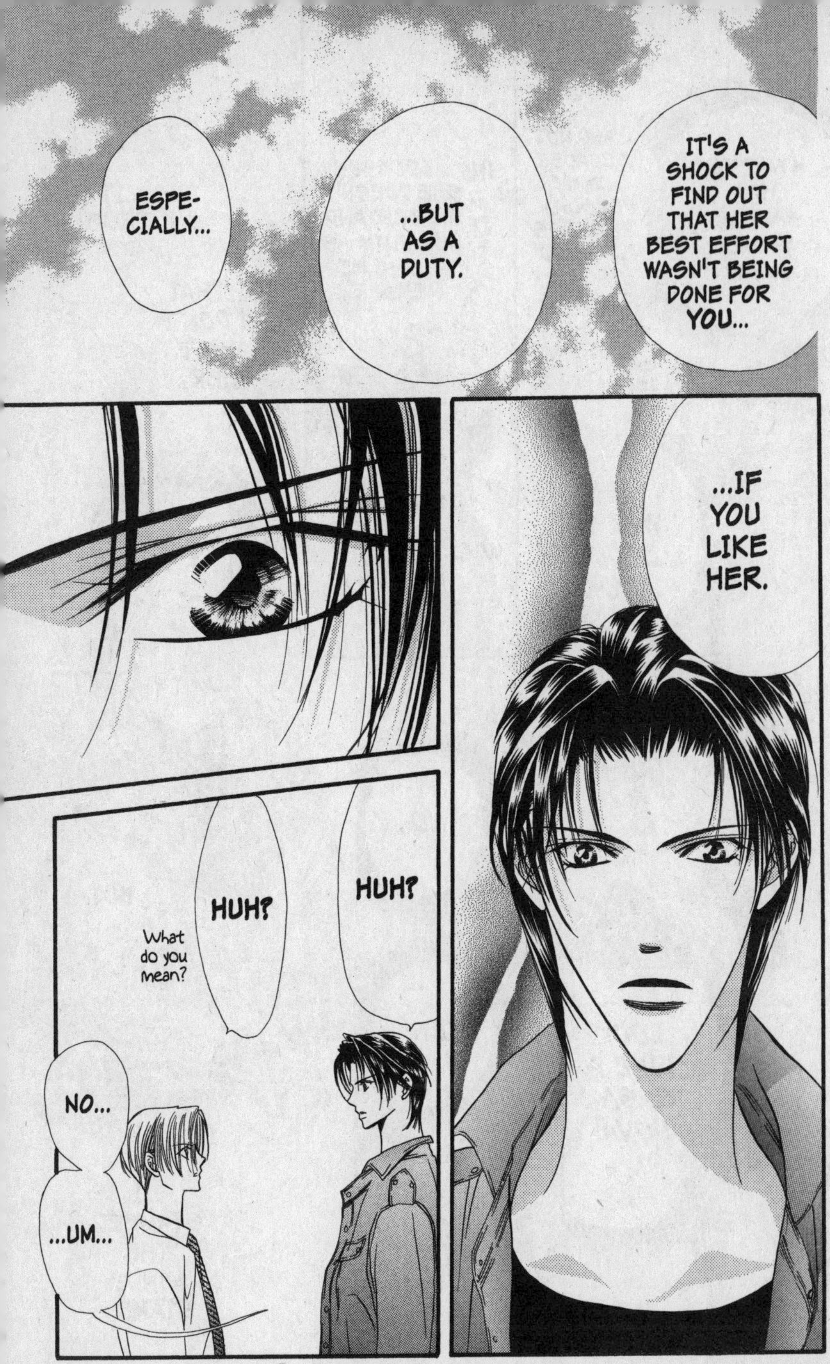
IT'S A SHOCK TO FIND OUT THAT HER BEST EFFORT WASN'T BEING DONE FOR YOU...
...BUT AS A DUTY.
ESPE-CIALLY...
...IF YOU LIKE HER.
HUH?
HUH?
What do you mean?
NO...
...UM...

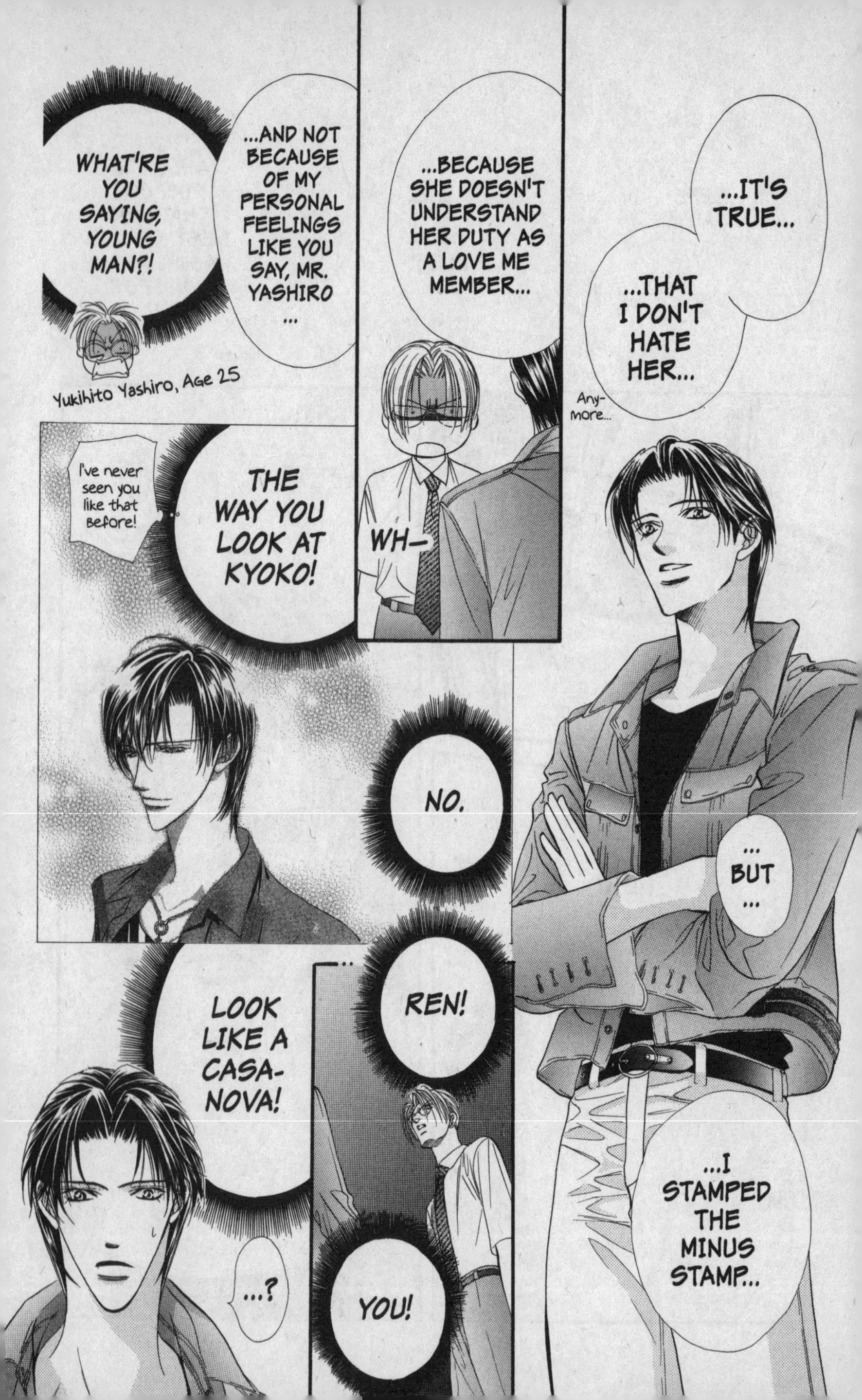
...IT'S TRUE...
...THAT I DON'T HATE HER...
Any-more...
... BUT ...
...I STAMPED THE MINUS STAMP...
...BECAUSE SHE DOESN'T UNDERSTAND HER DUTY AS A LOVE ME MEMBER...
WH—
...AND NOT BECAUSE OF MY PERSONAL FEELINGS LIKE YOU SAY, MR. YASHIRO ...
WHAT'RE YOU SAYING, YOUNG MAN?!
Yukihito Yashiro, Age 25
THE WAY YOU LOOK AT KYOKO!
I've never seen you like that before!
NO.
REN!
YOU!
LOOK LIKE A CASA-NOVA!
...?

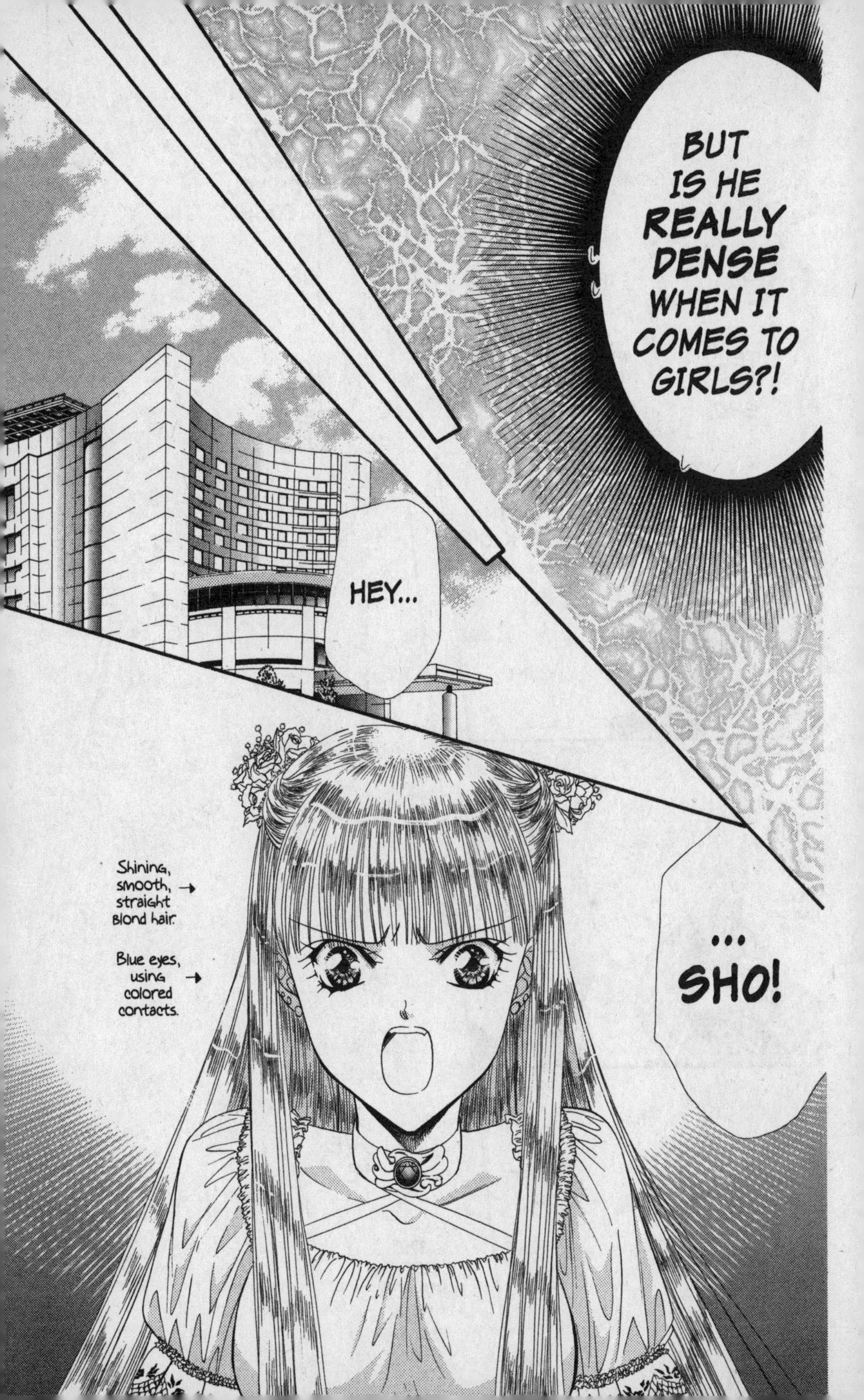
BUT IS HE REALLY DENSE WHEN IT COMES TO GIRLS?!
HEY...
...SHO!
Shining, smooth, straight blond hair.
Blue eyes, using colored contacts.

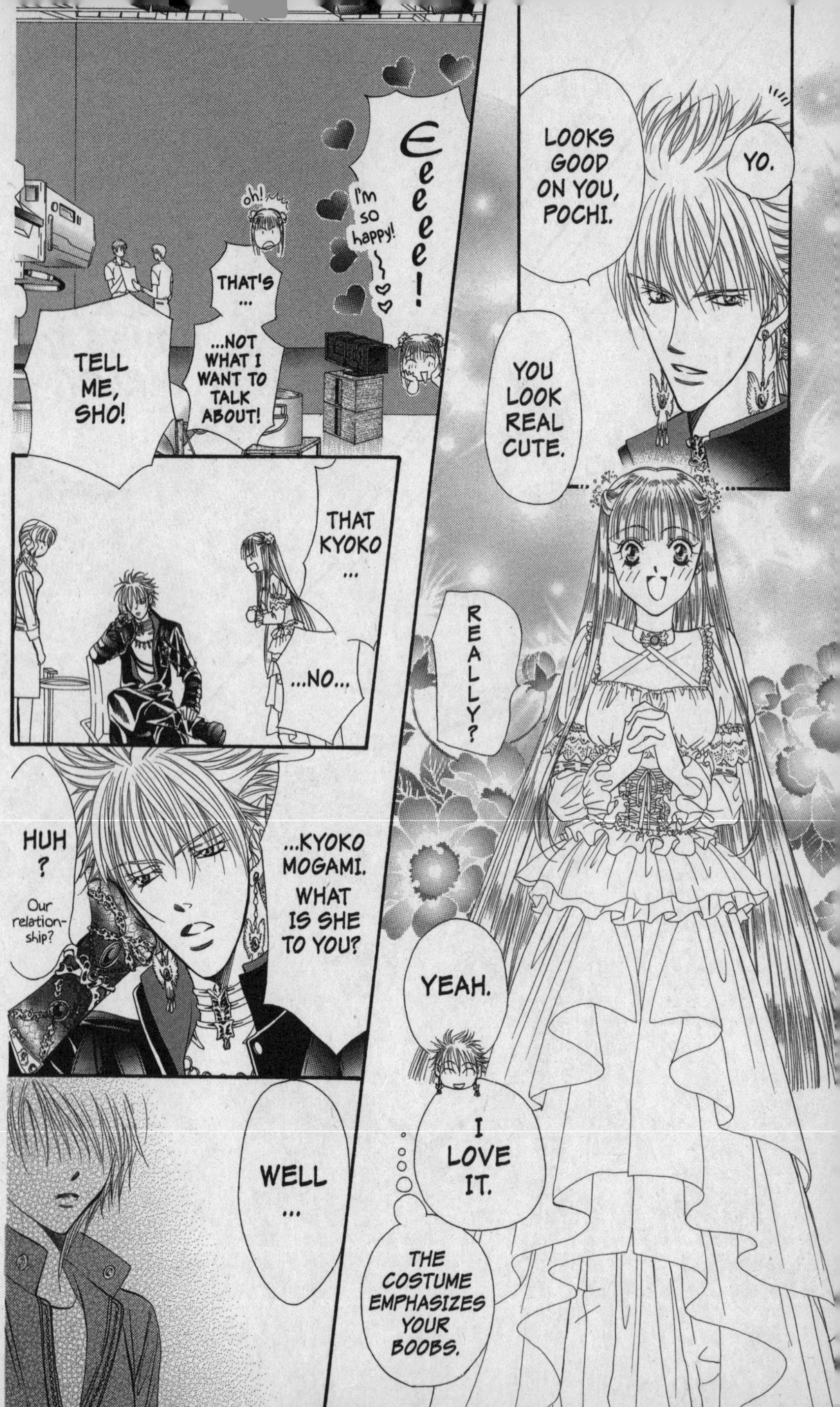
YO.
LOOKS GOOD ON YOU, POCHI.
YOU LOOK REAL CUTE.
REALLY?
YEAH.
I LOVE IT.
THE COSTUME EMPHASIZES YOUR BOOBS.
Eeeeee!
I'm so happy! ~♡
oh!
THAT'S...
...NOT WHAT I WANT TO TALK ABOUT!
TELL ME, SHO!
THAT KYOKO...
...NO...
...KYOKO MOGAMI. WHAT IS SHE TO YOU?
HUH?
Our relationship?
WELL...

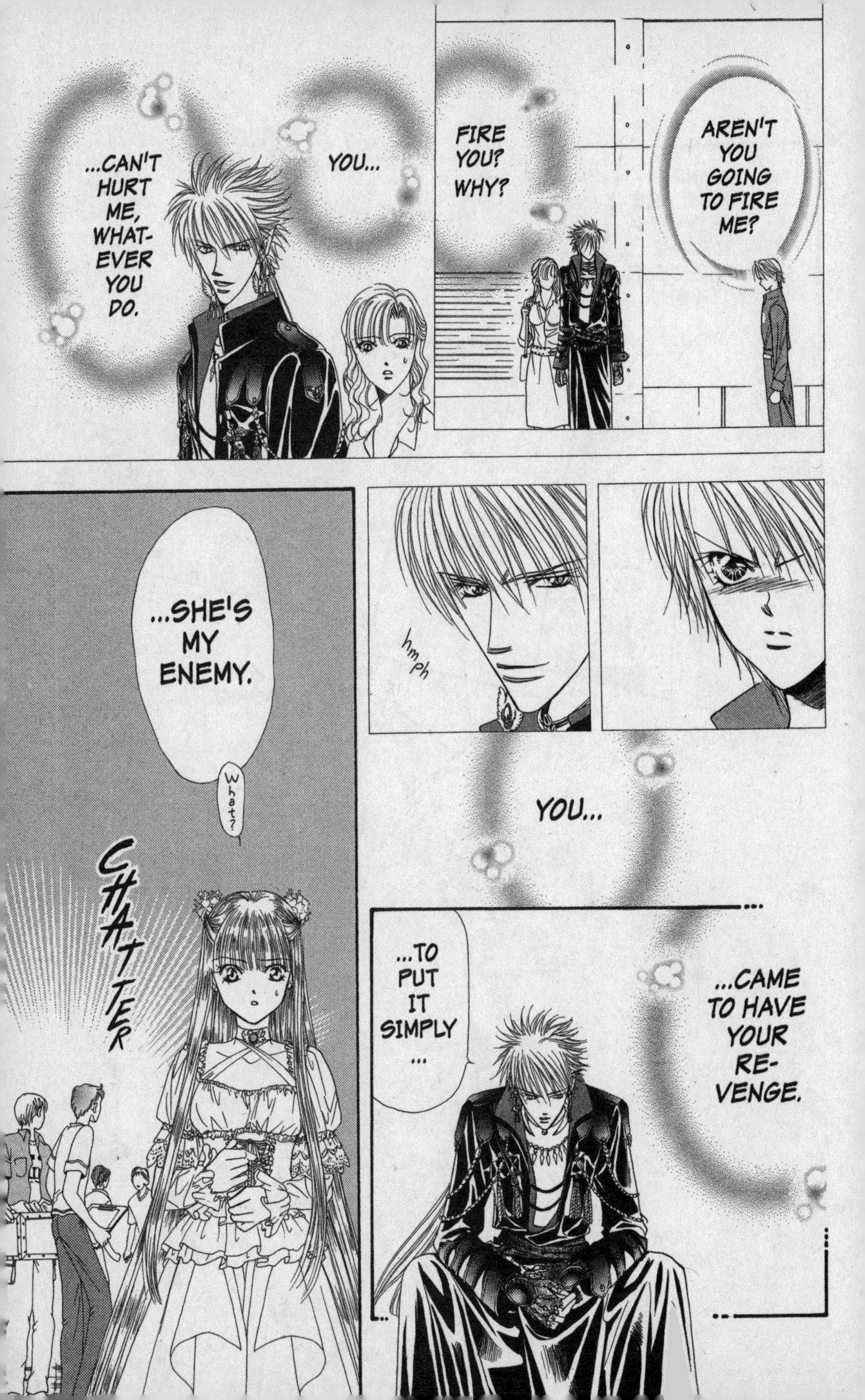
AREN'T YOU GOING TO FIRE ME?
FIRE YOU? WHY?
YOU...
...CAN'T HURT ME, WHAT-EVER YOU DO.
hmph
YOU...
...CAME TO HAVE YOUR RE-VENGE.
...TO PUT IT SIMPLY ...
...SHE'S MY ENEMY.
What?
CHATTER

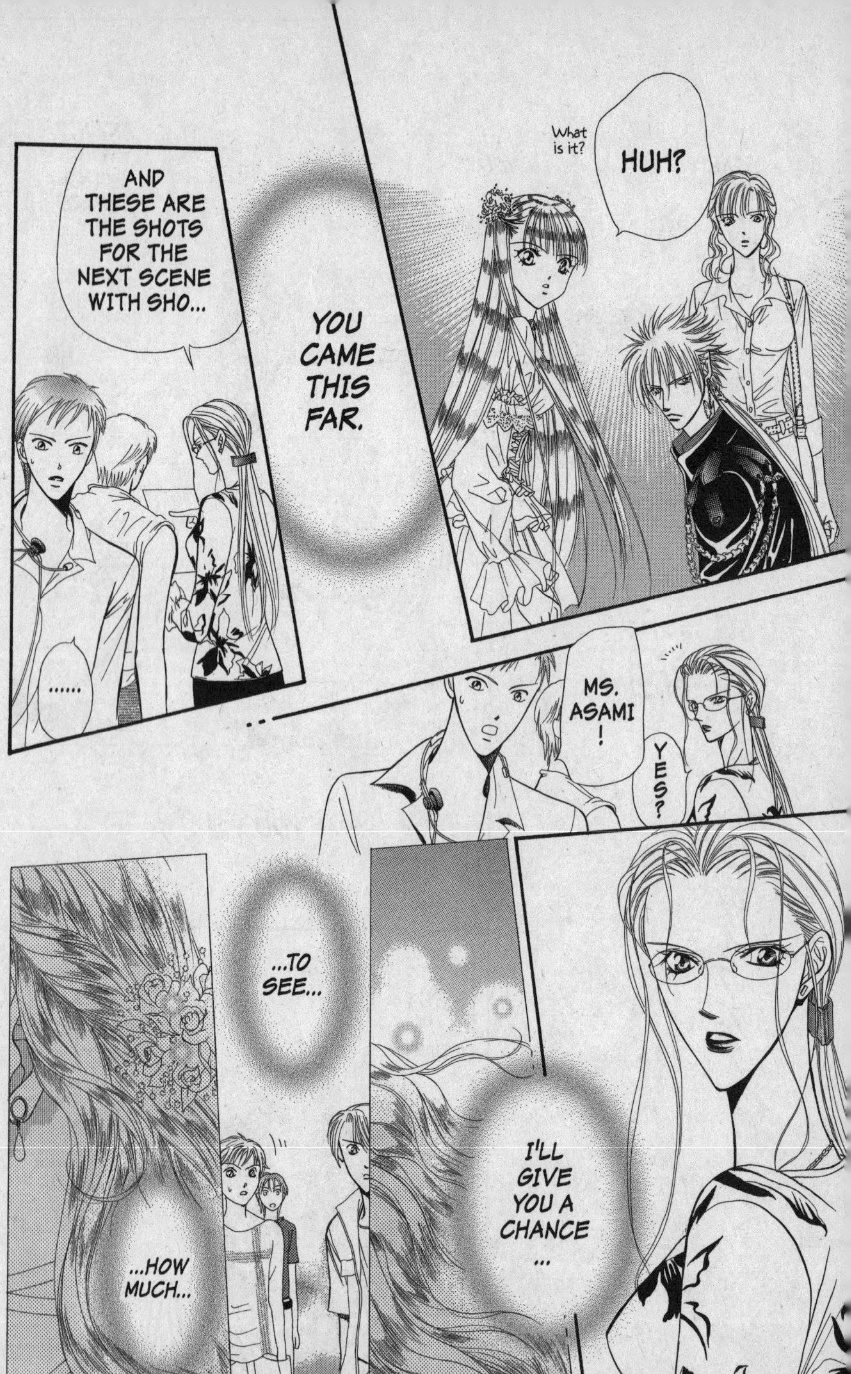
HUH?
What is it?
YOU CAME THIS FAR.
AND THESE ARE THE SHOTS FOR THE NEXT SCENE WITH SHO...
......
MS. ASAMI!
YES?
...
I'LL GIVE YOU A CHANCE ...
...TO SEE...
...HOW MUCH...

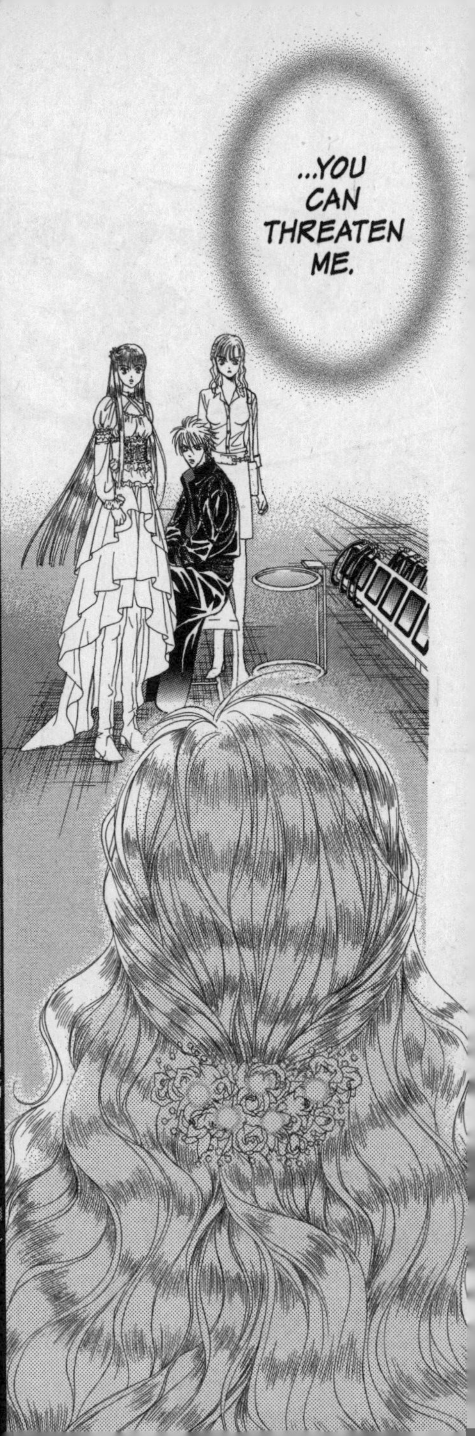
...YOU CAN THREATEN ME.

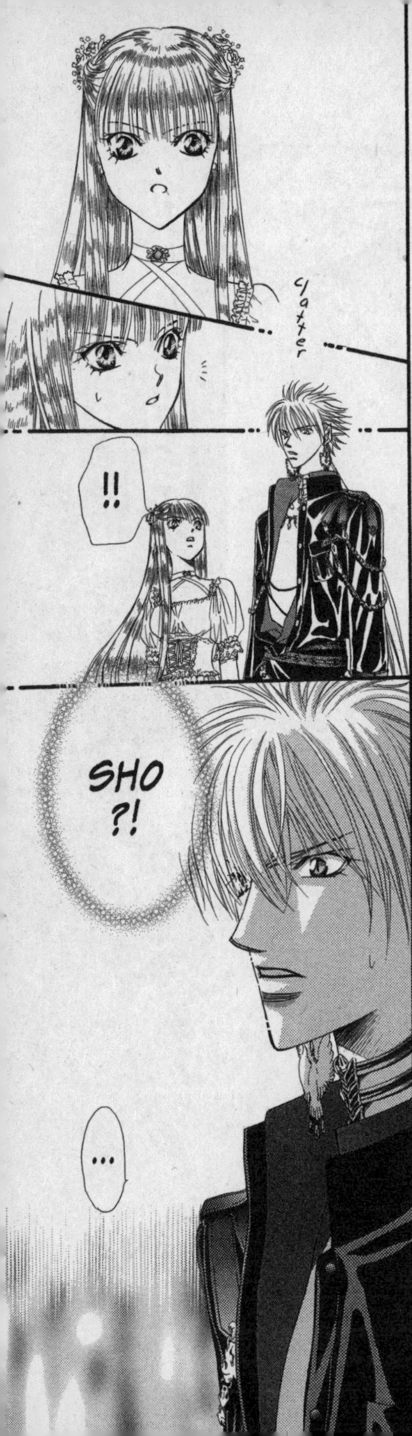
clatter
!!
SHO ?!
...

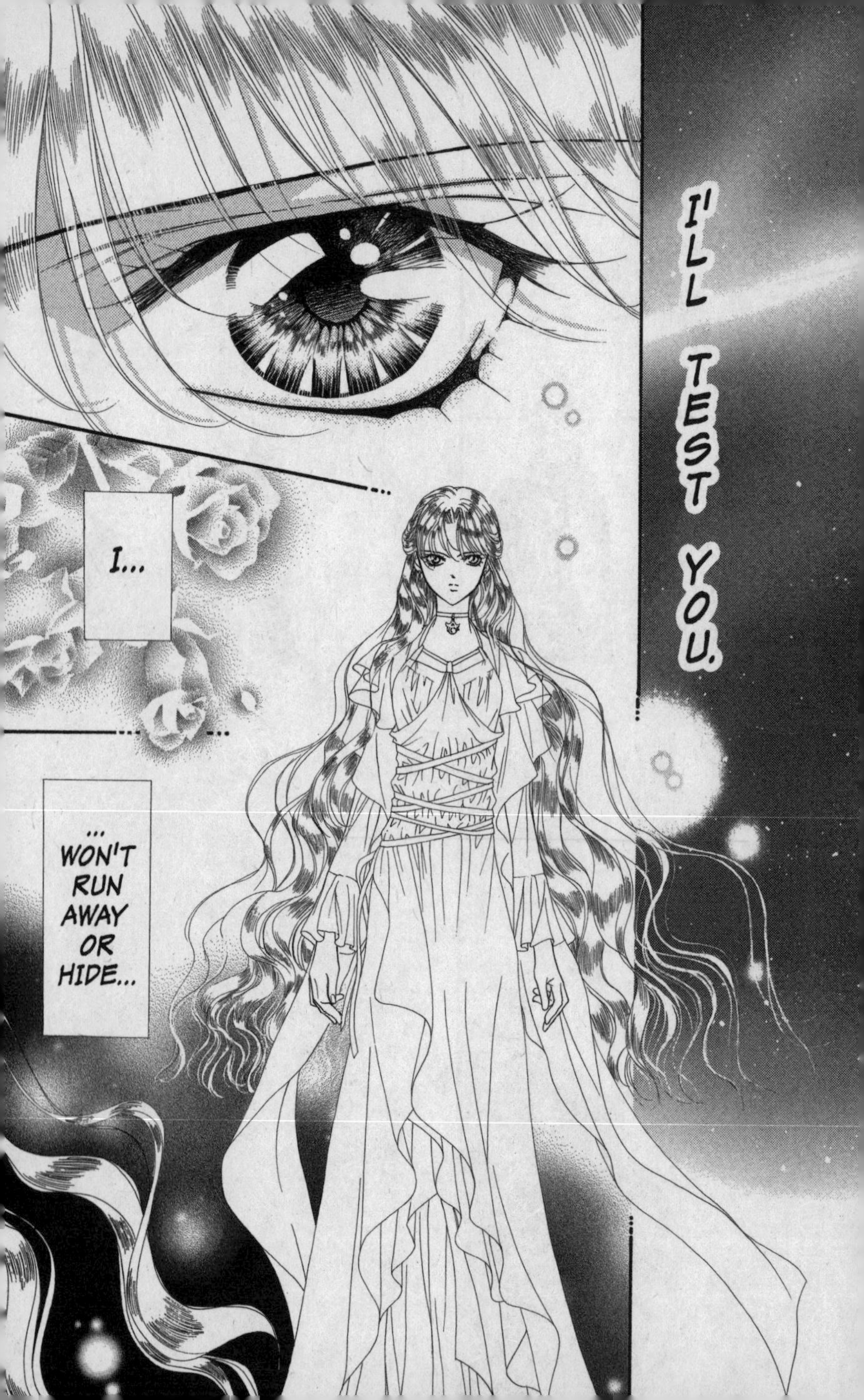
I'LL TEST YOU.
I...
...WON'T RUN AWAY OR HIDE...

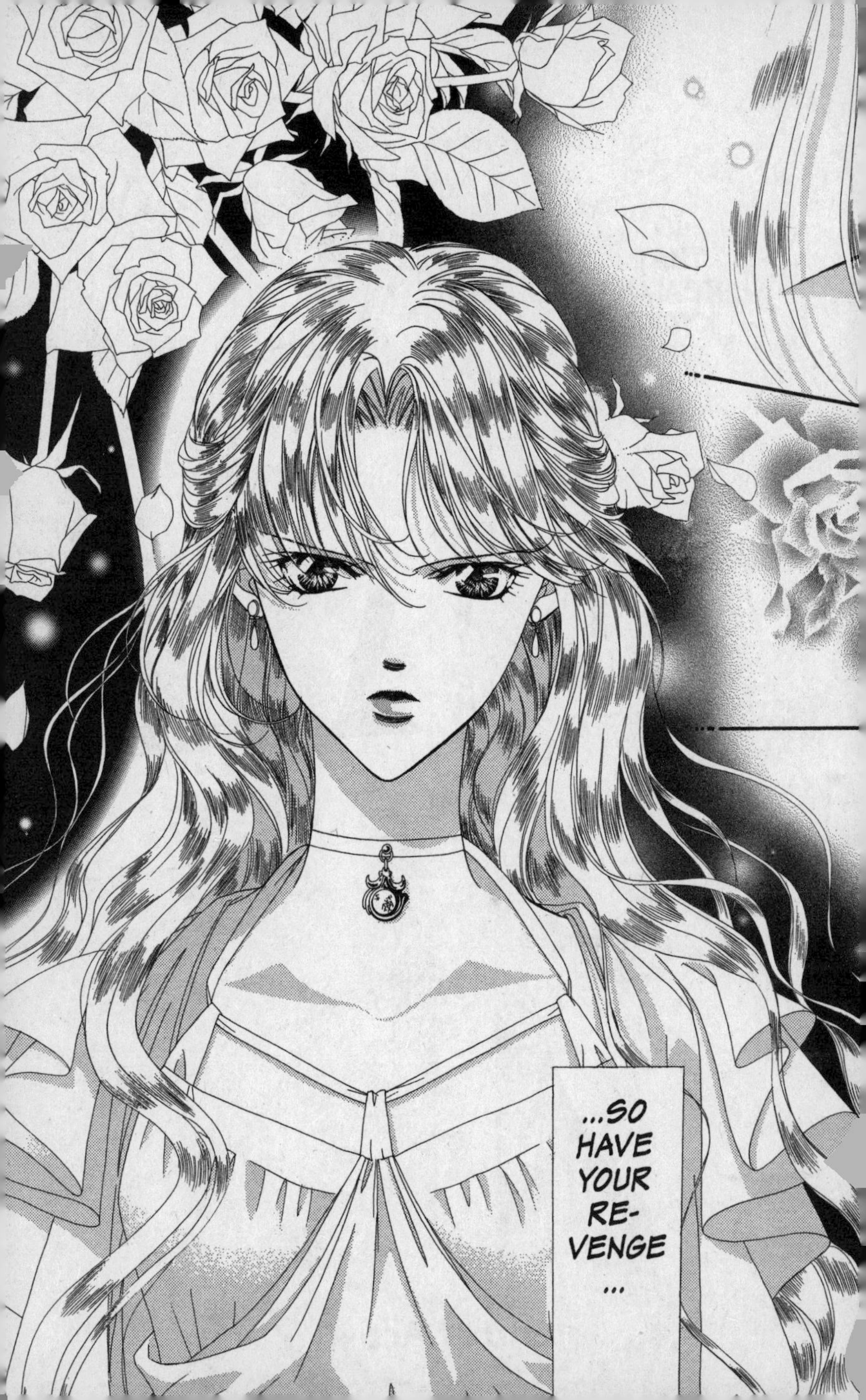
...SO HAVE YOUR RE-VENGE ...

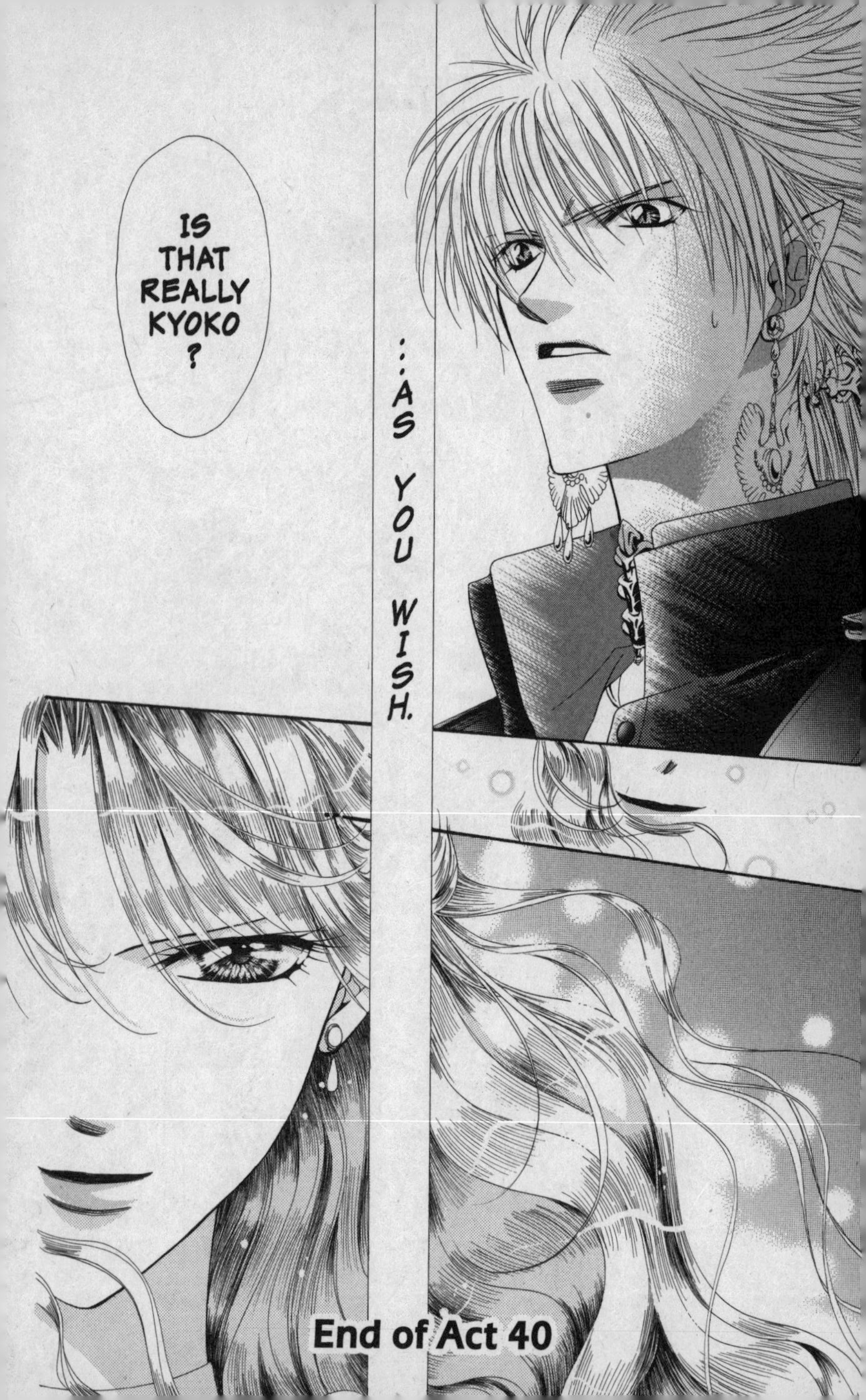
...AS YOU WISH.
IS THAT REALLY KYOKO?
End of Act 40

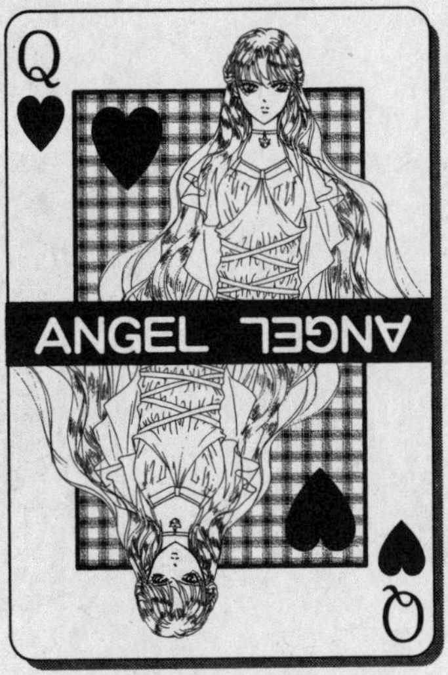
Q
ANGEL
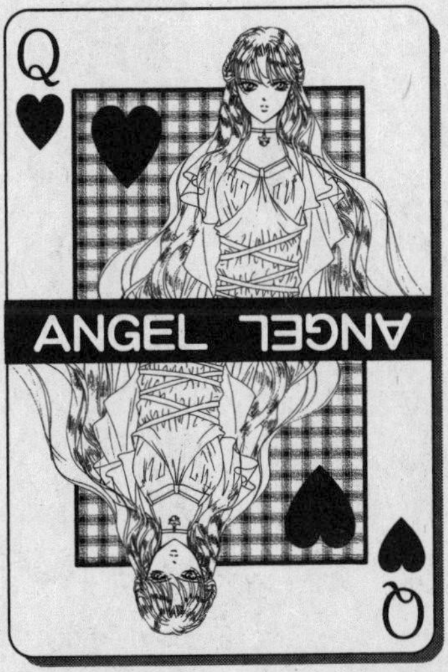
Q
ANGEL

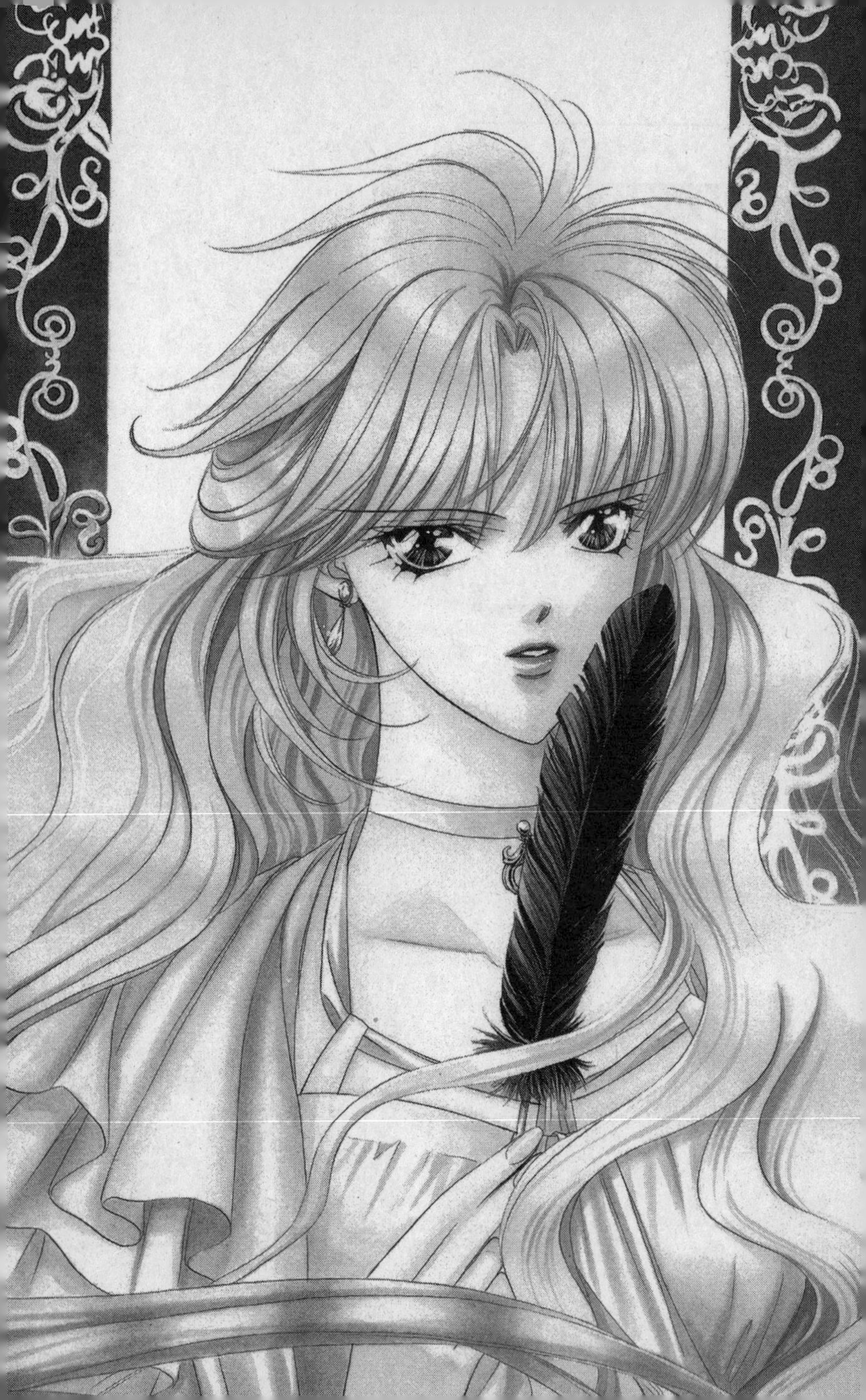

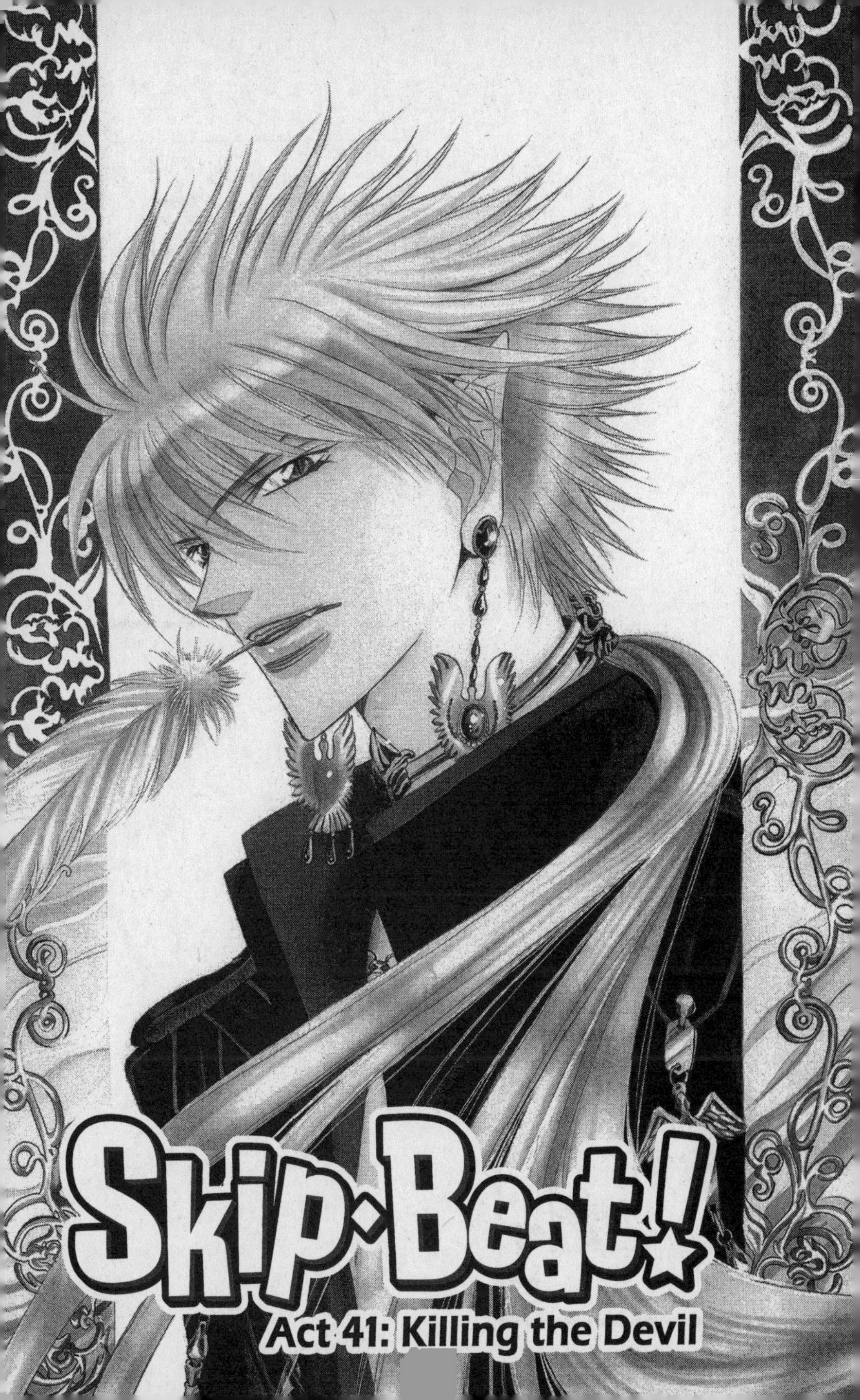
Skip·Beat!
Act 41: Killing the Devil

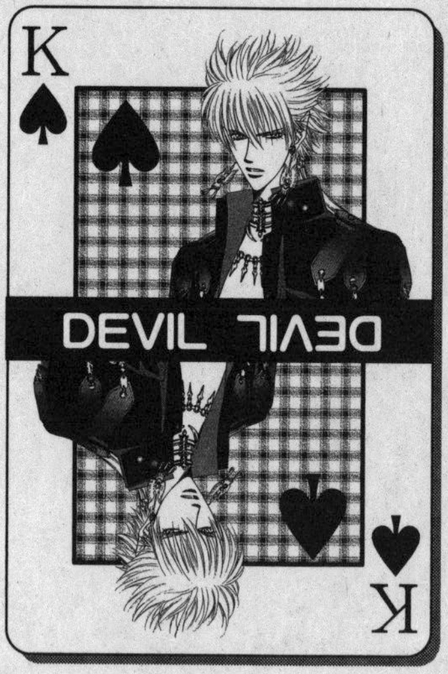
K
DEVIL
DEVIL
K

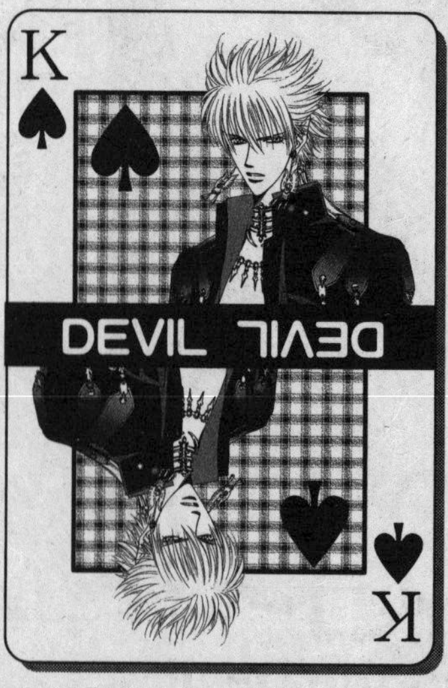
K
DEVIL
DEVIL
K

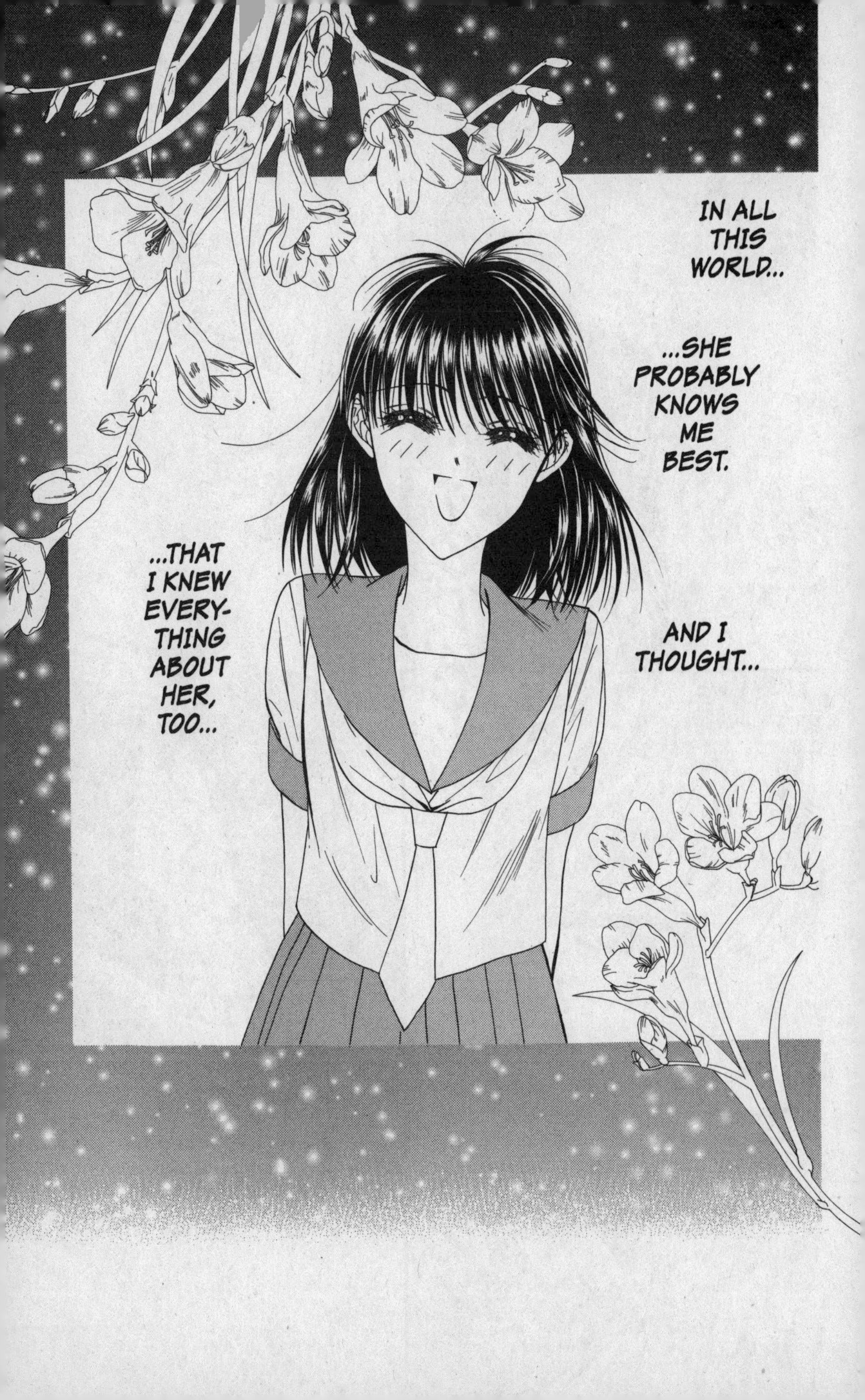
IN ALL THIS WORLD...
...SHE PROBABLY KNOWS ME BEST.
AND I THOUGHT...
...THAT I KNEW EVERY-THING ABOUT HER, TOO...

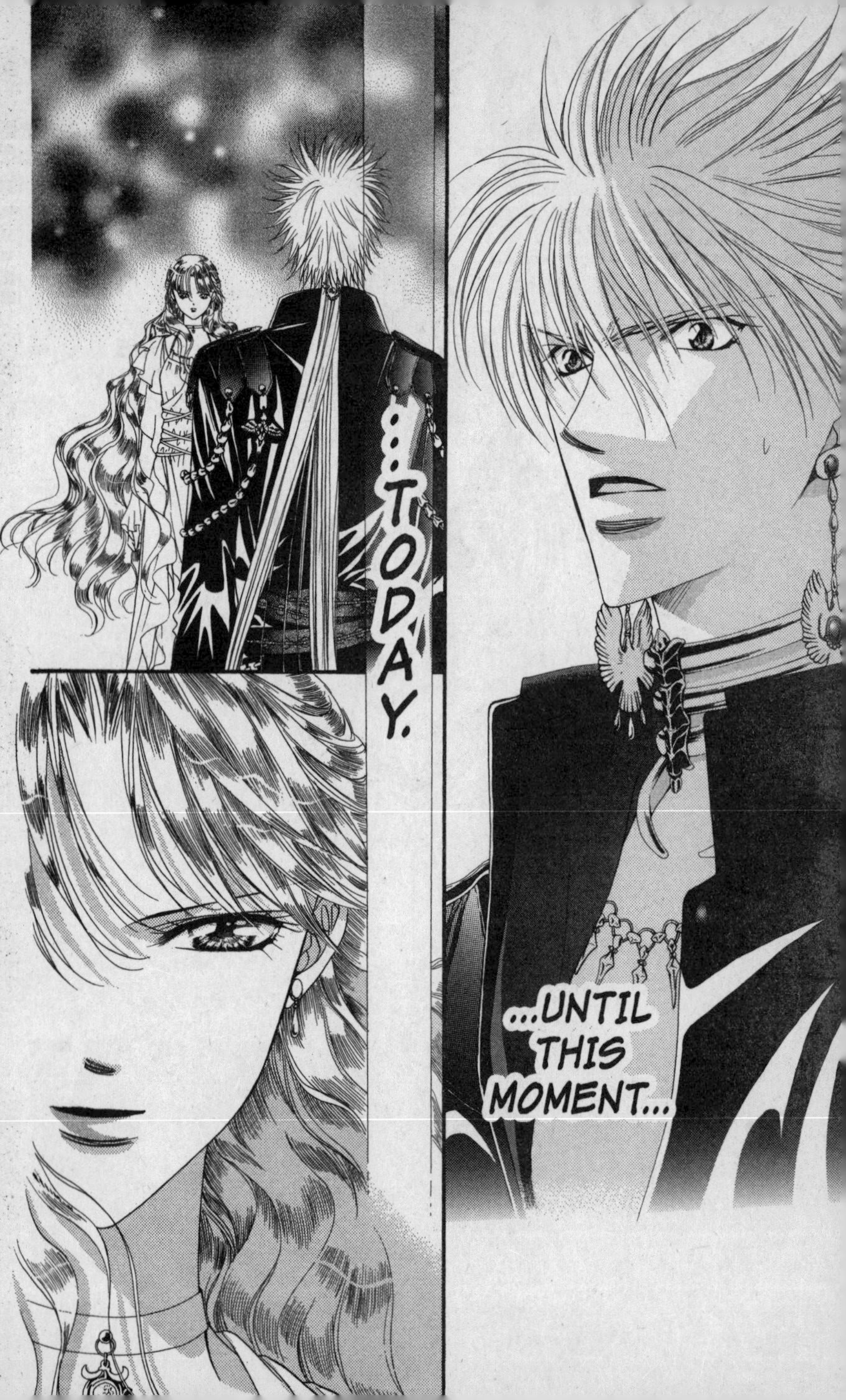
...UNTIL THIS MOMENT...
...TODAY.

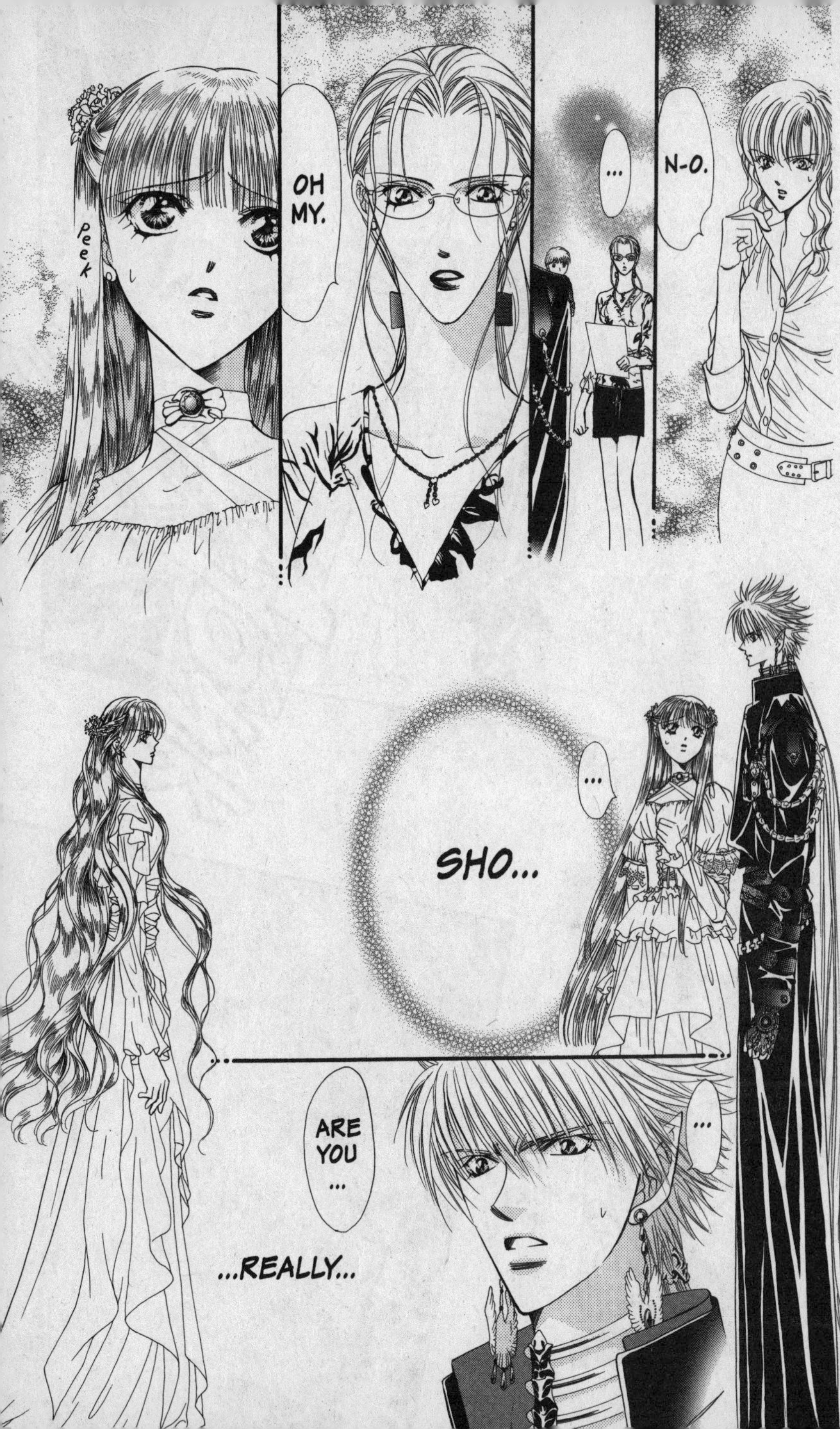
N-O.
...
OH MY.
Peek
...
SHO...
...
ARE YOU ...
...REALLY...

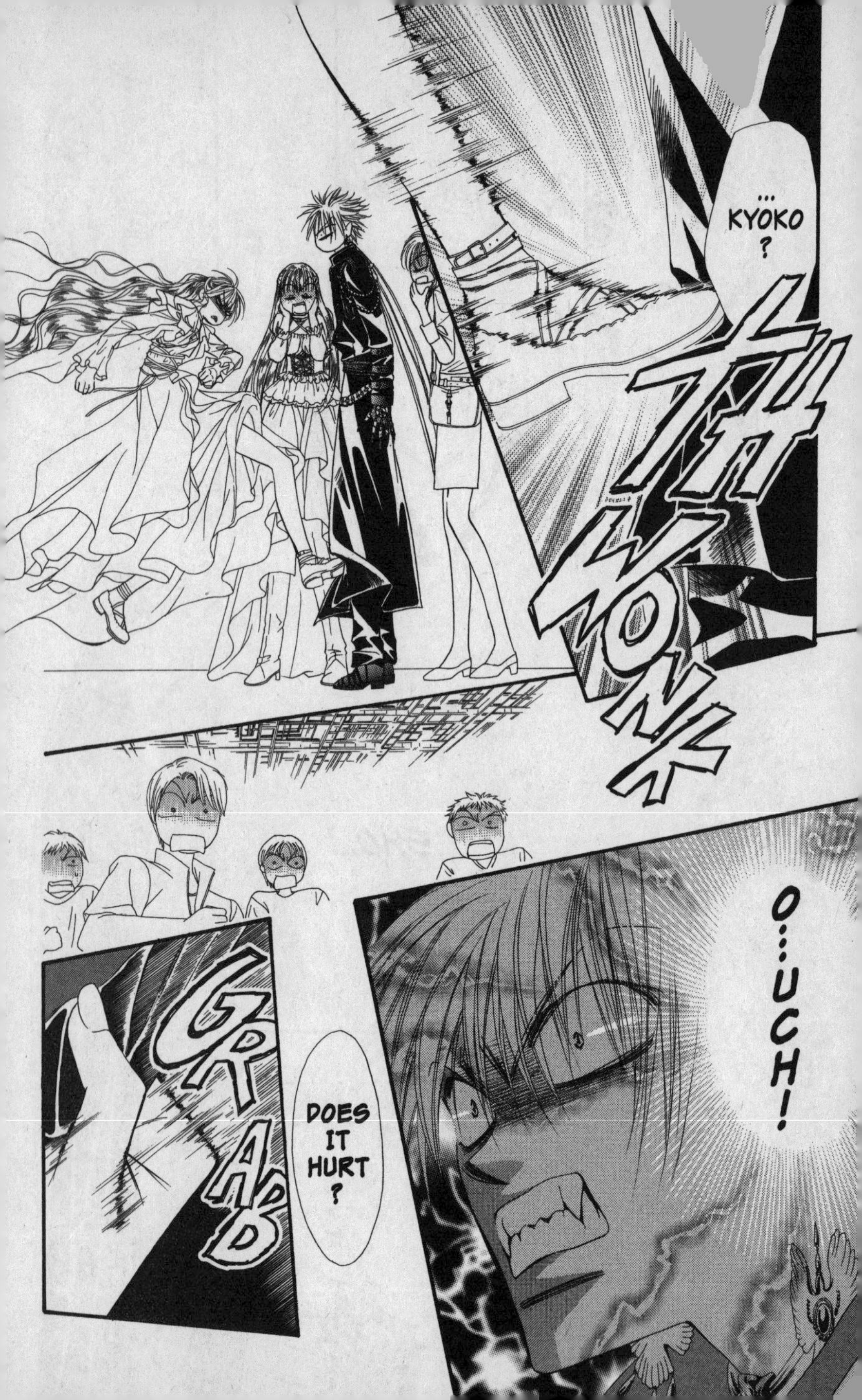
...KYOKO?
THWONK
O...UCH!
DOES IT HURT?
GRAB

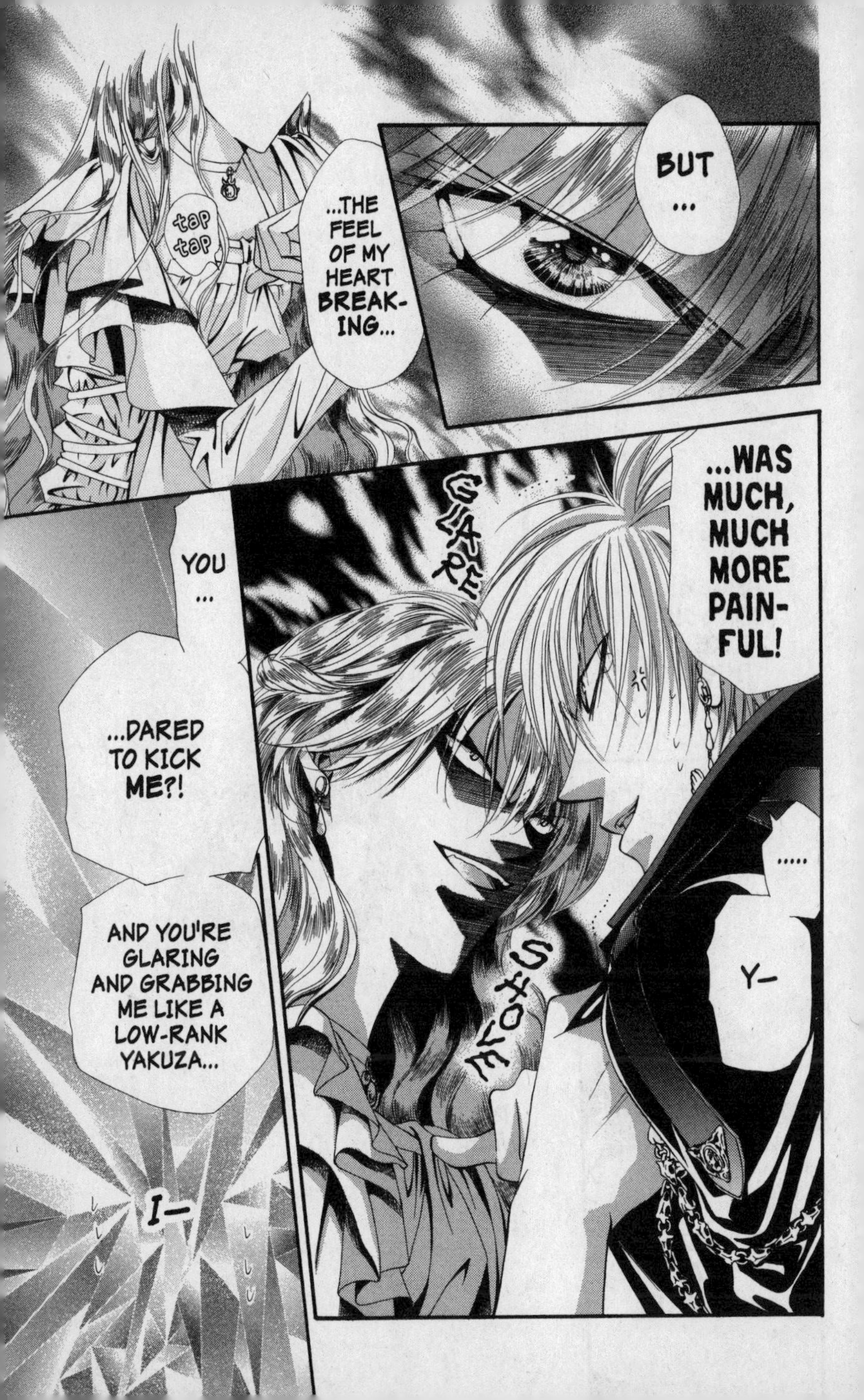
BUT ...
...THE FEEL OF MY HEART BREAKING...
tap tap
...WAS MUCH, MUCH MORE PAINFUL!
GLARE
.....
SHOVE
Y—
YOU ...
...DARED TO KICK ME?!
AND YOU'RE GLARING AND GRABBING ME LIKE A LOW-RANK YAKUZA...
I—

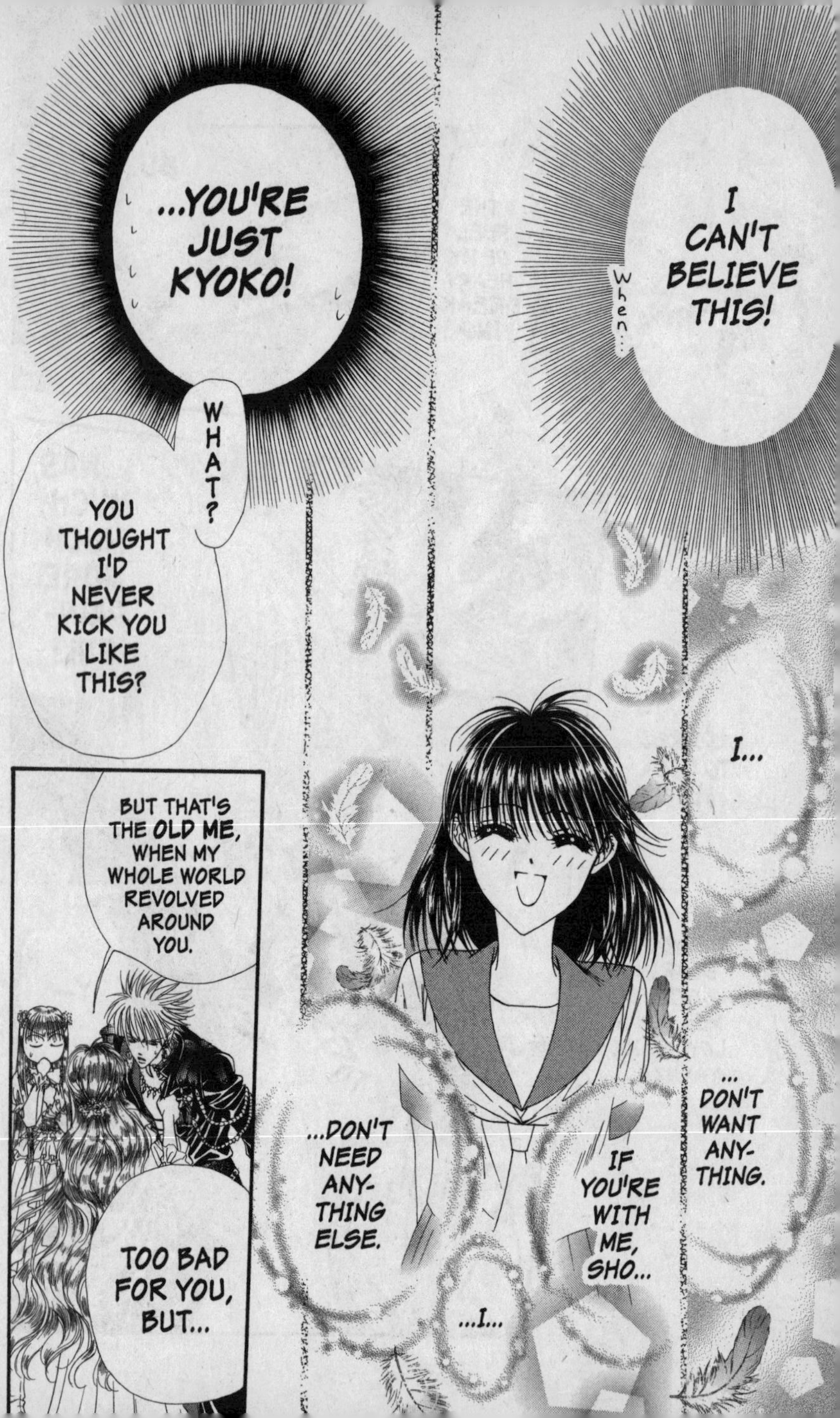

When...
I CAN'T BELIEVE THIS!
...YOU'RE JUST KYOKO!
WHAT?
YOU THOUGHT I'D NEVER KICK YOU LIKE THIS?
I...
...DON'T WANT ANYTHING.
IF YOU'RE WITH ME, SHO...
...I...
...DON'T NEED ANYTHING ELSE.
BUT THAT'S THE OLD ME, WHEN MY WHOLE WORLD REVOLVED AROUND YOU.
TOO BAD FOR YOU, BUT...

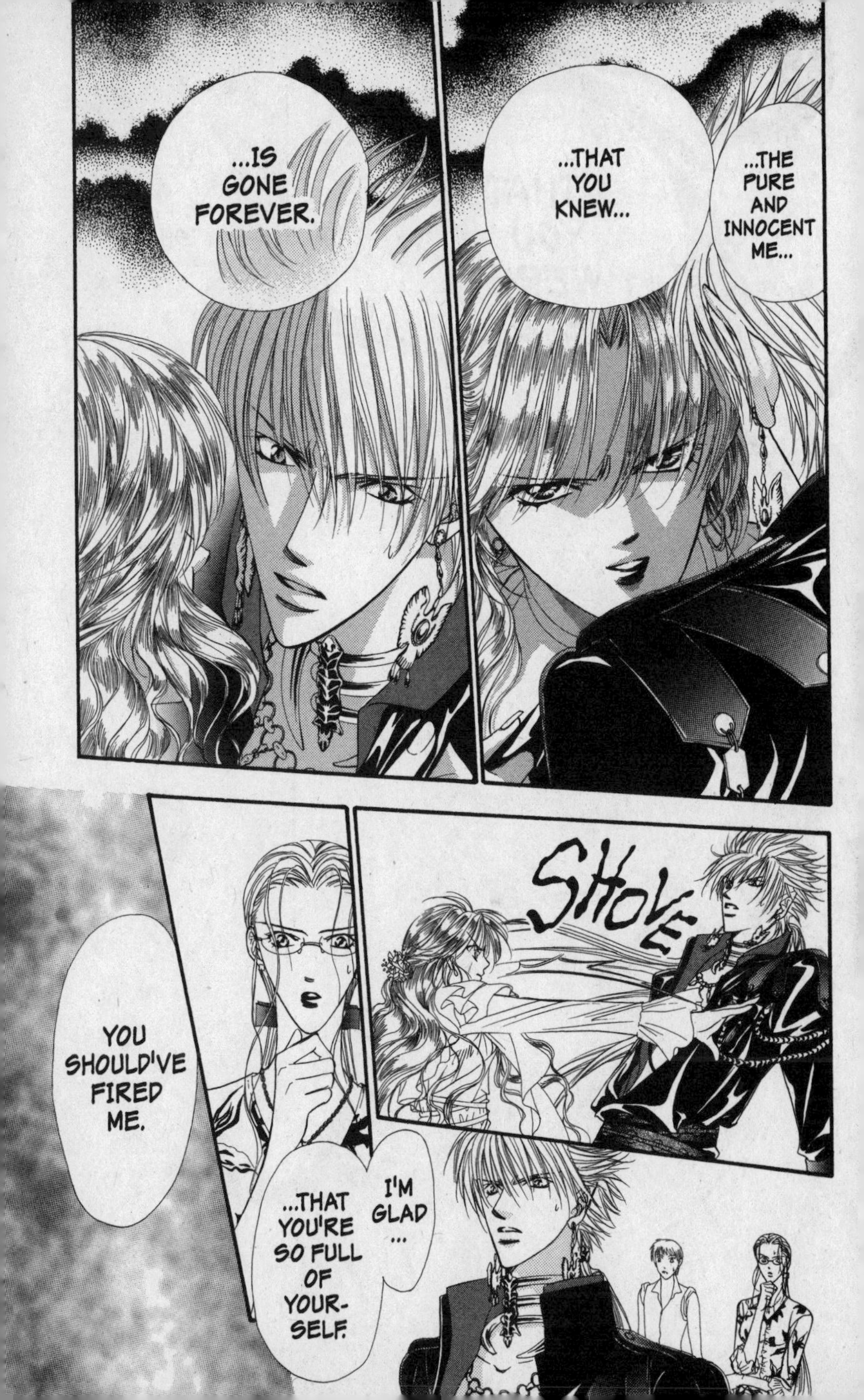
...THE PURE AND INNOCENT ME...
...THAT YOU KNEW...
...IS GONE FOREVER.
SHOVE
YOU SHOULD'VE FIRED ME.
I'M GLAD ...
...THAT YOU'RE SO FULL OF YOUR-SELF.

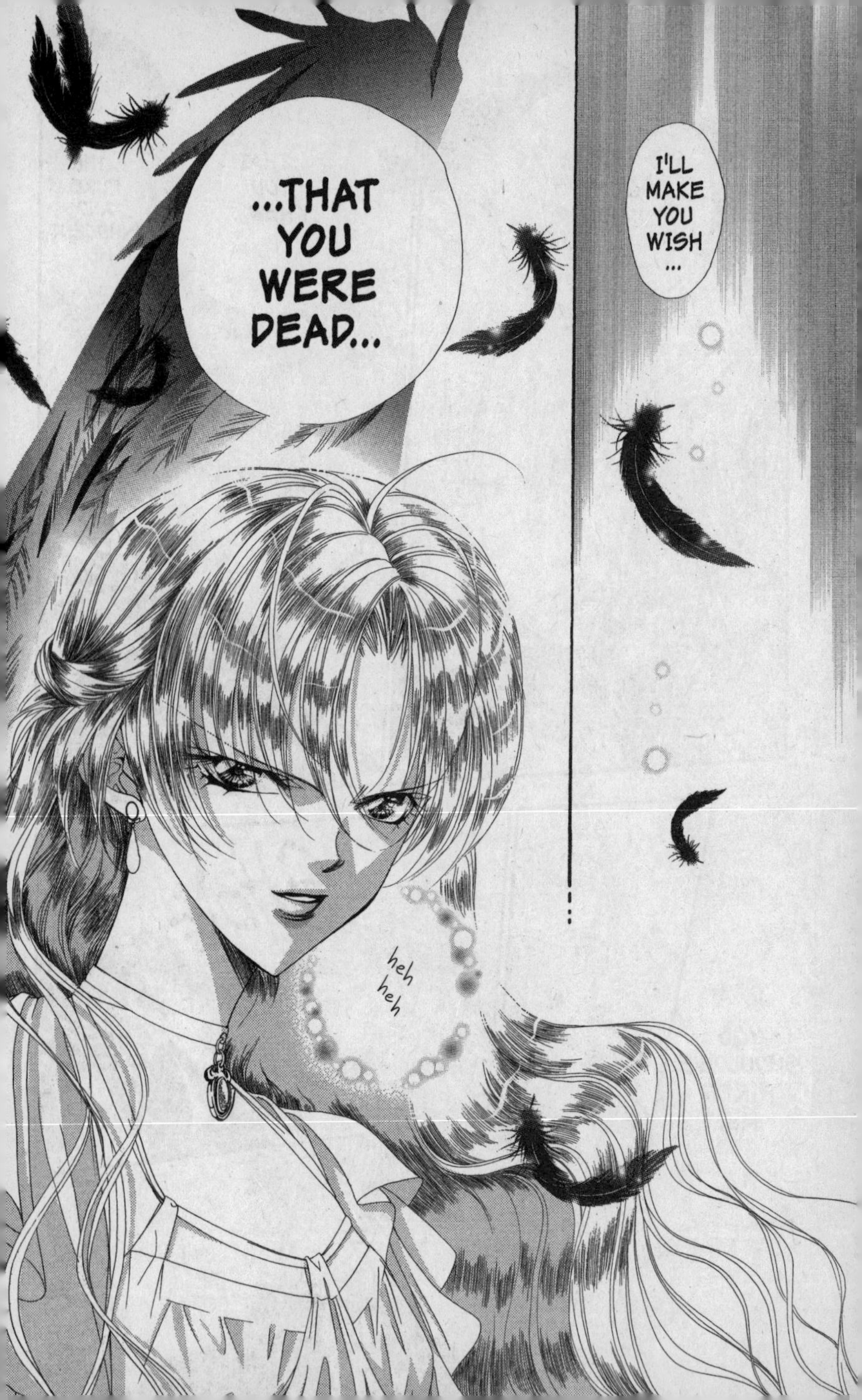
I'LL MAKE YOU WISH ...
...THAT YOU WERE DEAD...
heh heh

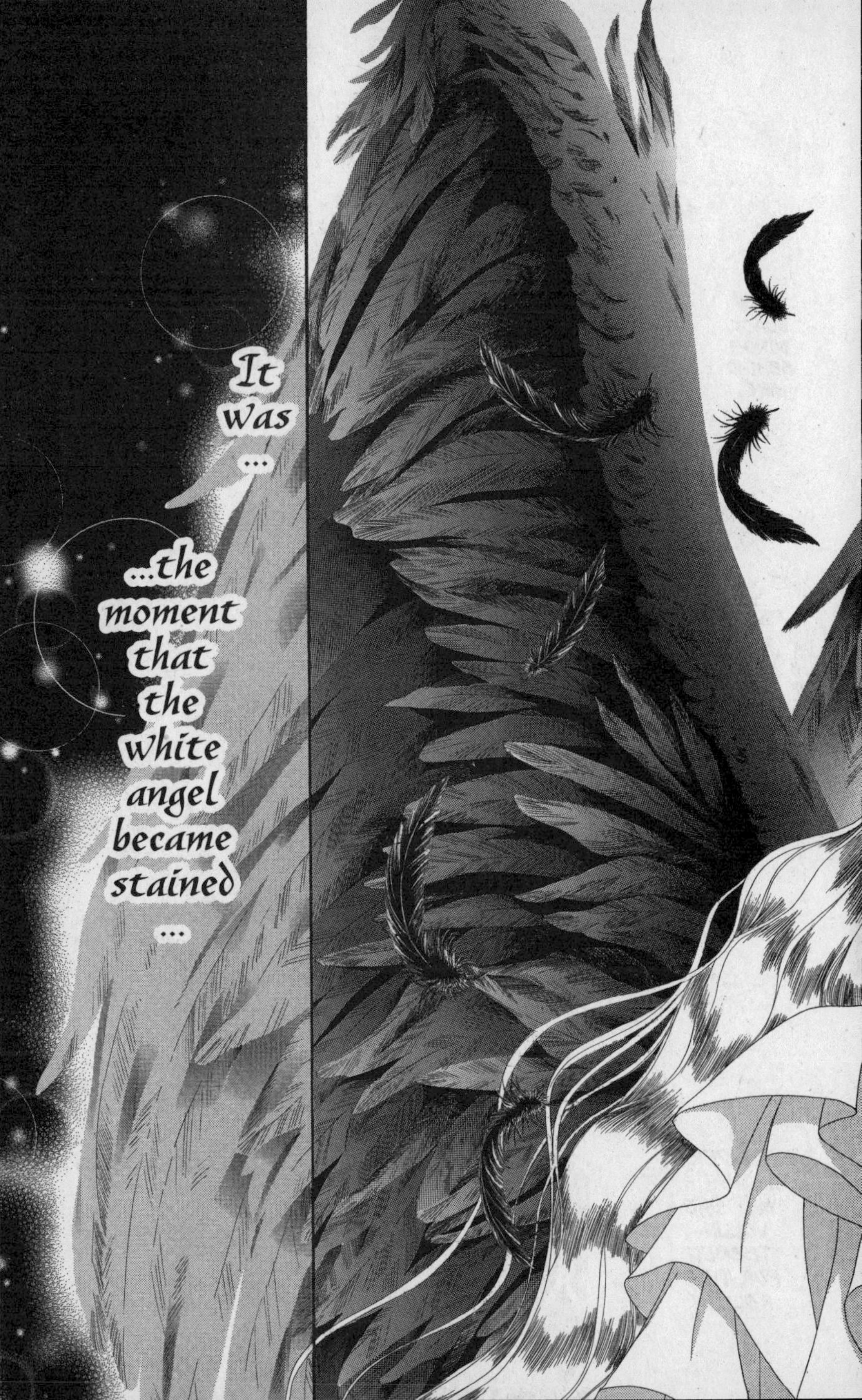
It was ...
...the moment that the white angel became stained ...

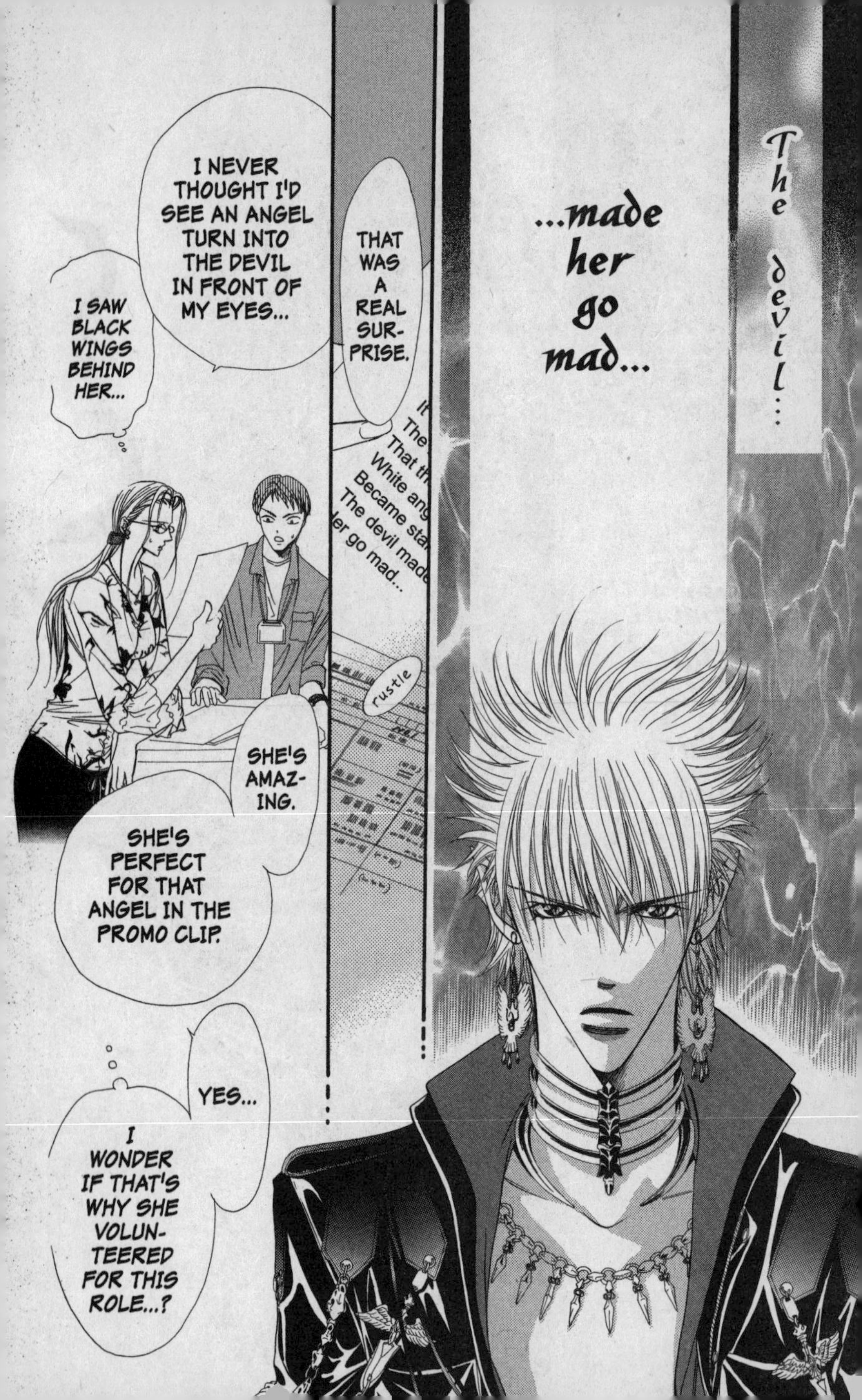
The devil...
...made her go mad...
THAT WAS A REAL SURPRISE.
I NEVER THOUGHT I'D SEE AN ANGEL TURN INTO THE DEVIL IN FRONT OF MY EYES...
I SAW BLACK WINGS BEHIND HER...
rustle
SHE'S AMAZING.
SHE'S PERFECT FOR THAT ANGEL IN THE PROMO CLIP.
YES...
I WONDER IF THAT'S WHY SHE VOLUNTEERED FOR THIS ROLE...?

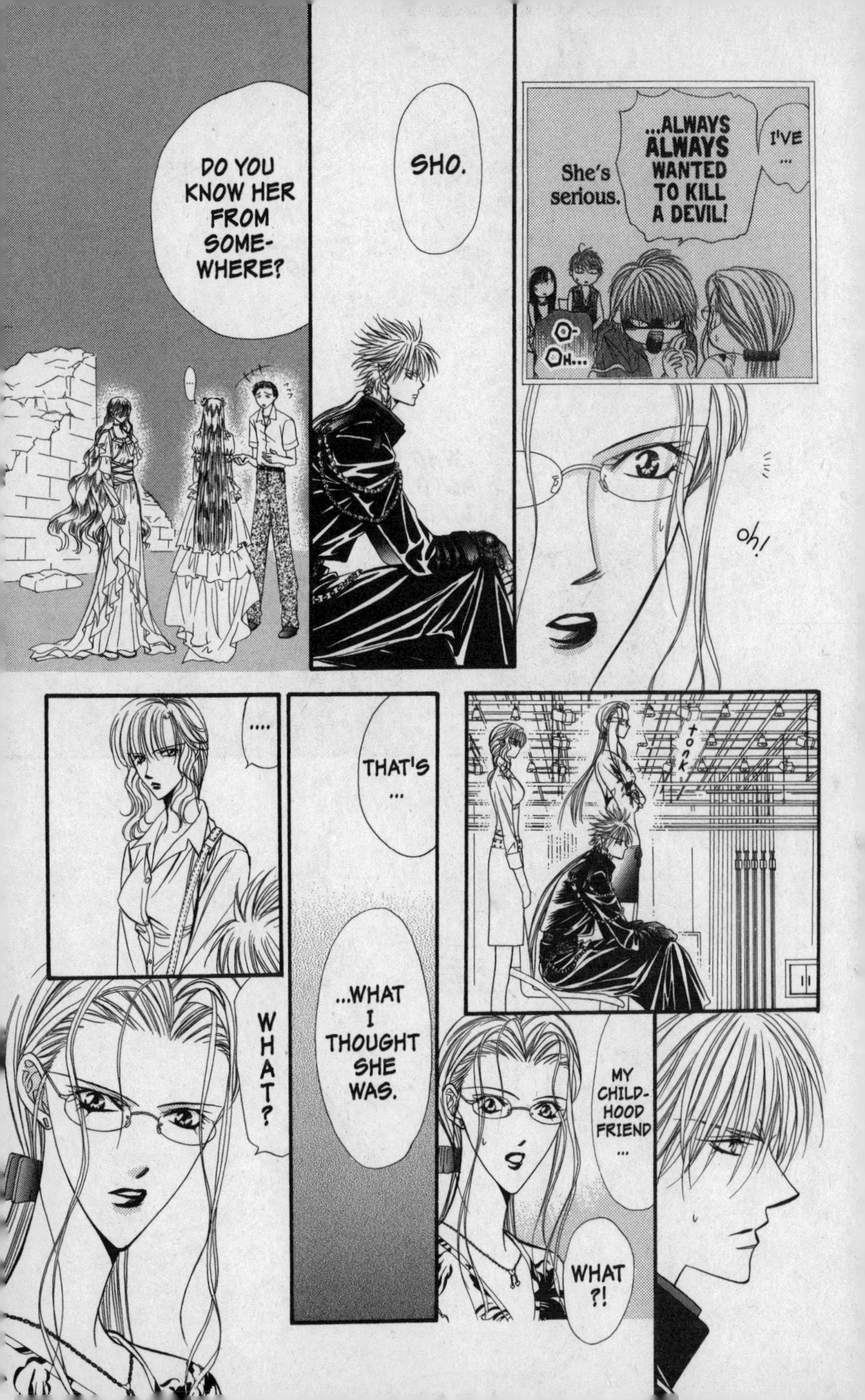

I'VE ...
...ALWAYS ALWAYS WANTED TO KILL A DEVIL!
She's serious.
O-OH...
oh!
SHO.
DO YOU KNOW HER FROM SOME-WHERE?
...
tonk
MY CHILD-HOOD FRIEND ...
WHAT ?!
THAT'S ...
...WHAT I THOUGHT SHE WAS.
....
WHAT?

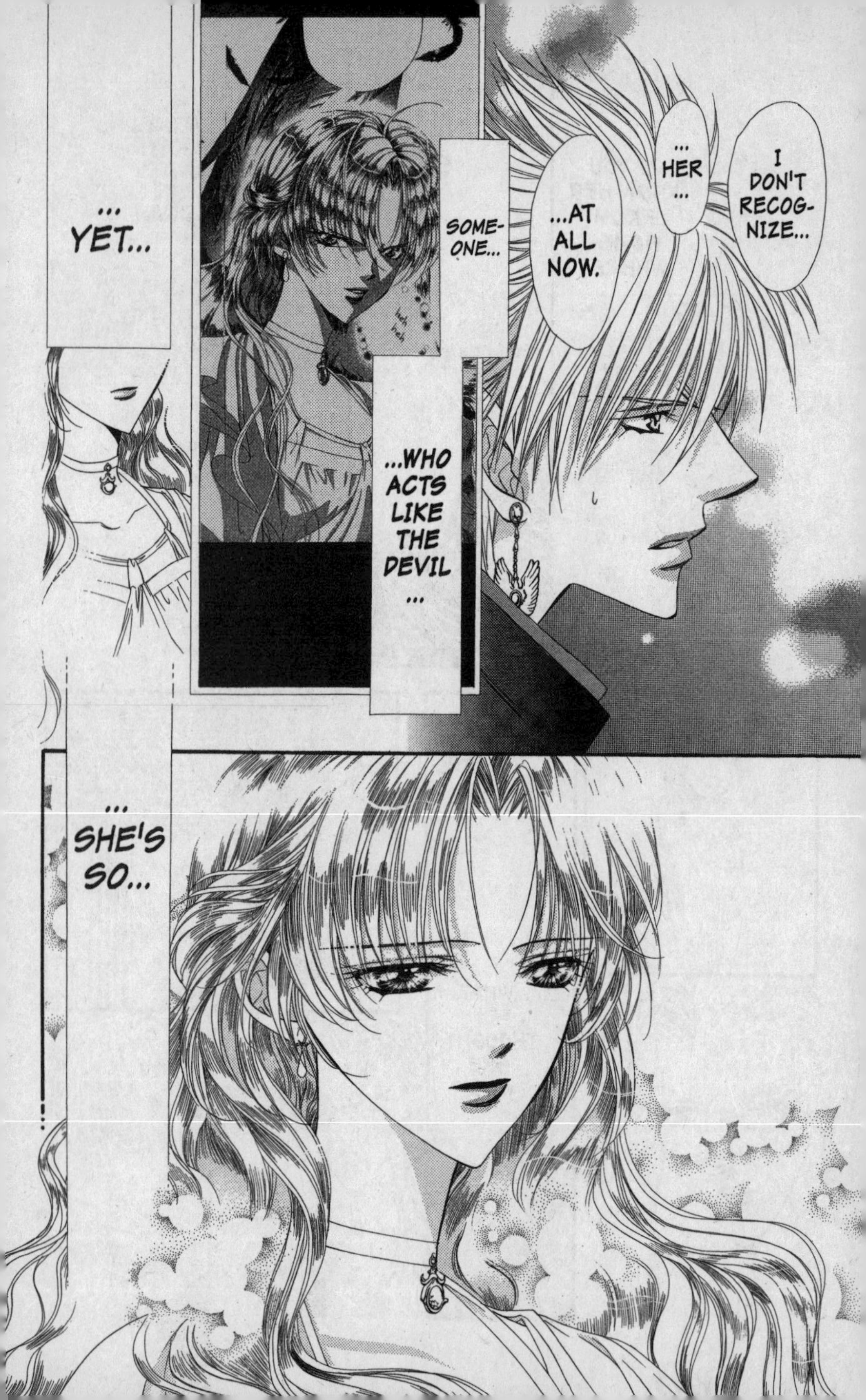
I DON'T RECOGNIZE...
...HER...
...AT ALL NOW.
SOME-ONE...
...WHO ACTS LIKE THE DEVIL...
...YET...
...SHE'S SO...

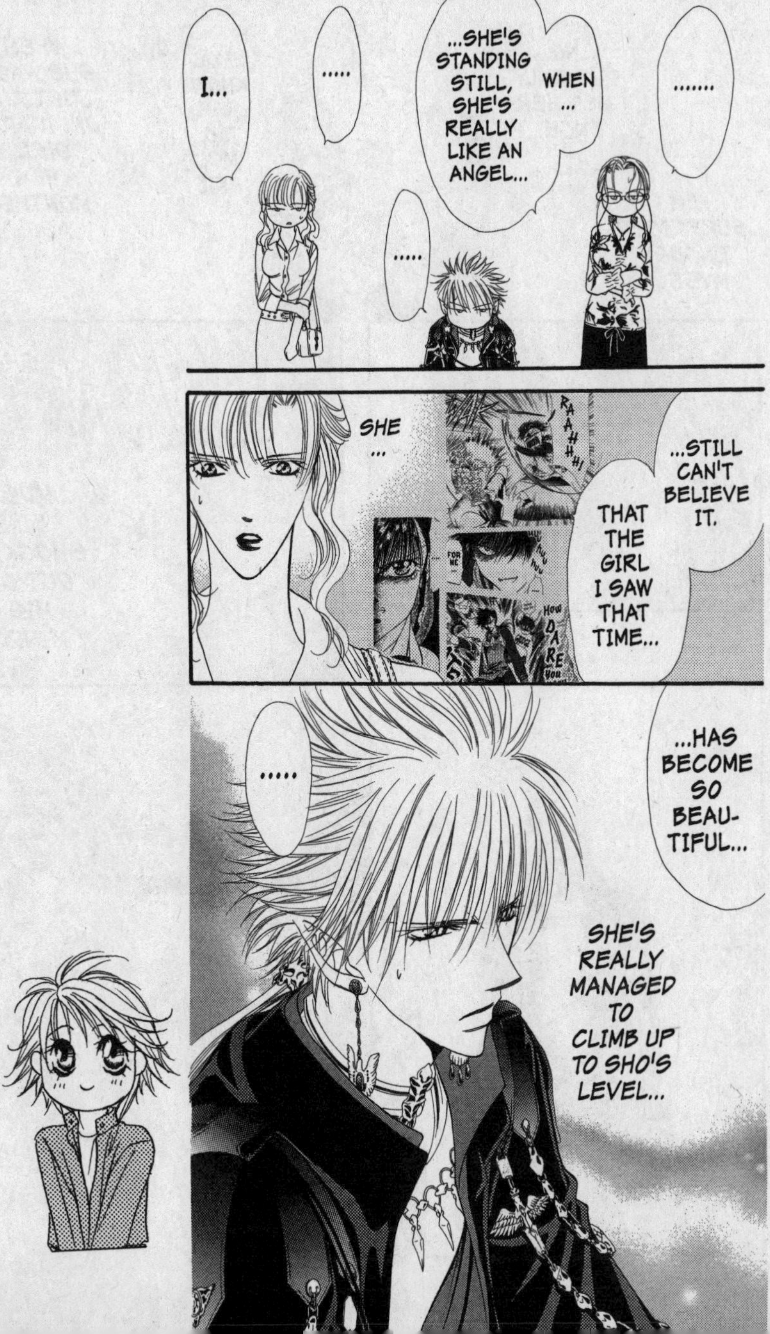
....
WHEN ...
...SHE'S STANDING STILL, SHE'S REALLY LIKE AN ANGEL...
.....
I...
.....
...STILL CAN'T BELIEVE IT.
THAT THE GIRL I SAW THAT TIME...
RAAHHH!
FOR ME ...
HOW DARE YOU
SHE ...
...HAS BECOME SO BEAU-TIFUL...
SHE'S REALLY MANAGED TO CLIMB UP TO SHO'S LEVEL...
.....

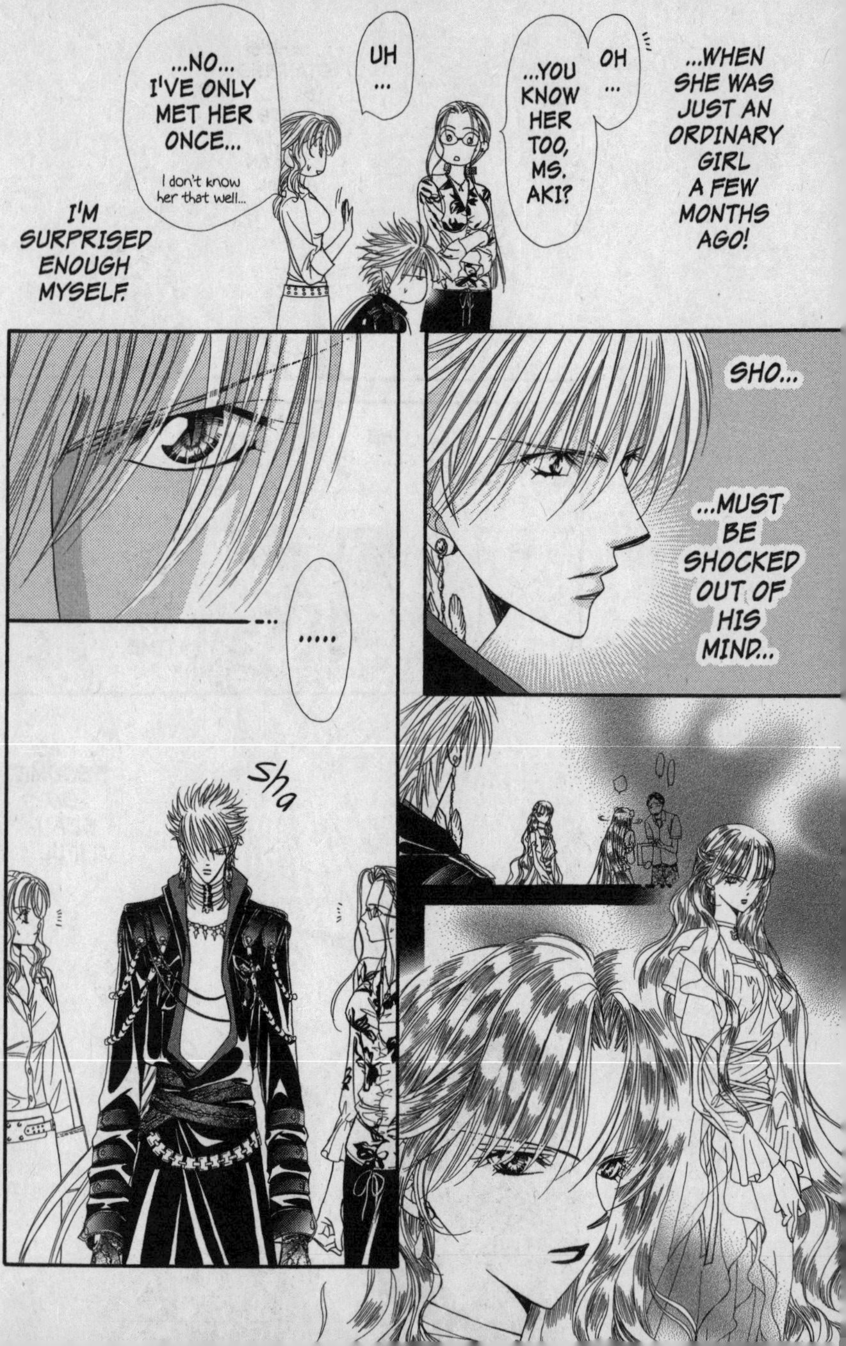
...WHEN SHE WAS JUST AN ORDINARY GIRL A FEW MONTHS AGO!
OH ...
...YOU KNOW HER TOO, MS. AKI?
UH ...
...NO... I'VE ONLY MET HER ONCE...
I don't know her that well...
I'M SURPRISED ENOUGH MYSELF.
SHO...
...MUST BE SHOCKED OUT OF HIS MIND...
.....
Sha

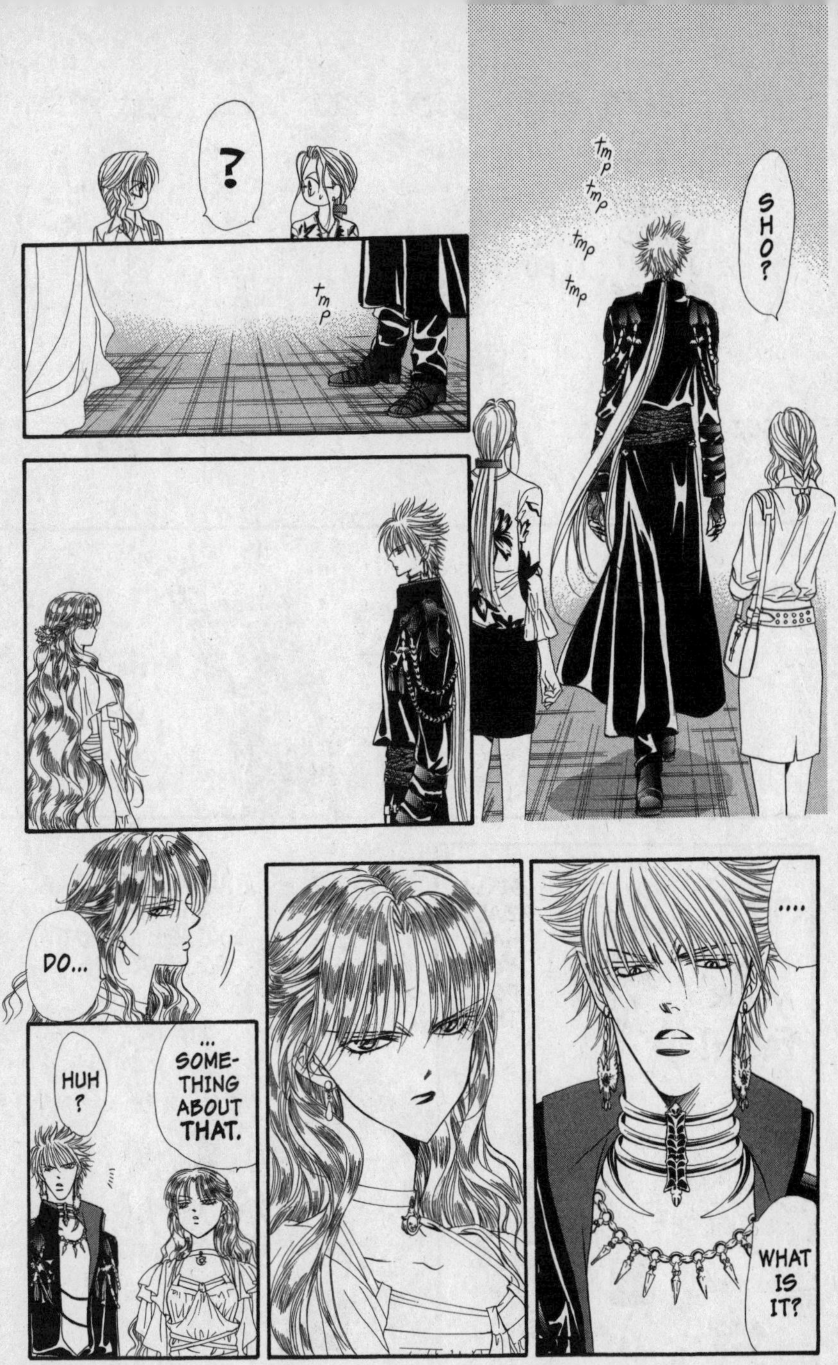
SHO?
tmp
tmp
tmp
tmp
?
tmp
....
WHAT IS IT?
DO...
... SOME-THING ABOUT THAT.
HUH?

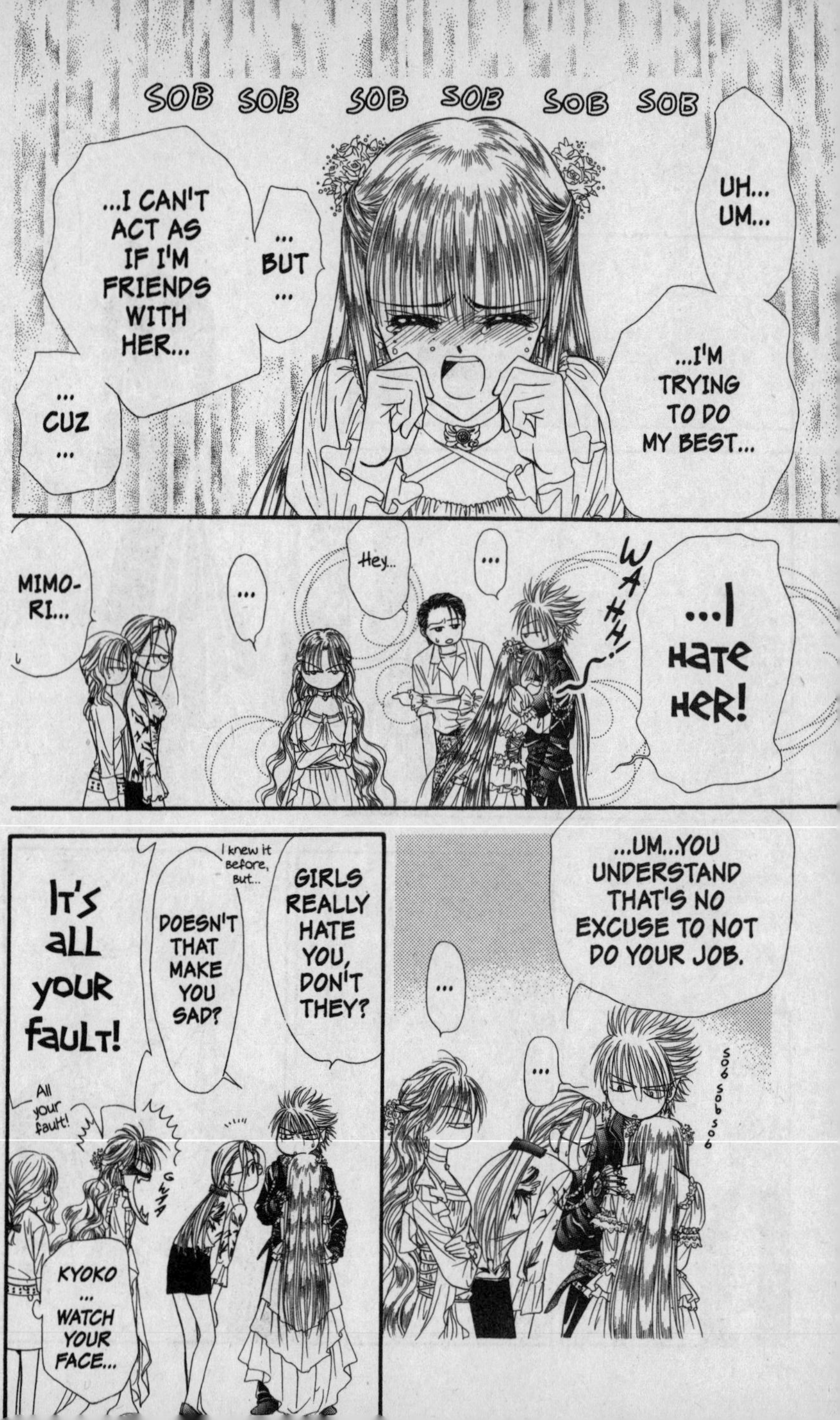
SOB SOB SOB SOB SOB SOB
UH... UM...
...I'M TRYING TO DO MY BEST...
... BUT ...
...I CAN'T ACT AS IF I'M FRIENDS WITH HER...
... CUZ ...
WAHH!
...I HATE HER!
...
Hey..
...
MIMORI...
...UM...YOU UNDERSTAND THAT'S NO EXCUSE TO NOT DO YOUR JOB.
SOB SOB SOB
...
...
GIRLS REALLY HATE YOU, DON'T THEY?
I knew it before, but...
DOESN'T THAT MAKE YOU SAD?
It's all your fault!
All your fault!
GWAA
KYOKO ... WATCH YOUR FACE...

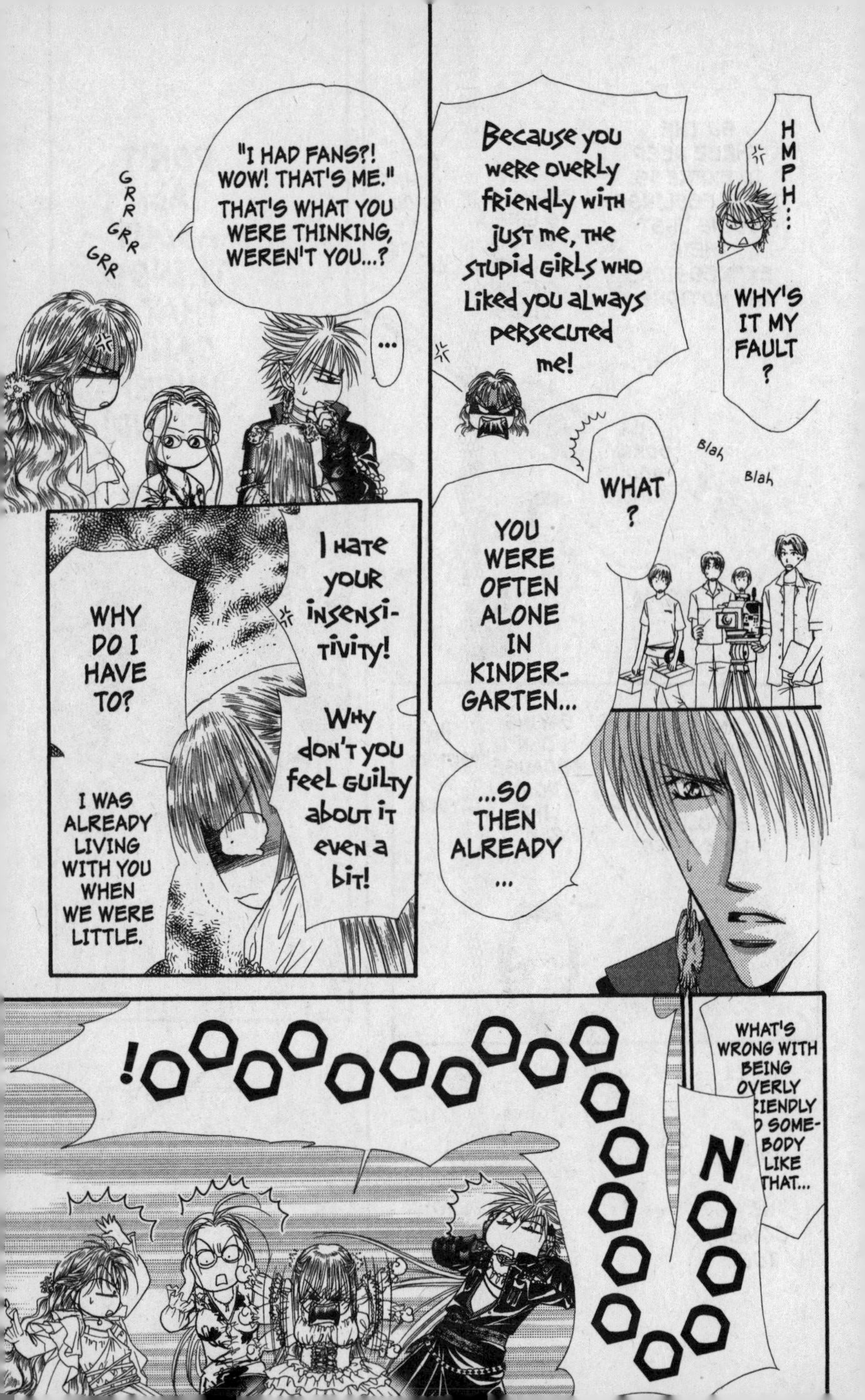

HMPH...
WHY'S IT MY FAULT?
Because you were overly friendly with just me, the stupid girls who liked you always persecuted me!
WHAT?
Blah
Blah
YOU WERE OFTEN ALONE IN KINDERGARTEN...
"I HAD FANS?! WOW! THAT'S ME." THAT'S WHAT YOU WERE THINKING, WEREN'T YOU...?
...
GRR GRR GRR
...SO THEN ALREADY...
I hate your insensitivity!
Why don't you feel guilty about it even a bit!
WHY DO I HAVE TO?
I WAS ALREADY LIVING WITH YOU WHEN WE WERE LITTLE.
WHAT'S WRONG WITH BEING OVERLY RIENDLY O SOME-BODY LIKE HAT...
NOOOOOOOOOOOOOOOOOOOOOOO!

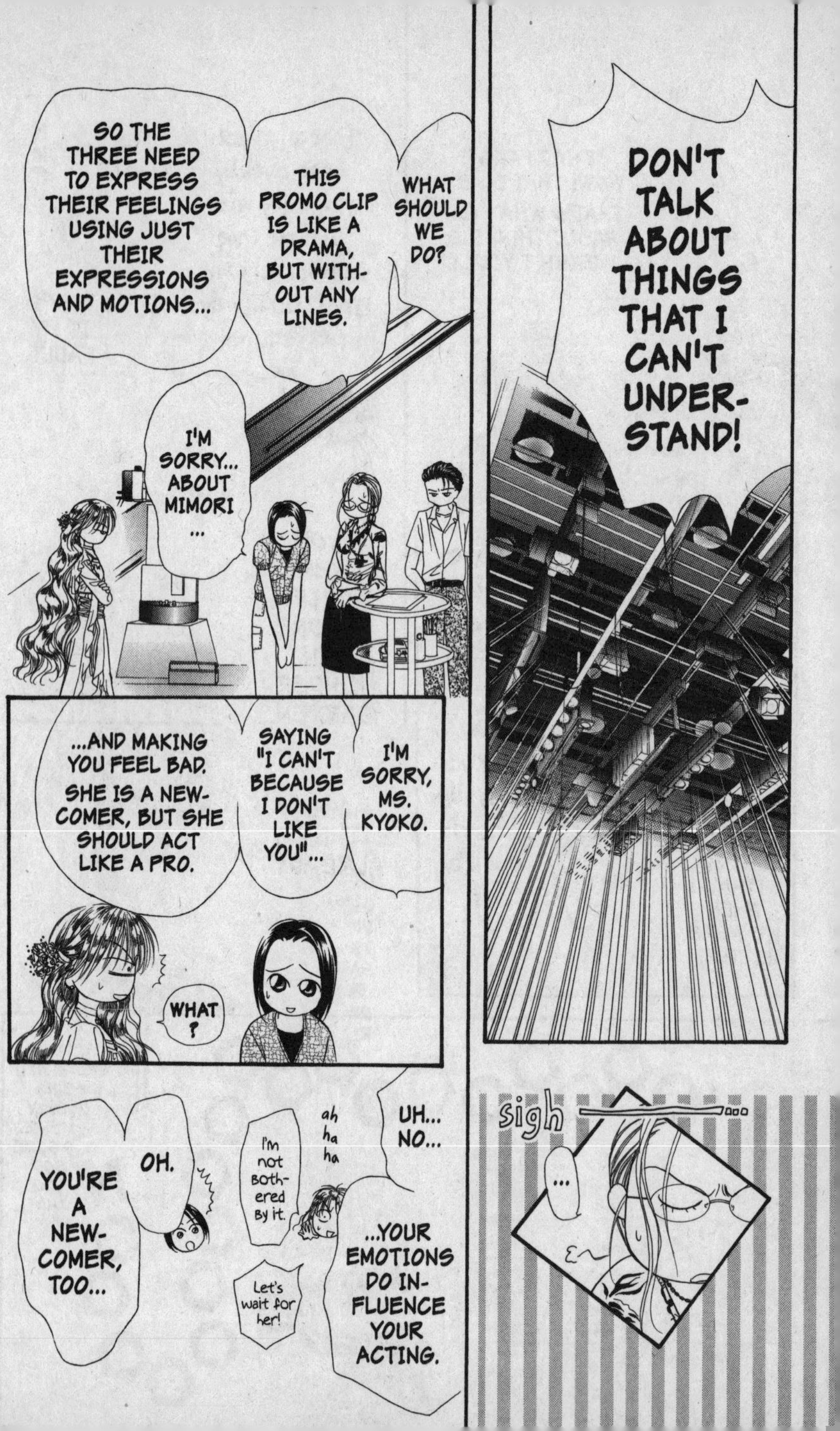
DON'T TALK ABOUT THINGS THAT I CAN'T UNDER-STAND!
WHAT SHOULD WE DO?
THIS PROMO CLIP IS LIKE A DRAMA, BUT WITH-OUT ANY LINES.
SO THE THREE NEED TO EXPRESS THEIR FEELINGS USING JUST THEIR EXPRESSIONS AND MOTIONS...
I'M SORRY... ABOUT MIMORI ...
I'M SORRY, MS. KYOKO.
SAYING "I CAN'T BECAUSE I DON'T LIKE YOU"...
...AND MAKING YOU FEEL BAD.
SHE IS A NEW-COMER, BUT SHE SHOULD ACT LIKE A PRO.
WHAT ?
sigh ——
...
UH... NO...
ah ha ha
I'm not both-ered by it.
OH.
YOU'RE A NEW-COMER, TOO...
...YOUR EMOTIONS DO IN-FLUENCE YOUR ACTING.
Let's wait for her!

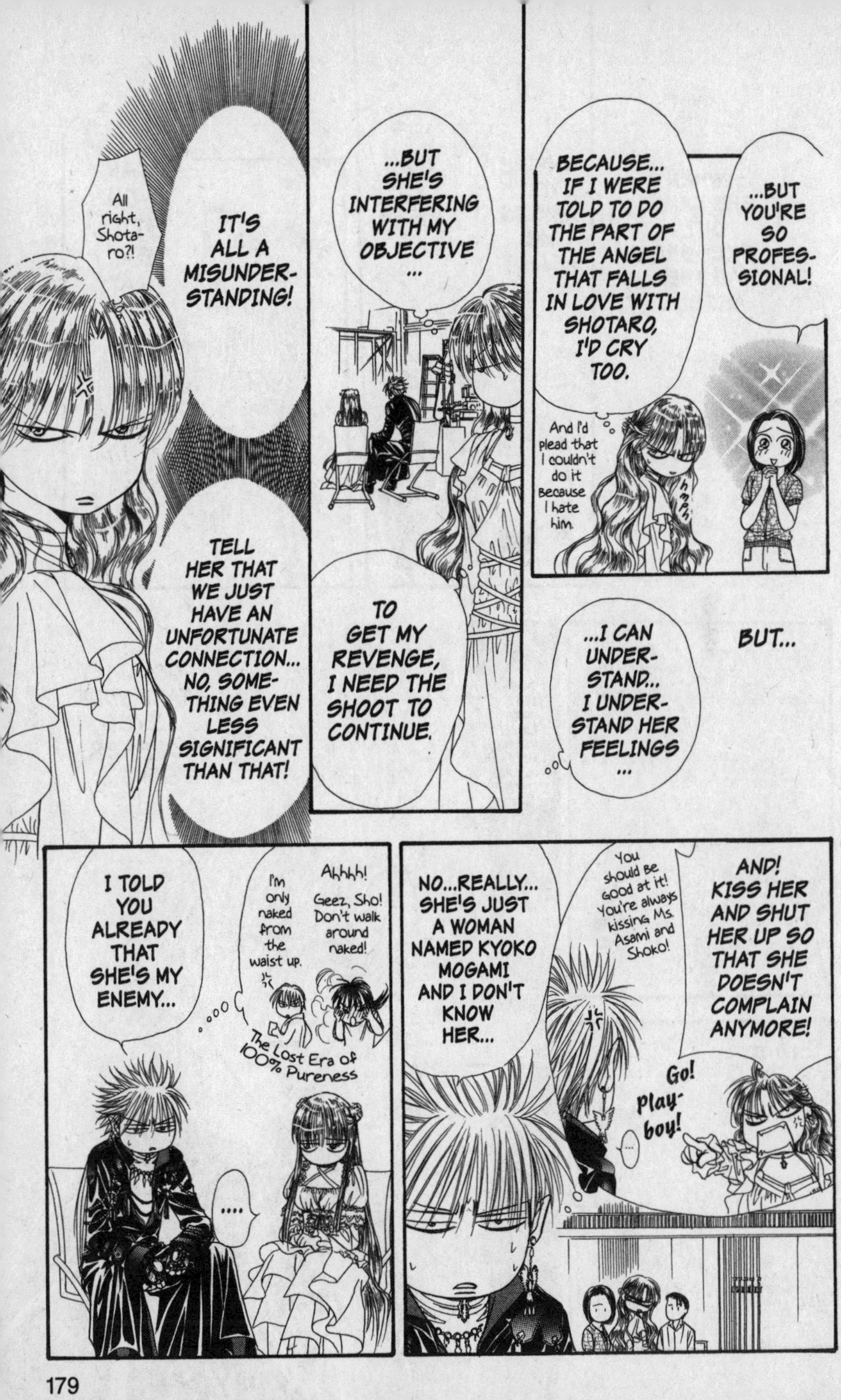
...BUT YOU'RE SO PROFESSIONAL!
BECAUSE... IF I WERE TOLD TO DO THE PART OF THE ANGEL THAT FALLS IN LOVE WITH SHOTARO, I'D CRY TOO.
And I'd plead that I couldn't do it because I hate him.
hmph
BUT...
...I CAN UNDERSTAND... I UNDERSTAND HER FEELINGS ...
...BUT SHE'S INTERFERING WITH MY OBJECTIVE ...
TO GET MY REVENGE, I NEED THE SHOOT TO CONTINUE.
IT'S ALL A MISUNDERSTANDING!
All right, Shotaro?!
TELL HER THAT WE JUST HAVE AN UNFORTUNATE CONNECTION... NO, SOMETHING EVEN LESS SIGNIFICANT THAN THAT!
AND! KISS HER AND SHUT HER UP SO THAT SHE DOESN'T COMPLAIN ANYMORE!
You should be good at it! You're always kissing Ms. Asami and Shoko!
NO...REALLY... SHE'S JUST A WOMAN NAMED KYOKO MOGAMI AND I DON'T KNOW HER...
Go! Playboy!
...
Ahhhh! Geez, Sho! Don't walk around naked!
I'm only naked from the waist up.
I TOLD YOU ALREADY THAT SHE'S MY ENEMY...
The Lost Era of 100% Pureness
....

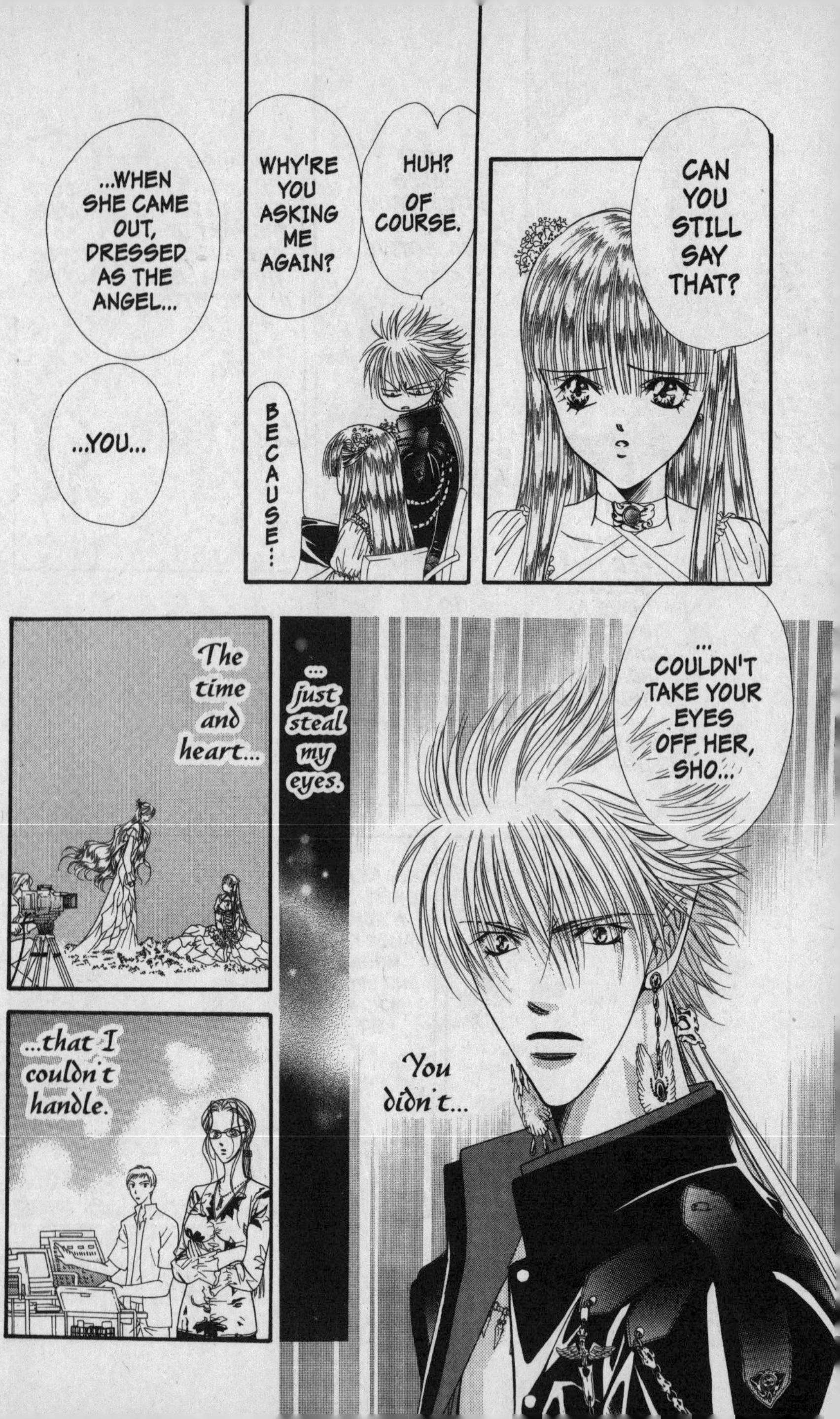
CAN YOU STILL SAY THAT?
HUH? OF COURSE.
WHY'RE YOU ASKING ME AGAIN?
BECAUSE...
...WHEN SHE CAME OUT, DRESSED AS THE ANGEL...
...YOU...
... COULDN'T TAKE YOUR EYES OFF HER, SHO...
You didn't...
... just steal my eyes.
The time and heart...
...that I couldn't handle.

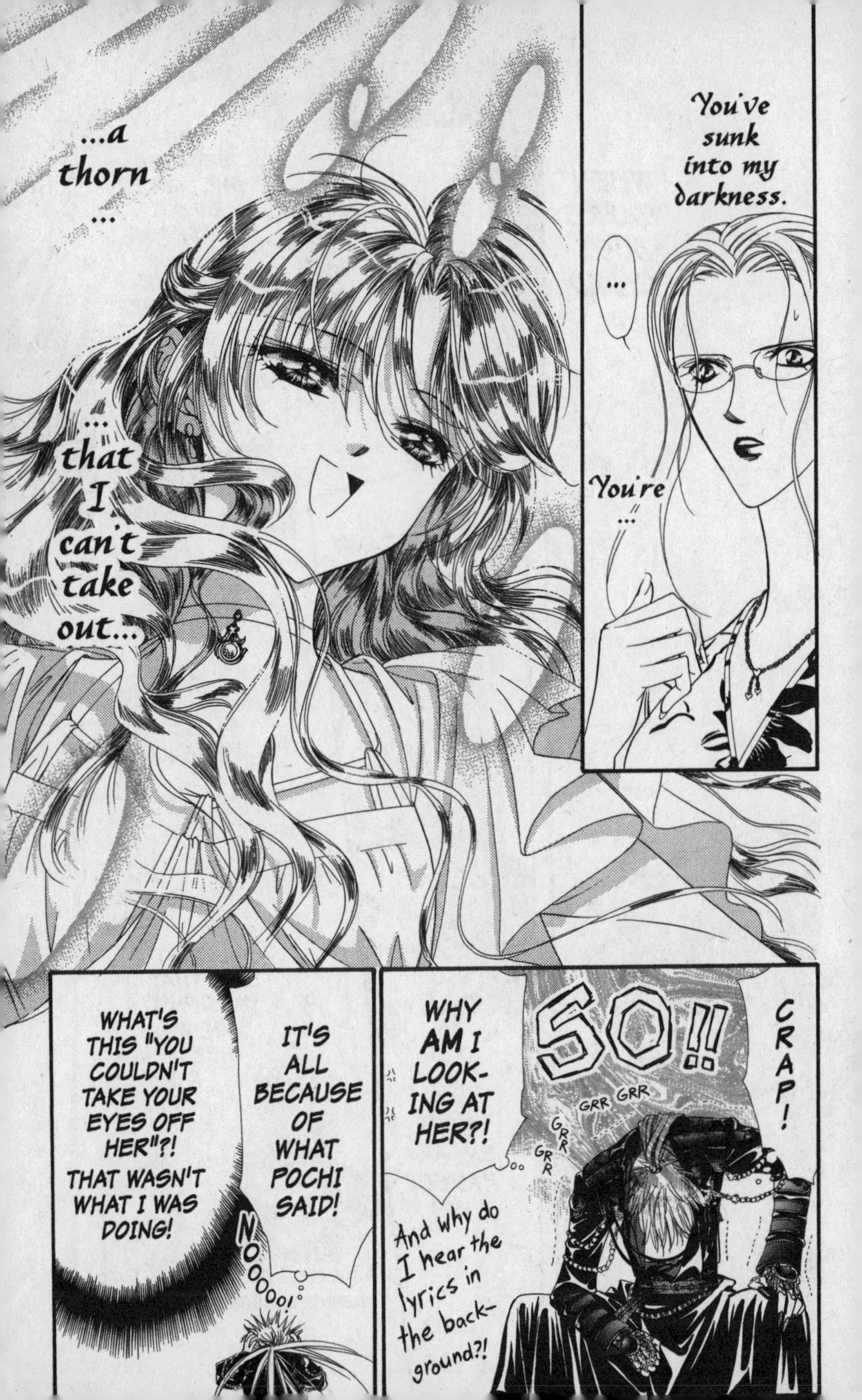
You've sunk into my darkness.
...
You're ...
...a thorn ...
...that I can't take out...
CRAP!
SO!!
GRR GRR
GRR
GRR
WHY AM I LOOKING AT HER?!
And why do I hear the lyrics in the background?!
IT'S ALL BECAUSE OF WHAT POCHI SAID!
WHAT'S THIS "YOU COULDN'T TAKE YOUR EYES OFF HER"?! THAT WASN'T WHAT I WAS DOING!
NOOOOOO!

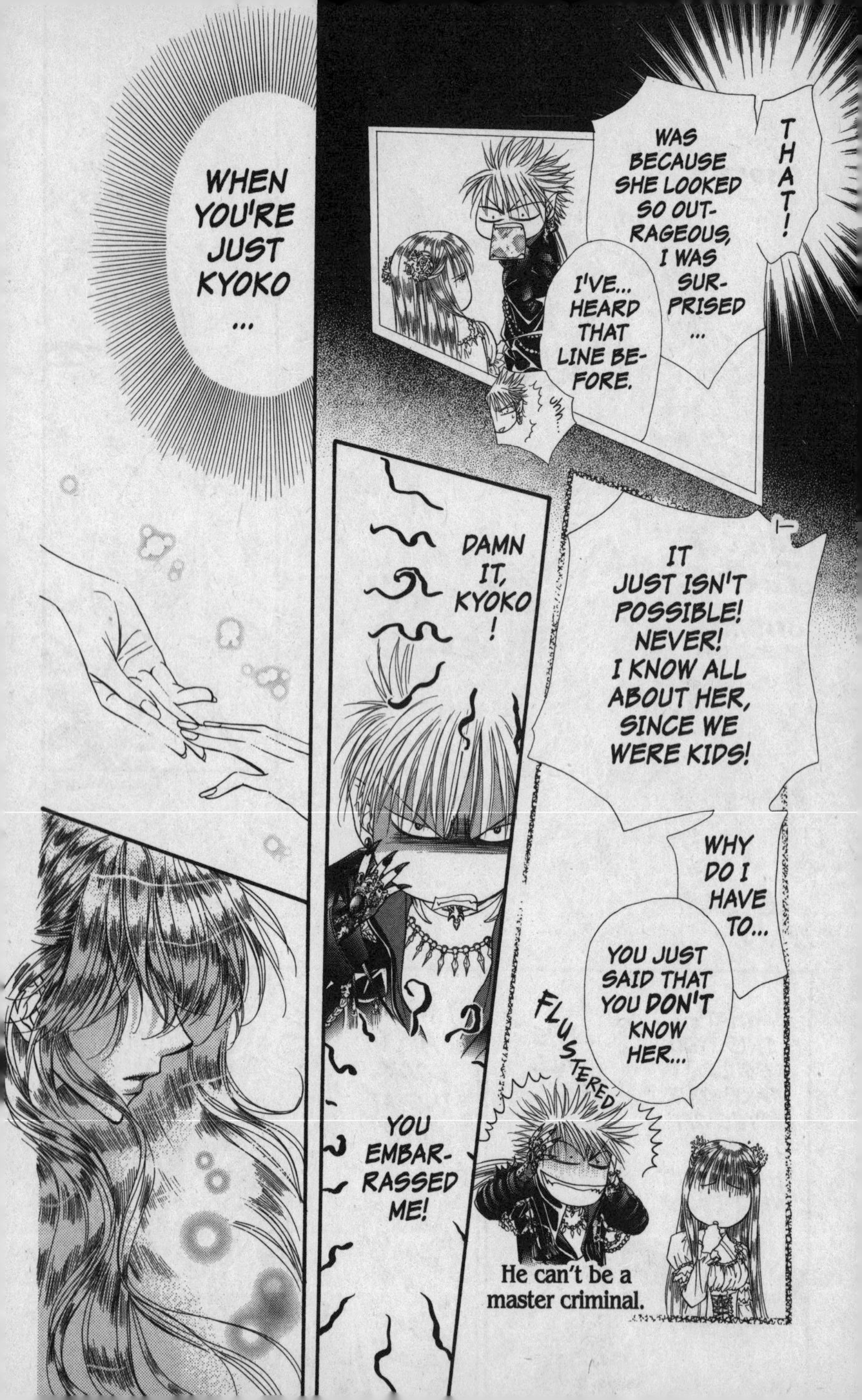
THAT!
WAS BECAUSE SHE LOOKED SO OUT-RAGEOUS, I WAS SUR-PRISED...
I'VE... HEARD THAT LINE BE-FORE.
IT JUST ISN'T POSSIBLE! NEVER! I KNOW ALL ABOUT HER, SINCE WE WERE KIDS!
WHY DO I HAVE TO...
YOU JUST SAID THAT YOU DON'T KNOW HER...
FLUSTERED
He can't be a master criminal.
DAMN IT, KYOKO!
YOU EMBAR-RASSED ME!
WHEN YOU'RE JUST KYOKO...

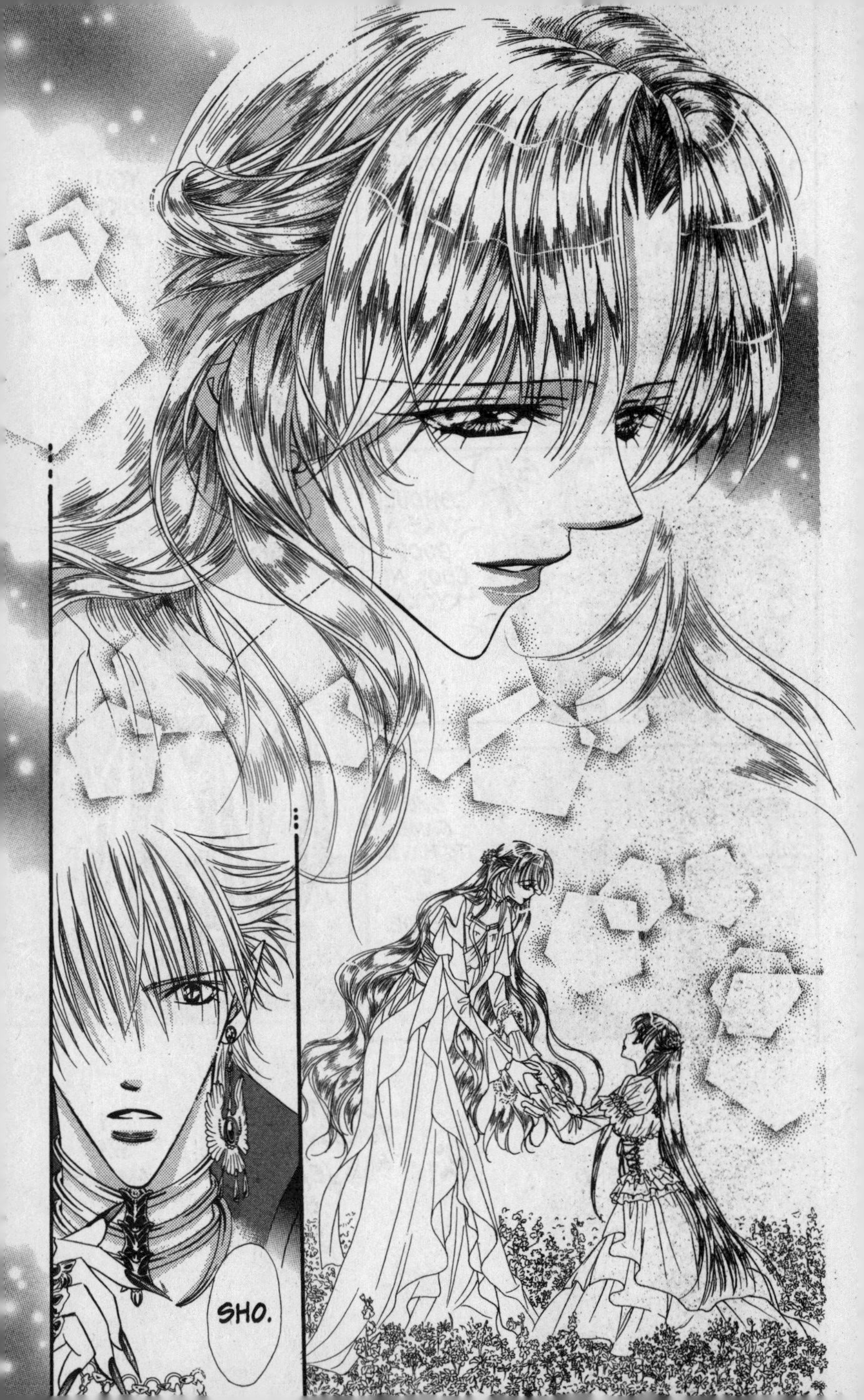
SHO.

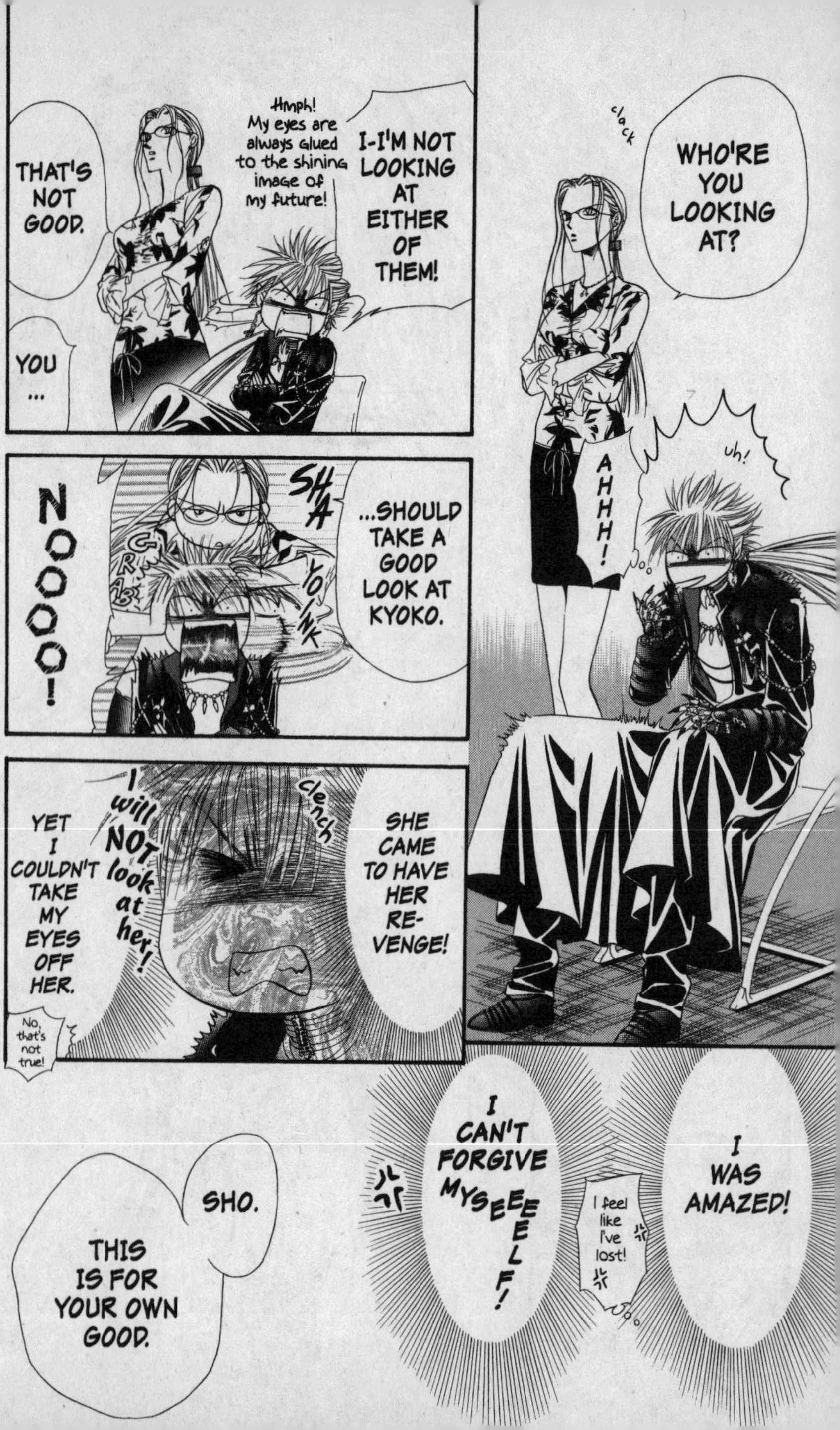
clack
WHO'RE YOU LOOKING AT?
uh!
AHHHH!
I-I'M NOT LOOKING AT EITHER OF THEM!
Hmph! My eyes are always glued to the shining image of my future!
THAT'S NOT GOOD.
YOU ...
...SHOULD TAKE A GOOD LOOK AT KYOKO.
SHA
YOINK
GRAB
NOOOOO!
clench
SHE CAME TO HAVE HER RE-VENGE!
I will NOT look at her!
YET I COULDN'T TAKE MY EYES OFF HER.
No, that's not true!
I WAS AMAZED!
I feel like I've lost!
I CAN'T FORGIVE MYSEEEELF!
SHO.
THIS IS FOR YOUR OWN GOOD.

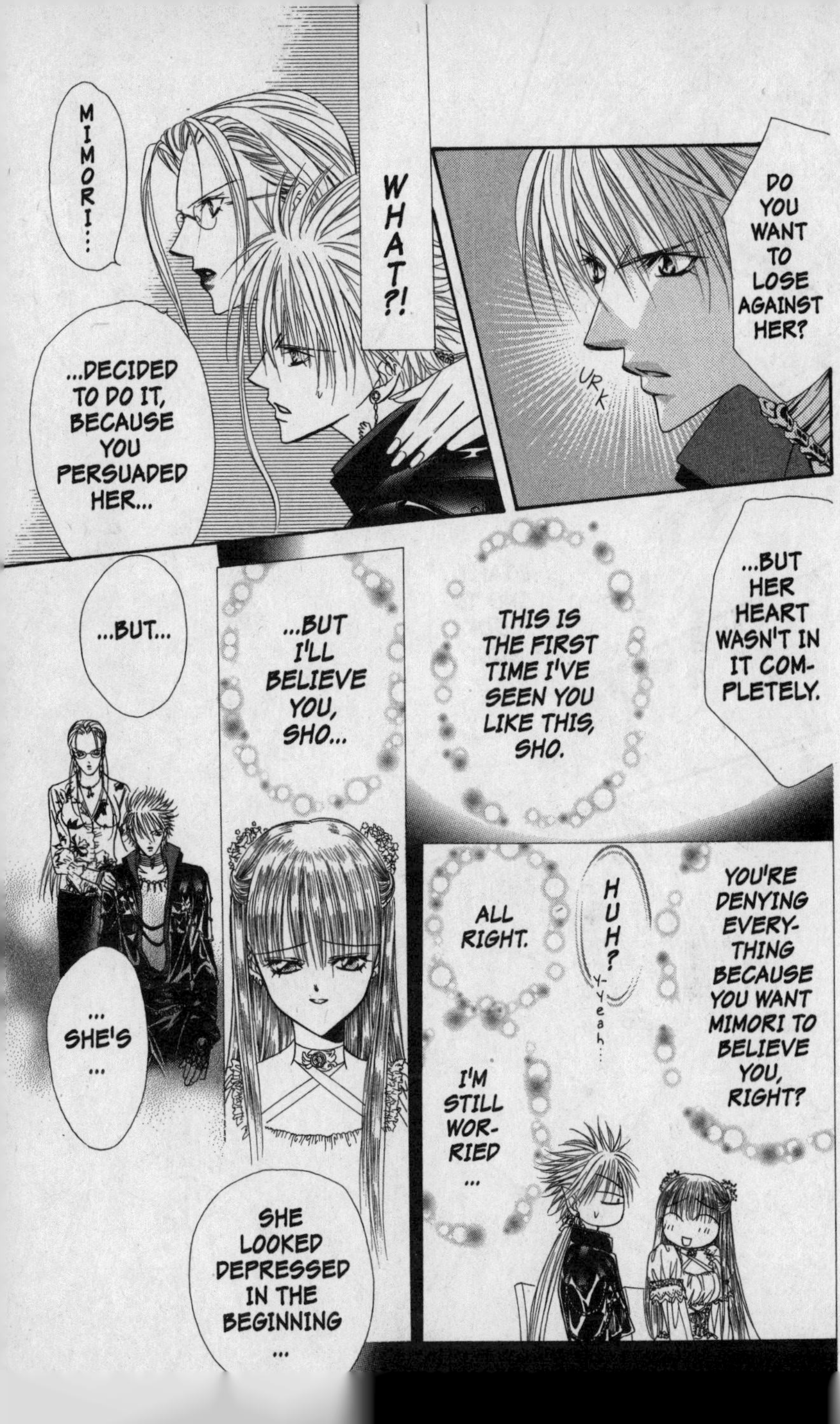
DO YOU WANT TO LOSE AGAINST HER?
URK
WHAT?!
MIMORI...
...DECIDED TO DO IT, BECAUSE YOU PERSUADED HER...
...BUT HER HEART WASN'T IN IT COMPLETELY.
THIS IS THE FIRST TIME I'VE SEEN YOU LIKE THIS, SHO.
YOU'RE DENYING EVERYTHING BECAUSE YOU WANT MIMORI TO BELIEVE YOU, RIGHT?
HUH?
Y-Yeah...
ALL RIGHT.
I'M STILL WORRIED...
...BUT I'LL BELIEVE YOU, SHO...
SHE LOOKED DEPRESSED IN THE BEGINNING...
...BUT...
...SHE'S...

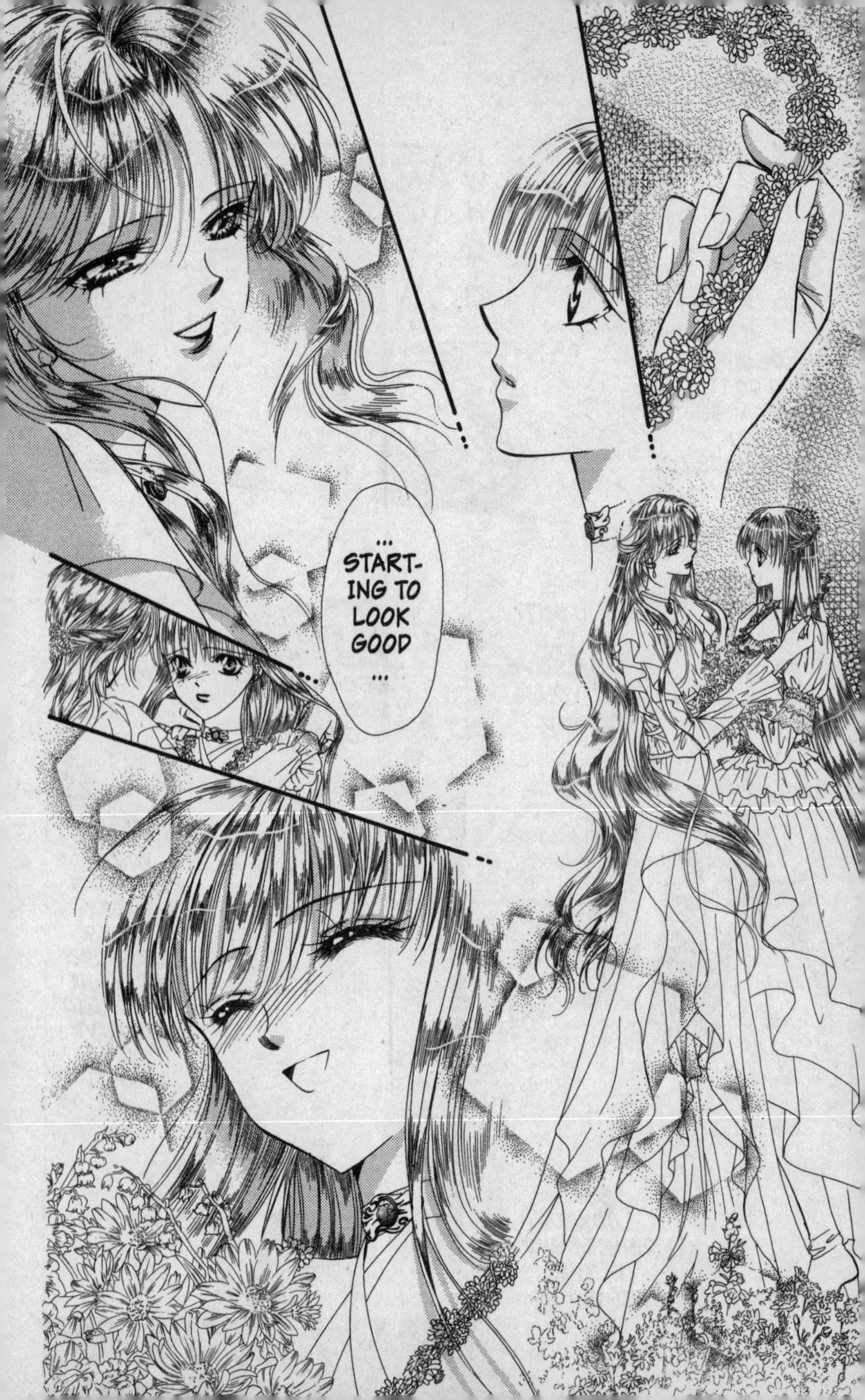
... STARTING TO LOOK GOOD ...

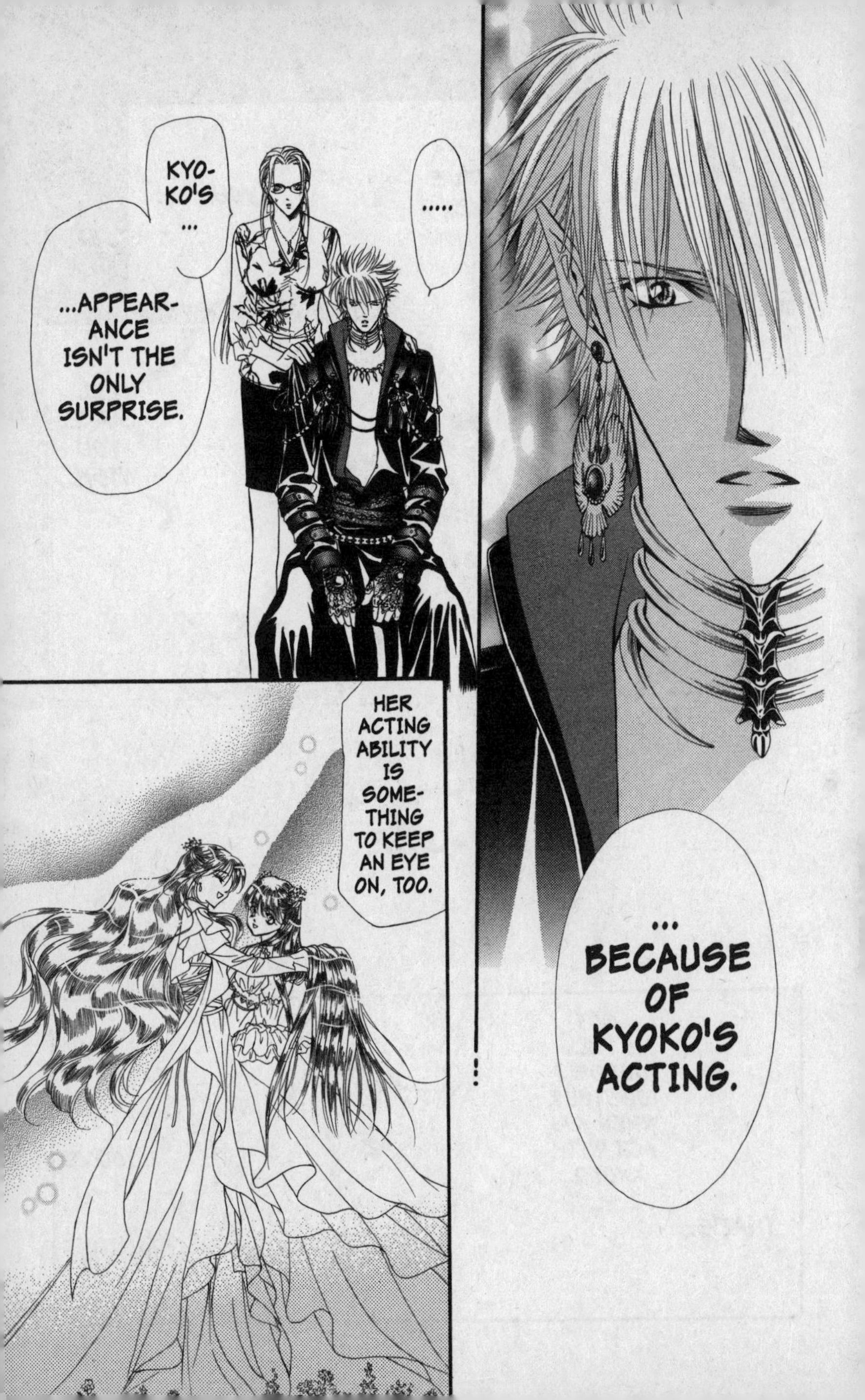
... BECAUSE OF KYOKO'S ACTING.
.....
KYO-KO'S ...
...APPEAR-ANCE ISN'T THE ONLY SURPRISE.
HER ACTING ABILITY IS SOME-THING TO KEEP AN EYE ON, TOO.

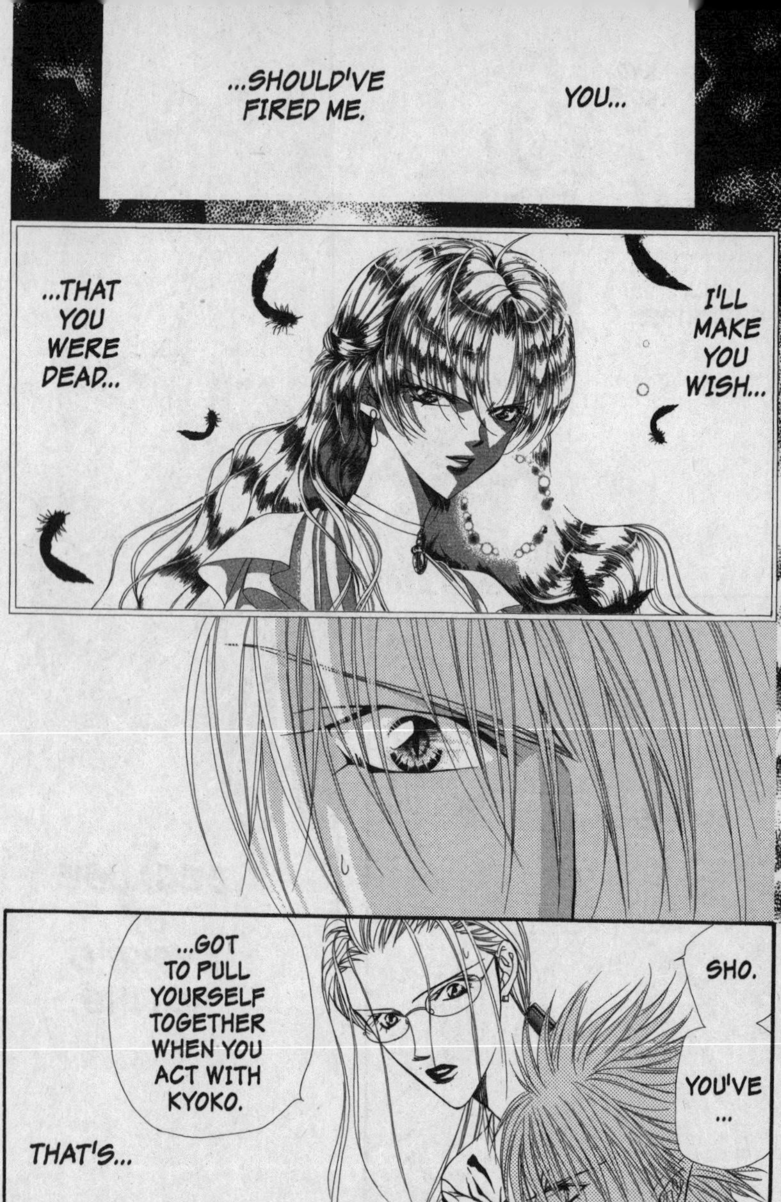
YOU...
...SHOULD'VE FIRED ME.
I'LL MAKE YOU WISH...
...THAT YOU WERE DEAD...
SHO.
YOU'VE ...
...GOT TO PULL YOURSELF TOGETHER WHEN YOU ACT WITH KYOKO.
THAT'S...

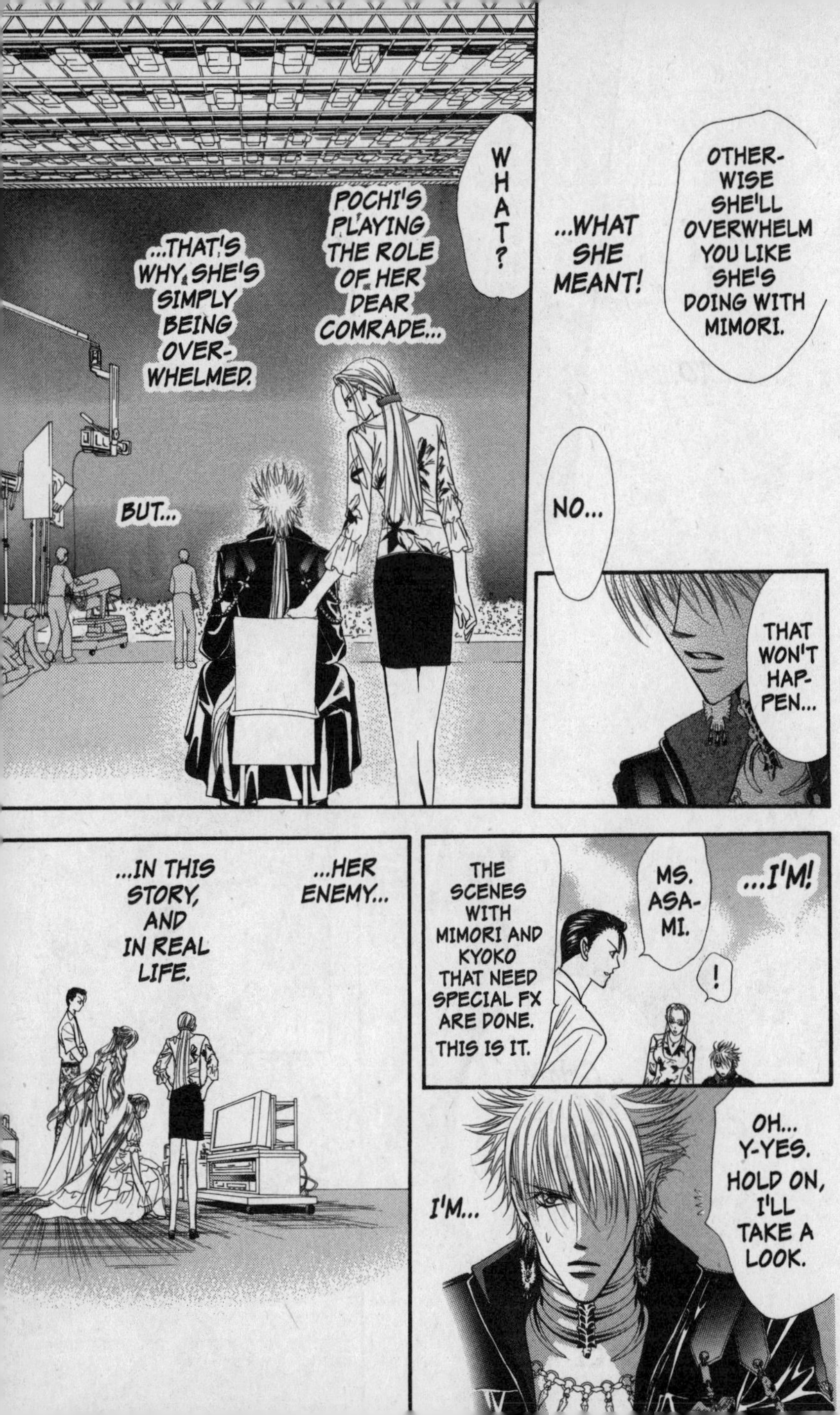
OTHER-WISE SHE'LL OVERWHELM YOU LIKE SHE'S DOING WITH MIMORI.
...WHAT SHE MEANT!
NO...
THAT WON'T HAP-PEN...
WHAT?
POCHI'S PLAYING THE ROLE OF HER DEAR COMRADE...
...THAT'S WHY SHE'S SIMPLY BEING OVER-WHELMED.
BUT...
...I'M!
MS. ASAMI.
!
THE SCENES WITH MIMORI AND KYOKO THAT NEED SPECIAL FX ARE DONE.
THIS IS IT.
OH... Y-YES.
HOLD ON, I'LL TAKE A LOOK.
I'M...
...HER ENEMY...
...IN THIS STORY, AND IN REAL LIFE.

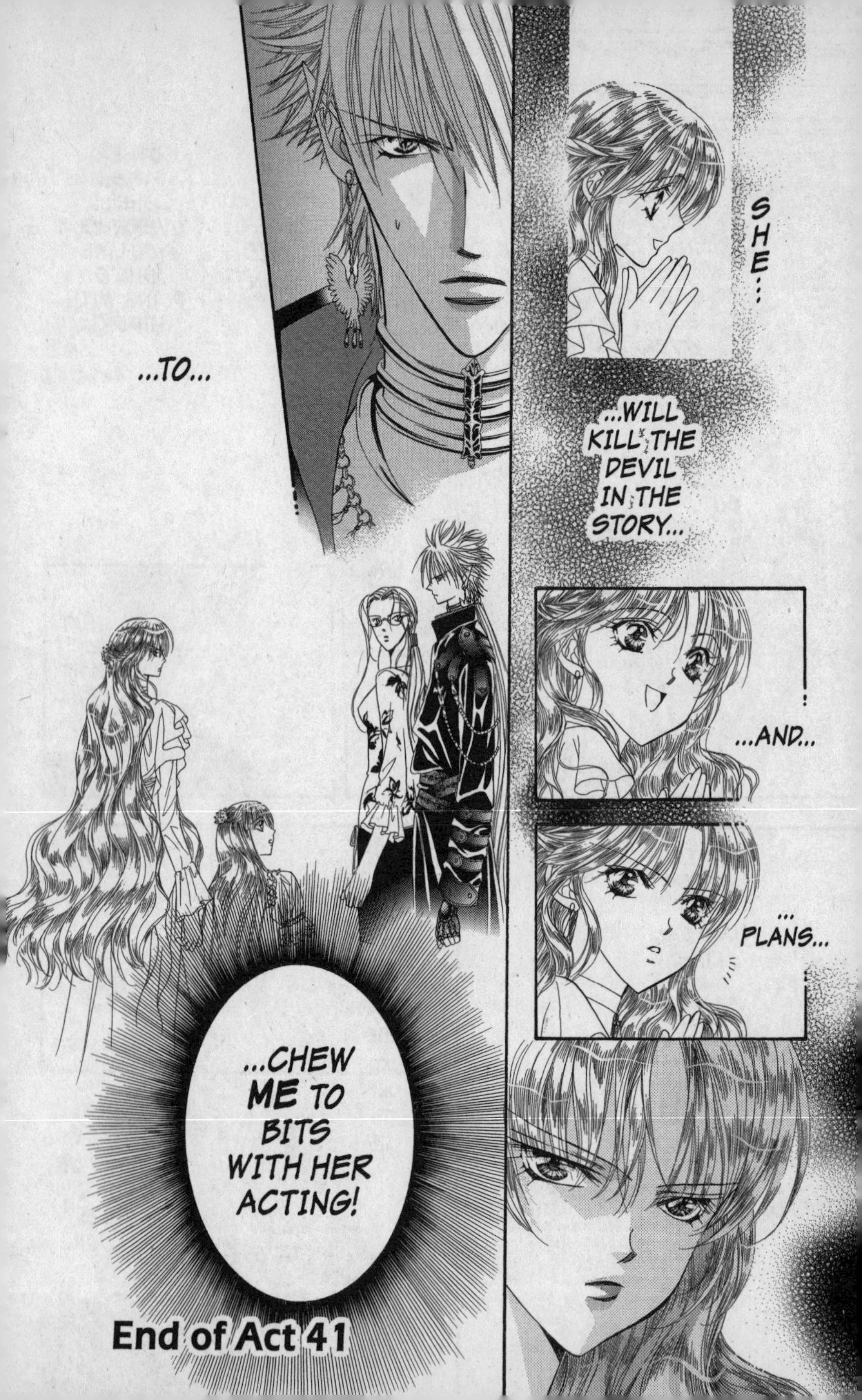
SHE...
...WILL KILL THE DEVIL IN THE STORY...
...AND...
...PLANS...
...TO...
...CHEW ME TO BITS WITH HER ACTING!
End of Act 41

Skip·Beat! End Notes

Everyone knows how to be a fan, but sometimes cool things from other cultures need a little help crossing the language barrier.

Page 28, panel 6: *Godfather* Theme
This song is typically used by motorbike gangs.

Page 39, panel 3: Taisho
Kyoko's boss and landlord. In traditional Japanese restaurants, the boss is called Taisho by employees and customers alike.

Page 39, panel 3: Okamisan
The Taisho's wife. In Japan, the *okami* acts as the face of the restaurant while her husband stays in the background to deal with cooking or managerial duties.

Page 43, panel 3: Itadakimasu
A little blessing or thank you before you eat.

Page 71, panel 3: Good Morning
Saying good morning regardless of the time is a custom in Japanese showbiz.

Page 73, panel 1: 2-hour drama
Two-hour dramas are the one-shots of the drama world. Many of them are mysteries, based on popular novels.

Page 82, panel 2: Pochi
Pochi is a popular name for dogs in Japan.

Page 103, panel 5: Kogal
Kogals are bleach-blonde, overly-bronzed girls who wear lots of makeup and accessories. They are similar to California Valley Girls in their use of slang and airhead personas.

Page 106, panel 4: Aso
The kanji for Asami can be read as Aso.

Page 124, panel 2: Tamagoyaki
A Japanese rolled omelet, sometimes called dashimaki. It's very popular in bento boxes, and can be either sweet or salty.

Page 132, panel 2: Throwing salt
The original Japanese is from the expression "To send the enemy salt," which is literally what Kyoko did, but also has the meaning of aiding the enemy.

Shojo Beat

Skip·Beat!

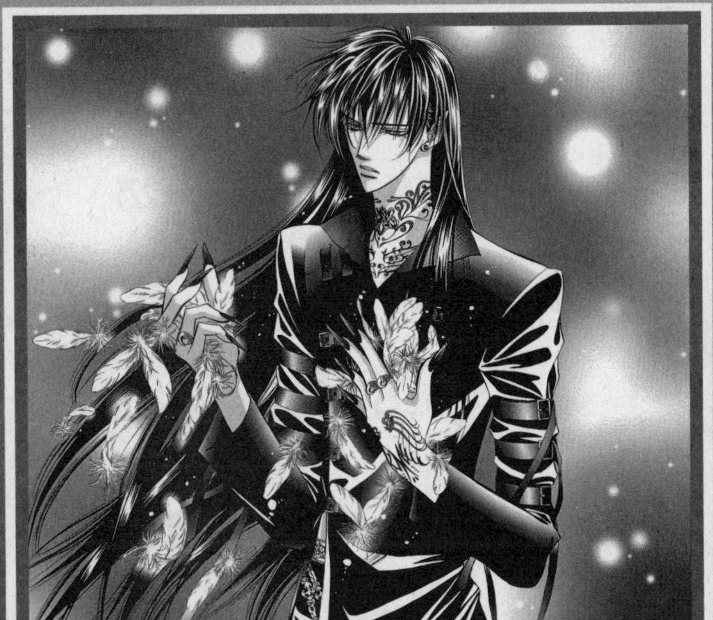

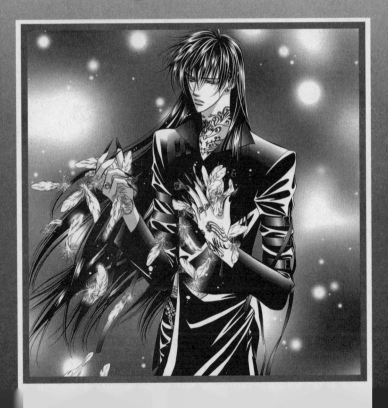

Skip·Beat!

Volume 8

CONTENTS

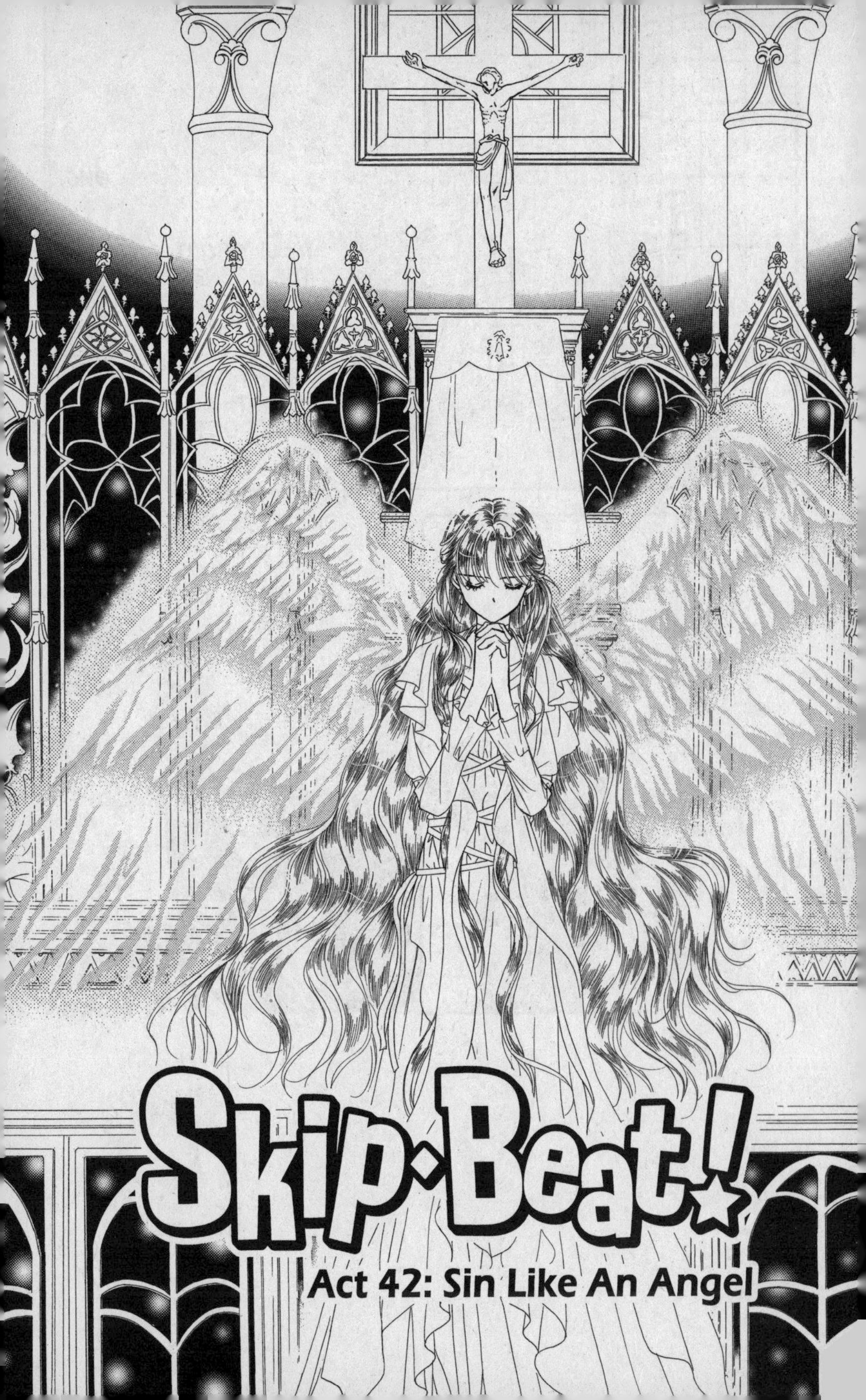
Skip·Beat!
Act 42: Sin Like An Angel

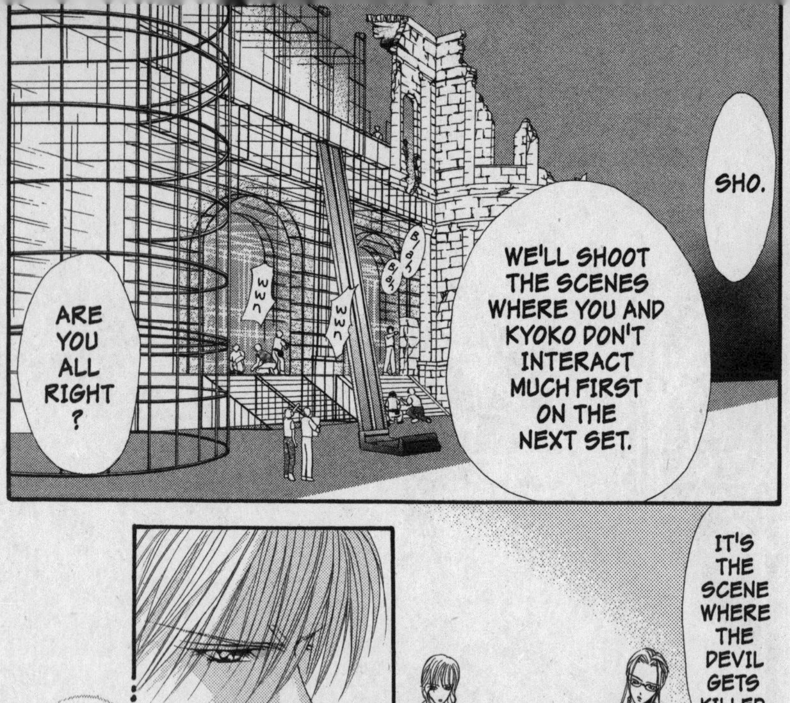
SHO.
WE'LL SHOOT THE SCENES WHERE YOU AND KYOKO DON'T INTERACT MUCH FIRST ON THE NEXT SET.
Blah Blah
ARE YOU ALL RIGHT?
IT'S THE SCENE WHERE THE DEVIL GETS KILLED.
....
I...

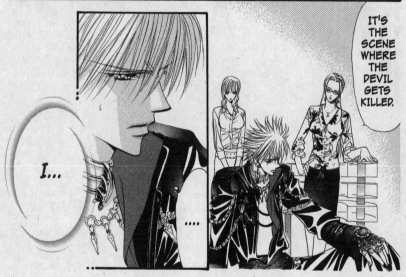

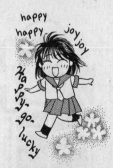

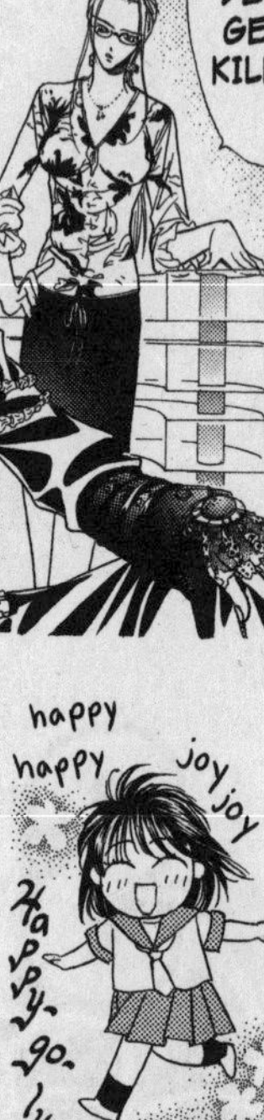
happy happy joy joy
Happy-go-lucky

SHO...

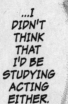

...I DIDN'T THINK THAT I'D BE STUDYING ACTING EITHER.

LAST YEAR...

...DIDN'T THINK THAT YOU COULD ACTUALLY ACT.

...MEAN BY THAT?

...WHAT DID KYOKO...

...I WOULDN'T HAVE BECOME INTERESTED IN ACTING.

IF YOU HADN'T DITCHED ME...

WERE YOU TWO...

"IF YOU HADN'T DITCHED ME."

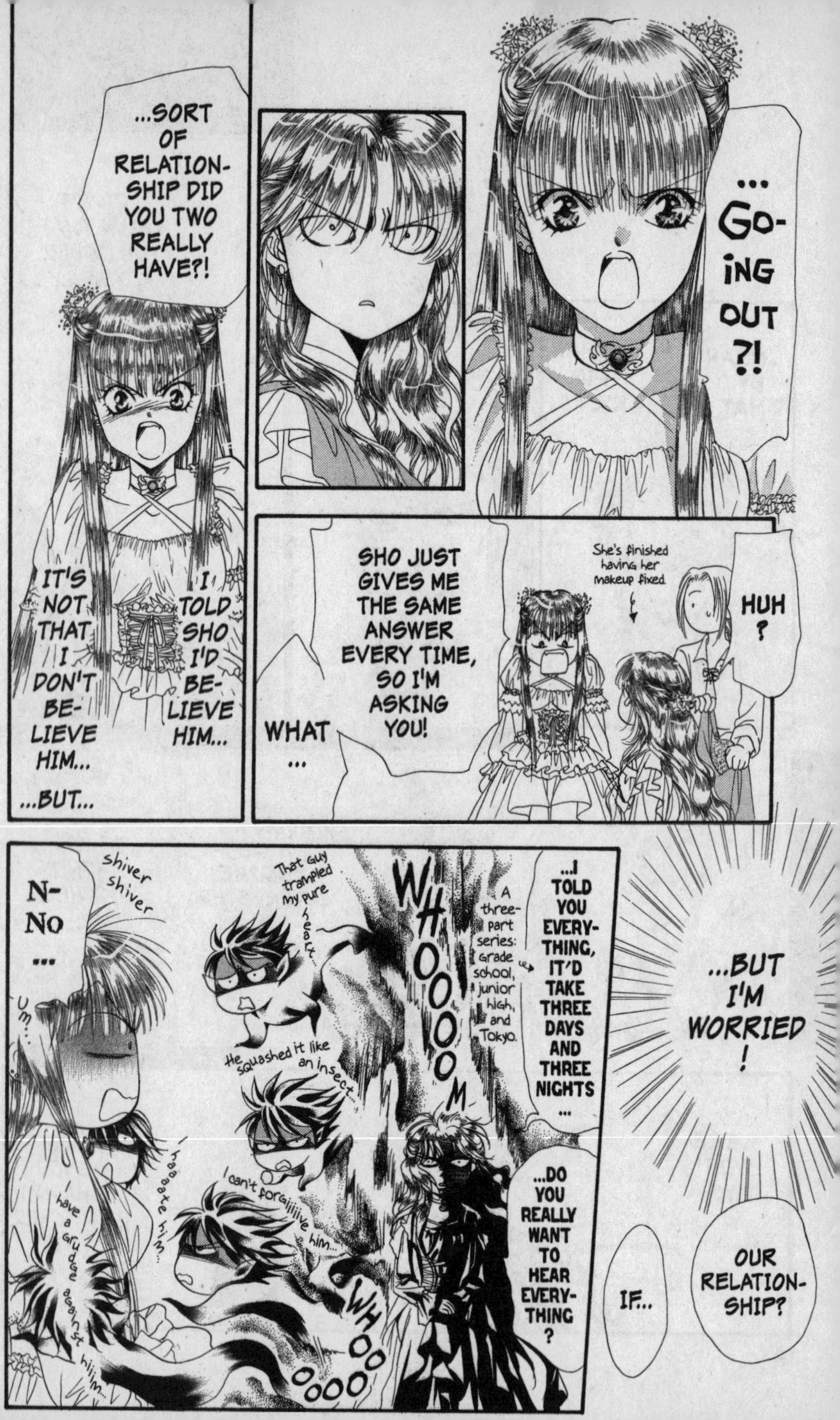
...GO-ING OUT?!
HUH?
She's finished having her makeup fixed.
WHAT ...
SHO JUST GIVES ME THE SAME ANSWER EVERY TIME, SO I'M ASKING YOU!
...SORT OF RELATION-SHIP DID YOU TWO REALLY HAVE?!
I TOLD SHO I'D BE-LIEVE HIM...
IT'S NOT THAT I DON'T BE-LIEVE HIM...
...BUT...
...BUT I'M WORRIED!
OUR RELATION-SHIP?
IF...
...I TOLD YOU EVERY-THING, IT'D TAKE THREE DAYS AND THREE NIGHTS...
A three-part series: Grade school, junior high, and Tokyo.
...DO YOU REALLY WANT TO HEAR EVERY-THING?
WHOOOOOM
WHOOOOOOO
That guy trampled my pure heart...
He squashed it like an insect...
I haaaate him...
I can't forgiiiiive him...
I have a grudge against hiiim...
shiver shiver
N-No...
Um...

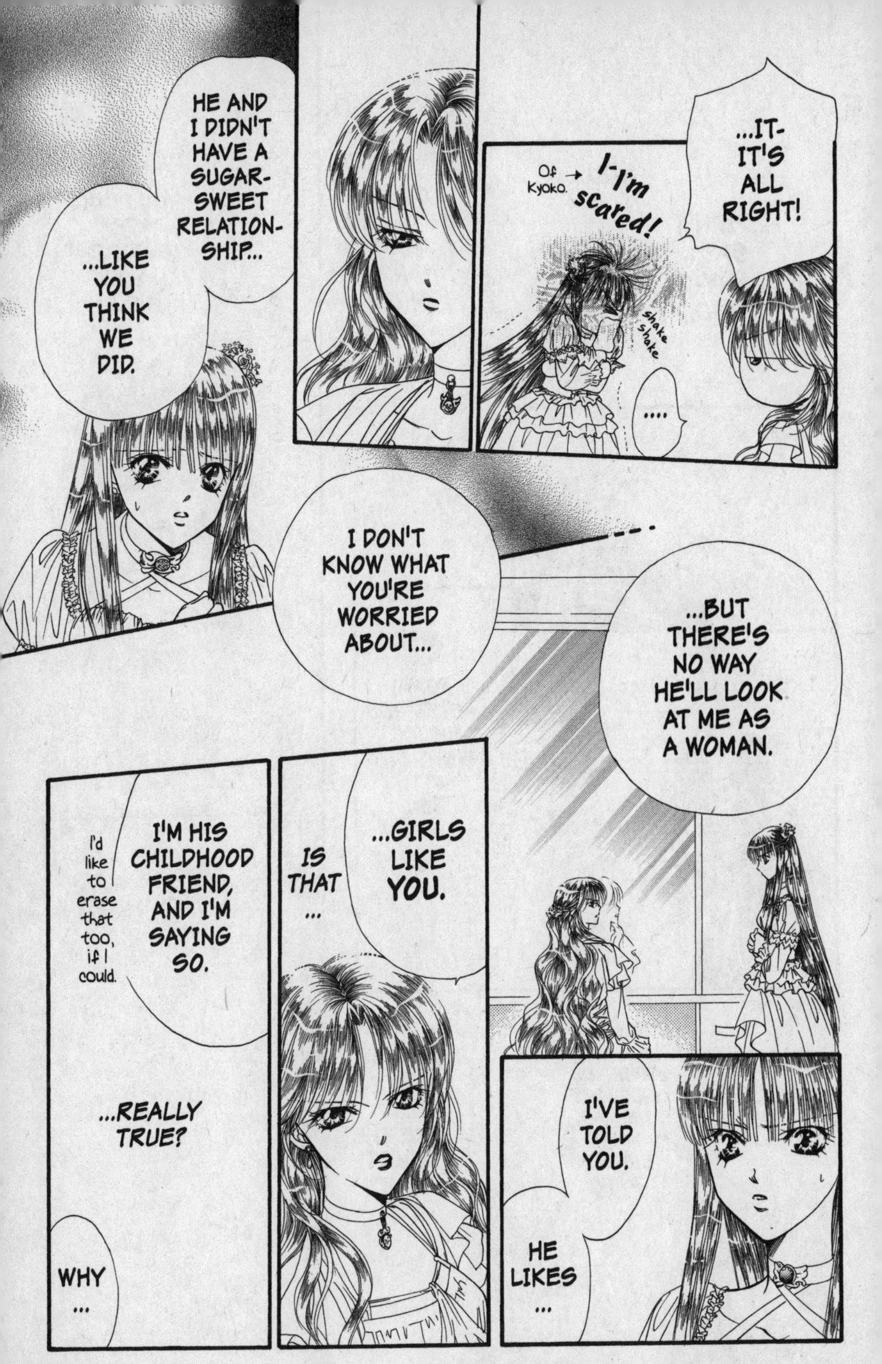
...IT- IT'S ALL RIGHT!
Of Kyoko. → I-I'm scared!
shake shake
....
HE AND I DIDN'T HAVE A SUGAR-SWEET RELATIONSHIP...
...LIKE YOU THINK WE DID.
I DON'T KNOW WHAT YOU'RE WORRIED ABOUT...
...BUT THERE'S NO WAY HE'LL LOOK AT ME AS A WOMAN.
I'VE TOLD YOU.
HE LIKES ...
...GIRLS LIKE YOU.
IS THAT ...
I'M HIS CHILDHOOD FRIEND, AND I'M SAYING SO.
I'd like to erase that too, if I could.
...REALLY TRUE?
WHY ...

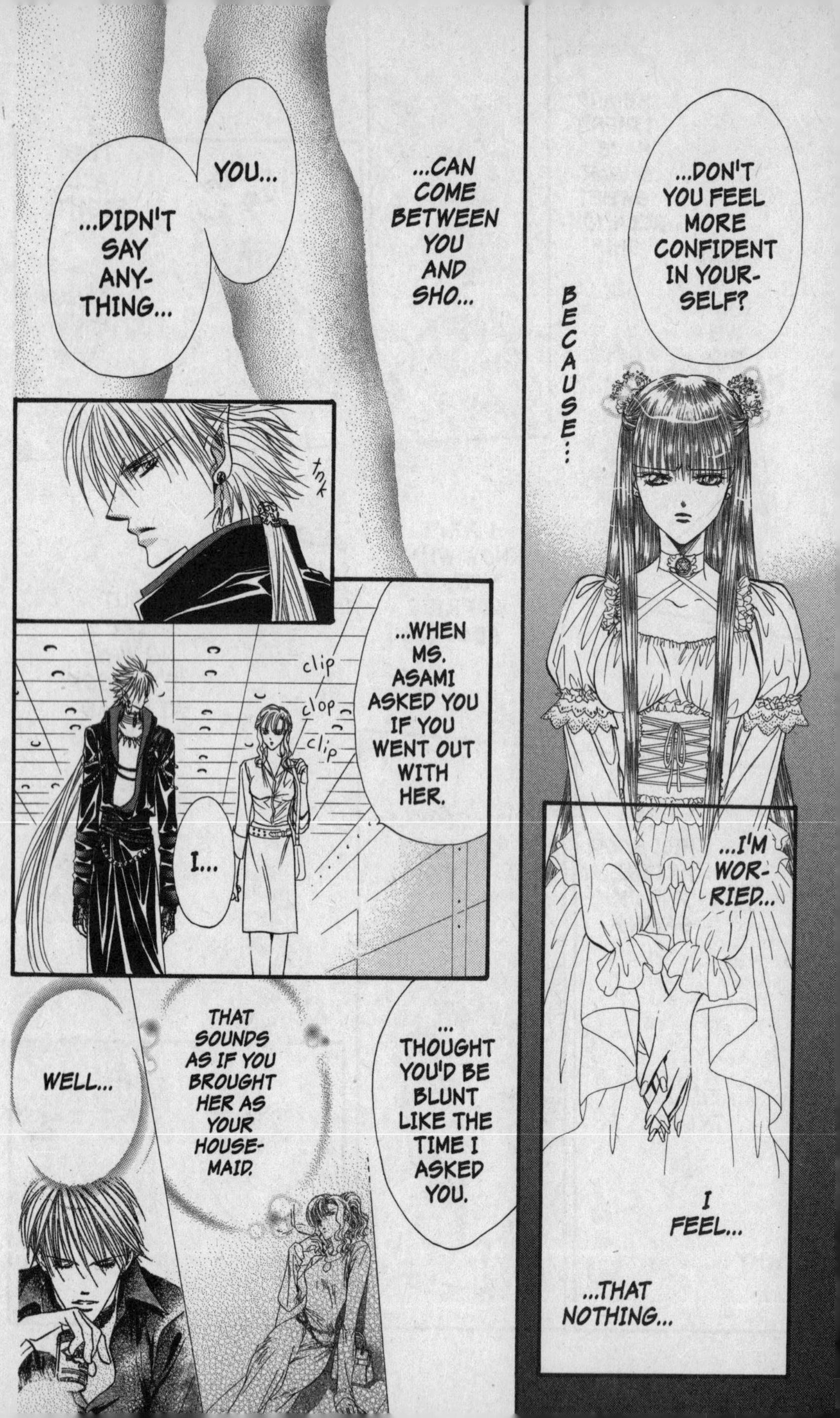
...DON'T YOU FEEL MORE CONFIDENT IN YOUR-SELF?
BECAUSE...
...I'M WOR-RIED...
I FEEL...
...THAT NOTHING...
...CAN COME BETWEEN YOU AND SHO...
YOU...
...DIDN'T SAY ANY-THING...
tnk
...WHEN MS. ASAMI ASKED YOU IF YOU WENT OUT WITH HER.
clip
clop
clip
I...
... THOUGHT YOU'D BE BLUNT LIKE THE TIME I ASKED YOU.
THAT SOUNDS AS IF YOU BROUGHT HER AS YOUR HOUSE-MAID.
WELL...

Greetings

Hello. I'm Nakamura. In Volume 7, the sad result was that the only new illustration was the one on the title page. I'm really sorry... ...But this time, my schedule is really tight too (It's my fault. I take too much time doing my storyboards, penciling, and inking) I believe that my editor would like me not to draw that much new stuff for Volume 8 too, if possible... ...therefore...I won't try to fill all the blank spaces like always...I'll just draw stuff that comes out naturally... Yes...the title page illustration. That was supposed to be included last time. I'd done the penciling, but didn't time to finish it. While I was drawing it, I thought that it looks like a character from a shonen manga that was really popular once... (No...I've never read the manga or watched the anime...)

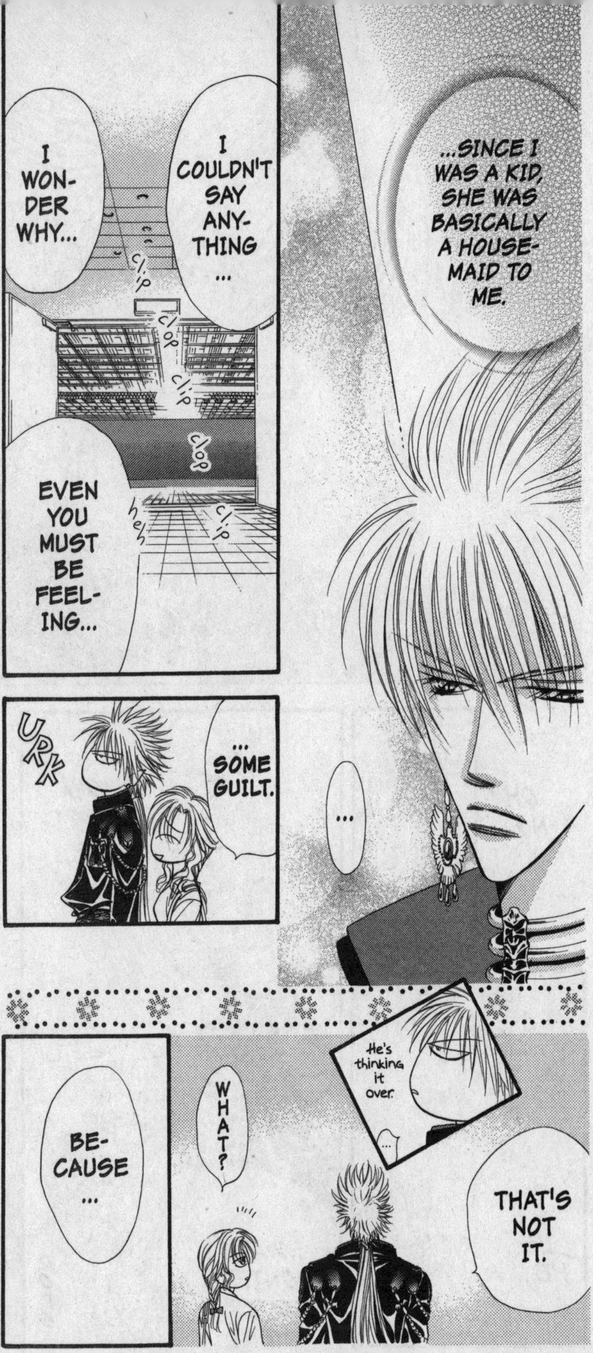
...SINCE I WAS A KID, SHE WAS BASICALLY A HOUSE-MAID TO ME.
...
I COULDN'T SAY ANY-THING ...
I WON-DER WHY...
clip clop clip clop clip
EVEN YOU MUST BE FEEL-ING...
heh
... SOME GUILT.
URK
He's thinking it over.
...
THAT'S NOT IT.
WHAT?
BE-CAUSE ...

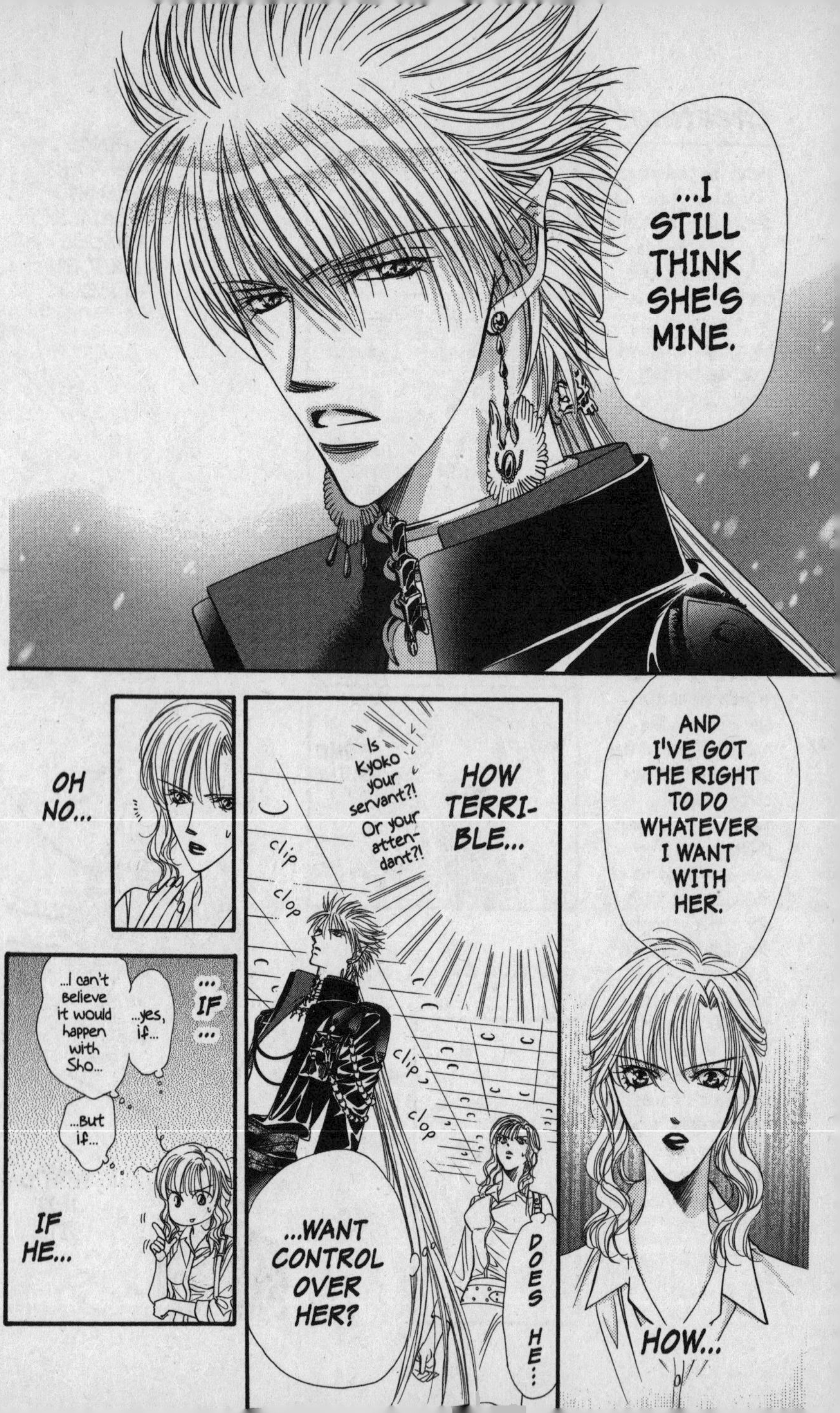
...I STILL THINK SHE'S MINE.
AND I'VE GOT THE RIGHT TO DO WHATEVER I WANT WITH HER.
HOW...
HOW TERRIBLE...
Is Kyoko your servant?! Or your attendant?!
clip clop
clip clop
DOES HE...
...WANT CONTROL OVER HER?
OH NO...
...IF...
...yes, if...
...I can't believe it would happen with Sho...
...But if...
IF HE...

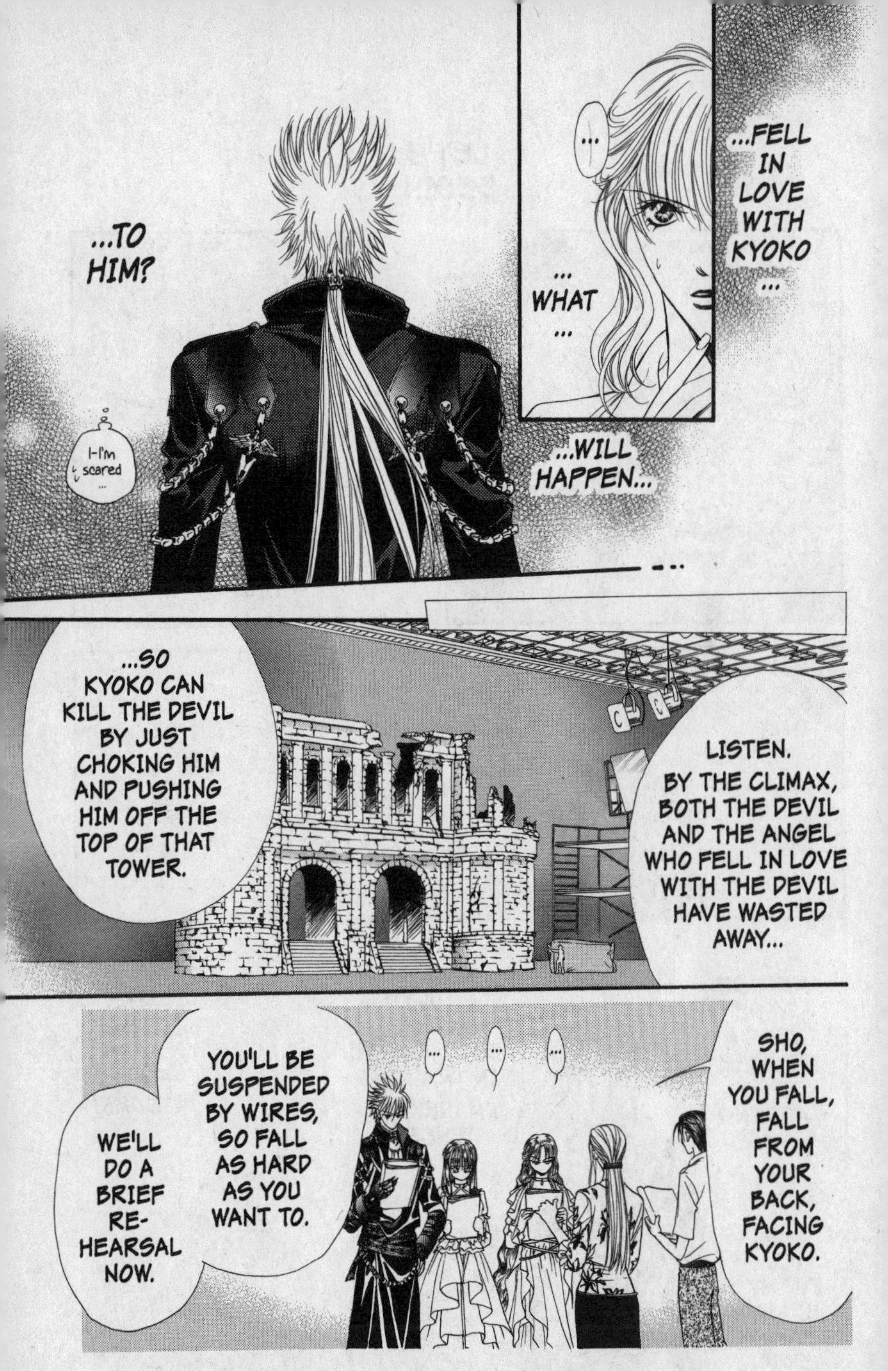
...
...FELL IN LOVE WITH KYOKO ...
... WHAT ...
...WILL HAPPEN...
...TO HIM?
I-I'm scared ...
LISTEN. BY THE CLIMAX, BOTH THE DEVIL AND THE ANGEL WHO FELL IN LOVE WITH THE DEVIL HAVE WASTED AWAY...
...SO KYOKO CAN KILL THE DEVIL BY JUST CHOKING HIM AND PUSHING HIM OFF THE TOP OF THAT TOWER.
SHO, WHEN YOU FALL, FALL FROM YOUR BACK, FACING KYOKO.
...
...
...
YOU'LL BE SUSPENDED BY WIRES, SO FALL AS HARD AS YOU WANT TO.
WE'LL DO A BRIEF RE-HEARSAL NOW.

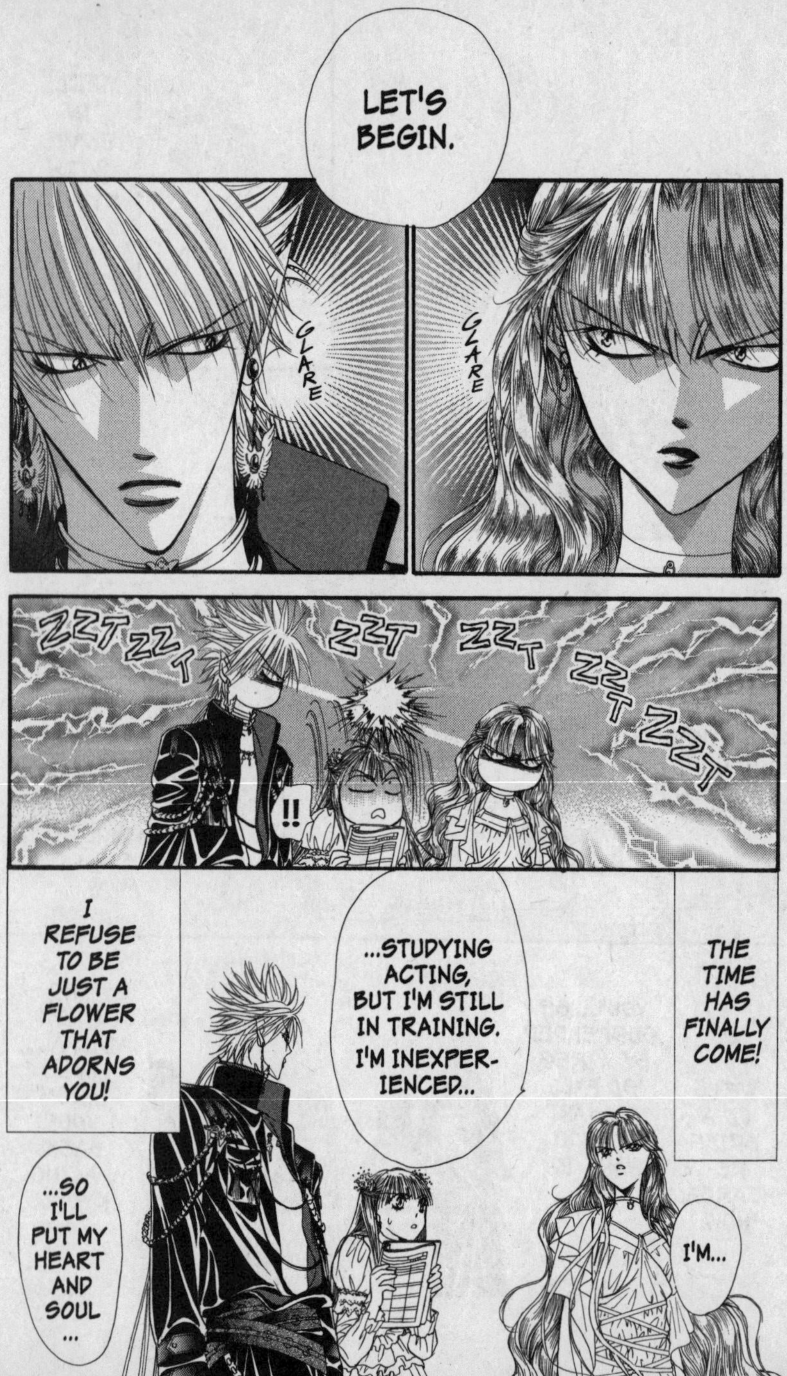
LET'S BEGIN.
GLARE
GLARE
ZZZT
ZZT
ZZT
ZZT
ZZT
ZZT
!!
THE TIME HAS FINALLY COME!
I'M...
...STUDYING ACTING, BUT I'M STILL IN TRAINING. I'M INEXPERIENCED...
I REFUSE TO BE JUST A FLOWER THAT ADORNS YOU!
...SO I'LL PUT MY HEART AND SOUL ...

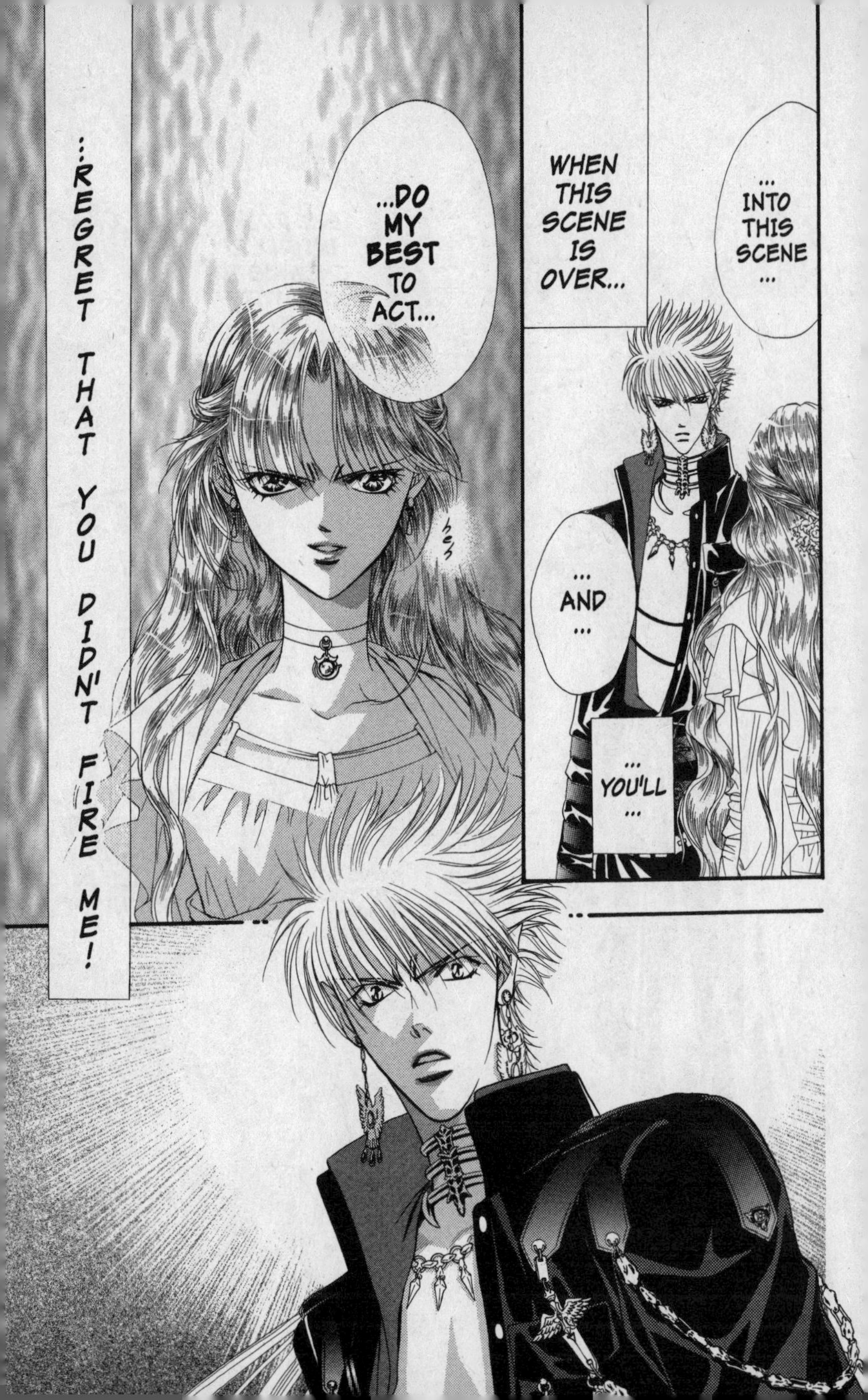
...INTO THIS SCENE...
WHEN THIS SCENE IS OVER...
...AND...
...YOU'LL...
...DO MY BEST TO ACT...
...REGRET THAT YOU DIDN'T FIRE ME!

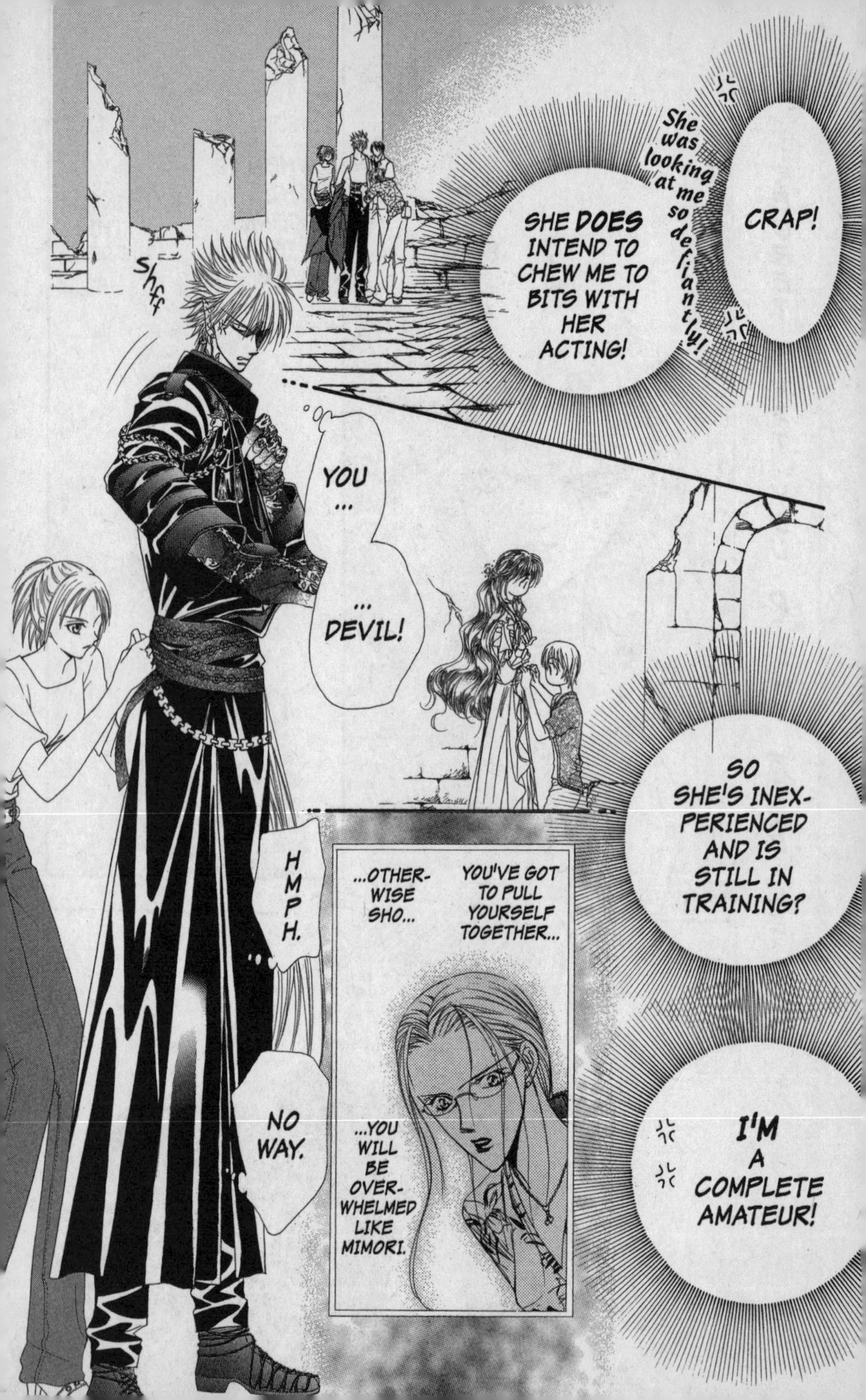
CRAP!
She was looking at me so defiantly!
SHE DOES INTEND TO CHEW ME TO BITS WITH HER ACTING!
Shff
YOU ...
... DEVIL!
SO SHE'S INEXPERIENCED AND IS STILL IN TRAINING?
I'M A COMPLETE AMATEUR!
YOU'VE GOT TO PULL YOURSELF TOGETHER...
...OTHERWISE SHO...
...YOU WILL BE OVERWHELMED LIKE MIMORI.
HMPH.
NO WAY.

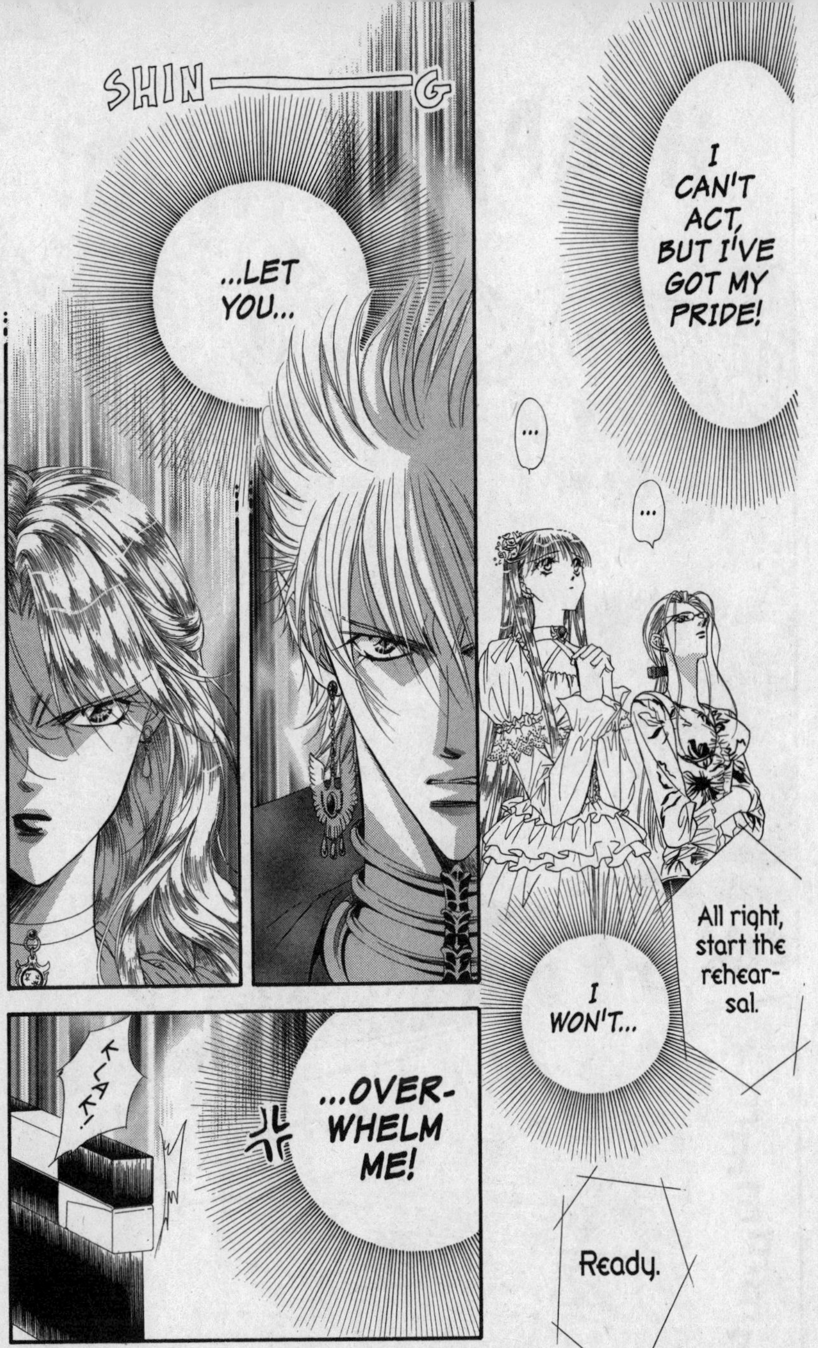
I CAN'T ACT, BUT I'VE GOT MY PRIDE!
...
...
All right, start the rehearsal.
I WON'T...
Ready.
SHIN——G
...LET YOU...
...OVER-WHELM ME!
KLAK!

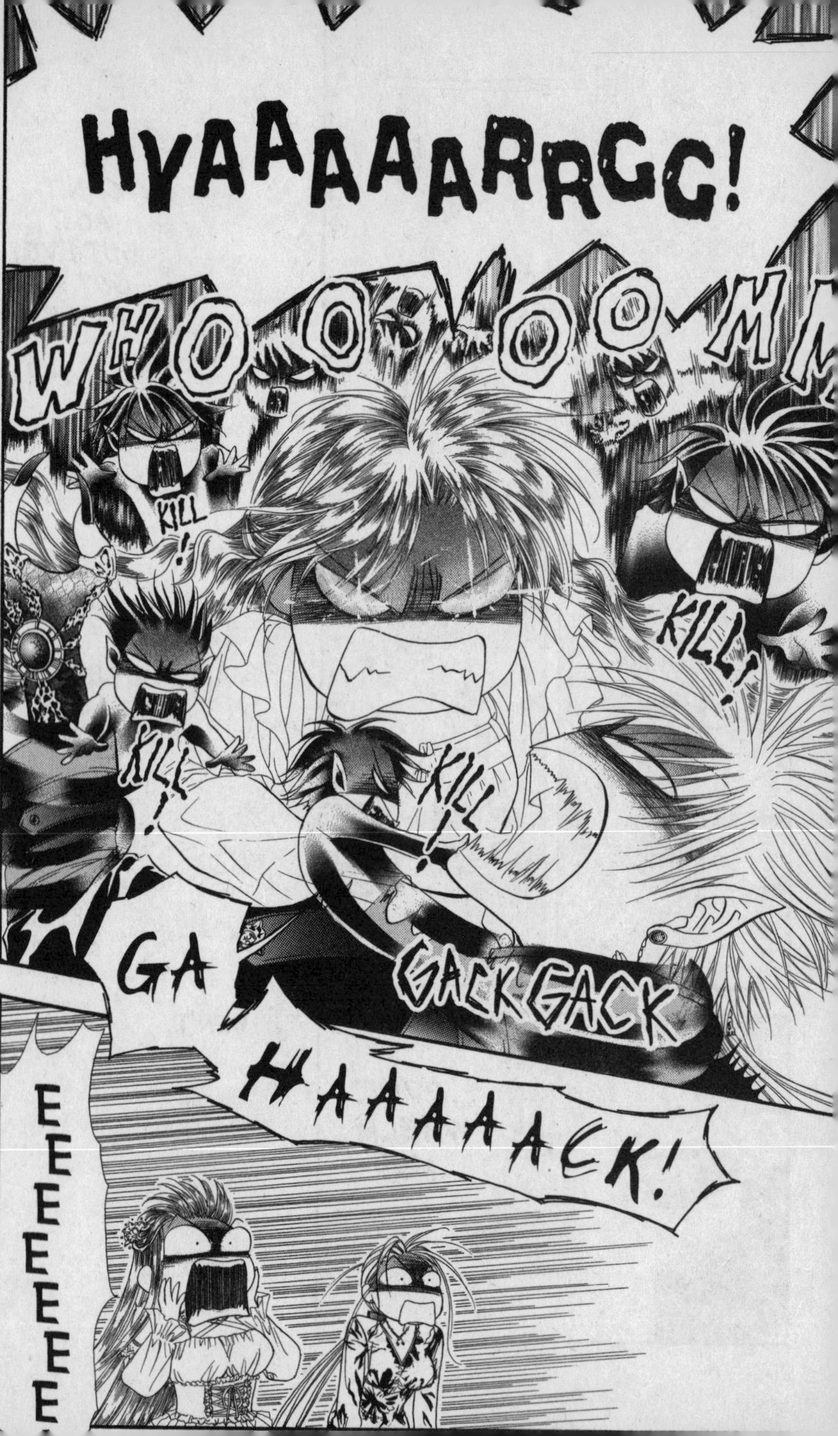
HYAAAAARRGG!
WHO-O-OO-MM
KILL!
KILL!
KILL!
KILL!
GA
GACK GACK
HAAAAAACK!
EEEEEEE

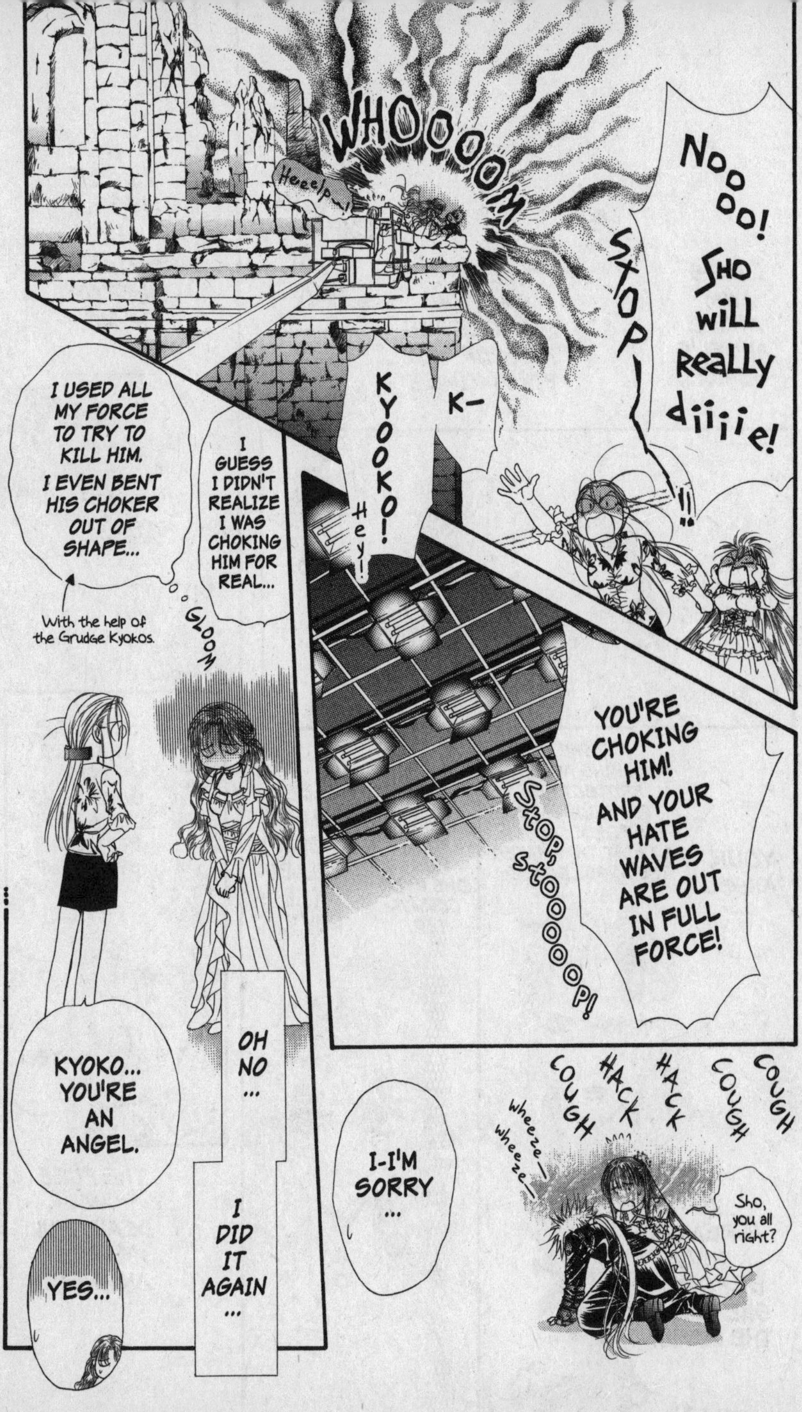
Noooo! Sho will really diiiie!
STOP!!
WHOOOOM
Heeelp...!
K-
KYOOKO!
Hey!
YOU'RE CHOKING HIM! AND YOUR HATE WAVES ARE OUT IN FULL FORCE!
Stop, stoooooop!
I GUESS I DIDN'T REALIZE I WAS CHOKING HIM FOR REAL...
GLOOM
I USED ALL MY FORCE TO TRY TO KILL HIM. I EVEN BENT HIS CHOKER OUT OF SHAPE...
With the help of the Grudge Kyokos.
COUGH COUGH HACK HACK COUGH
wheeze wheeze
Sho, you all right?
I-I'M SORRY...
OH NO... I DID IT AGAIN...
KYOKO... YOU'RE AN ANGEL.
YES...

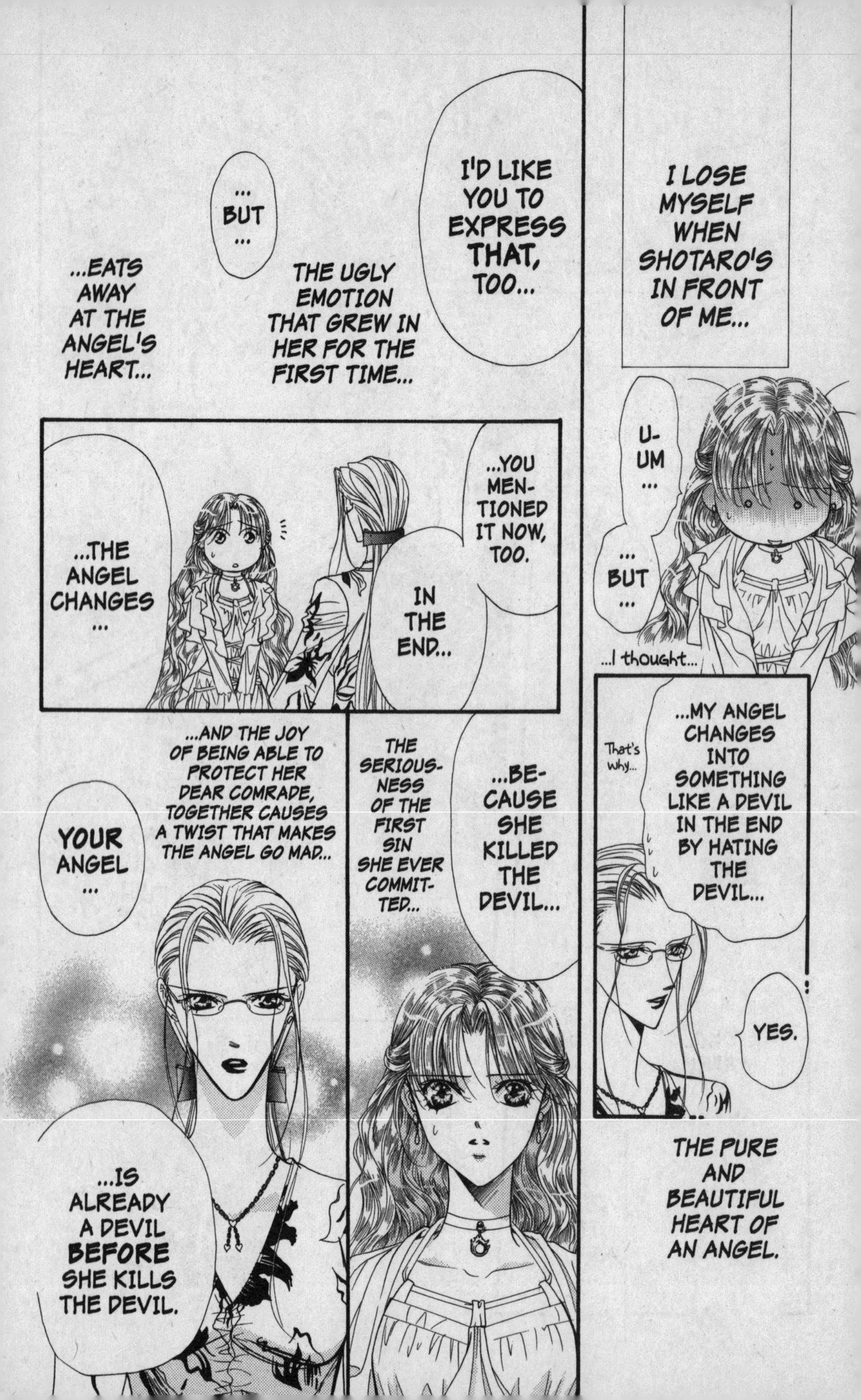
I LOSE MYSELF WHEN SHOTARO'S IN FRONT OF ME...
U-UM...
...BUT...
...I thought...
That's why...
...MY ANGEL CHANGES INTO SOMETHING LIKE A DEVIL IN THE END BY HATING THE DEVIL...
YES.
THE PURE AND BEAUTIFUL HEART OF AN ANGEL.
I'D LIKE YOU TO EXPRESS THAT, TOO...
...BUT...
THE UGLY EMOTION THAT GREW IN HER FOR THE FIRST TIME...
...EATS AWAY AT THE ANGEL'S HEART...
...YOU MEN-TIONED IT NOW, TOO.
IN THE END...
...THE ANGEL CHANGES...
...BE-CAUSE SHE KILLED THE DEVIL...
THE SERIOUS-NESS OF THE FIRST SIN SHE EVER COMMIT-TED...
...AND THE JOY OF BEING ABLE TO PROTECT HER DEAR COMRADE, TOGETHER CAUSES A TWIST THAT MAKES THE ANGEL GO MAD...
YOUR ANGEL...
...IS ALREADY A DEVIL BEFORE SHE KILLS THE DEVIL.

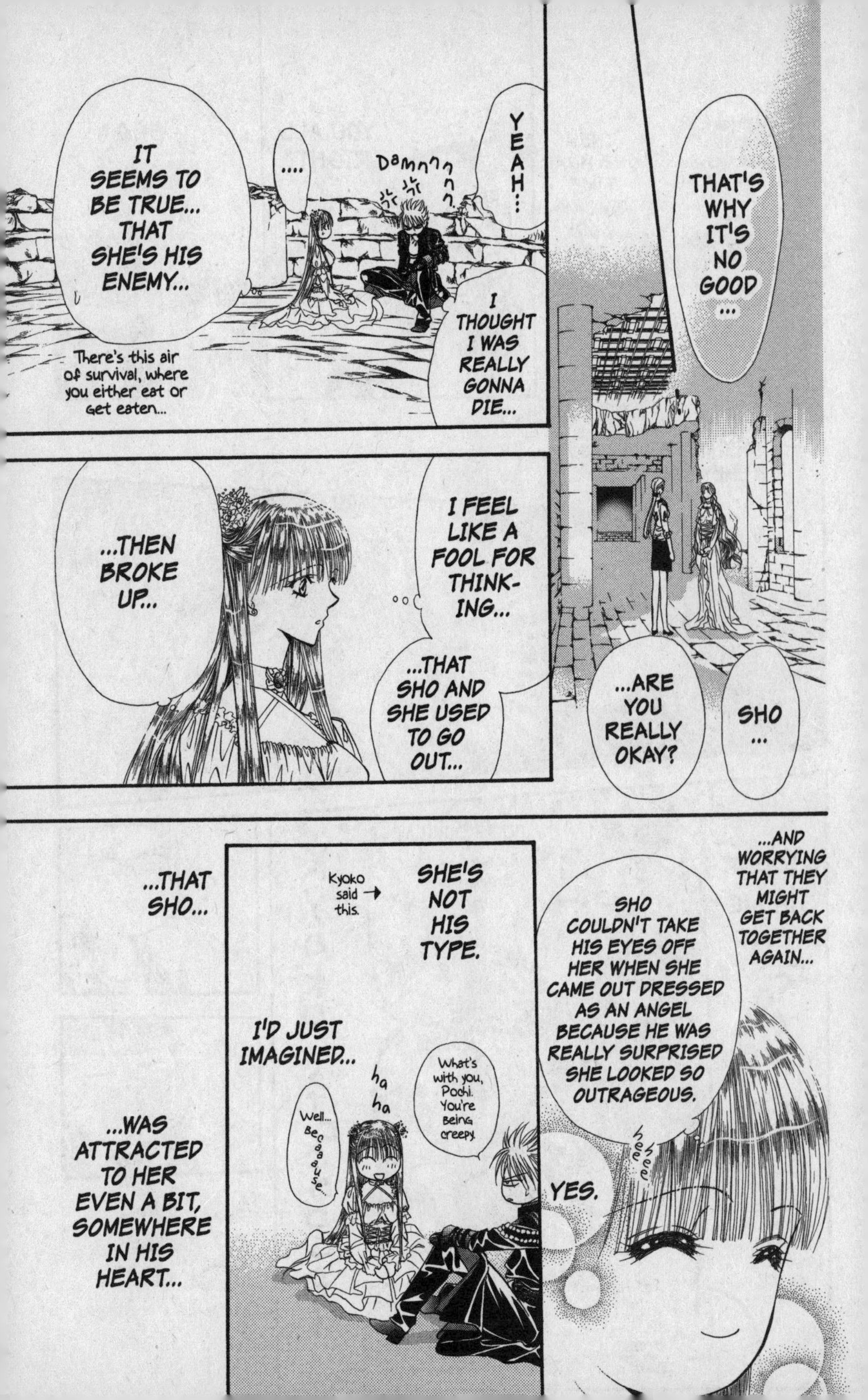
THAT'S WHY IT'S NO GOOD...
SHO...
...ARE YOU REALLY OKAY?
YEAH...
....
Damnnnnnn
IT SEEMS TO BE TRUE... THAT SHE'S HIS ENEMY...
I THOUGHT I WAS REALLY GONNA DIE...
There's this air of survival, where you either eat or get eaten...
I FEEL LIKE A FOOL FOR THINKING...
...THAT SHO AND SHE USED TO GO OUT...
...THEN BROKE UP...
...AND WORRYING THAT THEY MIGHT GET BACK TOGETHER AGAIN...
SHO COULDN'T TAKE HIS EYES OFF HER WHEN SHE CAME OUT DRESSED AS AN ANGEL BECAUSE HE WAS REALLY SURPRISED SHE LOOKED SO OUTRAGEOUS.
hee hee...
YES.
SHE'S NOT HIS TYPE.
Kyoko said this.
I'D JUST IMAGINED...
What's with you, Pochi. You're being creepy.
ha ha
Well... Becaaause...
...THAT SHO...
...WAS ATTRACTED TO HER EVEN A BIT, SOMEWHERE IN HIS HEART...

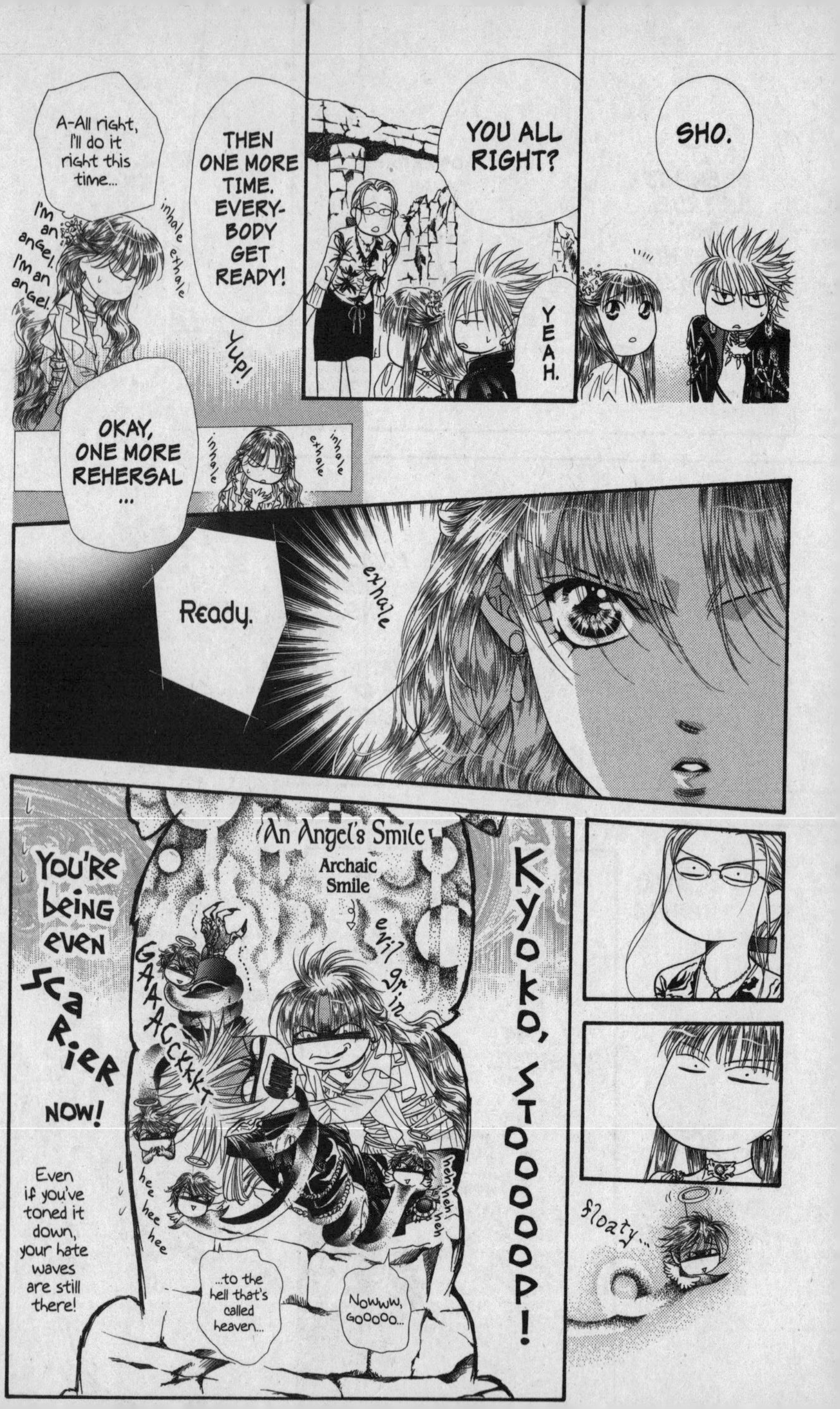
SHO.
YOU ALL RIGHT?
YEAH.
THEN ONE MORE TIME. EVERY-BODY GET READY!
Yup!
A-All right, I'll do it right this time...
inhale exhale
I'm an angel. I'm an angel.
OKAY, ONE MORE REHERSAL ...
inhale exhale inhale
exhale
Ready.
KYOKO, STOOOOOOP!
floaty...
An Angel's Smile
Archaic Smile
evil grin
GAAACKKKT
heh heh heh heh
hee hee hee
Nowww, Gooooo...
...to the hell that's called heaven...
You're being even scarier now!
Even if you've toned it down, your hate waves are still there!

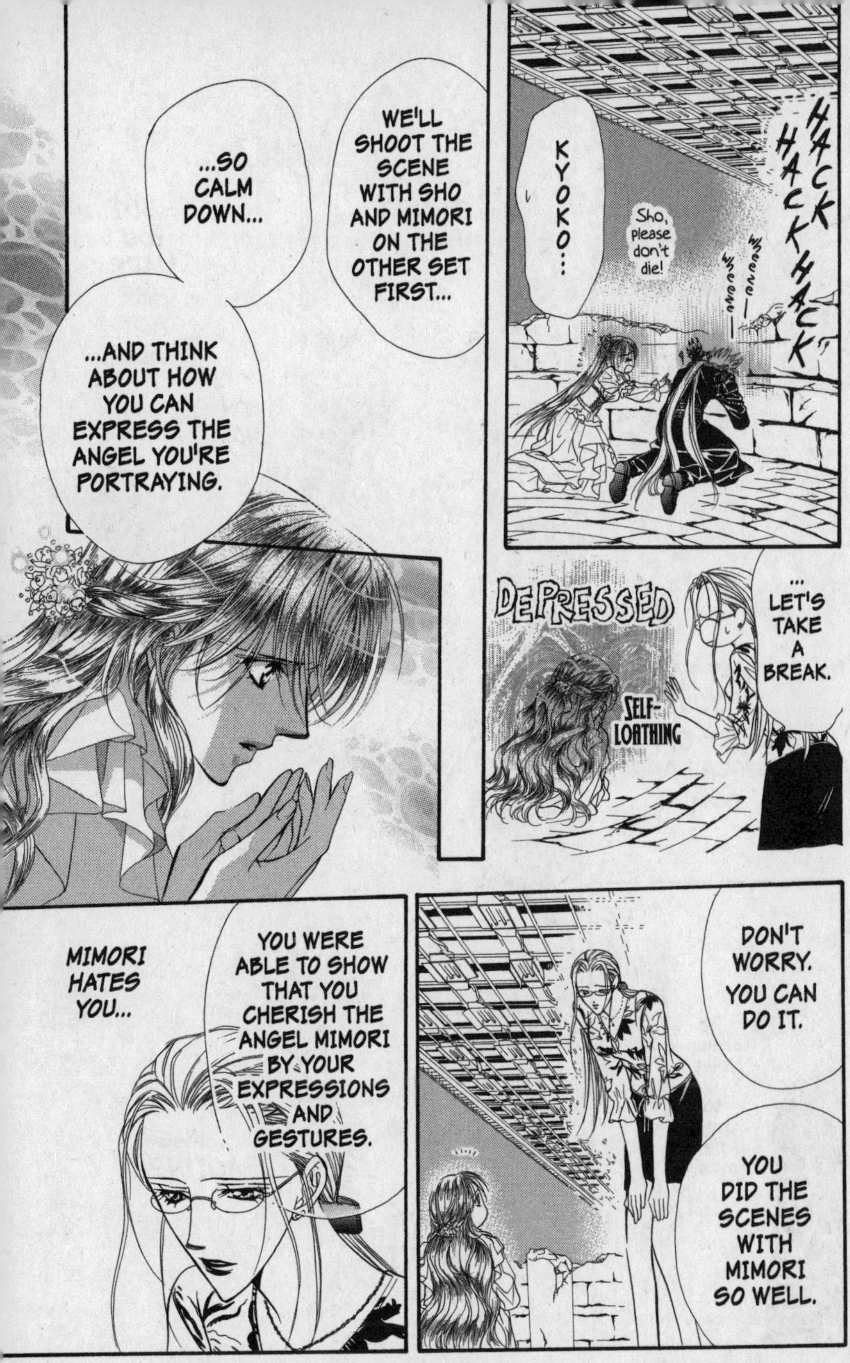
HACK HACK
HACK HACK
Wheeze— wheeze—
Sho, please don't die!
KYOKO...
DEPRESSED
... LET'S TAKE A BREAK.
SELF-LOATHING
WE'LL SHOOT THE SCENE WITH SHO AND MIMORI ON THE OTHER SET FIRST...
...SO CALM DOWN...
...AND THINK ABOUT HOW YOU CAN EXPRESS THE ANGEL YOU'RE PORTRAYING.
DON'T WORRY. YOU CAN DO IT.
YOU DID THE SCENES WITH MIMORI SO WELL.
YOU WERE ABLE TO SHOW THAT YOU CHERISH THE ANGEL MIMORI BY YOUR EXPRESSIONS AND GESTURES.
MIMORI HATES YOU...

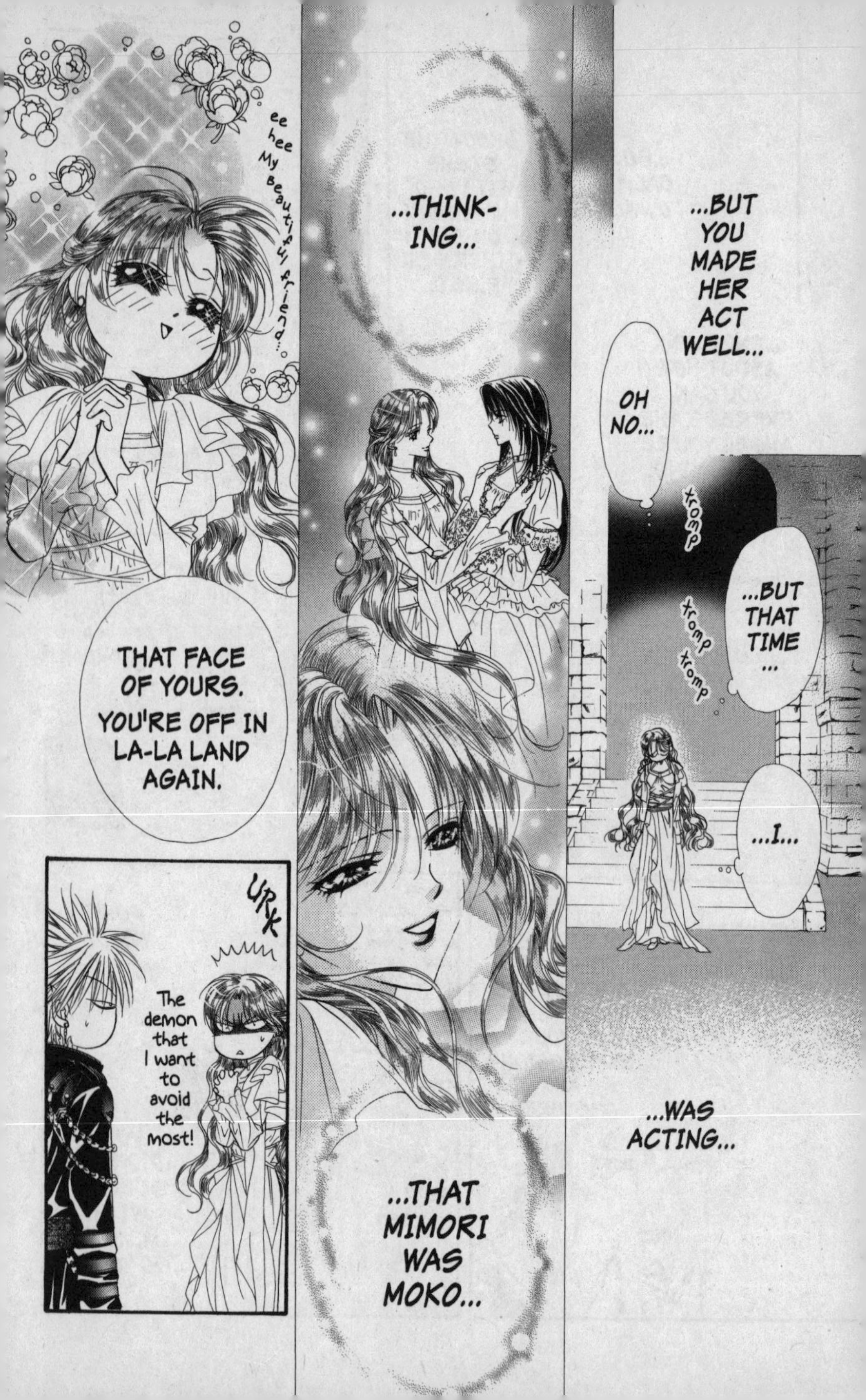
...BUT YOU MADE HER ACT WELL...
OH NO...
xromp
xromp
xromp
...BUT THAT TIME ...
...I...
...WAS ACTING...
...THINK-ING...
...THAT MIMORI WAS MOKO...
ee hee My beautiful friend...
THAT FACE OF YOURS. YOU'RE OFF IN LA-LA LAND AGAIN.
URK
The demon that I want to avoid the most!

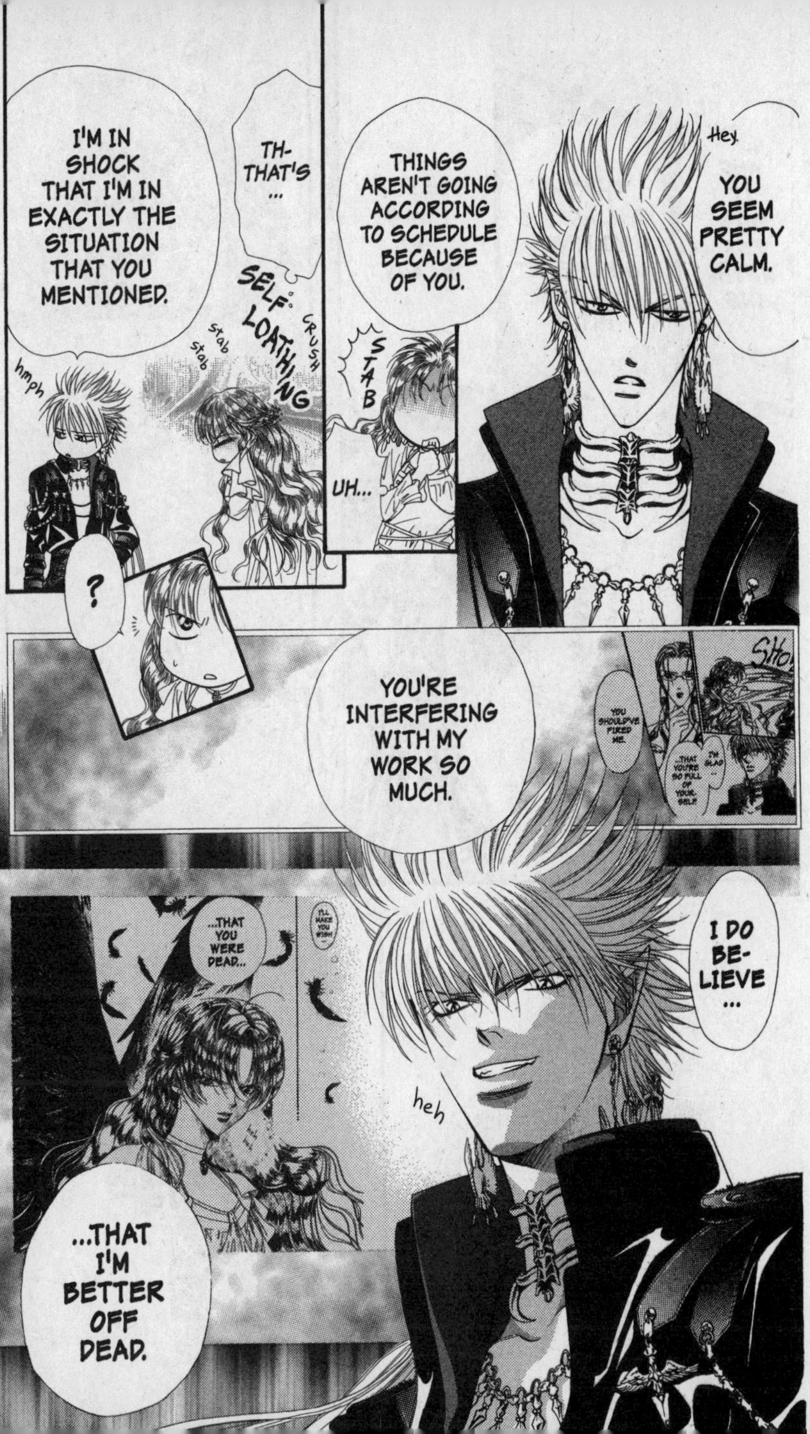
Hey.
YOU SEEM PRETTY CALM.
THINGS AREN'T GOING ACCORDING TO SCHEDULE BECAUSE OF YOU.
STAB
UH...
TH-THAT'S...
SELF-LOATHING
CRUSH
stab stab
I'M IN SHOCK THAT I'M IN EXACTLY THE SITUATION THAT YOU MENTIONED.
hmph
?
YOU SHOULD'VE FIRED ME.
I'M GLAD...
...THAT YOU'RE SO FULL OF YOURSELF.
YOU'RE INTERFERING WITH MY WORK SO MUCH.
I DO BE-LIEVE...
heh
I'LL MAKE YOU WISH...
...THAT YOU WERE DEAD...
...THAT I'M BETTER OFF DEAD.

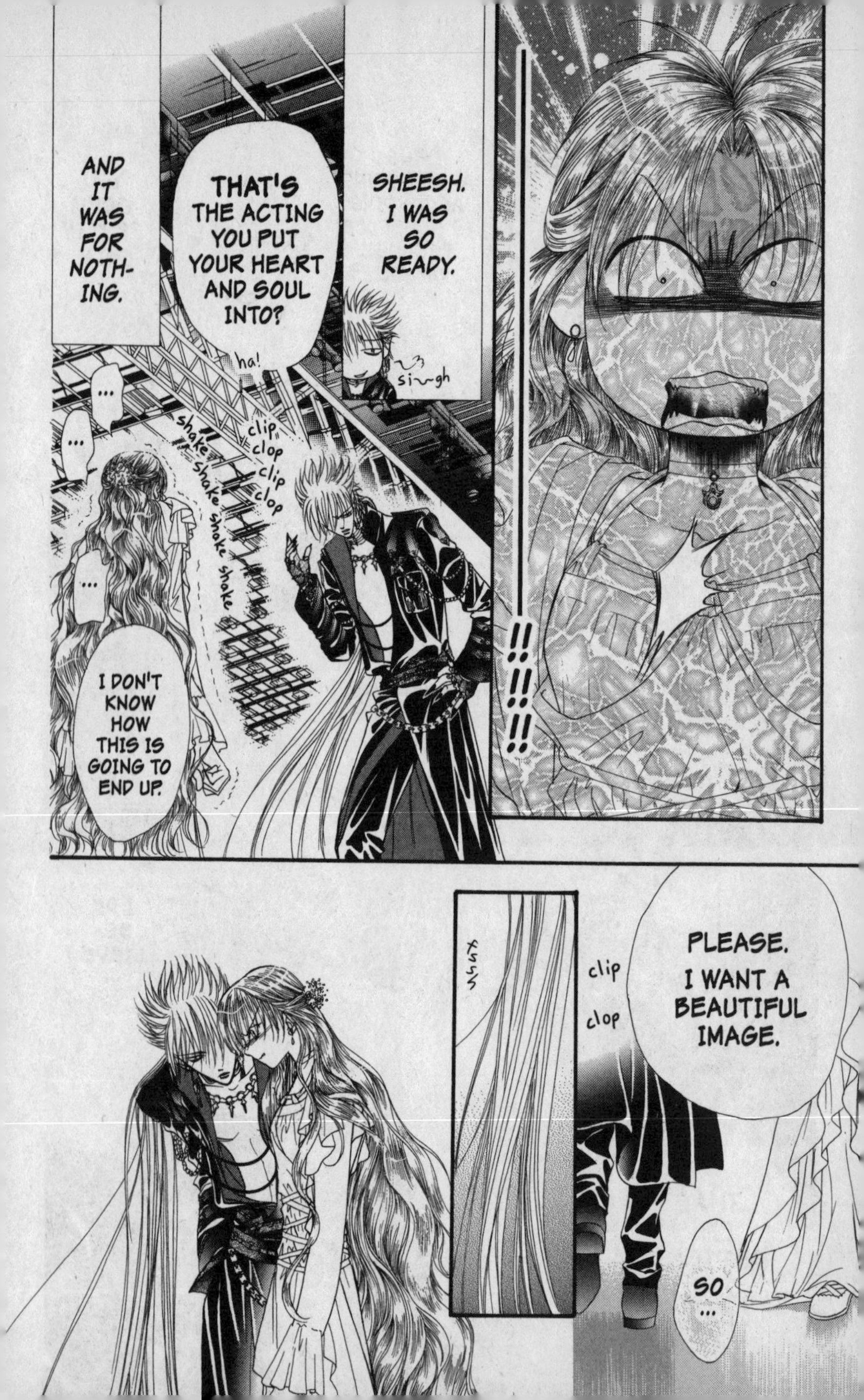
!!!!!!
SHEESH. I WAS SO READY.
si~gh
THAT'S THE ACTING YOU PUT YOUR HEART AND SOUL INTO?
ha!
AND IT WAS FOR NOTH-ING.
clip clop clip clop
...
...
shake shake shake shake
...
I DON'T KNOW HOW THIS IS GOING TO END UP.
PLEASE. I WANT A BEAUTIFUL IMAGE.
clip clop
SO ...

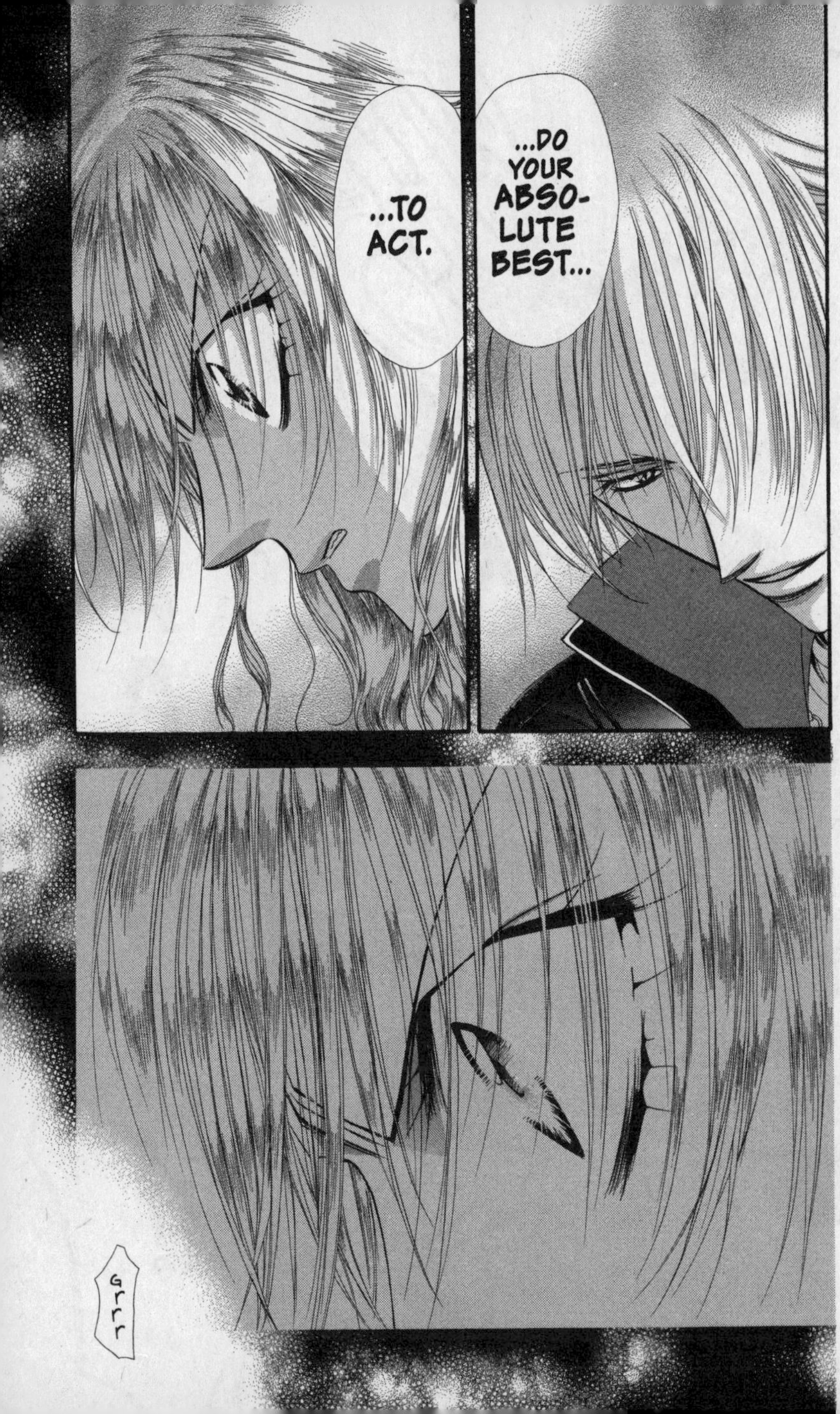
...DO YOUR ABSOLUTE BEST...
...TO ACT.
Grrr

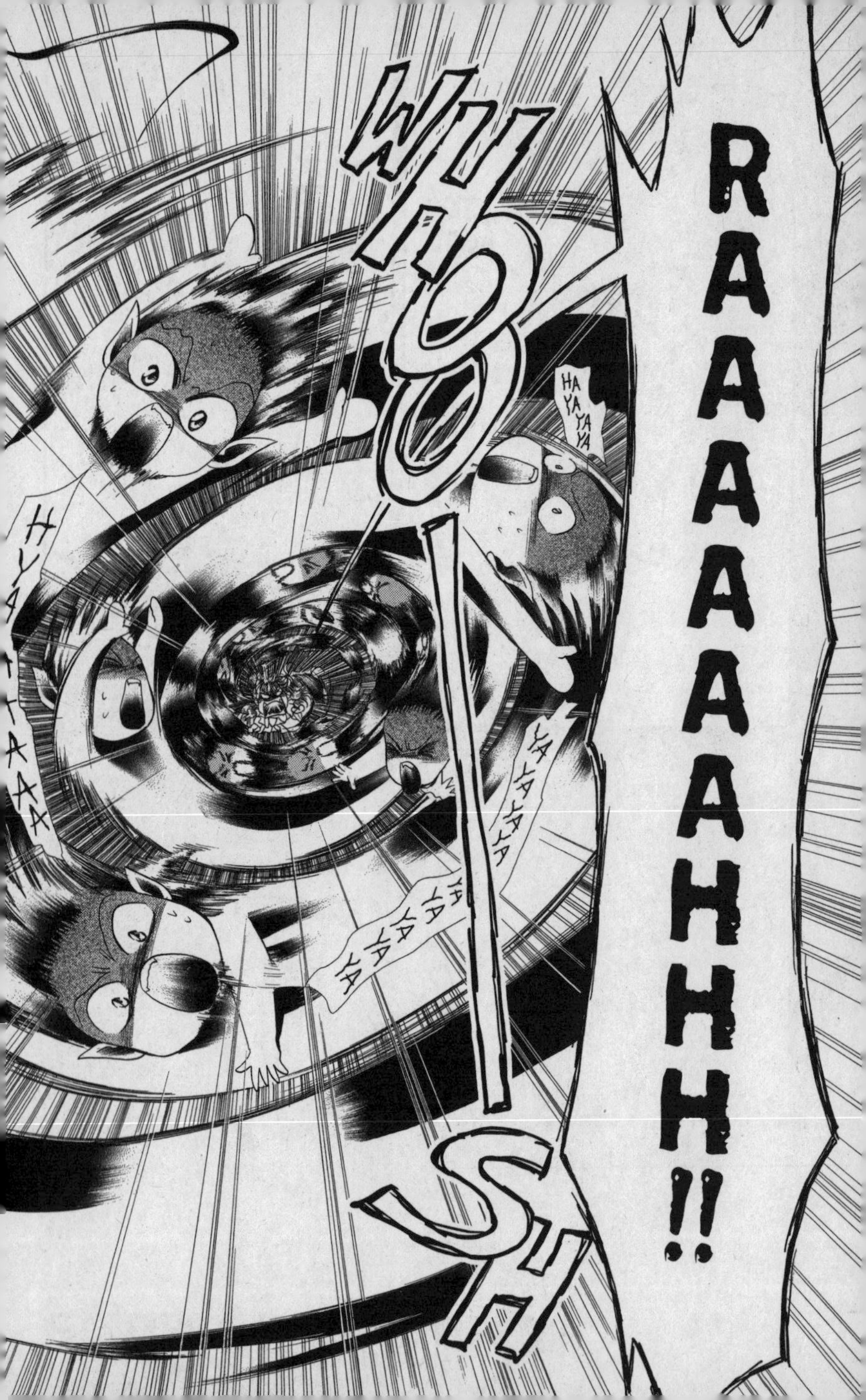

RAAAAAAHHH!!
WHOOOSH
HA YA YA YA YA
YA YA YA YA YA
HYAYAAAA
YA YA YA YA YA

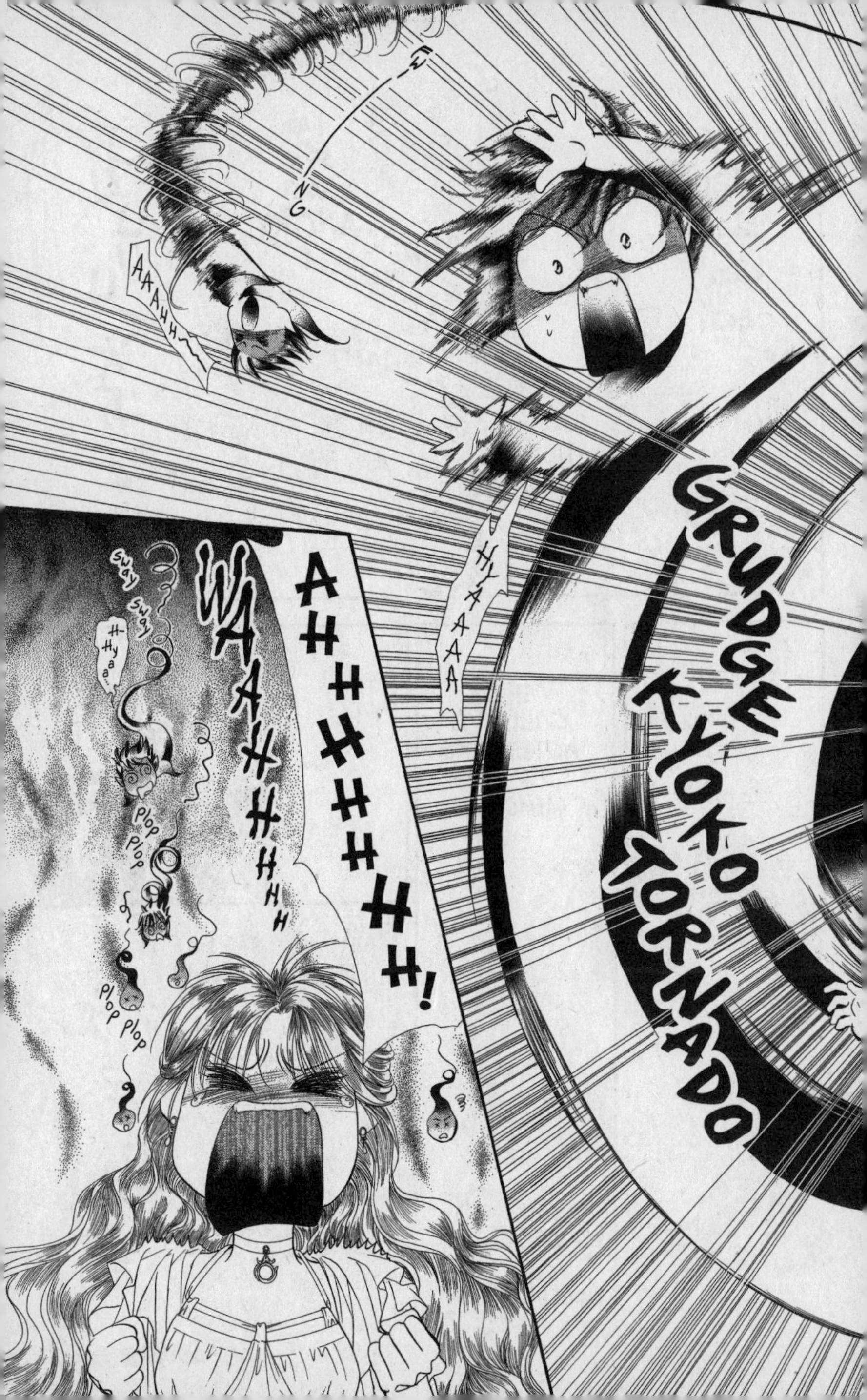
GRUDGE KYOKO TORNADO
FW—NG
AAAHH~
HYAAAAA
AHHHHHHH!
WAAHHHHHHH
Sway sway
H-Hyaa...
Plop plop
Plop plop

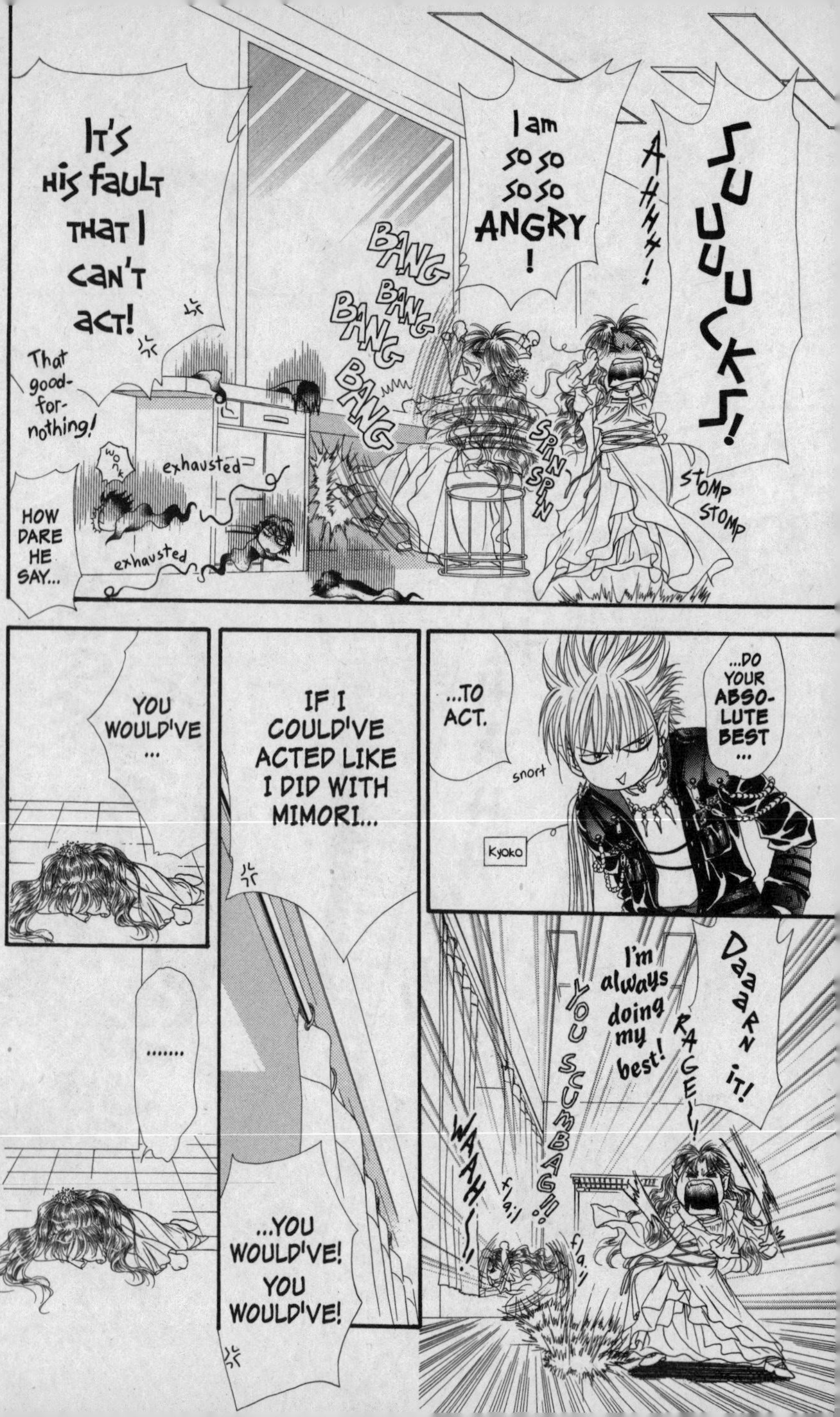
SUUUUCKS!
AHHHH!
I am so so so so ANGRY!
BANG BANG BANG BANG BANG
SPIN SPIN
STOMP STOMP
It's his fault that I can't act!
That good-for-nothing!
HOW DARE HE SAY...
wonk
exhausted
exhausted
...DO YOUR ABSOLUTE BEST...
...TO ACT.
snort
Kyoko
Daaarn it!
I'm always doing my best!
RAGE!!
YOU SCUMBAG!!
WAAAH!!
flail
flail
IF I COULD'VE ACTED LIKE I DID WITH MIMORI...
...YOU WOULD'VE! YOU WOULD'VE!
YOU WOULD'VE...
....

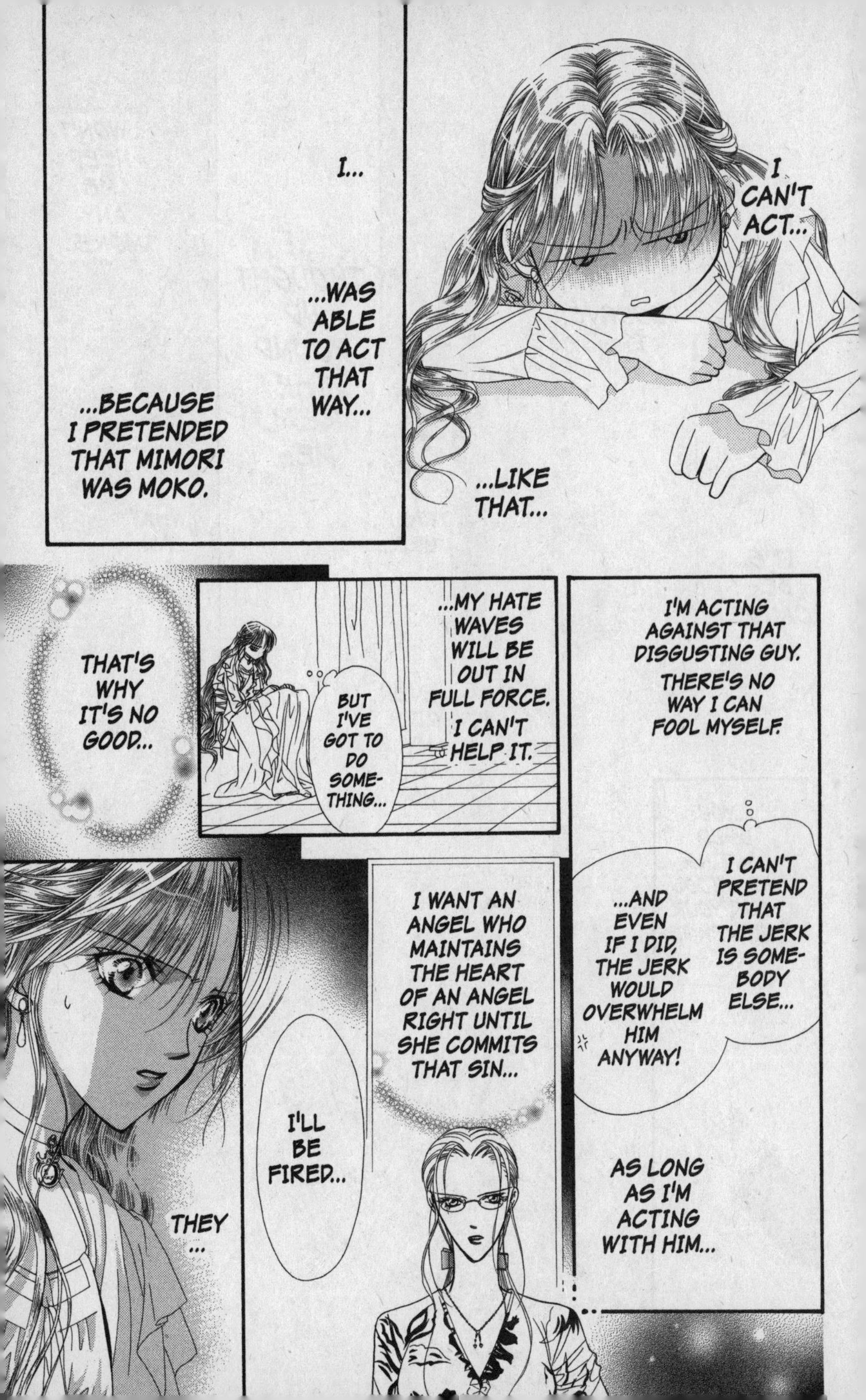
I CAN'T ACT...
...LIKE THAT...
I...
...WAS ABLE TO ACT THAT WAY...
...BECAUSE I PRETENDED THAT MIMORI WAS MOKO.
I'M ACTING AGAINST THAT DISGUSTING GUY.
THERE'S NO WAY I CAN FOOL MYSELF.
...MY HATE WAVES WILL BE OUT IN FULL FORCE.
I CAN'T HELP IT.
BUT I'VE GOT TO DO SOME-THING...
THAT'S WHY IT'S NO GOOD...
I CAN'T PRETEND THAT THE JERK IS SOME-BODY ELSE...
...AND EVEN IF I DID, THE JERK WOULD OVERWHELM HIM ANYWAY!
AS LONG AS I'M ACTING WITH HIM...
I WANT AN ANGEL WHO MAINTAINS THE HEART OF AN ANGEL RIGHT UNTIL SHE COMMITS THAT SIN...
I'LL BE FIRED...
THEY...

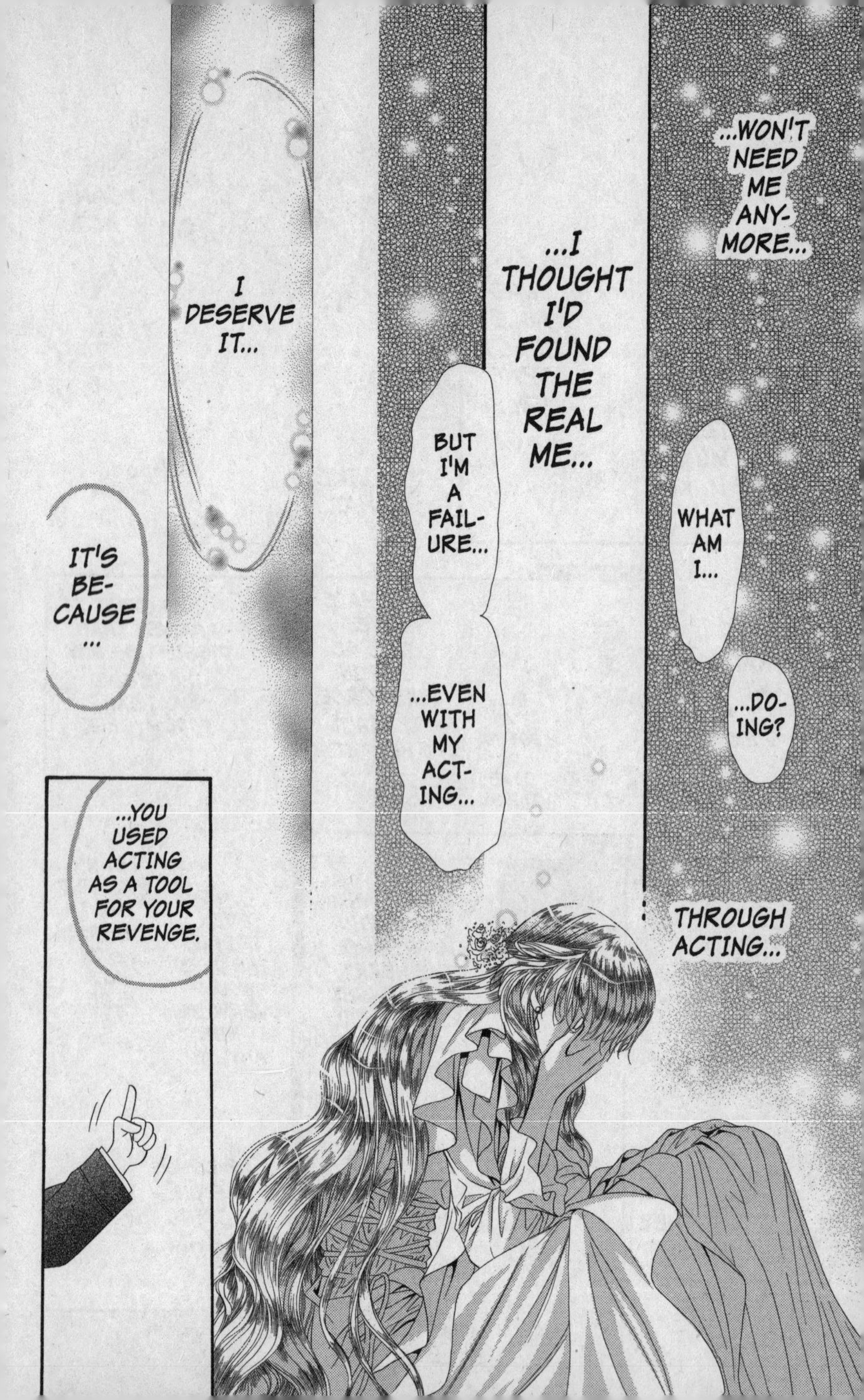
...WON'T NEED ME ANYMORE...
WHAT AM I...
...DOING?
...I THOUGHT I'D FOUND THE REAL ME...
THROUGH ACTING...
BUT I'M A FAILURE...
...EVEN WITH MY ACTING...
I DESERVE IT...
IT'S BECAUSE...
...YOU USED ACTING AS A TOOL FOR YOUR REVENGE.

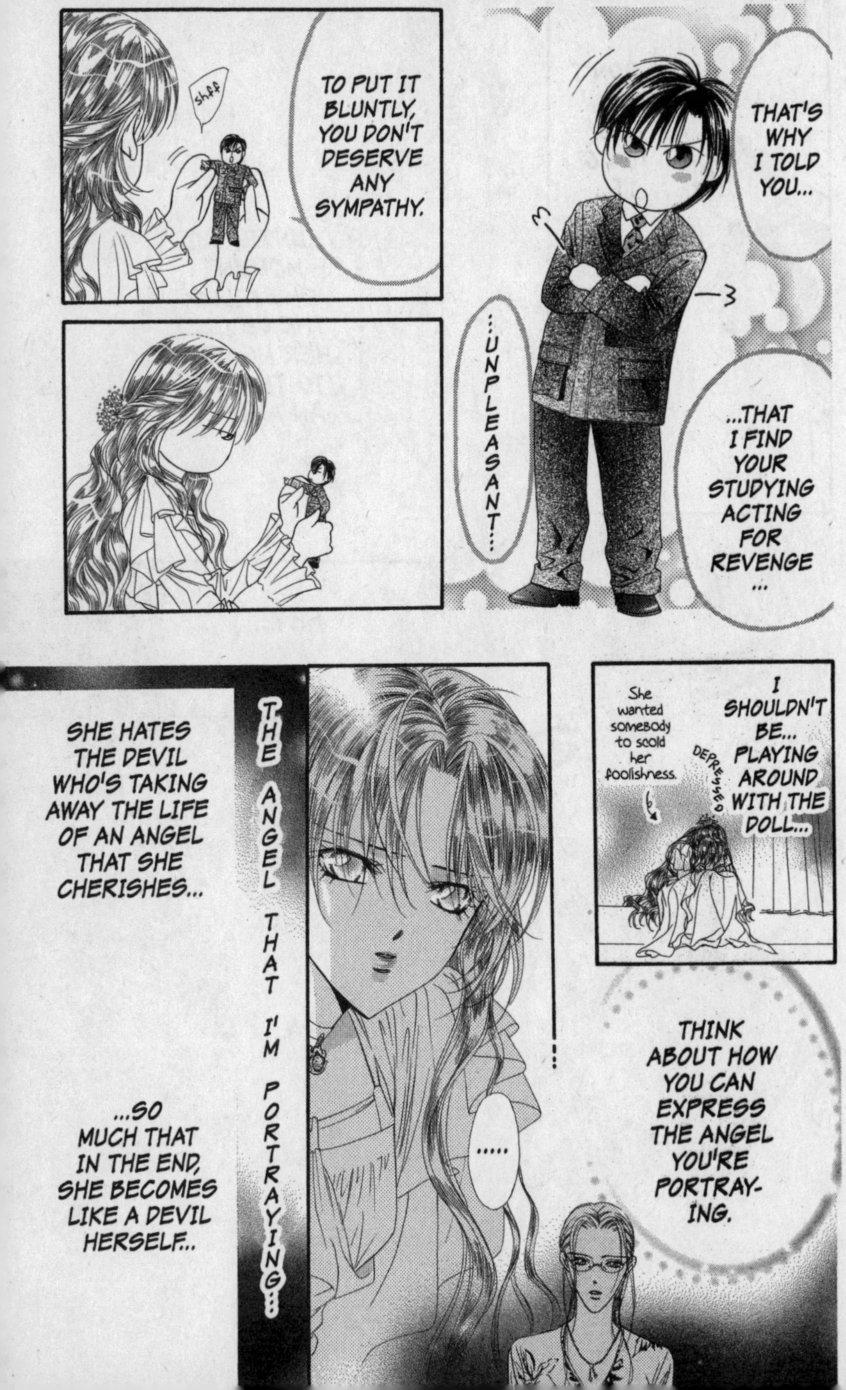
THAT'S WHY I TOLD YOU...
...THAT I FIND YOUR STUDYING ACTING FOR REVENGE ...
...UNPLEASANT...
TO PUT IT BLUNTLY, YOU DON'T DESERVE ANY SYMPATHY.
shff
I SHOULDN'T BE... PLAYING AROUND WITH THE DOLL...
She wanted somebody to scold her foolishness.
DEPRESSED
THINK ABOUT HOW YOU CAN EXPRESS THE ANGEL YOU'RE PORTRAYING.
!
.....
THE ANGEL THAT I'M PORTRAYING...
SHE HATES THE DEVIL WHO'S TAKING AWAY THE LIFE OF AN ANGEL THAT SHE CHERISHES...
...SO MUCH THAT IN THE END, SHE BECOMES LIKE A DEVIL HERSELF...

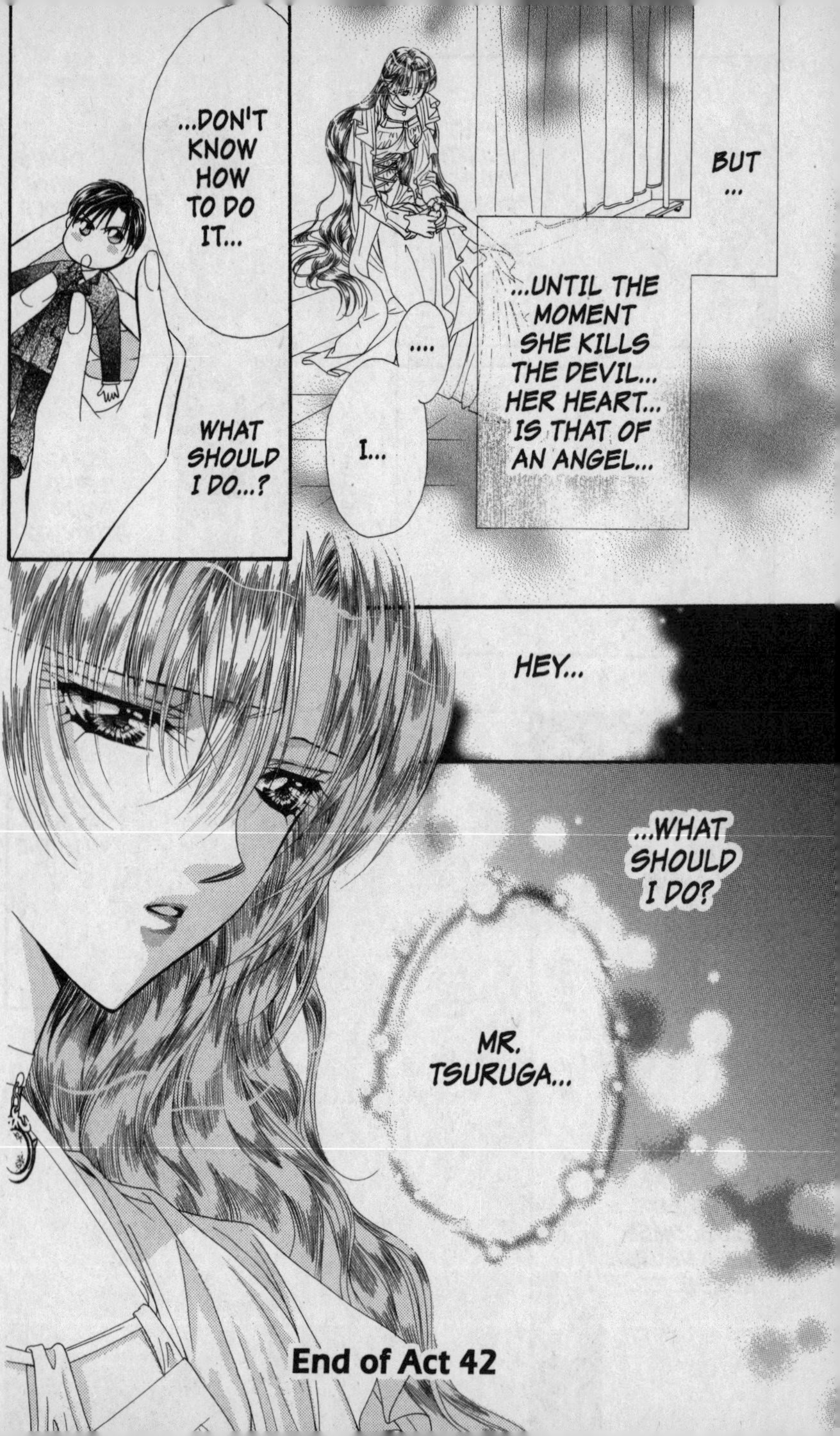
BUT ...
...UNTIL THE MOMENT SHE KILLS THE DEVIL... HER HEART... IS THAT OF AN ANGEL...
....
I...
...DON'T KNOW HOW TO DO IT...
WHAT SHOULD I DO...?
HEY...
...WHAT SHOULD I DO?
MR. TSURUGA...
End of Act 42

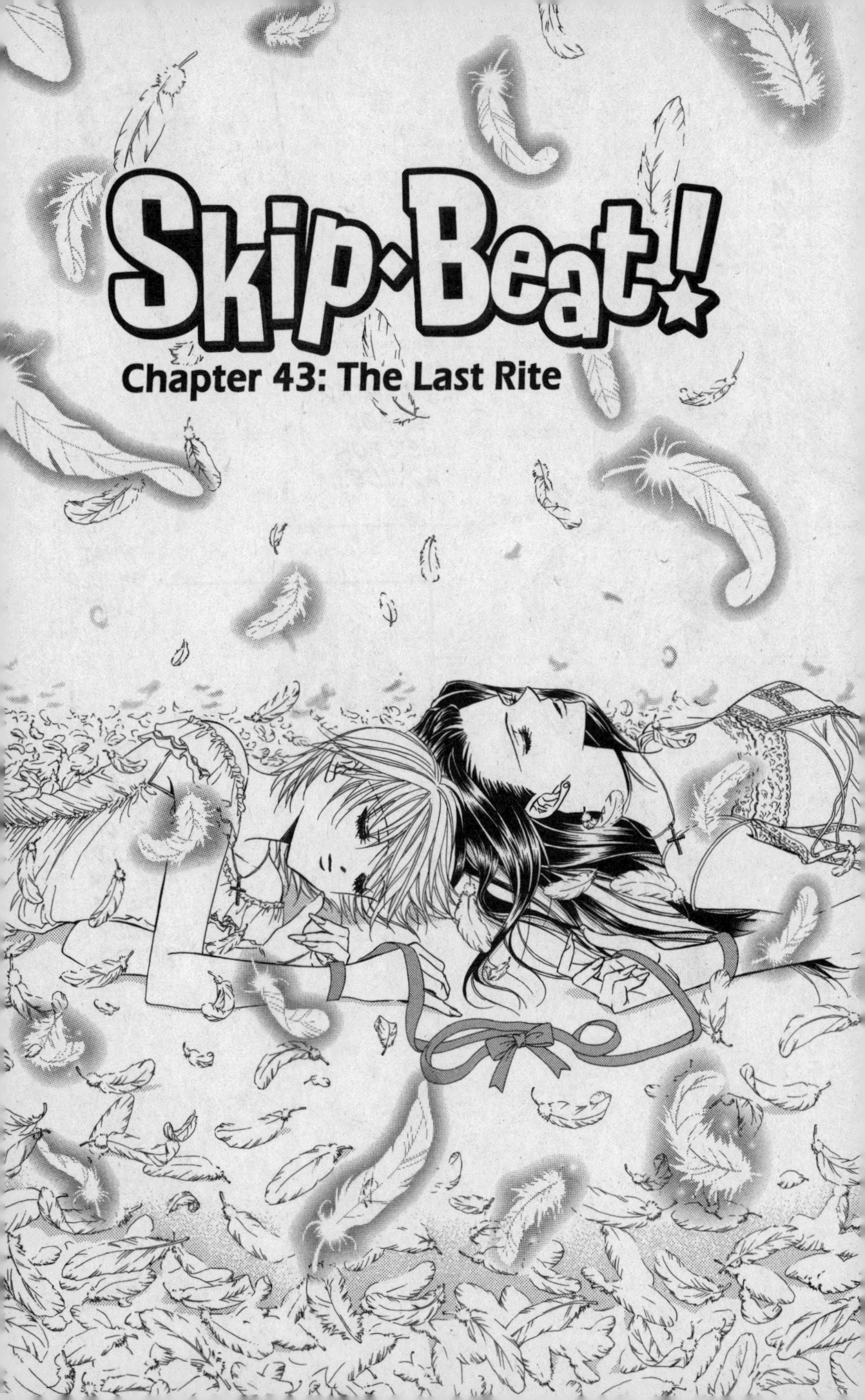
Skip·Beat!
Chapter 43: The Last Rite

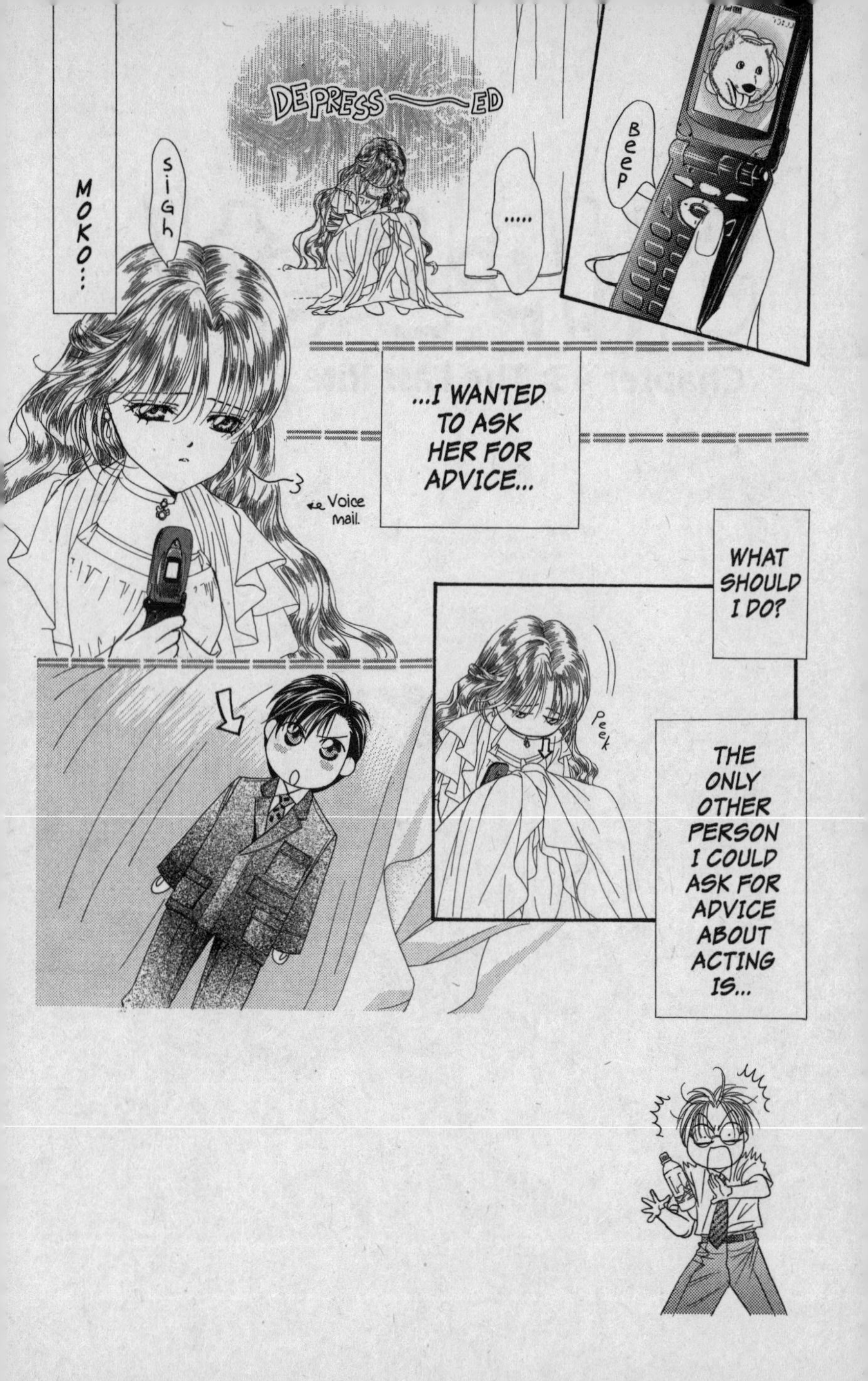
Beep
DEPRESS——ED
.....
MOKO...
Sigh
Voice mail.
...I WANTED TO ASK HER FOR ADVICE...
WHAT SHOULD I DO?
Peek
THE ONLY OTHER PERSON I COULD ASK FOR ADVICE ABOUT ACTING IS...

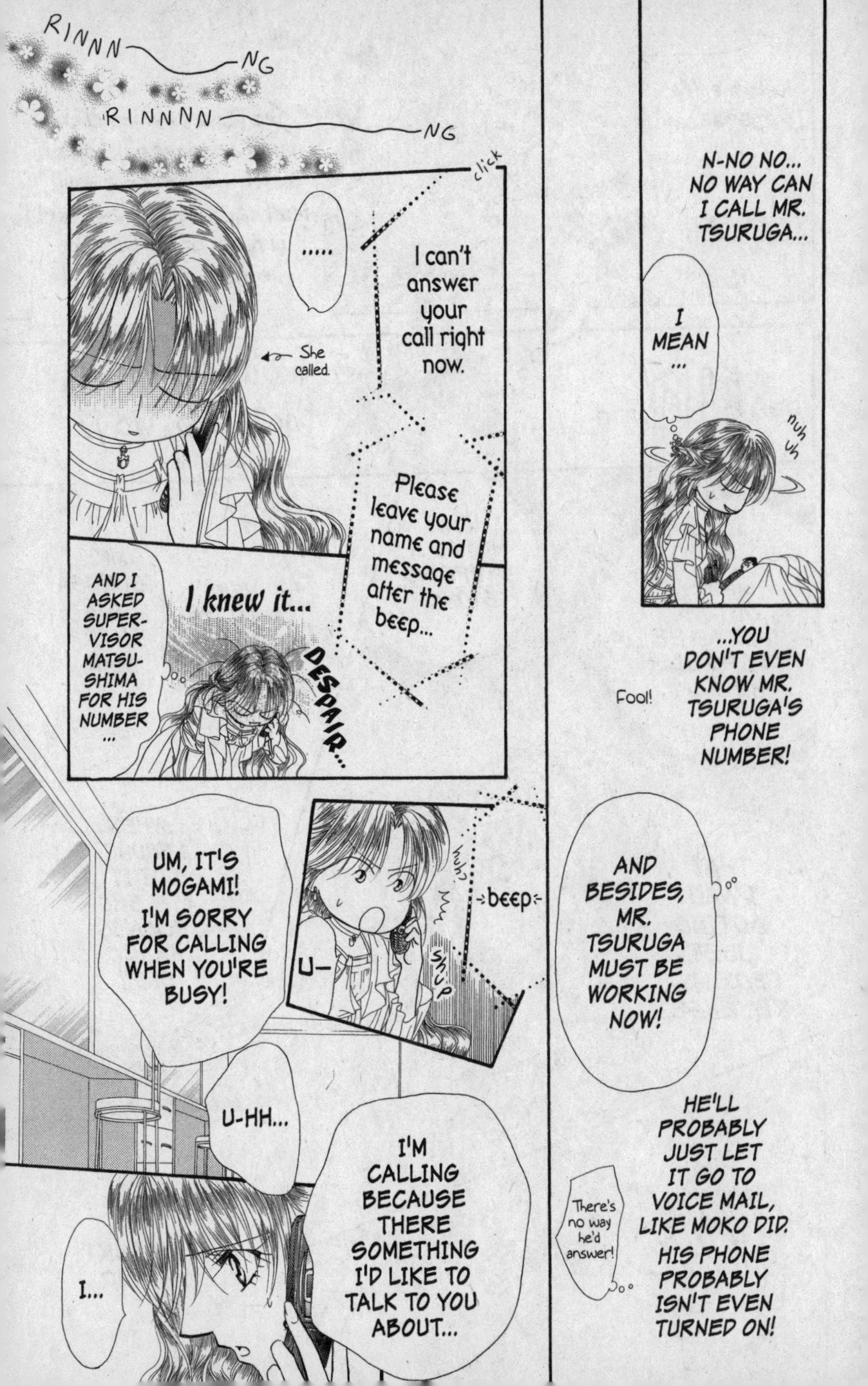
N-NO NO... NO WAY CAN I CALL MR. TSURUGA...
I MEAN ...
nuh uh
...YOU DON'T EVEN KNOW MR. TSURUGA'S PHONE NUMBER!
Fool!
AND BESIDES, MR. TSURUGA MUST BE WORKING NOW!
HE'LL PROBABLY JUST LET IT GO TO VOICE MAIL, LIKE MOKO DID.
HIS PHONE PROBABLY ISN'T EVEN TURNED ON!
There's no way he'd answer!
RINNN—NG
RINNNNN—NG
click
I can't answer your call right now.
.....
She called.
Please leave your name and message after the beep...
I knew it...
DESPAIR...
AND I ASKED SUPERVISOR MATSUSHIMA FOR HIS NUMBER...
-beep-
U—
UM, IT'S MOGAMI! I'M SORRY FOR CALLING WHEN YOU'RE BUSY!
U-HH...
I'M CALLING BECAUSE THERE SOMETHING I'D LIKE TO TALK TO YOU ABOUT...
I...

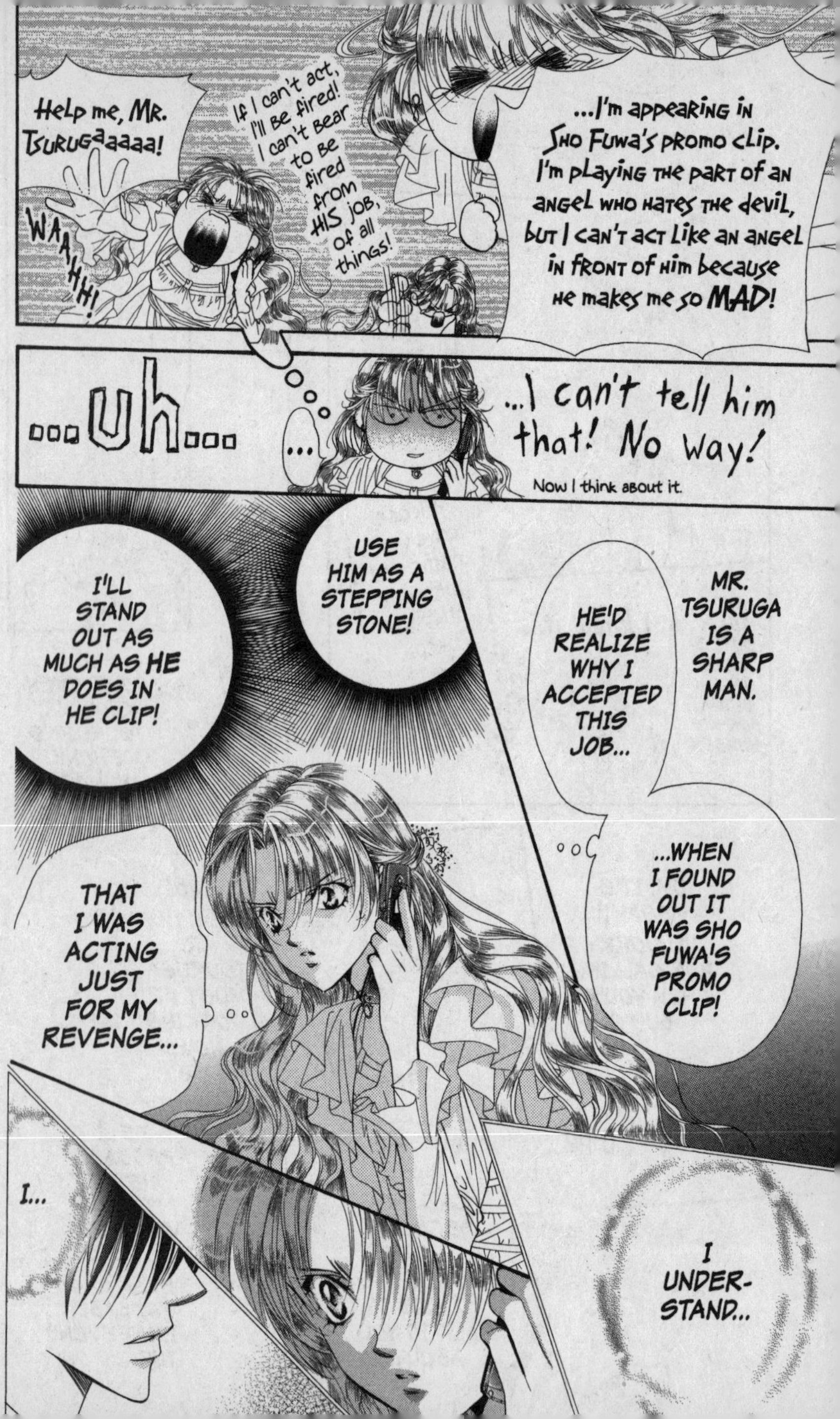
...I'm appearing in Sho Fuwa's promo clip. I'm playing the part of an angel who hates the devil, but I can't act like an angel in front of him because he makes me so MAD!
If I can't act, I'll be fired! I can't bear to be fired from HIS job, of all things!
Help me, Mr. Tsurugaaaaa!
WAAHH!
...I can't tell him that! No way!
Now I think about it.
...
...uh...
Mr. Tsuruga is a sharp man.
He'd realize why I accepted this job...
...when I found out it was Sho Fuwa's promo clip!
Use him as a stepping stone!
I'll stand out as much as he does in he clip!
That I was acting just for my revenge...
I understand...
I...

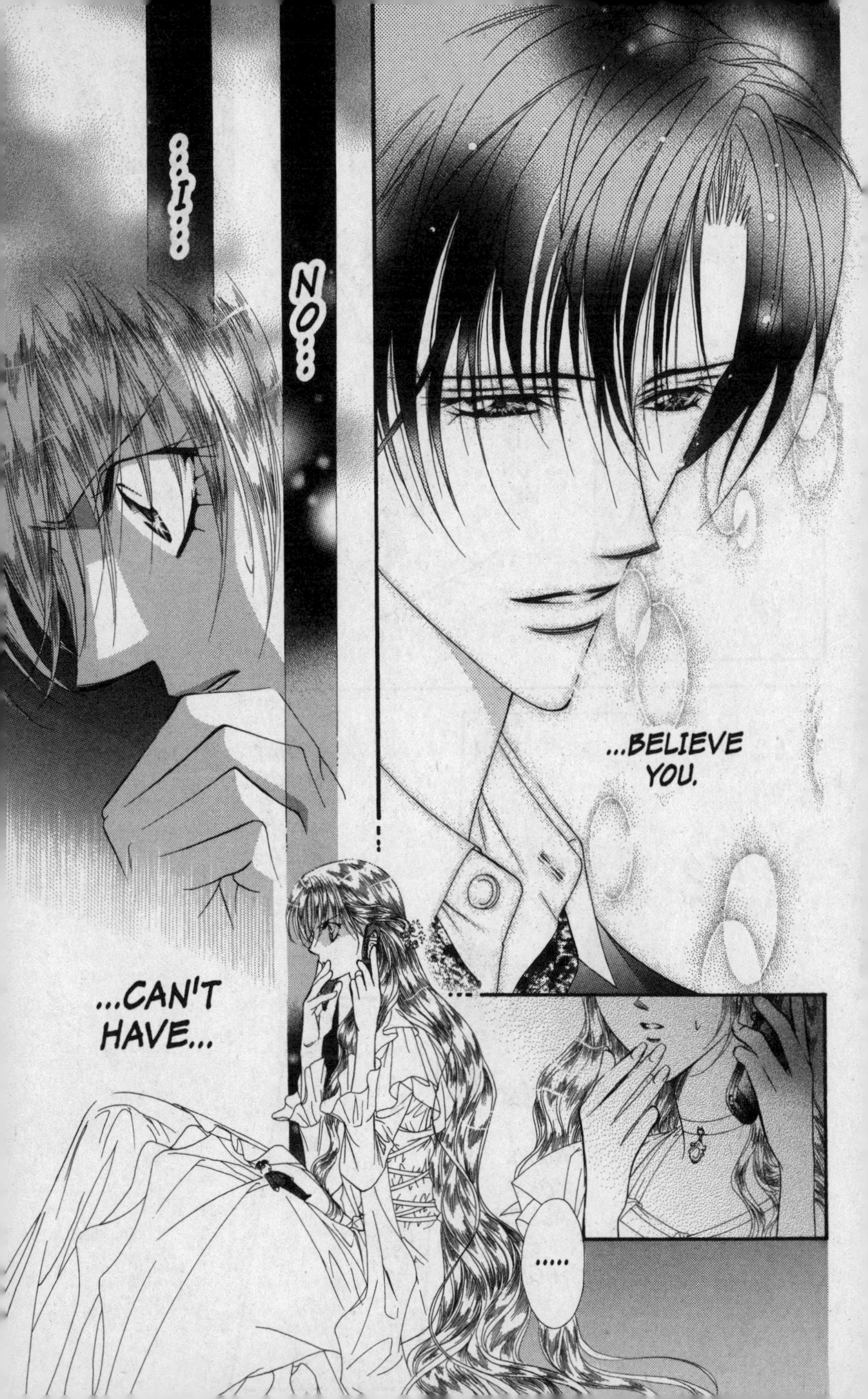
...BELIEVE YOU.
...
NO...
...I...
.....
...CAN'T HAVE...

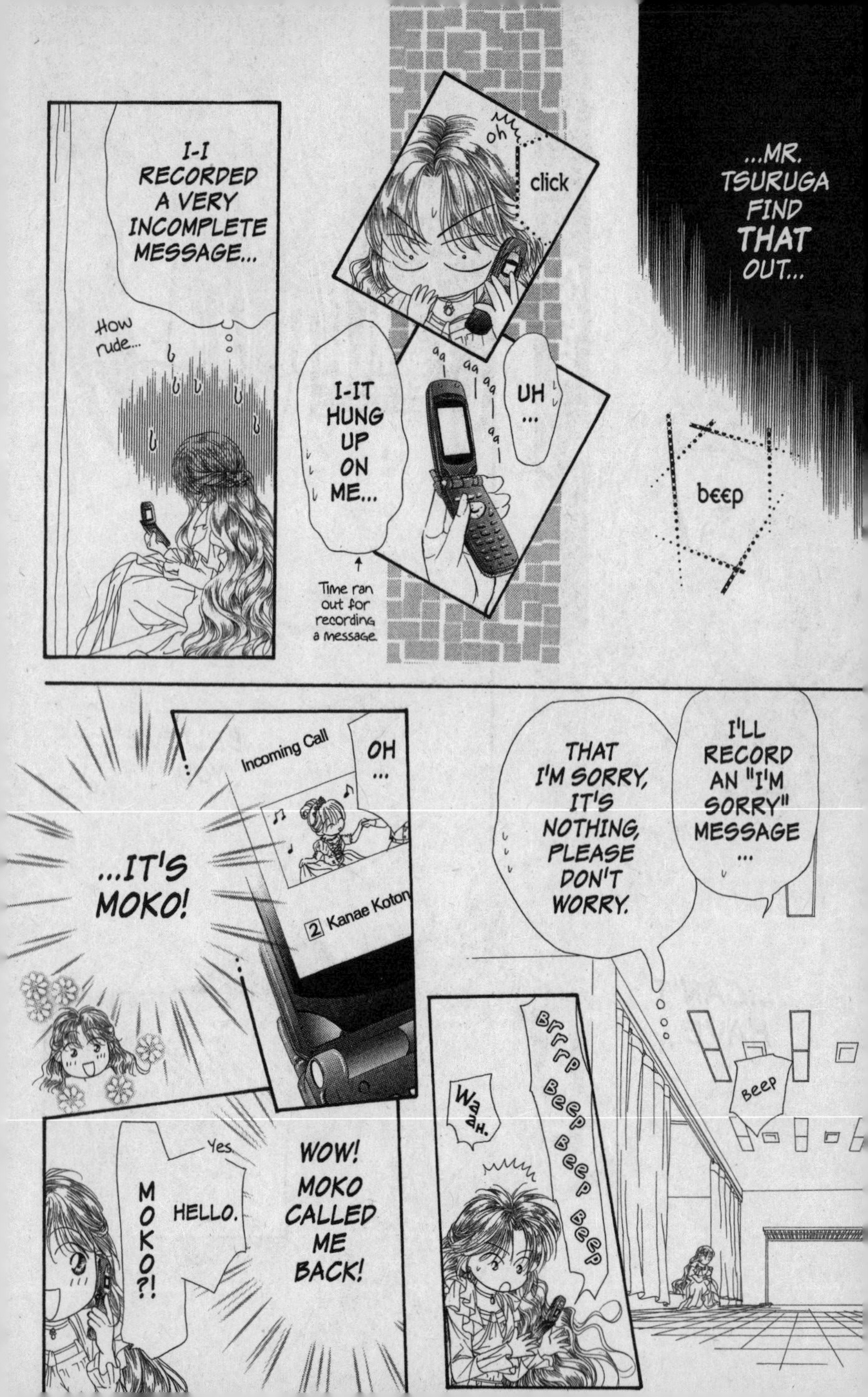
...MR. TSURUGA FIND THAT OUT...
bεεp
oh
click
UH ...
aa aa aa aa
I-IT HUNG UP ON ME...
Time ran out for recording a message.
I-I RECORDED A VERY INCOMPLETE MESSAGE...
How rude...
I'LL RECORD AN "I'M SORRY" MESSAGE ...
THAT I'M SORRY, IT'S NOTHING, PLEASE DON'T WORRY.
Beep
Brrrp Beep Beep Beep
Waah.
Incoming Call
2 Kanae Koton
OH ...
...IT'S MOKO!
WOW! MOKO CALLED ME BACK!
Yes.
HELLO.
MOKO?!

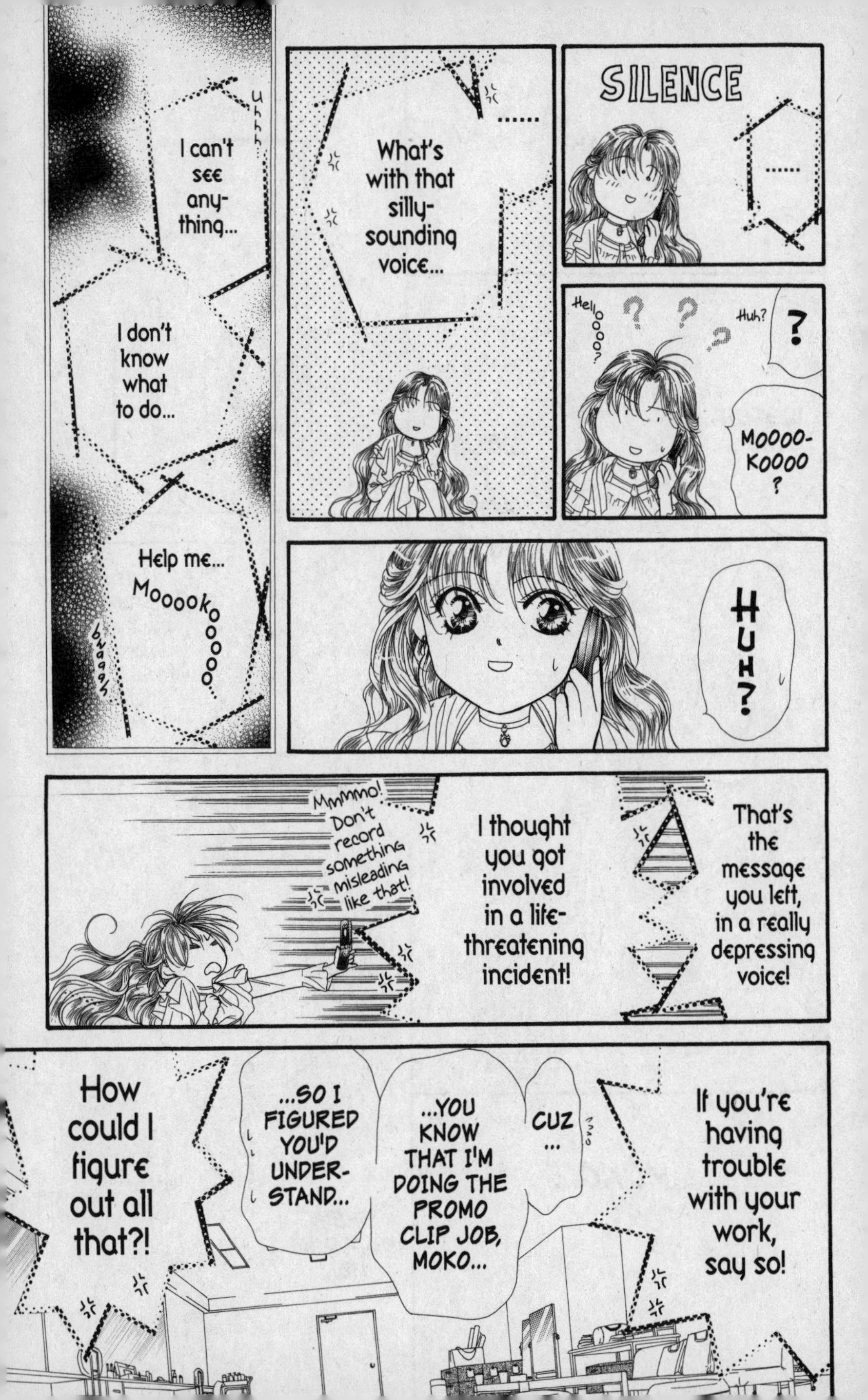
SILENCE
.....
?
Huh?
Hello0000?
MOOOO-KOOOO?
......
What's with that silly-sounding voice...
HUH?
Uhhh
I can't see anything...
I don't know what to do...
Help me... Mooookooooo
Bwaaah
That's the message you left, in a really depressing voice!
I thought you got involved in a life-threatening incident!
Mmmmo! Don't record something misleading like that!
If you're having trouble with your work, say so!
CUZ...
...YOU KNOW THAT I'M DOING THE PROMO CLIP JOB, MOKO...
...SO I FIGURED YOU'D UNDER-STAND...
How could I figure out all that?!

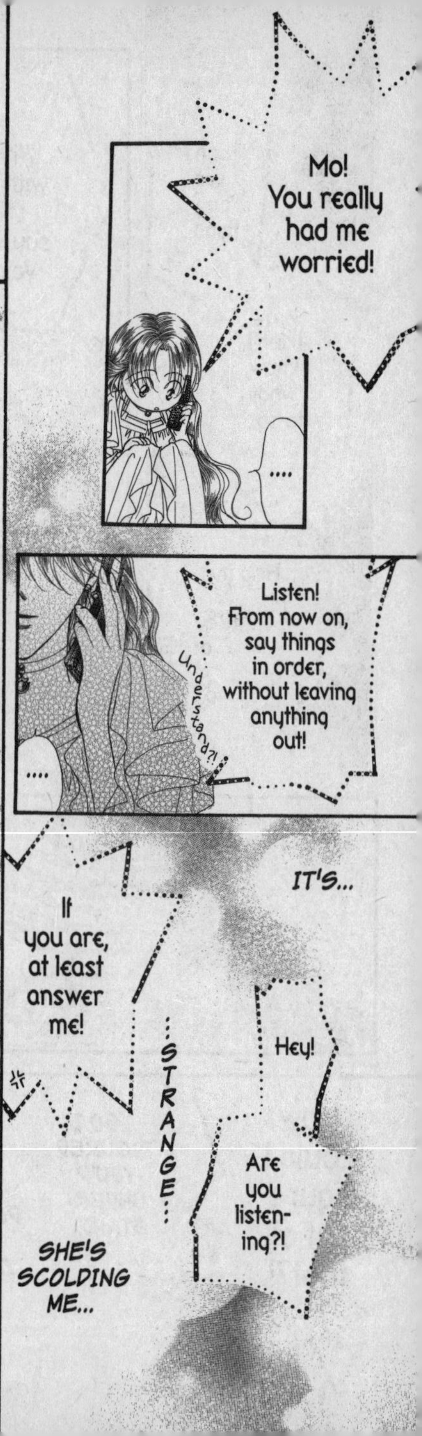
Mo! You really had me worried!
....
Listen! From now on, say things in order, without leaving anything out!
Understand?!
....
IT'S...
Hey!
Are you listening?!
If you are, at least answer me!
...STRANGE...
SHE'S SCOLDING ME...

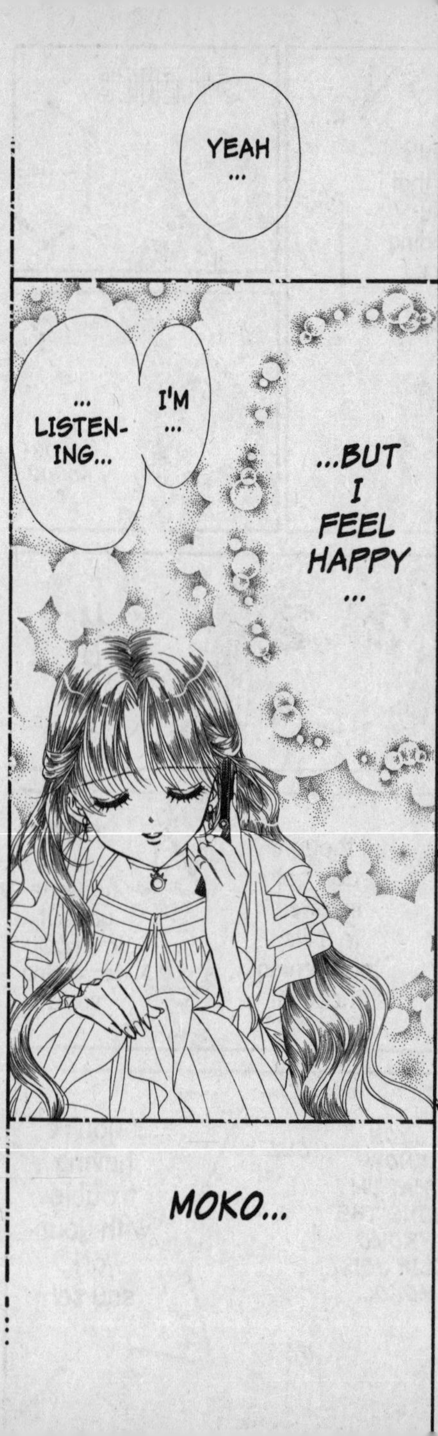
YEAH ...
...BUT I FEEL HAPPY ...
I'M ...
... LISTENING...
MOKO...

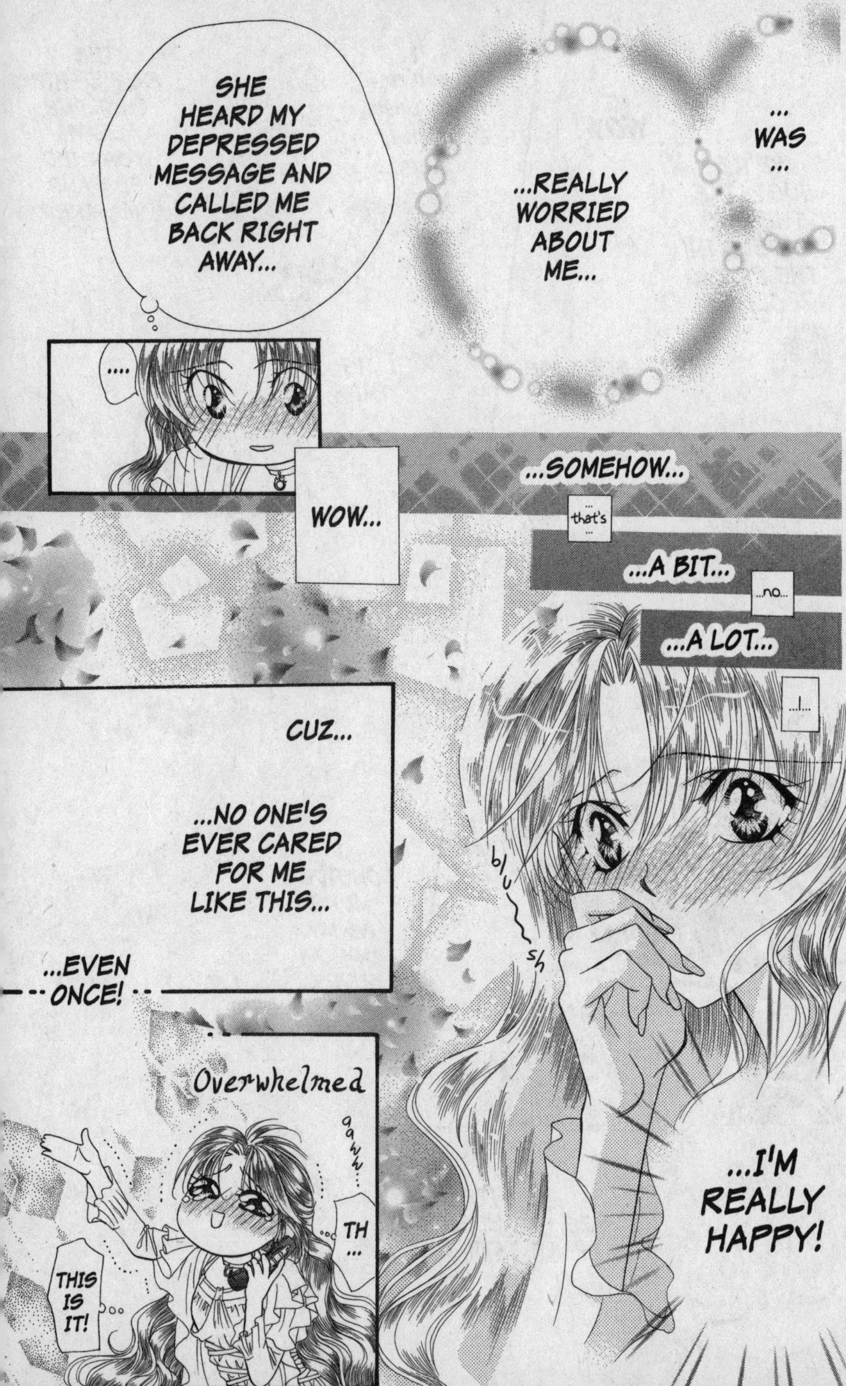

...WAS...
...REALLY WORRIED ABOUT ME...
SHE HEARD MY DEPRESSED MESSAGE AND CALLED ME BACK RIGHT AWAY...
....
...SOMEHOW...
...that's...
...A BIT...
...no...
...A LOT...
...I...
blush
...I'M REALLY HAPPY!
WOW...
CUZ...
...NO ONE'S EVER CARED FOR ME LIKE THIS...
...EVEN ONCE!
Overwhelmed
aaww...
TH...
THIS IS IT!

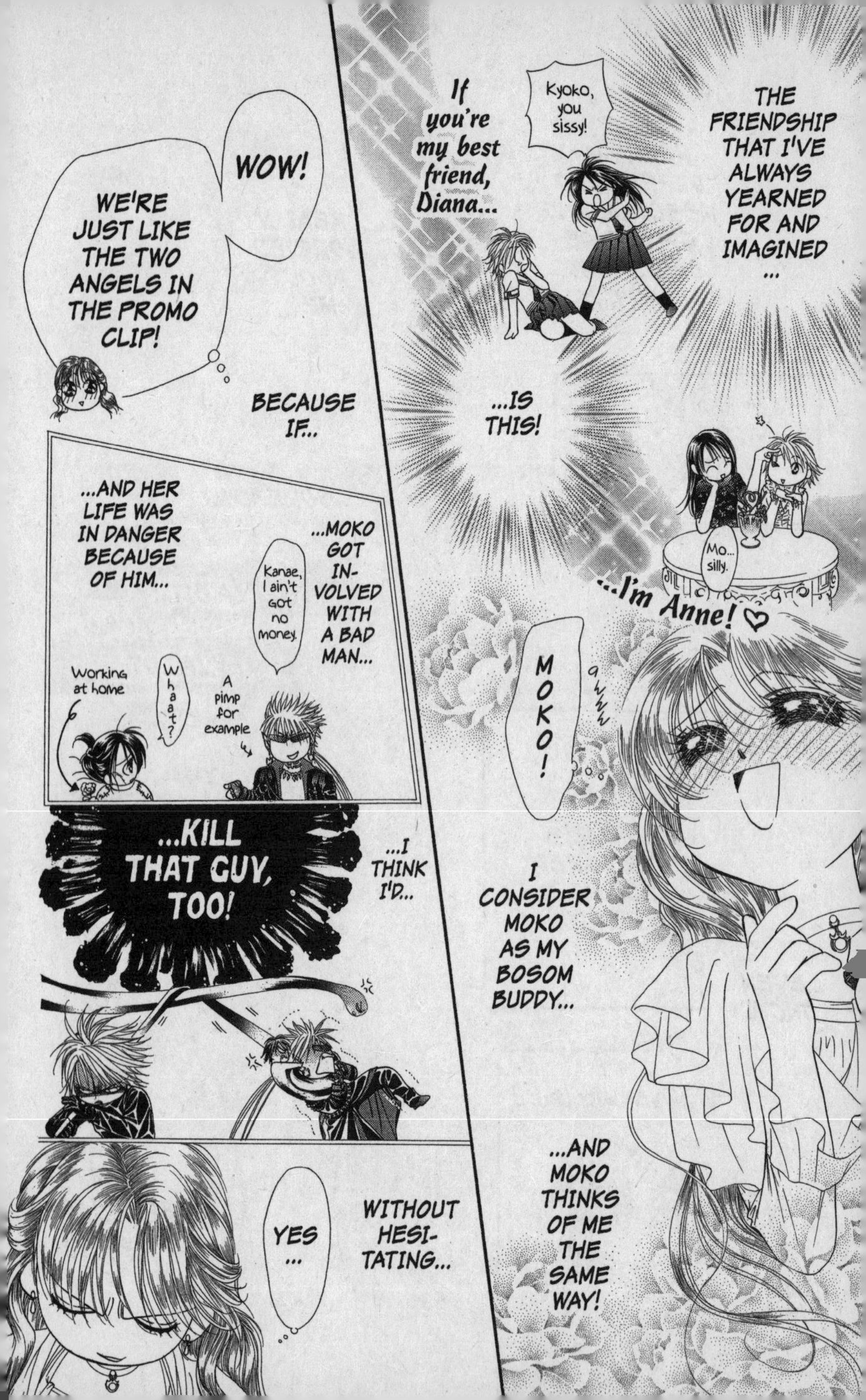
THE FRIENDSHIP THAT I'VE ALWAYS YEARNED FOR AND IMAGINED ...
Kyoko, you sissy!
If you're my best friend, Diana...
...IS THIS!
Mo... silly.
...I'm Anne! ♡
MOKO!
I CONSIDER MOKO AS MY BOSOM BUDDY...
...AND MOKO THINKS OF ME THE SAME WAY!
WOW!
WE'RE JUST LIKE THE TWO ANGELS IN THE PROMO CLIP!
BECAUSE IF...
...MOKO GOT IN-VOLVED WITH A BAD MAN...
Kanae, I ain't got no money.
...AND HER LIFE WAS IN DANGER BECAUSE OF HIM...
A pimp for example
Whaat?
Working at home
...I THINK I'D...
...KILL THAT GUY, TOO!
WITHOUT HESI-TATING...
YES...

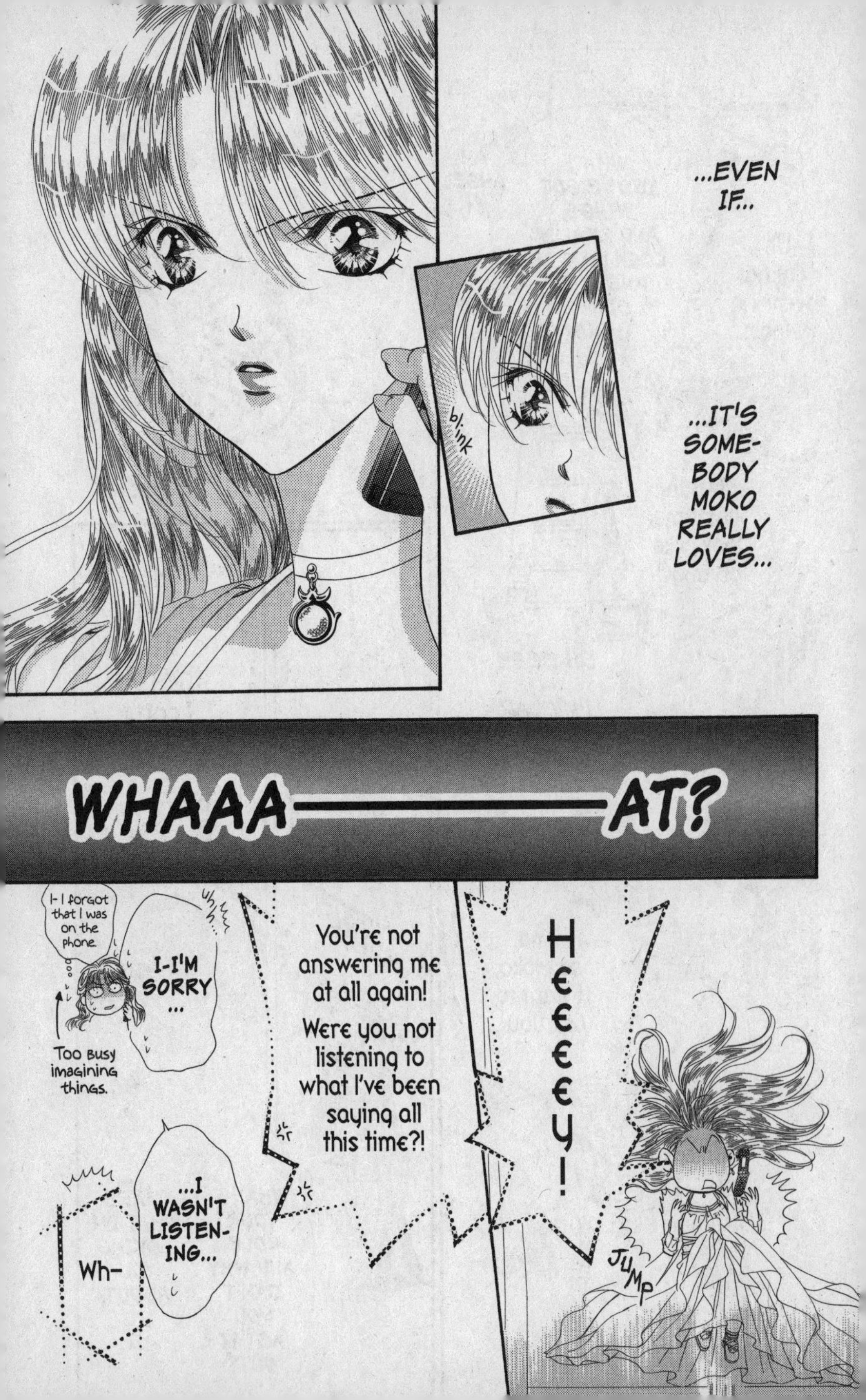

...EVEN IF...
...IT'S SOMEBODY MOKO REALLY LOVES...
blink
WHAAA——AT?
HEEEEY!
JUMP
You're not answering me at all again! Were you not listening to what I've been saying all this time?!
I-I'M SORRY...
I-I forgot that I was on the phone.
Too busy imagining things.
...I WASN'T LISTENING...
Wh-

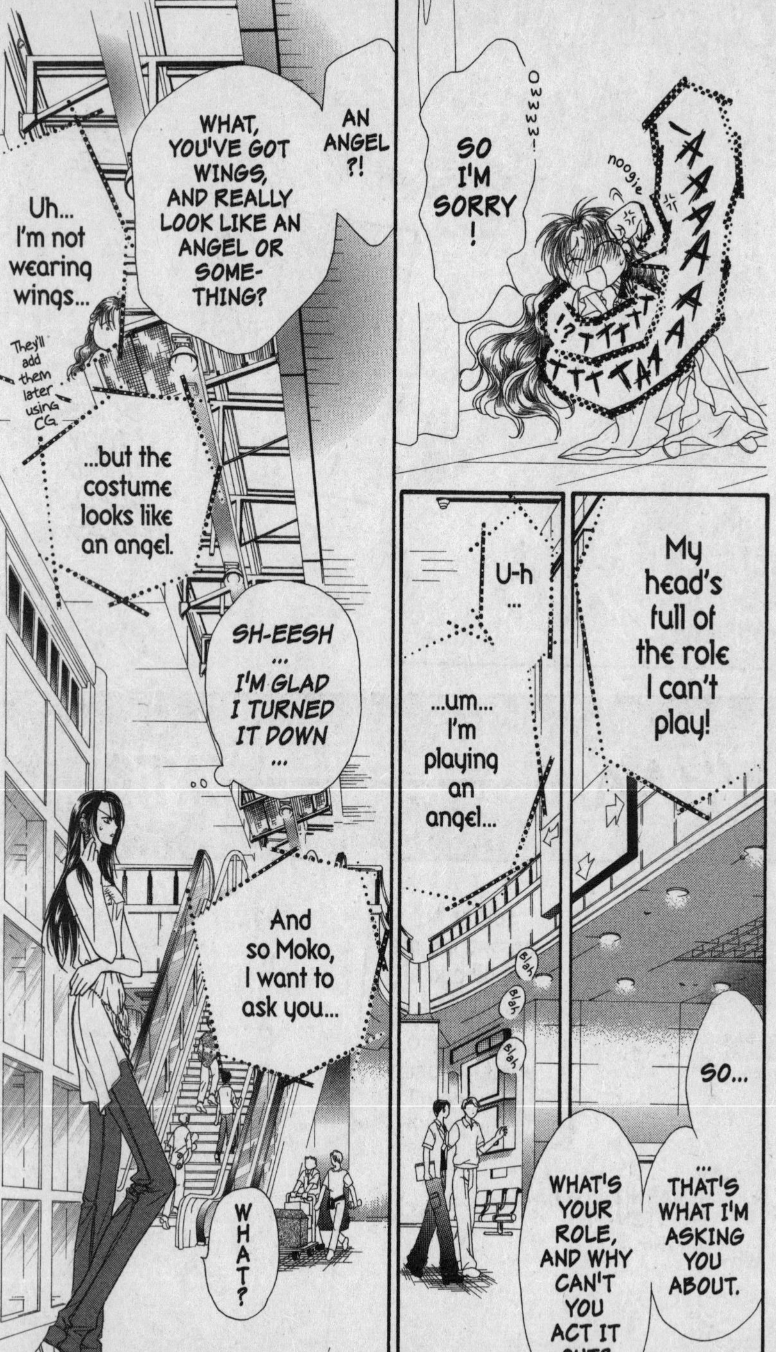
OWWWW!
SO I'M SORRY!
noogie
-AAAAAAAA
!? TTTTT TTTTTA
My head's full of the role I can't play!
U-h...
...um... I'm playing an angel...
Blah
Blah
Blah
SO...
...THAT'S WHAT I'M ASKING YOU ABOUT.
WHAT'S YOUR ROLE, AND WHY CAN'T YOU ACT IT OUT?
AN ANGEL?!
WHAT, YOU'VE GOT WINGS, AND REALLY LOOK LIKE AN ANGEL OR SOME-THING?
Uh... I'm not wearing wings...
They'll add them later using CG.
...but the costume looks like an angel.
SH-EESH... I'M GLAD I TURNED IT DOWN...
And so Moko, I want to ask you...
WHAT?

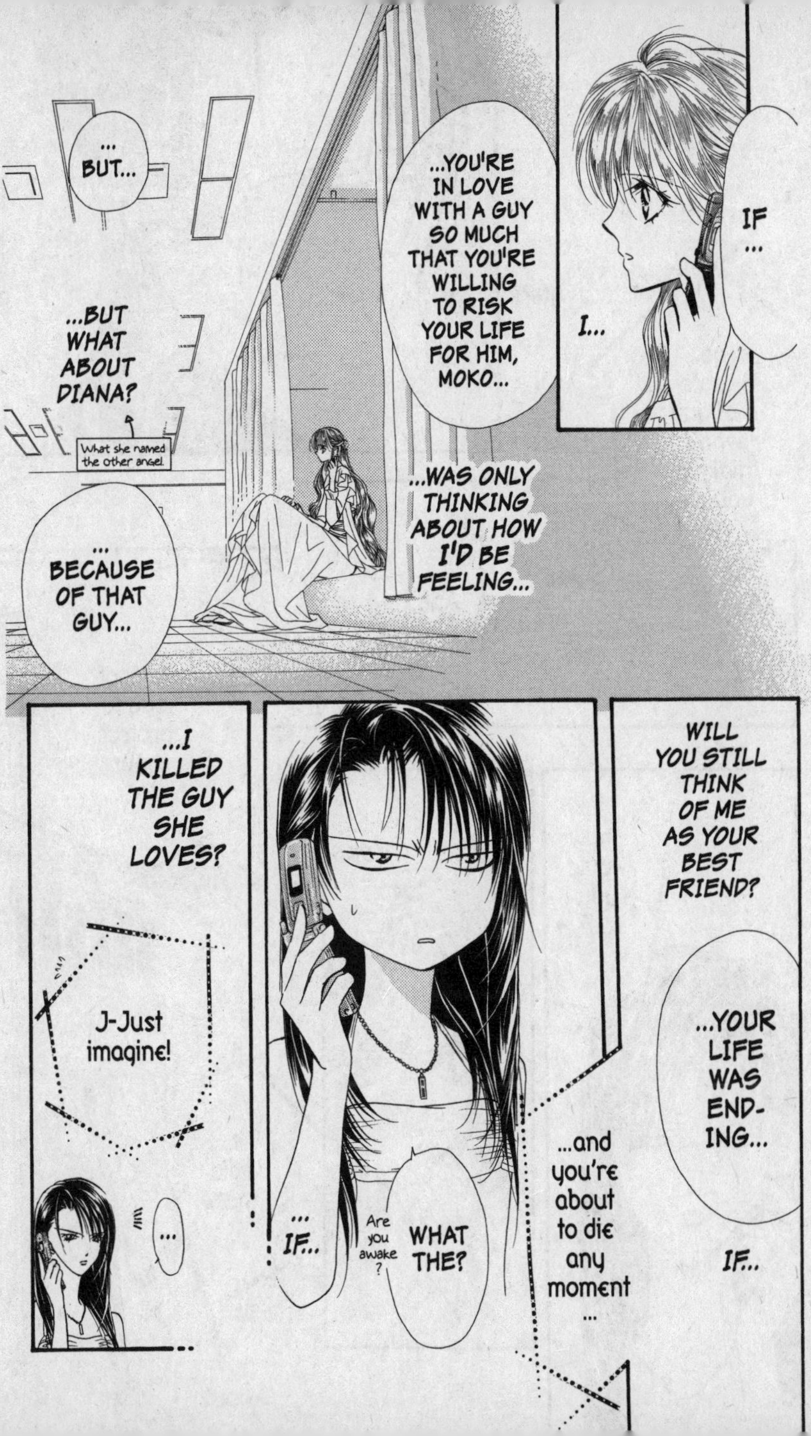
IF...
I...
...YOU'RE IN LOVE WITH A GUY SO MUCH THAT YOU'RE WILLING TO RISK YOUR LIFE FOR HIM, MOKO...
...WAS ONLY THINKING ABOUT HOW I'D BE FEELING...
... BUT...
...BUT WHAT ABOUT DIANA?
What she named the other angel.
... BECAUSE OF THAT GUY...
WILL YOU STILL THINK OF ME AS YOUR BEST FRIEND?
...YOUR LIFE WAS END-ING...
IF...
...and you're about to die any moment ...
WHAT THE?
Are you awake?
... IF...
...I KILLED THE GUY SHE LOVES?
J-Just imagine!
...

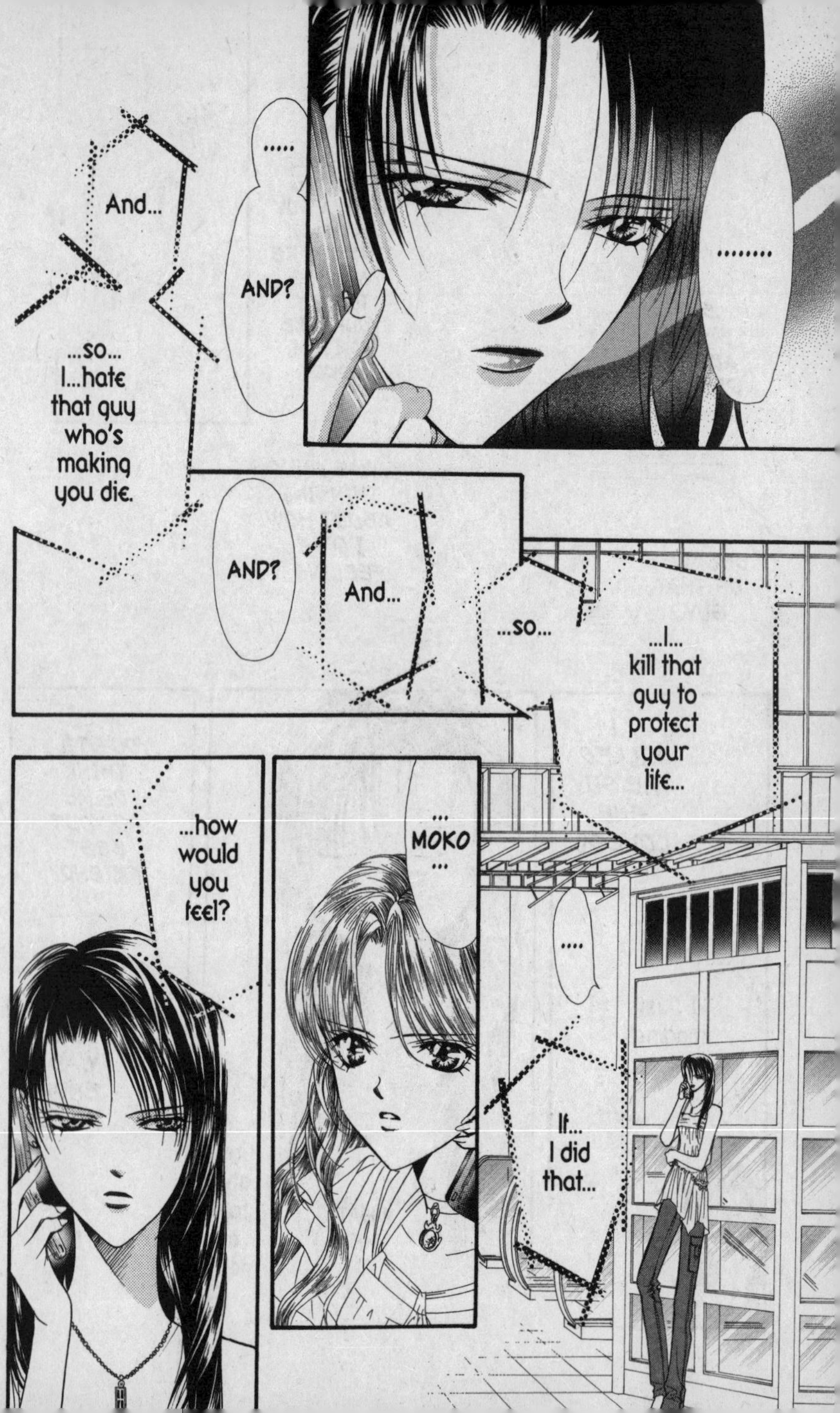
....
.....
AND?
And...
...so... I...hate that guy who's making you die.
AND?
And...
...so...
...I... kill that guy to protect your life...
....
If... I did that...
...MOKO...
...how would you feel?

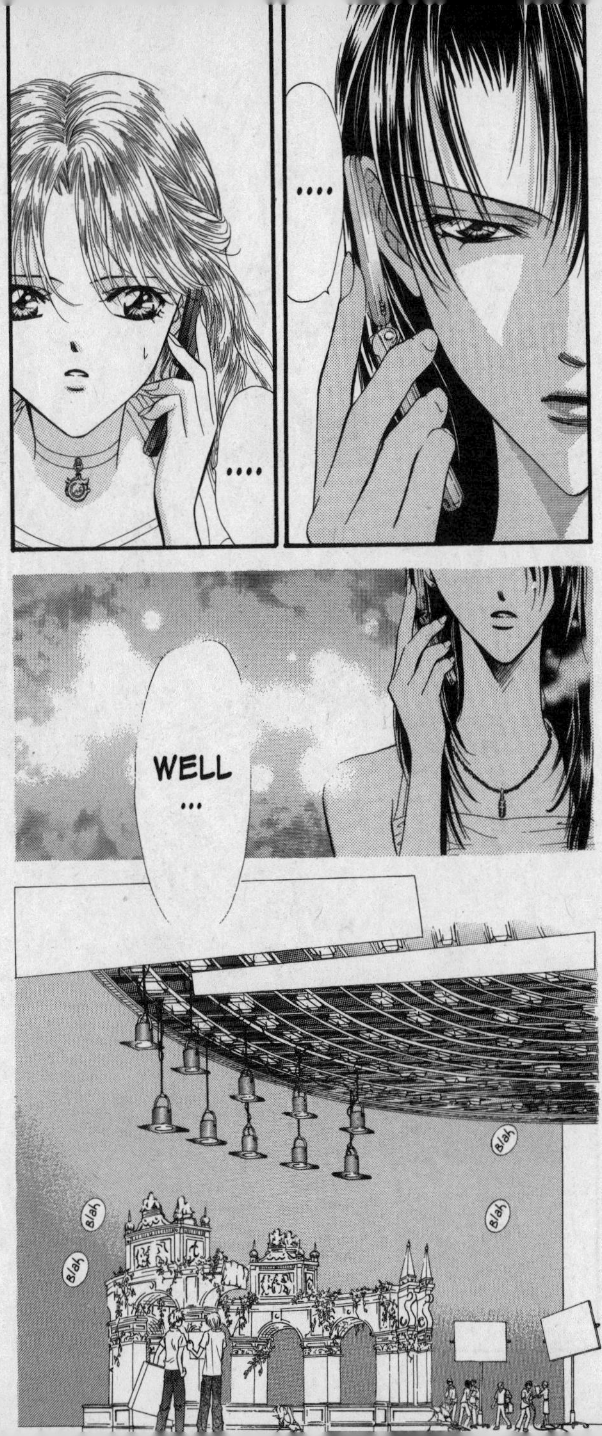
....
....
WELL ...
Blah
Blah
Blah
Blah

When I was drawing the promo clip arc, I was thinking that I wanted to do a little... of the devil version of Ren...But...I did it, But Sho looks Better in something like that..No...it's not just this time, But I always have trouble deciding what clothes Ren should wear in the story...Sho looks Good in anything, But with Ren, that doesn't work...(like Gaudy decorative stuff...)The range of clothes that he looks Good in is very narrow... especially summer clothes...I can only make him wear really simple clothes, and that's inconvenient...so with the devil Ren, the design of the clothes and accessories are very simple compared to Sho's...therefore, he doesn't look like a devil too much... oh dear... ...it's just a cosplay... ...one more thing I wanted to do was have Kanae wear the angel costume that Kyoko wore... if Kanae had accepted that job, Kanae would have worn the costume Kyoko wore...

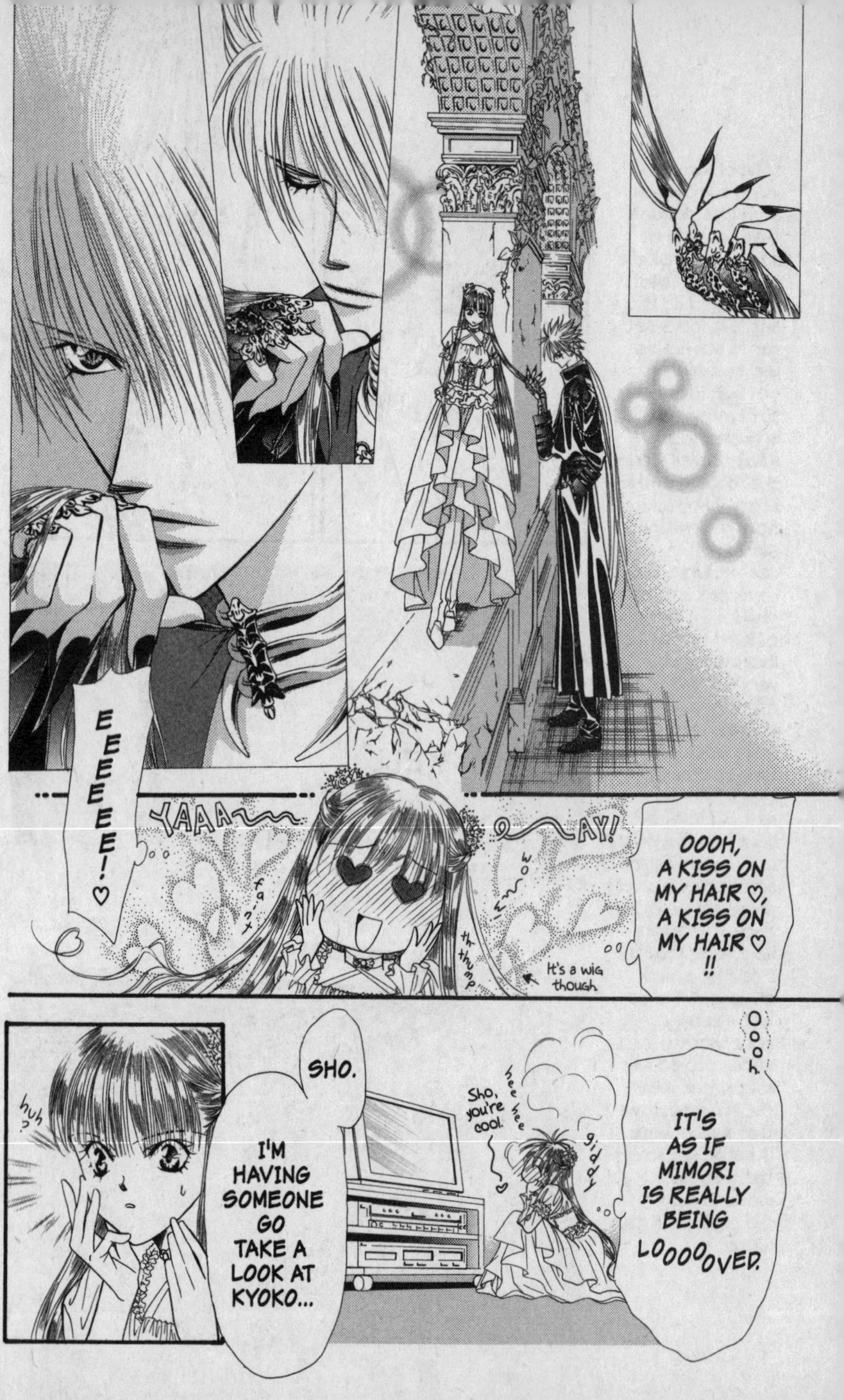
EEEEEE!♡
OOOH, A KISS ON MY HAIR ♡, A KISS ON MY HAIR ♡ !!
It's a wig though.
AY!
YAAA
faint
th-thump
Oooh
IT'S AS IF MIMORI IS REALLY BEING LOOOOOVED.
giddy
Sho, you're cool.
hee hee
SHO.
I'M HAVING SOMEONE GO TAKE A LOOK AT KYOKO...
huh?

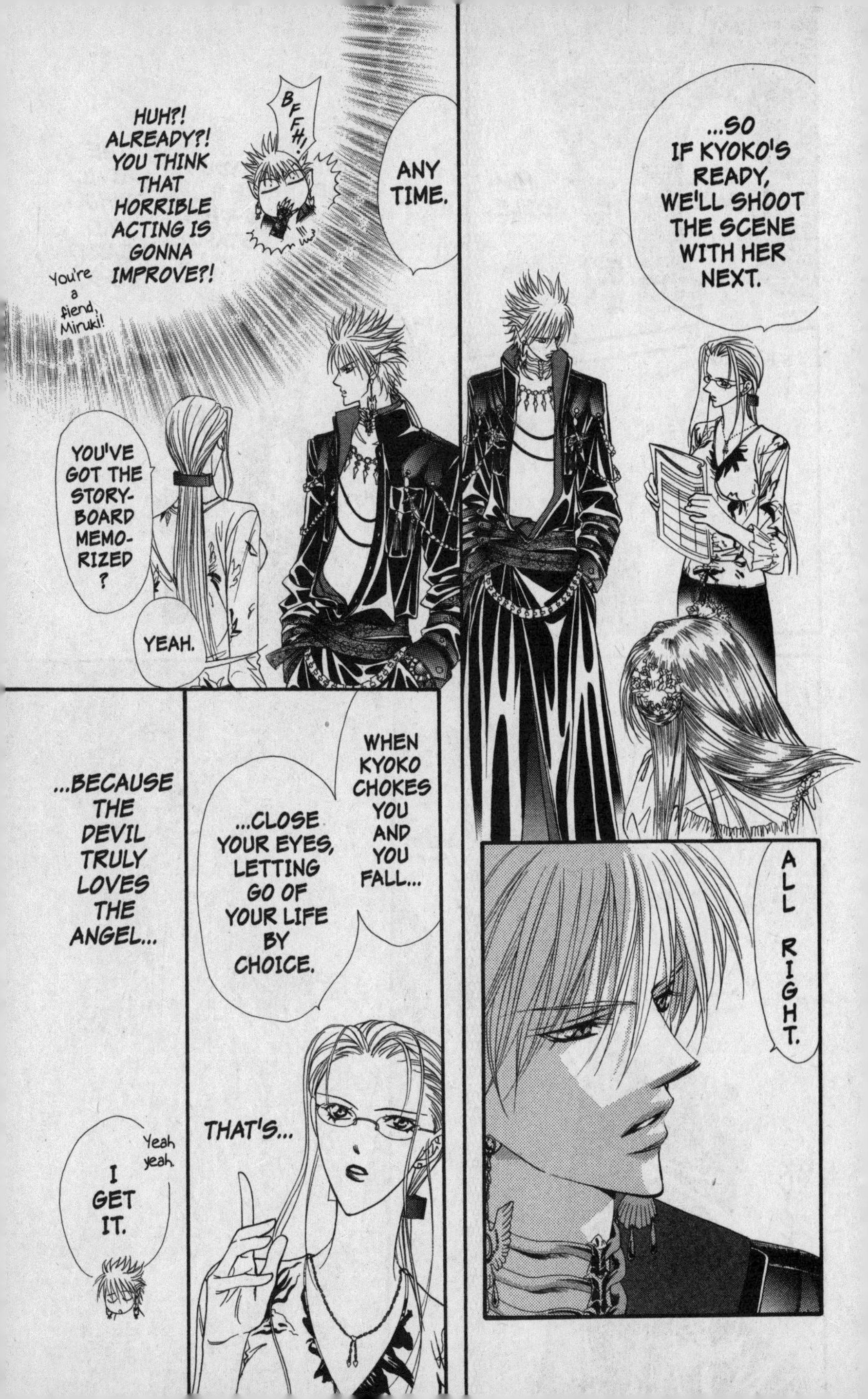
...SO IF KYOKO'S READY, WE'LL SHOOT THE SCENE WITH HER NEXT.
ANY TIME.
BFFH!!
HUH?! ALREADY?! YOU THINK THAT HORRIBLE ACTING IS GONNA IMPROVE?!
You're a fiend, Miruki!
YOU'VE GOT THE STORY-BOARD MEMO-RIZED?
YEAH.
WHEN KYOKO CHOKES YOU AND YOU FALL...
...CLOSE YOUR EYES, LETTING GO OF YOUR LIFE BY CHOICE.
THAT'S...
...BECAUSE THE DEVIL TRULY LOVES THE ANGEL...
I GET IT.
Yeah yeah.
ALL RIGHT.

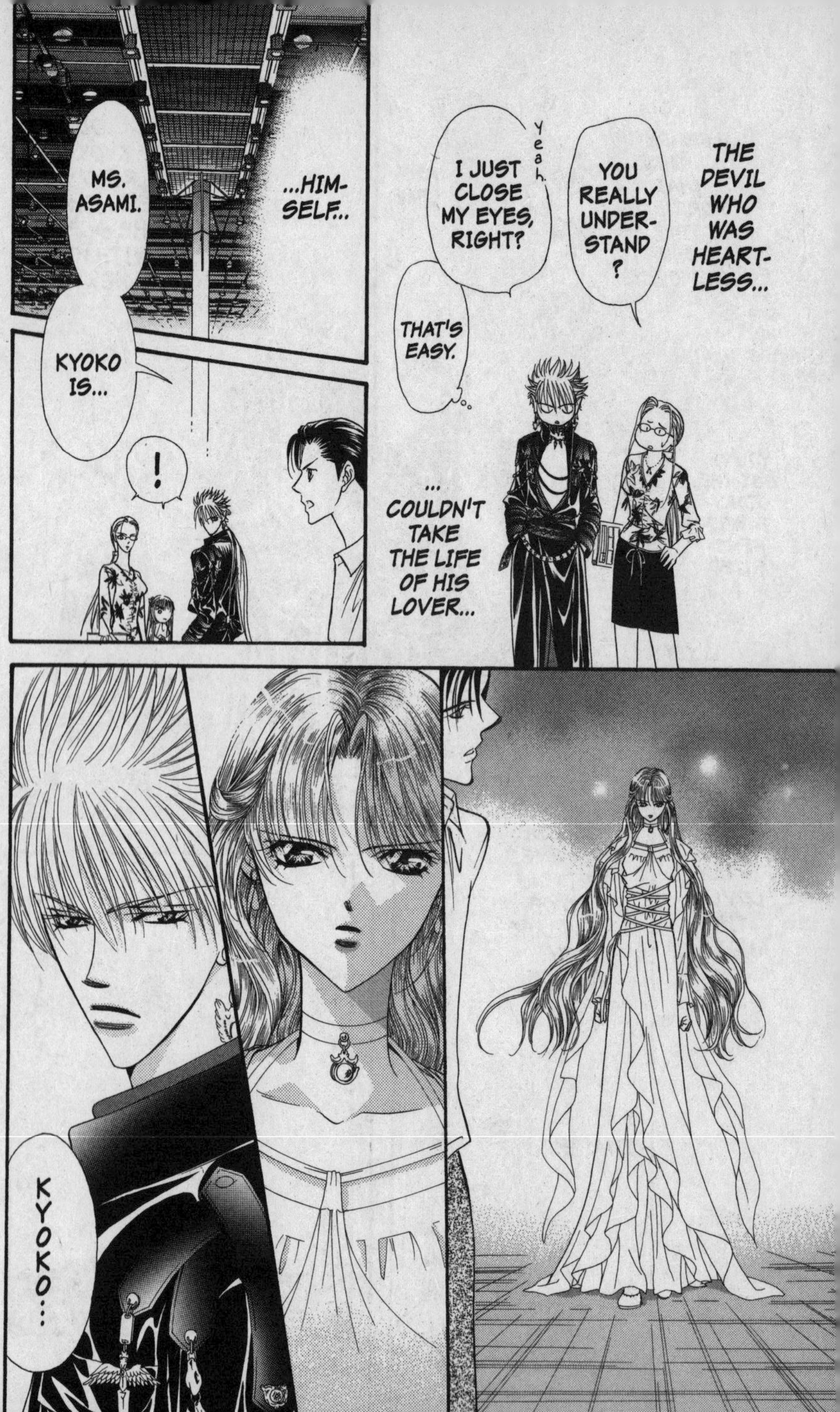
THE DEVIL WHO WAS HEARTLESS...
YOU REALLY UNDERSTAND?
Yeah.
I JUST CLOSE MY EYES, RIGHT?
THAT'S EASY.
...COULDN'T TAKE THE LIFE OF HIS LOVER...
...HIMSELF...
MS. ASAMI.
KYOKO IS...
!
KYOKO...

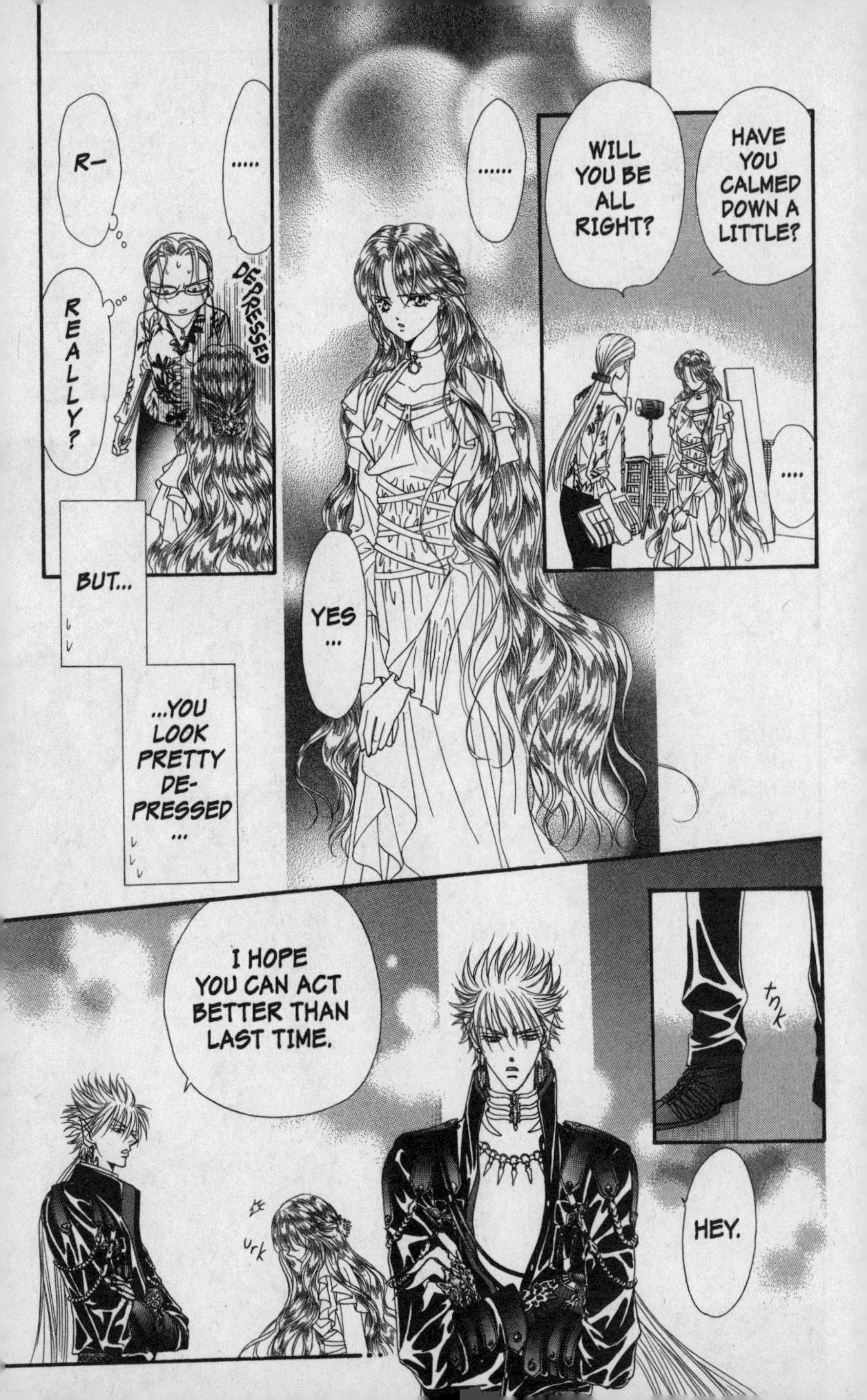

HAVE YOU CALMED DOWN A LITTLE?
WILL YOU BE ALL RIGHT?
....
......
YES ...
......
R—
REALLY?
DEPRESSED
BUT...
...YOU LOOK PRETTY DE-PRESSED ...
HEY.
I HOPE YOU CAN ACT BETTER THAN LAST TIME.
urk

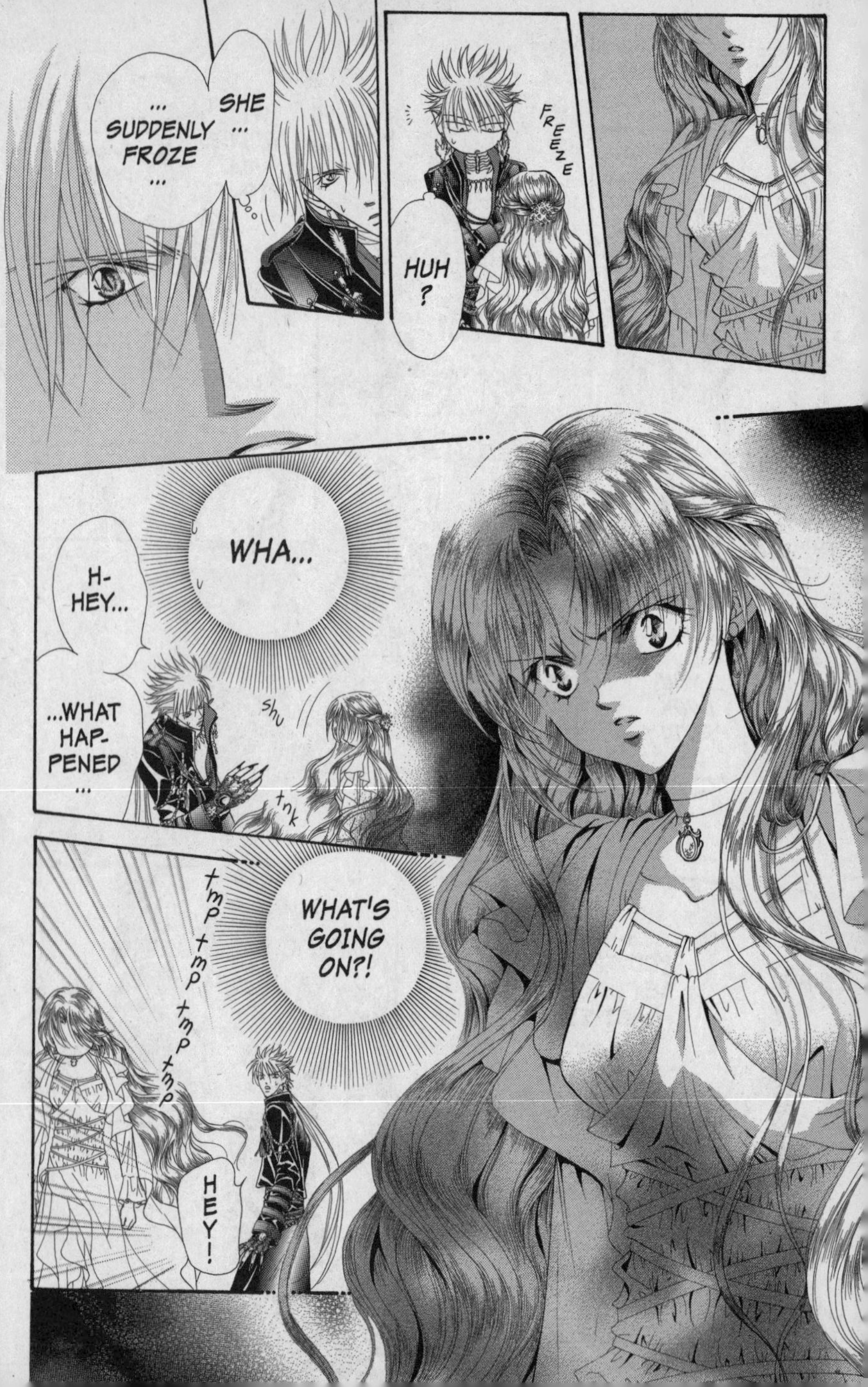
FREEZE
HUH?
SHE ...
... SUDDENLY FROZE ...
WHA...
H-HEY...
...WHAT HAPPENED ...
shu
tnk
WHAT'S GOING ON?!
tmp tmp tmp tmp tmp
HEY!

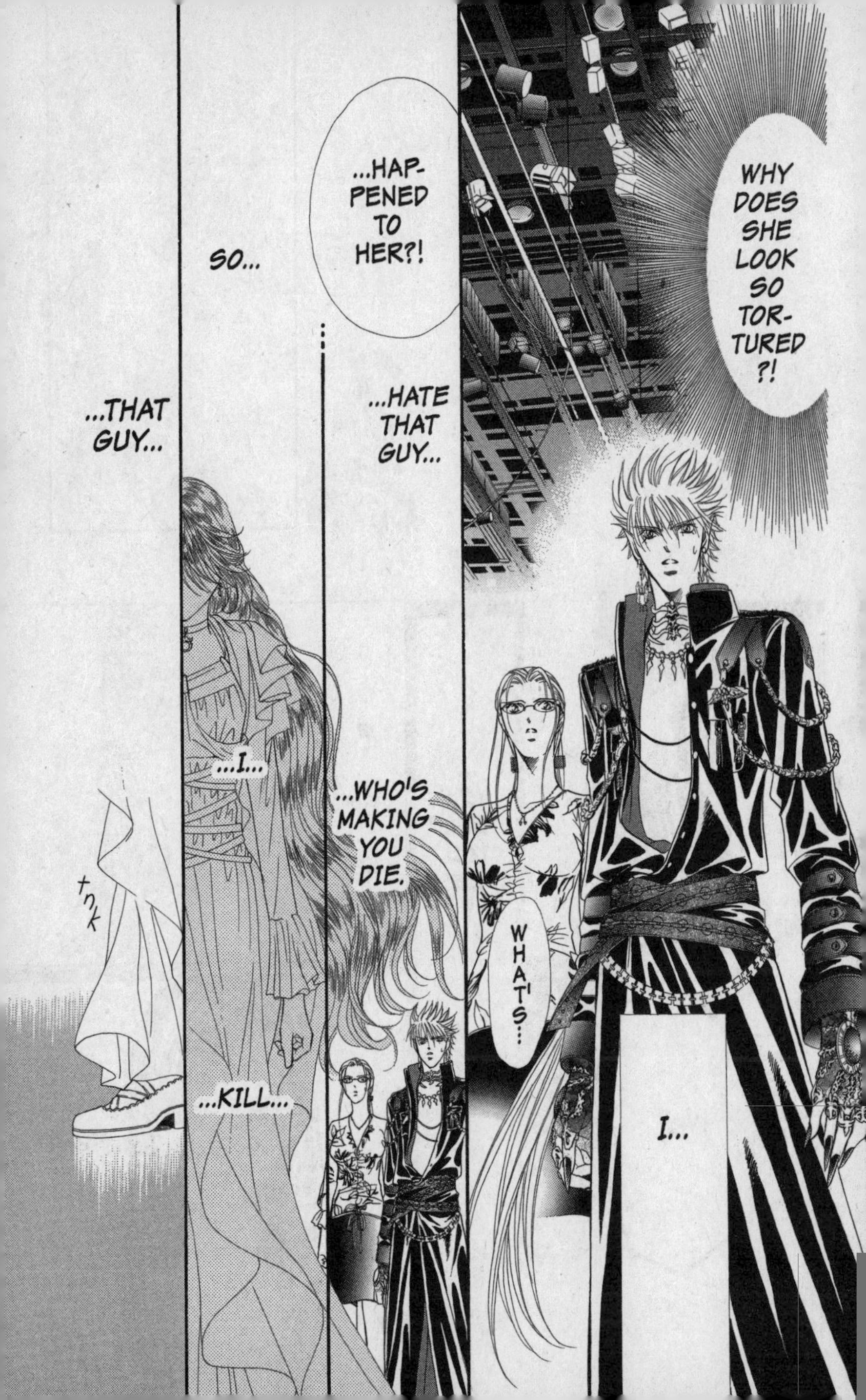
WHY DOES SHE LOOK SO TOR-TURED?!
WHAT'S...
I...
...HAP-PENED TO HER?!
...HATE THAT GUY...
...WHO'S MAKING YOU DIE.
SO...
...I...
...KILL...
...THAT GUY...
tnk

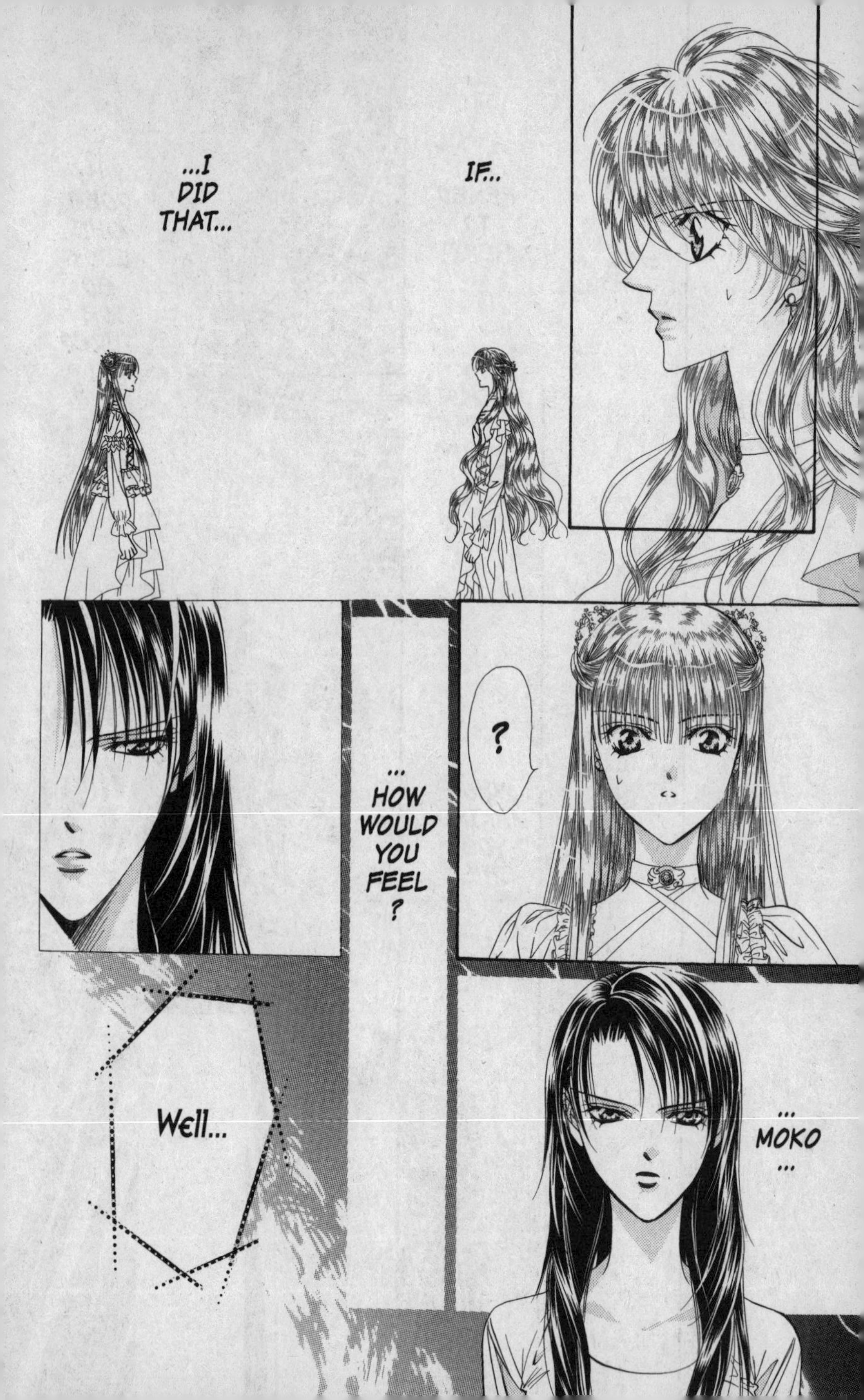
IF...
...I DID THAT...
?
...HOW WOULD YOU FEEL?
...MOKO...
Well...

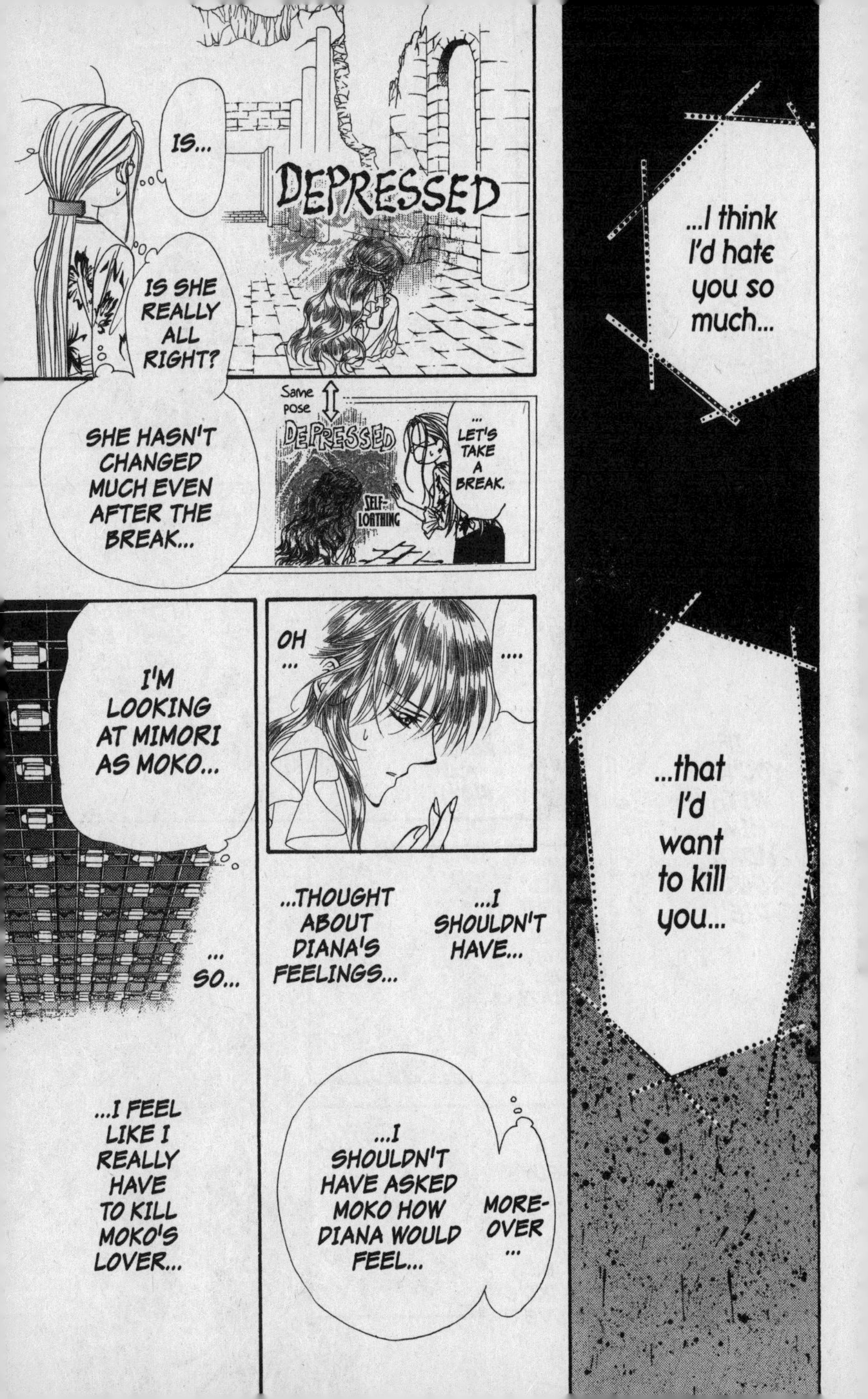
...I think I'd hate you so much...
...that I'd want to kill you...
IS...
DEPRESSED
IS SHE REALLY ALL RIGHT?
Same pose
DEPRESSED
... LET'S TAKE A BREAK.
SELF-LOATHING
SHE HASN'T CHANGED MUCH EVEN AFTER THE BREAK...
....
OH...
...I SHOULDN'T HAVE...
...THOUGHT ABOUT DIANA'S FEELINGS...
MORE-OVER...
...I SHOULDN'T HAVE ASKED MOKO HOW DIANA WOULD FEEL...
I'M LOOKING AT MIMORI AS MOKO...
...SO...
...I FEEL LIKE I REALLY HAVE TO KILL MOKO'S LOVER...

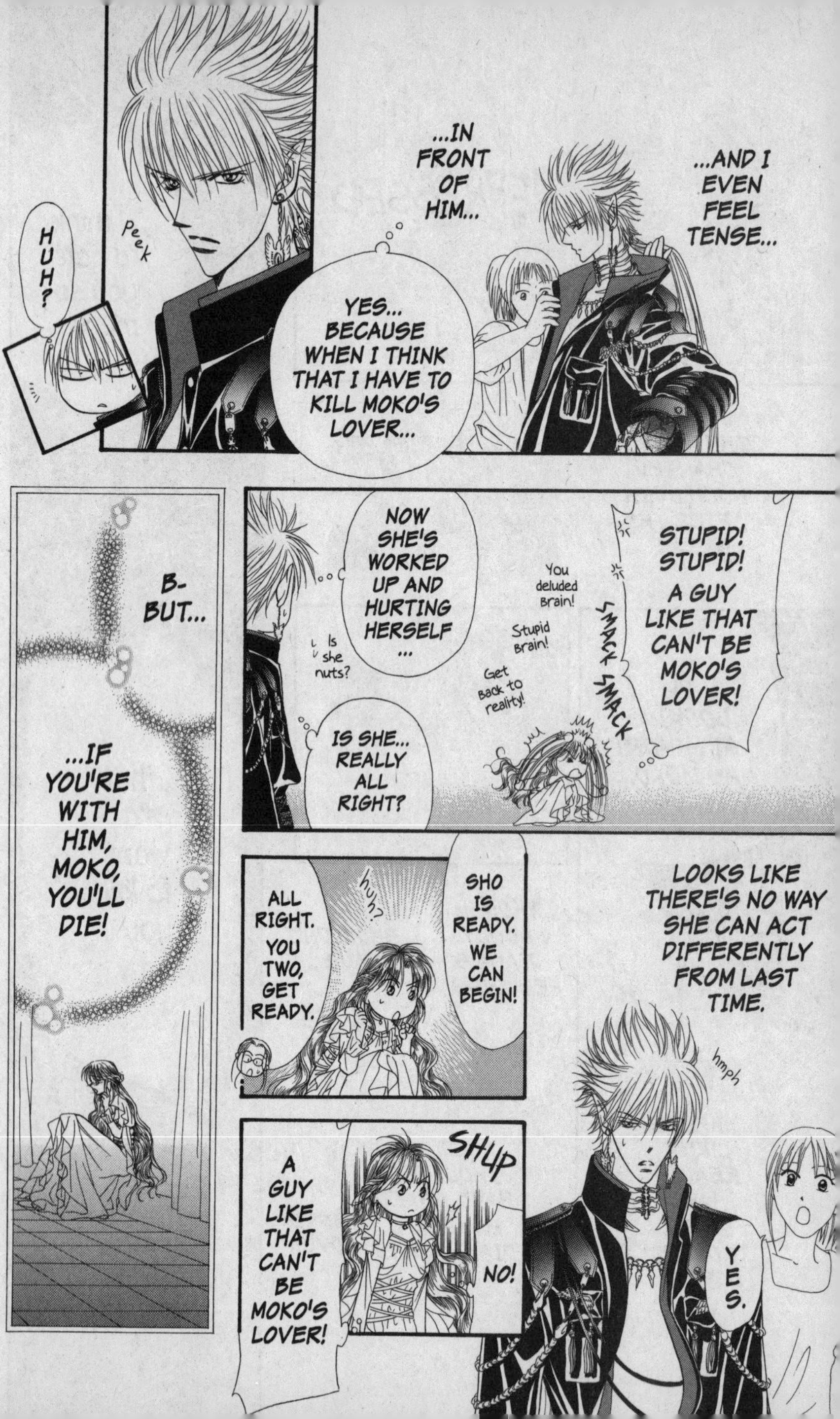
...AND I EVEN FEEL TENSE...
...IN FRONT OF HIM...
YES... BECAUSE WHEN I THINK THAT I HAVE TO KILL MOKO'S LOVER...
Peek
HUH?
STUPID! STUPID! A GUY LIKE THAT CAN'T BE MOKO'S LOVER!
SMACK SMACK
You deluded Brain!
Stupid Brain!
Get back to reality!
NOW SHE'S WORKED UP AND HURTING HERSELF...
Is she nuts?
IS SHE... REALLY ALL RIGHT?
LOOKS LIKE THERE'S NO WAY SHE CAN ACT DIFFERENTLY FROM LAST TIME.
hmph
SHO IS READY. WE CAN BEGIN!
huh?
ALL RIGHT. YOU TWO, GET READY.
YES.
NO!
SHUP
A GUY LIKE THAT CAN'T BE MOKO'S LOVER!
B-BUT...
...IF YOU'RE WITH HIM, MOKO, YOU'LL DIE!

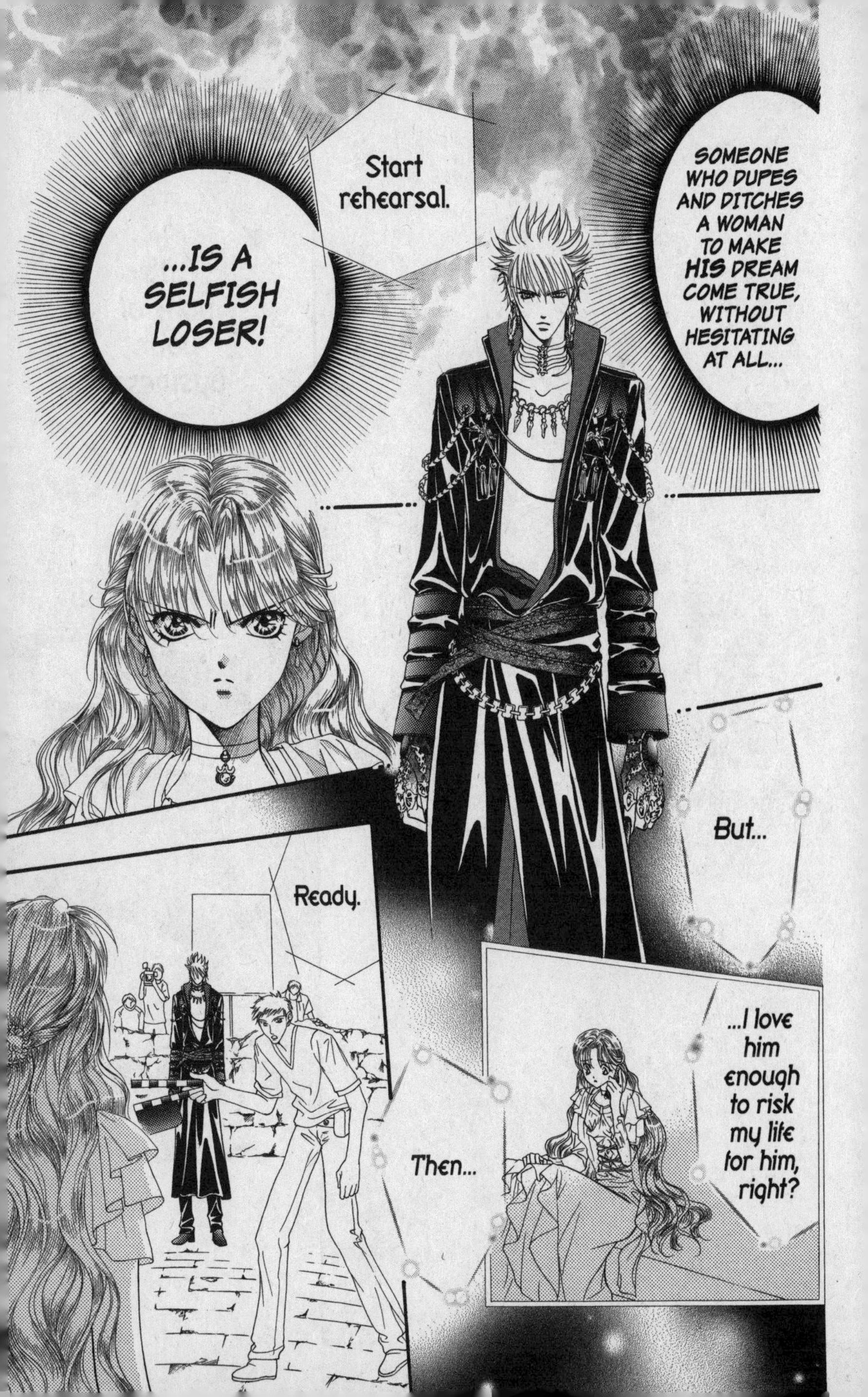

SOMEONE WHO DUPES AND DITCHES A WOMAN TO MAKE HIS DREAM COME TRUE, WITHOUT HESITATING AT ALL...
Start rehearsal.
...IS A SELFISH LOSER!
But...
...I love him enough to risk my life for him, right?
Then...
Ready.

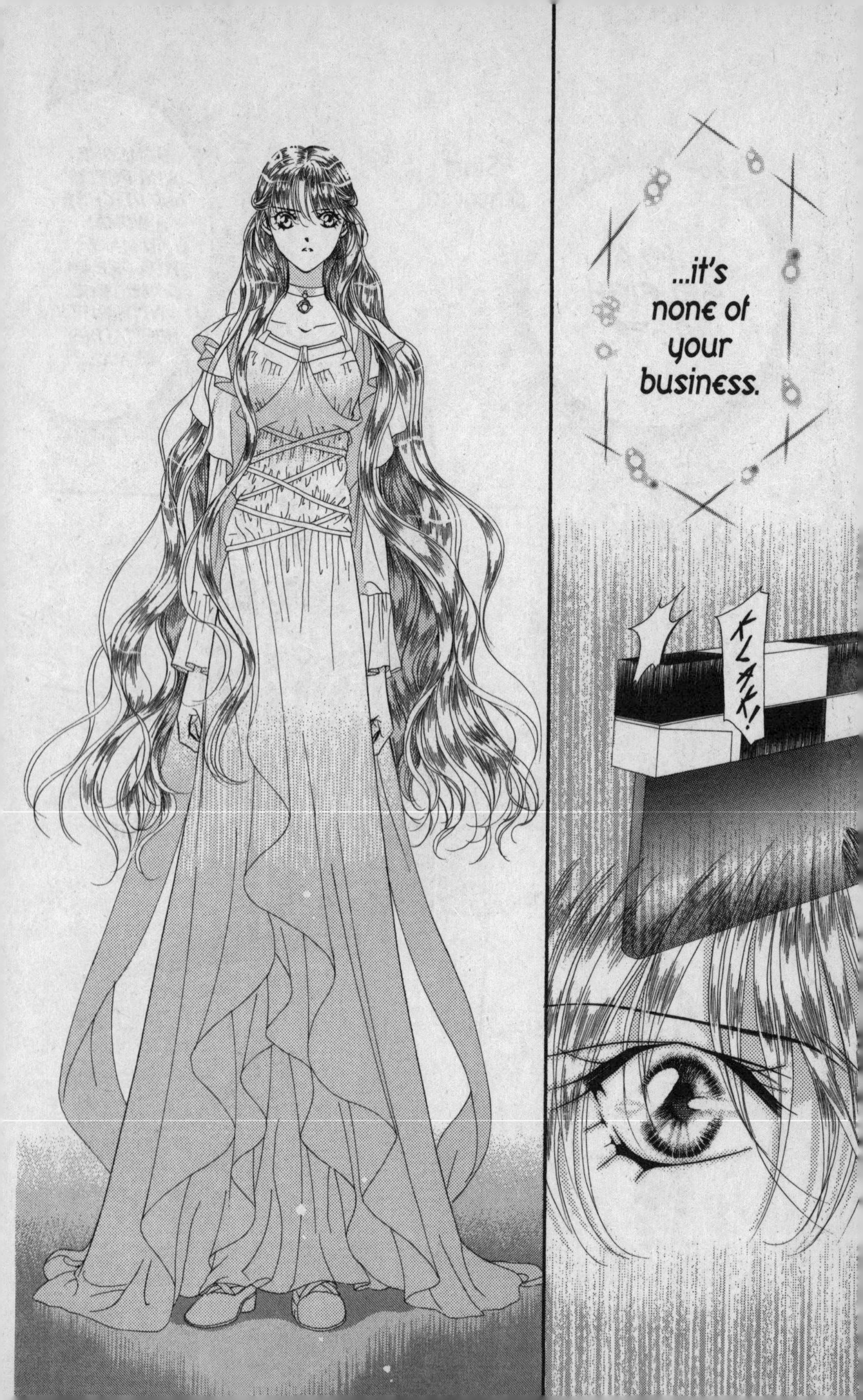
...it's none of your business.
KLAK!

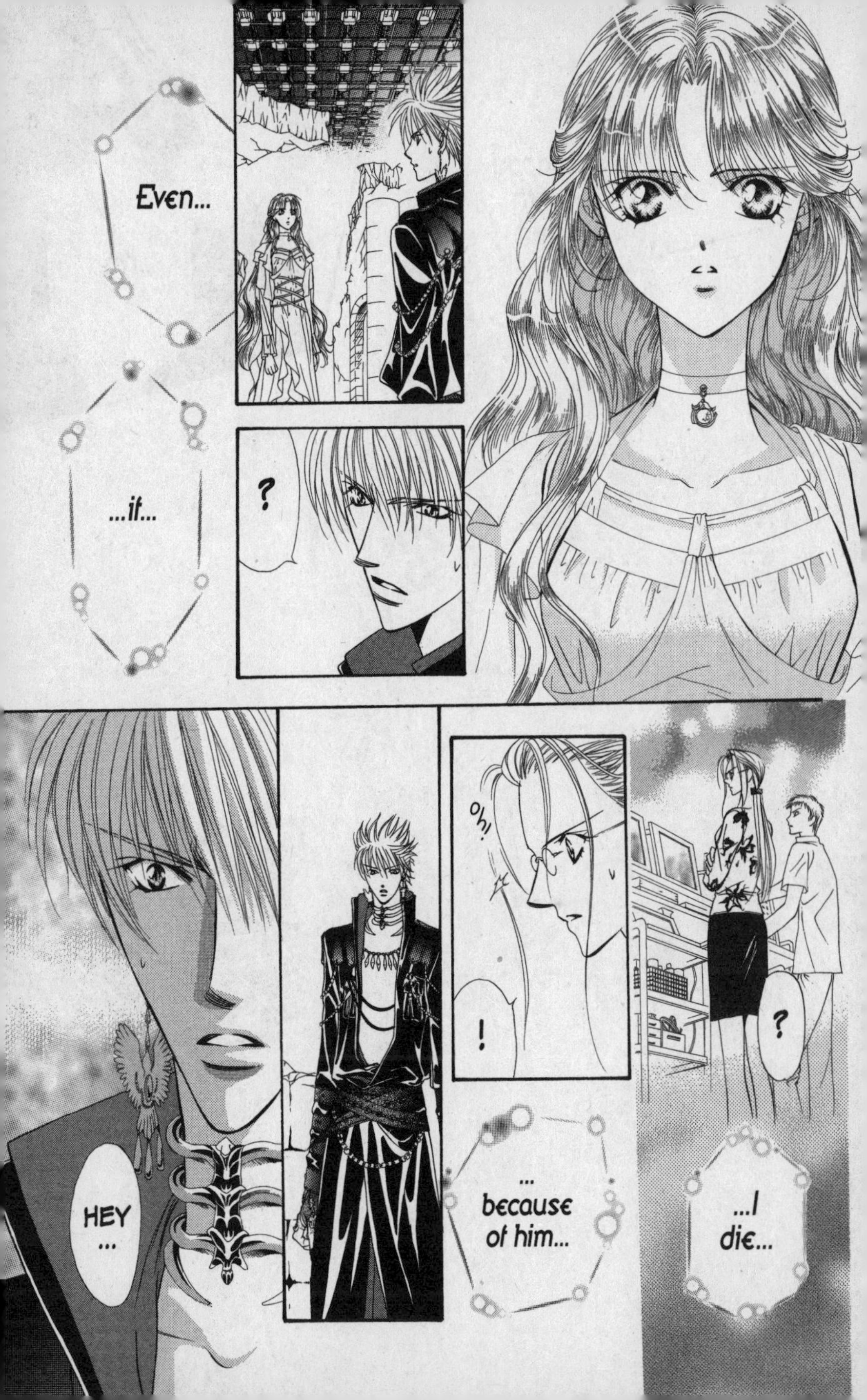
?
Even...
...if...
?
...I die...
oh!
!
... because of him...
HEY ...

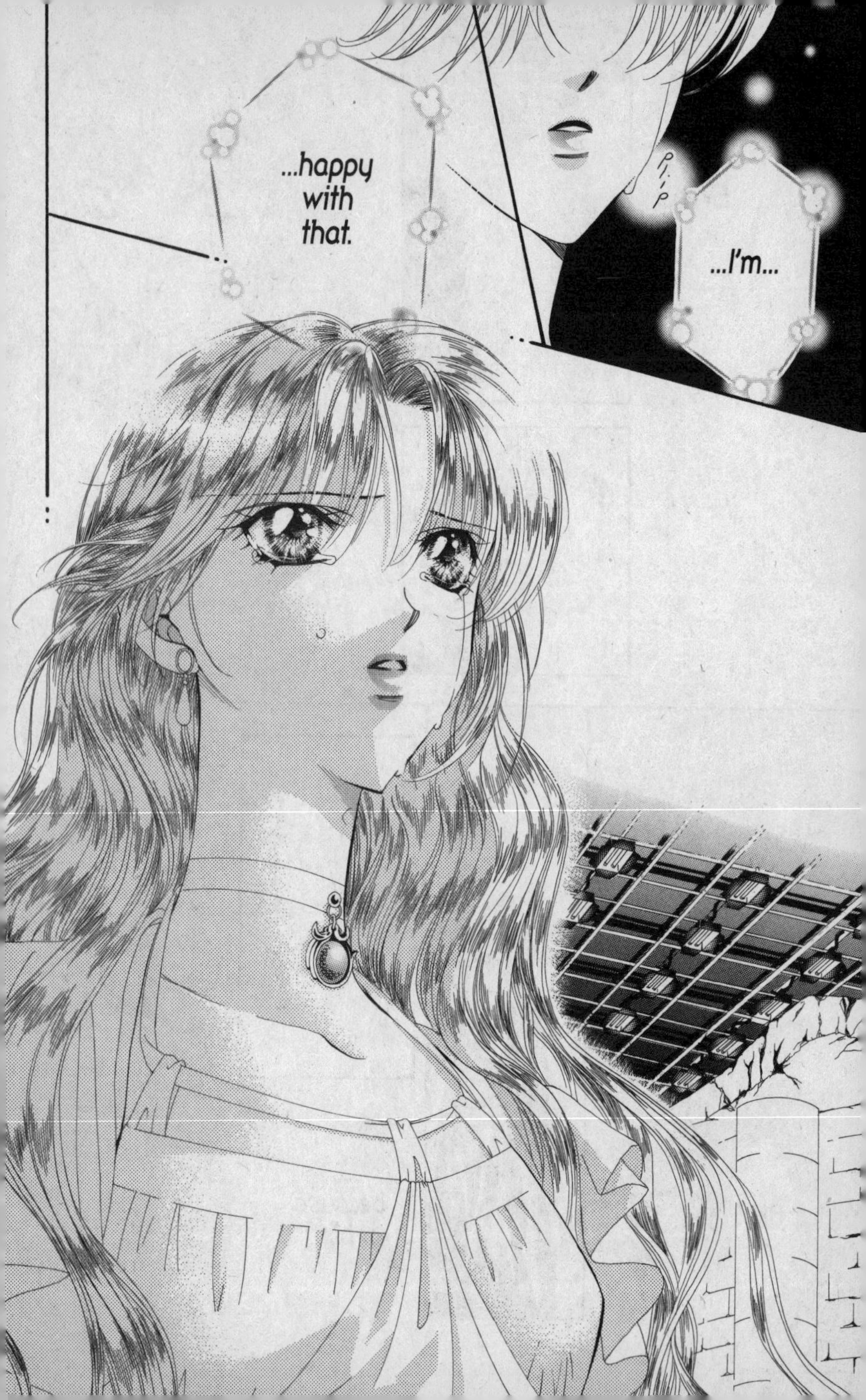
...I'm...
Plip
...happy with that.

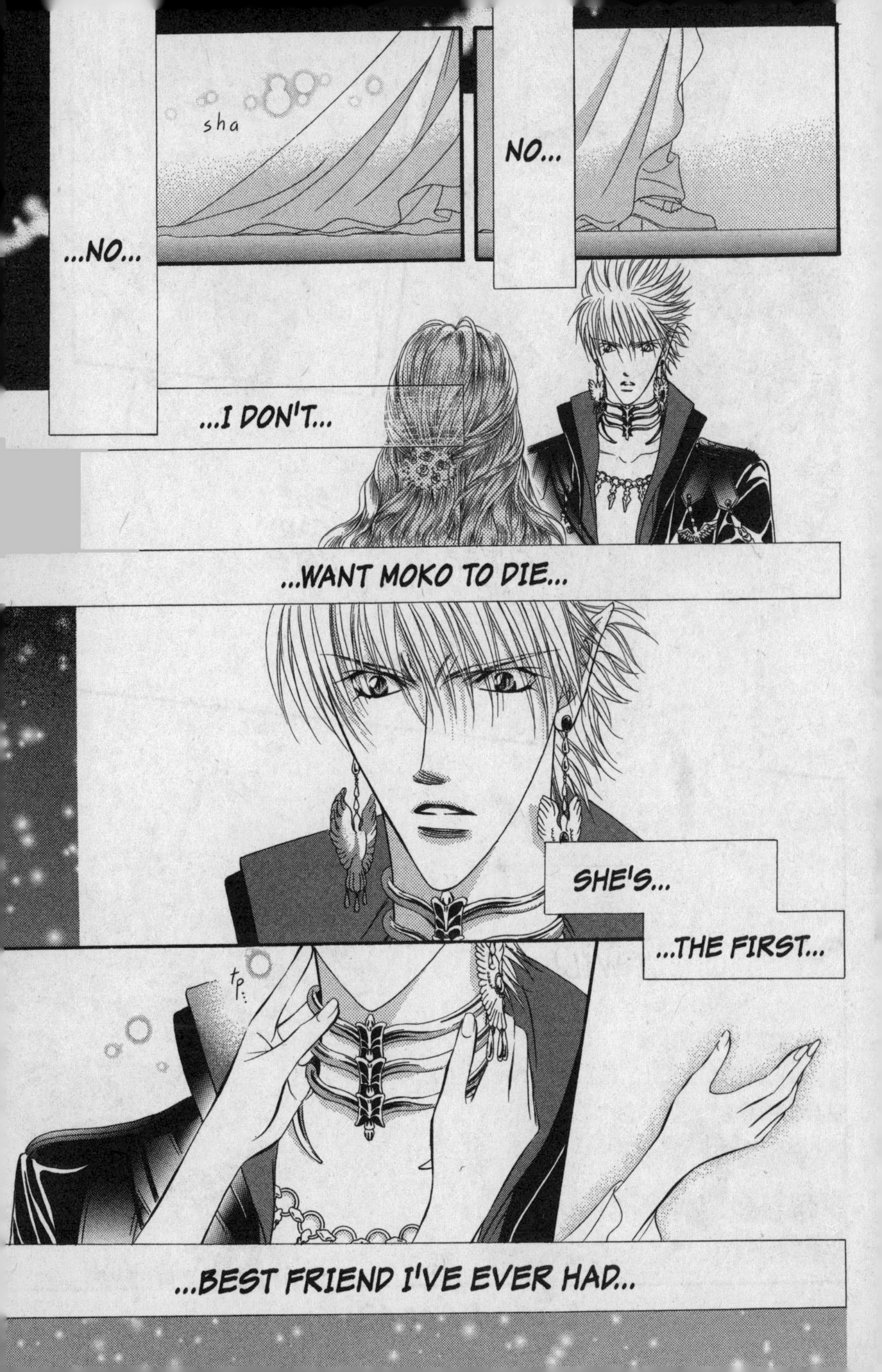
NO...
sha
...NO...
...I DON'T...
...WANT MOKO TO DIE...
SHE'S...
...THE FIRST...
tp...
...BEST FRIEND I'VE EVER HAD...

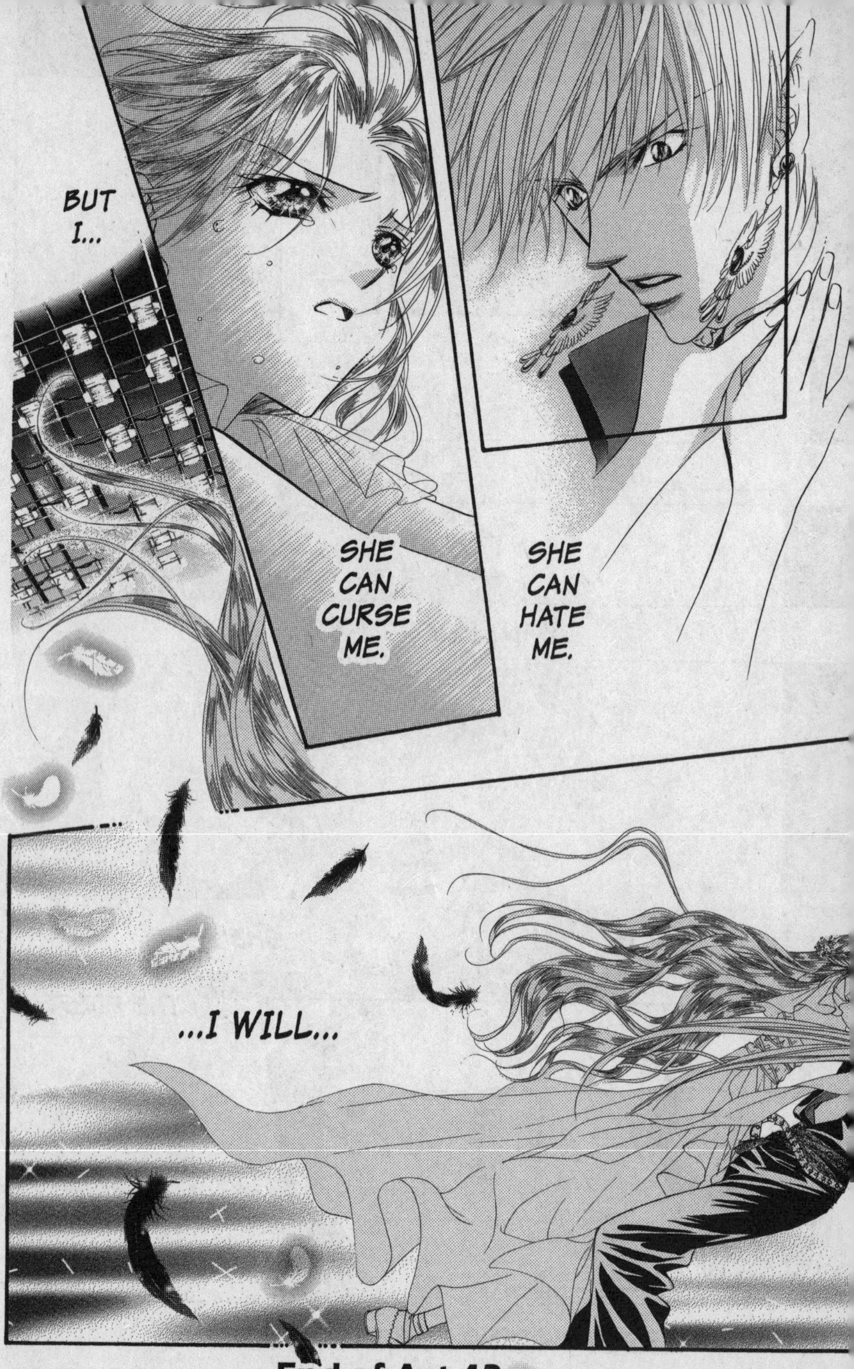
SHE CAN HATE ME.
SHE CAN CURSE ME.
BUT I...
...I WILL...

End of Act 43

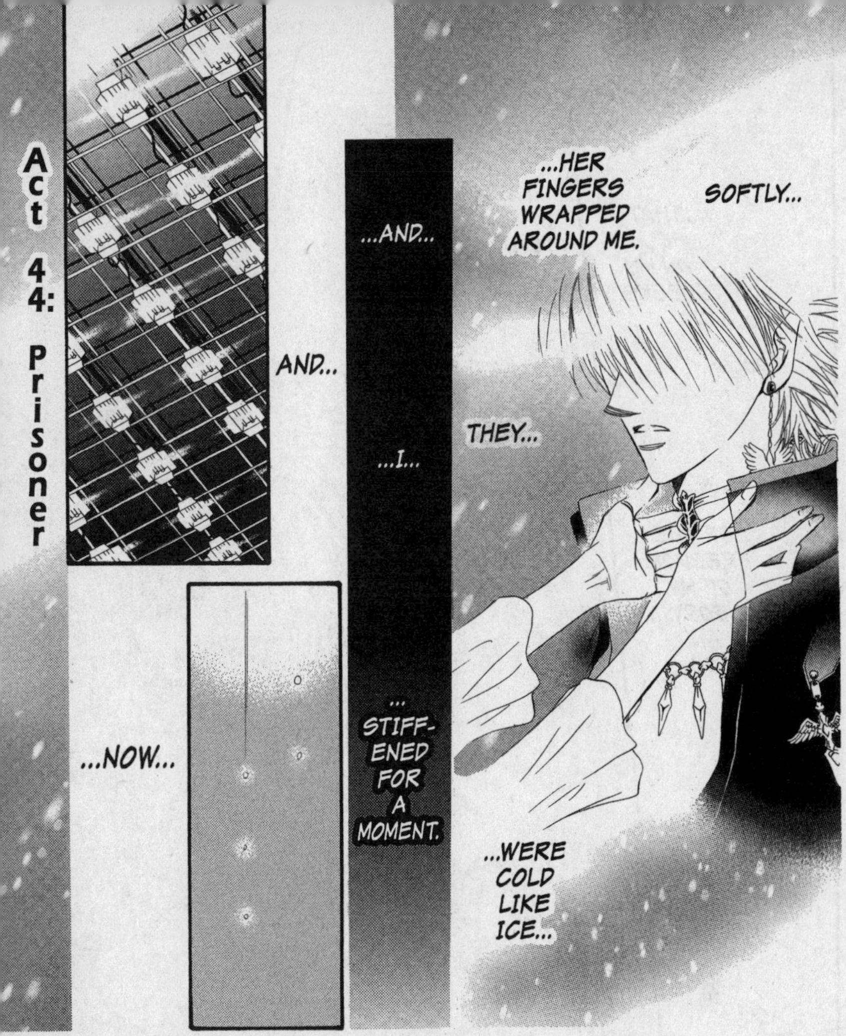
SOFTLY...
...HER FINGERS WRAPPED AROUND ME.
THEY...
...WERE COLD LIKE ICE...
...AND...
...I...
...STIFF-ENED FOR A MOMENT.
AND...
...NOW...
Act 44: Prisoner

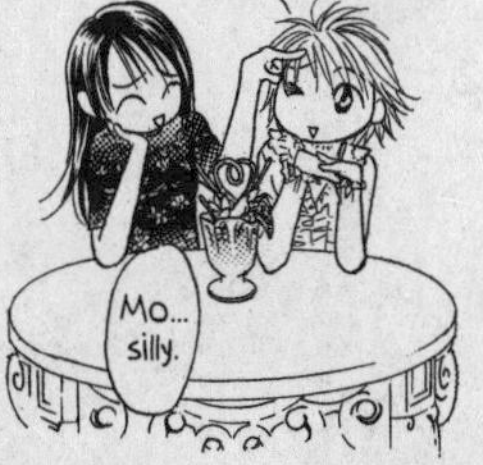
Mo... silly.

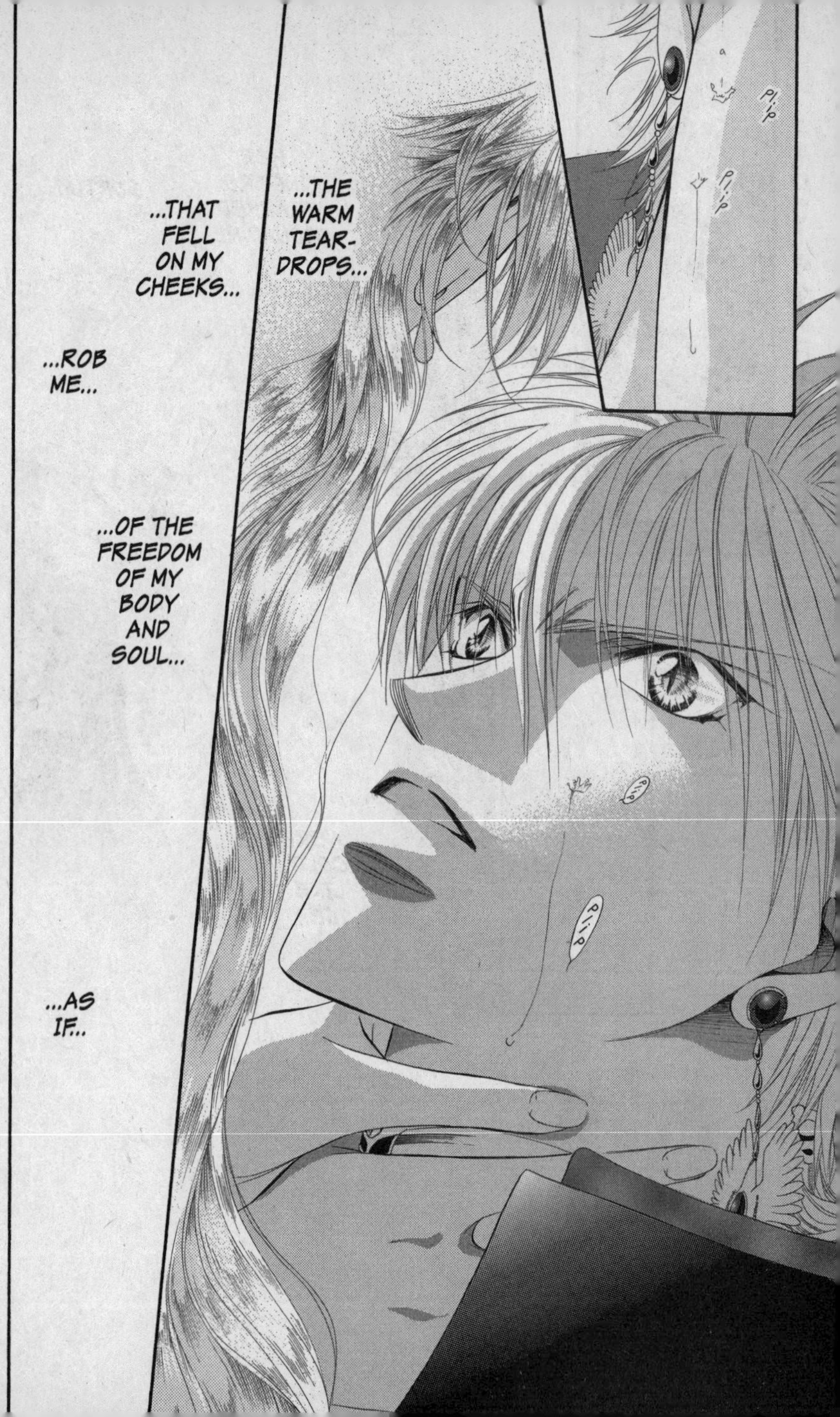
...THE WARM TEAR-DROPS...
...THAT FELL ON MY CHEEKS...
...ROB ME...
...OF THE FREEDOM OF MY BODY AND SOUL...
...AS IF...

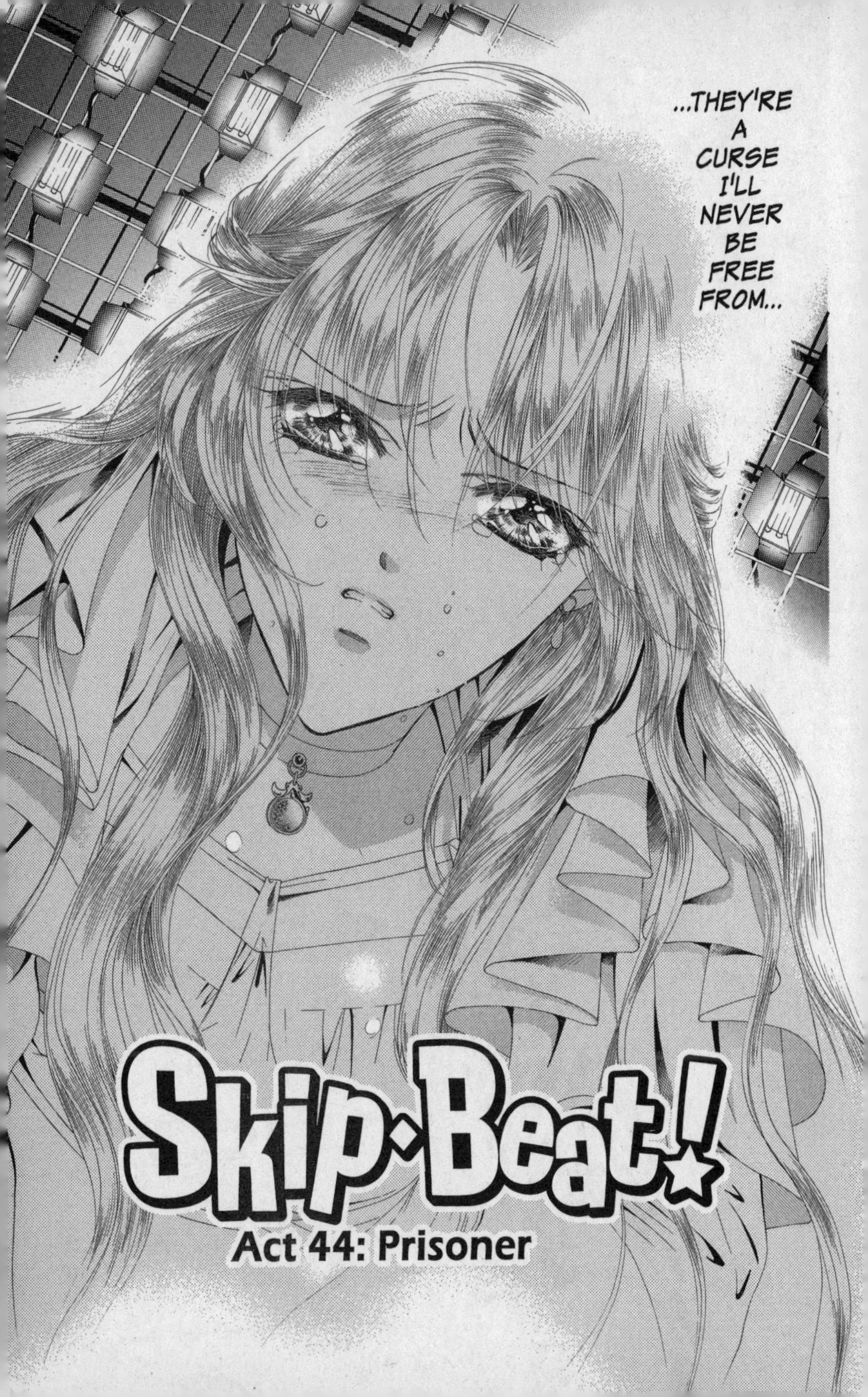
...THEY'RE A CURSE I'LL NEVER BE FREE FROM...
Skip·Beat!
Act 44: Prisoner

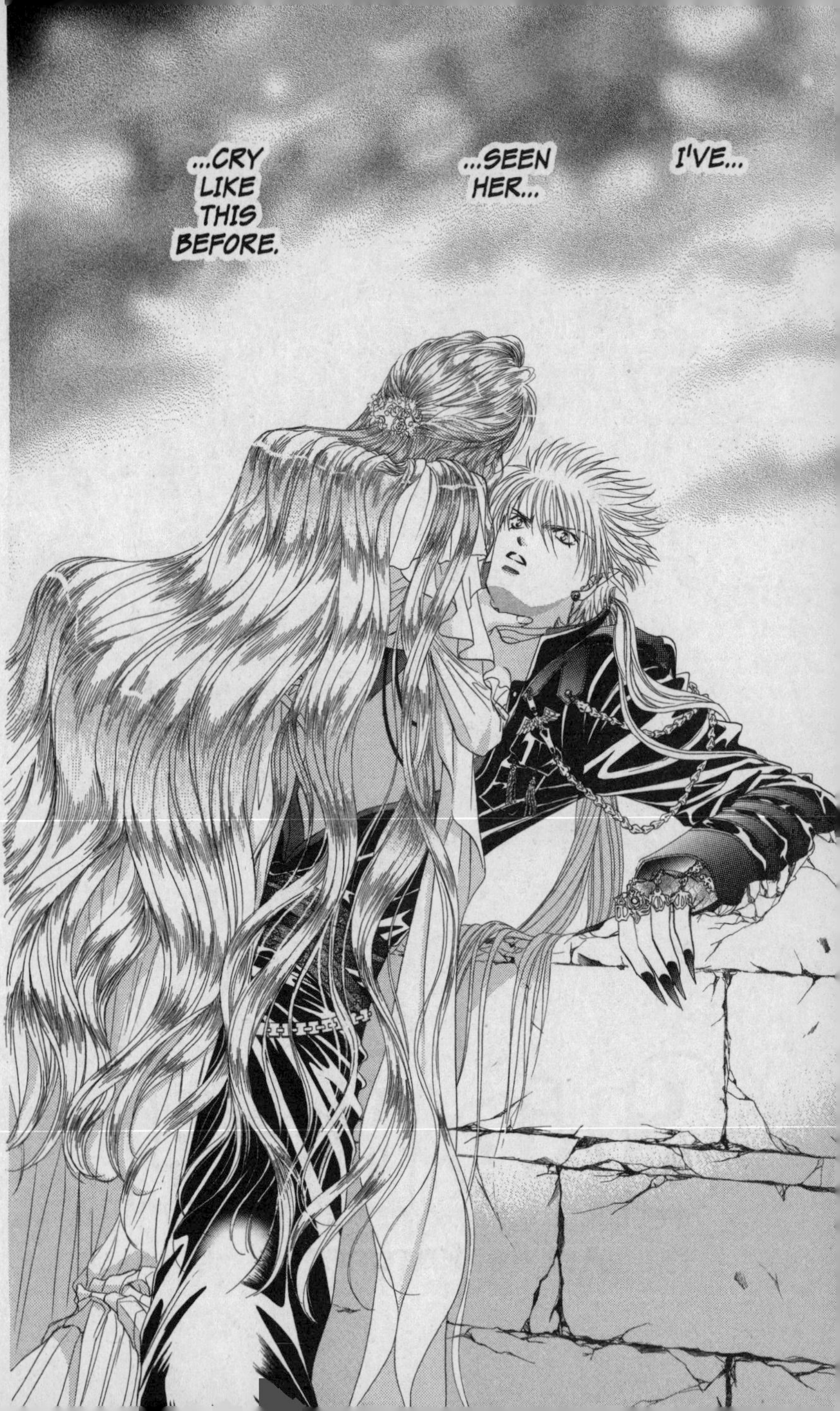
I'VE...
...SEEN HER...
...CRY LIKE THIS BEFORE.

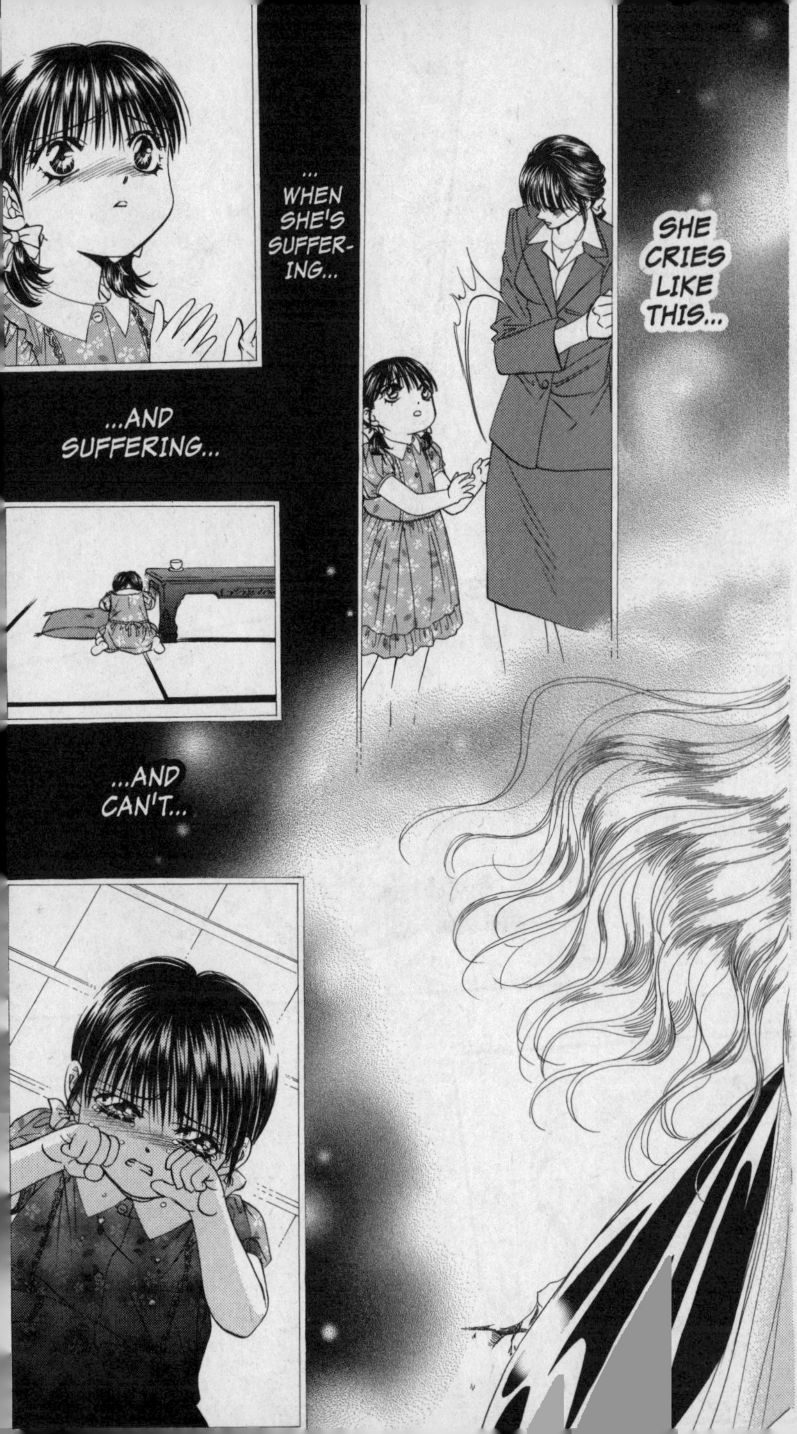
SHE CRIES LIKE THIS...
... WHEN SHE'S SUFFER-ING...
...AND SUFFERING...
...AND CAN'T...

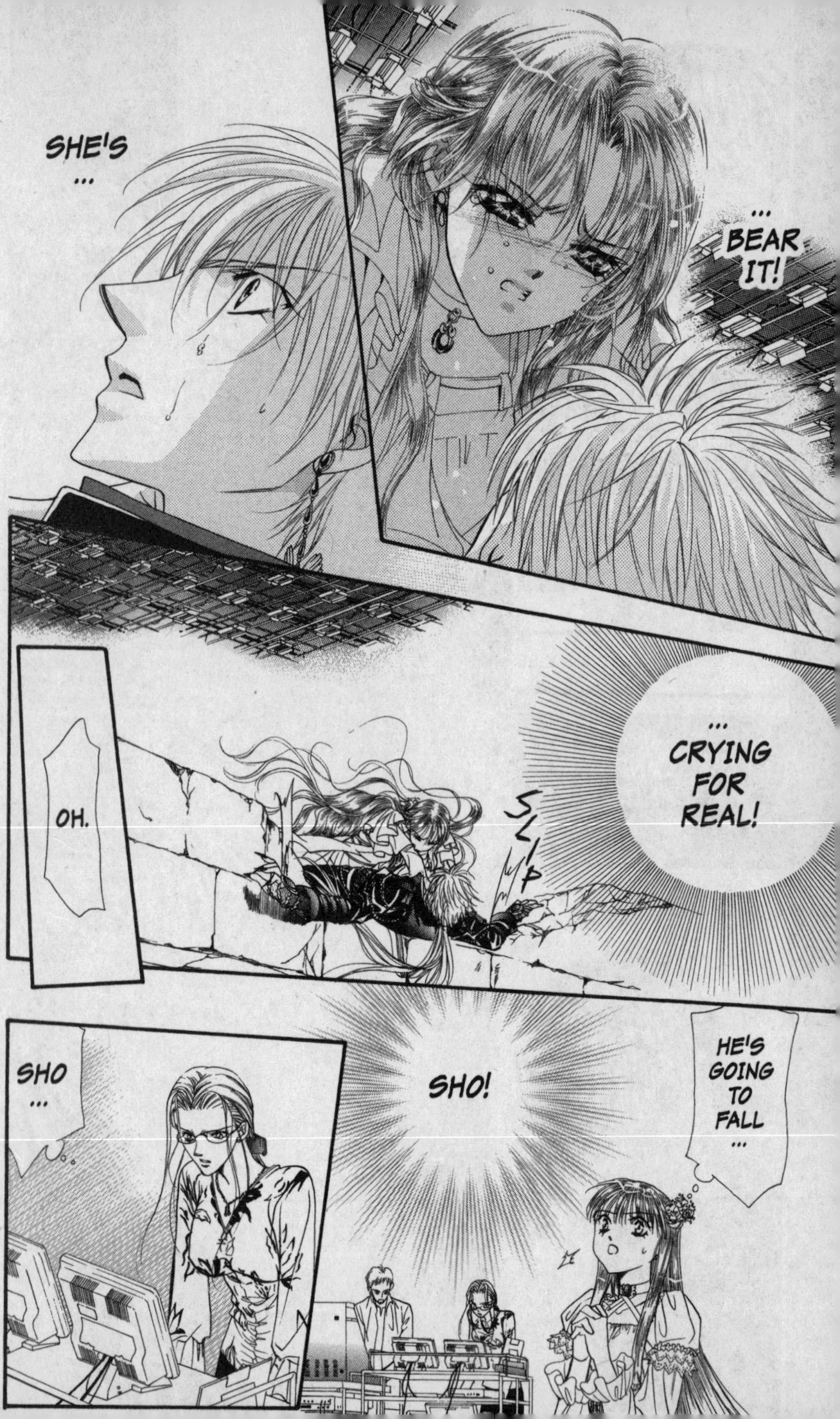
... BEAR IT!
SHE'S ...
... CRYING FOR REAL!
SLIP
OH.
HE'S GOING TO FALL ...
SHO!
SHO ...

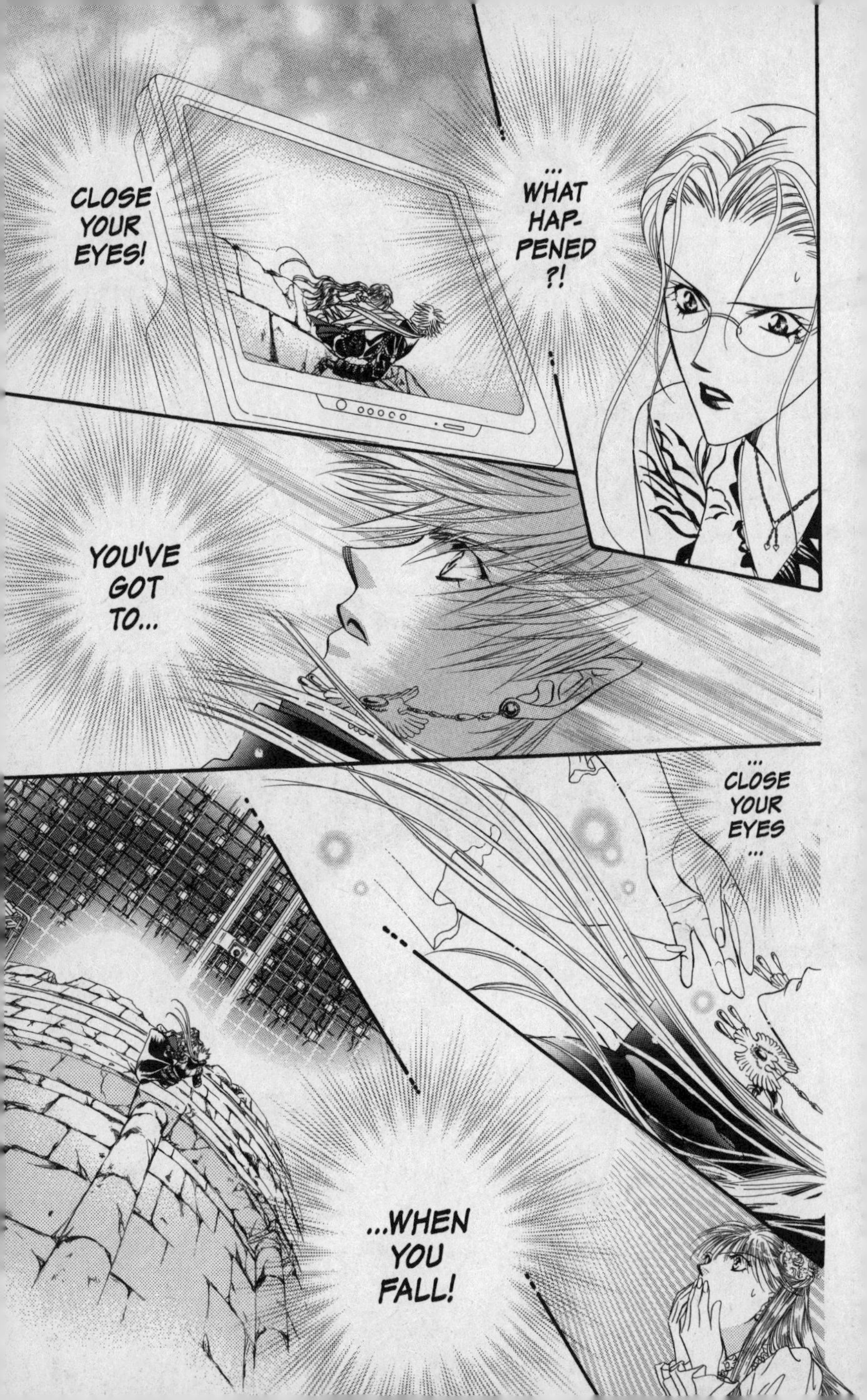
...WHAT HAP-PENED?!
CLOSE YOUR EYES!
YOU'VE GOT TO...
...CLOSE YOUR EYES...
...WHEN YOU FALL!

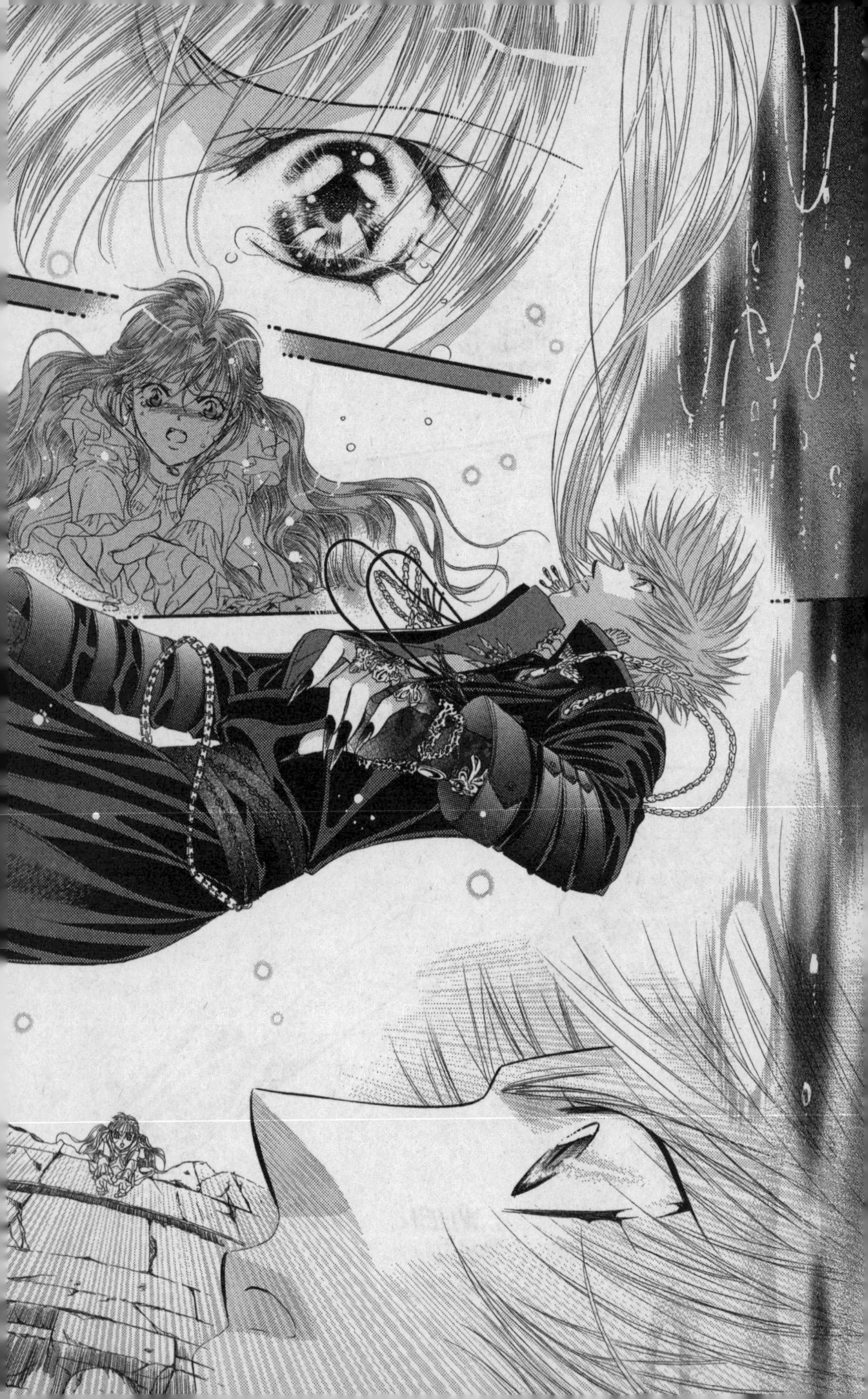

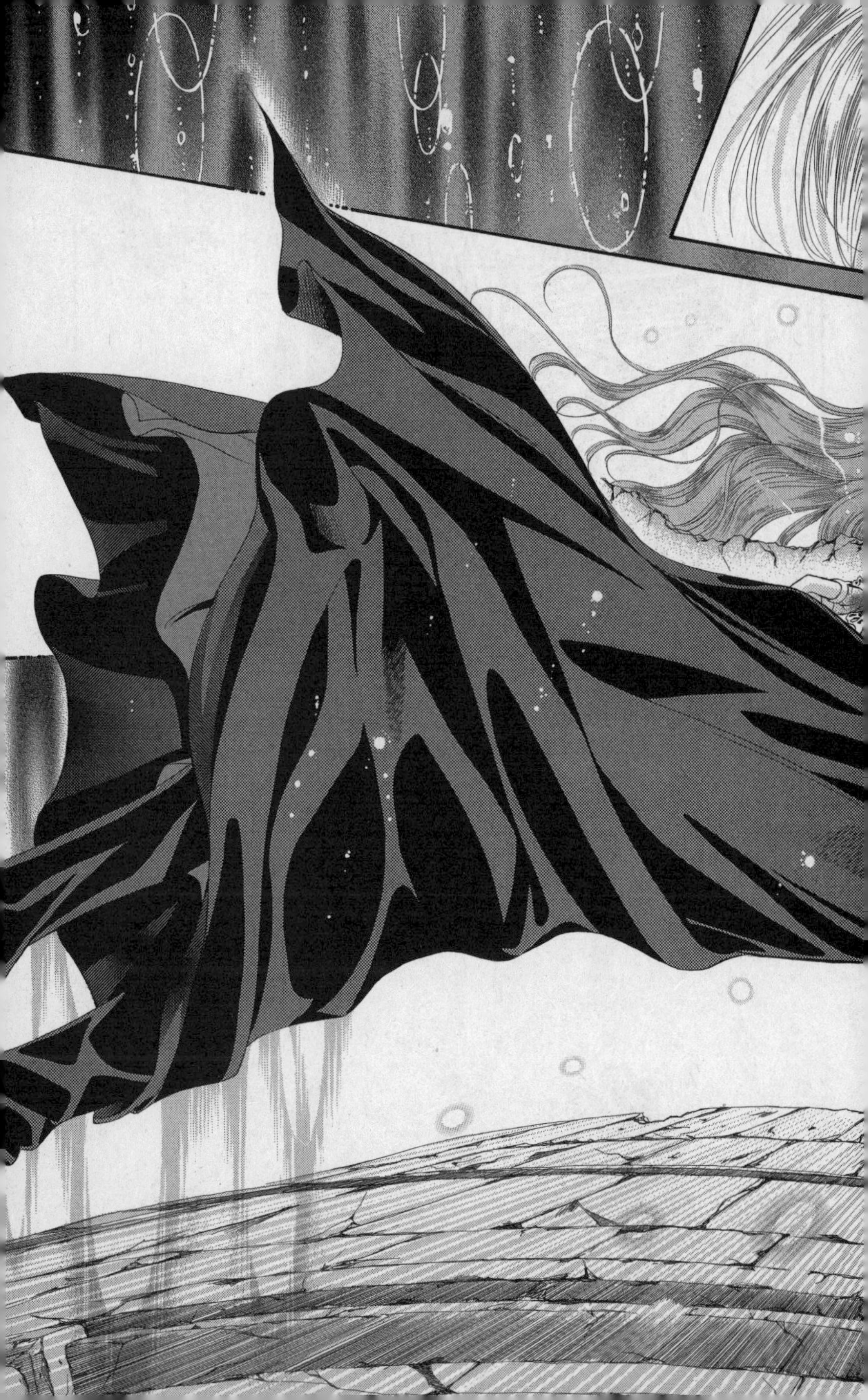

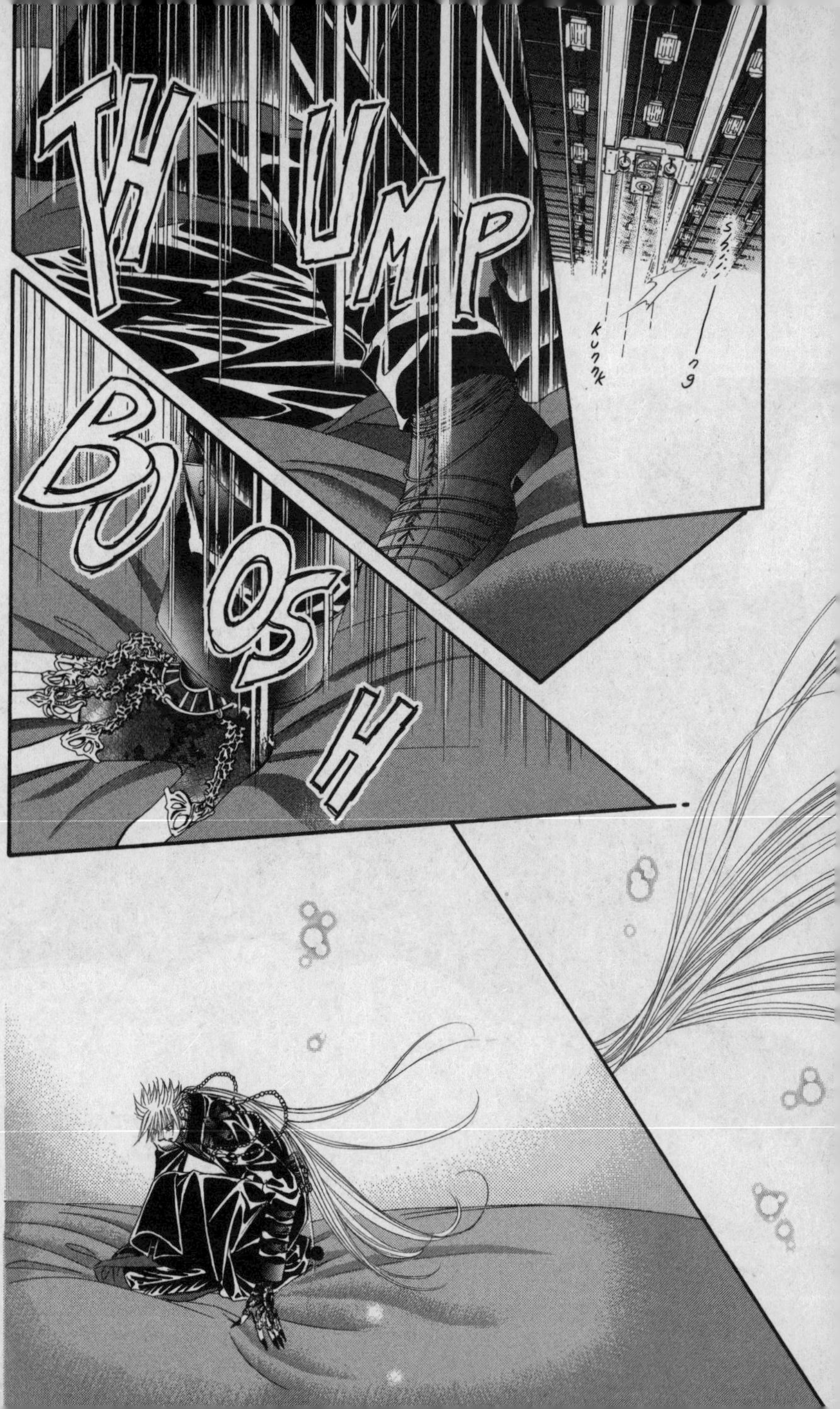
Shiiii—ng
kunnk
THUMP
BOOSH

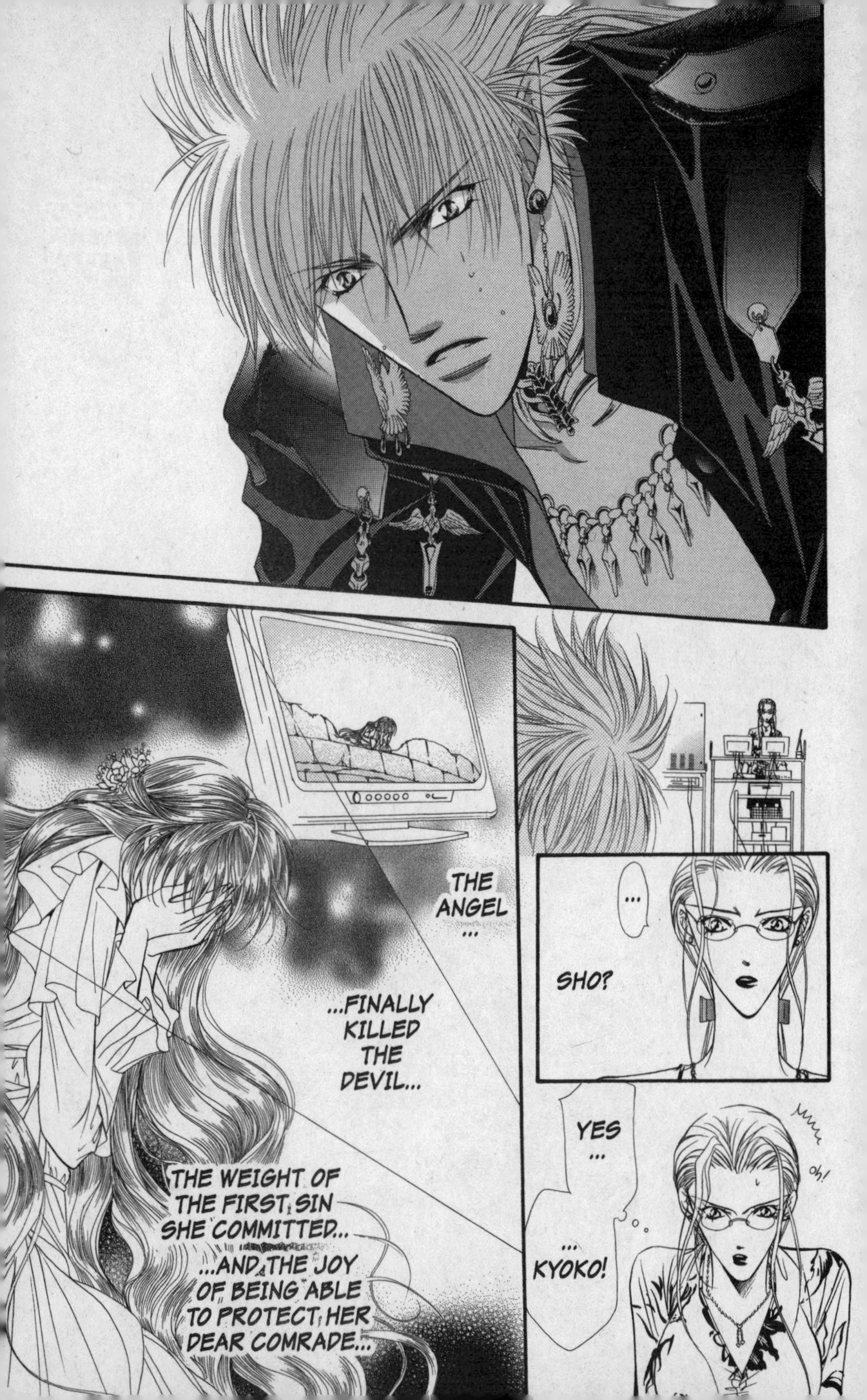
...
SHO?
YES ...
... KYOKO!
oh!
THE ANGEL ...
...FINALLY KILLED THE DEVIL...
THE WEIGHT OF THE FIRST SIN SHE COMMITTED...
...AND THE JOY OF BEING ABLE TO PROTECT HER DEAR COMRADE...

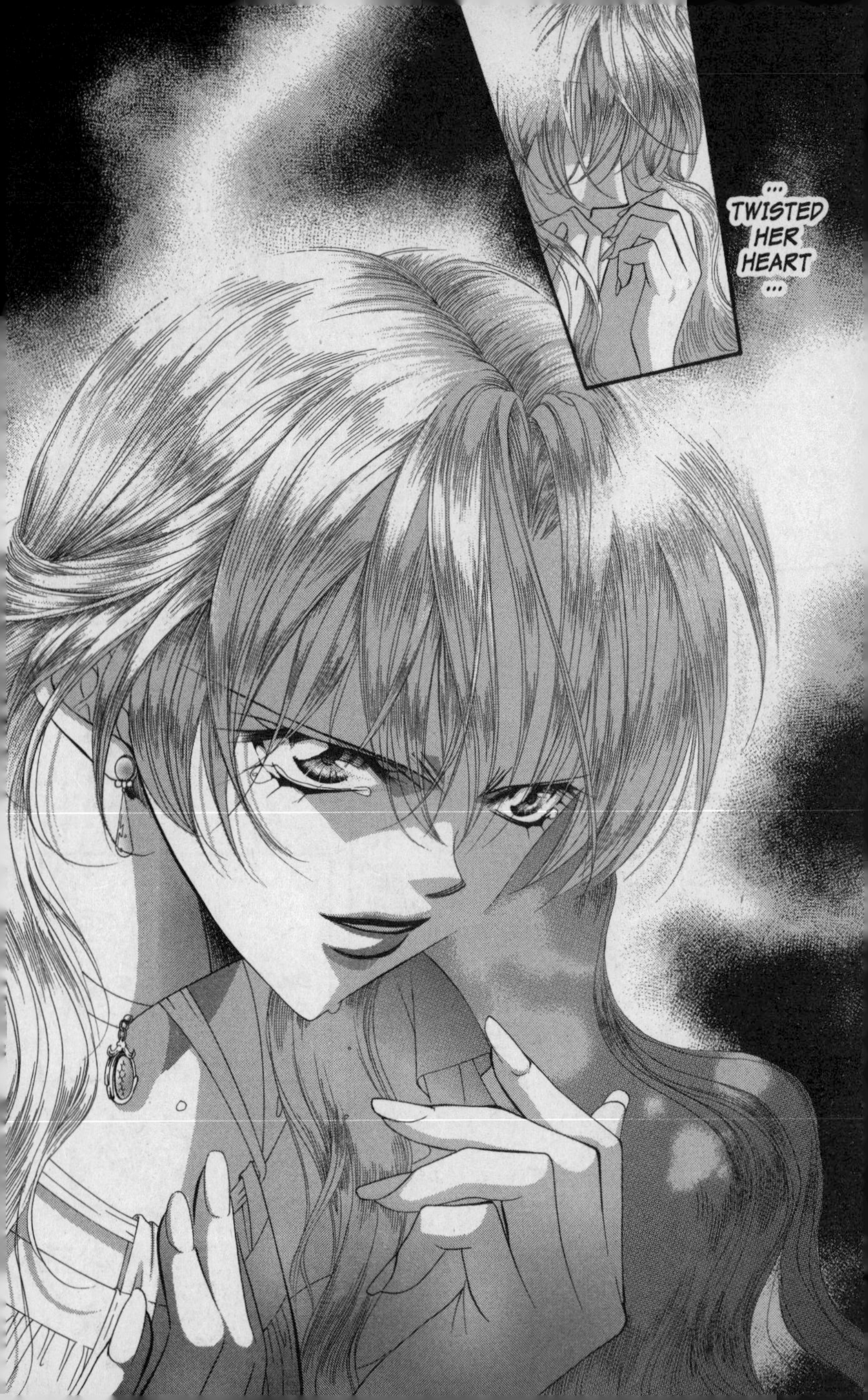
...TWISTED HER HEART...

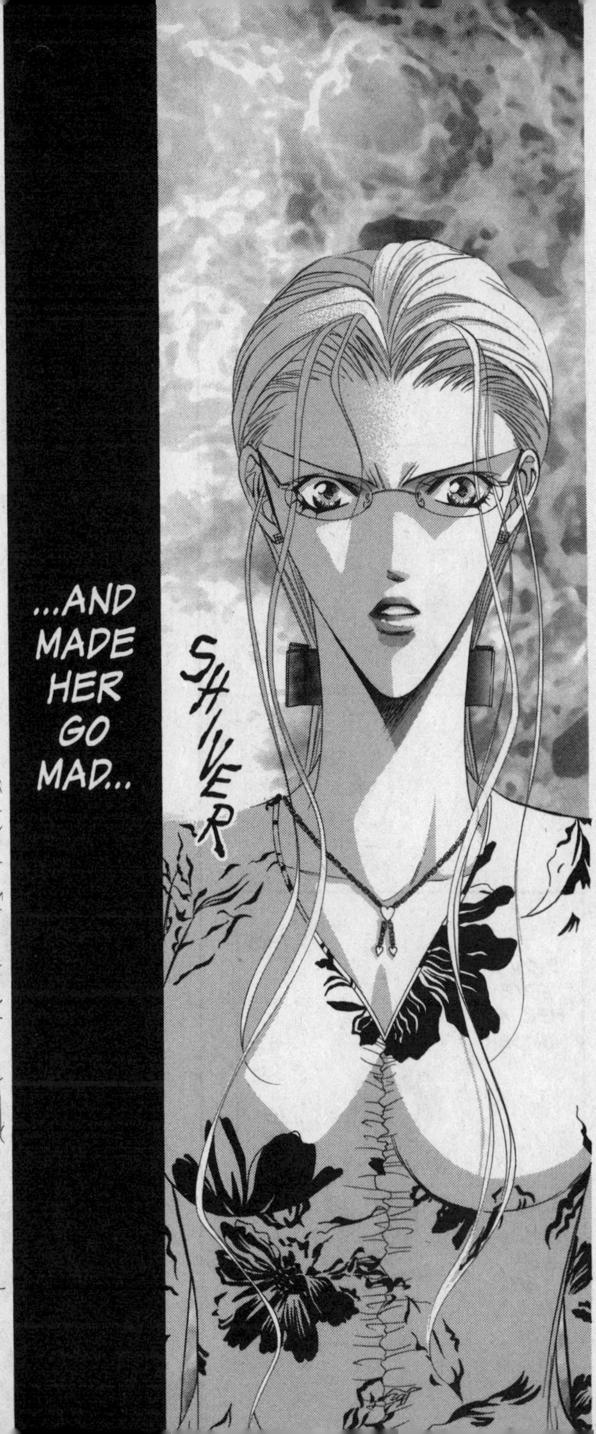
SHIVER
...AND MADE HER GO MAD...

...and Kyoko would have worn the costume Pochi wore...and when I thought about that, I wanted to draw it... but...a blonde Kanae... that's scary too, since she might not look good...

...therefore...

I tried drawing... Kyoko wearing Pochi's costume...

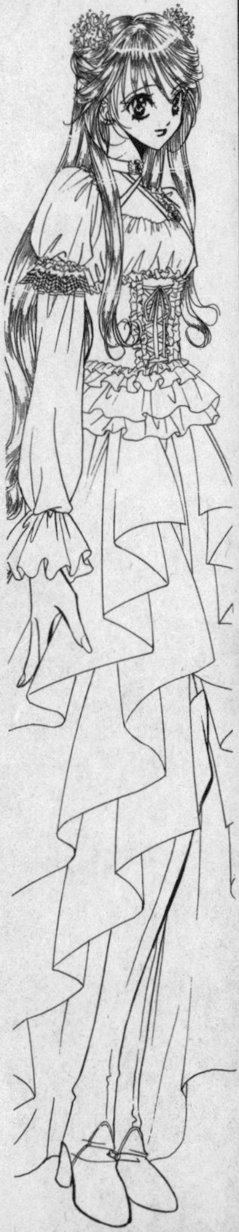

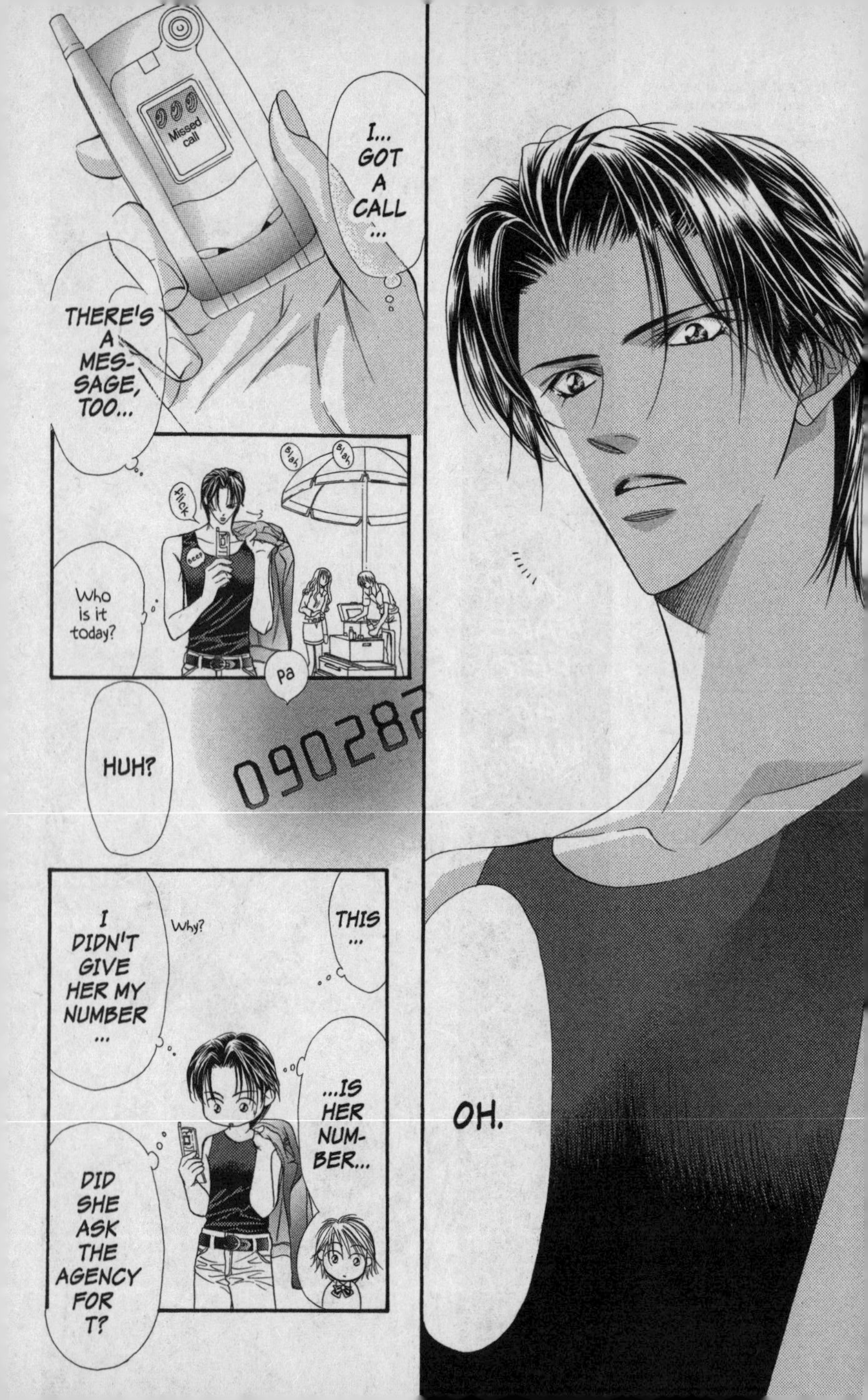
OH.
Missed call
I... GOT A CALL...
THERE'S A MES-SAGE, TOO...
Blah
Blah
Flick
Beep
Who is it today?
Pa
HUH?
090282
THIS...
...IS HER NUM-BER...
Why?
I DIDN'T GIVE HER MY NUMBER...
DID SHE ASK THE AGENCY FOR T?

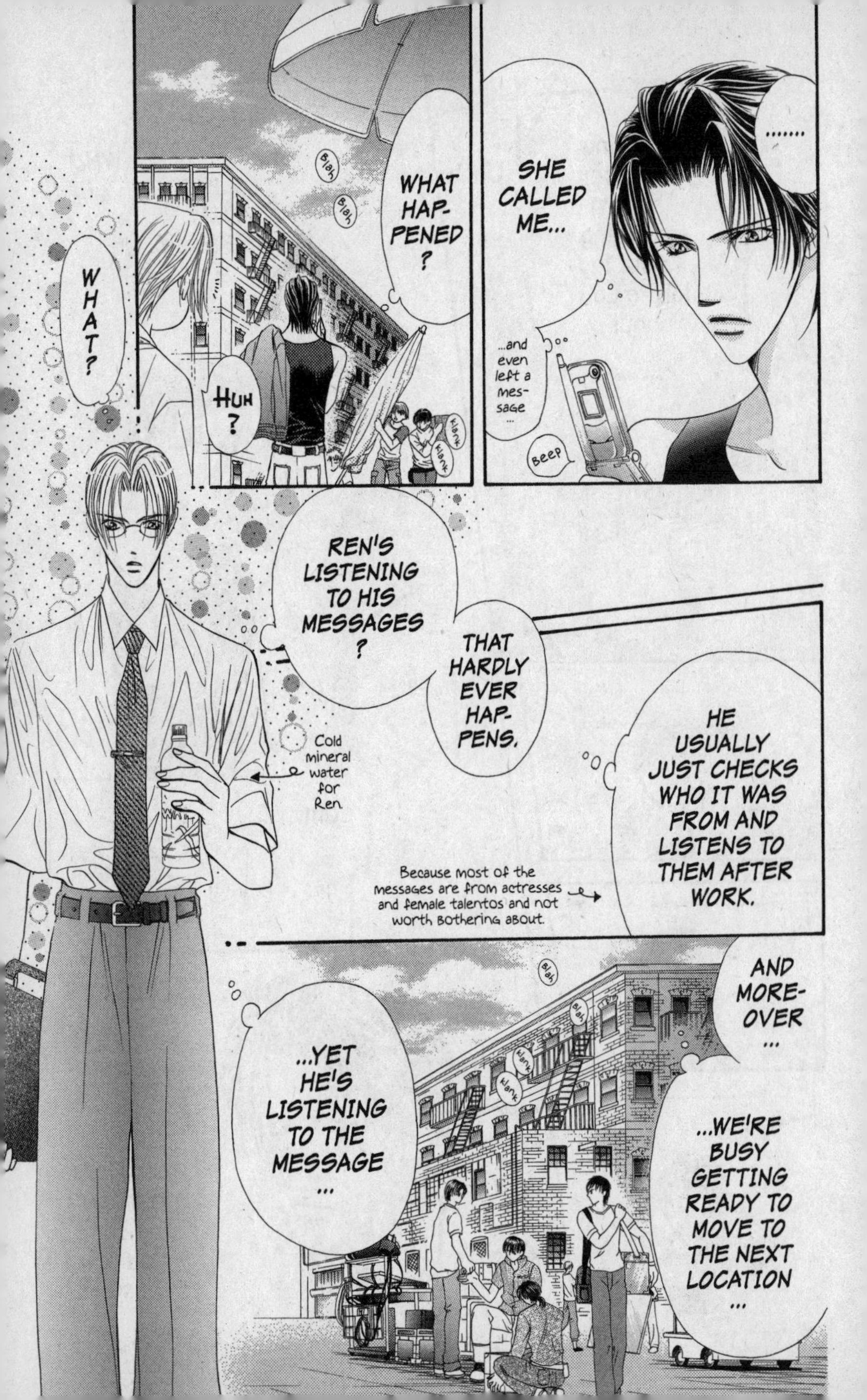
......
SHE CALLED ME...
...and even left a message...
Beep
WHAT HAPPENED?
Blah
Blah
HUH?
Klank
Klank
WHAT?
REN'S LISTENING TO HIS MESSAGES?
THAT HARDLY EVER HAPPENS.
HE USUALLY JUST CHECKS WHO IT WAS FROM AND LISTENS TO THEM AFTER WORK.
Because most of the messages are from actresses and female talentos and not worth bothering about.
Cold mineral water for Ren.
AND MOREOVER...
...WE'RE BUSY GETTING READY TO MOVE TO THE NEXT LOCATION...
Blah
Blah
Klank
Klank
...YET HE'S LISTENING TO THE MESSAGE...

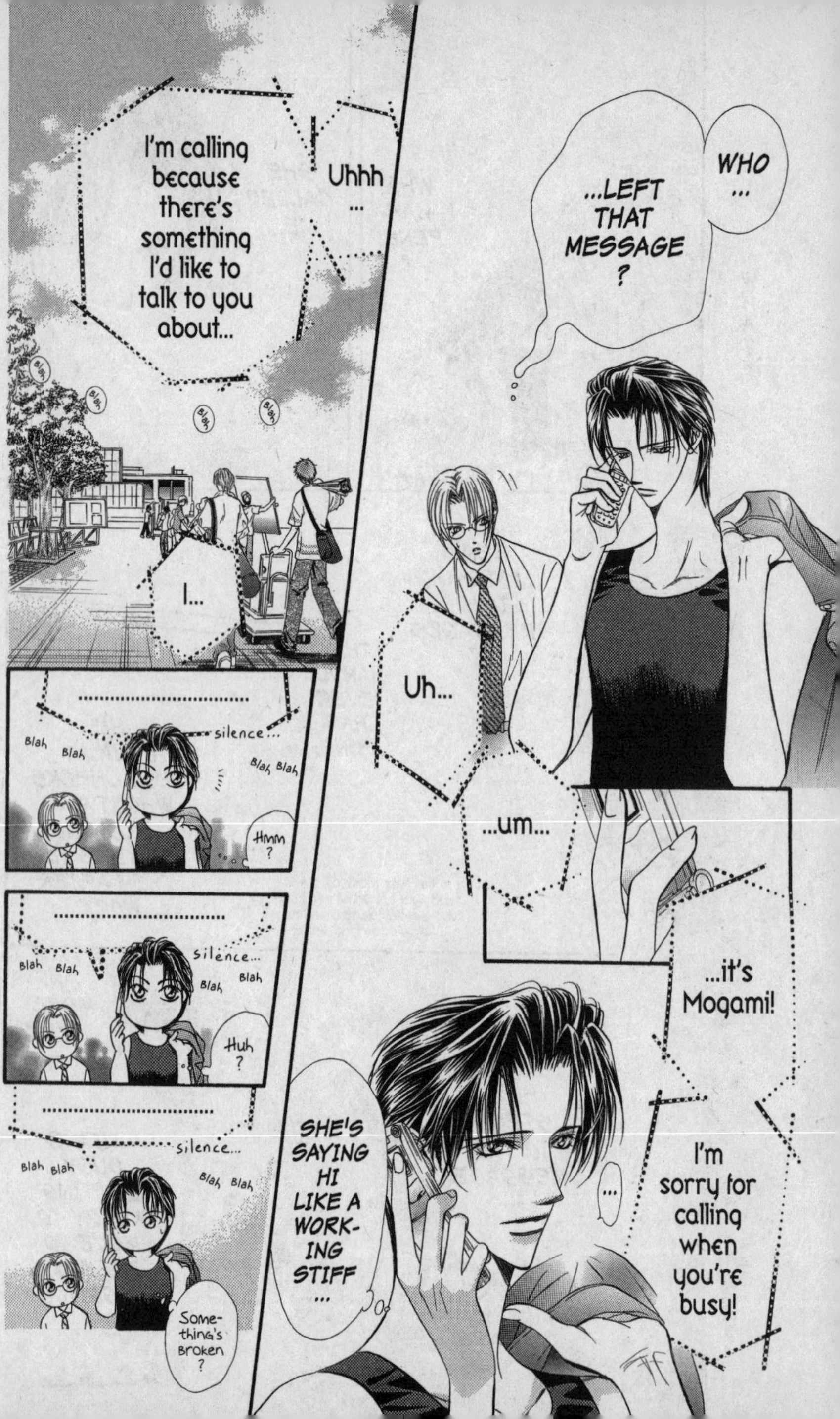
WHO ...
...LEFT THAT MESSAGE ?
Uh...
...um...
...it's Mogami!
I'm sorry for calling when you're busy!
...
SHE'S SAYING HI LIKE A WORKING STIFF ...
Uhhh ...
I'm calling because there's something I'd like to talk to you about...
Blah Blah Blah Blah
I...
....
silence...
Blah Blah Blah Blah
Hmm ?
....
silence...
Blah Blah Blah Blah
Huh ?
....
silence...
Blah Blah Blah Blah
Some-thing's Broken ?

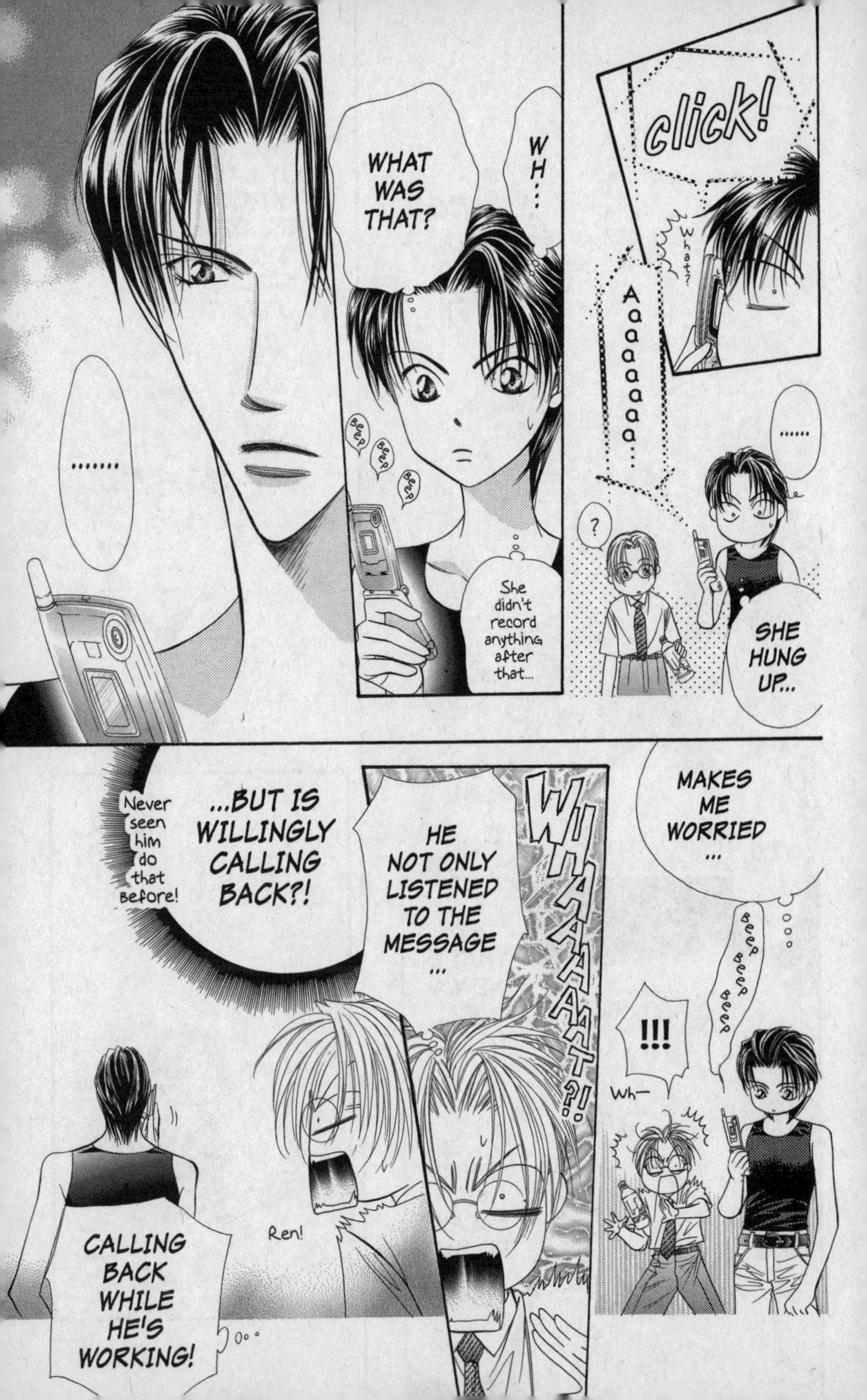
click!
What?
Aaaaaaaa...
......
?
SHE HUNG UP...
WH...
WHAT WAS THAT?
Beep
Beep
Beep
She didn't record anything after that...
....
MAKES ME WORRIED ...
Beep Beep Beep
!!!
Wh—
WHAAAAAT?!
HE NOT ONLY LISTENED TO THE MESSAGE ...
...BUT IS WILLINGLY CALLING BACK?!
Never seen him do that before!
Ren!
CALLING BACK WHILE HE'S WORKING!

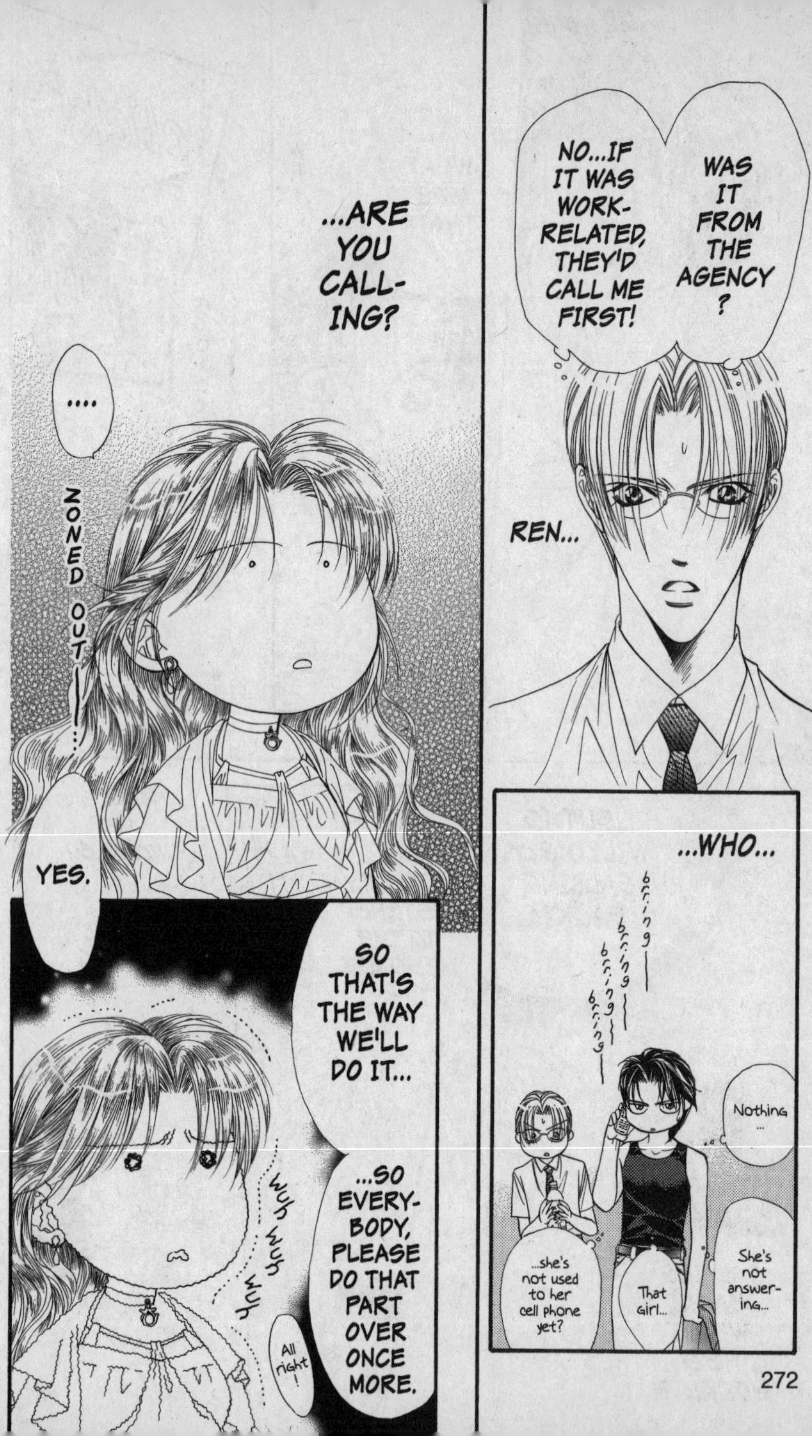
WAS IT FROM THE AGENCY?
NO...IF IT WAS WORK-RELATED, THEY'D CALL ME FIRST!
REN...
...WHO...
brring brring brring brring
Nothing...
She's not answering...
That girl...
...she's not used to her cell phone yet?
...ARE YOU CALLING?
....
ZONED OUT
YES.
SO THAT'S THE WAY WE'LL DO IT...
...SO EVERYBODY, PLEASE DO THAT PART OVER ONCE MORE.
wuh wuh wuh
All right!

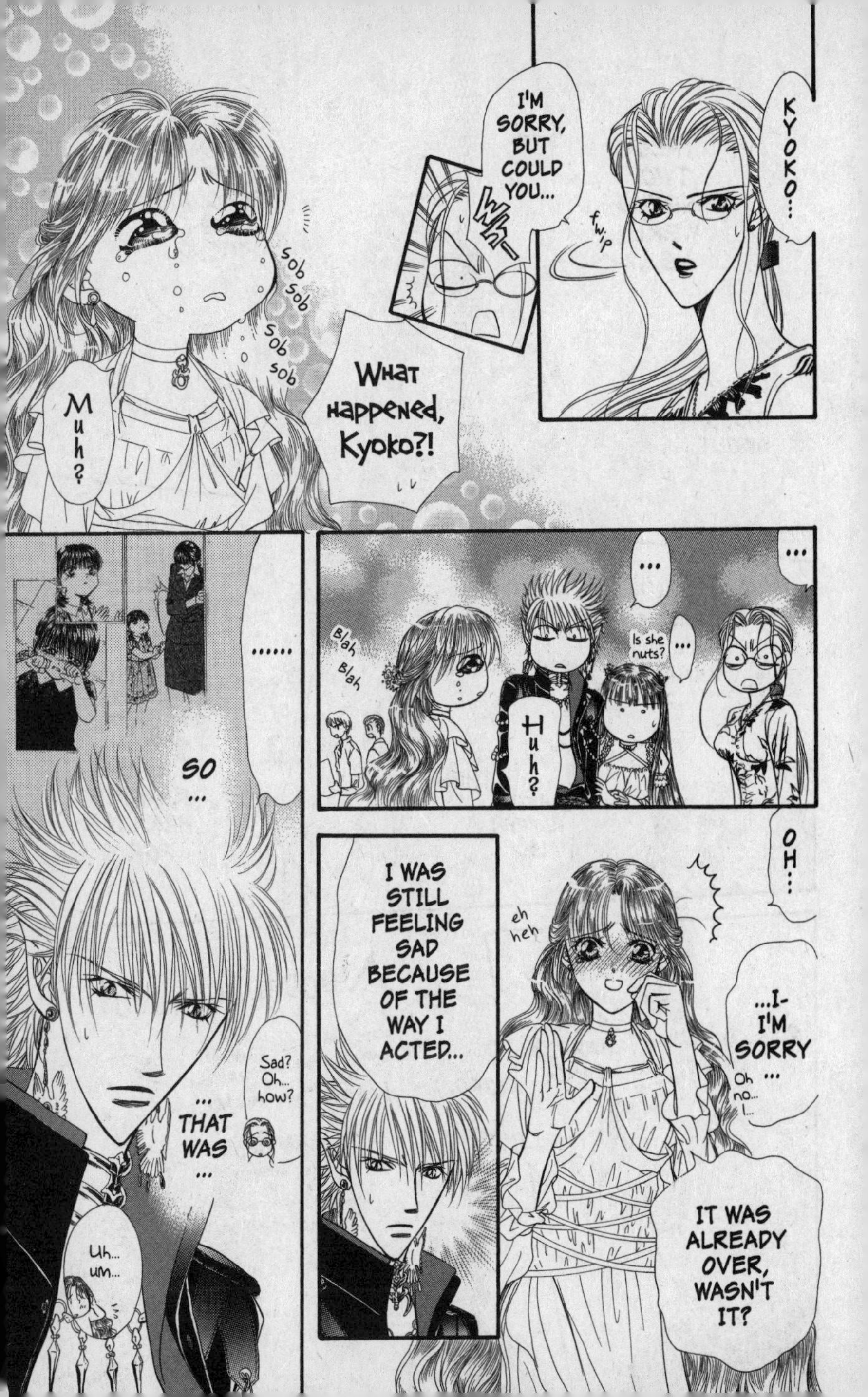
KYOKO...
I'M SORRY, BUT COULD YOU...
fwip
Wh—
What happened, Kyoko?!
sob sob sob sob
Muh?
...
...
Is she nuts?
...
Huh?
Blah Blah
OH...
...I- I'M SORRY ...
Oh no... I...
eh heh
I WAS STILL FEELING SAD BECAUSE OF THE WAY I ACTED...
IT WAS ALREADY OVER, WASN'T IT?
......
SO ...
... THAT WAS ...
Sad? Oh... how?
Uh... um...

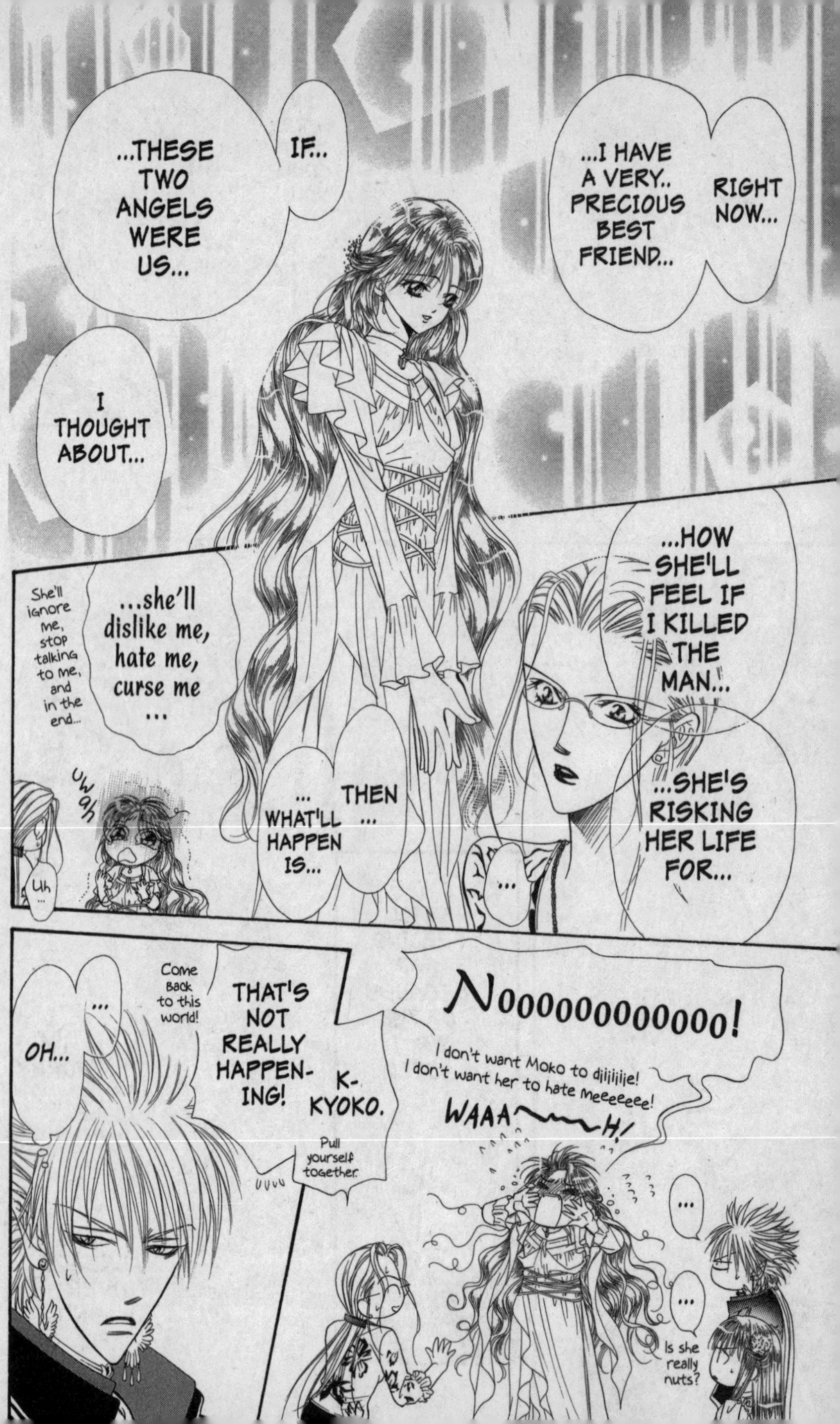
IF...
...THESE TWO ANGELS WERE US...
RIGHT NOW...
...I HAVE A VERY.. PRECIOUS BEST FRIEND...
I THOUGHT ABOUT...
...HOW SHE'LL FEEL IF I KILLED THE MAN...
...SHE'S RISKING HER LIFE FOR...
THEN ...
... WHAT'LL HAPPEN IS...
...
...she'll dislike me, hate me, curse me ...
She'll ignore me, stop talking to me, and in the end...
Uwah
Uh ...
Noooooooooooo!
I don't want Moko to diiiiiie! I don't want her to hate meeeeeee!
WAAA~~~H!
...
...
Is she really nuts?
K-KYOKO.
Pull yourself together.
THAT'S NOT REALLY HAPPEN-ING!
Come back to this world!
...
OH...

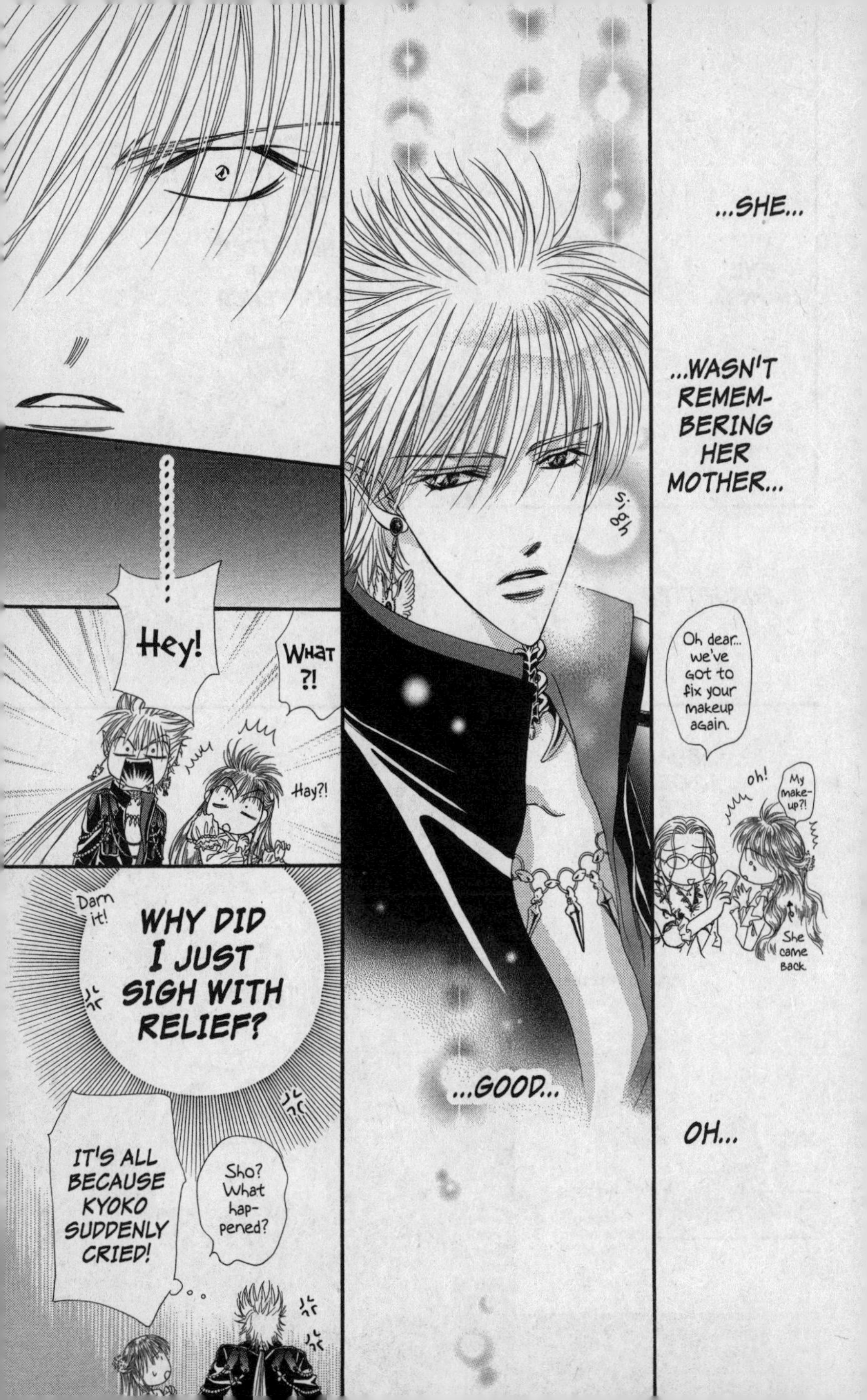
...SHE...
...WASN'T REMEMBERING HER MOTHER...
Oh dear... we've got to fix your makeup again.
Oh!
My make-up?!
She came back.
OH...
sigh
...GOOD...
......
Hey!
WHAT ?!
Hay?!
Darn it!
WHY DID I JUST SIGH WITH RELIEF?
IT'S ALL BECAUSE KYOKO SUDDENLY CRIED!
Sho? What hap-pened?

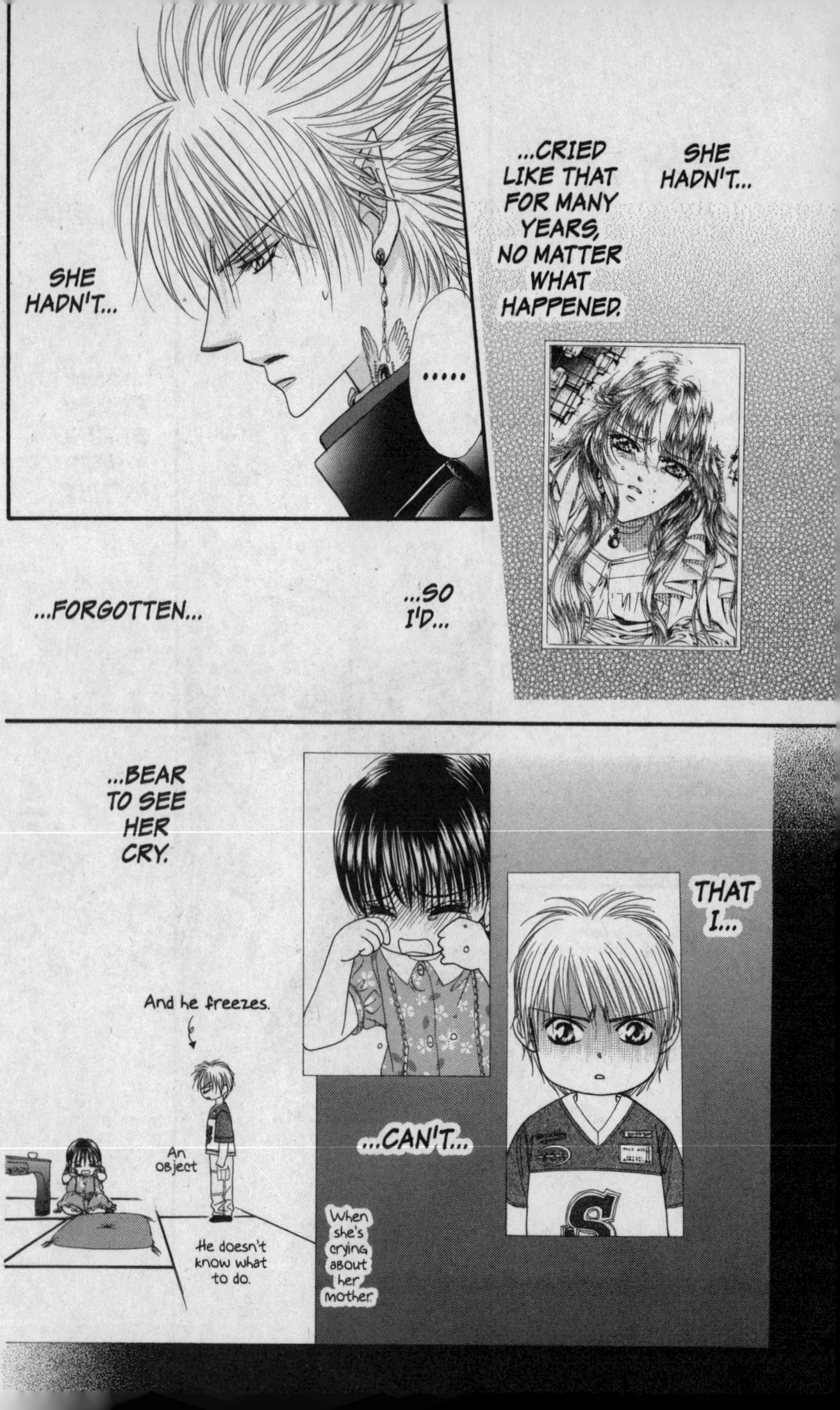
SHE HADN'T...
...CRIED LIKE THAT FOR MANY YEARS, NO MATTER WHAT HAPPENED.
SHE HADN'T...
.....
...SO I'D...
...FORGOTTEN...
THAT I...
...CAN'T...
...BEAR TO SEE HER CRY.
When she's crying about her mother.
And he freezes.
An object
He doesn't know what to do.

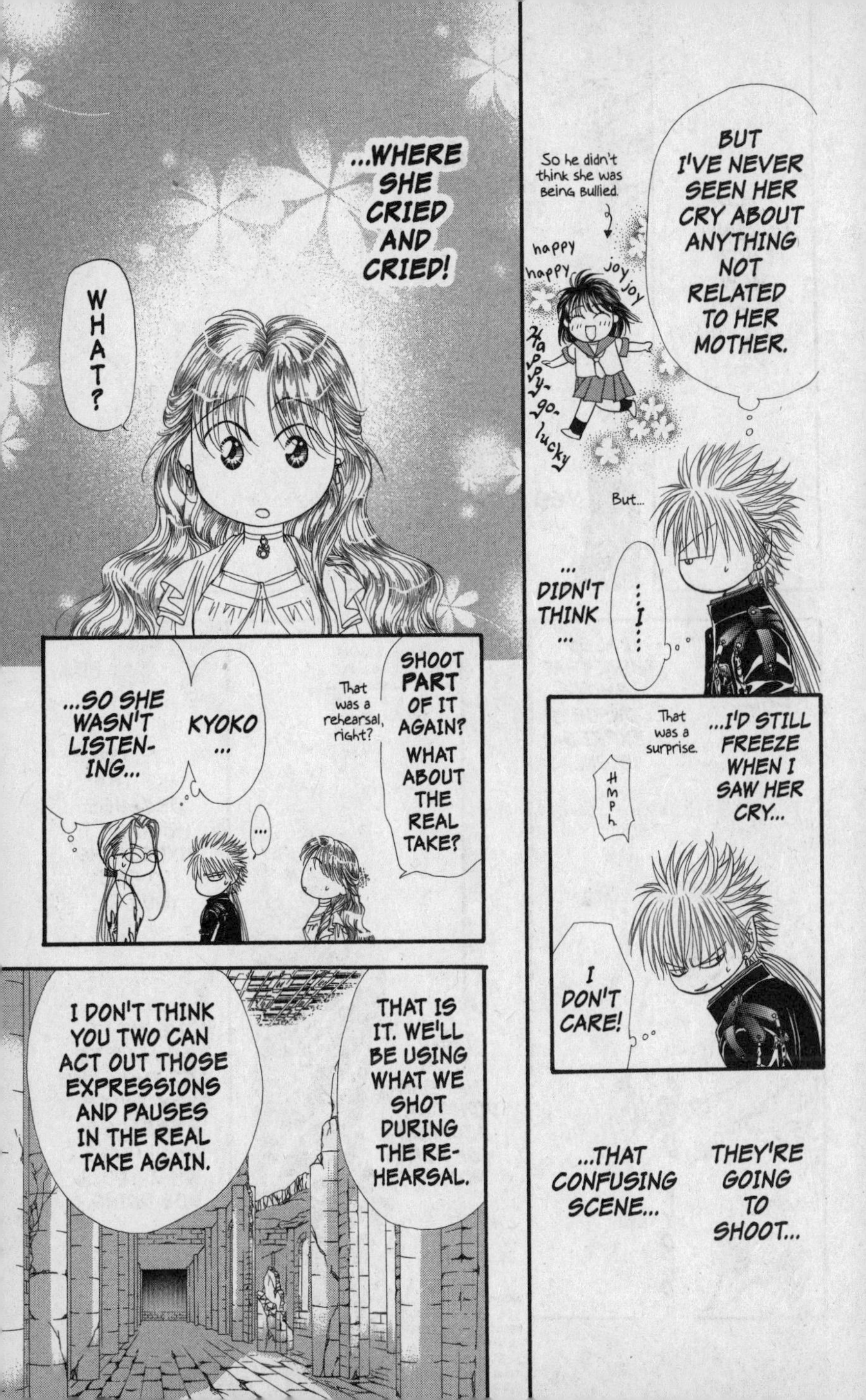
BUT I'VE NEVER SEEN HER CRY ABOUT ANYTHING NOT RELATED TO HER MOTHER.
So he didn't think she was being bullied.
happy happy
joy joy
Happy-go-lucky
But...
...I...
...DIDN'T THINK...
...I'D STILL FREEZE WHEN I SAW HER CRY...
That was a surprise.
Hmph.
I DON'T CARE!
THEY'RE GOING TO SHOOT...
...THAT CONFUSING SCENE...
...WHERE SHE CRIED AND CRIED!
WHAT?
SHOOT PART OF IT AGAIN? WHAT ABOUT THE REAL TAKE?
That was a rehearsal, right?
...
KYOKO...
...SO SHE WASN'T LISTENING...
THAT IS IT. WE'LL BE USING WHAT WE SHOT DURING THE RE-HEARSAL.
I DON'T THINK YOU TWO CAN ACT OUT THOSE EXPRESSIONS AND PAUSES IN THE REAL TAKE AGAIN.

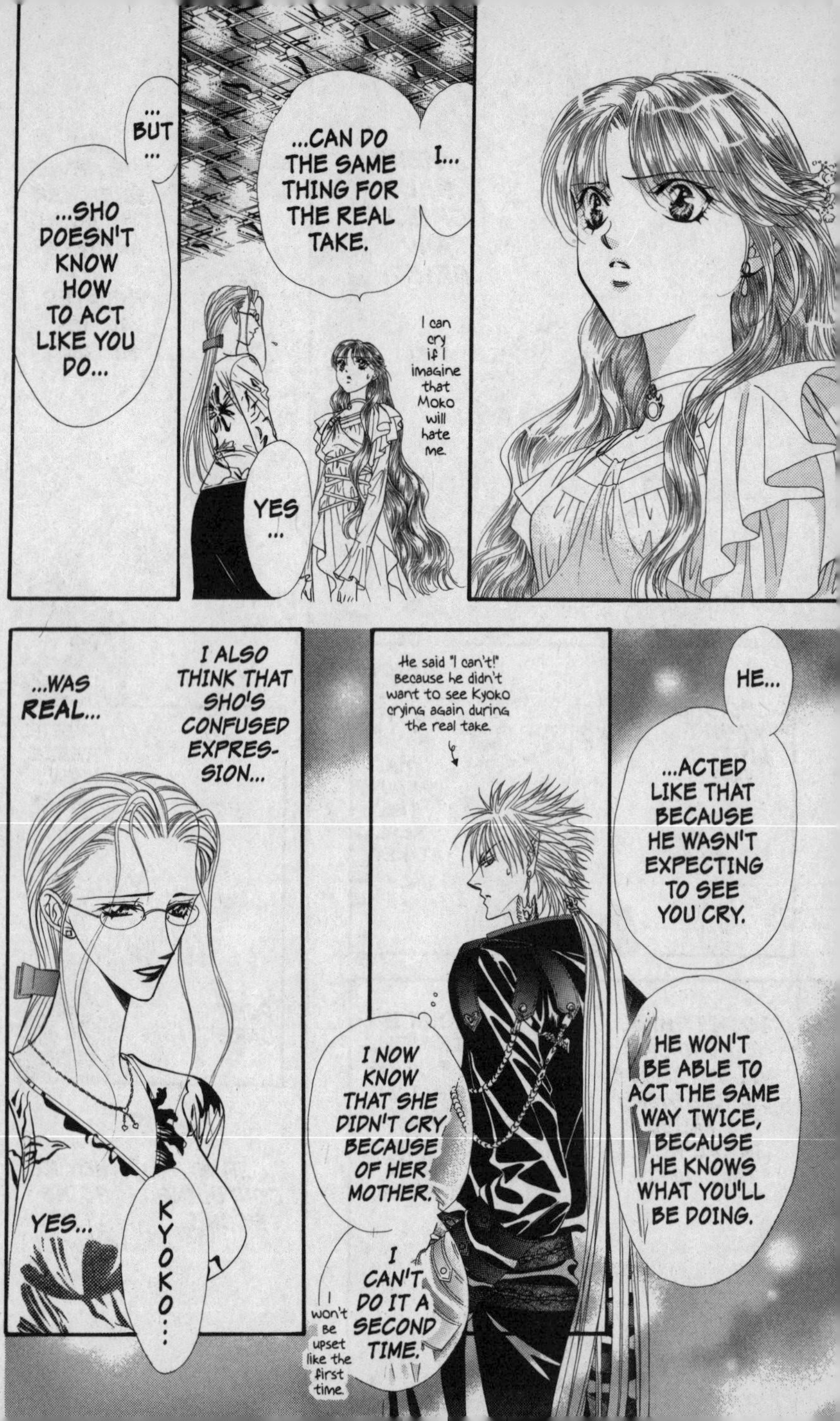
I...
...CAN DO THE SAME THING FOR THE REAL TAKE.
I can cry if I imagine that Moko will hate me.
YES...
...BUT...
...SHO DOESN'T KNOW HOW TO ACT LIKE YOU DO...
HE...
...ACTED LIKE THAT BECAUSE HE WASN'T EXPECTING TO SEE YOU CRY.
He said "I can't!" Because he didn't want to see Kyoko crying again during the real take.
HE WON'T BE ABLE TO ACT THE SAME WAY TWICE, BECAUSE HE KNOWS WHAT YOU'LL BE DOING.
I NOW KNOW THAT SHE DIDN'T CRY BECAUSE OF HER MOTHER.
I CAN'T DO IT A SECOND TIME.
I won't be upset like the first time.
I ALSO THINK THAT SHO'S CONFUSED EXPRESSION...
...WAS REAL...
KYOKO...
YES...

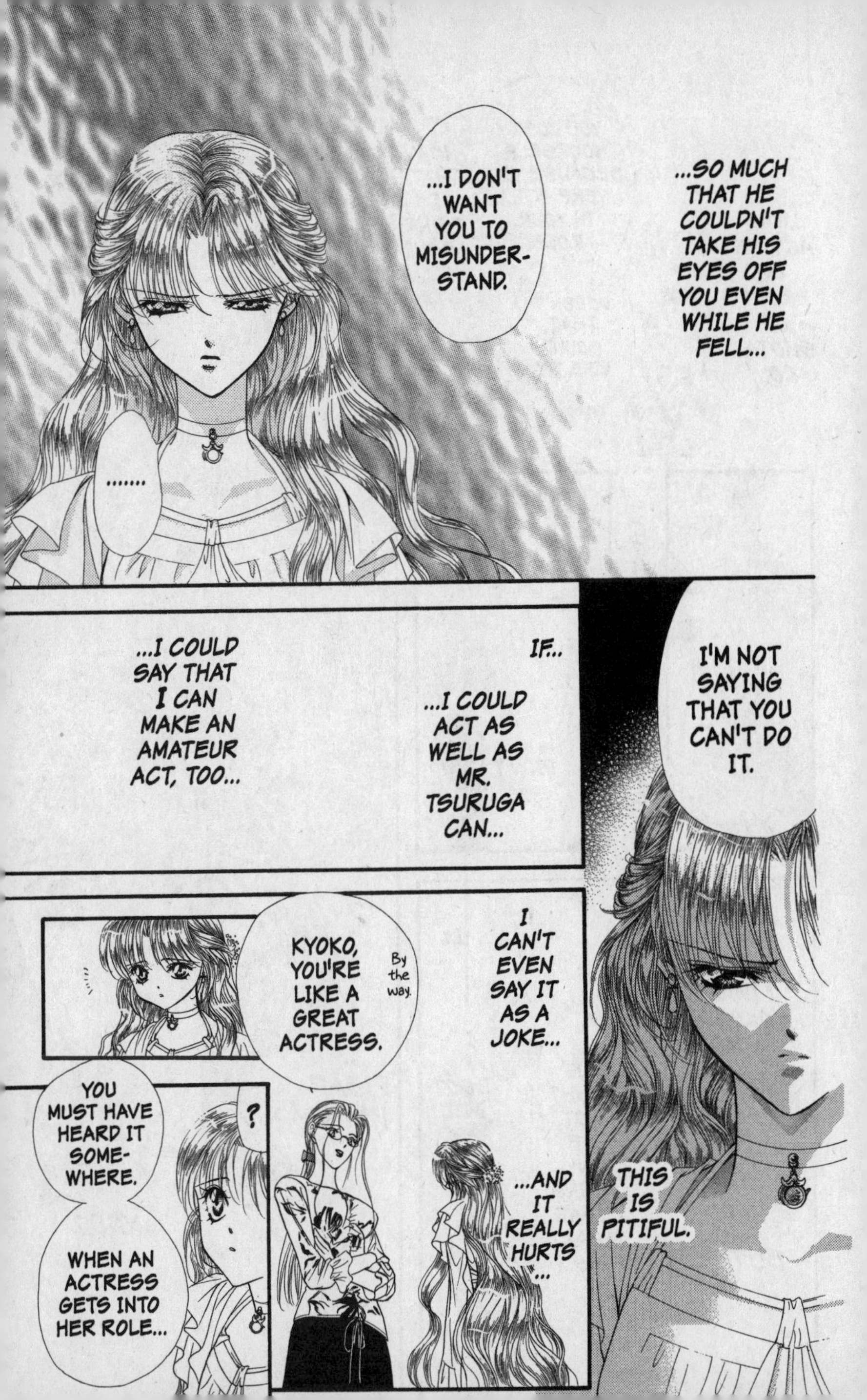
...SO MUCH THAT HE COULDN'T TAKE HIS EYES OFF YOU EVEN WHILE HE FELL...
...I DON'T WANT YOU TO MISUNDERSTAND.
....
I'M NOT SAYING THAT YOU CAN'T DO IT.
IF...
...I COULD ACT AS WELL AS MR. TSURUGA CAN...
...I COULD SAY THAT I CAN MAKE AN AMATEUR ACT, TOO...
I CAN'T EVEN SAY IT AS A JOKE...
...AND IT REALLY HURTS...
THIS IS PITIFUL.
By the way.
KYOKO, YOU'RE LIKE A GREAT ACTRESS.
?
YOU MUST HAVE HEARD IT SOMEWHERE.
WHEN AN ACTRESS GETS INTO HER ROLE...

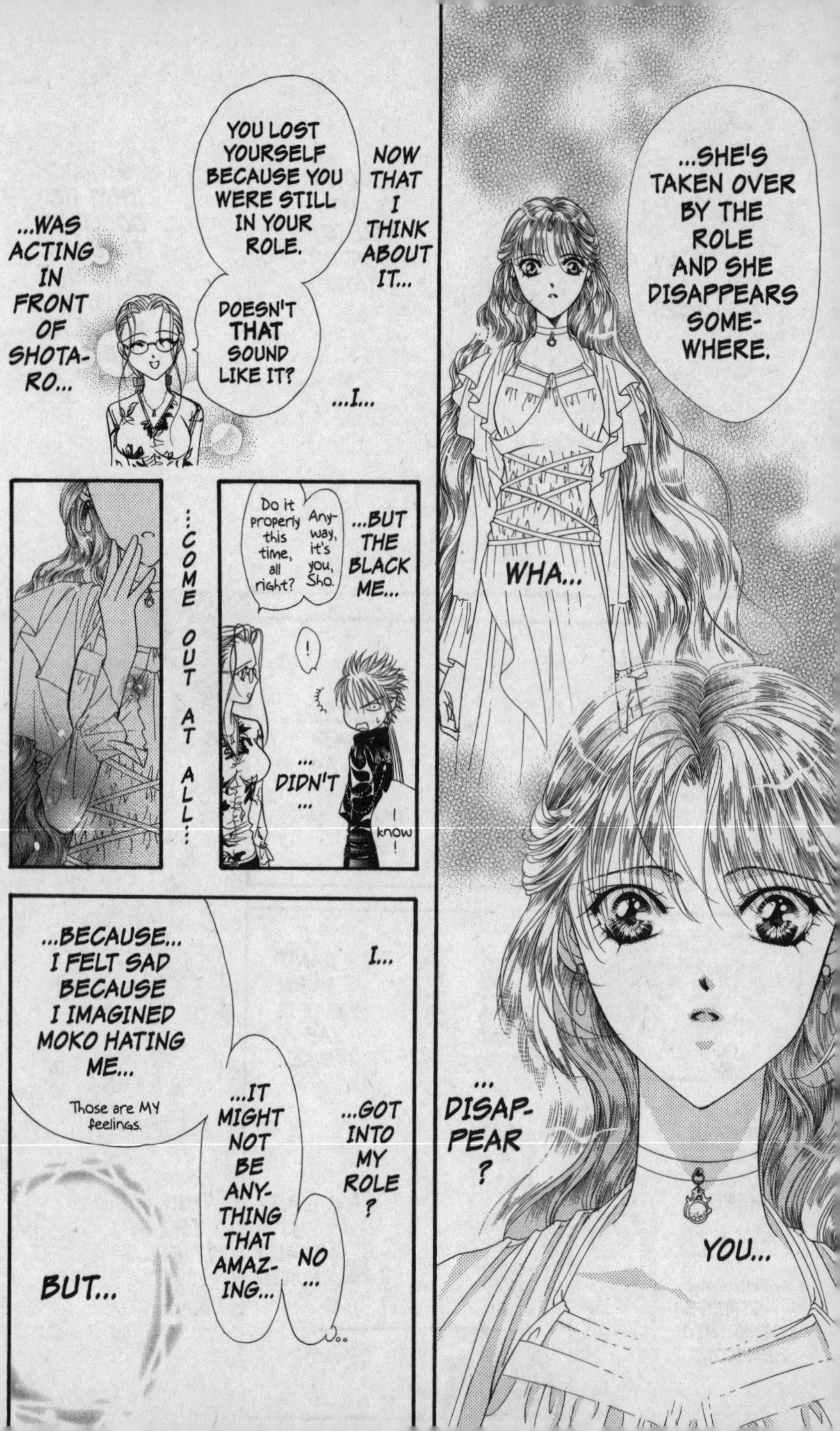
...SHE'S TAKEN OVER BY THE ROLE AND SHE DISAPPEARS SOME-WHERE.
WHA...
...DISAP-PEAR?
YOU...
NOW THAT I THINK ABOUT IT...
YOU LOST YOURSELF BECAUSE YOU WERE STILL IN YOUR ROLE.
DOESN'T THAT SOUND LIKE IT?
...I...
...WAS ACTING IN FRONT OF SHOTA-RO...
...BUT THE BLACK ME...
Any-way, it's you, Sho.
Do it properly this time, all right?
!
...DIDN'T...
I know!
...COME OUT AT ALL...
I...
...GOT INTO MY ROLE?
...IT MIGHT NOT BE ANY-THING THAT AMAZ-ING...
NO...
...BECAUSE... I FELT SAD BECAUSE I IMAGINED MOKO HATING ME...
Those are MY feelings.
BUT...

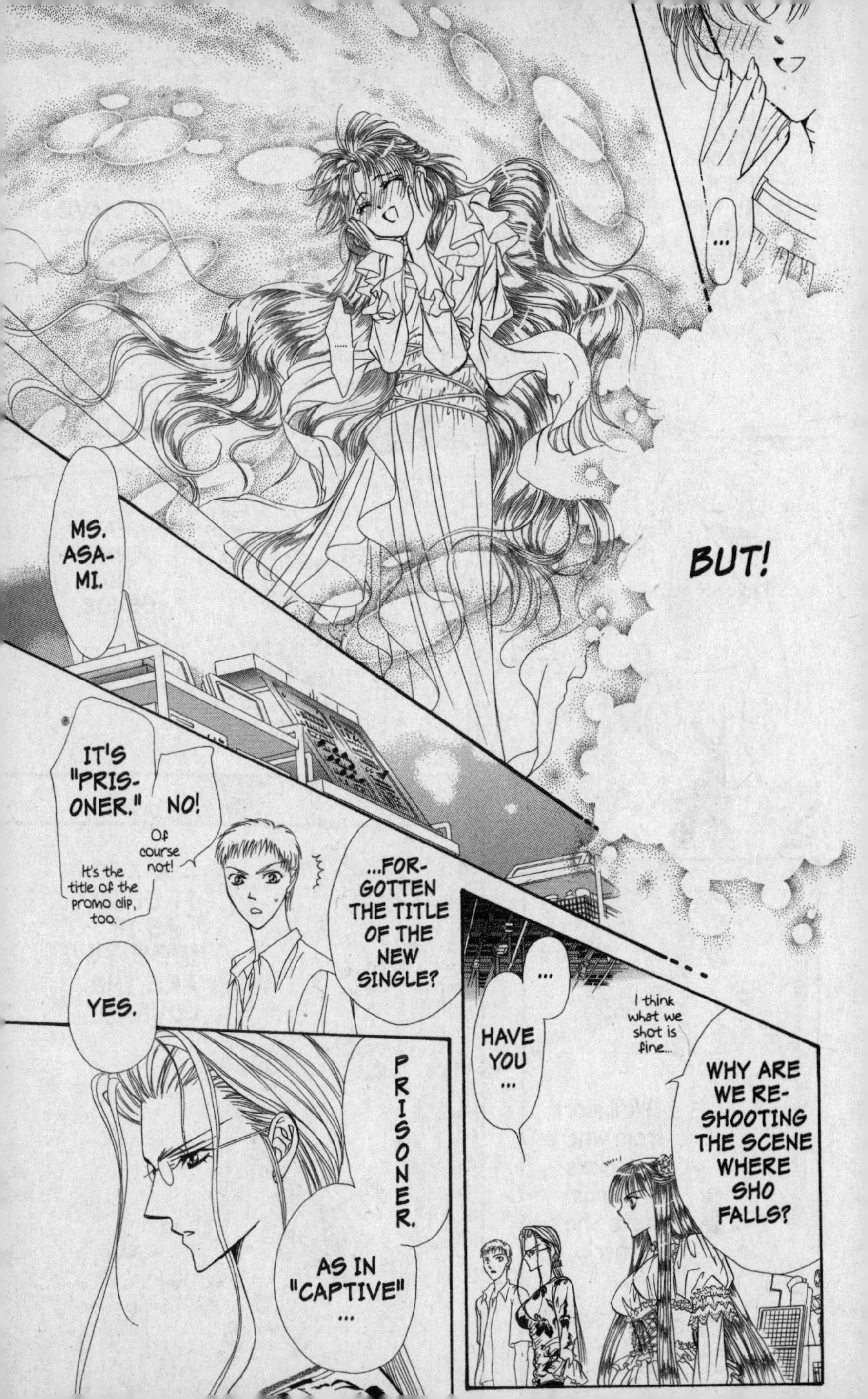
...
BUT!
MS. ASA-MI.
WHY ARE WE RE-SHOOTING THE SCENE WHERE SHO FALLS?
I think what we shot is fine...
...
HAVE YOU ...
...FOR-GOTTEN THE TITLE OF THE NEW SINGLE?
NO!
Of course not!
IT'S "PRIS-ONER."
It's the title of the promo clip, too.
YES.
PRISONER.
AS IN "CAPTIVE" ...

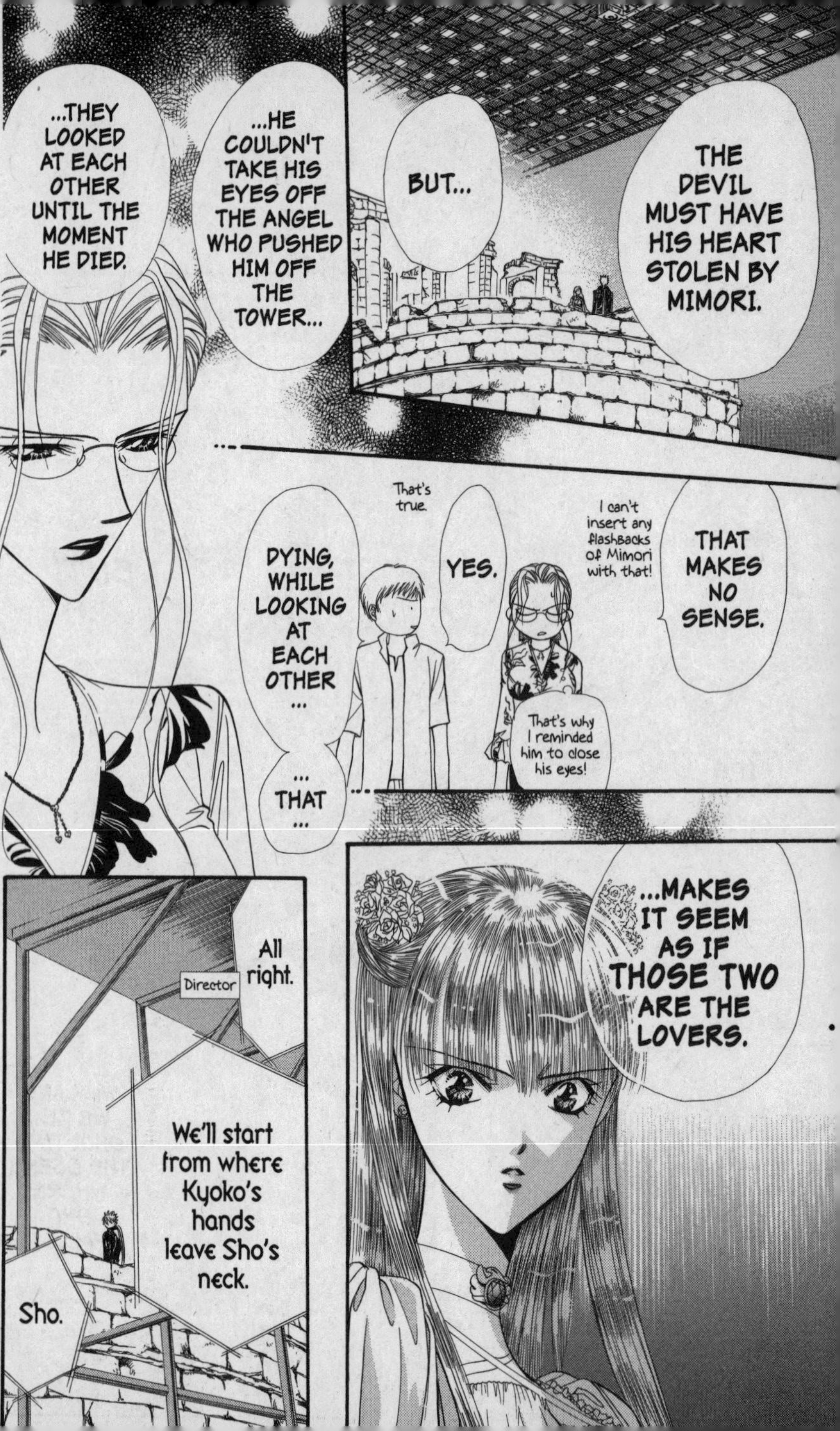
THE DEVIL MUST HAVE HIS HEART STOLEN BY MIMORI.
BUT...
...HE COULDN'T TAKE HIS EYES OFF THE ANGEL WHO PUSHED HIM OFF THE TOWER...
...THEY LOOKED AT EACH OTHER UNTIL THE MOMENT HE DIED.
THAT MAKES NO SENSE.
I can't insert any flashbacks of Mimori with that!
That's why I reminded him to close his eyes!
YES.
That's true.
DYING, WHILE LOOKING AT EACH OTHER...
...THAT...
...MAKES IT SEEM AS IF THOSE TWO ARE THE LOVERS.
Director
All right.
We'll start from where Kyoko's hands leave Sho's neck.
Sho.

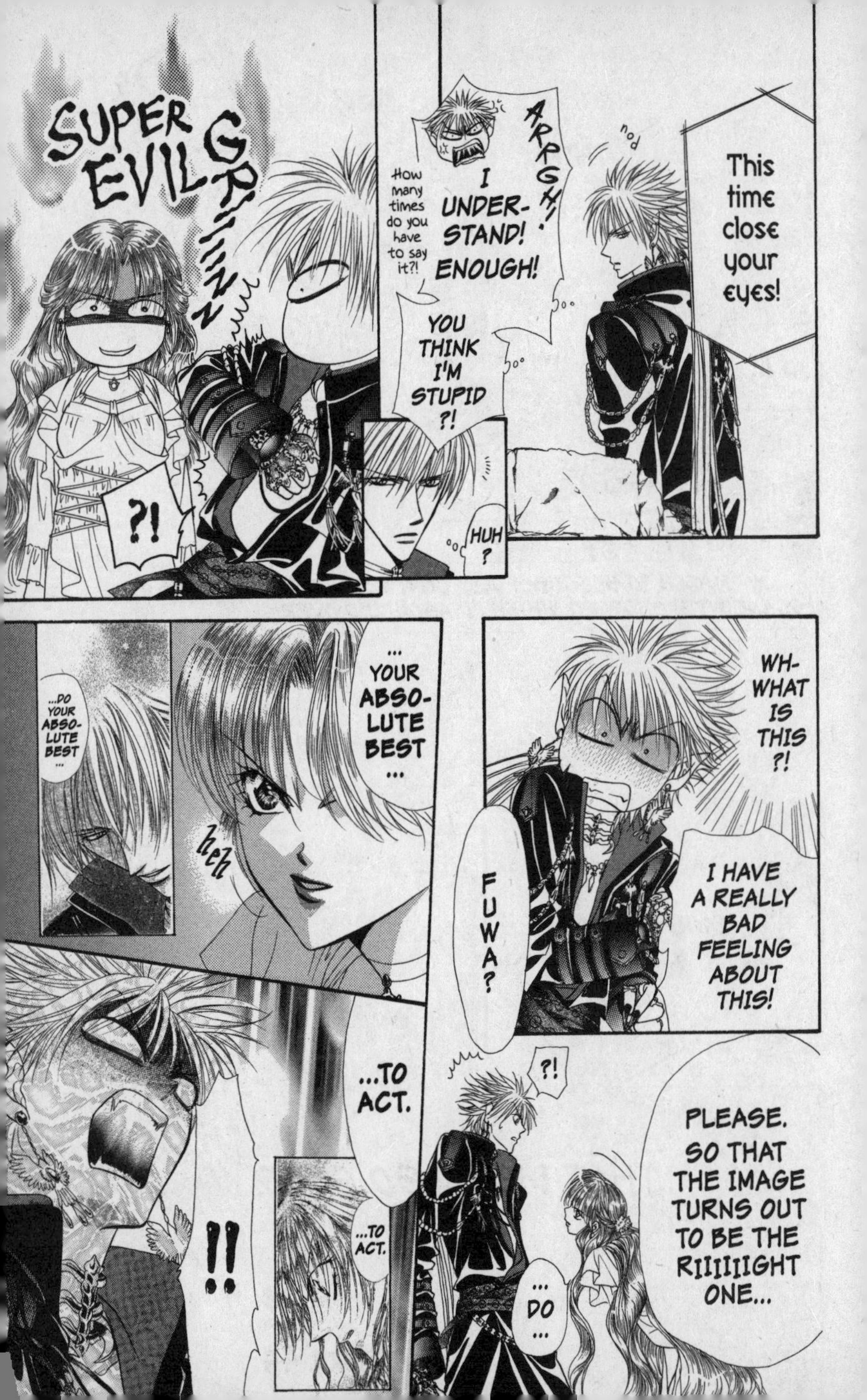
nod
This time close your eyes!
ARRGH!
I UNDER-STAND! ENOUGH!
How many times do you have to say it?!
YOU THINK I'M STUPID?!
HUH?
SUPER EVIL GRIIIINN
?!
WH-WHAT IS THIS?!
I HAVE A REALLY BAD FEELING ABOUT THIS!
FUWA?
...YOUR ABSO-LUTE BEST...
heh
...DO YOUR ABSO-LUTE BEST...
PLEASE. SO THAT THE IMAGE TURNS OUT TO BE THE RIIIIIIGHT ONE...
?!
...DO...
...TO ACT.
...TO ACT.
!!

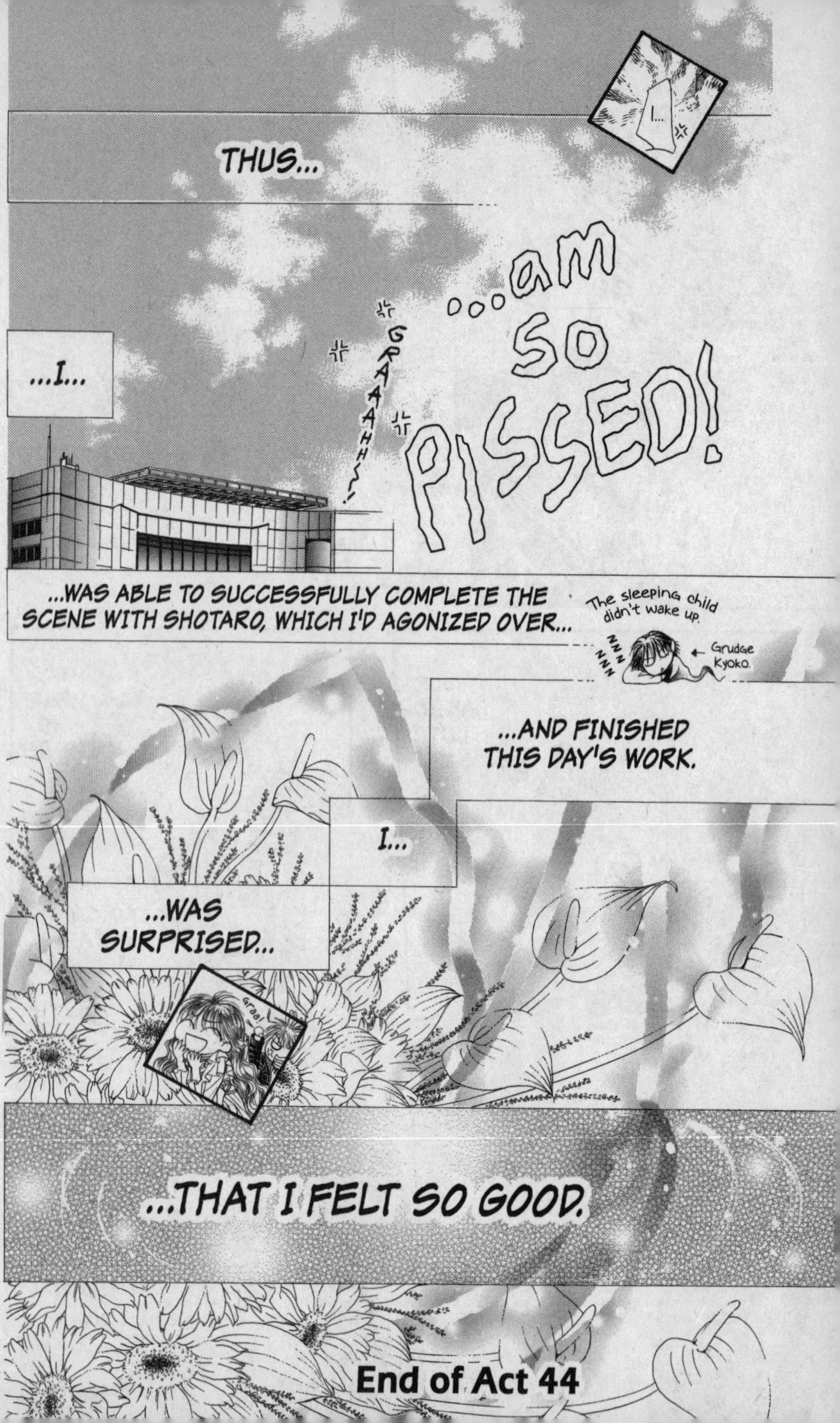
I...
THUS...
...am SO PISSED!
GRAAAHH~!
...I...
...WAS ABLE TO SUCCESSFULLY COMPLETE THE SCENE WITH SHOTARO, WHICH I'D AGONIZED OVER...
The sleeping child didn't wake up.
Grudge Kyoko.
...AND FINISHED THIS DAY'S WORK.
I...
...WAS SURPRISED...
Graa!
...THAT I FELT SO GOOD.
End of Act 44

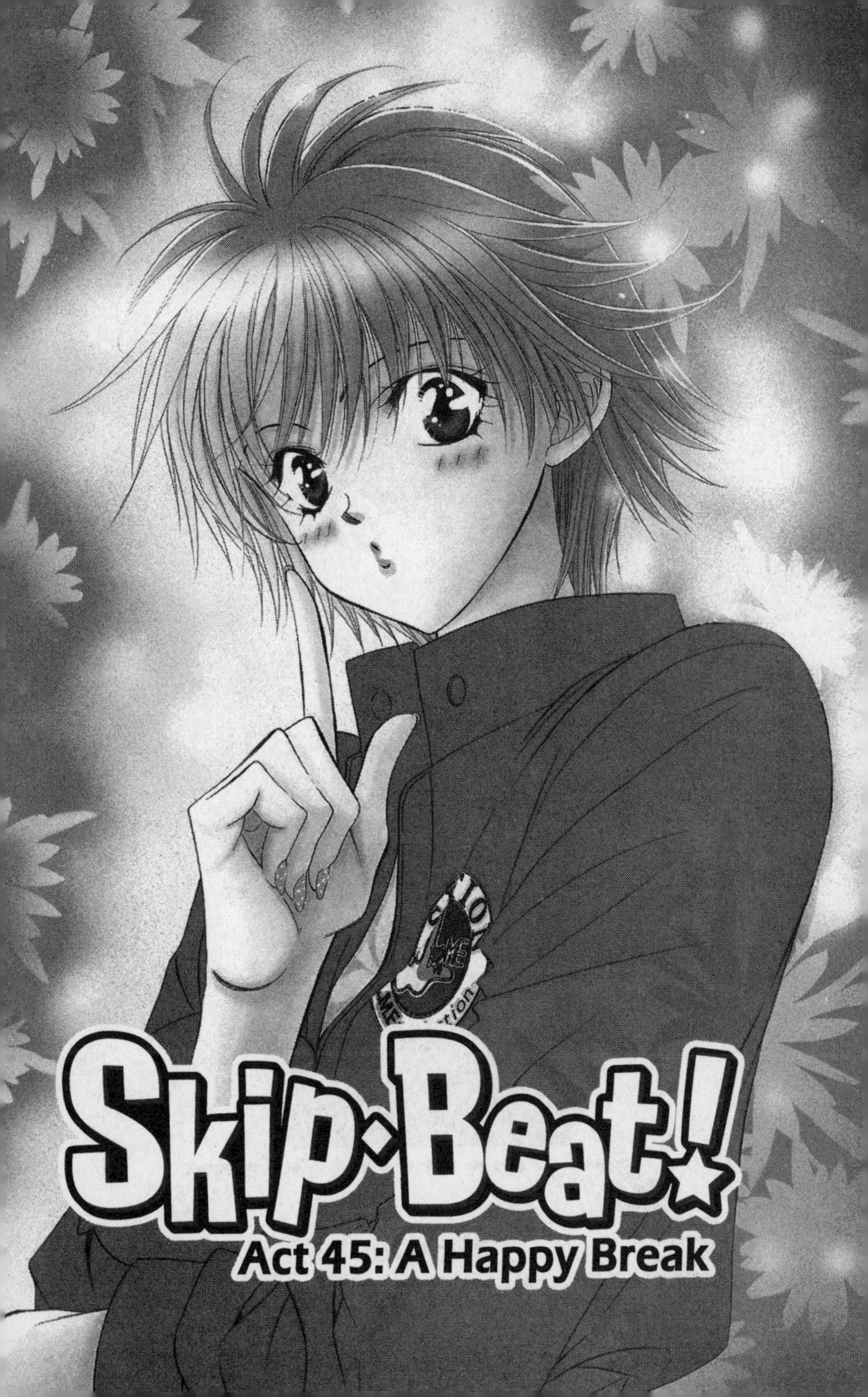
Skip·Beat!
Act 45: A Happy Break

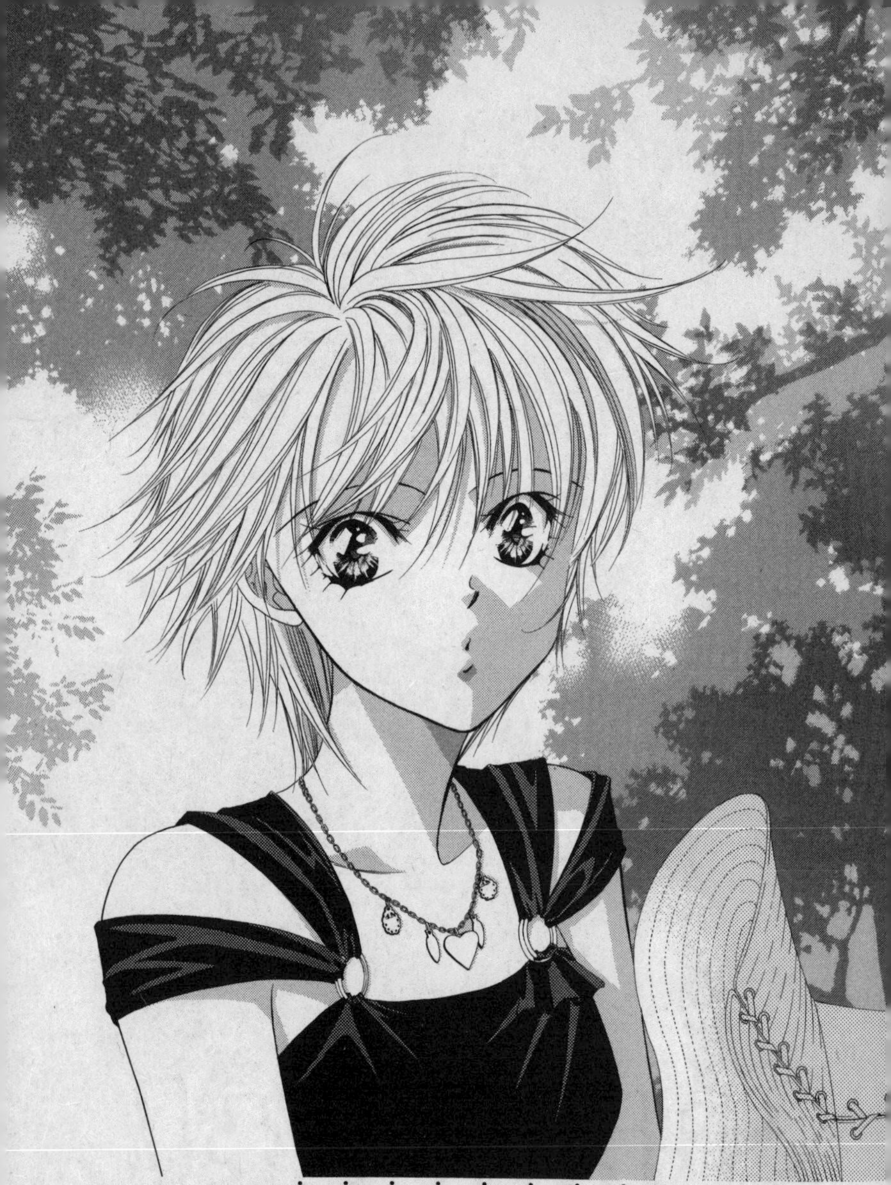

Skip·Beat!

Volume 8

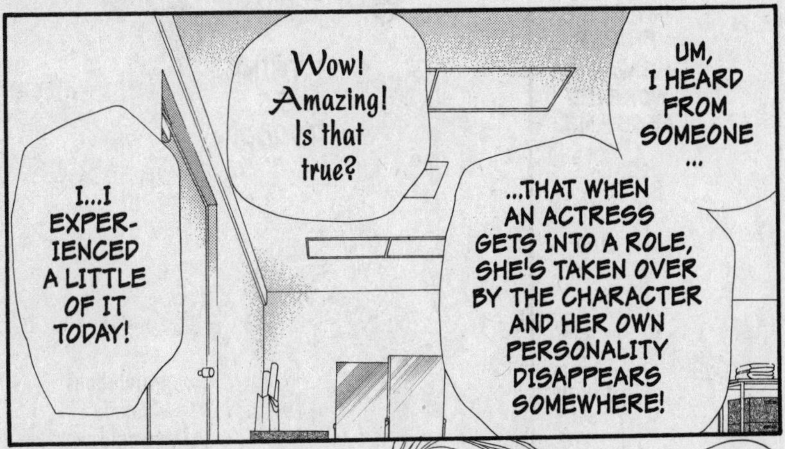
UM, I HEARD FROM SOMEONE ...
...THAT WHEN AN ACTRESS GETS INTO A ROLE, SHE'S TAKEN OVER BY THE CHARACTER AND HER OWN PERSONALITY DISAPPEARS SOMEWHERE!
Wow! Amazing! Is that true?
I...I EXPER-IENCED A LITTLE OF IT TODAY!
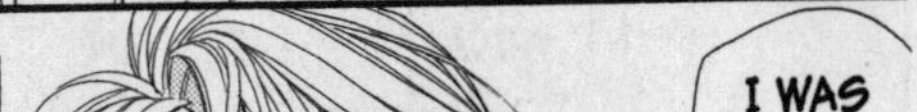
I WAS ACTING IN FRONT OF HIM...
...BUT THE DARK ME THAT ALWAYS APPEARS DIDN'T COME OUT AT AAAAAALL!
eee hee hee
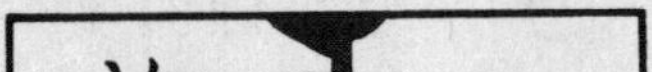
Wow! That's great, Ms. Kyoko!
You must have grown as an actress then!
...
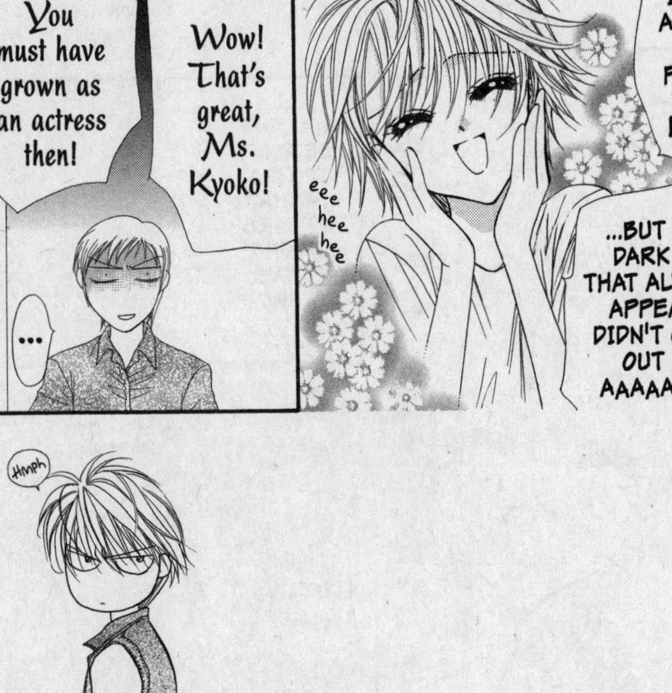
Hmph

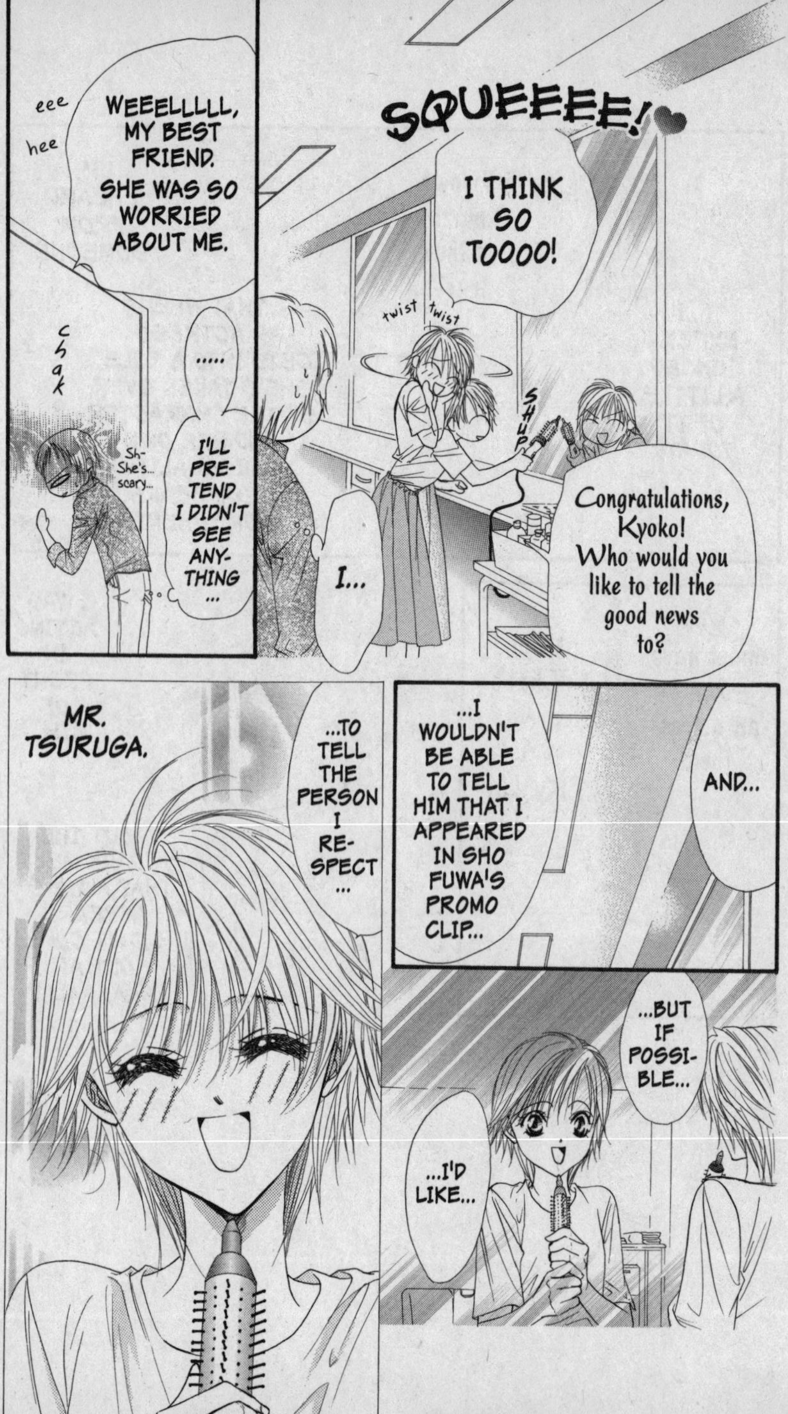
SQUEEEE!
I THINK SO TOOOO!
twist twist
SHUP
Congratulations, Kyoko! Who would you like to tell the good news to?
I...
WEEELLLLL, MY BEST FRIEND. SHE WAS SO WORRIED ABOUT ME.
eee hee
chak
.....
I'LL PRETEND I DIDN'T SEE ANYTHING...
Sh-She's... scary...
AND...
...I WOULDN'T BE ABLE TO TELL HIM THAT I APPEARED IN SHO FUWA'S PROMO CLIP...
...BUT IF POSSIBLE...
...I'D LIKE...
...TO TELL THE PERSON I RESPECT...
MR. TSURUGA.

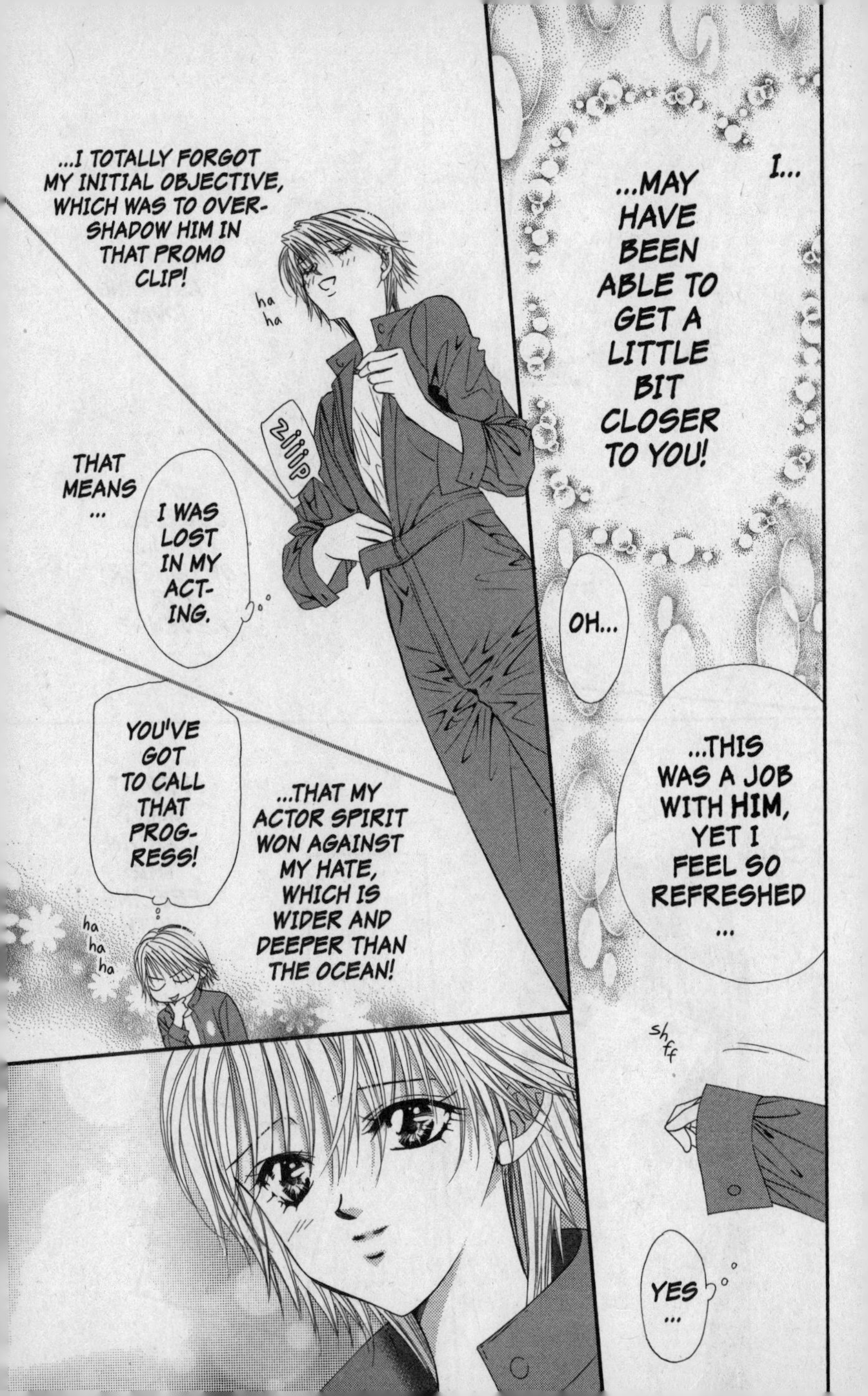
I...
...MAY HAVE BEEN ABLE TO GET A LITTLE BIT CLOSER TO YOU!
OH...
...THIS WAS A JOB WITH HIM, YET I FEEL SO REFRESHED...
...I TOTALLY FORGOT MY INITIAL OBJECTIVE, WHICH WAS TO OVER-SHADOW HIM IN THAT PROMO CLIP!
ha ha
ziiip
THAT MEANS...
I WAS LOST IN MY ACT-ING.
...THAT MY ACTOR SPIRIT WON AGAINST MY HATE, WHICH IS WIDER AND DEEPER THAN THE OCEAN!
YOU'VE GOT TO CALL THAT PROG-RESS!
ha ha ha
shff
YES...

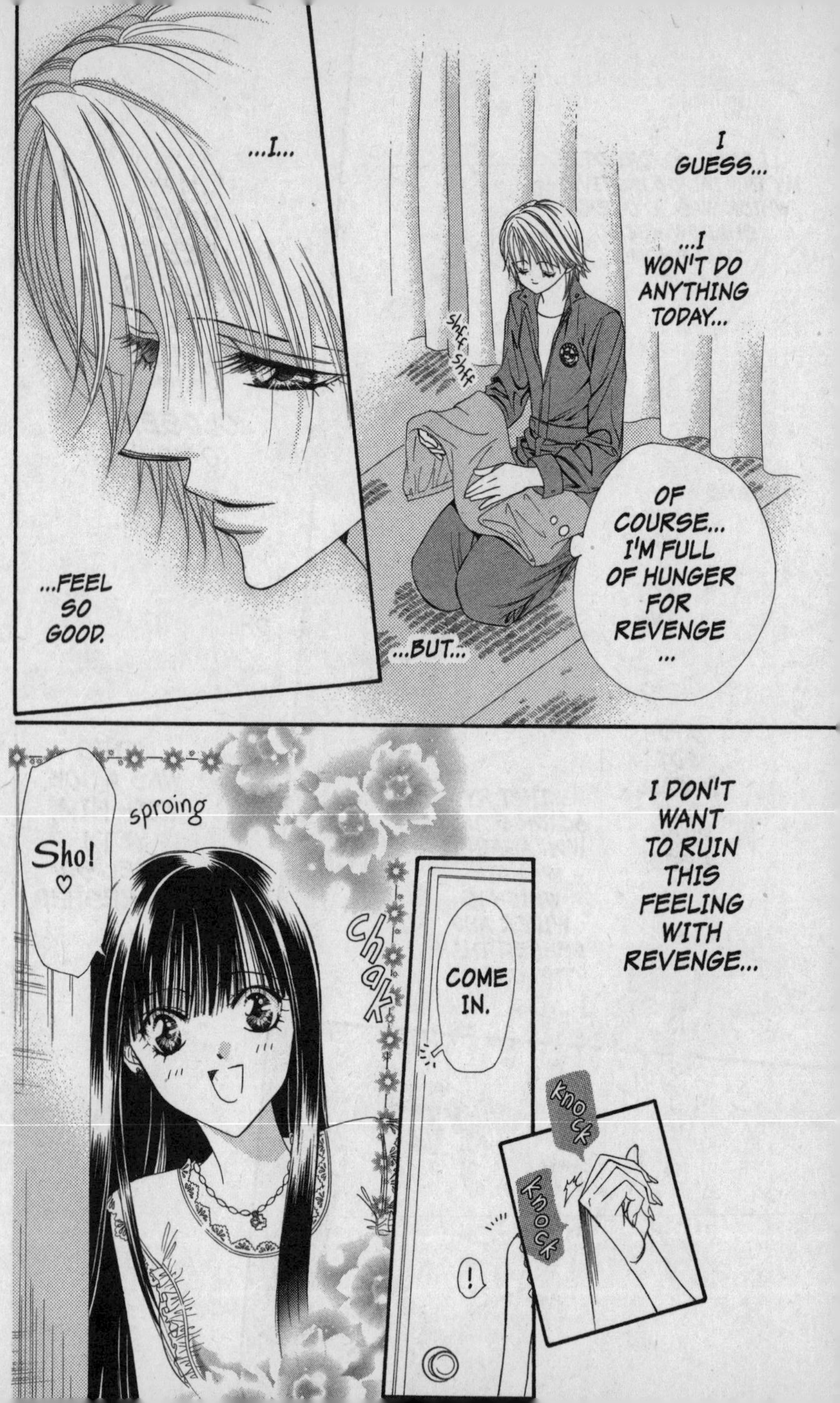
I GUESS...
...I WON'T DO ANYTHING TODAY...
shff shff
OF COURSE... I'M FULL OF HUNGER FOR REVENGE...
...BUT...
...I...
...FEEL SO GOOD.
I DON'T WANT TO RUIN THIS FEELING WITH REVENGE...
knock knock
!
COME IN.
chak
sproing
Sho! ♡

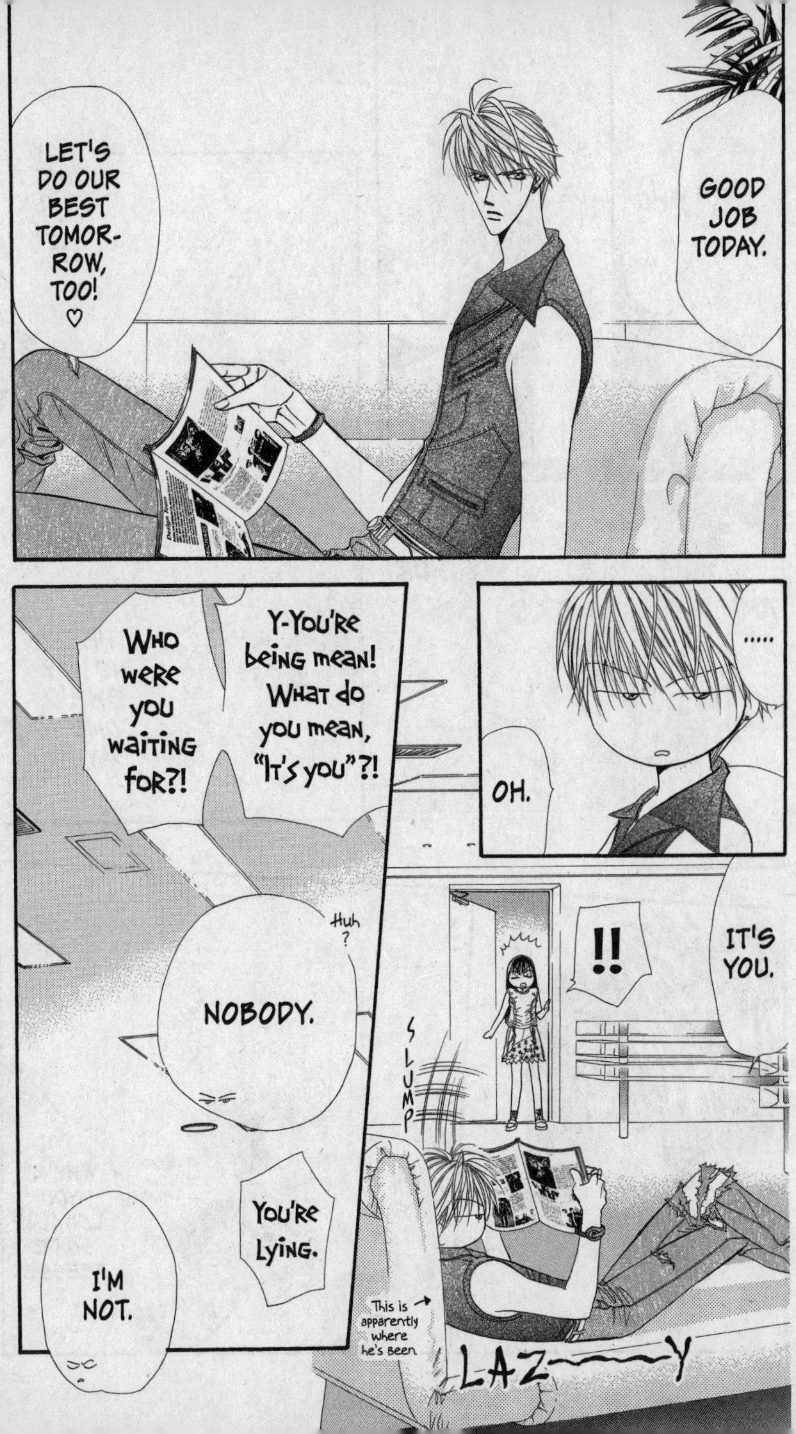
GOOD JOB TODAY.
LET'S DO OUR BEST TOMOR-ROW, TOO! ♡
.....
OH.
IT'S YOU.
!!
SLUMP
This is apparently where he's been
LAZ-----Y
Y-You're being mean! What do you mean, "It's you"?!
Who were you waiting for?!
Huh?
NOBODY.
You're lying.
I'M NOT.

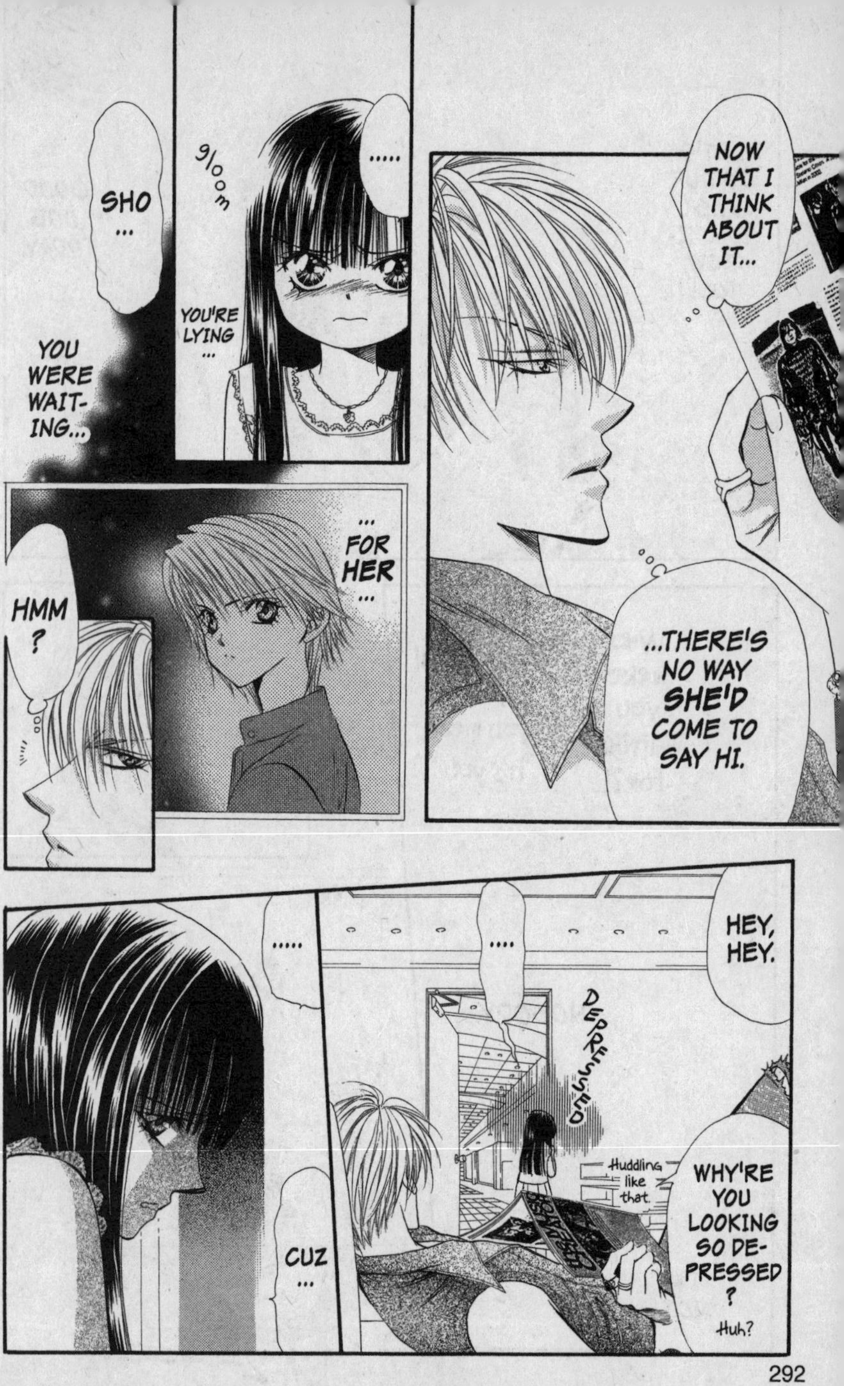

NOW THAT I THINK ABOUT IT...
...THERE'S NO WAY SHE'D COME TO SAY HI.
.....
gloom
YOU'RE LYING...
SHO...
YOU WERE WAIT-ING...
...FOR HER...
HMM?
HEY, HEY.
WHY'RE YOU LOOKING SO DE-PRESSED?
Huh?
Huddling like that.
DEPRESSED
....
.....
CUZ...

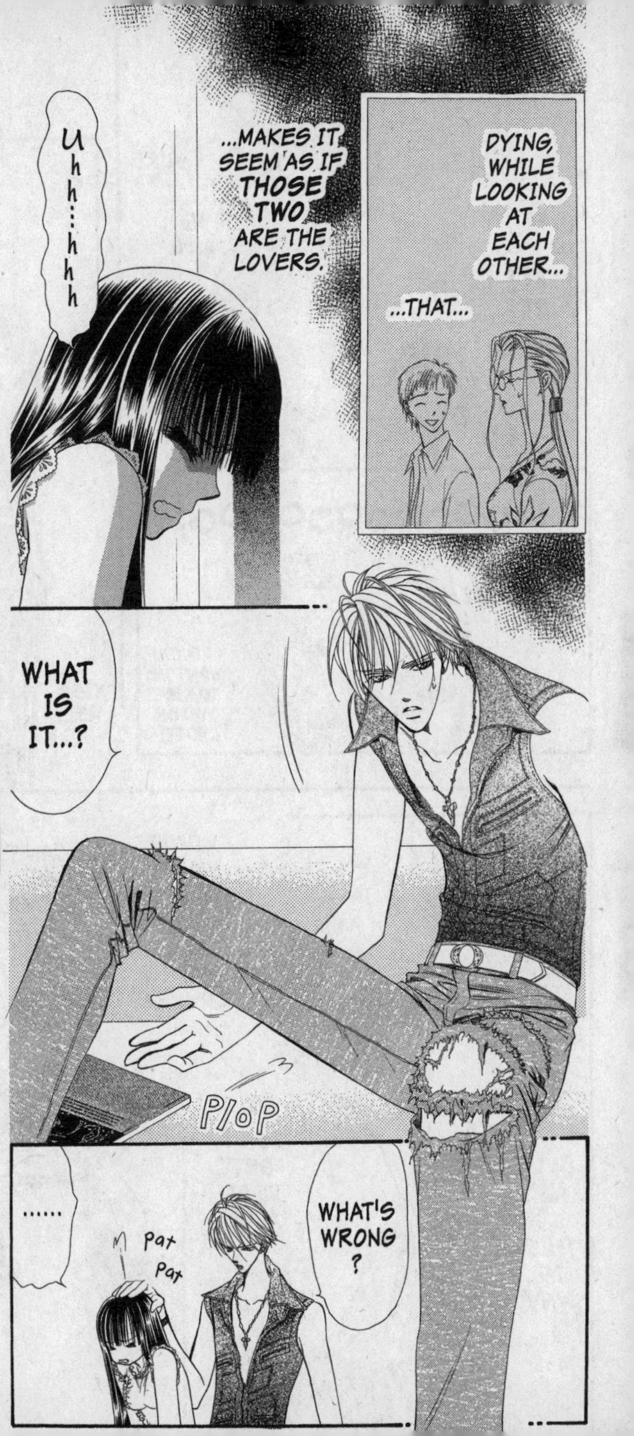
DYING, WHILE LOOKING AT EACH OTHER...
...THAT...
...MAKES IT SEEM AS IF THOSE TWO ARE THE LOVERS.
Uhh...hhh
WHAT IS IT...?
PLOP
WHAT'S WRONG?
M
Pat Pat
......

Mimori Nanokura

For some reason, my assistants liked her...I myself don't hate her either, so I'm thinking about having her appear in Kyoko's school scenes again...

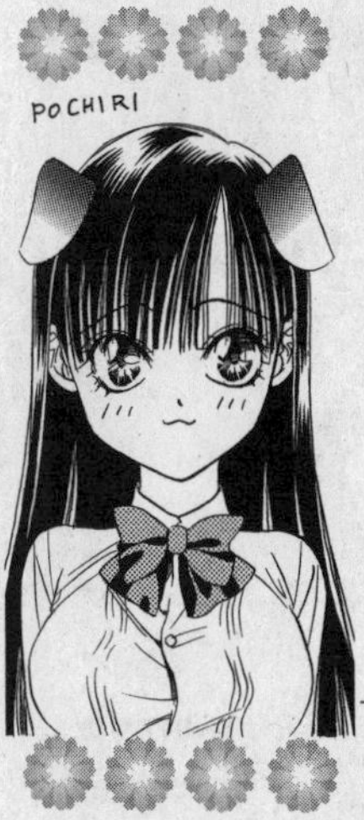
POCHIRI

If I have the time to have Pochi, who has nothing to do with the main story, interact and play around with Kyoko... That is...in my case, I'm so obsessed with the "ending" of each chapter, I run out of pages, so I cut things here and there...and episodes disappear often... 6

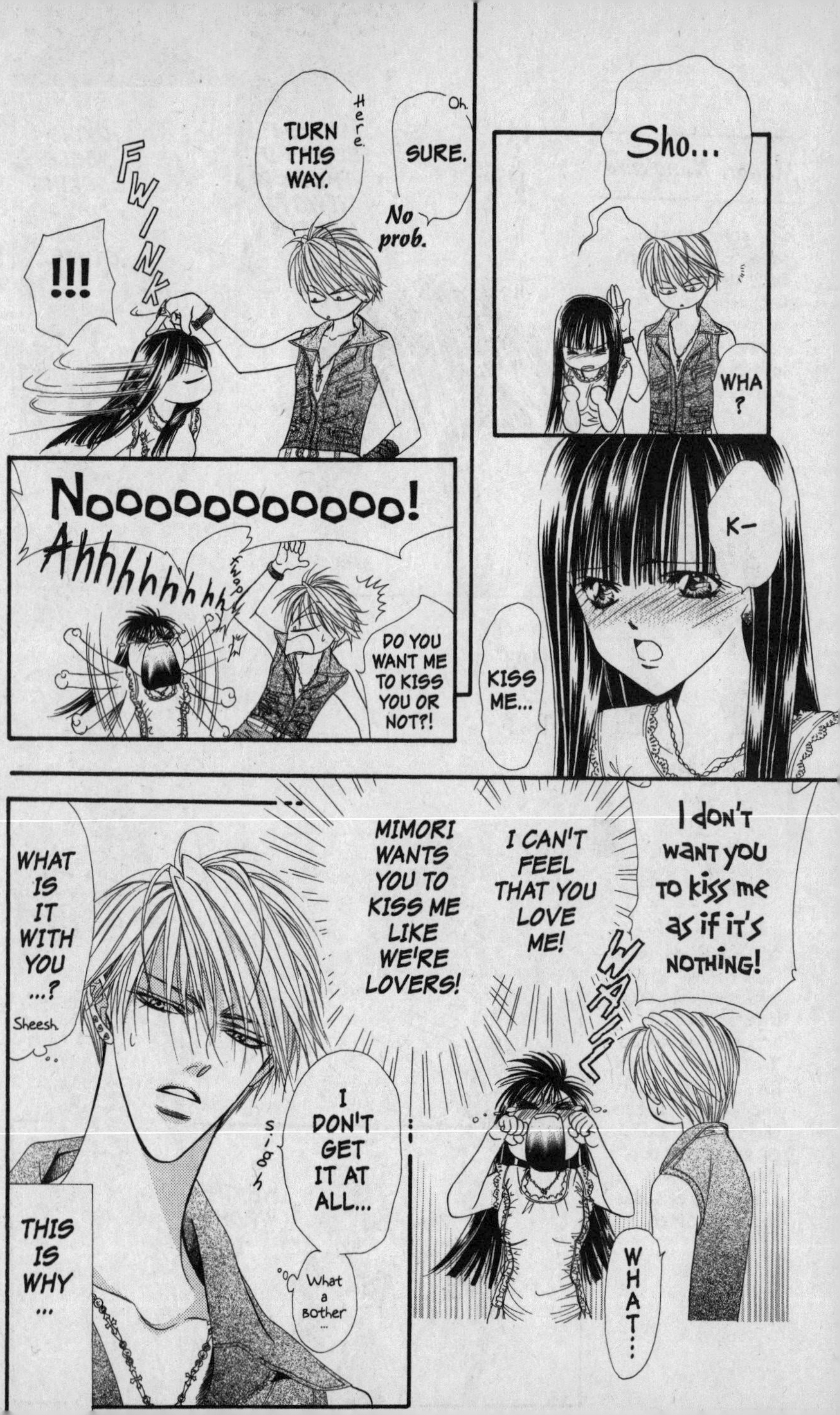

Sho...
WHA?
K-
KISS ME...
Oh.
SURE.
No prob.
Here.
TURN THIS WAY.
FWINK
!!!
Nooooooooooo!
Ahhhhhhhh
twap
DO YOU WANT ME TO KISS YOU OR NOT?!
I don't want you to kiss me as if it's nothing!
WAIL
I CAN'T FEEL THAT YOU LOVE ME!
MIMORI WANTS YOU TO KISS ME LIKE WE'RE LOVERS!
WHAT...
I DON'T GET IT AT ALL...
sigh
What a bother...
WHAT IS IT WITH YOU...?
Sheesh.
THIS IS WHY...

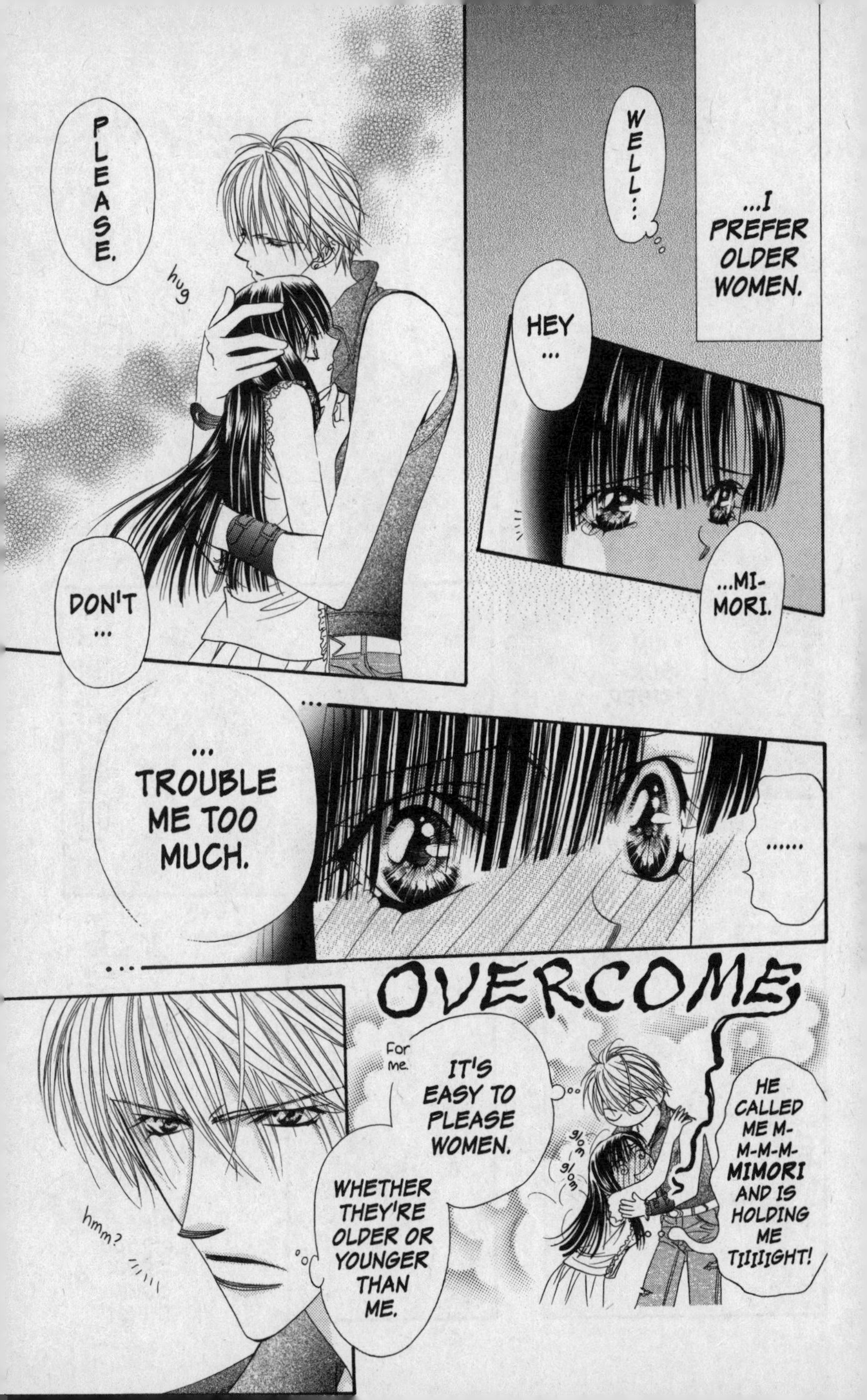

...I PREFER OLDER WOMEN.
WELL...
HEY...
...MI-MORI.
PLEASE.
hug
DON'T...
......
...TROUBLE ME TOO MUCH.
OVERCOME
HE CALLED ME M-M-M-M-MIMORI AND IS HOLDING ME TIIIIIGHT!
glom glom
IT'S EASY TO PLEASE WOMEN.
For me.
WHETHER THEY'RE OLDER OR YOUNGER THAN ME.
hmm?

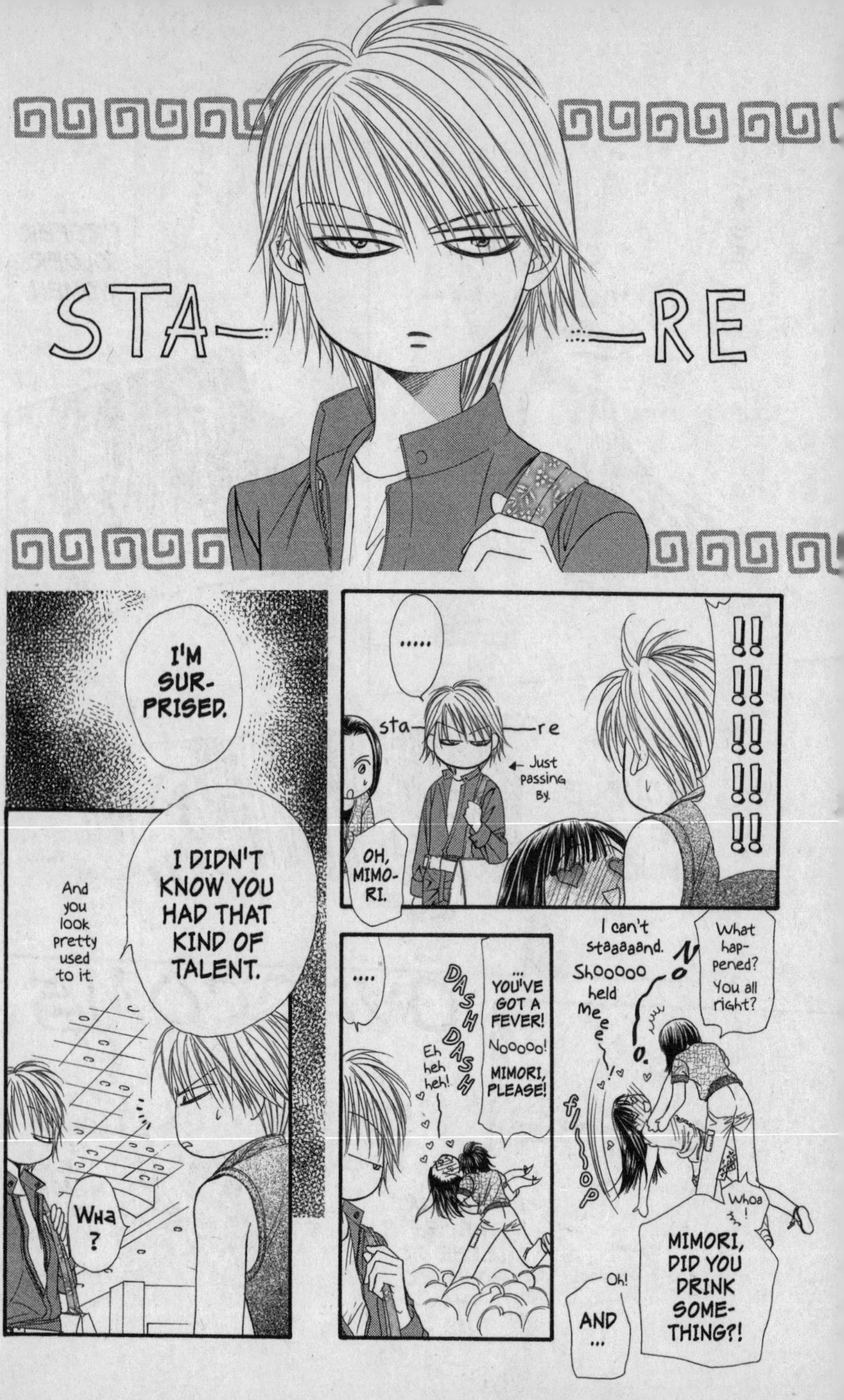
STA— —RE
!! !! !! !! !!
.....
sta— —re
Just passing by.
OH, MIMORI.
What happened? You all right?
I can't staaaaand. Shoooooo held meeee~!
NO
fl~op
Whoa!
MIMORI, DID YOU DRINK SOMETHING?!
Oh! AND ...
... YOU'VE GOT A FEVER! Nooooo! MIMORI, PLEASE!
DASH DASH
Eh heh heh!
....
I'M SURPRISED.
I DIDN'T KNOW YOU HAD THAT KIND OF TALENT.
And you look pretty used to it.
Wha?

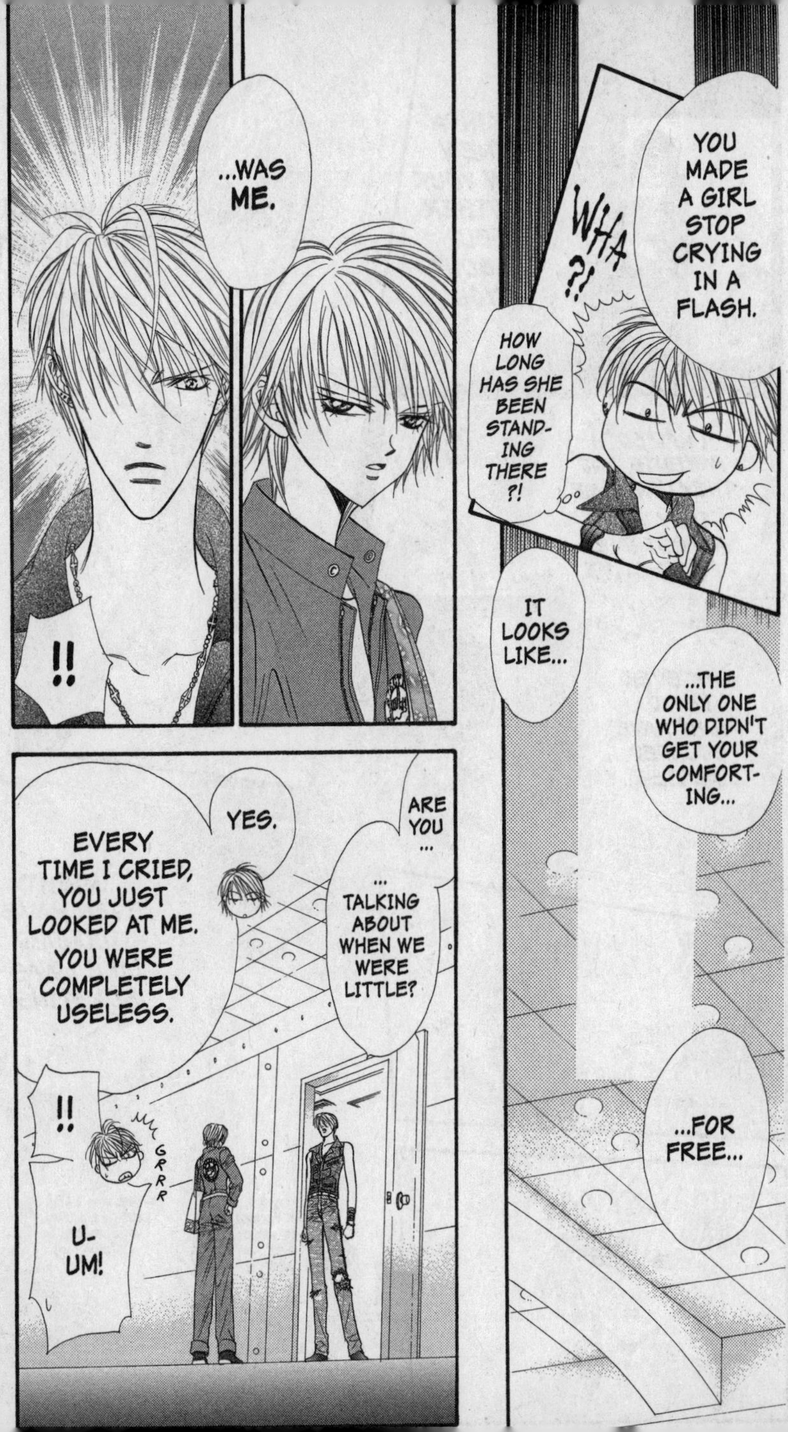
YOU MADE A GIRL STOP CRYING IN A FLASH.
WHA ?!
HOW LONG HAS SHE BEEN STANDING THERE ?!
IT LOOKS LIKE...
...THE ONLY ONE WHO DIDN'T GET YOUR COMFORTING...
...FOR FREE...
...WAS ME.
!!
ARE YOU ...
... TALKING ABOUT WHEN WE WERE LITTLE?
YES.
EVERY TIME I CRIED, YOU JUST LOOKED AT ME. YOU WERE COMPLETELY USELESS.
!!
GRRR
U-UM!

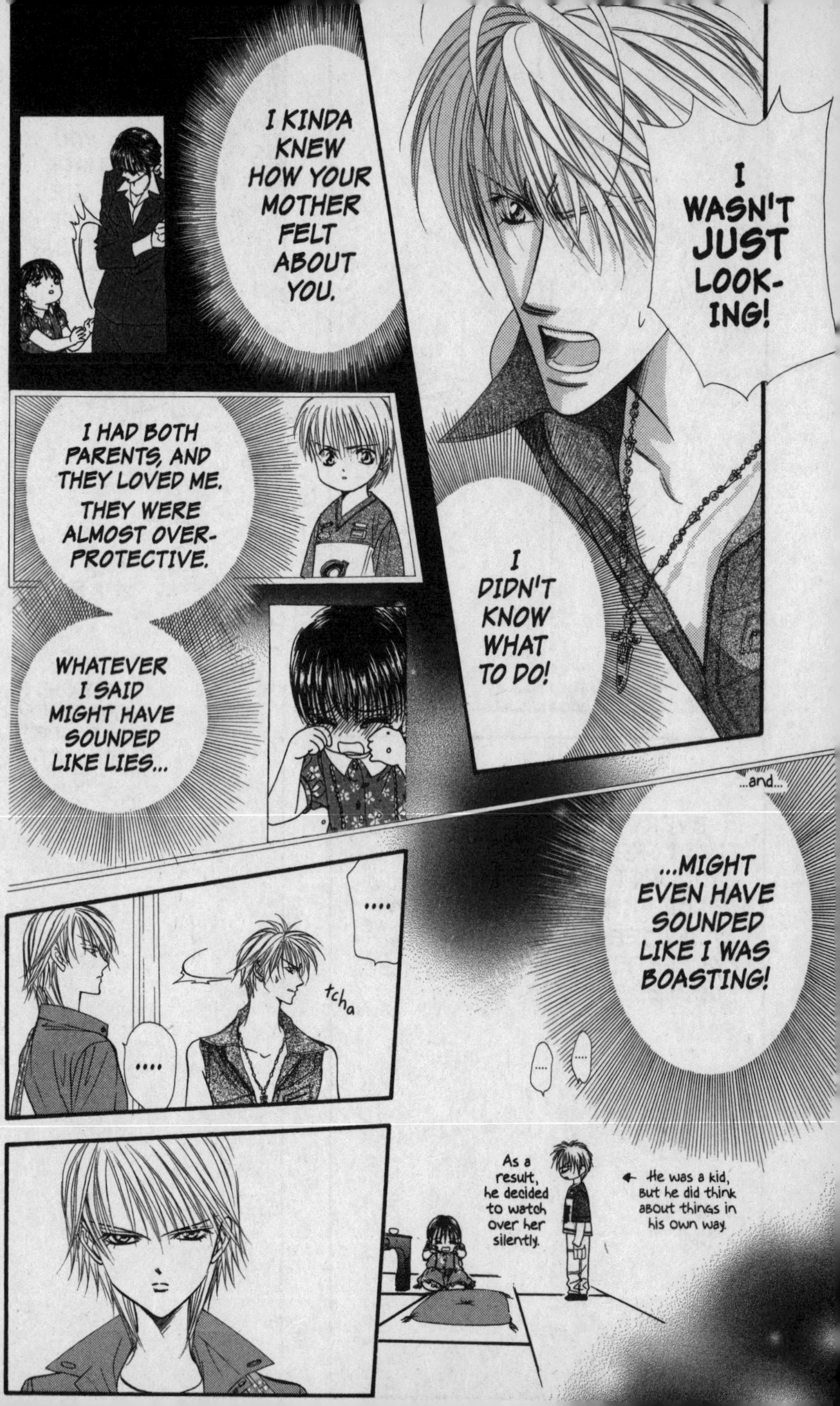
I WASN'T JUST LOOKING!
I DIDN'T KNOW WHAT TO DO!
I KINDA KNEW HOW YOUR MOTHER FELT ABOUT YOU.
I HAD BOTH PARENTS, AND THEY LOVED ME. THEY WERE ALMOST OVER-PROTECTIVE.
WHATEVER I SAID MIGHT HAVE SOUNDED LIKE LIES...
...and...
...MIGHT EVEN HAVE SOUNDED LIKE I WAS BOASTING!
....
....
....
tcha
....
He was a kid, but he did think about things in his own way.
As a result, he decided to watch over her silently.

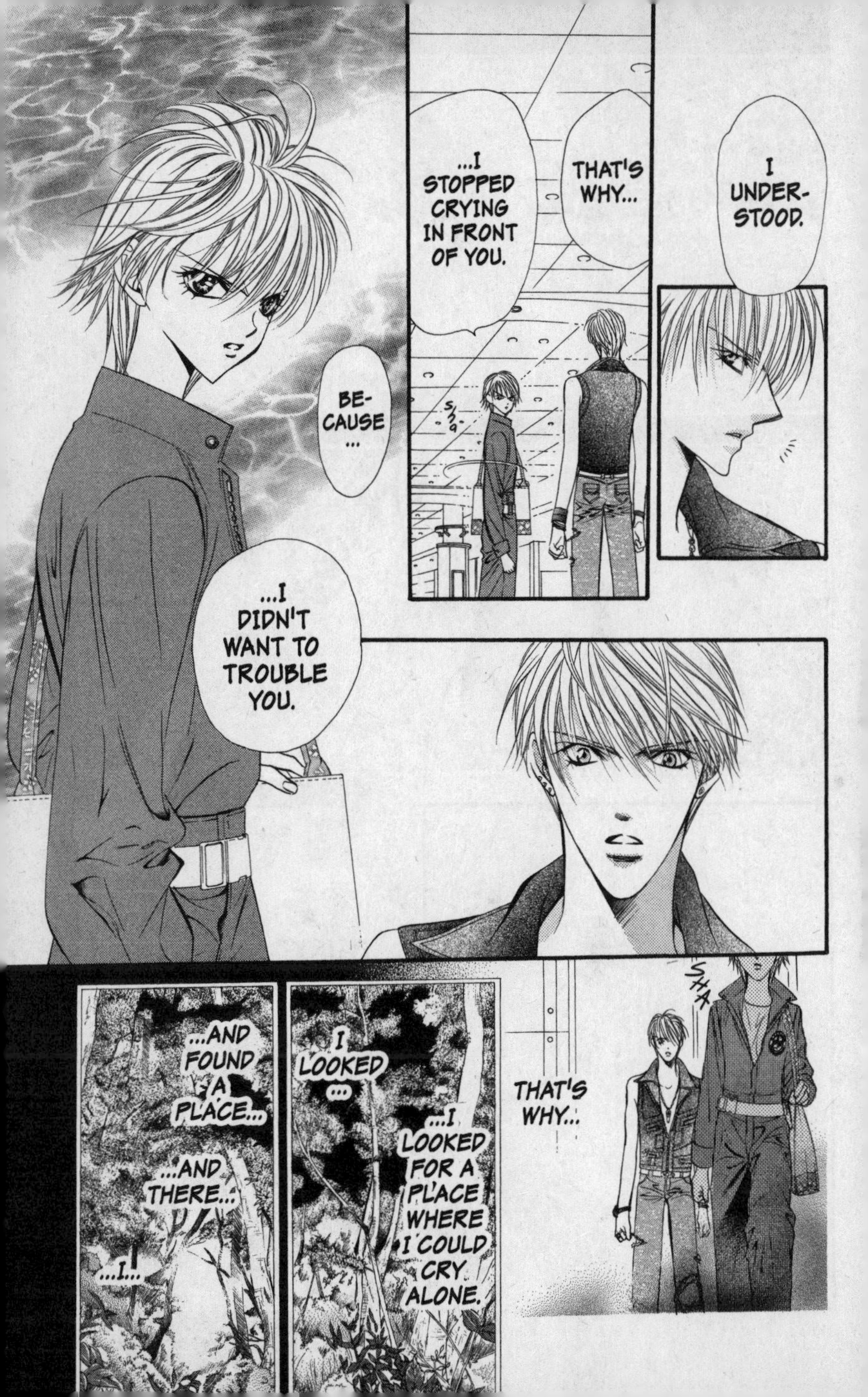
I UNDERSTOOD.
THAT'S WHY...
...I STOPPED CRYING IN FRONT OF YOU.
BECAUSE...
...I DIDN'T WANT TO TROUBLE YOU.
SHA
THAT'S WHY...
I LOOKED...
...I LOOKED FOR A PLACE WHERE I COULD CRY ALONE.
...AND FOUND A PLACE...
...AND THERE...
...I...

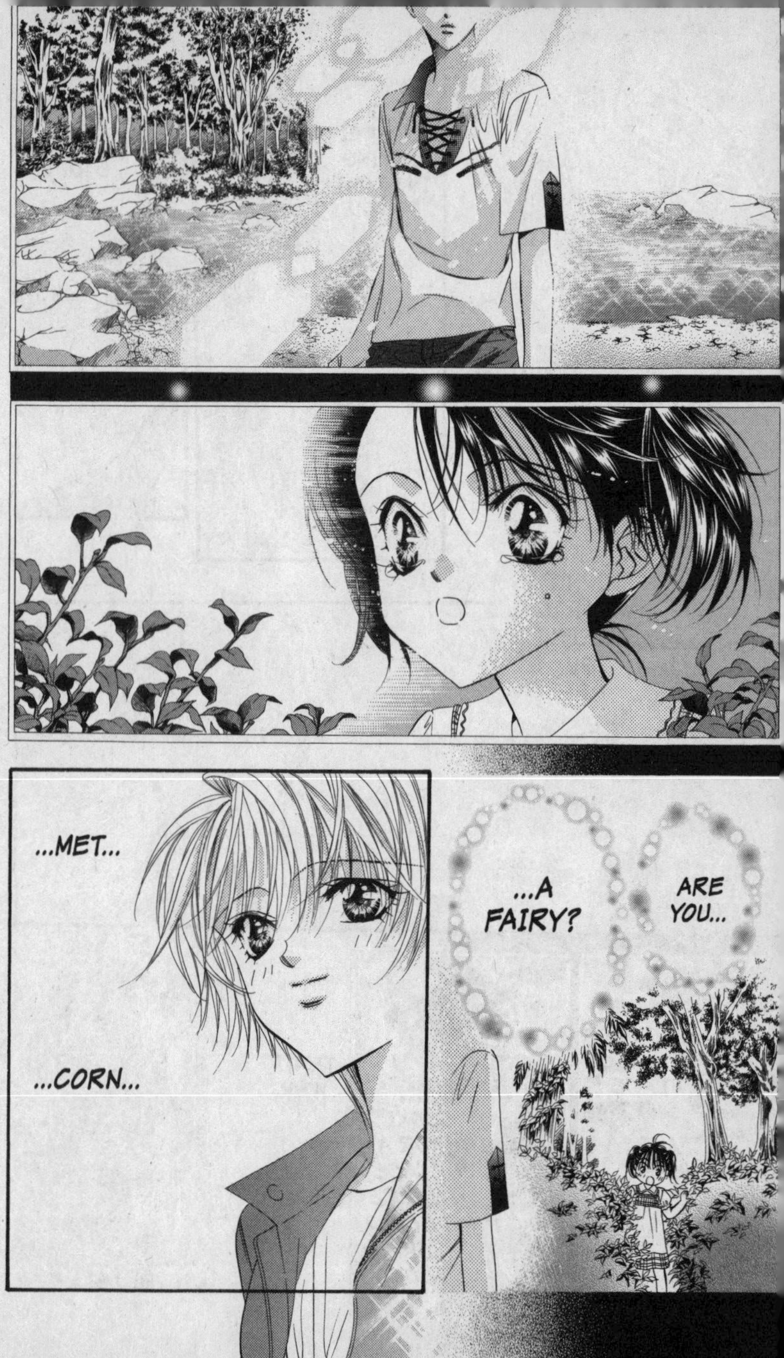
ARE YOU...
...A FAIRY?
...MET...
...CORN...

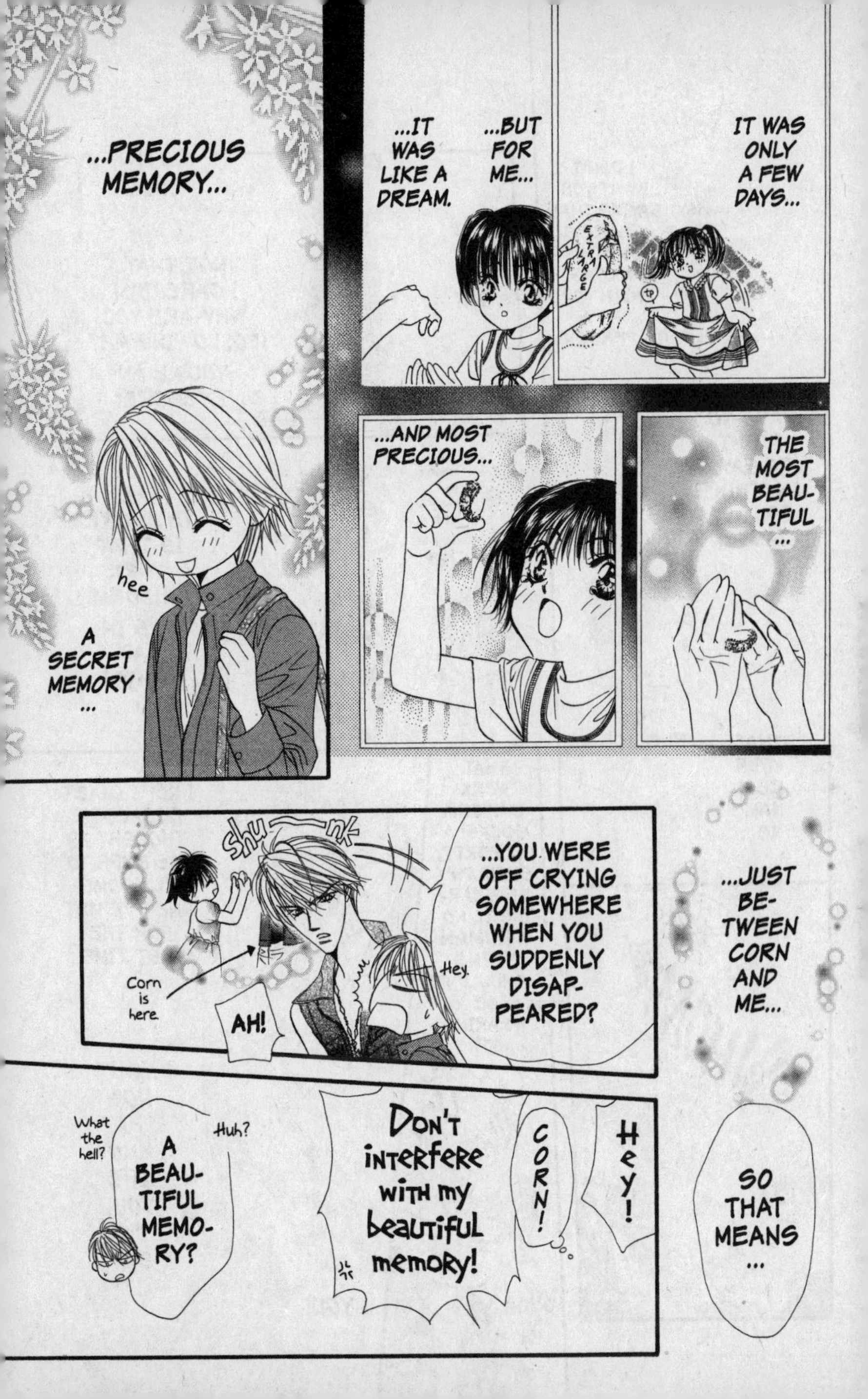
IT WAS ONLY A FEW DAYS...
EXTRA LARGE
tp
...BUT FOR ME...
...IT WAS LIKE A DREAM.
THE MOST BEAUTIFUL...
...AND MOST PRECIOUS...
...PRECIOUS MEMORY...
hee
A SECRET MEMORY...
...JUST BETWEEN CORN AND ME...
...YOU WERE OFF CRYING SOMEWHERE WHEN YOU SUDDENLY DISAPPEARED?
Hey.
shu—nk
AH!
Corn is here.
SO THAT MEANS...
Hey!
CORN!
Don't interfere with my beautiful memory!
Huh?
A BEAUTIFUL MEMORY?
What the hell?

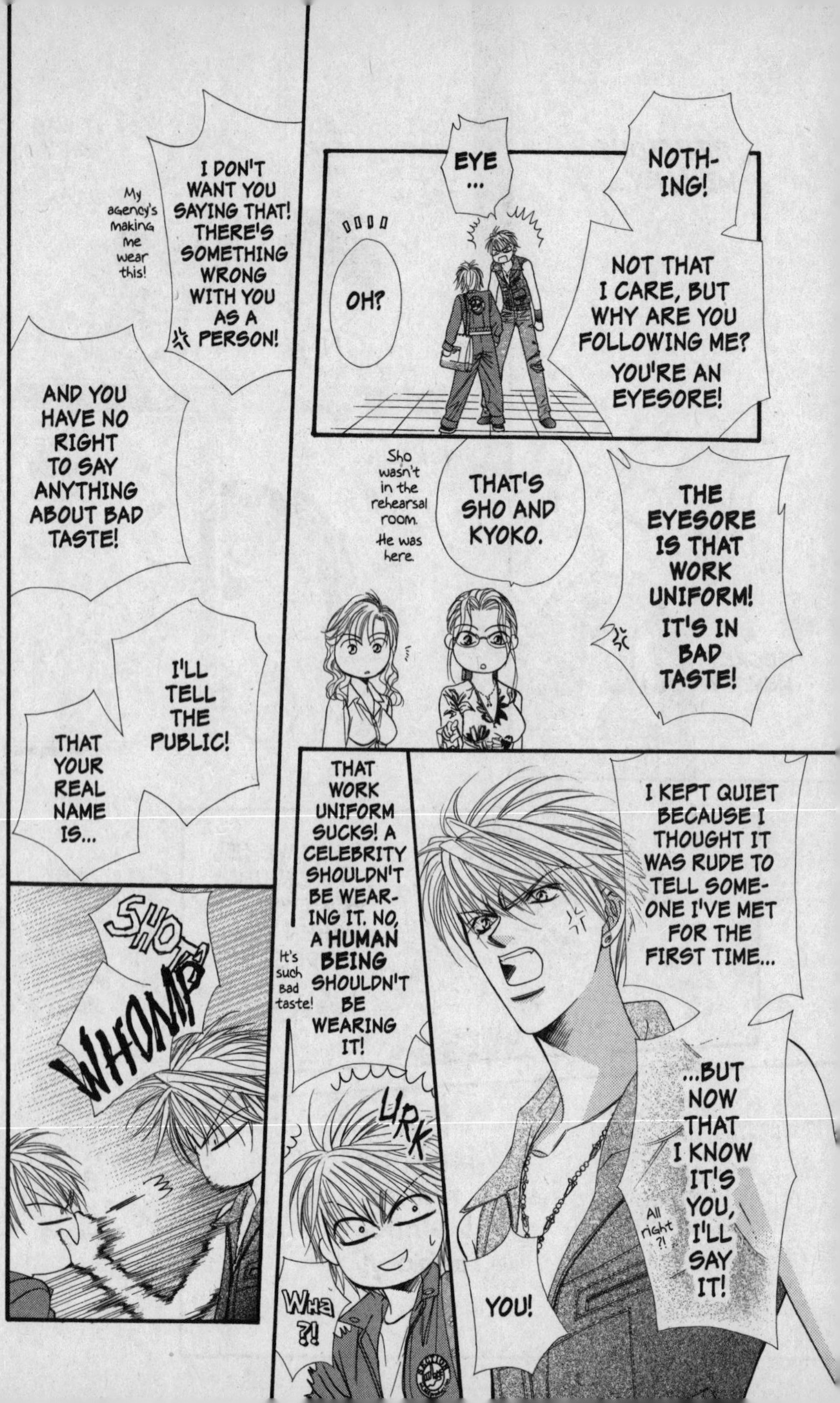
NOTH-ING!
NOT THAT I CARE, BUT WHY ARE YOU FOLLOWING ME? YOU'RE AN EYESORE!
EYE ...
OH?
THE EYESORE IS THAT WORK UNIFORM! IT'S IN BAD TASTE!
THAT'S SHO AND KYOKO.
Sho wasn't in the rehearsal room. He was here.
I KEPT QUIET BECAUSE I THOUGHT IT WAS RUDE TO TELL SOME-ONE I'VE MET FOR THE FIRST TIME...
...BUT NOW THAT I KNOW IT'S YOU, I'LL SAY IT!
All right ?!
YOU!
THAT WORK UNIFORM SUCKS! A CELEBRITY SHOULDN'T BE WEAR-ING IT. NO, A HUMAN BEING SHOULDN'T BE WEARING IT!
It's such bad taste!
URK
WHA ?!
I DON'T WANT YOU SAYING THAT! THERE'S SOMETHING WRONG WITH YOU AS A PERSON!
My agency's making me wear this!
AND YOU HAVE NO RIGHT TO SAY ANYTHING ABOUT BAD TASTE!
I'LL TELL THE PUBLIC!
THAT YOUR REAL NAME IS...
SHOTA
WHOMP

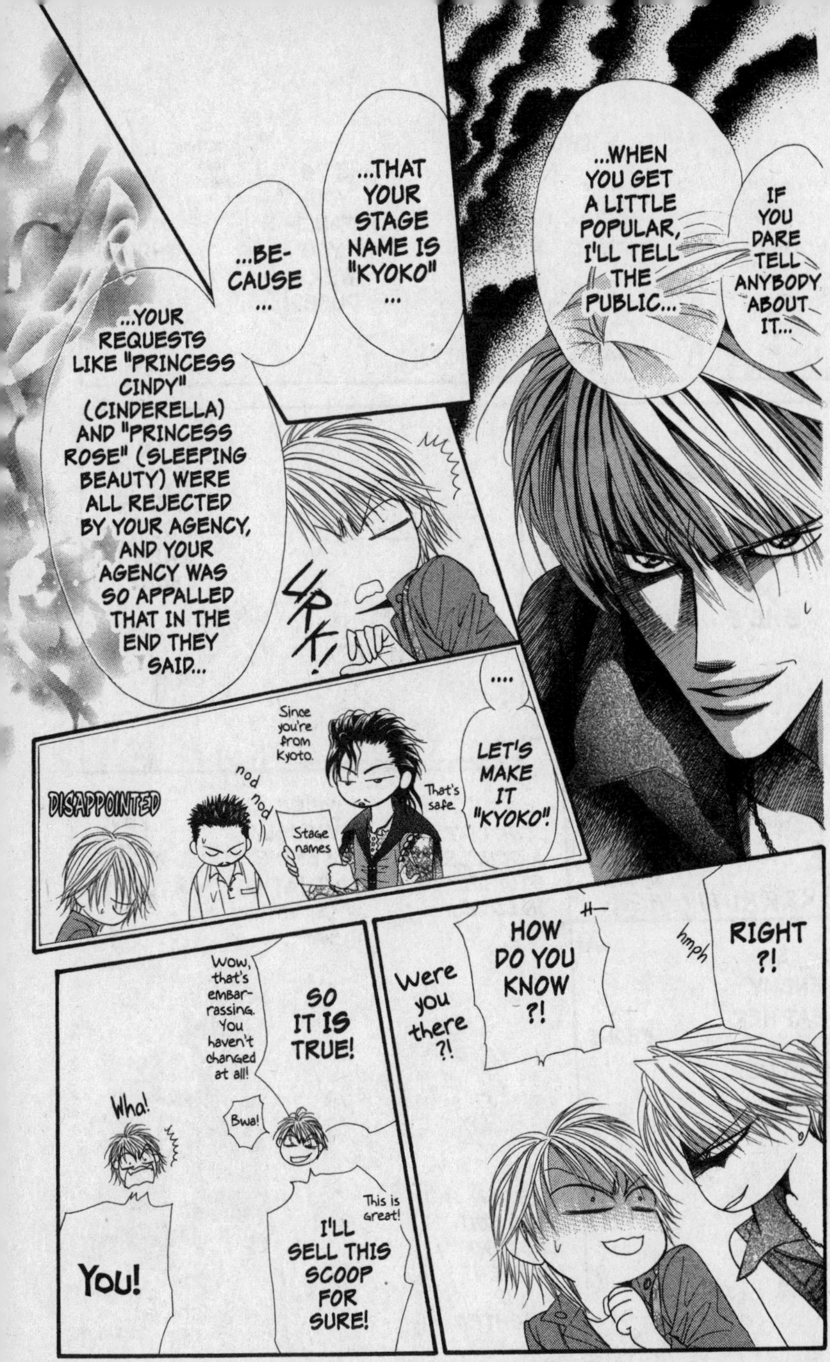
IF YOU DARE TELL ANYBODY ABOUT IT...
...WHEN YOU GET A LITTLE POPULAR, I'LL TELL THE PUBLIC...
...THAT YOUR STAGE NAME IS "KYOKO"...
...BE-CAUSE...
...YOUR REQUESTS LIKE "PRINCESS CINDY" (CINDERELLA) AND "PRINCESS ROSE" (SLEEPING BEAUTY) WERE ALL REJECTED BY YOUR AGENCY, AND YOUR AGENCY WAS SO APPALLED THAT IN THE END THEY SAID...
URK!
....
LET'S MAKE IT "KYOKO".
That's safe.
Since you're from Kyoto.
Stage names
nod nod
DISAPPOINTED
RIGHT?!
hmph
HOW DO YOU KNOW?!
H—
Were you there?!
SO IT IS TRUE!
Wow, that's embarrassing. You haven't changed at all!
Wha!
Bwa!
This is great!
I'LL SELL THIS SCOOP FOR SURE!
YOU!

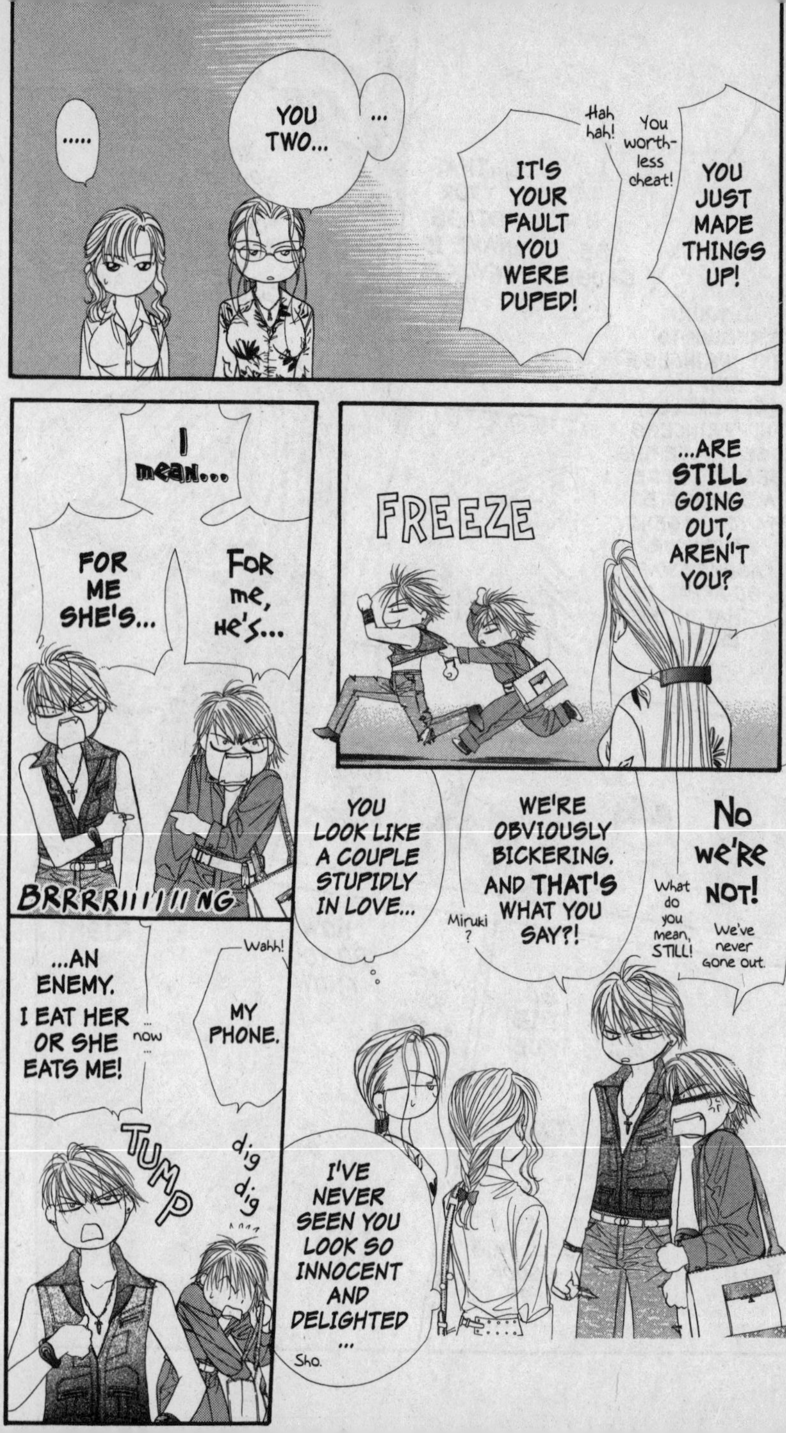
YOU JUST MADE THINGS UP!
You worthless cheat!
Hah hah!
IT'S YOUR FAULT YOU WERE DUPED!
...
YOU TWO...
.....
...ARE STILL GOING OUT, AREN'T YOU?
FREEZE
No we're NOT!
We've never gone out.
What do you mean, STILL!
WE'RE OBVIOUSLY BICKERING. AND THAT'S WHAT YOU SAY?!
Miruki?
YOU LOOK LIKE A COUPLE STUPIDLY IN LOVE...
I'VE NEVER SEEN YOU LOOK SO INNOCENT AND DELIGHTED...
Sho.
I mean...
For me, he's...
FOR ME SHE'S...
BRRRRIIIIIING
MY PHONE.
Wahh!
...now...
...AN ENEMY. I EAT HER OR SHE EATS ME!
TUMP
dig dig

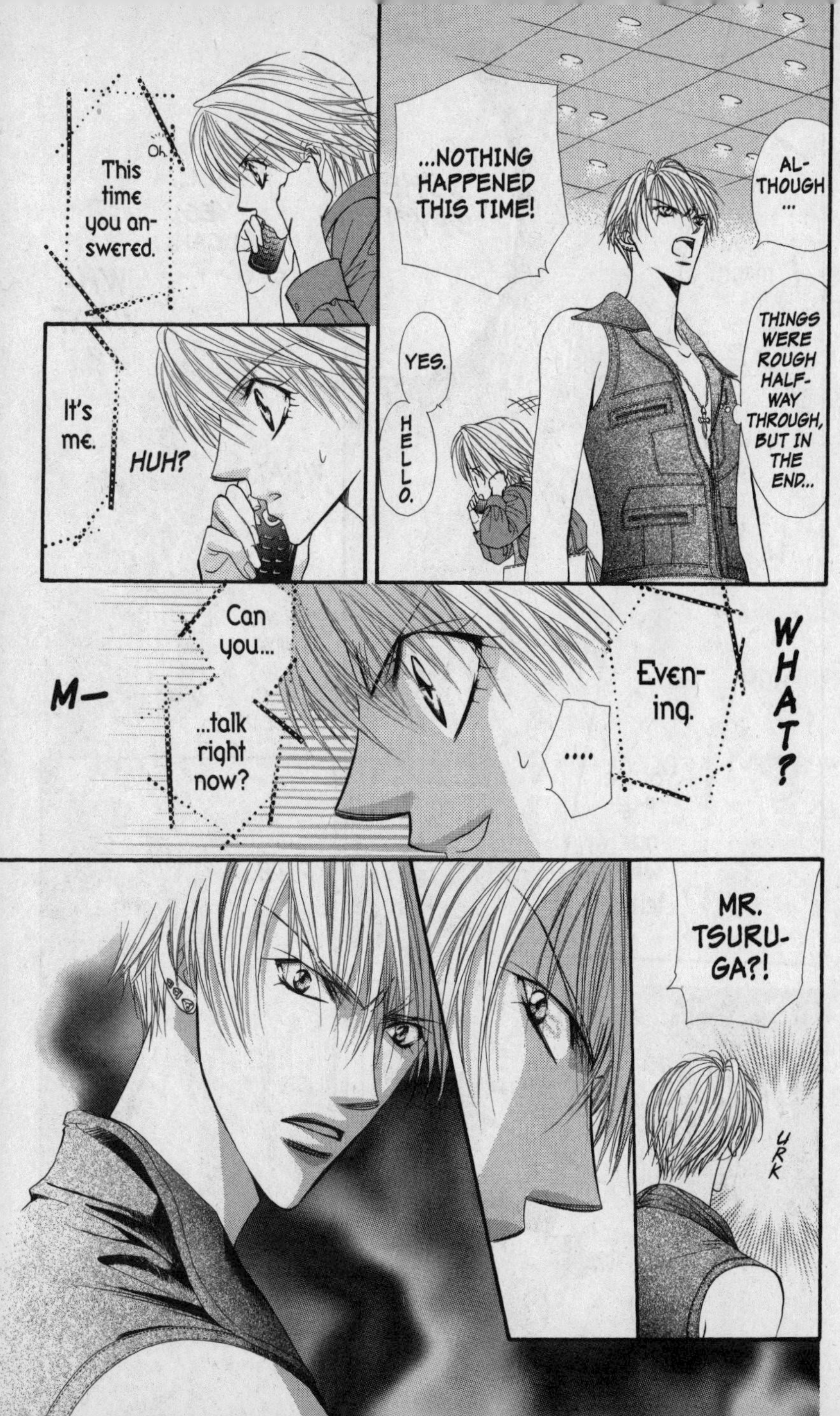
AL-THOUGH...
...NOTHING HAPPENED THIS TIME!
THINGS WERE ROUGH HALF-WAY THROUGH, BUT IN THE END...
YES.
HELLO.
Oh.
This time you an-swered.
It's me.
HUH?
WHAT?
Even-ing.
....
Can you...
...talk right now?
M—
MR. TSURU-GA?!
URK

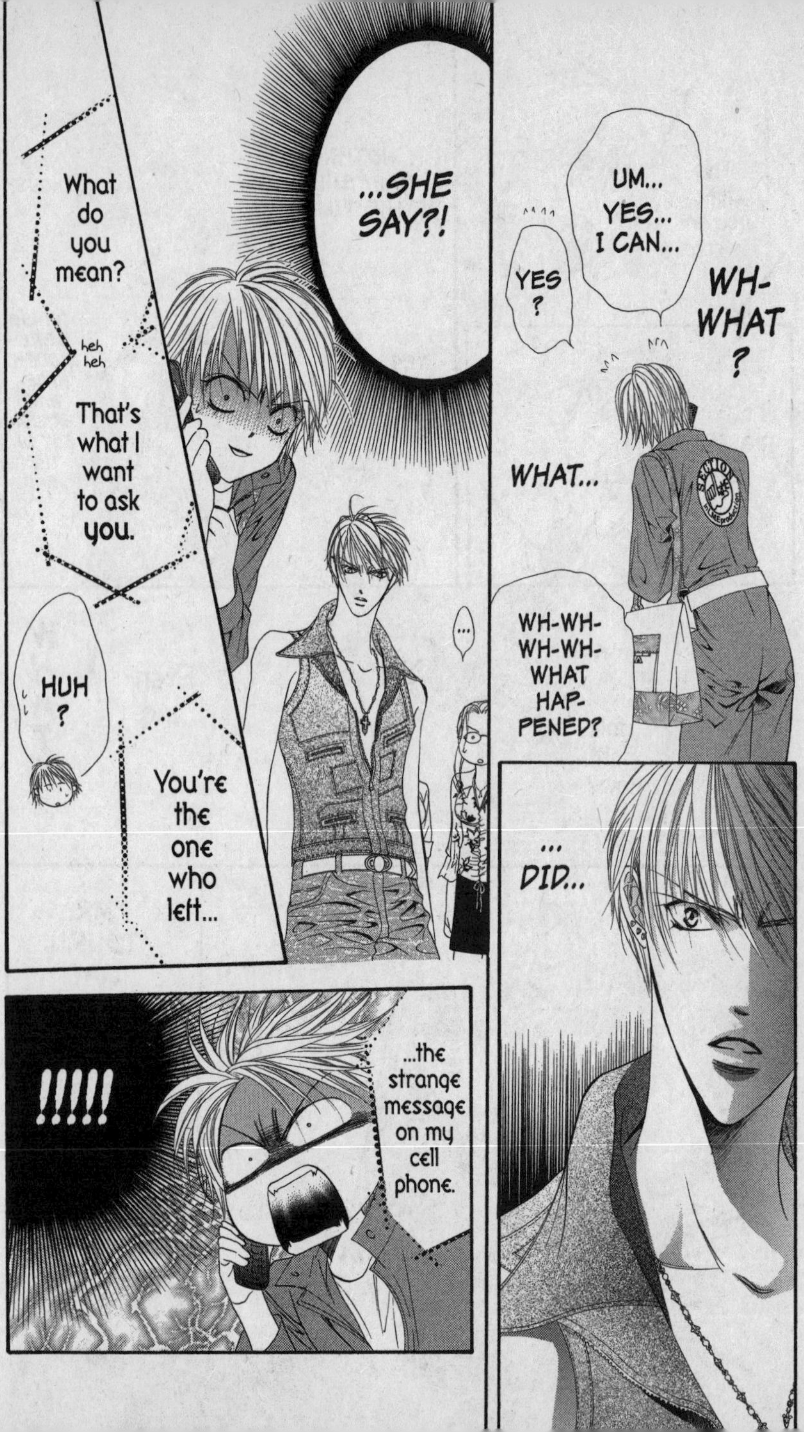
WH-WHAT?
UM... YES... I CAN...
YES?
WHAT...
WH-WH-WH-WH-WHAT HAPPENED?
...DID...
...SHE SAY?!
What do you mean?
heh heh
That's what I want to ask you.
...
HUH?
You're the one who left...
...the strange message on my cell phone.
!!!!!

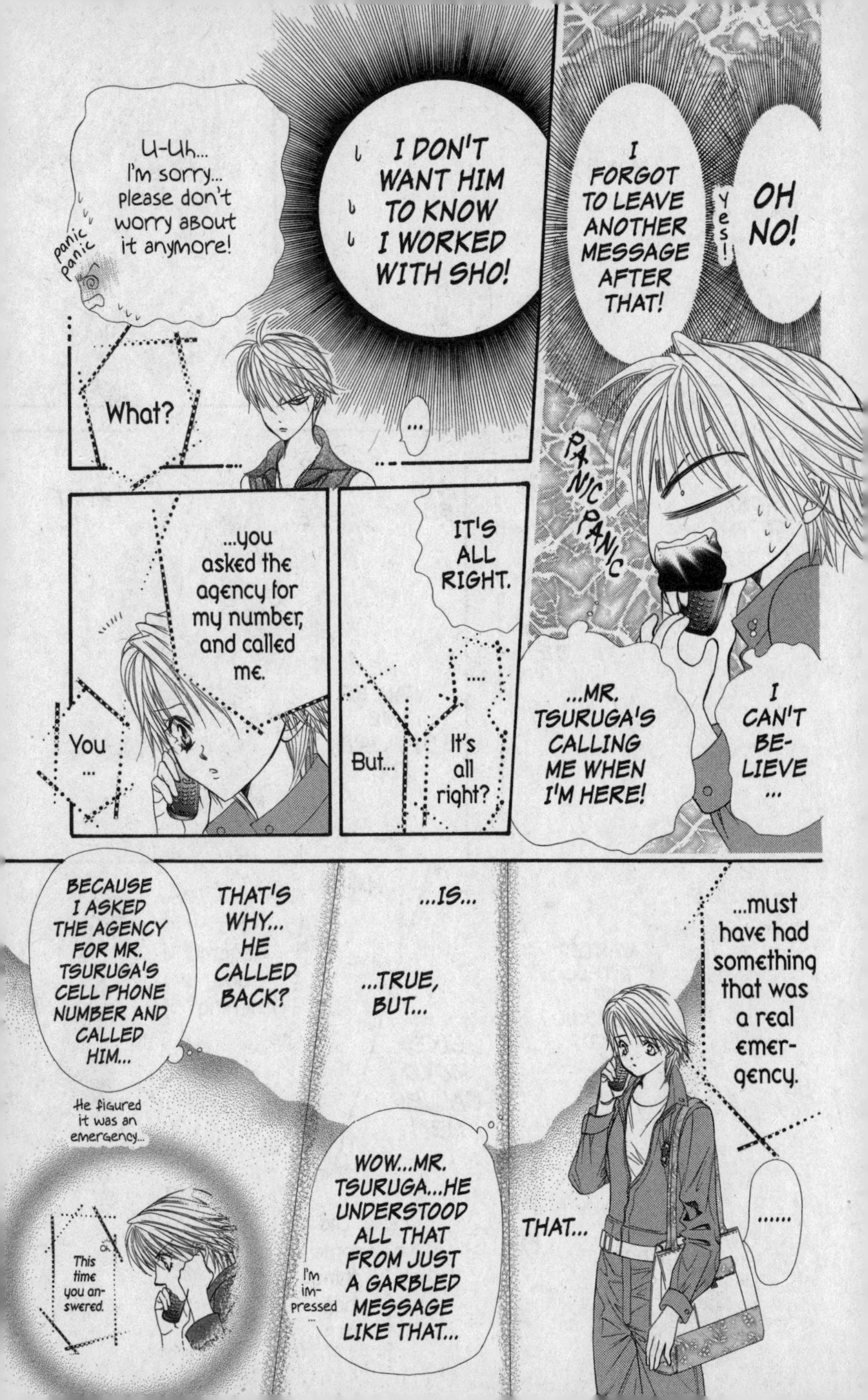

OH NO!
Yes!
I FORGOT TO LEAVE ANOTHER MESSAGE AFTER THAT!
PANIC PANIC
I CAN'T BE-LIEVE ...
...MR. TSURUGA'S CALLING ME WHEN I'M HERE!
I DON'T WANT HIM TO KNOW I WORKED WITH SHO!
U-Uh... I'm sorry... please don't worry about it anymore!
panic panic
...
What?
IT'S ALL RIGHT.
...
It's all right?
But...
...you asked the agency for my number, and called me.
You ...
...must have had something that was a real emergency.
......
THAT...
...IS...
...TRUE, BUT...
THAT'S WHY... HE CALLED BACK?
BECAUSE I ASKED THE AGENCY FOR MR. TSURUGA'S CELL PHONE NUMBER AND CALLED HIM...
WOW...MR. TSURUGA...HE UNDERSTOOD ALL THAT FROM JUST A GARBLED MESSAGE LIKE THAT...
I'm im-pressed ...
He figured it was an emergency...
Oh
This time you an-swered.

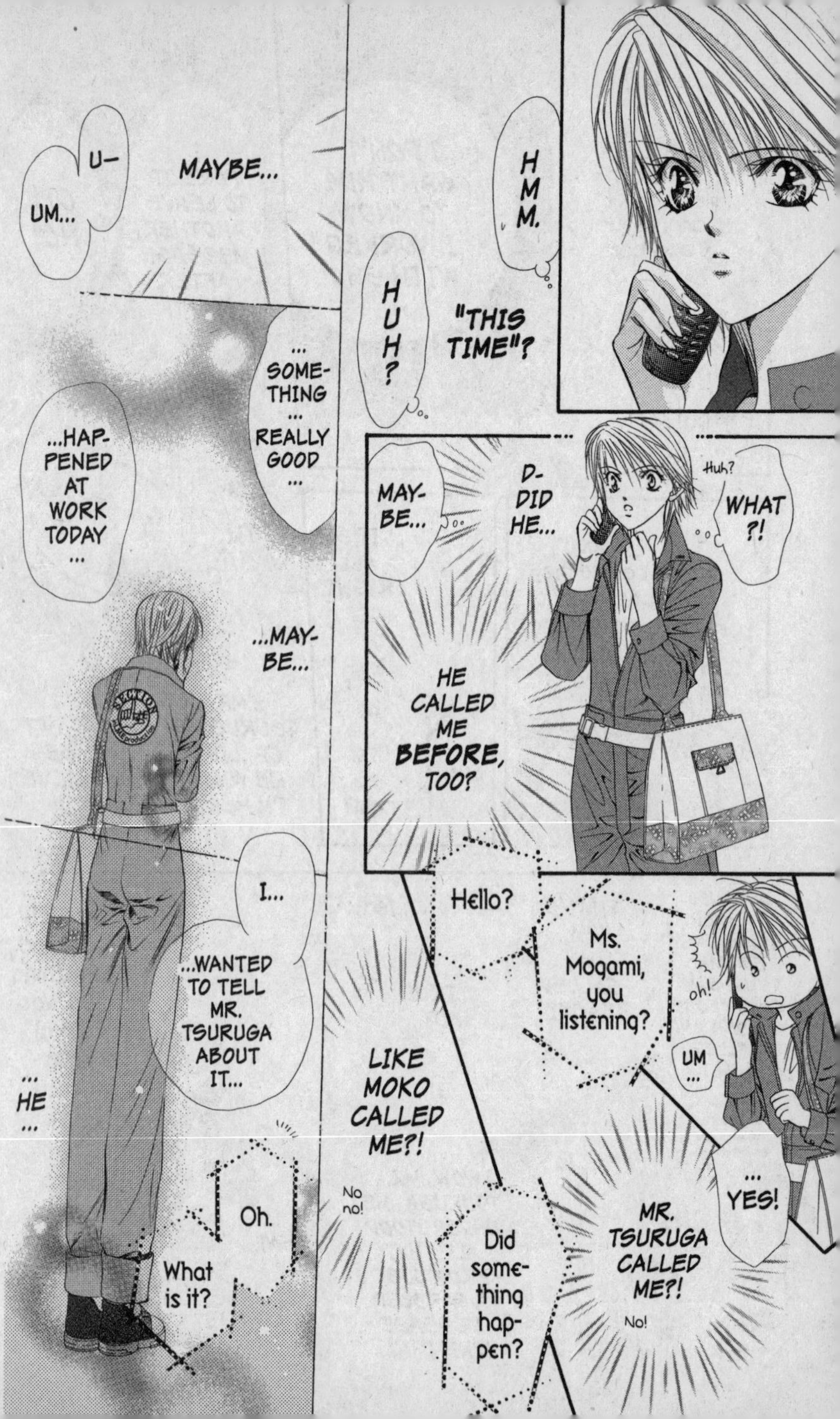
HMM.
"THIS TIME"?
HUH?
Huh?
WHAT?!
D-DID HE...
MAYBE...
HE CALLED ME BEFORE, TOO?
Hello?
Ms. Mogami, you listening?
oh!
UM...
...YES!
MR. TSURUGA CALLED ME?!
No!
Did something happen?
LIKE MOKO CALLED ME?!
No no!
MAYBE...
U-
UM...
...SOMETHING...REALLY GOOD...
...HAPPENED AT WORK TODAY...
...MAYBE...
I...
...WANTED TO TELL MR. TSURUGA ABOUT IT...
...HE...
Oh.
What is it?

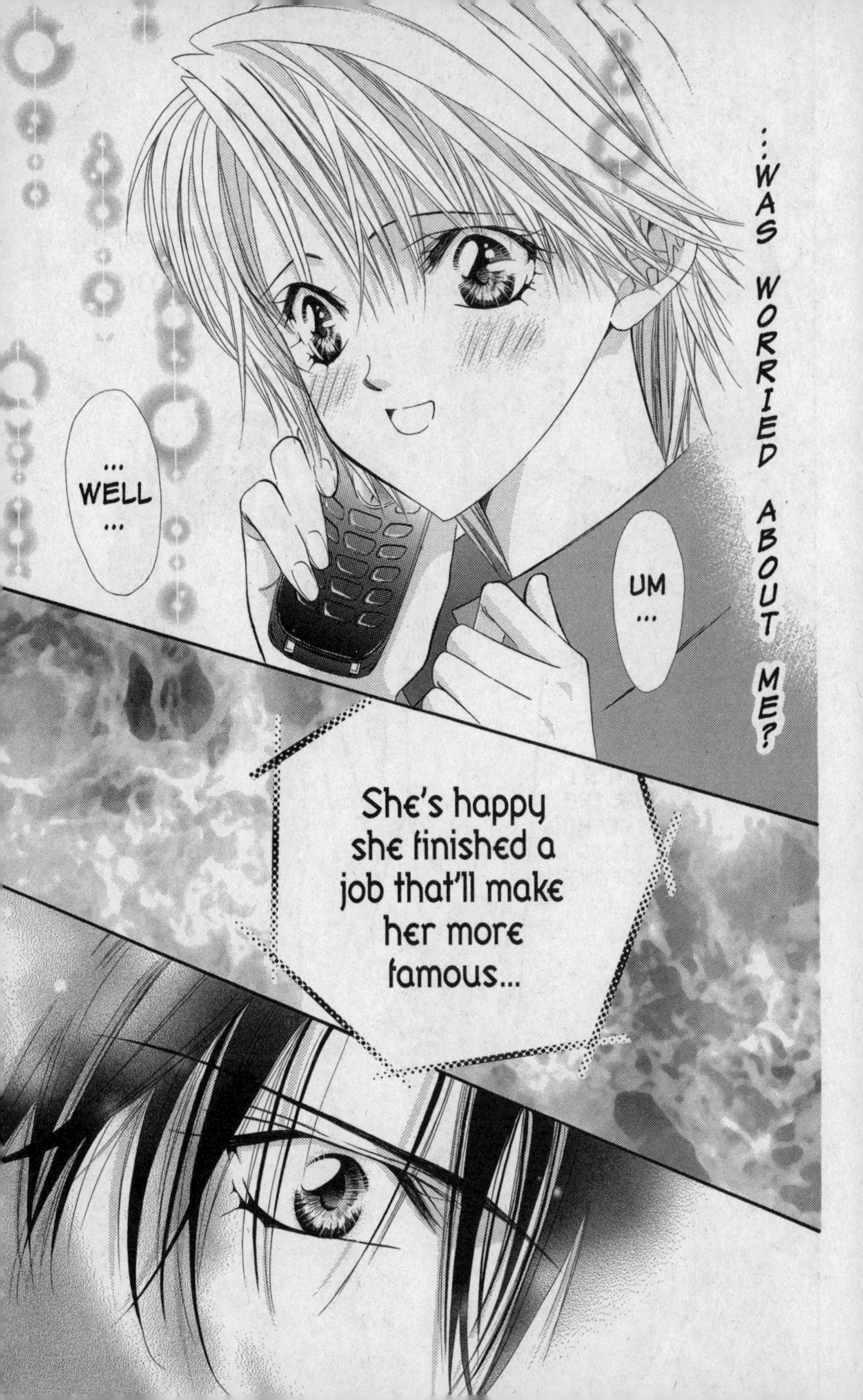
...WAS WORRIED ABOUT ME?
UM ...
... WELL ...
She's happy she finished a job that'll make her more famous...

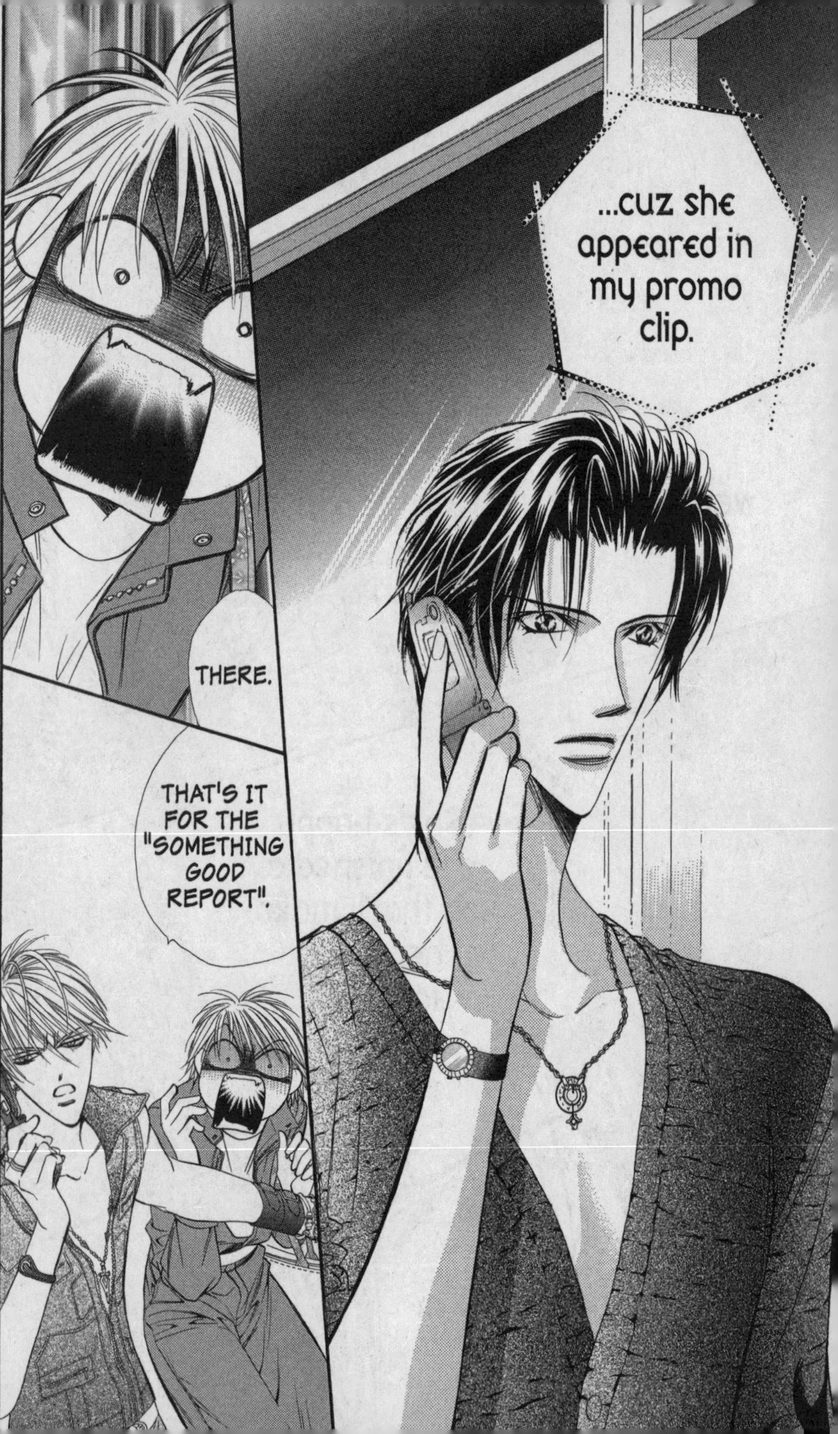
...cuz she appeared in my promo clip.
THERE.
THAT'S IT FOR THE "SOMETHING GOOD REPORT".

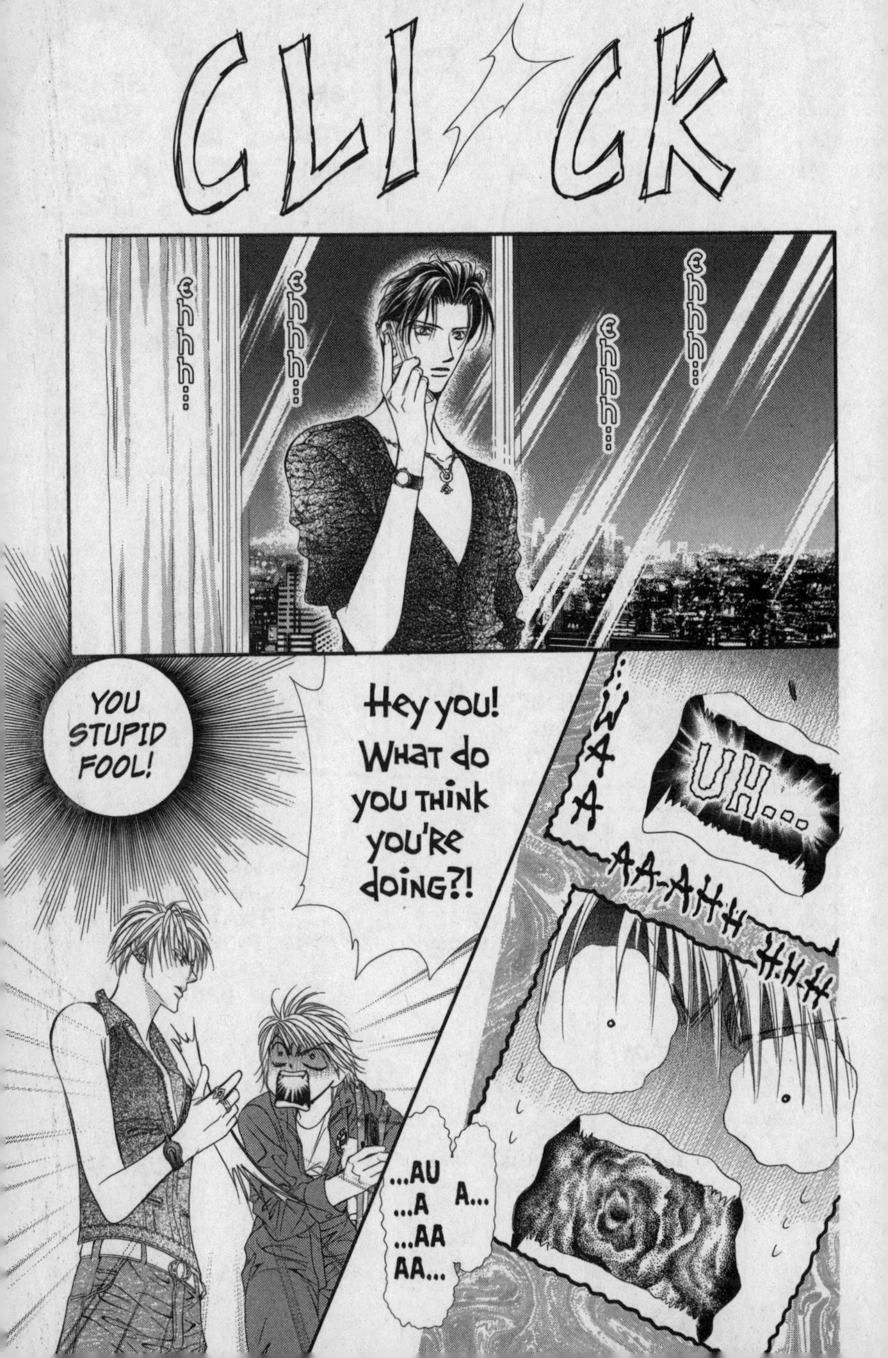
CLICK
UH...
...WAAA-AA-AHH HHH
...AU ...A ...AA AA... A...
Hey you! What do you think you're doing?!
YOU STUPID FOOL!

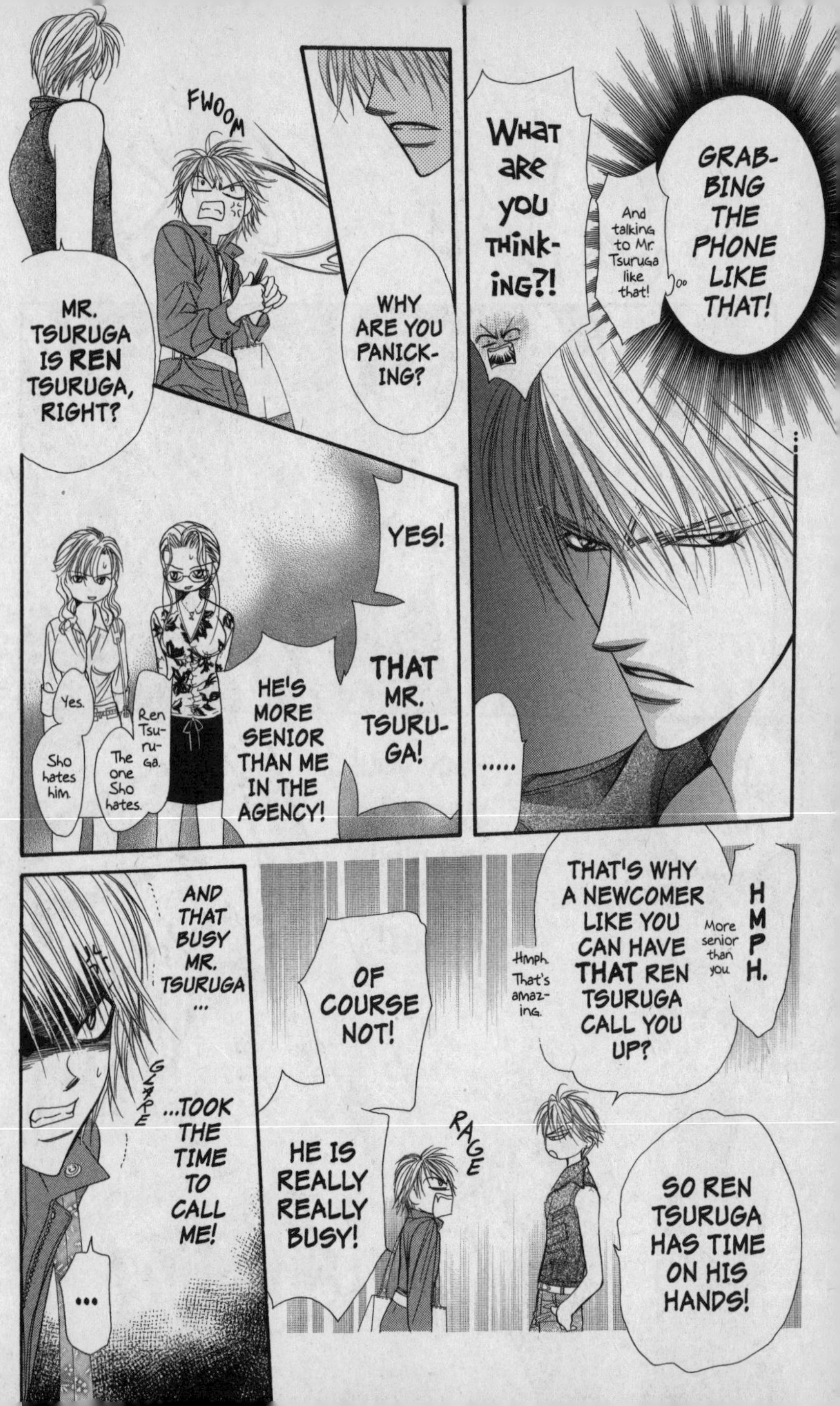
GRAB-BING THE PHONE LIKE THAT!
And talking to Mr. Tsuruga like that!
What are you THINK-ING?!
.....
WHY ARE YOU PANICK-ING?
FWOOM
MR. TSURUGA IS REN TSURUGA, RIGHT?
YES!
THAT MR. TSURU-GA!
HE'S MORE SENIOR THAN ME IN THE AGENCY!
Ren Tsu-ru-ga.
The one Sho hates.
Yes.
Sho hates him.
THAT'S WHY A NEWCOMER LIKE YOU CAN HAVE THAT REN TSURUGA CALL YOU UP?
HMPH.
More senior than you.
Hmph. That's amaz-ing.
SO REN TSURUGA HAS TIME ON HIS HANDS!
OF COURSE NOT!
RAGE
HE IS REALLY REALLY BUSY!
AND THAT BUSY MR. TSURUGA ...
GLARE
...TOOK THE TIME TO CALL ME!
...

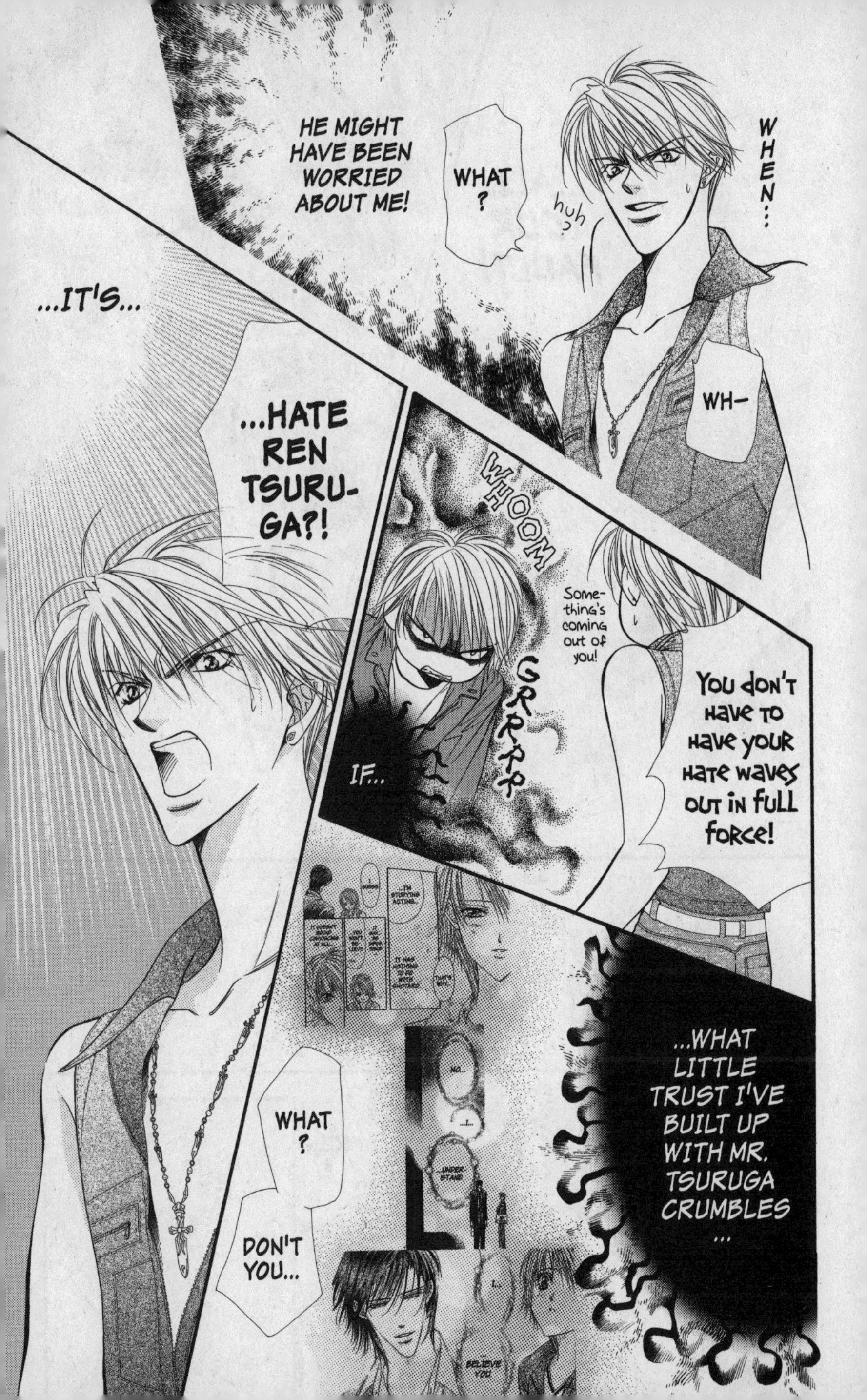

WHEN...
huh?
WHAT?
HE MIGHT HAVE BEEN WORRIED ABOUT ME!
WH—
You don't have to have your hate waves out in full force!
Something's coming out of you!
WHOOM
GRRRR
IF...
...IT'S...
...HATE REN TSURUGA?!
...WHAT LITTLE TRUST I'VE BUILT UP WITH MR. TSURUGA CRUMBLES...
WHAT?
DON'T YOU...

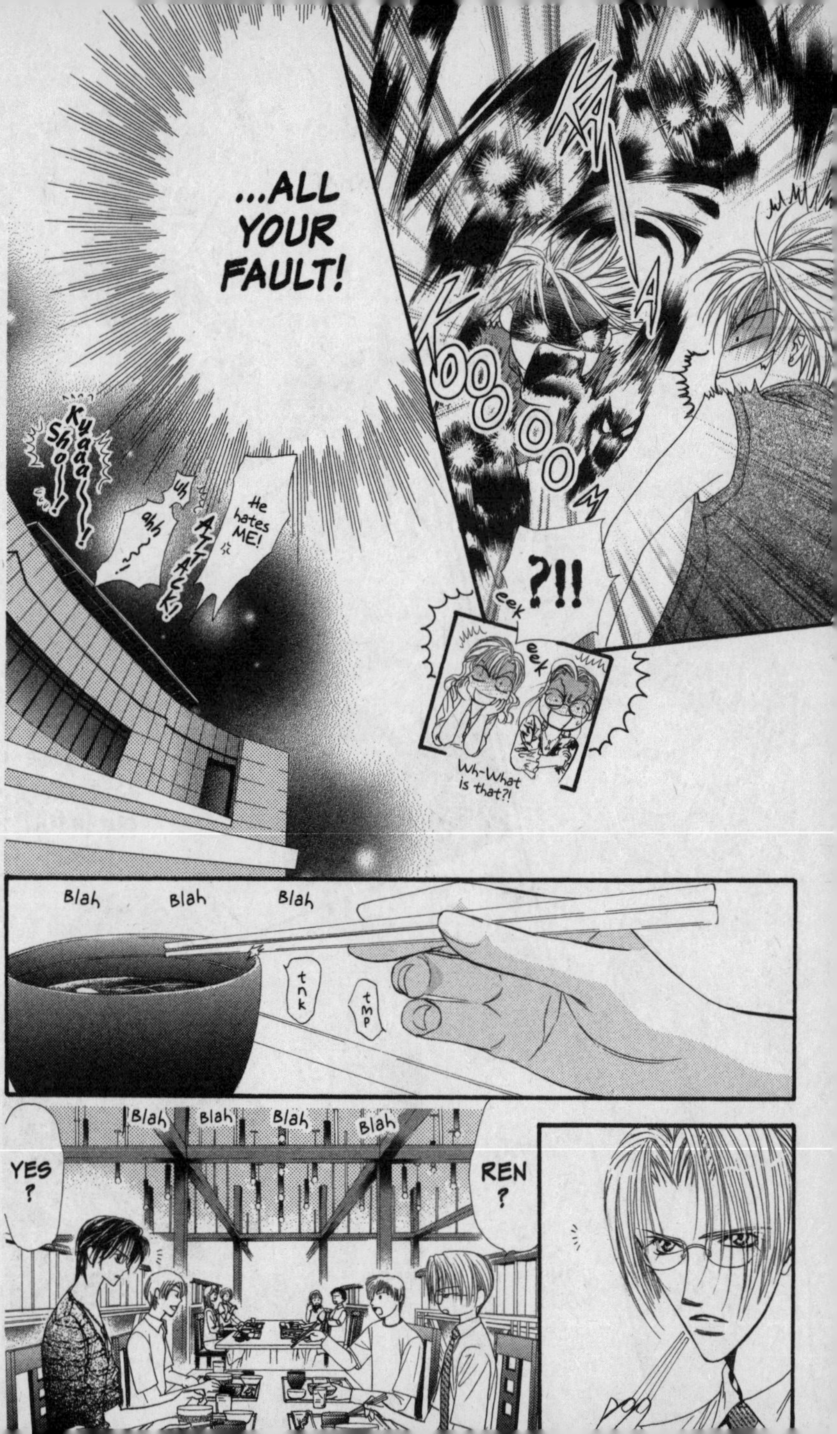
KAAA
KOOOOOOM
?!!
eek
eek
Wh-What is that?!
...ALL YOUR FAULT!
He hates ME!
ATTACK!
uh ahh~!
Kyaaa~!
Sho~!
Blah Blah Blah
tnk
tmp
Blah Blah Blah Blah
REN?
YES?

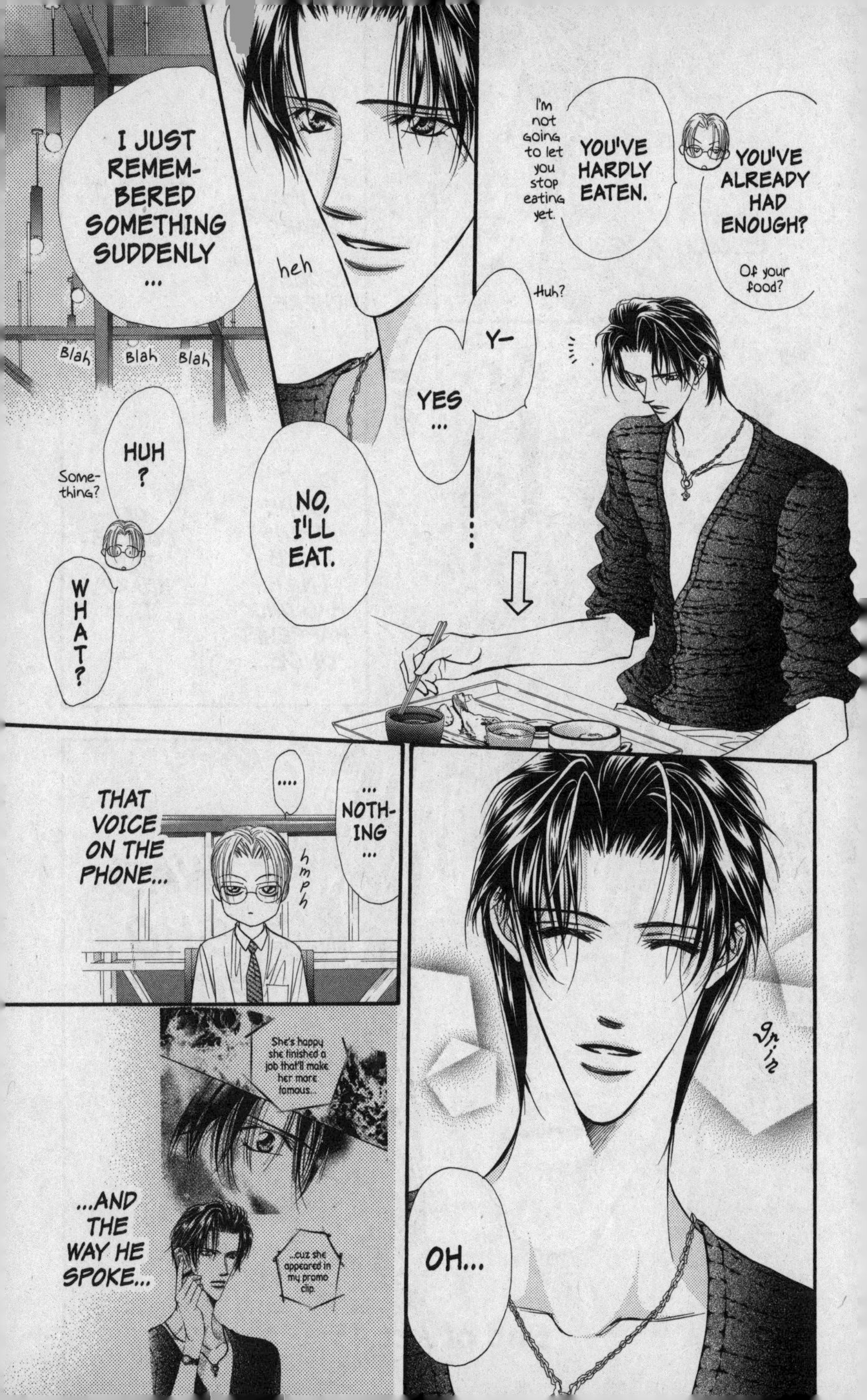

YOU'VE ALREADY HAD ENOUGH?
Of your food?
YOU'VE HARDLY EATEN.
I'm not going to let you stop eating yet.
Huh?
Y-
YES ...
...
NO, I'LL EAT.
heh
I JUST REMEMBERED SOMETHING SUDDENLY ...
Blah Blah Blah
HUH?
Something?
WHAT?
grin
OH...
... NOTHING ...
....
hmph
THAT VOICE ON THE PHONE...
She's happy she finished a job that'll make her more famous...
...AND THE WAY HE SPOKE...
...cuz she appeared in my promo clip.

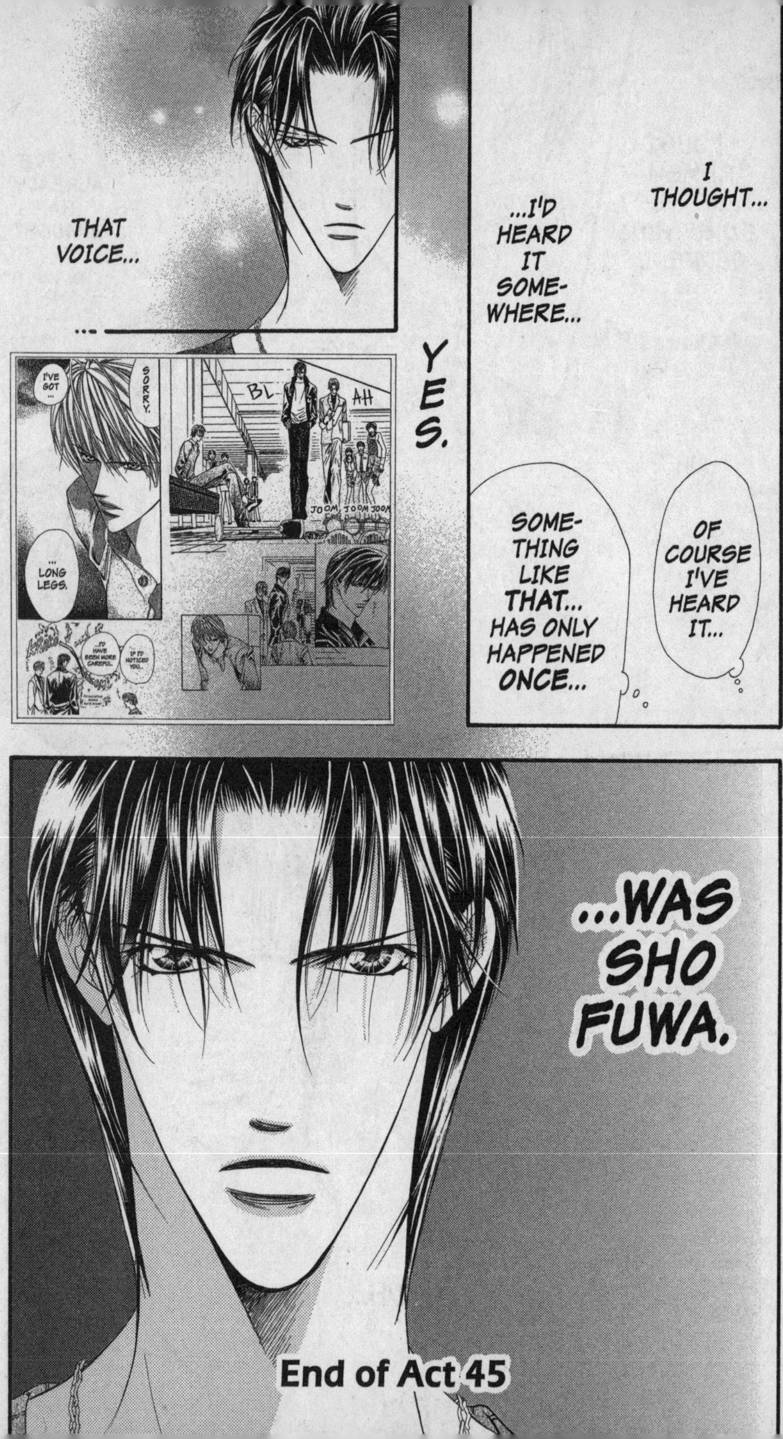
I THOUGHT...
...I'D HEARD IT SOMEWHERE...
OF COURSE I'VE HEARD IT...
SOMETHING LIKE THAT... HAS ONLY HAPPENED ONCE...
THAT VOICE...
...—
YES.
BL
AH
JOOM JOOM JOOM
SORRY.
I'VE GOT...
... LONG LEGS.
IF I'D NOTICED YOU...
...I'D HAVE BEEN MORE CAREFUL
...WAS SHO FUWA.
End of Act 45

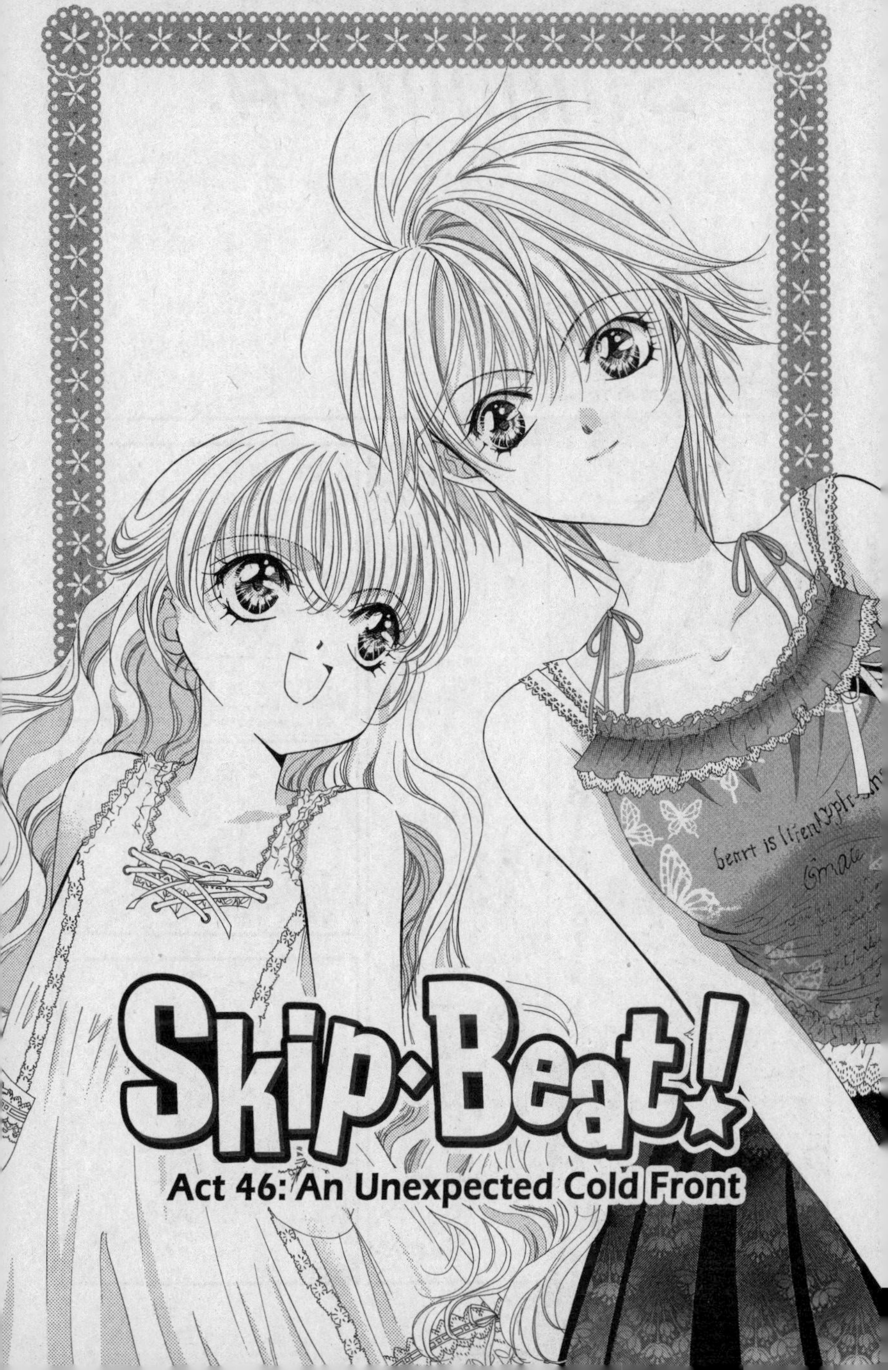
Skip·Beat!
Act 46: An Unexpected Cold Front

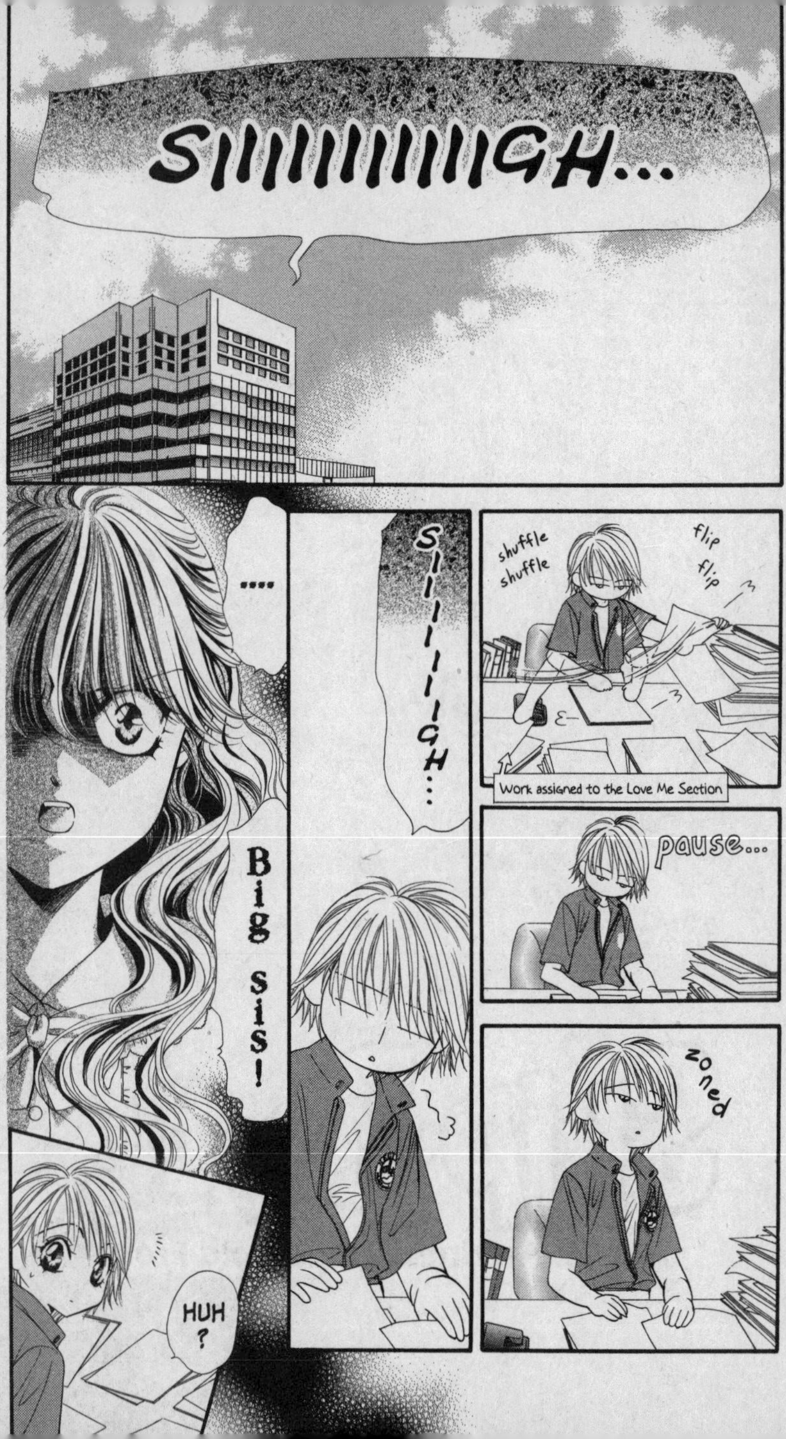

SIIIIIIIIIIGH...
shuffle shuffle
flip flip
Work assigned to the Love Me Section
pause...
zoned
SIIIIIIIGH...
....
Big sis!
HUH?

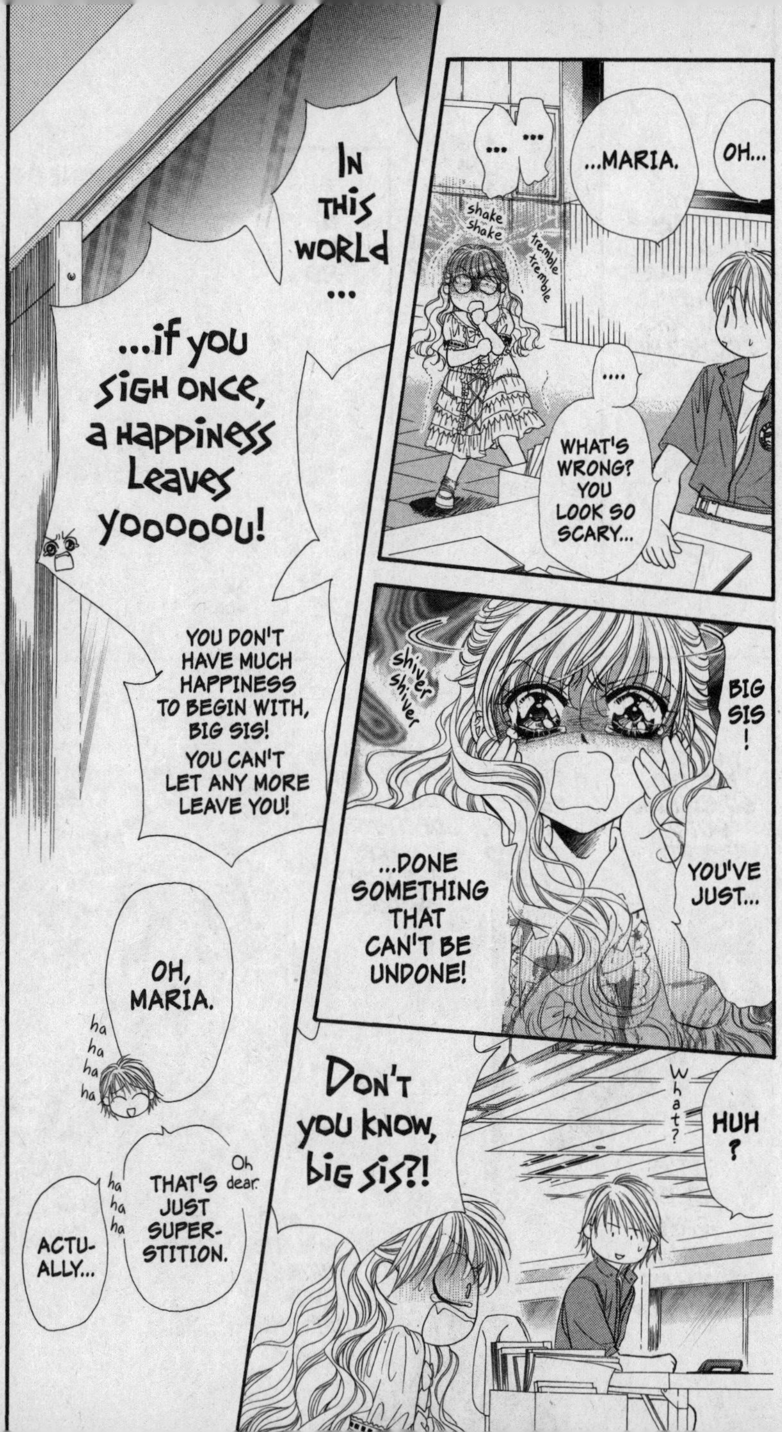
OH...
...MARIA.
...
...
shake shake
tremble tremble
....
WHAT'S WRONG? YOU LOOK SO SCARY...
BIG SIS!
YOU'VE JUST...
...DONE SOMETHING THAT CAN'T BE UNDONE!
shiver shiver
HUH?
What?
Don't you know, big sis?!
In this world...
...if you sigh once, a happiness leaves yoooooou!
YOU DON'T HAVE MUCH HAPPINESS TO BEGIN WITH, BIG SIS! YOU CAN'T LET ANY MORE LEAVE YOU!
OH, MARIA.
ha ha ha ha
Oh dear.
THAT'S JUST SUPER-STITION.
ha ha ha
ACTU-ALLY...

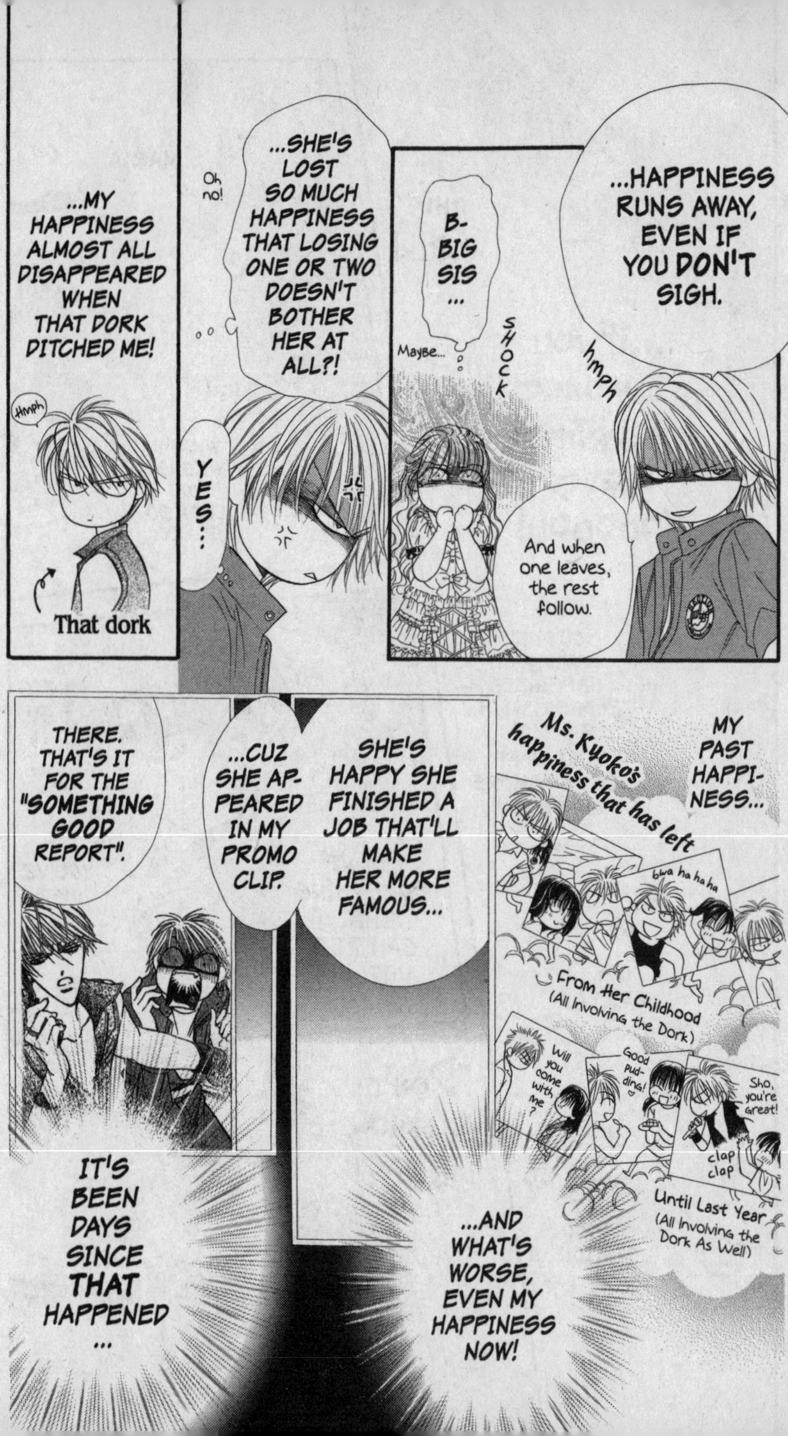
...HAPPINESS RUNS AWAY, EVEN IF YOU DON'T SIGH.
hmph
And when one leaves, the rest follow.
SHOCK
B-BIG SIS...
Maybe...
...SHE'S LOST SO MUCH HAPPINESS THAT LOSING ONE OR TWO DOESN'T BOTHER HER AT ALL?!
Oh no!
YES...
...MY HAPPINESS ALMOST ALL DISAPPEARED WHEN THAT DORK DITCHED ME!
Hmph
That dork
MY PAST HAPPI-NESS...
Ms. Kyoko's happiness that has left
bwa ha ha ha
From Her Childhood (All Involving the Dork)
Sho, you're Great!
Good pud-ding!
Will you come with me?
clap clap
Until Last Year (All Involving the Dork As Well)
SHE'S HAPPY SHE FINISHED A JOB THAT'LL MAKE HER MORE FAMOUS...
...CUZ SHE AP-PEARED IN MY PROMO CLIP.
THERE. THAT'S IT FOR THE "SOMETHING GOOD REPORT".
...AND WHAT'S WORSE, EVEN MY HAPPINESS NOW!
IT'S BEEN DAYS SINCE THAT HAPPENED...

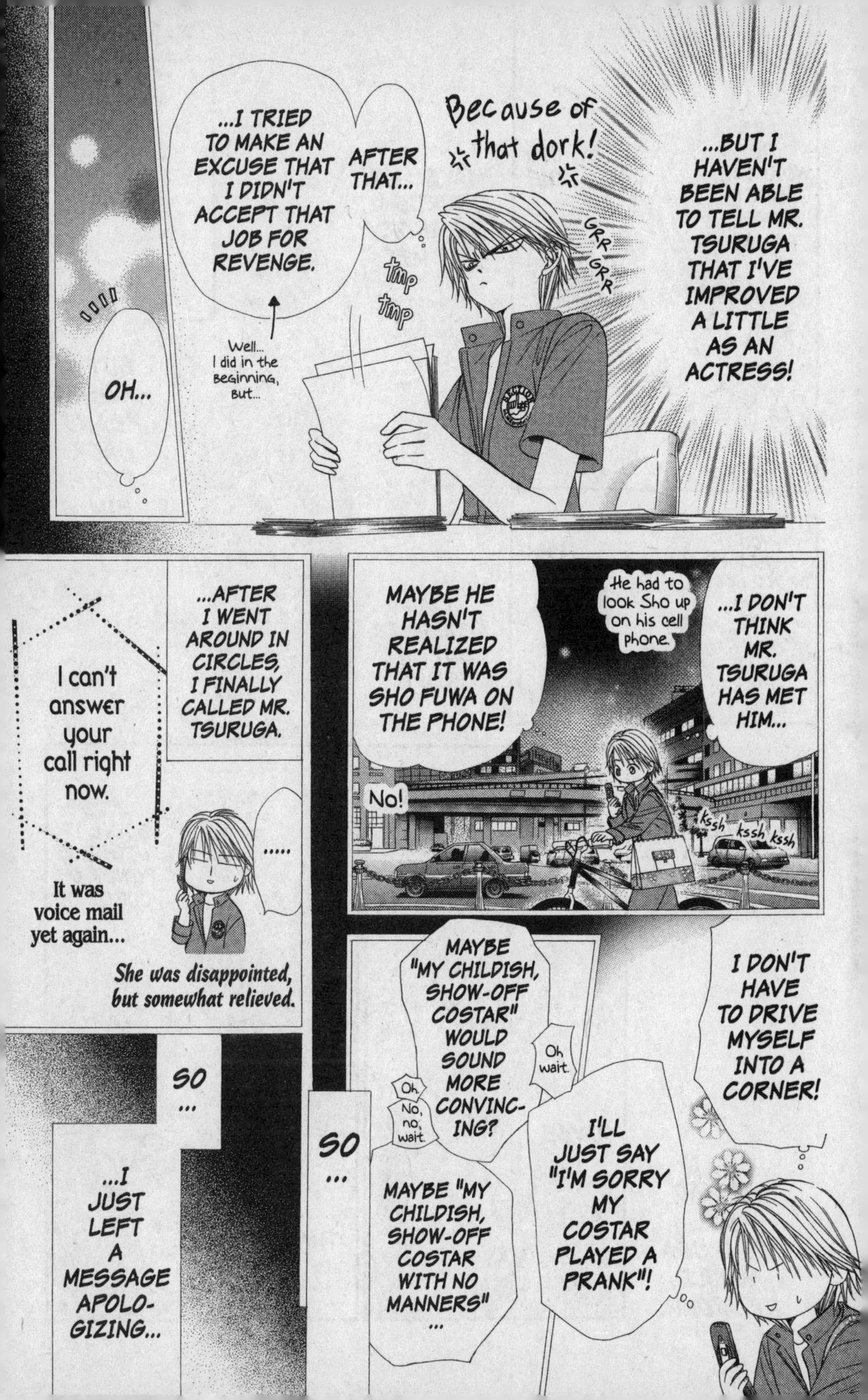

...BUT I HAVEN'T BEEN ABLE TO TELL MR. TSURUGA THAT I'VE IMPROVED A LITTLE AS AN ACTRESS!
Because of that dork!
GRR GRR
tmp tmp
AFTER THAT...
...I TRIED TO MAKE AN EXCUSE THAT I DIDN'T ACCEPT THAT JOB FOR REVENGE.
Well... I did in the beginning, but...
OH...
...I DON'T THINK MR. TSURUGA HAS MET HIM...
He had to look Sho up on his cell phone.
MAYBE HE HASN'T REALIZED THAT IT WAS SHO FUWA ON THE PHONE!
No!
kssh kssh kssh
...AFTER I WENT AROUND IN CIRCLES, I FINALLY CALLED MR. TSURUGA.
I can't answer your call right now.
.....
It was voice mail yet again...
She was disappointed, but somewhat relieved.
I DON'T HAVE TO DRIVE MYSELF INTO A CORNER!
MAYBE "MY CHILDISH, SHOW-OFF COSTAR" WOULD SOUND MORE CONVINCING?
Oh wait.
I'LL JUST SAY "I'M SORRY MY COSTAR PLAYED A PRANK"!
Oh.
No, no, wait.
SO...
MAYBE "MY CHILDISH, SHOW-OFF COSTAR WITH NO MANNERS"...
SO...
...I JUST LEFT A MESSAGE APOLOGIZING...

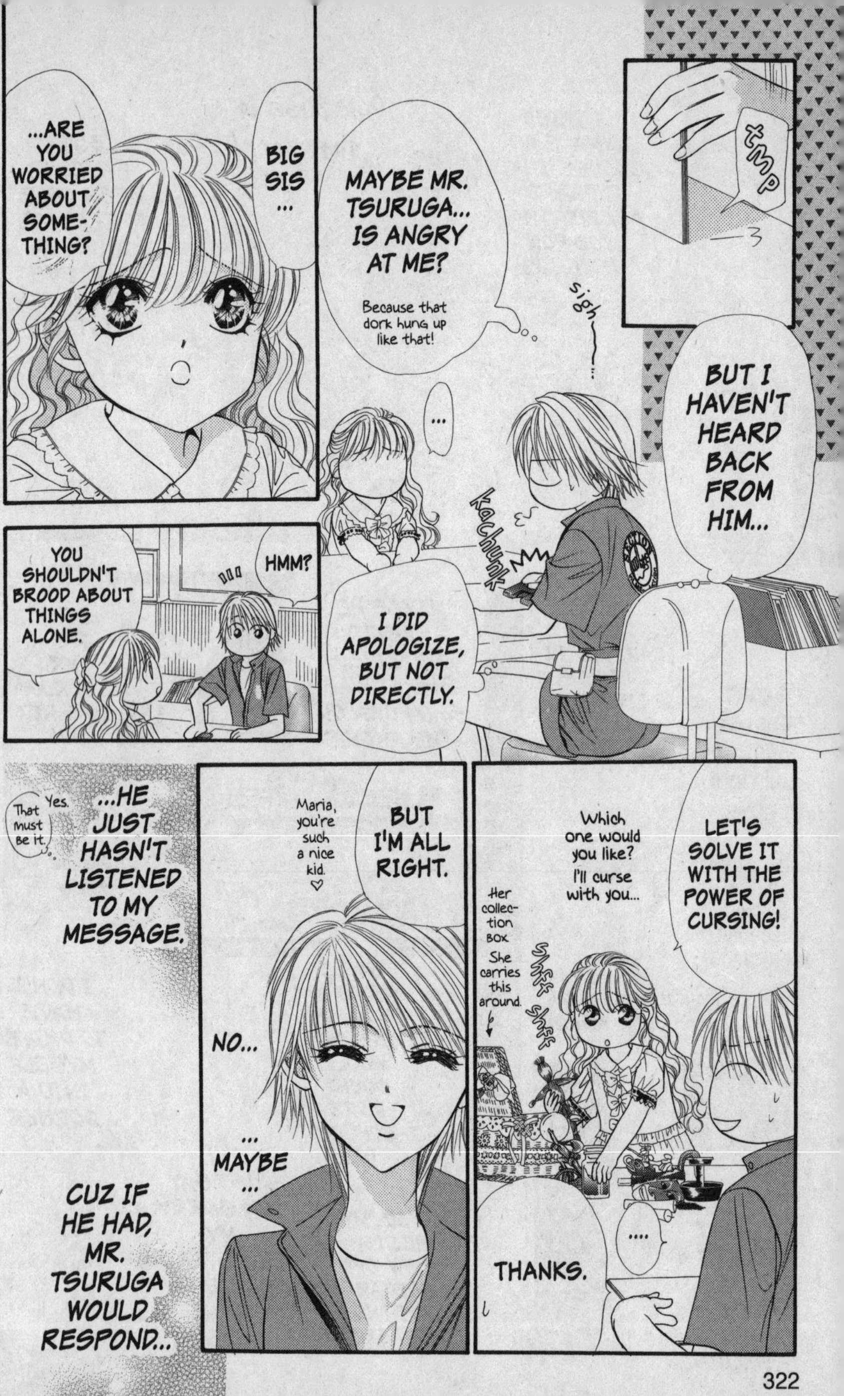
tmp
sigh
BUT I HAVEN'T HEARD BACK FROM HIM...
MAYBE MR. TSURUGA... IS ANGRY AT ME?
Because that dork hung up like that!
kachunk
I DID APOLOGIZE, BUT NOT DIRECTLY.
...
BIG SIS ...
...ARE YOU WORRIED ABOUT SOMETHING?
HMM?
YOU SHOULDN'T BROOD ABOUT THINGS ALONE.
LET'S SOLVE IT WITH THE POWER OF CURSING!
Which one would you like? I'll curse with you...
Her collection box
She carries this around.
shff shff
....
THANKS.
BUT I'M ALL RIGHT.
Maria, you're such a nice kid ♡
NO...
... MAYBE ...
...HE JUST HASN'T LISTENED TO MY MESSAGE.
Yes. That must be it.
CUZ IF HE HAD, MR. TSURUGA WOULD RESPOND...

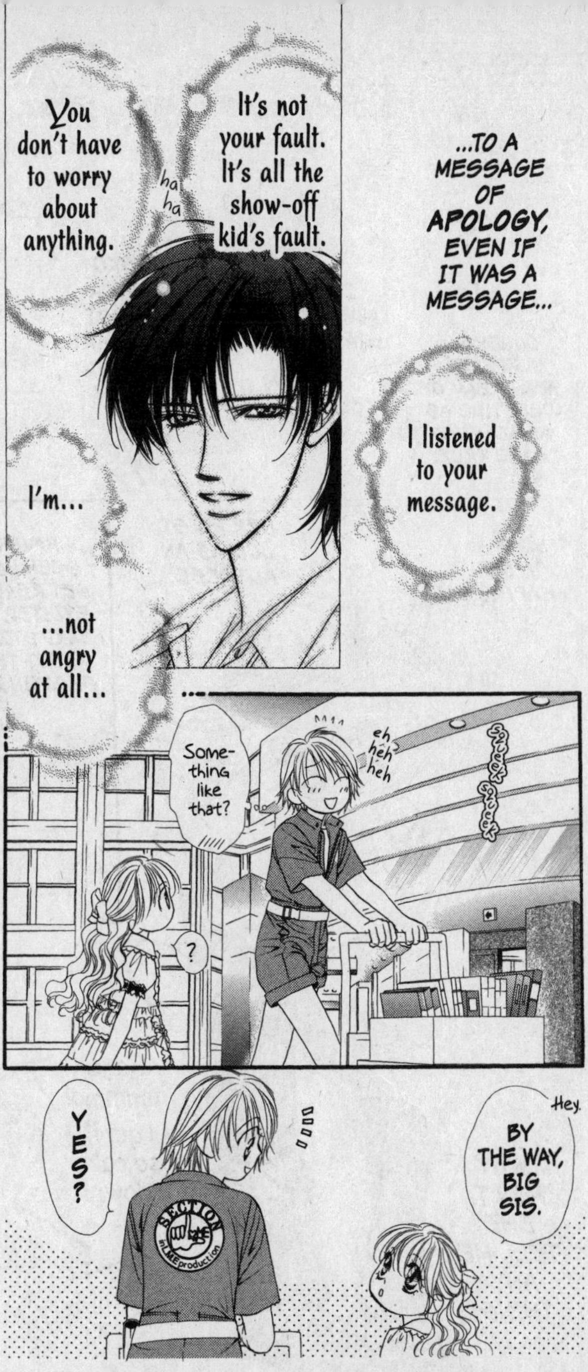
...TO A MESSAGE OF APOLOGY, EVEN IF IT WAS A MESSAGE...
I listened to your message.
It's not your fault. It's all the show-off kid's fault.
ha ha
You don't have to worry about anything.
I'm...
...not angry at all...
eh heh heh
squeek squeek
Some-thing like that?
?
Hey.
BY THE WAY, BIG SIS.
YES?

Haruki Asami

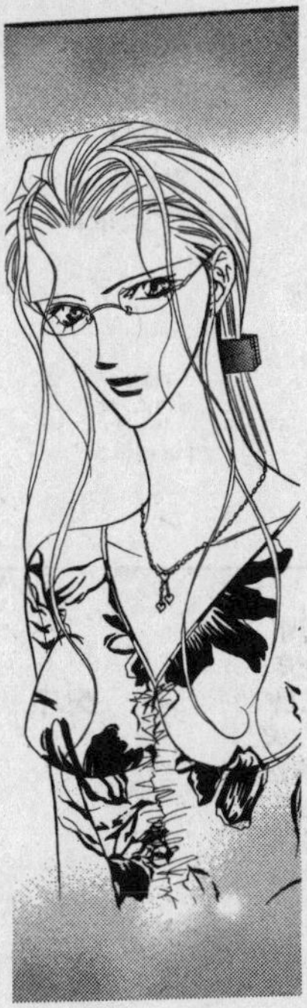

This woman... I basically prefer women to have breasts than have none at all...but if they're this big... her shoulders become wide, and I'm scared she looks like a sumo wrestler...and...as I continue drawing her, I feel that her breasts are getting even bigger, so I'm even more scared... anyway, like Ren, this woman is a bother, because I have to pay attention to her...

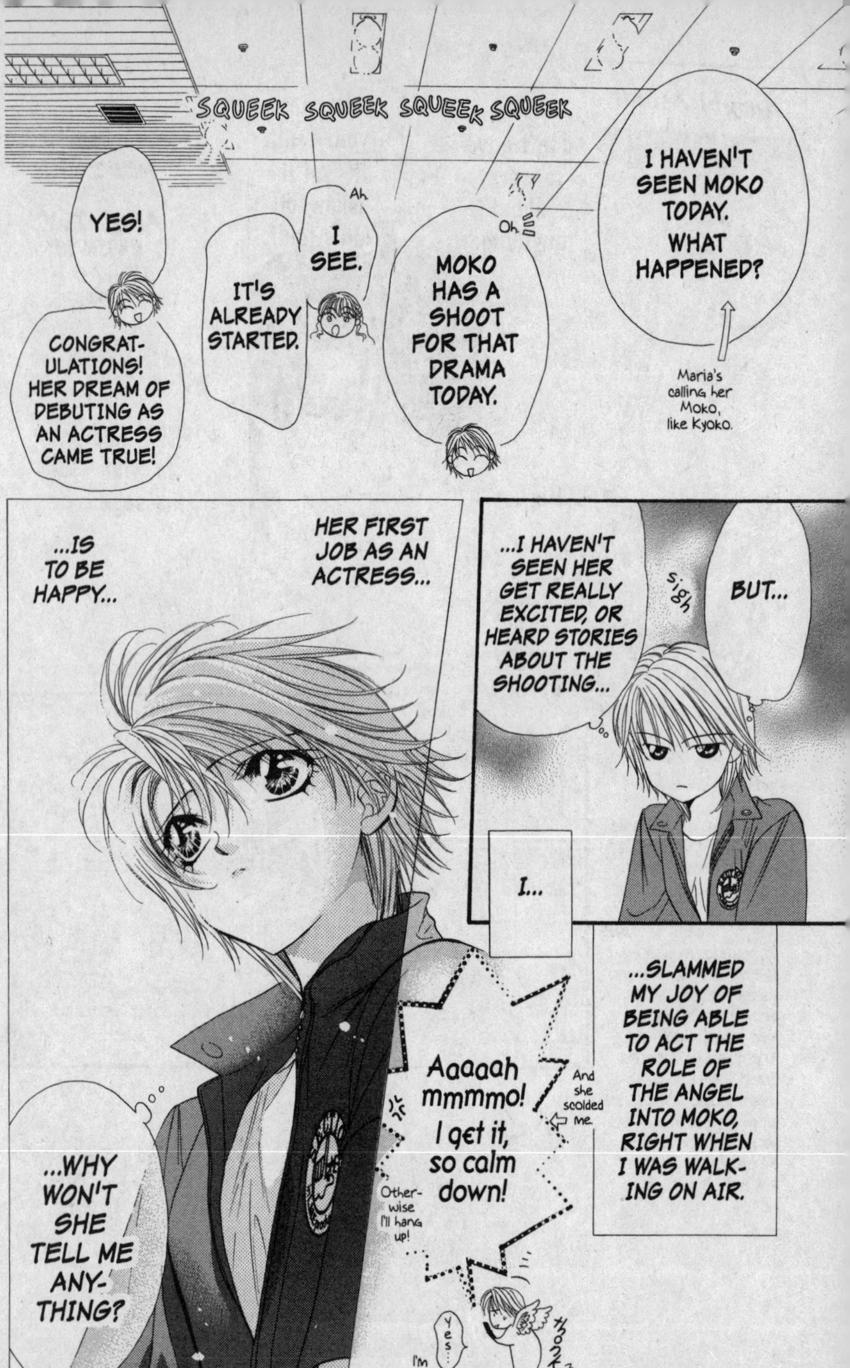

SQUEEK SQUEEK SQUEEK SQUEEK
I HAVEN'T SEEN MOKO TODAY. WHAT HAPPENED?
Maria's calling her Moko, like Kyoko.
Oh.
MOKO HAS A SHOOT FOR THAT DRAMA TODAY.
Ah.
I SEE.
IT'S ALREADY STARTED.
YES!
CONGRATULATIONS! HER DREAM OF DEBUTING AS AN ACTRESS CAME TRUE!
BUT...
sigh
...I HAVEN'T SEEN HER GET REALLY EXCITED, OR HEARD STORIES ABOUT THE SHOOTING...
I...
...SLAMMED MY JOY OF BEING ABLE TO ACT THE ROLE OF THE ANGEL INTO MOKO, RIGHT WHEN I WAS WALKING ON AIR.
And she scolded me.
Aaaaah mmmmo! I get it, so calm down!
Otherwise I'll hang up!
Yes...
I'm sorry...
thonk
And she came back down to earth.
HER FIRST JOB AS AN ACTRESS...
...IS TO BE HAPPY...
...WHY WON'T SHE TELL ME ANYTHING?

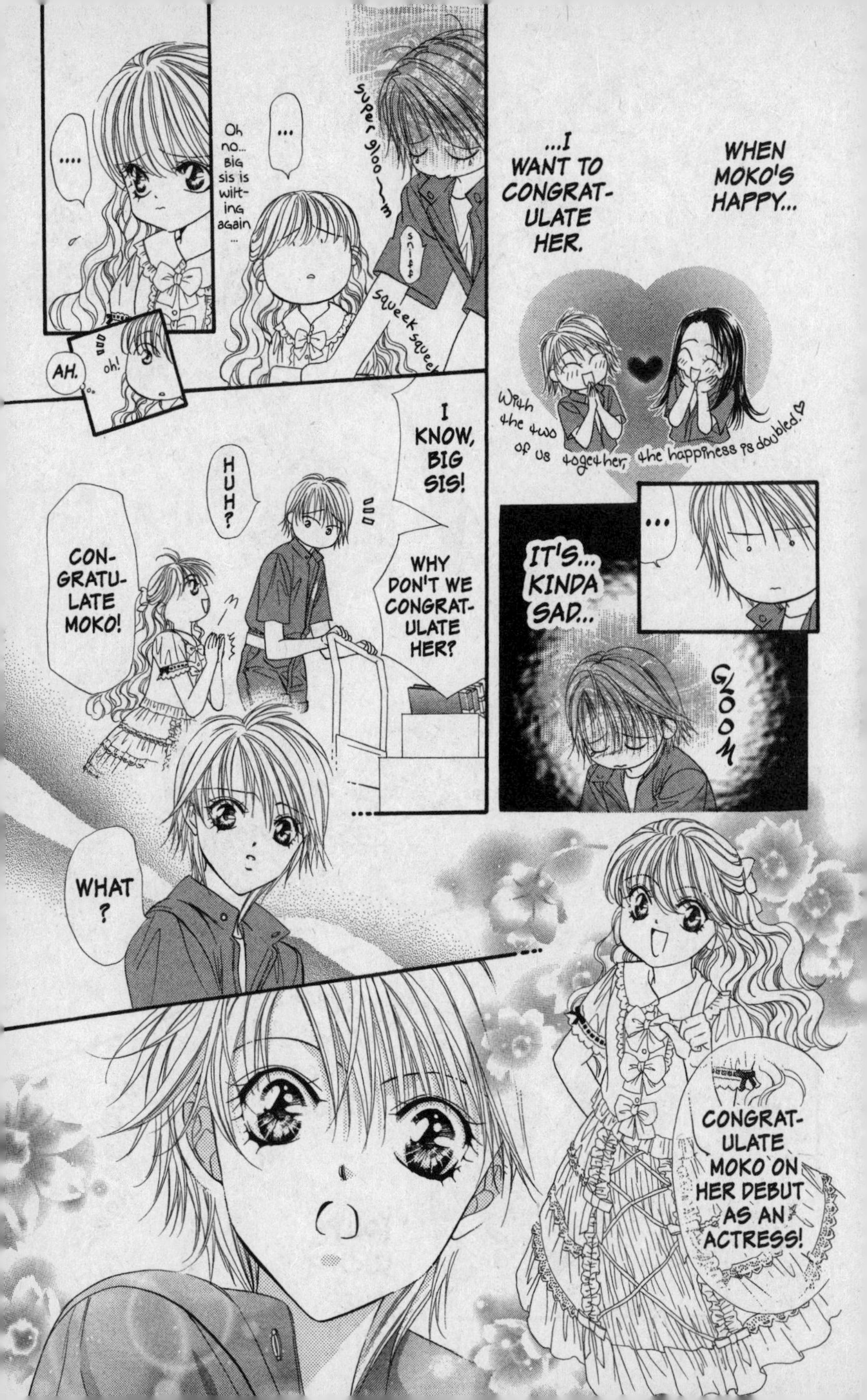
WHEN MOKO'S HAPPY...
...I WANT TO CONGRATULATE HER.
With the two of us together, the happiness is doubled♡
...
IT'S... KINDA SAD...
GLOOM
super gloo~m
...
sniff
squeek squeek
Oh no... BIG sis is wilting again...
....
AH.
oh!
I KNOW, BIG SIS!
WHY DON'T WE CONGRATULATE HER?
HUH?
CON-GRATU-LATE MOKO!
....
WHAT?
....
CONGRAT-ULATE MOKO ON HER DEBUT AS AN ACTRESS!

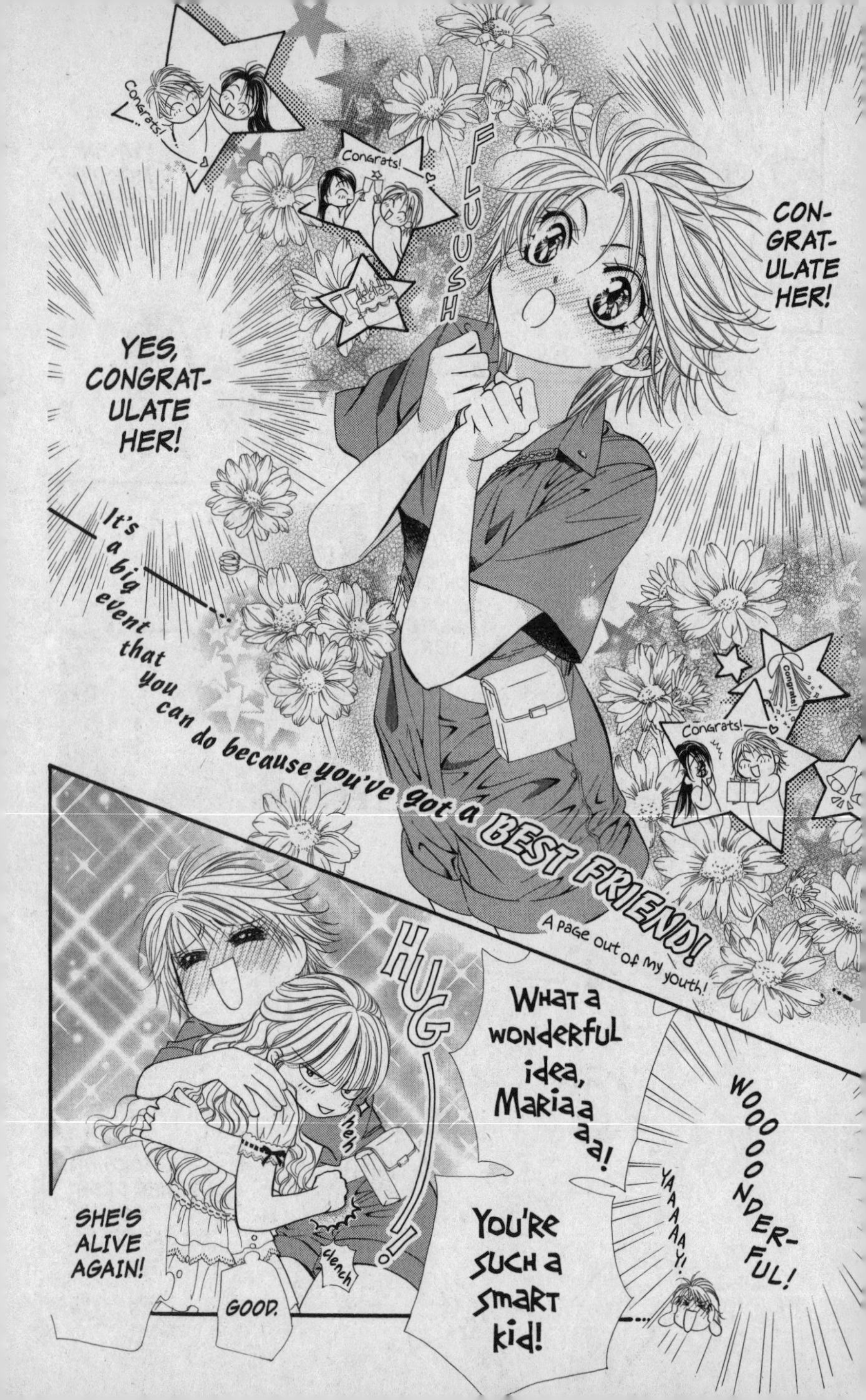
CON-GRAT-ULATE HER!
Congrats!
Congrats!
Congrats!
Congrats!
FLUUSH
YES, CONGRAT-ULATE HER!
It's a big event that you can do because you've got a BEST FRIEND!
A page out of my youth!
...
WOOOOONDER-FUL!
YAAAAAY!
What a wonderful idea, Mariaaaaa!
You're such a smart kid!
...
HUG!!
heh
clench
GOOD.
SHE'S ALIVE AGAIN!

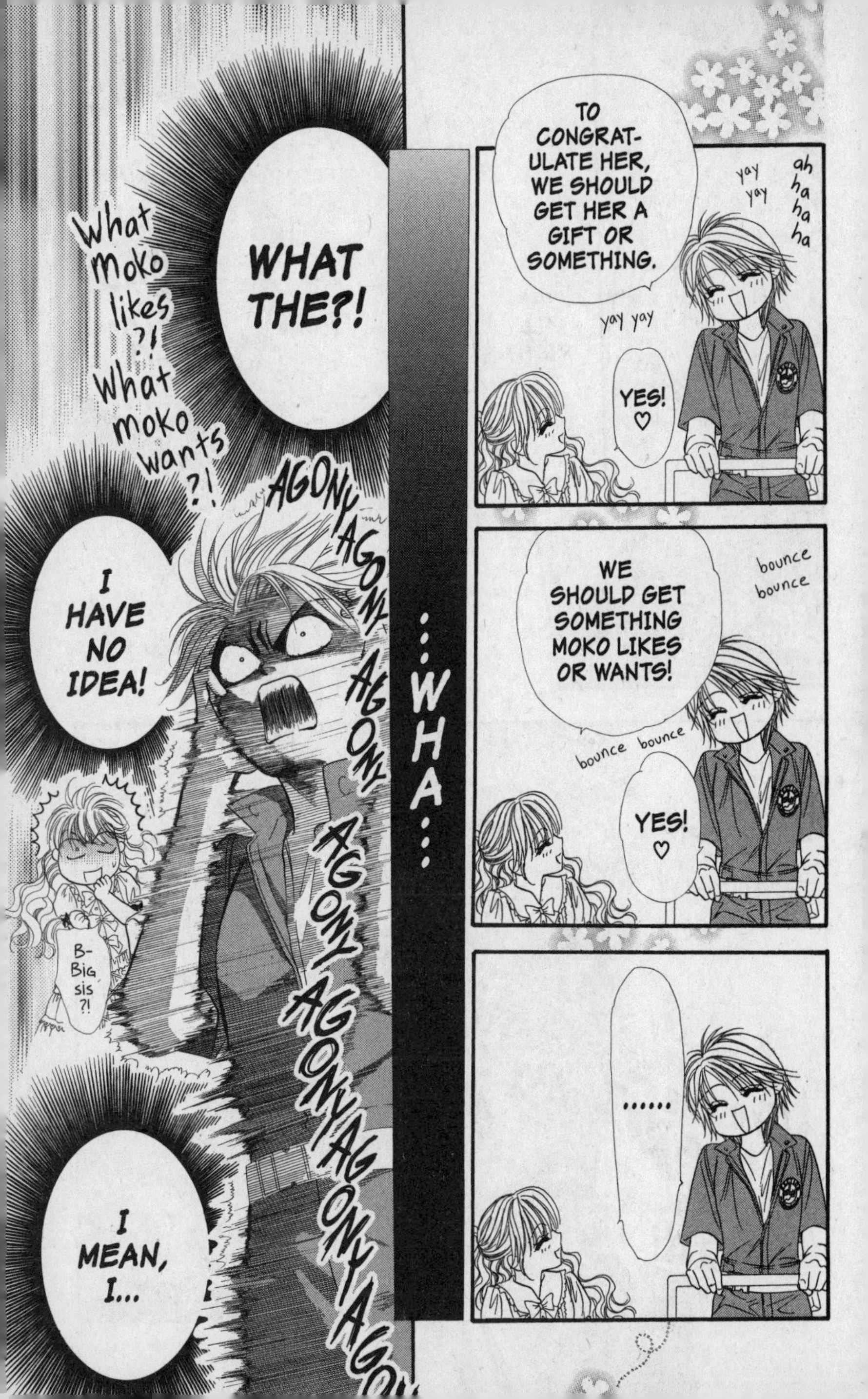
TO CONGRAT-ULATE HER, WE SHOULD GET HER A GIFT OR SOMETHING.
ah ha ha ha
yay yay
yay yay
YES! ♡
bounce bounce
WE SHOULD GET SOMETHING MOKO LIKES OR WANTS!
bounce bounce
YES! ♡
......
...WHA...
WHAT THE?!
What moko likes?! What moko wants?!
AGONY AGONY AGONY AGONY AGONY AGONY AGONY AGONY AGONY AGO
I HAVE NO IDEA!
B-Big sis?!
I MEAN, I...

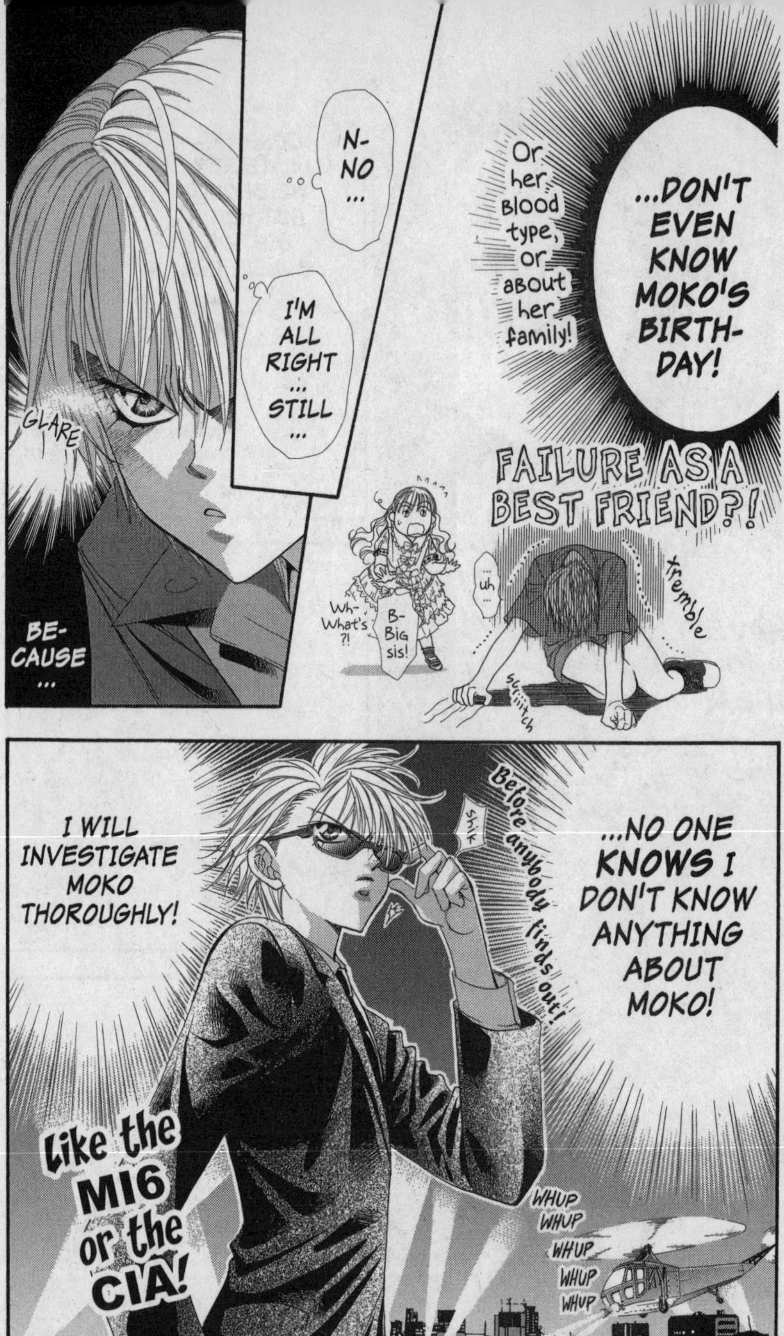
...DON'T EVEN KNOW MOKO'S BIRTHDAY!
Or her blood type, or about her family!
FAILURE AS A BEST FRIEND?!
tremble
...uh...
B- Big sis!
Wh- What's ?!
scriiitch
N-NO...
I'M ALL RIGHT... STILL...
GLARE
BE-CAUSE...
...NO ONE KNOWS I DON'T KNOW ANYTHING ABOUT MOKO!
Before anybody finds out!
stik
I WILL INVESTIGATE MOKO THOROUGHLY!
WHUP WHUP WHUP WHUP WHUP
Like the MI6 or the CIA!
...

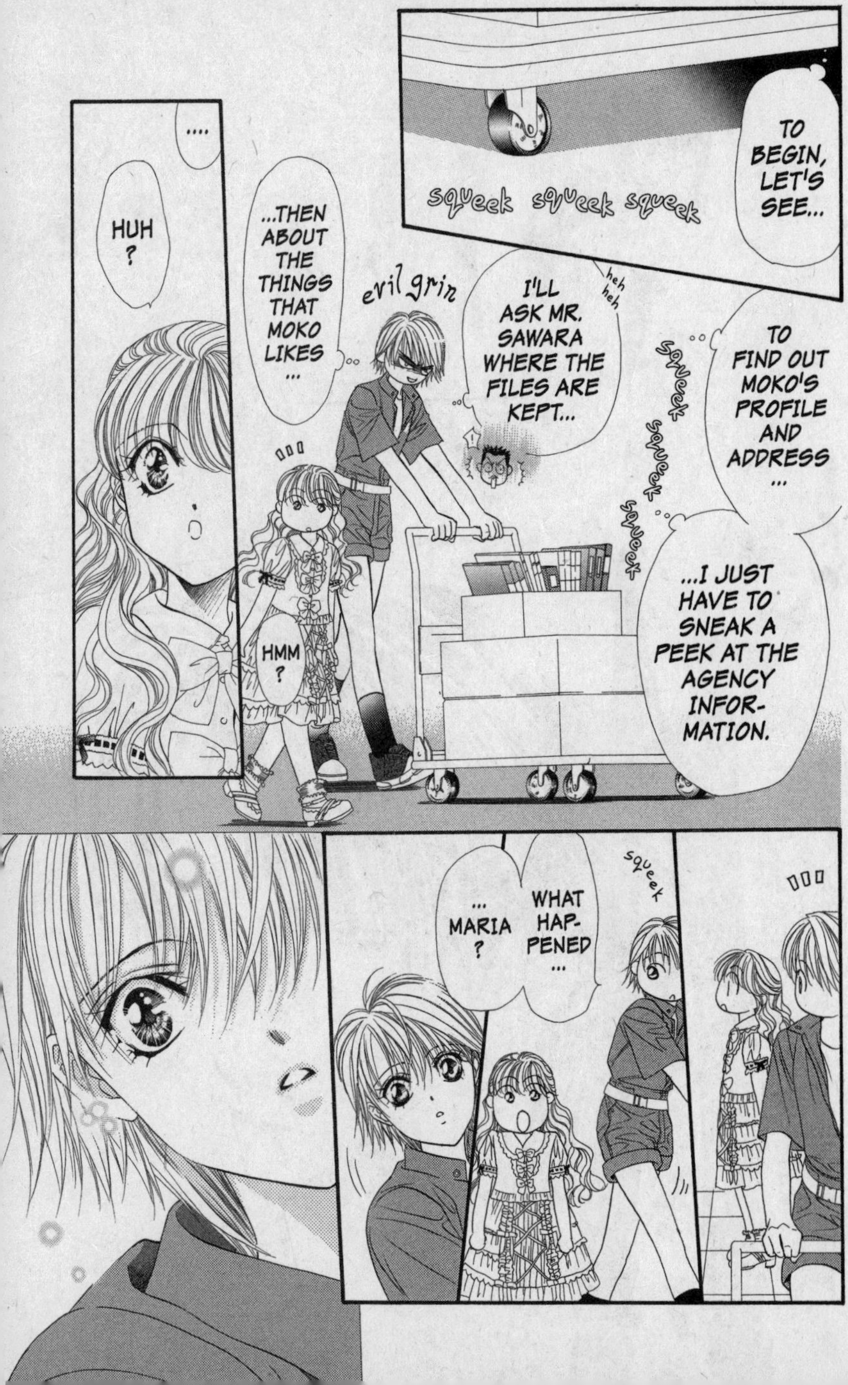
TO BEGIN, LET'S SEE...
squeek squeek squeek
TO FIND OUT MOKO'S PROFILE AND ADDRESS...
...I JUST HAVE TO SNEAK A PEEK AT THE AGENCY INFORMATION.
squeek squeek squeek
heh heh
I'LL ASK MR. SAWARA WHERE THE FILES ARE KEPT...
evil grin
...THEN ABOUT THE THINGS THAT MOKO LIKES...
HMM?
....
HUH?
squeek
WHAT HAPPENED...
...MARIA?

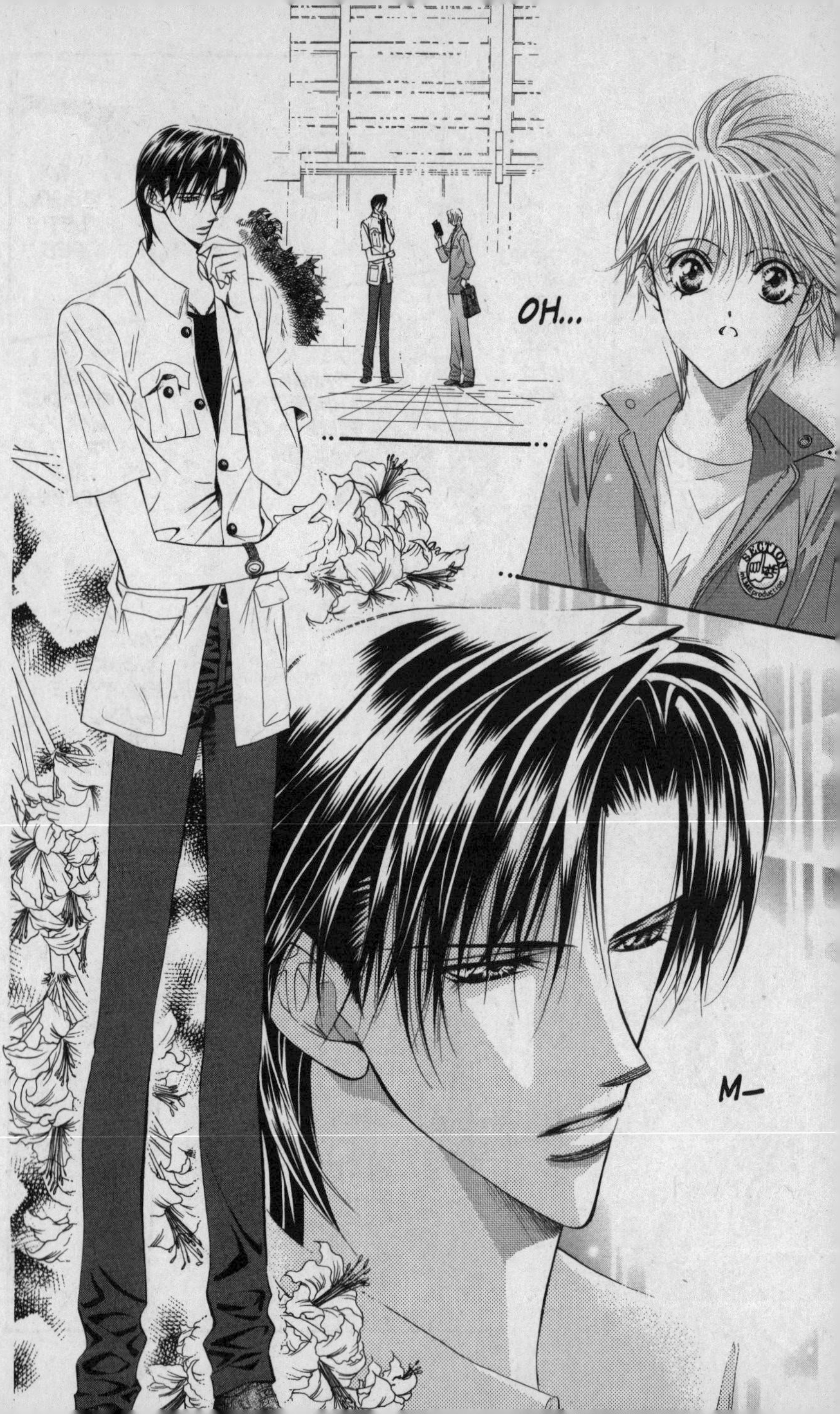
OH...
...
..——..
M—

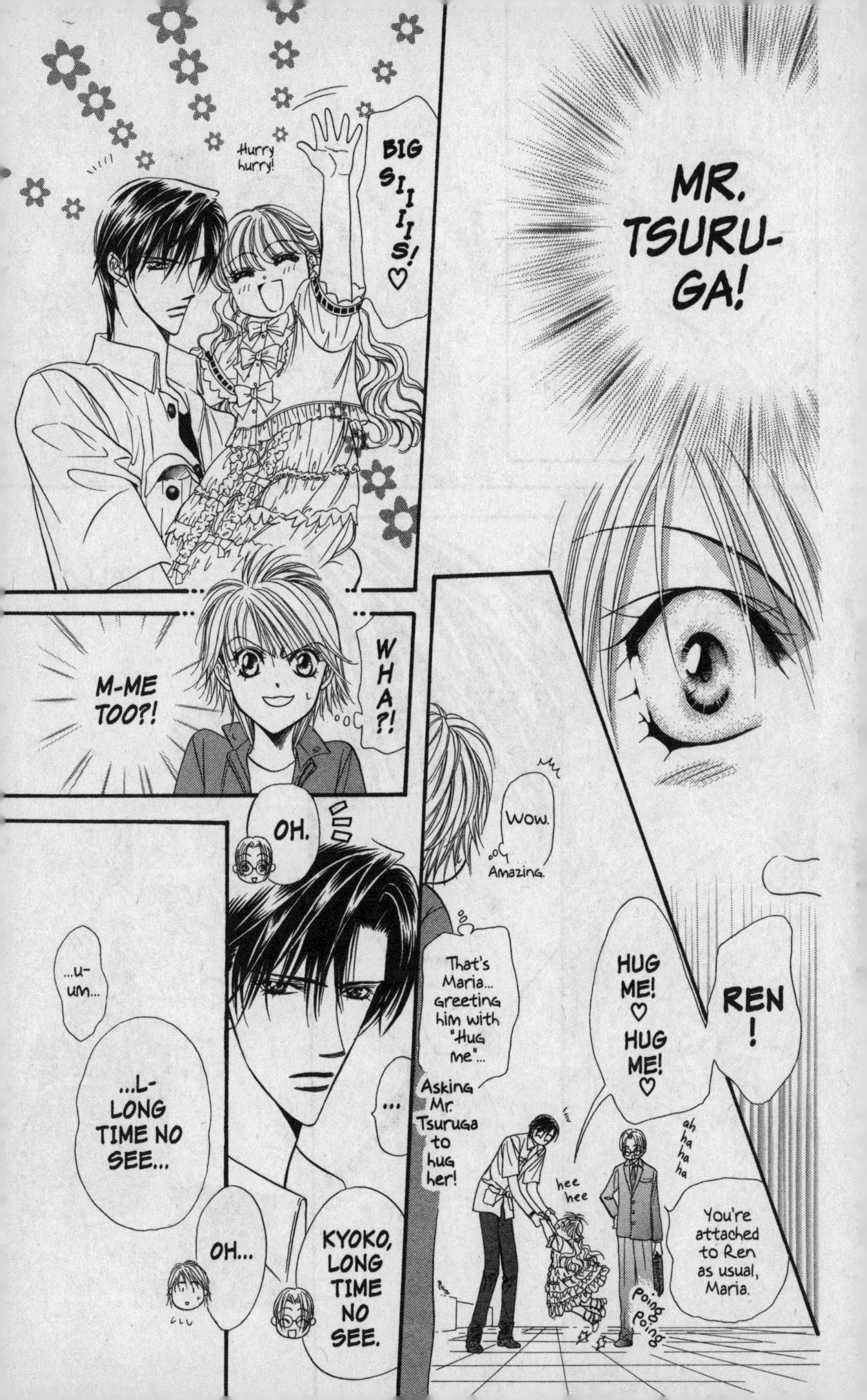
MR. TSURUGA!
REN!
HUG ME! ♡ HUG ME! ♡
Wow.
Amazing.
That's Maria... greeting him with "Hug me"...
Asking Mr. Tsuruga to hug her!
ah ha ha ha
You're attached to Ren as usual, Maria.
hee hee
Poing Poing
BIG SIIIIS! ♡
Hurry hurry!
WHA?!
M-ME TOO?!
OH.
...
KYOKO, LONG TIME NO SEE.
OH...
...u-um...
...L-LONG TIME NO SEE...

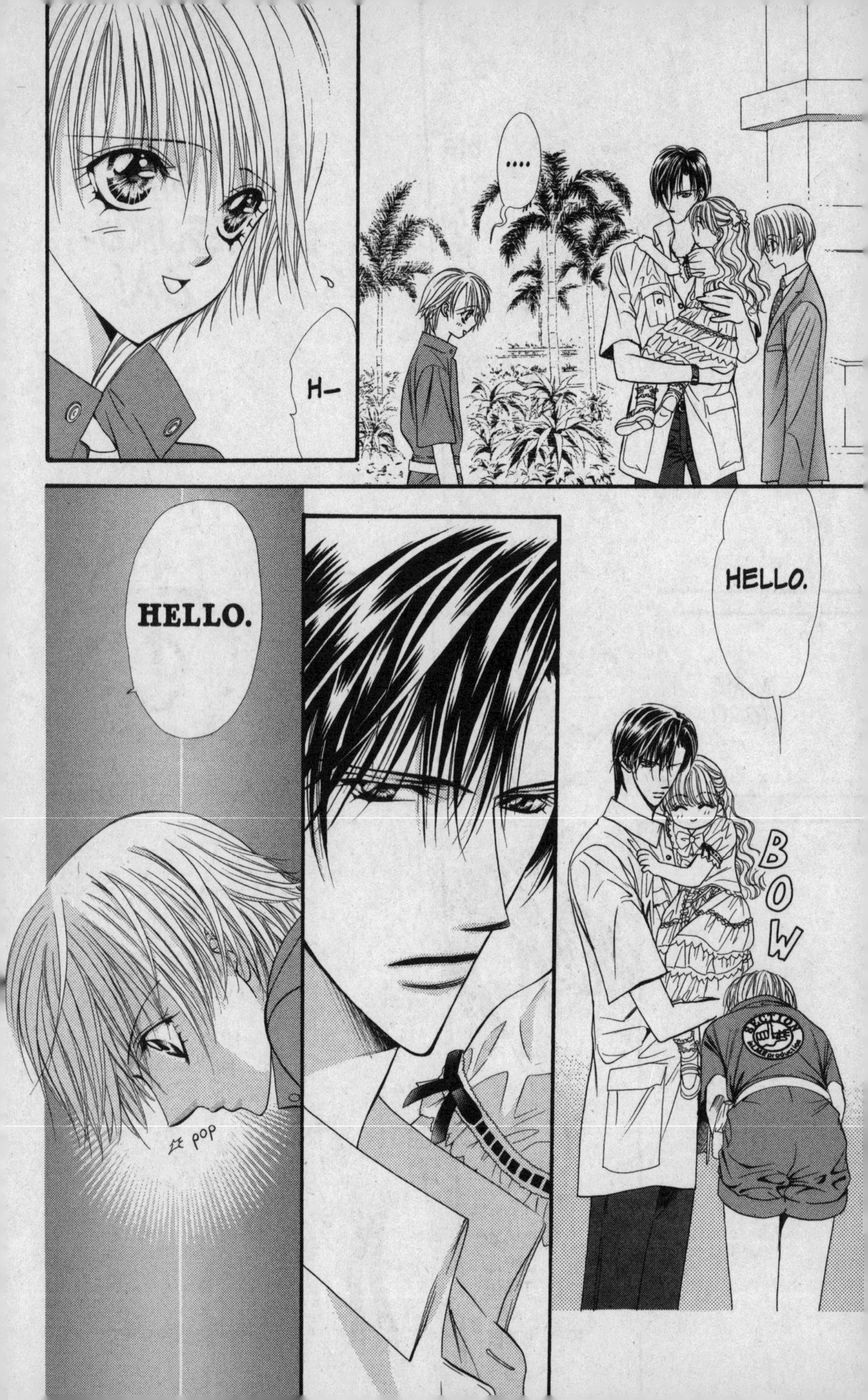
....
H–
HELLO.
BOW
HELLO.
pop

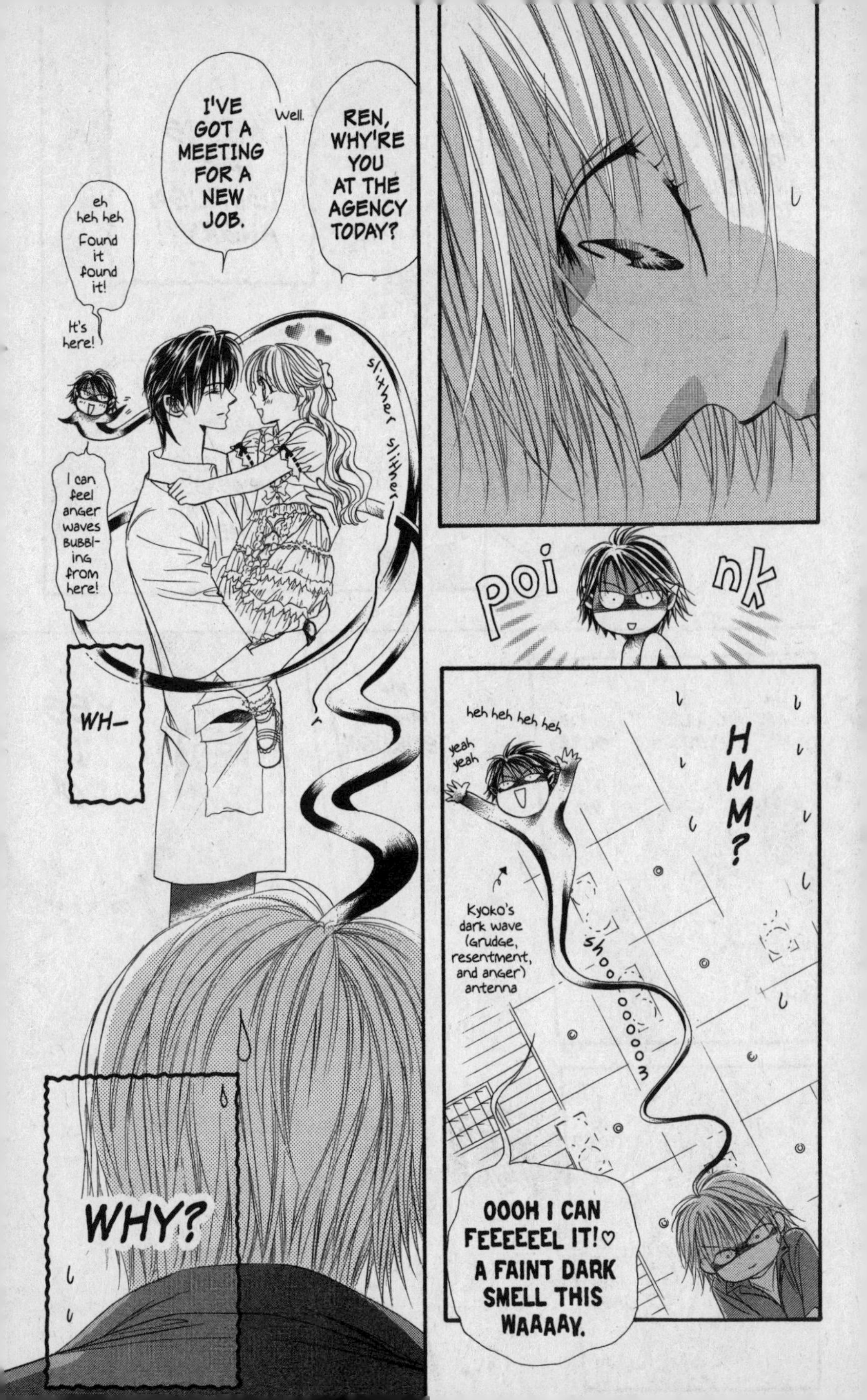

poi nk
HMM?
heh heh heh heh
yeah yeah
Kyoko's dark wave (grudge, resentment, and anger) antenna
shoooooooom
OOOH I CAN FEEEEEEL IT! ♡ A FAINT DARK SMELL THIS WAAAAY.
REN, WHY'RE YOU AT THE AGENCY TODAY?
Well.
I'VE GOT A MEETING FOR A NEW JOB.
eh heh heh Found it found it!
It's here!
slither slither
I can feel anger waves bubbling from here!
WH—
WHY?

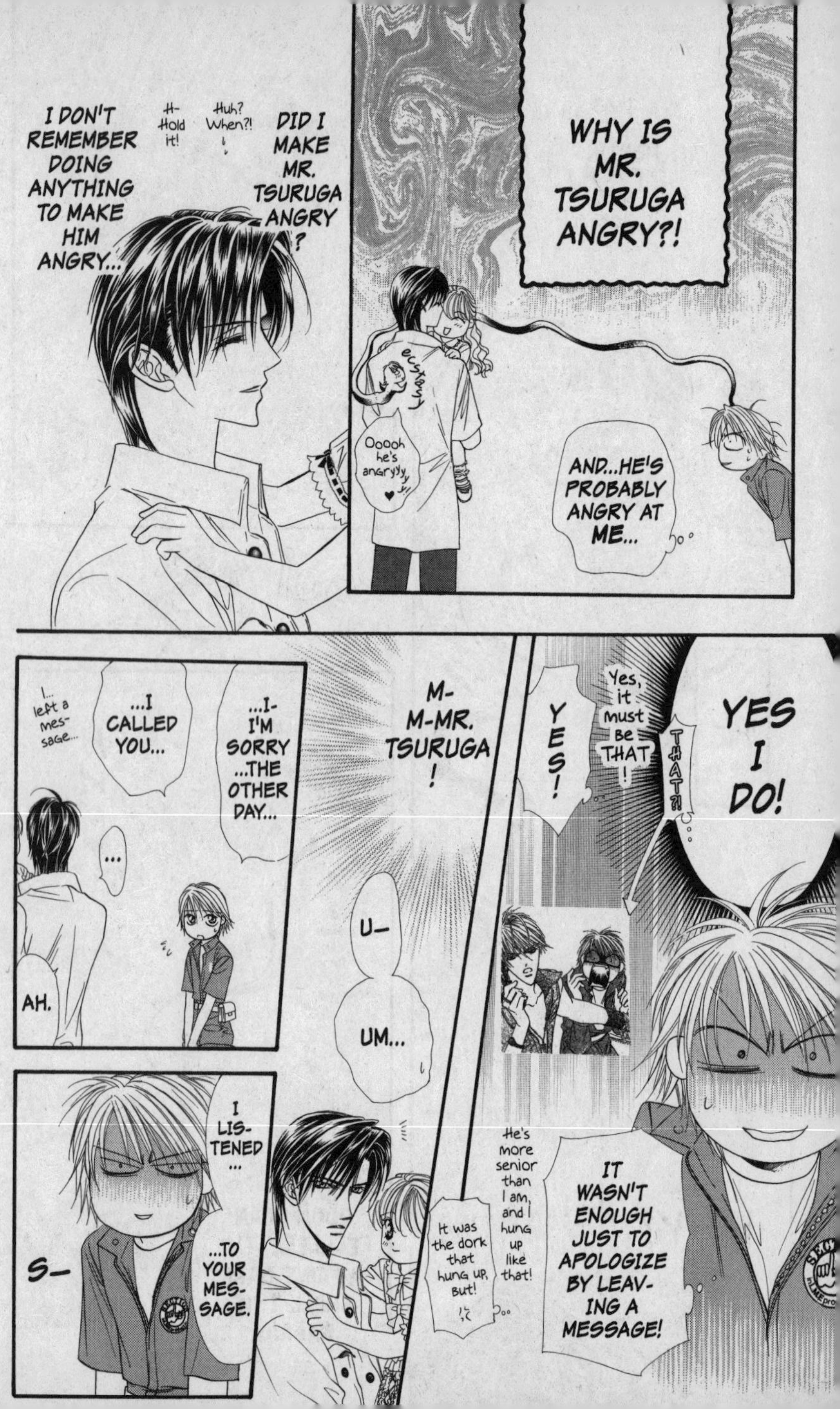
WHY IS MR. TSURUGA ANGRY?!
AND...HE'S PROBABLY ANGRY AT ME...
ecstasy
Ooooh he's angryyyy!! ♥
DID I MAKE MR. TSURUGA ANGRY?
Huh? When?!
H-Hold it!
I DON'T REMEMBER DOING ANYTHING TO MAKE HIM ANGRY...
YES I DO!
THAT?!
Yes, it must be THAT!
YES!
IT WASN'T ENOUGH JUST TO APOLOGIZE BY LEAVING A MESSAGE!
He's more senior than I am, and I hung up like that!
It was the dork that hung up, but!
M-M-MR. TSURUGA!
...I-I'M SORRY ...THE OTHER DAY...
...I CALLED YOU...
I... left a message...
...
AH.
U—
UM...
I LISTENED...
...TO YOUR MESSAGE.
S—

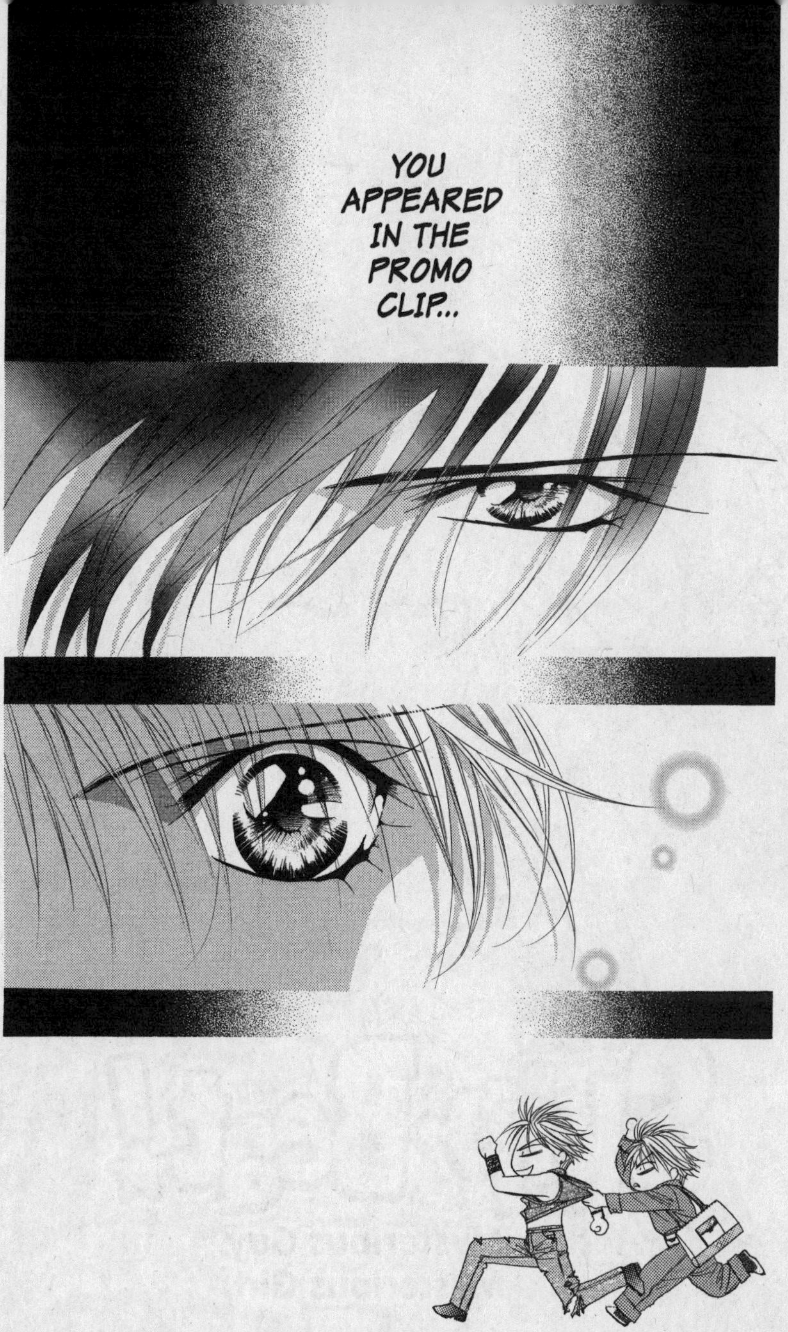
YOU APPEARED IN THE PROMO CLIP...

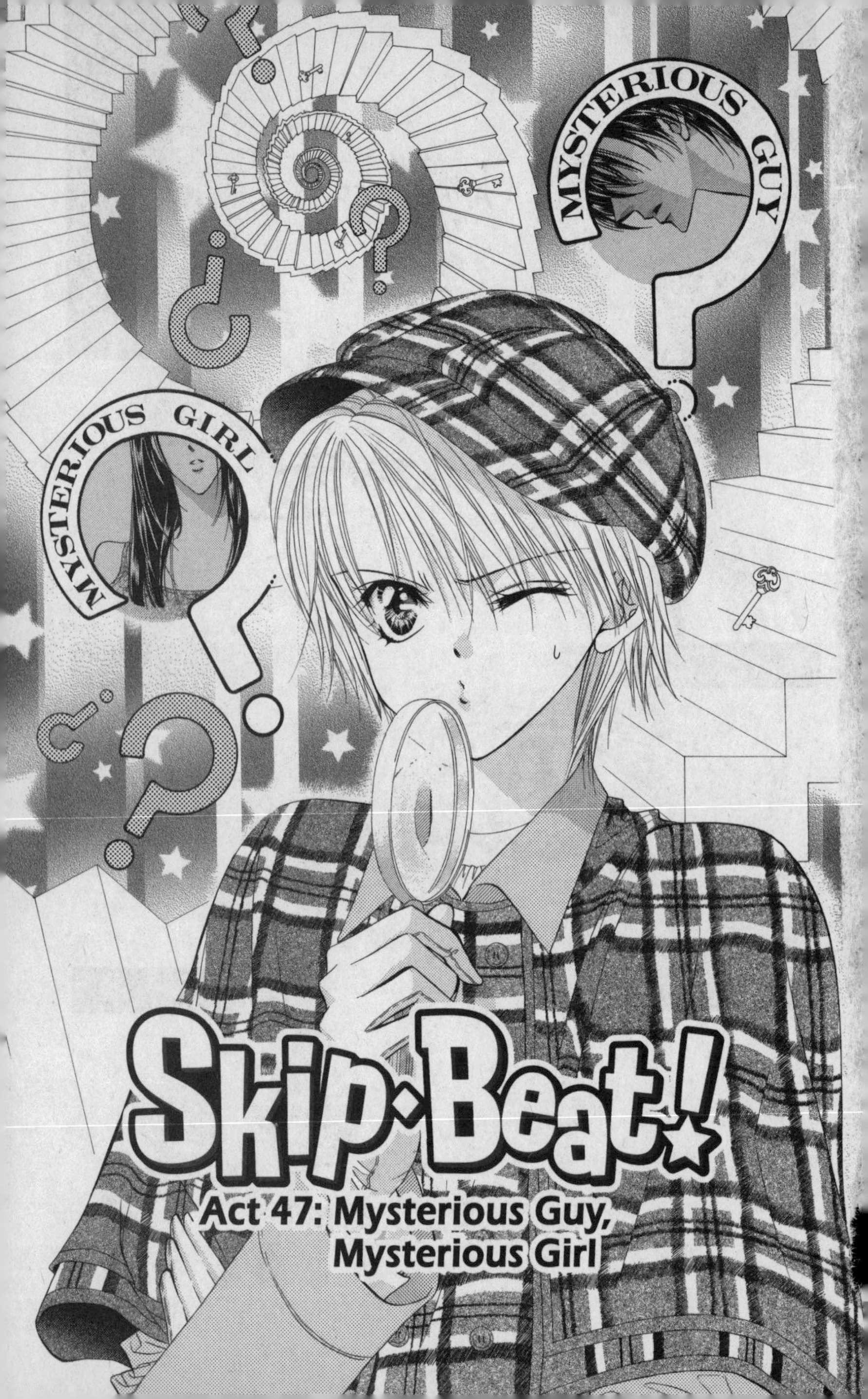
MYSTERIOUS GUY
MYSTERIOUS GIRL
Skip·Beat!
Act 47: Mysterious Guy, Mysterious Girl

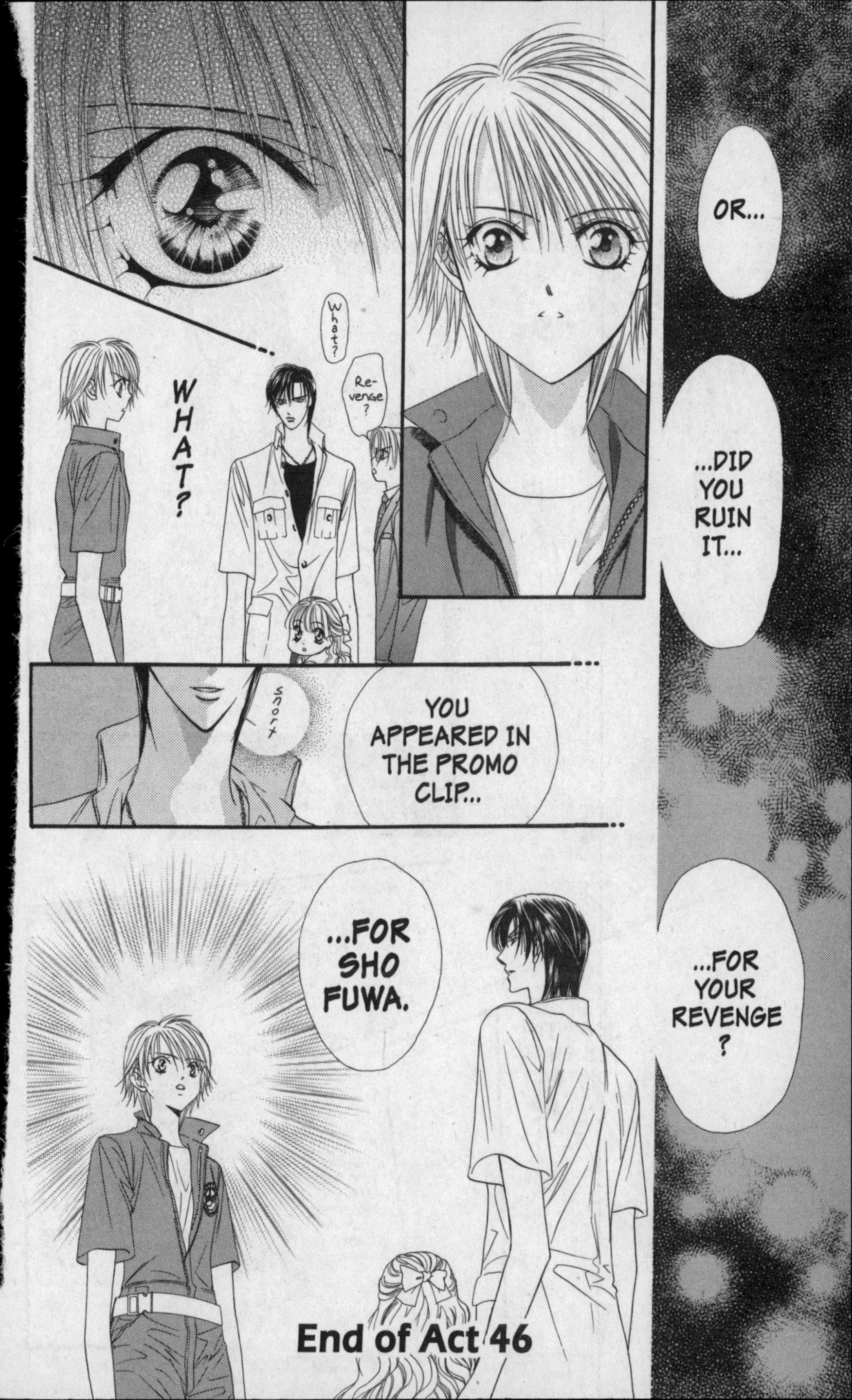
OR...
...DID YOU RUIN IT...
...FOR YOUR REVENGE?
What?
Re-venge?
WHAT?
snort
YOU APPEARED IN THE PROMO CLIP...
...FOR SHO FUWA.
End of Act 46

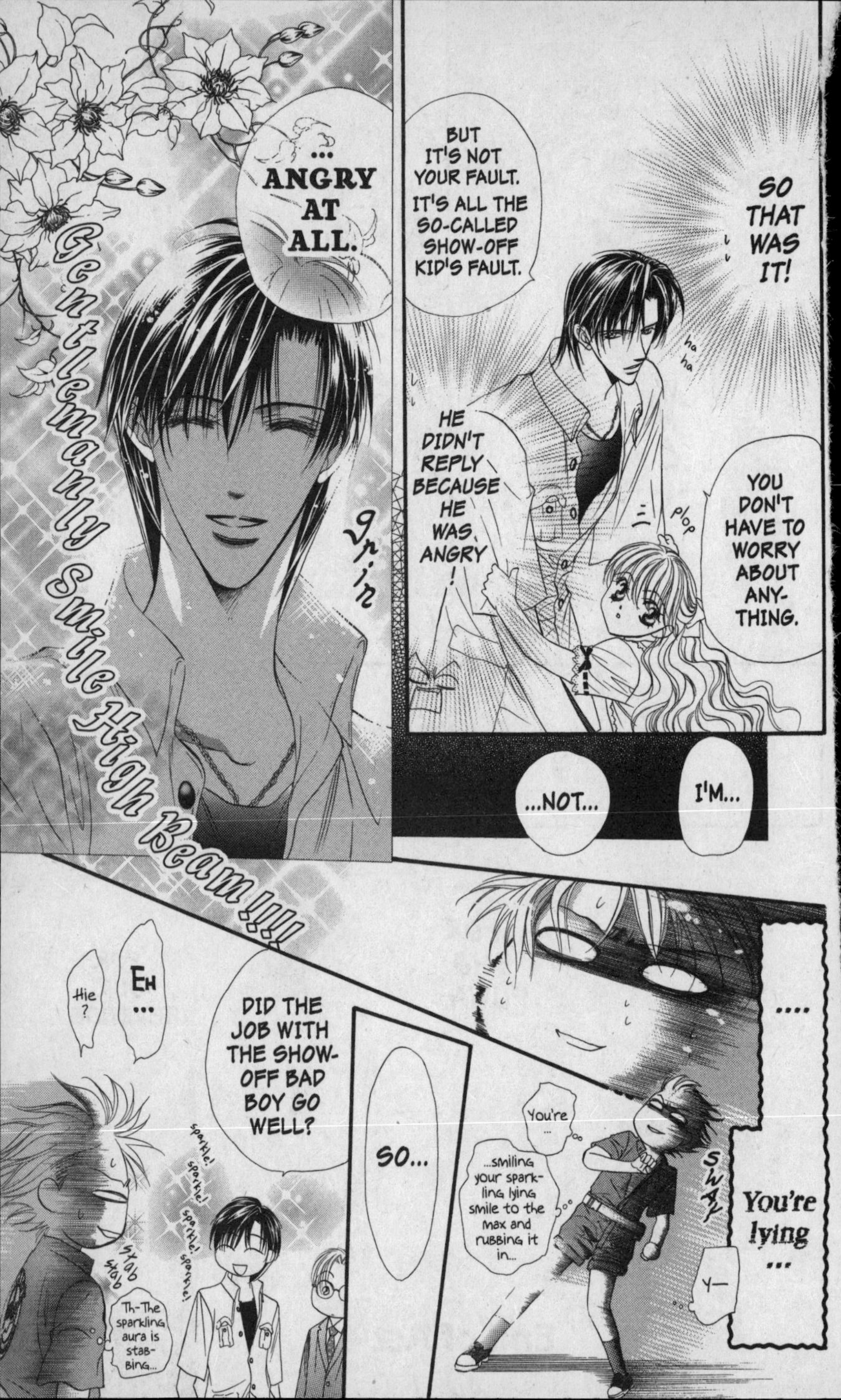

SO THAT WAS IT!
BUT IT'S NOT YOUR FAULT. IT'S ALL THE SO-CALLED SHOW-OFF KID'S FAULT.
ha ha
YOU DON'T HAVE TO WORRY ABOUT ANYTHING.
plop
HE DIDN'T REPLY BECAUSE HE WAS ANGRY!
I'M...
...NOT...
...ANGRY AT ALL.
Gentlemanly Smile High Beam!!!!
grin
....
You're lying...
Y—
SWAY
You're...
...smiling your sparkling lying smile to the max and rubbing it in...
SO...
DID THE JOB WITH THE SHOW-OFF BAD BOY GO WELL?
EH...
Hie?
sparkle! sparkle! sparkle! sparkle!
stab stab
Th-The sparkling aura is stabbing...

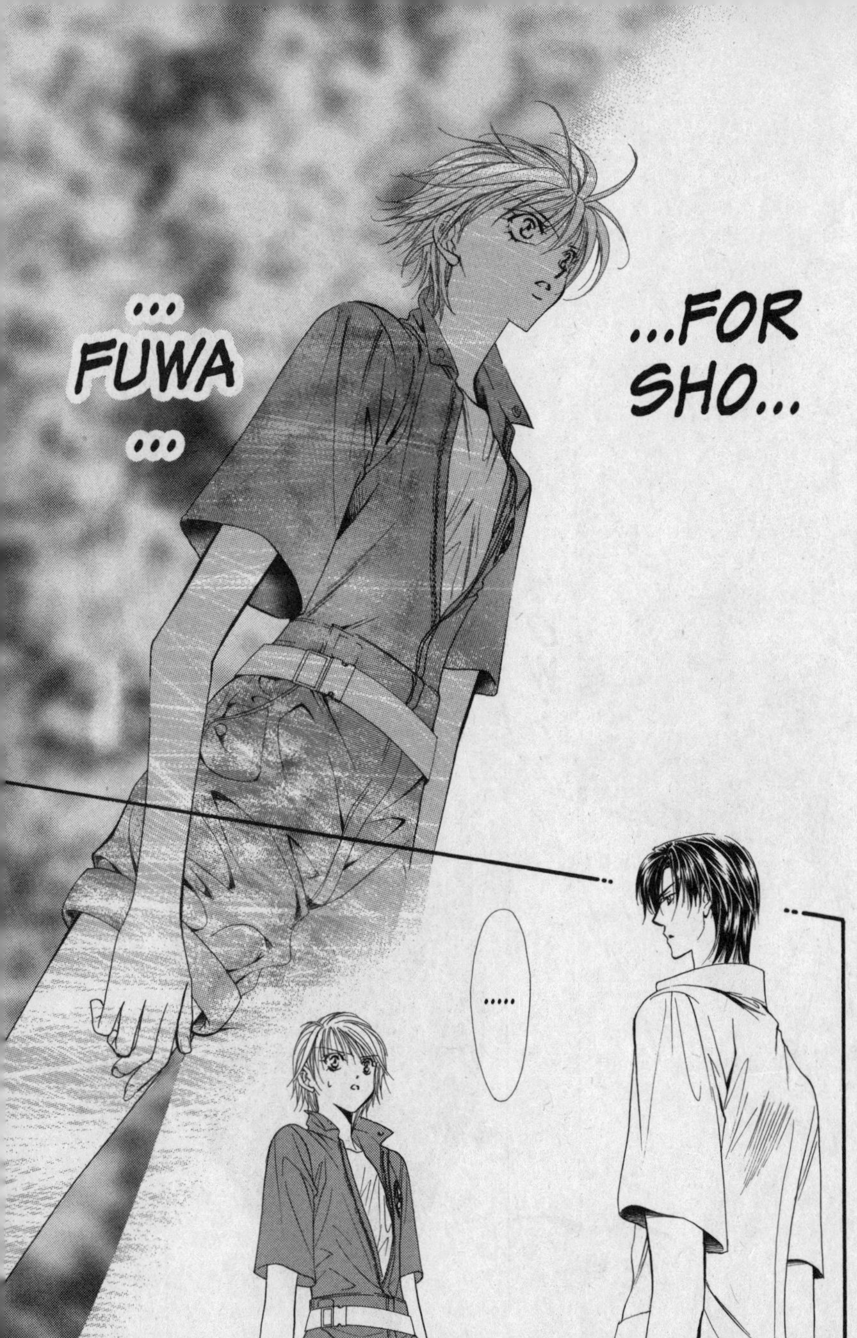
...FOR SHO...
...FUWA...
.....

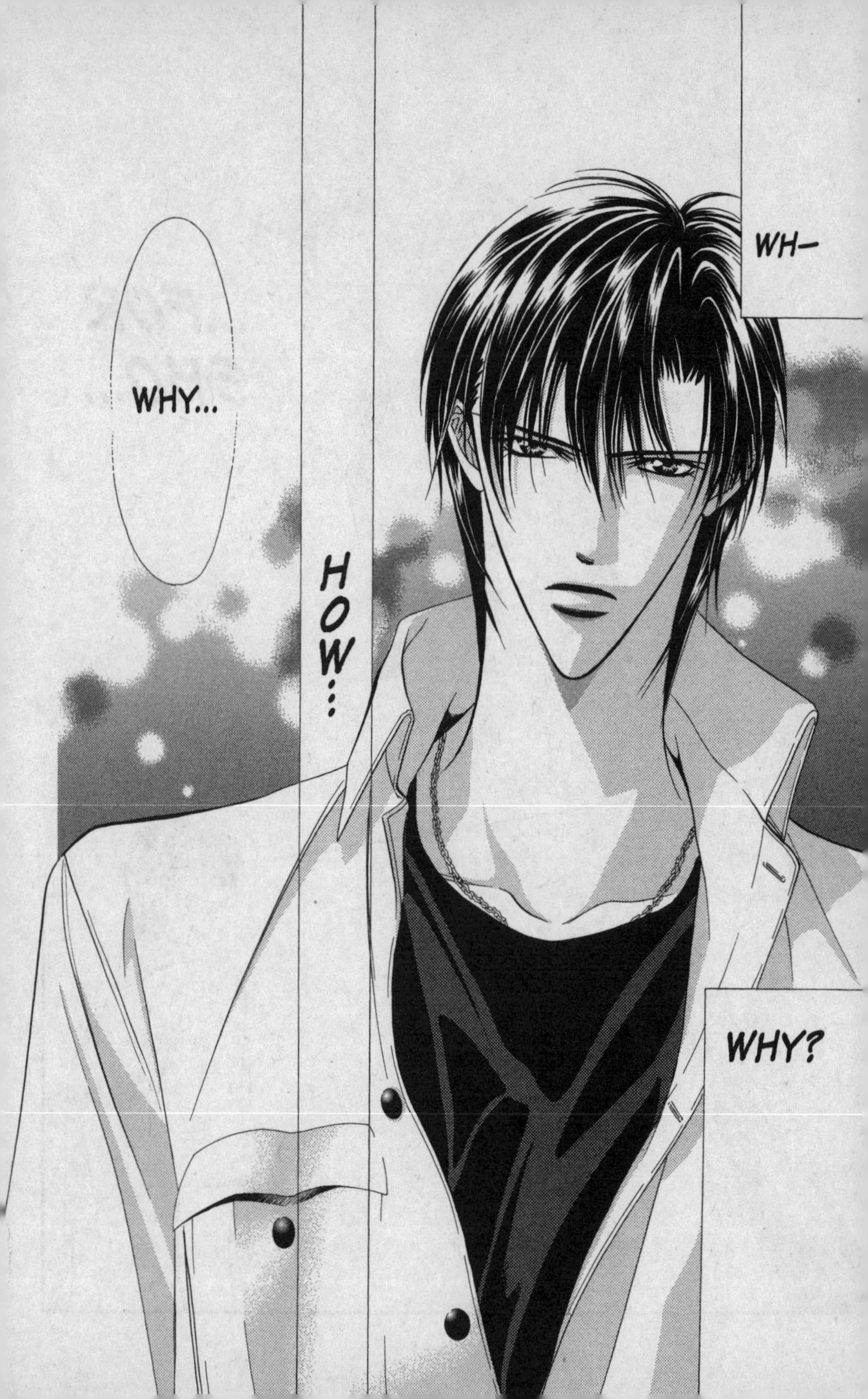
WH–
WHY?
HOW...
WHY...

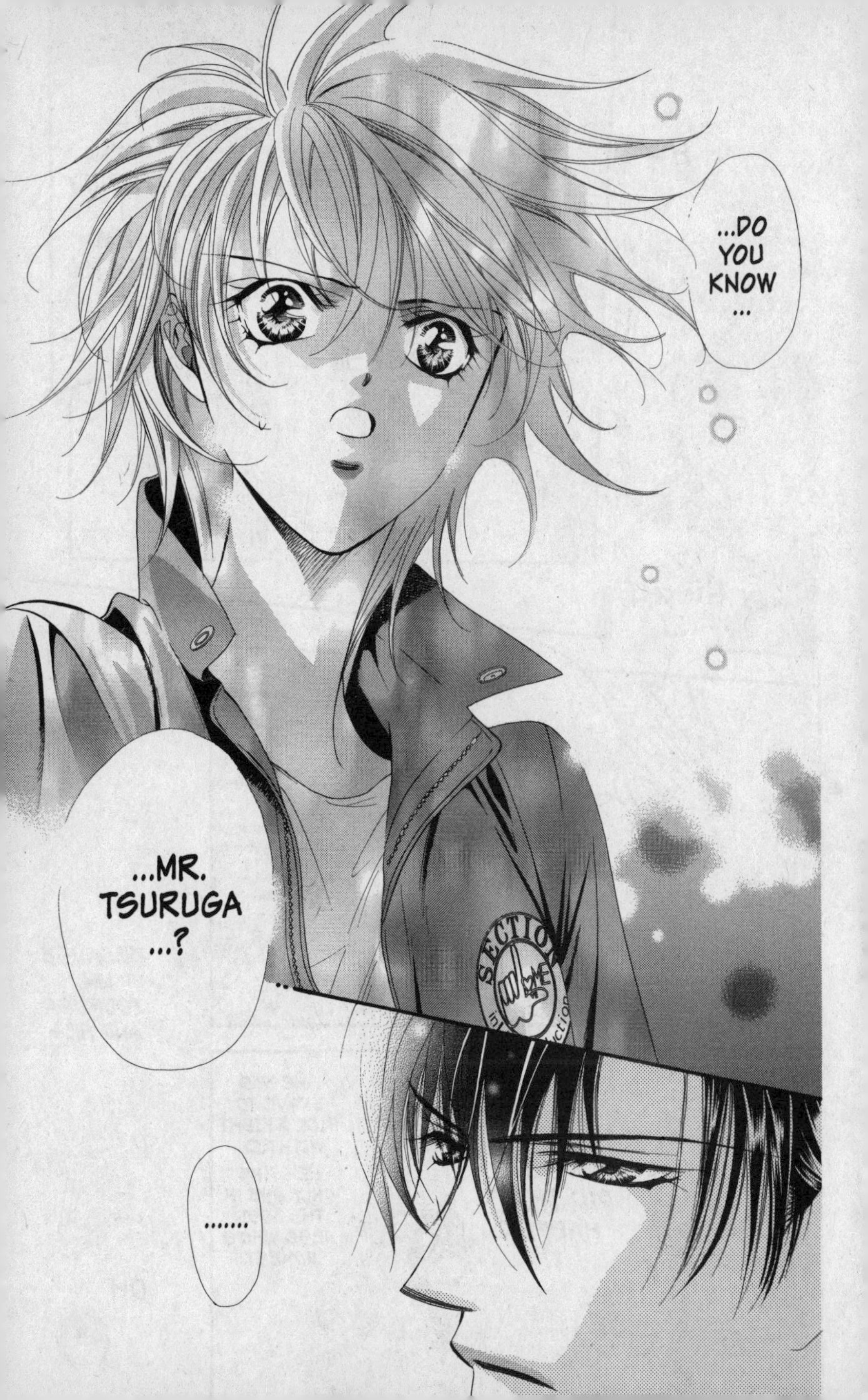
...DO YOU KNOW ...
...MR. TSURUGA ...?
....

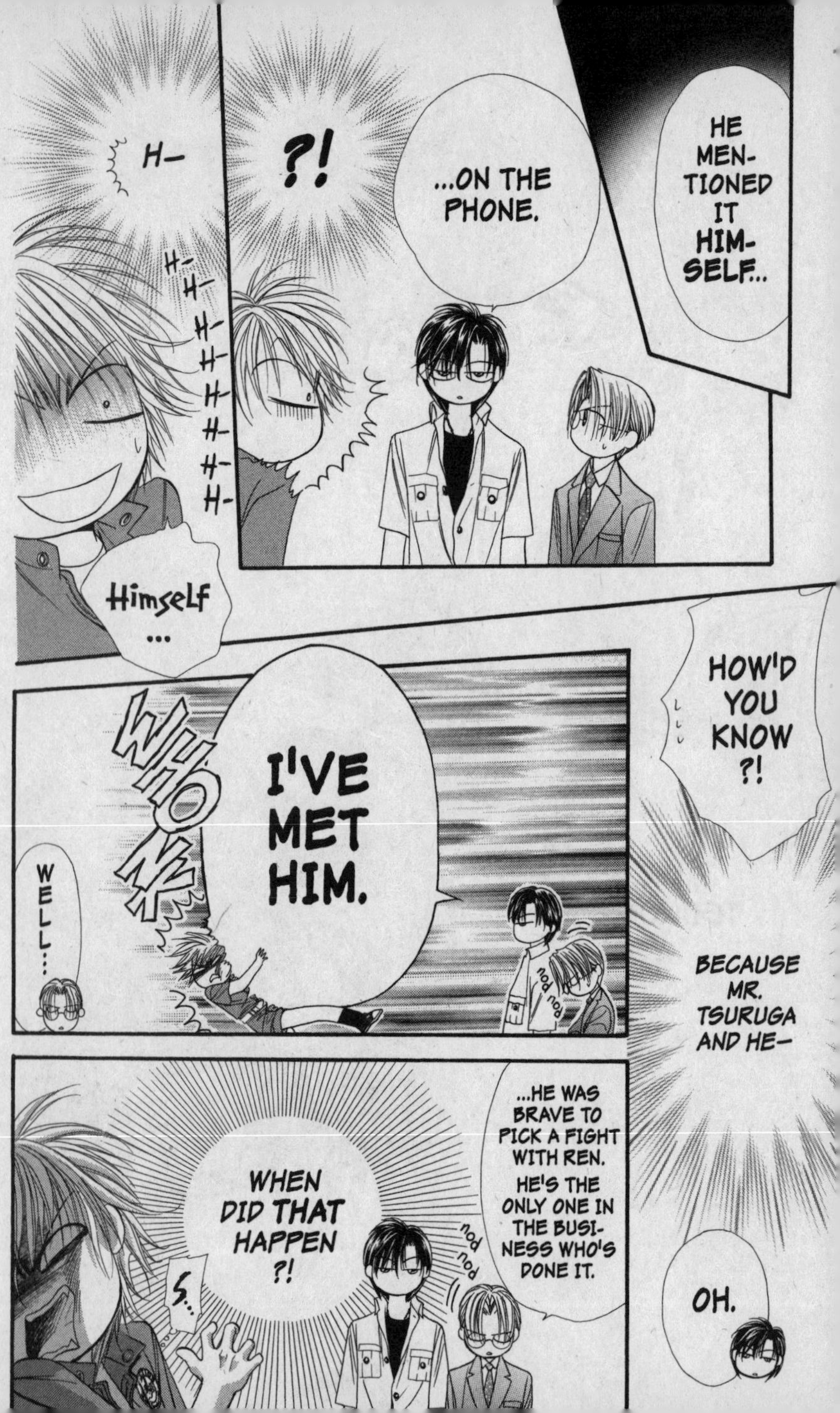
HE MEN- TIONED IT HIM- SELF...
...ON THE PHONE.
?!
H-
H- H- H- H- H- H- H- H- H-
Himself ...
HOW'D YOU KNOW ?!
I'VE MET HIM.
WHOMP
pou pou
WELL...
BECAUSE MR. TSURUGA AND HE—
OH.
...HE WAS BRAVE TO PICK A FIGHT WITH REN.
HE'S THE ONLY ONE IN THE BUSI- NESS WHO'S DONE IT.
pou pou
WHEN DID THAT HAPPEN ?!
S...

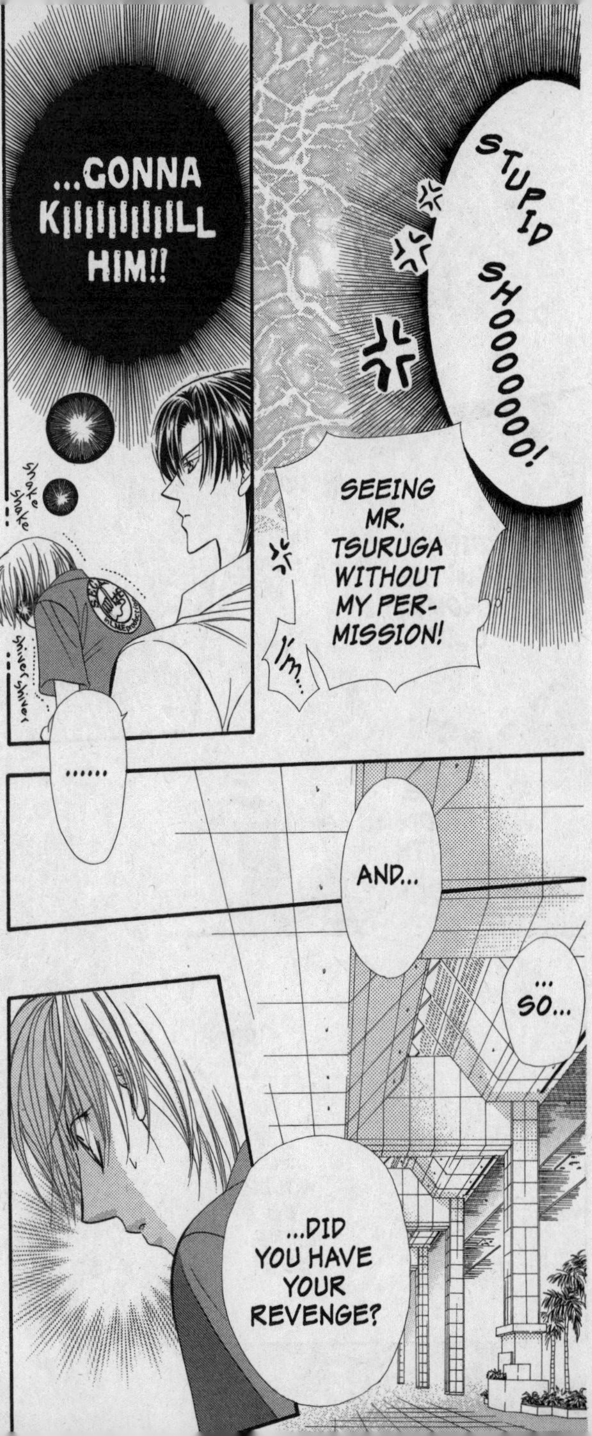
STUPID SHOOOOOOO!
I'm...
SEEING MR. TSURUGA WITHOUT MY PERMISSION!
...GONNA KIIIIIIIIILL HIM!!
shake shake
shiver shiver
......
AND...
...SO...
...DID YOU HAVE YOUR REVENGE?

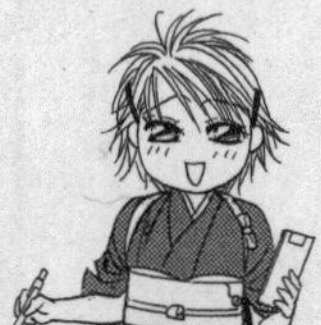

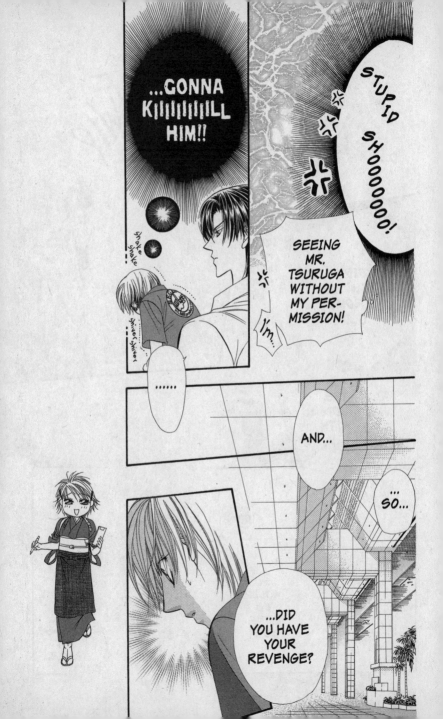

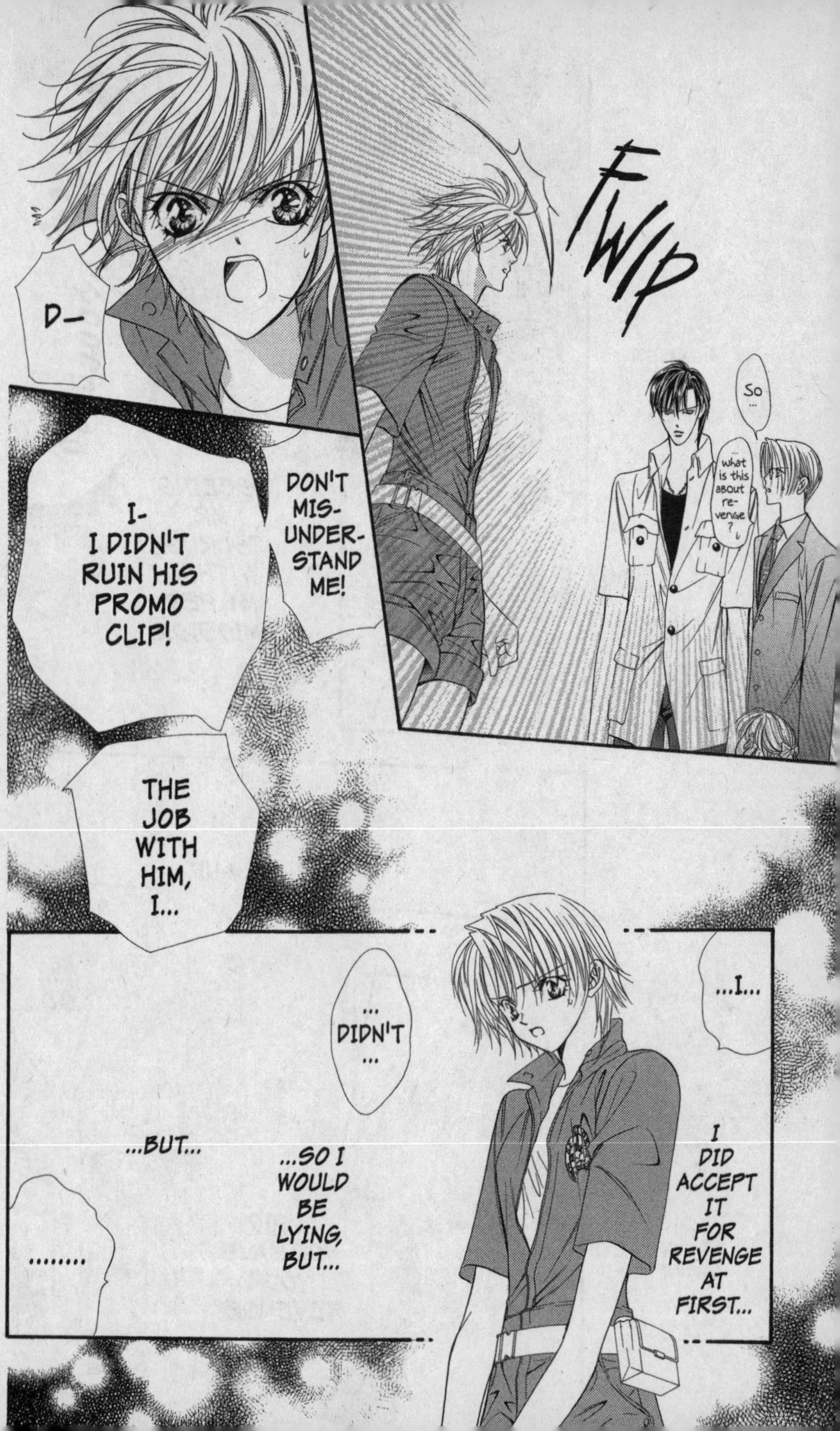
FWIP
So ...
... what is this about re-venge?
D—
DON'T MIS-UNDER-STAND ME!
I- I DIDN'T RUIN HIS PROMO CLIP!
THE JOB WITH HIM, I...
...I...
... DIDN'T ...
I DID ACCEPT IT FOR REVENGE AT FIRST...
...SO I WOULD BE LYING, BUT...
...BUT...
....

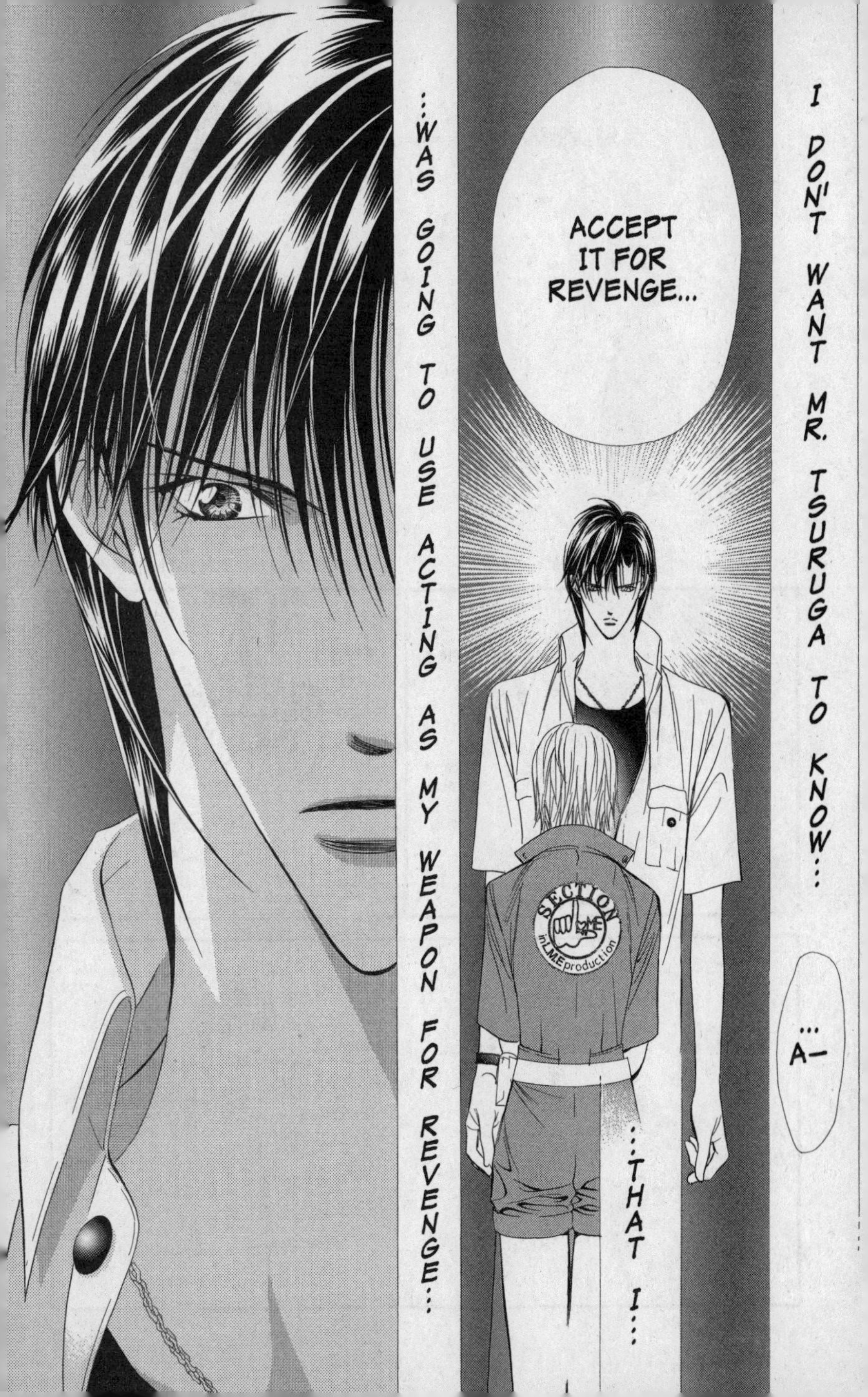
I DON'T WANT MR. TSURUGA TO KNOW...
...A—
ACCEPT IT FOR REVENGE...
SECTION inLME production
...THAT I...
...WAS GOING TO USE ACTING AS MY WEAPON FOR REVENGE...

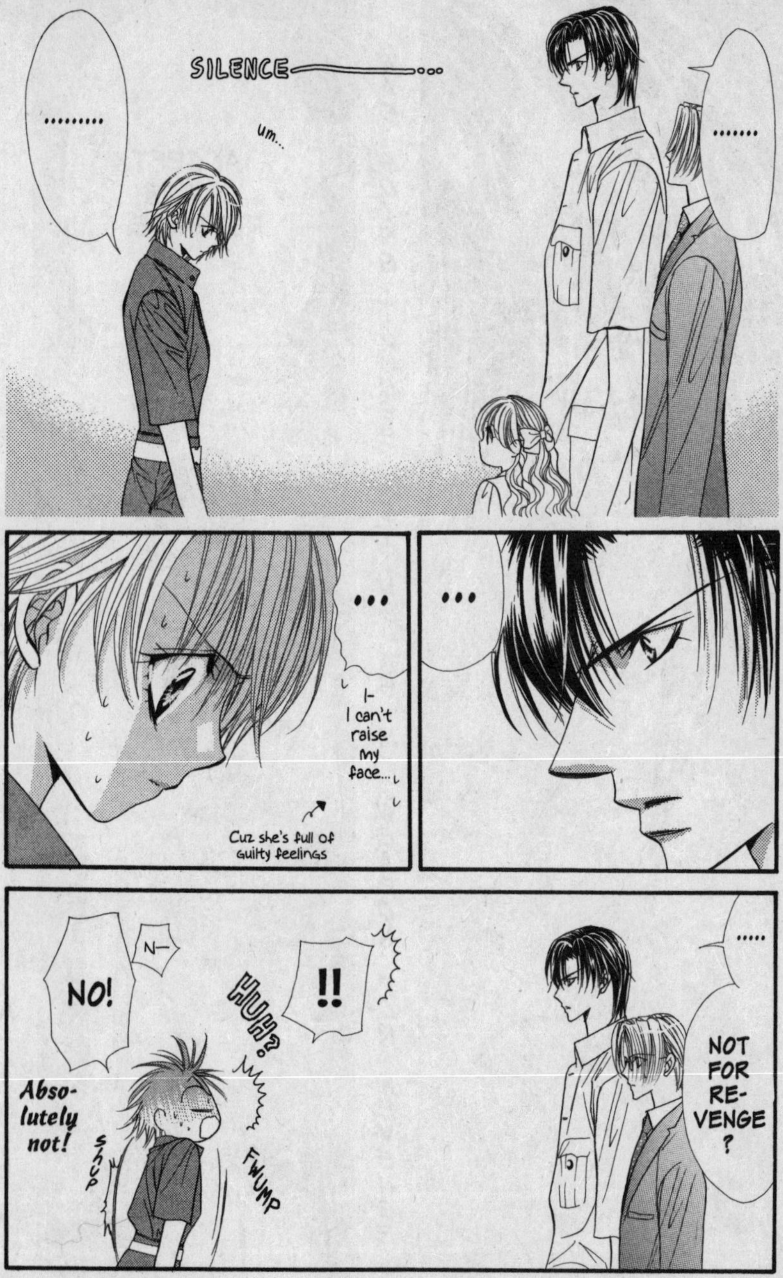

....
SILENCE———...
um...
....
...
...
I- I can't raise my face...
Cuz she's full of guilty feelings
.....
NOT FOR RE-VENGE?
!!
HUH?
N—
NO!
Abso-lutely not!
FWUMP
SHUP

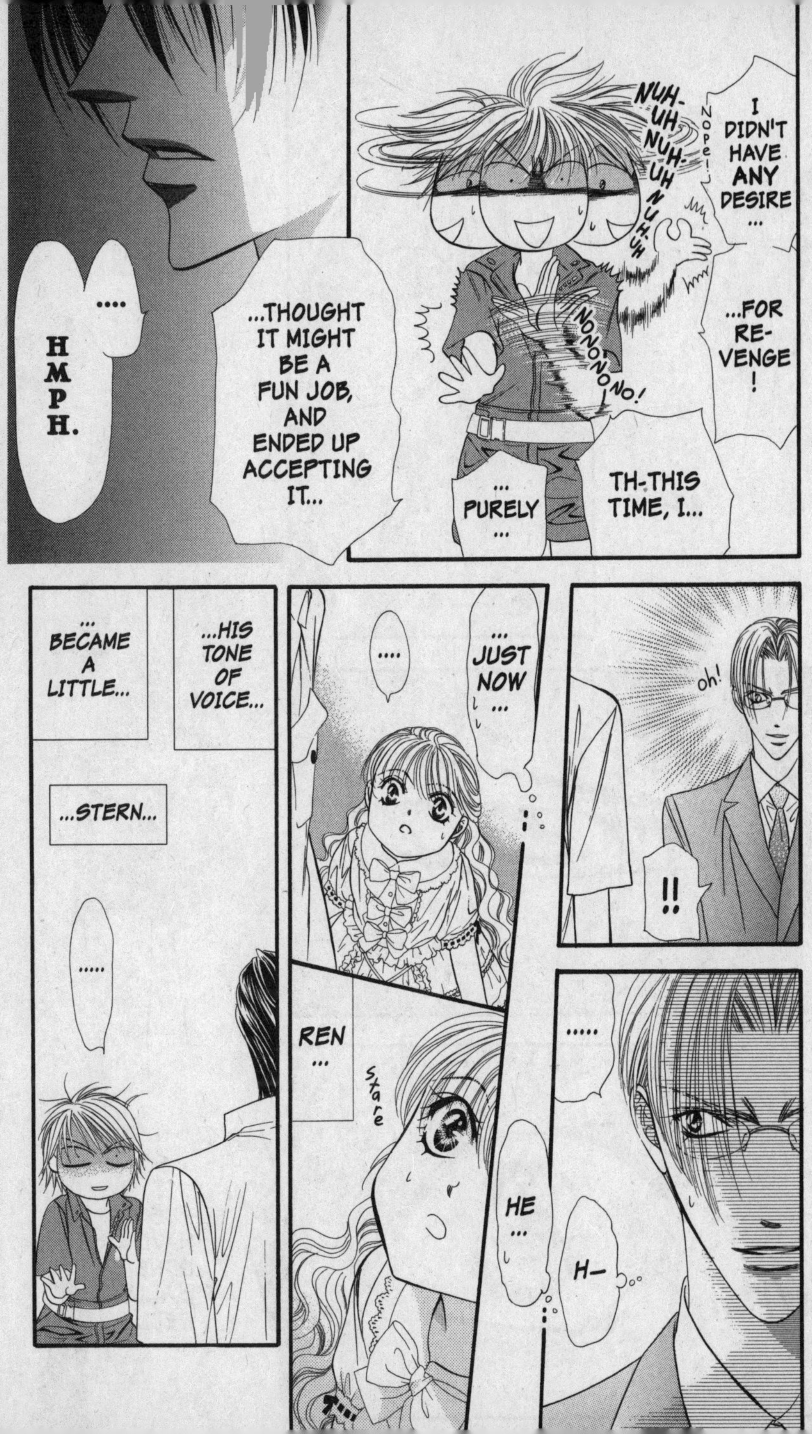

I DIDN'T HAVE ANY DESIRE ...
...FOR REVENGE!
NUH-UH NUH-UH NUH-UH
Nope!
NONONONO NO!
TH-THIS TIME, I...
... PURELY ...
...THOUGHT IT MIGHT BE A FUN JOB, AND ENDED UP ACCEPTING IT...
....
HMPH.
oh!
!!
... JUST NOW ...
....
...HIS TONE OF VOICE...
... BECAME A LITTLE...
...STERN...
.....
.....
H—
HE ...
REN ...
stare

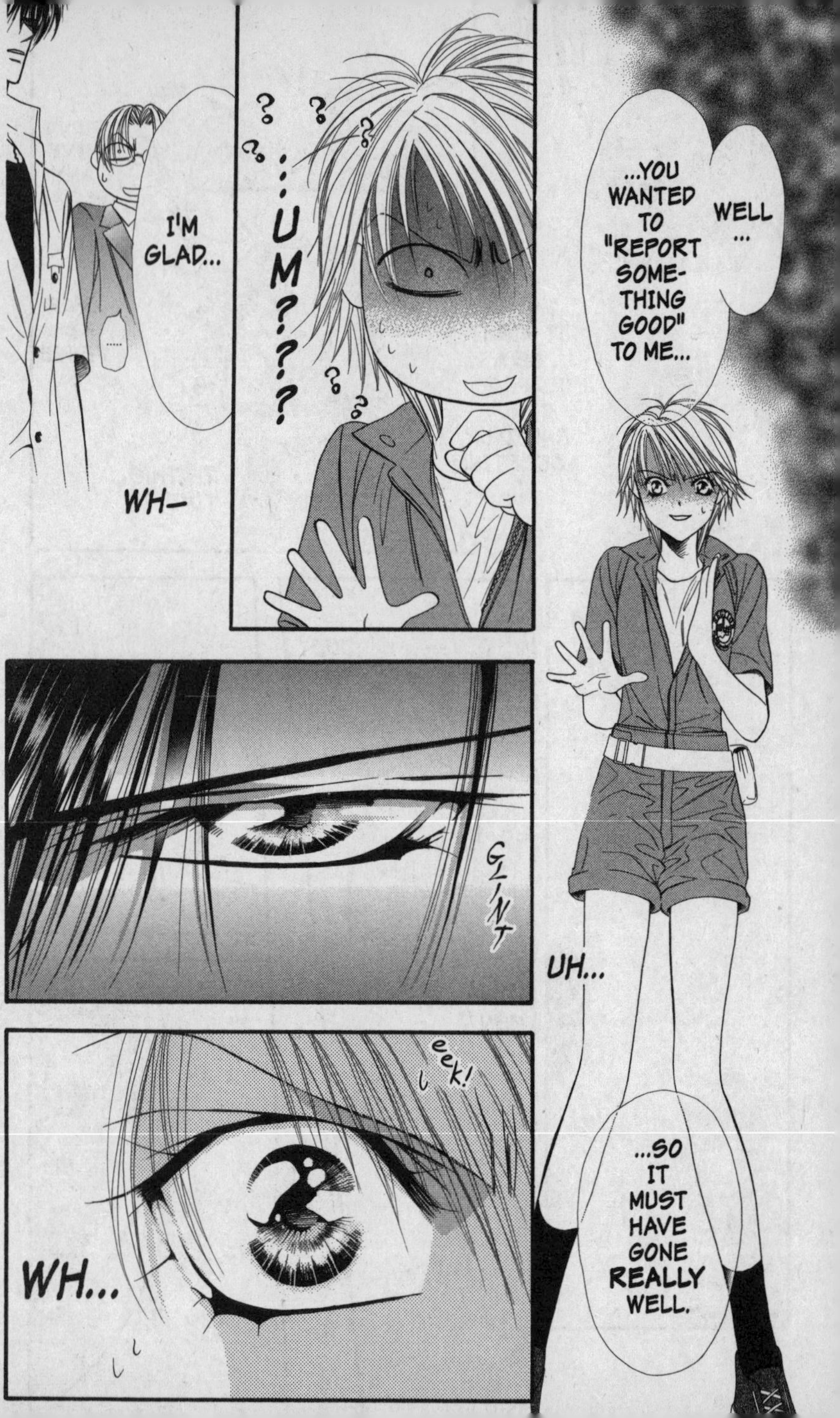
WELL...
...YOU WANTED TO "REPORT SOMETHING GOOD" TO ME...
UH...
...SO IT MUST HAVE GONE REALLY WELL.
...UM????
I'M GLAD...
.....
WH–
GLINT
eek!
WH...

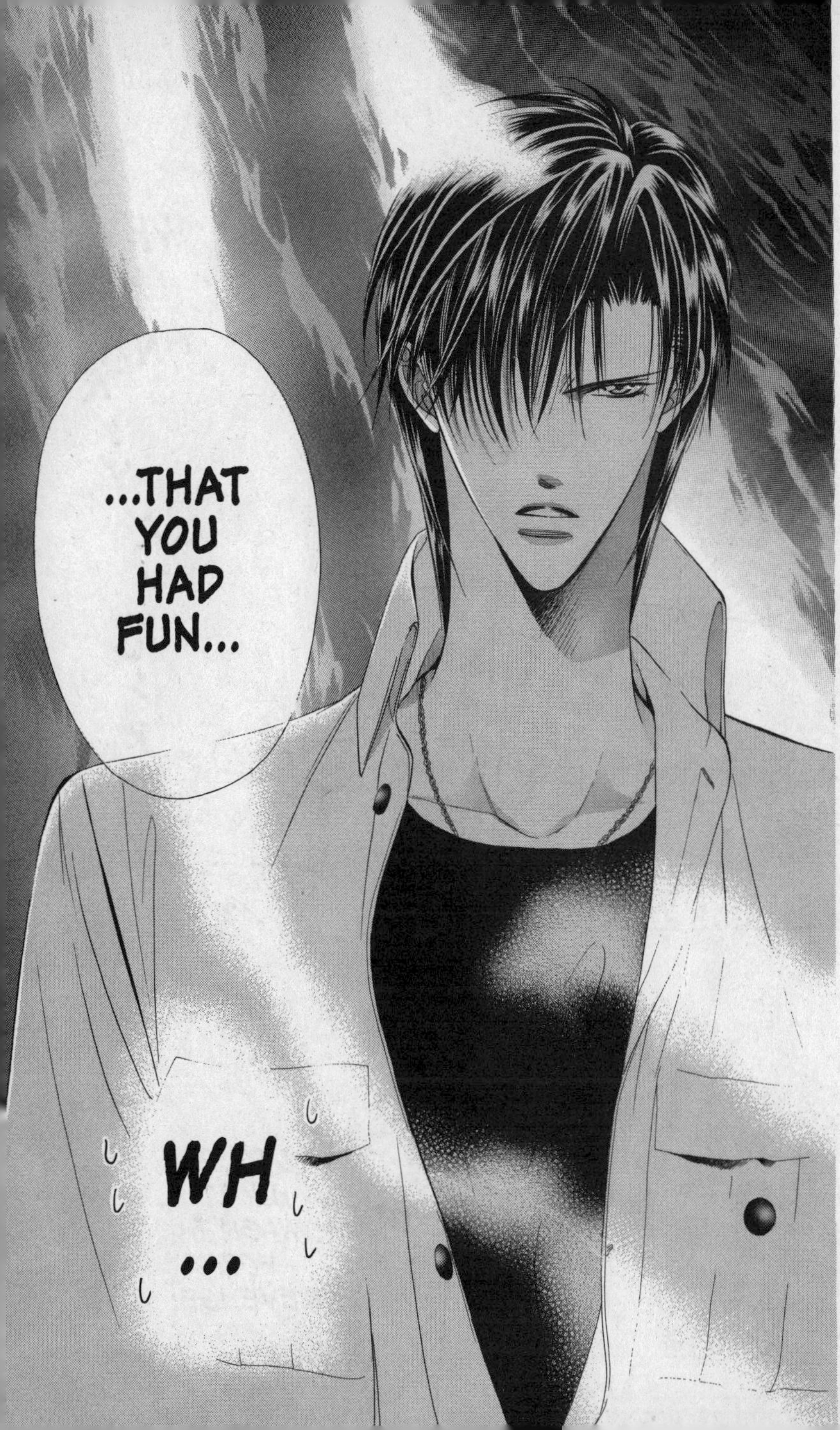
...THAT YOU HAD FUN...
WH...

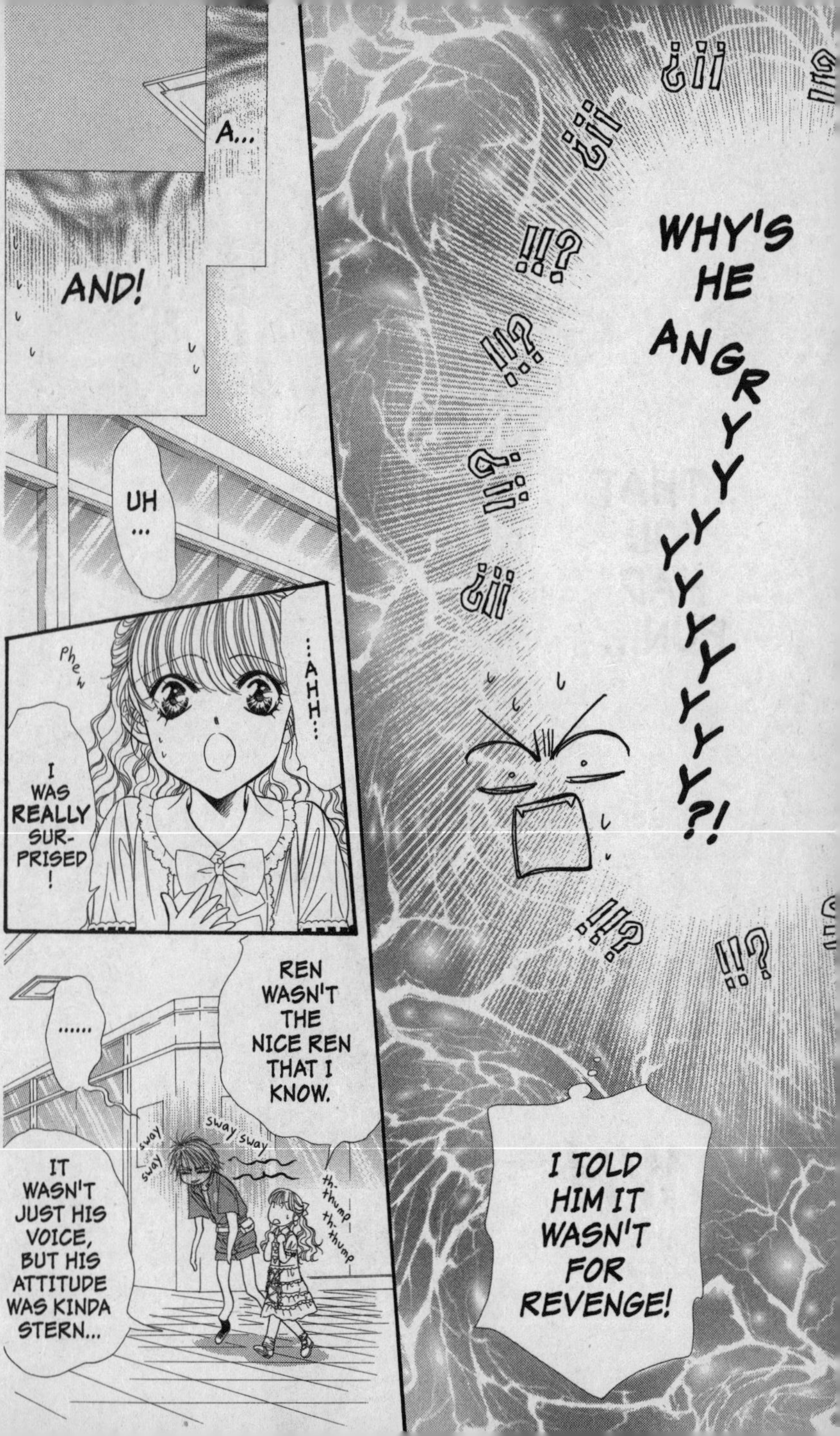
WHY'S HE ANGRYYYYYYYYYY?!
!!?
!!?
!!?
!!?
!!?
!!?
!!?
!!?
I TOLD HIM IT WASN'T FOR REVENGE!
A...
AND!
UH...
...AHH...
Phew
I WAS REALLY SURPRISED!
REN WASN'T THE NICE REN THAT I KNOW.
......
sway sway
sway sway
th-thump th-thump
IT WASN'T JUST HIS VOICE, BUT HIS ATTITUDE WAS KINDA STERN...

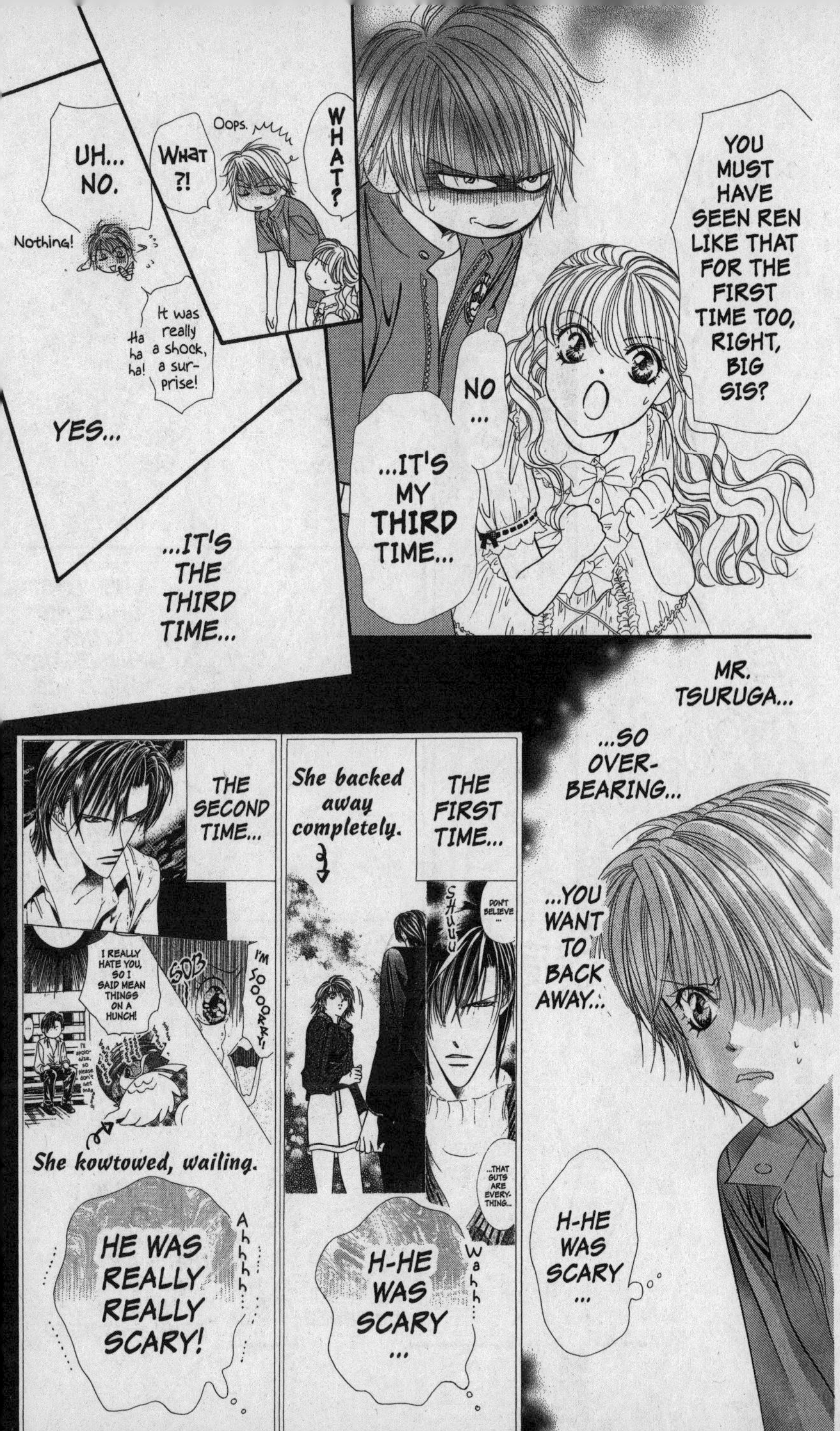
YOU MUST HAVE SEEN REN LIKE THAT FOR THE FIRST TIME TOO, RIGHT, BIG SIS?
NO ...
...IT'S MY THIRD TIME...
WHAT?
Oops.
WHAT ?!
UH... NO.
Nothing!
It was really a shock, a surprise!
Ha ha ha!
YES...
...IT'S THE THIRD TIME...
MR. TSURUGA...
...SO OVER-BEARING...
...YOU WANT TO BACK AWAY...
H-HE WAS SCARY ...
THE FIRST TIME...
SHUUU
DON'T BELIEVE ...
...THAT GUTS ARE EVERYTHING...
She backed away completely.
H-HE WAS SCARY ...
Wahh...
THE SECOND TIME...
I'M SOOOORRY!
SOB
I REALLY HATE YOU, SO I SAID MEAN THINGS ON A HUNCH!
She kowtowed, wailing.
HE WAS REALLY REALLY SCARY!
Ahhhh...

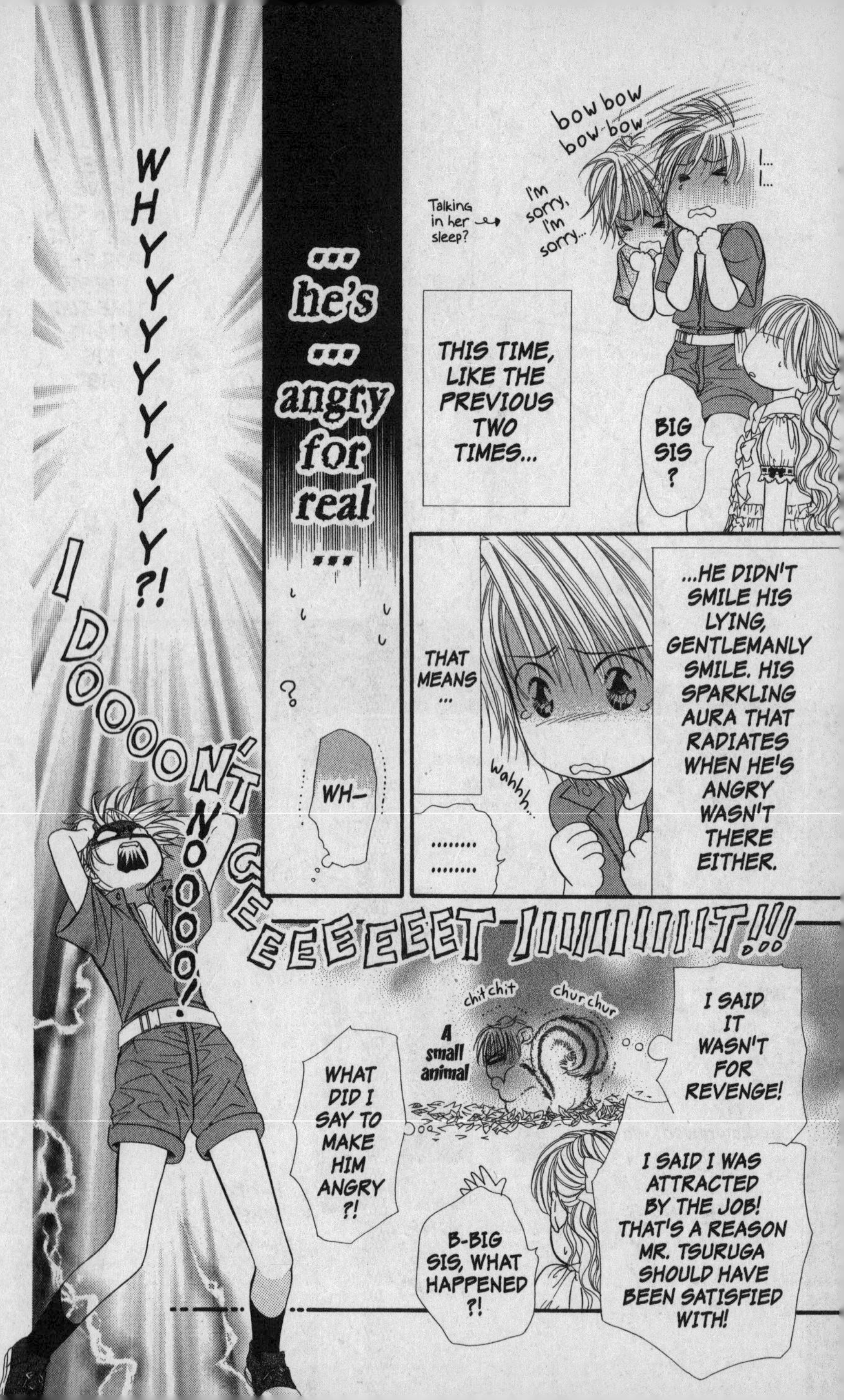

bow bow
bow bow
I... I...
I'm sorry, I'm sorry...
Talking in her sleep?
BIG SIS?
THIS TIME, LIKE THE PREVIOUS TWO TIMES...
...he's ...angry for real...
...HE DIDN'T SMILE HIS LYING, GENTLEMANLY SMILE. HIS SPARKLING AURA THAT RADIATES WHEN HE'S ANGRY WASN'T THERE EITHER.
THAT MEANS...
wahhh...
....
....
?
WH-
WHYYYYYYYYY?!
I DOOOON'T GEEEEEET IIIIIIIIIT!!!
NOOOOOOO!
I SAID IT WASN'T FOR REVENGE!
chur chur
chit chit
A small animal
WHAT DID I SAY TO MAKE HIM ANGRY?!
I SAID I WAS ATTRACTED BY THE JOB! THAT'S A REASON MR. TSURUGA SHOULD HAVE BEEN SATISFIED WITH!
B-BIG SIS, WHAT HAPPENED?!

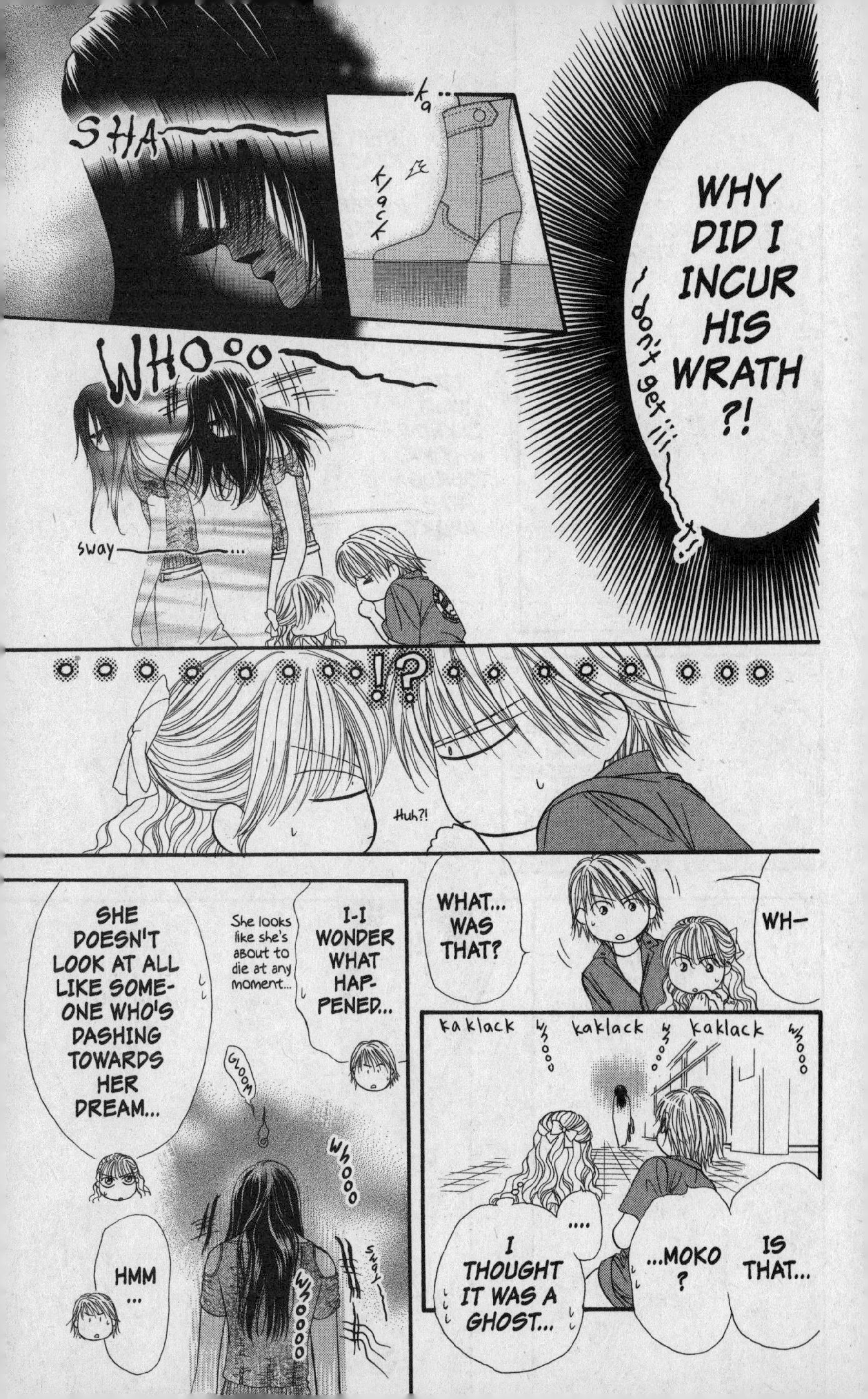
WHY DID I INCUR HIS WRATH?!
I don't get it!!
ka...
klack
SHA
WHOOO
sway...
!?
Huh?!
WH-
WHAT... WAS THAT?
kaklack whooo kaklack whooo kaklack whooo
IS THAT...
...MOKO?
....
I THOUGHT IT WAS A GHOST...
I-I WONDER WHAT HAPPENED...
She looks like she's about to die at any moment...
SHE DOESN'T LOOK AT ALL LIKE SOMEONE WHO'S DASHING TOWARDS HER DREAM...
GLOOM
whooo
sway
HMM...
whooooo

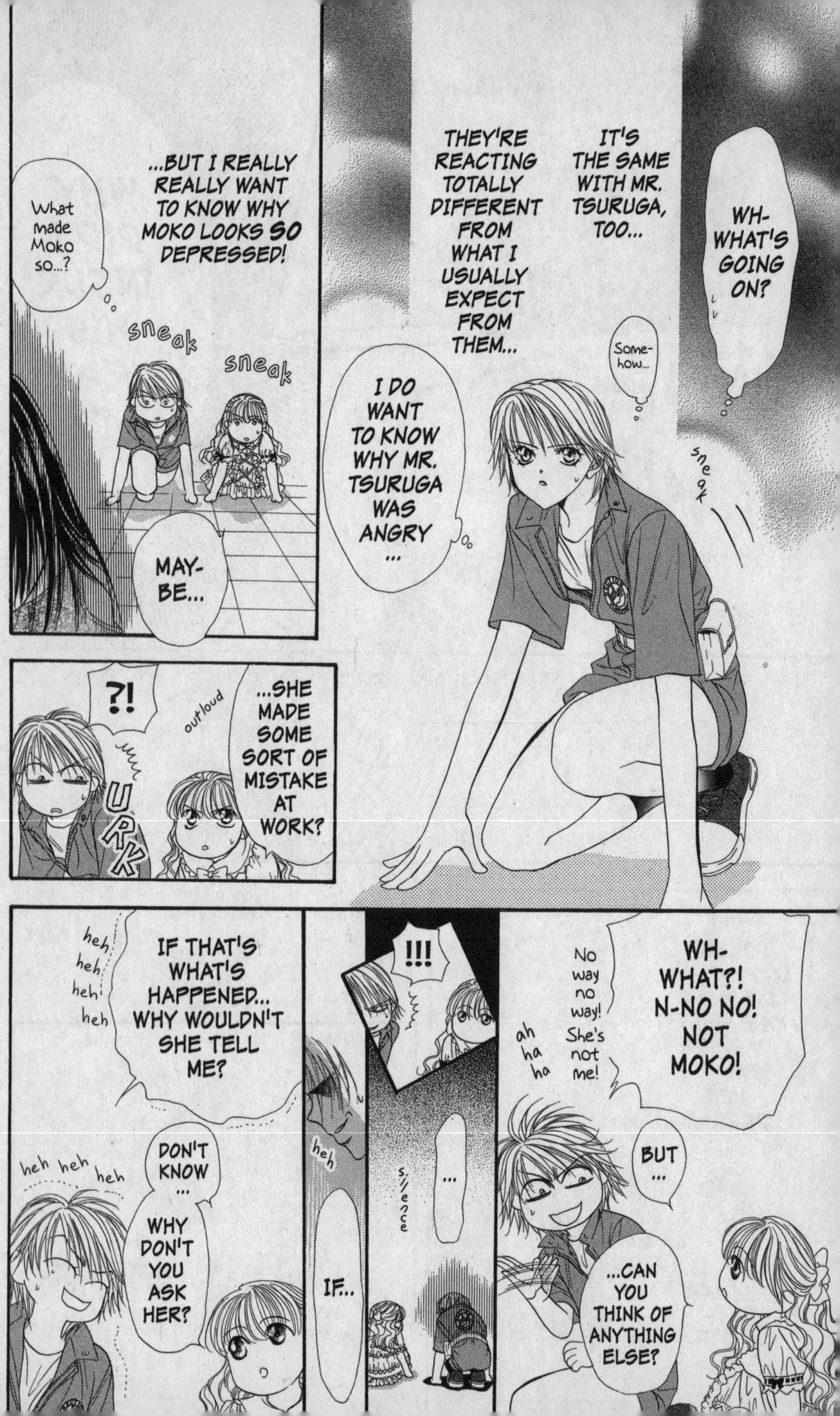
WH-WHAT'S GOING ON?
IT'S THE SAME WITH MR. TSURUGA, TOO...
THEY'RE REACTING TOTALLY DIFFERENT FROM WHAT I USUALLY EXPECT FROM THEM...
Some-how...
I DO WANT TO KNOW WHY MR. TSURUGA WAS ANGRY...
sneak
...BUT I REALLY REALLY WANT TO KNOW WHY MOKO LOOKS SO DEPRESSED!
What made Moko so...?
sneak
sneak
MAY-BE...
...SHE MADE SOME SORT OF MISTAKE AT WORK?
outloud
?!
URK
WH-WHAT?! N-NO NO! NOT MOKO!
No way no way! She's not me!
ah ha ha
BUT...
...CAN YOU THINK OF ANYTHING ELSE?
!!!
heh
...
silence
IF...
IF THAT'S WHAT'S HAPPENED... WHY WOULDN'T SHE TELL ME?
heh heh heh heh
DON'T KNOW... WHY DON'T YOU ASK HER?
heh heh heh

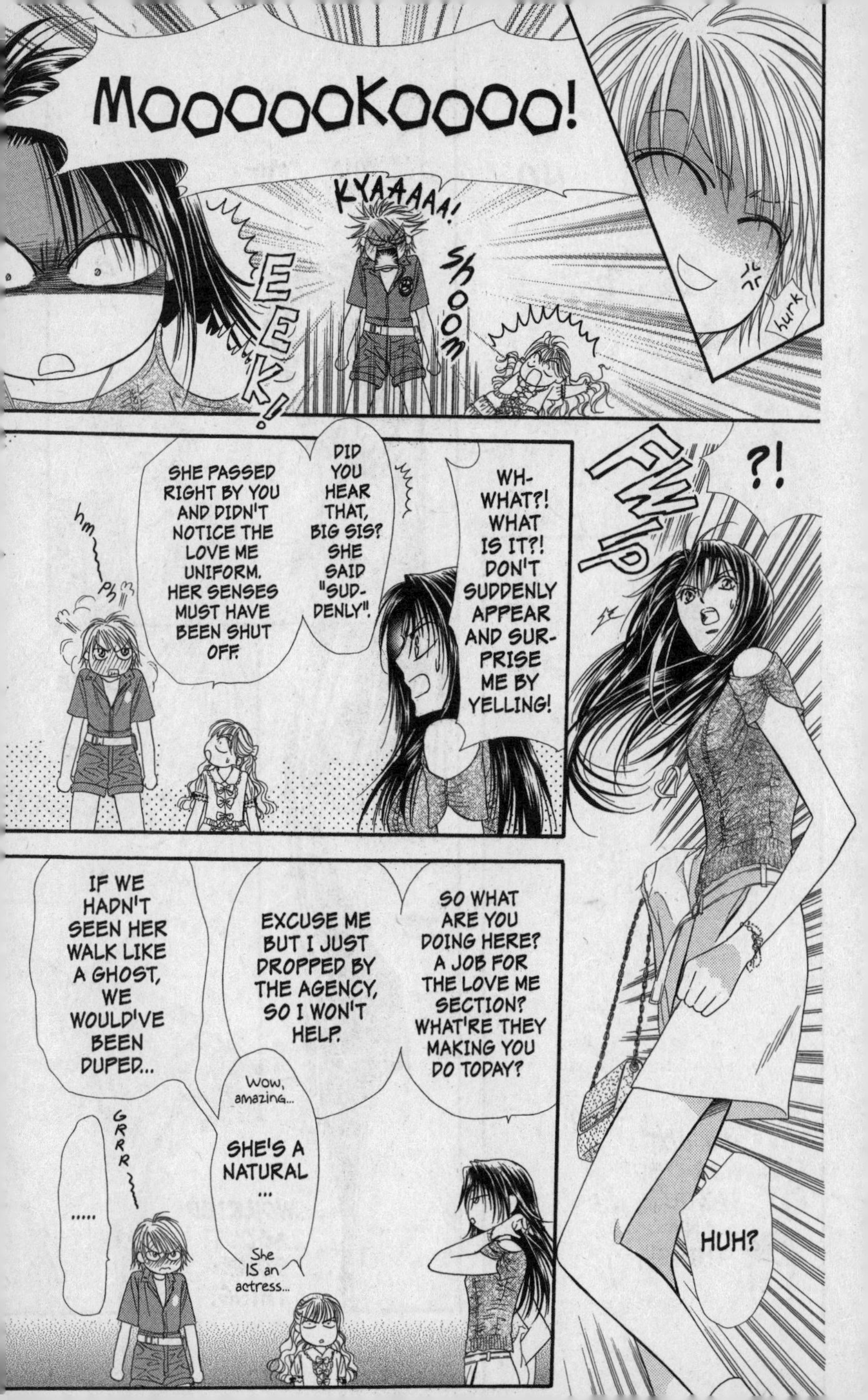
hurk
MOOOOOKOOOOO!
KYAAAAA!
EEEK!
SHOOOM
?!
FWIP
HUH?
WH-WHAT?! WHAT IS IT?! DON'T SUDDENLY APPEAR AND SURPRISE ME BY YELLING!
DID YOU HEAR THAT, BIG SIS? SHE SAID "SUDDENLY".
SHE PASSED RIGHT BY YOU AND DIDN'T NOTICE THE LOVE ME UNIFORM. HER SENSES MUST HAVE BEEN SHUT OFF.
hm~~ph
SO WHAT ARE YOU DOING HERE? A JOB FOR THE LOVE ME SECTION? WHAT'RE THEY MAKING YOU DO TODAY?
EXCUSE ME BUT I JUST DROPPED BY THE AGENCY, SO I WON'T HELP.
IF WE HADN'T SEEN HER WALK LIKE A GHOST, WE WOULD'VE BEEN DUPED...
Wow, amazing...
SHE'S A NATURAL...
She IS an actress...
GRRR
.....

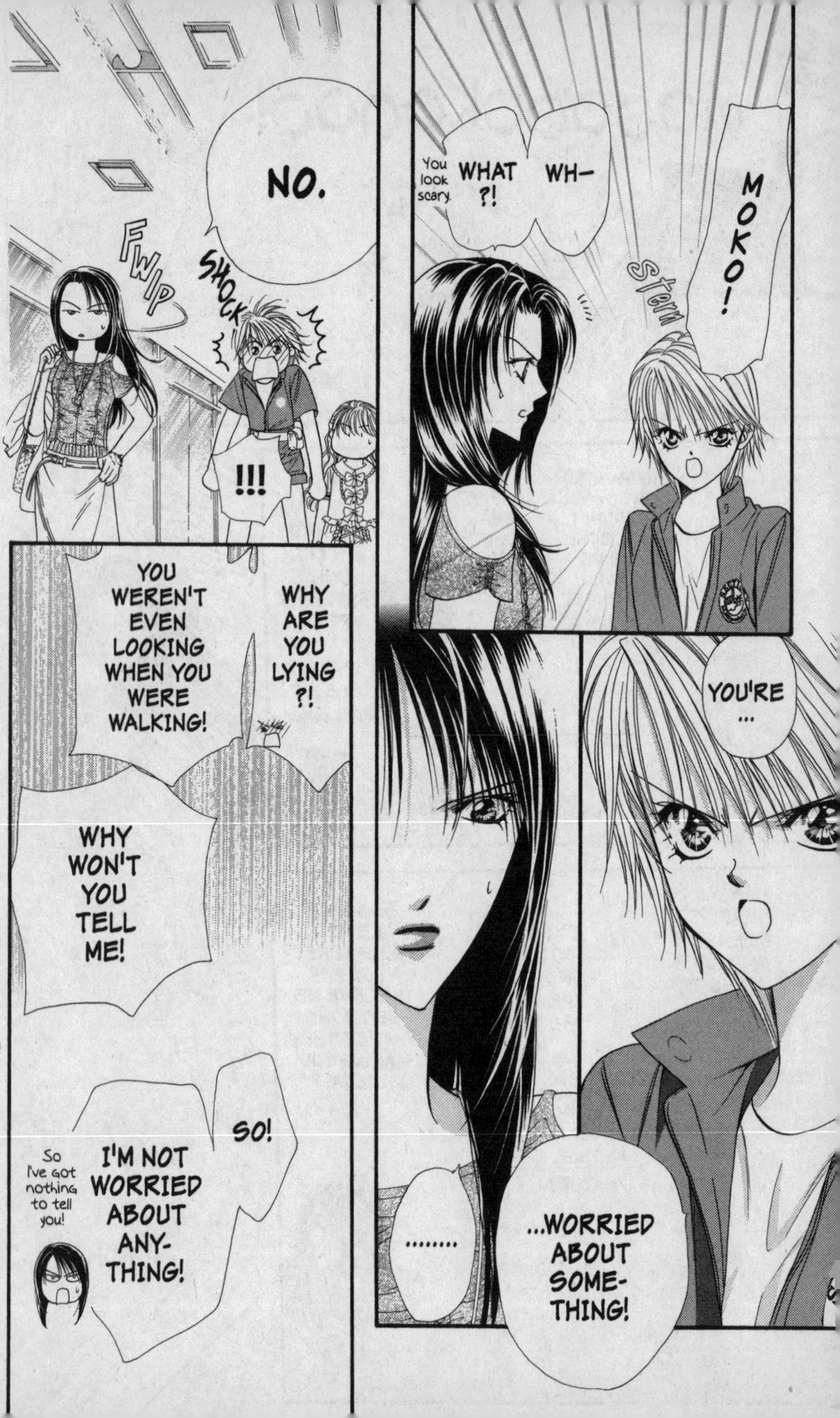

MOKO!
Stern
WH-
WHAT ?!
You look scary.
YOU'RE ...
...WORRIED ABOUT SOME-THING!
....
NO.
FWIP
SHOCK
!!!
WHY ARE YOU LYING ?!
YOU WEREN'T EVEN LOOKING WHEN YOU WERE WALKING!
WHY WON'T YOU TELL ME!
SO!
I'M NOT WORRIED ABOUT ANY-THING!
So I've got nothing to tell you!

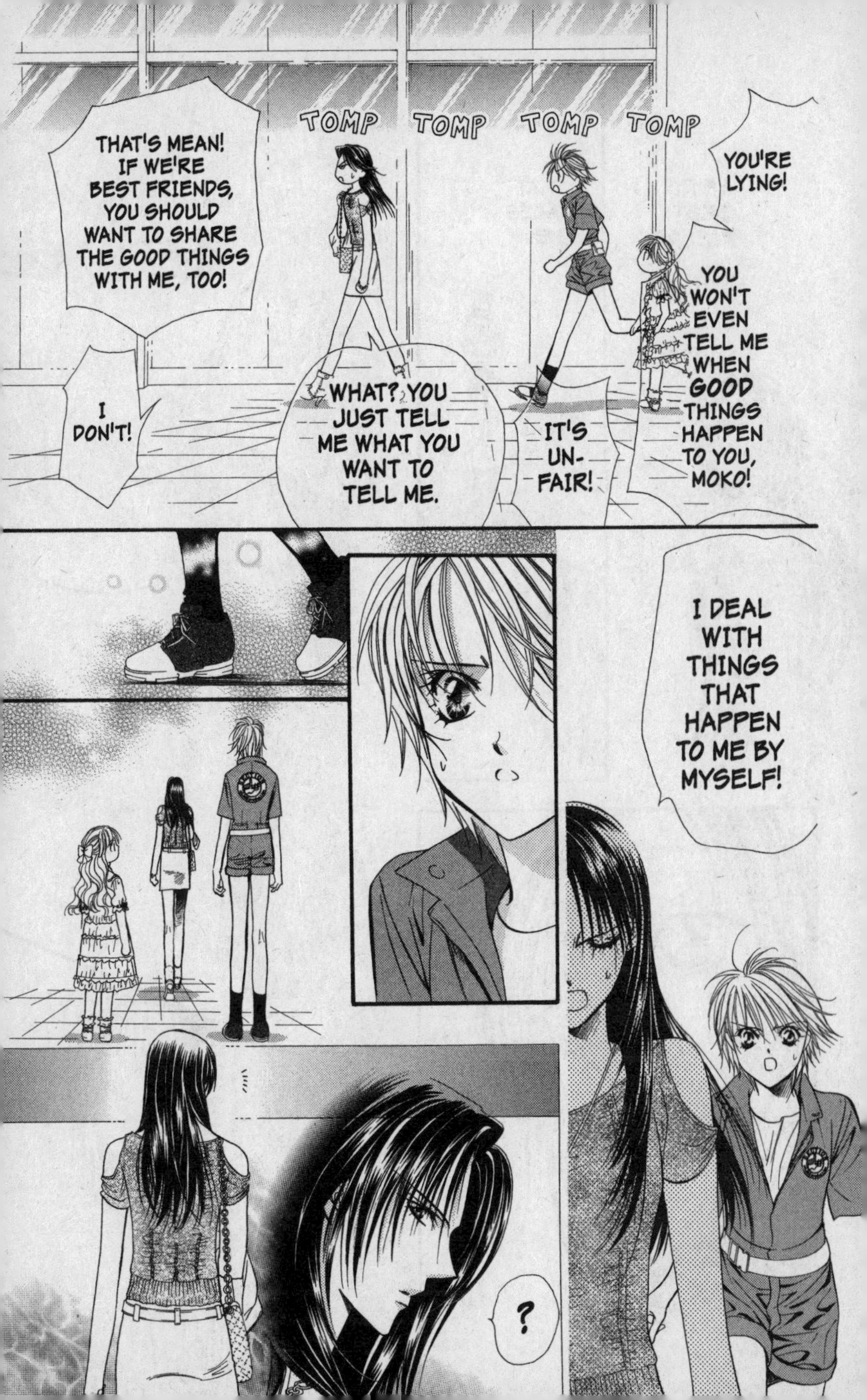
TOMP TOMP TOMP TOMP
YOU'RE LYING!
YOU WON'T EVEN TELL ME WHEN GOOD THINGS HAPPEN TO YOU, MOKO!
IT'S UN-FAIR!
WHAT? YOU JUST TELL ME WHAT YOU WANT TO TELL ME.
THAT'S MEAN! IF WE'RE BEST FRIENDS, YOU SHOULD WANT TO SHARE THE GOOD THINGS WITH ME, TOO!
I DON'T!
I DEAL WITH THINGS THAT HAPPEN TO ME BY MYSELF!
?

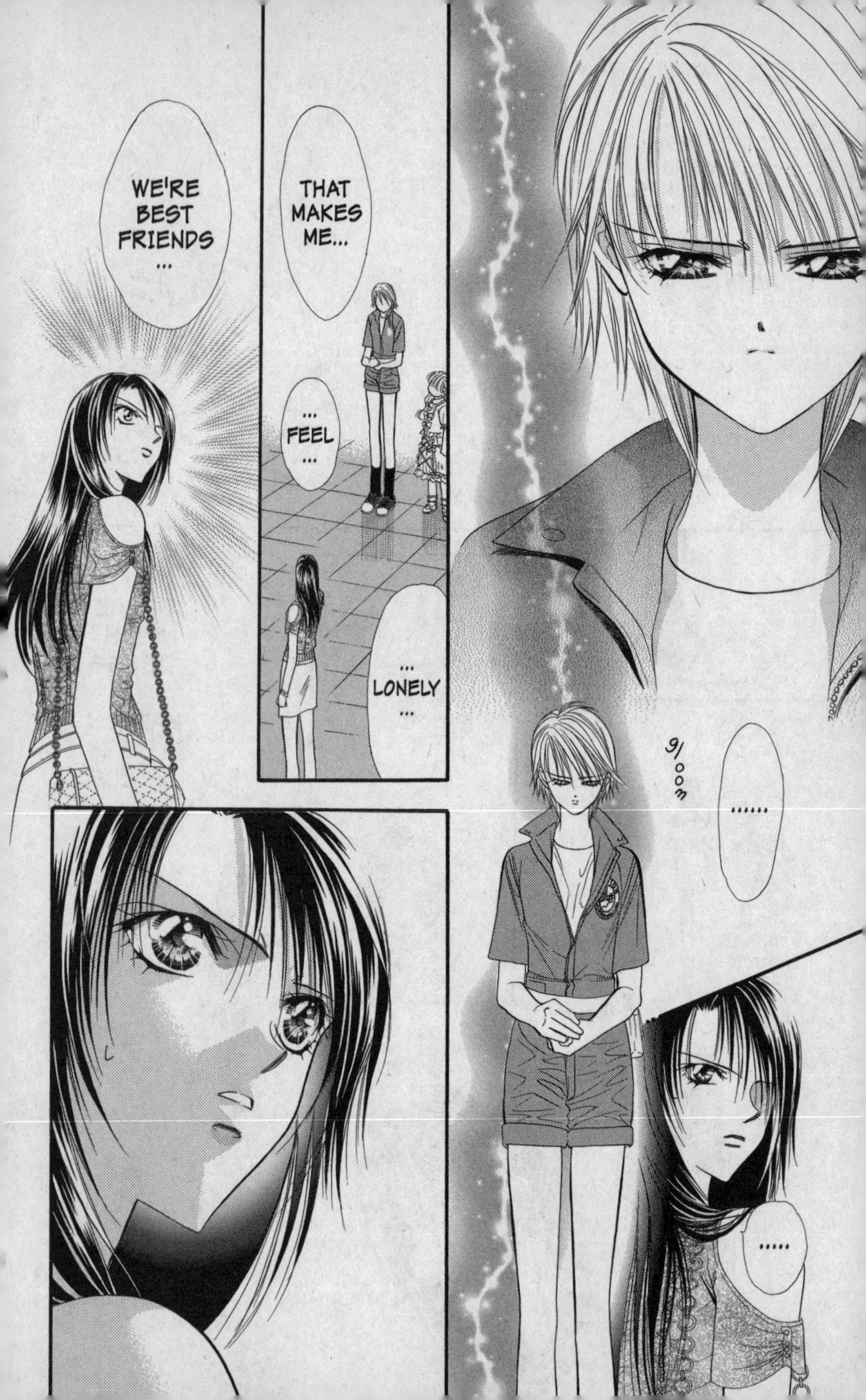

THAT MAKES ME...
... FEEL ...
... LONELY ...
WE'RE BEST FRIENDS ...
gloom
......
.....

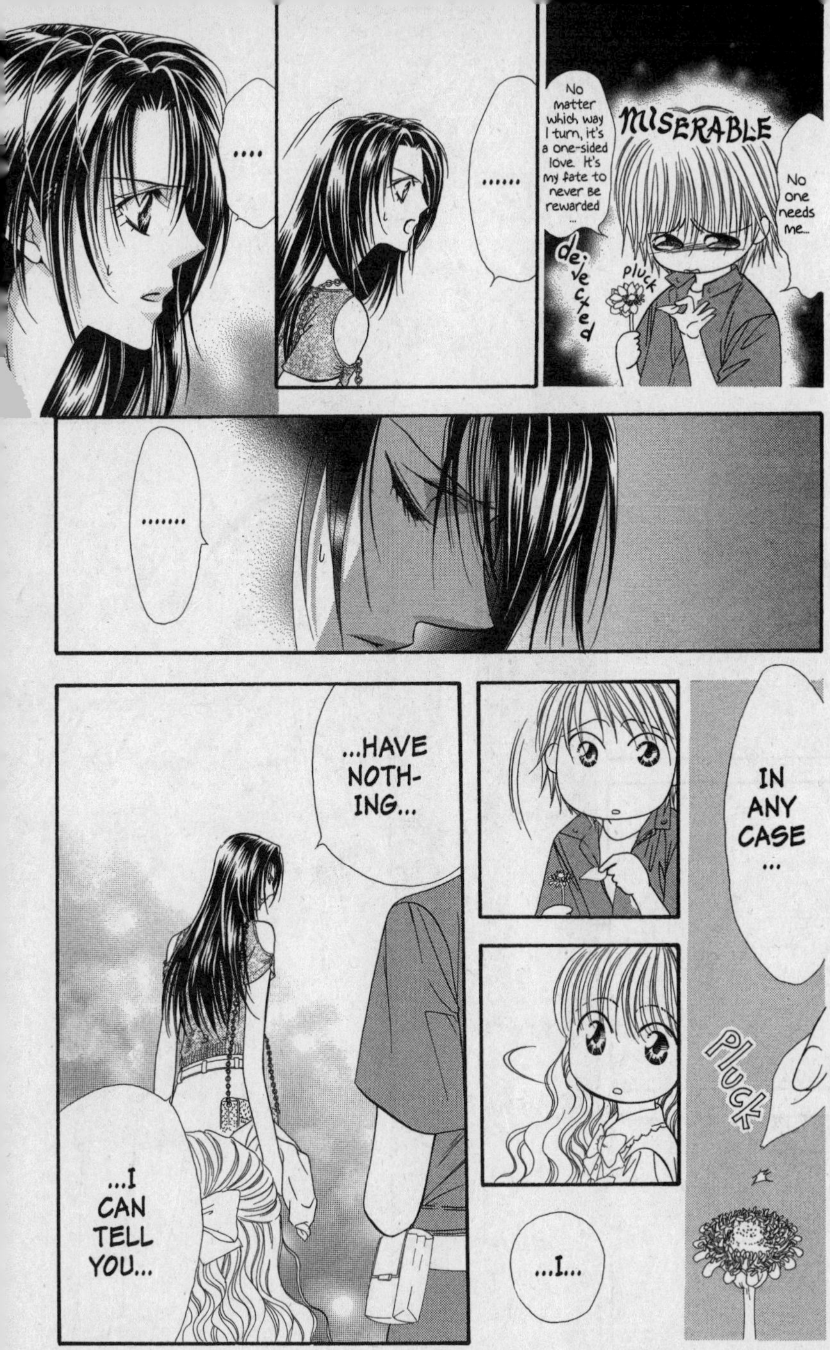
MISERABLE
No one needs me...
No matter which way I turn, it's a one-sided love. It's my fate to never be rewarded ...
dejected
pluck
......
....
....
IN ANY CASE ...
Pluck
...I...
...HAVE NOTH-ING...
...I CAN TELL YOU...

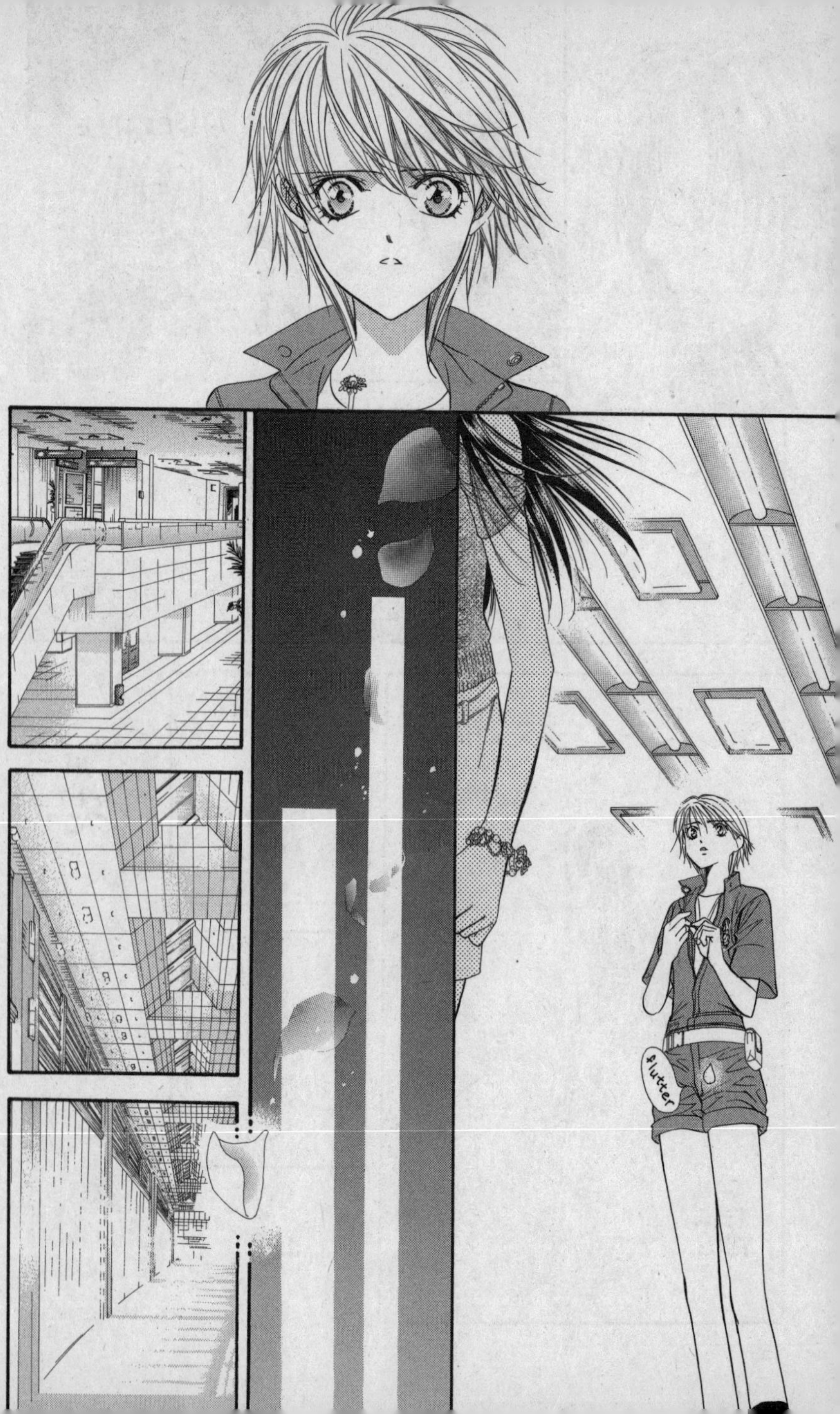
flutter

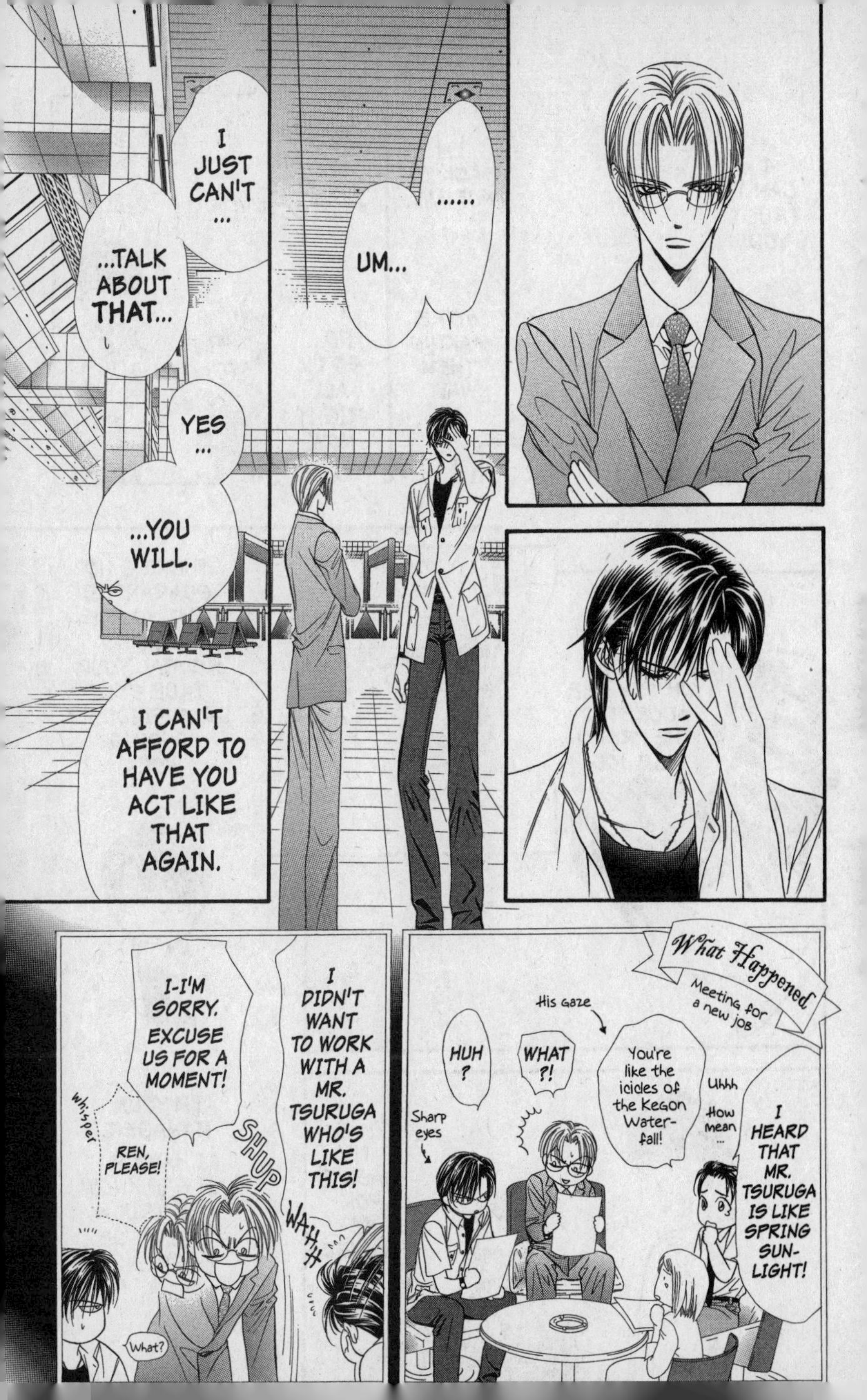
......
UM...
I JUST CAN'T ...
...TALK ABOUT THAT...
YES ...
...YOU WILL.
I CAN'T AFFORD TO HAVE YOU ACT LIKE THAT AGAIN.
What Happened
Meeting for a new job
I HEARD THAT MR. TSURUGA IS LIKE SPRING SUN-LIGHT!
Uhhh
How mean ...
His gaze
You're like the icicles of the Kegon Water-fall!
WHAT ?!
HUH ?
Sharp eyes
I DIDN'T WANT TO WORK WITH A MR. TSURUGA WHO'S LIKE THIS!
I-I'M SORRY. EXCUSE US FOR A MOMENT!
SHUP
WAH
whisper
REN, PLEASE!
What?

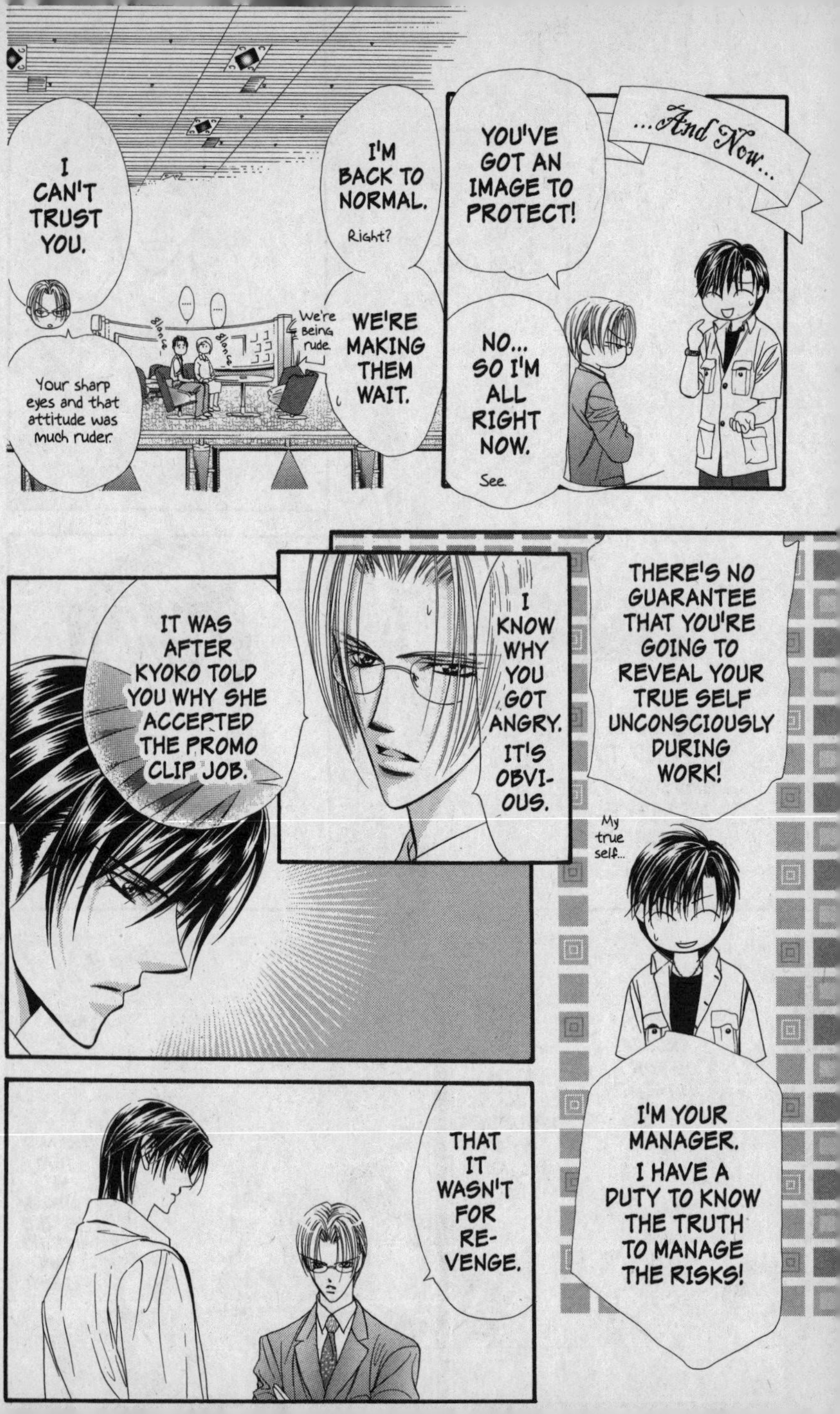
...And Now...
YOU'VE GOT AN IMAGE TO PROTECT!
NO... SO I'M ALL RIGHT NOW.
See.
I'M BACK TO NORMAL.
Right?
WE'RE MAKING THEM WAIT.
We're being rude.
glance
glance
I CAN'T TRUST YOU.
Your sharp eyes and that attitude was much ruder.
THERE'S NO GUARANTEE THAT YOU'RE GOING TO REVEAL YOUR TRUE SELF UNCONSCIOUSLY DURING WORK!
My true self...
I'M YOUR MANAGER.
I HAVE A DUTY TO KNOW THE TRUTH TO MANAGE THE RISKS!
I KNOW WHY YOU GOT ANGRY.
IT'S OBVIOUS.
IT WAS AFTER KYOKO TOLD YOU WHY SHE ACCEPTED THE PROMO CLIP JOB.
THAT IT WASN'T FOR REVENGE.

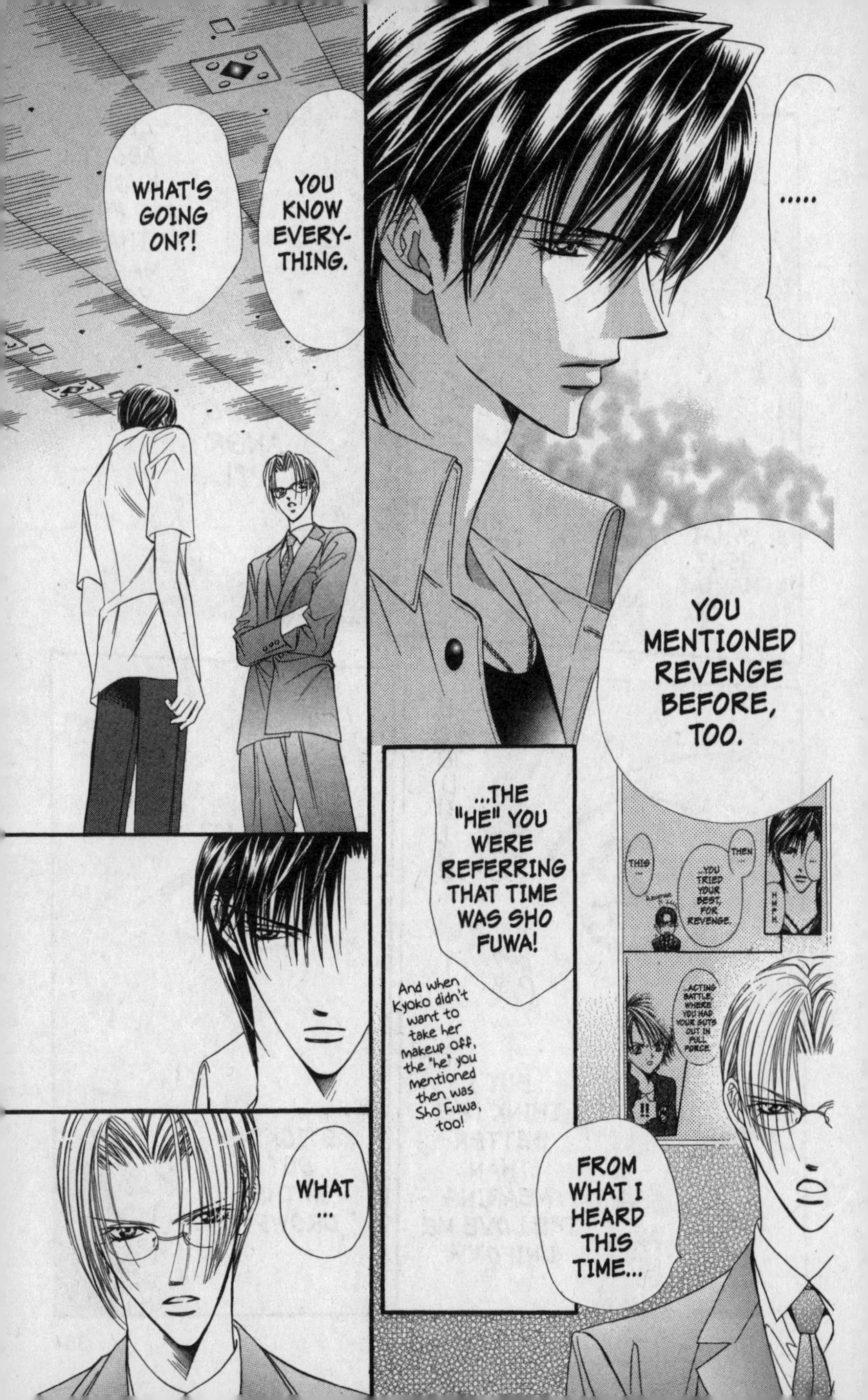
.....
YOU MENTIONED REVENGE BEFORE, TOO.
YOU KNOW EVERYTHING.
WHAT'S GOING ON?!
...THE "HE" YOU WERE REFERRING THAT TIME WAS SHO FUWA!
And when Kyoko didn't want to take her makeup off, the "he" you mentioned then was Sho Fuwa, too!
THEN ...
THIS ...
...YOU TRIED YOUR BEST, FOR REVENGE.
HMPH.
...ACTING BATTLE, WHERE YOU HAD YOUR GUTS OUT IN FULL FORCE.
!!
FROM WHAT I HEARD THIS TIME...
WHAT ...

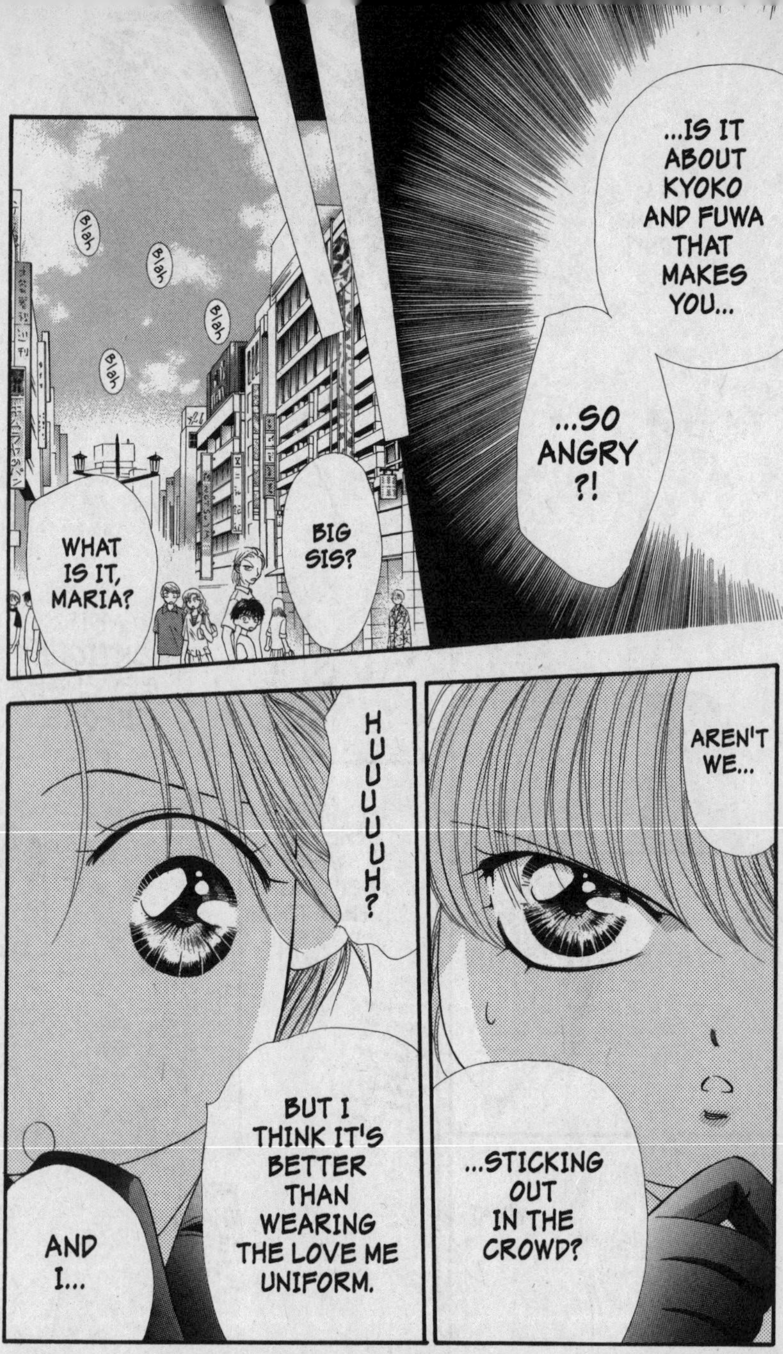
...IS IT ABOUT KYOKO AND FUWA THAT MAKES YOU...
...SO ANGRY?!
Blah
Blah
Blah
Blah
BIG SIS?
WHAT IS IT, MARIA?
AREN'T WE...
...STICKING OUT IN THE CROWD?
HUUUUUH?
BUT I THINK IT'S BETTER THAN WEARING THE LOVE ME UNIFORM.
AND I...

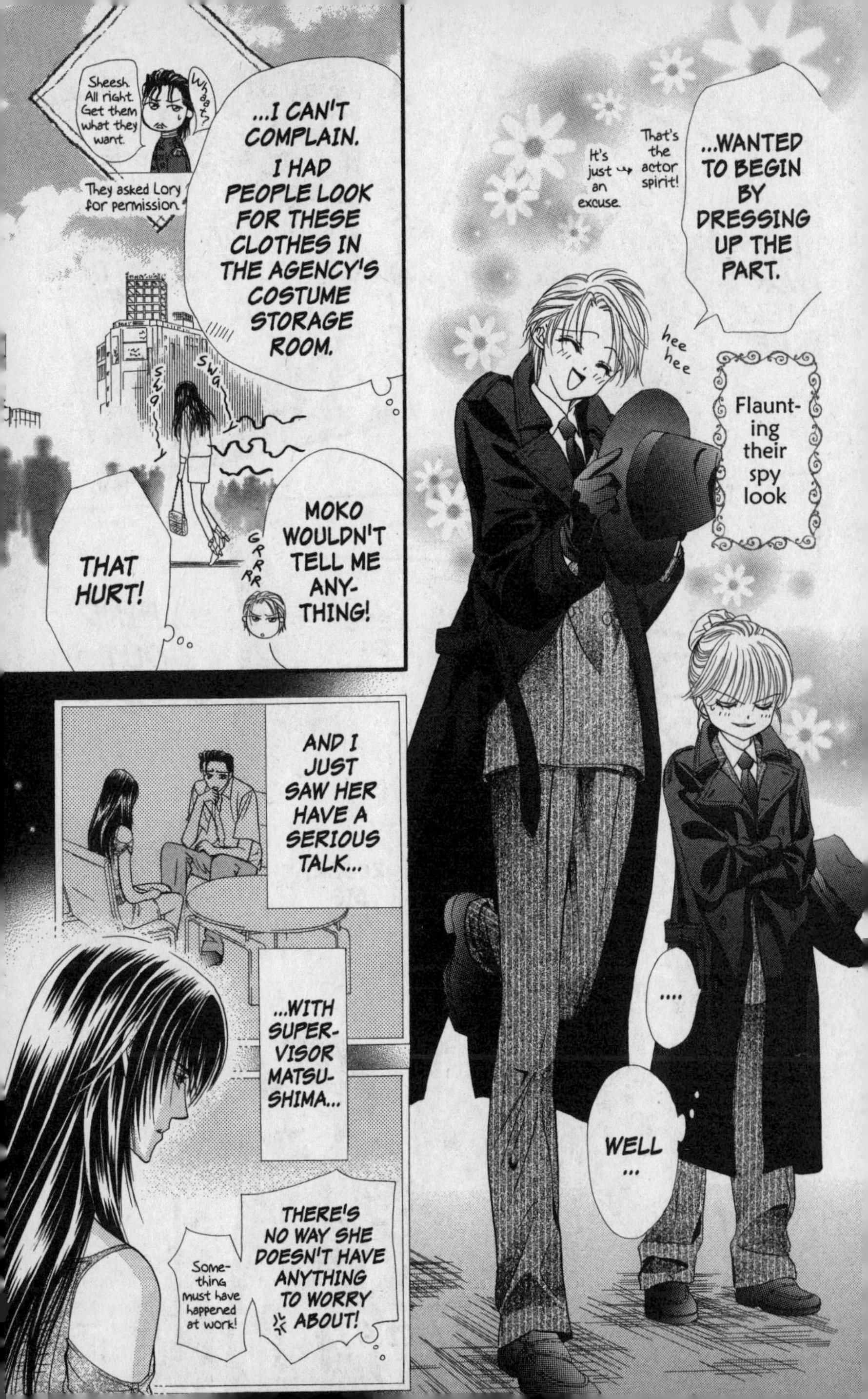
...WANTED TO BEGIN BY DRESSING UP THE PART.
That's the actor spirit!
It's just an excuse.
hee hee
Flaunt-ing their spy look
....
WELL ...
...I CAN'T COMPLAIN. I HAD PEOPLE LOOK FOR THESE CLOTHES IN THE AGENCY'S COSTUME STORAGE ROOM.
Whaaa?
Sheesh. All right. Get them what they want.
They asked Lory for permission.
MOKO WOULDN'T TELL ME ANY-THING!
GRRRR
THAT HURT!
AND I JUST SAW HER HAVE A SERIOUS TALK...
...WITH SUPER-VISOR MATSU-SHIMA...
THERE'S NO WAY SHE DOESN'T HAVE ANYTHING TO WORRY ABOUT!
Some-thing must have happened at work!

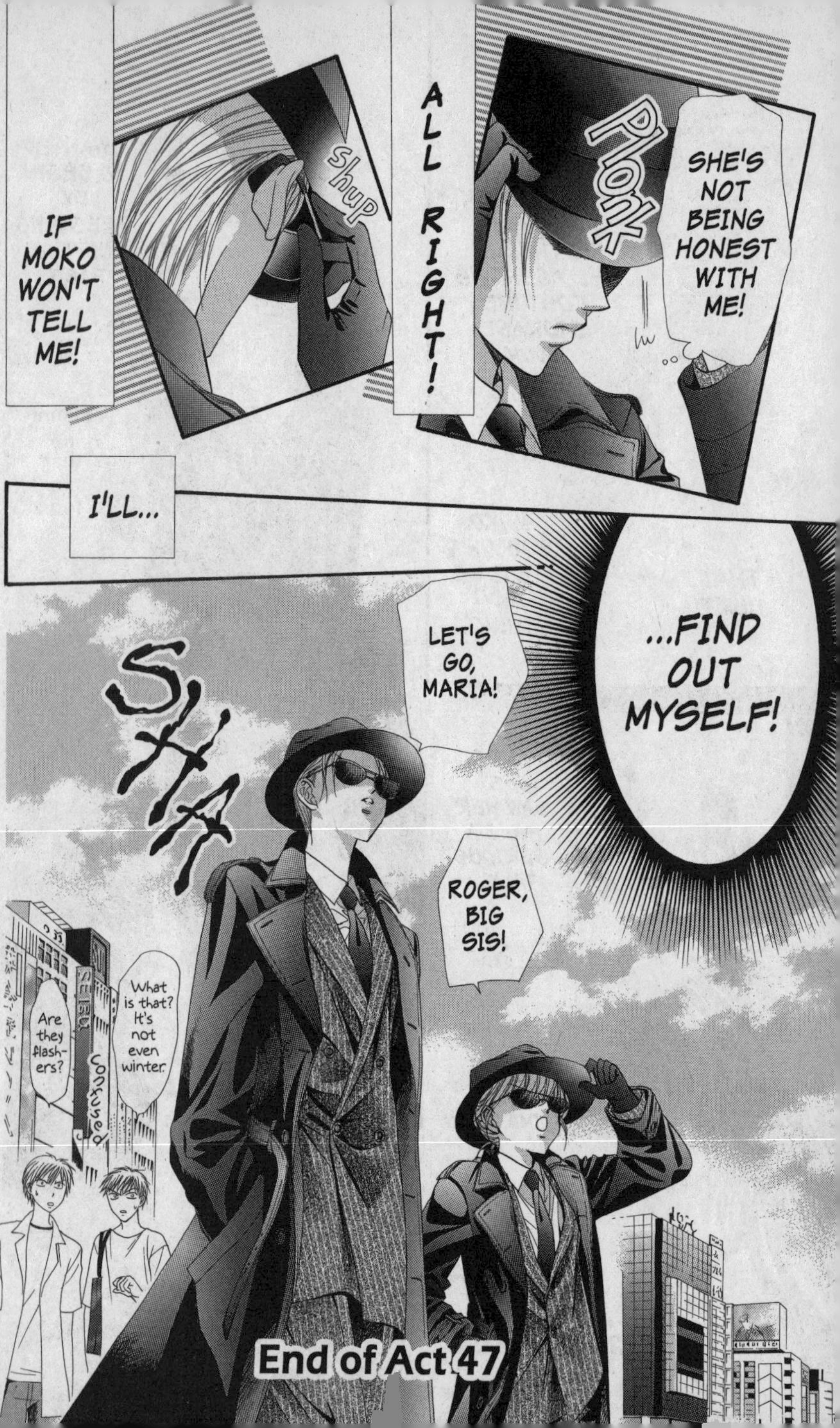
Plonk
SHE'S NOT BEING HONEST WITH ME!
ALL RIGHT!
shup
IF MOKO WON'T TELL ME!
I'LL...
...FIND OUT MYSELF!
LET'S GO, MARIA!
SHA
ROGER, BIG SIS!
What is that? It's not even winter.
Are they flashers?
confused
End of Act 47

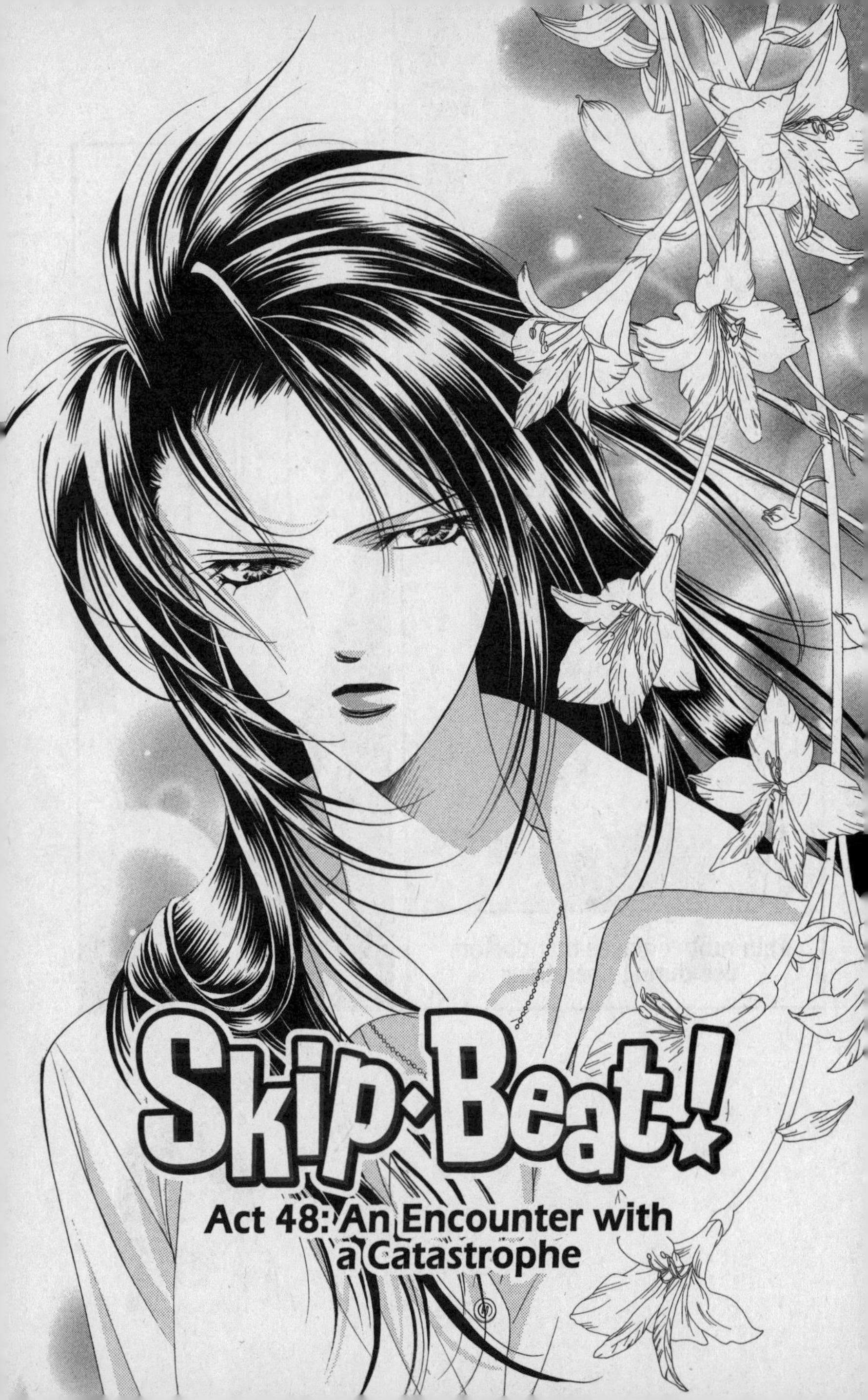
Skip·Beat!
Act 48: An Encounter with a Catastrophe

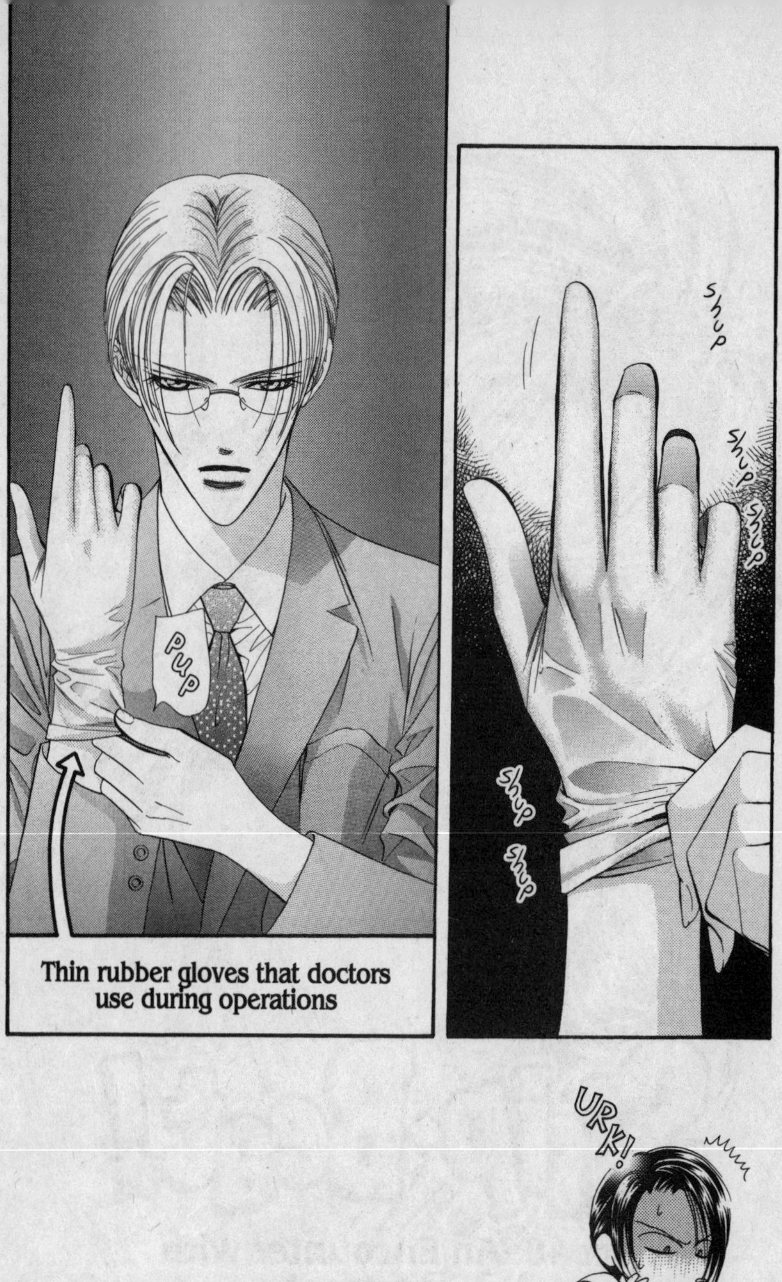
shup
shup shup
shup shup
Pup
Thin rubber gloves that doctors use during operations
URK!

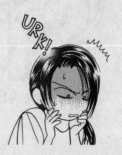

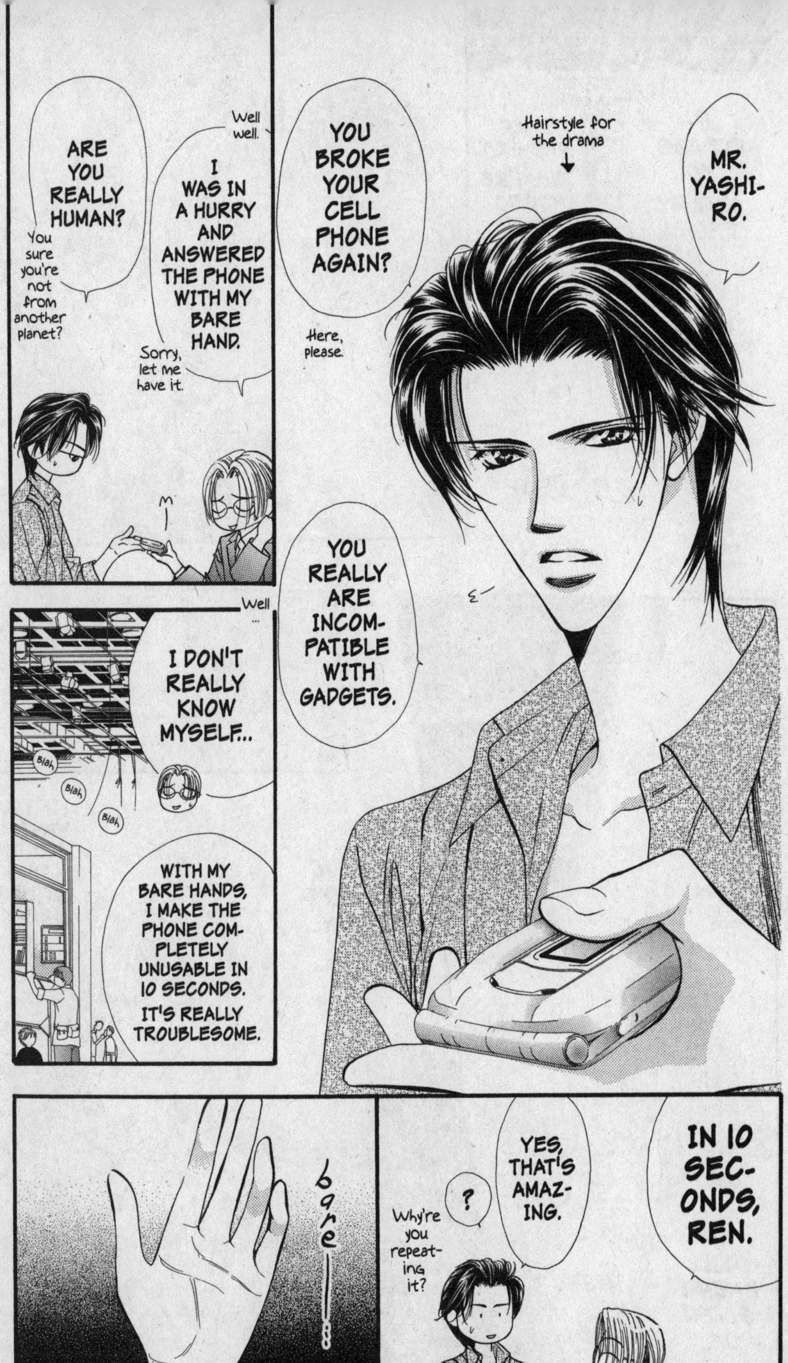
Hairstyle for the drama
MR. YASHIRO.
YOU BROKE YOUR CELL PHONE AGAIN?
Here, please.
YOU REALLY ARE INCOMPATIBLE WITH GADGETS.
Well well.
I WAS IN A HURRY AND ANSWERED THE PHONE WITH MY BARE HAND.
Sorry, let me have it.
ARE YOU REALLY HUMAN?
You sure you're not from another planet?
Well...
I DON'T REALLY KNOW MYSELF...
Blah
Blah
Blah
WITH MY BARE HANDS, I MAKE THE PHONE COMPLETELY UNUSABLE IN 10 SECONDS.
IT'S REALLY TROUBLESOME.
IN 10 SECONDS, REN.
YES, THAT'S AMAZING.
?
Why're you repeating it?
bare......

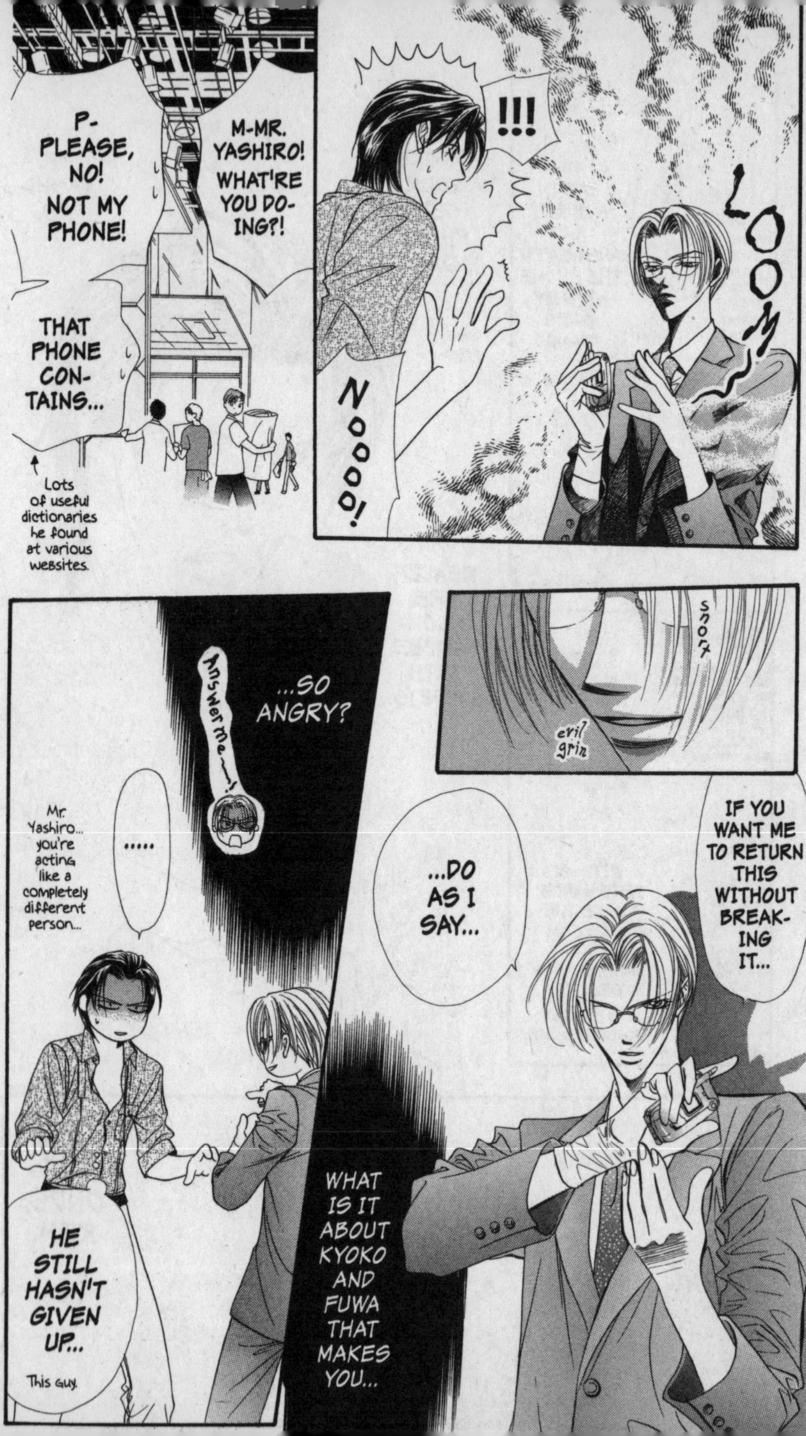
!!!
LOOM
NOOOO!
M-MR. YASHIRO! WHAT'RE YOU DO-ING?!
P-PLEASE, NO! NOT MY PHONE!
THAT PHONE CON-TAINS...
Lots of useful dictionaries he found at various websites.
snort
evil grin
IF YOU WANT ME TO RETURN THIS WITHOUT BREAK-ING IT...
...DO AS I SAY...
WHAT IS IT ABOUT KYOKO AND FUWA THAT MAKES YOU...
...SO ANGRY?
Answer me—!
.....
Mr. Yashiro... you're acting like a completely different person...
HE STILL HASN'T GIVEN UP...
This guy.

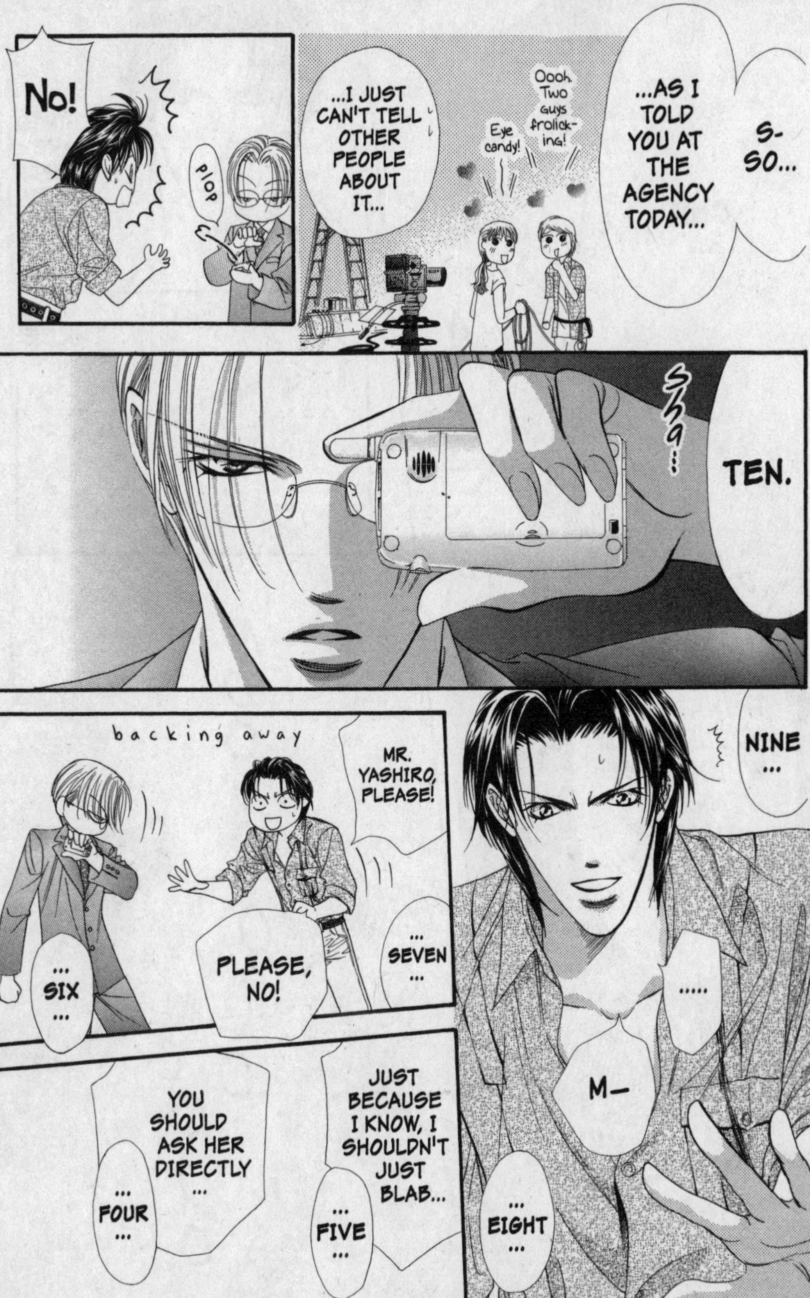
S-SO...
...AS I TOLD YOU AT THE AGENCY TODAY...
Oooh. Two guys frolicking!
Eye candy!
...I JUST CAN'T TELL OTHER PEOPLE ABOUT IT...
No!
PLOP
Shag...
TEN.
NINE...
.....
M—
...EIGHT...
MR. YASHIRO, PLEASE!
...SEVEN...
backing away
PLEASE, NO!
...SIX...
JUST BECAUSE I KNOW, I SHOULDN'T JUST BLAB...
...FIVE...
YOU SHOULD ASK HER DIRECTLY...
...FOUR...

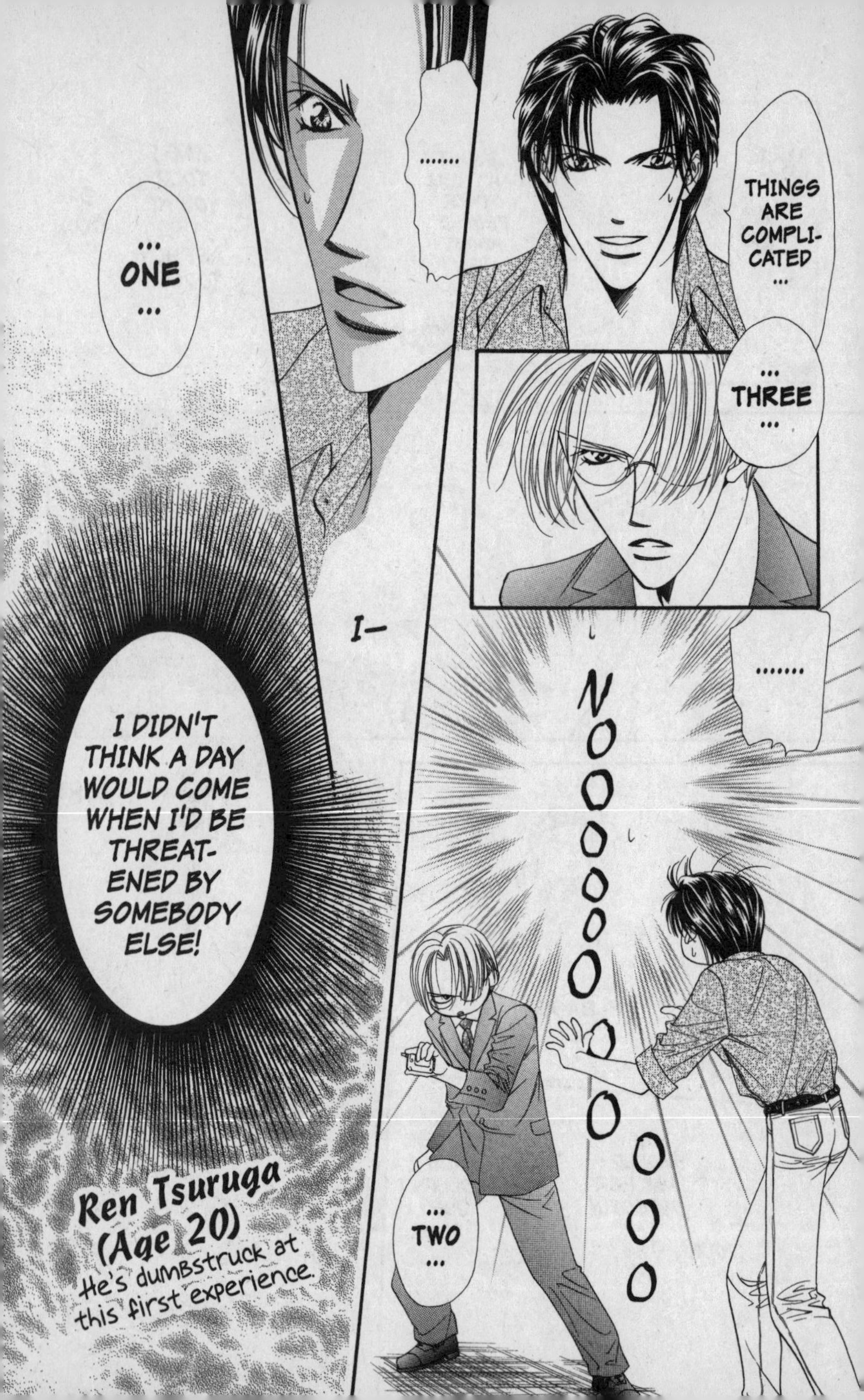
THINGS ARE COMPLICATED...
......
...THREE...
......
NOOOOOOOOOOOOOO
...TWO...
...ONE...
I—
I DIDN'T THINK A DAY WOULD COME WHEN I'D BE THREATENED BY SOMEBODY ELSE!
Ren Tsuruga (Age 20)
He's dumbstruck at this first experience.

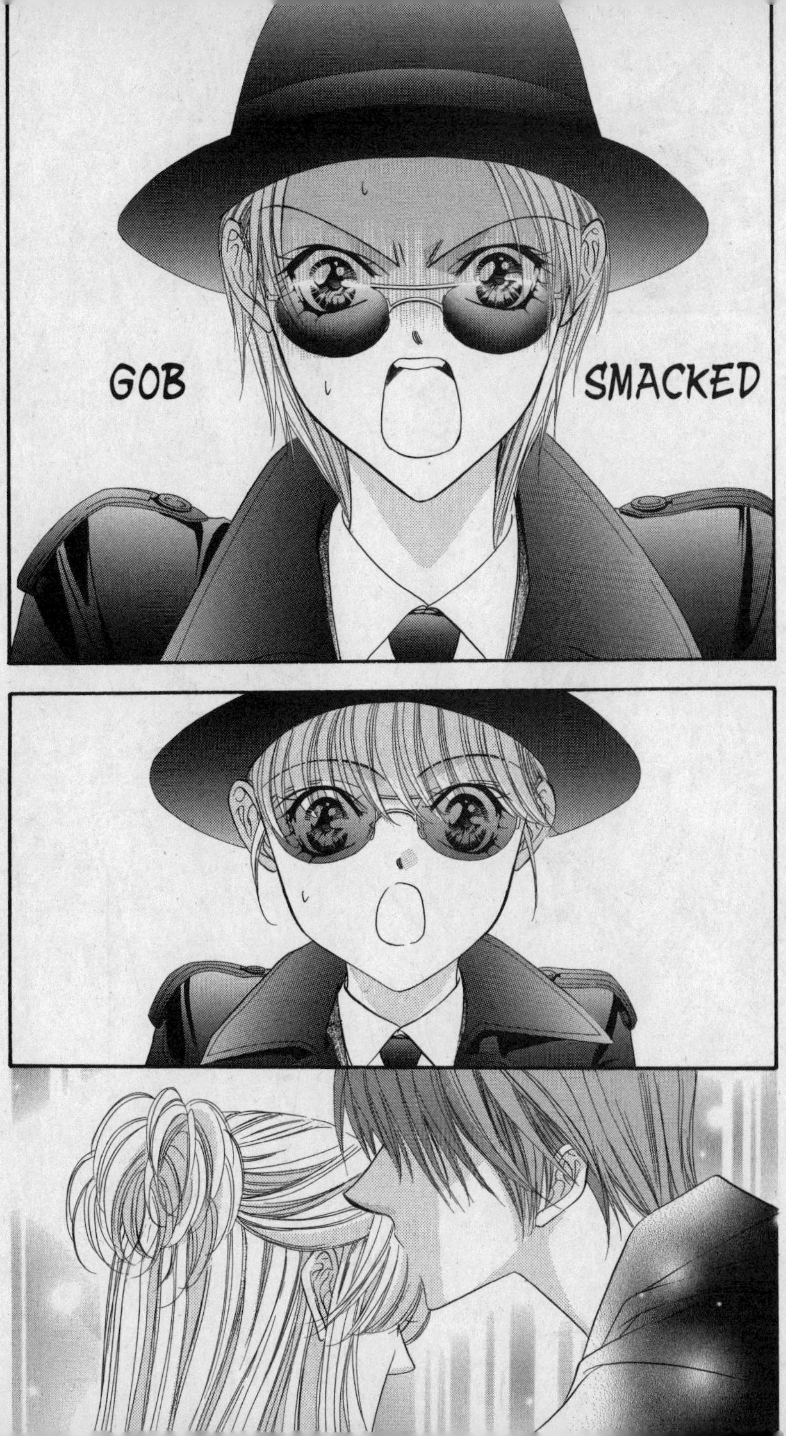
GOB
SMACKED

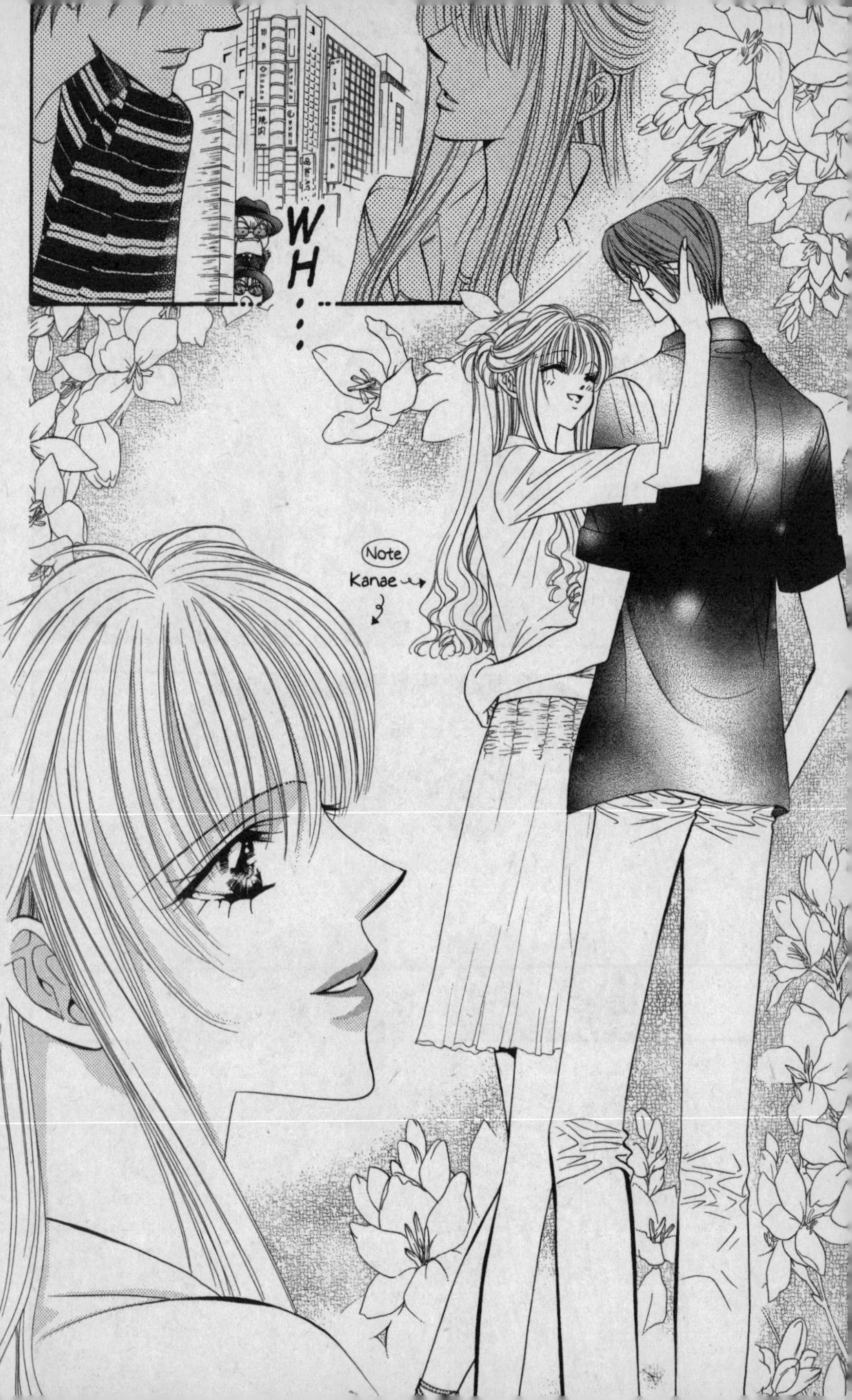
WH...
Note
Kanae

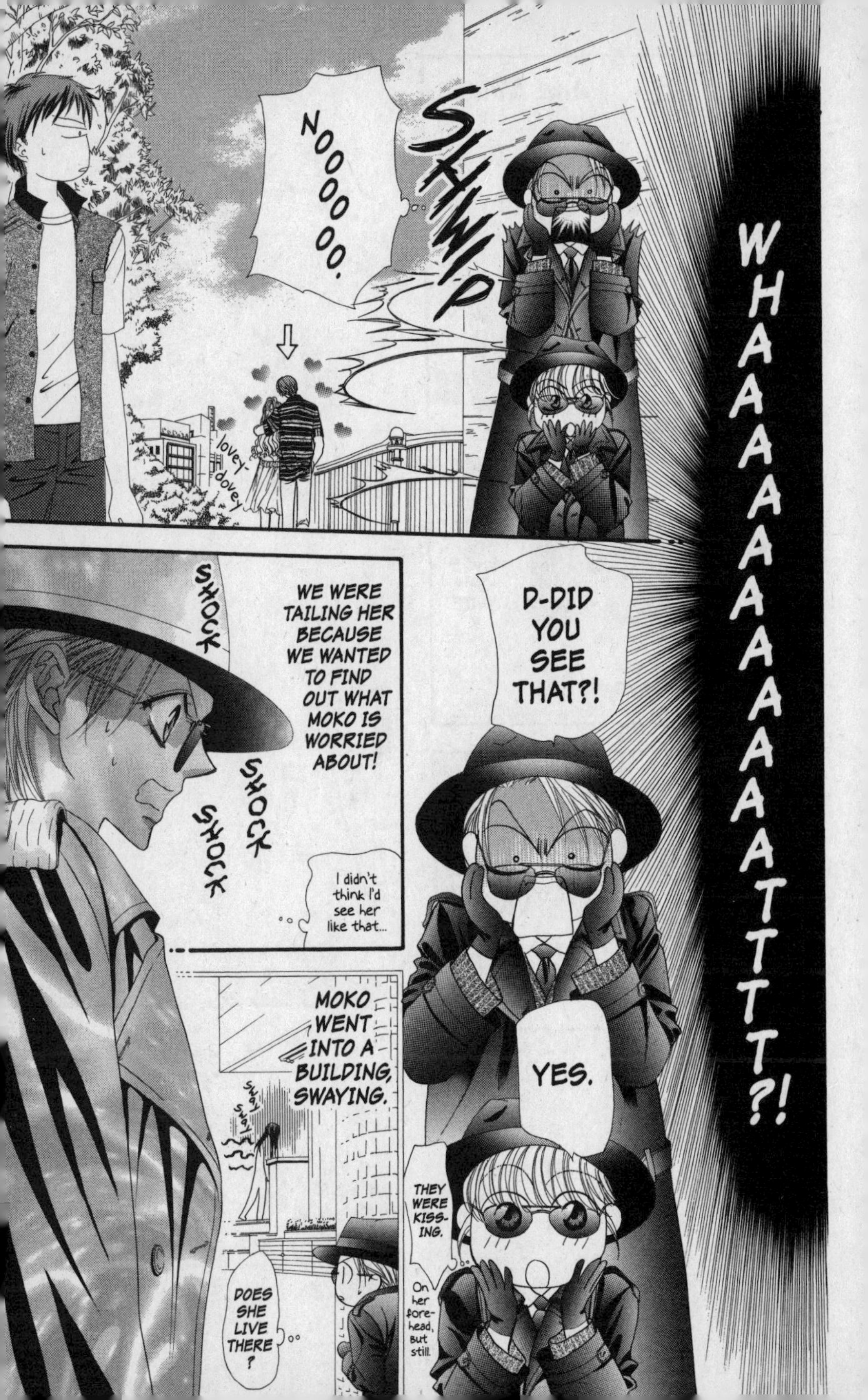
SHWIP
NOOOOOO.
lovey-dovey
WHAAAAAAAAAAAAAATTTT?!
D-DID YOU SEE THAT?!
YES.
THEY WERE KISS-ING.
On her fore-head, but still.
WE WERE TAILING HER BECAUSE WE WANTED TO FIND OUT WHAT MOKO IS WORRIED ABOUT!
SHOCK
SHOCK
SHOCK
I didn't think I'd see her like that...
MOKO WENT INTO A BUILDING, SWAYING.
sway sway
DOES SHE LIVE THERE?

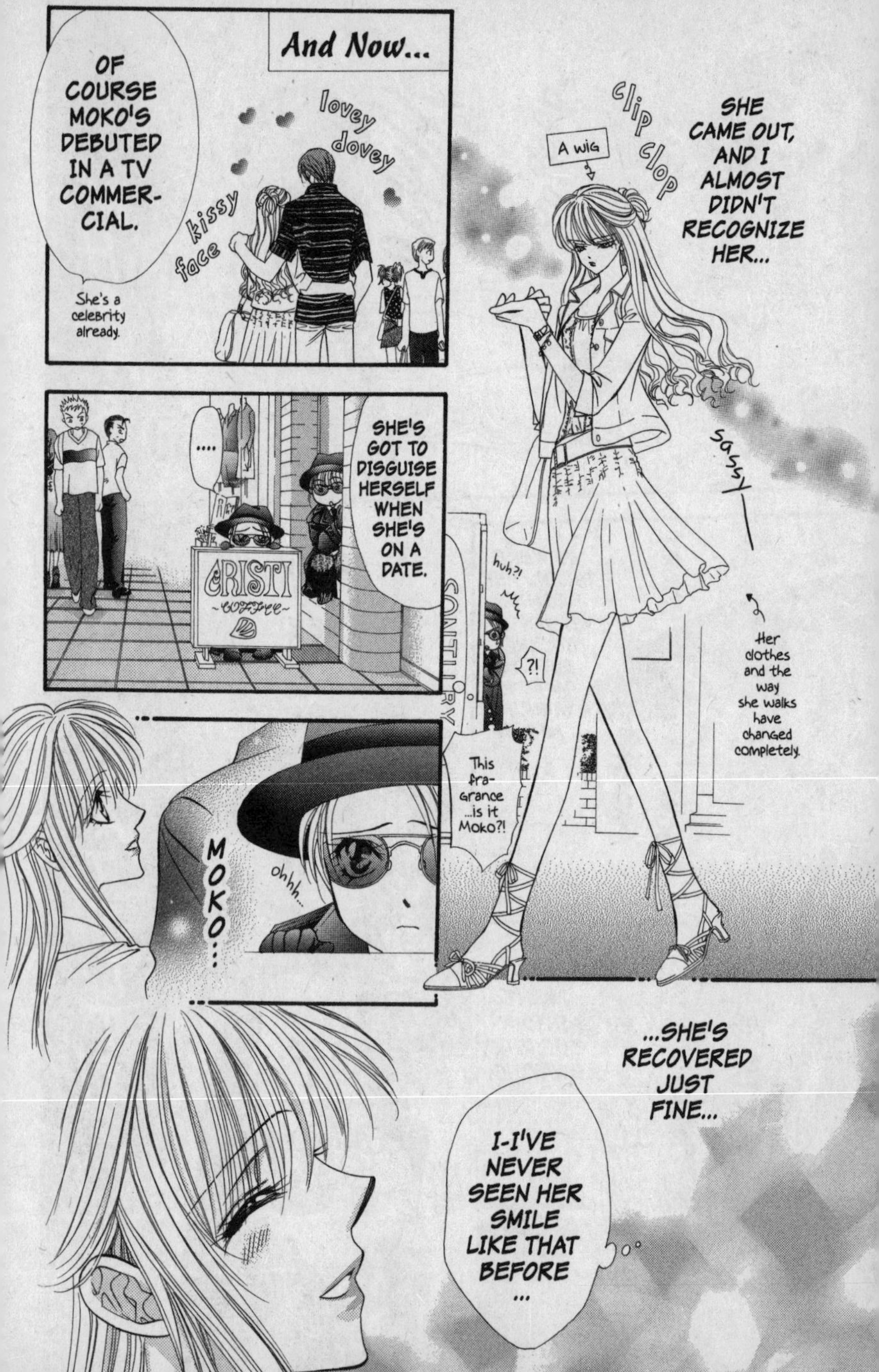
SHE CAME OUT, AND I ALMOST DIDN'T RECOGNIZE HER...
clip clop
A wig
sassy
Her clothes and the way she walks have changed completely.
huh?!
?!
This fra-grance ...is it Moko?!
And Now...
OF COURSE MOKO'S DEBUTED IN A TV COMMER-CIAL.
lovey dovey
kissy face
She's a celebrity already.
SHE'S GOT TO DISGUISE HERSELF WHEN SHE'S ON A DATE.
....
CRISTI
MOKO...
ohhh...
...SHE'S RECOVERED JUST FINE...
I-I'VE NEVER SEEN HER SMILE LIKE THAT BEFORE ...

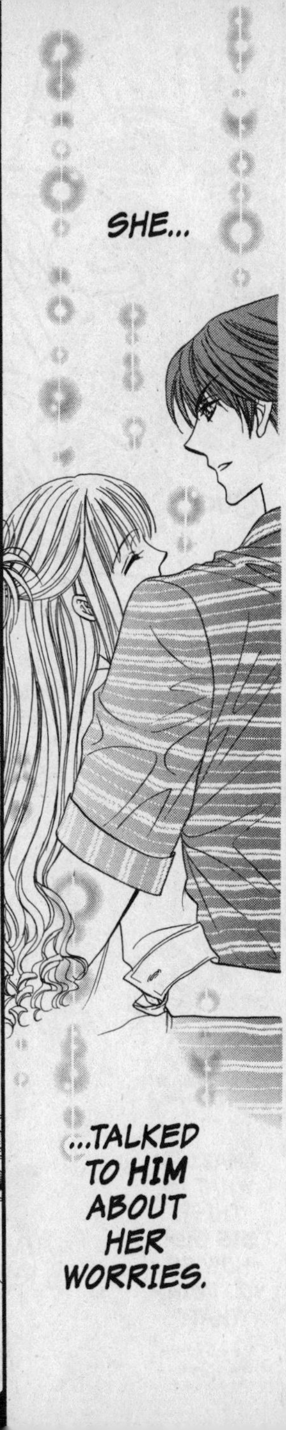
SHE...
...TALKED TO HIM ABOUT HER WORRIES.

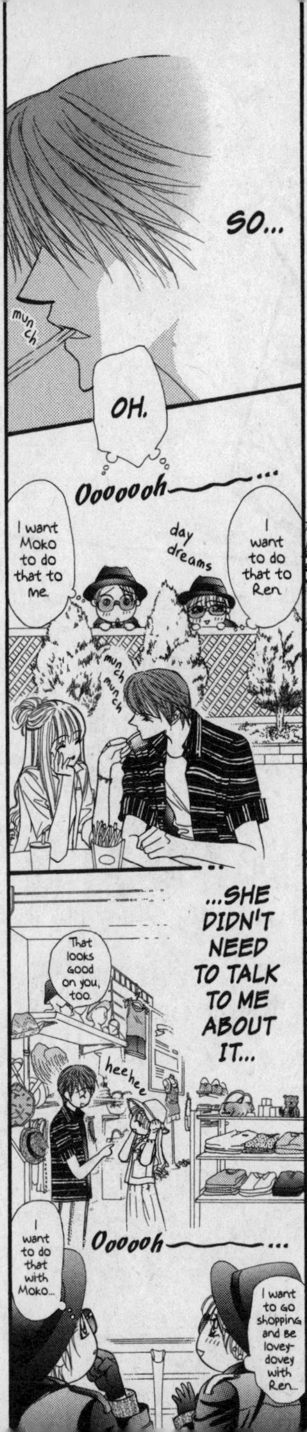
SO...
munch
OH.
Oooooh———...
I want to do that to Ren.
day dreams
I want Moko to do that to me.
munch munch
...SHE DIDN'T NEED TO TALK TO ME ABOUT IT...
That looks good on you, too.
heehee
Ooooh———...
I want to go shopping and be lovey-dovey with Ren...
I want to do that with Moko...

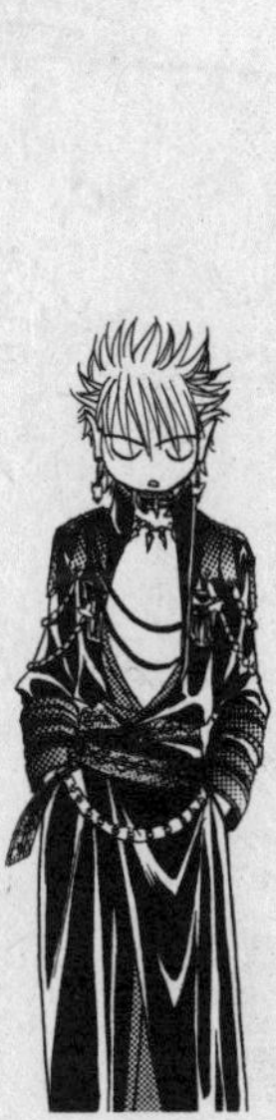

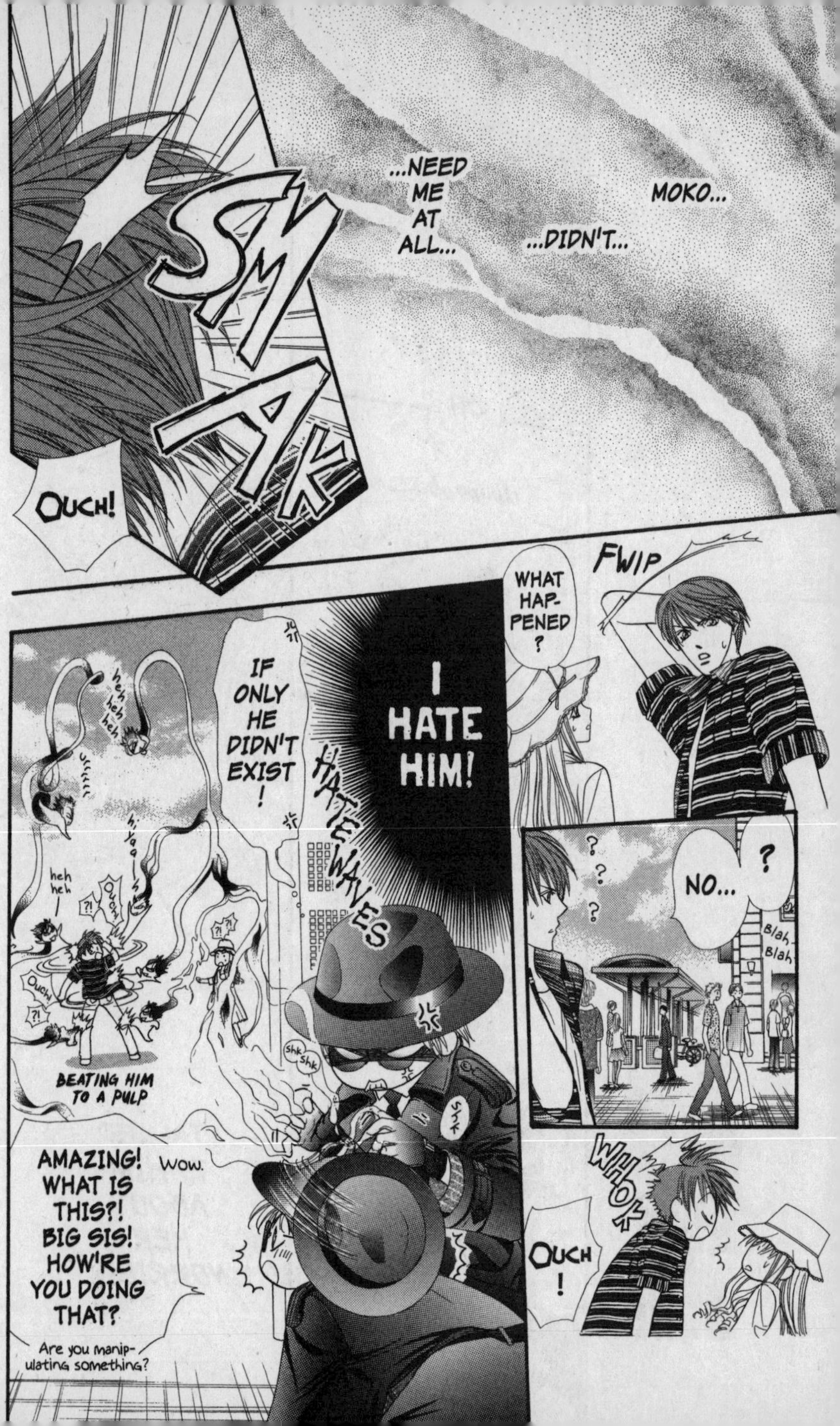
MOKO...
...DIDN'T...
...NEED ME AT ALL...
SMACK
OUCH!
FWIP
WHAT HAP-PENED?
I HATE HIM!
IF ONLY HE DIDN'T EXIST!
HATE WAVES
heh heh heh
hi yaa
heh heh
Ouch
Ouch
?!
?!
?!
BEATING HIM TO A PULP
Shk Shk
NO...
?
? ? ?
Blah, Blah
WHOK
OUCH!
AMAZING! WHAT IS THIS?! BIG SIS! HOW'RE YOU DOING THAT?
Wow.
Are you manip-ulating something?

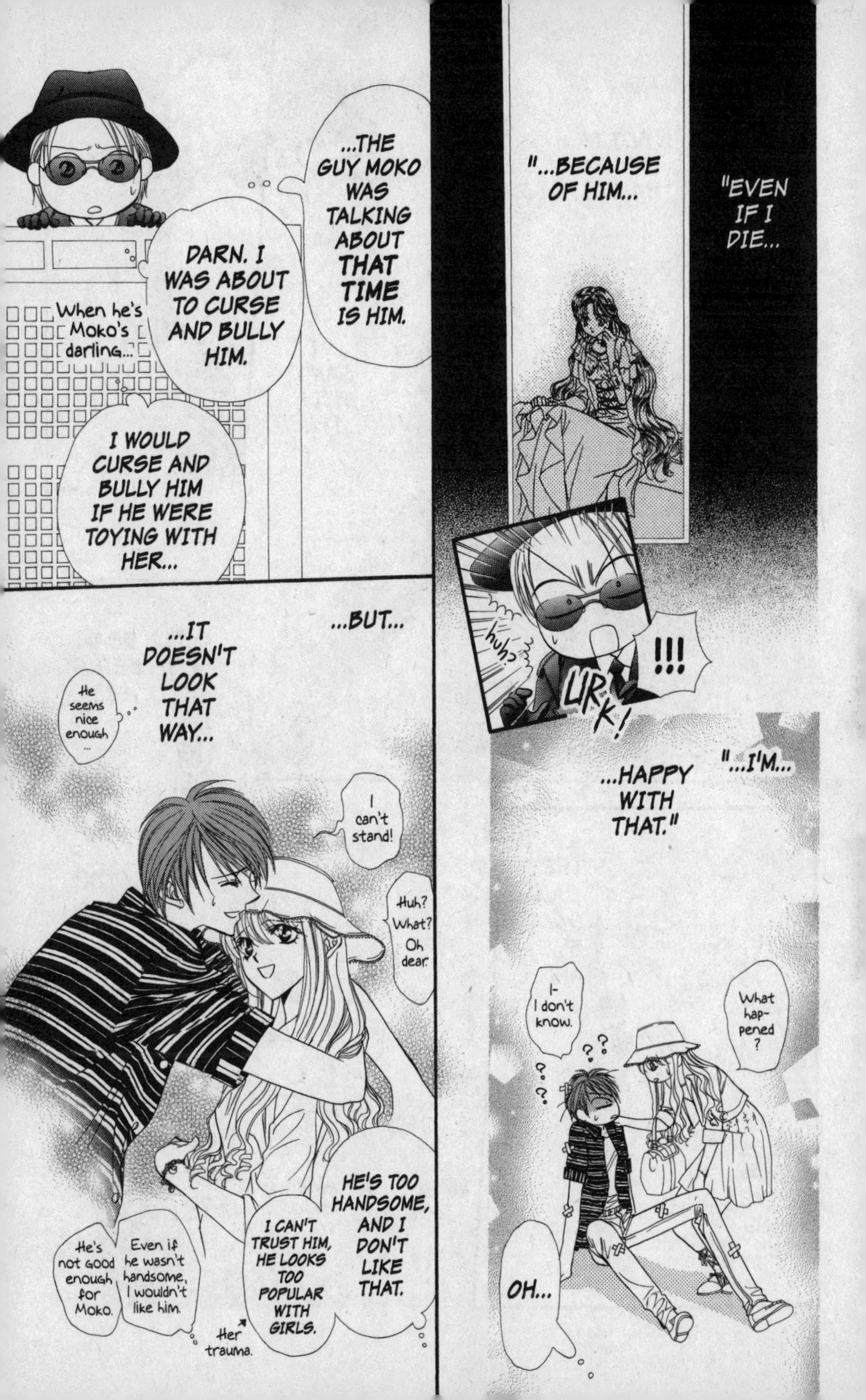
"EVEN IF I DIE...
"...BECAUSE OF HIM...
huh?
!!!
URK!
"...I'M...
...HAPPY WITH THAT."
What hap-pened?
I- I don't know.
OH...
...THE GUY MOKO WAS TALKING ABOUT THAT TIME IS HIM.
DARN. I WAS ABOUT TO CURSE AND BULLY HIM.
When he's Moko's darling...
I WOULD CURSE AND BULLY HIM IF HE WERE TOYING WITH HER...
...BUT...
...IT DOESN'T LOOK THAT WAY...
He seems nice enough...
I can't stand!
Huh? What? Oh dear.
HE'S TOO HANDSOME, AND I DON'T LIKE THAT.
I CAN'T TRUST HIM, HE LOOKS TOO POPULAR WITH GIRLS.
Her trauma.
Even if he wasn't handsome, I wouldn't like him.
He's not good enough for Moko.

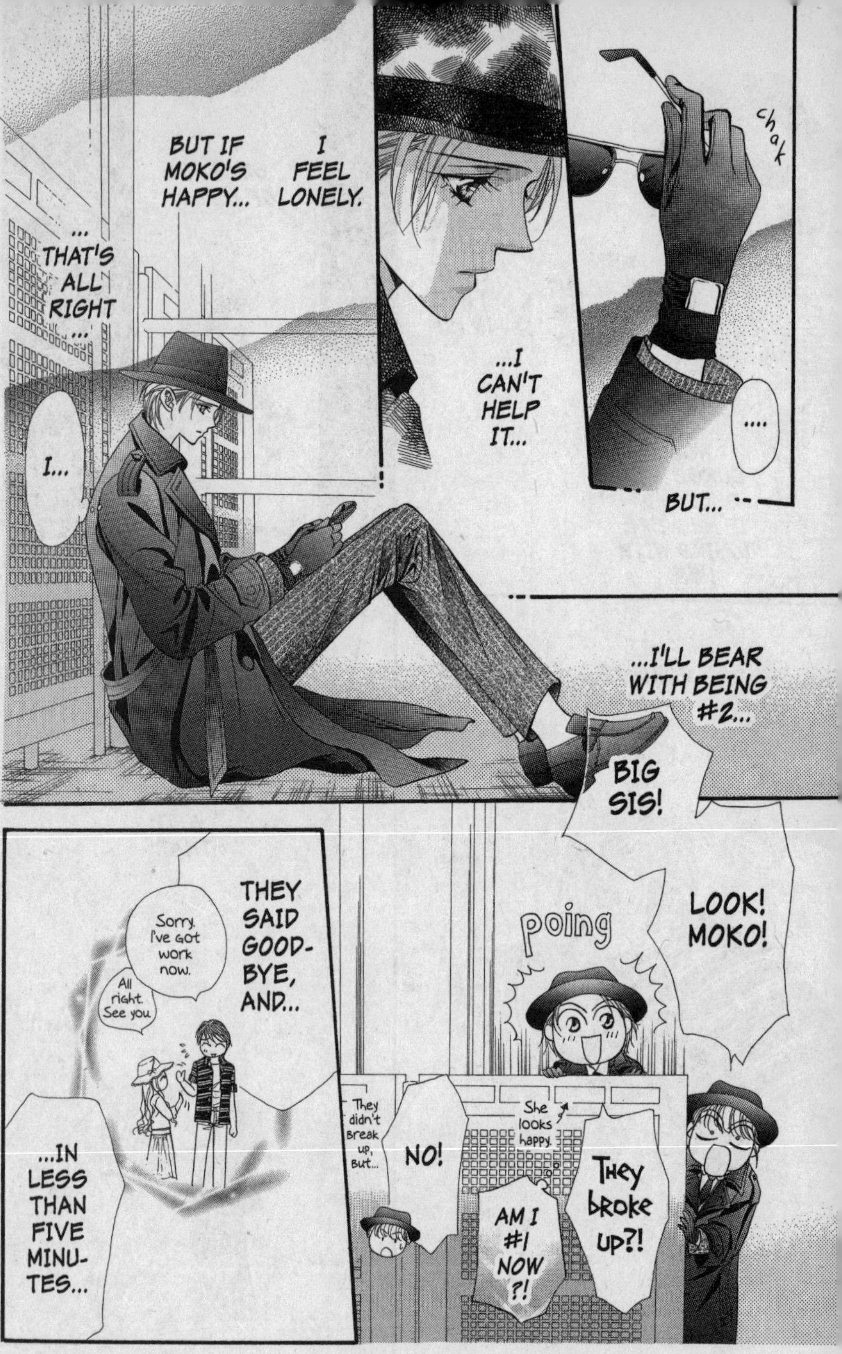
chak
....
BUT...
...I CAN'T HELP IT...
I FEEL LONELY.
BUT IF MOKO'S HAPPY...
...THAT'S ALL RIGHT...
I...
...I'LL BEAR WITH BEING #2...
BIG SIS!
LOOK! MOKO!
poing
They broke up?!
AM I #1 NOW?!
She looks happy.
NO!
They didn't break up, but...
THEY SAID GOOD-BYE, AND...
Sorry. I've got work now.
All right. See you.
...IN LESS THAN FIVE MINU-TES...

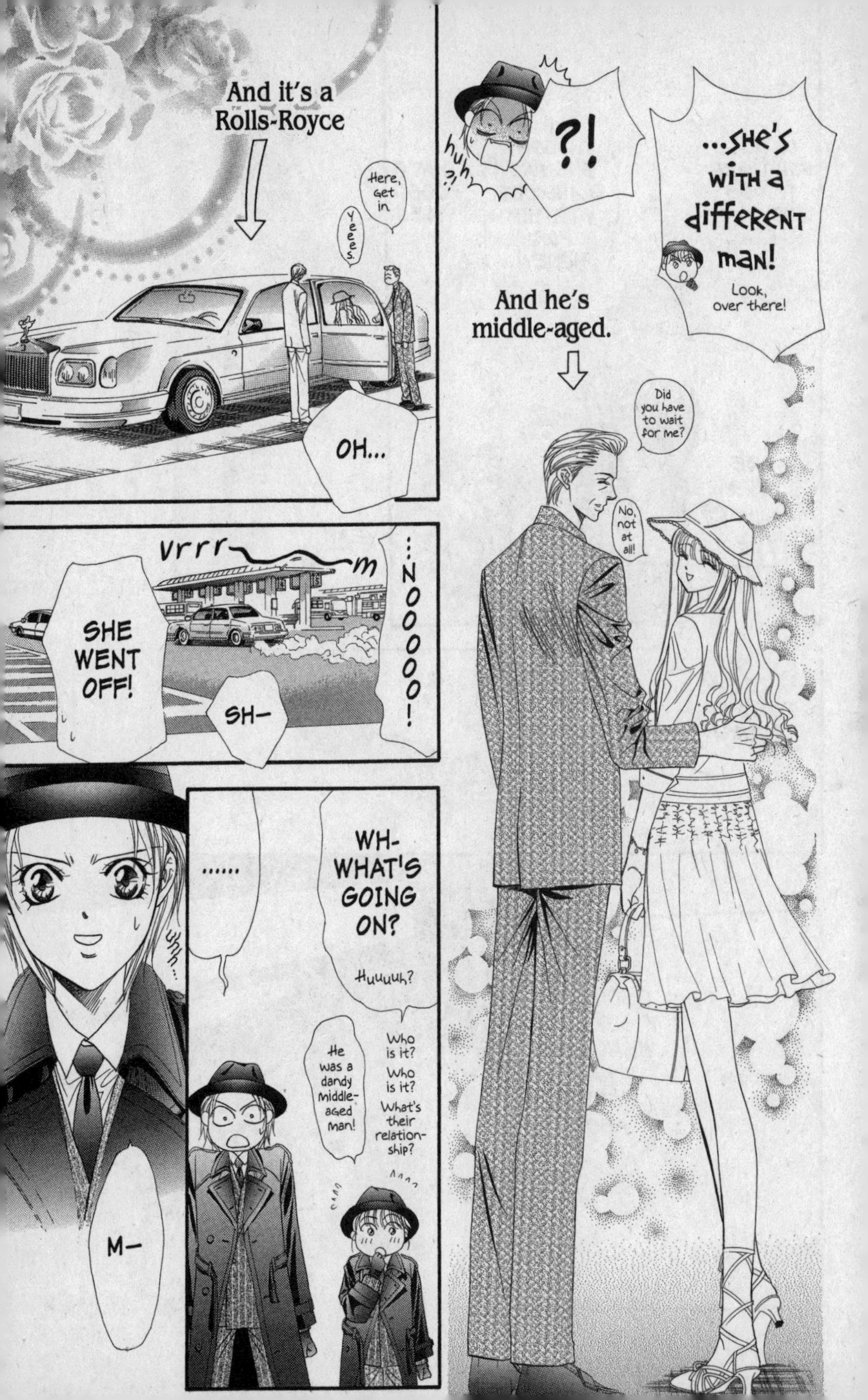
...SHE'S WITH A DIFFERENT MAN!
Look, over there!
?!
huh?!
And he's middle-aged.
Did you have to wait for me?
No, not at all!
And it's a Rolls-Royce
Here, get in.
Yeees.
OH...
...NOOOOOO!
vrrr—m
SH-
SHE WENT OFF!
WH-WHAT'S GOING ON?
Huuuuh?
......
Who is it? Who is it? What's their relationship?
He was a dandy middle-aged man!
uhh...
M-

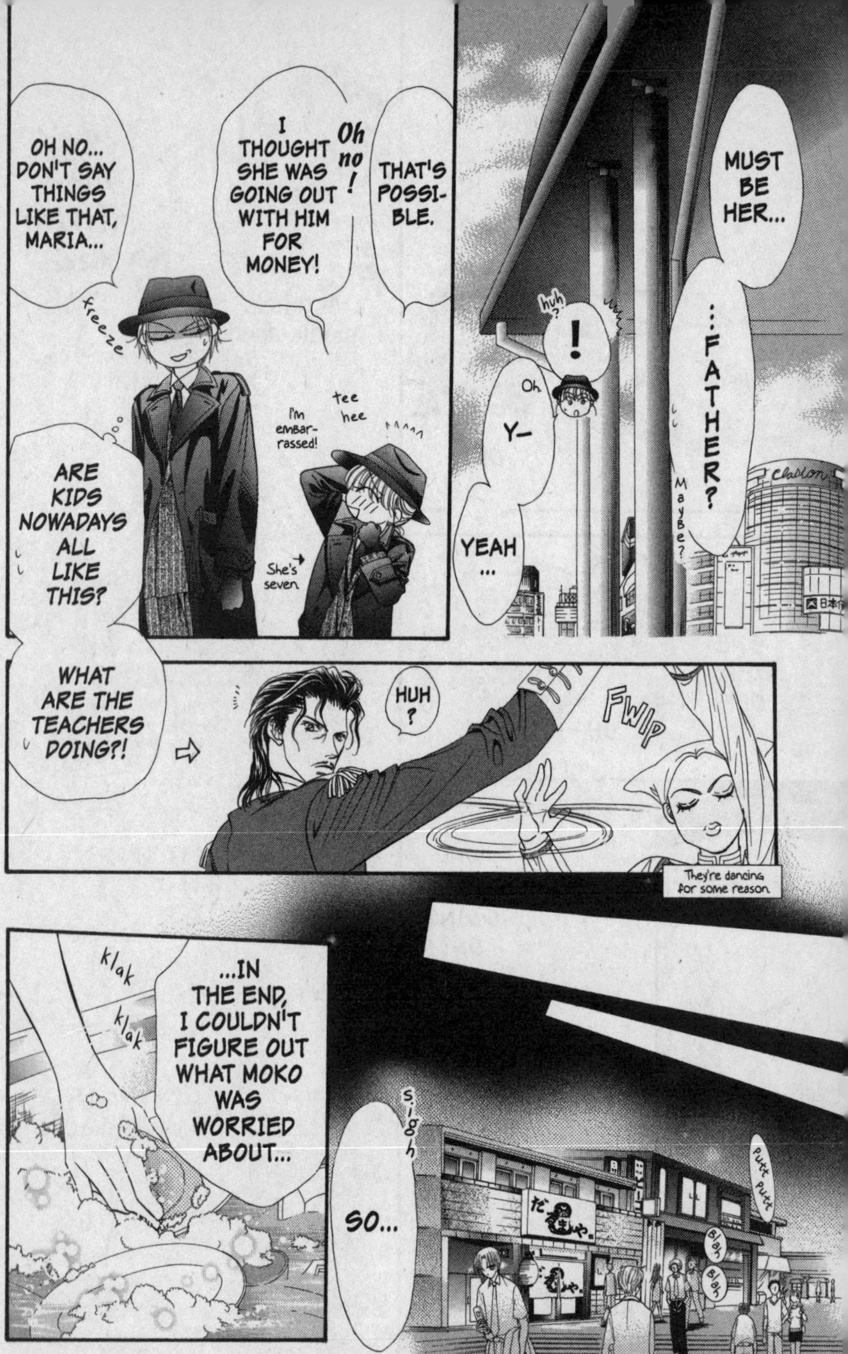
MUST BE HER...
...FATHER?
Maybe?
huh?
!
Oh.
Y—
YEAH...
THAT'S POSSIBLE.
Oh no!
I THOUGHT SHE WAS GOING OUT WITH HIM FOR MONEY!
OH NO... DON'T SAY THINGS LIKE THAT, MARIA...
freeze
tee hee
I'm embarrassed!
She's seven
ARE KIDS NOWADAYS ALL LIKE THIS?
WHAT ARE THE TEACHERS DOING?!
FWIP
HUH?
They're dancing for some reason.
Putt putt
Blah
Blah
sigh
SO...
...IN THE END, I COULDN'T FIGURE OUT WHAT MOKO WAS WORRIED ABOUT...
klak
klak

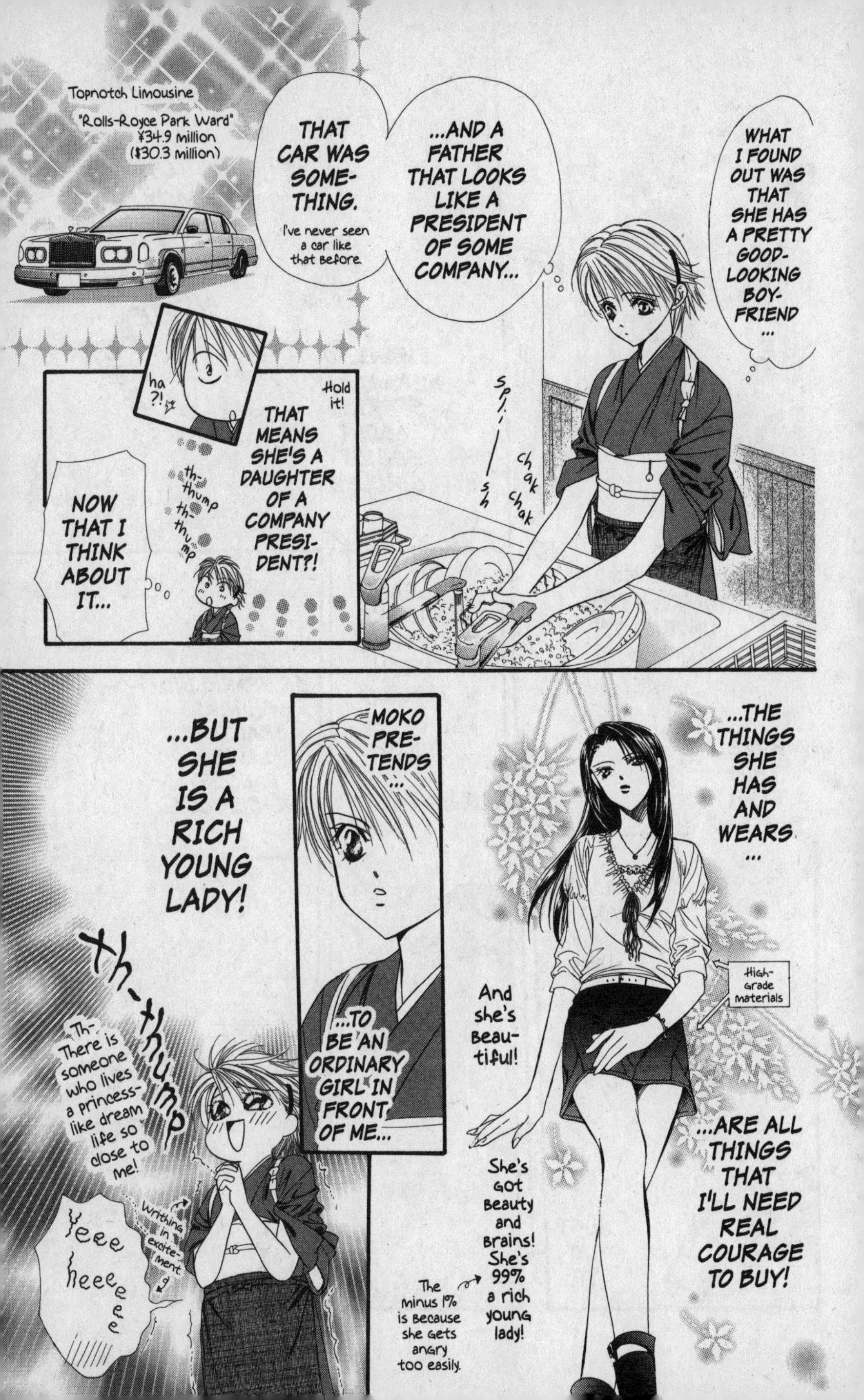
WHAT I FOUND OUT WAS THAT SHE HAS A PRETTY GOOD-LOOKING BOY-FRIEND...
...AND A FATHER THAT LOOKS LIKE A PRESIDENT OF SOME COMPANY...
THAT CAR WAS SOME-THING.
I've never seen a car like that before.
Topnotch Limousine
"Rolls-Royce Park Ward" ¥34.9 million ($30.3 million)
spli-sh
chak chak
Hold it!
ha ?!
THAT MEANS SHE'S A DAUGHTER OF A COMPANY PRESI-DENT?!
NOW THAT I THINK ABOUT IT...
th-thump th-thump
...THE THINGS SHE HAS AND WEARS...
High-Grade materials
And she's Beau-tiful!
...ARE ALL THINGS THAT I'LL NEED REAL COURAGE TO BUY!
She's Got Beauty and Brains! She's 99% a rich young lady!
The minus 1% is because she gets angry too easily.
MOKO PRE-TENDS...
...TO BE AN ORDINARY GIRL IN FRONT OF ME...
...BUT SHE IS A RICH YOUNG LADY!
th-thump
Th-There is someone who lives a princess-like dream life so close to me!
Writhing in excite-ment
Yeee heeeeeee

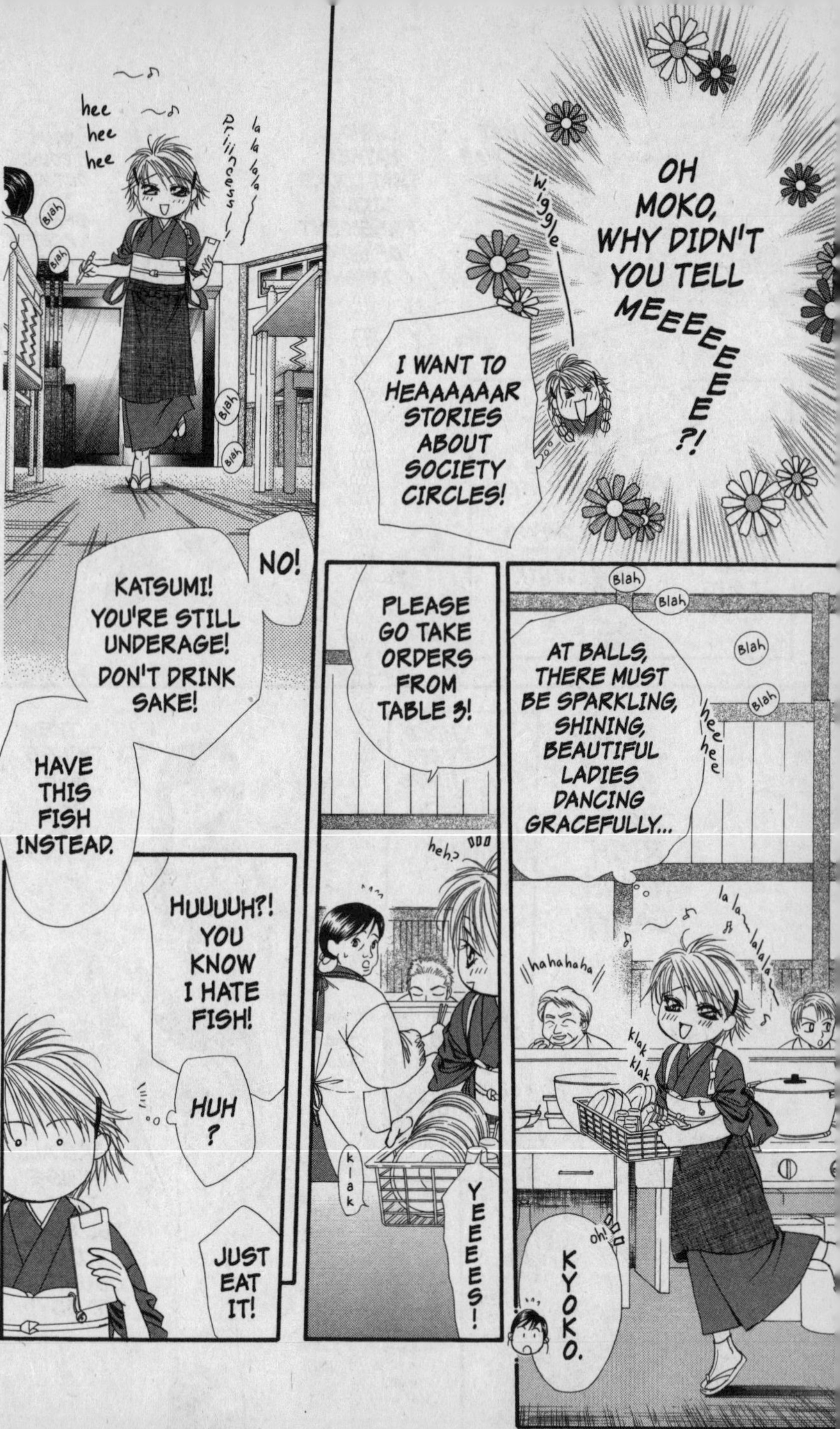
OH MOKO, WHY DIDN'T YOU TELL MEEEEEEEE?!
wiggle
I WANT TO HEAAAAAAR STORIES ABOUT SOCIETY CIRCLES!
Blah
Blah
Blah
Blah
AT BALLS, THERE MUST BE SPARKLING, SHINING, BEAUTIFUL LADIES DANCING GRACEFULLY...
hee hee
la la lalala
hahahaha
klak klak
oh!
KYOKO.
PLEASE GO TAKE ORDERS FROM TABLE 3!
heh?
klak
YEEEES!
hee hee hee
la la la la
Priiincess
Blah
Blah
Blah
Blah
NO!
KATSUMI! YOU'RE STILL UNDERAGE! DON'T DRINK SAKE!
HAVE THIS FISH INSTEAD.
HUUUUH?! YOU KNOW I HATE FISH!
HUH?
JUST EAT IT!

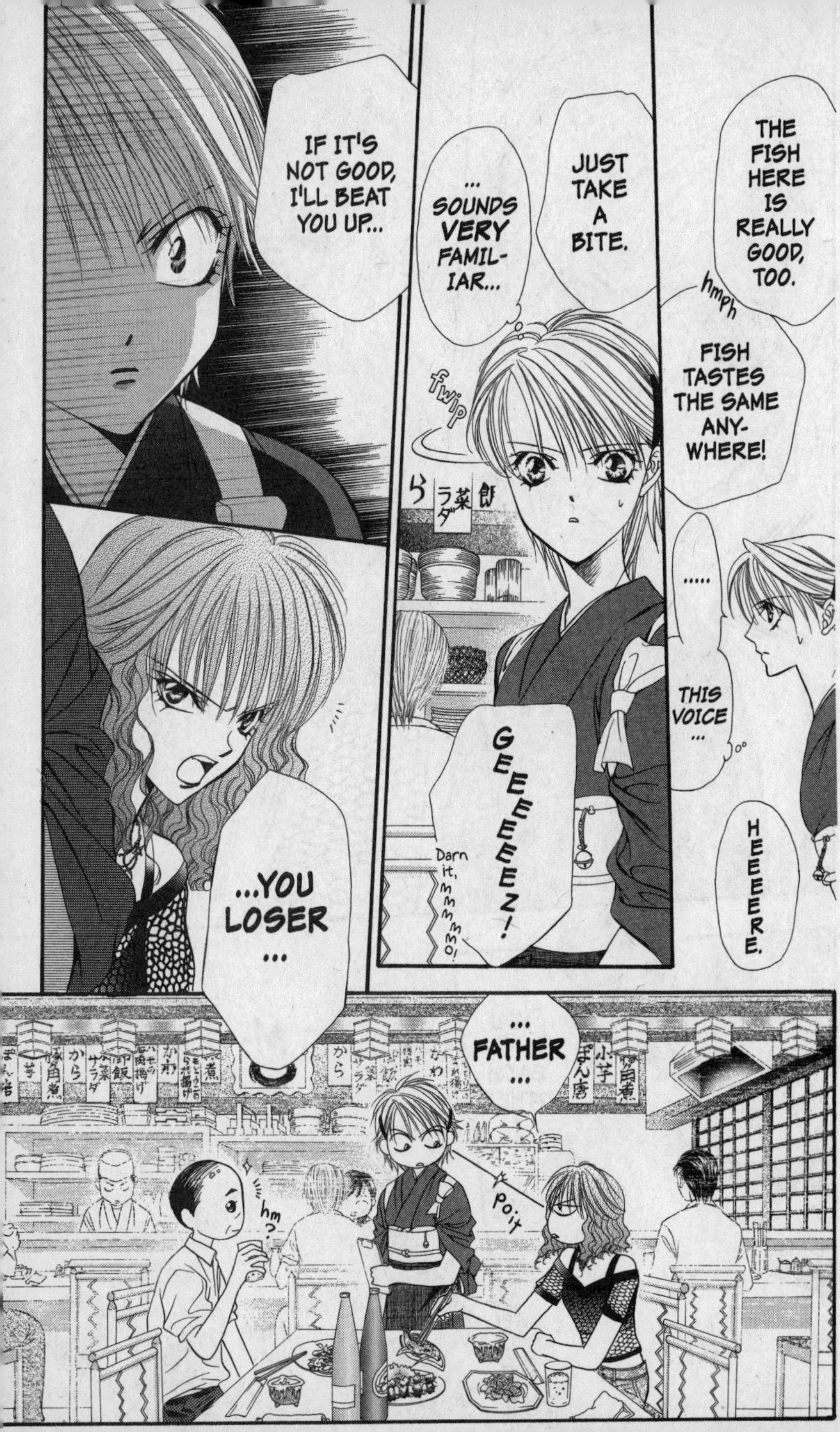
THE FISH HERE IS REALLY GOOD, TOO.
hmph
FISH TASTES THE SAME ANYWHERE!
.....
THIS VOICE...
HEEEERE.
JUST TAKE A BITE.
...SOUNDS VERY FAMILIAR...
fwip
GEEEEEZ!
Darn it, mmmmmo!
IF IT'S NOT GOOD, I'LL BEAT YOU UP...
...YOU LOSER...
...FATHER...
hm?
Poit

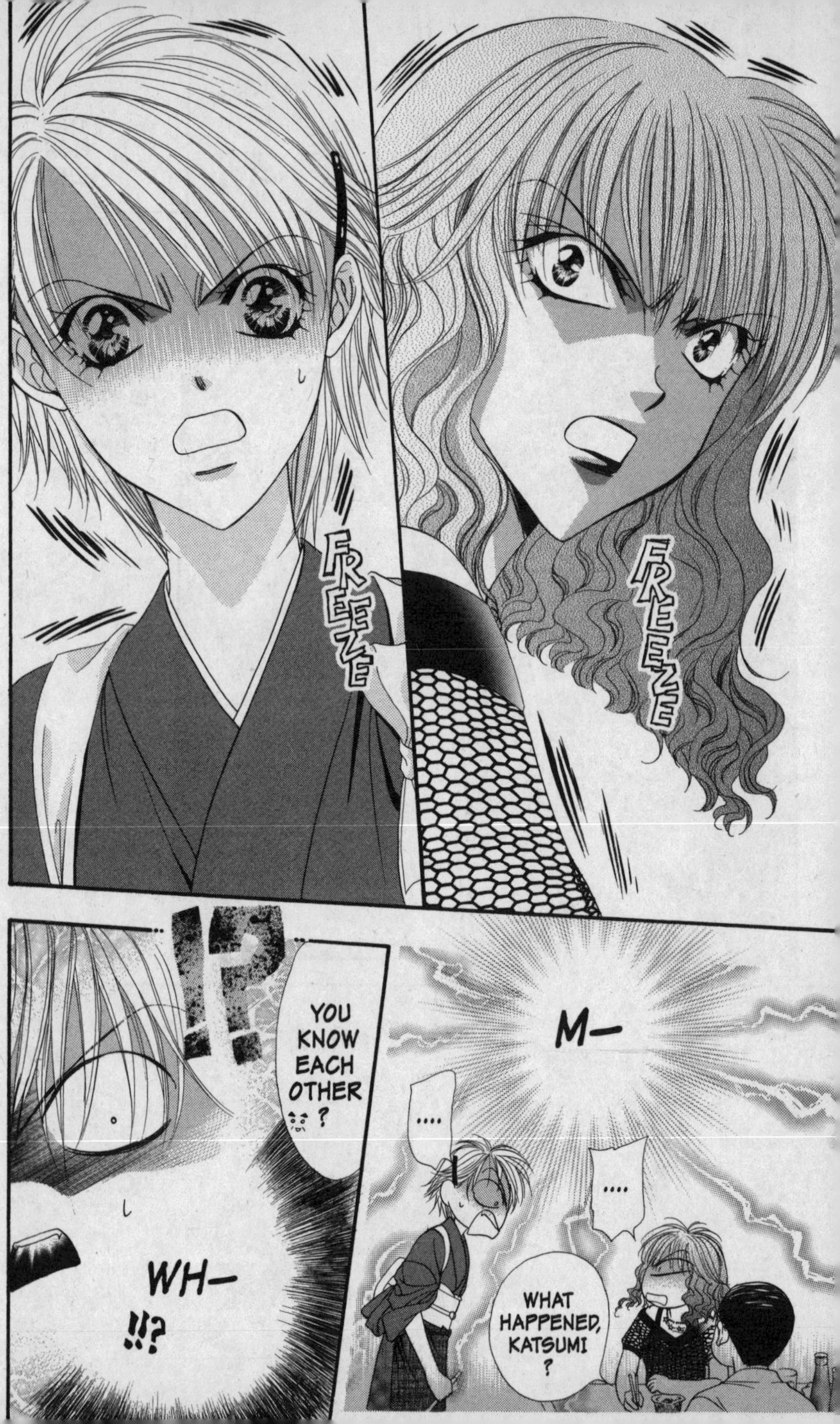
FREEZE
FREEZE
M—
....
....
WHAT HAPPENED, KATSUMI?
...!?...
YOU KNOW EACH OTHER?
WH— !!?

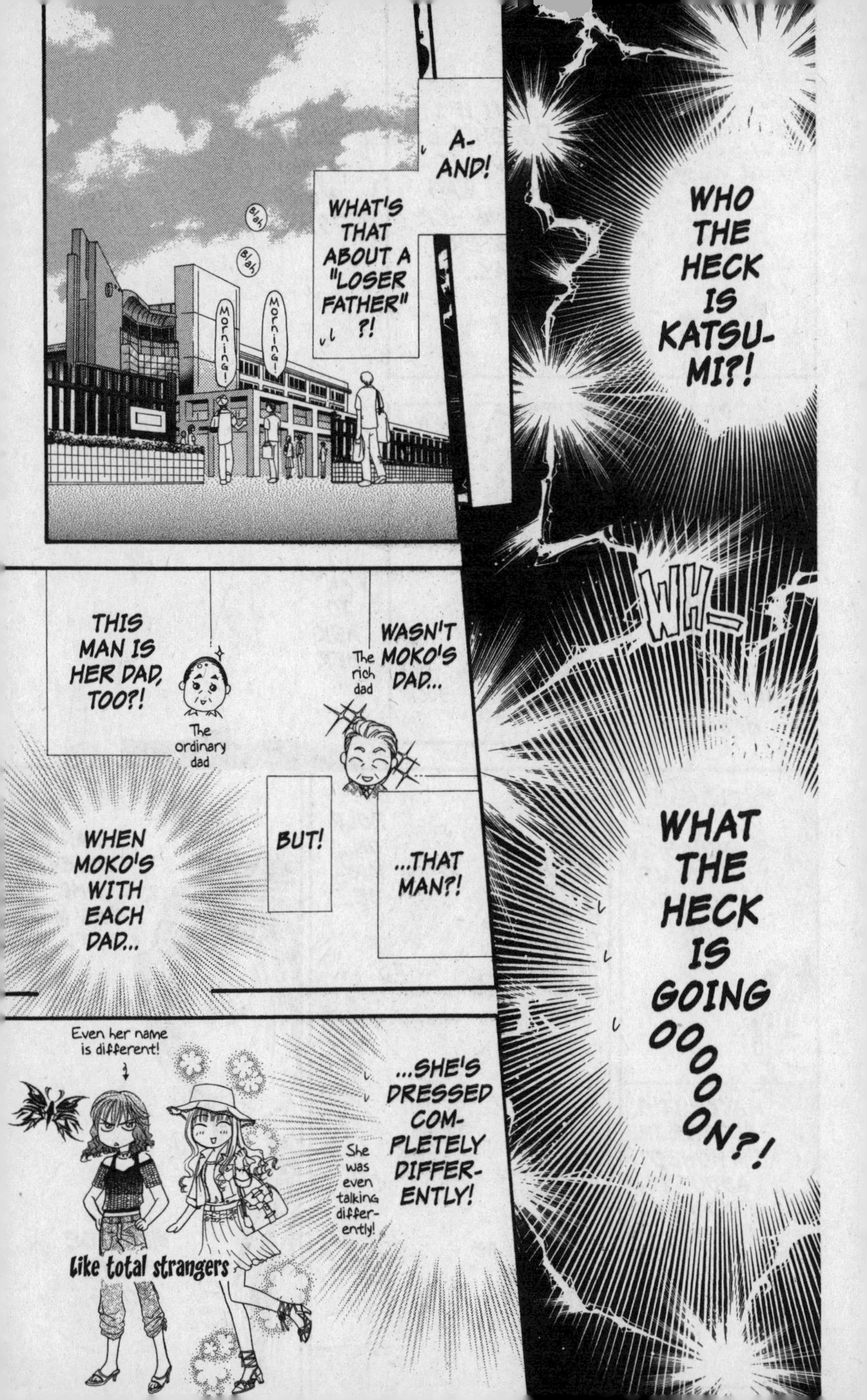

WHO THE HECK IS KATSUMI?!
WH-
WHAT THE HECK IS GOING OOOOOON?!
A-AND!
WHAT'S THAT ABOUT A "LOSER FATHER"?!
Blah
Blah
Morning!
Morning!
WASN'T MOKO'S DAD...
The rich dad
...THAT MAN?!
BUT!
THIS MAN IS HER DAD, TOO?!
The ordinary dad
WHEN MOKO'S WITH EACH DAD...
...SHE'S DRESSED COMPLETELY DIFFERENTLY!
She was even talking differently!
Even her name is different!
Like total strangers

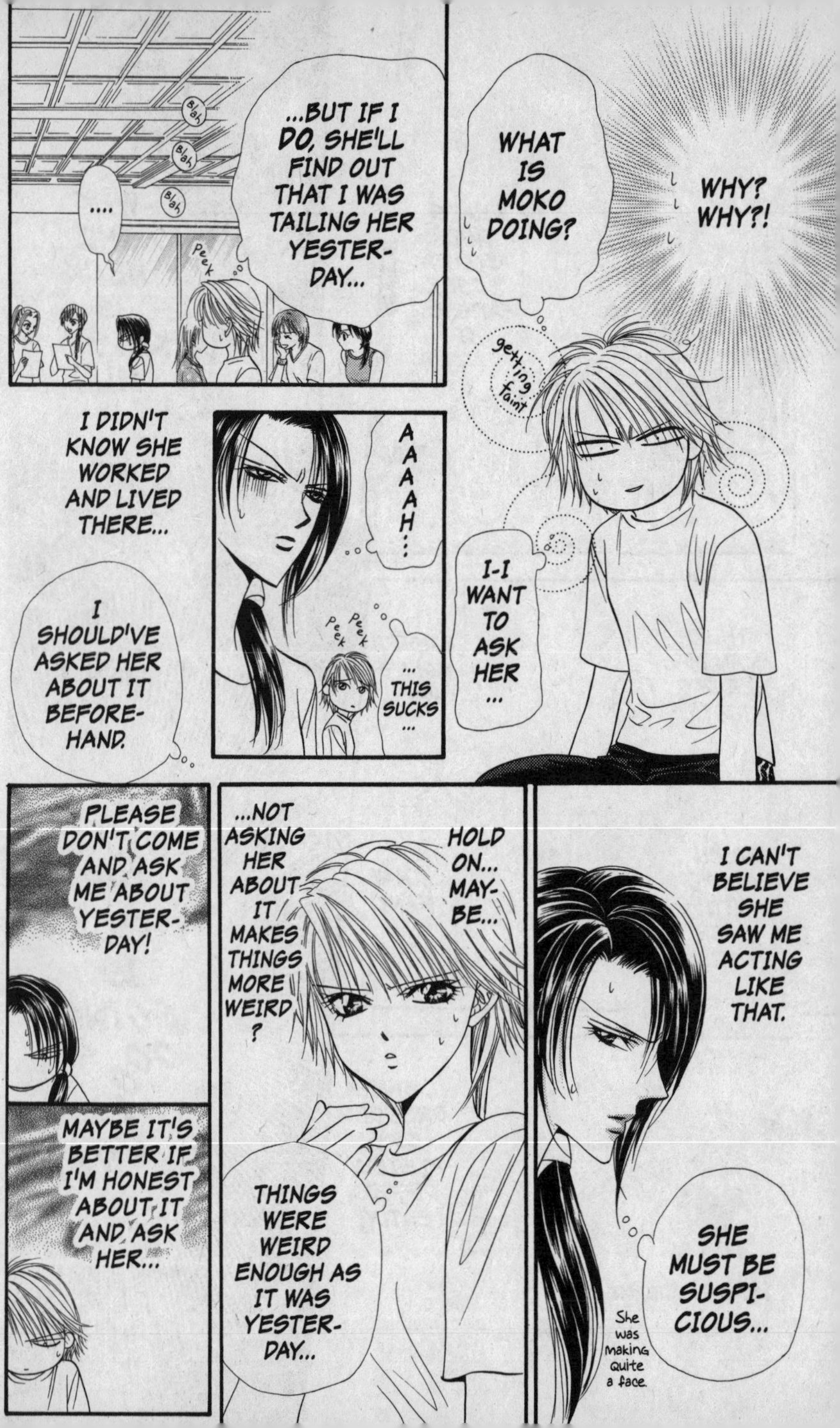
WHY? WHY?!
WHAT IS MOKO DOING?
getting faint
I-I WANT TO ASK HER...
...BUT IF I DO, SHE'LL FIND OUT THAT I WAS TAILING HER YESTER-DAY...
Blah
Blah
Blah
Peek
....
AAAAH...
Peek Peek
...THIS SUCKS...
I DIDN'T KNOW SHE WORKED AND LIVED THERE...
I SHOULD'VE ASKED HER ABOUT IT BEFORE-HAND.
I CAN'T BELIEVE SHE SAW ME ACTING LIKE THAT.
SHE MUST BE SUSPI-CIOUS...
She was making quite a face.
HOLD ON... MAY-BE...
...NOT ASKING HER ABOUT IT MAKES THINGS MORE WEIRD?
THINGS WERE WEIRD ENOUGH AS IT WAS YESTER-DAY...
PLEASE DON'T COME AND ASK ME ABOUT YESTER-DAY!
MAYBE IT'S BETTER IF I'M HONEST ABOUT IT AND ASK HER...

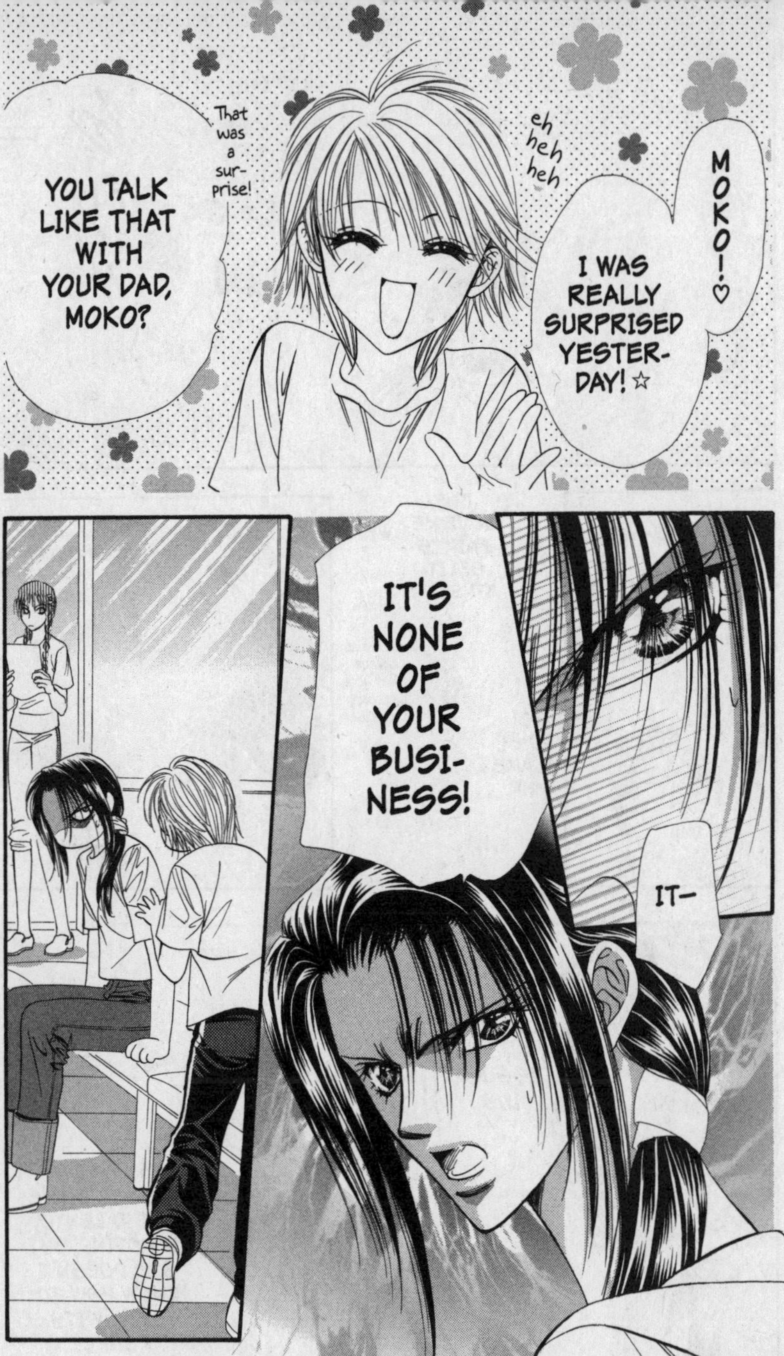
MOKO!♡
I WAS REALLY SURPRISED YESTERDAY! ☆
eh heh heh
That was a surprise!
YOU TALK LIKE THAT WITH YOUR DAD, MOKO?
IT—
IT'S NONE OF YOUR BUSINESS!

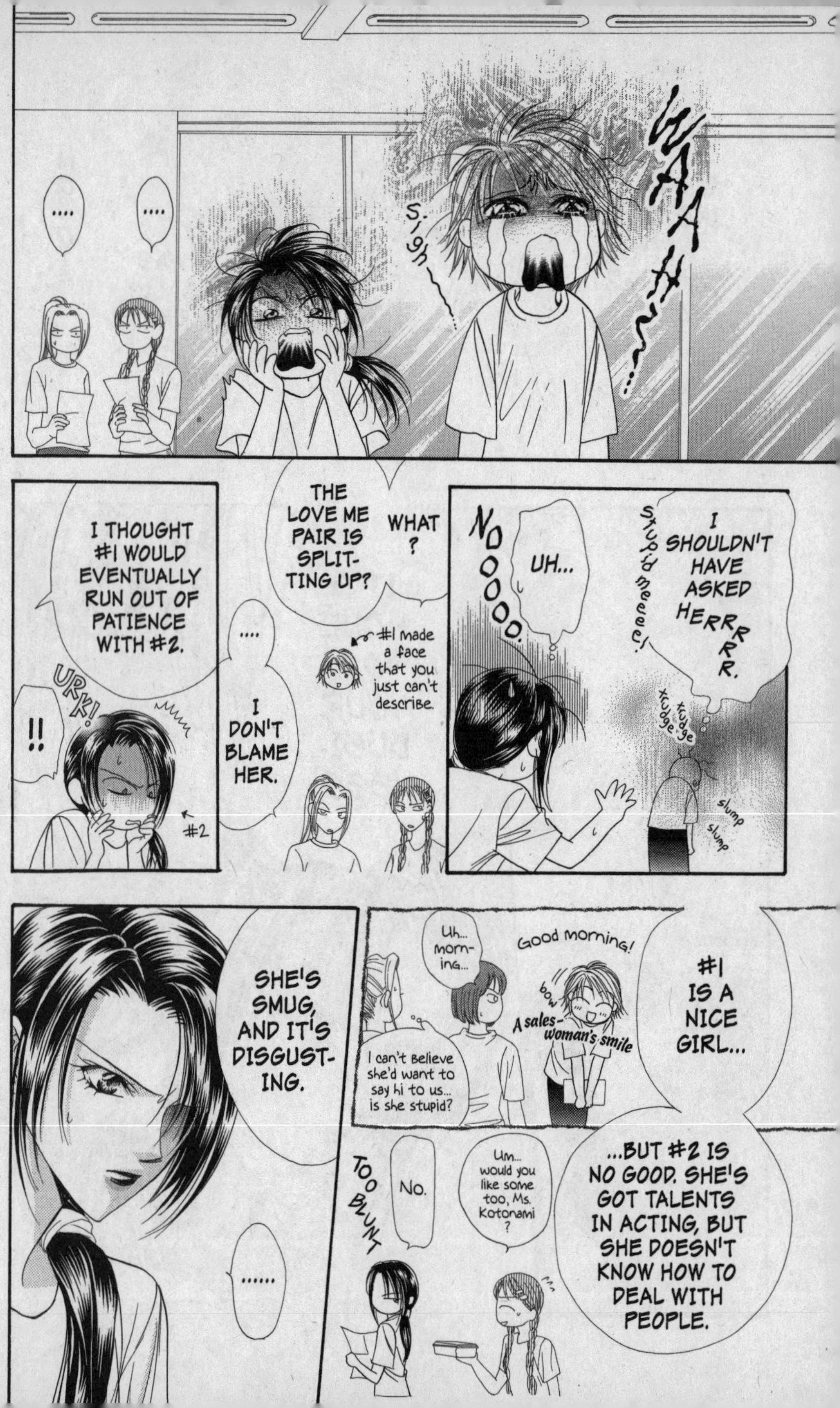
WAAHH~...
sigh~
....
....
I SHOULDN'T HAVE ASKED HERRRRR.
stupid meeee!
NOOOOO.
UH...
trudge trudge
slump slump
WHAT?
THE LOVE ME PAIR IS SPLITTING UP?
#1 made a face that you just can't describe.
....
I DON'T BLAME HER.
I THOUGHT #1 WOULD EVENTUALLY RUN OUT OF PATIENCE WITH #2.
URK!
!!
#2
#1 IS A NICE GIRL...
Good morning!
Uh... morning...
bow
A saleswoman's smile
I can't believe she'd want to say hi to us... is she stupid?
...BUT #2 IS NO GOOD. SHE'S GOT TALENTS IN ACTING, BUT SHE DOESN'T KNOW HOW TO DEAL WITH PEOPLE.
Um... would you like some too, Ms. Kotonami?
No.
TOO BLUNT
......
SHE'S SMUG, AND IT'S DISGUSTING.

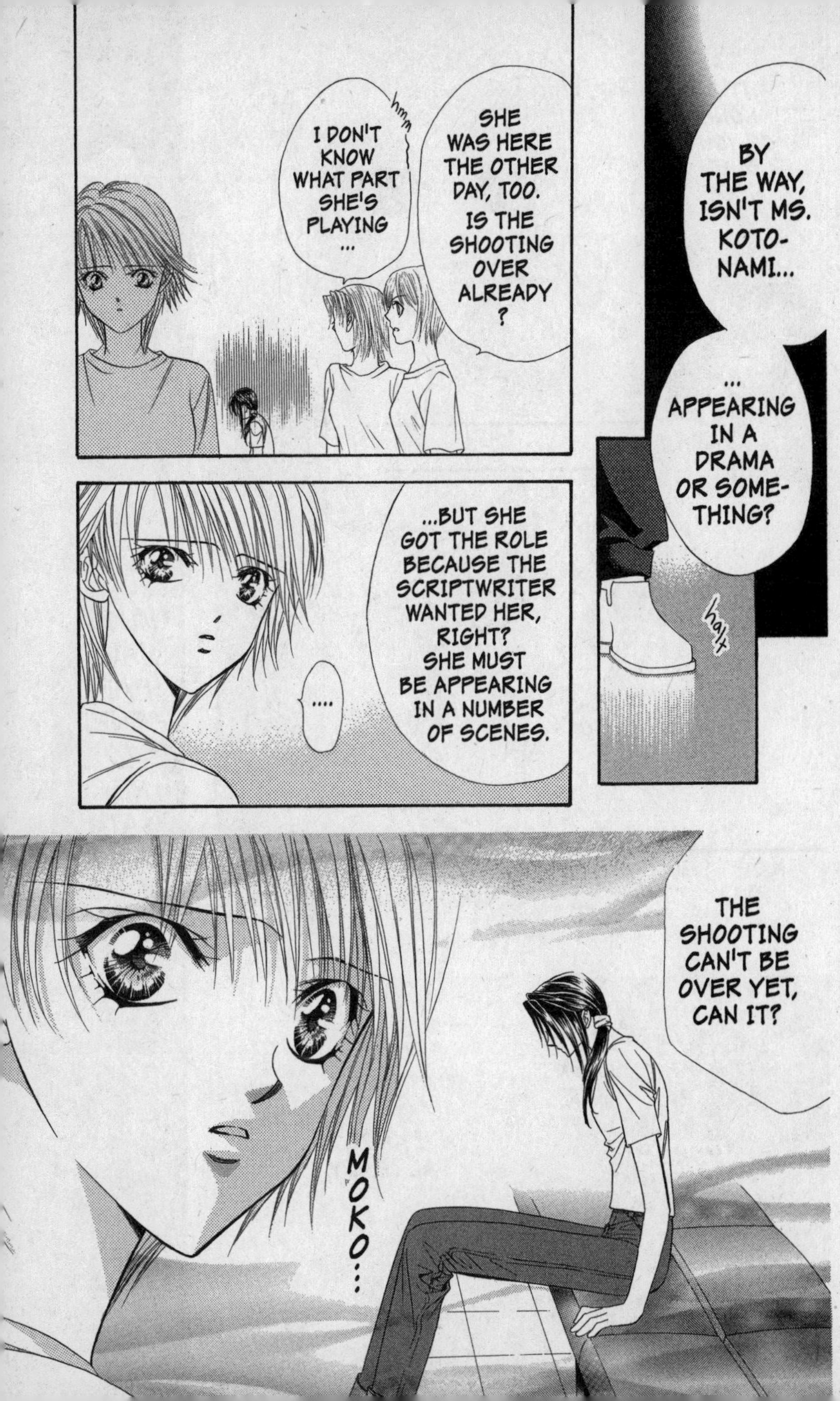
BY THE WAY, ISN'T MS. KOTO-NAMI...
... APPEARING IN A DRAMA OR SOME-THING?
halt
SHE WAS HERE THE OTHER DAY, TOO. IS THE SHOOTING OVER ALREADY?
hmm
I DON'T KNOW WHAT PART SHE'S PLAYING ...
...BUT SHE GOT THE ROLE BECAUSE THE SCRIPTWRITER WANTED HER, RIGHT? SHE MUST BE APPEARING IN A NUMBER OF SCENES.
....
THE SHOOTING CAN'T BE OVER YET, CAN IT?
MOKO...

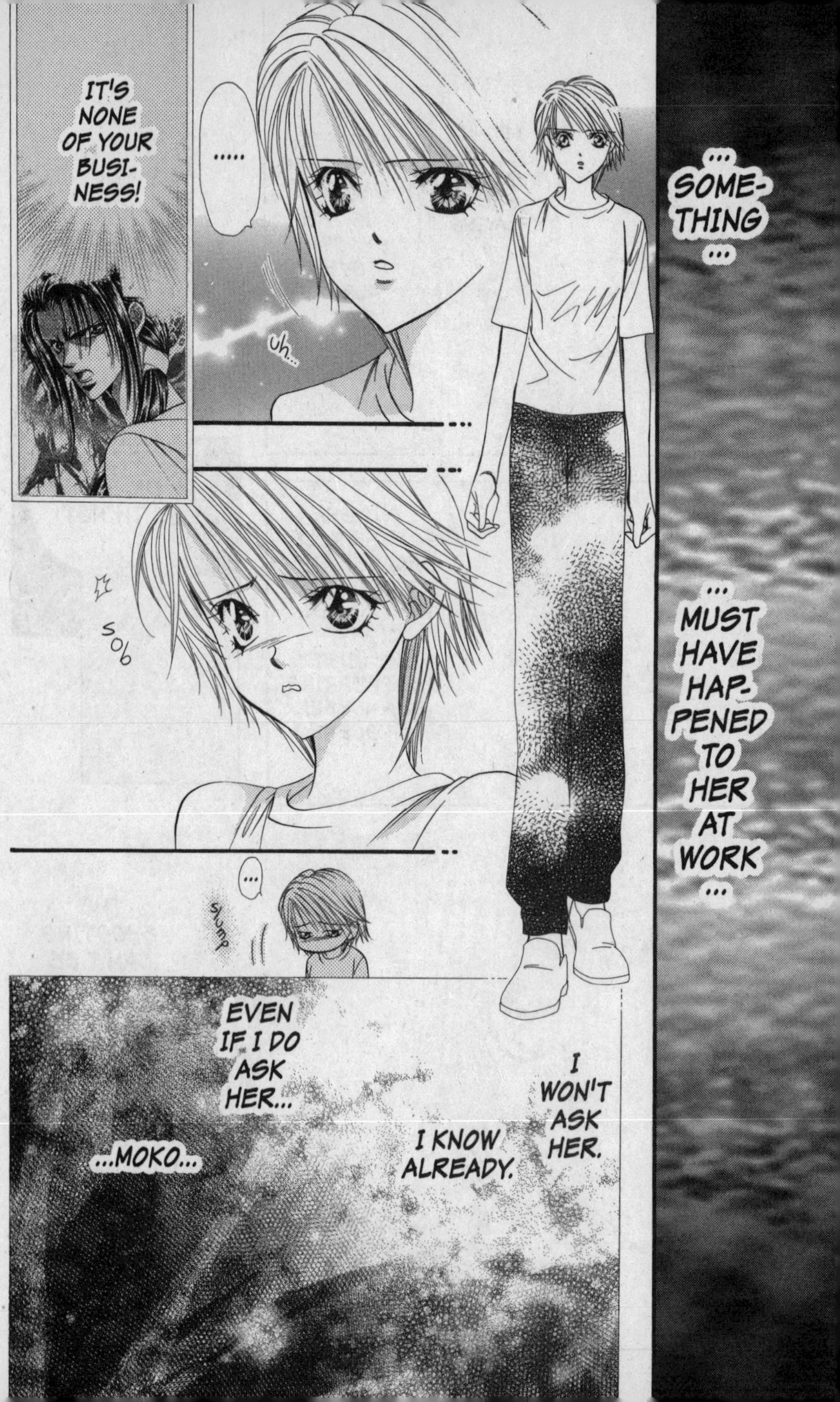

...SOMETHING...
...MUST HAVE HAPPENED TO HER AT WORK...
.....
uh...
IT'S NONE OF YOUR BUSINESS!
sob
...
slump
I WON'T ASK HER.
EVEN IF I DO ASK HER...
I KNOW ALREADY.
...MOKO...

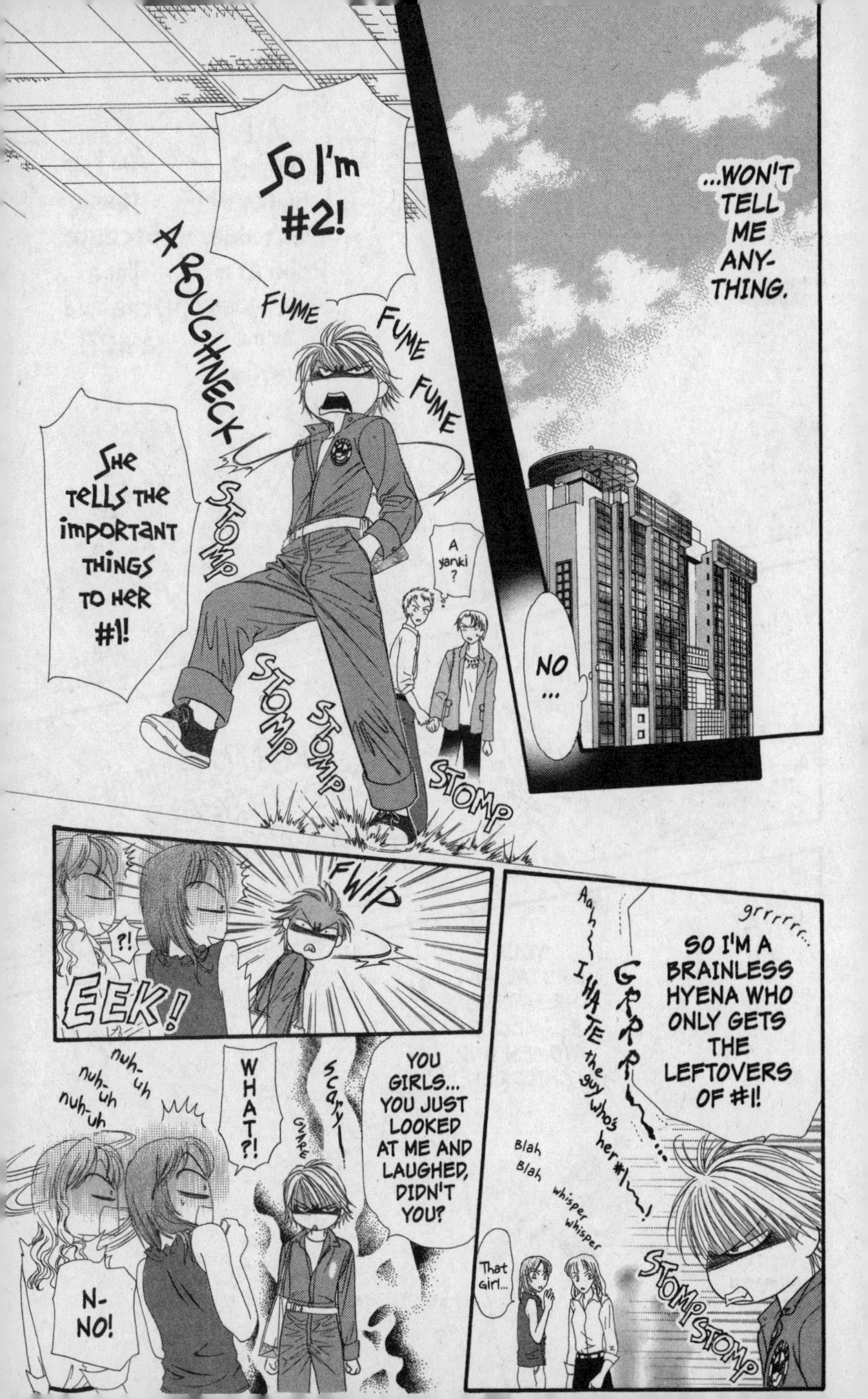
...WON'T TELL ME ANYTHING.
NO...
So I'm #2!
A ROUGHNECK
FUME
FUME
FUME
She tells the important things to her #1!
STOMP
A yanki?
STOMP
STOMP
STOMP
grrrrrr...
SO I'M A BRAINLESS HYENA WHO ONLY GETS THE LEFTOVERS OF #1!
GRRR...
Aah~ I HATE the guy who's her #1~!
Blah Blah
whisper whisper
That girl...
STOMP STOMP
FWIP
?!
EEK!
YOU GIRLS... YOU JUST LOOKED AT ME AND LAUGHED, DIDN'T YOU?
Scary~!
GLARE
WHAT?!
nuh-uh
nuh-uh
nuh-uh
N-NO!

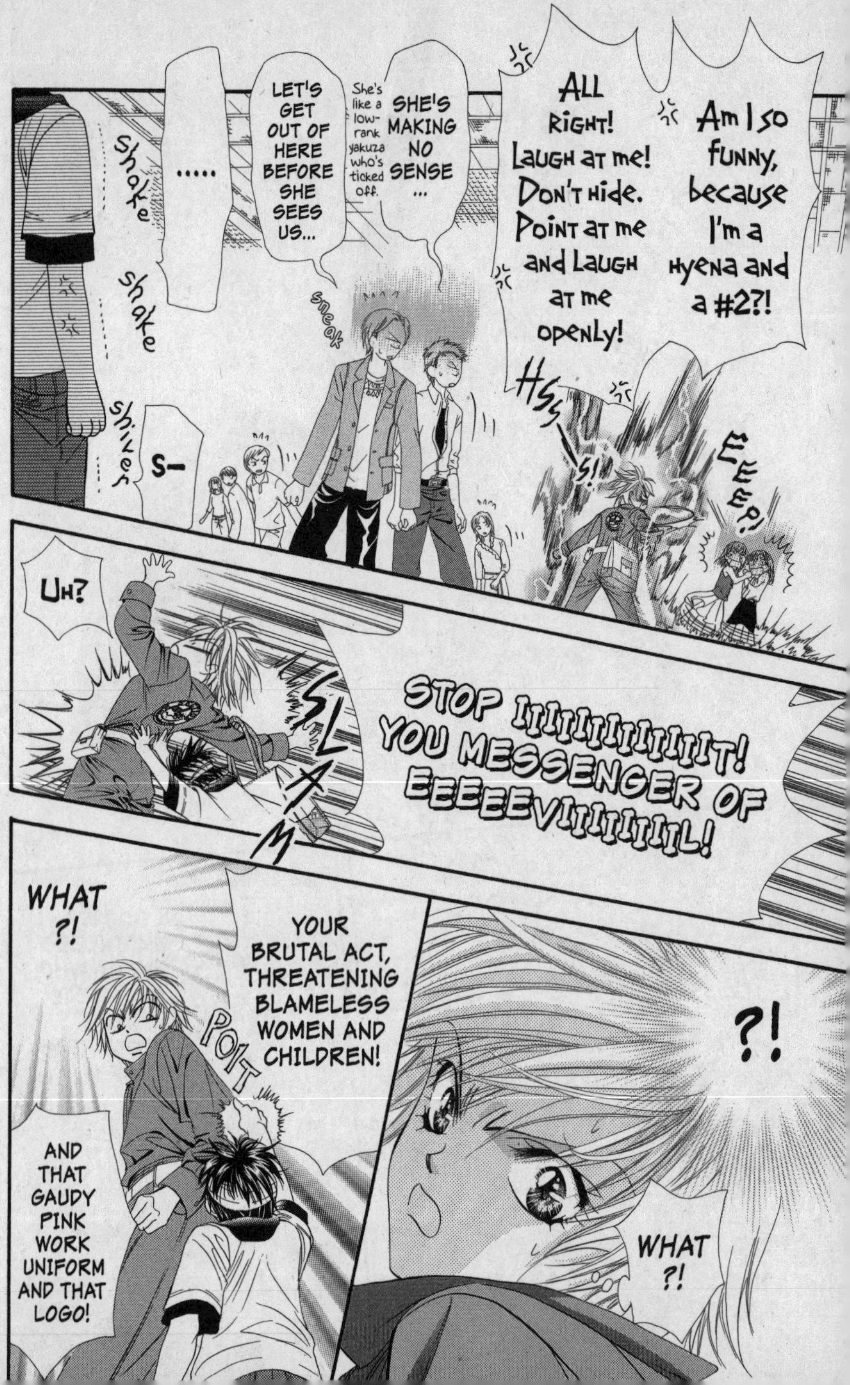

Am I so funny, because I'm a hyena and a #2?!
All right! Laugh at me! Don't hide. Point at me and laugh at me openly!
HSSS!
EEEEP!
SHE'S MAKING NO SENSE...
She's like a low-rank yakuza who's ticked off.
sneak
LET'S GET OUT OF HERE BEFORE SHE SEES US...
.....
shake
shake
shiver
S-
STOP IIIIIIIIIIIIT! YOU MESSENGER OF EEEEEVIIIIIIIIL!
SLAM
UH?
?!
WHAT ?!
YOUR BRUTAL ACT, THREATENING BLAMELESS WOMEN AND CHILDREN!
WHAT ?!
POIT
AND THAT GAUDY PINK WORK UNIFORM AND THAT LOGO!

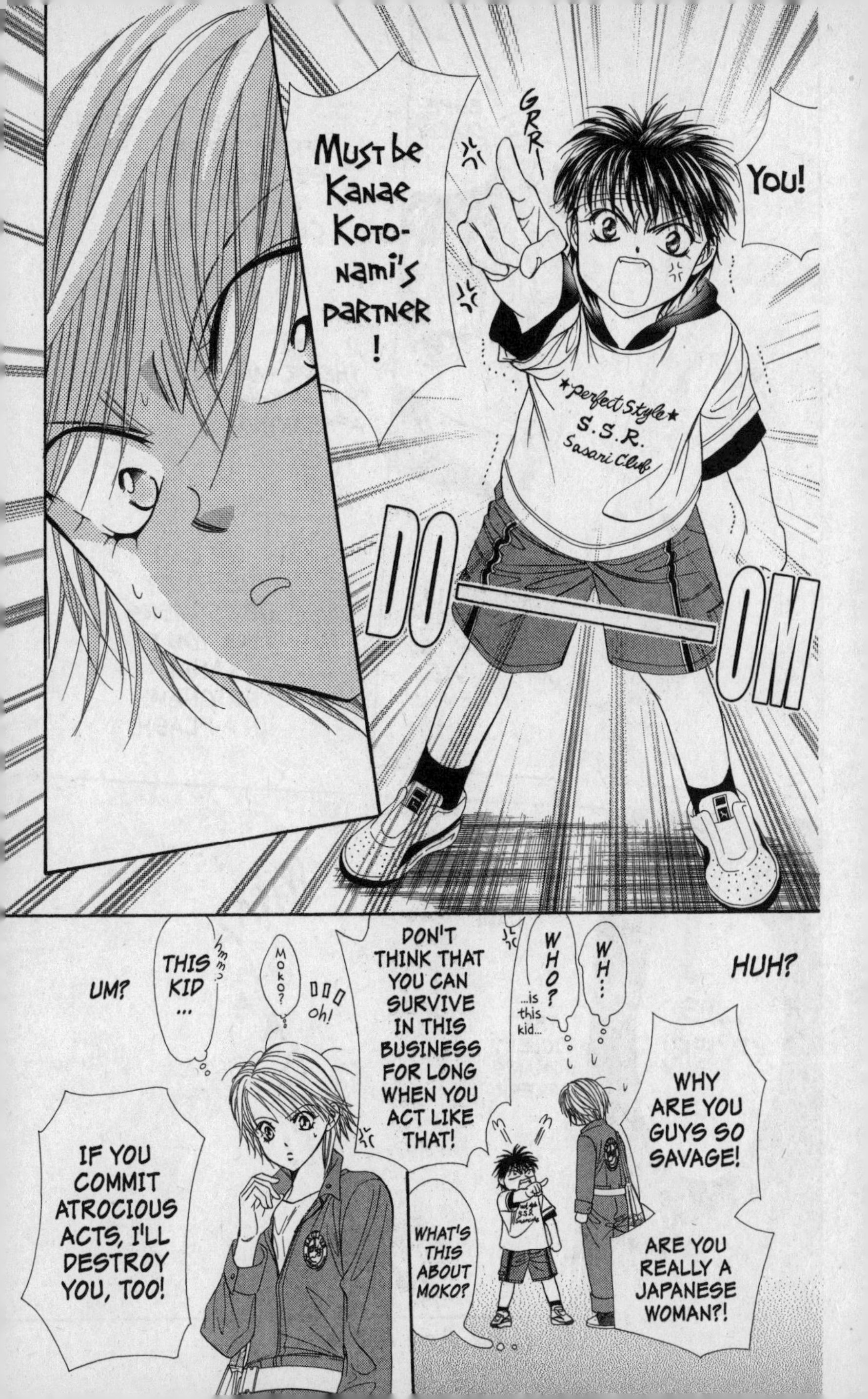
YOU!
GRR!
Must be Kanae Koto-nami's partner!
DOOM
HUH?
WH...
WHO?
...is this kid...
DON'T THINK THAT YOU CAN SURVIVE IN THIS BUSINESS FOR LONG WHEN YOU ACT LIKE THAT!
Moko?
oh!
THIS KID...
hmm?
UM?
WHY ARE YOU GUYS SO SAVAGE!
ARE YOU REALLY A JAPANESE WOMAN?!
WHAT'S THIS ABOUT MOKO?
IF YOU COMMIT ATROCIOUS ACTS, I'LL DESTROY YOU, TOO!

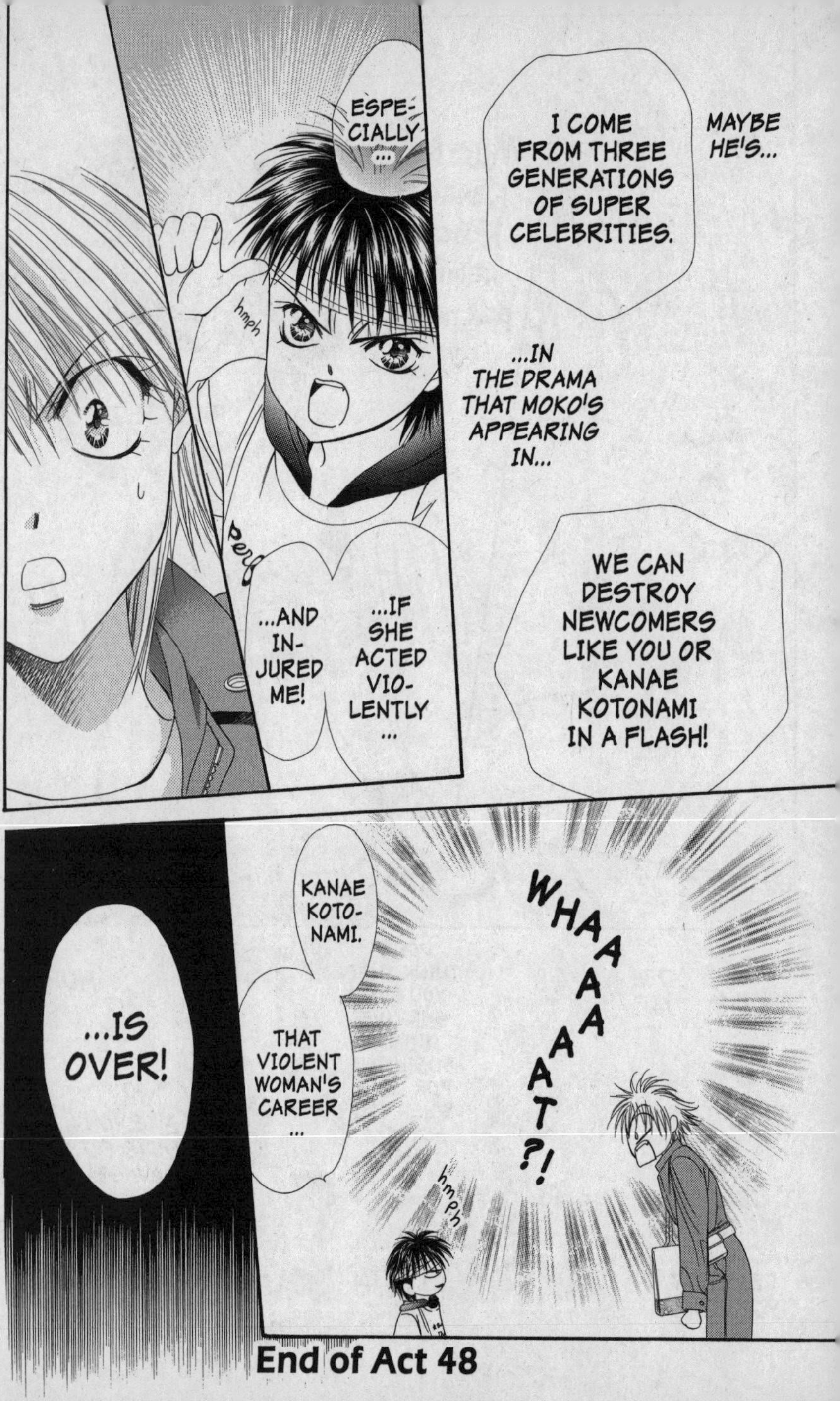
MAYBE HE'S...
I COME FROM THREE GENERATIONS OF SUPER CELEBRITIES.
...IN THE DRAMA THAT MOKO'S APPEARING IN...
WE CAN DESTROY NEWCOMERS LIKE YOU OR KANAE KOTONAMI IN A FLASH!
ESPE-CIALLY...
hmph
...IF SHE ACTED VIO-LENTLY...
...AND IN-JURED ME!
WHAAAAAAT?!
hmph
KANAE KOTO-NAMI.
THAT VIOLENT WOMAN'S CAREER...
...IS OVER!

End of Act 48

Shojo Beat

Skip·Beat!☆

Skip·Beat!

Volume 9

CONTENTS

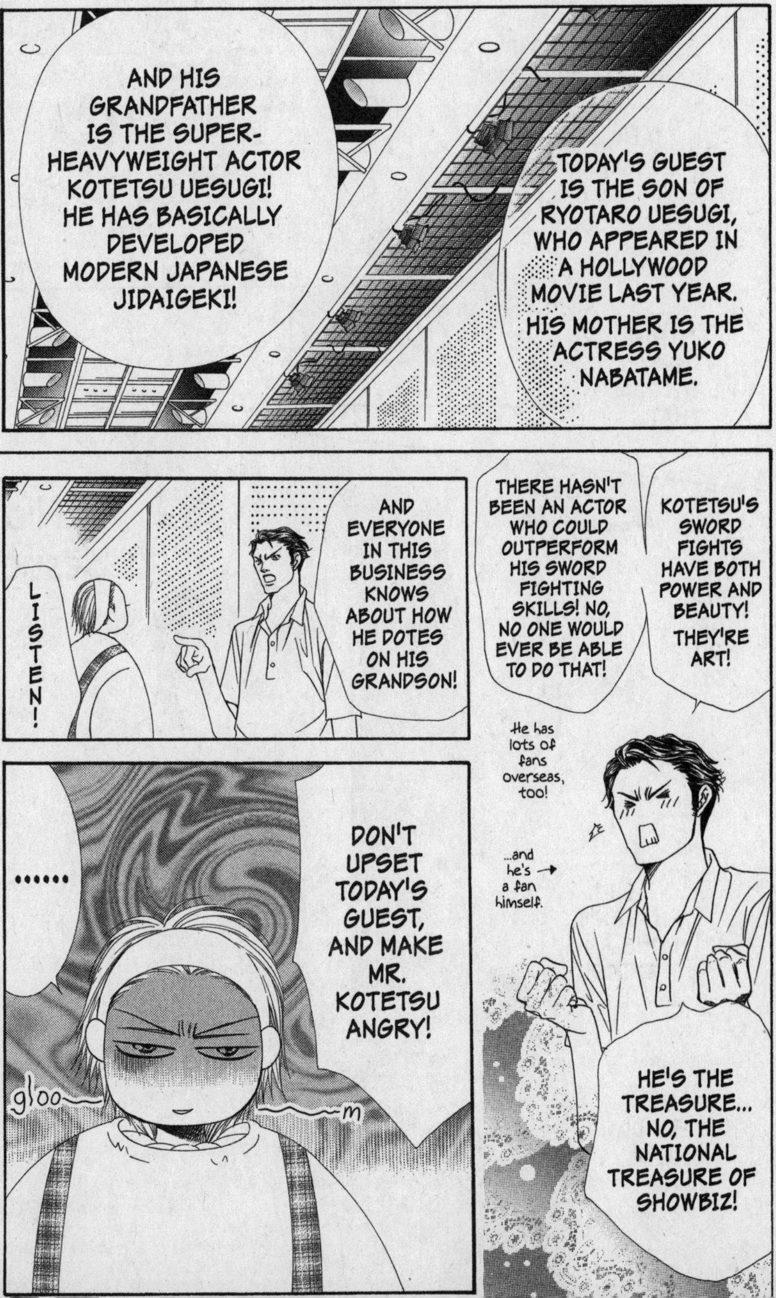
TODAY'S GUEST IS THE SON OF RYOTARO UESUGI, WHO APPEARED IN A HOLLYWOOD MOVIE LAST YEAR. HIS MOTHER IS THE ACTRESS YUKO NABATAME.
AND HIS GRANDFATHER IS THE SUPER-HEAVYWEIGHT ACTOR KOTETSU UESUGI! HE HAS BASICALLY DEVELOPED MODERN JAPANESE JIDAIGEKI!
KOTETSU'S SWORD FIGHTS HAVE BOTH POWER AND BEAUTY! THEY'RE ART!
THERE HASN'T BEEN AN ACTOR WHO COULD OUTPERFORM HIS SWORD FIGHTING SKILLS! NO, NO ONE WOULD EVER BE ABLE TO DO THAT!
He has lots of fans overseas, too!
...and he's → a fan himself.
HE'S THE TREASURE... NO, THE NATIONAL TREASURE OF SHOWBIZ!
AND EVERYONE IN THIS BUSINESS KNOWS ABOUT HOW HE DOTES ON HIS GRANDSON!
LISTEN!
DON'T UPSET TODAY'S GUEST, AND MAKE MR. KOTETSU ANGRY!
......
gloo~~ ~~~m

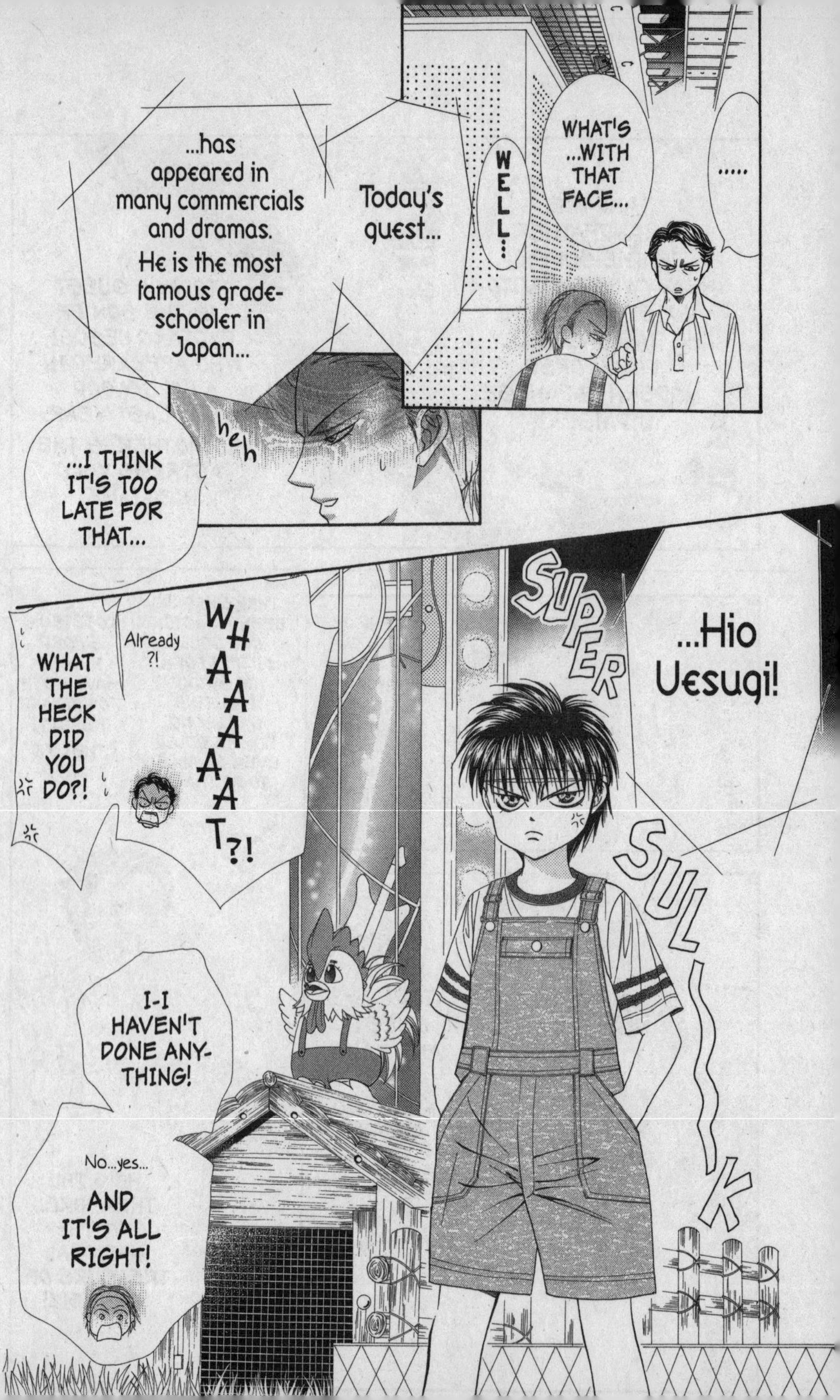
.....
WHAT'S ...WITH THAT FACE...
WELL...
Today's guest...
...has appeared in many commercials and dramas. He is the most famous grade-schooler in Japan...
heh
...I THINK IT'S TOO LATE FOR THAT...
SUPER
...Hio Uesugi!
SULK
WHAAAAAT?!
Already ?!
WHAT THE HECK DID YOU DO?!
I-I HAVEN'T DONE ANY-THING!
No...yes...
AND IT'S ALL RIGHT!

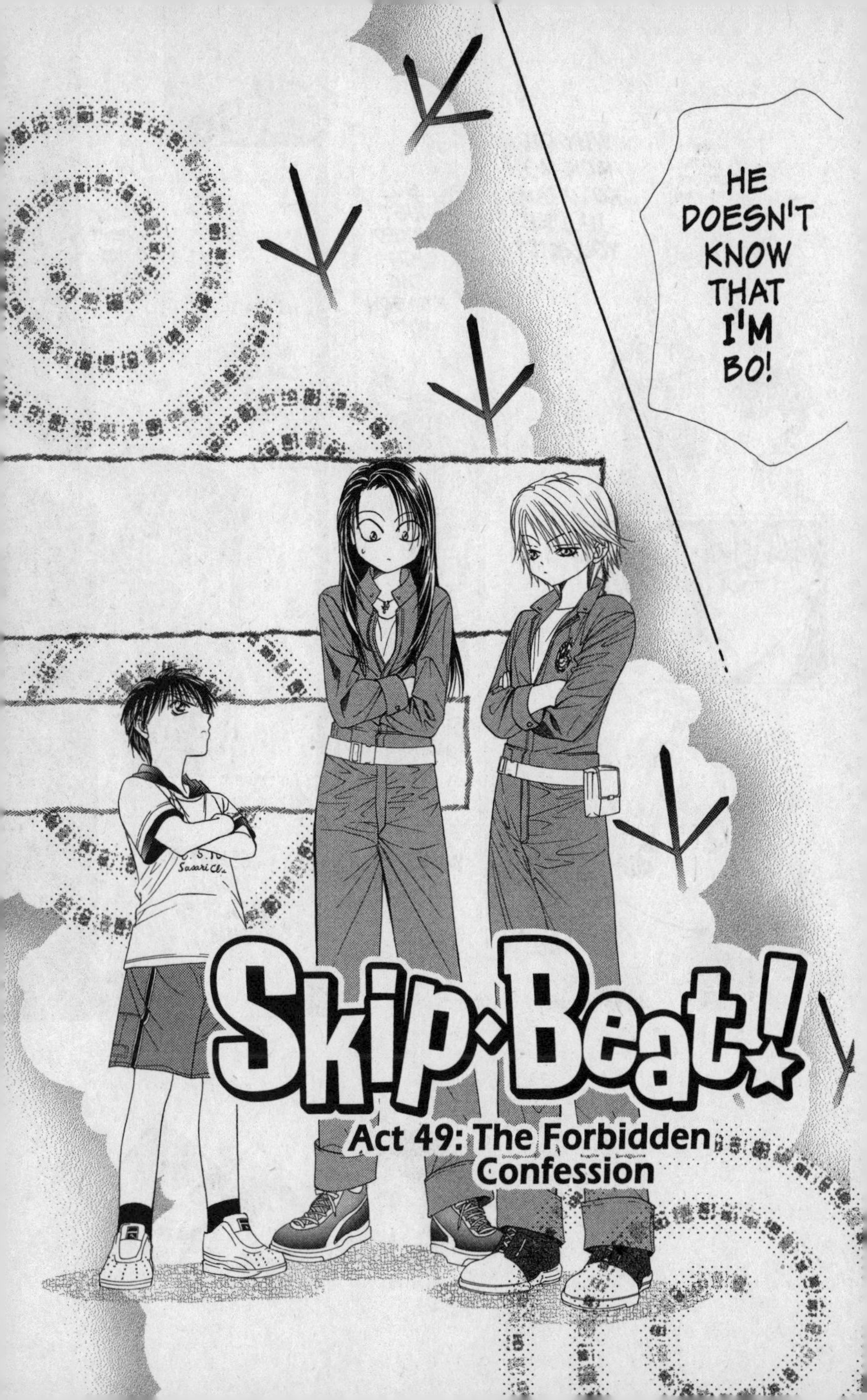
HE DOESN'T KNOW THAT I'M BO!
Skip·Beat!
Act 49: The Forbidden Confession

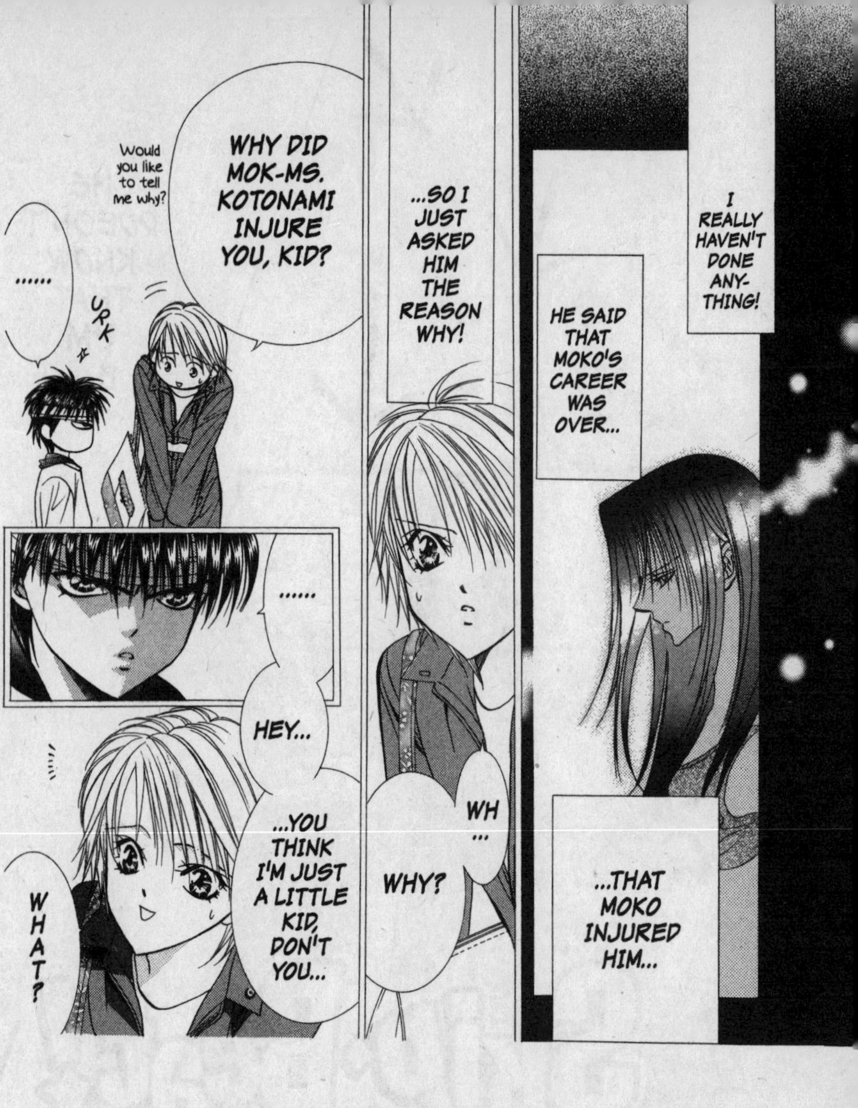
I REALLY HAVEN'T DONE ANY-THING!
HE SAID THAT MOKO'S CAREER WAS OVER...
...THAT MOKO INJURED HIM...
...SO I JUST ASKED HIM THE REASON WHY!
WH...
WHY?
WHY DID MOK-MS. KOTONAMI INJURE YOU, KID?
Would you like to tell me why?
URK
......
......
HEY...
...YOU THINK I'M JUST A LITTLE KID, DON'T YOU...
WHAT?
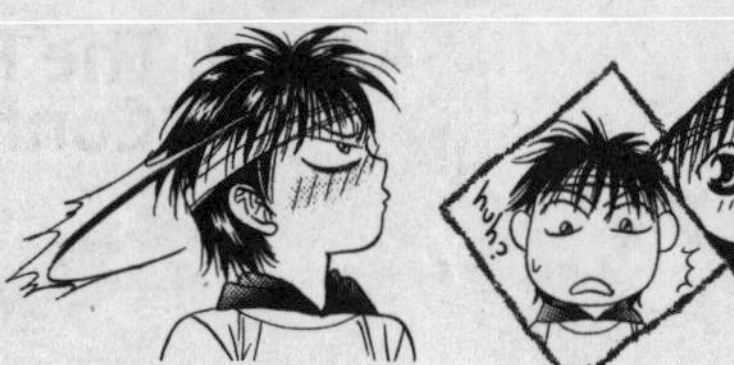
huh?

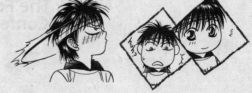

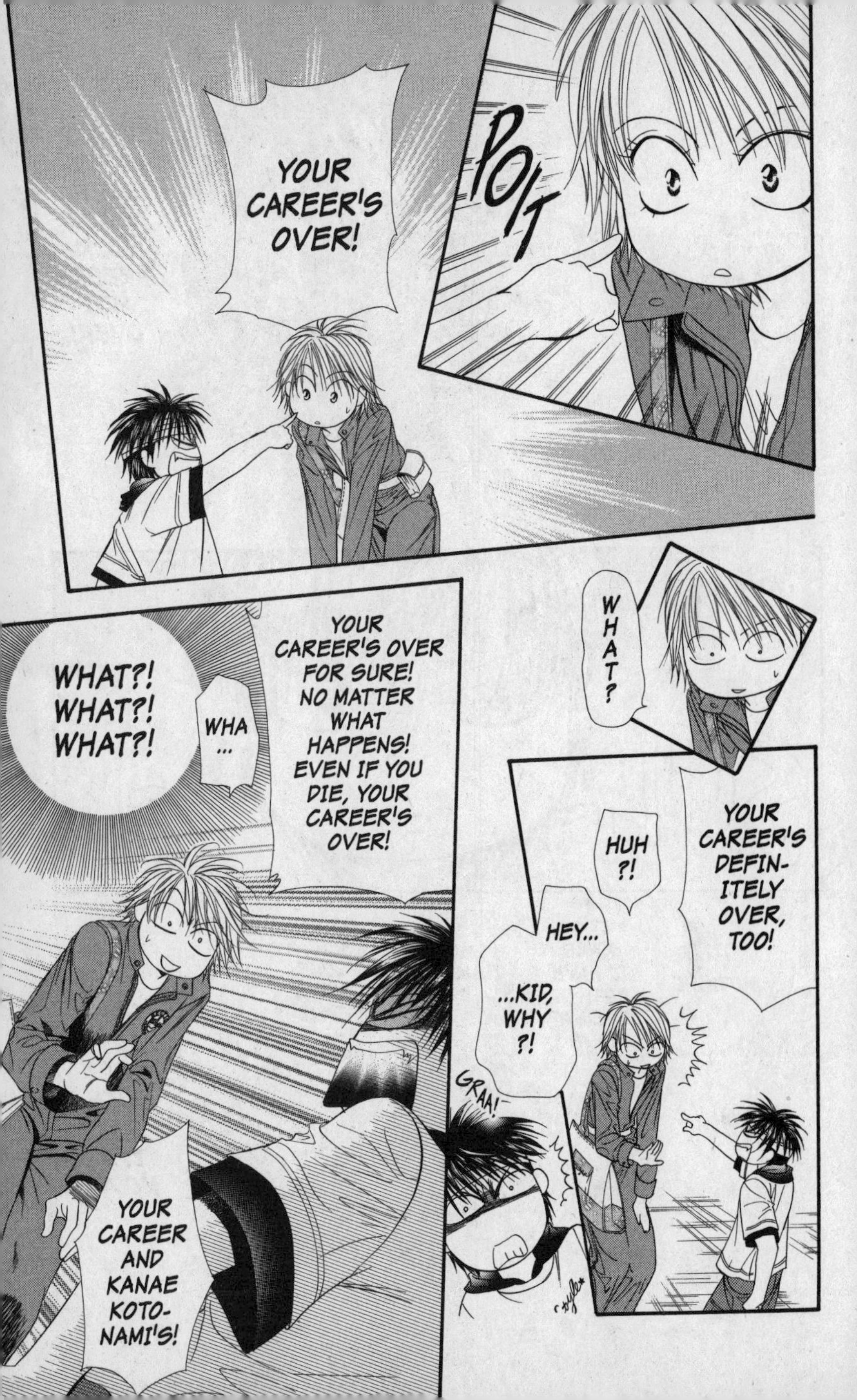
POIT
YOUR CAREER'S OVER!
WHAT?
YOUR CAREER'S DEFINITELY OVER, TOO!
HUH?!
HEY...
...KID, WHY?!
GRAA!
YOUR CAREER'S OVER FOR SURE! NO MATTER WHAT HAPPENS! EVEN IF YOU DIE, YOUR CAREER'S OVER!
WHA...
WHAT?! WHAT?! WHAT?!
YOUR CAREER AND KANAE KOTONAMI'S!

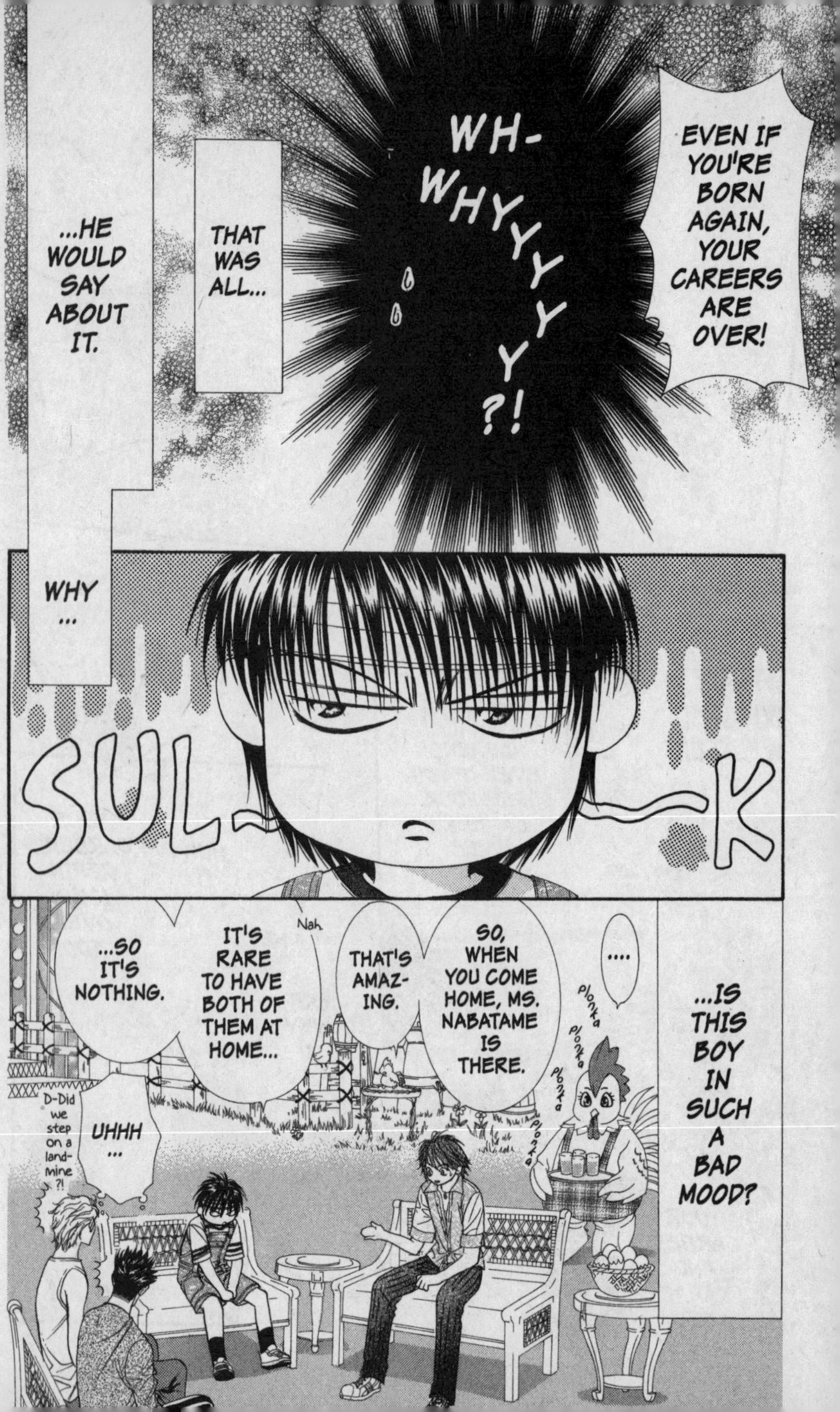

EVEN IF YOU'RE BORN AGAIN, YOUR CAREERS ARE OVER!
WH-WHYYYYYY?!
THAT WAS ALL...
...HE WOULD SAY ABOUT IT.
WHY ...
SUL—K
...IS THIS BOY IN SUCH A BAD MOOD?
....
SO, WHEN YOU COME HOME, MS. NABATAME IS THERE.
Plonka Plonka Plonka Plonka
THAT'S AMAZ-ING.
Nah.
IT'S RARE TO HAVE BOTH OF THEM AT HOME...
...SO IT'S NOTHING.
UHHH ...
D-Did we step on a land-mine ?!

Greetings

I'll start by apologizing... the blank spaces haven't been filled this time as well... And I think this volume I spent the most time fixing things...

I tend to take time fixing things for the tankobon. This time I did them in bits, because I had three manuscripts to do for the magazine, so the total was about nine days...(that's too long...) Usually, I go over the typesetting, redraw the cuts I don't like, and add effects that I couldn't do when the manuscript was first printed in the magazine. However, this time, the obvious reason is that due to certain circumstances, I re-applied screentones for most of the characters' shadows in this volume. I really want to say thanks to my assistants. Thank yoooooooou!!

The third round of fixing was for the pages before and after the 2-page Ren cover illustration (the extra episodes), the title page illustration and filling in the blank spaces...I wasn't going to do them because I didn't have the time...but I ended up doing them...without telling my editor... (Well...since I submit them to the editorial department, they find out anyway... Wry smile...

So this Vol. 9 really consists of blood, sweat, and tears...I would be very happy if all you readers enjoy it...

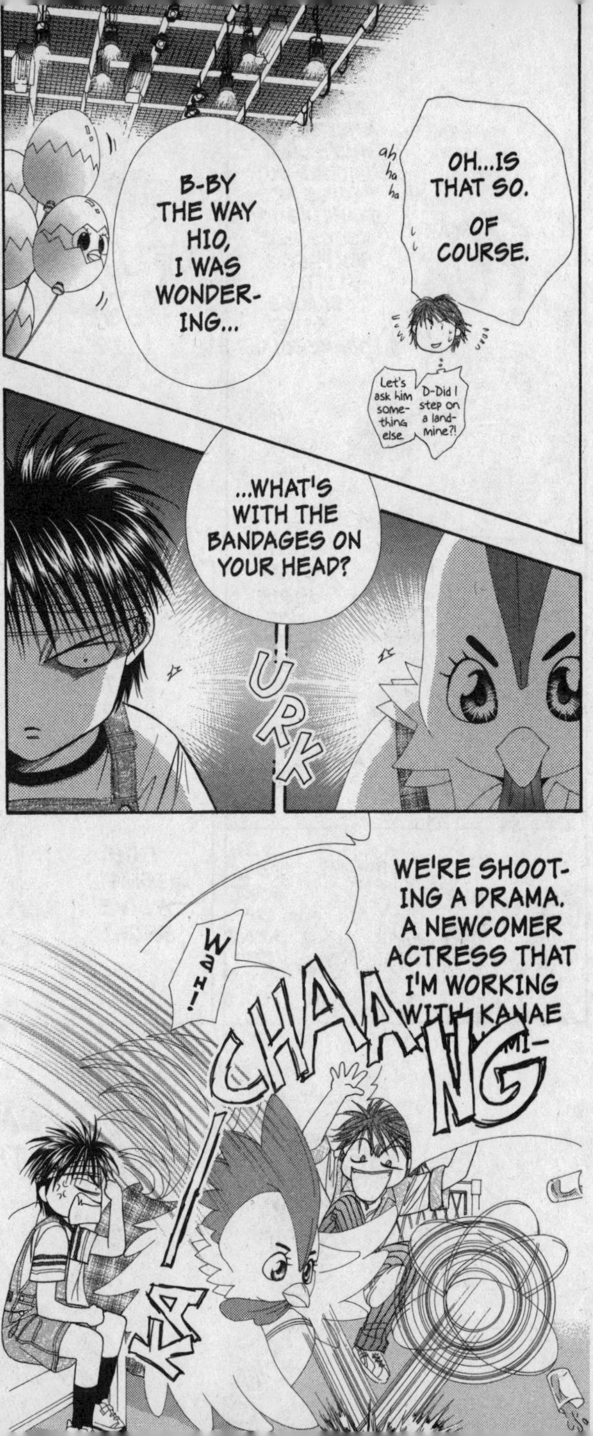
ah ha ha
OH...IS THAT SO. OF COURSE.
D-Did I step on a land-mine?!
Let's ask him something else.
B-BY THE WAY HIO, I WAS WONDERING...
...WHAT'S WITH THE BANDAGES ON YOUR HEAD?
URK
WE'RE SHOOTING A DRAMA. A NEWCOMER ACTRESS THAT I'M WORKING WITH KANAE MI-
CHAANG
WAH!
KA

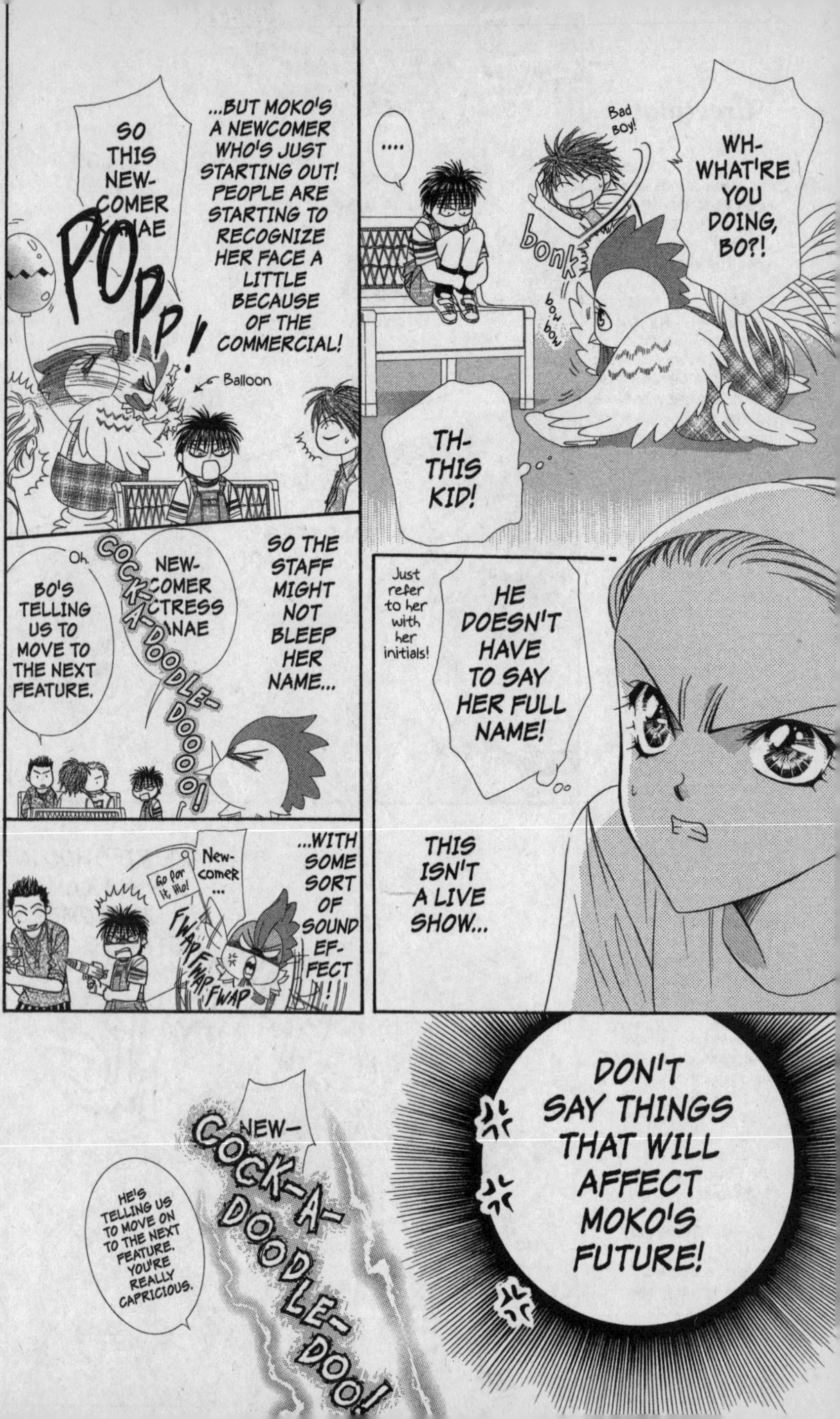
WH-WHAT'RE YOU DOING, BO?!
Bad boy!
bonk
bow bow
....
TH-THIS KID!
SO THIS NEWCOMER KANAE
...BUT MOKO'S A NEWCOMER WHO'S JUST STARTING OUT! PEOPLE ARE STARTING TO RECOGNIZE HER FACE A LITTLE BECAUSE OF THE COMMERCIAL!
POPP!
Balloon
Just refer to her with her initials!
HE DOESN'T HAVE TO SAY HER FULL NAME!
THIS ISN'T A LIVE SHOW...
SO THE STAFF MIGHT NOT BLEEP HER NAME...
NEWCOMER ACTRESS KANAE
COCK-A-DOODLE-DOOOOO!
Oh.
BO'S TELLING US TO MOVE TO THE NEXT FEATURE.
...WITH SOME SORT OF SOUND EFFECT!
Newcomer...
FWAP FWAP FWAP
Go for It, Hio!
DON'T SAY THINGS THAT WILL AFFECT MOKO'S FUTURE!
NEW-
COCK-A-DOODLE-DOO!
HE'S TELLING US TO MOVE ON TO THE NEXT FEATURE. YOU'RE REALLY CAPRICIOUS.

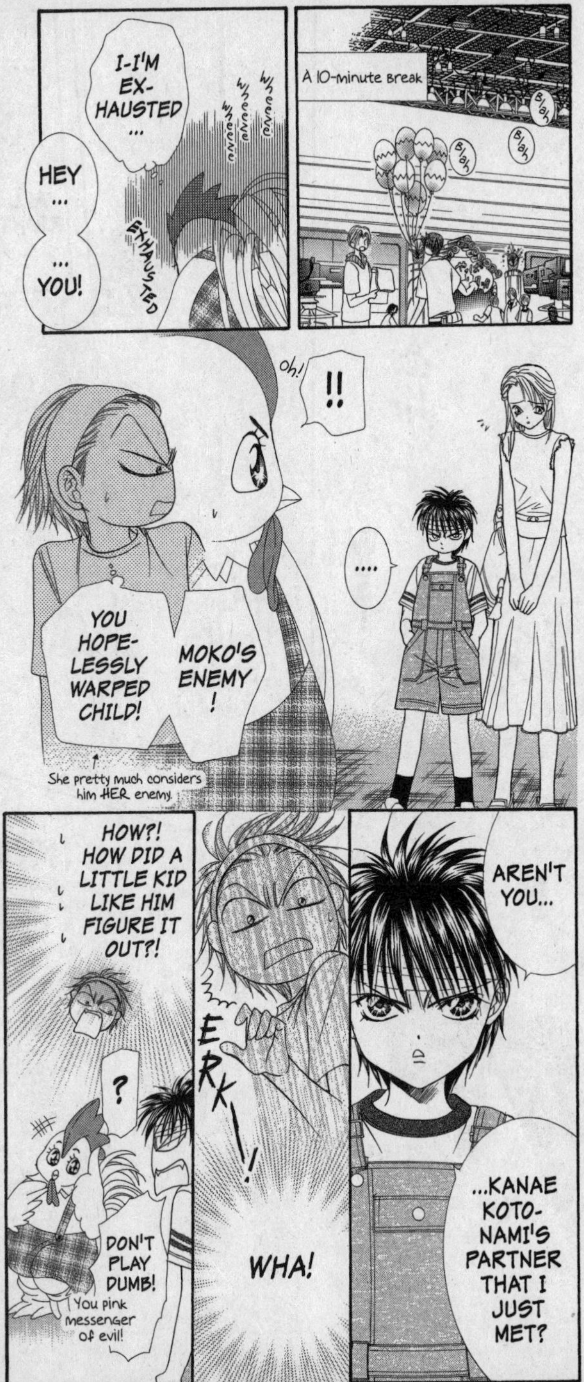
A 10-minute break
Blah
Blah
Blah
I-I'M EX-HAUSTED...
wheeze wheeze wheeze wheeze
HEY...
...YOU!
EXHAUSTED
oh!
!!
....
MOKO'S ENEMY!
YOU HOPELESSLY WARPED CHILD!
She pretty much considers him HER enemy.
AREN'T YOU...
...KANAE KOTONAMI'S PARTNER THAT I JUST MET?
ERK!!
WHA!
HOW?! HOW DID A LITTLE KID LIKE HIM FIGURE IT OUT?!
?
DON'T PLAY DUMB!
You pink messenger of evil!
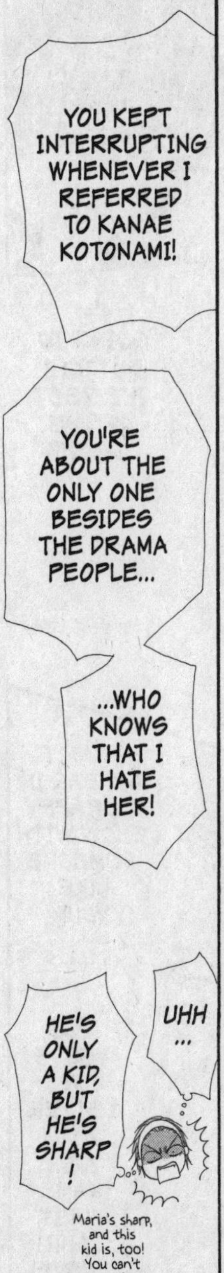
YOU KEPT INTERRUPTING WHENEVER I REFERRED TO KANAE KOTONAMI!
YOU'RE ABOUT THE ONLY ONE BESIDES THE DRAMA PEOPLE...
...WHO KNOWS THAT I HATE HER!
UHH...
HE'S ONLY A KID, BUT HE'S SHARP!
Maria's sharp, and this kid is, too! You can't underestimate them!

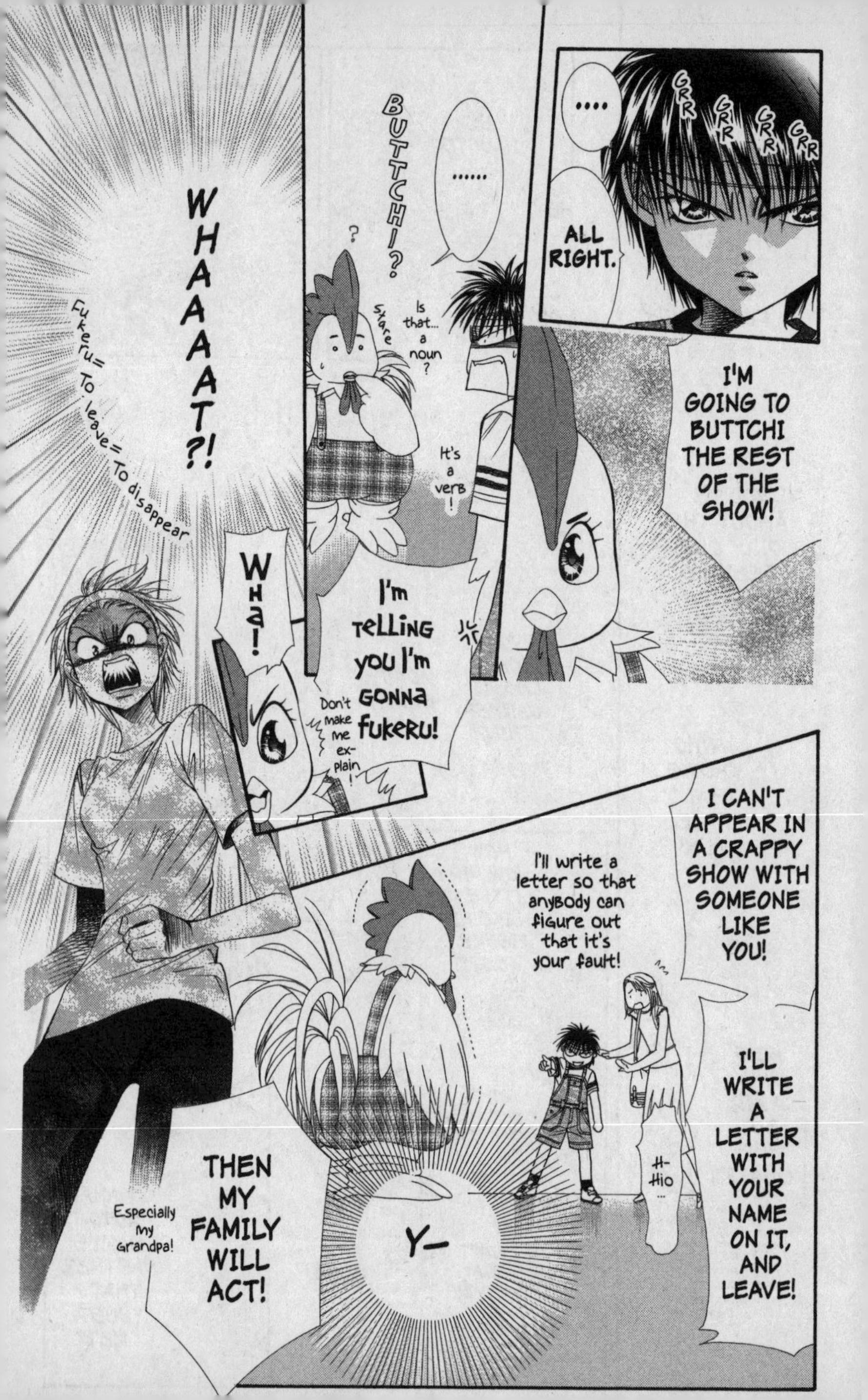
....
ALL RIGHT.
GRR GRR GRR GRR
I'M GOING TO BUTTCHI THE REST OF THE SHOW!
BUTTCHI?
......
?
Stare
Is that... a noun?
It's a verb!
I'm telling you I'm gonna fukeru!
Don't make me ex-plain!
Wha!
WHAAAAAT?!
Fukeru= To leave= To disappear
I CAN'T APPEAR IN A CRAPPY SHOW WITH SOMEONE LIKE YOU!
I'LL WRITE A LETTER WITH YOUR NAME ON IT, AND LEAVE!
I'll write a letter so that anybody can figure out that it's your fault!
H-Hio...
Y-
THEN MY FAMILY WILL ACT!
Especially my Grandpa!

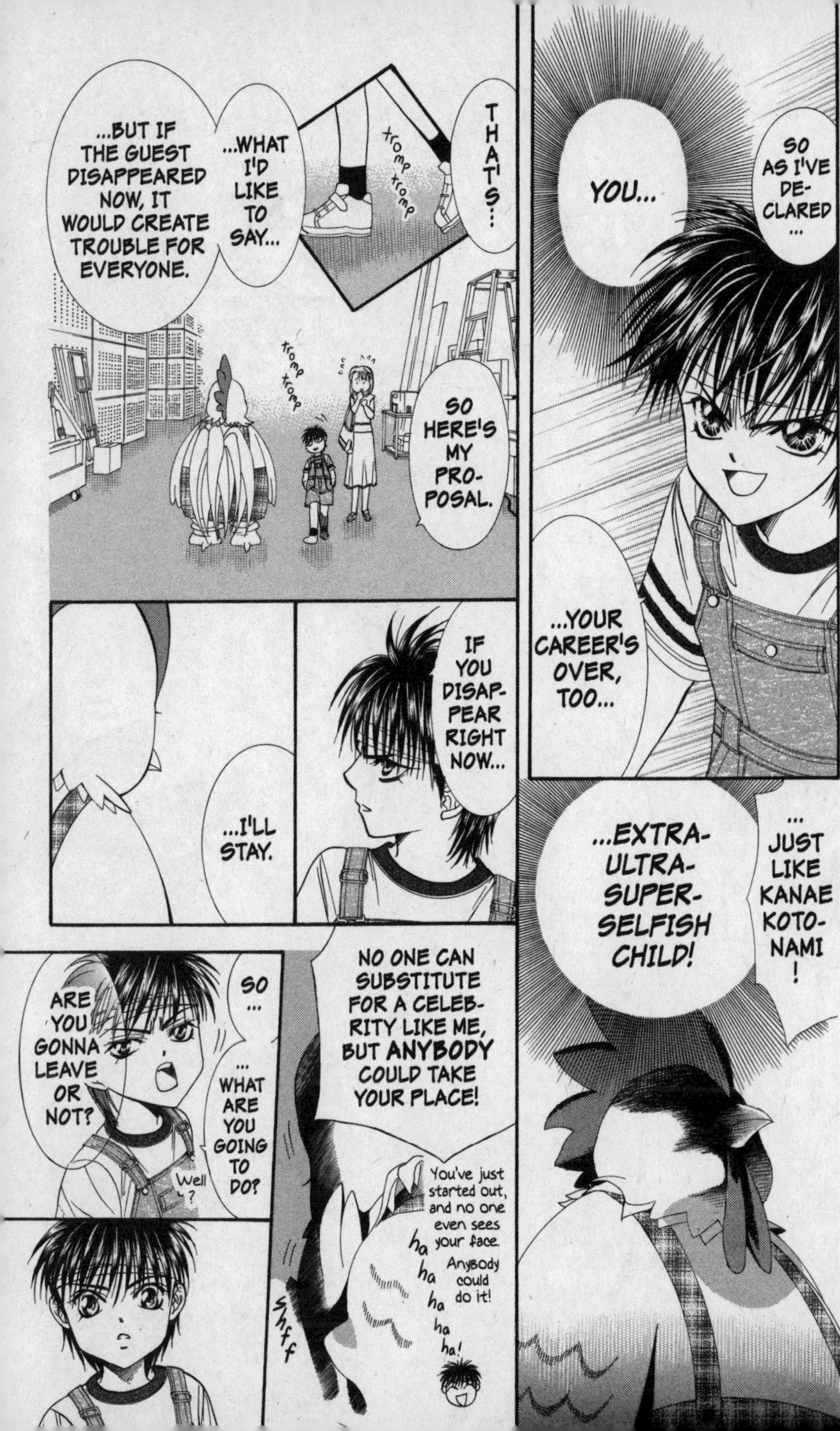

SO AS I'VE DECLARED...
YOU...
...YOUR CAREER'S OVER, TOO...
...JUST LIKE KANAE KOTONAMI!
...EXTRA-ULTRA-SUPER-SELFISH CHILD!
THAT'S...
xromp xromp
...WHAT I'D LIKE TO SAY...
...BUT IF THE GUEST DISAPPEARED NOW, IT WOULD CREATE TROUBLE FOR EVERYONE.
xromp xromp
SO HERE'S MY PROPOSAL.
IF YOU DISAPPEAR RIGHT NOW...
...I'LL STAY.
NO ONE CAN SUBSTITUTE FOR A CELEBRITY LIKE ME, BUT ANYBODY COULD TAKE YOUR PLACE!
You've just started out, and no one even sees your face.
Anybody could do it!
ha ha ha ha ha!
Shff
SO...
...WHAT ARE YOU GOING TO DO?
ARE YOU GONNA LEAVE OR NOT?
Well?

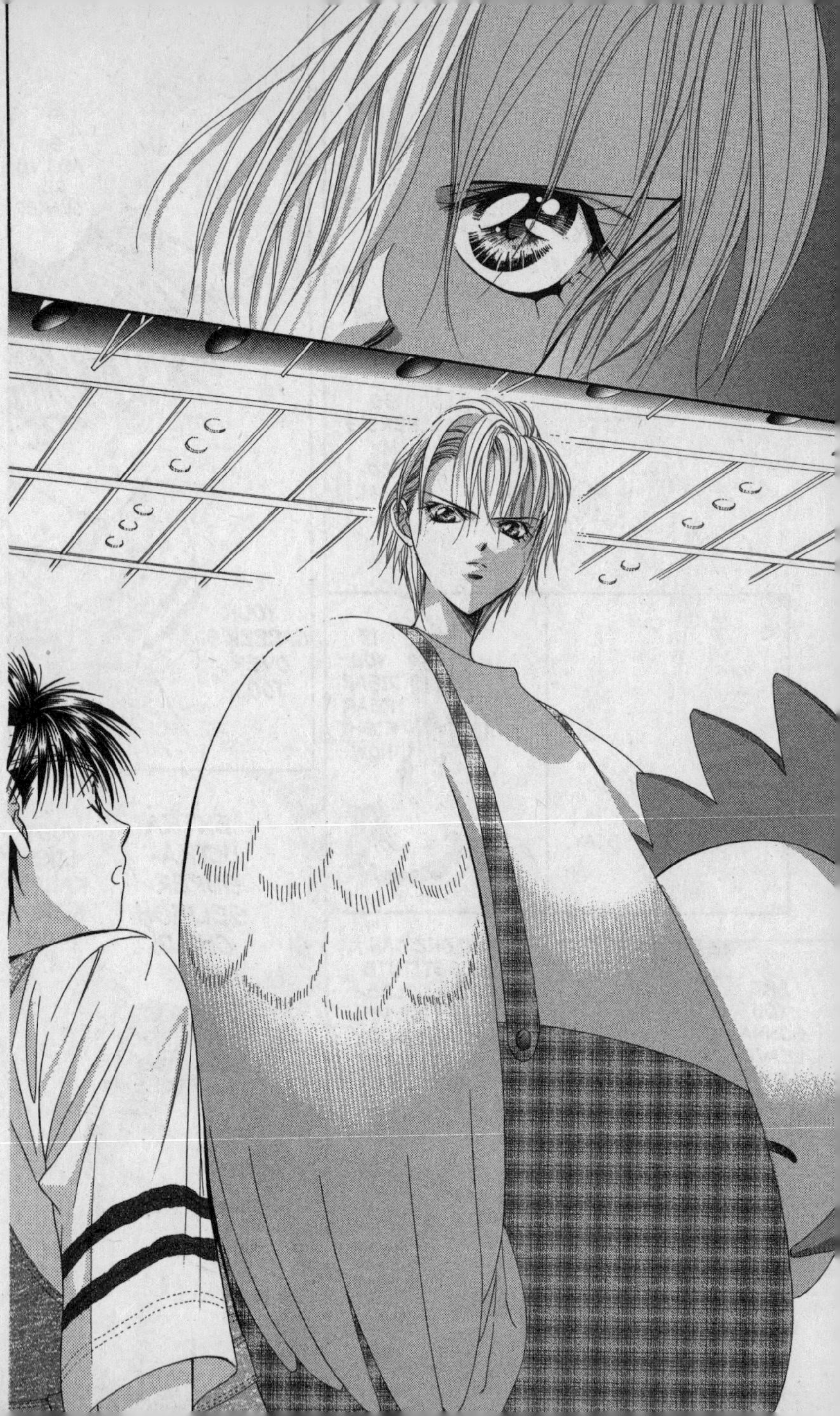

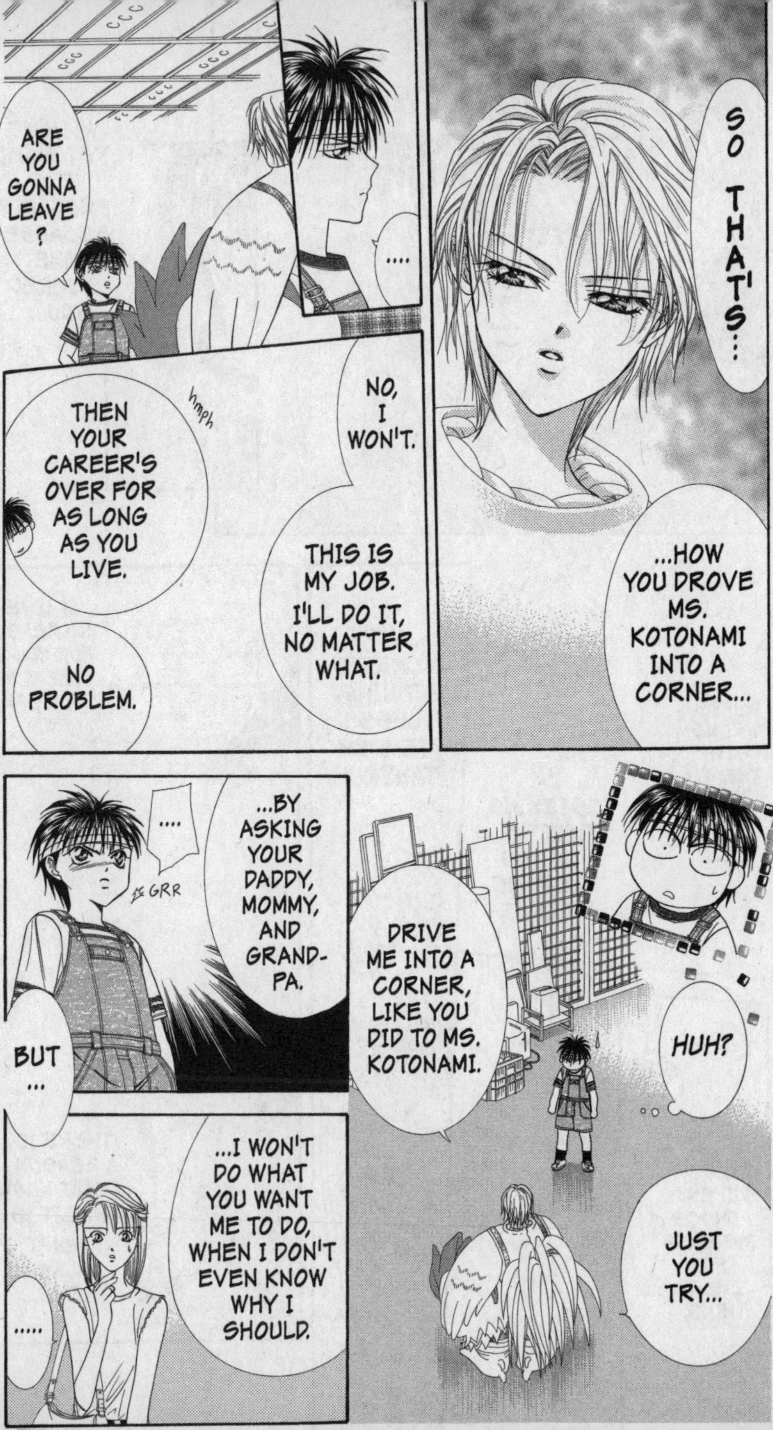
SO THAT'S...
...HOW YOU DROVE MS. KOTONAMI INTO A CORNER...
ARE YOU GONNA LEAVE?
....
NO, I WON'T.
hmph
THEN YOUR CAREER'S OVER FOR AS LONG AS YOU LIVE.
THIS IS MY JOB. I'LL DO IT, NO MATTER WHAT.
NO PROBLEM.
HUH?
JUST YOU TRY...
DRIVE ME INTO A CORNER, LIKE YOU DID TO MS. KOTONAMI.
....
...BY ASKING YOUR DADDY, MOMMY, AND GRAND-PA.
GRR
BUT...
...I WON'T DO WHAT YOU WANT ME TO DO, WHEN I DON'T EVEN KNOW WHY I SHOULD.
.....

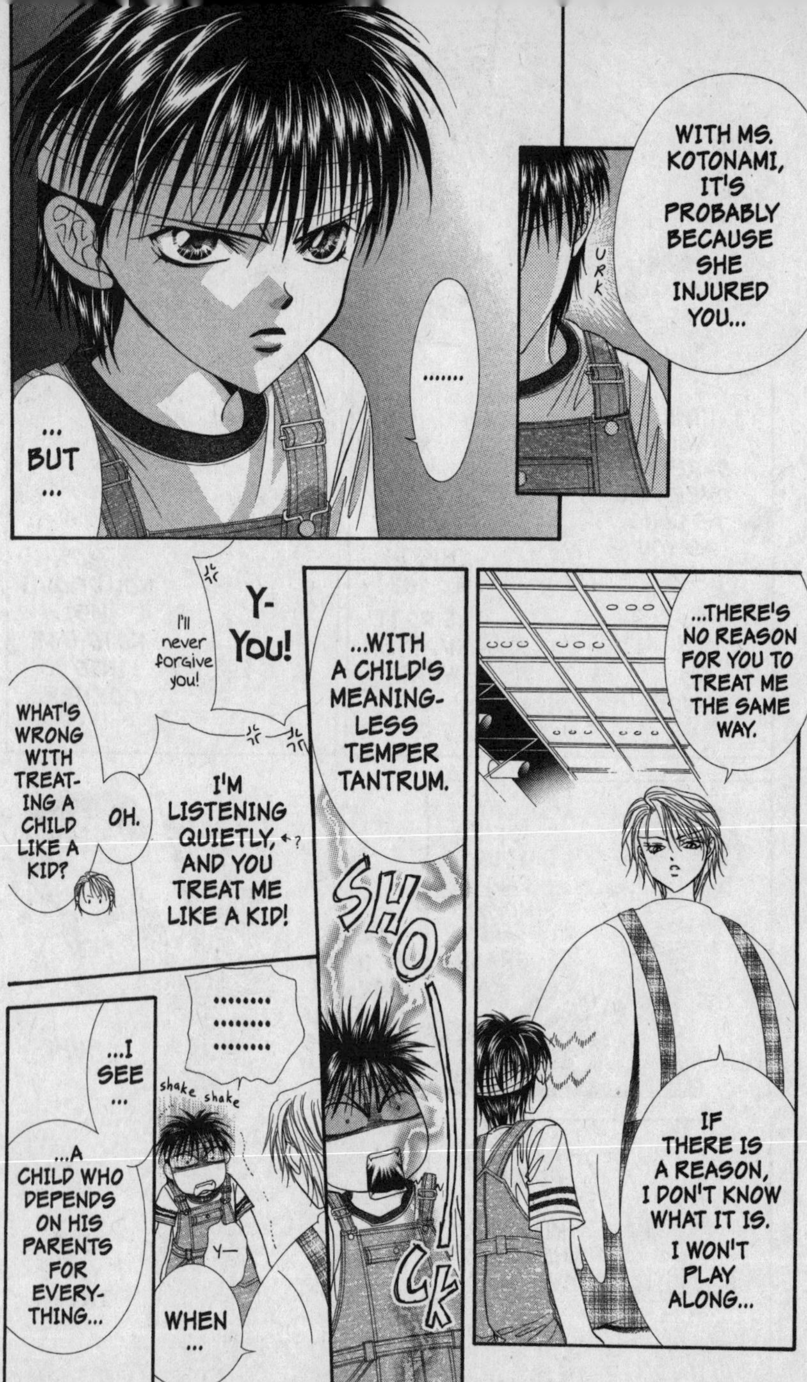

WITH MS. KOTONAMI, IT'S PROBABLY BECAUSE SHE INJURED YOU...
URK
....
...BUT...
...THERE'S NO REASON FOR YOU TO TREAT ME THE SAME WAY.
IF THERE IS A REASON, I DON'T KNOW WHAT IT IS.
I WON'T PLAY ALONG...
...WITH A CHILD'S MEANING-LESS TEMPER TANTRUM.
SHOCK
Y-YOU!
I'll never forgive you!
I'M LISTENING QUIETLY, AND YOU TREAT ME LIKE A KID!
?
OH.
WHAT'S WRONG WITH TREAT-ING A CHILD LIKE A KID?
....
...I SEE...
shake shake
...A CHILD WHO DEPENDS ON HIS PARENTS FOR EVERY-THING...
Y—
WHEN...

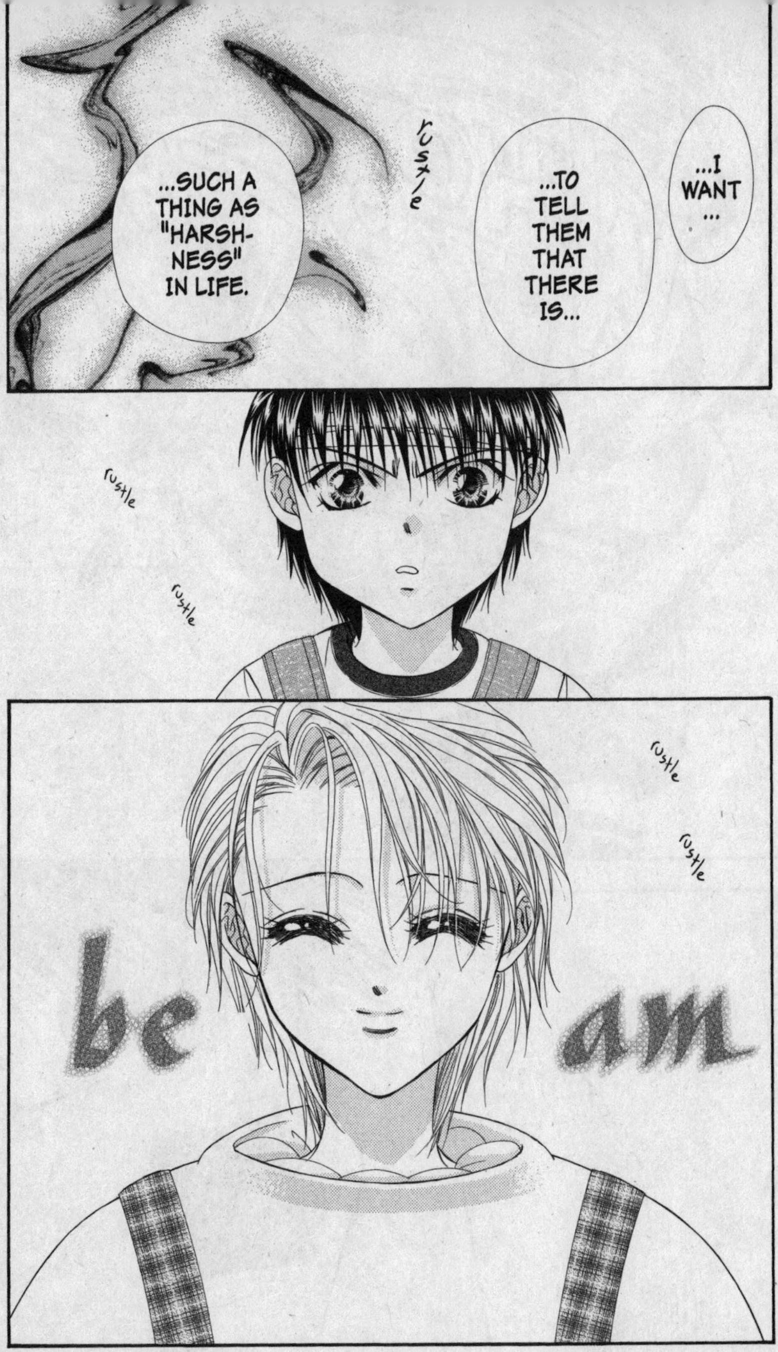
...I WANT...
...TO TELL THEM THAT THERE IS...
rustle
...SUCH A THING AS "HARSHNESS" IN LIFE.
rustle
rustle
rustle
rustle
be am

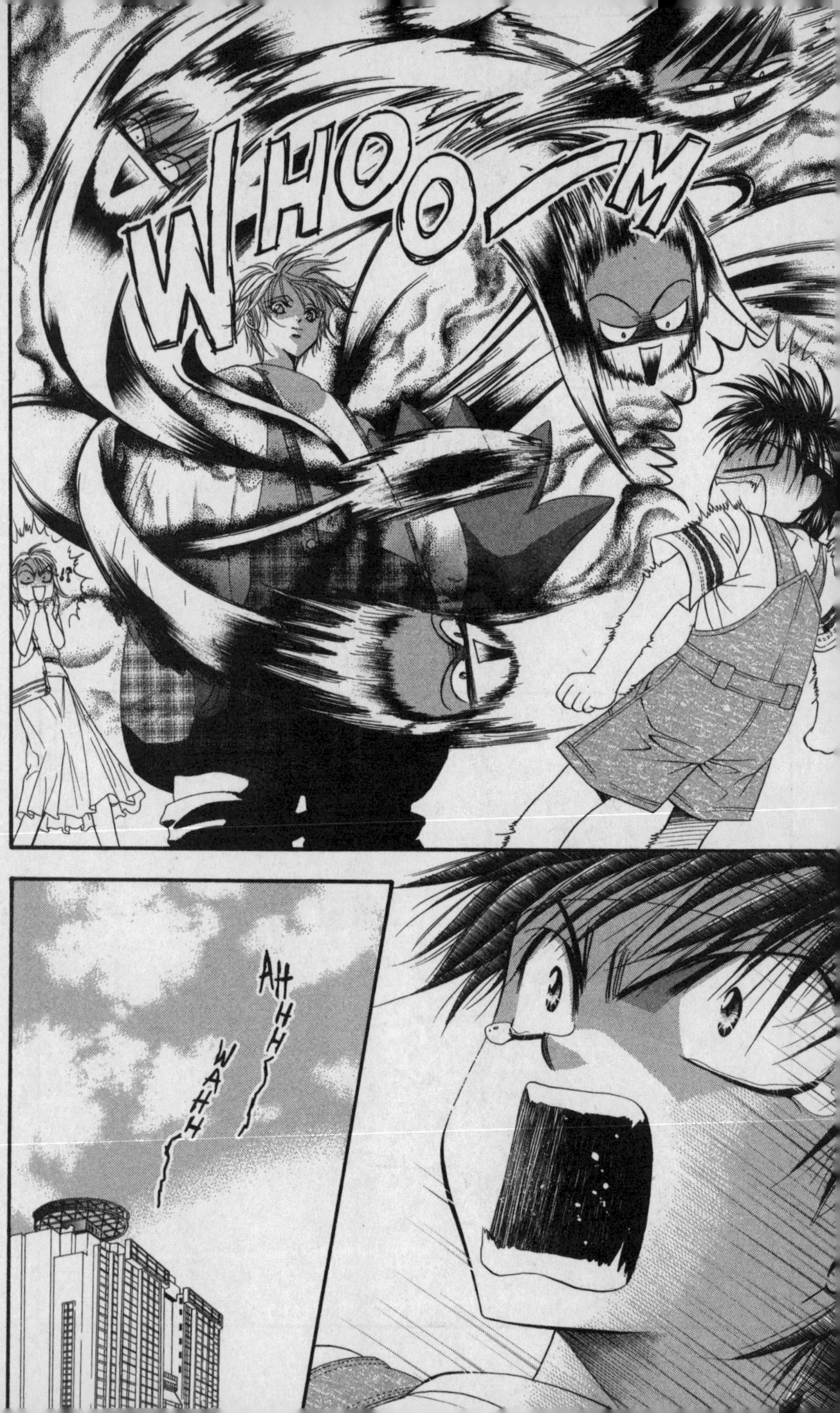
WHOO—M
AHHHH—
WAHHH—

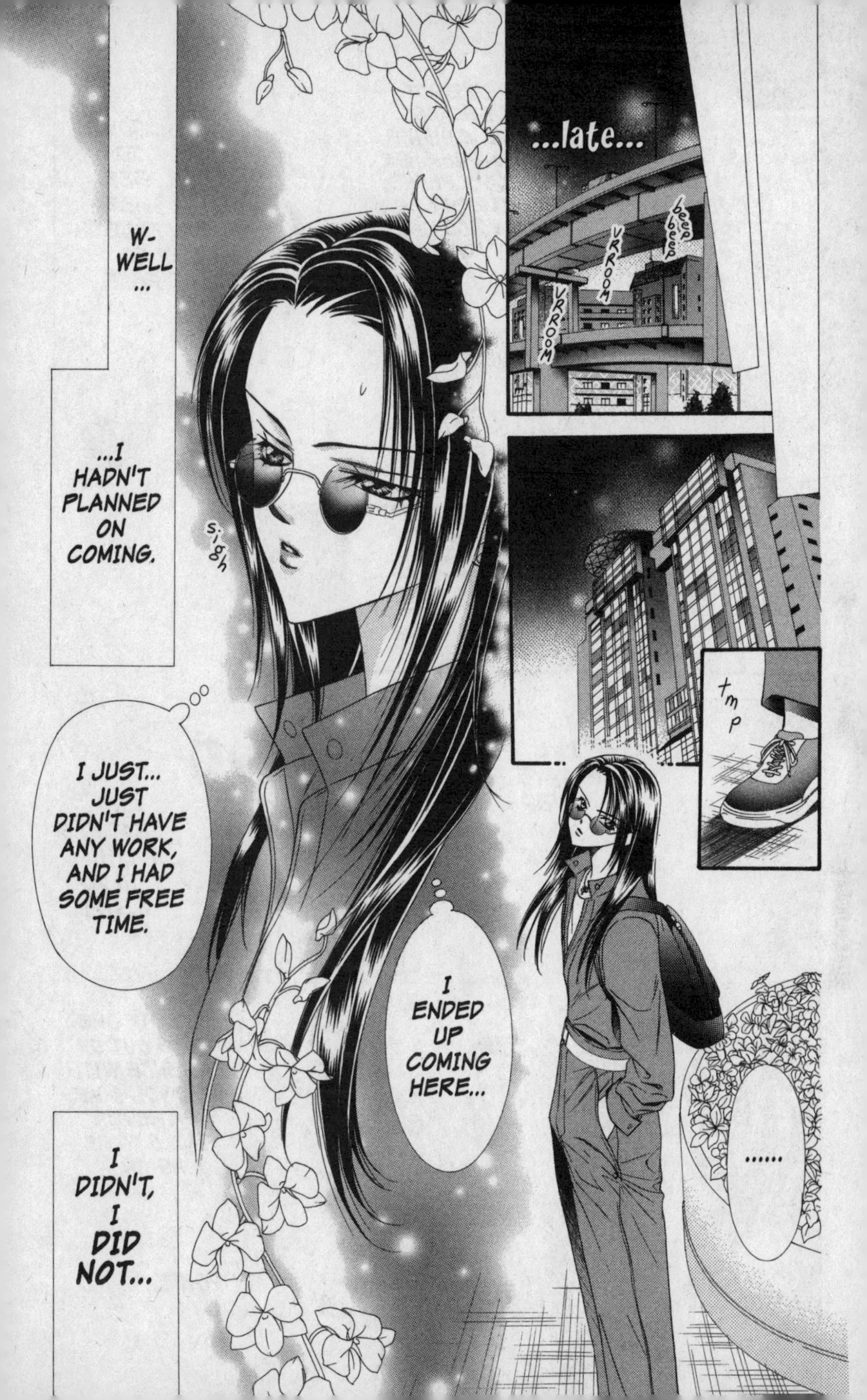
...late...
beep beep
VRROOM
VRROOM
tmp
W-WELL ...
...I HADN'T PLANNED ON COMING.
sigh
I JUST... JUST DIDN'T HAVE ANY WORK, AND I HAD SOME FREE TIME.
......
I ENDED UP COMING HERE...
I DIDN'T, I DID NOT...

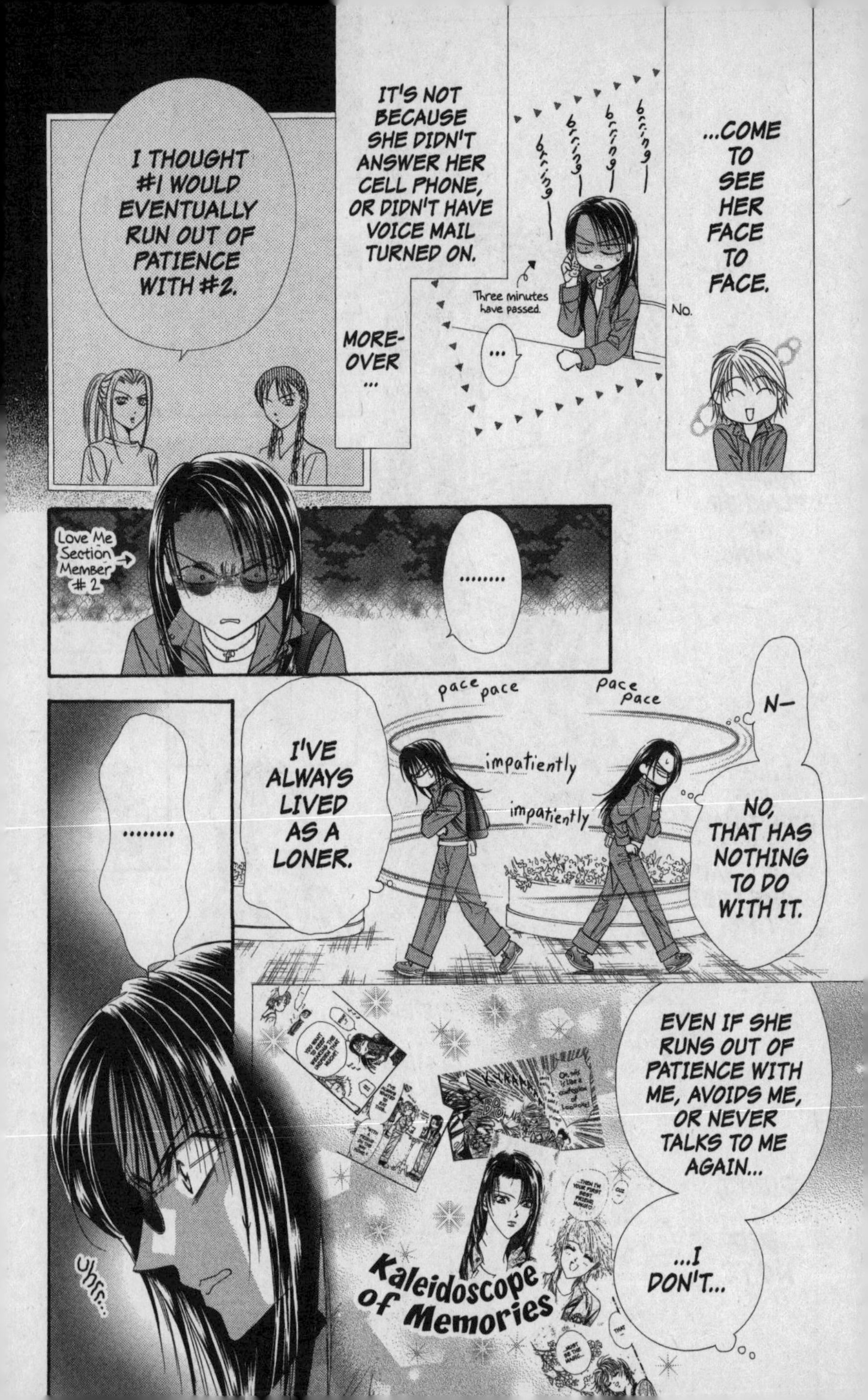
...COME TO SEE HER FACE TO FACE.
No.
IT'S NOT BECAUSE SHE DIDN'T ANSWER HER CELL PHONE, OR DIDN'T HAVE VOICE MAIL TURNED ON.
brring brring brring brring
Three minutes have passed.
MORE-OVER...
...
I THOUGHT #1 WOULD EVENTUALLY RUN OUT OF PATIENCE WITH #2.
....
Love Me Section Member #2
pace pace
pace pace
N—
NO, THAT HAS NOTHING TO DO WITH IT.
impatiently
impatiently
I'VE ALWAYS LIVED AS A LONER.
EVEN IF SHE RUNS OUT OF PATIENCE WITH ME, AVOIDS ME, OR NEVER TALKS TO ME AGAIN...
...I DON'T...
Kaleidoscope of Memories
....
uhrr...

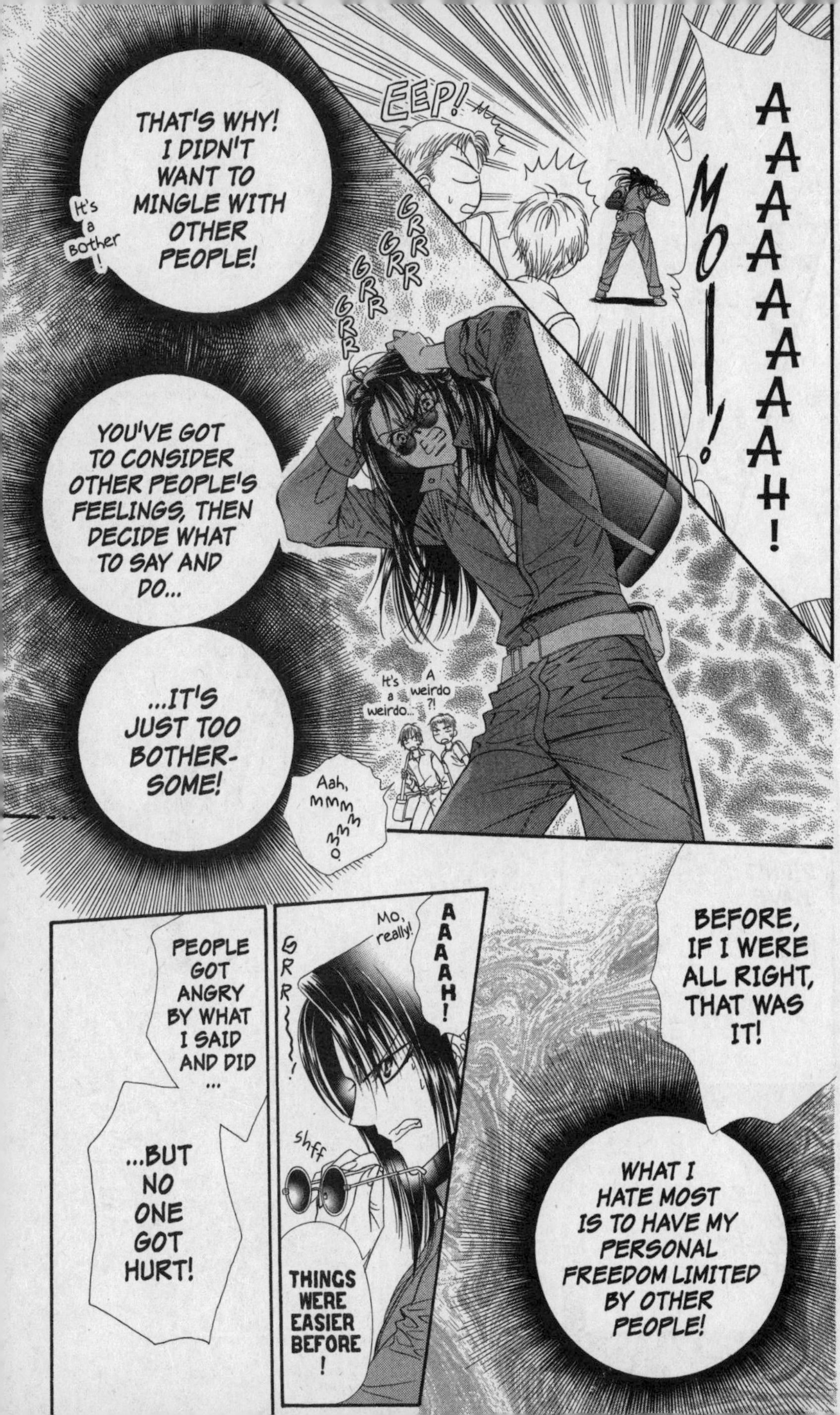
AAAAAAAAAH!
MO!!
EEP!
GRR GRR GRR GRR
THAT'S WHY! I DIDN'T WANT TO MINGLE WITH OTHER PEOPLE!
It's a bother!
YOU'VE GOT TO CONSIDER OTHER PEOPLE'S FEELINGS, THEN DECIDE WHAT TO SAY AND DO...
...IT'S JUST TOO BOTHER-SOME!
A weirdo?!
It's a weirdo...
Aah, mmmmmmo.
BEFORE, IF I WERE ALL RIGHT, THAT WAS IT!
WHAT I HATE MOST IS TO HAVE MY PERSONAL FREEDOM LIMITED BY OTHER PEOPLE!
AAAAH!
Mo, really!
GRR~!
shff
THINGS WERE EASIER BEFORE!
PEOPLE GOT ANGRY BY WHAT I SAID AND DID...
...BUT NO ONE GOT HURT!

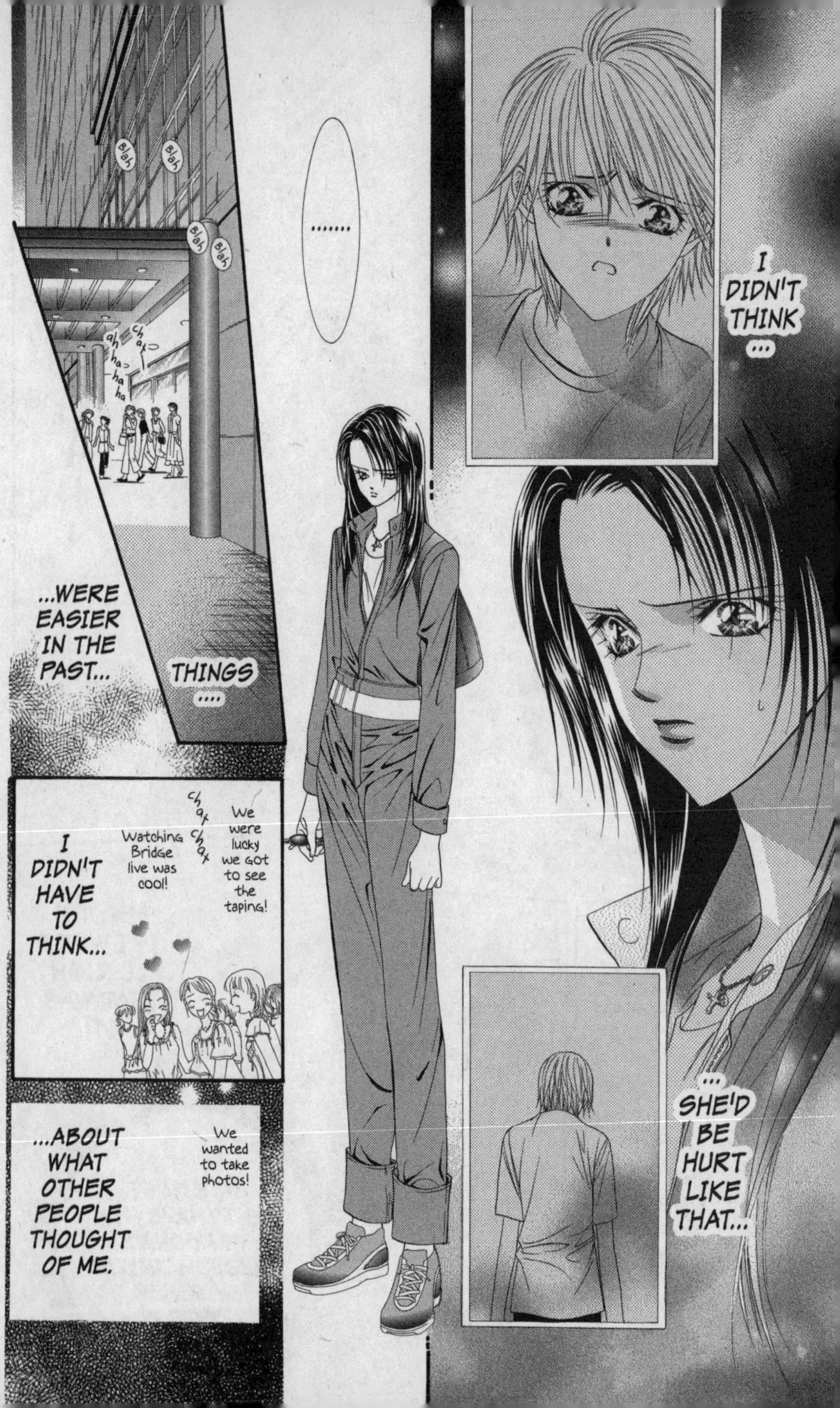
I DIDN'T THINK...
...SHE'D BE HURT LIKE THAT...
....
Blah Blah
Blah Blah
chat
ah ha ha ha
THINGS....
...WERE EASIER IN THE PAST...
I DIDN'T HAVE TO THINK...
We were lucky we got to see the taping!
chat chat
Watching Bridge live was cool!
...ABOUT WHAT OTHER PEOPLE THOUGHT OF ME.
We wanted to take photos!

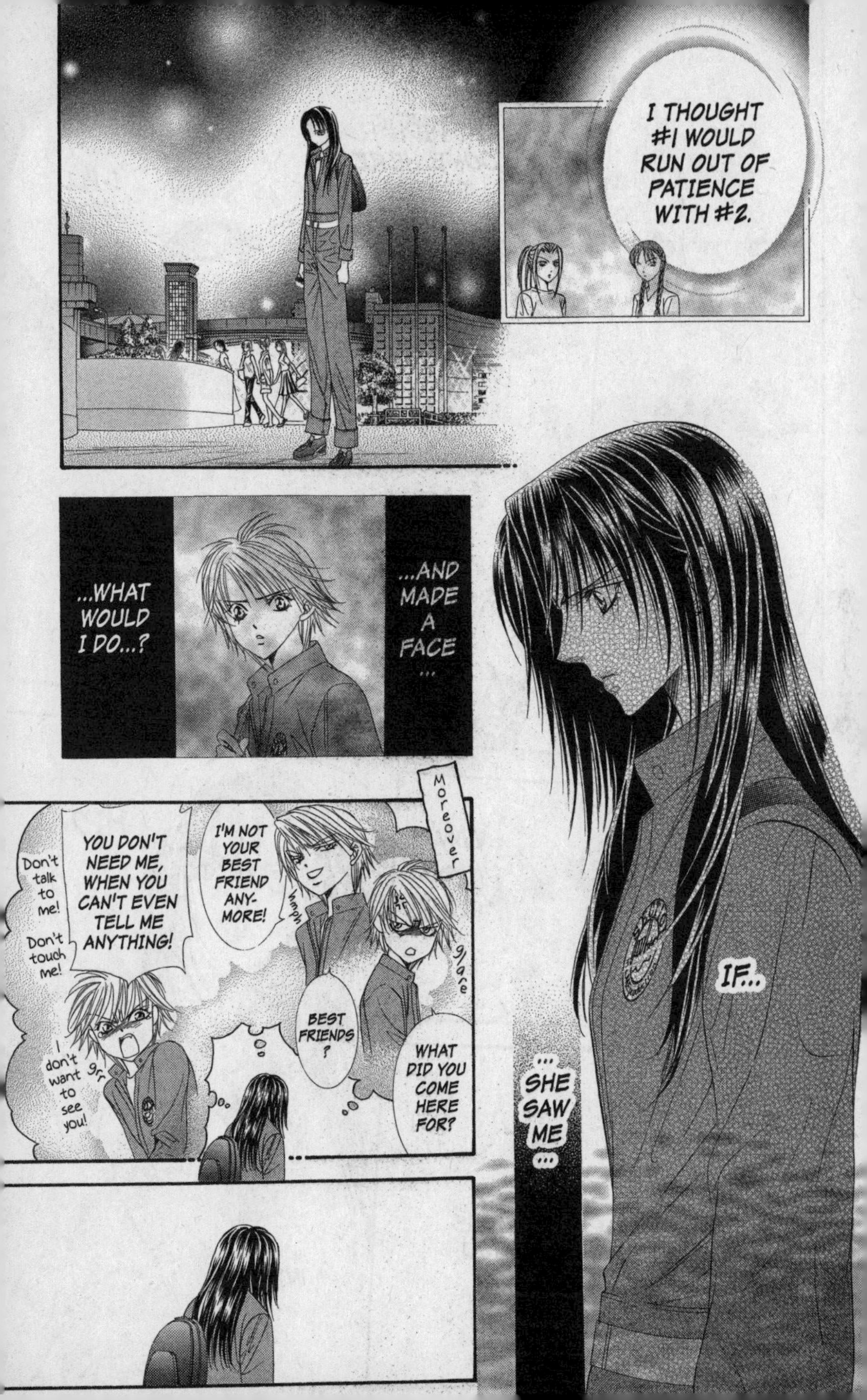
I THOUGHT #1 WOULD RUN OUT OF PATIENCE WITH #2.
IF...
...SHE SAW ME...
...AND MADE A FACE...
...WHAT WOULD I DO...?
Moreover
I'M NOT YOUR BEST FRIEND ANY-MORE!
hmph
glare
YOU DON'T NEED ME, WHEN YOU CAN'T EVEN TELL ME ANYTHING!
Don't talk to me!
Don't touch me!
grr
I don't want to see you!
WHAT DID YOU COME HERE FOR?
BEST FRIENDS?

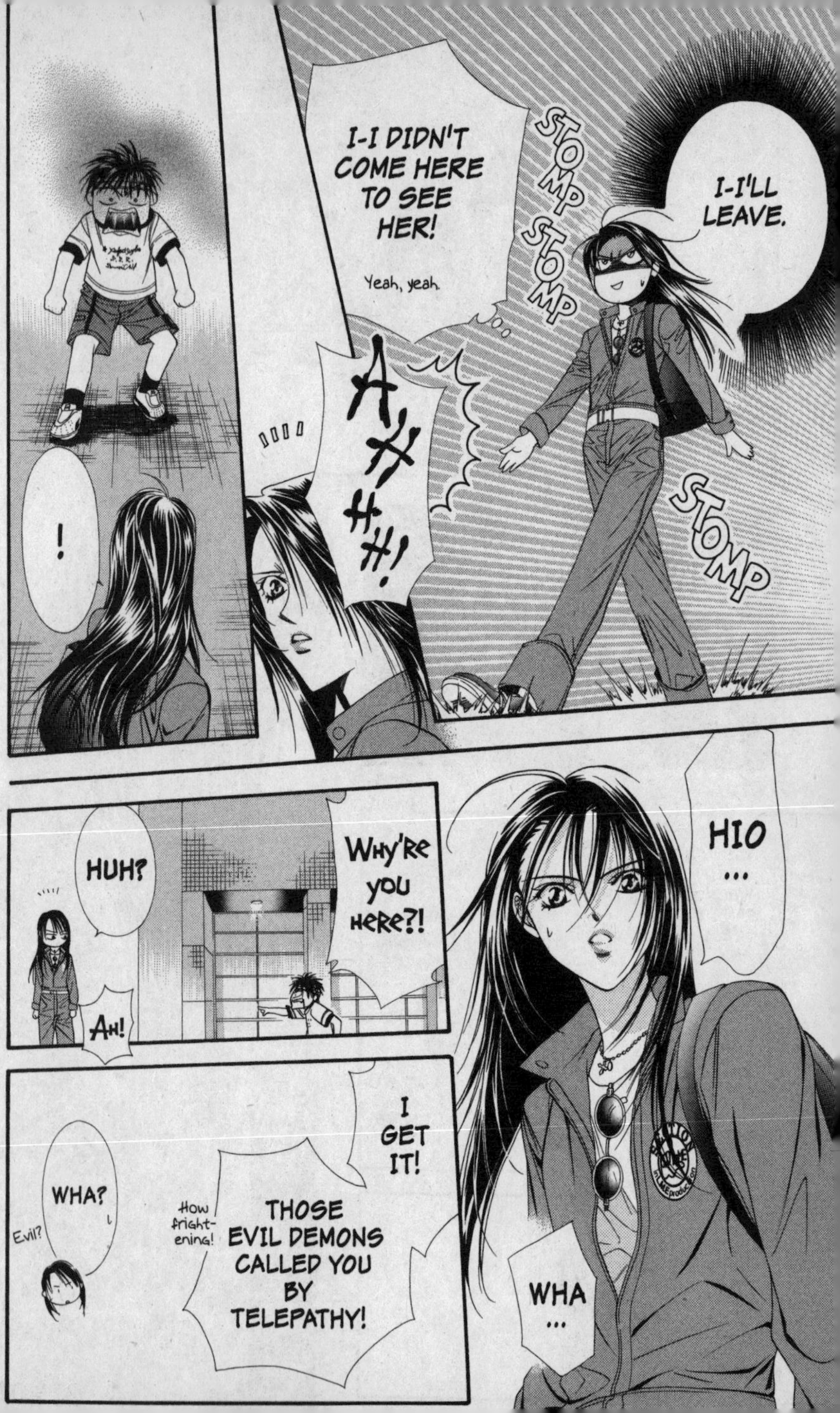
I-I'LL LEAVE.
STOMP STOMP
I-I DIDN'T COME HERE TO SEE HER!
Yeah, yeah.
STOMP
AHHHH!
!
HIO ...
WHA ...
WHY'RE YOU HERE?!
HUH?
AH!
I GET IT!
THOSE EVIL DEMONS CALLED YOU BY TELEPATHY!
How fright-ening!
WHA?
Evil?

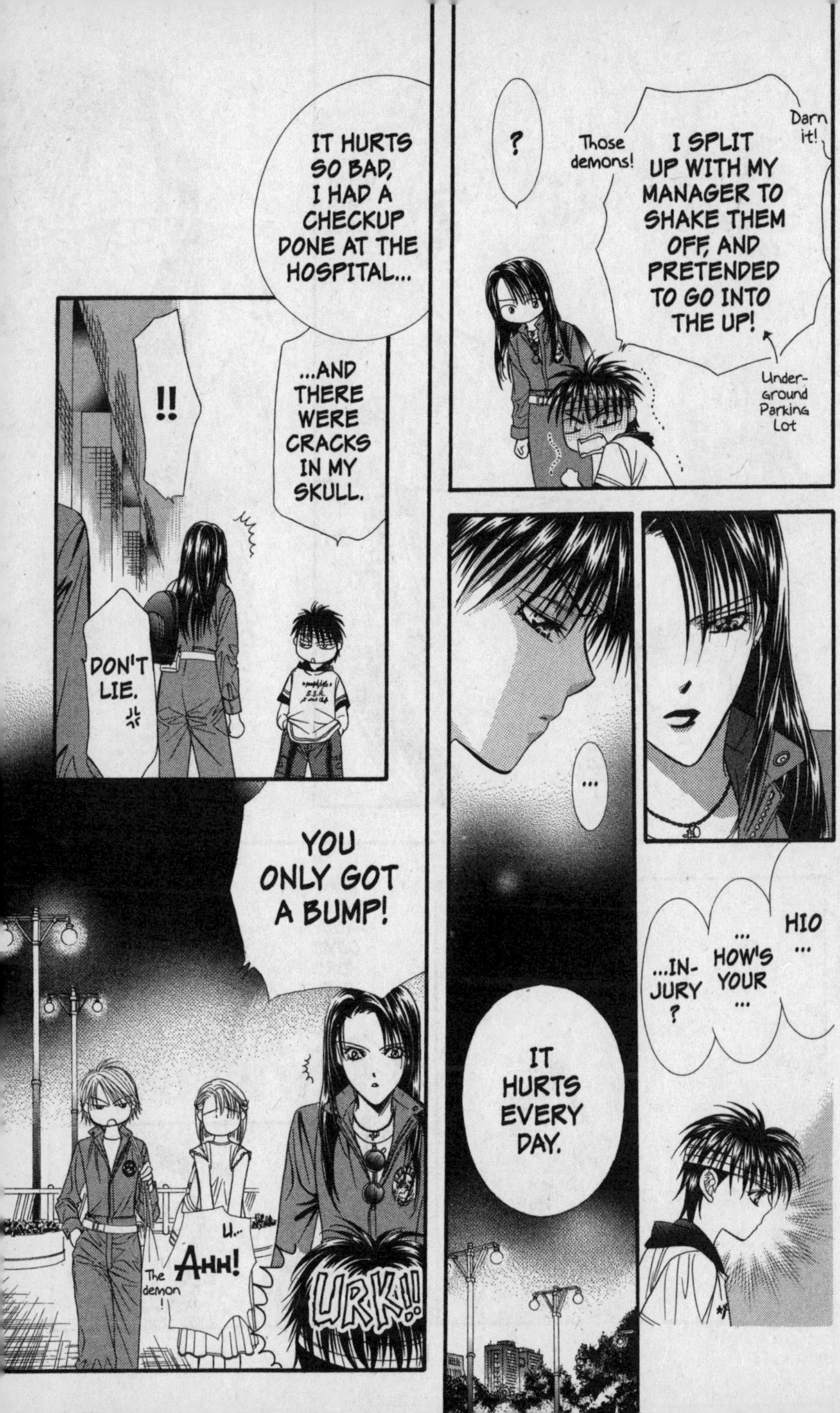
Darn it!
I SPLIT UP WITH MY MANAGER TO SHAKE THEM OFF, AND PRETENDED TO GO INTO THE UP!
Those demons!
?
Under-ground Parking Lot
...
HIO ...
... HOW'S YOUR ...
...IN-JURY?
IT HURTS EVERY DAY.
IT HURTS SO BAD, I HAD A CHECKUP DONE AT THE HOSPITAL...
...AND THERE WERE CRACKS IN MY SKULL.
!!
DON'T LIE.
YOU ONLY GOT A BUMP!
U...
AHH!
The demon!
URK!!

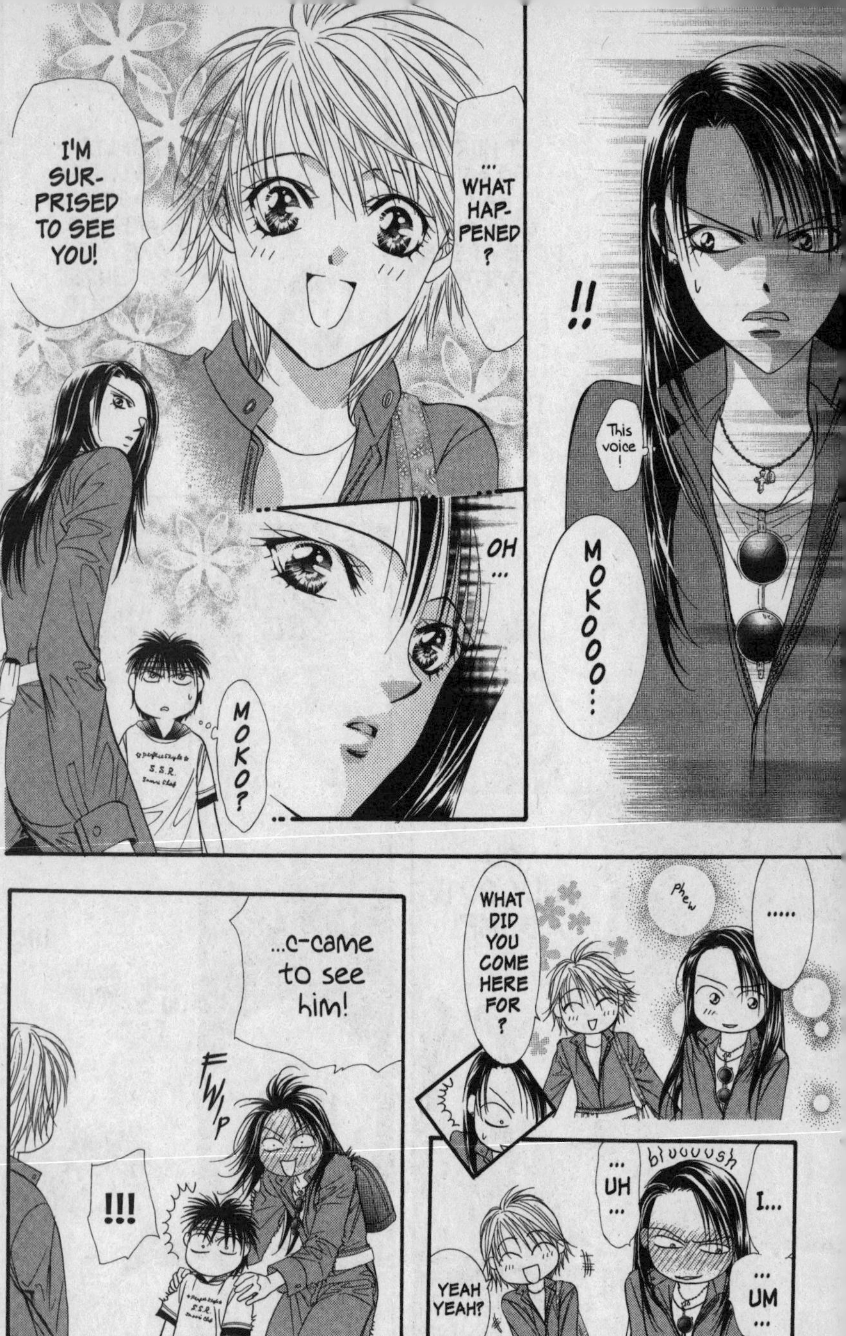
!!
This voice!
MOKOOOO...
...WHAT HAP-PENED?
I'M SUR-PRISED TO SEE YOU!
OH...
MOKO?
.....
Phew
WHAT DID YOU COME HERE FOR?
bluuuush
I...
...UH...
...UM...
YEAH YEAH?
...c-came to see him!
FWIP
!!!

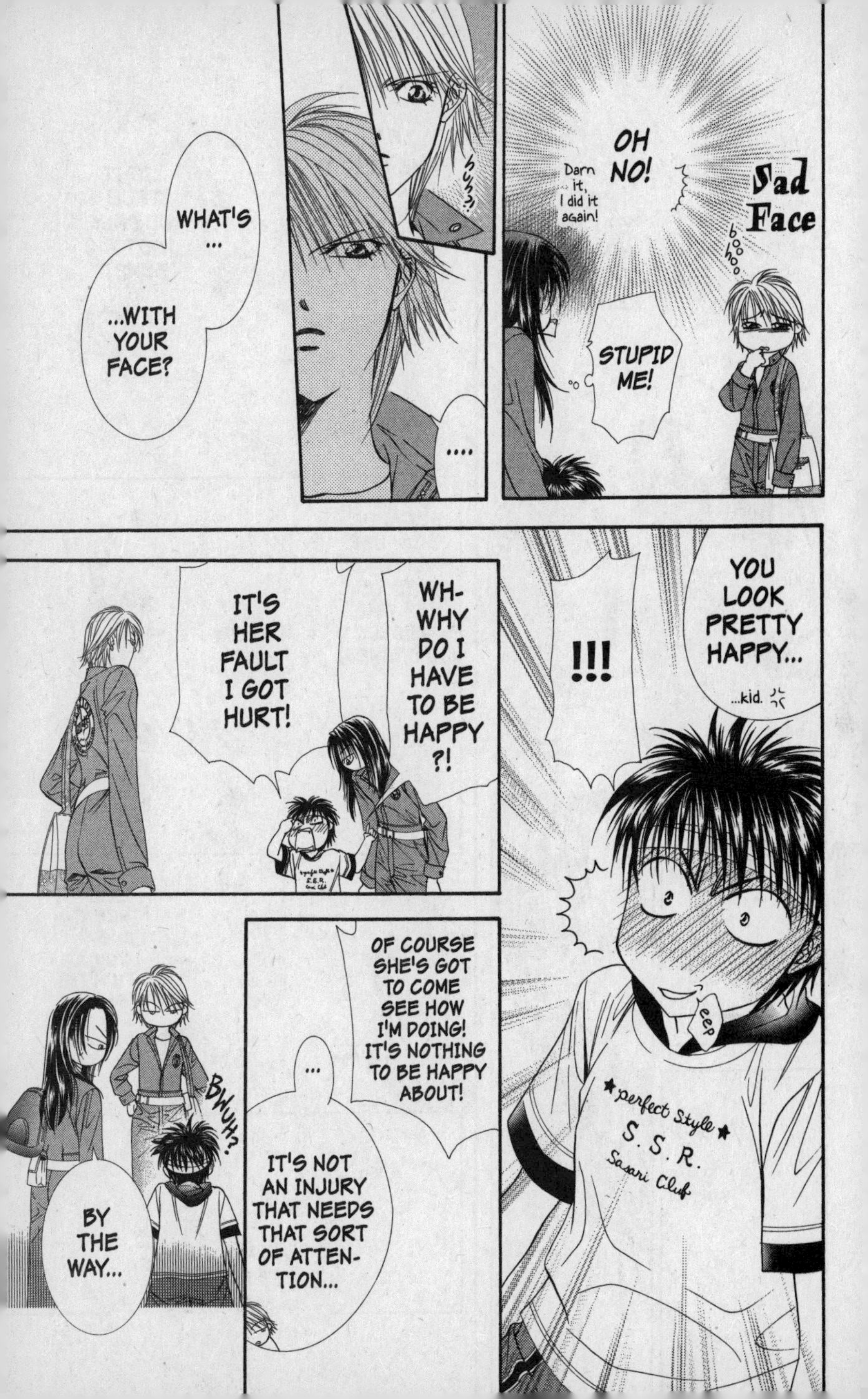
OH NO!
Darn it, I did it again!
Sad Face
boo hoo
STUPID ME!
huh?!
....
WHAT'S ...
...WITH YOUR FACE?
YOU LOOK PRETTY HAPPY...
...kid.
!!!
eep
★ perfect Style ★ S.S.R. Sasari Club
WH-WHY DO I HAVE TO BE HAPPY?!
IT'S HER FAULT I GOT HURT!
OF COURSE SHE'S GOT TO COME SEE HOW I'M DOING! IT'S NOTHING TO BE HAPPY ABOUT!
...
IT'S NOT AN INJURY THAT NEEDS THAT SORT OF ATTEN-TION...
BWUH?
BY THE WAY...

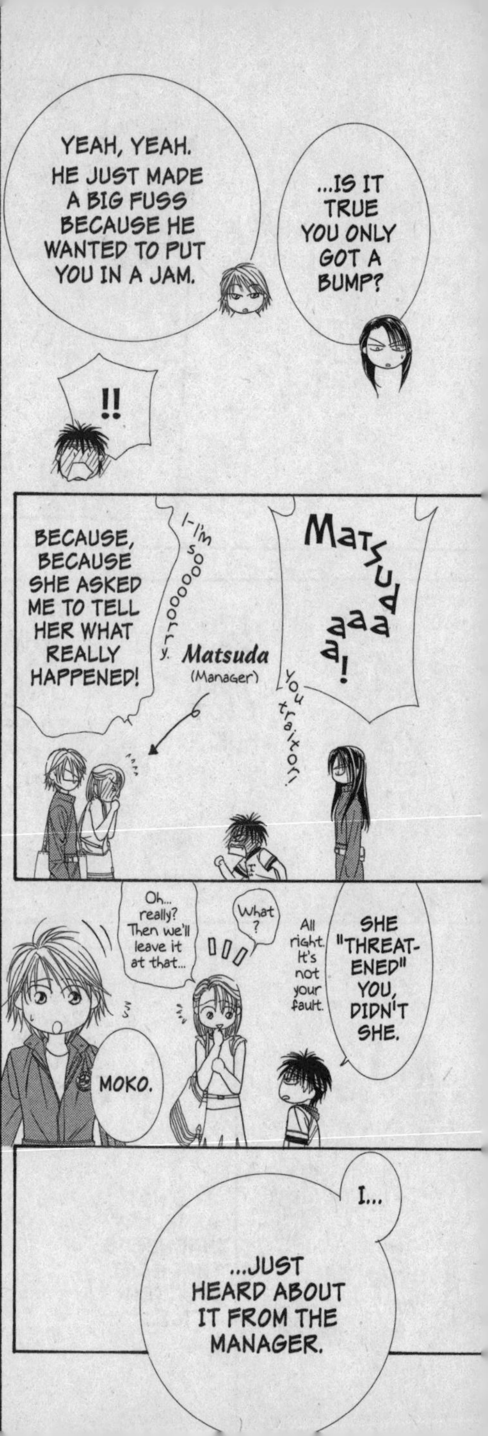
...IS IT TRUE YOU ONLY GOT A BUMP?
YEAH, YEAH. HE JUST MADE A BIG FUSS BECAUSE HE WANTED TO PUT YOU IN A JAM.
!!
Matsudaaaaa!
You traitor!
I-I'm soooooorry.
BECAUSE, BECAUSE SHE ASKED ME TO TELL HER WHAT REALLY HAPPENED!
Matsuda (Manager)
SHE "THREATENED" YOU, DIDN'T SHE.
All right. It's not your fault.
What?
Oh... really? Then we'll leave it at that...
MOKO.
I...
...JUST HEARD ABOUT IT FROM THE MANAGER.
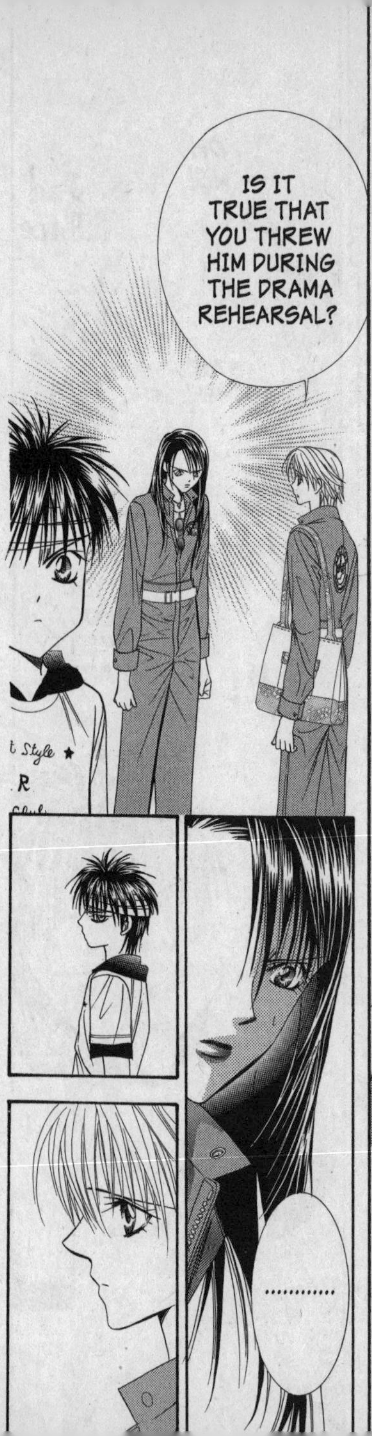
IS IT TRUE THAT YOU THREW HIM DURING THE DRAMA REHEARSAL?
....

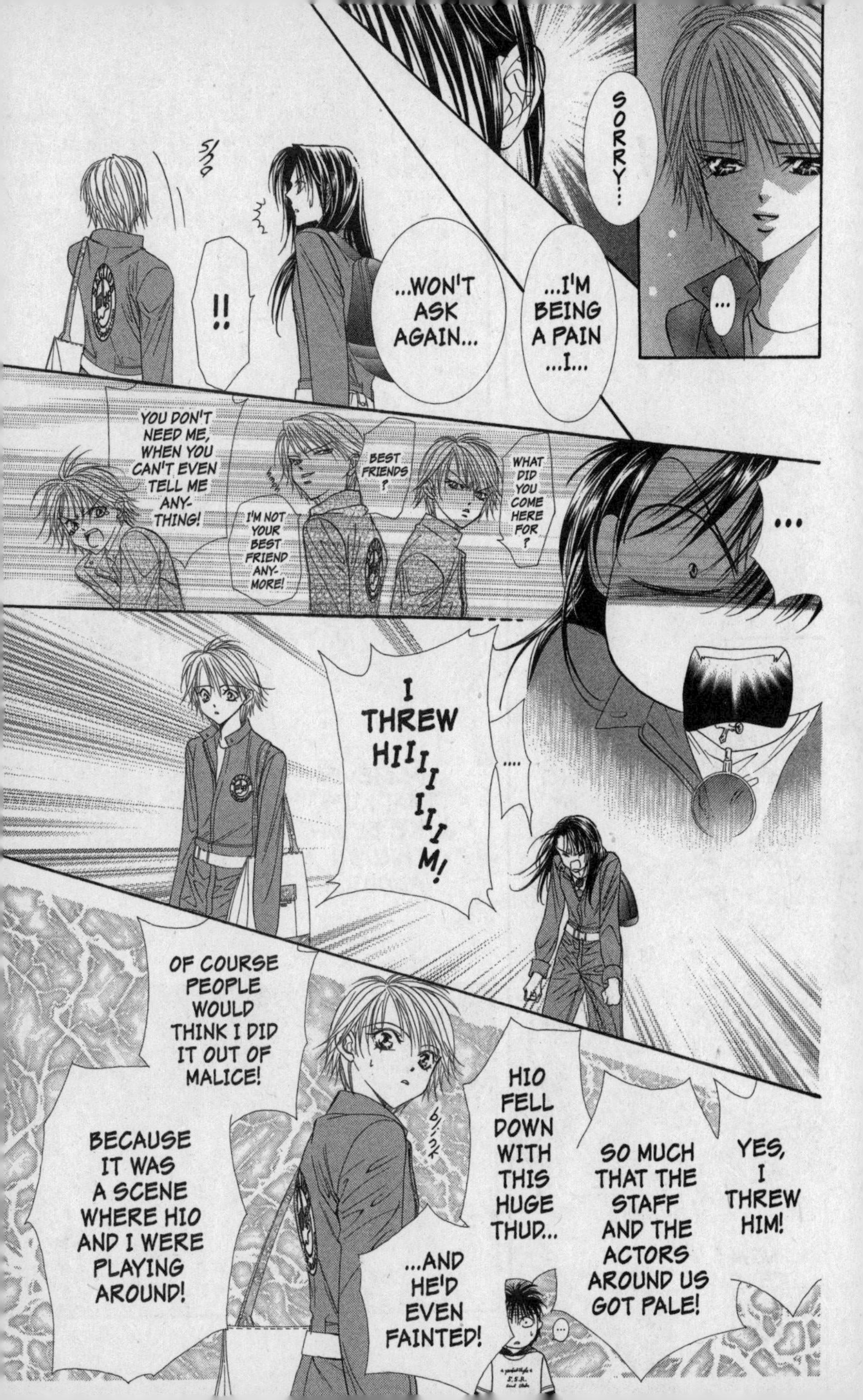
SORRY...
...
...I'M BEING A PAIN ...I...
...WON'T ASK AGAIN...
!!
...
WHAT DID YOU COME HERE FOR?
BEST FRIENDS?
I'M NOT YOUR BEST FRIEND ANYMORE!
YOU DON'T NEED ME, WHEN YOU CAN'T EVEN TELL ME ANYTHING!
I THREW HIIIIIIIIM!
....
YES, I THREW HIM!
SO MUCH THAT THE STAFF AND THE ACTORS AROUND US GOT PALE!
HIO FELL DOWN WITH THIS HUGE THUD...
...AND HE'D EVEN FAINTED!
...
OF COURSE PEOPLE WOULD THINK I DID IT OUT OF MALICE!
BECAUSE IT WAS A SCENE WHERE HIO AND I WERE PLAYING AROUND!

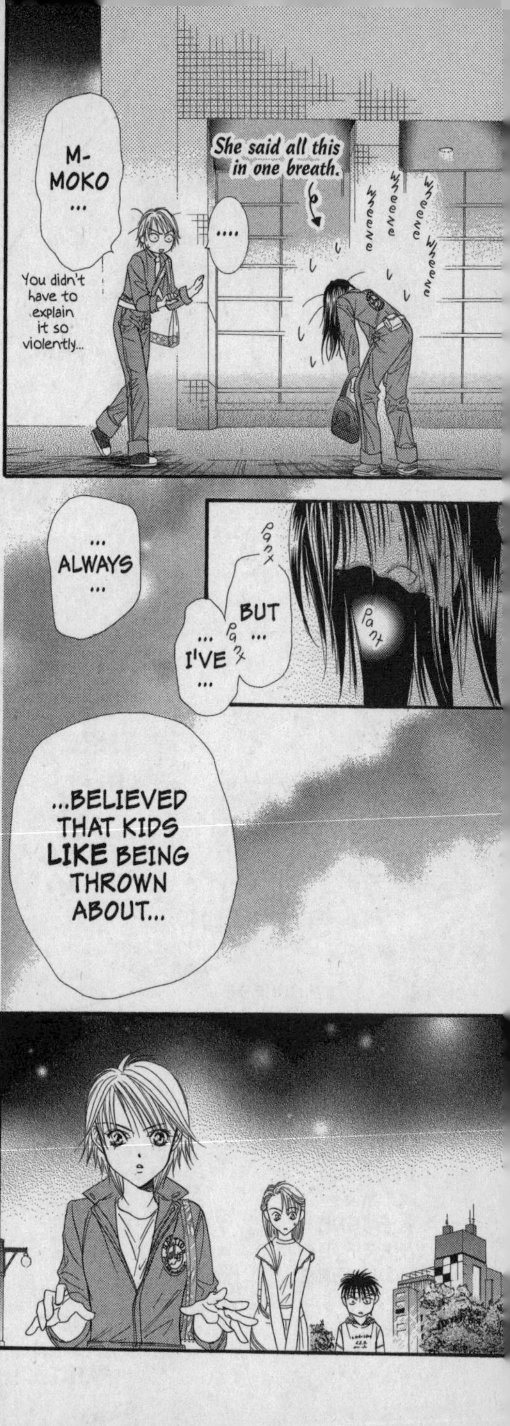
She said all this in one breath.
Wheeze wheeze
Wheeze wheeze
....
M-MOKO ...
You didn't have to explain it so violently...
Pant
BUT ... I'VE ...
Pant
Pant
... ALWAYS ...
...BELIEVED THAT KIDS LIKE BEING THROWN ABOUT...

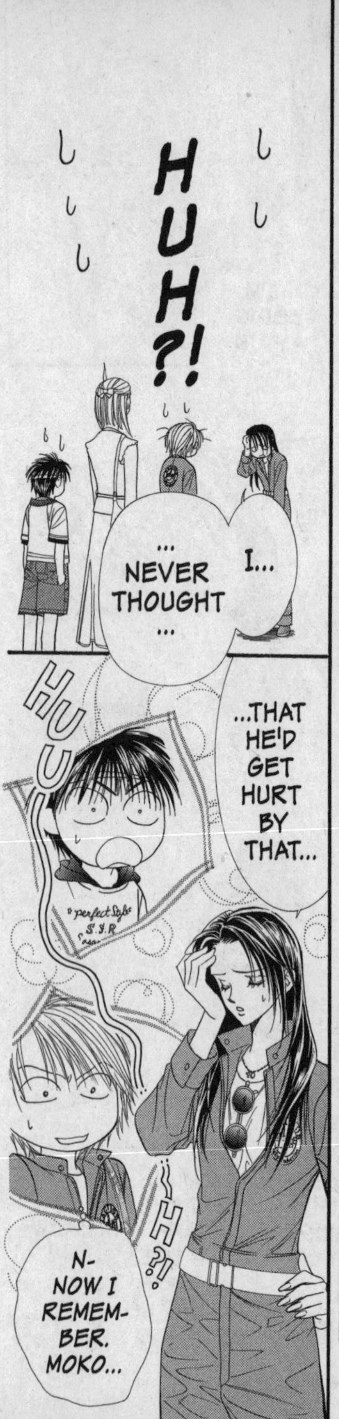
HUH?!
I... NEVER THOUGHT ...
...THAT HE'D GET HURT BY THAT...
HUH?!
HUH?!
N-NOW I REMEMBER. MOKO...

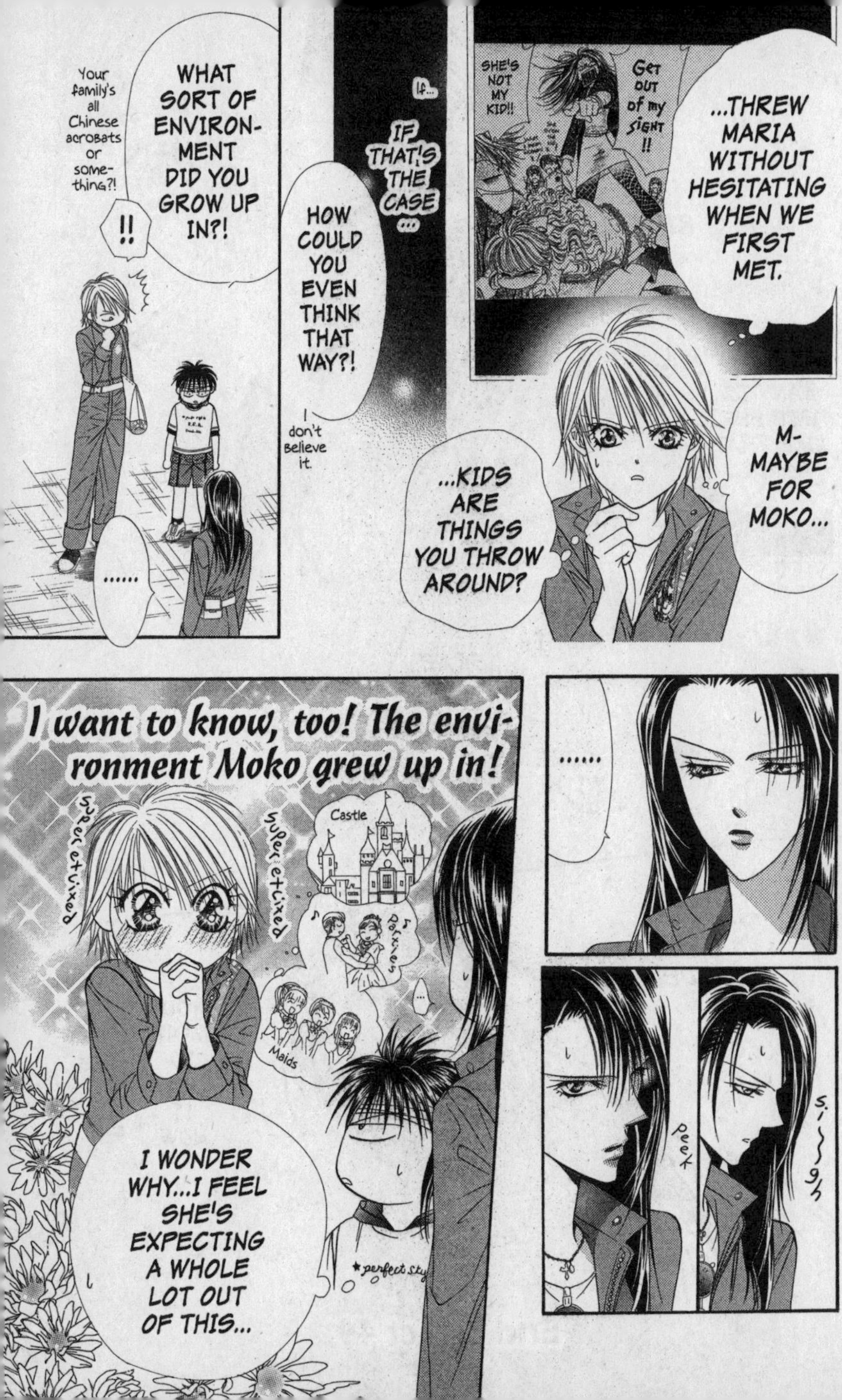
...THREW MARIA WITHOUT HESITATING WHEN WE FIRST MET.
Get out of my sight!!
SHE'S NOT MY KID!!
M-MAYBE FOR MOKO...
...KIDS ARE THINGS YOU THROW AROUND?
If...
IF THAT'S THE CASE...
HOW COULD YOU EVEN THINK THAT WAY?!
I don't believe it.
WHAT SORT OF ENVIRONMENT DID YOU GROW UP IN?!
Your family's all Chinese acrobats or something?!
!!
......
......
Peek
Si~gh
I want to know, too! The environment Moko grew up in!
super excited
super excited
Castle
Parties
Maids
...
I WONDER WHY...I FEEL SHE'S EXPECTING A WHOLE LOT OUT OF THIS...
★perfect sty

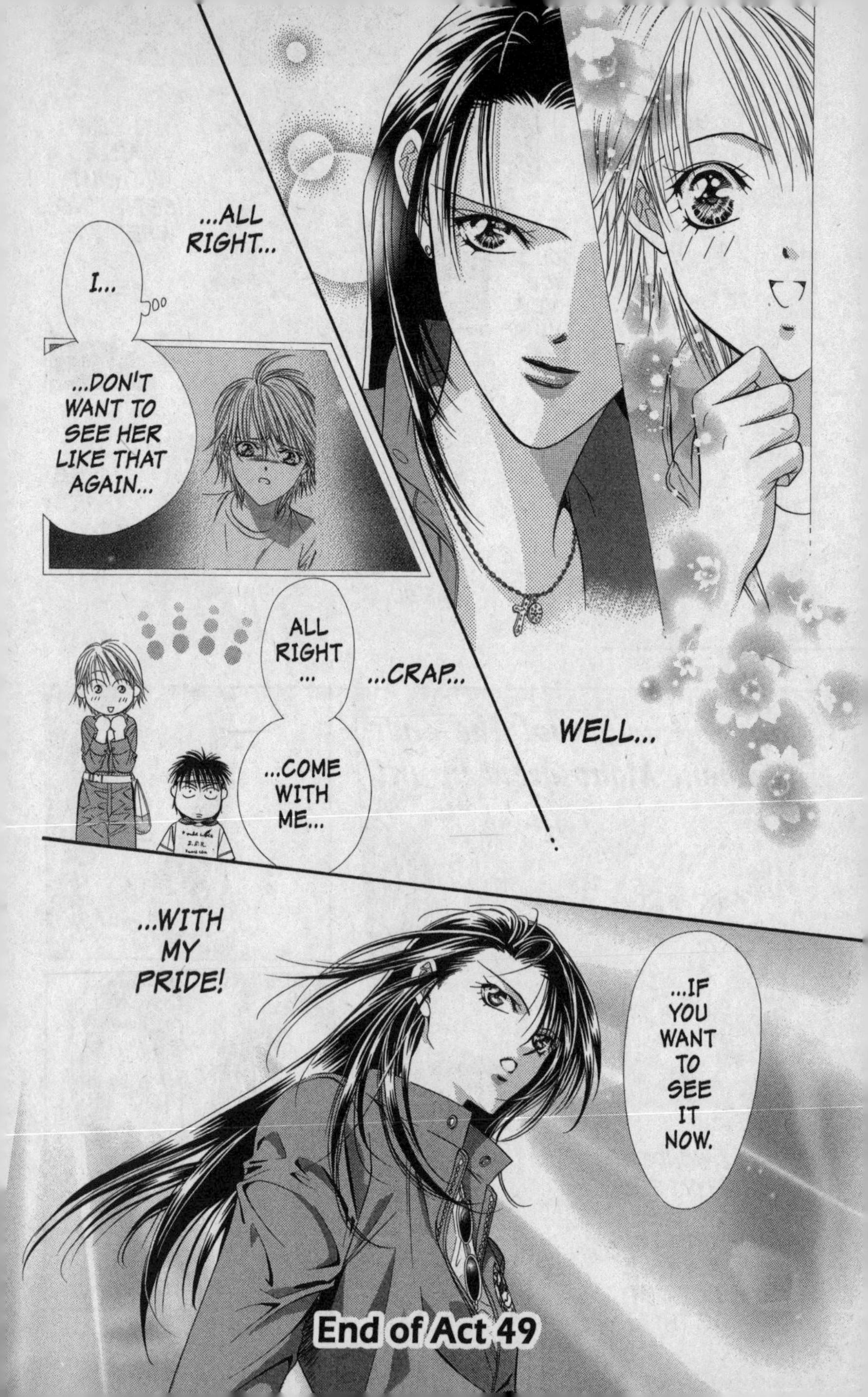
...ALL RIGHT...
I...
...DON'T WANT TO SEE HER LIKE THAT AGAIN...
WELL...
ALL RIGHT ...
...COME WITH ME...
...CRAP...
...IF YOU WANT TO SEE IT NOW.
...WITH MY PRIDE!
End of Act 49

A Little Episode: This story was an episode that was sadly cut out from the storyboard due to page constraints.

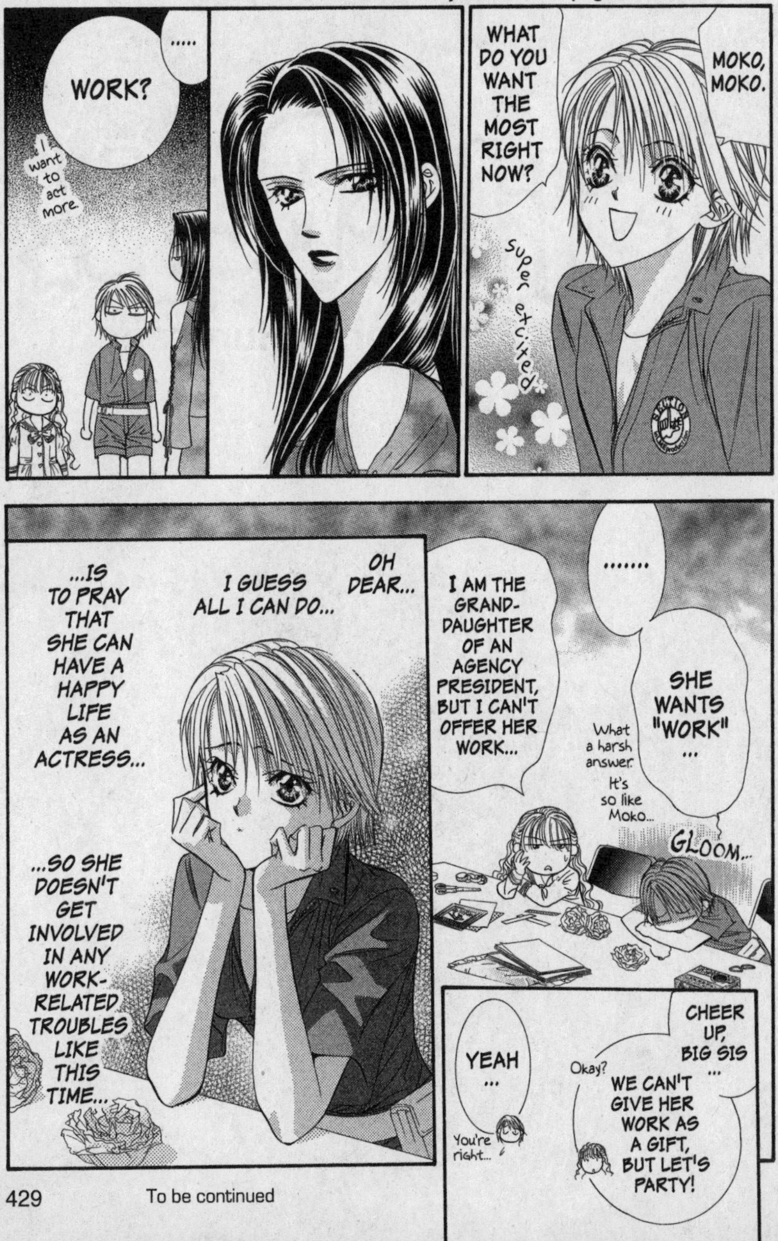
MOKO, MOKO.
WHAT DO YOU WANT THE MOST RIGHT NOW?
super excited
.....
WORK?
I want to act more.
....
SHE WANTS "WORK" ...
What a harsh answer. It's so like Moko...
I AM THE GRAND-DAUGHTER OF AN AGENCY PRESIDENT, BUT I CAN'T OFFER HER WORK...
GLOOM...
CHEER UP, BIG SIS ...
Okay?
WE CAN'T GIVE HER WORK AS A GIFT, BUT LET'S PARTY!
YEAH ...
You're right...
OH DEAR...
I GUESS ALL I CAN DO...
...IS TO PRAY THAT SHE CAN HAVE A HAPPY LIFE AS AN ACTRESS...
...SO SHE DOESN'T GET INVOLVED IN ANY WORK-RELATED TROUBLES LIKE THIS TIME...

To be continued

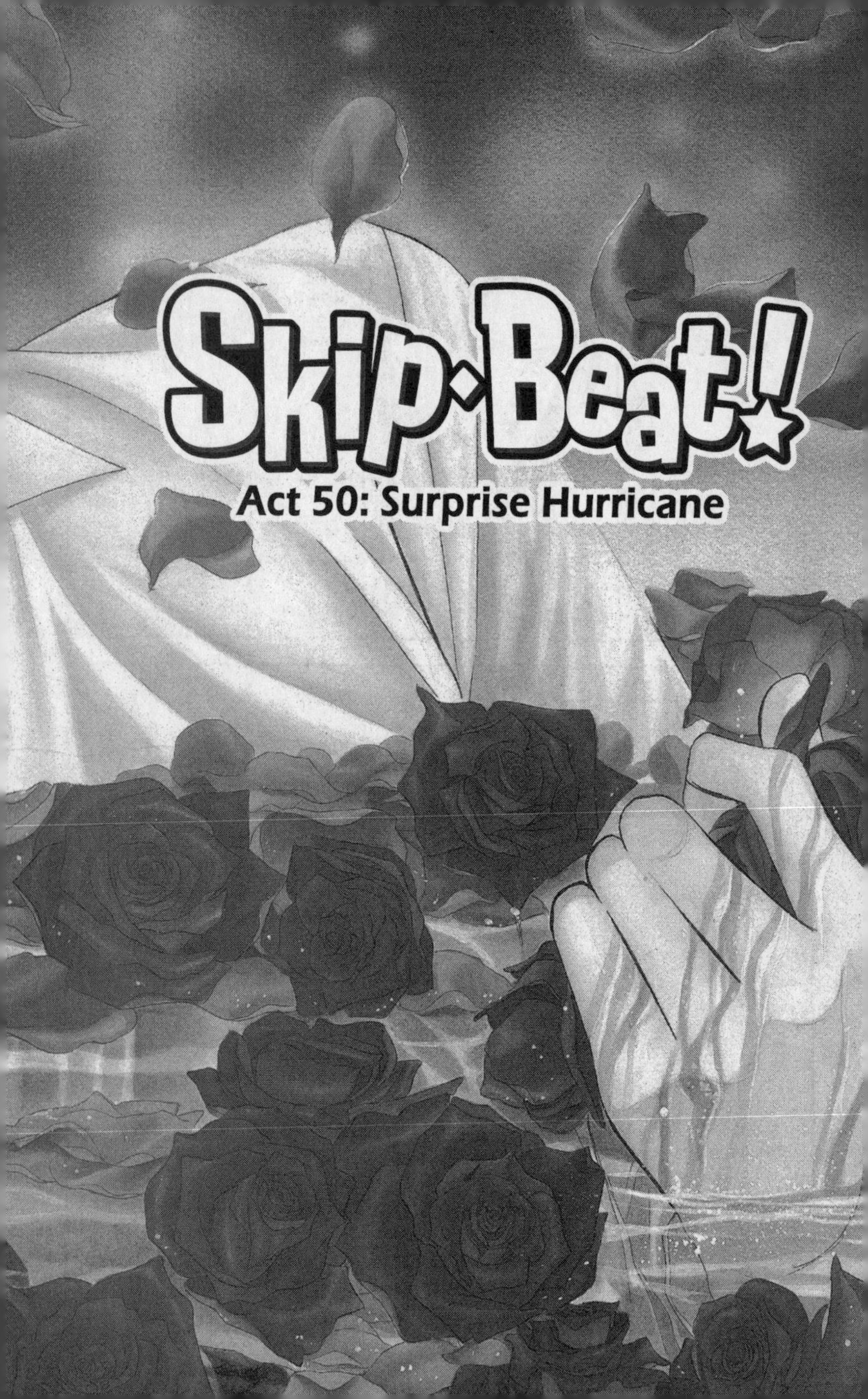
Skip·Beat!
Act 50: Surprise Hurricane

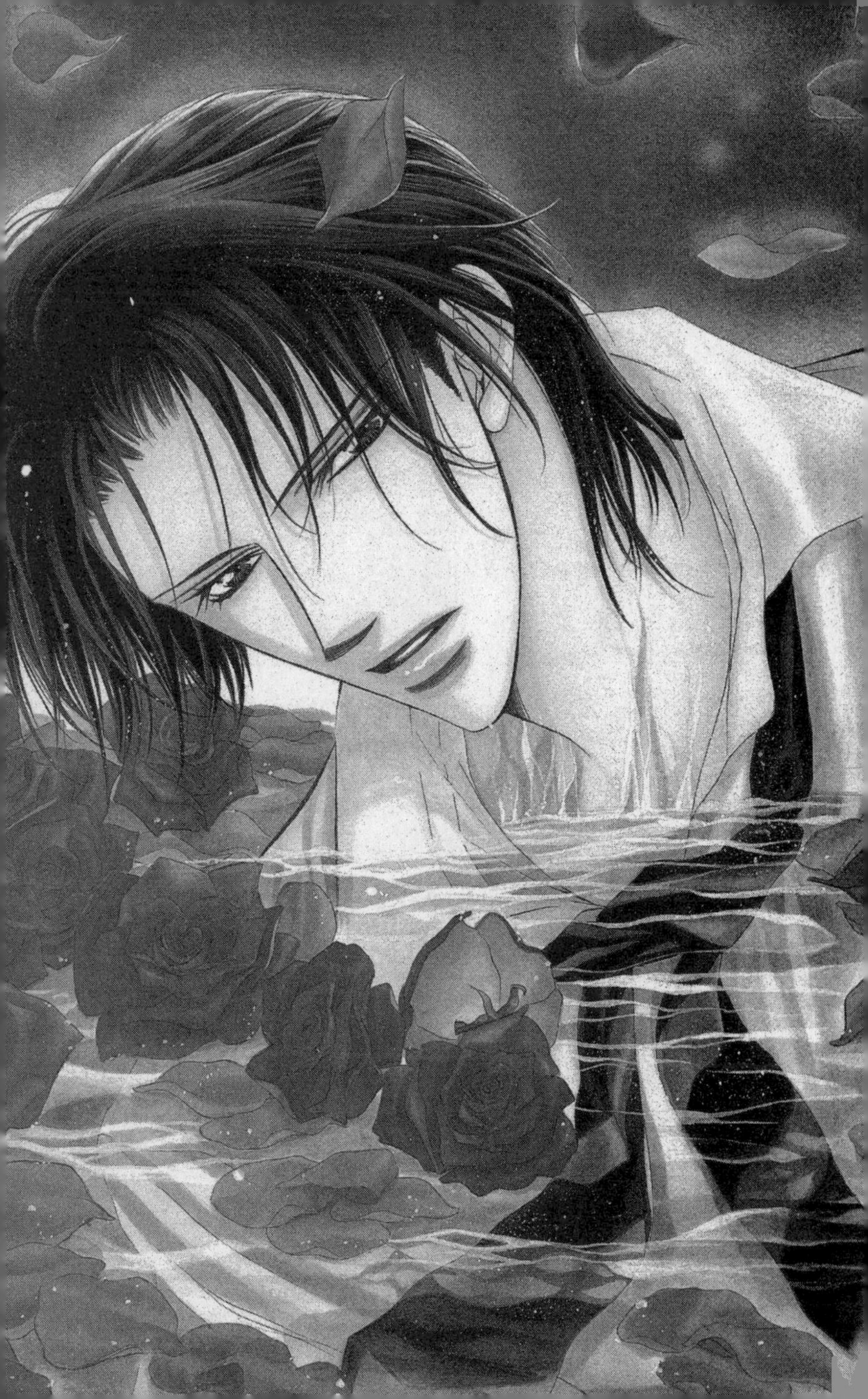

A Little Episode: Continued

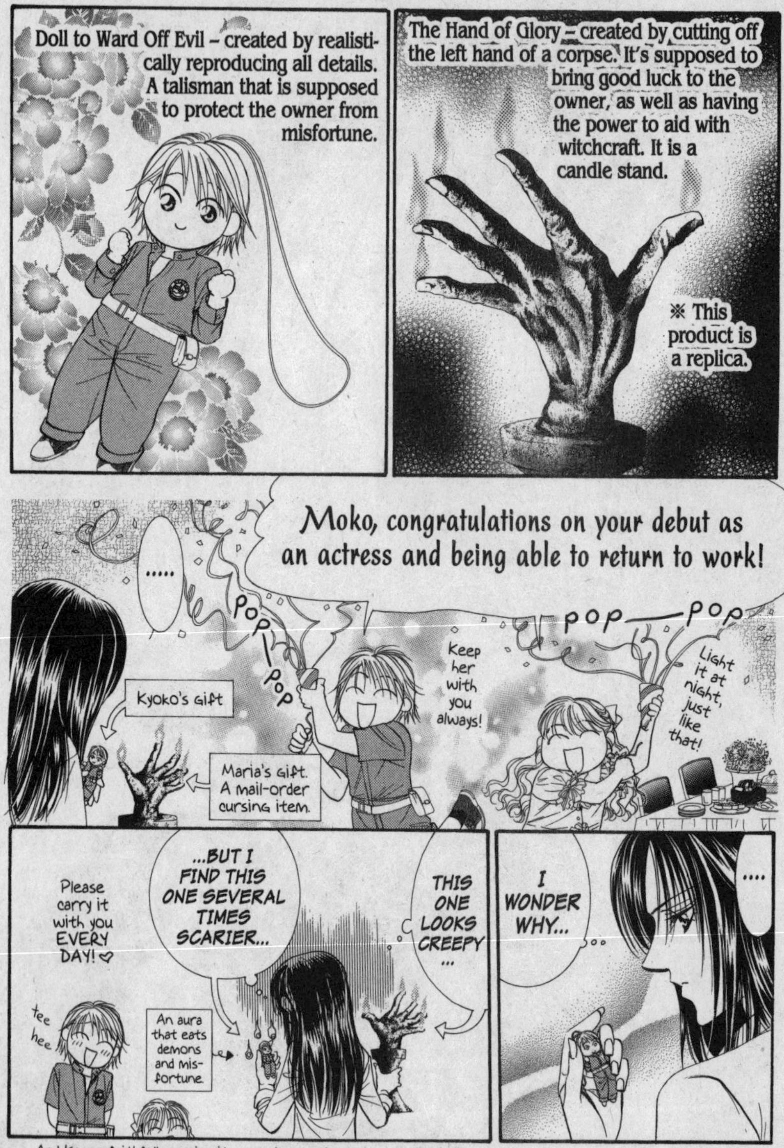
The Hand of Glory – created by cutting off the left hand of a corpse. It's supposed to bring good luck to the owner, as well as having the power to aid with witchcraft. It is a candle stand.
※ This product is a replica.
Doll to Ward Off Evil – created by realistically reproducing all details. A talisman that is supposed to protect the owner from misfortune.
Moko, congratulations on your debut as an actress and being able to return to work!
pop—pop
Light it at night, just like that!
Keep her with you always!
pop pop
......
Kyoko's gift
Maria's gift. A mail-order cursing item.
....
I WONDER WHY...
THIS ONE LOOKS CREEPY ...
...BUT I FIND THIS ONE SEVERAL TIMES SCARIER...
Please carry it with you EVERY DAY!
tee hee
An aura that eats demons and misfortune.

And Kanae faithfully carries it around every day, because she is afraid of being cursed by it...

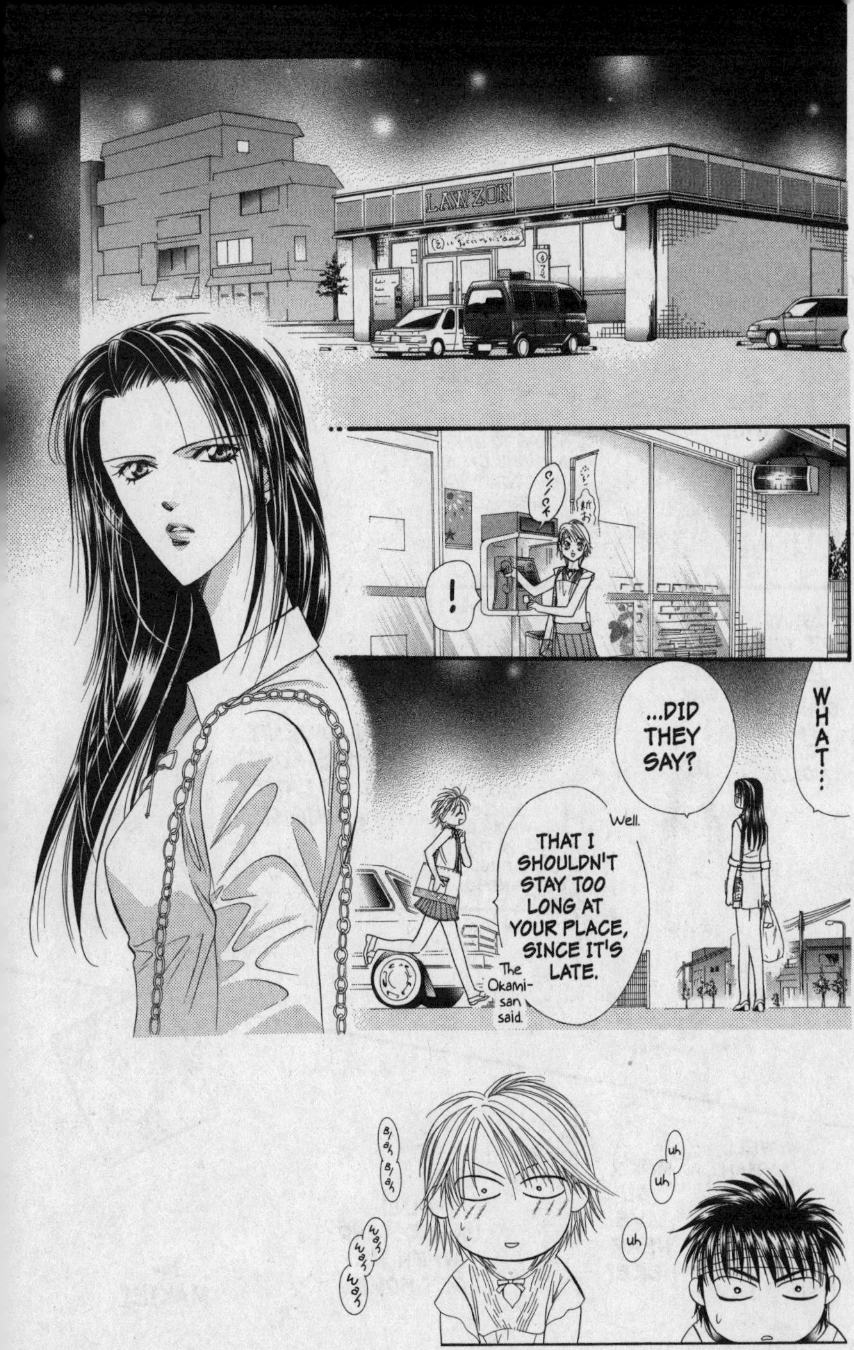
LAWZON
CLICK
!
WHAT...
...DID THEY SAY?
Well.
THAT I SHOULDN'T STAY TOO LONG AT YOUR PLACE, SINCE IT'S LATE.
The Okami-san said.
uh uh
uh
Blah Blah
wah wah wah

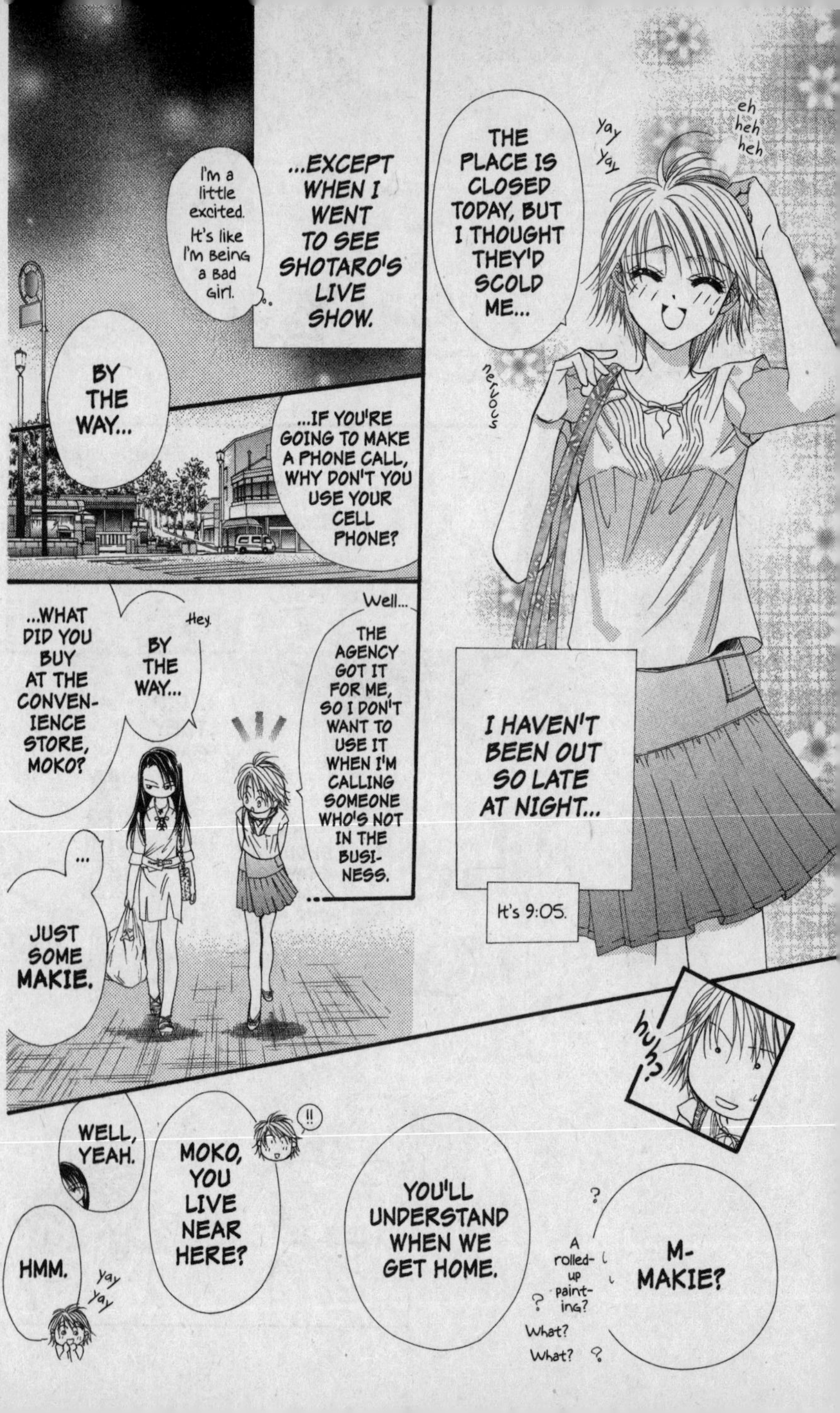
eh heh heh
yay yay
THE PLACE IS CLOSED TODAY, BUT I THOUGHT THEY'D SCOLD ME...
nervous
I HAVEN'T BEEN OUT SO LATE AT NIGHT...
It's 9:05.
...EXCEPT WHEN I WENT TO SEE SHOTARO'S LIVE SHOW.
I'm a little excited. It's like I'm being a bad girl.
BY THE WAY...
...IF YOU'RE GOING TO MAKE A PHONE CALL, WHY DON'T YOU USE YOUR CELL PHONE?
Well...
THE AGENCY GOT IT FOR ME, SO I DON'T WANT TO USE IT WHEN I'M CALLING SOMEONE WHO'S NOT IN THE BUSINESS.
Hey.
BY THE WAY...
...WHAT DID YOU BUY AT THE CONVENIENCE STORE, MOKO?
...
JUST SOME MAKIE.
huh?
M-MAKIE?
A rolled-up painting?
What?
What?
YOU'LL UNDERSTAND WHEN WE GET HOME.
!!
MOKO, YOU LIVE NEAR HERE?
WELL, YEAH.
HMM.
yay yay

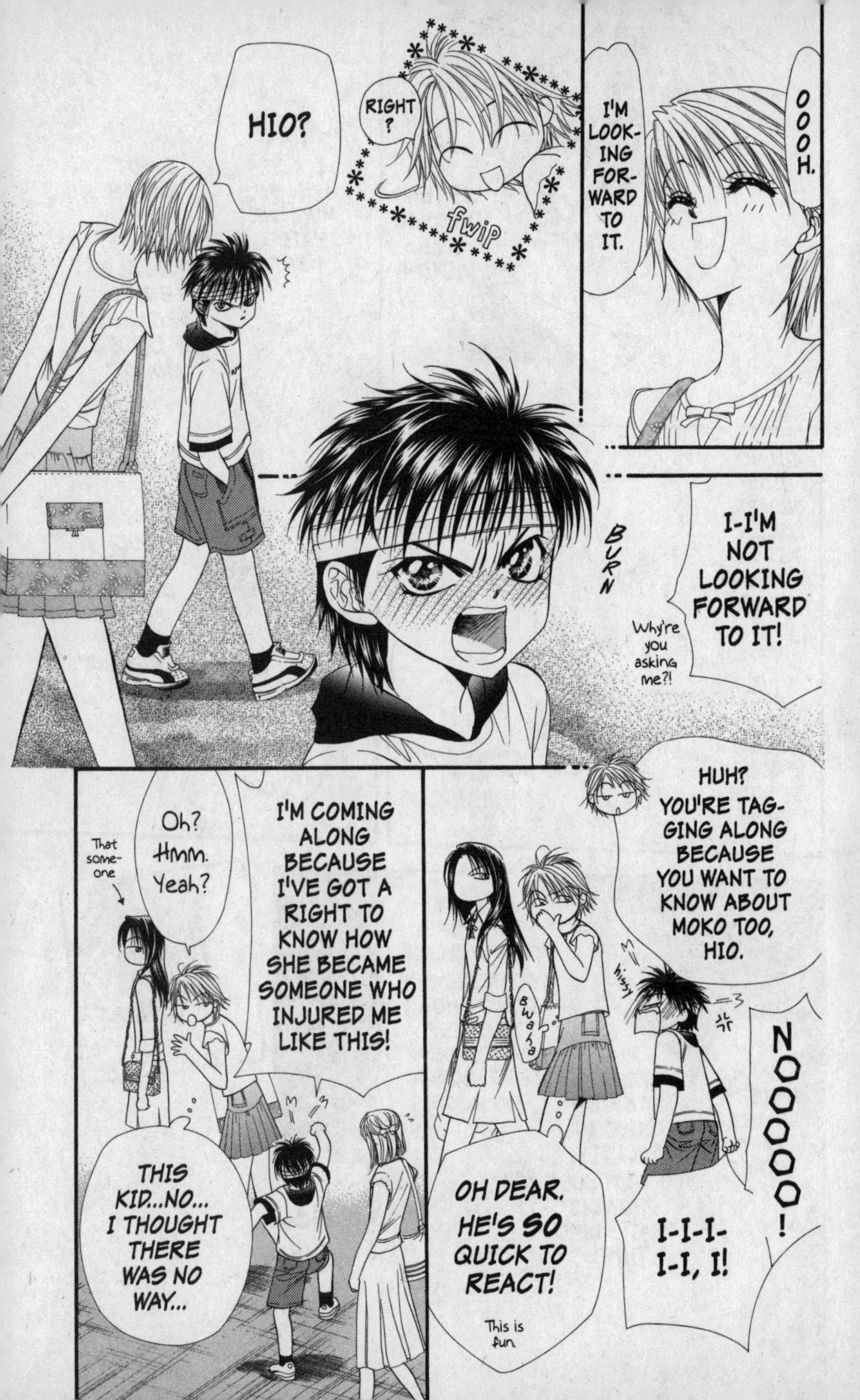
OOOH.
I'M LOOKING FORWARD TO IT.
RIGHT?
fwip
HIO?
I-I'M NOT LOOKING FORWARD TO IT!
Why're you asking me?!
BURN
HUH? YOU'RE TAGGING ALONG BECAUSE YOU WANT TO KNOW ABOUT MOKO TOO, HIO.
hissy
Bwaha
NOOOOO!
I-I-I-I-I, I!
OH DEAR. HE'S SO QUICK TO REACT!
This is fun.
I'M COMING ALONG BECAUSE I'VE GOT A RIGHT TO KNOW HOW SHE BECAME SOMEONE WHO INJURED ME LIKE THIS!
Oh? Hmm. Yeah?
That someone
THIS KID...NO... I THOUGHT THERE WAS NO WAY...

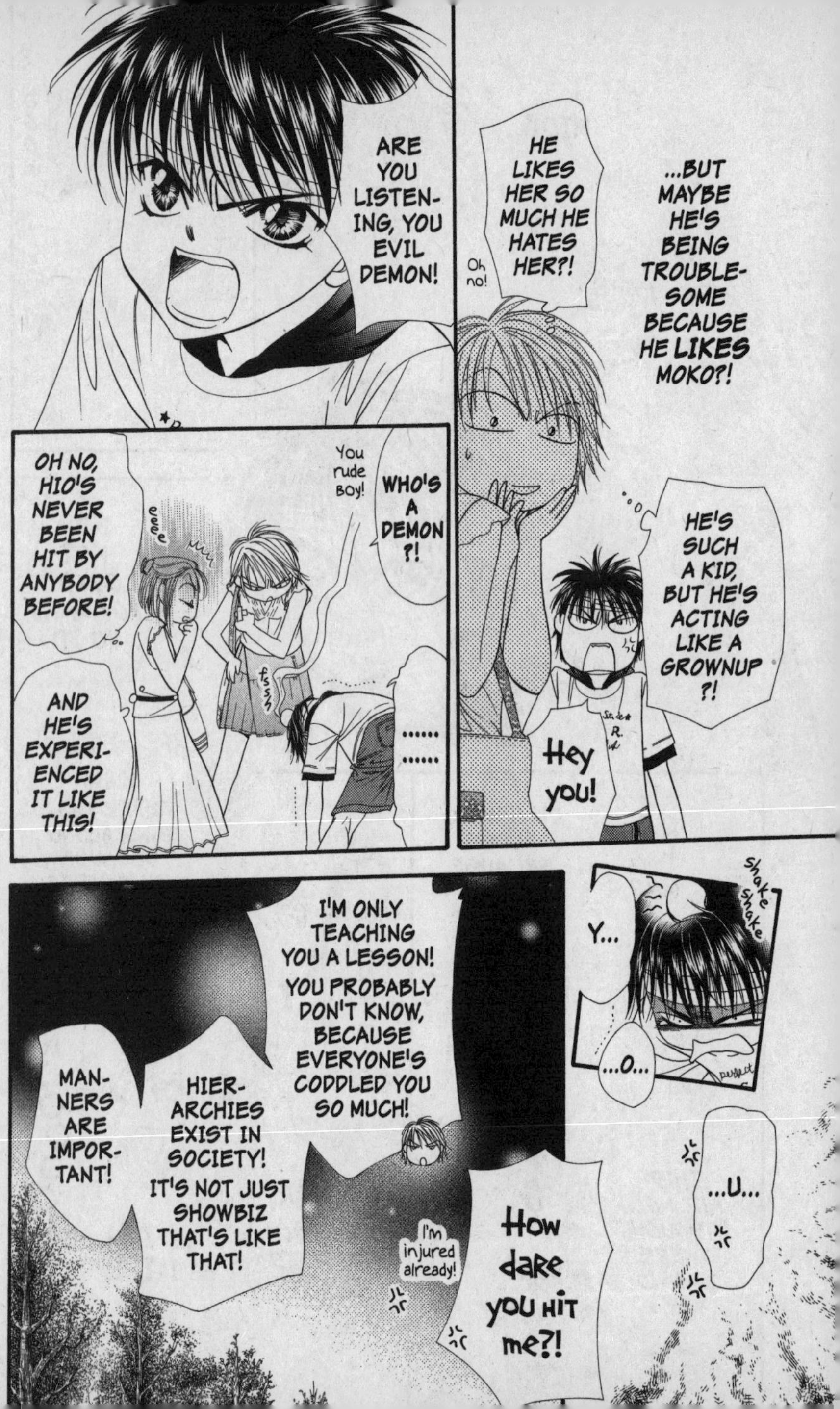
...BUT MAYBE HE'S BEING TROUBLE-SOME BECAUSE HE LIKES MOKO?!
HE LIKES HER SO MUCH HE HATES HER?!
Oh no!
HE'S SUCH A KID, BUT HE'S ACTING LIKE A GROWNUP?!
Hey you!
ARE YOU LISTEN-ING, YOU EVIL DEMON!
WHO'S A DEMON?!
You rude boy!
OH NO, HIO'S NEVER BEEN HIT BY ANYBODY BEFORE!
eeee
fsss
......
......
AND HE'S EXPERI-ENCED IT LIKE THIS!
shake shake
Y...
...O...
...U...
How dare you hit me?!
I'm injured already!
I'M ONLY TEACHING YOU A LESSON!
YOU PROBABLY DON'T KNOW, BECAUSE EVERYONE'S CODDLED YOU SO MUCH!
HIER-ARCHIES EXIST IN SOCIETY!
IT'S NOT JUST SHOWBIZ THAT'S LIKE THAT!
MAN-NERS ARE IMPOR-TANT!

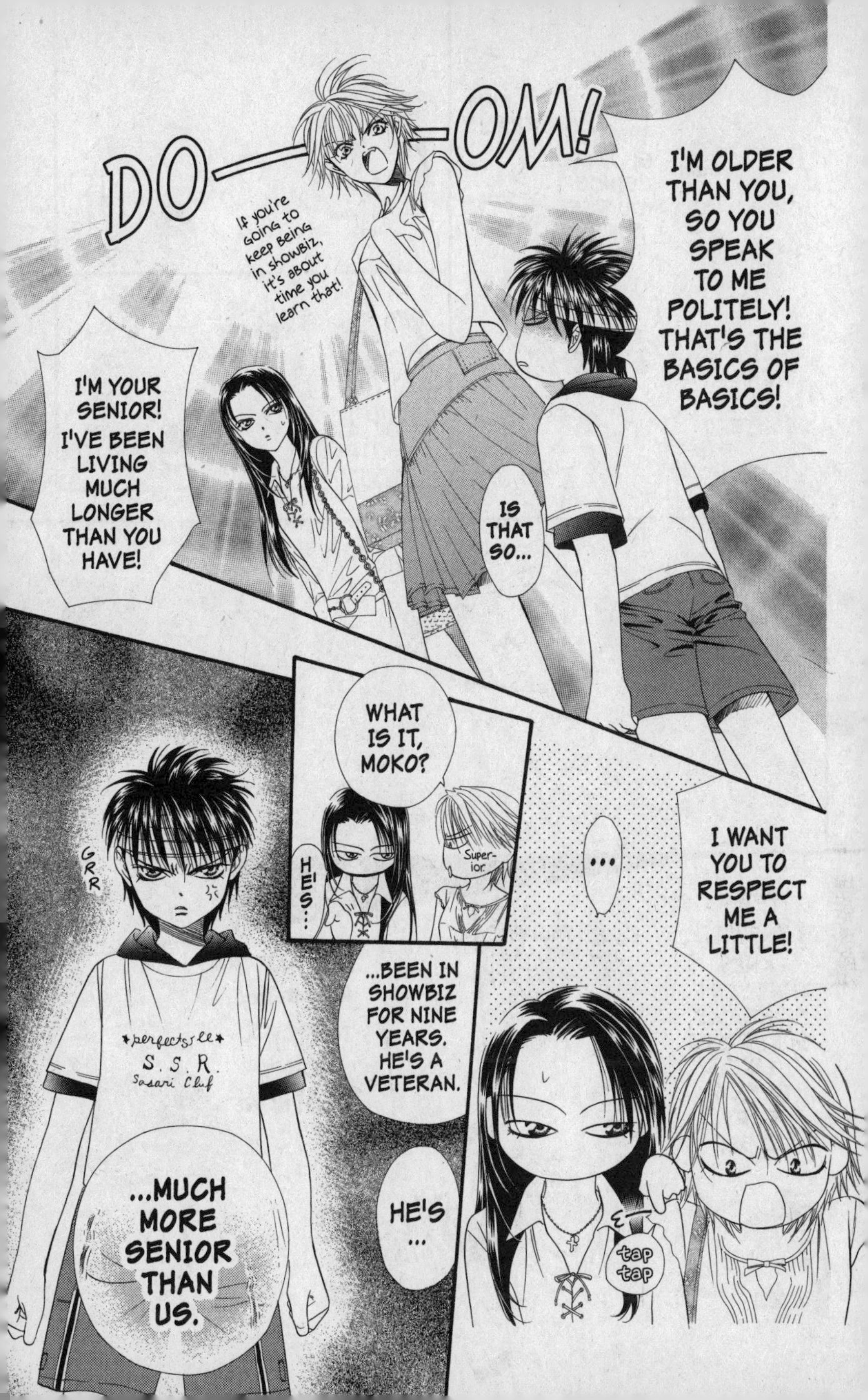
DO—OM!
I'M OLDER THAN YOU, SO YOU SPEAK TO ME POLITELY! THAT'S THE BASICS OF BASICS!
If you're going to keep being in showbiz, it's about time you learn that!
IS THAT SO...
I'M YOUR SENIOR! I'VE BEEN LIVING MUCH LONGER THAN YOU HAVE!
I WANT YOU TO RESPECT ME A LITTLE!
...
tap tap
WHAT IS IT, MOKO?
Super-ior.
HE'S...
...BEEN IN SHOWBIZ FOR NINE YEARS. HE'S A VETERAN.
HE'S ...
GRR
...MUCH MORE SENIOR THAN US.
perfect S.S.R. Sasari Club

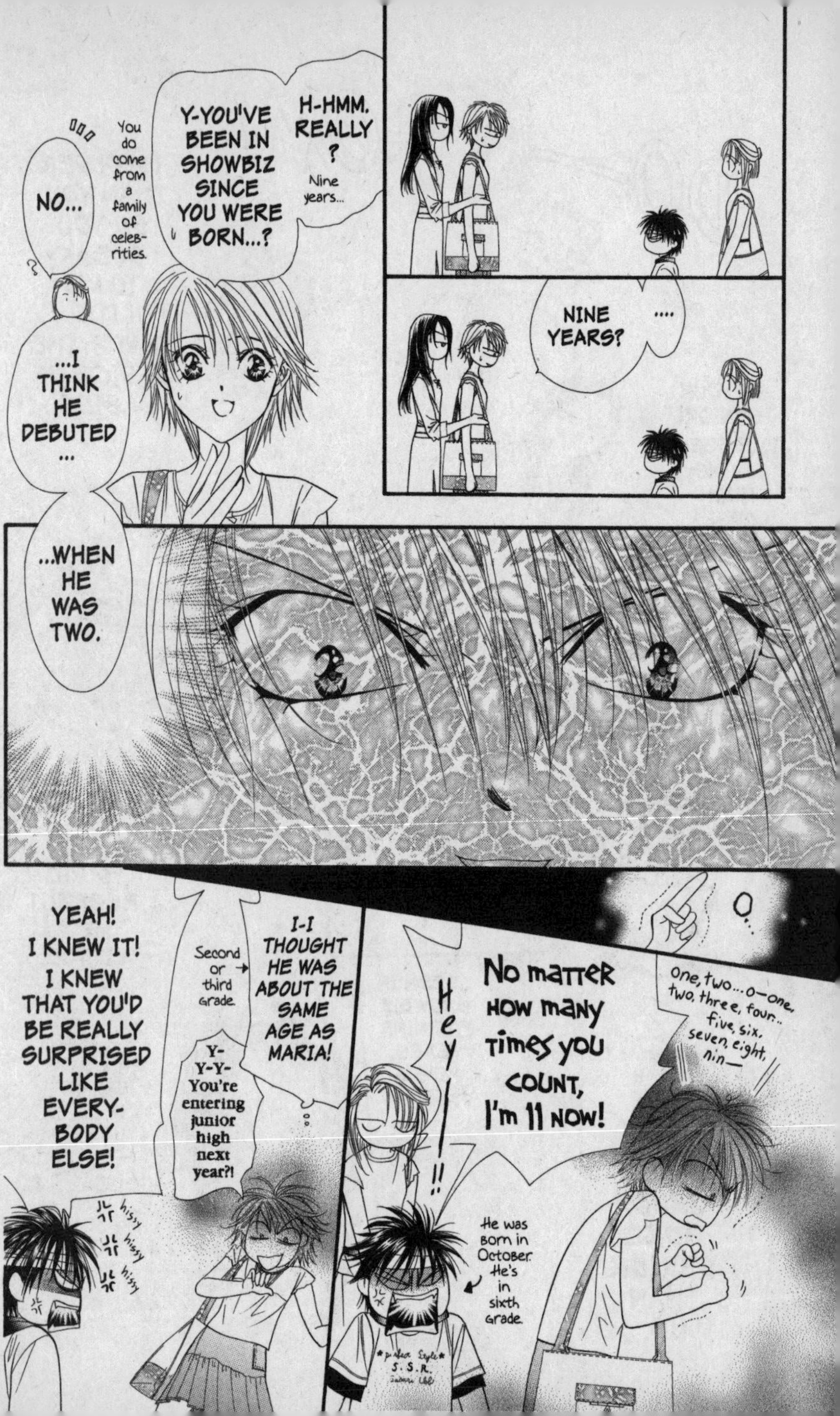
NINE YEARS?
....
H-HMM. REALLY?
Nine years...
Y-YOU'VE BEEN IN SHOWBIZ SINCE YOU WERE BORN...?
You do come from a family of celebrities.
NO...
...I THINK HE DEBUTED...
...WHEN HE WAS TWO.
O...
One, two... o-one, two, three, four... five, six, seven, eight, nin—
No matter how many times you count, I'm 11 now!
Hey!!!
He was born in October. He's in sixth grade.
I-I THOUGHT HE WAS ABOUT THE SAME AGE AS MARIA!
Second or third grade.
Y-Y-Y-You're entering junior high next year?!
YEAH! I KNEW IT! I KNEW THAT YOU'D BE REALLY SURPRISED LIKE EVERYBODY ELSE!
hissy
hissy
hissy

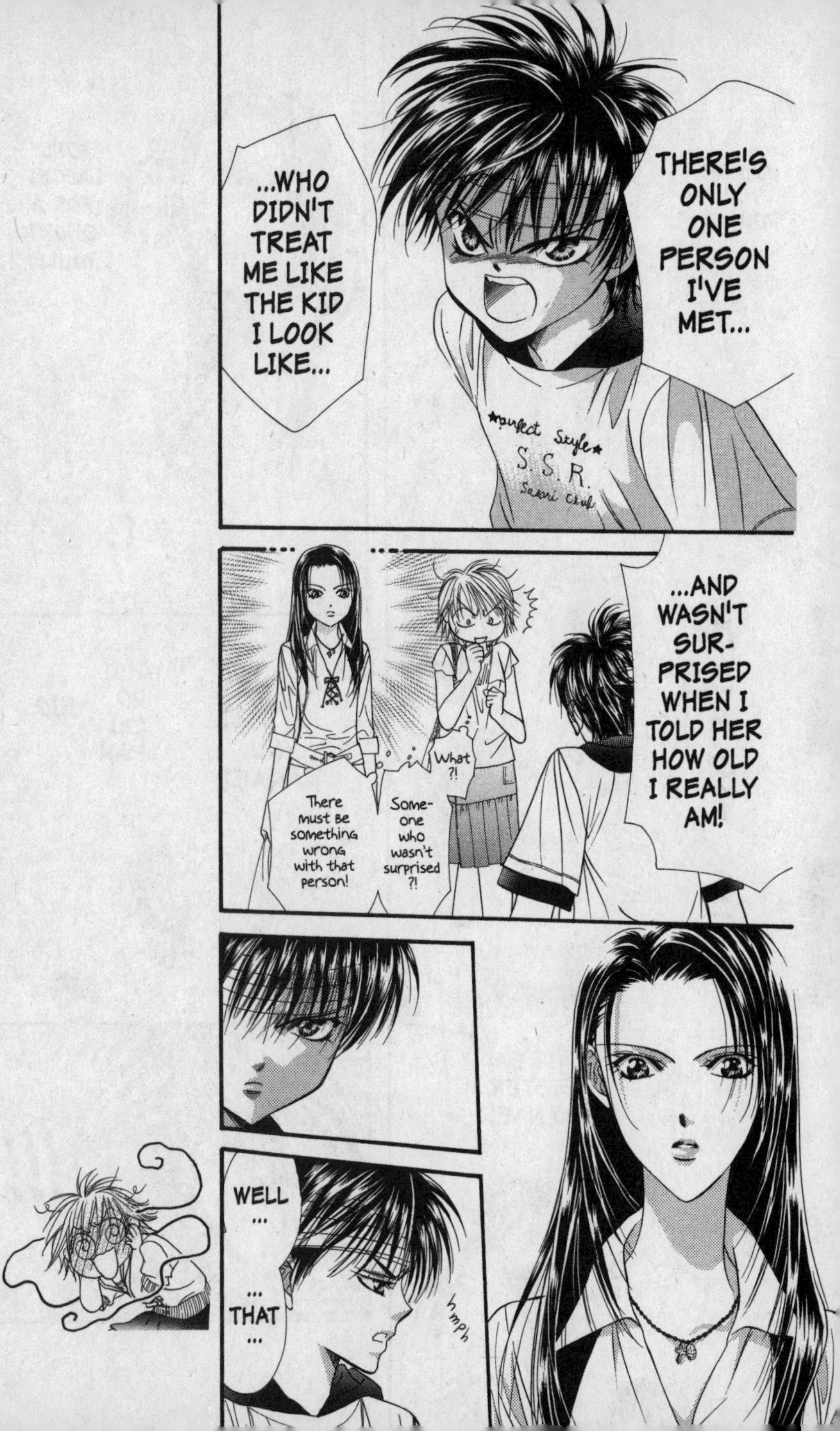
THERE'S ONLY ONE PERSON I'VE MET...
...WHO DIDN'T TREAT ME LIKE THE KID I LOOK LIKE...
...AND WASN'T SUR-PRISED WHEN I TOLD HER HOW OLD I REALLY AM!
What?!
Some-one who wasn't surprised?!
There must be something wrong with that person!
WELL...
...THAT...
hmph

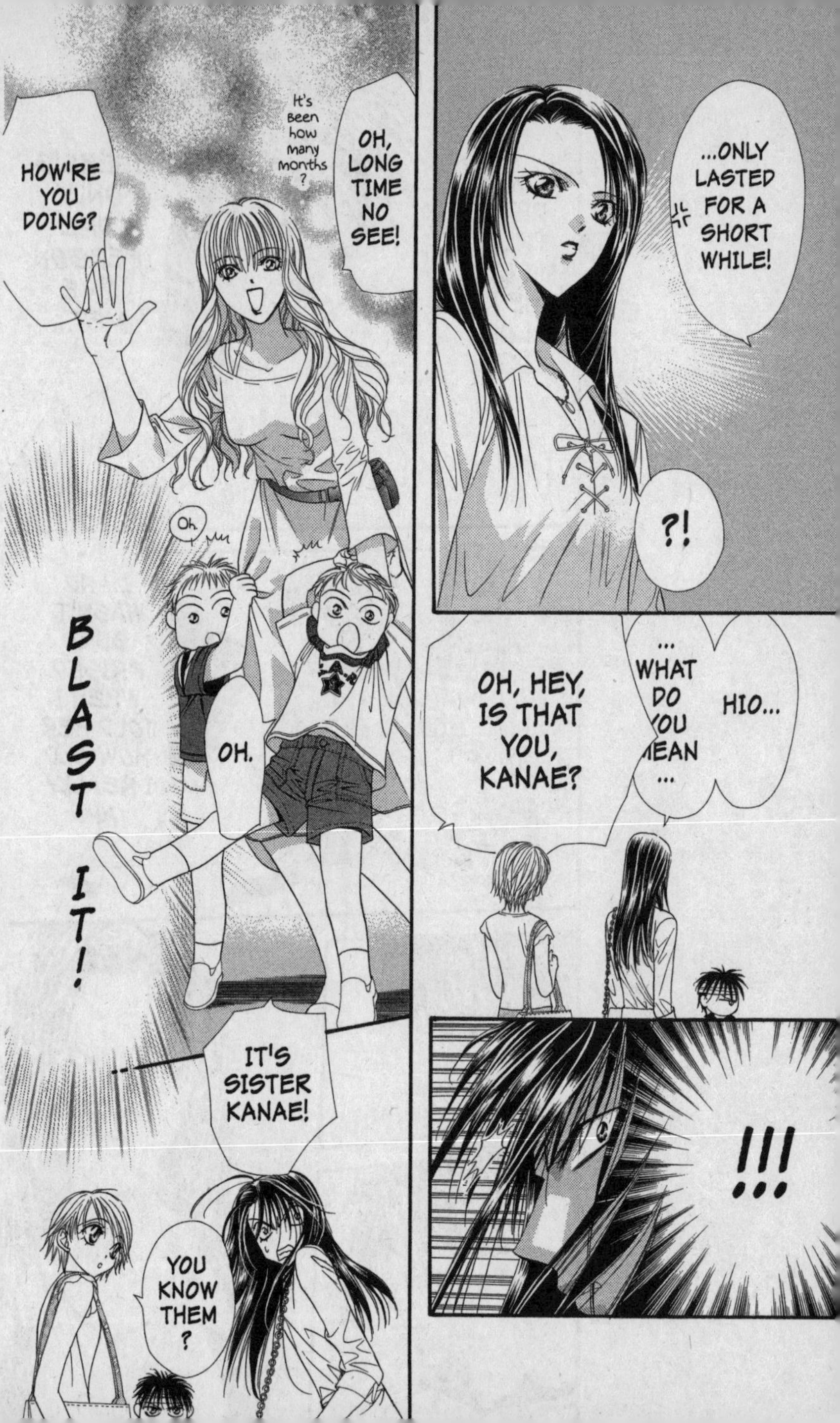

...ONLY LASTED FOR A SHORT WHILE!
?!
HIO...
... WHAT DO YOU MEAN ...
OH, HEY, IS THAT YOU, KANAE?
!!!
OH, LONG TIME NO SEE!
It's been how many months?
HOW'RE YOU DOING?
Oh.
BLAST IT!
OH.
IT'S SISTER KANAE!
YOU KNOW THEM?

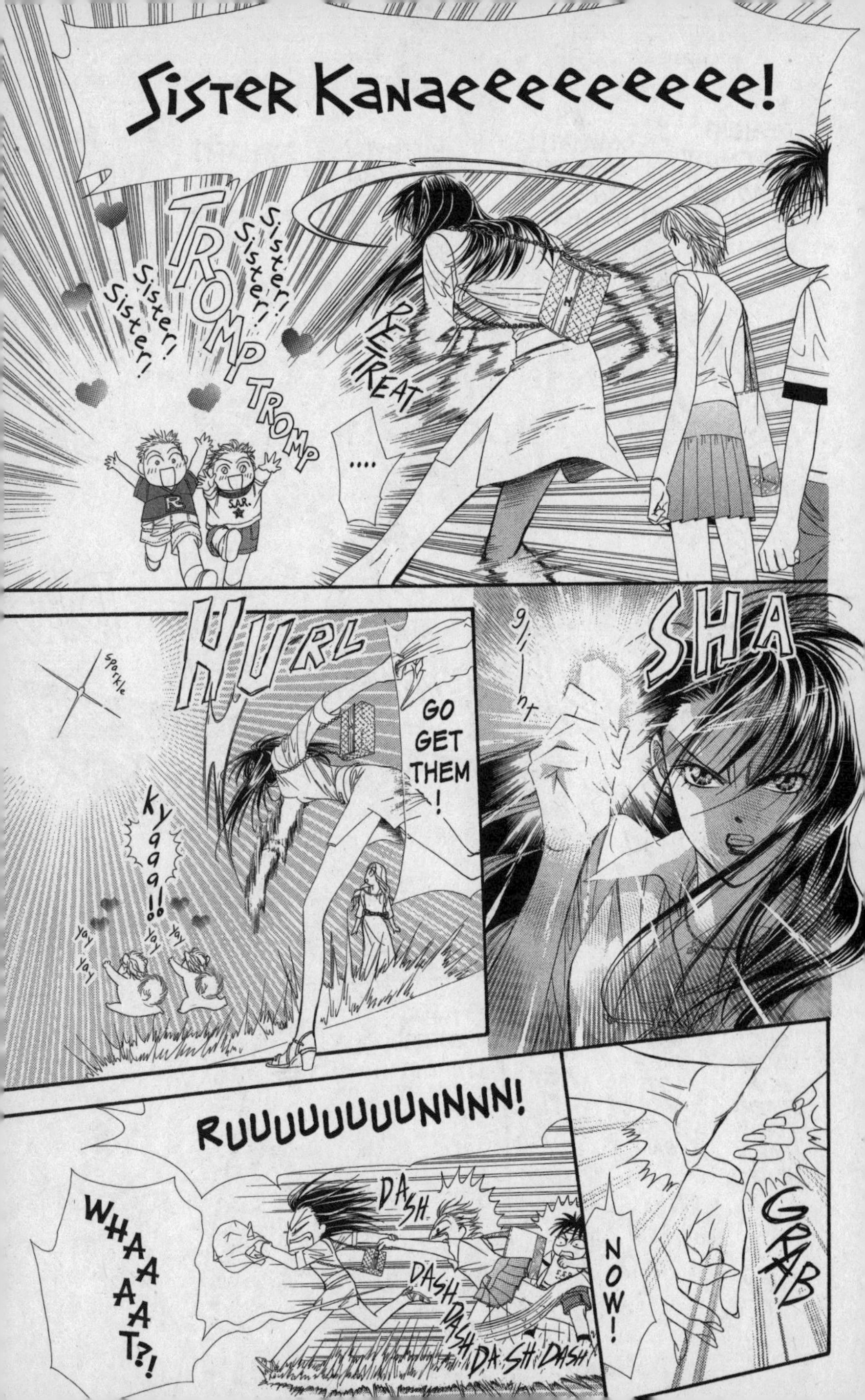
Sister Kanaeeeeeeeeee!
Sister! Sister! Sister! Sister!
TROMP TROMP
RETREAT
....
SHA
glint
HURL
GO GET THEM!
sparkle
Kyaaa!!
yay yay yay yay
GRAB
NOW!
RUUUUUUUUNNNN!
DASH DASH DASH DASH DASH DASH
WHAAAAAT?!

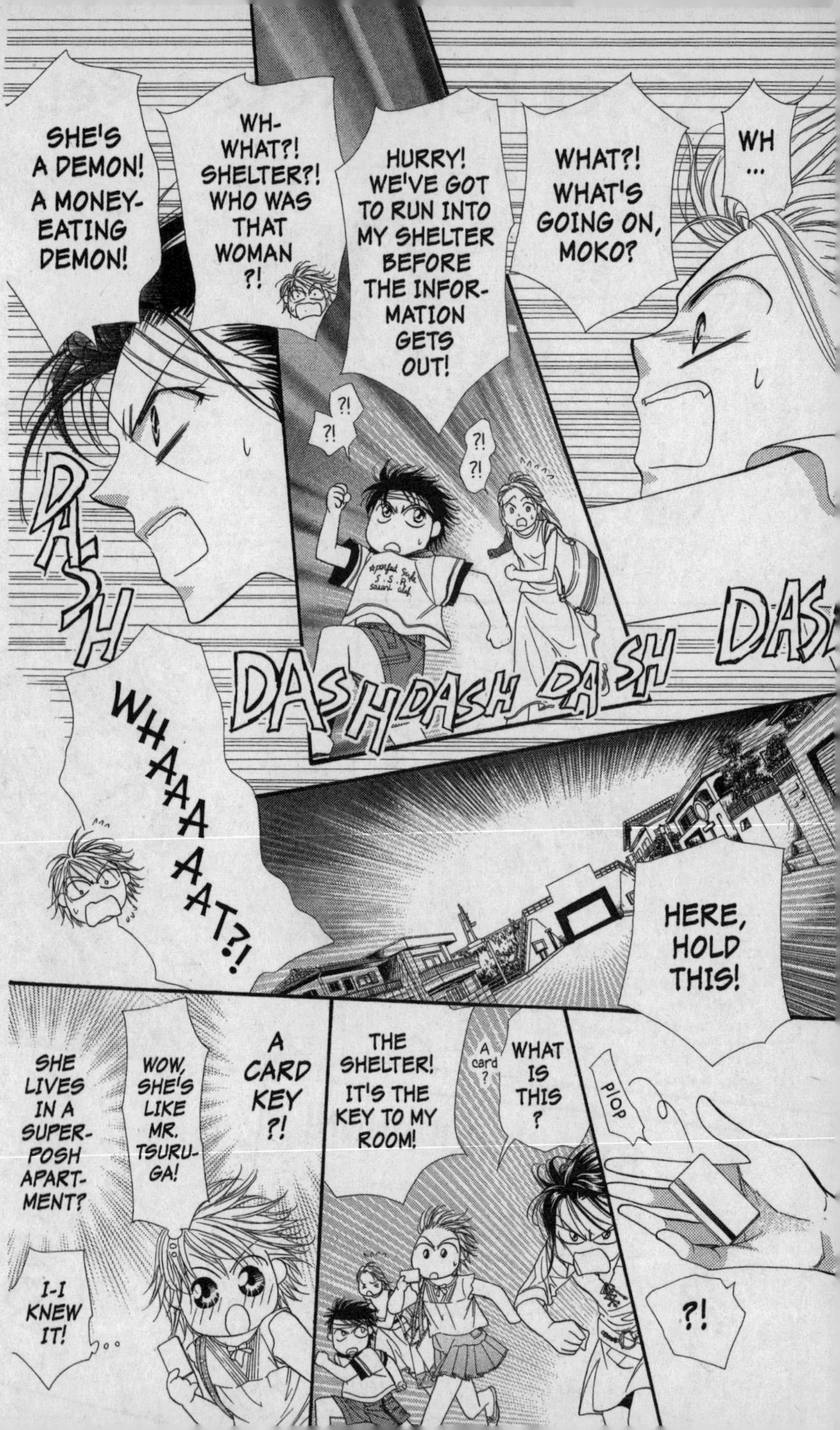
WH ...
WHAT?! WHAT'S GOING ON, MOKO?
HURRY! WE'VE GOT TO RUN INTO MY SHELTER BEFORE THE INFORMATION GETS OUT!
?! ?!
?! ?!
WH-WHAT?! SHELTER?! WHO WAS THAT WOMAN ?!
SHE'S A DEMON! A MONEY-EATING DEMON!
DASH
DASH DASH DASH DASH
WHAAAAAAT?!
HERE, HOLD THIS!
?!
WHAT IS THIS ?
A card ?
THE SHELTER! IT'S THE KEY TO MY ROOM!
A CARD KEY ?!
WOW, SHE'S LIKE MR. TSURUGA!
SHE LIVES IN A SUPER-POSH APARTMENT?
I-I KNEW IT!

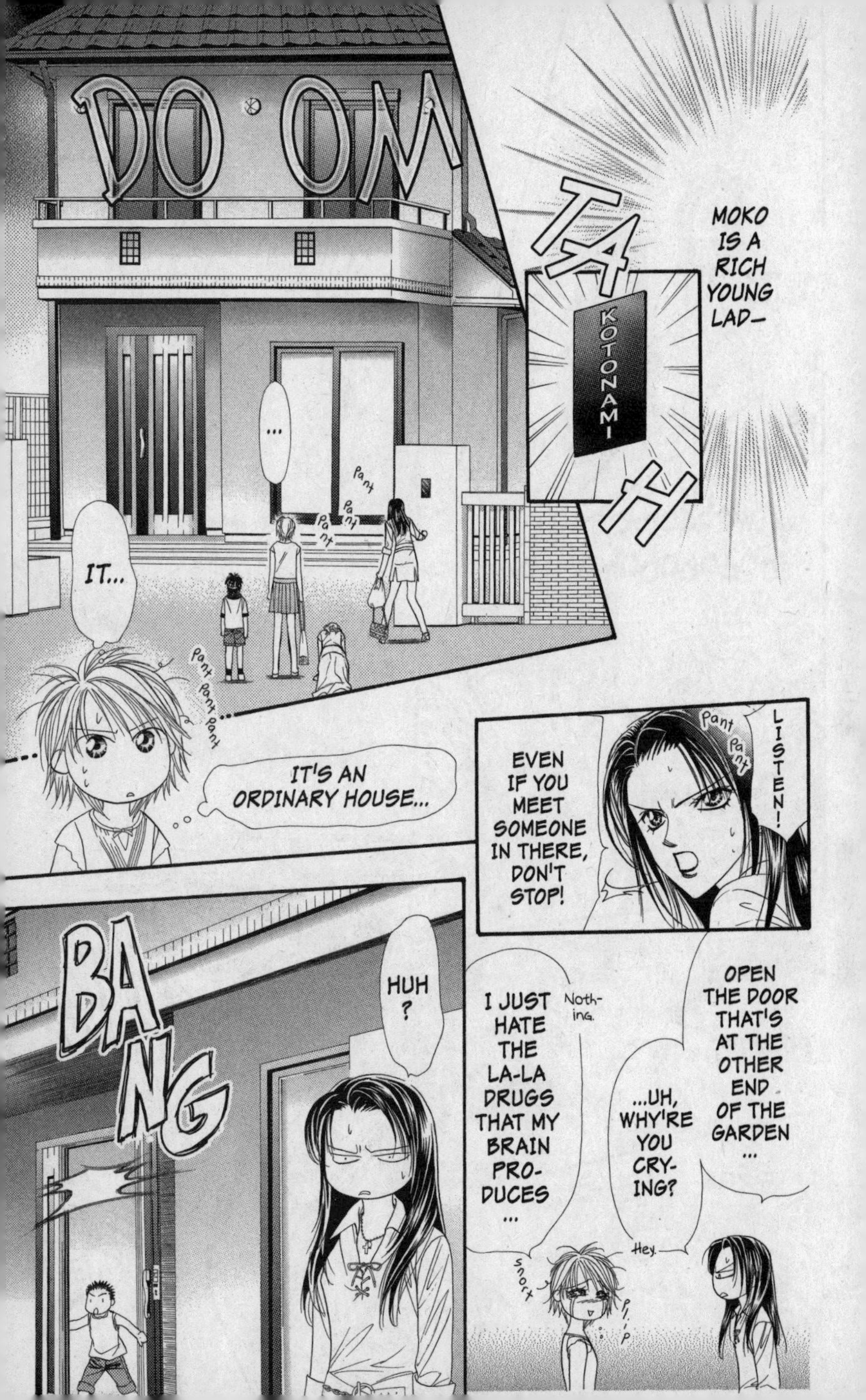
MOKO IS A RICH YOUNG LAD—
TAH
KOTONAMI
DO OM
...
Pant Pant Pant
IT...
Pant Pant Pant
IT'S AN ORDINARY HOUSE...
LISTEN!
Pant Pant
EVEN IF YOU MEET SOMEONE IN THERE, DON'T STOP!
OPEN THE DOOR THAT'S AT THE OTHER END OF THE GARDEN ...
...UH, WHY'RE YOU CRYING?
Hey.
Noth-ing.
I JUST HATE THE LA-LA DRUGS THAT MY BRAIN PRO-DUCES ...
snort
Plip
BANG
HUH ?

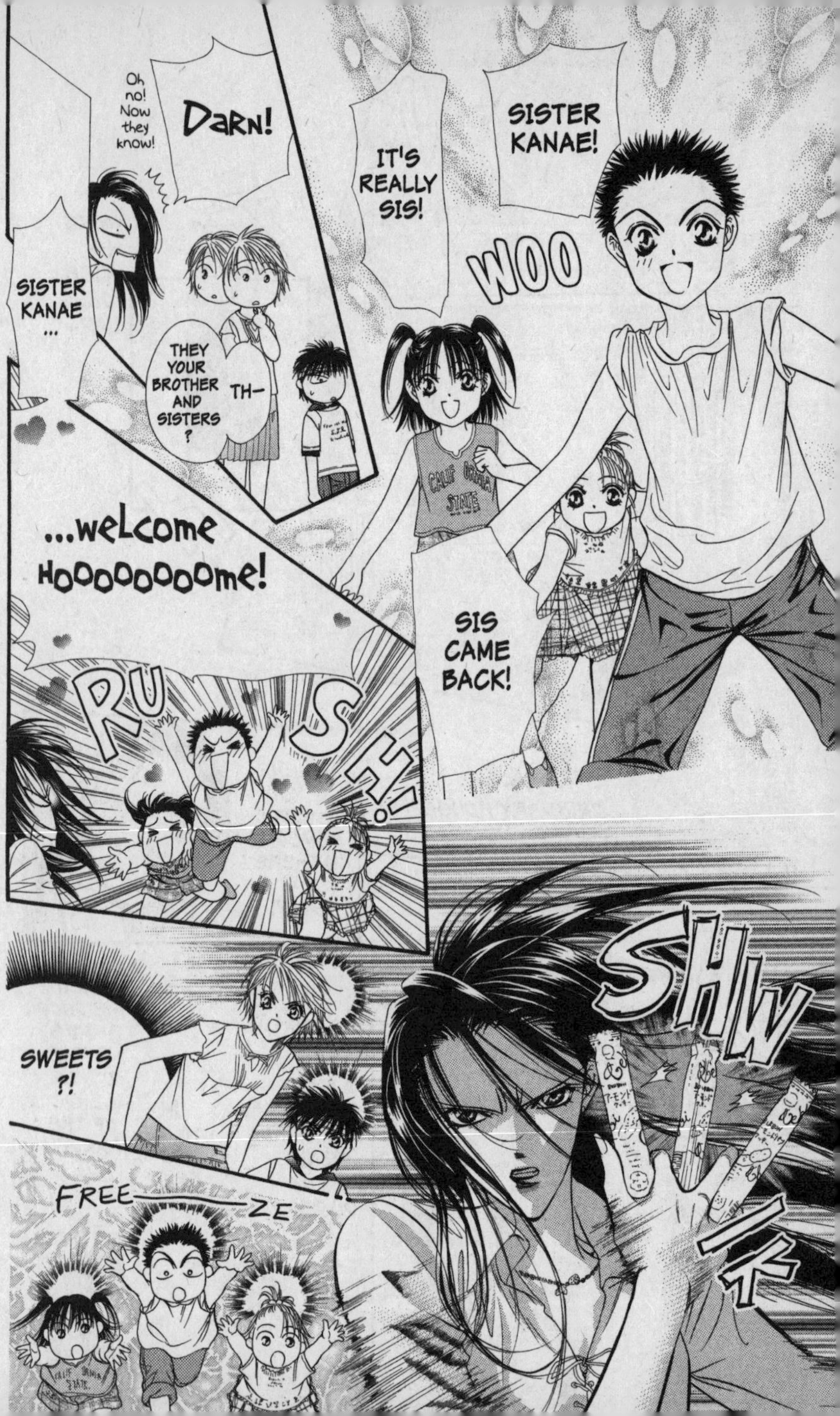
SISTER KANAE!
IT'S REALLY SIS!
WOO
SIS CAME BACK!
Darn!
Oh no! Now they know!
SISTER KANAE ...
TH—
THEY YOUR BROTHER AND SISTERS?
...welcome HOOOOOOOOme!
RUSH!
SHW
SWEETS ?!
FREE—ZE

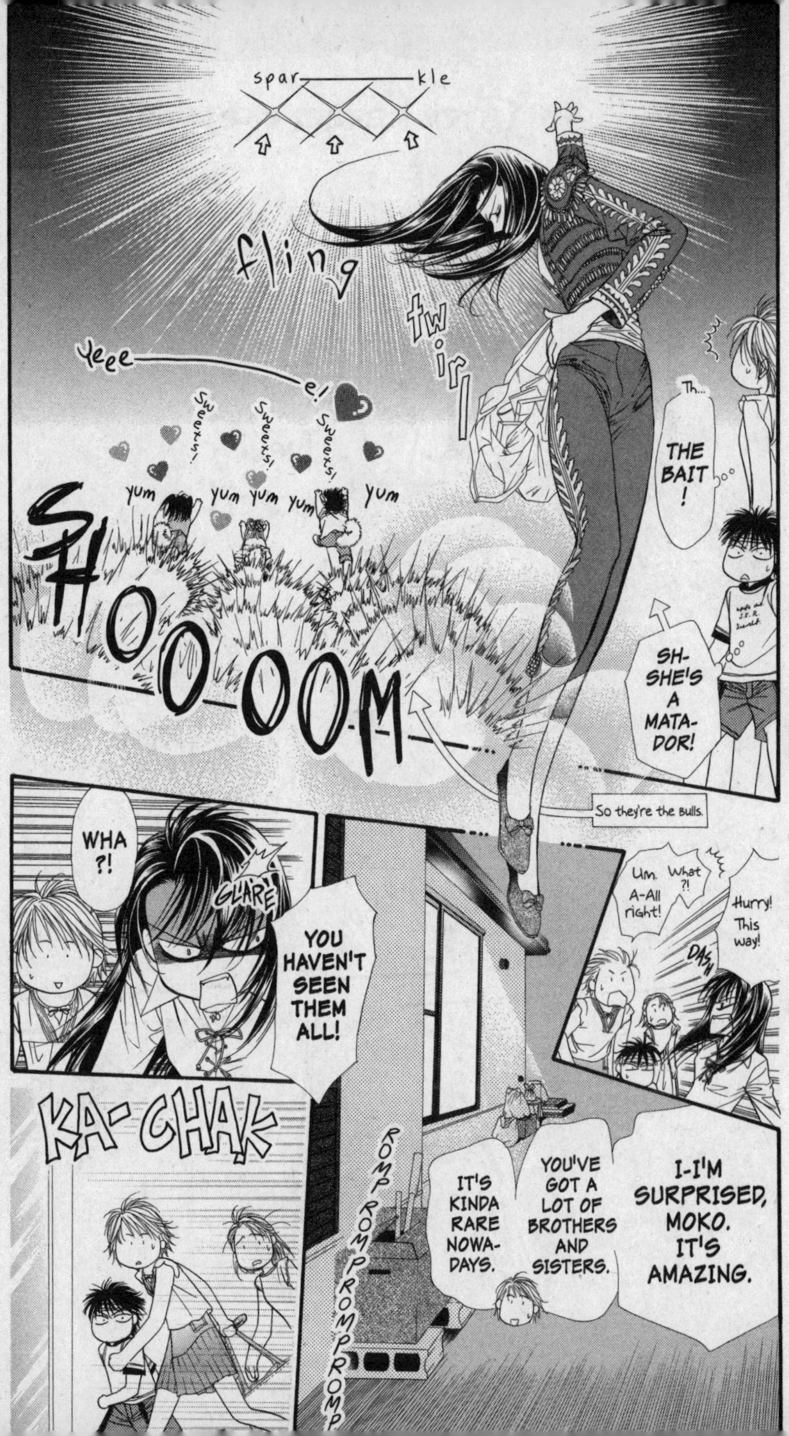
spar——kle
Th... THE BAIT!
fling
twirl
Yeee——e!
Sweets!
Sweets!
Sweets!
yum yum yum yum yum
SHOOOOM
SH-SHE'S A MATADOR!
So they're the bulls.
Hurry! This way!
What?!
Um. A-All right!
DASH
WHA?!
GLARE
YOU HAVEN'T SEEN THEM ALL!
I-I'M SURPRISED, MOKO. IT'S AMAZING.
YOU'VE GOT A LOT OF BROTHERS AND SISTERS.
IT'S KINDA RARE NOWA-DAYS.
ROMP ROMP ROMP ROMP
KA-CHAK

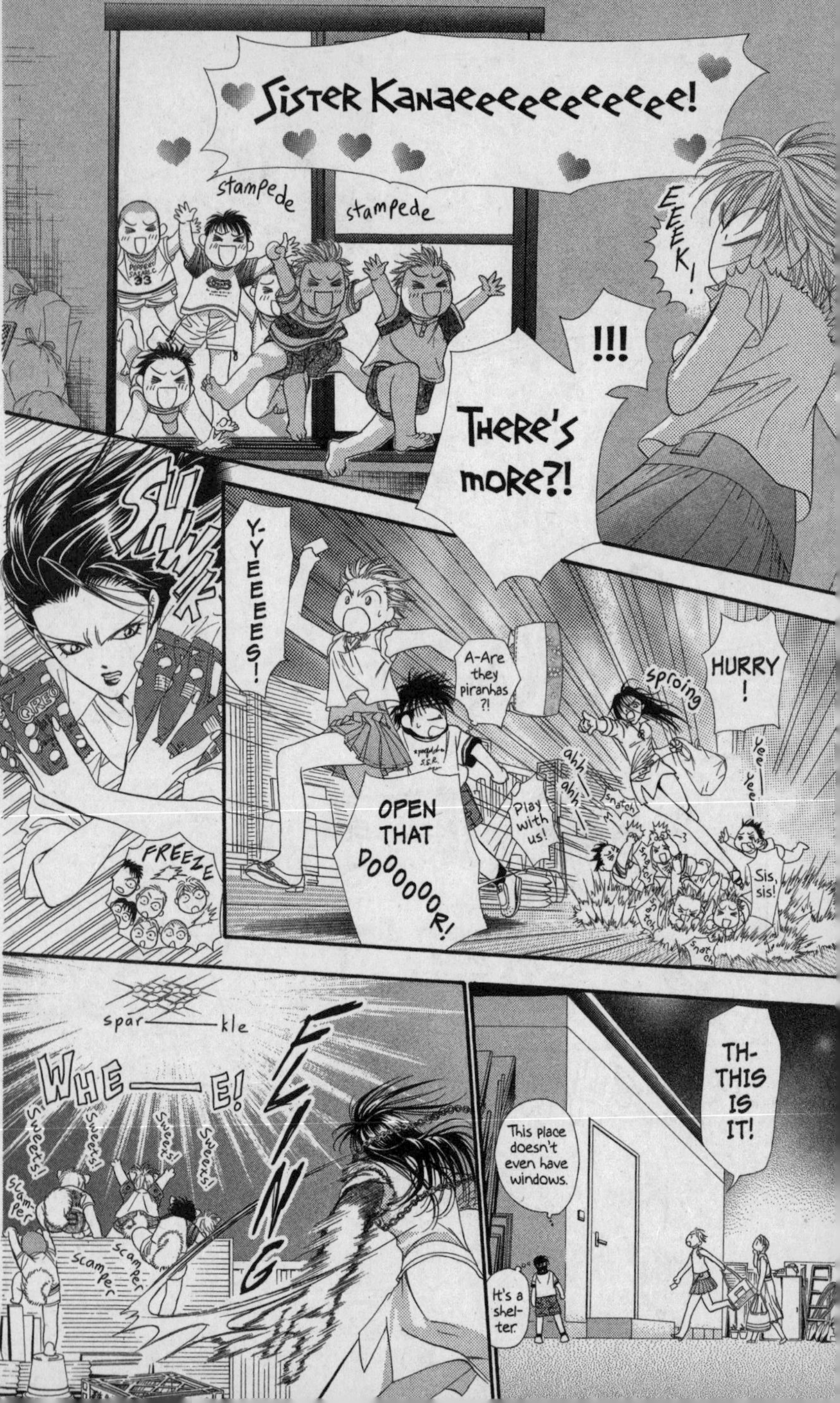
Sister Kanaeeeeeeeeeeee!
stampede
stampede
EEEEK!
!!!
There's more?!
HURRY!
sproing
Yee yee
Sis, sis!
snatch
snatch
ahh ahh
Play with us!
A-Are they piranhas?!
Y-YEEEEES!
OPEN THAT DOOOOOOR!
SHWIK
FREEZE
TH-THIS IS IT!
This place doesn't even have windows.
It's a shelter.
sparkle
WHE—E!
FLING
Sweets!
Sweets!
Sweets!
Sweets!
scamper
scamper
scamper

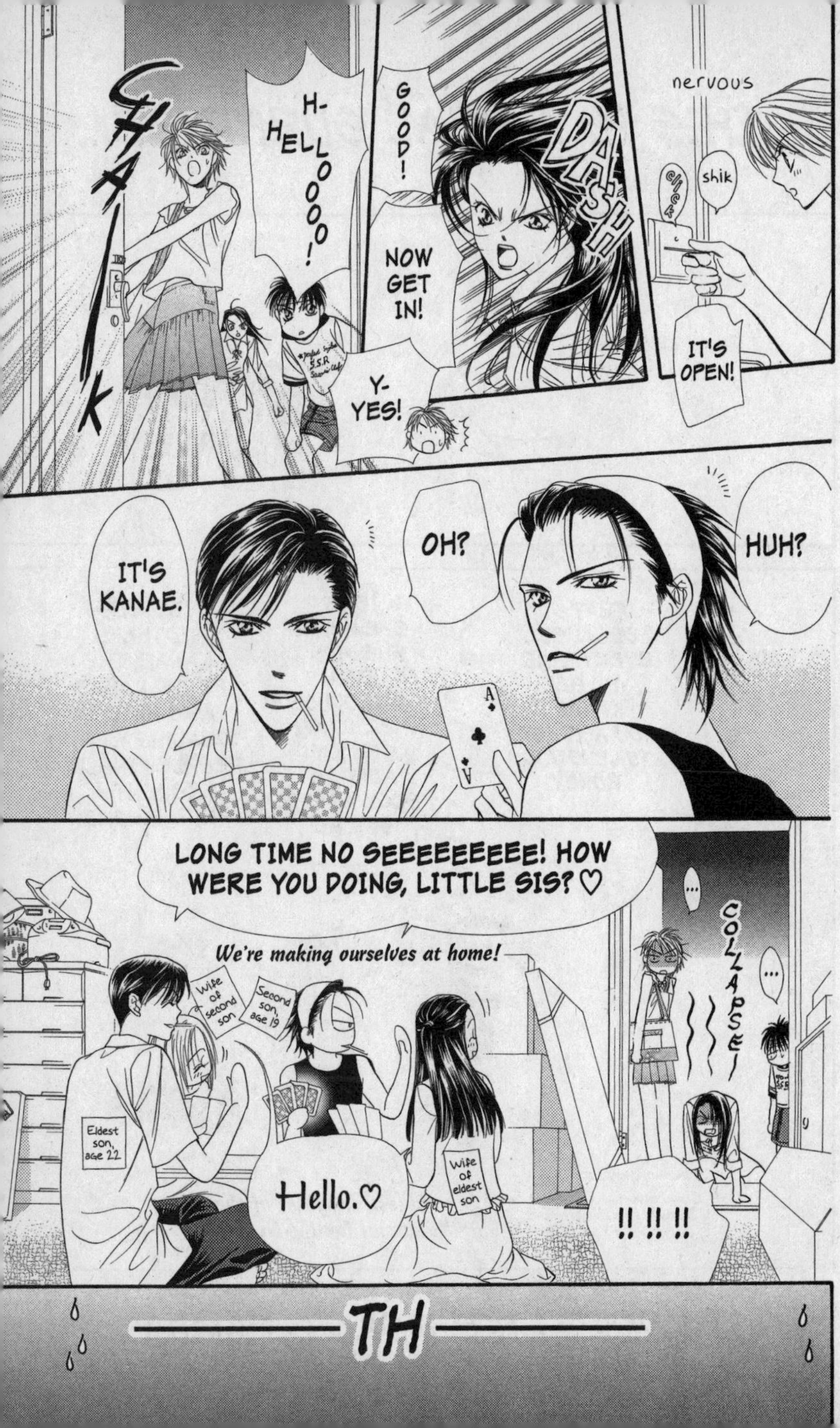

nervous
click
shik
IT'S OPEN!
DASH
GOOD!
NOW GET IN!
Y-YES!
SHAK
H-HELLOOOO!
HUH?
OH?
IT'S KANAE.
...
COLLAPSE!
...
!! !! !!
LONG TIME NO SEEEEEEEEE! HOW WERE YOU DOING, LITTLE SIS? ♡
We're making ourselves at home!
Wife of eldest son
Second son, age 19
Wife of second son
Eldest son, age 22
Hello.♡
TH

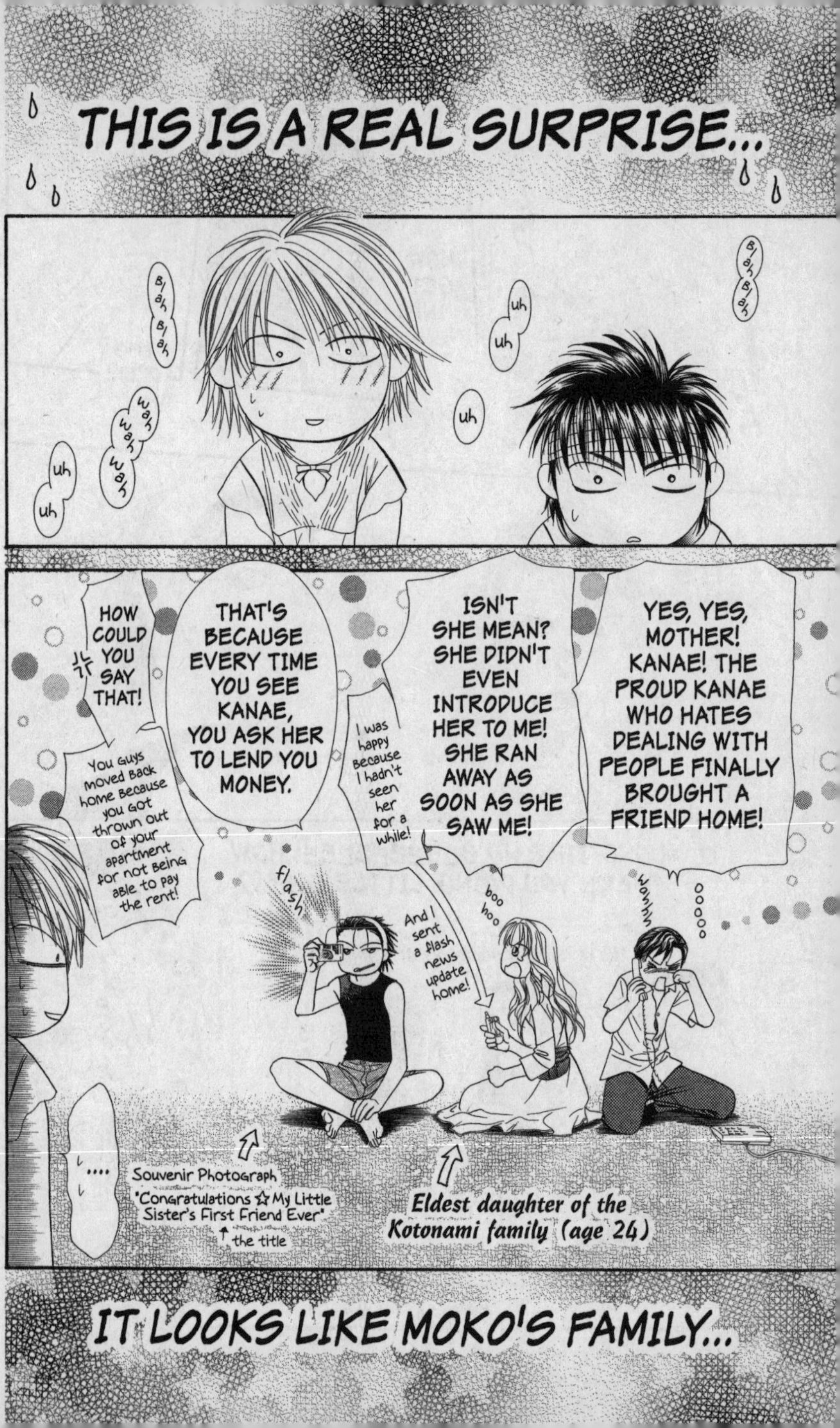
THIS IS A REAL SURPRISE...
Blah Blah
uh
uh
uh
Blah Blah
wah wah wah
uh
uh
YES, YES, MOTHER! KANAE! THE PROUD KANAE WHO HATES DEALING WITH PEOPLE FINALLY BROUGHT A FRIEND HOME!
ISN'T SHE MEAN? SHE DIDN'T EVEN INTRODUCE HER TO ME! SHE RAN AWAY AS SOON AS SHE SAW ME!
I was happy because I hadn't seen her for a while!
THAT'S BECAUSE EVERY TIME YOU SEE KANAE, YOU ASK HER TO LEND YOU MONEY.
HOW COULD YOU SAY THAT!
You guys moved back home because you got thrown out of your apartment for not being able to pay the rent!
Waahh
ooooo
boo hoo
And I sent a flash news update home!
flash
Eldest daughter of the Kotonami family (age 24)
Souvenir Photograph "Congratulations ☆ My Little Sister's First Friend Ever"
↑ the title
....
IT LOOKS LIKE MOKO'S FAMILY...

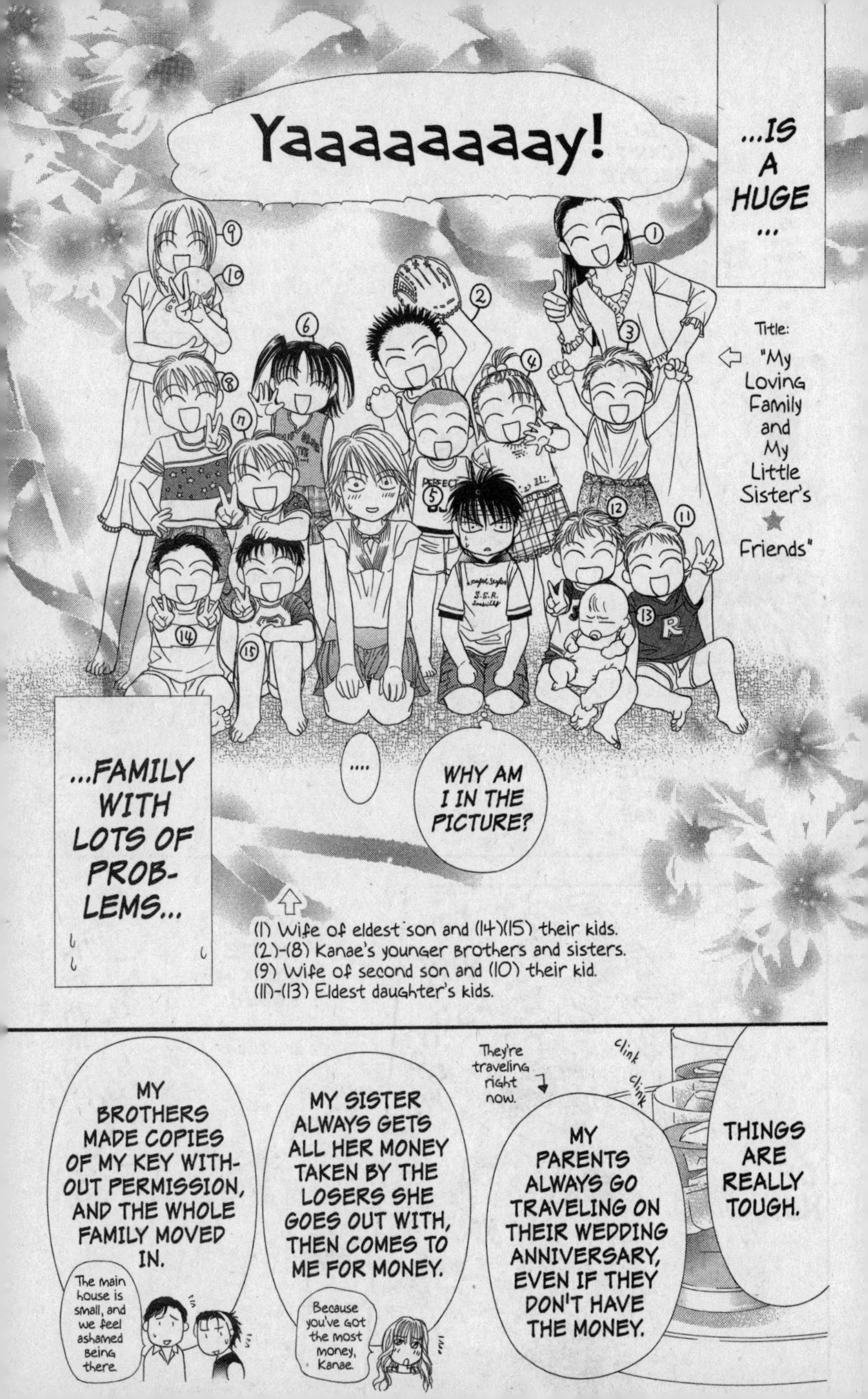
...IS A HUGE ...
Title: "My Loving Family and My Little Sister's ★ Friends"
Yaaaaaaaaay!
WHY AM I IN THE PICTURE?
....
...FAMILY WITH LOTS OF PROB-LEMS...
(1) Wife of eldest son and (14)(15) their kids.
(2)-(8) Kanae's younger brothers and sisters.
(9) Wife of second son and (10) their kid.
(11)-(13) Eldest daughter's kids.
THINGS ARE REALLY TOUGH.
clink
clink
They're traveling right now.
MY PARENTS ALWAYS GO TRAVELING ON THEIR WEDDING ANNIVERSARY, EVEN IF THEY DON'T HAVE THE MONEY.
MY SISTER ALWAYS GETS ALL HER MONEY TAKEN BY THE LOSERS SHE GOES OUT WITH, THEN COMES TO ME FOR MONEY.
Because you've got the most money, Kanae.
MY BROTHERS MADE COPIES OF MY KEY WITH-OUT PERMISSION, AND THE WHOLE FAMILY MOVED IN.
The main house is small, and we feel ashamed being there.

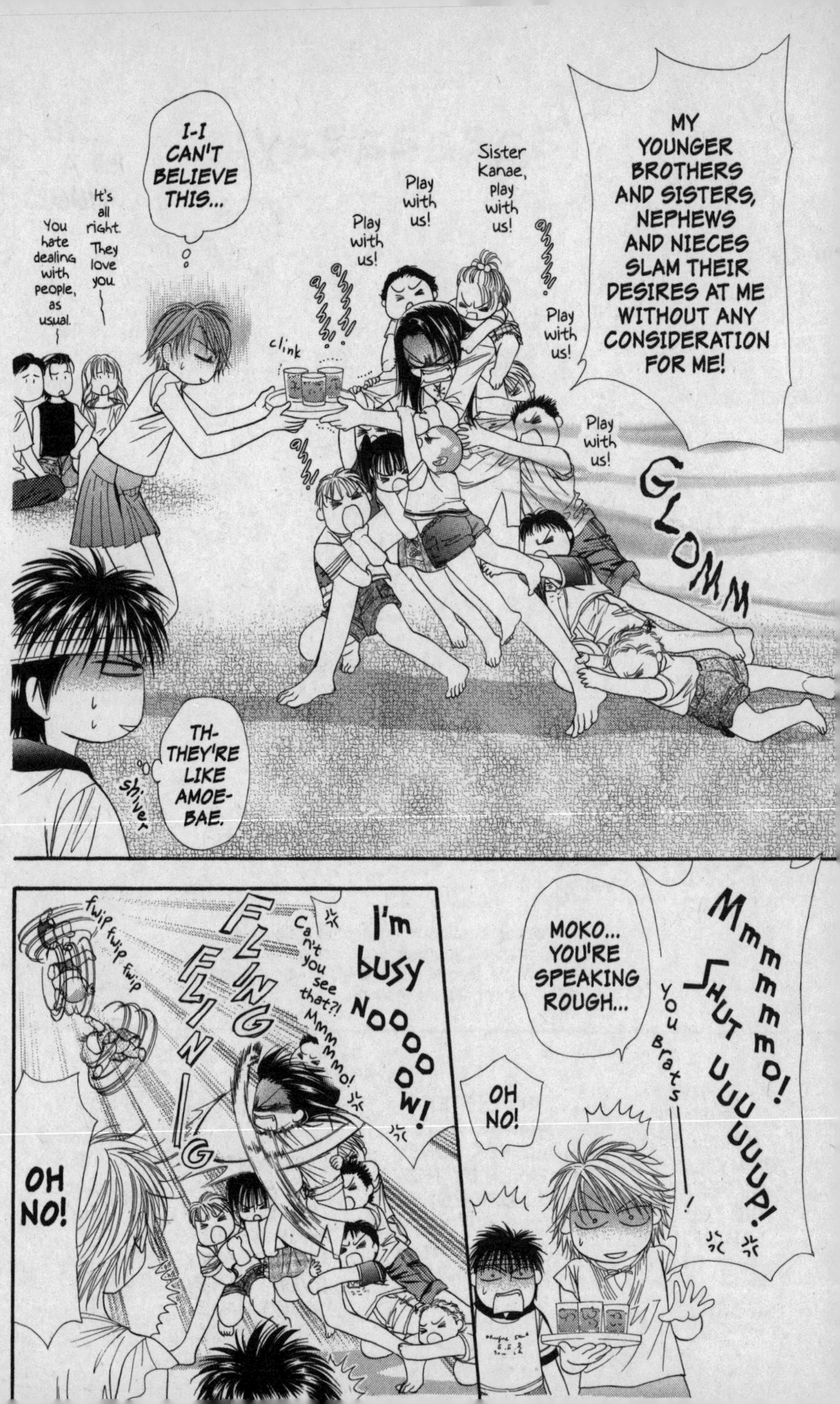
MY YOUNGER BROTHERS AND SISTERS, NEPHEWS AND NIECES SLAM THEIR DESIRES AT ME WITHOUT ANY CONSIDERATION FOR ME!
Sister Kanae, play with us!
Play with us!
Play with us!
I-I CAN'T BELIEVE THIS...
It's all right. They love you.
You hate dealing with people, as usual.
ahhhh!
Play with us!
ahhhh!
ahhhh!
clink
Play with us!
ahh!
GLOMM
TH-THEY'RE LIKE AMOE-BAE.
shiver
Mmmmmo! SHUT UUUUUUP!
You Brats—!
MOKO... YOU'RE SPEAKING ROUGH...
OH NO!
I'm busy NOOOOOOW!
Can't you see that?! Mmmmmo!
FLING
FLING
fwip fwip fwip
OH NO!

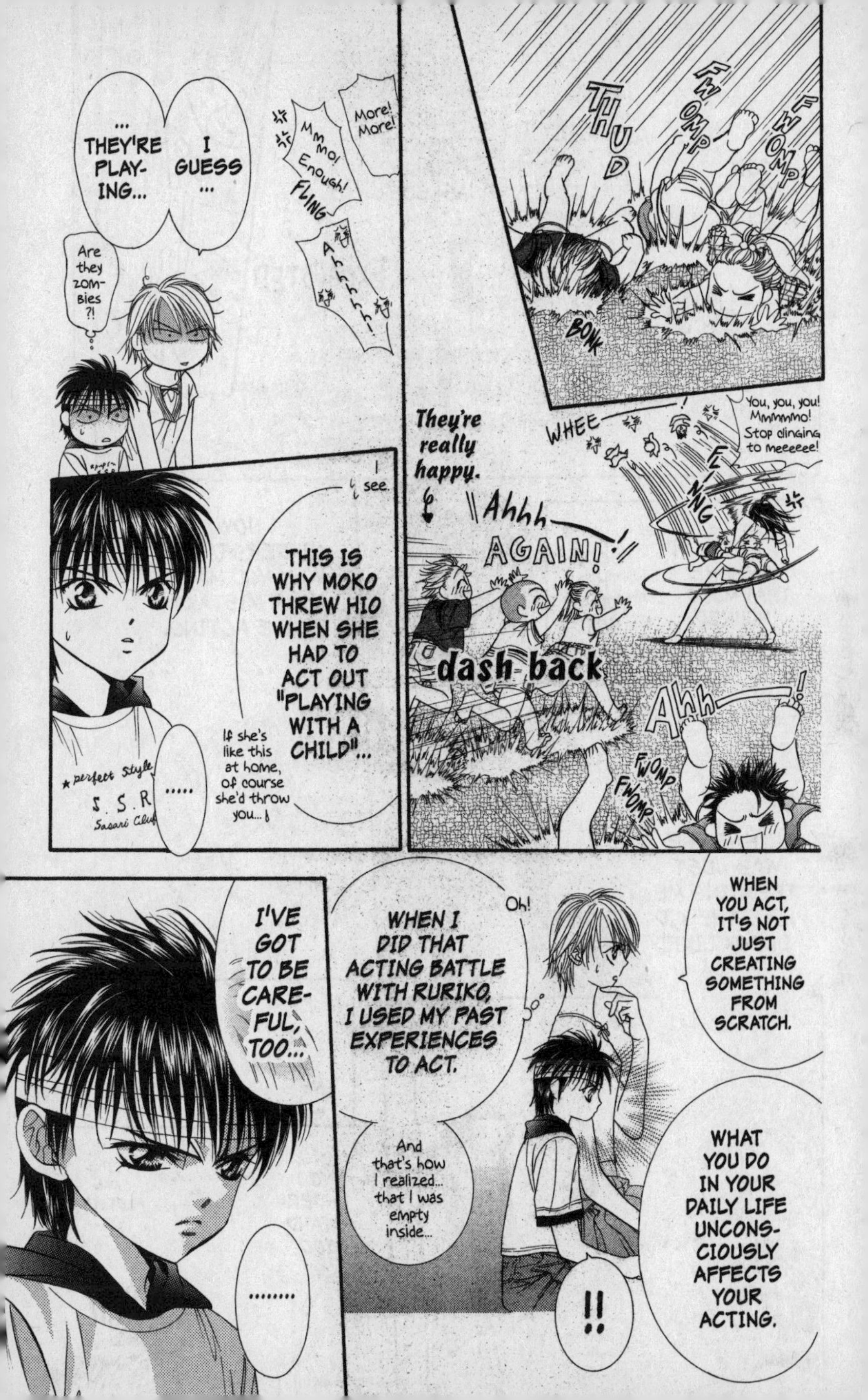
FWOMP
FWOMP
THUD
BONK
More! More!
Mmmo! Enough!
FLING
Ahhhhhh!
I GUESS...
... THEY'RE PLAYING...
Are they zombies?!
You, you, you! Mmmmmo! Stop clinging to meeeeee!
FLING
WHEE
Ahhh AGAIN!
They're really happy.
dash back
Ahh—!
FWOMP
FWOMP
I see.
THIS IS WHY MOKO THREW HIO WHEN SHE HAD TO ACT OUT "PLAYING WITH A CHILD"...
If she's like this at home, of course she'd throw you...
.....
★perfect Style S.S.R Sasari Club
WHEN YOU ACT, IT'S NOT JUST CREATING SOMETHING FROM SCRATCH.
WHAT YOU DO IN YOUR DAILY LIFE UNCONSCIOUSLY AFFECTS YOUR ACTING.
!!
Oh!
WHEN I DID THAT ACTING BATTLE WITH RURIKO, I USED MY PAST EXPERIENCES TO ACT.
And that's how I realized... that I was empty inside...
I'VE GOT TO BE CAREFUL, TOO...
....

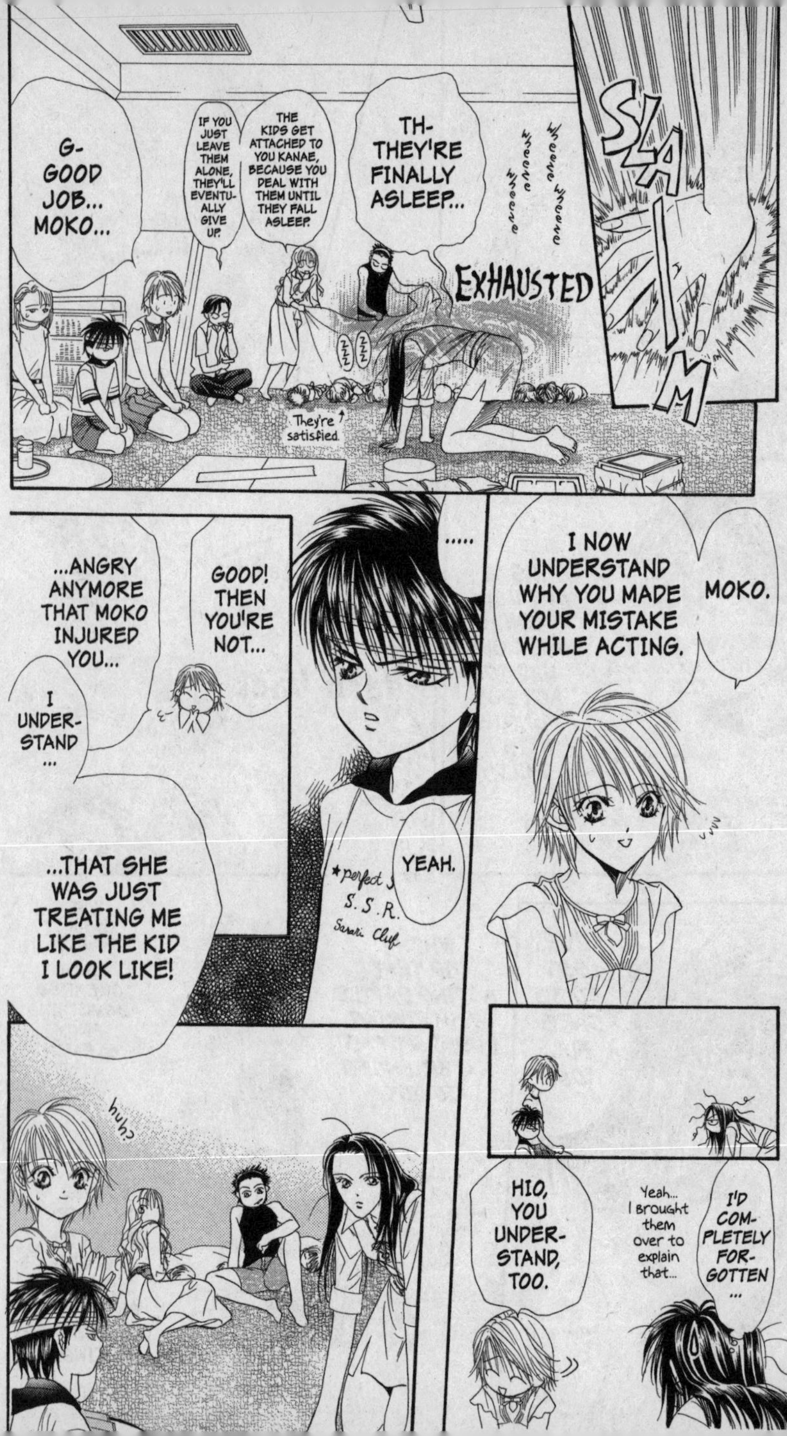
SLAM
TH- THEY'RE FINALLY ASLEEP...
wheeze wheeze wheeze wheeze
EXHAUSTED
THE KIDS GET ATTACHED TO YOU KANAE, BECAUSE YOU DEAL WITH THEM UNTIL THEY FALL ASLEEP.
IF YOU JUST LEAVE THEM ALONE, THEY'LL EVENTUALLY GIVE UP.
G- GOOD JOB... MOKO...
They're satisfied.
MOKO.
I NOW UNDERSTAND WHY YOU MADE YOUR MISTAKE WHILE ACTING.
.....
YEAH.
GOOD! THEN YOU'RE NOT...
...ANGRY ANYMORE THAT MOKO INJURED YOU...
I UNDERSTAND...
...THAT SHE WAS JUST TREATING ME LIKE THE KID I LOOK LIKE!
I'D COMPLETELY FORGOTTEN...
Yeah... I brought them over to explain that...
HIO, YOU UNDERSTAND, TOO.
huh?

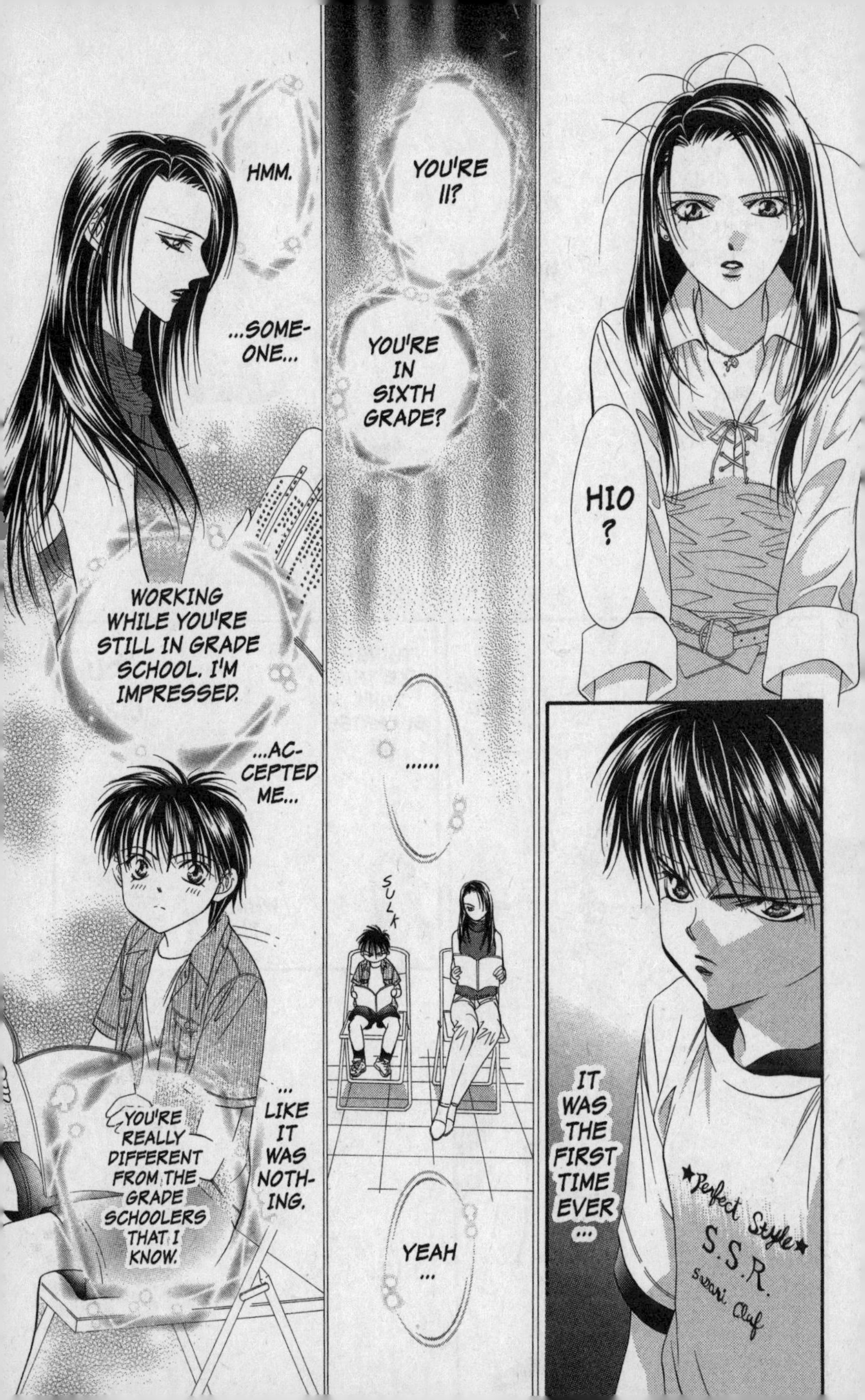
HIO ?
IT WAS THE FIRST TIME EVER ...
★Perfect Style★ S.S.R.
YOU'RE 11?
YOU'RE IN SIXTH GRADE?
......
SULK
YEAH ...
HMM.
...SOME-ONE...
WORKING WHILE YOU'RE STILL IN GRADE SCHOOL. I'M IMPRESSED.
...AC-CEPTED ME...
... LIKE IT WAS NOTH-ING.
YOU'RE REALLY DIFFERENT FROM THE GRADE SCHOOLERS THAT I KNOW.

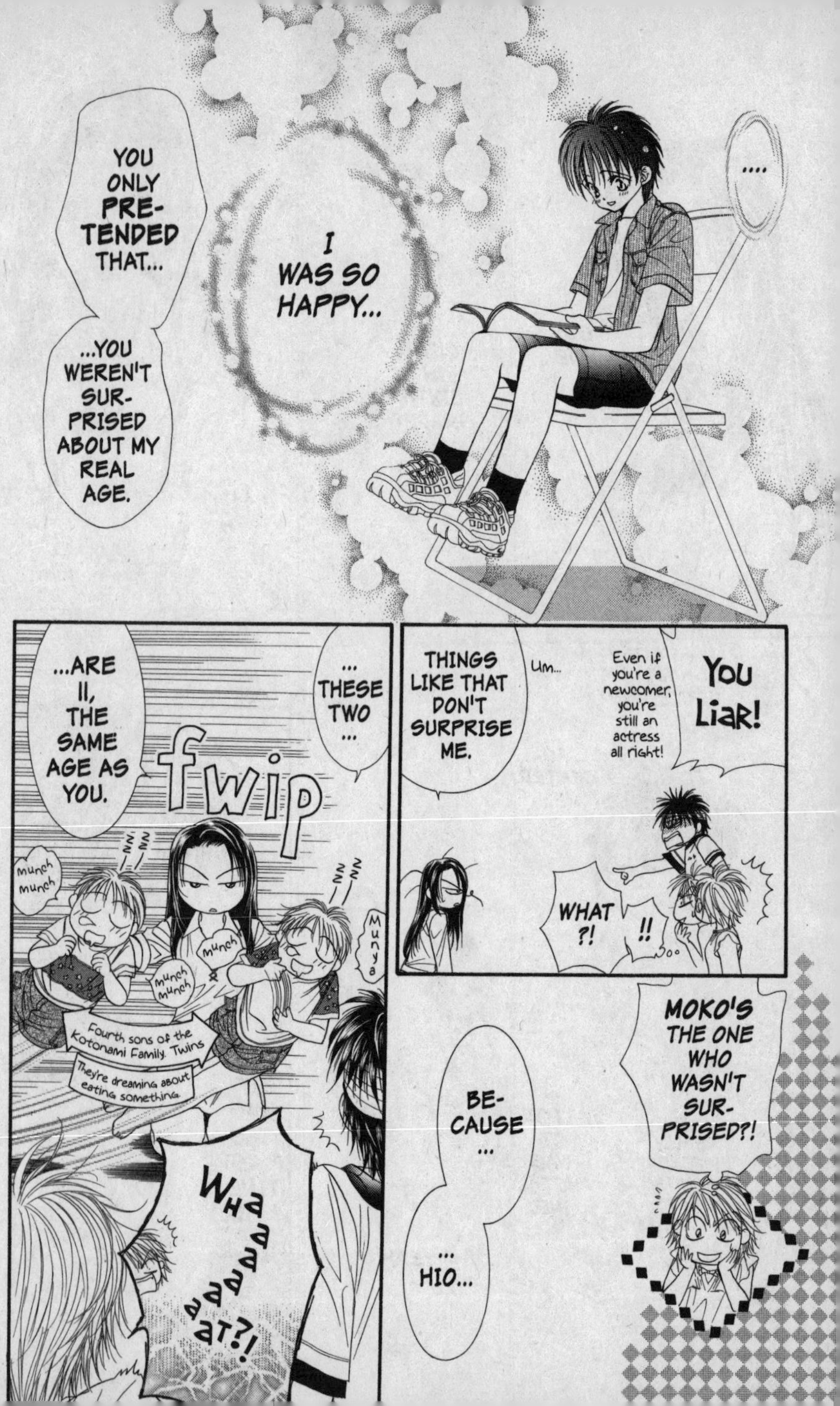
....
I WAS SO HAPPY...
YOU ONLY PRE-TENDED THAT...
...YOU WEREN'T SUR-PRISED ABOUT MY REAL AGE.
YOU LIAR!
Even if you're a newcomer, you're still an actress all right!
Um...
THINGS LIKE THAT DON'T SURPRISE ME.
WHAT?!
!!
MOKO'S THE ONE WHO WASN'T SUR-PRISED?!
BE-CAUSE ...
... HIO...
... THESE TWO ...
...ARE 11, THE SAME AGE AS YOU.
fwip
munch munch
munch
munch munch
Munya
Fourth sons of the Kotonami Family. Twins
They're dreaming about eating something.
Whaaaaaaat?!

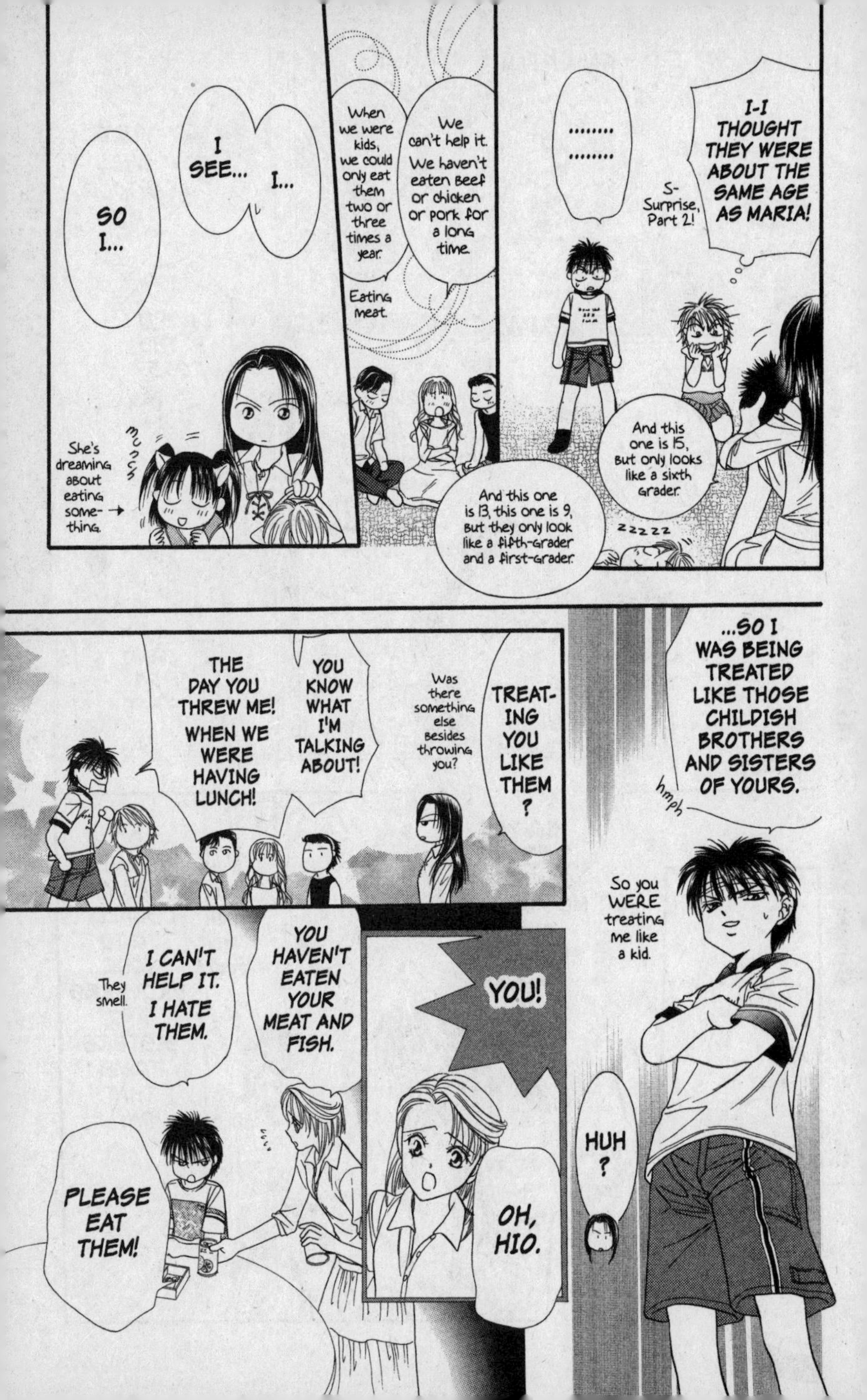
I-I THOUGHT THEY WERE ABOUT THE SAME AGE AS MARIA!
S-Surprise, Part 2!
....
....
And this one is 15, but only looks like a sixth grader.
And this one is 13, this one is 9, but they only look like a fifth-grader and a first-grader.
zzzzz
We can't help it. We haven't eaten beef or chicken or pork for a long time.
When we were kids, we could only eat them two or three times a year.
Eating meat.
I SEE... I...
SO I...
munch
She's dreaming about eating some-thing.
...SO I WAS BEING TREATED LIKE THOSE CHILDISH BROTHERS AND SISTERS OF YOURS.
hmph
So you WERE treating me like a kid.
HUH ?
TREATING YOU LIKE THEM ?
Was there something else besides throwing you?
YOU KNOW WHAT I'M TALKING ABOUT!
THE DAY YOU THREW ME! WHEN WE WERE HAVING LUNCH!
YOU!
OH, HIO.
YOU HAVEN'T EATEN YOUR MEAT AND FISH.
I CAN'T HELP IT. I HATE THEM.
They smell.
PLEASE EAT THEM!

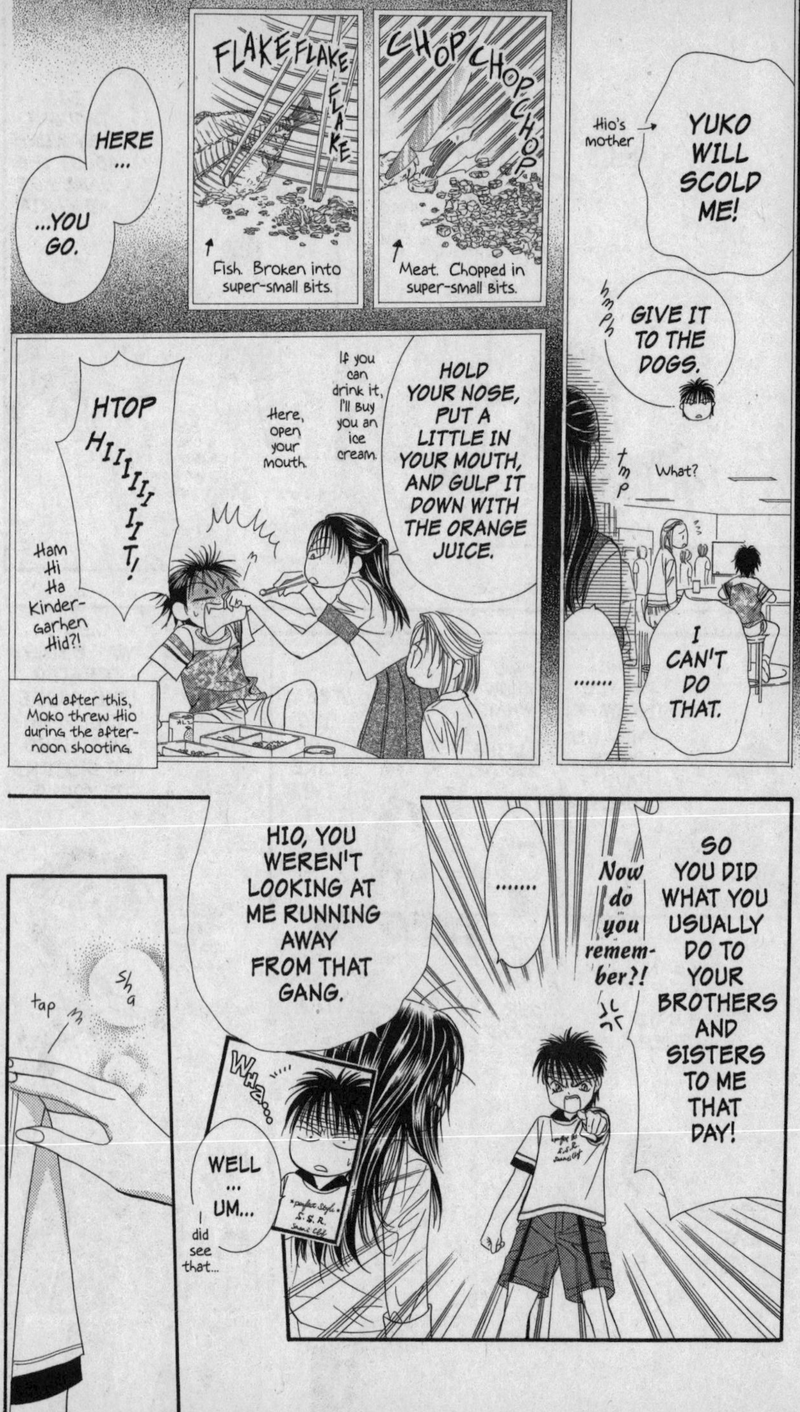
Hio's mother
YUKO WILL SCOLD ME!
hmph
GIVE IT TO THE DOGS.
tmp
What?
I CAN'T DO THAT.
....
CHOP CHOP CHOP CHOP
Meat. Chopped in super-small bits.
FLAKE FLAKE FLAKE
Fish. Broken into super-small bits.
HERE...
...YOU GO.
HOLD YOUR NOSE, PUT A LITTLE IN YOUR MOUTH, AND GULP IT DOWN WITH THE ORANGE JUICE.
If you can drink it, I'll buy you an ice cream.
Here, open your mouth.
HTOP HIIIIIIIT!
Ham Hi Ha Kinder-Garhen Hid?!
And after this, Moko threw Hio during the after-noon shooting.
SO YOU DID WHAT YOU USUALLY DO TO YOUR BROTHERS AND SISTERS TO ME THAT DAY!
Now do you remem-ber?!
....
HIO, YOU WEREN'T LOOKING AT ME RUNNING AWAY FROM THAT GANG.
Wha...
WELL... UM...
I did see that...
Sha
tap

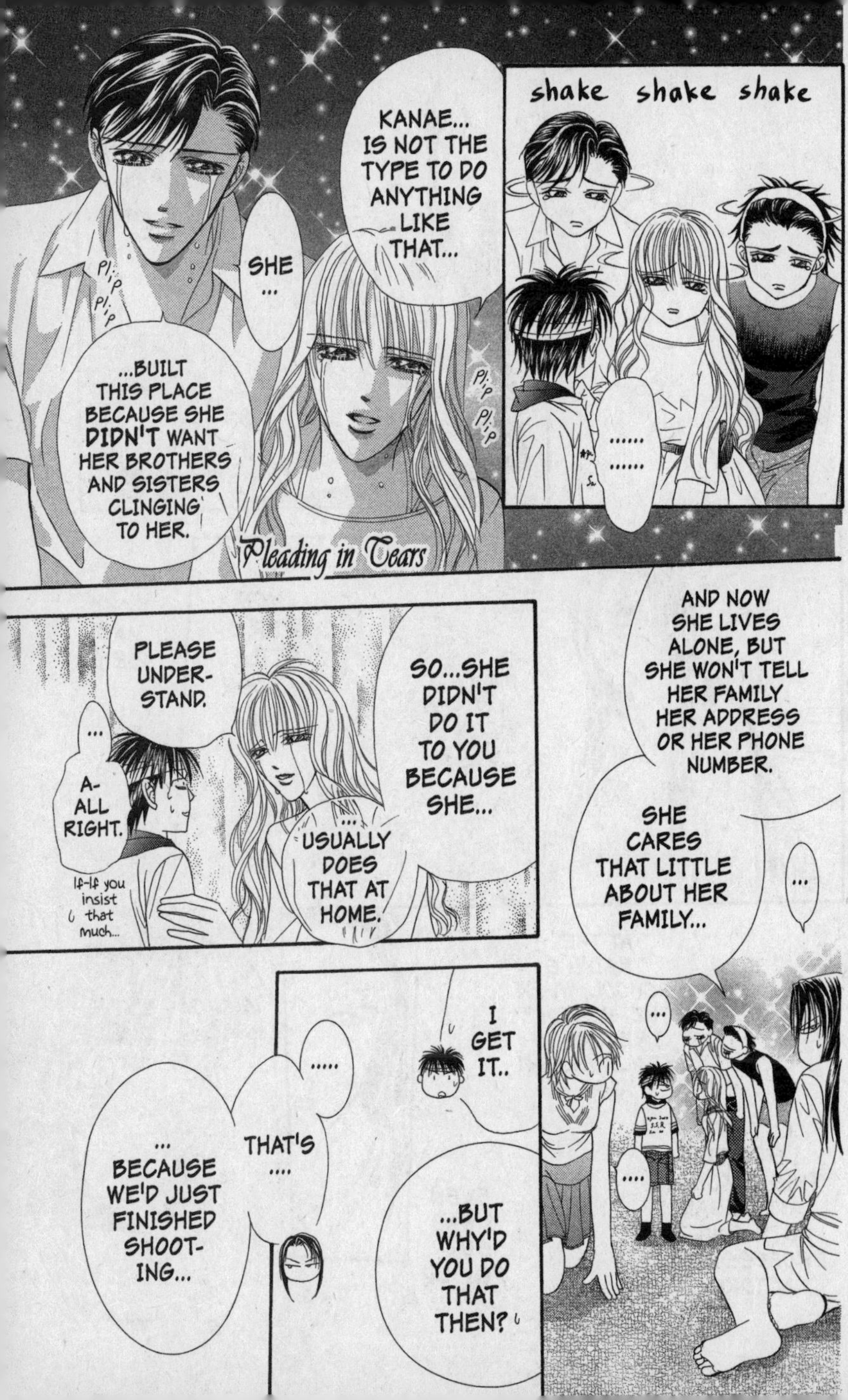
KANAE... IS NOT THE TYPE TO DO ANYTHING LIKE THAT...
SHE ...
...BUILT THIS PLACE BECAUSE SHE DIDN'T WANT HER BROTHERS AND SISTERS CLINGING TO HER.
Pl.p Pl.p
Pl.p Pl.p
Pleading in Tears
shake shake shake
....
AND NOW SHE LIVES ALONE, BUT SHE WON'T TELL HER FAMILY HER ADDRESS OR HER PHONE NUMBER.
SHE CARES THAT LITTLE ABOUT HER FAMILY...
...
SO...SHE DIDN'T DO IT TO YOU BECAUSE SHE...
...USUALLY DOES THAT AT HOME.
PLEASE UNDER-STAND.
...
A- ALL RIGHT.
If-If you insist that much...
...
....
I GET IT..
...BUT WHY'D YOU DO THAT THEN?
.....
THAT'S ....
... BECAUSE WE'D JUST FINISHED SHOOT-ING...

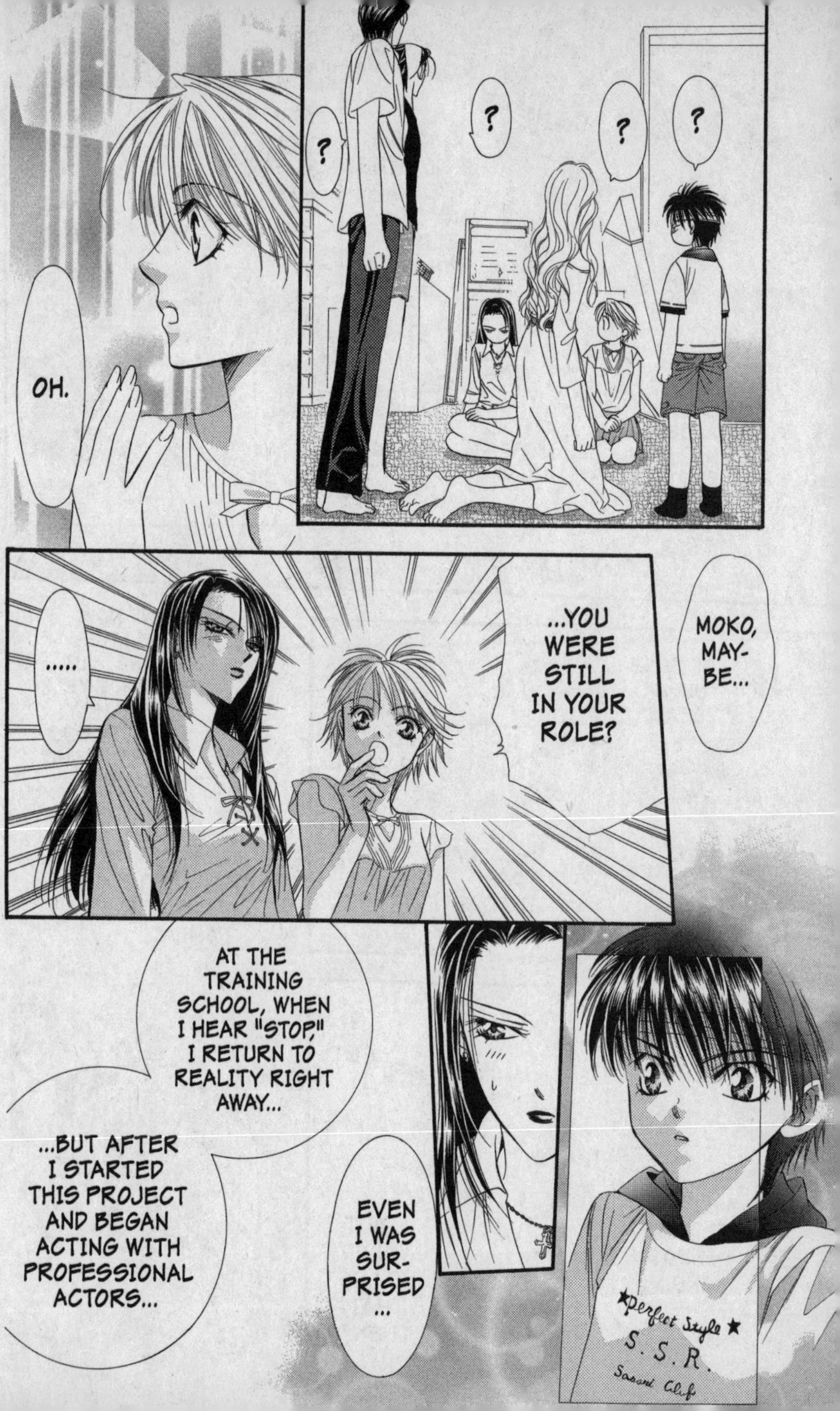
?
?
?
?
OH.
MOKO, MAY-BE...
...YOU WERE STILL IN YOUR ROLE?
.....
EVEN I WAS SUR-PRISED...
AT THE TRAINING SCHOOL, WHEN I HEAR "STOP," I RETURN TO REALITY RIGHT AWAY...
...BUT AFTER I STARTED THIS PROJECT AND BEGAN ACTING WITH PROFESSIONAL ACTORS...
★Perfect Style★
S.S.R.

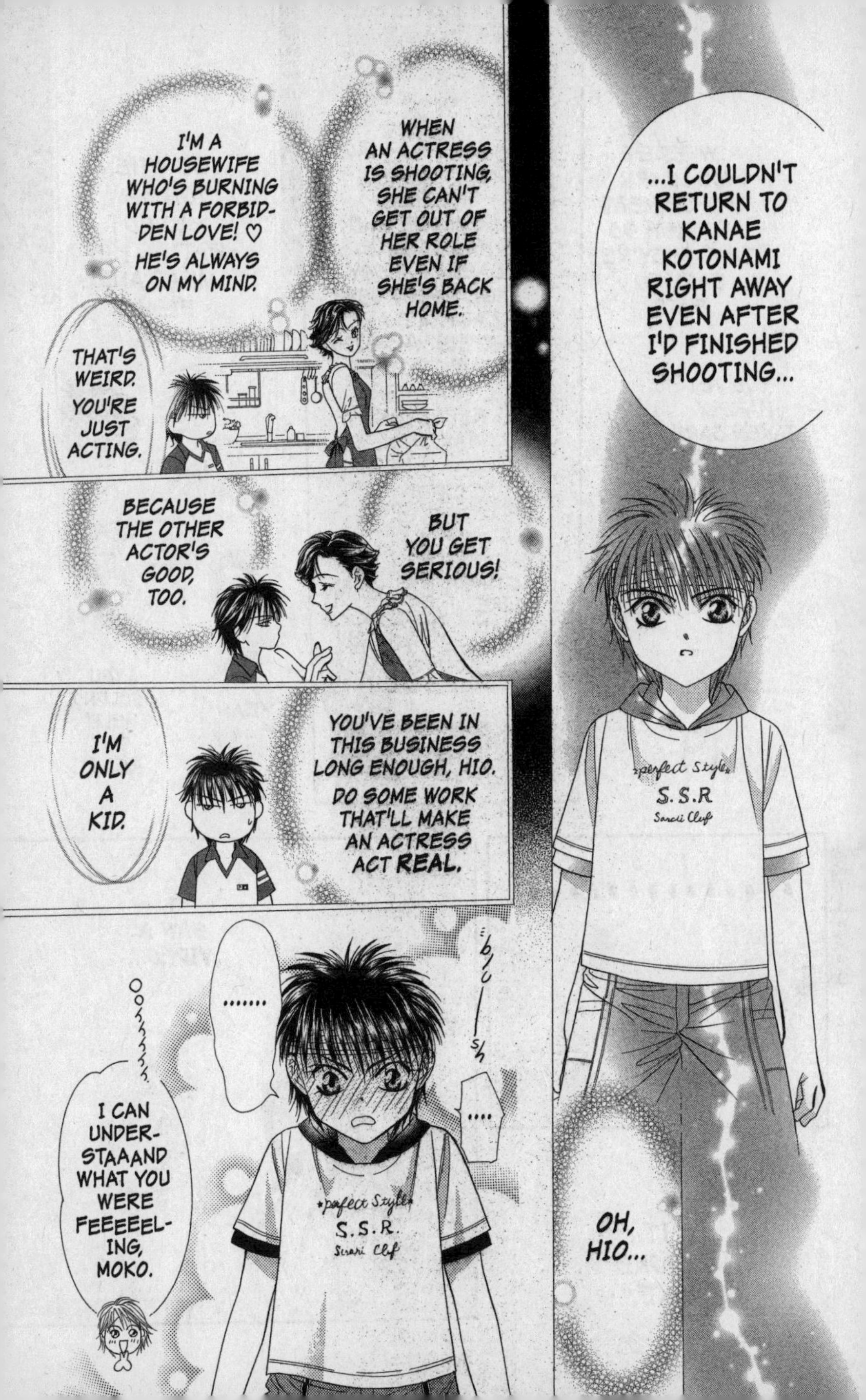
...I COULDN'T RETURN TO KANAE KOTONAMI RIGHT AWAY EVEN AFTER I'D FINISHED SHOOTING...
OH, HIO...
WHEN AN ACTRESS IS SHOOTING, SHE CAN'T GET OUT OF HER ROLE EVEN IF SHE'S BACK HOME.
I'M A HOUSEWIFE WHO'S BURNING WITH A FORBID-DEN LOVE! ♡ HE'S ALWAYS ON MY MIND.
THAT'S WEIRD. YOU'RE JUST ACTING.
BUT YOU GET SERIOUS!
BECAUSE THE OTHER ACTOR'S GOOD, TOO.
YOU'VE BEEN IN THIS BUSINESS LONG ENOUGH, HIO. DO SOME WORK THAT'LL MAKE AN ACTRESS ACT REAL.
I'M ONLY A KID.
blu-sh
....
....
Oohhhhh
I CAN UNDER-STAAAND WHAT YOU WERE FEEEEEL-ING, MOKO.

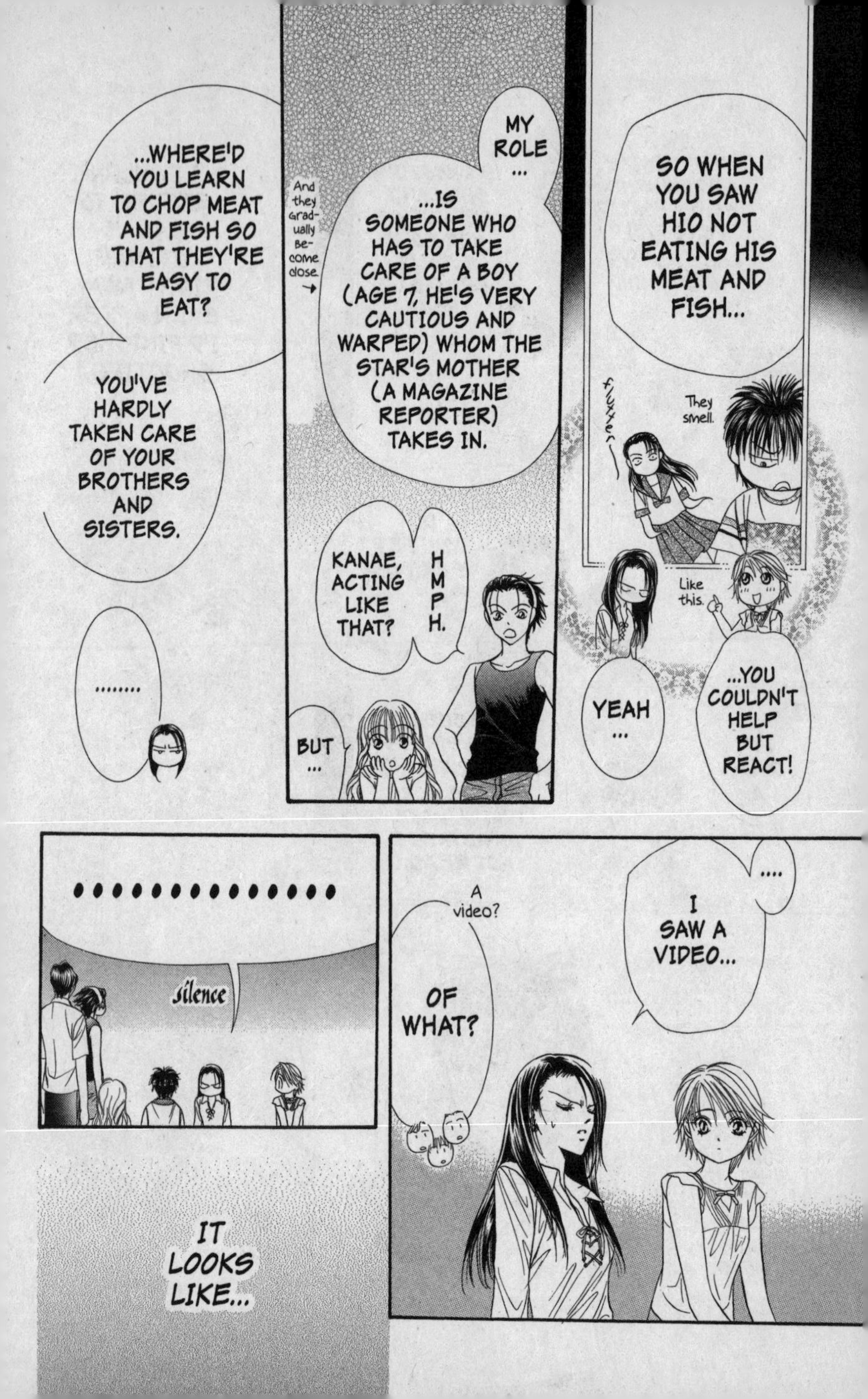
SO WHEN YOU SAW HIO NOT EATING HIS MEAT AND FISH...
flutter
They smell.
Like this.
...YOU COULDN'T HELP BUT REACT!
YEAH ...
MY ROLE ...
...IS SOMEONE WHO HAS TO TAKE CARE OF A BOY (AGE 7, HE'S VERY CAUTIOUS AND WARPED) WHOM THE STAR'S MOTHER (A MAGAZINE REPORTER) TAKES IN.
And they Gradually Become close. →
HMPH.
KANAE, ACTING LIKE THAT?
BUT ...
...WHERE'D YOU LEARN TO CHOP MEAT AND FISH SO THAT THEY'RE EASY TO EAT?
YOU'VE HARDLY TAKEN CARE OF YOUR BROTHERS AND SISTERS.
....
....
I SAW A VIDEO...
A video?
OF WHAT?
....
silence
IT LOOKS LIKE...

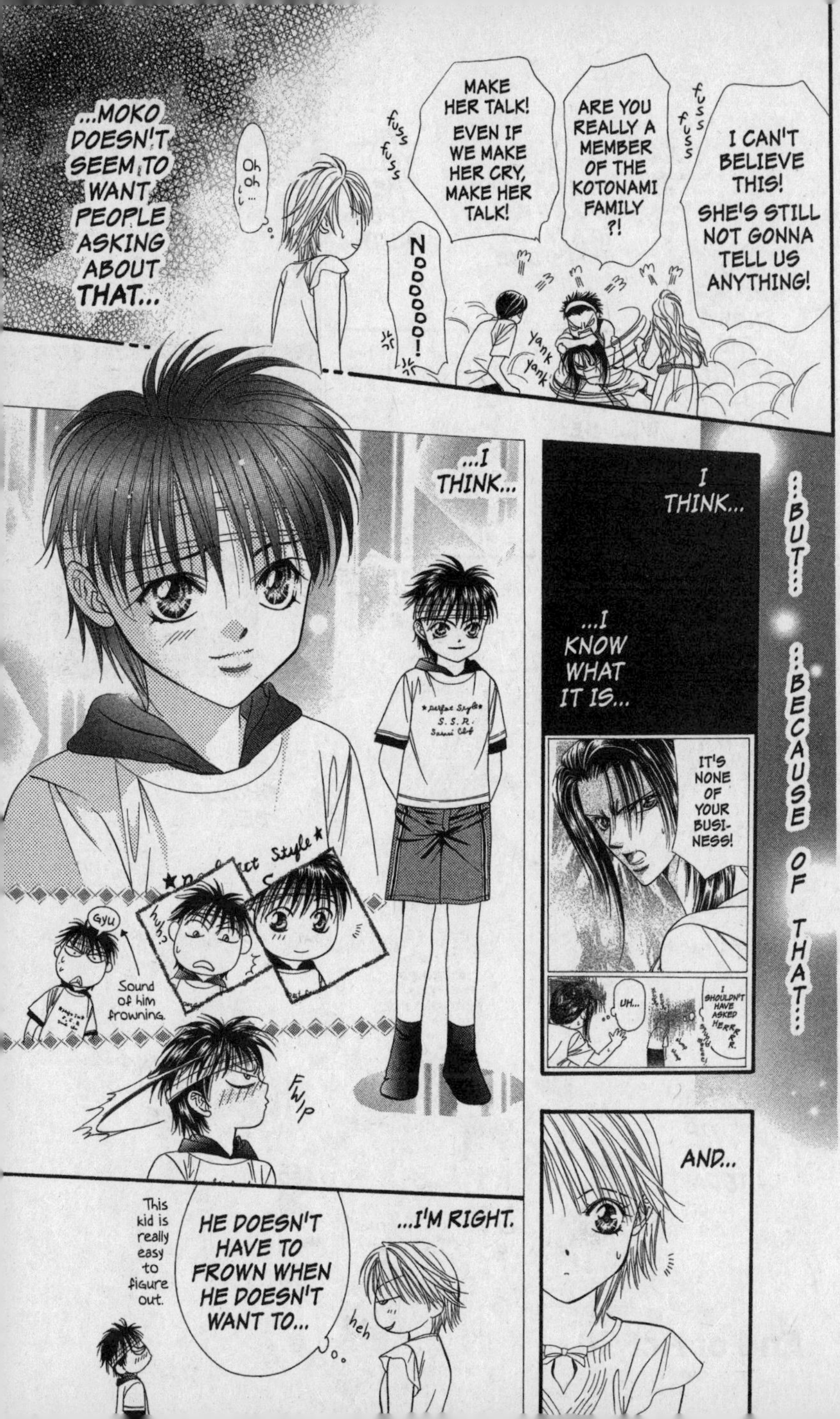
I CAN'T BELIEVE THIS! SHE'S STILL NOT GONNA TELL US ANYTHING!
fuss fuss
ARE YOU REALLY A MEMBER OF THE KOTONAMI FAMILY?!
MAKE HER TALK! EVEN IF WE MAKE HER CRY, MAKE HER TALK!
fuss fuss
yank yank
NOOOOOOO!
Oh oh...
...MOKO DOESN'T SEEM TO WANT PEOPLE ASKING ABOUT THAT...
...BUT... ...BECAUSE OF THAT...
I THINK...
...I KNOW WHAT IT IS...
IT'S NONE OF YOUR BUSINESS!
UH...
I SHOULDN'T HAVE ASKED HERRRR.
...I THINK...
Gyu
Sound of him frowning.
huh?
FWIP
AND...
...I'M RIGHT.
heh
HE DOESN'T HAVE TO FROWN WHEN HE DOESN'T WANT TO...
This kid is really easy to figure out.

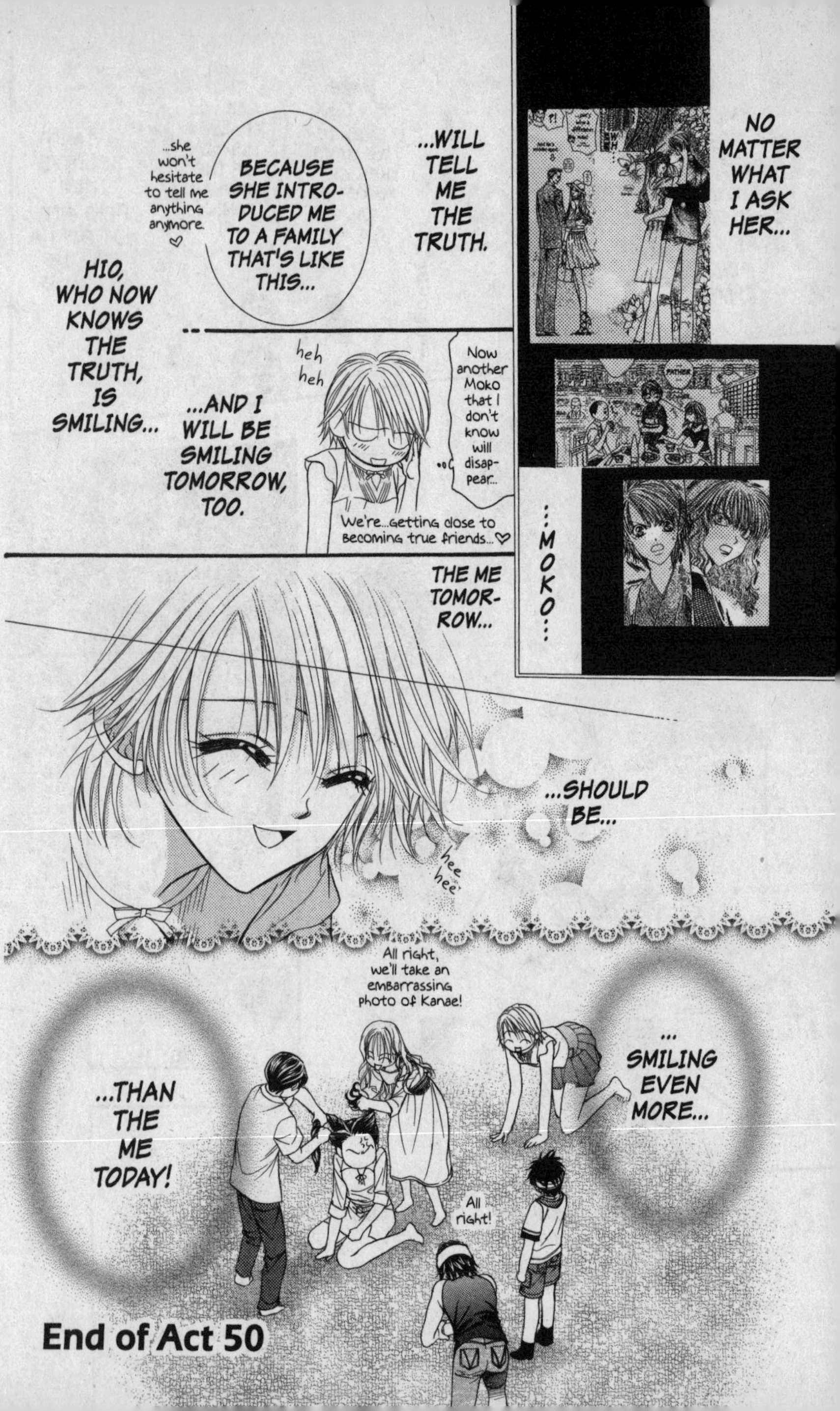
NO MATTER WHAT I ASK HER...
...MOKO...
...WILL TELL ME THE TRUTH.
BECAUSE SHE INTRODUCED ME TO A FAMILY THAT'S LIKE THIS...
...she won't hesitate to tell me anything anymore. ♡
HIO, WHO NOW KNOWS THE TRUTH, IS SMILING...
Now another Moko that I don't know will disappear...
heh heh
...AND I WILL BE SMILING TOMORROW, TOO.
We're...getting close to becoming true friends...♡
THE ME TOMORROW...
...SHOULD BE...
hee hee
...SMILING EVEN MORE...
All right, we'll take an embarrassing photo of Kanae!
All right!
...THAN THE ME TODAY!

End of Act 50

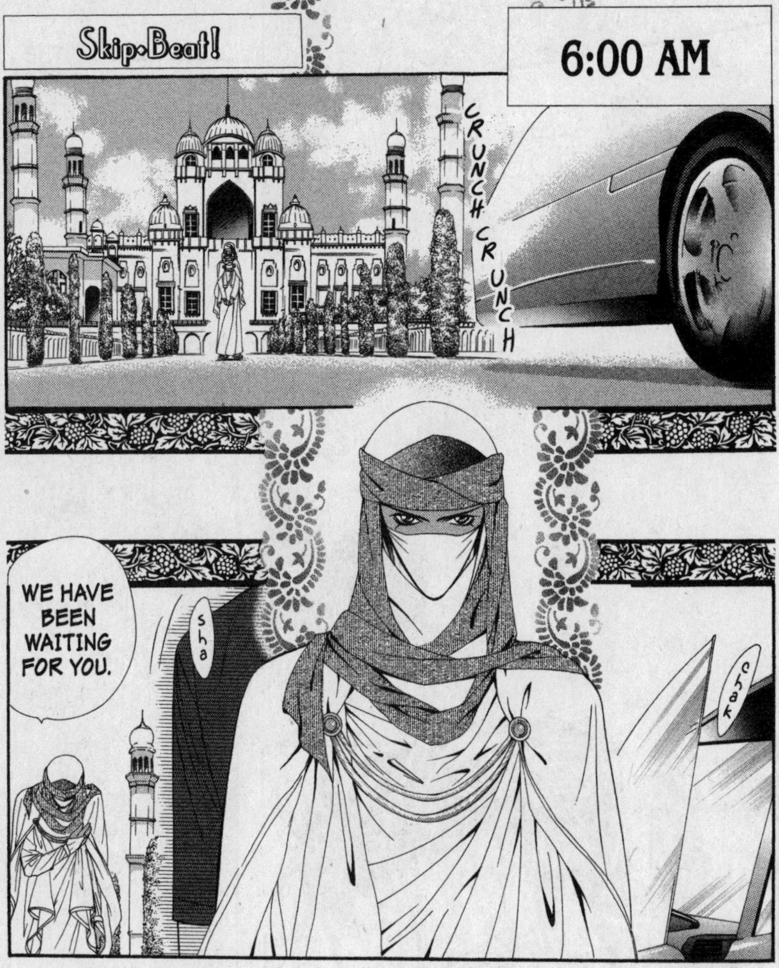
6:00 AM
CRUNCH CRUNCH
chak
sha
WE HAVE BEEN WAITING FOR YOU.

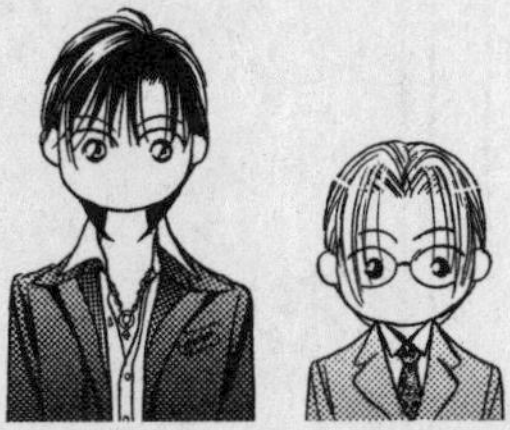

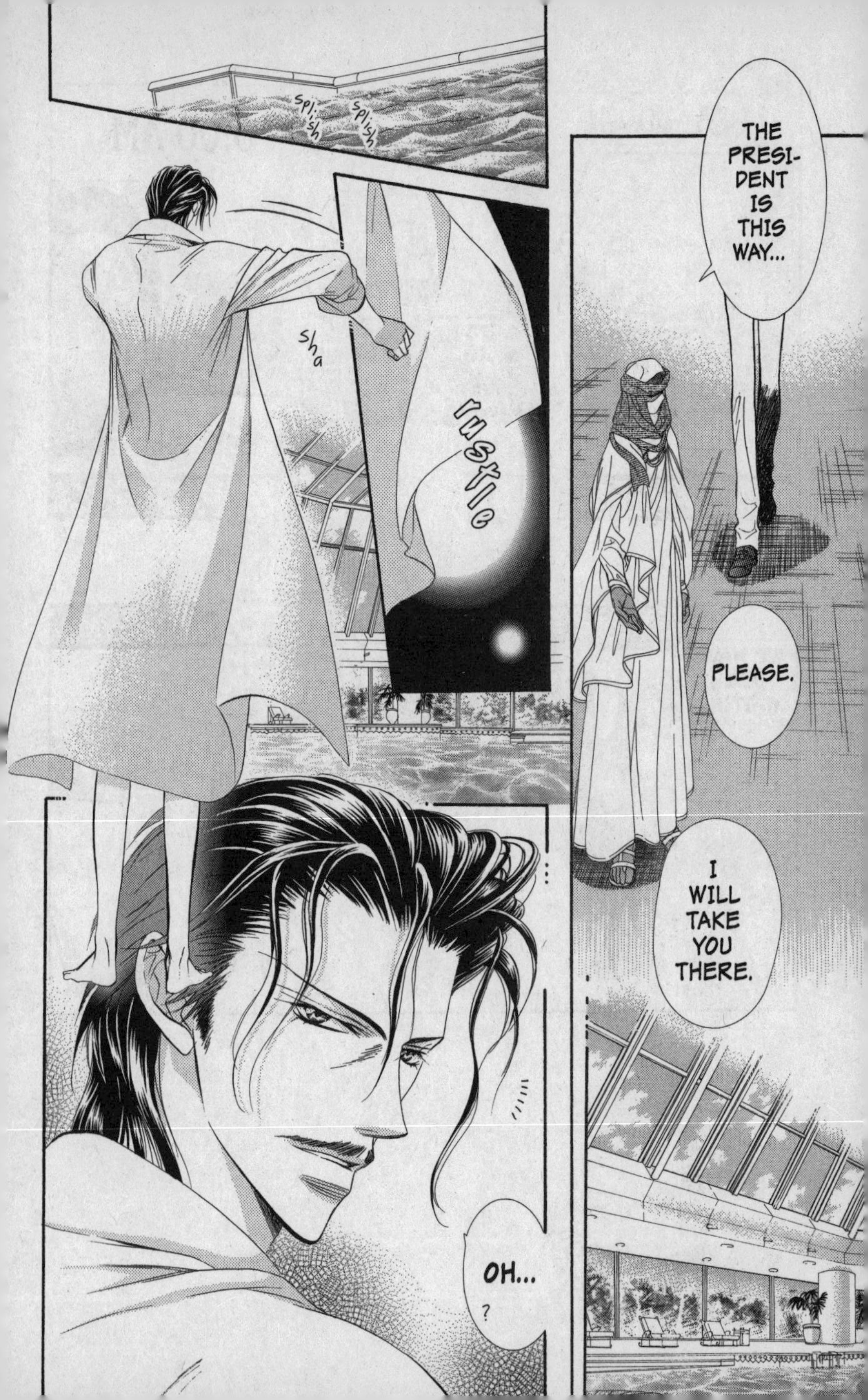
THE PRESIDENT IS THIS WAY...
PLEASE.
I WILL TAKE YOU THERE.
splish
splish
sha
rustle
...
OH...
?

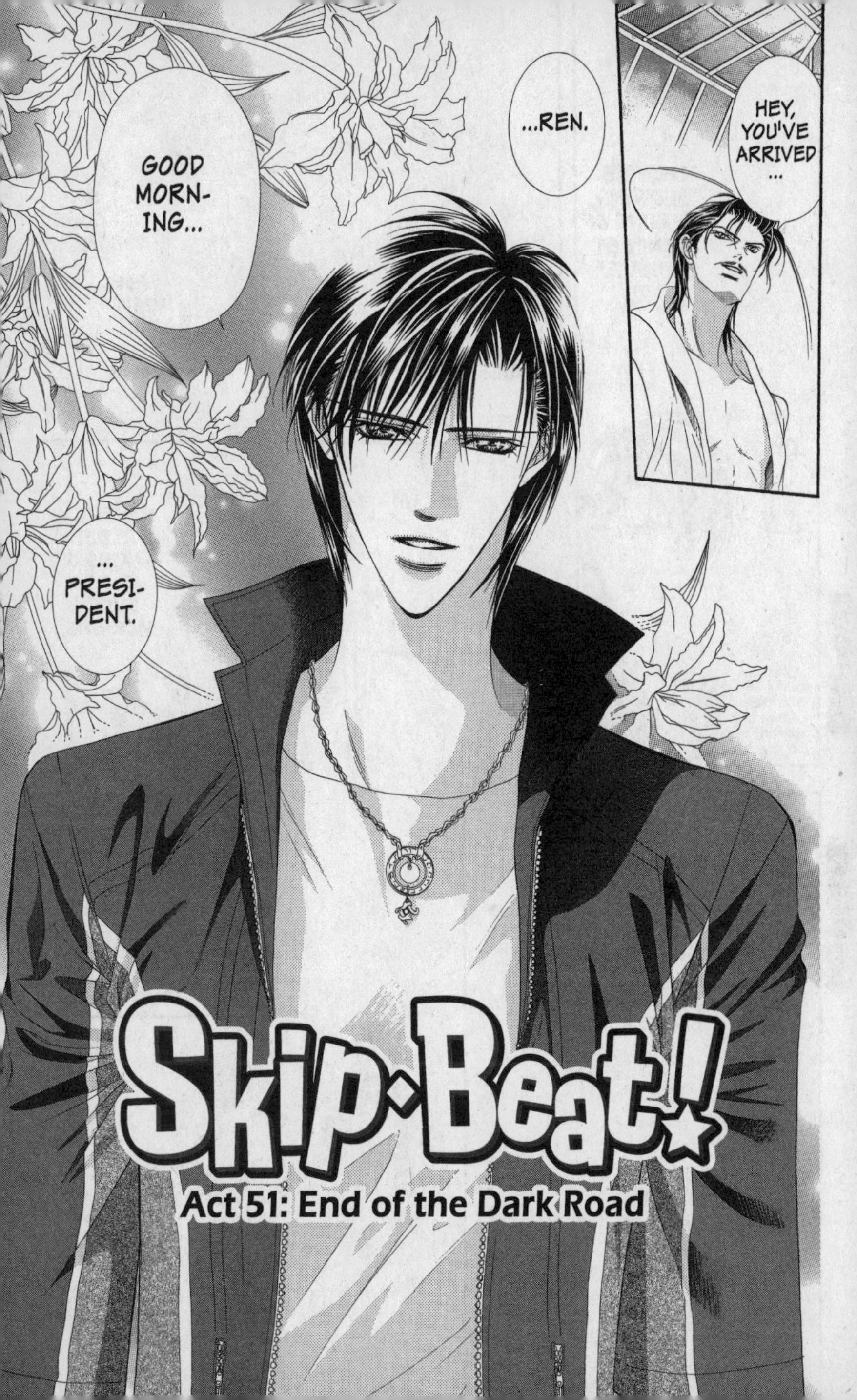
HEY, YOU'VE ARRIVED ...
...REN.
GOOD MORN-ING...
... PRESI-DENT.
Skip·Beat!
Act 51: End of the Dark Road

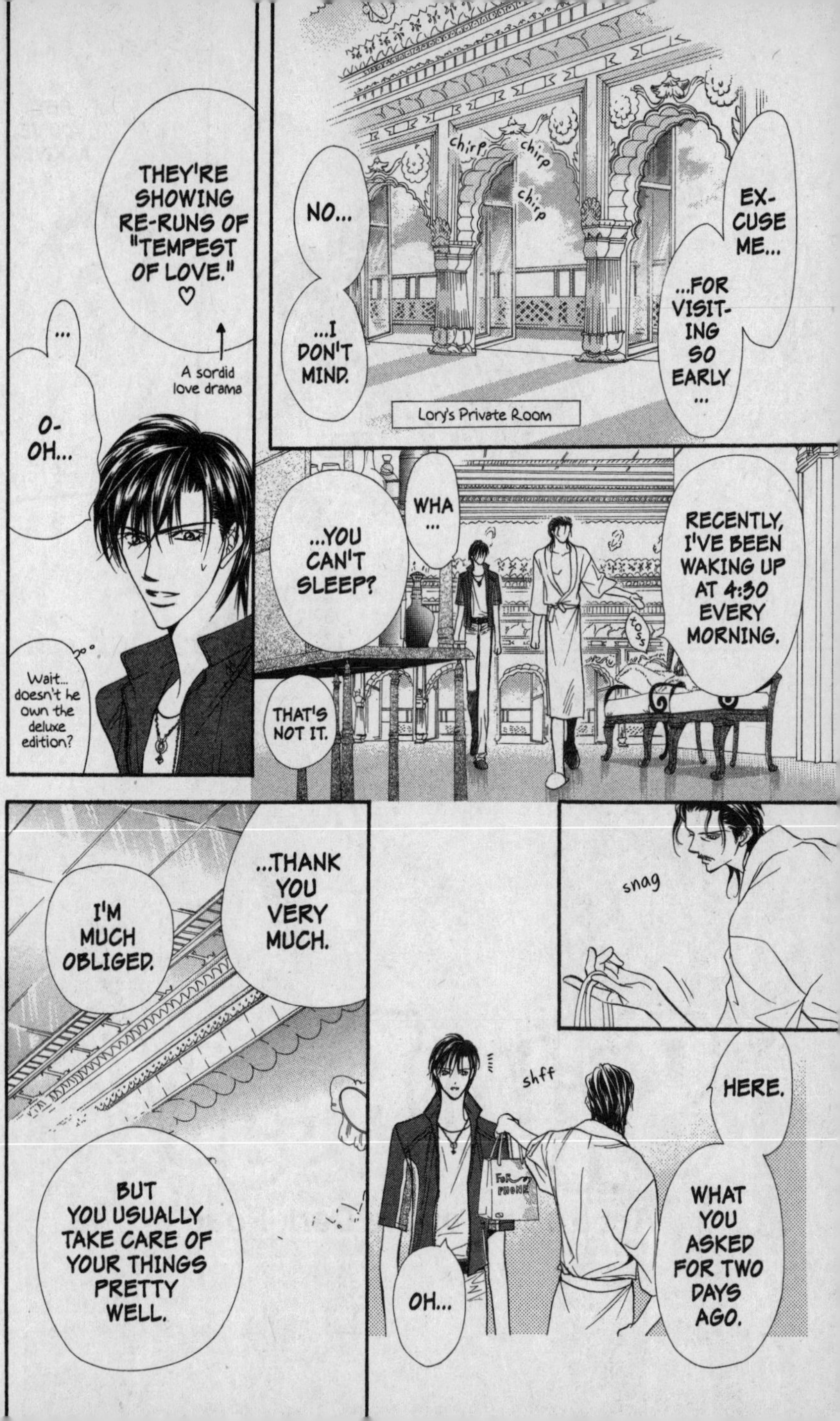
EX-CUSE ME...
...FOR VISIT-ING SO EARLY...
chirp
chirp
chirp
NO...
...I DON'T MIND.
Lory's Private Room
RECENTLY, I'VE BEEN WAKING UP AT 4:30 EVERY MORNING.
toss
WHA...
...YOU CAN'T SLEEP?
THAT'S NOT IT.
THEY'RE SHOWING RE-RUNS OF "TEMPEST OF LOVE." ♡
A sordid love drama
...
O-OH...
Wait... doesn't he own the deluxe edition?
snag
HERE.
WHAT YOU ASKED FOR TWO DAYS AGO.
shft
OH...
...THANK YOU VERY MUCH.
I'M MUCH OBLIGED.
BUT YOU USUALLY TAKE CARE OF YOUR THINGS PRETTY WELL.

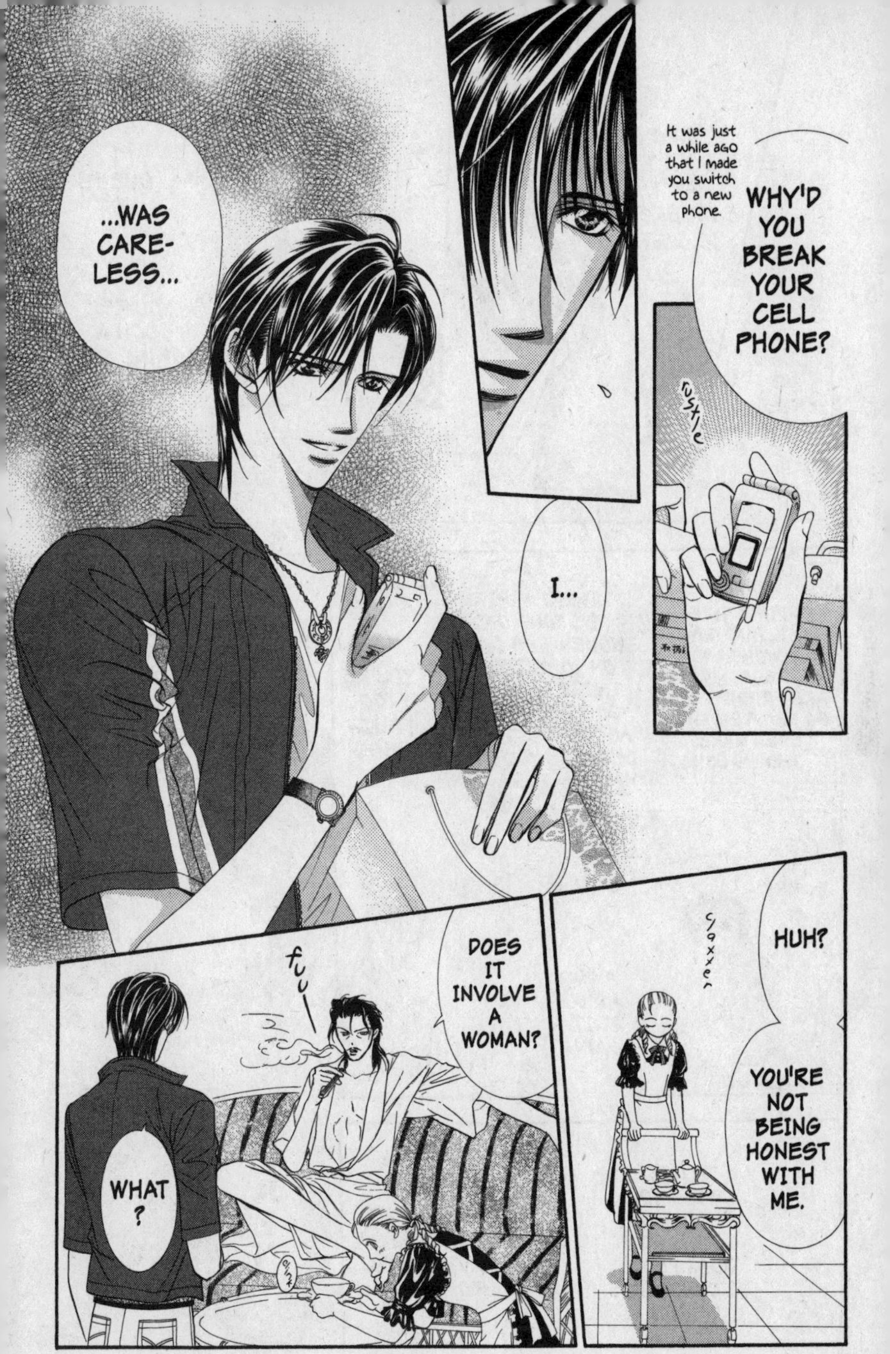
It was just a while ago that I made you switch to a new phone.
WHY'D YOU BREAK YOUR CELL PHONE?
rustle
I...
...WAS CARELESS...
clatter
HUH?
YOU'RE NOT BEING HONEST WITH ME.
DOES IT INVOLVE A WOMAN?
fuu
WHAT?
clink

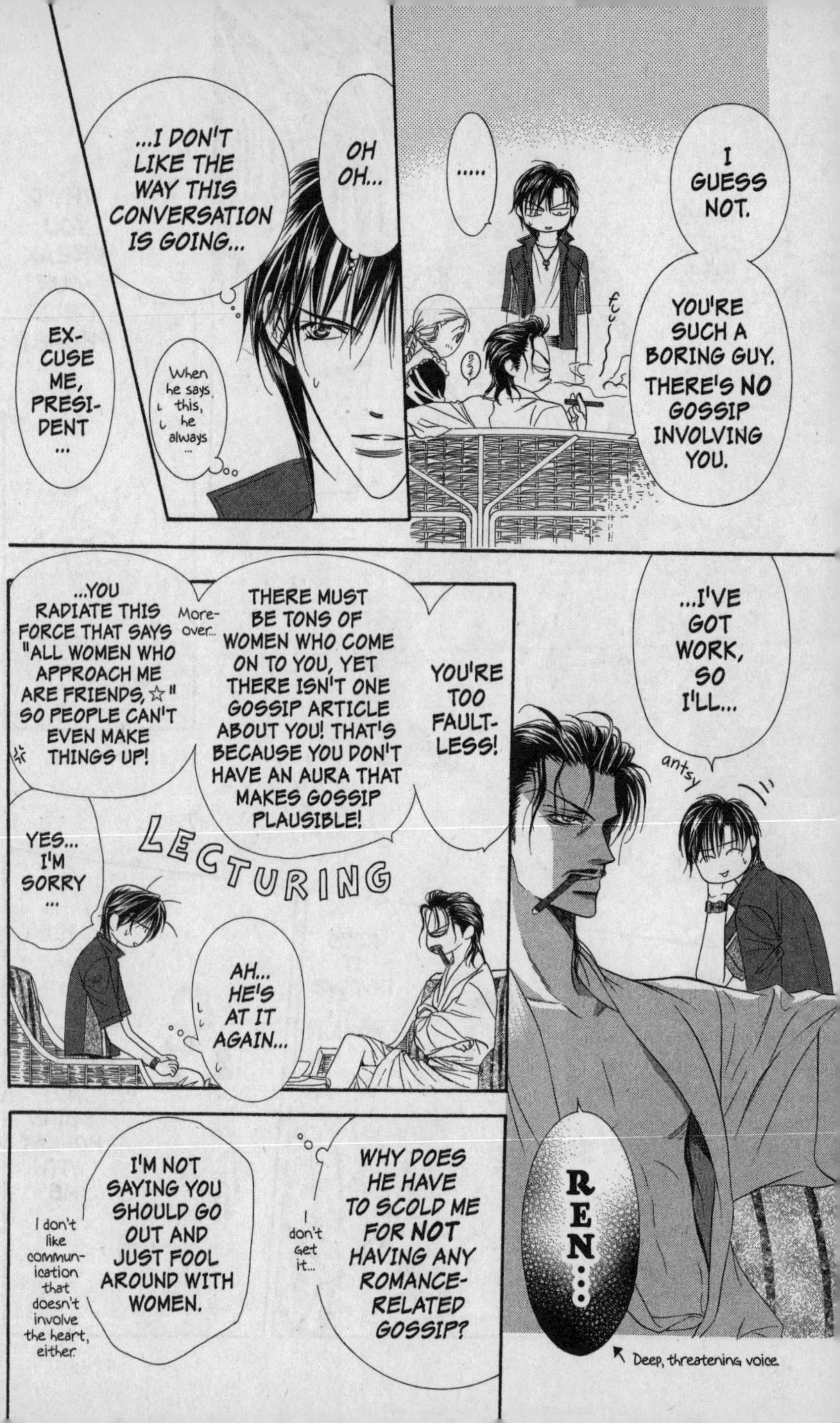
I GUESS NOT.
YOU'RE SUCH A BORING GUY. THERE'S NO GOSSIP INVOLVING YOU.
.....
OH OH...
...I DON'T LIKE THE WAY THIS CONVERSATION IS GOING...
When he says this, he always...
EX-CUSE ME, PRESI-DENT...
...I'VE GOT WORK, SO I'LL...
antsy
REN...
Deep, threatening voice.
YOU'RE TOO FAULT-LESS!
THERE MUST BE TONS OF WOMEN WHO COME ON TO YOU, YET THERE ISN'T ONE GOSSIP ARTICLE ABOUT YOU! THAT'S BECAUSE YOU DON'T HAVE AN AURA THAT MAKES GOSSIP PLAUSIBLE!
More-over...
...YOU RADIATE THIS FORCE THAT SAYS "ALL WOMEN WHO APPROACH ME ARE FRIENDS,☆" SO PEOPLE CAN'T EVEN MAKE THINGS UP!
LECTURING
YES... I'M SORRY...
AH... HE'S AT IT AGAIN...
WHY DOES HE HAVE TO SCOLD ME FOR NOT HAVING ANY ROMANCE-RELATED GOSSIP?
I don't get it...
I'M NOT SAYING YOU SHOULD GO OUT AND JUST FOOL AROUND WITH WOMEN.
I don't like communi-cation that doesn't involve the heart, either.

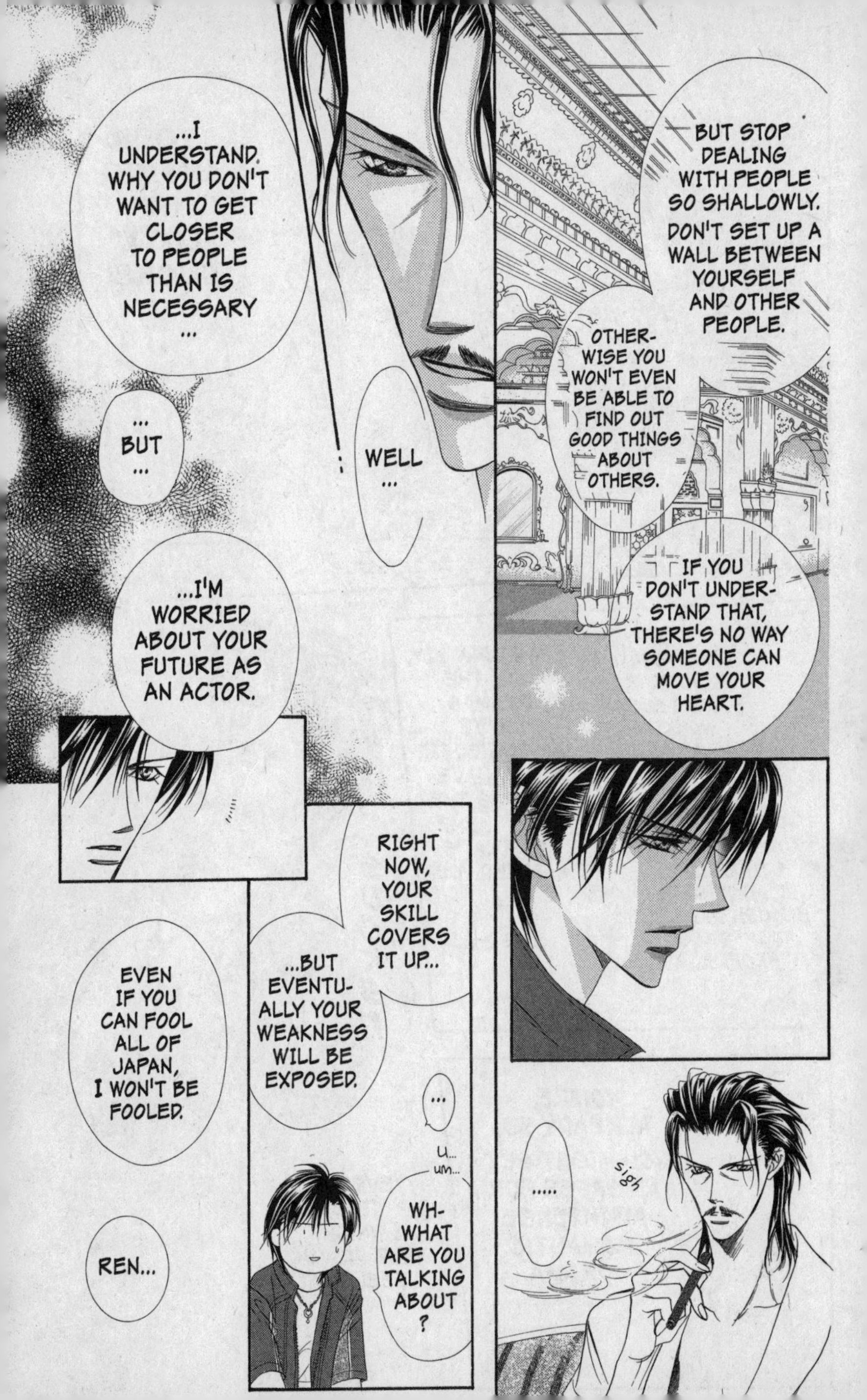
BUT STOP DEALING WITH PEOPLE SO SHALLOWLY. DON'T SET UP A WALL BETWEEN YOURSELF AND OTHER PEOPLE.
OTHER-WISE YOU WON'T EVEN BE ABLE TO FIND OUT GOOD THINGS ABOUT OTHERS.
IF YOU DON'T UNDER-STAND THAT, THERE'S NO WAY SOMEONE CAN MOVE YOUR HEART.
.....
sigh
WELL ...
...I UNDERSTAND. WHY YOU DON'T WANT TO GET CLOSER TO PEOPLE THAN IS NECESSARY ...
... BUT ...
...I'M WORRIED ABOUT YOUR FUTURE AS AN ACTOR.
RIGHT NOW, YOUR SKILL COVERS IT UP...
...BUT EVENTU-ALLY YOUR WEAKNESS WILL BE EXPOSED.
EVEN IF YOU CAN FOOL ALL OF JAPAN, I WON'T BE FOOLED.
...
U... um...
WH-WHAT ARE YOU TALKING ABOUT ?
REN...

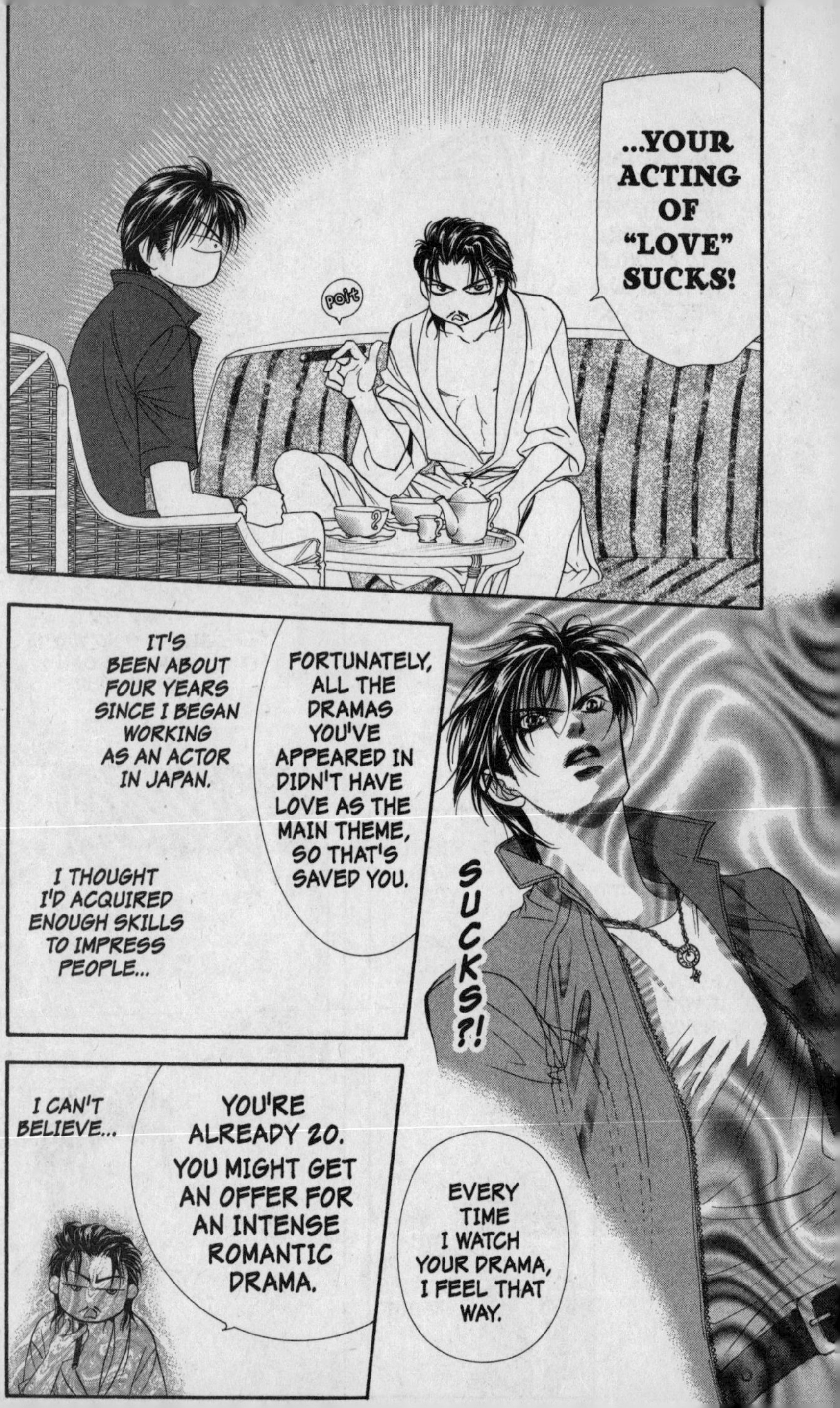
...YOUR ACTING OF "LOVE" SUCKS!
poit
SUCKS?!
FORTUNATELY, ALL THE DRAMAS YOU'VE APPEARED IN DIDN'T HAVE LOVE AS THE MAIN THEME, SO THAT'S SAVED YOU.
IT'S BEEN ABOUT FOUR YEARS SINCE I BEGAN WORKING AS AN ACTOR IN JAPAN.
I THOUGHT I'D ACQUIRED ENOUGH SKILLS TO IMPRESS PEOPLE...
EVERY TIME I WATCH YOUR DRAMA, I FEEL THAT WAY.
YOU'RE ALREADY 20. YOU MIGHT GET AN OFFER FOR AN INTENSE ROMANTIC DRAMA.
I CAN'T BELIEVE...

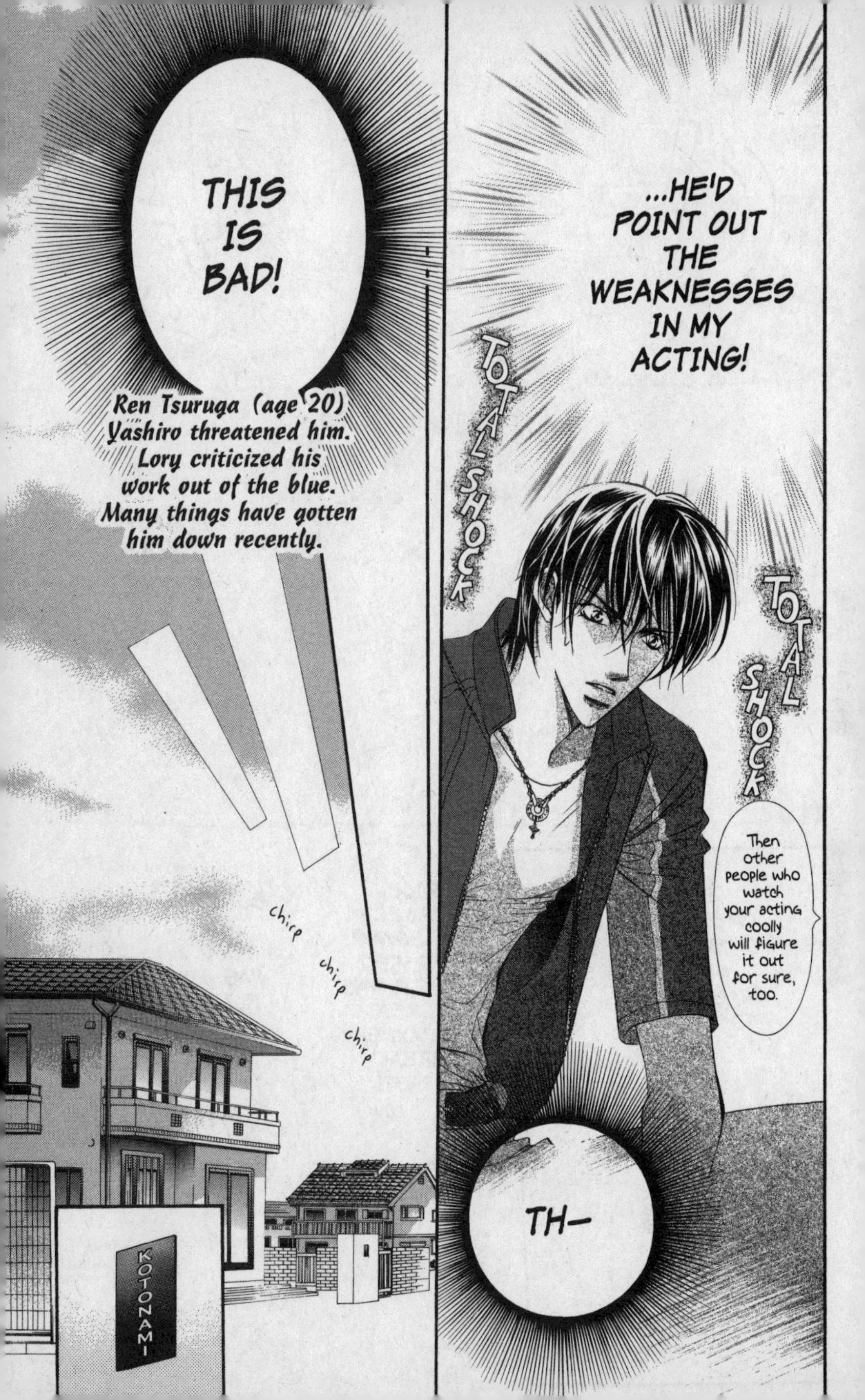
...HE'D POINT OUT THE WEAKNESSES IN MY ACTING!
TOTAL SHOCK
TOTAL SHOCK
Then other people who watch your acting coolly will figure it out for sure, too.
TH–
THIS IS BAD!
Ren Tsuruga (age 20) Yashiro threatened him. Lory criticized his work out of the blue. Many things have gotten him down recently.
chirp
chirp
chirp
KOTONAMI

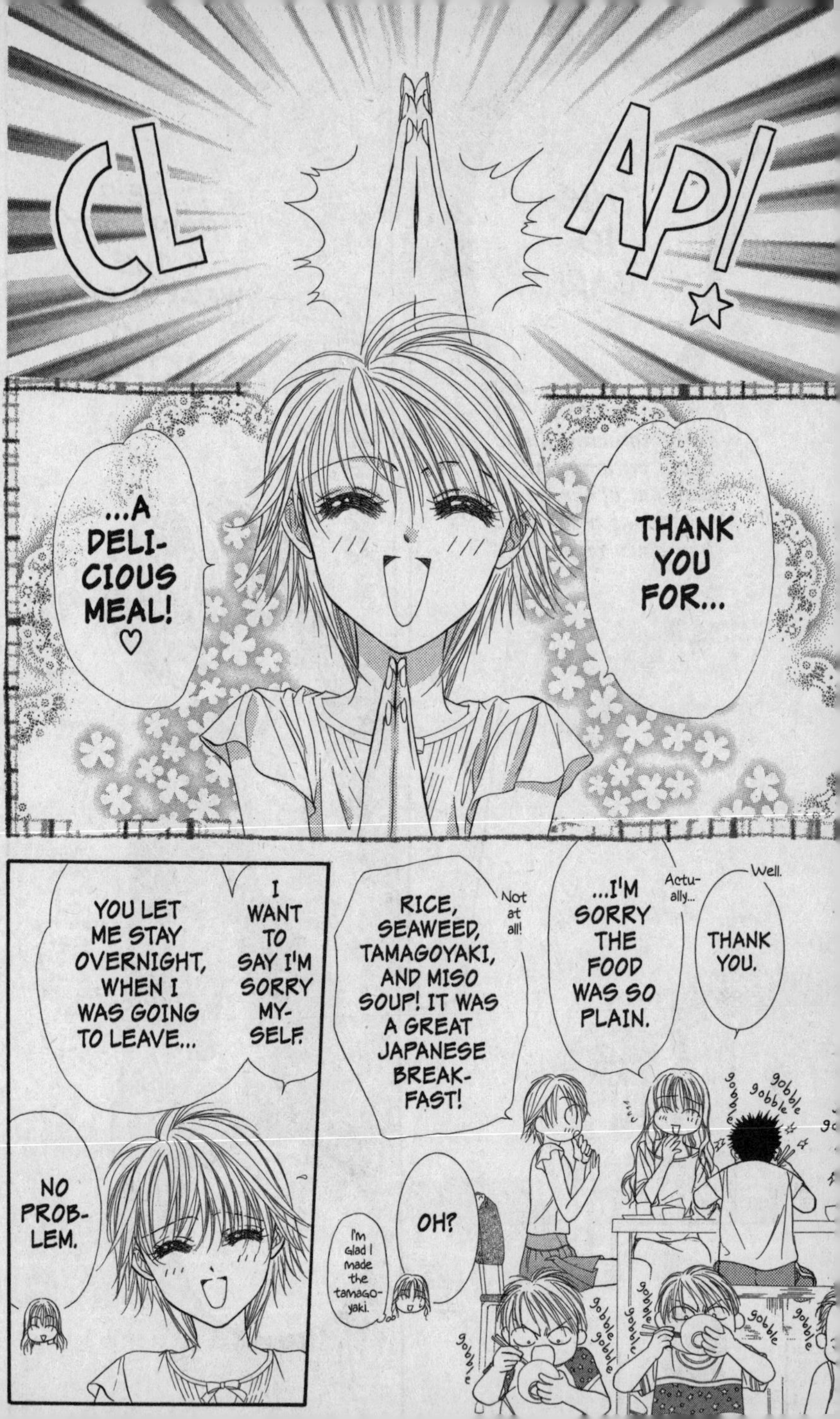
CLAP!
THANK YOU FOR...
...A DELICIOUS MEAL! ♡
Well.
THANK YOU.
Actually...
...I'M SORRY THE FOOD WAS SO PLAIN.
Not at all!
RICE, SEAWEED, TAMAGOYAKI, AND MISO SOUP! IT WAS A GREAT JAPANESE BREAKFAST!
gobble gobble gobble
OH?
I'm Glad I made the tamagoyaki.
gobble gobble gobble gobble gobble gobble
I WANT TO SAY I'M SORRY MYSELF.
YOU LET ME STAY OVERNIGHT, WHEN I WAS GOING TO LEAVE...
NO PROBLEM.

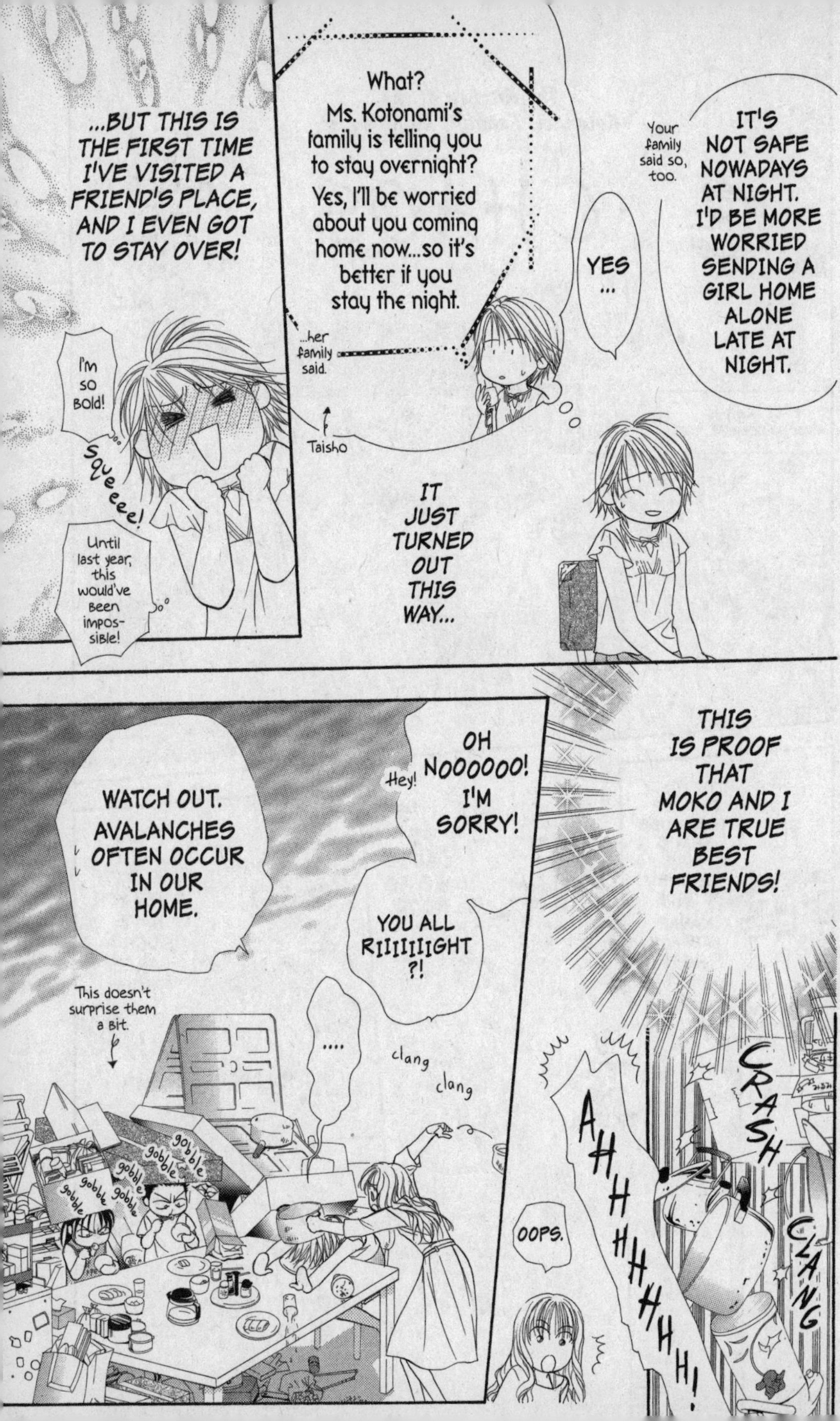
Your family said so, too.
IT'S NOT SAFE NOWADAYS AT NIGHT. I'D BE MORE WORRIED SENDING A GIRL HOME ALONE LATE AT NIGHT.
YES...
What? Ms. Kotonami's family is telling you to stay overnight? Yes, I'll be worried about you coming home now...so it's better if you stay the night.
...her family said.
Taisho
IT JUST TURNED OUT THIS WAY...
...BUT THIS IS THE FIRST TIME I'VE VISITED A FRIEND'S PLACE, AND I EVEN GOT TO STAY OVER!
I'm so bold!
Squeeeee!
Until last year, this would've been impossible!
THIS IS PROOF THAT MOKO AND I ARE TRUE BEST FRIENDS!
CRASH
CLANG
AHHHHHHHH!
OOPS.
OH NOOOOOO! I'M SORRY!
Hey!
WATCH OUT. AVALANCHES OFTEN OCCUR IN OUR HOME.
YOU ALL RIIIIIIIGHT ?!
....
clang
clang
This doesn't surprise them a bit.
gobble
gobble
gobble
gobble
gobble

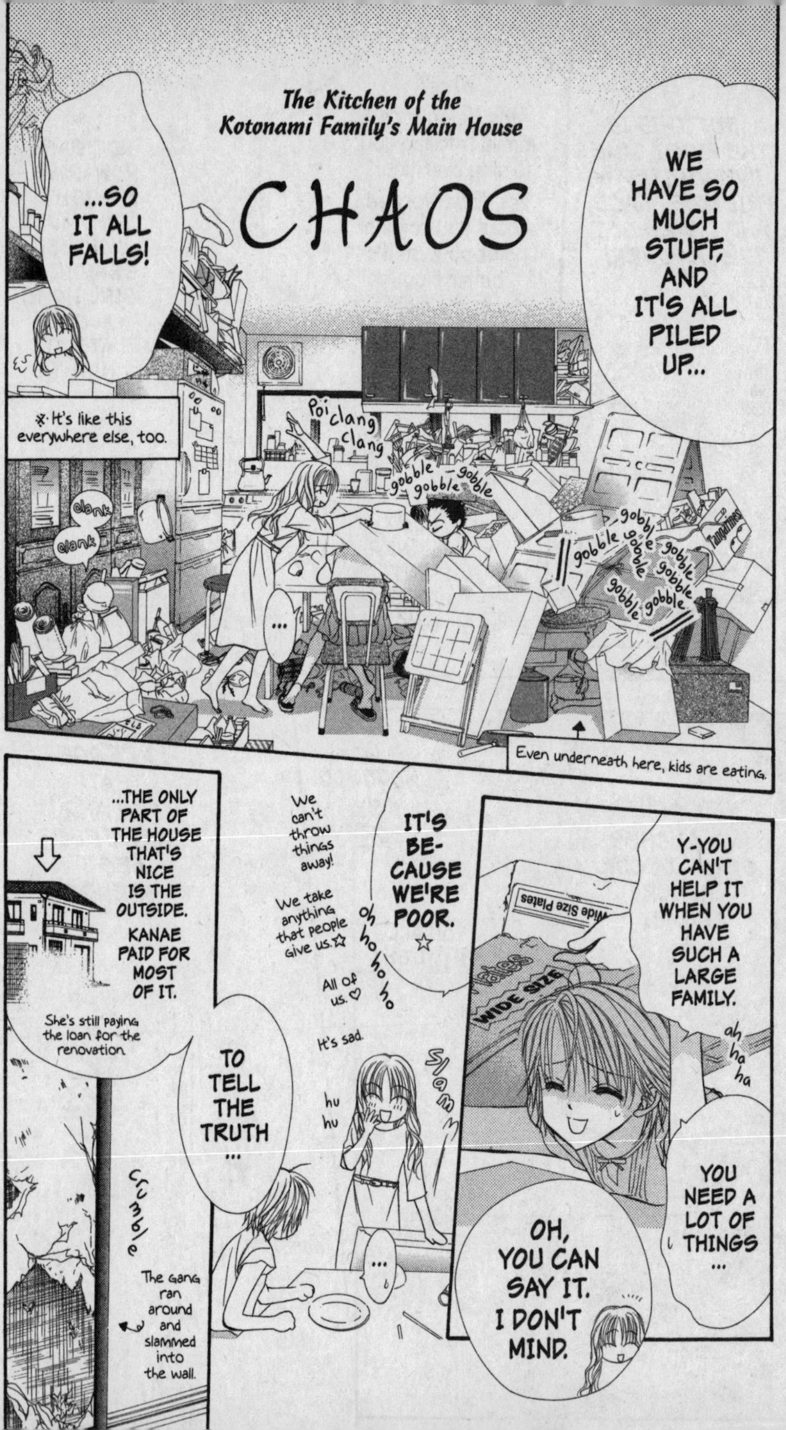
The Kitchen of the Kotonami Family's Main House
CHAOS
WE HAVE SO MUCH STUFF, AND IT'S ALL PILED UP...
...SO IT ALL FALLS!
※ It's like this everywhere else, too.
Poi
clang clang
gobble gobble gobble
gobble gobble gobble gobble gobble gobble gobble
Tangerines
clank clank
...
Even underneath here, kids are eating.
Y-YOU CAN'T HELP IT WHEN YOU HAVE SUCH A LARGE FAMILY.
Wide Size Plates
WIDE SIZE
ah ha ha
YOU NEED A LOT OF THINGS...
OH, YOU CAN SAY IT. I DON'T MIND.
IT'S BE-CAUSE WE'RE POOR. ☆
We can't throw things away!
We take anything that people give us.☆
oh ho ho ho
All of us.♡
It's sad.
Slam
hu hu
TO TELL THE TRUTH...
...
...THE ONLY PART OF THE HOUSE THAT'S NICE IS THE OUTSIDE. KANAE PAID FOR MOST OF IT.
She's still paying the loan for the renovation.
crumble
The gang ran around and slammed into the wall.

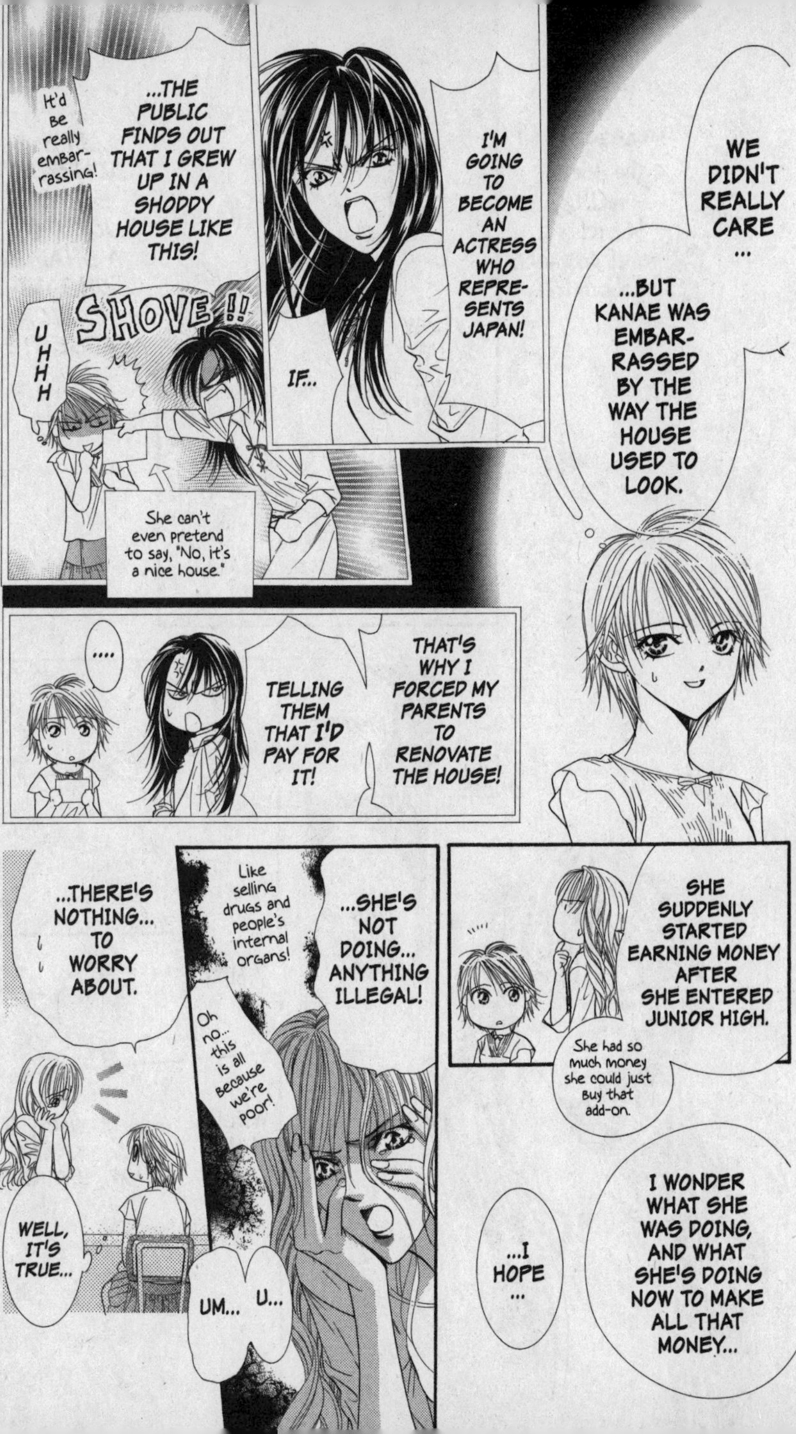
WE DIDN'T REALLY CARE...
...BUT KANAE WAS EMBARRASSED BY THE WAY THE HOUSE USED TO LOOK.
I'M GOING TO BECOME AN ACTRESS WHO REPRESENTS JAPAN!
IF...
...THE PUBLIC FINDS OUT THAT I GREW UP IN A SHODDY HOUSE LIKE THIS!
It'd be really embarrassing!
SHOVE!!
UHHH
She can't even pretend to say, "No, it's a nice house."
THAT'S WHY I FORCED MY PARENTS TO RENOVATE THE HOUSE!
TELLING THEM THAT I'D PAY FOR IT!
....
SHE SUDDENLY STARTED EARNING MONEY AFTER SHE ENTERED JUNIOR HIGH.
She had so much money she could just buy that add-on.
I WONDER WHAT SHE WAS DOING, AND WHAT SHE'S DOING NOW TO MAKE ALL THAT MONEY...
...I HOPE...
...SHE'S NOT DOING... ANYTHING ILLEGAL!
Like selling drugs and people's internal organs!
Oh no... this is all because we're poor!
UM... U...
...THERE'S NOTHING... TO WORRY ABOUT.
WELL, IT'S TRUE...

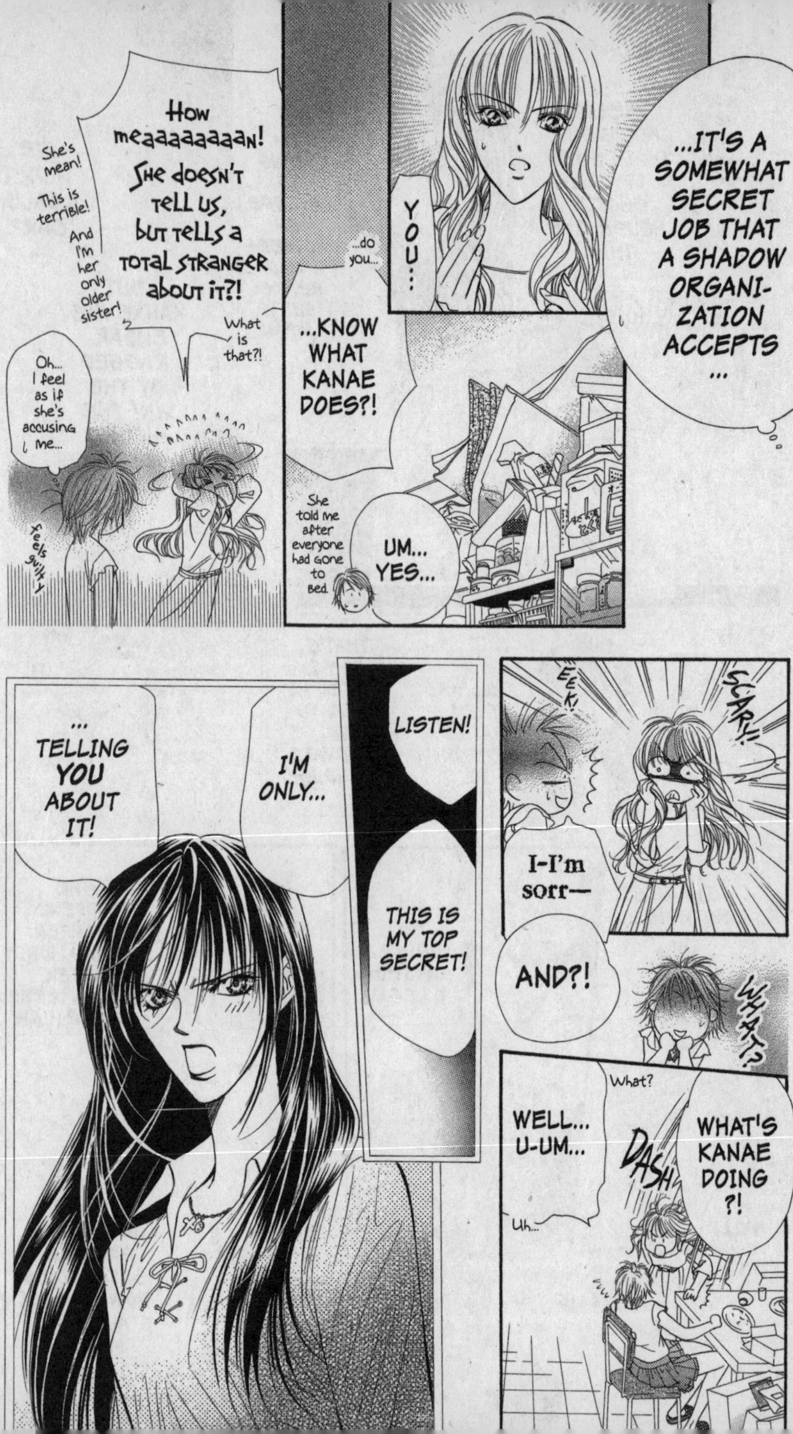
YOU...
...do you...
...KNOW WHAT KANAE DOES?!
UM... YES...
She told me after everyone had gone to bed.
...IT'S A SOMEWHAT SECRET JOB THAT A SHADOW ORGANIZATION ACCEPTS...
How meaaaaaaaan!
She doesn't tell us, but tells a total stranger about it?!
She's mean!
This is terrible!
And I'm her only older sister!
What is that?!
Oh... I feel as if she's accusing me...
feels guilty
SCARY!!
EEK!
I-I'm sorr—
AND?!
WHAT?!
WHAT'S KANAE DOING?!
What?
WELL... U-UM...
DASH
Uh...
LISTEN!
THIS IS MY TOP SECRET!
I'M ONLY...
...TELLING YOU ABOUT IT!

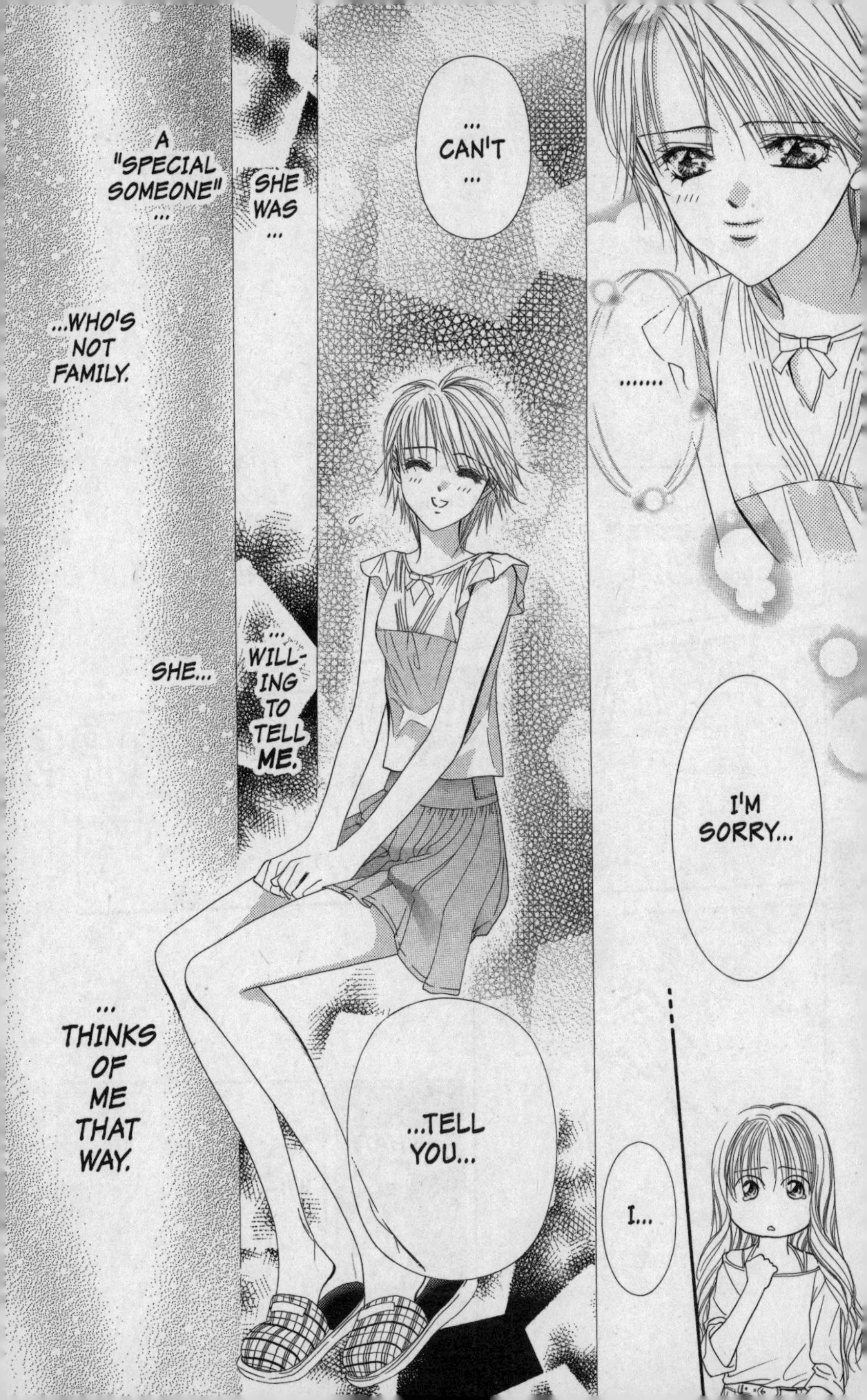
....
I'M SORRY...
I...
...
CAN'T
...
...TELL YOU...
SHE WAS...
...WILL-ING TO TELL ME.
A "SPECIAL SOMEONE"...
...WHO'S NOT FAMILY.
SHE...
...THINKS OF ME THAT WAY.

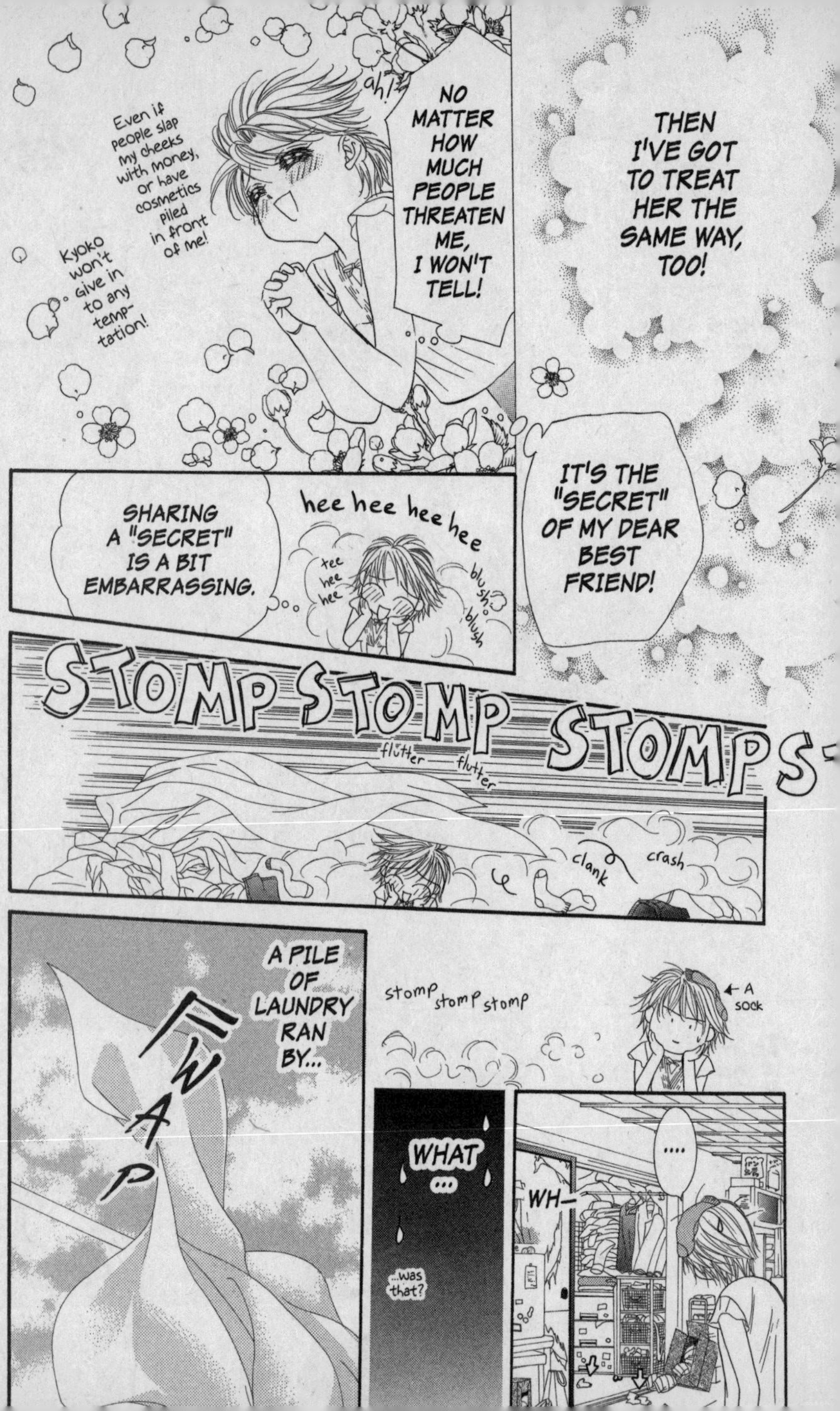
THEN I'VE GOT TO TREAT HER THE SAME WAY, TOO!
IT'S THE "SECRET" OF MY DEAR BEST FRIEND!
ah!
NO MATTER HOW MUCH PEOPLE THREATEN ME, I WON'T TELL!
Even if people slap my cheeks with money, or have cosmetics piled in front of me!
Kyoko won't give in to any temptation!
hee hee hee hee
SHARING A "SECRET" IS A BIT EMBARRASSING.
blush blush
tee hee hee
STOMP STOMP STOMPS
flutter flutter
crash
clank
stomp stomp stomp
← A sock
....
WH–
WHAT...
...was that?
A PILE OF LAUNDRY RAN BY...
FWAP

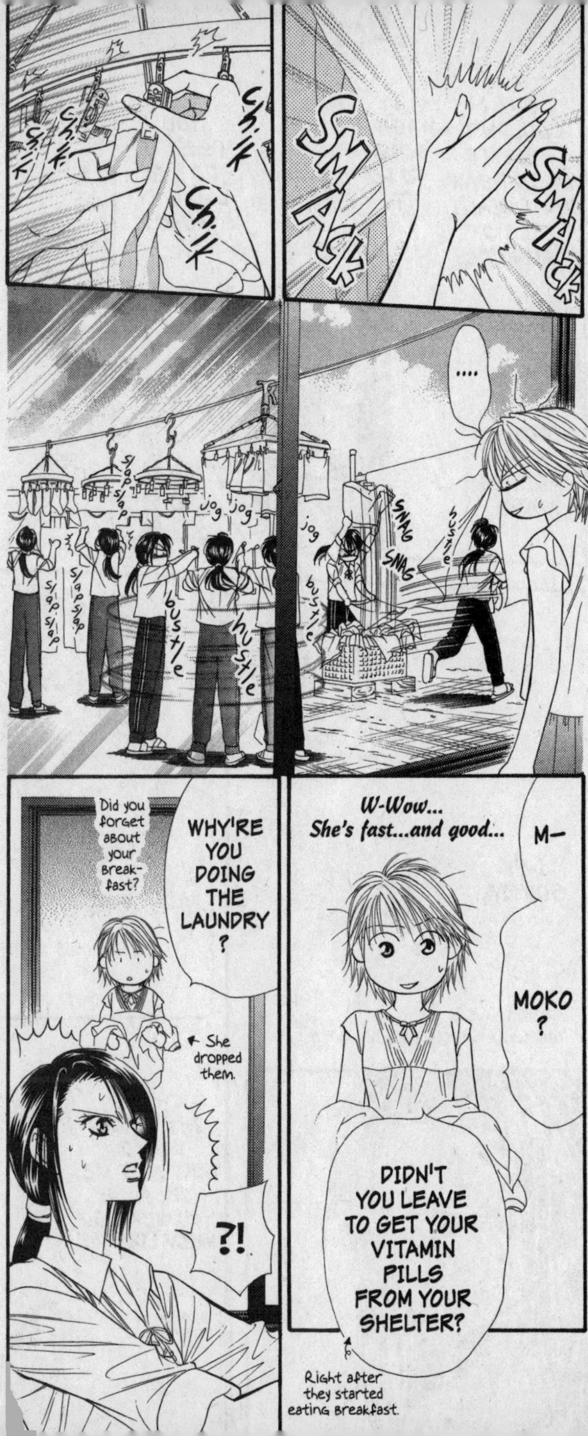
SMACK
SMACK
chik
chik
chik
chik
chik
....
SNAG
SNAG
hustle
jog
bustle
slap slap
jog jog
slap slap slap
bustle
hustle
M—
MOKO?
W-Wow... She's fast...and good...
DIDN'T YOU LEAVE TO GET YOUR VITAMIN PILLS FROM YOUR SHELTER?
Right after they started eating breakfast.
WHY'RE YOU DOING THE LAUNDRY?
Did you forget about your breakfast?
She dropped them.
?!

Hio Uesugi

The last time, I wrote that I would just draw stuff that come out naturally...but I'd forgotten... that there was a chapter where he appears... (And the reason is the same one I mentioned in the Greeting this time... I like having the Hio+Kanae pair and the Hio+Kyoko pair interacting quite a bit, so I'd like to have him appear again if possible...

The hawk cowers at the chicken...

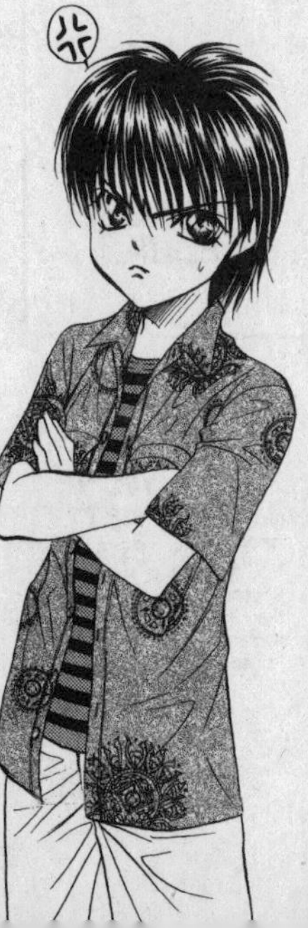

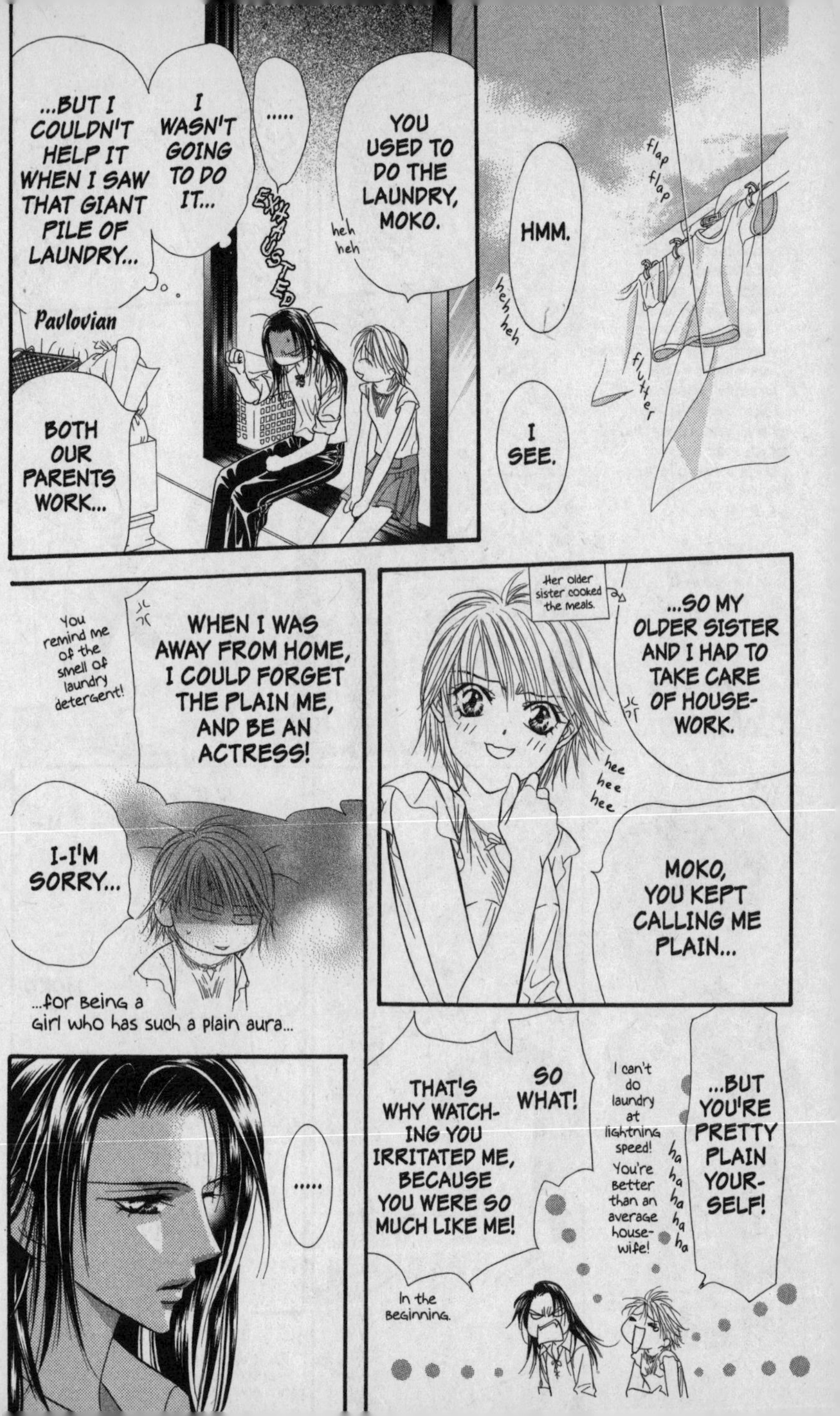
flap flap
HMM.
heh heh
flutter
I SEE.
YOU USED TO DO THE LAUNDRY, MOKO.
heh heh
.....
EXHAUSTED
I WASN'T GOING TO DO IT...
...BUT I COULDN'T HELP IT WHEN I SAW THAT GIANT PILE OF LAUNDRY...
Pavlovian
BOTH OUR PARENTS WORK...
Her older sister cooked the meals.
...SO MY OLDER SISTER AND I HAD TO TAKE CARE OF HOUSE-WORK.
hee hee hee
MOKO, YOU KEPT CALLING ME PLAIN...
WHEN I WAS AWAY FROM HOME, I COULD FORGET THE PLAIN ME, AND BE AN ACTRESS!
You remind me of the smell of laundry detergent!
I-I'M SORRY...
...for being a girl who has such a plain aura...
...BUT YOU'RE PRETTY PLAIN YOUR-SELF!
ha ha ha ha ha ha
I can't do laundry at lightning speed! You're better than an average house-wife!
SO WHAT!
THAT'S WHY WATCH-ING YOU IRRITATED ME, BECAUSE YOU WERE SO MUCH LIKE ME!
In the beginning.
.....

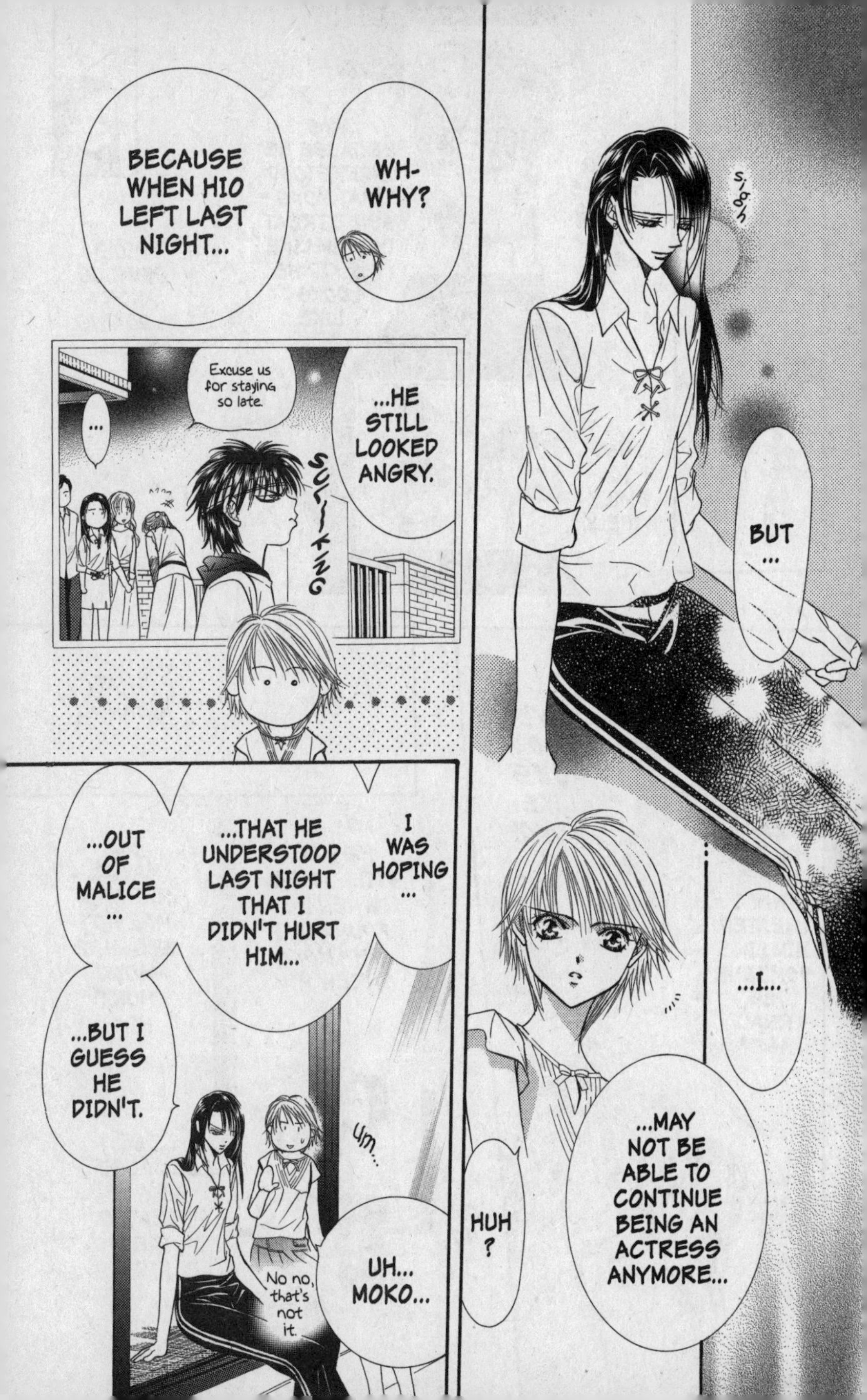
WH-WHY?
BECAUSE WHEN HIO LEFT LAST NIGHT...
...HE STILL LOOKED ANGRY.
SULKING
Excuse us for staying so late.
...
I WAS HOPING...
...THAT HE UNDERSTOOD LAST NIGHT THAT I DIDN'T HURT HIM...
...OUT OF MALICE...
...BUT I GUESS HE DIDN'T.
UH... MOKO...
No no, that's not it.
um...
sigh
BUT...
...I...
...MAY NOT BE ABLE TO CONTINUE BEING AN ACTRESS ANYMORE...
HUH?

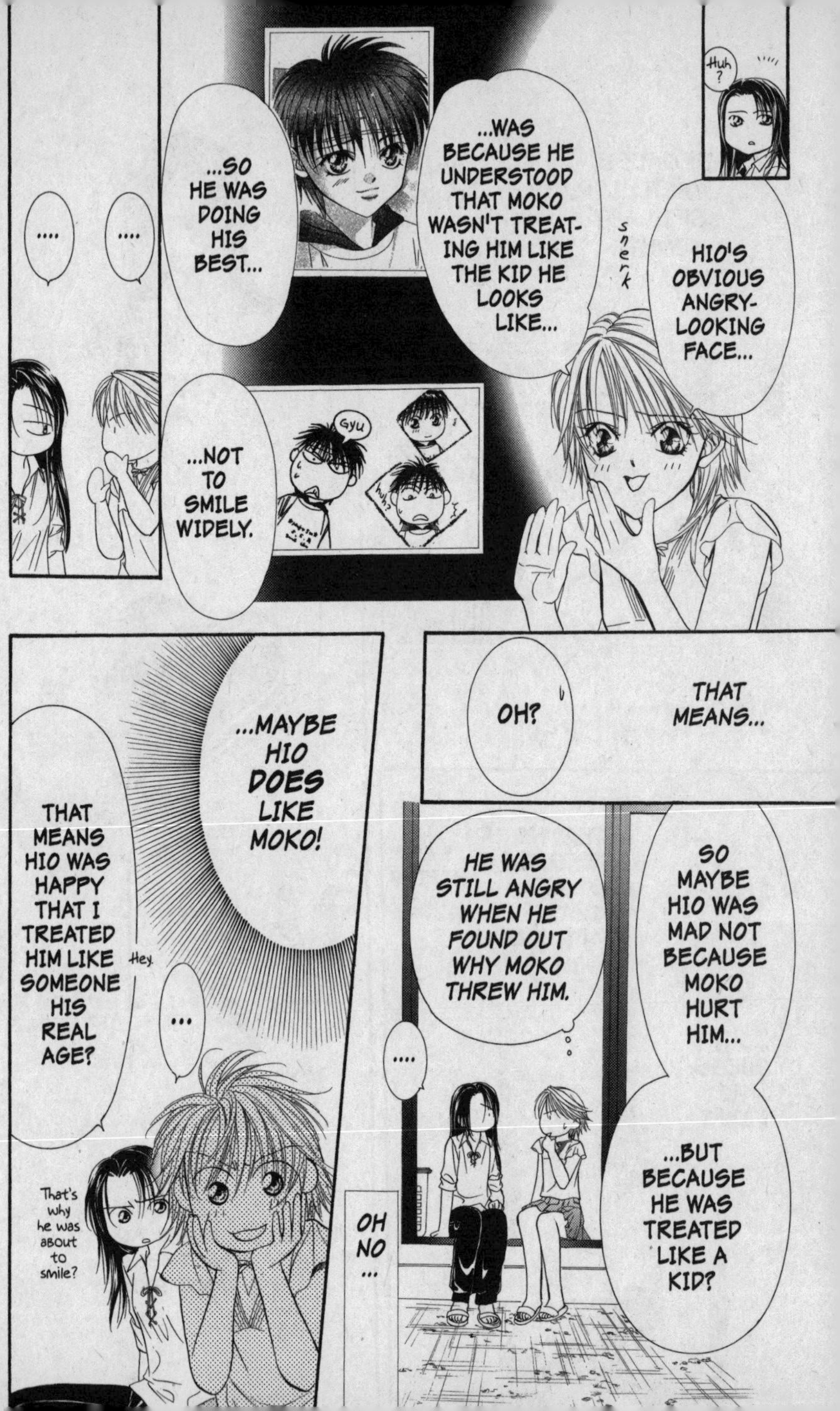
Huh?
HIO'S OBVIOUS ANGRY-LOOKING FACE...
snerk
...WAS BECAUSE HE UNDERSTOOD THAT MOKO WASN'T TREATING HIM LIKE THE KID HE LOOKS LIKE...
...SO HE WAS DOING HIS BEST...
...NOT TO SMILE WIDELY.
Gyu
huh?
....
....
THAT MEANS...
OH?
SO MAYBE HIO WAS MAD NOT BECAUSE MOKO HURT HIM...
...BUT BECAUSE HE WAS TREATED LIKE A KID?
HE WAS STILL ANGRY WHEN HE FOUND OUT WHY MOKO THREW HIM.
....
OH NO ...
...MAYBE HIO DOES LIKE MOKO!
THAT MEANS HIO WAS HAPPY THAT I TREATED HIM LIKE SOMEONE HIS REAL AGE?
Hey.
...
That's why he was about to smile?

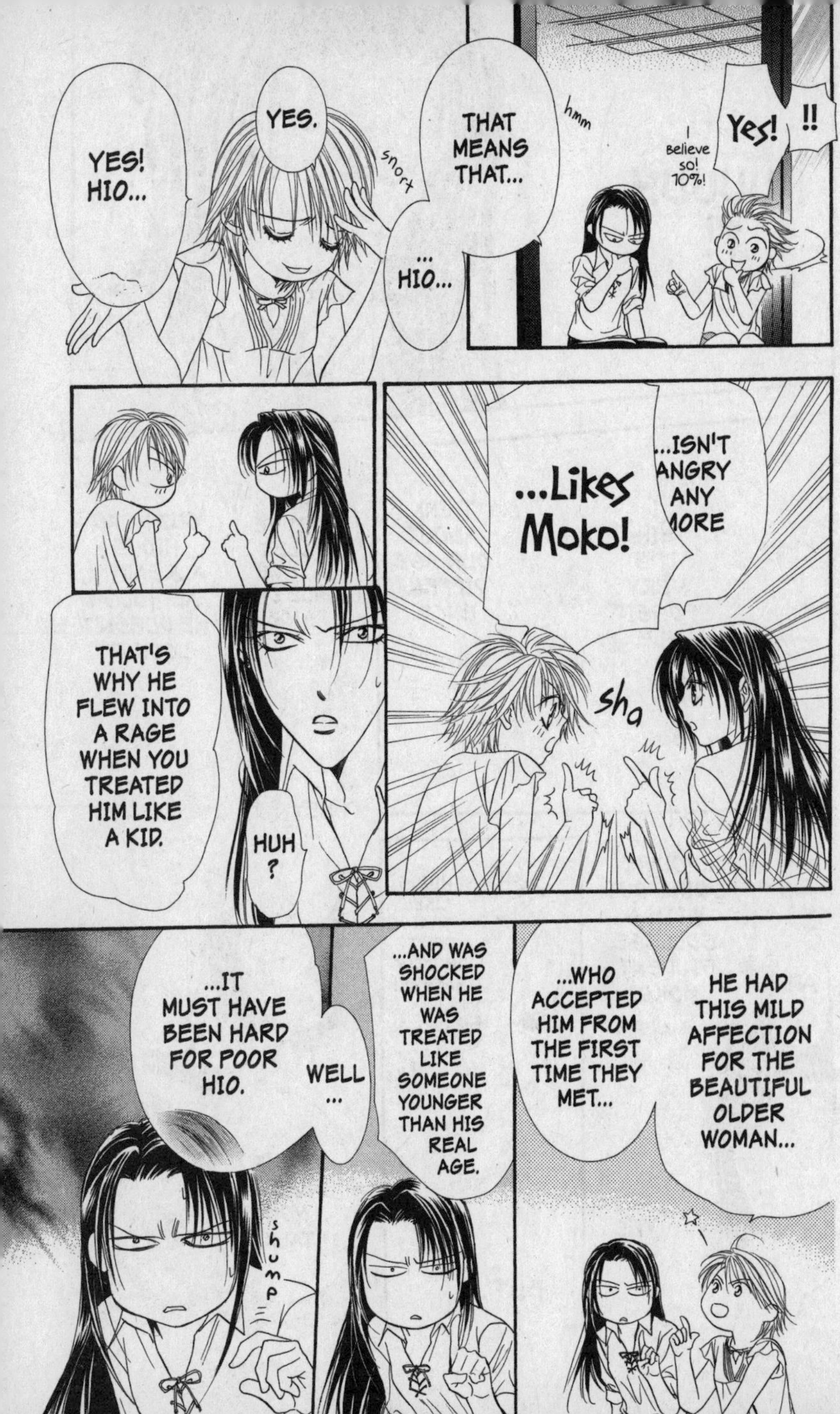
!!
Yes!
I believe so! 10%!
hmm
THAT MEANS THAT...
... HIO...
snort
YES.
YES! HIO...
...ISN'T ANGRY ANY MORE
...Likes Moko!
sha
THAT'S WHY HE FLEW INTO A RAGE WHEN YOU TREATED HIM LIKE A KID.
HUH?
HE HAD THIS MILD AFFECTION FOR THE BEAUTIFUL OLDER WOMAN...
...WHO ACCEPTED HIM FROM THE FIRST TIME THEY MET...
...AND WAS SHOCKED WHEN HE WAS TREATED LIKE SOMEONE YOUNGER THAN HIS REAL AGE.
WELL ...
...IT MUST HAVE BEEN HARD FOR POOR HIO.
shump

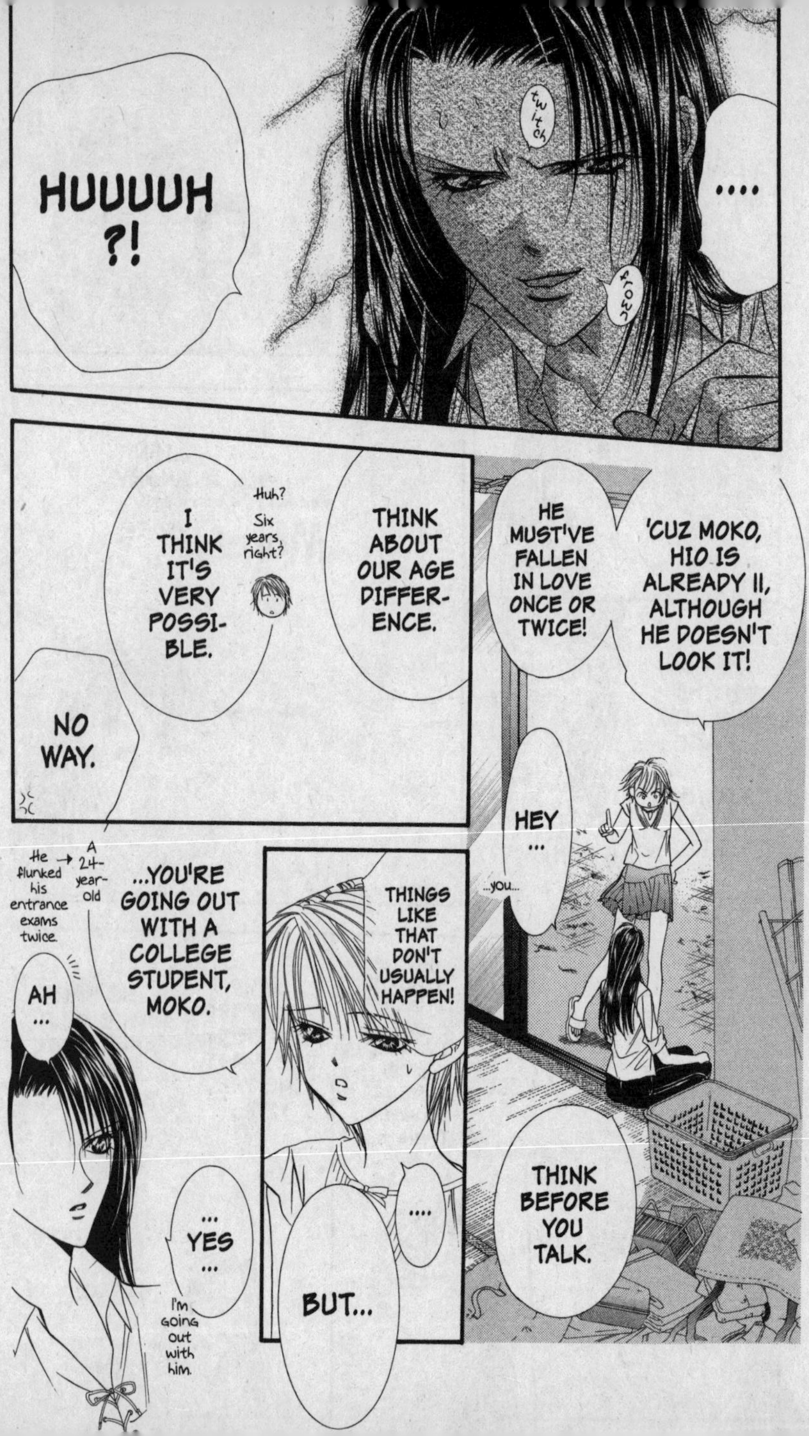

....
twitch
frown
HUUUUH ?!
'CUZ MOKO, HIO IS ALREADY 11, ALTHOUGH HE DOESN'T LOOK IT!
HE MUST'VE FALLEN IN LOVE ONCE OR TWICE!
HEY ...
...you...
THINK BEFORE YOU TALK.
THINK ABOUT OUR AGE DIFFER-ENCE.
Huh? Six years, right?
I THINK IT'S VERY POSSI-BLE.
NO WAY.
THINGS LIKE THAT DON'T USUALLY HAPPEN!
....
BUT...
A 24-year-old
He flunked his entrance exams twice.
...YOU'RE GOING OUT WITH A COLLEGE STUDENT, MOKO.
AH ...
... YES ...
I'm going out with him.

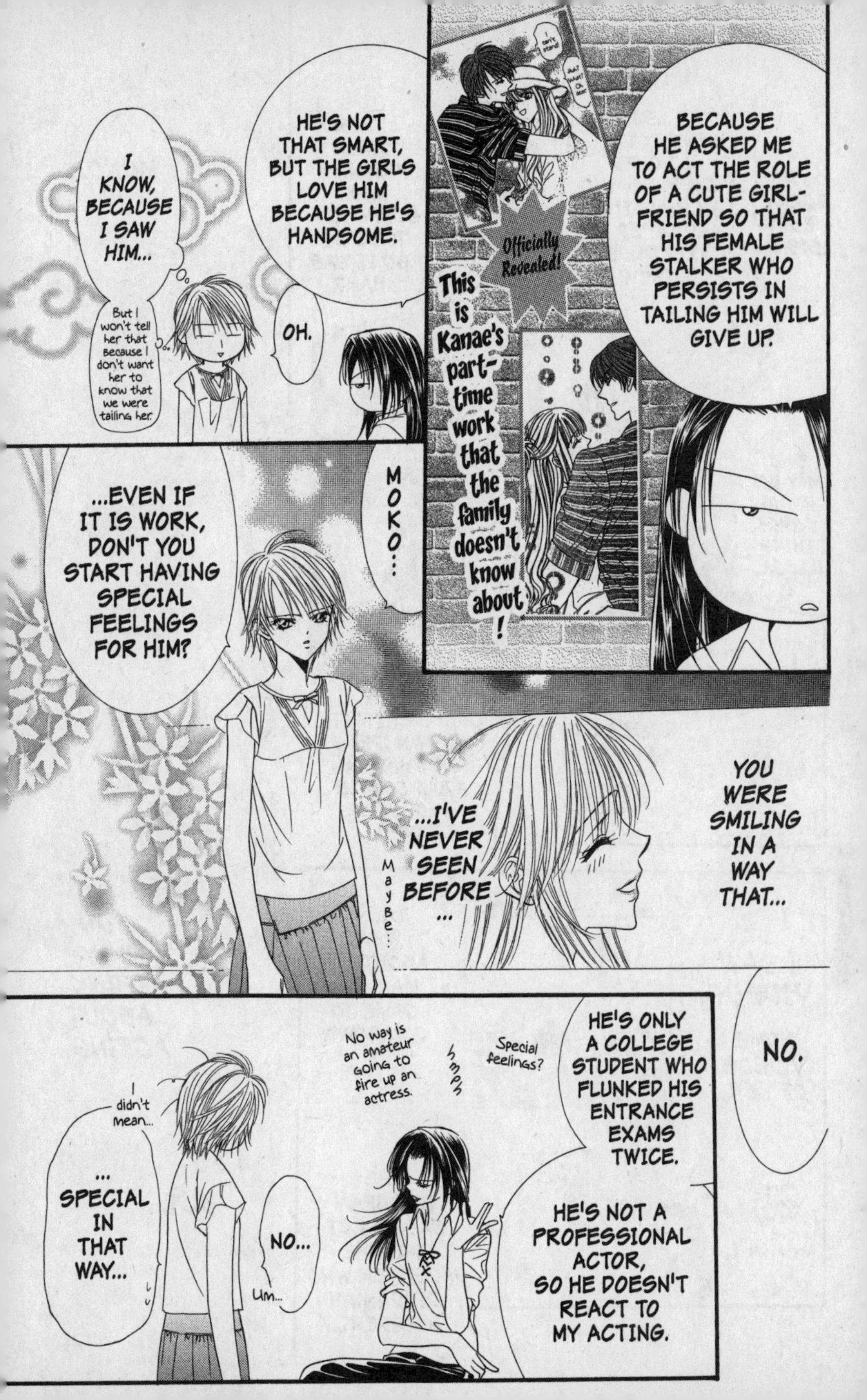
BECAUSE HE ASKED ME TO ACT THE ROLE OF A CUTE GIRL-FRIEND SO THAT HIS FEMALE STALKER WHO PERSISTS IN TAILING HIM WILL GIVE UP.
Officially Revealed!
This is Kanae's part-time work that the family doesn't know about!
HE'S NOT THAT SMART, BUT THE GIRLS LOVE HIM BECAUSE HE'S HANDSOME.
OH.
I KNOW, BECAUSE I SAW HIM...
But I won't tell her that because I don't want her to know that we were tailing her.
MOKO...
...EVEN IF IT IS WORK, DON'T YOU START HAVING SPECIAL FEELINGS FOR HIM?
YOU WERE SMILING IN A WAY THAT...
...I'VE NEVER SEEN BEFORE...
Maybe...
NO.
HE'S ONLY A COLLEGE STUDENT WHO FLUNKED HIS ENTRANCE EXAMS TWICE.
HE'S NOT A PROFESSIONAL ACTOR, SO HE DOESN'T REACT TO MY ACTING.
Special feelings?
hmph
No way is an amateur going to fire up an actress.
NO...
Um...
I didn't mean...
...SPECIAL IN THAT WAY...

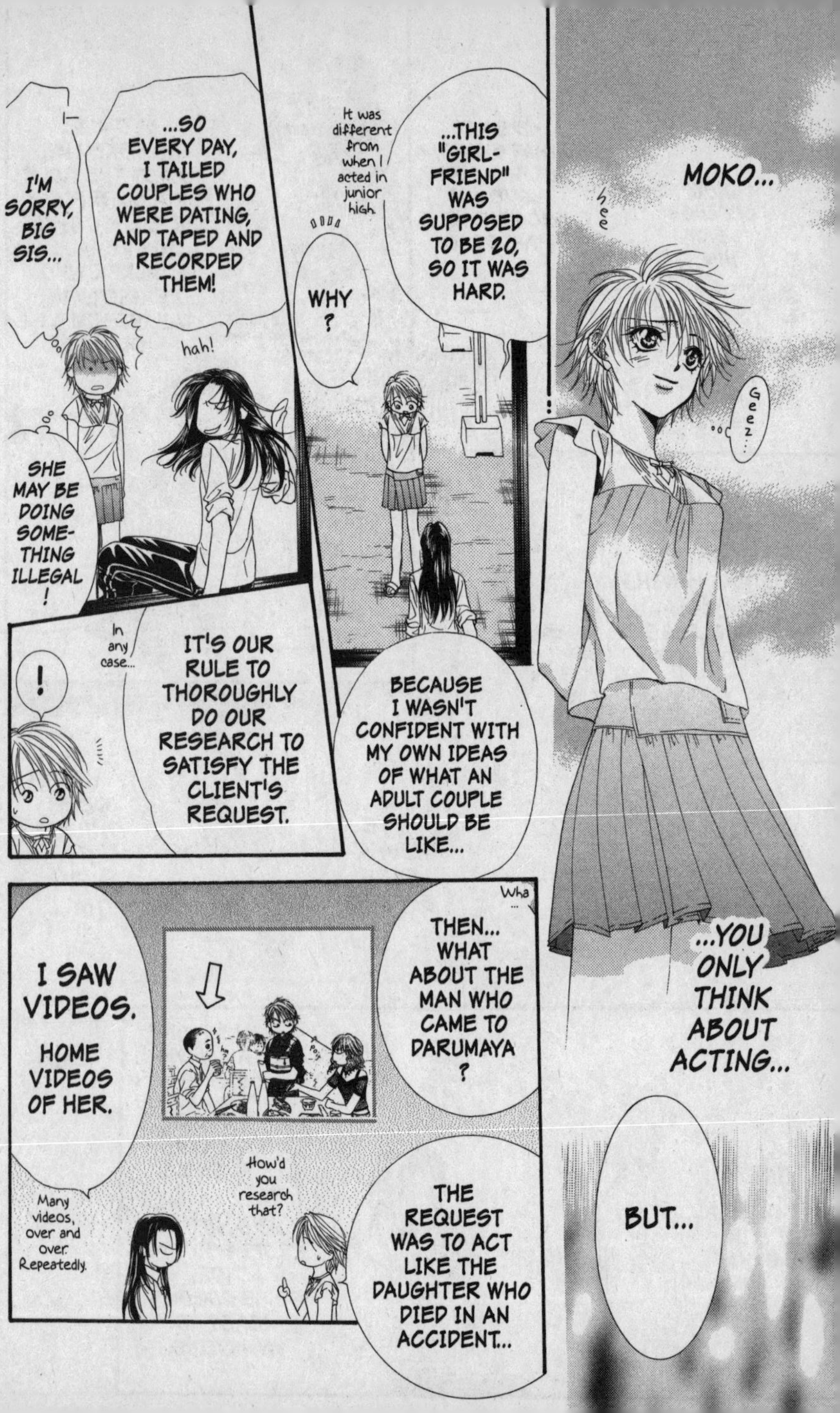

hee
MOKO...
Geez...
...YOU ONLY THINK ABOUT ACTING...
BUT...
It was different from when I acted in junior high.
...THIS "GIRL-FRIEND" WAS SUPPOSED TO BE 20, SO IT WAS HARD.
WHY?
BECAUSE I WASN'T CONFIDENT WITH MY OWN IDEAS OF WHAT AN ADULT COUPLE SHOULD BE LIKE...
...SO EVERY DAY, I TAILED COUPLES WHO WERE DATING, AND TAPED AND RECORDED THEM!
I—
I'M SORRY, BIG SIS...
hah!
SHE MAY BE DOING SOME-THING ILLEGAL!
!
In any case...
IT'S OUR RULE TO THOROUGHLY DO OUR RESEARCH TO SATISFY THE CLIENT'S REQUEST.
Wha...
THEN... WHAT ABOUT THE MAN WHO CAME TO DARUMAYA?
THE REQUEST WAS TO ACT LIKE THE DAUGHTER WHO DIED IN AN ACCIDENT...
How'd you research that?
I SAW VIDEOS.
HOME VIDEOS OF HER.
Many videos, over and over. Repeatedly.

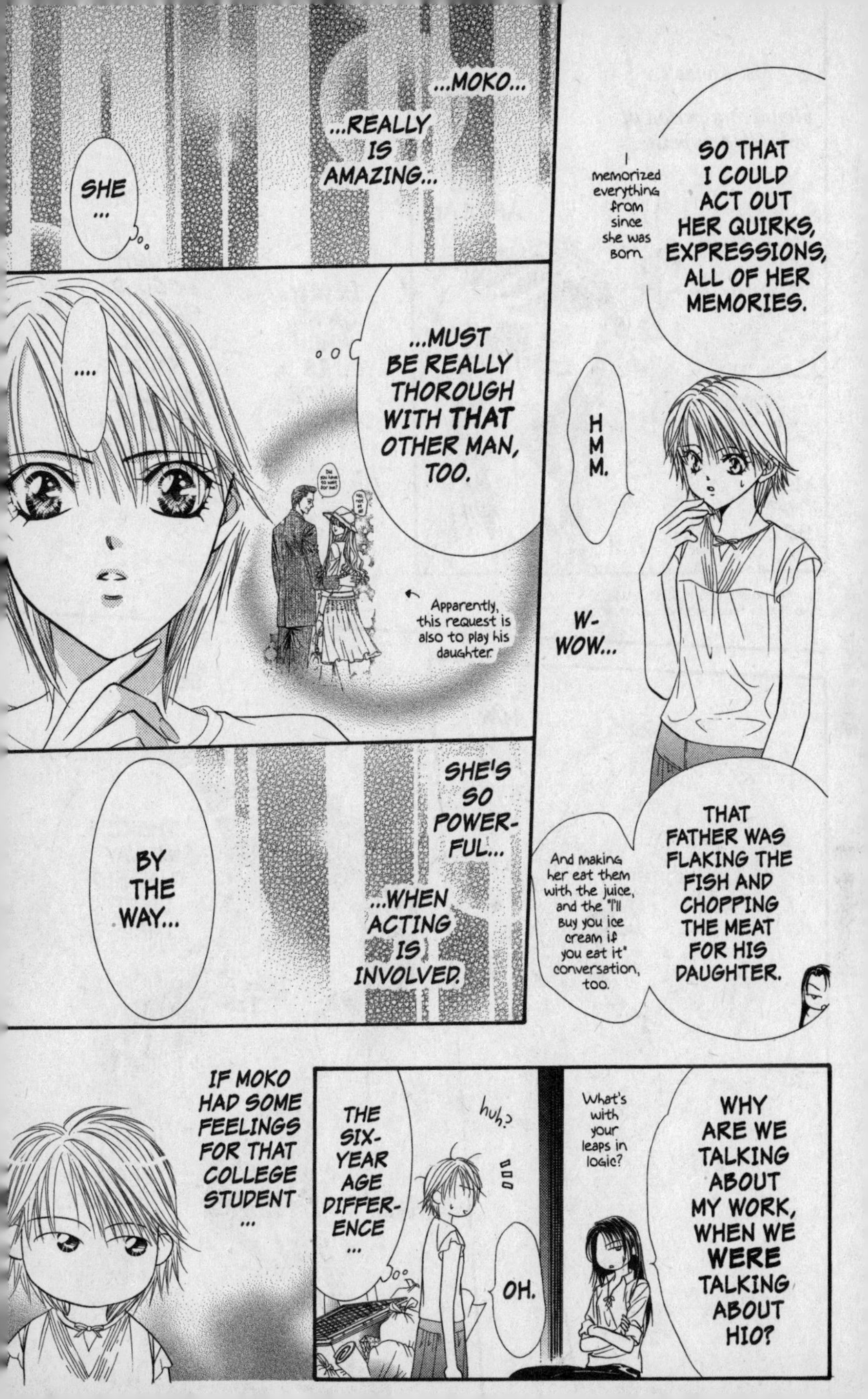

SO THAT I COULD ACT OUT HER QUIRKS, EXPRESSIONS, ALL OF HER MEMORIES.
I memorized everything from since she was born.
HMM.
W-WOW...
THAT FATHER WAS FLAKING THE FISH AND CHOPPING THE MEAT FOR HIS DAUGHTER.
And making her eat them with the juice, and the "I'll buy you ice cream if you eat it" conversation, too.
...MOKO...
...REALLY IS AMAZING...
SHE ...
...MUST BE REALLY THOROUGH WITH THAT OTHER MAN, TOO.
Apparently, this request is also to play his daughter.
....
SHE'S SO POWERFUL...
...WHEN ACTING IS INVOLVED.
BY THE WAY...
WHY ARE WE TALKING ABOUT MY WORK, WHEN WE WERE TALKING ABOUT HIO?
What's with your leaps in logic?
THE SIX-YEAR AGE DIFFERENCE ...
huh?
OH.
IF MOKO HAD SOME FEELINGS FOR THAT COLLEGE STUDENT ...

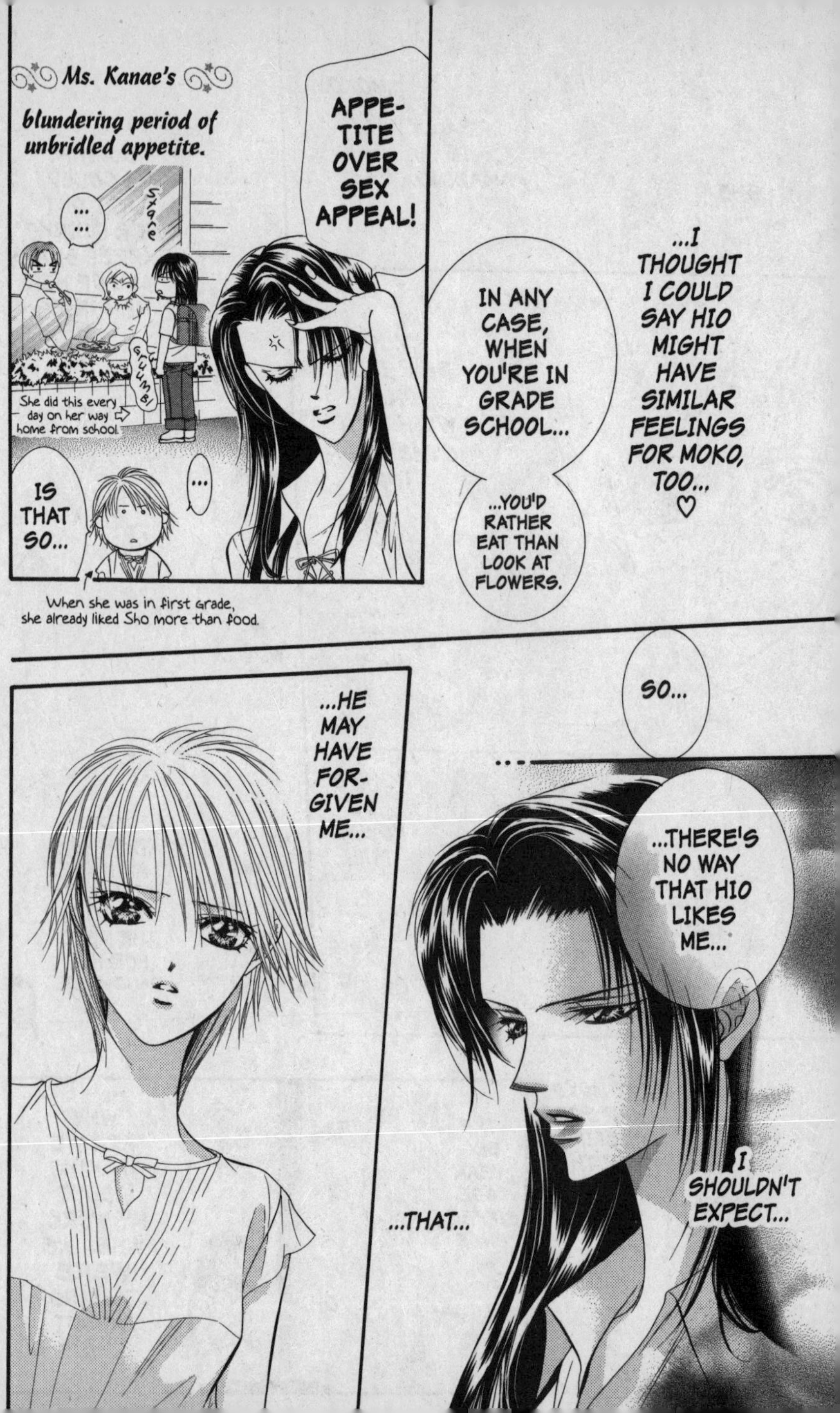
...I THOUGHT I COULD SAY HIO MIGHT HAVE SIMILAR FEELINGS FOR MOKO, TOO...♡
IN ANY CASE, WHEN YOU'RE IN GRADE SCHOOL...
...YOU'D RATHER EAT THAN LOOK AT FLOWERS.
APPE-TITE OVER SEX APPEAL!
Ms. Kanae's blundering period of unbridled appetite.
...
...
Stare
GRUUMBL
She did this every day on her way home from school.
...
IS THAT SO...
When she was in first grade, she already liked Sho more than food.
SO...
...THERE'S NO WAY THAT HIO LIKES ME...
I SHOULDN'T EXPECT...
...THAT...
...HE MAY HAVE FOR-GIVEN ME...

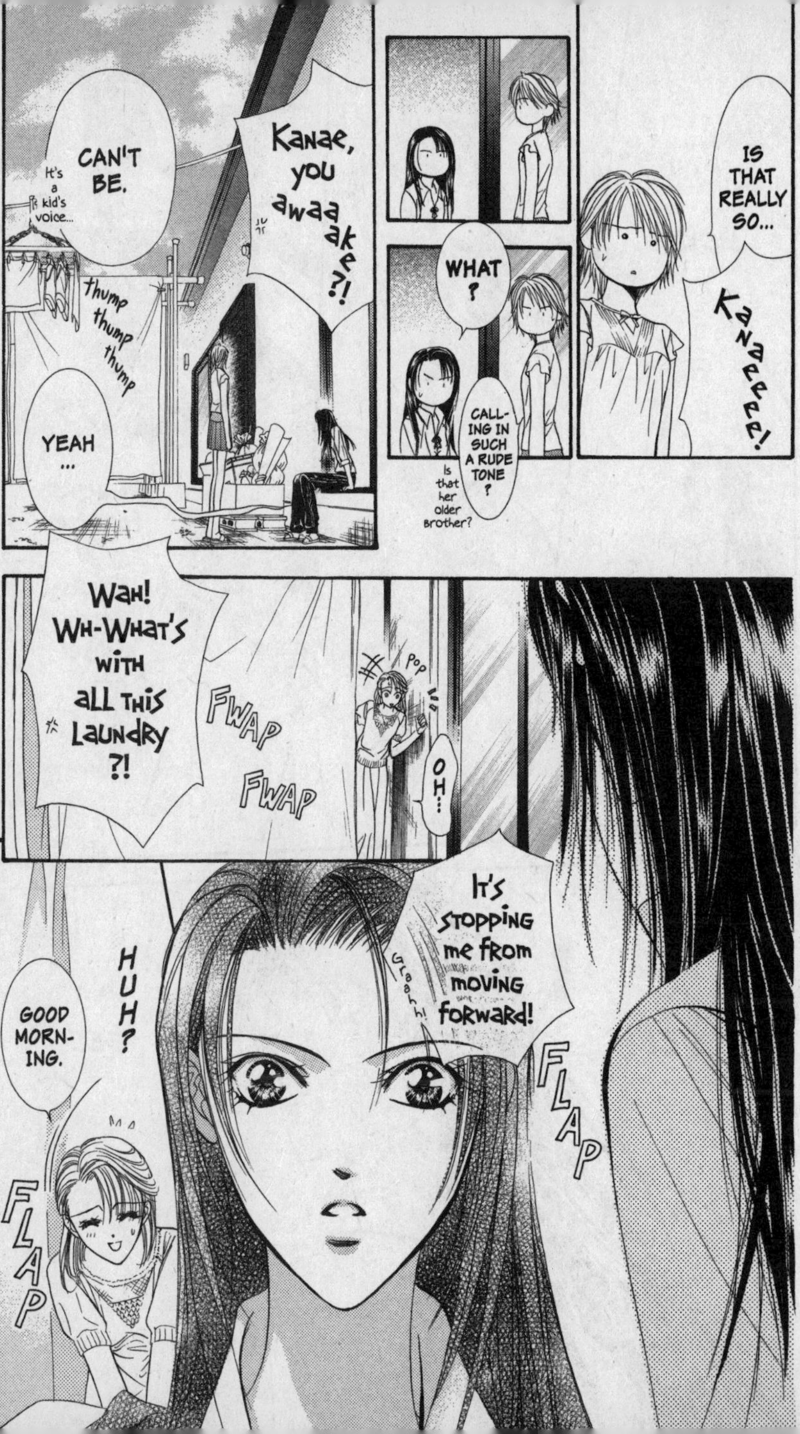
IS THAT REALLY SO...
Kanaeee!
WHAT?
CALLING IN SUCH A RUDE TONE?
Is that her older brother?
Kanae, you awaaake?!
CAN'T BE.
It's a kid's voice...
thump thump thump
YEAH...
Pop
Wah! Wh-What's with all this laundry?!
FWAP
FWAP
OH...
It's stopping me from moving forward!
Graahh!
FLAP
HUH?
GOOD MORNING.
FLAP

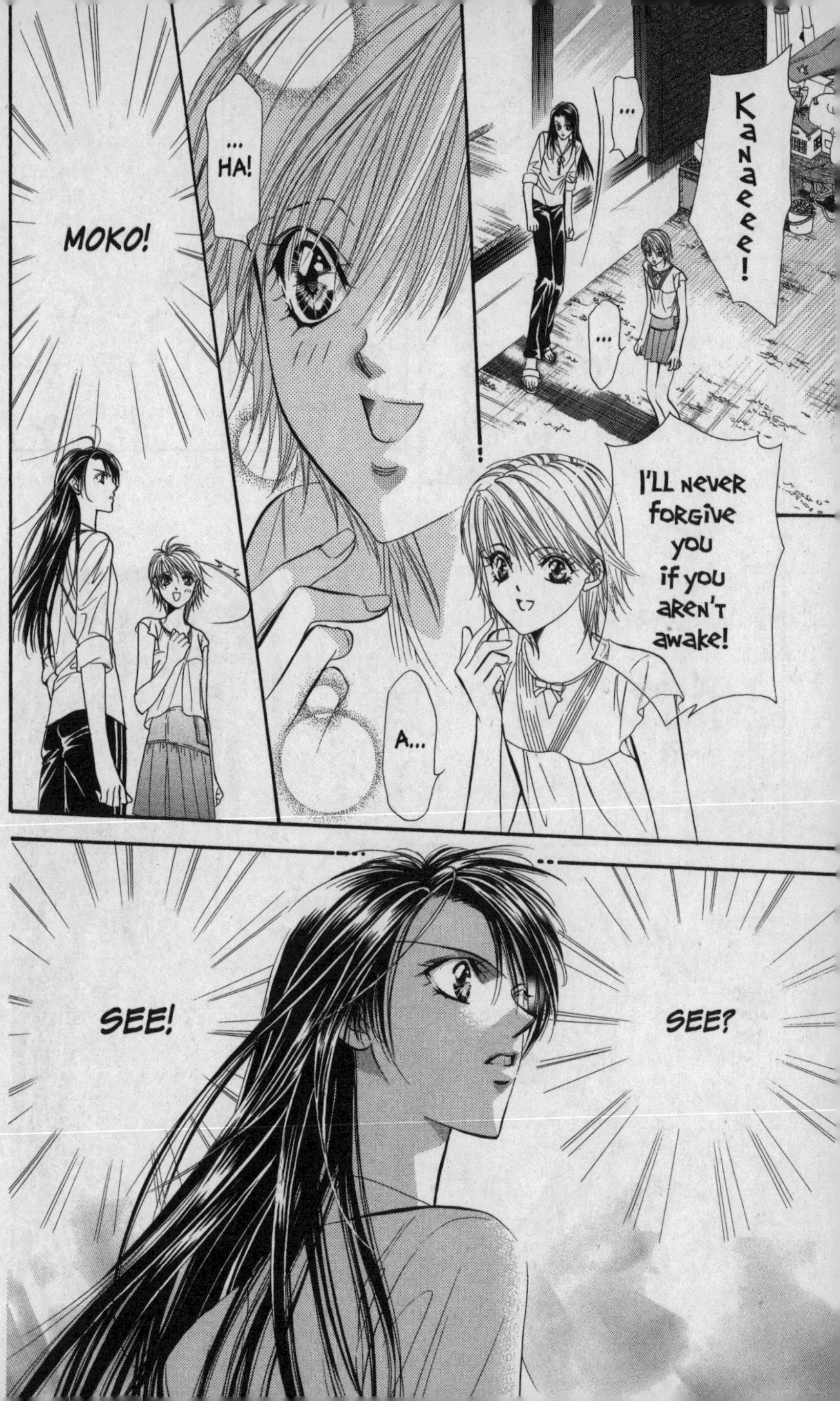
Kanaeee!
...
...
I'LL never forgive you if you aren't awake!
...HA!
A...
MOKO!
SEE?
SEE!

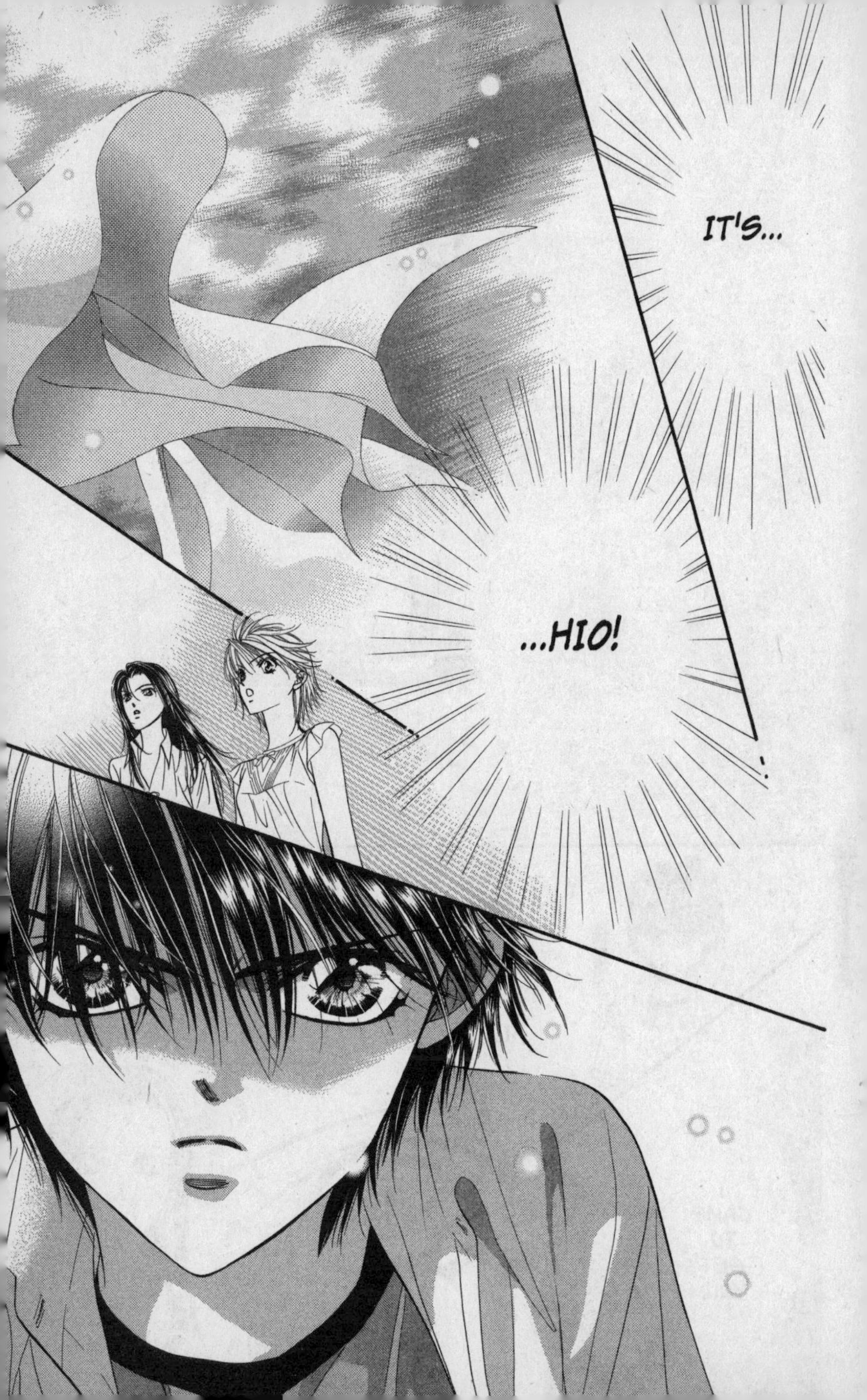
IT'S...
...HIO!

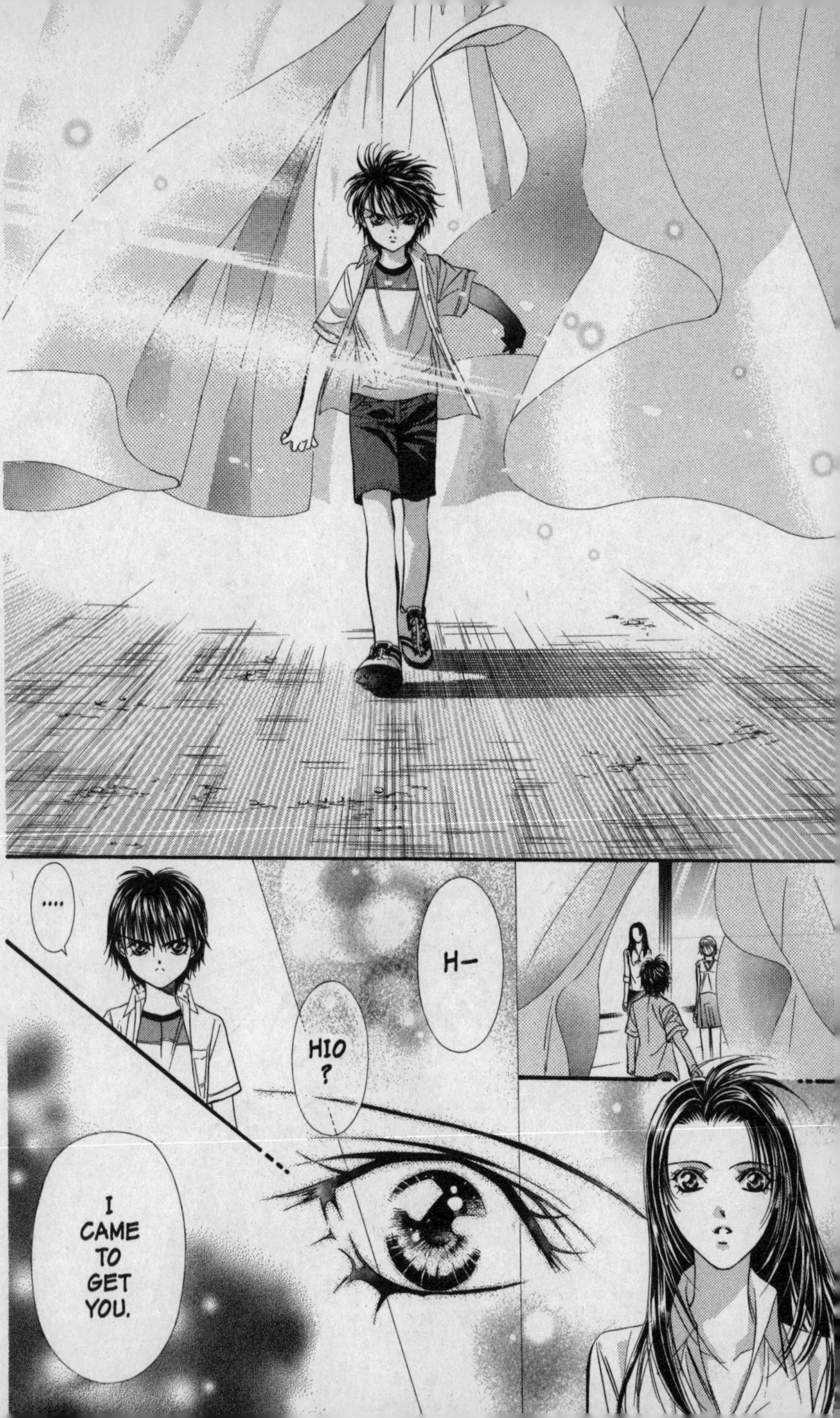
H–
HIO?
....
I CAME TO GET YOU.

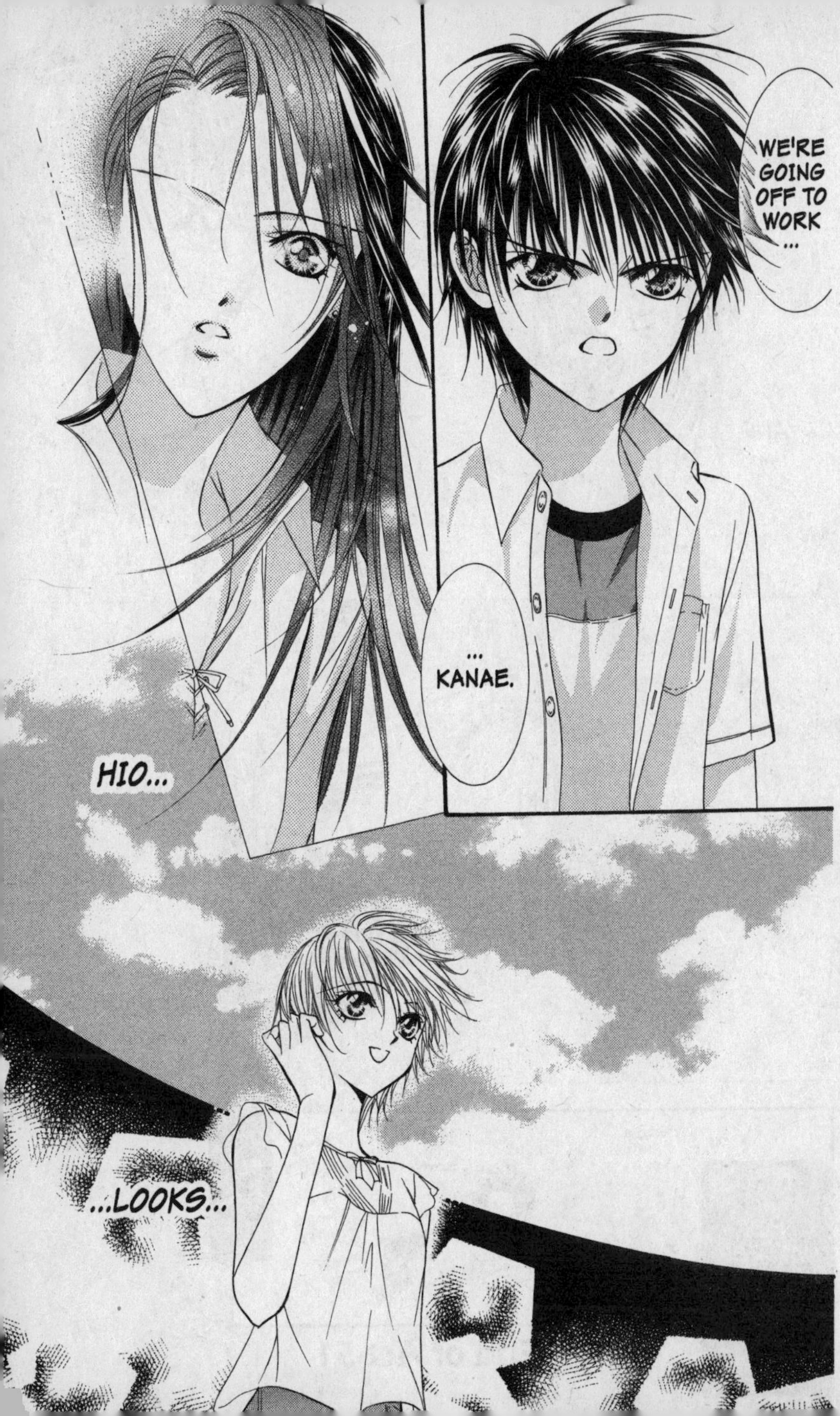
WE'RE GOING OFF TO WORK ...
... KANAE.
HIO...
...LOOKS...

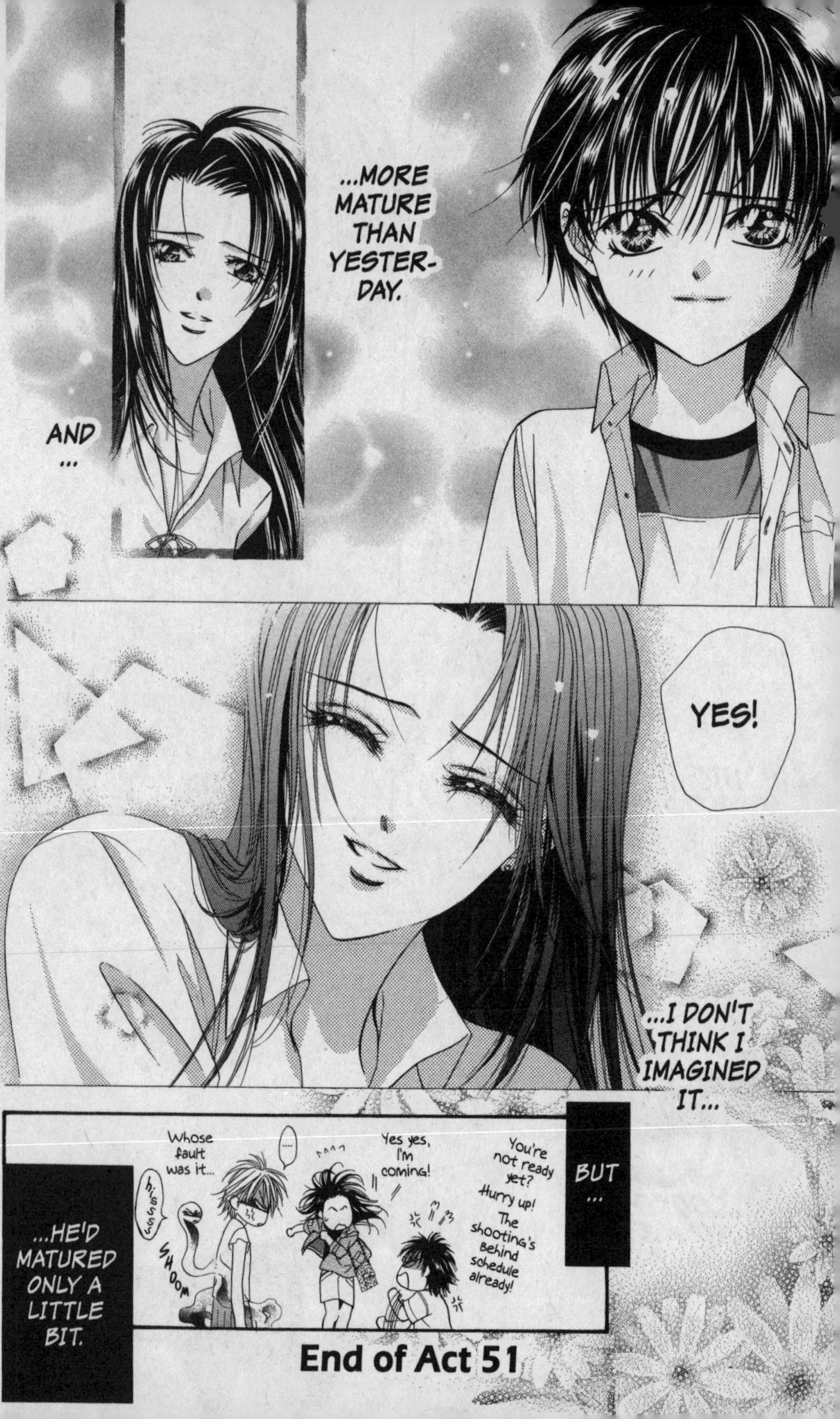
...MORE MATURE THAN YESTER-DAY.
AND ...
YES!
...I DON'T THINK I IMAGINED IT...
BUT ...
You're not ready yet? Hurry up! The shooting's behind schedule already!
Yes yes, I'm coming!
....
Whose fault was it...
hiss
SHOOM
...HE'D MATURED ONLY A LITTLE BIT.
End of Act 51

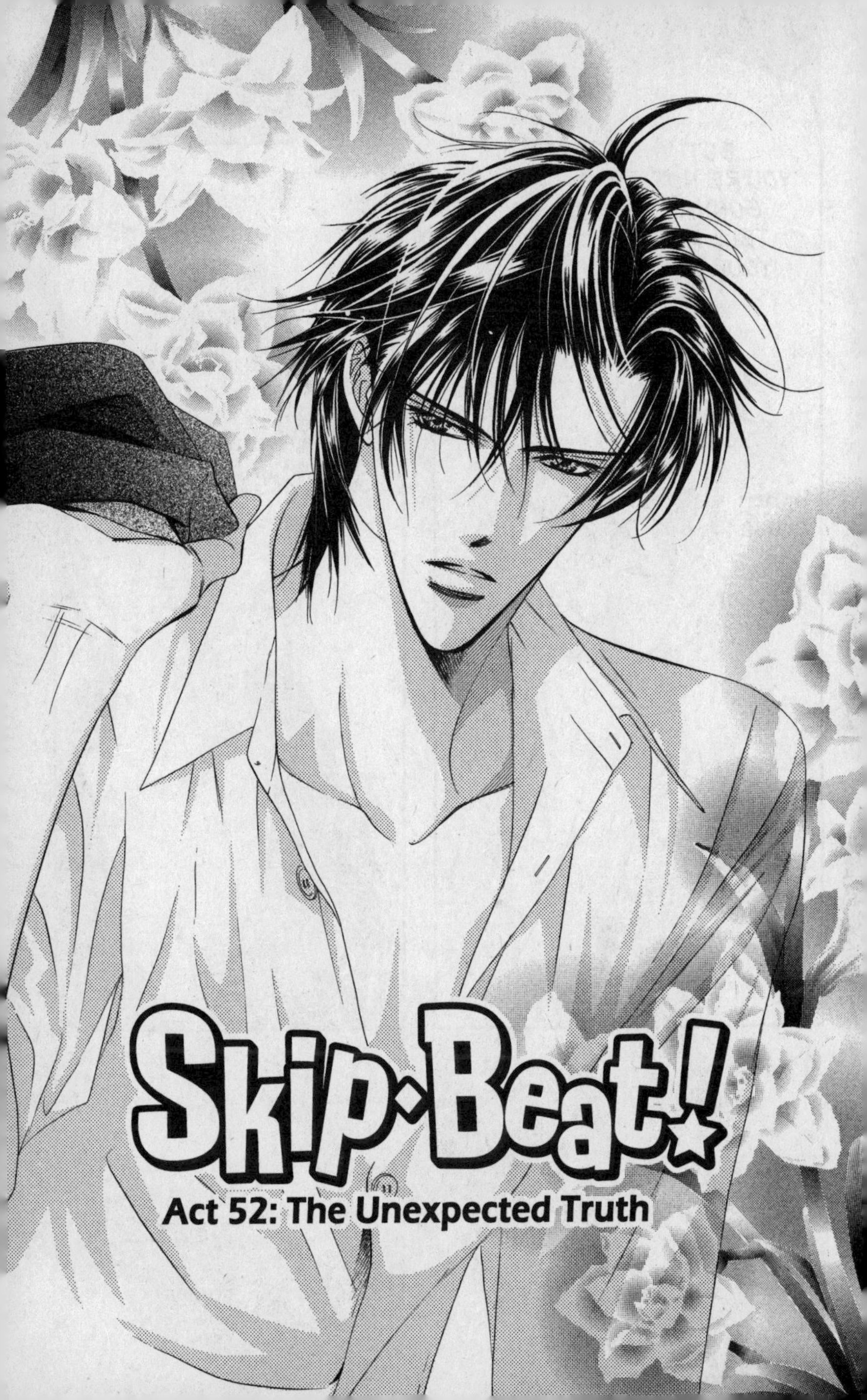
Skip·Beat!
Act 52: The Unexpected Truth

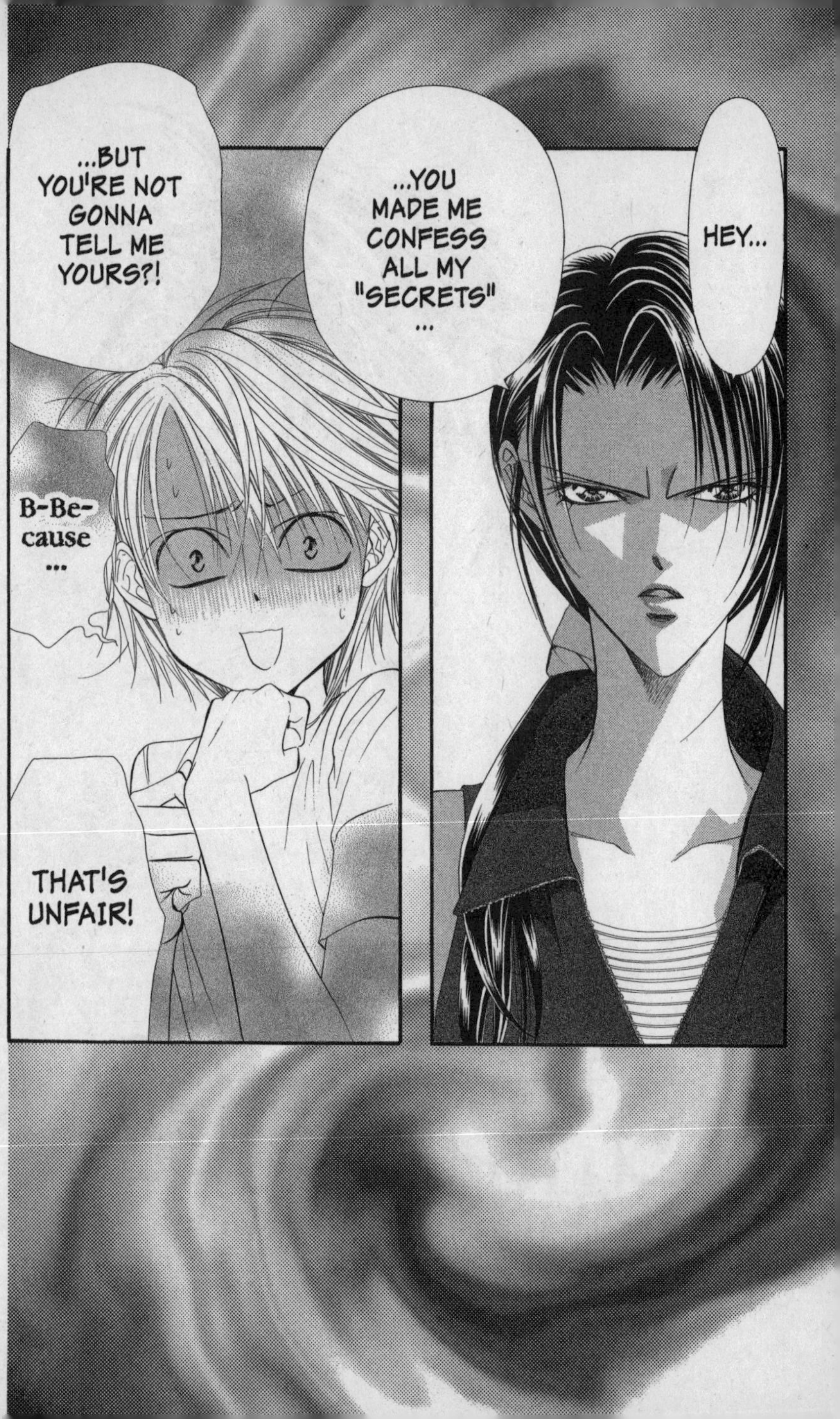
HEY...
...YOU MADE ME CONFESS ALL MY "SECRETS" ...
...BUT YOU'RE NOT GONNA TELL ME YOURS?!
B-Be-cause ...
THAT'S UNFAIR!

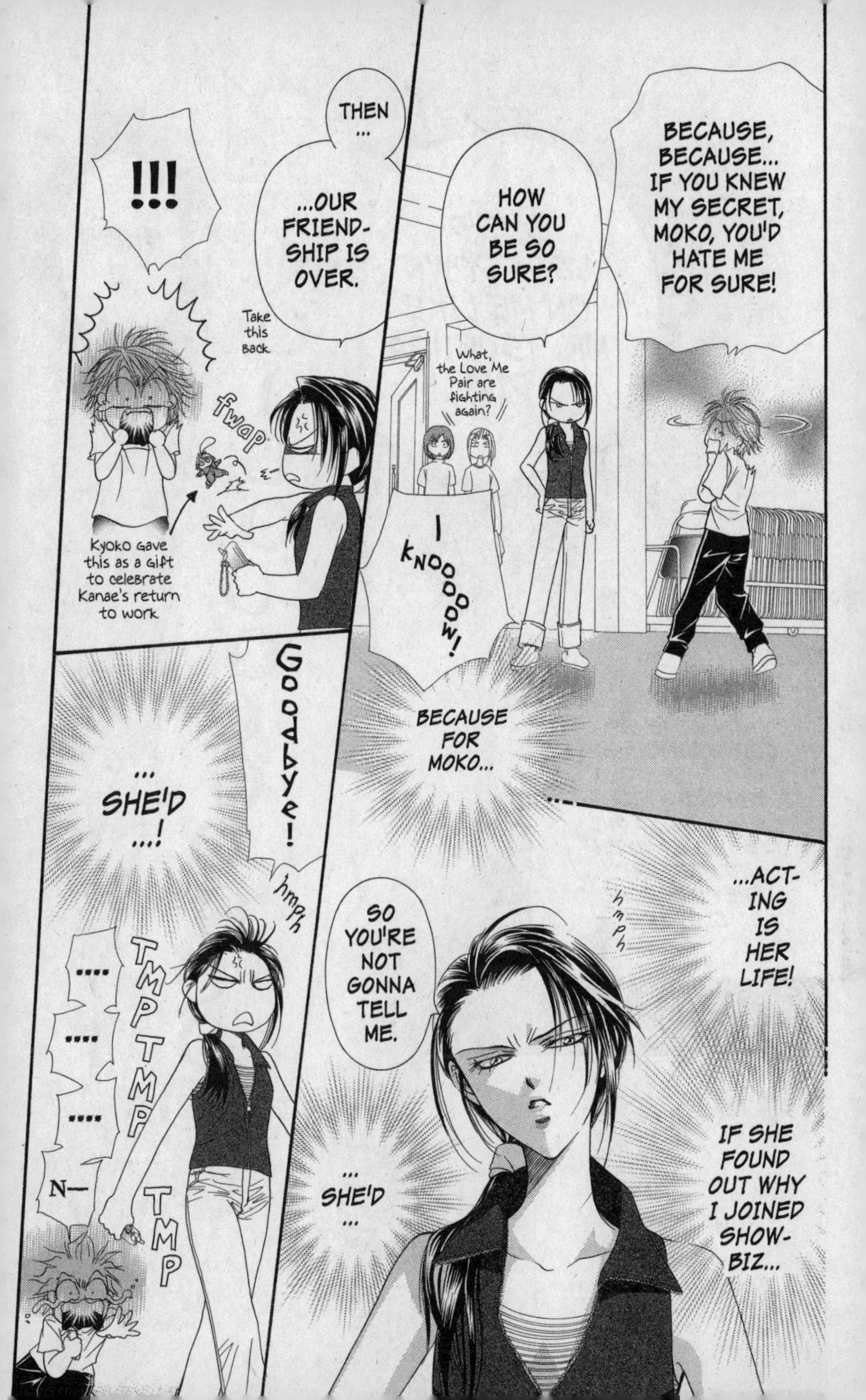
BECAUSE, BECAUSE... IF YOU KNEW MY SECRET, MOKO, YOU'D HATE ME FOR SURE!
HOW CAN YOU BE SO SURE?
What, the Love Me Pair are fighting again?
I KNOOOOOOW!
BECAUSE FOR MOKO...
THEN...
...OUR FRIENDSHIP IS OVER.
Take this back.
fwap
!!!
Kyoko gave this as a gift to celebrate Kanae's return to work.
...ACTING IS HER LIFE!
hmph
SO YOU'RE NOT GONNA TELL ME.
IF SHE FOUND OUT WHY I JOINED SHOW-BIZ...
...SHE'D...
...SHE'D...!
Goodbye!
hmph
TMP TMP TMP TMP
....
....
....
N—

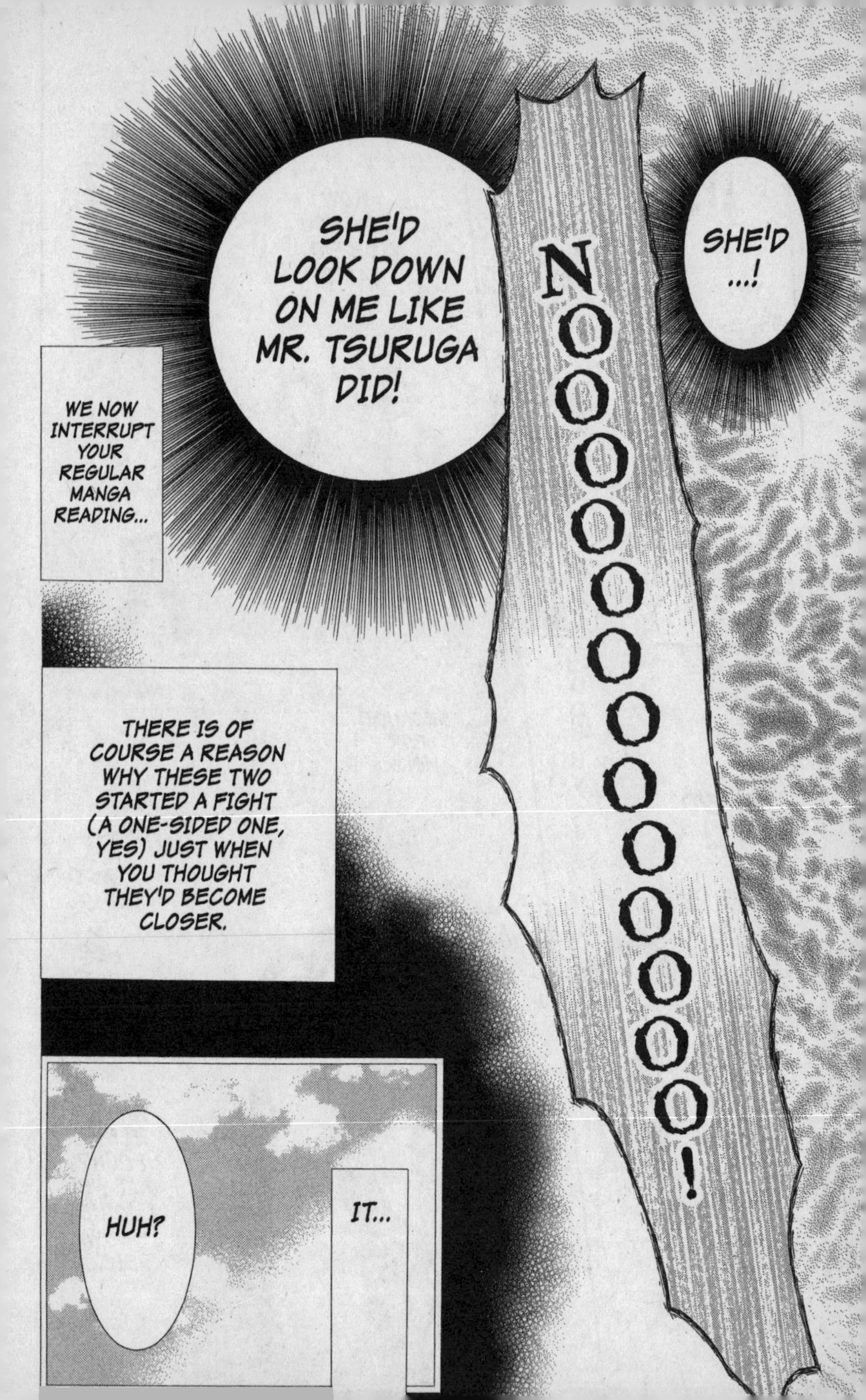
SHE'D ...!
SHE'D LOOK DOWN ON ME LIKE MR. TSURUGA DID!
NOOOOOOOOOOOOOO!
WE NOW INTERRUPT YOUR REGULAR MANGA READING...
THERE IS OF COURSE A REASON WHY THESE TWO STARTED A FIGHT (A ONE-SIDED ONE, YES) JUST WHEN YOU THOUGHT THEY'D BECOME CLOSER.
IT...
HUH?

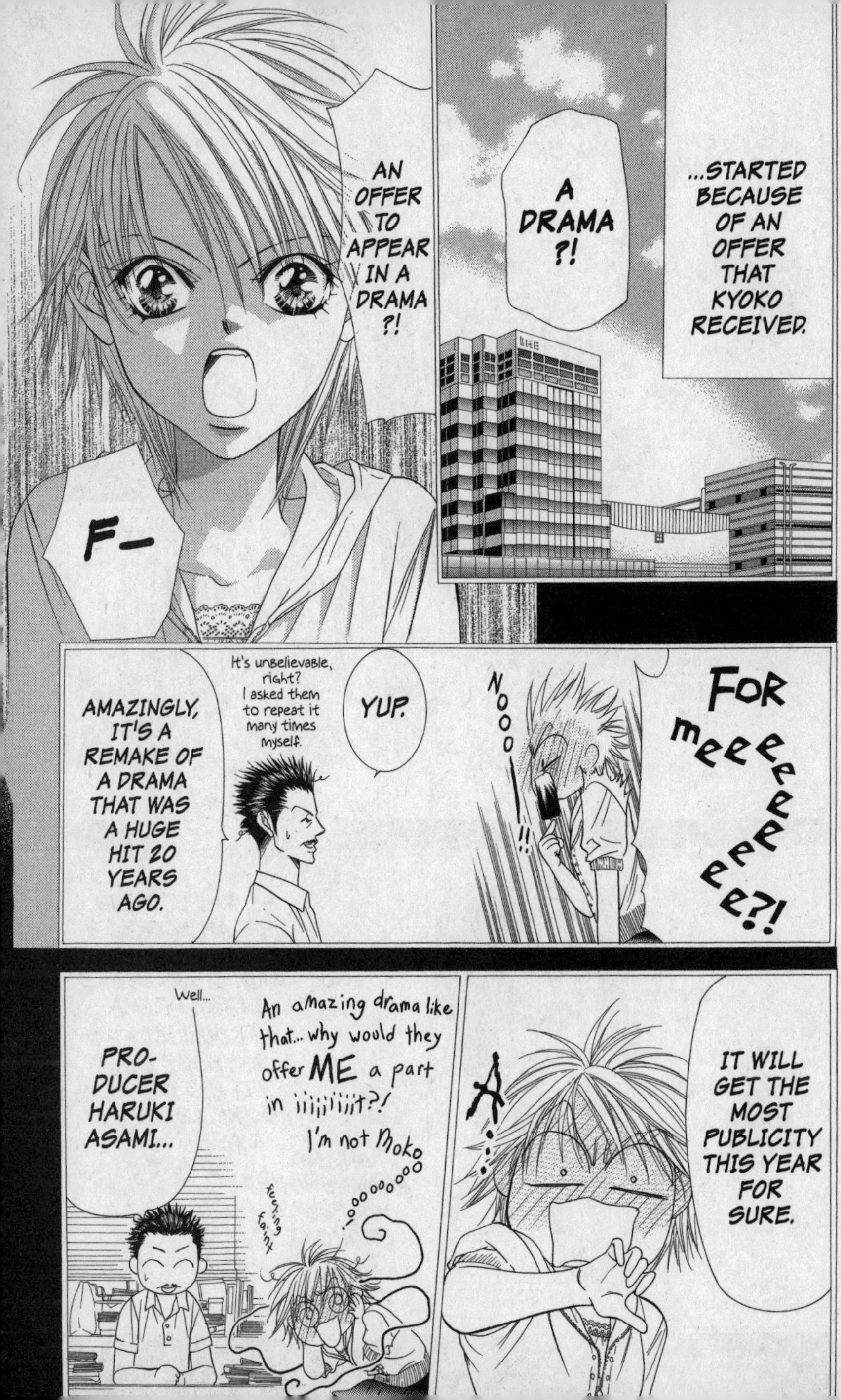
...STARTED BECAUSE OF AN OFFER THAT KYOKO RECEIVED.
A DRAMA ?!
AN OFFER TO APPEAR IN A DRAMA ?!
F—
FOR meeeeeeeeee?!
Nooo—!!
YUP.
It's unbelievable, right? I asked them to repeat it many times myself.
AMAZINGLY, IT'S A REMAKE OF A DRAMA THAT WAS A HUGE HIT 20 YEARS AGO.
IT WILL GET THE MOST PUBLICITY THIS YEAR FOR SURE.
A...
An amazing drama like that... why would they offer ME a part in iiiiiiiit?!
I'm not Mokoooooooooo...
reeling faint
Well...
PRODUCER HARUKI ASAMI...

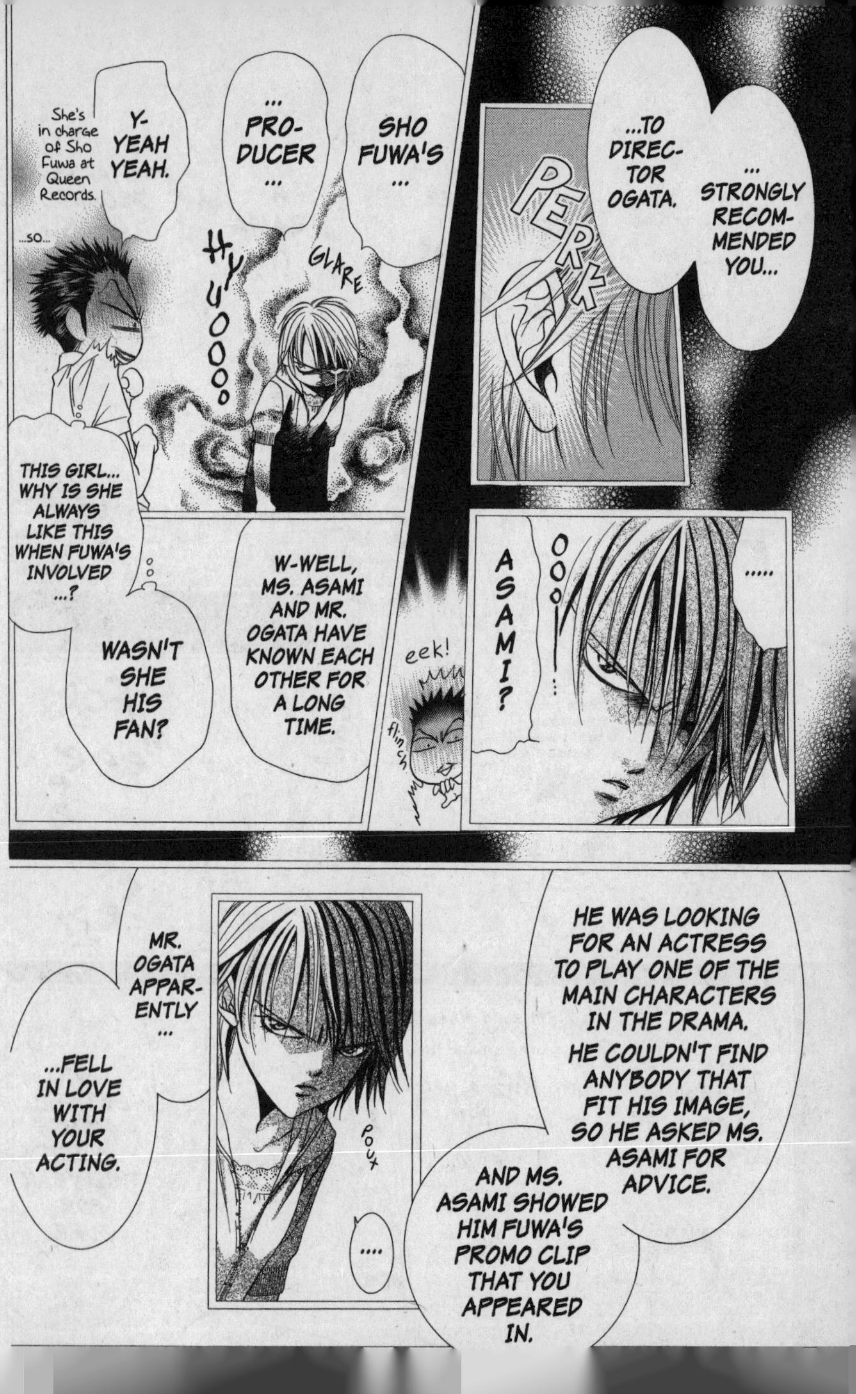

... STRONGLY RECOMMENDED YOU...
...TO DIRECTOR OGATA.
PERK
SHO FUWA'S ...
... PRODUCER ...
Y-YEAH YEAH.
She's in charge of Sho Fuwa at Queen Records.
...so...
GLARE
HYUOOOO
THIS GIRL... WHY IS SHE ALWAYS LIKE THIS WHEN FUWA'S INVOLVED ...?
.....
OOO...!
ASAMI?
eek!
flinch
W-WELL, MS. ASAMI AND MR. OGATA HAVE KNOWN EACH OTHER FOR A LONG TIME.
WASN'T SHE HIS FAN?
HE WAS LOOKING FOR AN ACTRESS TO PLAY ONE OF THE MAIN CHARACTERS IN THE DRAMA. HE COULDN'T FIND ANYBODY THAT FIT HIS IMAGE, SO HE ASKED MS. ASAMI FOR ADVICE.
AND MS. ASAMI SHOWED HIM FUWA'S PROMO CLIP THAT YOU APPEARED IN.
POUT
....
MR. OGATA APPARENTLY ...
...FELL IN LOVE WITH YOUR ACTING.

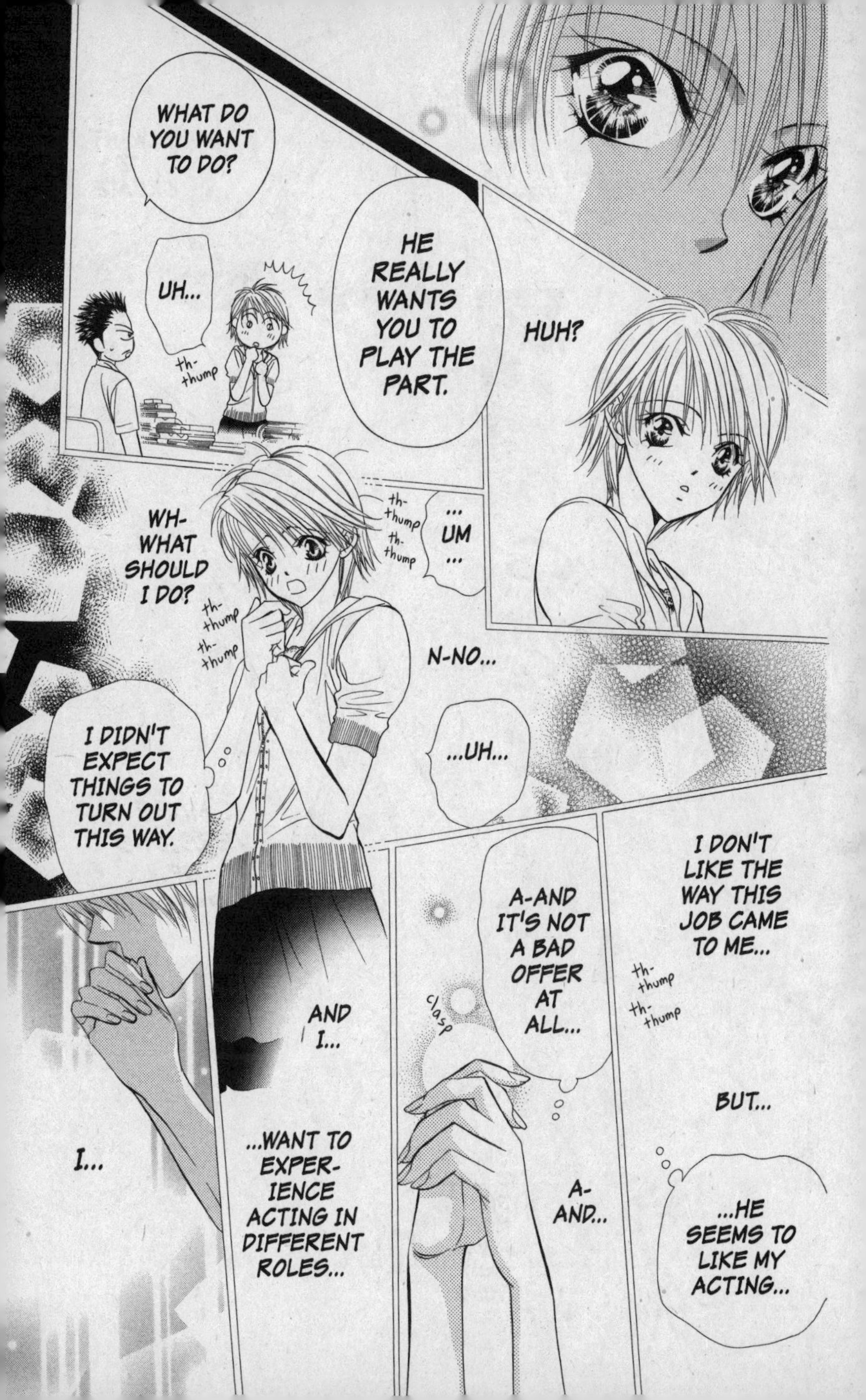
WHAT DO YOU WANT TO DO?
UH...
th-thump
HE REALLY WANTS YOU TO PLAY THE PART.
HUH?
... UM ...
th-thump th-thump
WH-WHAT SHOULD I DO?
th-thump th-thump
N-NO...
...UH...
I DIDN'T EXPECT THINGS TO TURN OUT THIS WAY.
I DON'T LIKE THE WAY THIS JOB CAME TO ME...
th-thump th-thump
BUT...
...HE SEEMS TO LIKE MY ACTING...
A-AND IT'S NOT A BAD OFFER AT ALL...
clasp
A-AND...
AND I...
...WANT TO EXPER-IENCE ACTING IN DIFFERENT ROLES...
I...

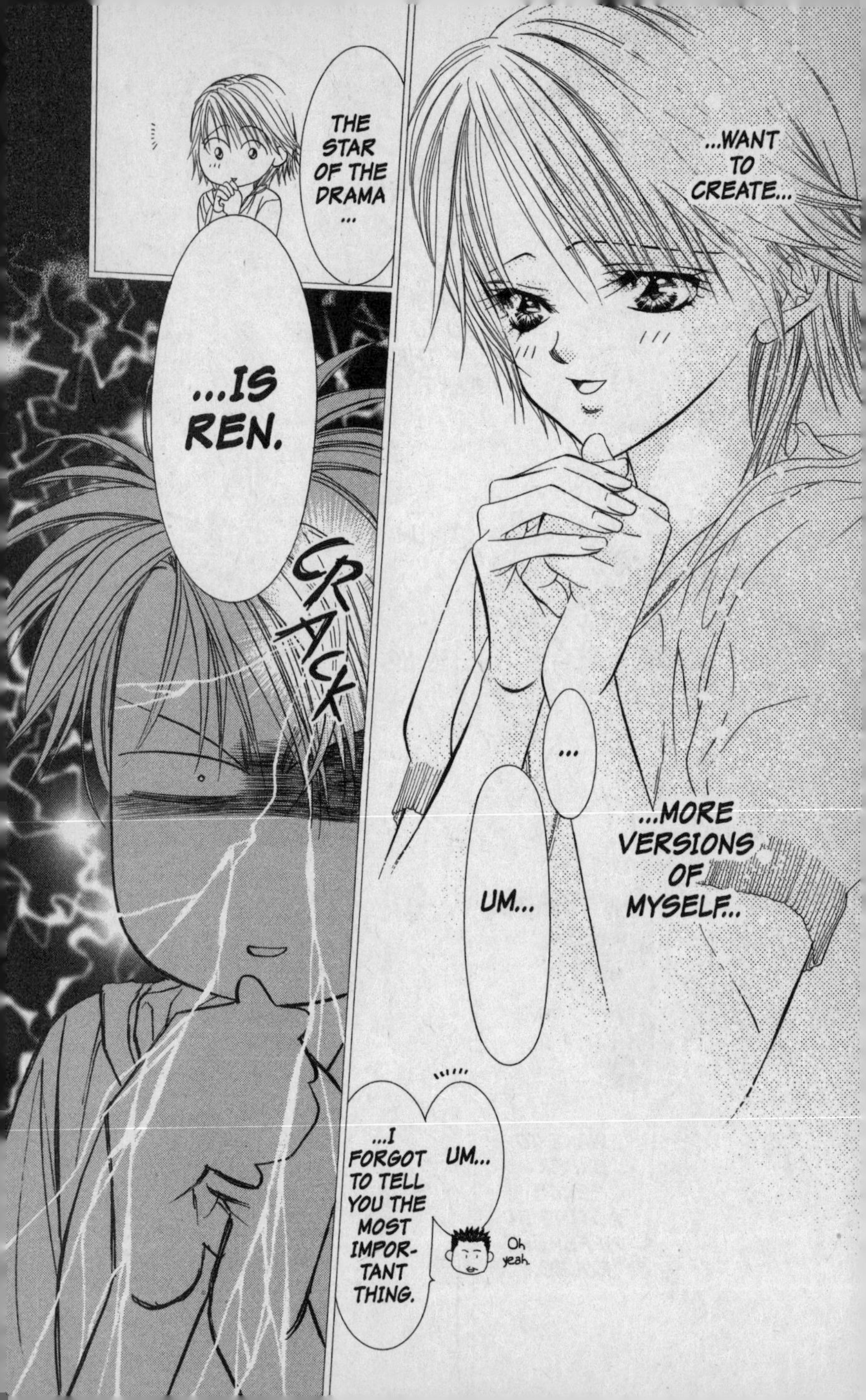
...WANT TO CREATE...
...MORE VERSIONS OF MYSELF...
...
UM...
UM...
...I FORGOT TO TELL YOU THE MOST IMPORTANT THING.
Oh yeah.
THE STAR OF THE DRAMA...
...IS REN.
CRACK

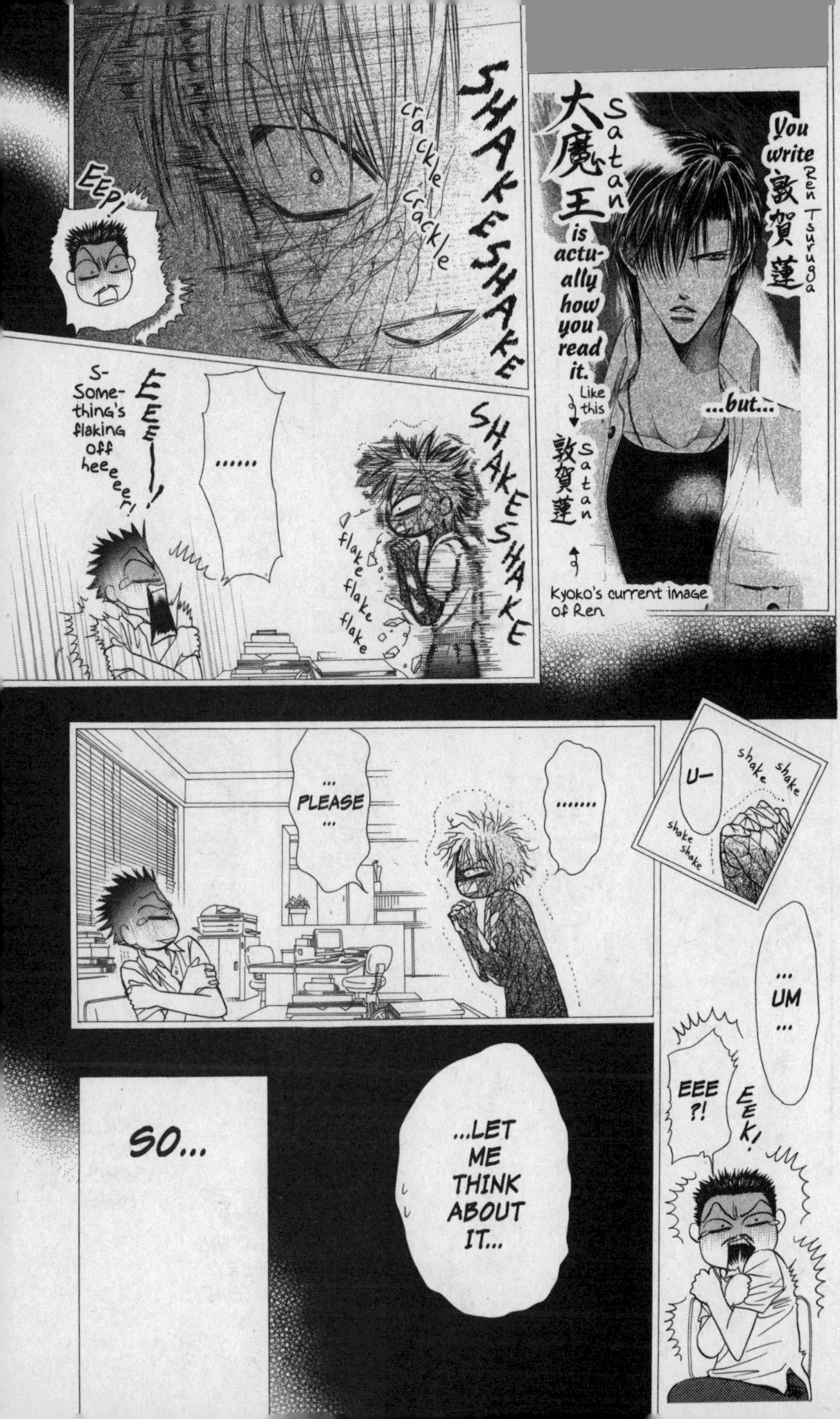
You write 敦賀蓮 Ren Tsuruga
...but...
大魔王 Satan is actually how you read it.
Like this
敦賀蓮 Satan
Kyoko's current image of Ren
SHAKESHAKE
crackle crackle
EEP!
SHAKESHAKE
flake flake flake
......
EEEE—!
S-Something's flaking off heeeeer!
U—
shake shake
shake shake
....
...PLEASE...
...UM...
EEE?!
EEK!
...LET ME THINK ABOUT IT...
SO...

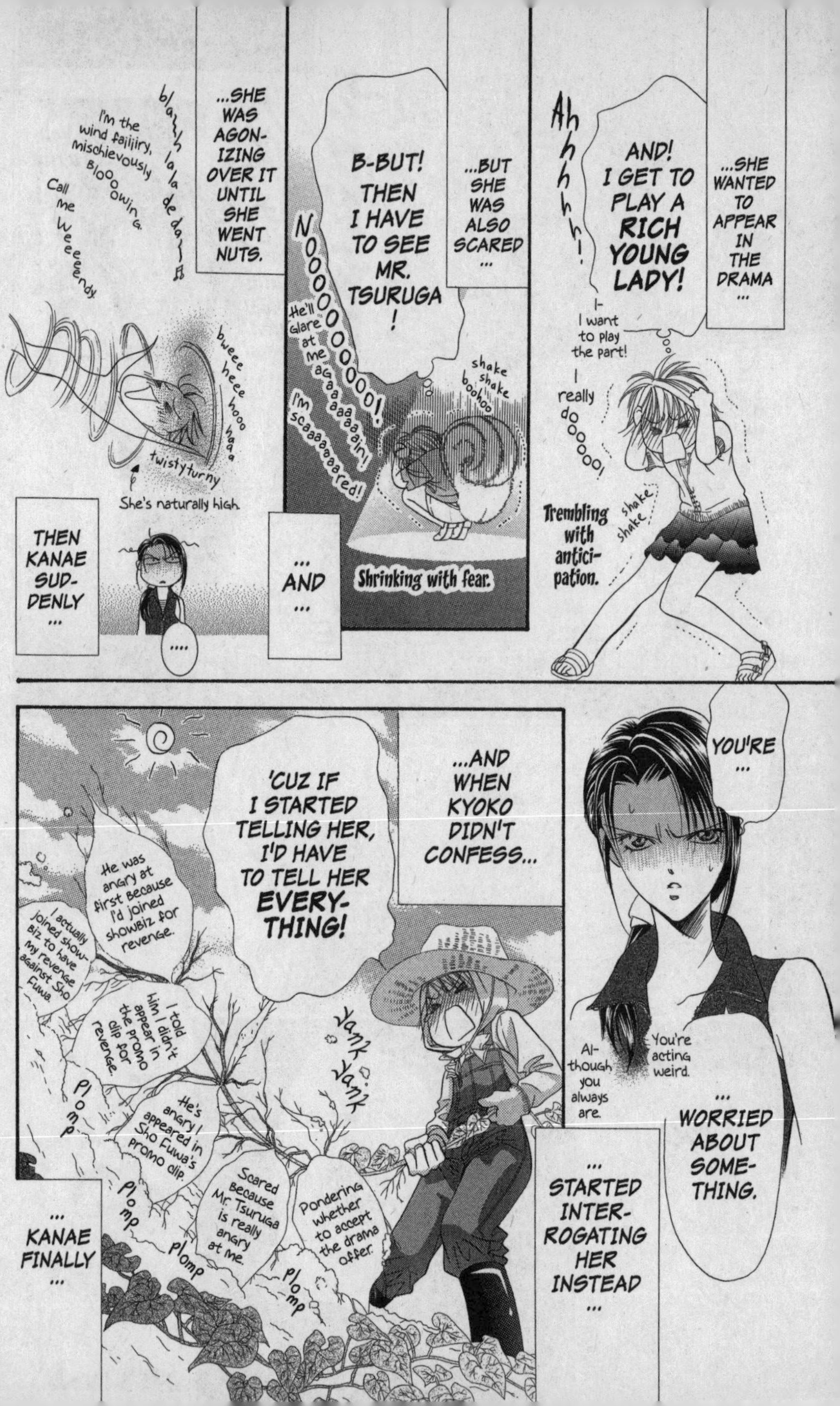
...SHE WANTED TO APPEAR IN THE DRAMA ...
AND! I GET TO PLAY A RICH YOUNG LADY!
Ahhhhh!
I- I want to play the part!
I really doooooo!
shake shake
Trembling with antici-pation.
...BUT SHE WAS ALSO SCARED ...
B-BUT! THEN I HAVE TO SEE MR. TSURUGA!
Nooooooooooo!
He'll Glare at me aGaaaaaaain!
I'm scaaaaaaaared!
shake shake boohoo
Shrinking with fear.
... AND ...
...SHE WAS AGONIZING OVER IT UNTIL SHE WENT NUTS.
blaaah lala de da
I'm the wind faiiiiry, mischievously blooowing.
Call me Weeeeendy.
bweee heee hooo haaa
twistyturny
She's naturally high.
THEN KANAE SUDDENLY ...
....
YOU'RE ...
... WORRIED ABOUT SOMETHING.
You're acting weird.
Although you always are.
... STARTED INTERROGATING HER INSTEAD ...
...AND WHEN KYOKO DIDN'T CONFESS...
'CUZ IF I STARTED TELLING HER, I'D HAVE TO TELL HER EVERYTHING!
Yank Yank
Pondering whether to accept the drama offer.
Scared because Mr. Tsuruga is really angry at me.
He's angry I appeared in Sho Fuwa's promo clip.
I told him I didn't appear in the promo clip for revenge.
He was angry at first because I'd joined showbiz for revenge.
I actually joined show-biz to have my revenge against Sho Fuwa.
Plomp
Plomp
Plomp
Plomp
... KANAE FINALLY ...

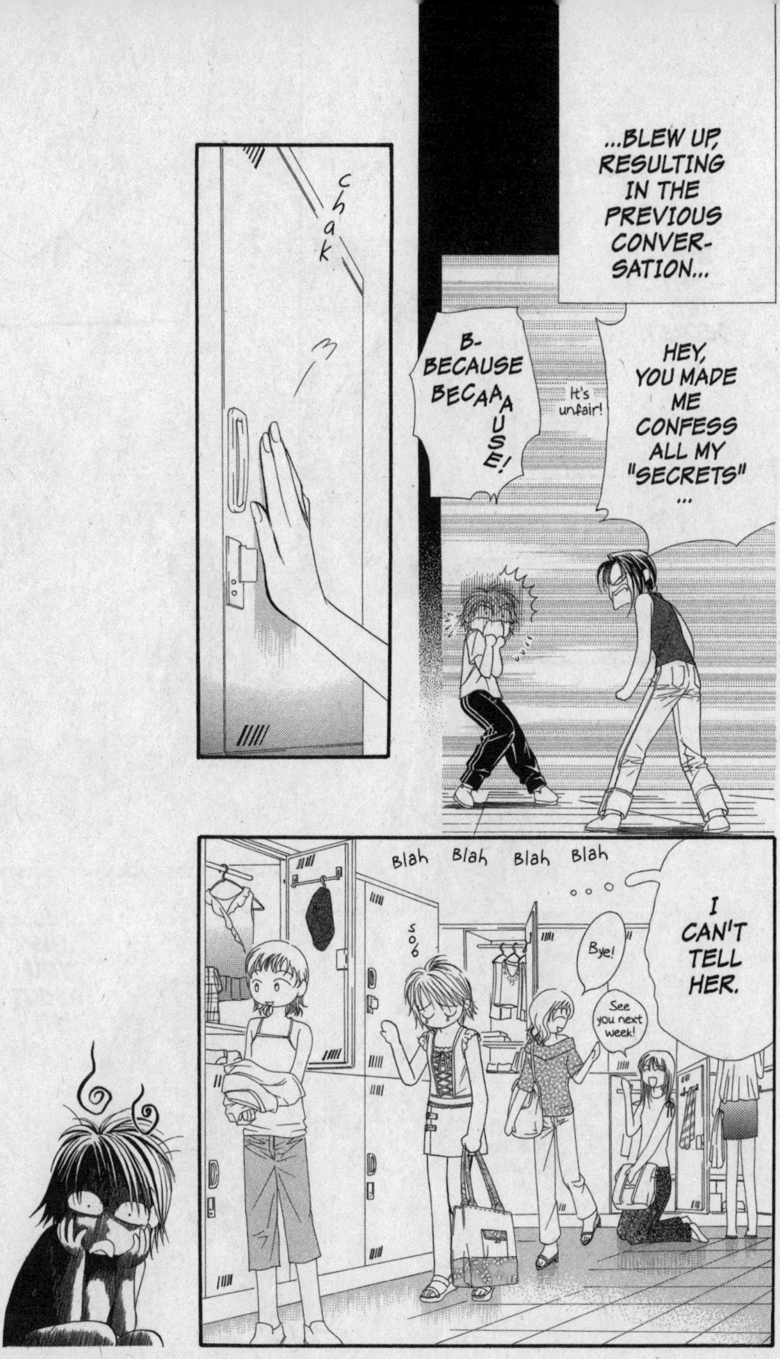
...BLEW UP, RESULTING IN THE PREVIOUS CONVER-SATION...
HEY, YOU MADE ME CONFESS ALL MY "SECRETS" ...
It's unfair!
B-BECAUSE BECAAAAUSE!
chak
I CAN'T TELL HER.
Blah Blah Blah Blah
See you next week!
Bye!
sob

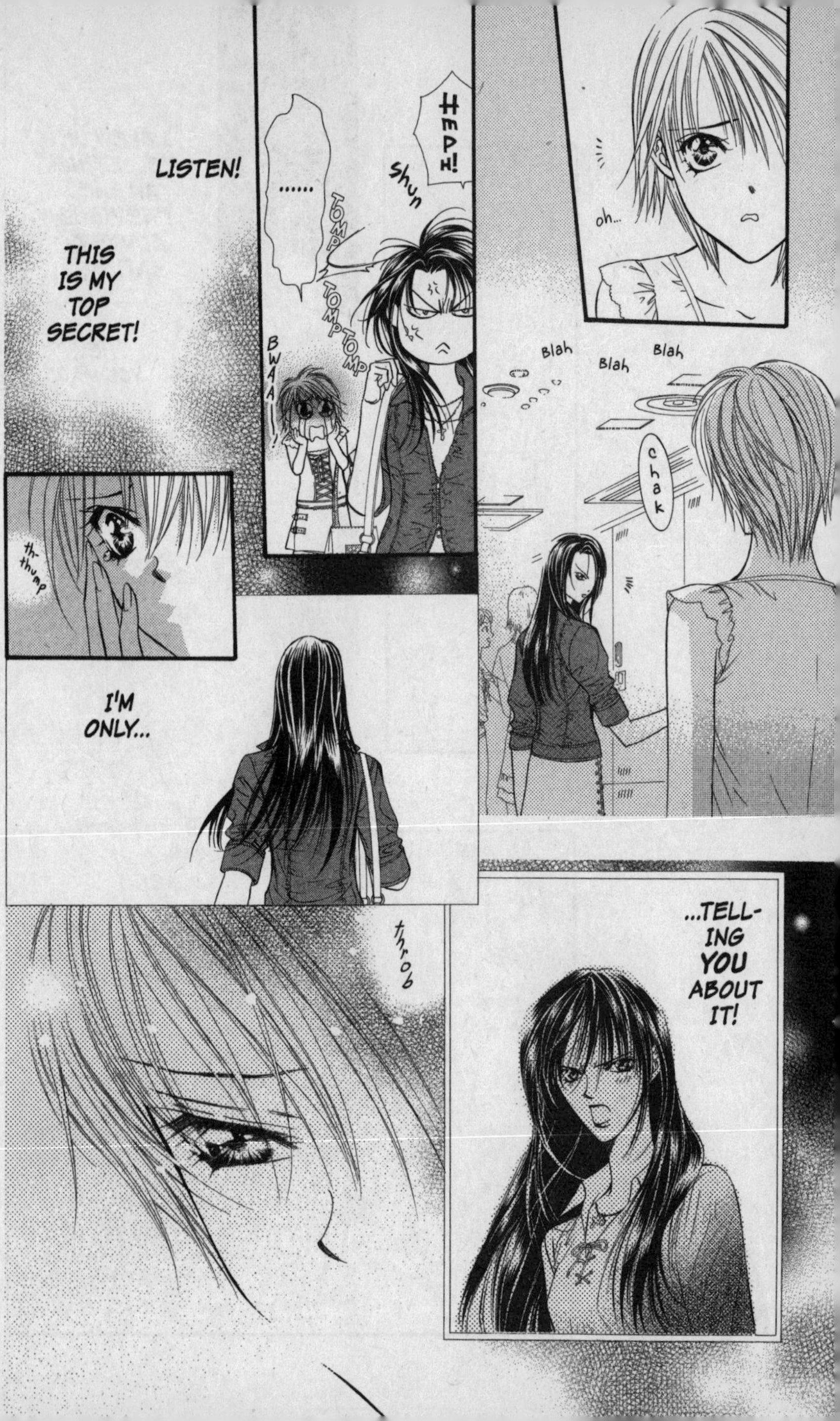
oh...
HMPH!
Shun
......
TOMP TOMP TOMP TOMP
BWAAA
LISTEN!
THIS IS MY TOP SECRET!
Blah Blah Blah
chak
th-thump
I'M ONLY...
...TELLING YOU ABOUT IT!
throb

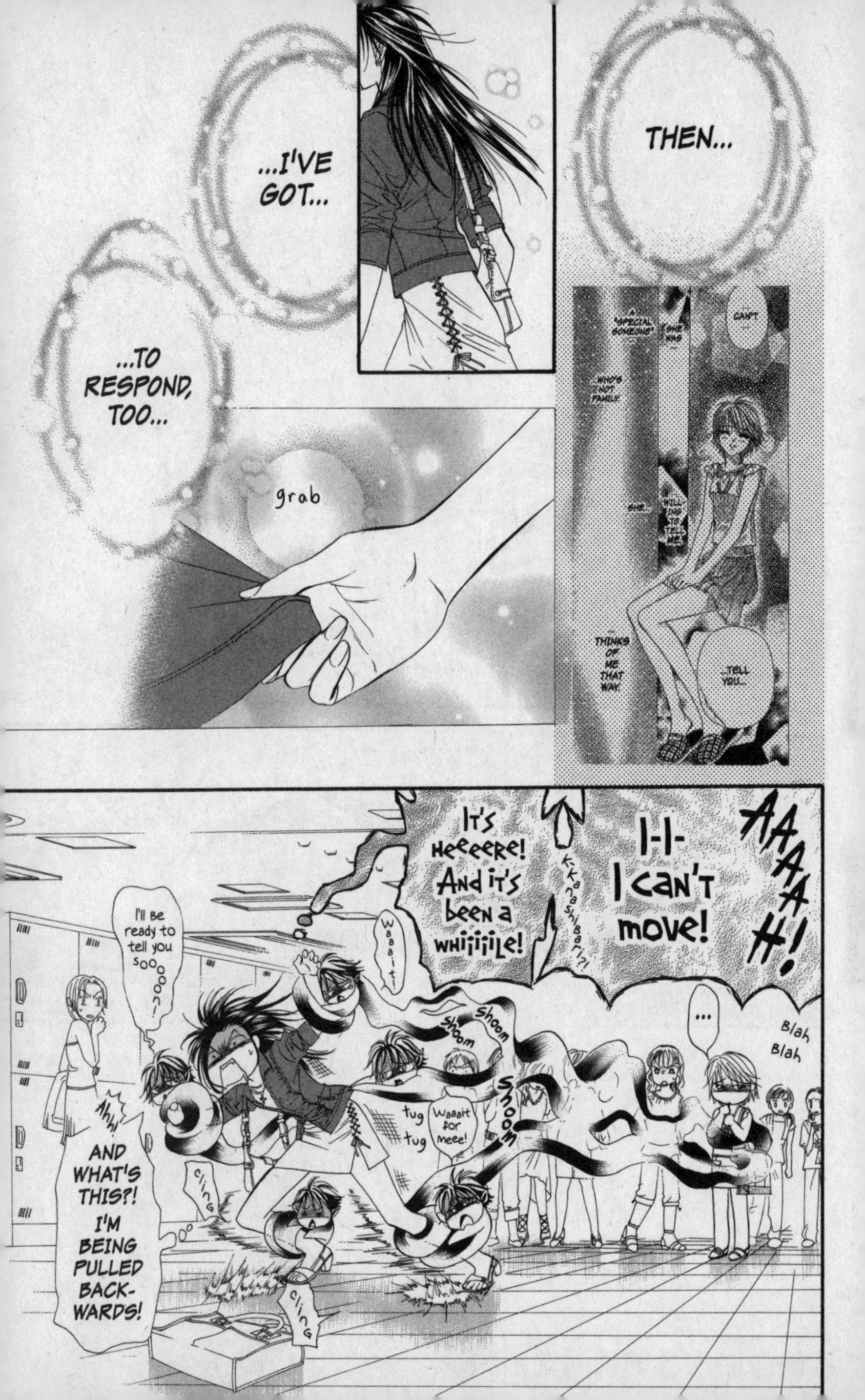
THEN...
...I'VE GOT...
...TO RESPOND, TOO...
...CAN'T...
"SHE" WAS...
A "SPECIAL SOMEONE"...
...WHO'S NOT FAMILY.
...WILLING TO TELL ME.
SHE...
...TELL YOU...
...THINKS OF ME THAT WAY.
grab
AAAAAH!
I-I- I can't move!
K-Kanashibari?!
It's heeeere! And it's been a whiiiiile!
Waaait!
I'll be ready to tell you sooooon!
...
Blah Blah
Shoom Shoom
Shoom
Waaait for meee!
tug tug
Ahh!
AND WHAT'S THIS?! I'M BEING PULLED BACKWARDS!
cling
cling

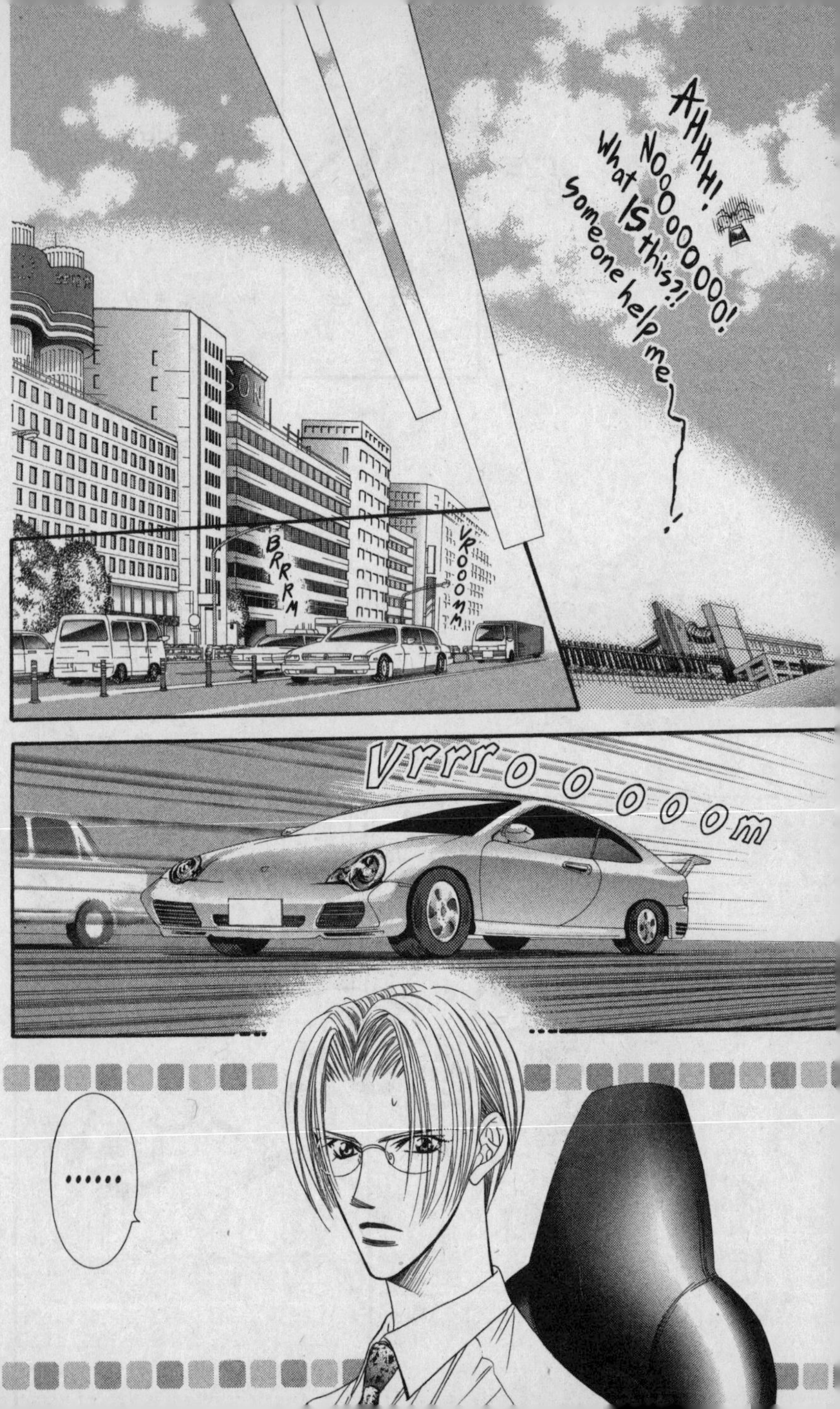
AHHH! NOOOOOOOOO!
What IS this?!
Someone help me—!
BRRRM
VROOOMM
Vrrroooom
......

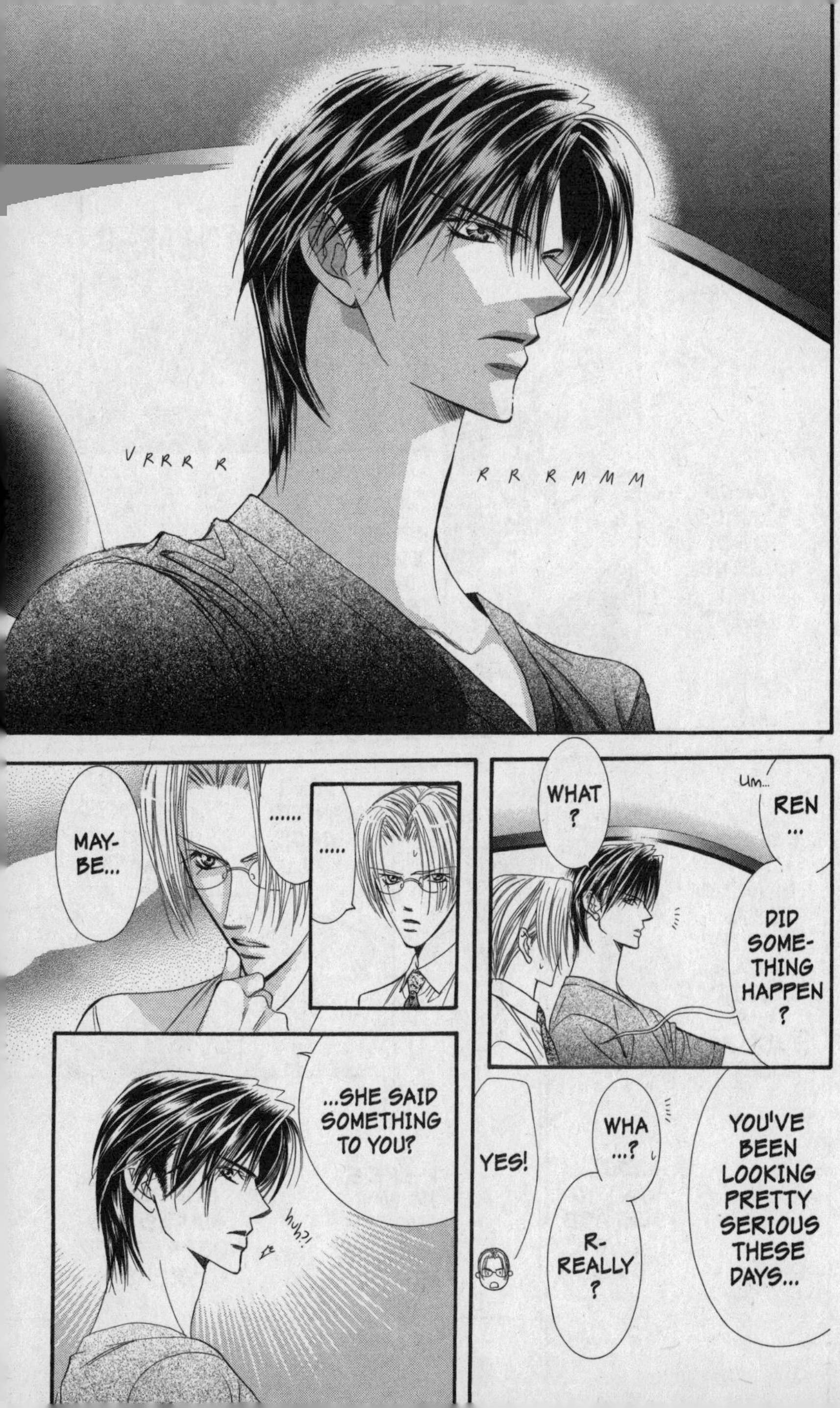
VRRRR R
R R RMMM
Um...
REN ...
DID SOMETHING HAPPEN ?
WHAT ?
.....
......
MAYBE...
YOU'VE BEEN LOOKING PRETTY SERIOUS THESE DAYS...
WHA ...?
R-REALLY ?
YES!
...SHE SAID SOMETHING TO YOU?
huh?!

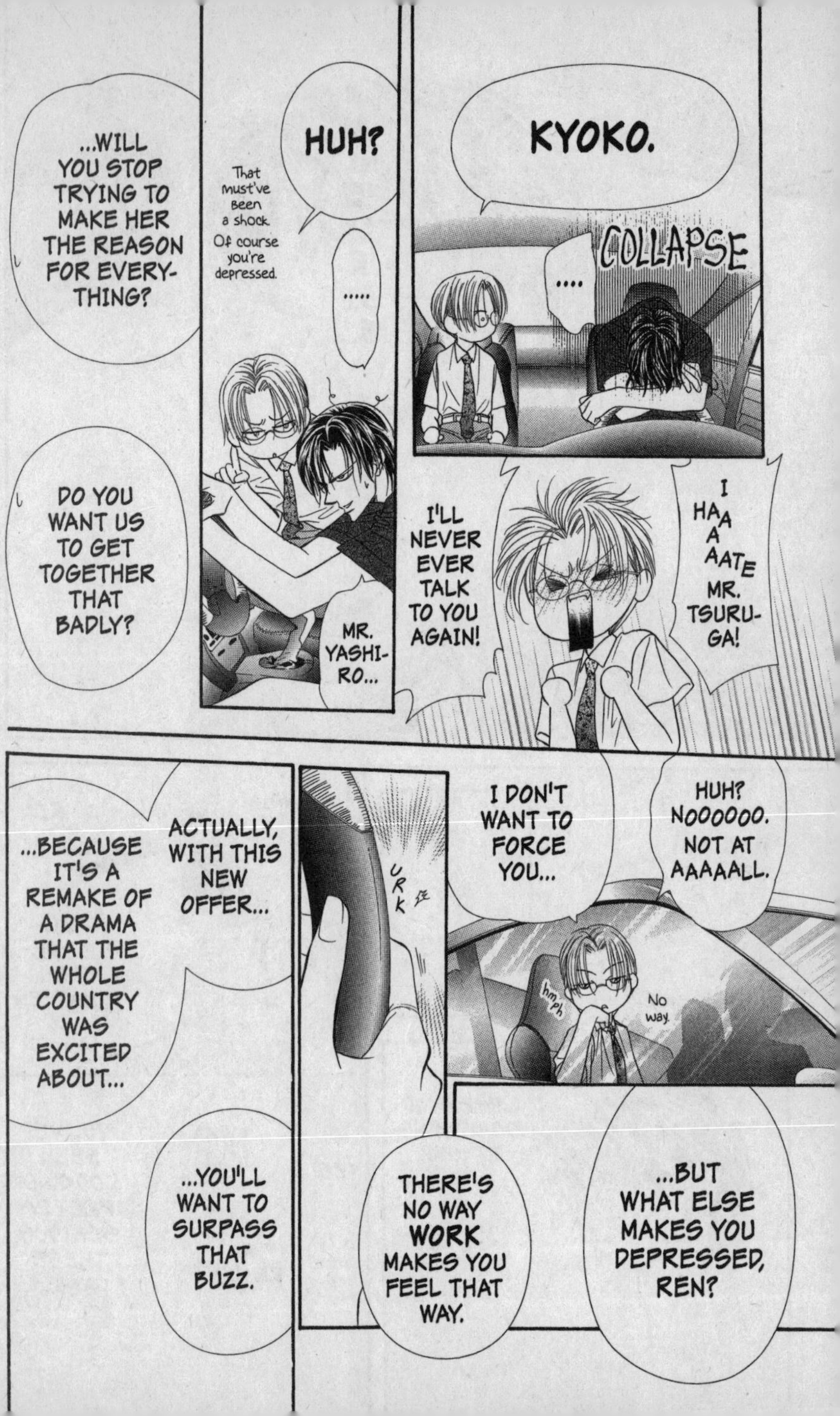
KYOKO.
....
COLLAPSE
I HAAAAATE MR. TSURUGA!
I'LL NEVER EVER TALK TO YOU AGAIN!
HUH?
That must've been a shock. Of course you're depressed.
.....
MR. YASHIRO...
...WILL YOU STOP TRYING TO MAKE HER THE REASON FOR EVERYTHING?
DO YOU WANT US TO GET TOGETHER THAT BADLY?
HUH? NOOOOOO. NOT AT AAAAALL.
I DON'T WANT TO FORCE YOU...
hmph
No way.
...BUT WHAT ELSE MAKES YOU DEPRESSED, REN?
THERE'S NO WAY WORK MAKES YOU FEEL THAT WAY.
URK
ACTUALLY, WITH THIS NEW OFFER...
...BECAUSE IT'S A REMAKE OF A DRAMA THAT THE WHOLE COUNTRY WAS EXCITED ABOUT...
...YOU'LL WANT TO SURPASS THAT BUZZ.

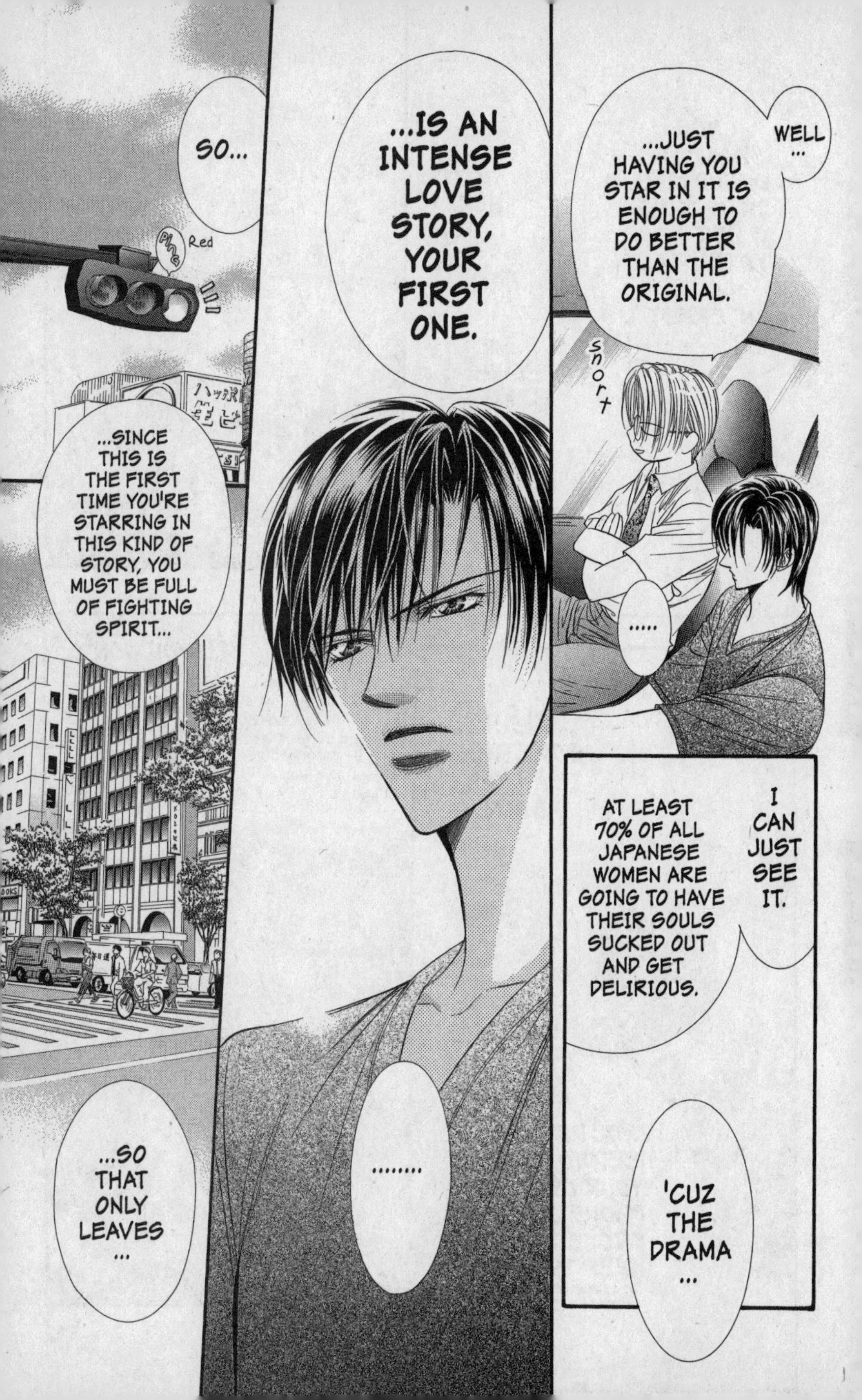
WELL ...
...JUST HAVING YOU STAR IN IT IS ENOUGH TO DO BETTER THAN THE ORIGINAL.
snort
.....
I CAN JUST SEE IT.
AT LEAST 70% OF ALL JAPANESE WOMEN ARE GOING TO HAVE THEIR SOULS SUCKED OUT AND GET DELIRIOUS.
'CUZ THE DRAMA ...
...IS AN INTENSE LOVE STORY, YOUR FIRST ONE.
....
SO...
Ping
Red
...SINCE THIS IS THE FIRST TIME YOU'RE STARRING IN THIS KIND OF STORY, YOU MUST BE FULL OF FIGHTING SPIRIT...
...SO THAT ONLY LEAVES ...

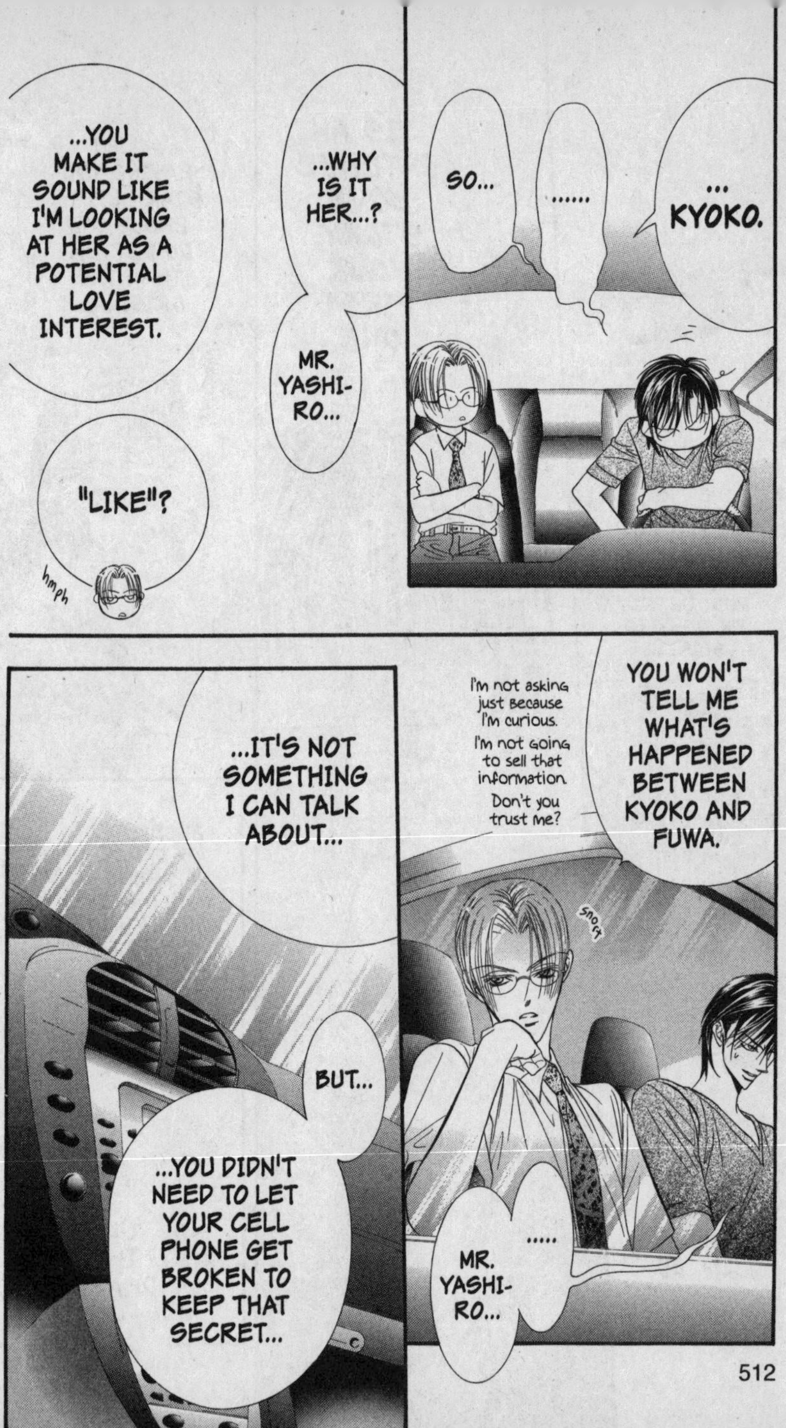
... KYOKO.
......
SO...
...WHY IS IT HER...?
MR. YASHIRO...
...YOU MAKE IT SOUND LIKE I'M LOOKING AT HER AS A POTENTIAL LOVE INTEREST.
"LIKE"?
hmph
YOU WON'T TELL ME WHAT'S HAPPENED BETWEEN KYOKO AND FUWA.
I'm not asking just because I'm curious.
I'm not going to sell that information.
Don't you trust me?
snort
.....
MR. YASHIRO...
...IT'S NOT SOMETHING I CAN TALK ABOUT...
BUT...
...YOU DIDN'T NEED TO LET YOUR CELL PHONE GET BROKEN TO KEEP THAT SECRET...

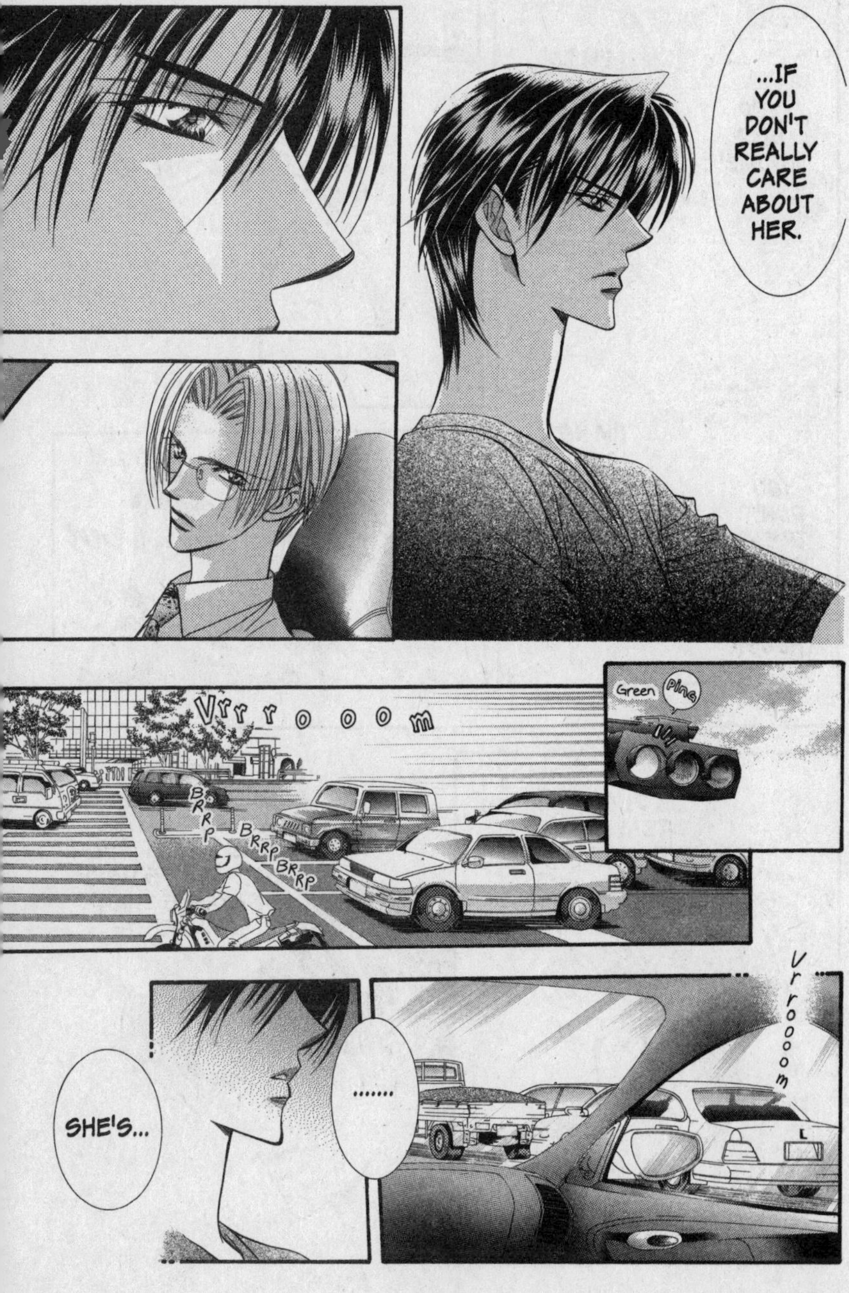
...IF YOU DON'T REALLY CARE ABOUT HER.
Green
Pinc
Vrr r o o o m
BRRP
BRRP
BRRP
Vrroooom
......
SHE'S...

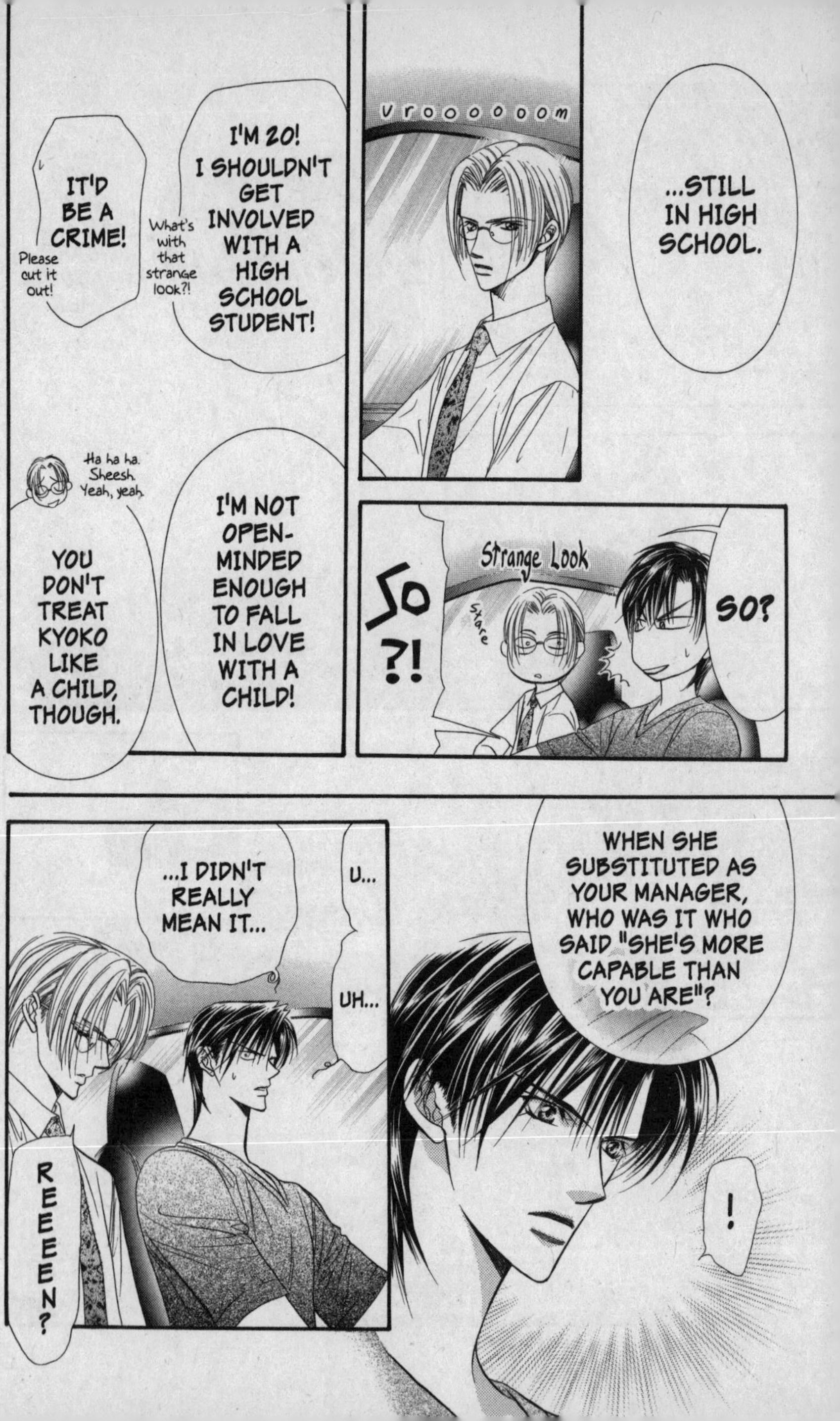
...STILL IN HIGH SCHOOL.
Vrooooooom
SO?
Strange Look
Stare
SO ?!
I'M 20! I SHOULDN'T GET INVOLVED WITH A HIGH SCHOOL STUDENT!
What's with that strange look?!
IT'D BE A CRIME!
Please cut it out!
I'M NOT OPEN-MINDED ENOUGH TO FALL IN LOVE WITH A CHILD!
Ha ha ha. Sheesh. Yeah, yeah.
YOU DON'T TREAT KYOKO LIKE A CHILD, THOUGH.
WHEN SHE SUBSTITUTED AS YOUR MANAGER, WHO WAS IT WHO SAID "SHE'S MORE CAPABLE THAN YOU ARE"?
!
U...
UH...
...I DIDN'T REALLY MEAN IT...
REEEEEN?

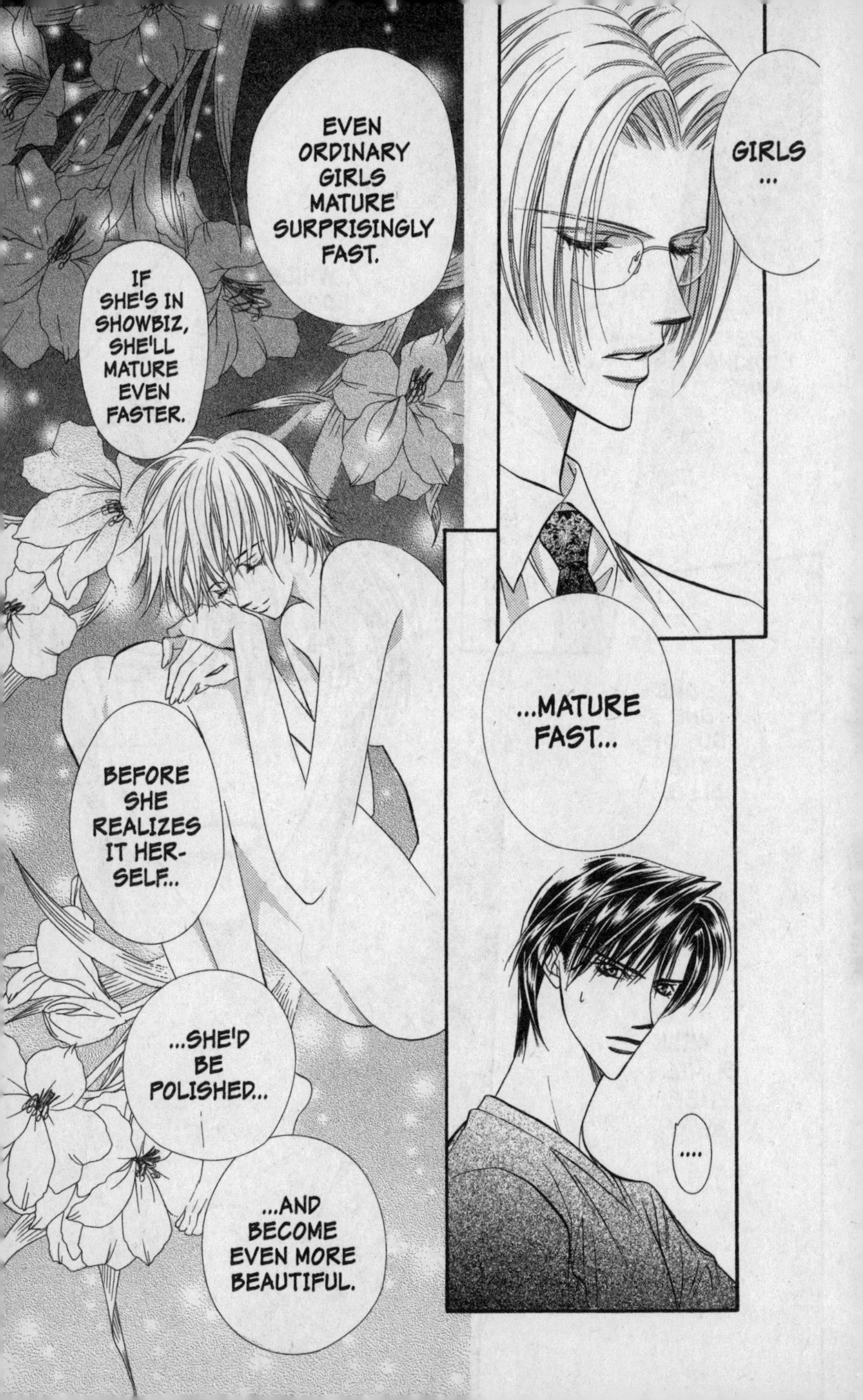
GIRLS ...
...MATURE FAST...
....
EVEN ORDINARY GIRLS MATURE SURPRISINGLY FAST.
IF SHE'S IN SHOWBIZ, SHE'LL MATURE EVEN FASTER.
BEFORE SHE REALIZES IT HER-SELF...
...SHE'D BE POLISHED...
...AND BECOME EVEN MORE BEAUTIFUL.

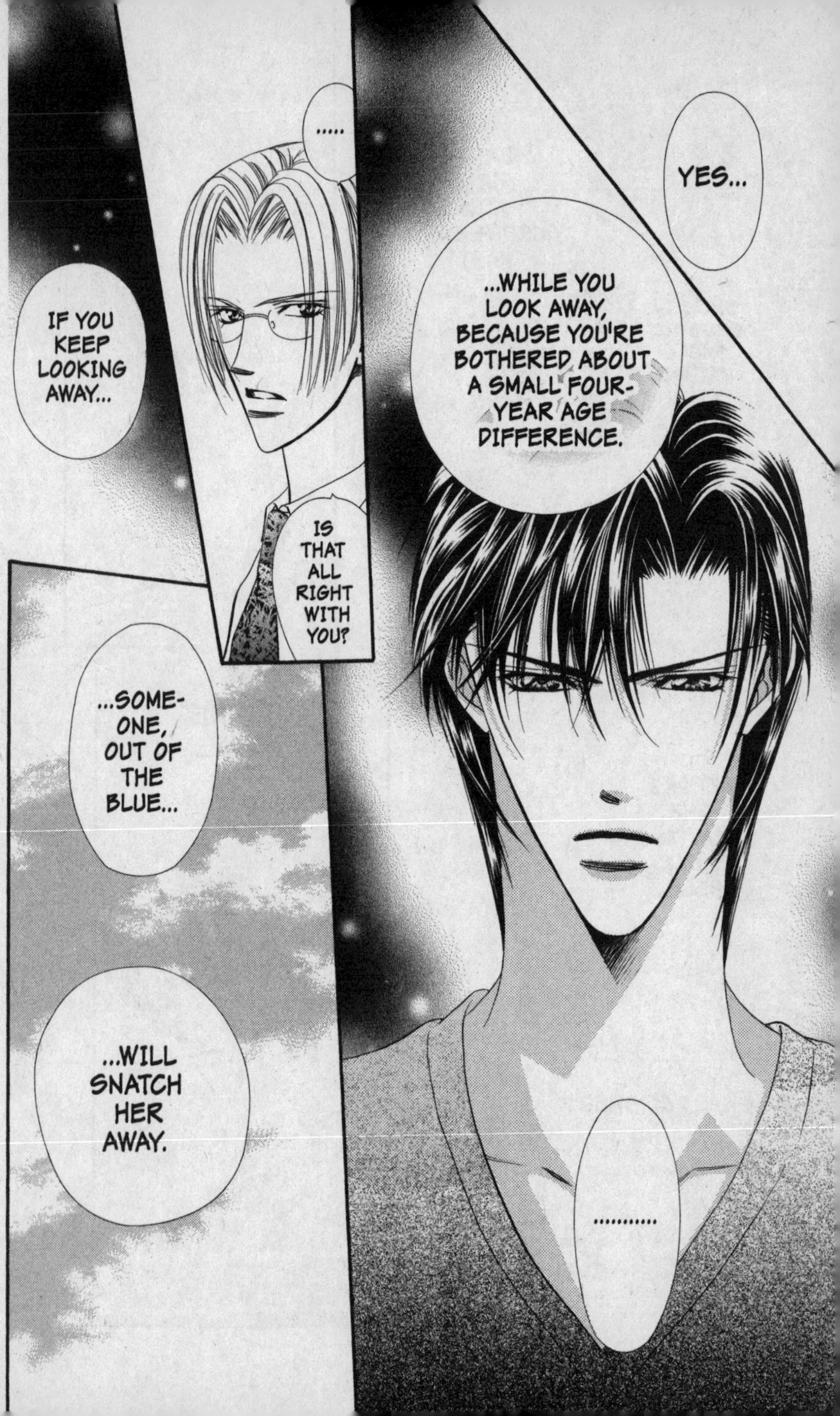
YES...
...WHILE YOU LOOK AWAY, BECAUSE YOU'RE BOTHERED ABOUT A SMALL FOUR-YEAR AGE DIFFERENCE.
....
.....
IF YOU KEEP LOOKING AWAY...
IS THAT ALL RIGHT WITH YOU?
...SOME-ONE, OUT OF THE BLUE...
...WILL SNATCH HER AWAY.

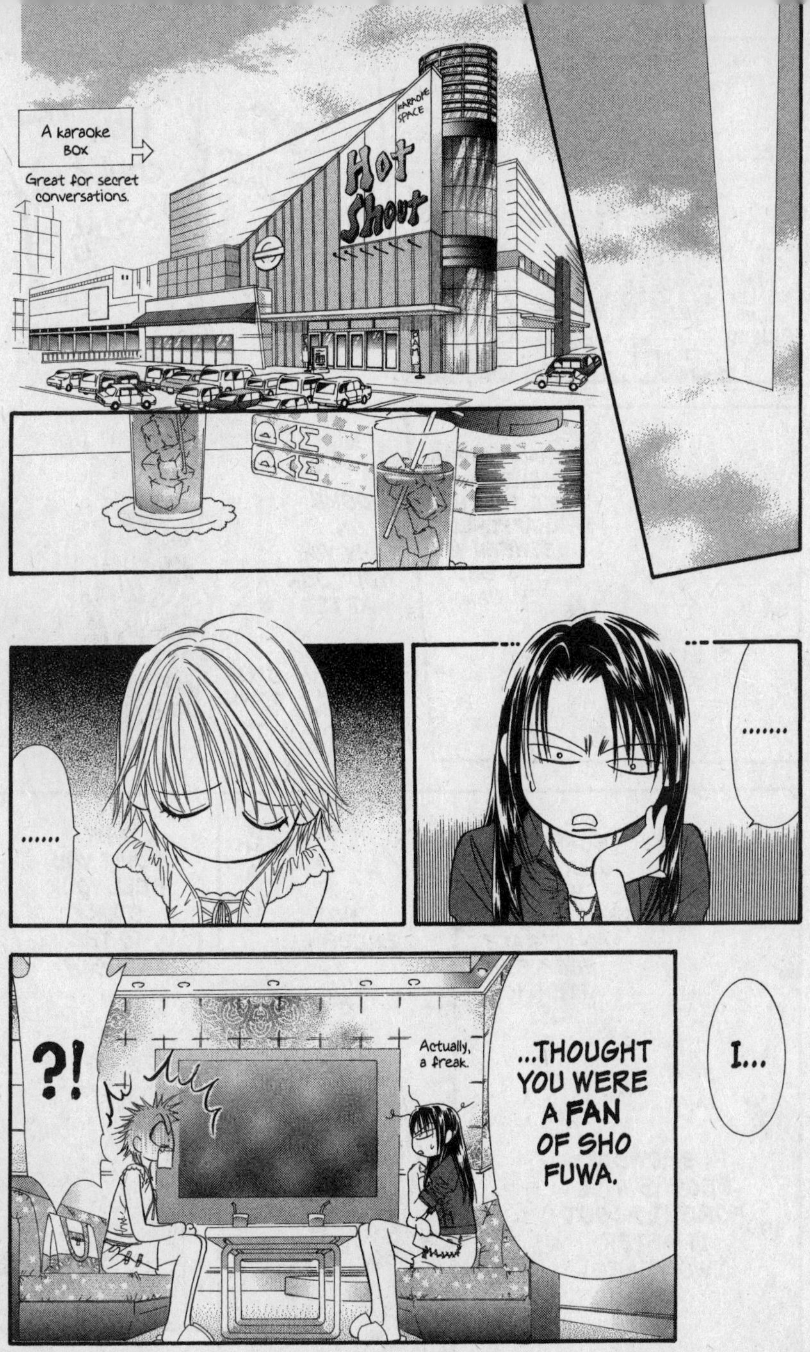
KARAOKE SPACE
Hot Shout
A karaoke BOX
Great for secret conversations.
......
......
I...
...THOUGHT YOU WERE A FAN OF SHO FUWA.
Actually, a freak.
?!

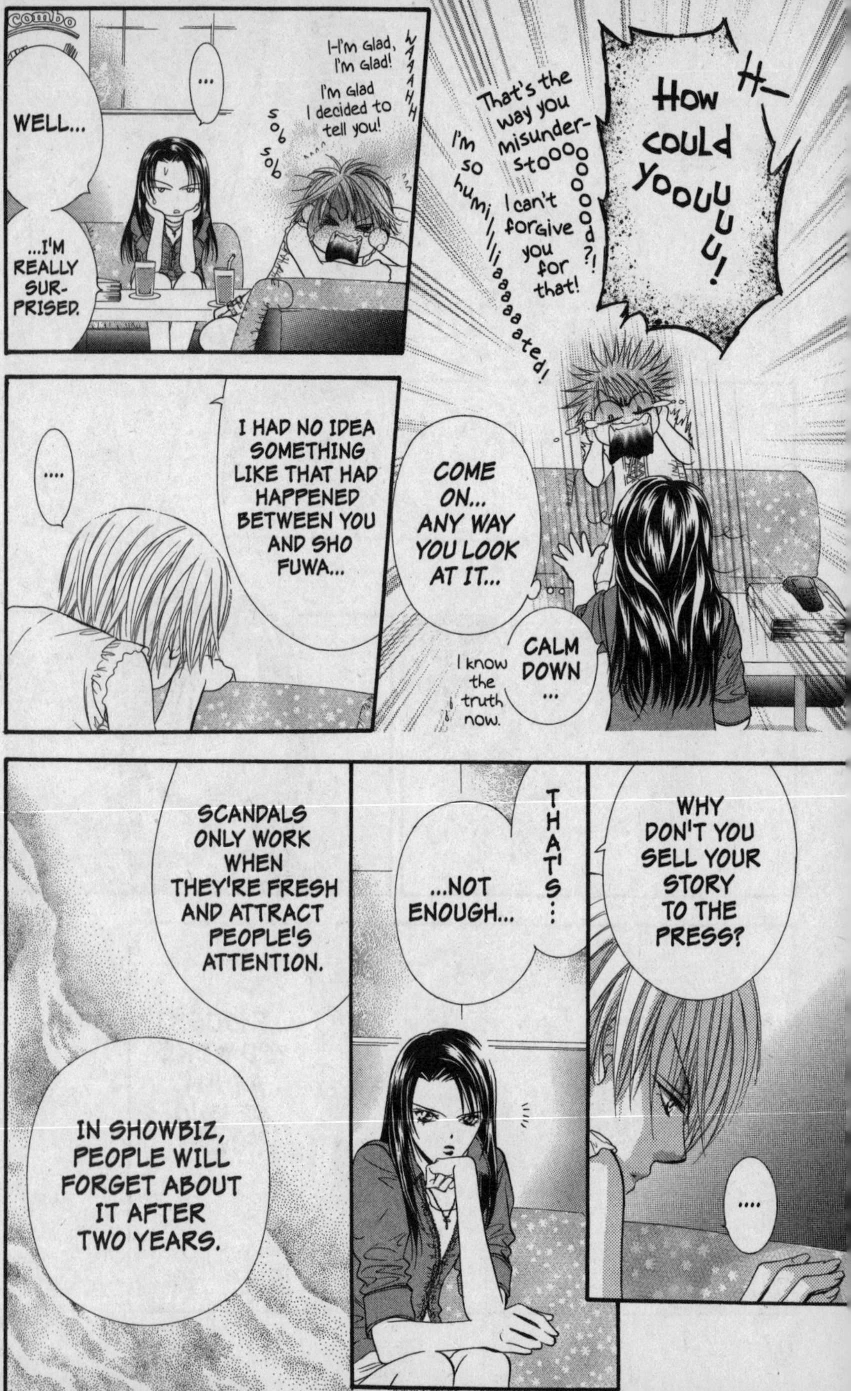
H—
How could yoouuuuu!
That's the way you misunder-stooooooood?!
I can't forgive you for that!
I'm so humillliaaaaated!
COME ON... ANY WAY YOU LOOK AT IT...
CALM DOWN...
I know the truth now.
combo
I-I'm Glad, I'm Glad!
I'm Glad I decided to tell you!
WAAAAHH
sob sob
...
WELL...
...I'M REALLY SURPRISED.
I HAD NO IDEA SOMETHING LIKE THAT HAD HAPPENED BETWEEN YOU AND SHO FUWA...
....
WHY DON'T YOU SELL YOUR STORY TO THE PRESS?
....
THAT'S...
...NOT ENOUGH...
SCANDALS ONLY WORK WHEN THEY'RE FRESH AND ATTRACT PEOPLE'S ATTENTION.
IN SHOWBIZ, PEOPLE WILL FORGET ABOUT IT AFTER TWO YEARS.

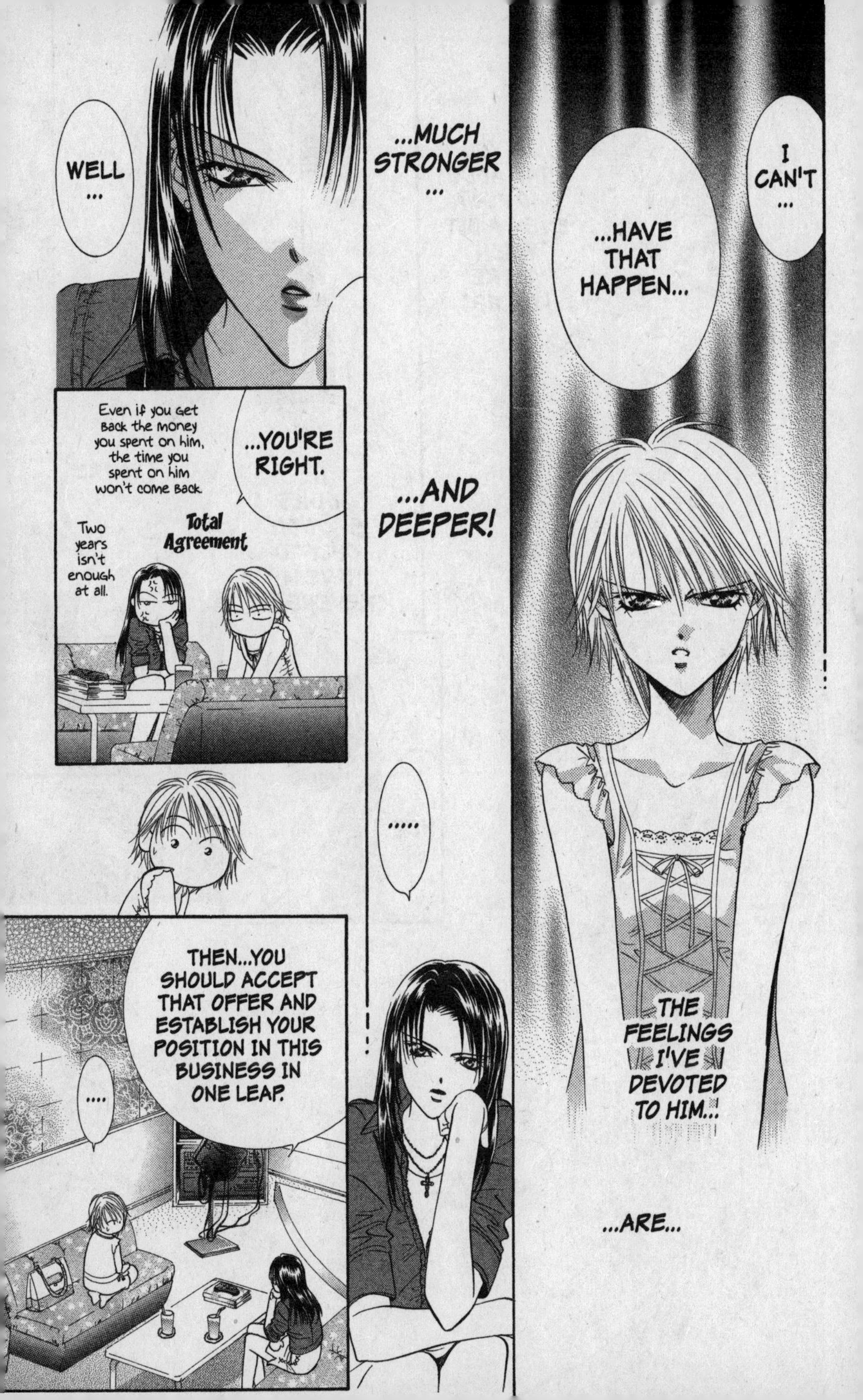
I CAN'T ...
...HAVE THAT HAPPEN...
THE FEELINGS I'VE DEVOTED TO HIM...!
...ARE...
...MUCH STRONGER ...
...AND DEEPER!
.....
WELL ...
...YOU'RE RIGHT.
Even if you get back the money you spent on him, the time you spent on him won't come back.
Total Agreement
Two years isn't enough at all.
THEN...YOU SHOULD ACCEPT THAT OFFER AND ESTABLISH YOUR POSITION IN THIS BUSINESS IN ONE LEAP.
....

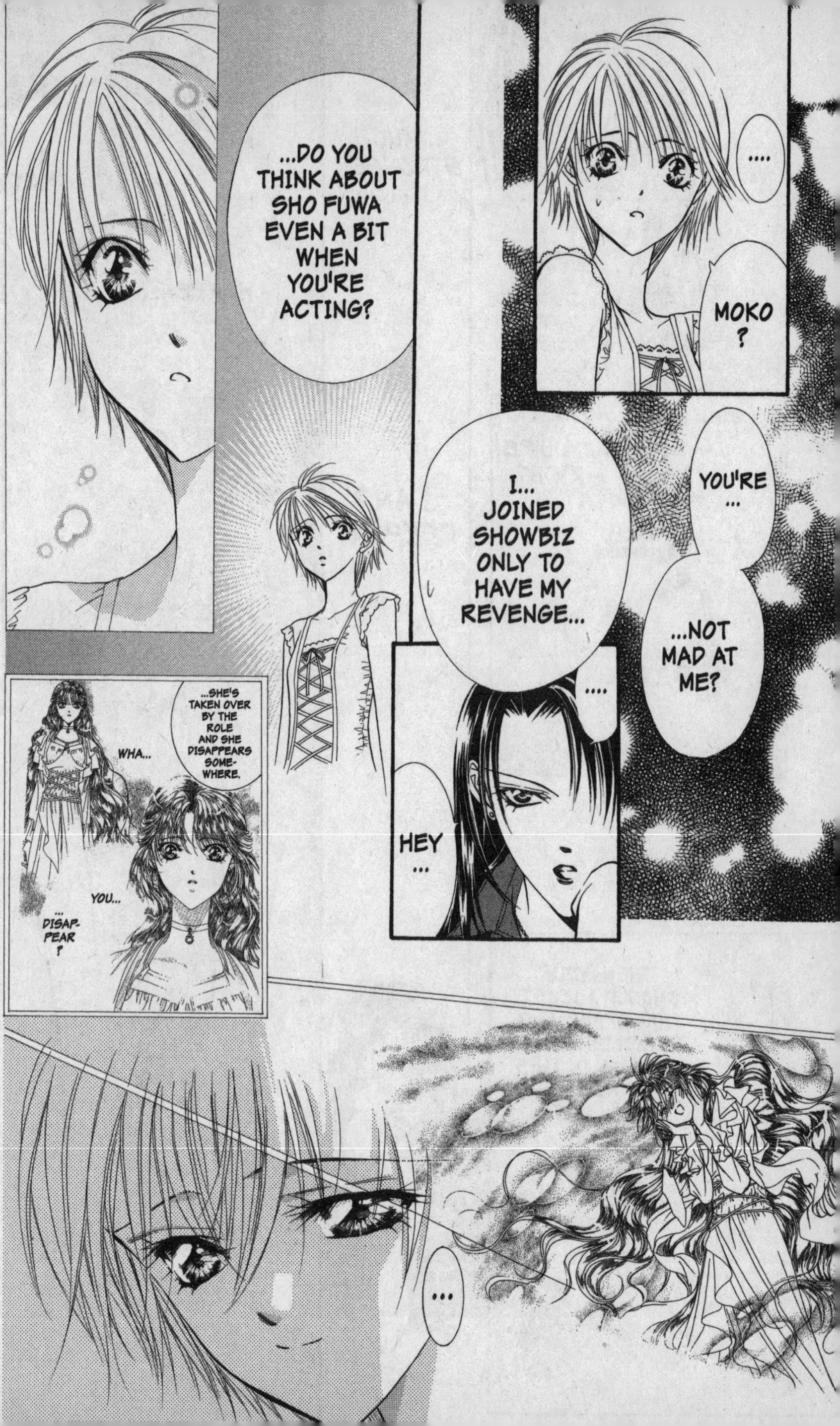
....
MOKO ?
YOU'RE ...
...NOT MAD AT ME?
I... JOINED SHOWBIZ ONLY TO HAVE MY REVENGE...
....
HEY ...
...DO YOU THINK ABOUT SHO FUWA EVEN A BIT WHEN YOU'RE ACTING?
...SHE'S TAKEN OVER BY THE ROLE AND SHE DISAPPEARS SOME-WHERE.
WHA...
YOU...
...DISAP-PEAR ?
...

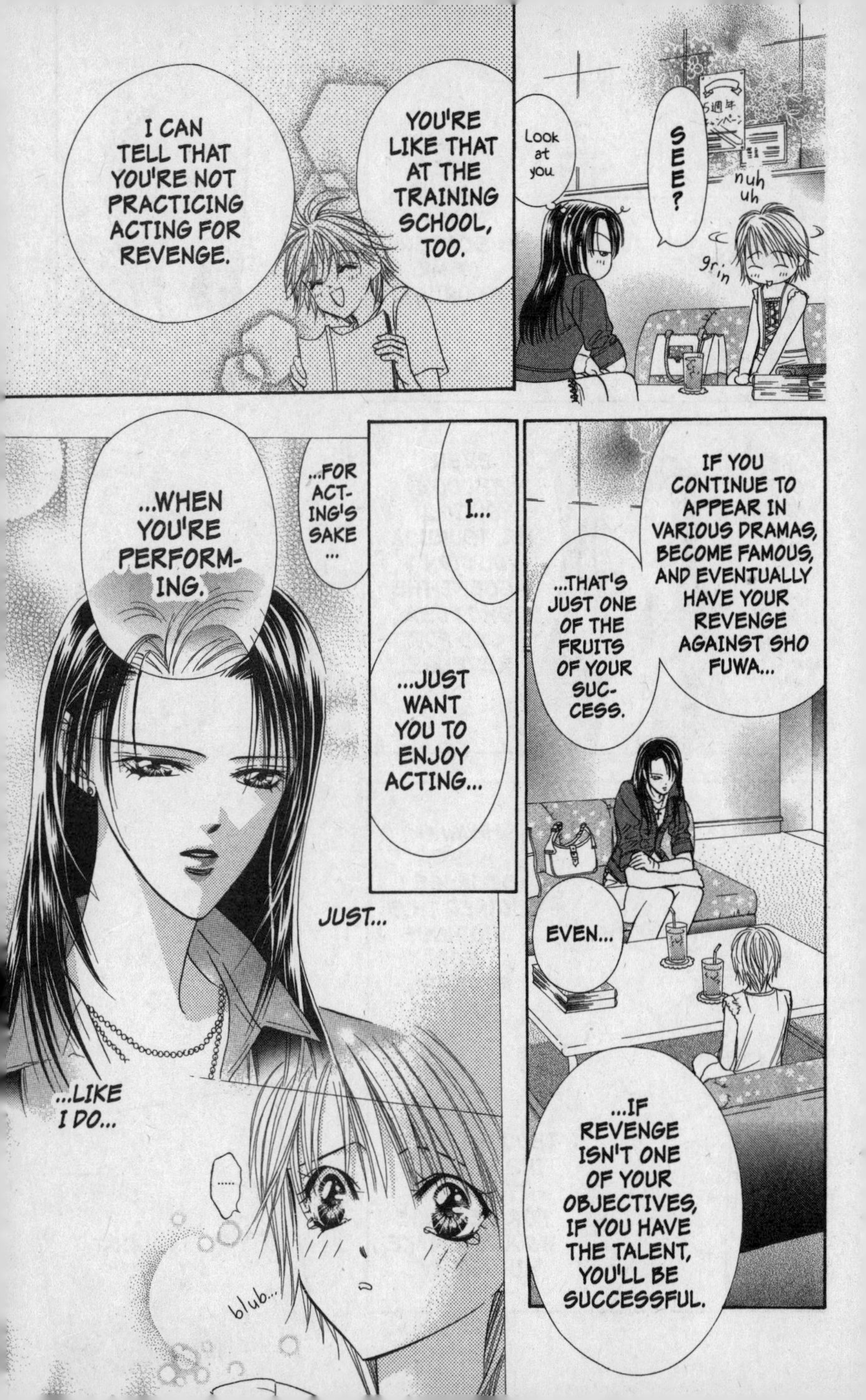

SEE?
Look at you
nuh uh
grin
YOU'RE LIKE THAT AT THE TRAINING SCHOOL, TOO.
I CAN TELL THAT YOU'RE NOT PRACTICING ACTING FOR REVENGE.
IF YOU CONTINUE TO APPEAR IN VARIOUS DRAMAS, BECOME FAMOUS, AND EVENTUALLY HAVE YOUR REVENGE AGAINST SHO FUWA...
...THAT'S JUST ONE OF THE FRUITS OF YOUR SUCCESS.
EVEN...
...IF REVENGE ISN'T ONE OF YOUR OBJECTIVES, IF YOU HAVE THE TALENT, YOU'LL BE SUCCESSFUL.
I...
...JUST WANT YOU TO ENJOY ACTING...
...FOR ACTING'S SAKE...
...WHEN YOU'RE PERFORMING.
JUST...
...LIKE I DO...
.....
blub...

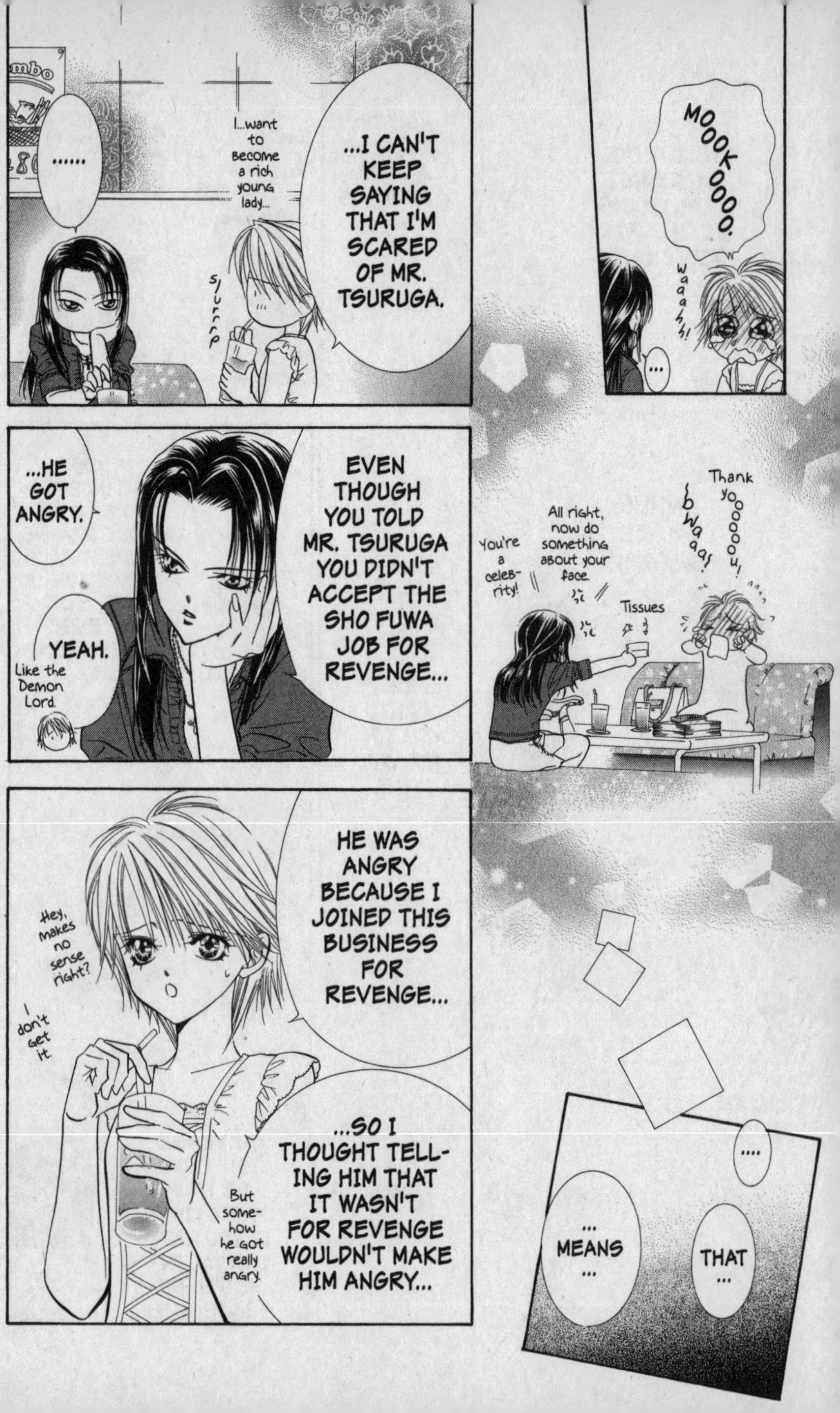
MOOKOOOO.
Waaahh!
...
...I CAN'T KEEP SAYING THAT I'M SCARED OF MR. TSURUGA.
I...want to become a rich young lady...
slurrp
......
Thank yoooooou!
bwaaa!
All right, now do something about your face.
You're a celeb-rity!
Tissues
EVEN THOUGH YOU TOLD MR. TSURUGA YOU DIDN'T ACCEPT THE SHO FUWA JOB FOR REVENGE...
...HE GOT ANGRY.
YEAH.
Like the Demon Lord.
....
THAT...
...MEANS...
HE WAS ANGRY BECAUSE I JOINED THIS BUSINESS FOR REVENGE...
...SO I THOUGHT TELL-ING HIM THAT IT WASN'T FOR REVENGE WOULDN'T MAKE HIM ANGRY...
But some-how he got really angry.
Hey, makes no sense right?
I don't get it.

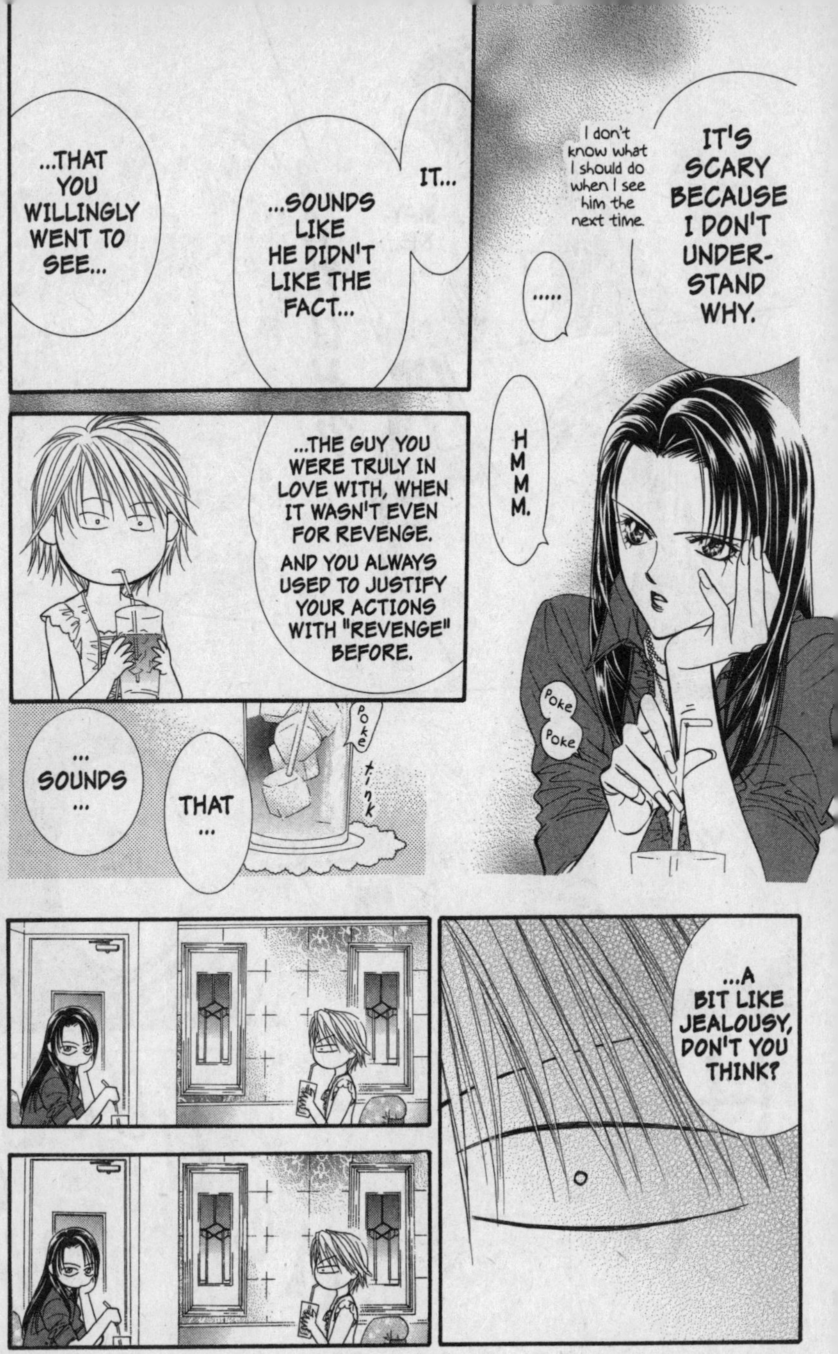
IT'S SCARY BECAUSE I DON'T UNDERSTAND WHY.
I don't know what I should do when I see him the next time.
.....
HMMM.
Poke
Poke
IT...
...SOUNDS LIKE HE DIDN'T LIKE THE FACT...
...THAT YOU WILLINGLY WENT TO SEE...
...THE GUY YOU WERE TRULY IN LOVE WITH, WHEN IT WASN'T EVEN FOR REVENGE.
AND YOU ALWAYS USED TO JUSTIFY YOUR ACTIONS WITH "REVENGE" BEFORE.
Poke
tink
THAT ...
... SOUNDS ...
...A BIT LIKE JEALOUSY, DON'T YOU THINK?

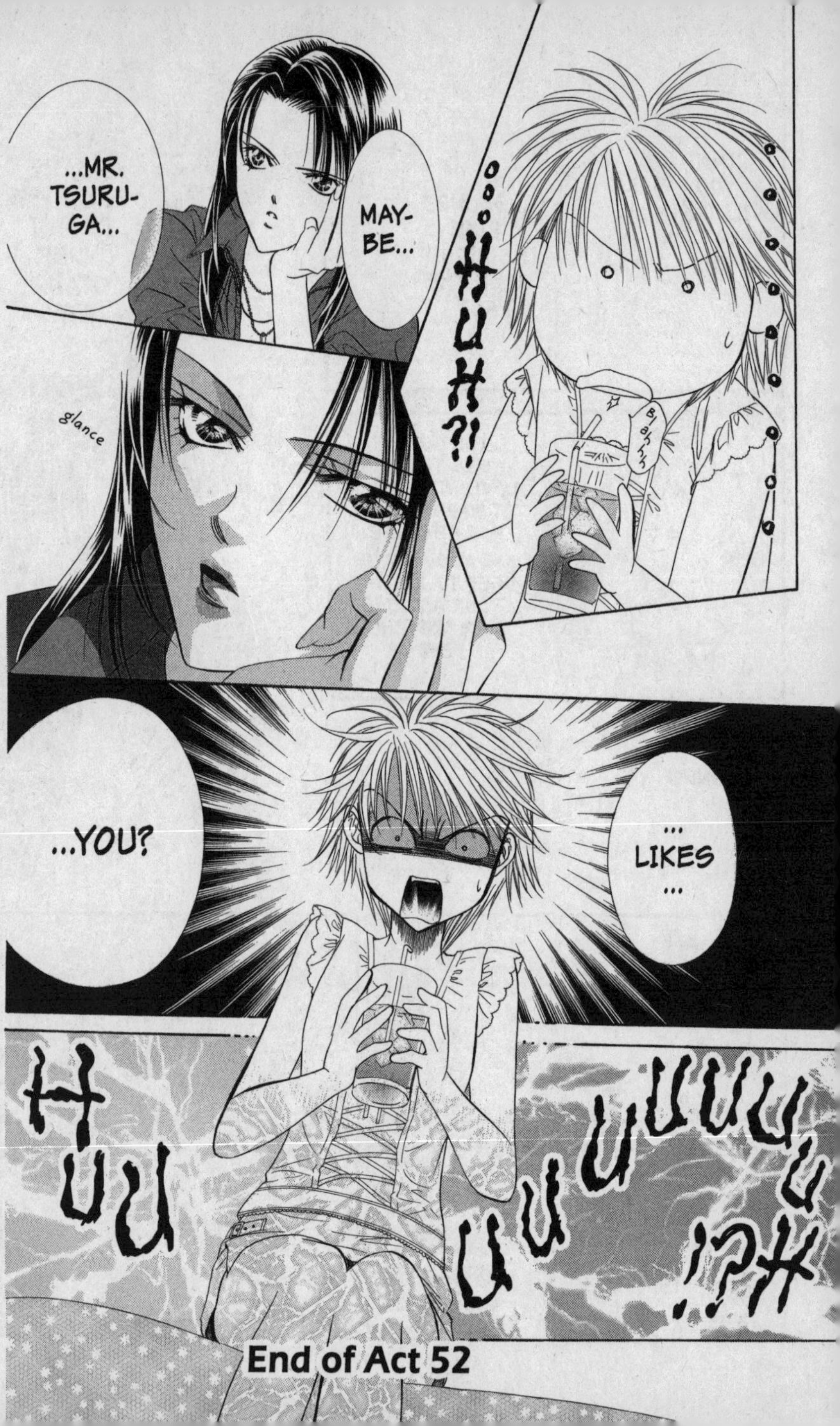
HUH?!
Blahhh
MAY-BE...
...MR. TSURUGA...
glance
...LIKES...
...YOU?
HUUUUUUUUUUUH?!

End of Act 52

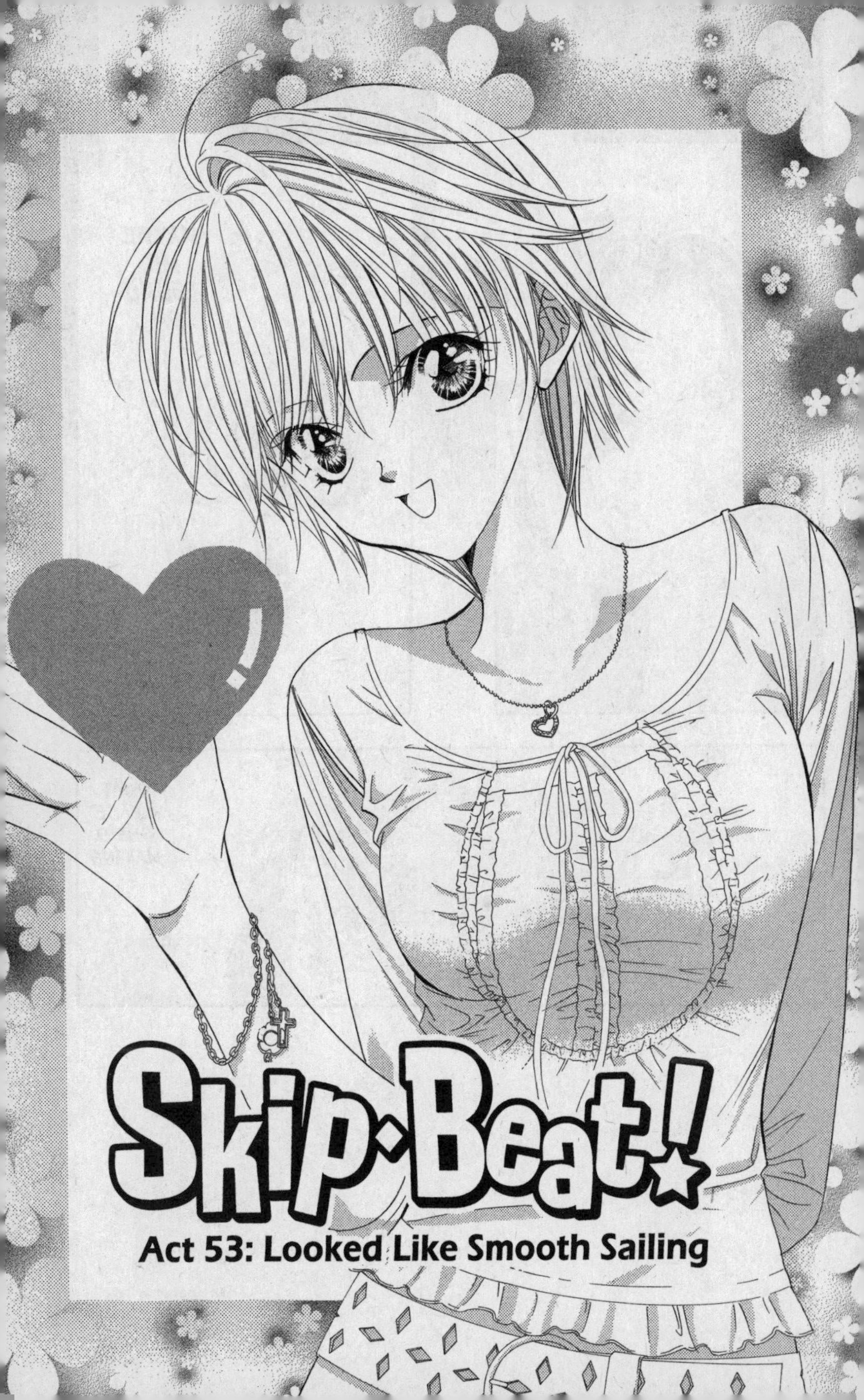
Skip·Beat!
Act 53: Looked Like Smooth Sailing

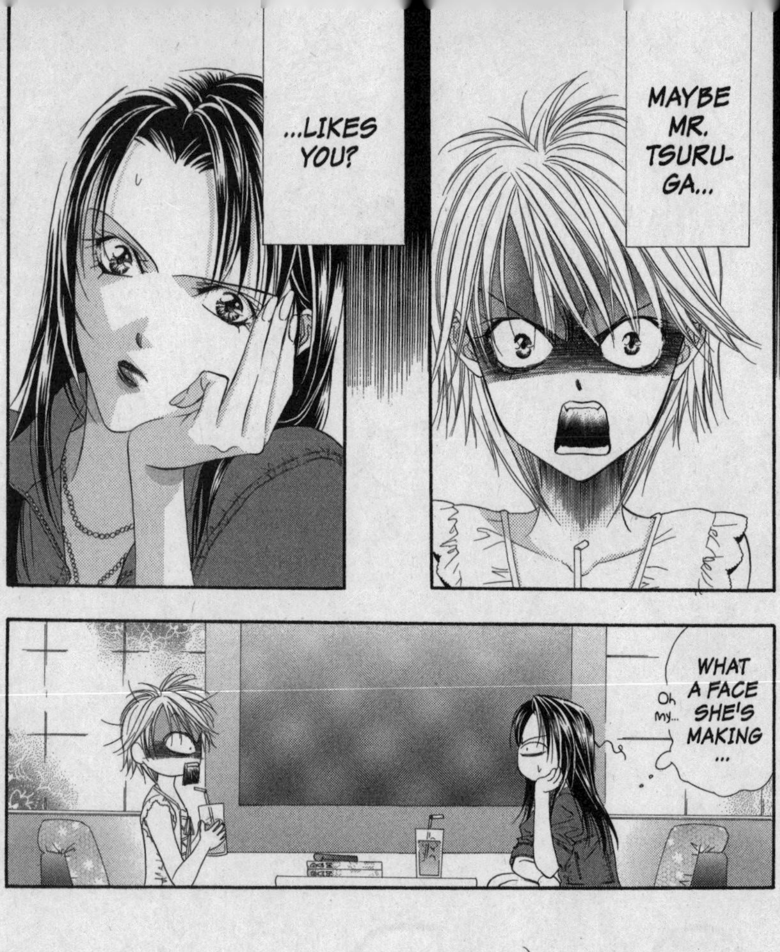
MAYBE MR. TSURUGA...
...LIKES YOU?
WHAT A FACE SHE'S MAKING ...
Oh my...
bweee heee hooo haaa
twistyturny
She's naturally high.

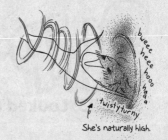

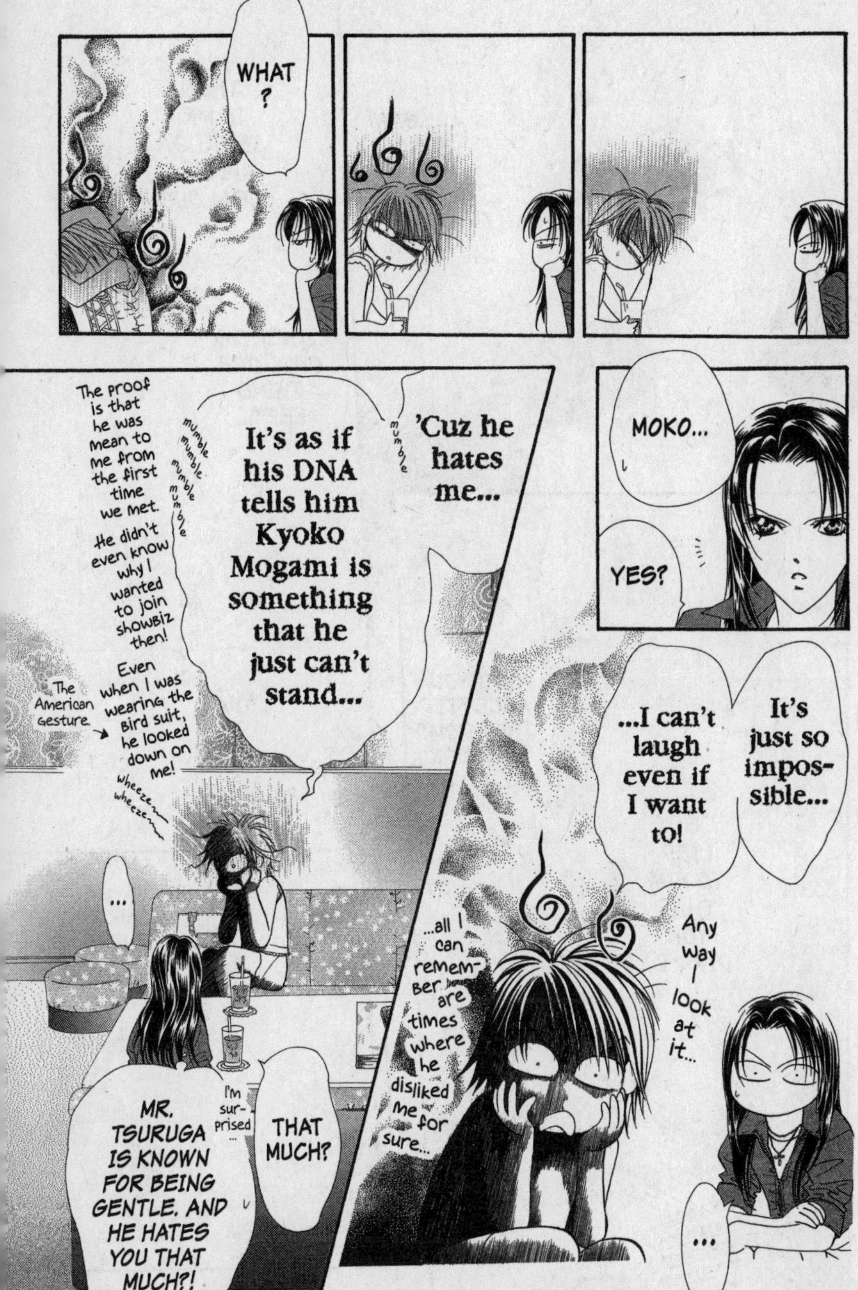
WHAT?
MOKO...
YES?
It's just so impossible...
...I can't laugh even if I want to!
Any way I look at it...
...all I can remember are times where he disliked me for sure...
...
'Cuz he hates me...
mumble
It's as if his DNA tells him Kyoko Mogami is something that he just can't stand...
mumble mumble mumble mumble
The proof is that he was mean to me from the first time we met. He didn't even know why I wanted to join showbiz then! Even when I was wearing the Bird suit, he looked down on me!
The American Gesture.
wheeze wheeze
...
THAT MUCH?
I'm surprised...
MR. TSURUGA IS KNOWN FOR BEING GENTLE. AND HE HATES YOU THAT MUCH?!

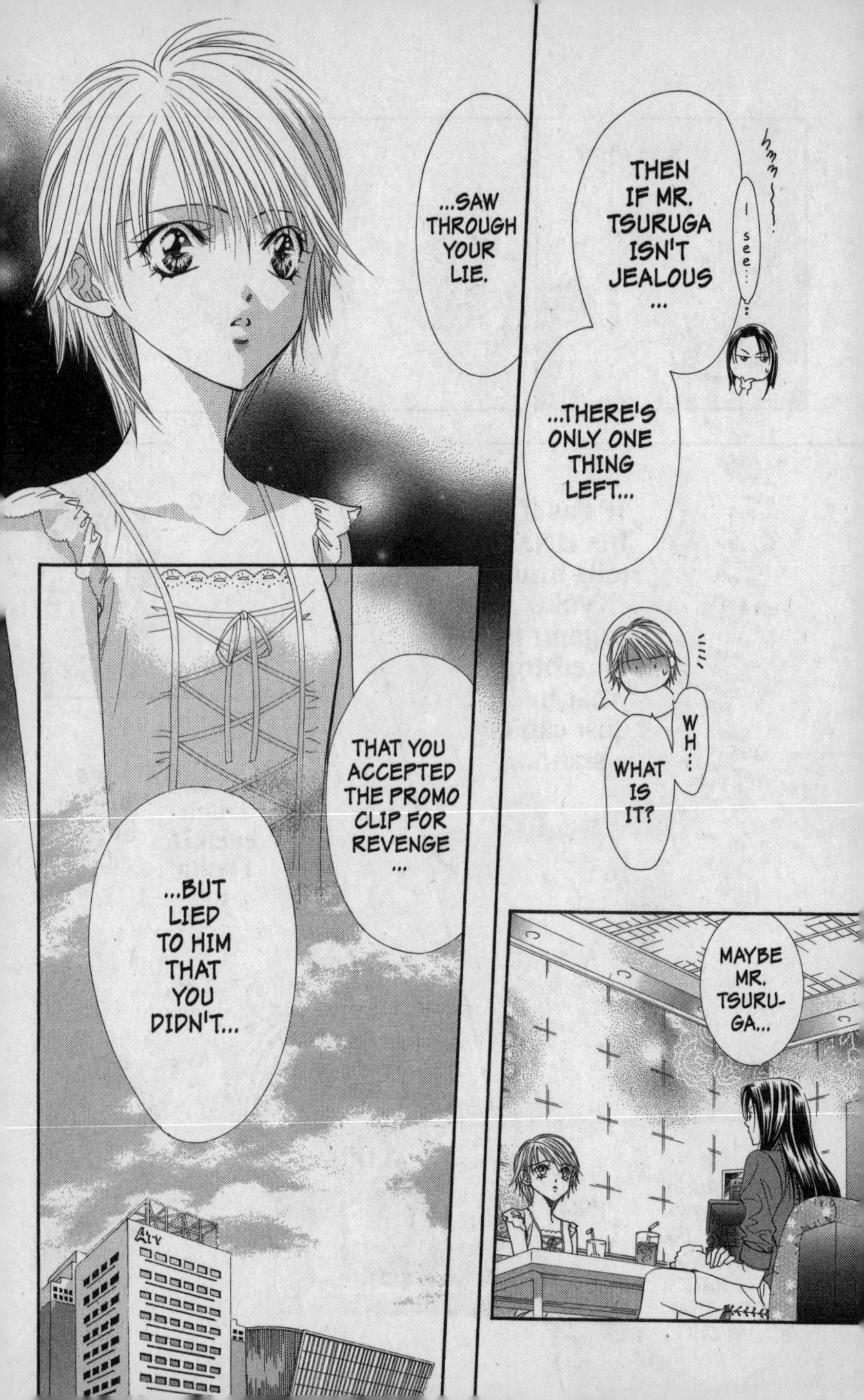

hmm~~~!
I see...
THEN IF MR. TSURUGA ISN'T JEALOUS ...
...THERE'S ONLY ONE THING LEFT...
WH...
WHAT IS IT?
MAYBE MR. TSURU-GA...
...SAW THROUGH YOUR LIE.
THAT YOU ACCEPTED THE PROMO CLIP FOR REVENGE ...
...BUT LIED TO HIM THAT YOU DIDN'T...

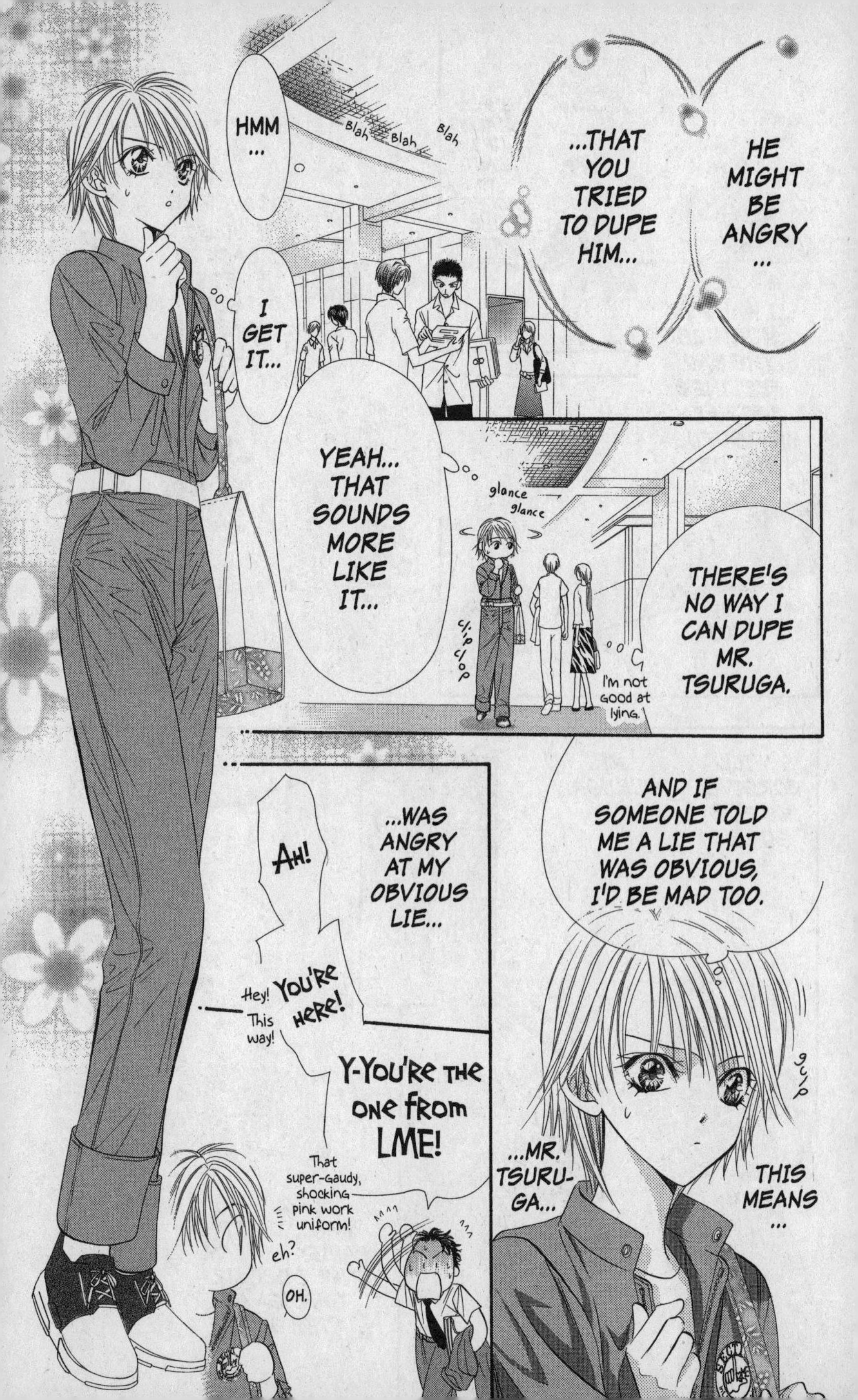
HE MIGHT BE ANGRY...
...THAT YOU TRIED TO DUPE HIM...
Blah Blah Blah
HMM...
I GET IT...
THERE'S NO WAY I CAN DUPE MR. TSURUGA.
I'm not good at lying.
glance glance
clip clop
YEAH... THAT SOUNDS MORE LIKE IT...
AND IF SOMEONE TOLD ME A LIE THAT WAS OBVIOUS, I'D BE MAD TOO.
gulp
THIS MEANS...
...MR. TSURUGA...
...WAS ANGRY AT MY OBVIOUS LIE...
AH!
Hey! This way!
YOU'RE HERE!
Y-YOU'RE THE ONE FROM LME!
That super-gaudy, shocking pink work uniform!
eh?
OH.

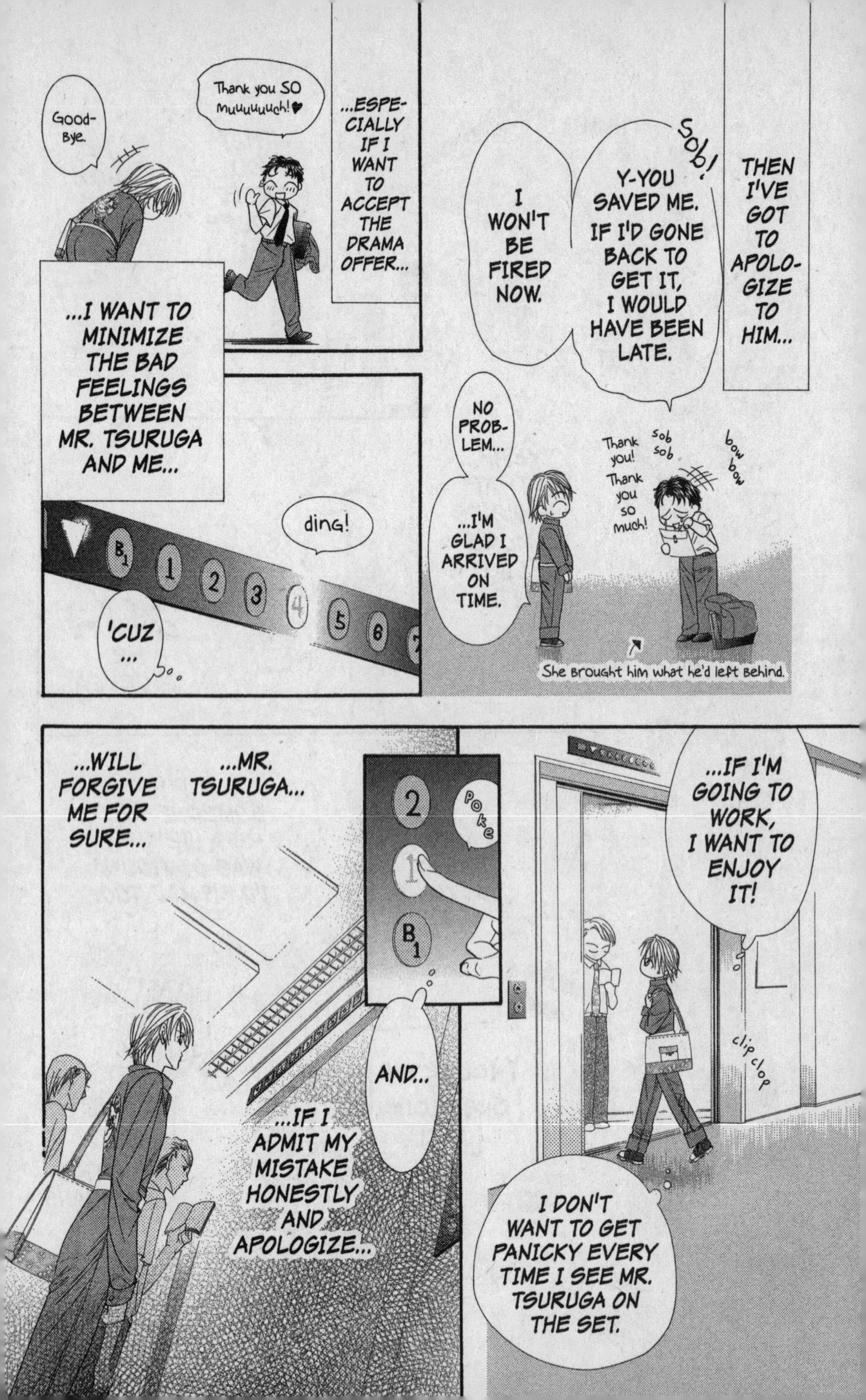
THEN I'VE GOT TO APOLOGIZE TO HIM...
Sob!
Y-YOU SAVED ME. IF I'D GONE BACK TO GET IT, I WOULD HAVE BEEN LATE.
I WON'T BE FIRED NOW.
bow bow
sob sob
Thank you! Thank you so much!
NO PROBLEM...
...I'M GLAD I ARRIVED ON TIME.
She brought him what he'd left behind.
...ESPECIALLY IF I WANT TO ACCEPT THE DRAMA OFFER...
Thank you SO Muuuuuuch!♥
Good-Bye.
...I WANT TO MINIMIZE THE BAD FEELINGS BETWEEN MR. TSURUGA AND ME...
ding!
'CUZ...
...IF I'M GOING TO WORK, I WANT TO ENJOY IT!
clip clop
I DON'T WANT TO GET PANICKY EVERY TIME I SEE MR. TSURUGA ON THE SET.
...MR. TSURUGA...
...WILL FORGIVE ME FOR SURE...
Poke
AND...
...IF I ADMIT MY MISTAKE HONESTLY AND APOLOGIZE...

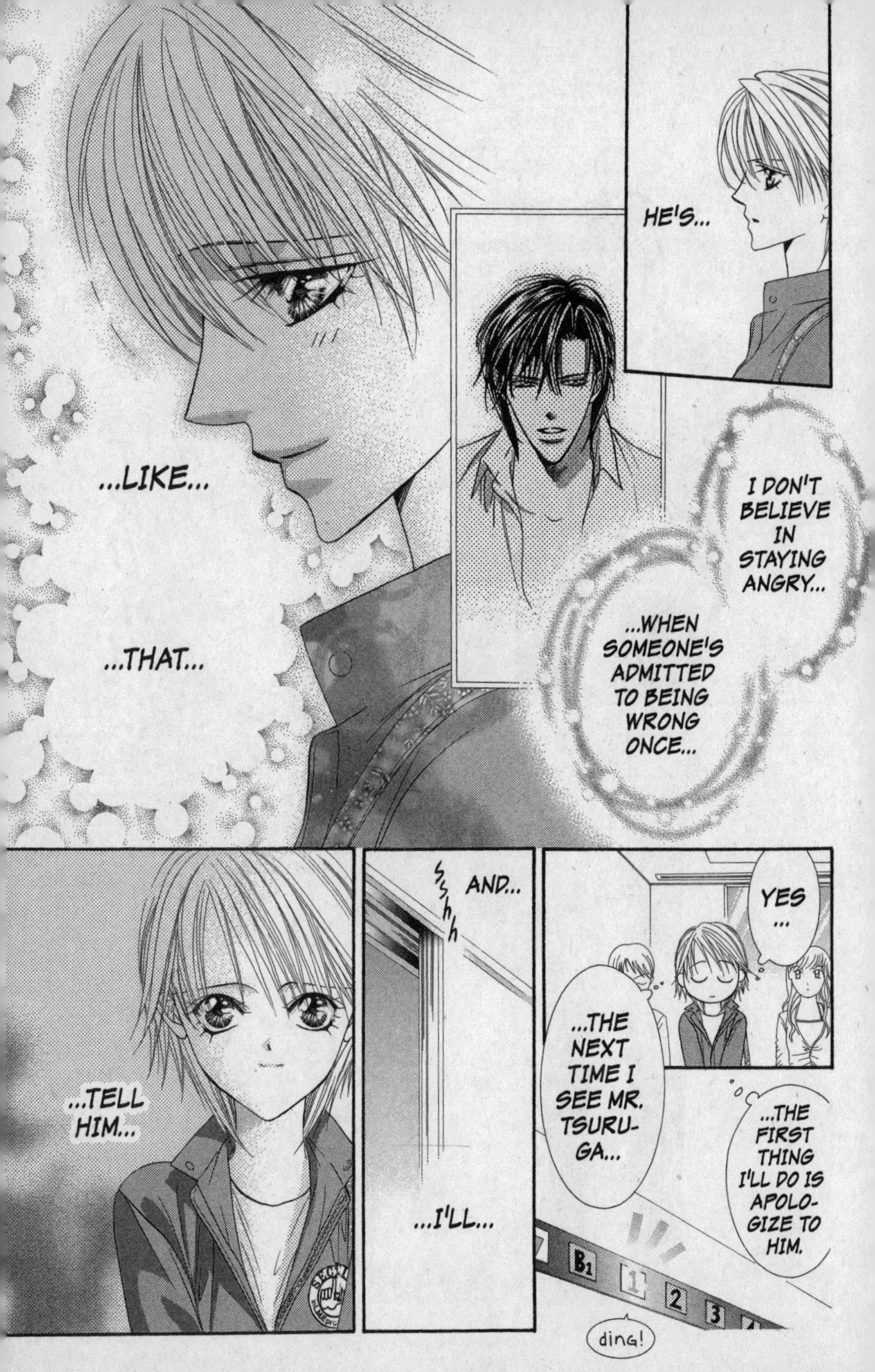

HE'S...
I DON'T BELIEVE IN STAYING ANGRY...
...WHEN SOMEONE'S ADMITTED TO BEING WRONG ONCE...
...LIKE...
...THAT...
YES ...
...THE NEXT TIME I SEE MR. TSURU-GA...
...THE FIRST THING I'LL DO IS APOLO-GIZE TO HIM.
ding!
AND...
sshh
...I'LL...
...TELL HIM...

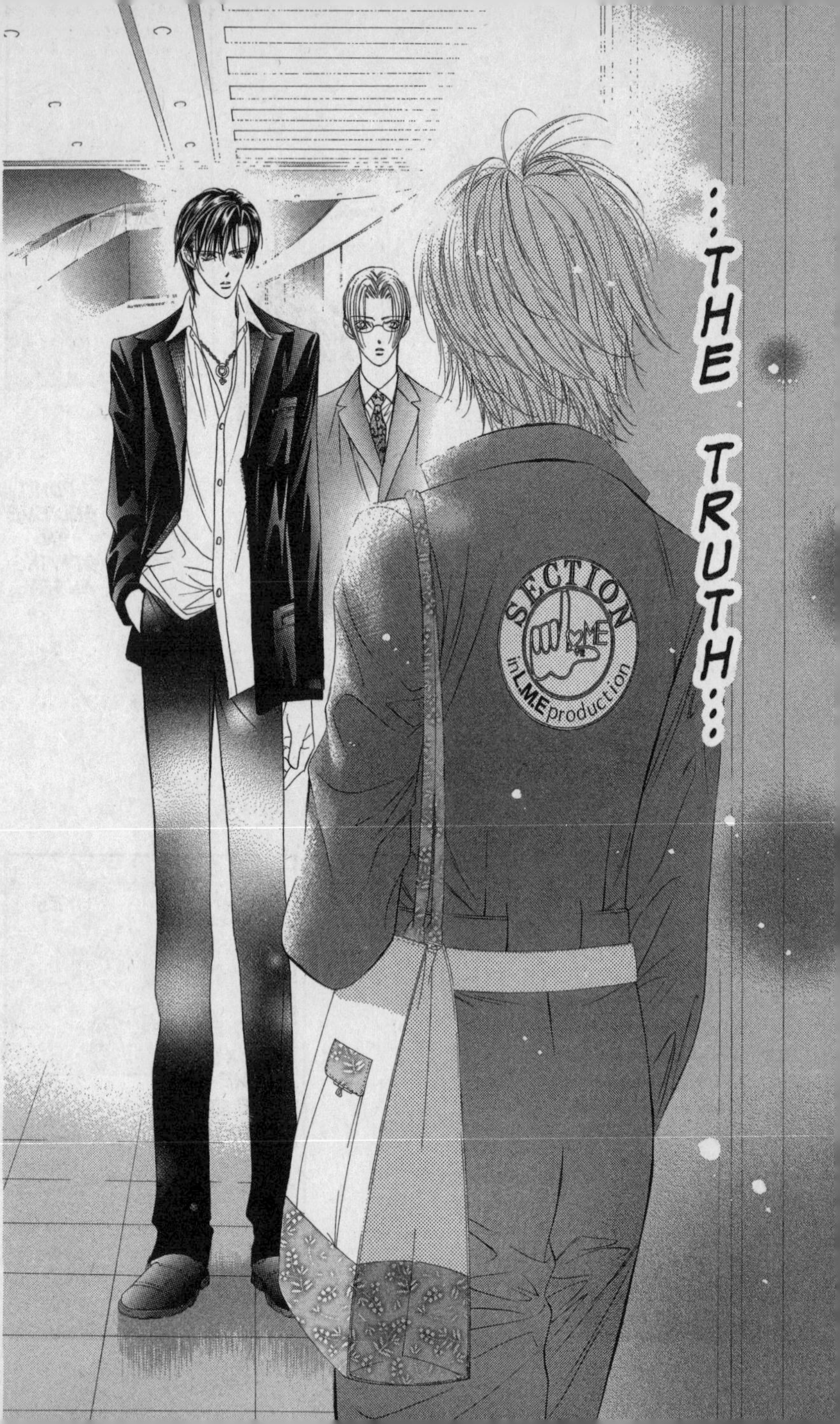
...THE TRUTH...
SECTION
L.M.E
in L.M.E production

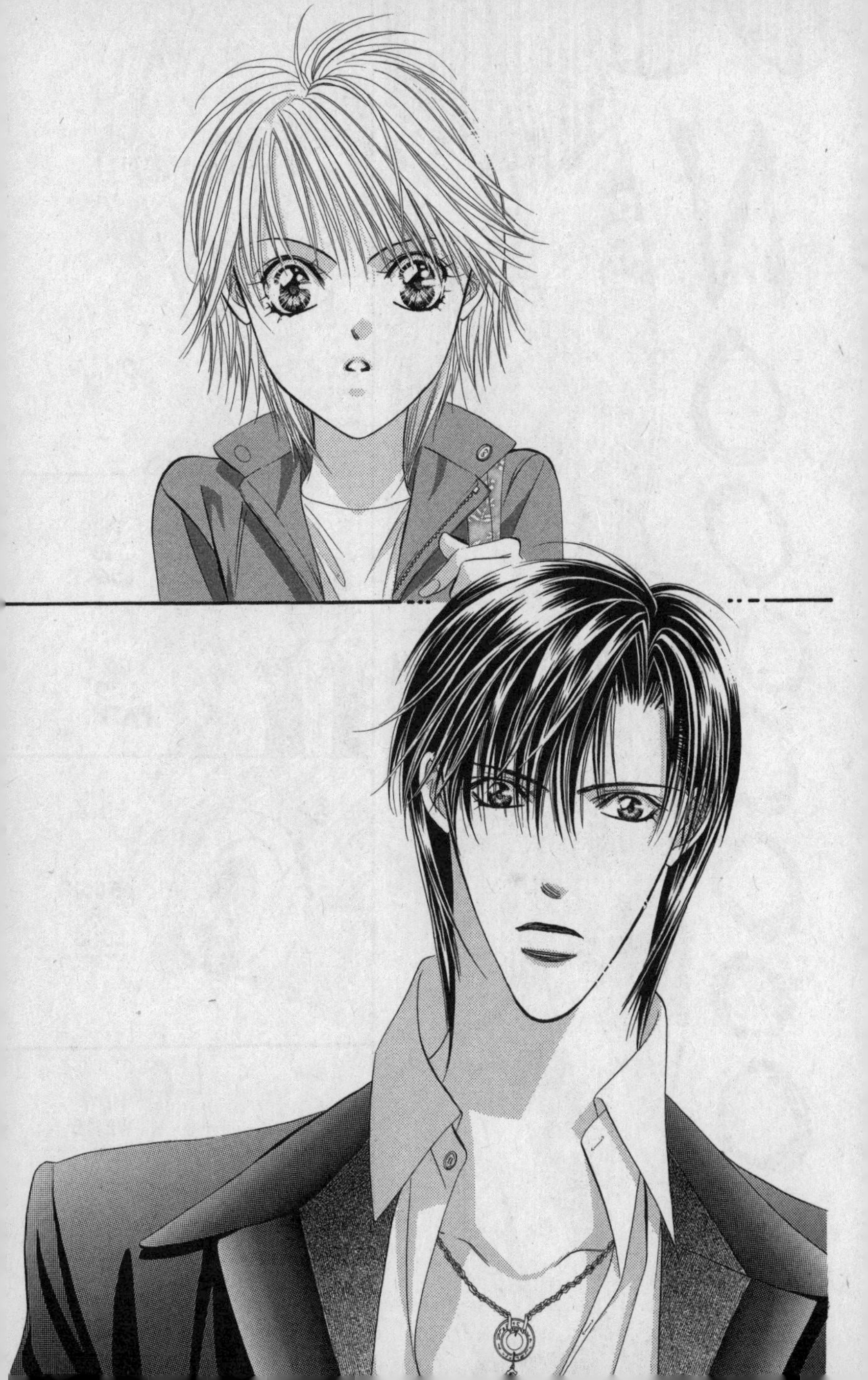

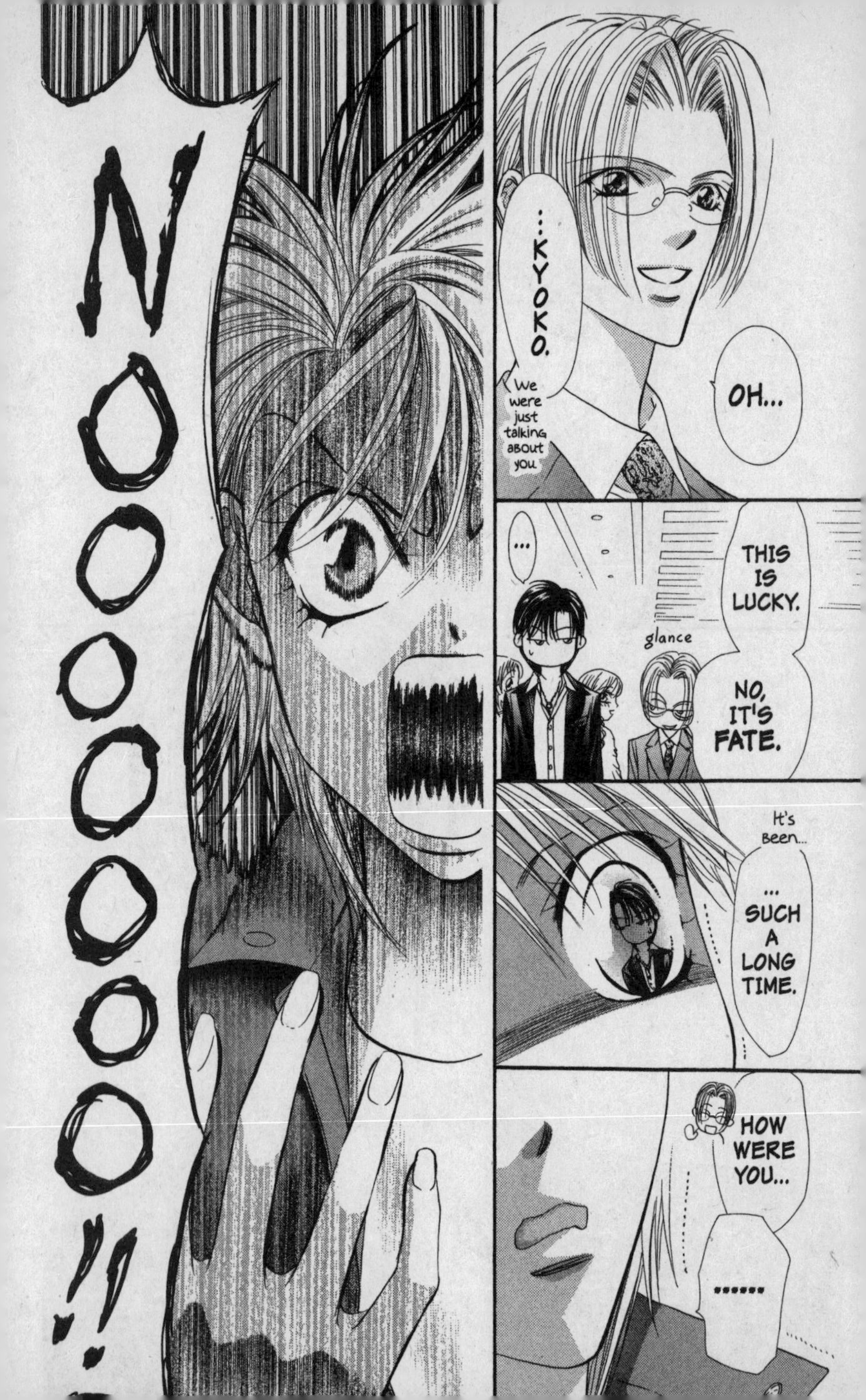
OH...
...KYOKO.
We were just talking about you.
THIS IS LUCKY.
NO, IT'S FATE.
...
glance
It's Been...
... SUCH A LONG TIME.
HOW WERE YOU...
......
NOOOOOOOOO!!

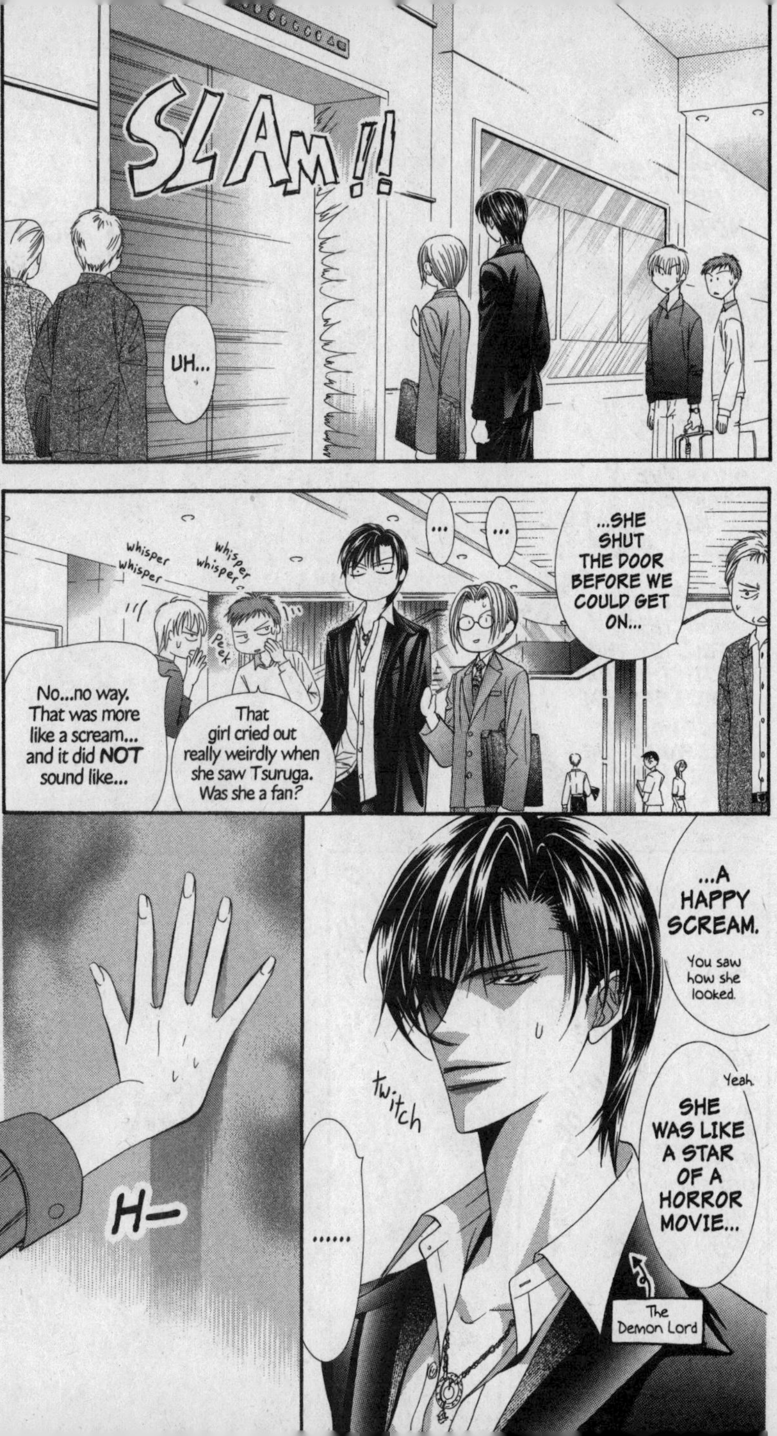
SLAM!!
UH...
...SHE SHUT THE DOOR BEFORE WE COULD GET ON...
...
...
whisper whisper
whisper whisper
Peek
That girl cried out really weirdly when she saw Tsuruga. Was she a fan?
No...no way. That was more like a scream... and it did **NOT** sound like...
...A HAPPY SCREAM.
You saw how she looked.
Yeah.
SHE WAS LIKE A STAR OF A HORROR MOVIE...
twitch
......
The Demon Lord
H—

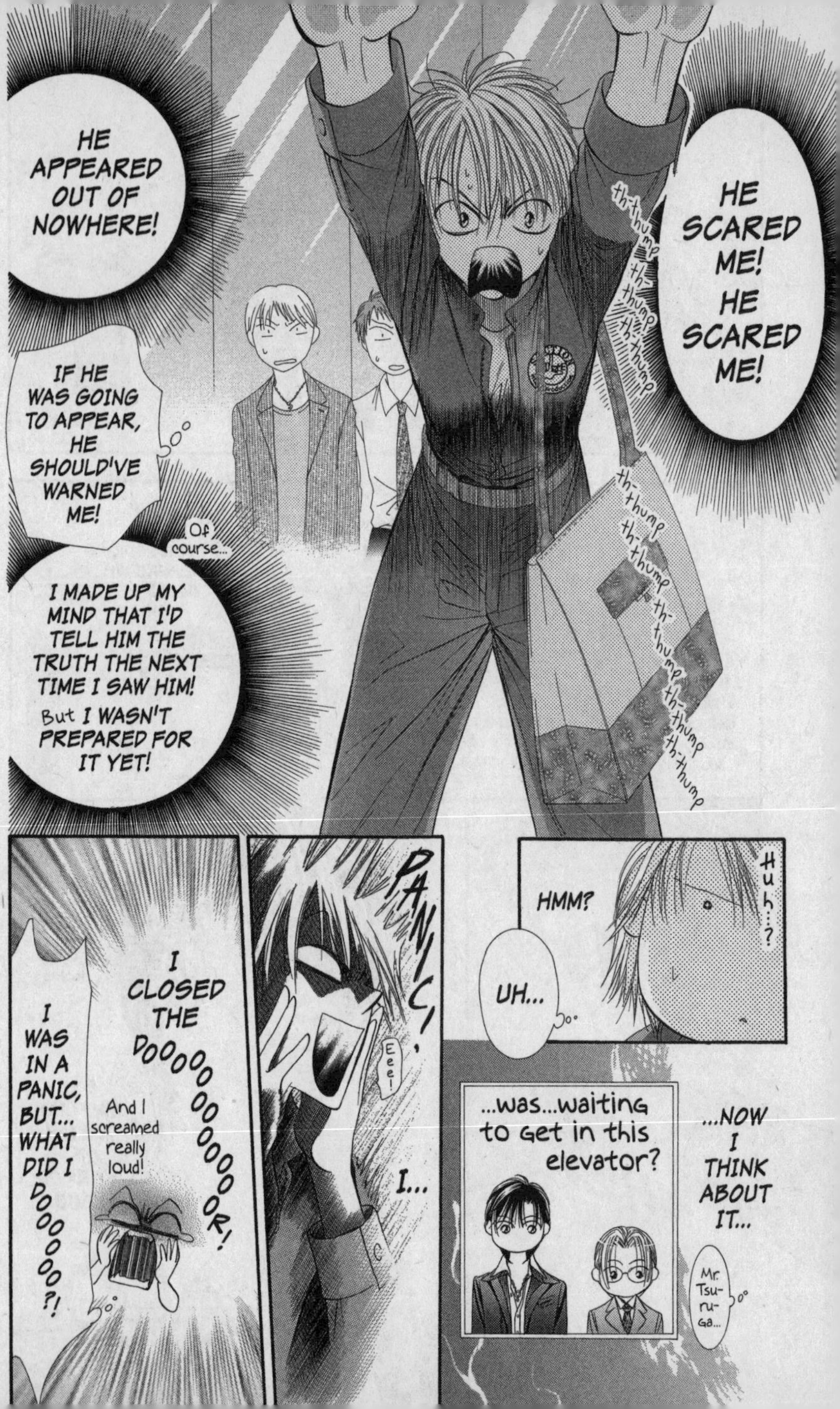
HE SCARED ME! HE SCARED ME!
th-thump th-thump th-thump
HE APPEARED OUT OF NOWHERE!
IF HE WAS GOING TO APPEAR, HE SHOULD'VE WARNED ME!
Of course...
I MADE UP MY MIND THAT I'D TELL HIM THE TRUTH THE NEXT TIME I SAW HIM! But I WASN'T PREPARED FOR IT YET!
th-thump th-thump th-thump th-thump th-thump
Huh...?
HMM?
UH...
...NOW I THINK ABOUT IT...
...was...waiting to get in this elevator?
Mr. Tsu-ru-ga...
PANIC,
Eee!
I...
I CLOSED THE DOOOOOOOOOOOR!
I WAS IN A PANIC, BUT... WHAT DID I DOOOOOOOO?!
And I screamed really loud!

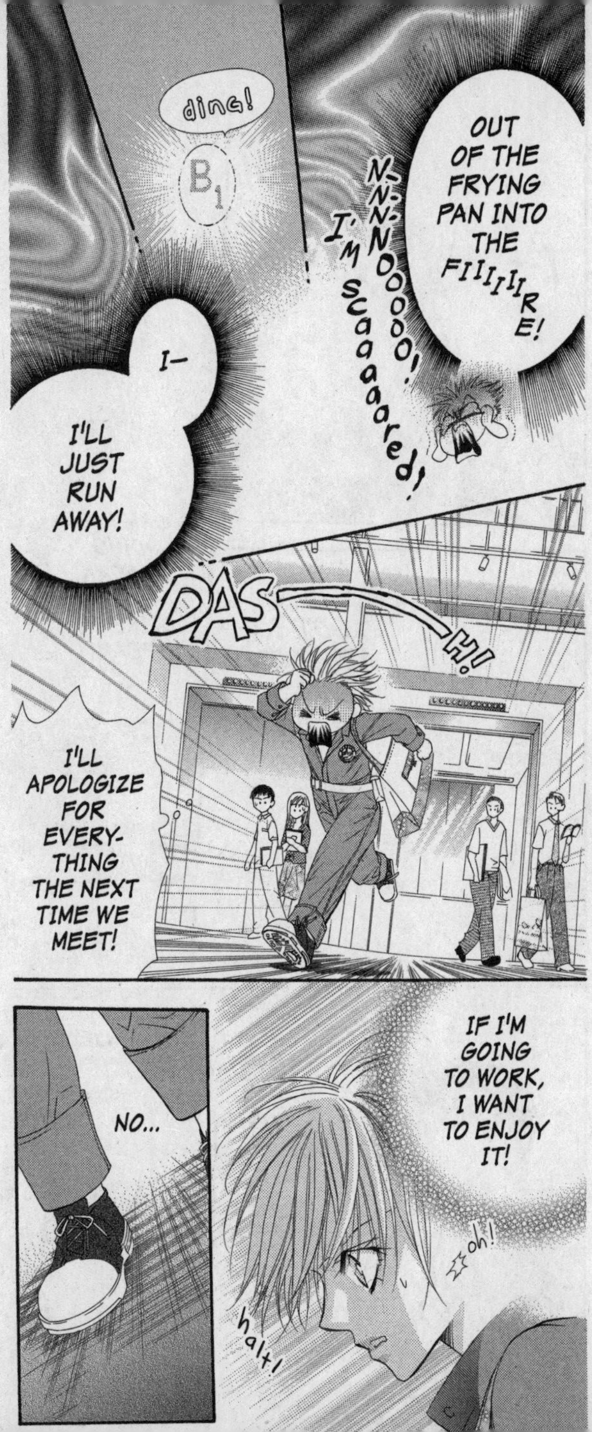
ding!
B1
OUT OF THE FRYING PAN INTO THE FIIIIIIRE!
N-N-N-NOOOOO! I'M SCaaaaared!
I—
I'LL JUST RUN AWAY!
DASH!
I'LL APOLOGIZE FOR EVERYTHING THE NEXT TIME WE MEET!
IF I'M GOING TO WORK, I WANT TO ENJOY IT!
oh!
halt!
NO...
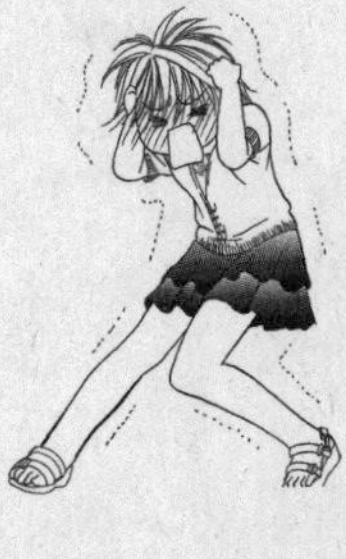

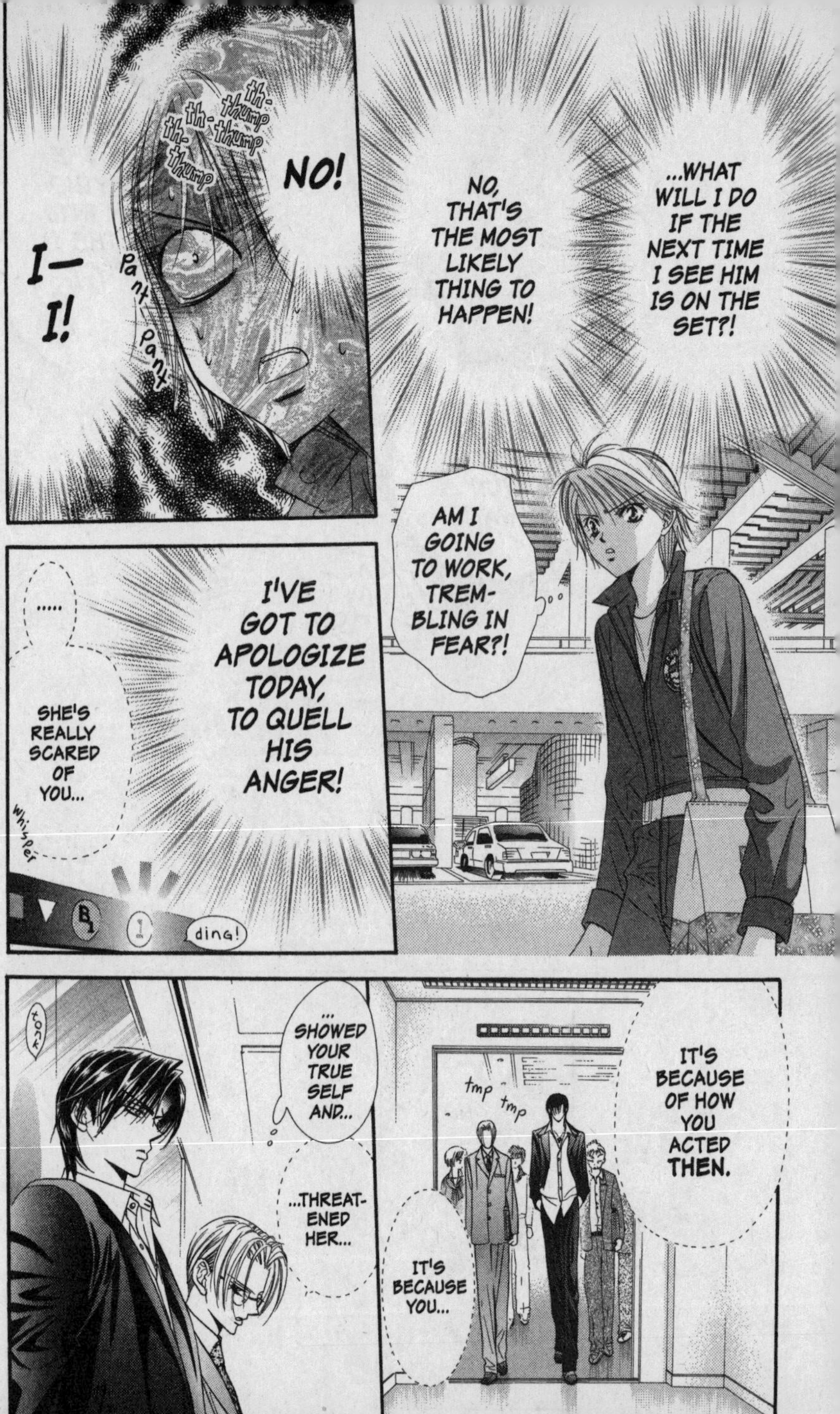
...WHAT WILL I DO IF THE NEXT TIME I SEE HIM IS ON THE SET?!
NO, THAT'S THE MOST LIKELY THING TO HAPPEN!
AM I GOING TO WORK, TREMBLING IN FEAR?!
NO!
th-thump th-thump th-thump
pant pant
I— I!
I'VE GOT TO APOLOGIZE TODAY, TO QUELL HIS ANGER!
.....
SHE'S REALLY SCARED OF YOU...
whisper
ding!
IT'S BECAUSE OF HOW YOU ACTED THEN.
tmp tmp
IT'S BECAUSE YOU...
...SHOWED YOUR TRUE SELF AND...
...THREATENED HER...
tonk

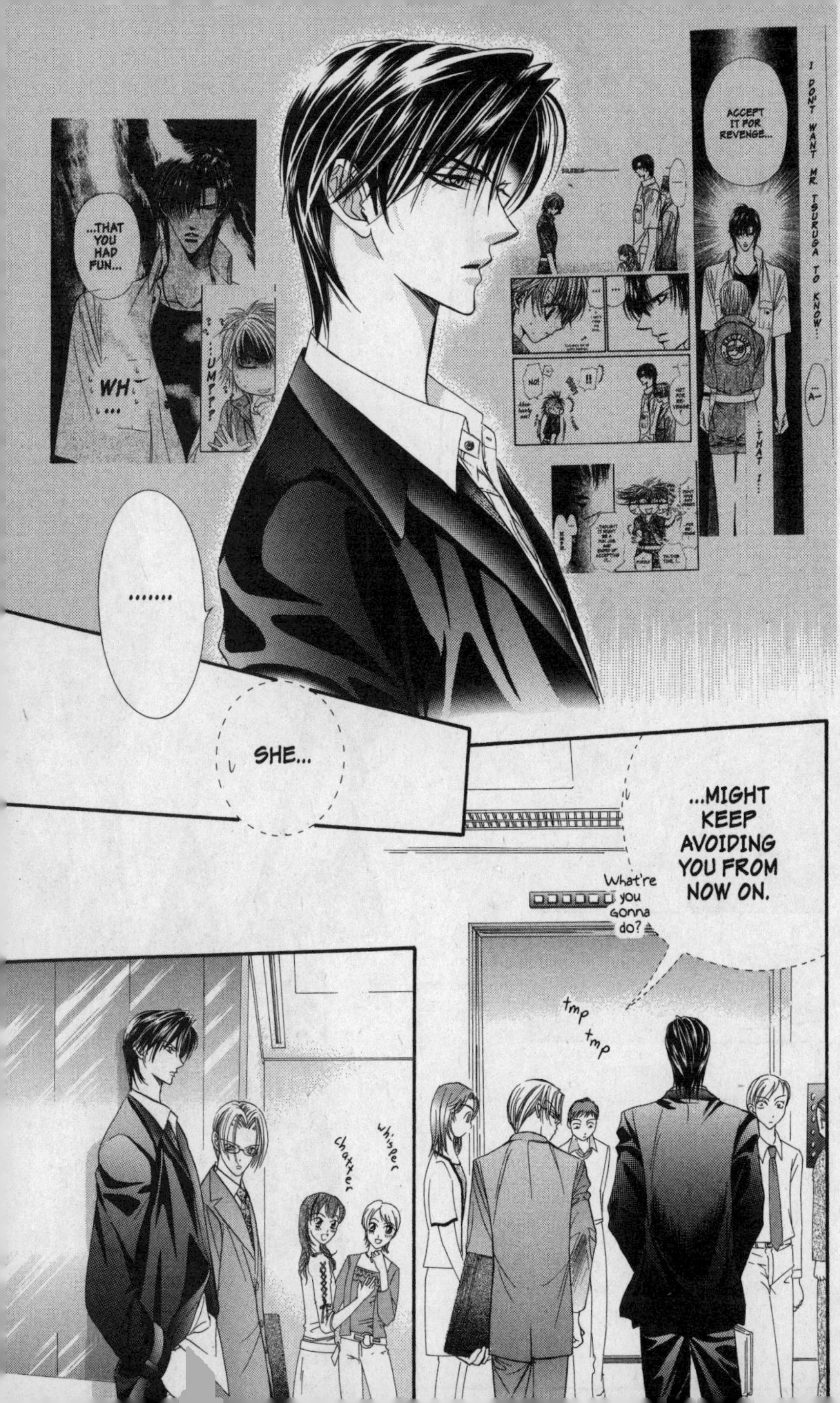
ACCEPT IT FOR REVENGE...
I DON'T WANT MR TSURUGA TO KNOW...
...THAT I...
A—
...THAT YOU HAD FUN...
...UMP??
WH...
....
SHE...
...MIGHT KEEP AVOIDING YOU FROM NOW ON.
What're you gonna do?
tmp tmp
whisper
chatter

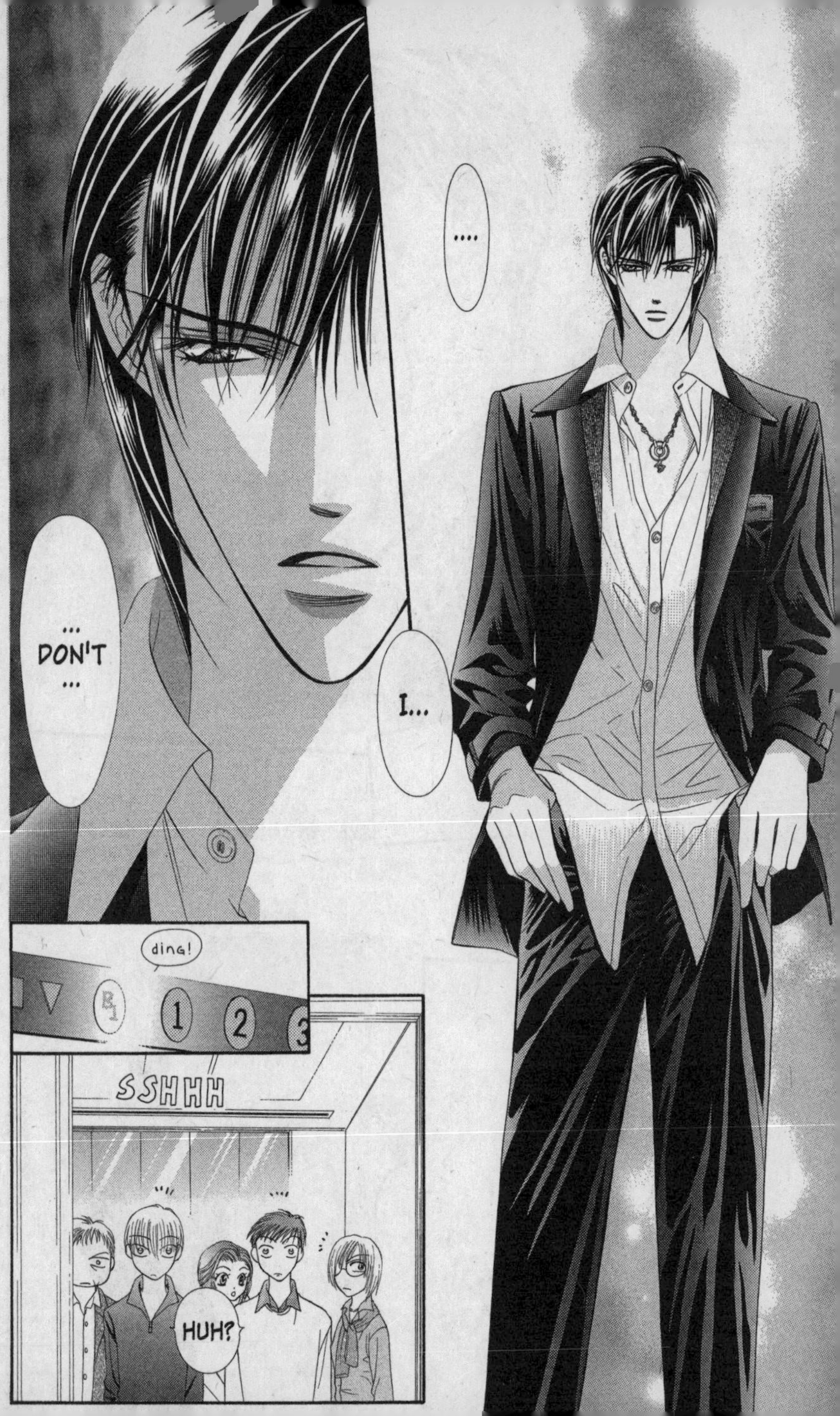
....
I...
... DON'T ...
ding!
SSHHH
HUH?

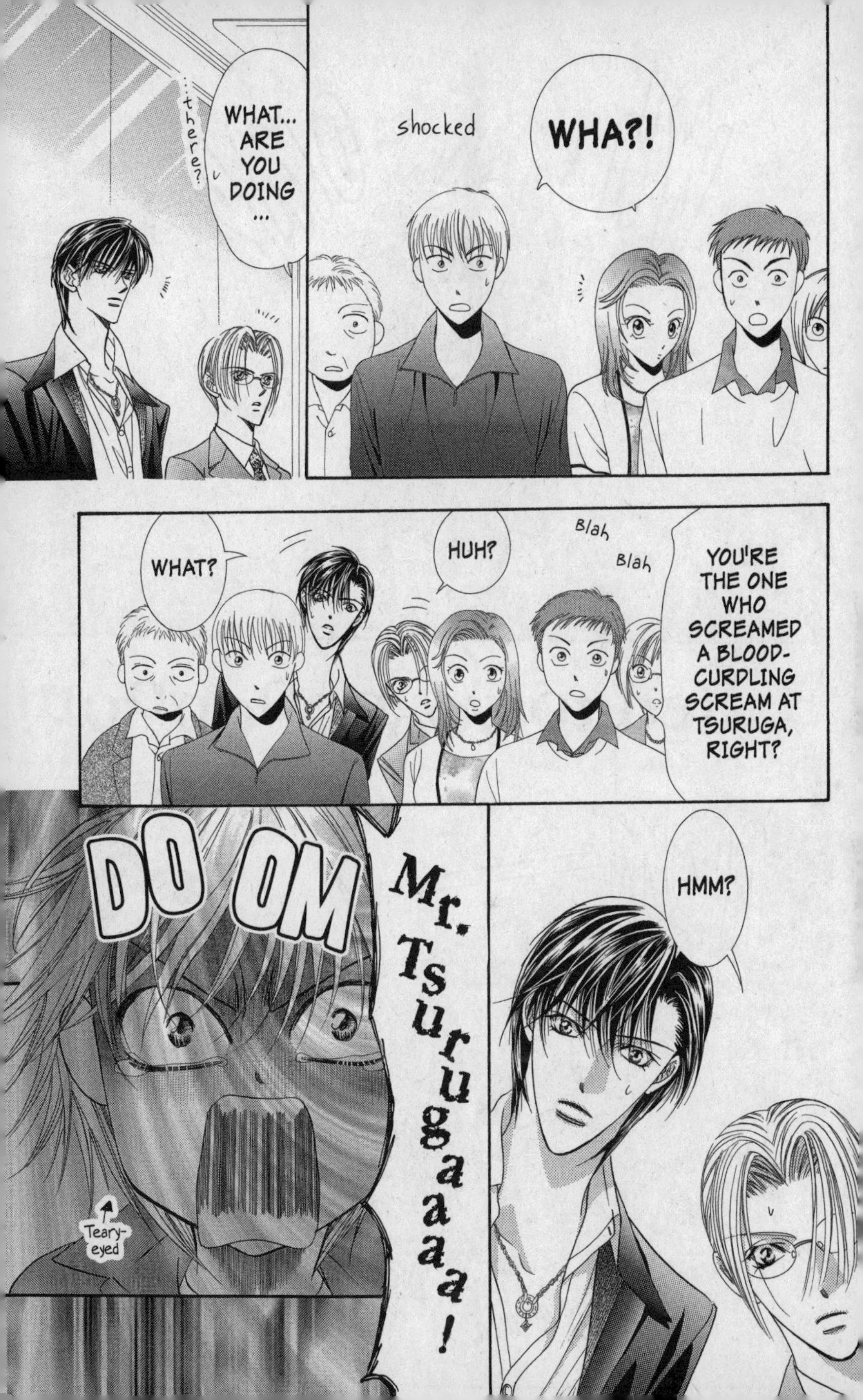
WHA?!
shocked
WHAT... ARE YOU DOING ...
...there?
YOU'RE THE ONE WHO SCREAMED A BLOOD-CURDLING SCREAM AT TSURUGA, RIGHT?
Blah Blah
HUH?
WHAT?
HMM?
Mr. Tsurugaaaaa!
DO OM
Teary-eyed

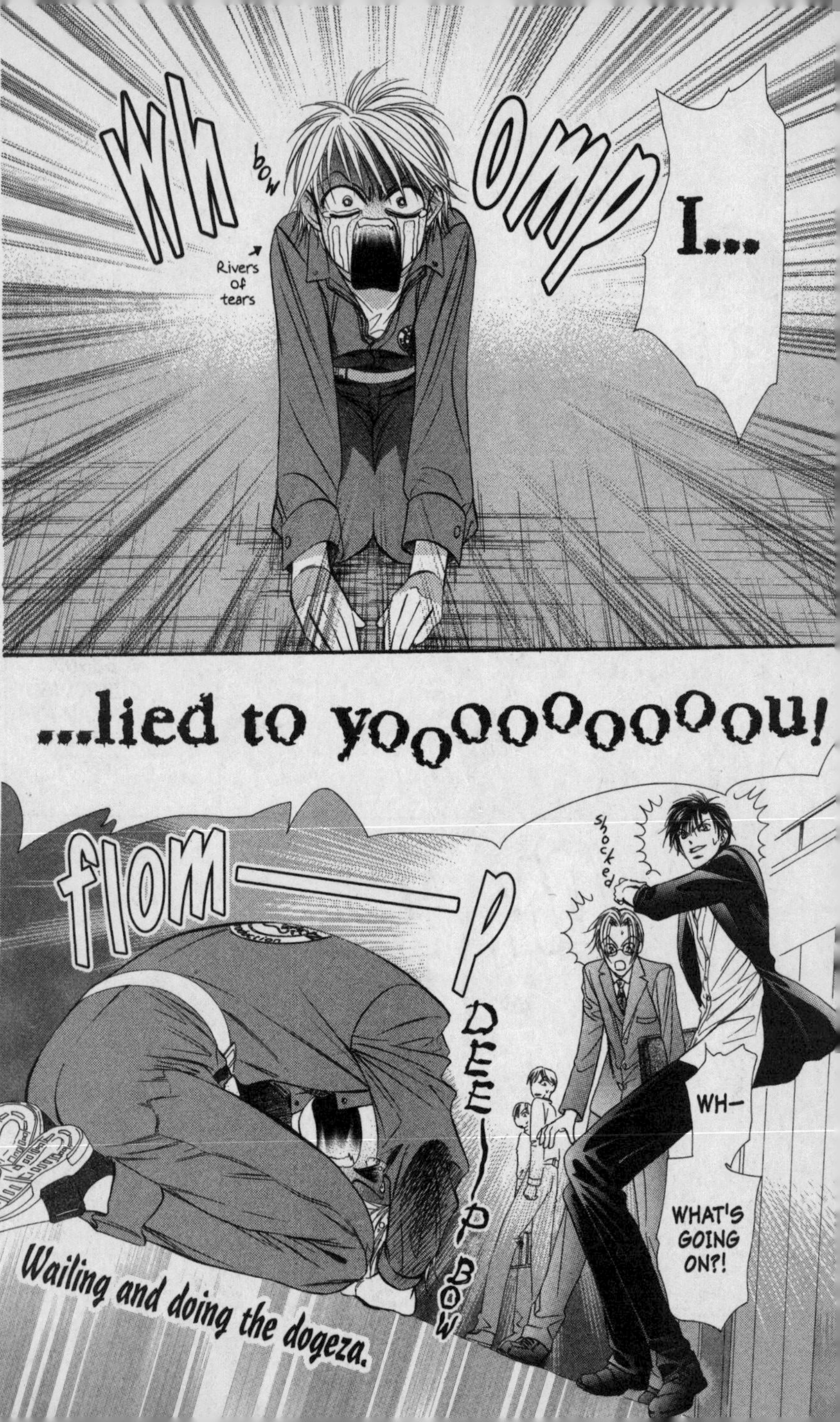
I...
Whomp
bow
Rivers of tears
...lied to yooooooooou!
shocked
WH—
WHAT'S GOING ON?!
flom—p
DEE—P BOW
Wailing and doing the dogeza.

PRESI-
DENT.

HMM
...

chilling

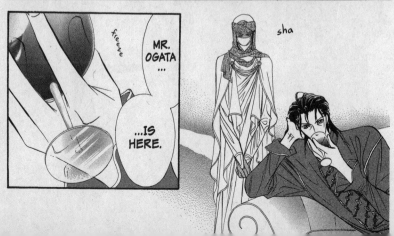

freeze

MR.
OGATA
...

...IS
HERE.

sha

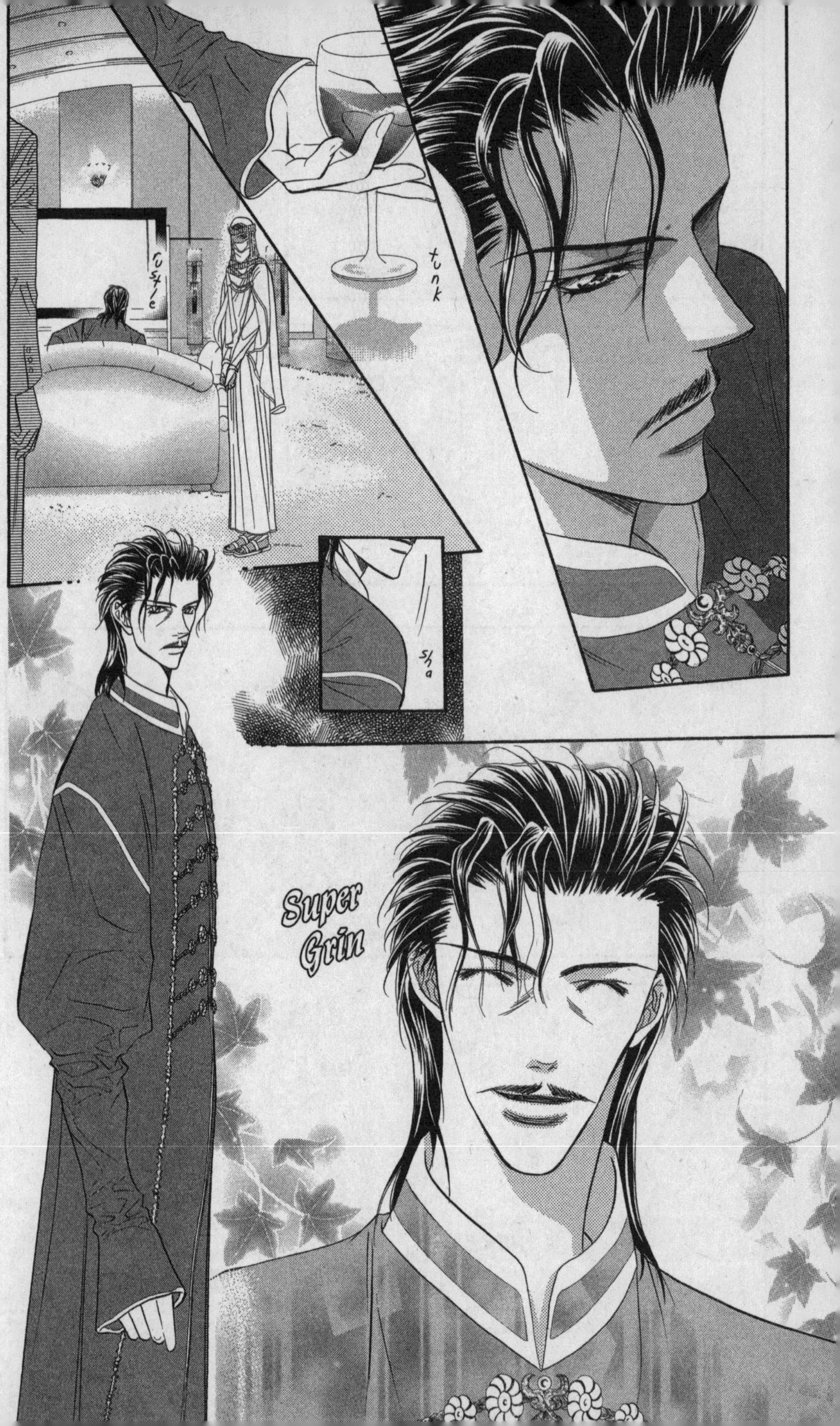
tunk
rustle
sha
Super Grin

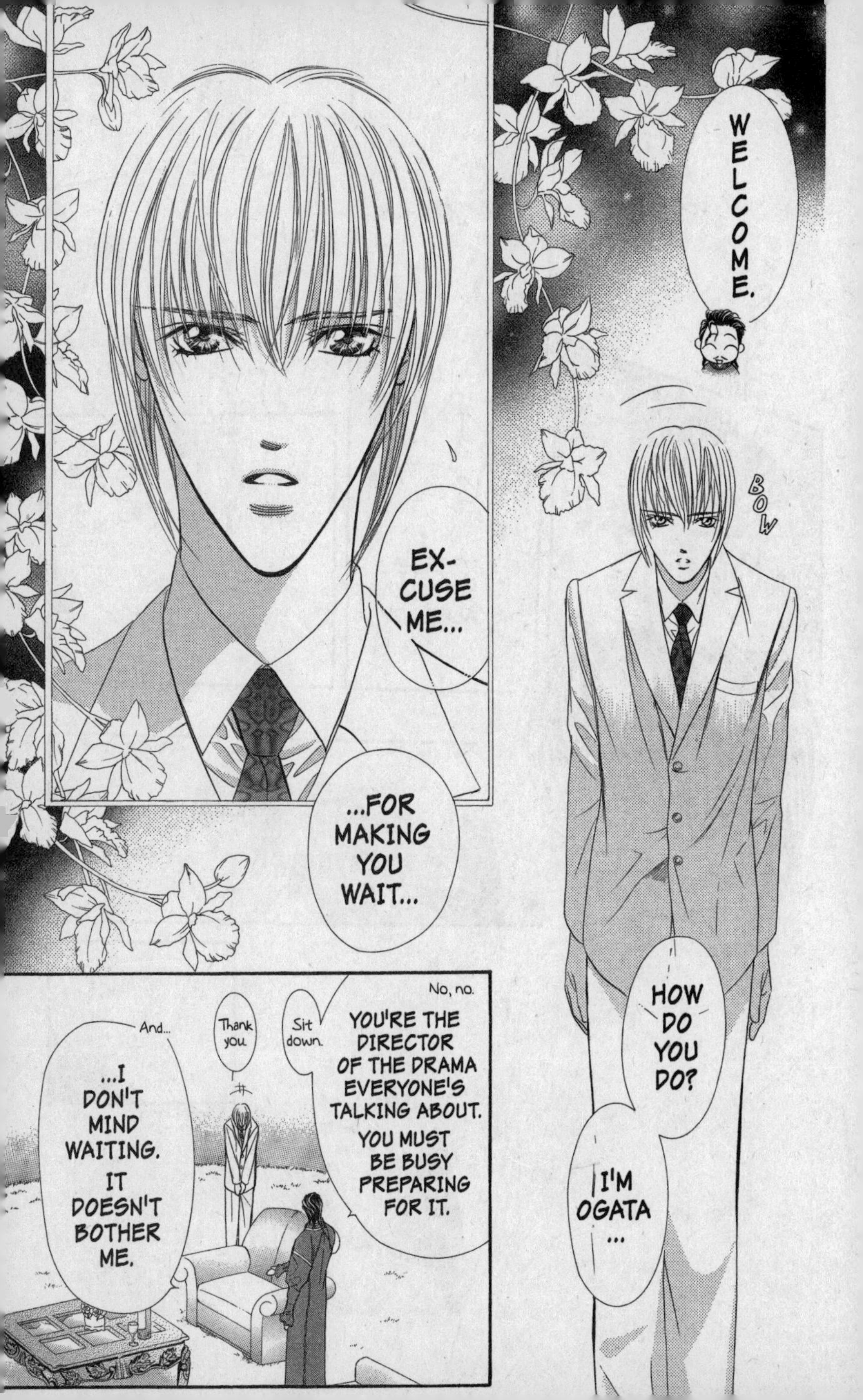
WELCOME.
BOW
HOW DO YOU DO?
I'M OGATA...
EX-CUSE ME...
...FOR MAKING YOU WAIT...
No, no.
YOU'RE THE DIRECTOR OF THE DRAMA EVERYONE'S TALKING ABOUT.
YOU MUST BE BUSY PREPARING FOR IT.
Sit down.
Thank you
And...
...I DON'T MIND WAITING.
IT DOESN'T BOTHER ME.

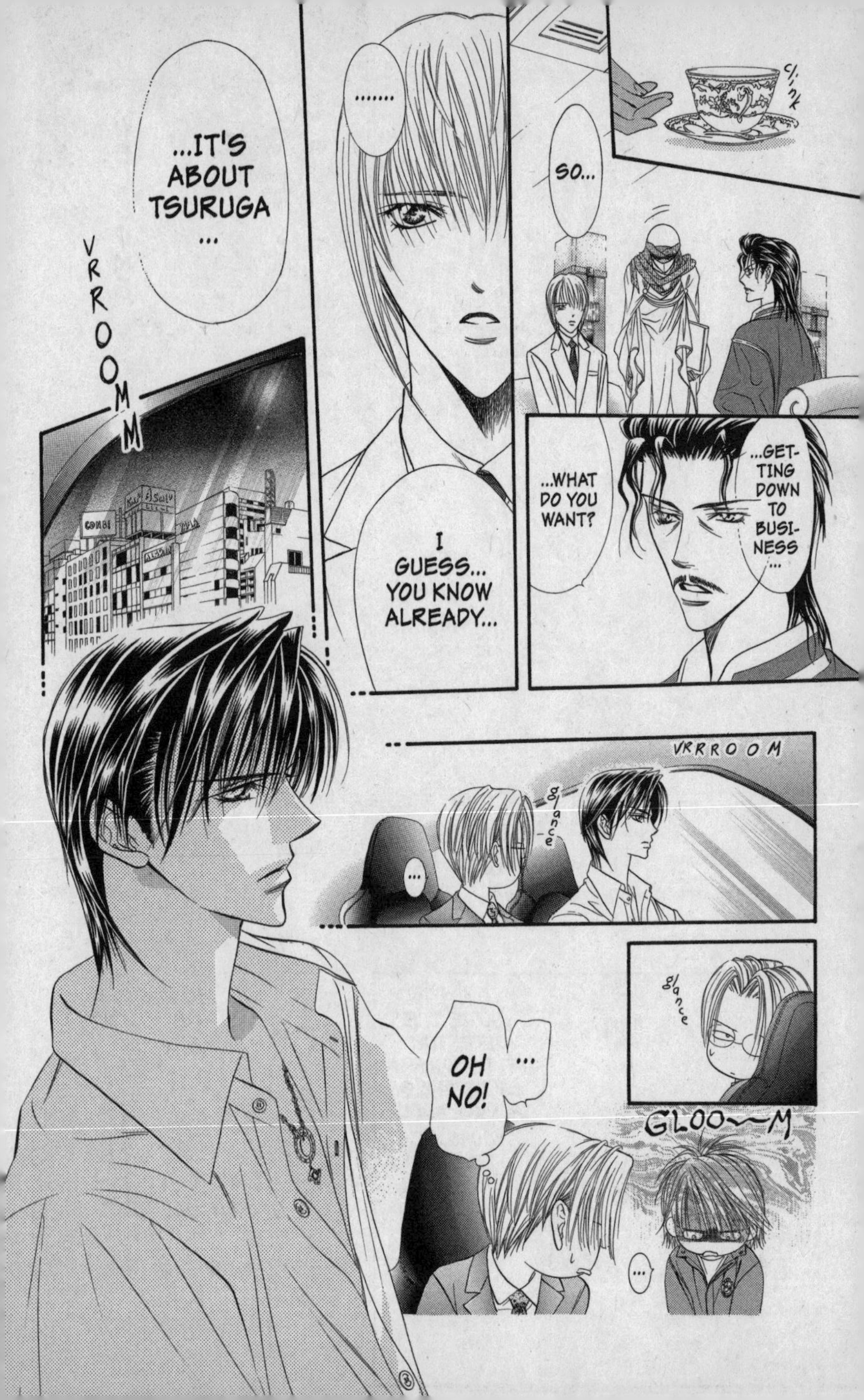
clink
SO...
...GETTING DOWN TO BUSINESS...
...WHAT DO YOU WANT?
....
I GUESS... YOU KNOW ALREADY...
...IT'S ABOUT TSURUGA...
VRROOMM
VRRROOM
glance
...
glance
GLOO~M
OH NO! ...
...

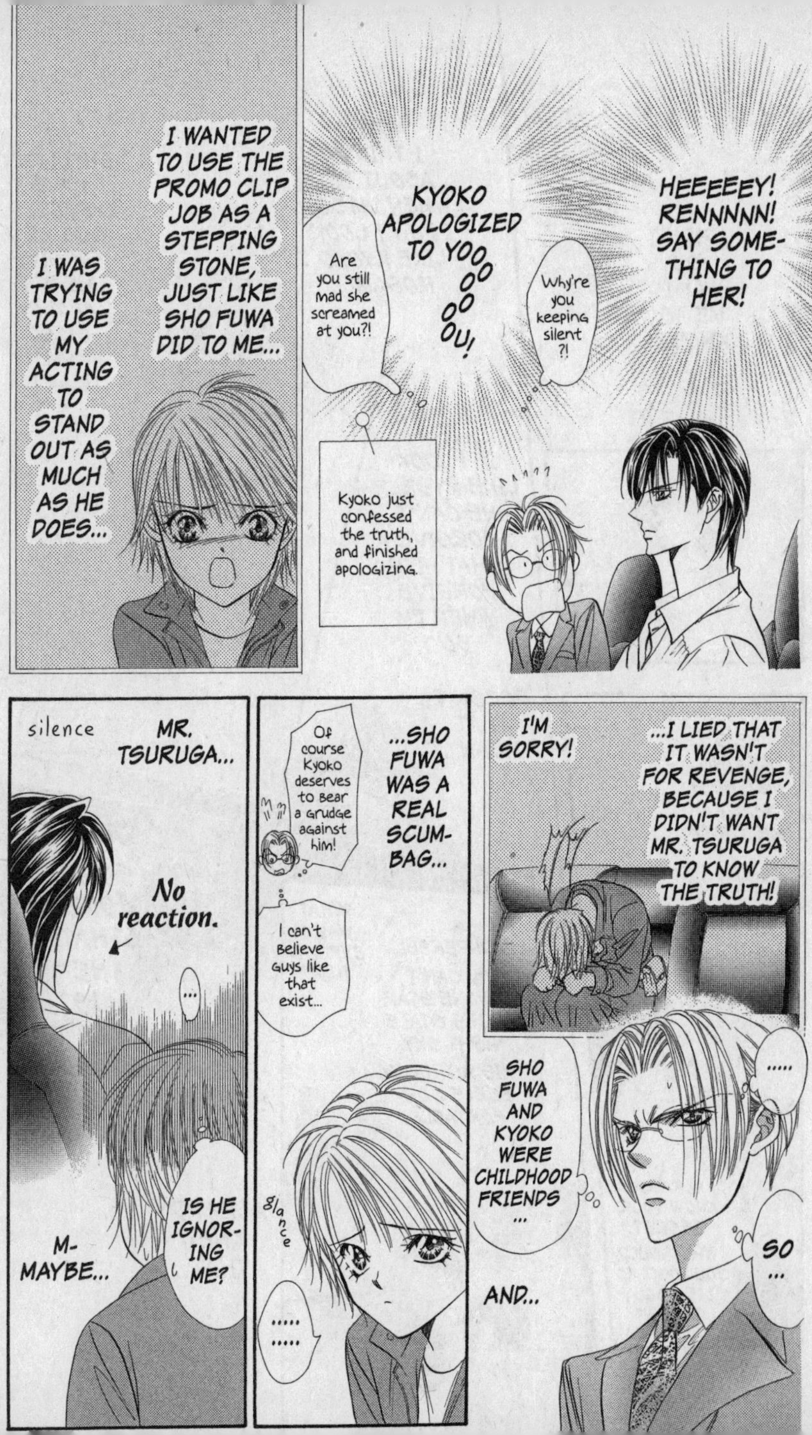
HEEEEEY! RENNNNN! SAY SOME-THING TO HER!
Why're you keeping silent?!
KYOKO APOLOGIZED TO YOOOOOOOU!
Are you still mad she screamed at you?!
Kyoko just confessed the truth, and finished apologizing.
I WANTED TO USE THE PROMO CLIP JOB AS A STEPPING STONE, JUST LIKE SHO FUWA DID TO ME...
I WAS TRYING TO USE MY ACTING TO STAND OUT AS MUCH AS HE DOES...
...I LIED THAT IT WASN'T FOR REVENGE, BECAUSE I DIDN'T WANT MR. TSURUGA TO KNOW THE TRUTH!
I'M SORRY!
.....
SO ...
SHO FUWA AND KYOKO WERE CHILDHOOD FRIENDS ...
AND...
...SHO FUWA WAS A REAL SCUM-BAG...
Of course Kyoko deserves to bear a grudge against him!
I can't believe guys like that exist...
glance
....
MR. TSURUGA...
silence
No reaction.
...
IS HE IGNORING ME?
M-MAYBE...

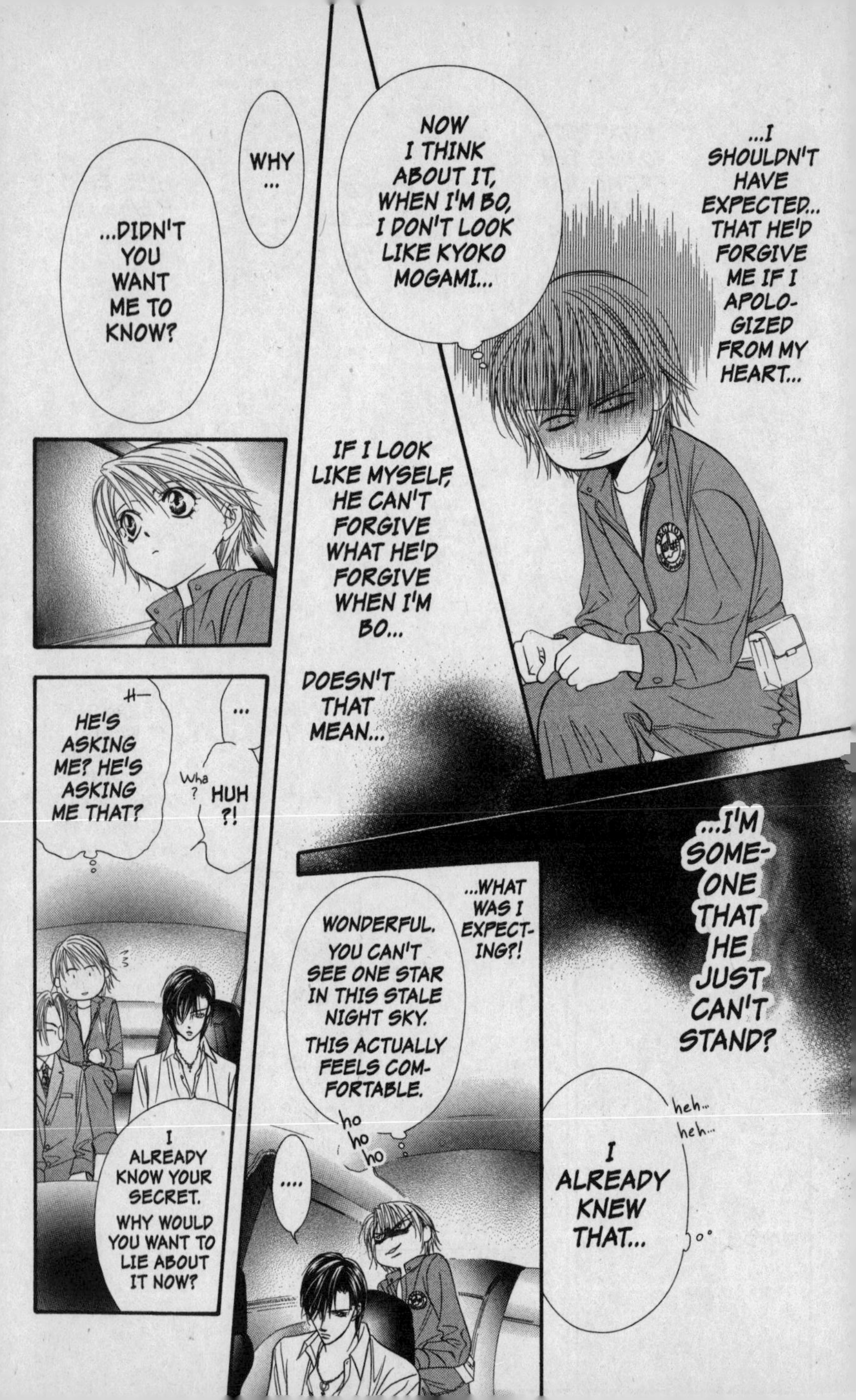
...I SHOULDN'T HAVE EXPECTED... THAT HE'D FORGIVE ME IF I APOLOGIZED FROM MY HEART...
NOW I THINK ABOUT IT, WHEN I'M BO, I DON'T LOOK LIKE KYOKO MOGAMI...
IF I LOOK LIKE MYSELF, HE CAN'T FORGIVE WHAT HE'D FORGIVE WHEN I'M BO...
DOESN'T THAT MEAN...
...I'M SOMEONE THAT HE JUST CAN'T STAND?
I ALREADY KNEW THAT...
heh... heh...
...WHAT WAS I EXPECTING?!
WONDERFUL. YOU CAN'T SEE ONE STAR IN THIS STALE NIGHT SKY. THIS ACTUALLY FEELS COMFORTABLE.
ho ho ho
....
WHY...
...DIDN'T YOU WANT ME TO KNOW?
...
HUH?!
Wha?
H— HE'S ASKING ME? HE'S ASKING ME THAT?
I ALREADY KNOW YOUR SECRET. WHY WOULD YOU WANT TO LIE ABOUT IT NOW?

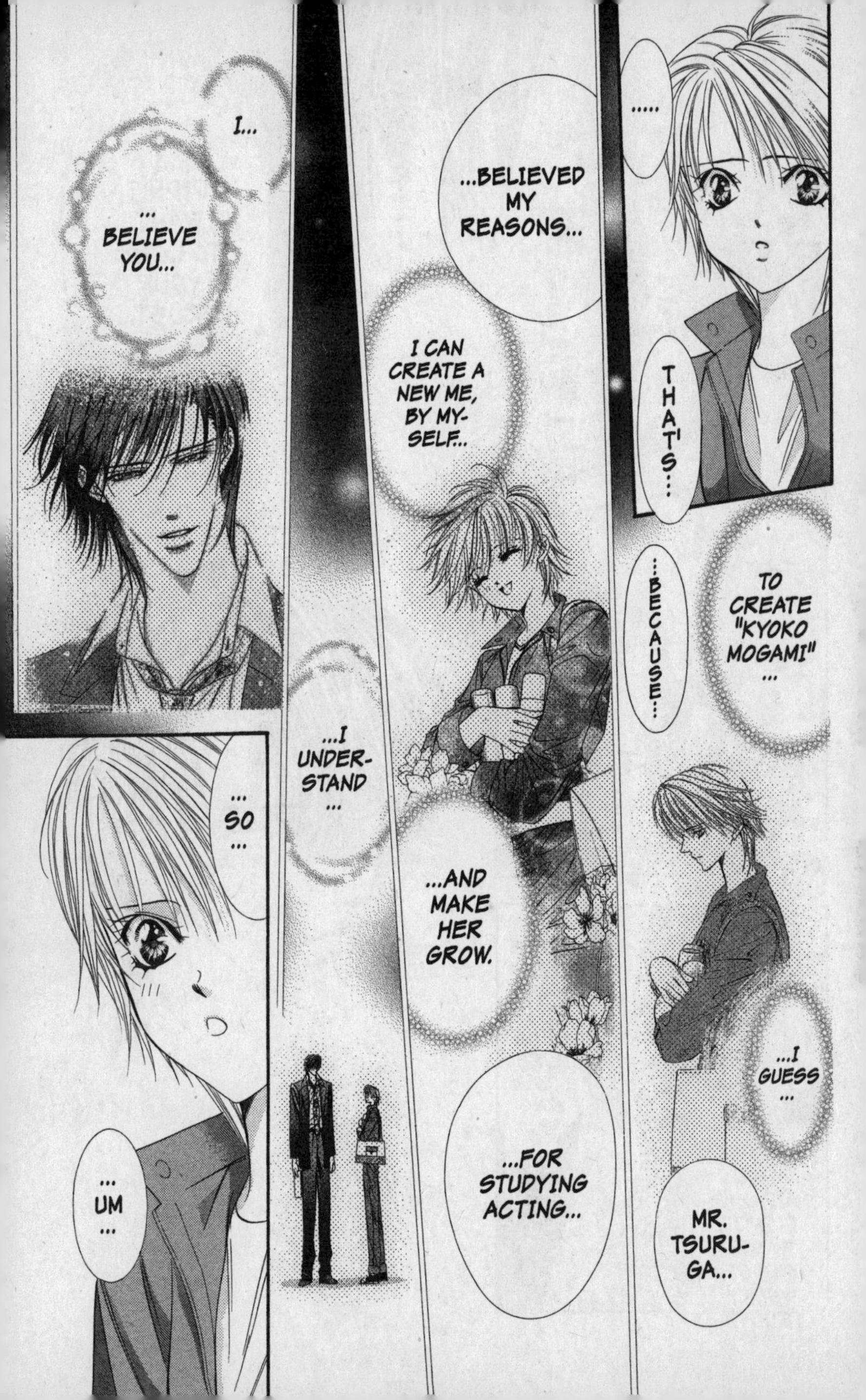
.....
THAT'S...
TO CREATE "KYOKO MOGAMI"...
...BECAUSE...
...I GUESS...
MR. TSURUGA...
...BELIEVED MY REASONS...
I CAN CREATE A NEW ME, BY MY-SELF..
...AND MAKE HER GROW.
...FOR STUDYING ACTING...
...I UNDER-STAND...
I...
...BELIEVE YOU...
...SO...
...UM...

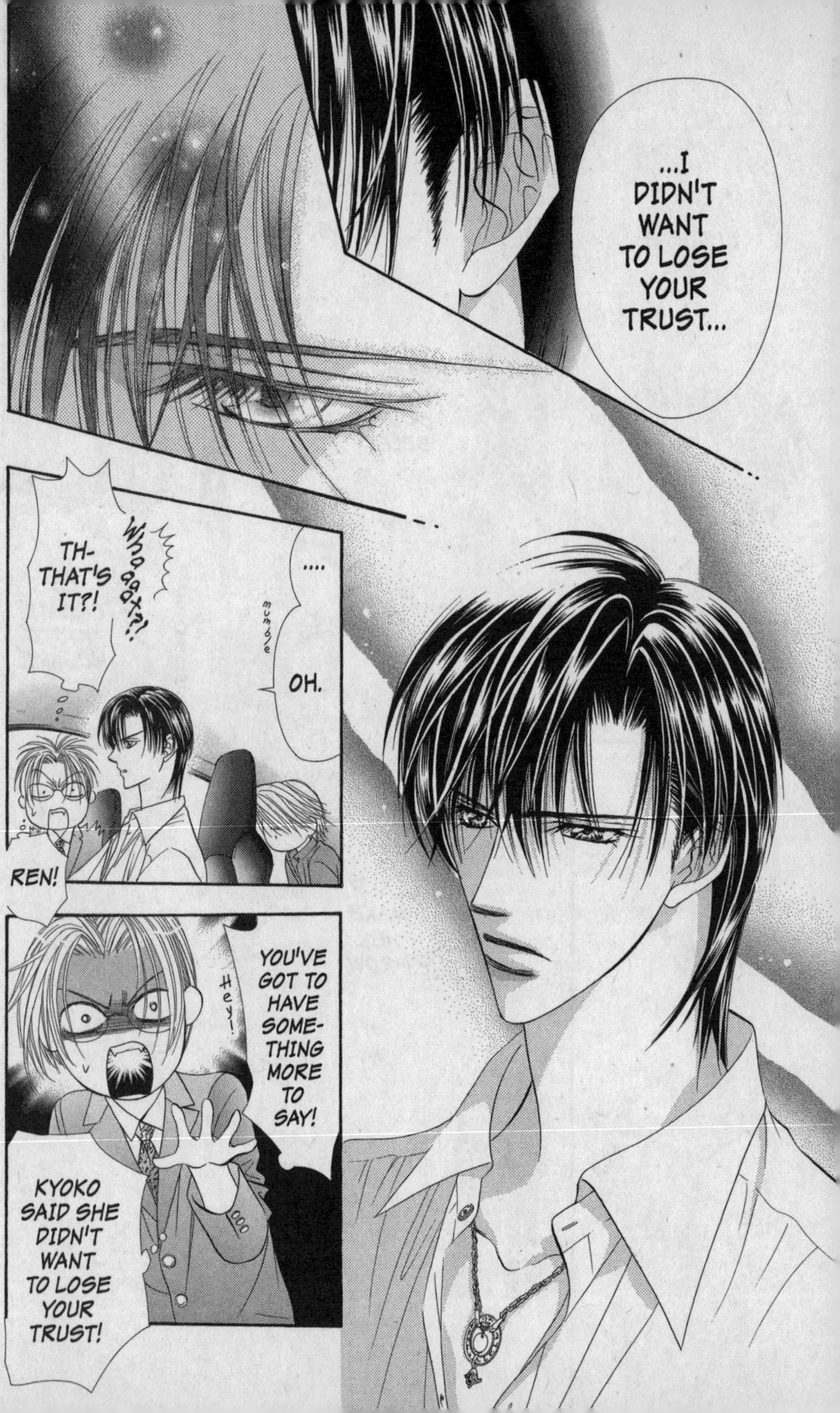
...I DIDN'T WANT TO LOSE YOUR TRUST...
....
mumble
OH.
TH-THAT'S IT?!
Whaaat?!
REN!
YOU'VE GOT TO HAVE SOMETHING MORE TO SAY!
Hey!
KYOKO SAID SHE DIDN'T WANT TO LOSE YOUR TRUST!

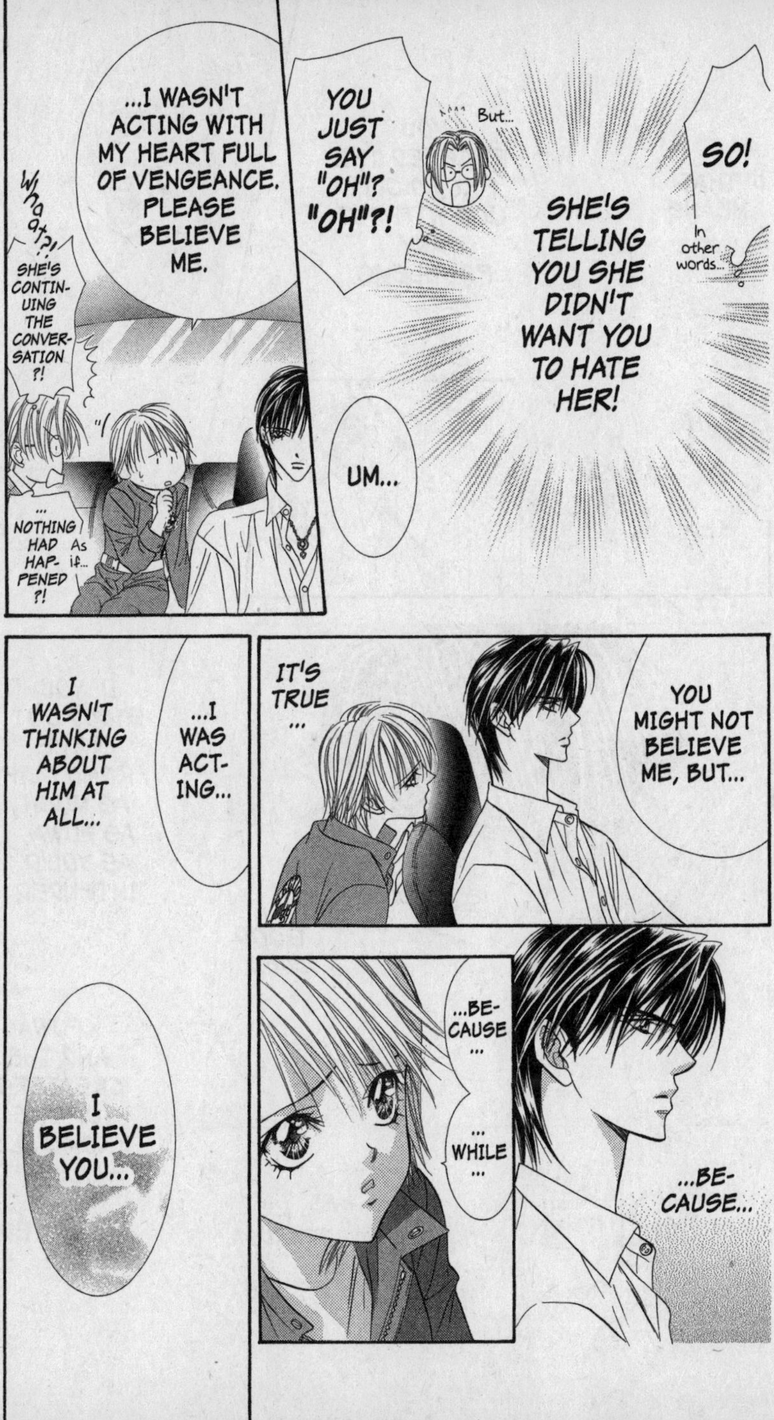
SO!
In other words...
SHE'S TELLING YOU SHE DIDN'T WANT YOU TO HATE HER!
But...
YOU JUST SAY "OH"? "OH"?!
UM...
...I WASN'T ACTING WITH MY HEART FULL OF VENGEANCE. PLEASE BELIEVE ME.
Whaat?!
SHE'S CONTINUING THE CONVERSATION?!
As if...
...NOTHING HAD HAPPENED?!
YOU MIGHT NOT BELIEVE ME, BUT...
IT'S TRUE...
...BECAUSE...
...BECAUSE...
...WHILE...
...I WAS ACTING...
I WASN'T THINKING ABOUT HIM AT ALL...
I BELIEVE YOU...

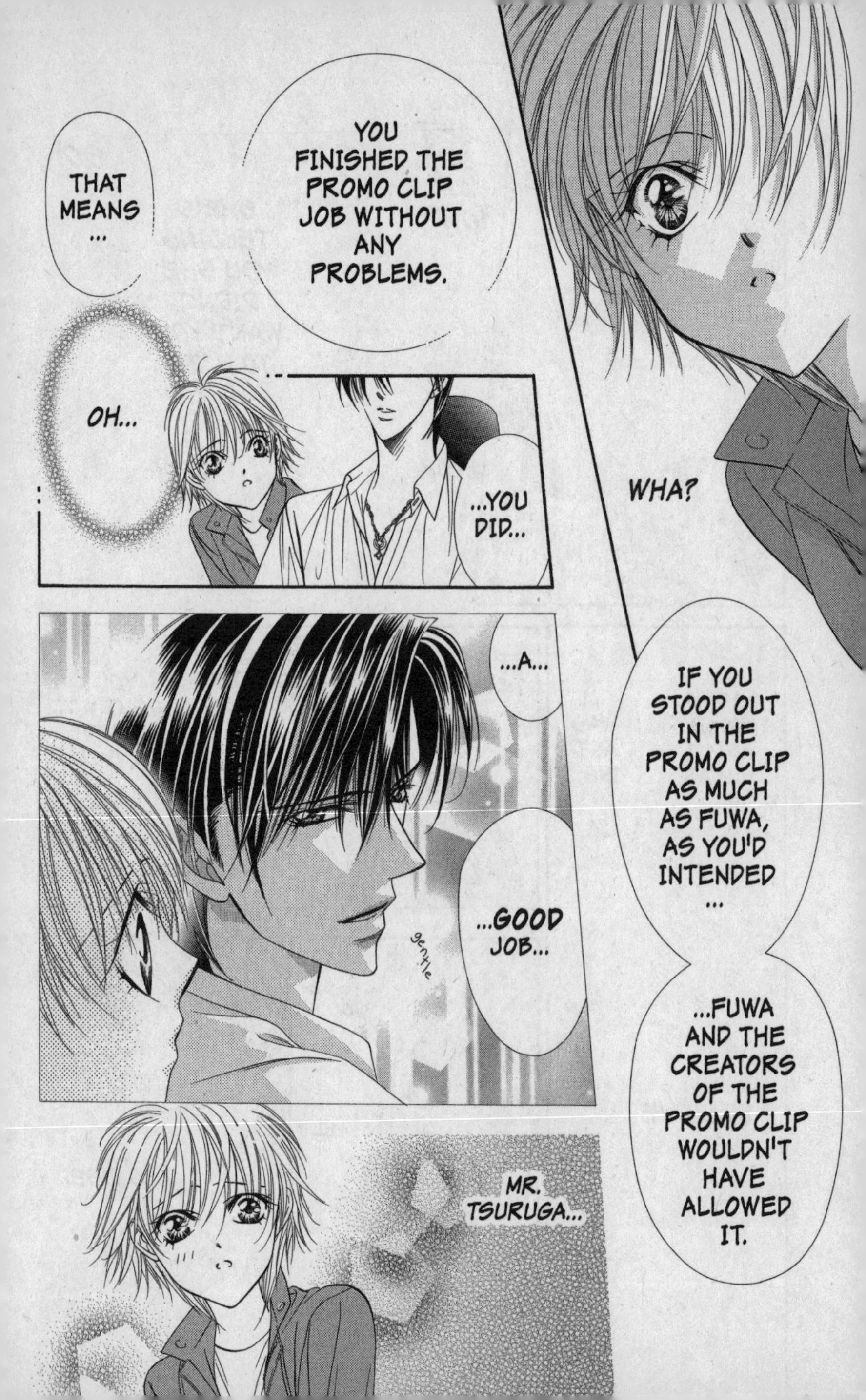
WHA?
IF YOU STOOD OUT IN THE PROMO CLIP AS MUCH AS FUWA, AS YOU'D INTENDED ...
...FUWA AND THE CREATORS OF THE PROMO CLIP WOULDN'T HAVE ALLOWED IT.
YOU FINISHED THE PROMO CLIP JOB WITHOUT ANY PROBLEMS.
THAT MEANS ...
...YOU DID...
OH...
...A...
...GOOD JOB...
gentle
MR. TSURUGA...

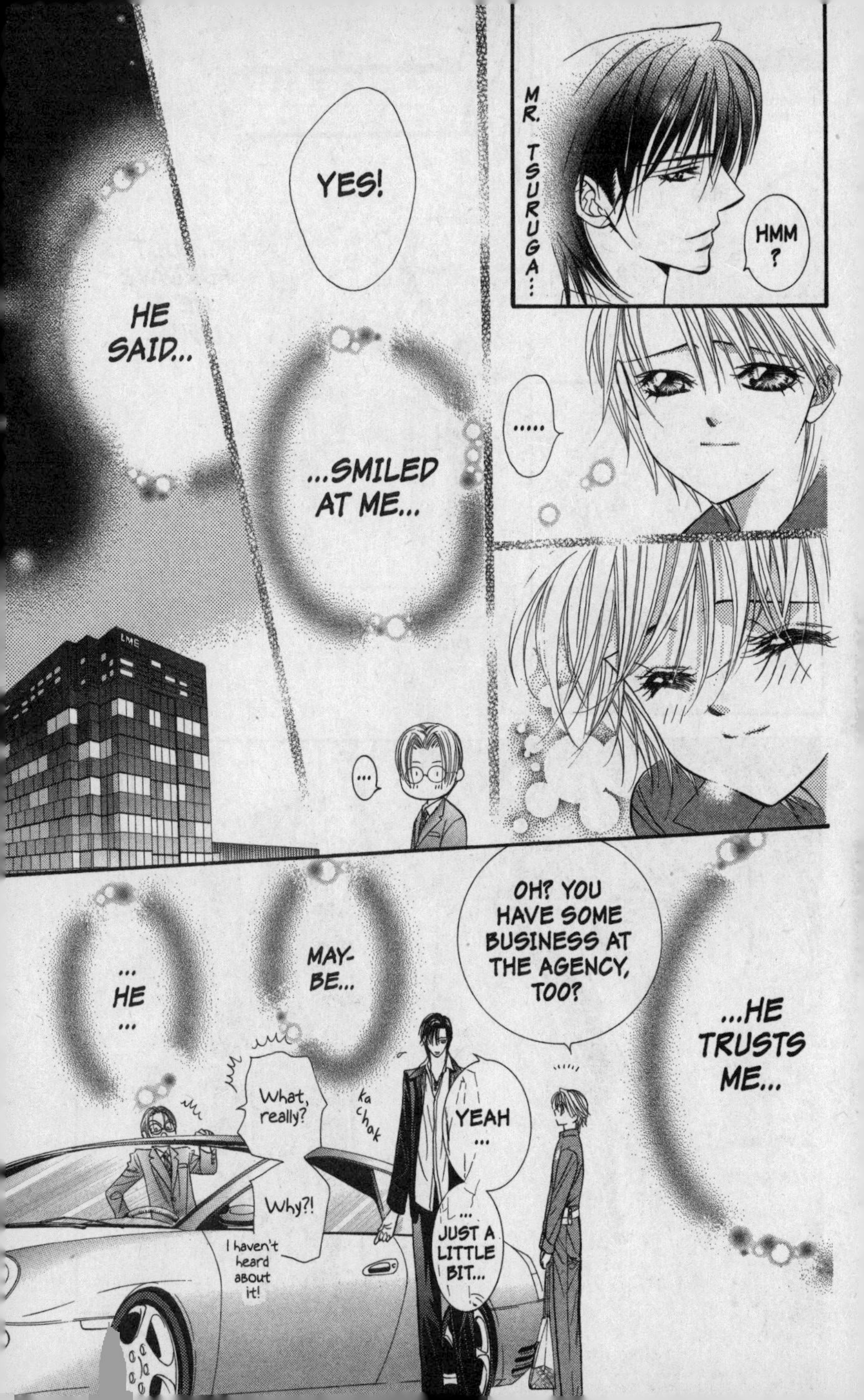
MR. TSURUGA...
HMM?
......
YES!
...SMILED AT ME...
....
HE SAID...
...HE TRUSTS ME...
OH? YOU HAVE SOME BUSINESS AT THE AGENCY, TOO?
YEAH...
...JUST A LITTLE BIT...
MAY-BE...
...HE...
What, really?
ka chak
Why?!
I haven't heard about it!

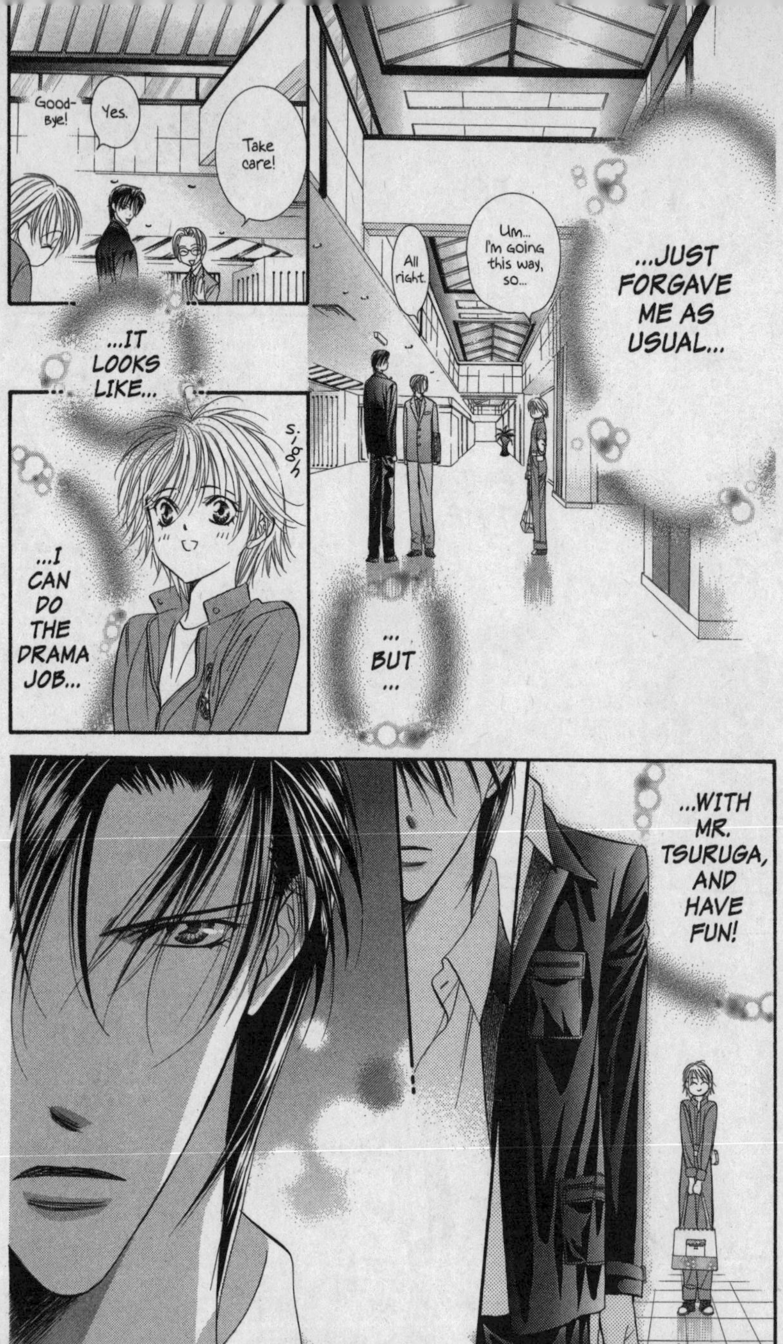
...JUST FORGAVE ME AS USUAL...
Um... I'm going this way, so...
All right.
... BUT ...
Take care!
Yes.
Good-bye!
...IT LOOKS LIKE...
sigh
...I CAN DO THE DRAMA JOB...
...WITH MR. TSURUGA, AND HAVE FUN!

End of Act 53

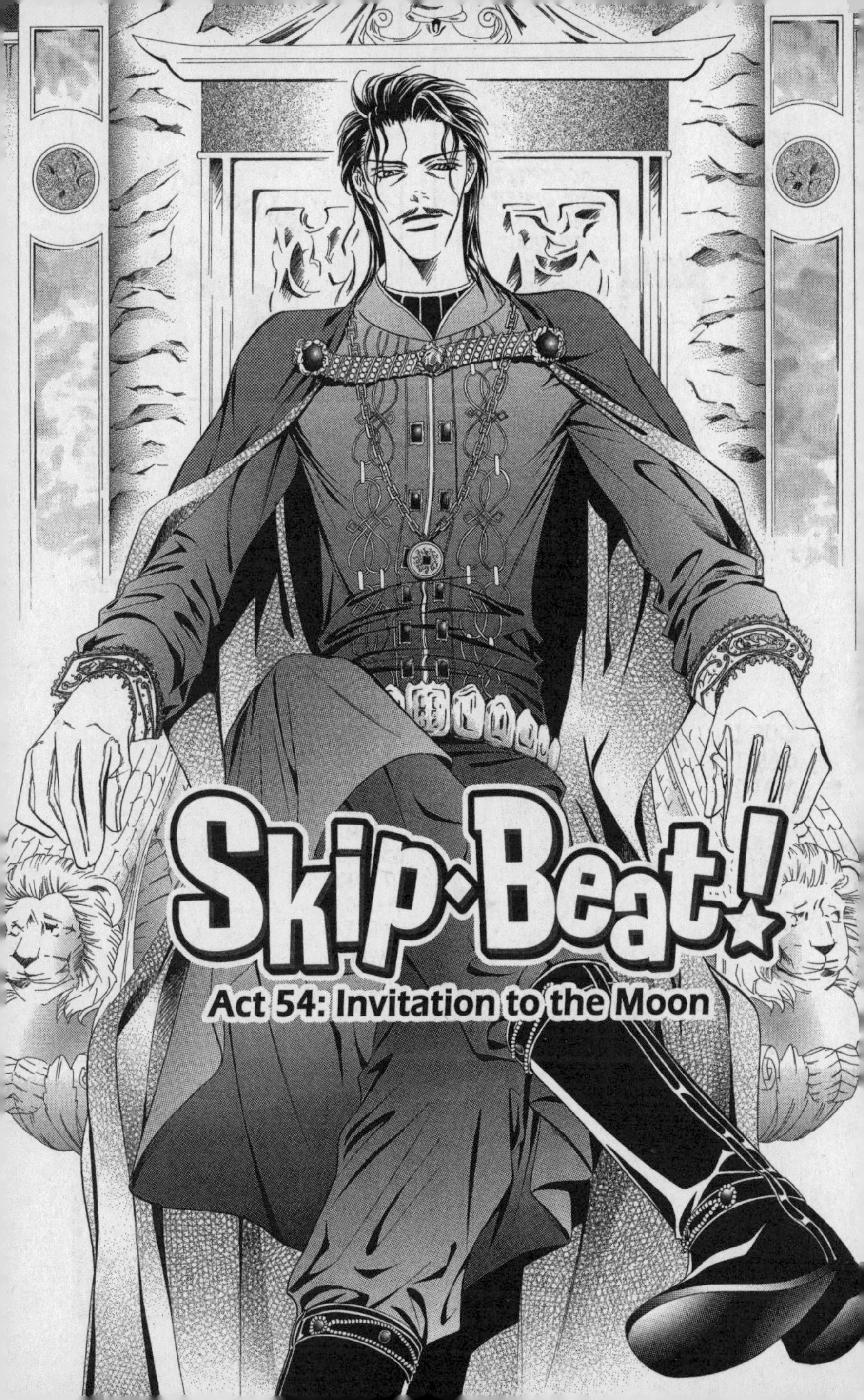
Skip·Beat!
Act 54: Invitation to the Moon

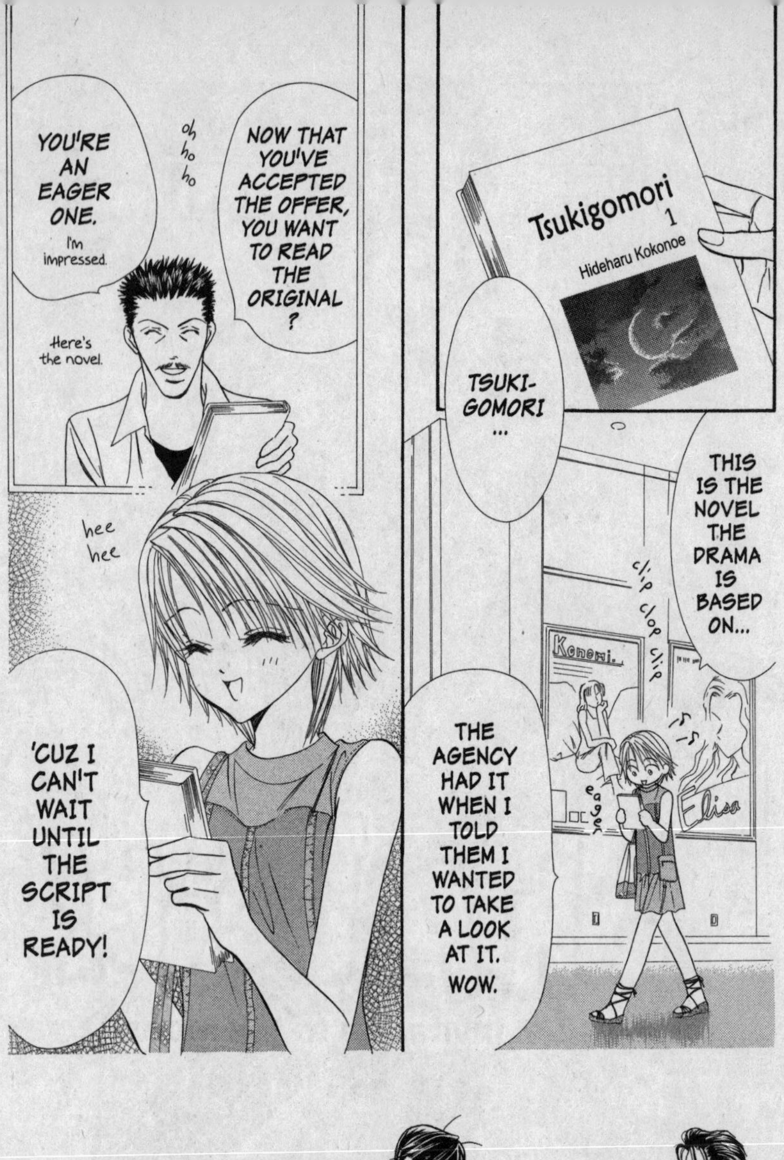
Tsukigomori 1
Hideharu Kokonoe
TSUKI-GOMORI ...
THIS IS THE NOVEL THE DRAMA IS BASED ON...
clip clop clip
Konomi.
Elisa
eager
THE AGENCY HAD IT WHEN I TOLD THEM I WANTED TO TAKE A LOOK AT IT.
WOW.
NOW THAT YOU'VE ACCEPTED THE OFFER, YOU WANT TO READ THE ORIGINAL ?
oh ho ho
YOU'RE AN EAGER ONE.
I'm impressed.
Here's the novel.
hee hee
'CUZ I CAN'T WAIT UNTIL THE SCRIPT IS READY!

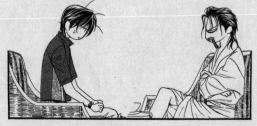

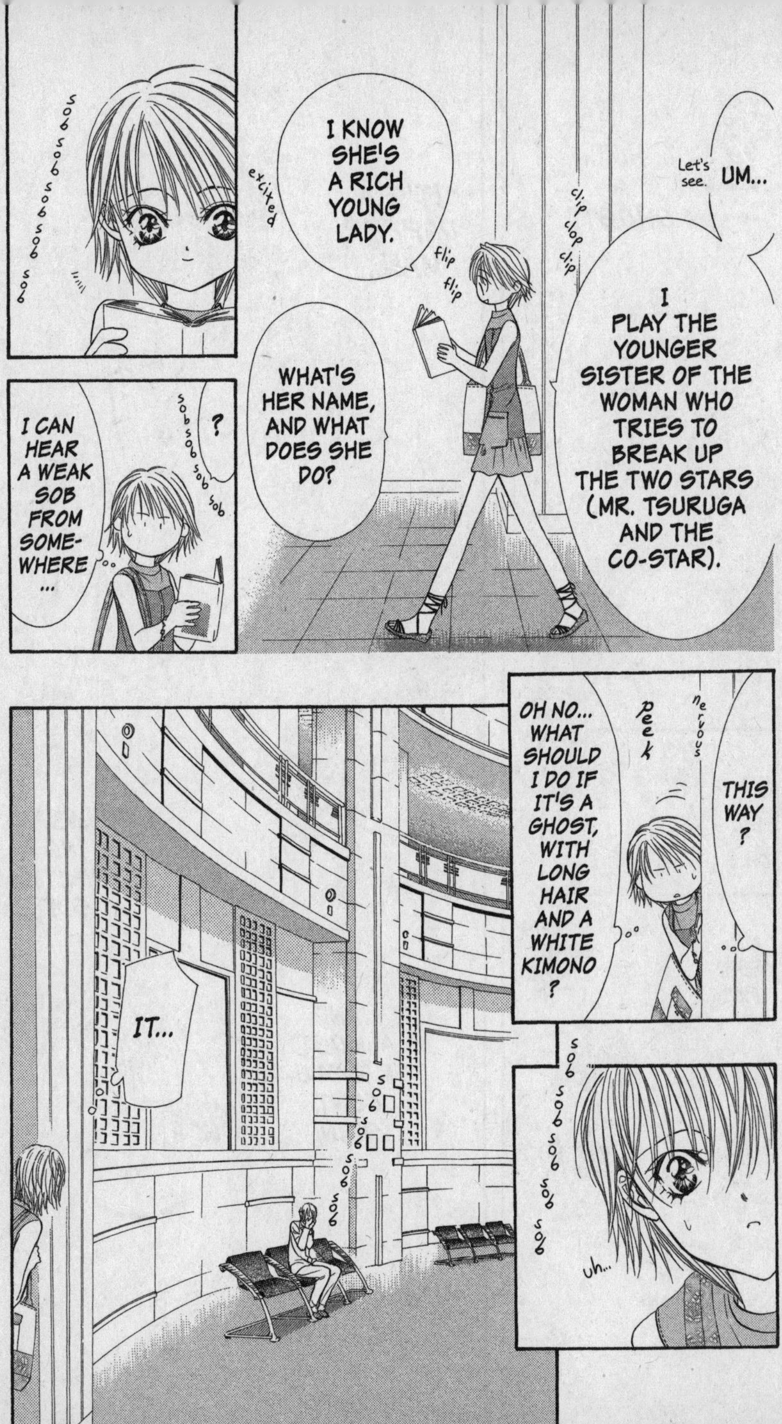
Let's see.
UM...
I PLAY THE YOUNGER SISTER OF THE WOMAN WHO TRIES TO BREAK UP THE TWO STARS (MR. TSURUGA AND THE CO-STAR).
clip clop clip
flip flip
I KNOW SHE'S A RICH YOUNG LADY.
excited
WHAT'S HER NAME, AND WHAT DOES SHE DO?
sob sob sob sob sob sob
?
sob sob sob sob
I CAN HEAR A WEAK SOB FROM SOME-WHERE...
THIS WAY?
nervous
peek
OH NO... WHAT SHOULD I DO IF IT'S A GHOST, WITH LONG HAIR AND A WHITE KIMONO?
sob sob sob sob sob
uh...
IT...
sob sob sob sob sob

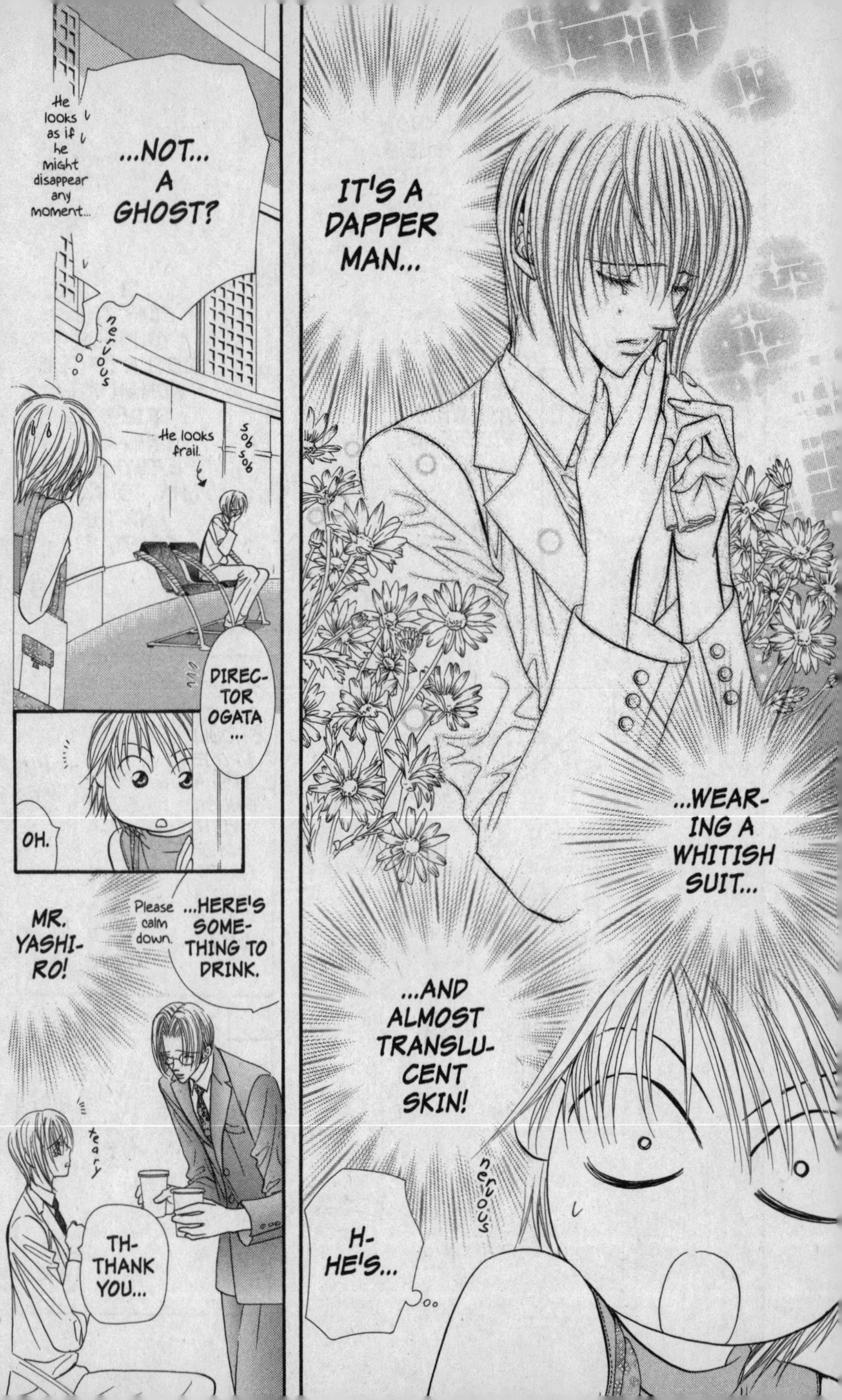
IT'S A DAPPER MAN...
...WEARING A WHITISH SUIT...
...AND ALMOST TRANSLUCENT SKIN!
nervous
H-HE'S...
...NOT... A GHOST?
He looks as if he might disappear any moment...
nervous
He looks frail.
sob sob
DIRECTOR OGATA...
OH.
MR. YASHIRO!
...HERE'S SOMETHING TO DRINK.
Please calm down.
teary
TH-THANK YOU...

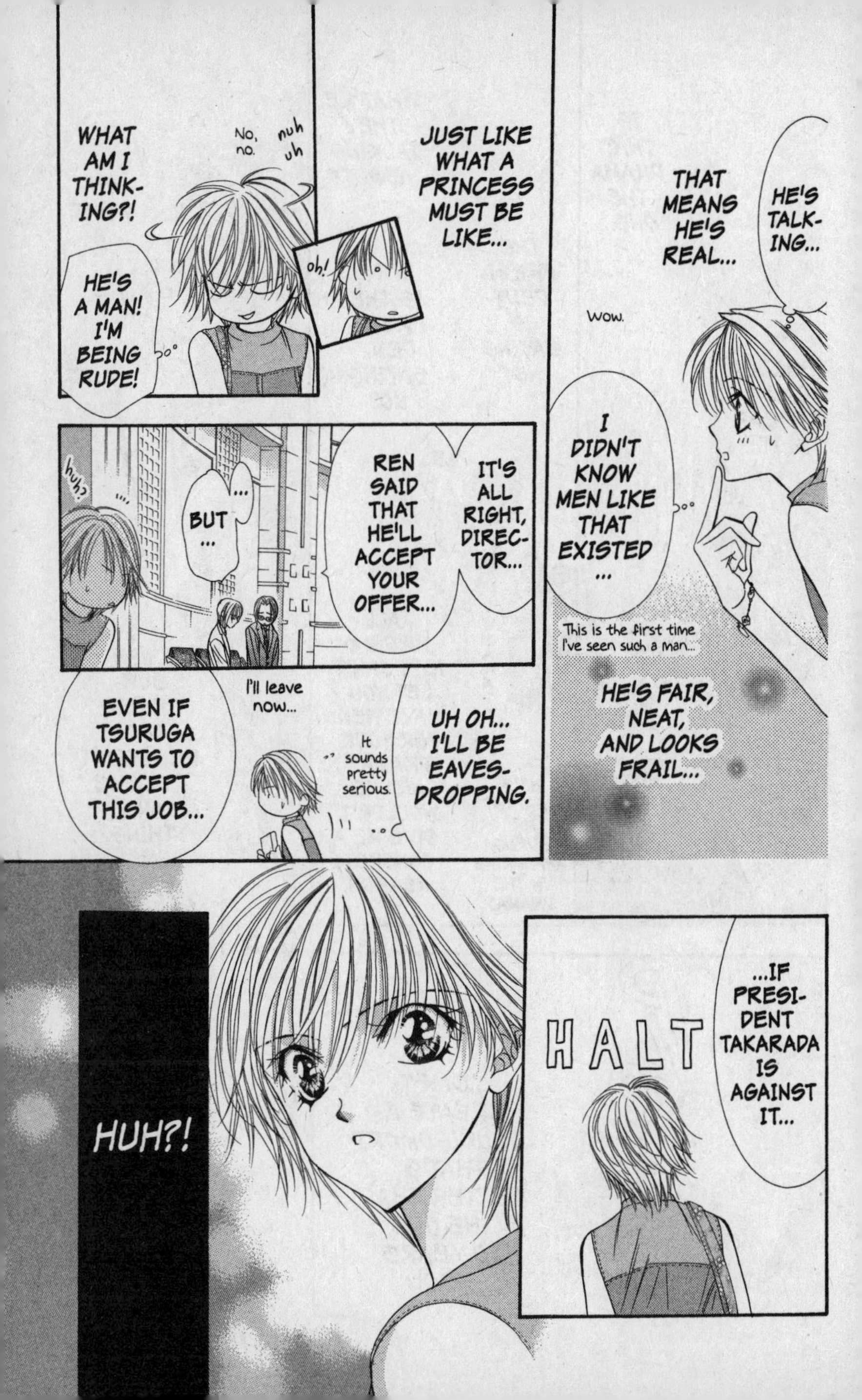
HE'S TALKING...
THAT MEANS HE'S REAL...
Wow.
I DIDN'T KNOW MEN LIKE THAT EXISTED...
This is the first time I've seen such a man...
HE'S FAIR, NEAT, AND LOOKS FRAIL...
JUST LIKE WHAT A PRINCESS MUST BE LIKE...
oh!
nuh uh
No, no.
WHAT AM I THINKING?!
HE'S A MAN! I'M BEING RUDE!
IT'S ALL RIGHT, DIRECTOR...
REN SAID THAT HE'LL ACCEPT YOUR OFFER...
...
BUT ...
huh?
UH OH... I'LL BE EAVESDROPPING.
It sounds pretty serious.
I'll leave now...
EVEN IF TSURUGA WANTS TO ACCEPT THIS JOB...
...IF PRESIDENT TAKARADA IS AGAINST IT...
HALT
HUH?!

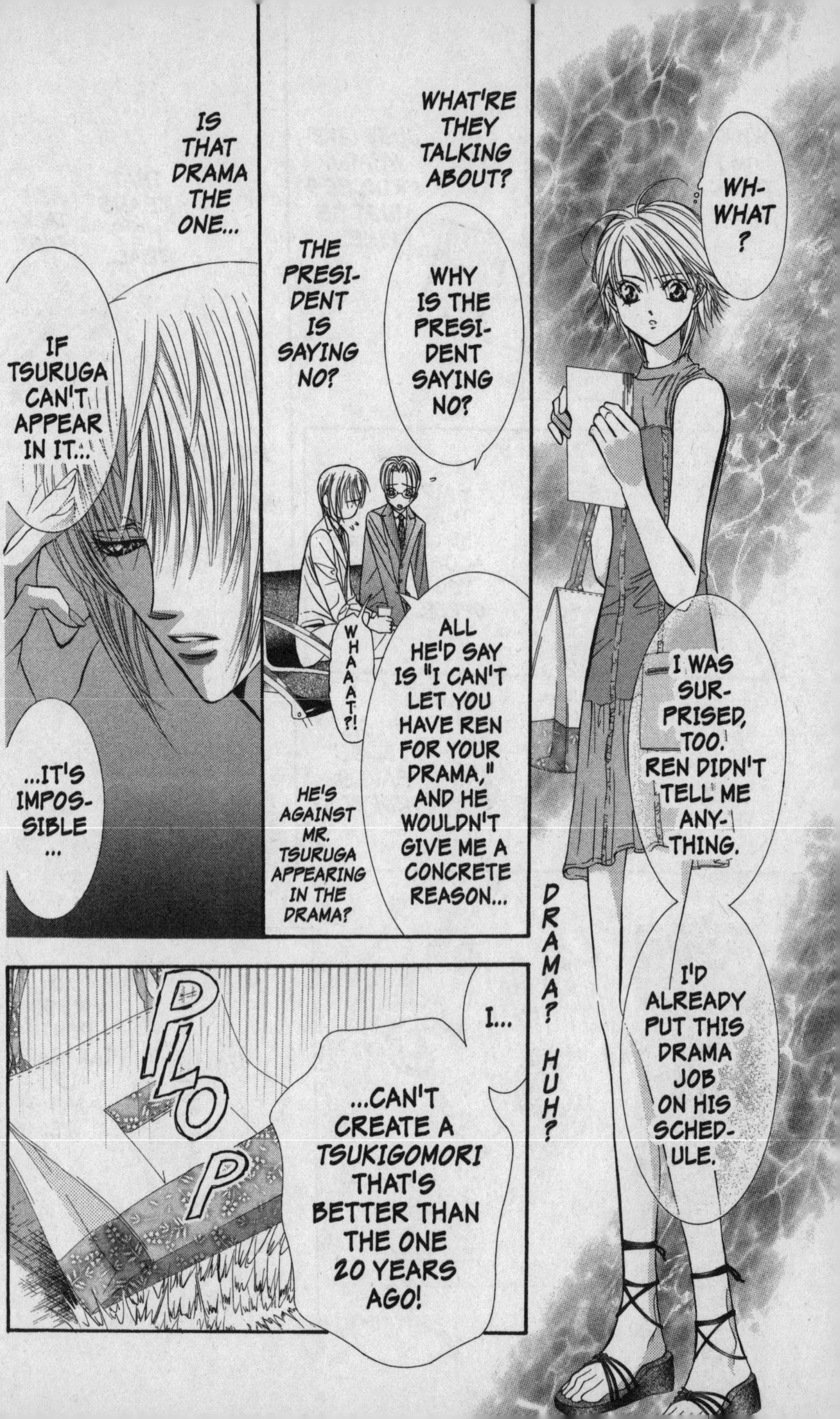
WH-WHAT?
I WAS SURPRISED, TOO. REN DIDN'T TELL ME ANYTHING.
I'D ALREADY PUT THIS DRAMA JOB ON HIS SCHEDULE.
DRAMA? HUH?
WHAT'RE THEY TALKING ABOUT?
WHY IS THE PRESIDENT SAYING NO?
THE PRESIDENT IS SAYING NO?
ALL HE'D SAY IS "I CAN'T LET YOU HAVE REN FOR YOUR DRAMA," AND HE WOULDN'T GIVE ME A CONCRETE REASON...
WHAAAAT?!
HE'S AGAINST MR. TSURUGA APPEARING IN THE DRAMA?
IS THAT DRAMA THE ONE...
IF TSURUGA CAN'T APPEAR IN IT...
...IT'S IMPOSSIBLE...
I...
...CAN'T CREATE A TSUKIGOMORI THAT'S BETTER THAN THE ONE 20 YEARS AGO!
PLOP

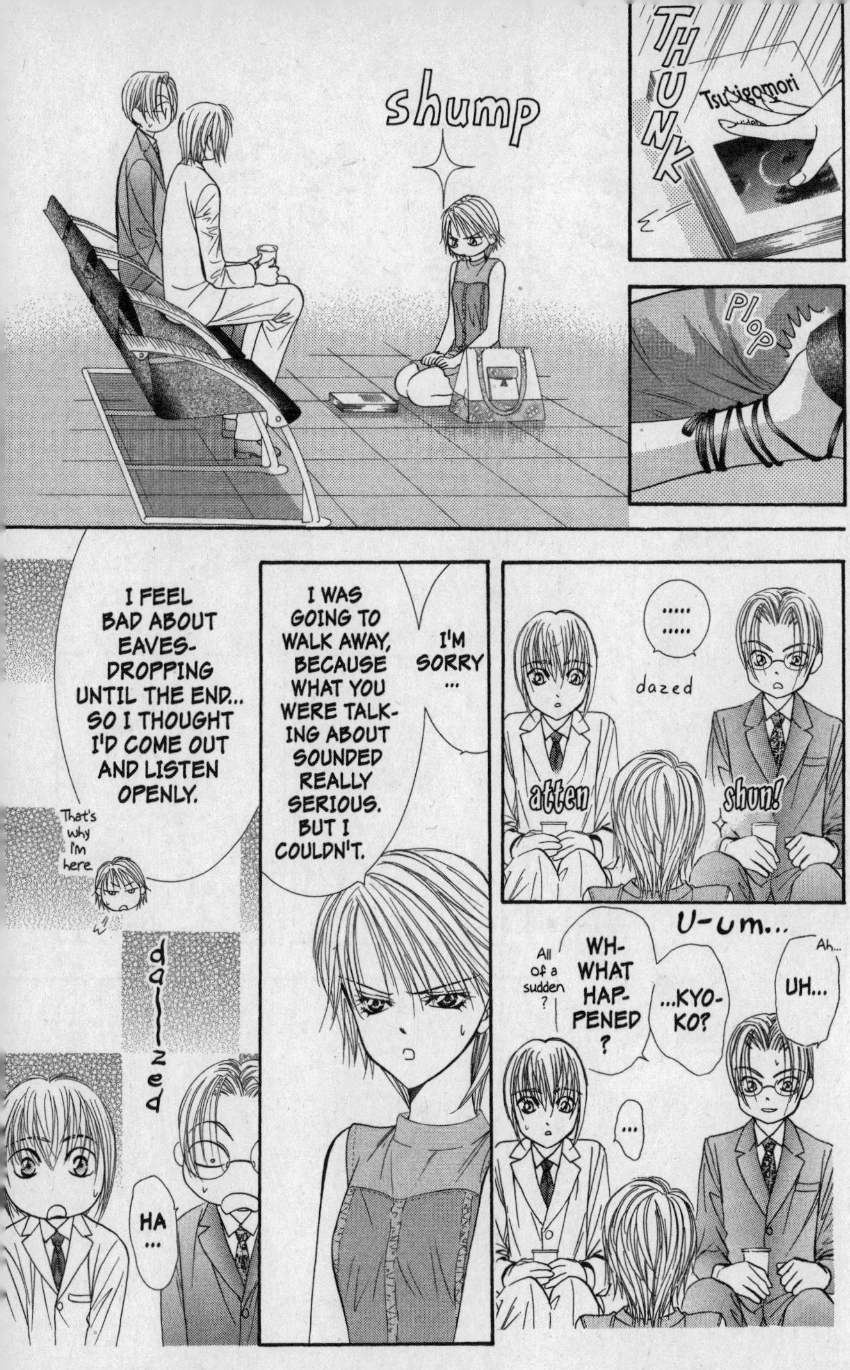
THUNK
Tsukigomori
PLOP
shump
.....
.....
dazed
atten
shun!
U-um...
Ah...
UH...
...KYO-KO?
WH-WHAT HAP-PENED?
All of a sudden?
...
I'M SORRY...
I WAS GOING TO WALK AWAY, BECAUSE WHAT YOU WERE TALK-ING ABOUT SOUNDED REALLY SERIOUS. BUT I COULDN'T.
I FEEL BAD ABOUT EAVES-DROPPING UNTIL THE END... SO I THOUGHT I'D COME OUT AND LISTEN OPENLY.
That's why I'm here
dazed
HA...

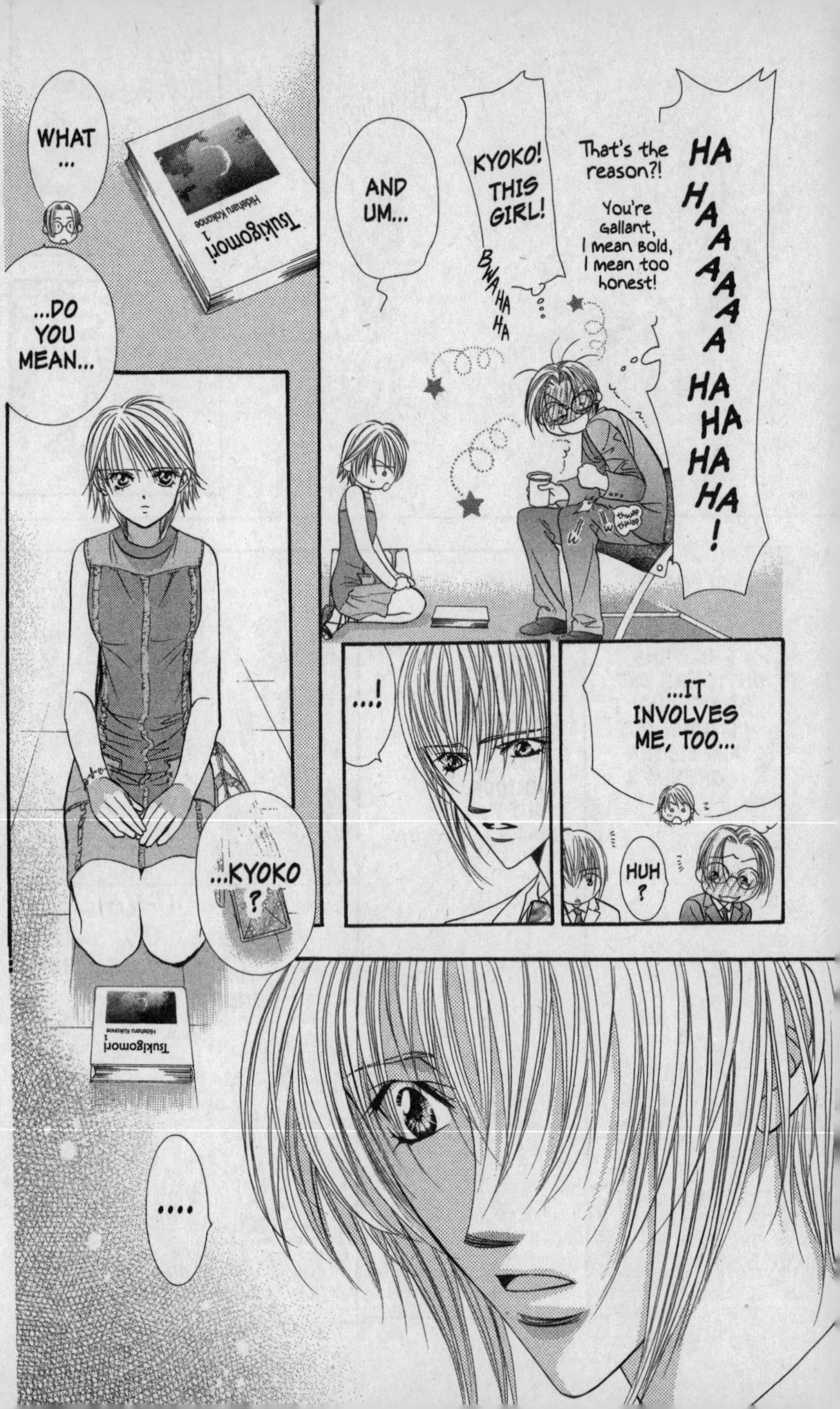
HA HAAAAAA HA HA HA HA!
That's the reason?!
You're gallant, I mean bold, I mean too honest!
KYOKO! THIS GIRL!
BWAHAHAHA
AND UM...
...IT INVOLVES ME, TOO...
HUH?
...!
WHAT...
Tsukigomori 1
Hidenaru Kokonoe
...DO YOU MEAN...
...KYOKO?
Tsukigomori 1
Hidenaru Kokonoe
....

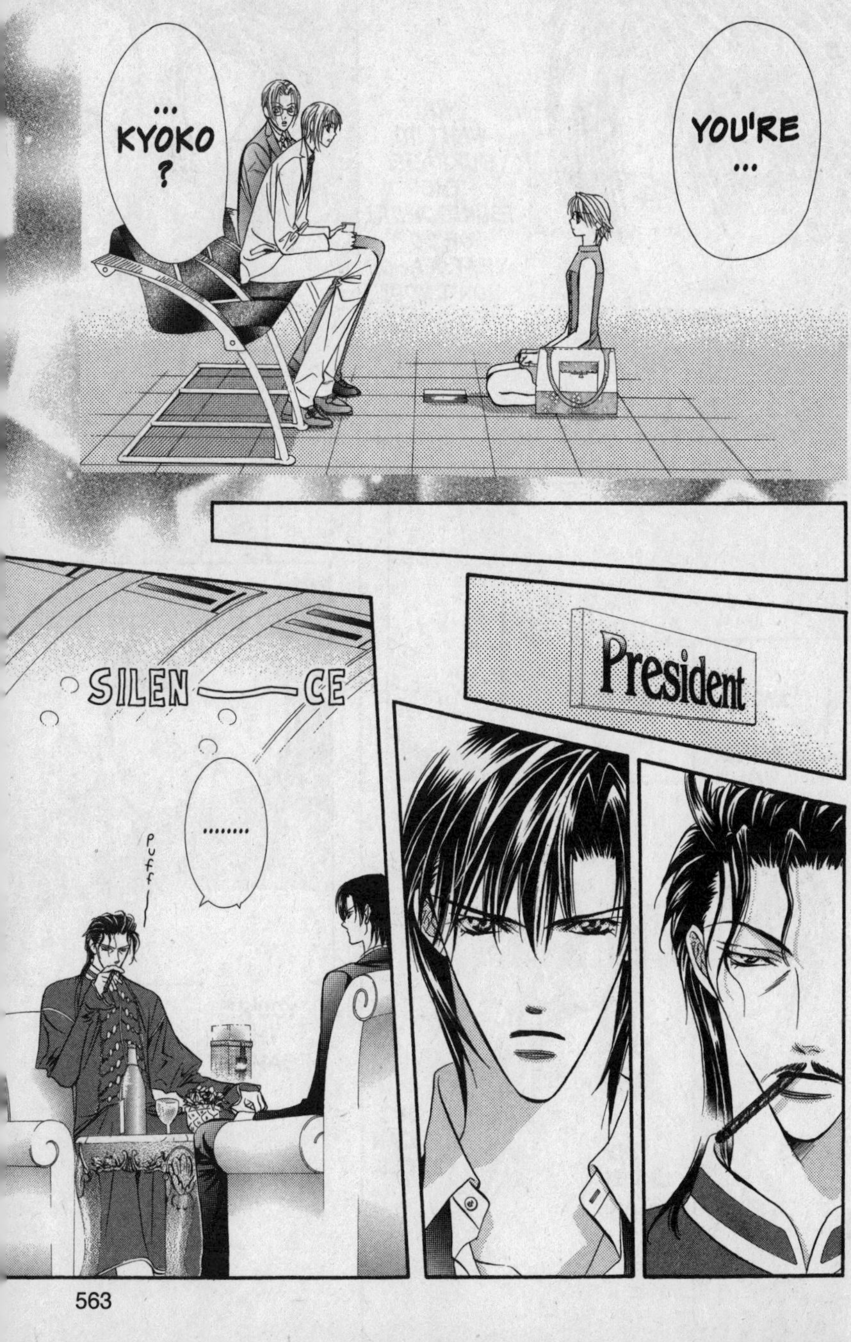
YOU'RE ...
... KYOKO ?
President
SILEN——CE
....
puff

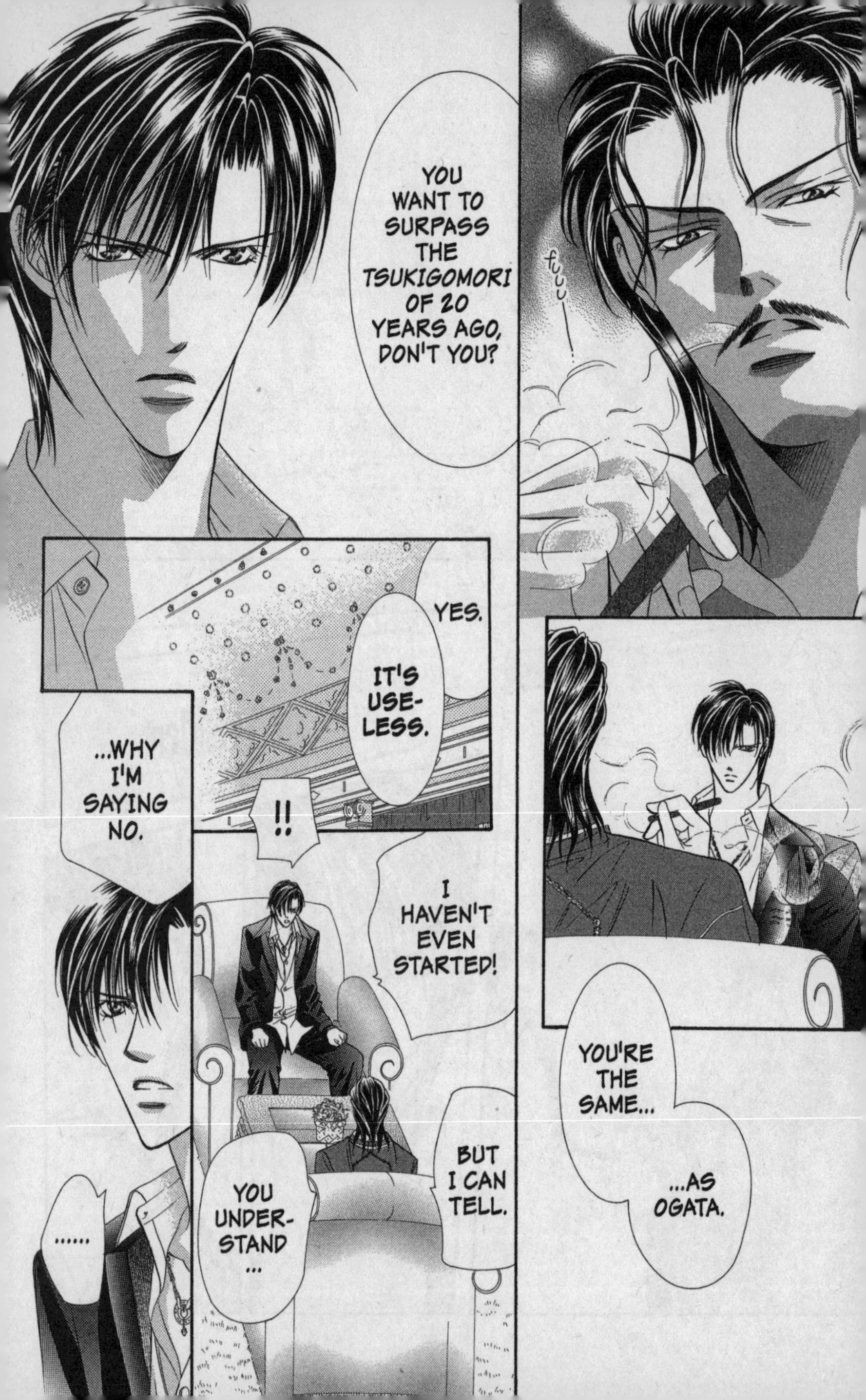

FUUU
YOU'RE THE SAME...
...AS OGATA.
YOU WANT TO SURPASS THE TSUKIGOMORI OF 20 YEARS AGO, DON'T YOU?
YES.
IT'S USE-LESS.
!!
I HAVEN'T EVEN STARTED!
BUT I CAN TELL.
YOU UNDER-STAND ...
...WHY I'M SAYING NO.
......

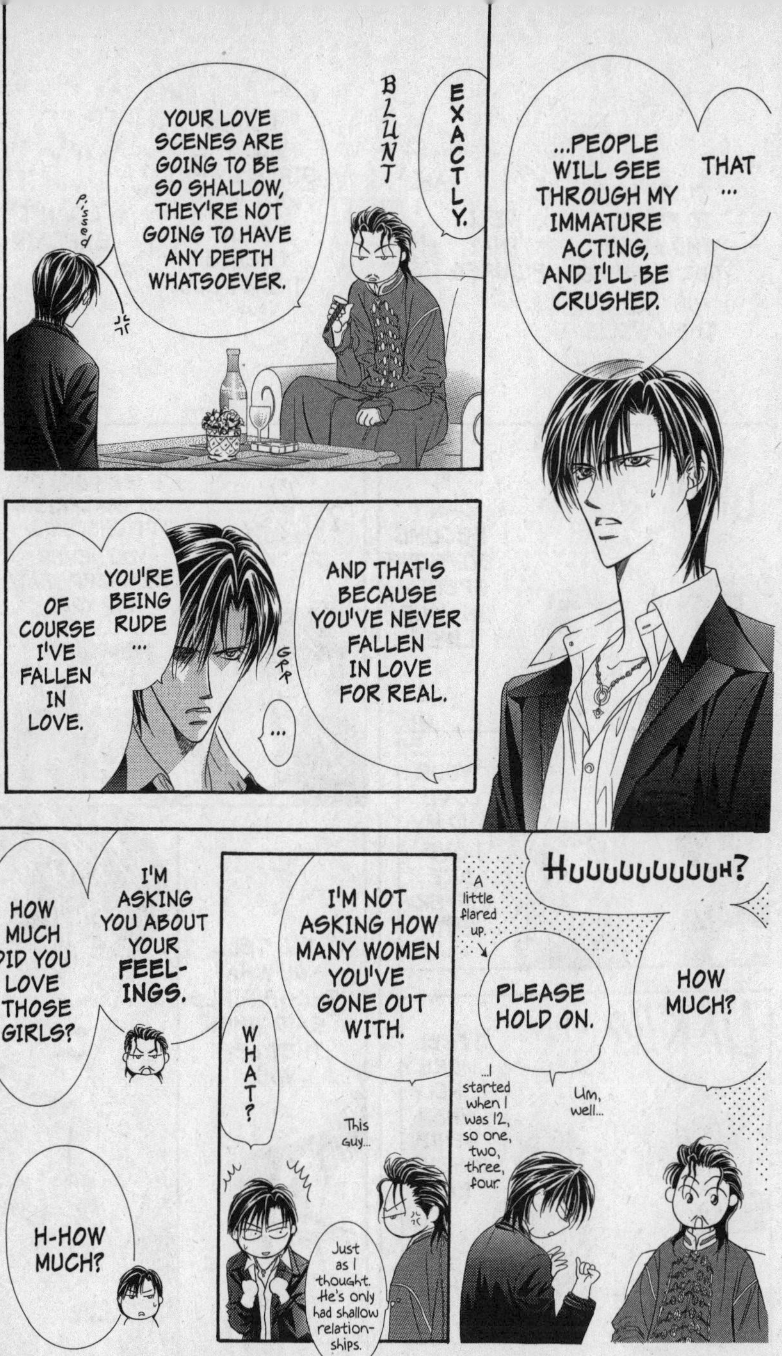
THAT ...
...PEOPLE WILL SEE THROUGH MY IMMATURE ACTING, AND I'LL BE CRUSHED.
EXACTLY.
BLUNT
YOUR LOVE SCENES ARE GOING TO BE SO SHALLOW, THEY'RE NOT GOING TO HAVE ANY DEPTH WHATSOEVER.
Pissed
AND THAT'S BECAUSE YOU'VE NEVER FALLEN IN LOVE FOR REAL.
...
GRR
YOU'RE BEING RUDE ...
OF COURSE I'VE FALLEN IN LOVE.
HUUUUUUUUUH?
HOW MUCH?
A little flared up.
PLEASE HOLD ON.
Um, well...
...I started when I was 12, so one, two, three, four.
I'M NOT ASKING HOW MANY WOMEN YOU'VE GONE OUT WITH.
WHAT?
This guy...
Just as I thought. He's only had shallow relation-ships.
I'M ASKING YOU ABOUT YOUR FEEL-INGS.
HOW MUCH DID YOU LOVE THOSE GIRLS?
H-HOW MUCH?

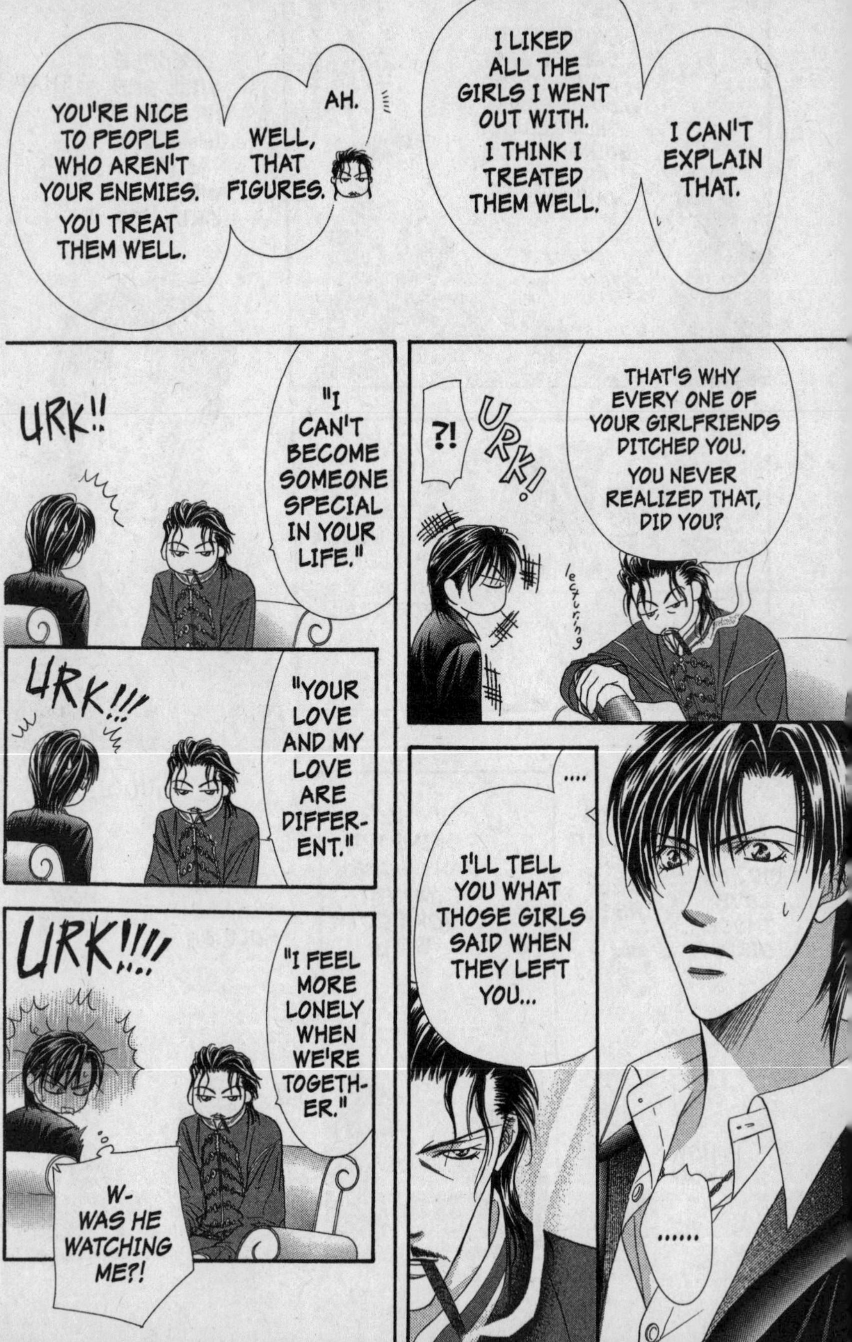

I CAN'T EXPLAIN THAT.
I LIKED ALL THE GIRLS I WENT OUT WITH.
I THINK I TREATED THEM WELL.
AH.
WELL, THAT FIGURES.
YOU'RE NICE TO PEOPLE WHO AREN'T YOUR ENEMIES.
YOU TREAT THEM WELL.
THAT'S WHY EVERY ONE OF YOUR GIRLFRIENDS DITCHED YOU.
YOU NEVER REALIZED THAT, DID YOU?
URK!
?!
lecturing
....
I'LL TELL YOU WHAT THOSE GIRLS SAID WHEN THEY LEFT YOU...
......
"I CAN'T BECOME SOMEONE SPECIAL IN YOUR LIFE."
URK!!
"YOUR LOVE AND MY LOVE ARE DIFFER-ENT."
URK!!!
"I FEEL MORE LONELY WHEN WE'RE TOGETH-ER."
URK!!!!
W-WAS HE WATCHING ME?!

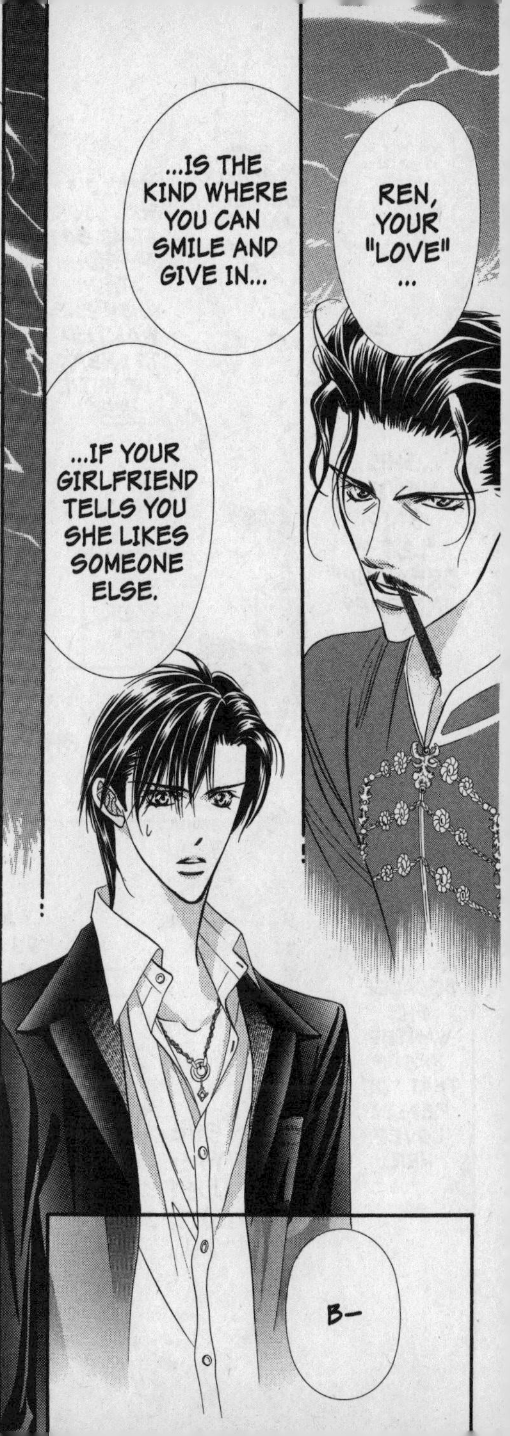
REN, YOUR "LOVE" ...
...IS THE KIND WHERE YOU CAN SMILE AND GIVE IN...
...IF YOUR GIRLFRIEND TELLS YOU SHE LIKES SOMEONE ELSE.
B—

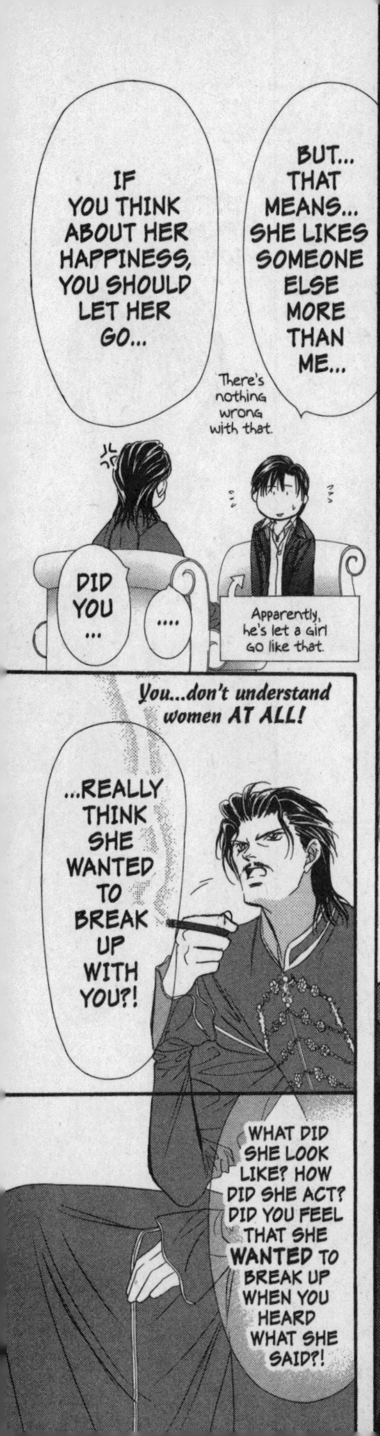
BUT... THAT MEANS... SHE LIKES SOMEONE ELSE MORE THAN ME...
IF YOU THINK ABOUT HER HAPPINESS, YOU SHOULD LET HER GO...
There's nothing wrong with that.
Apparently, he's let a girl go like that.
....
DID YOU ...
You...don't understand women AT ALL!
...REALLY THINK SHE WANTED TO BREAK UP WITH YOU?!
WHAT DID SHE LOOK LIKE? HOW DID SHE ACT? DID YOU FEEL THAT SHE WANTED TO BREAK UP WHEN YOU HEARD WHAT SHE SAID?!

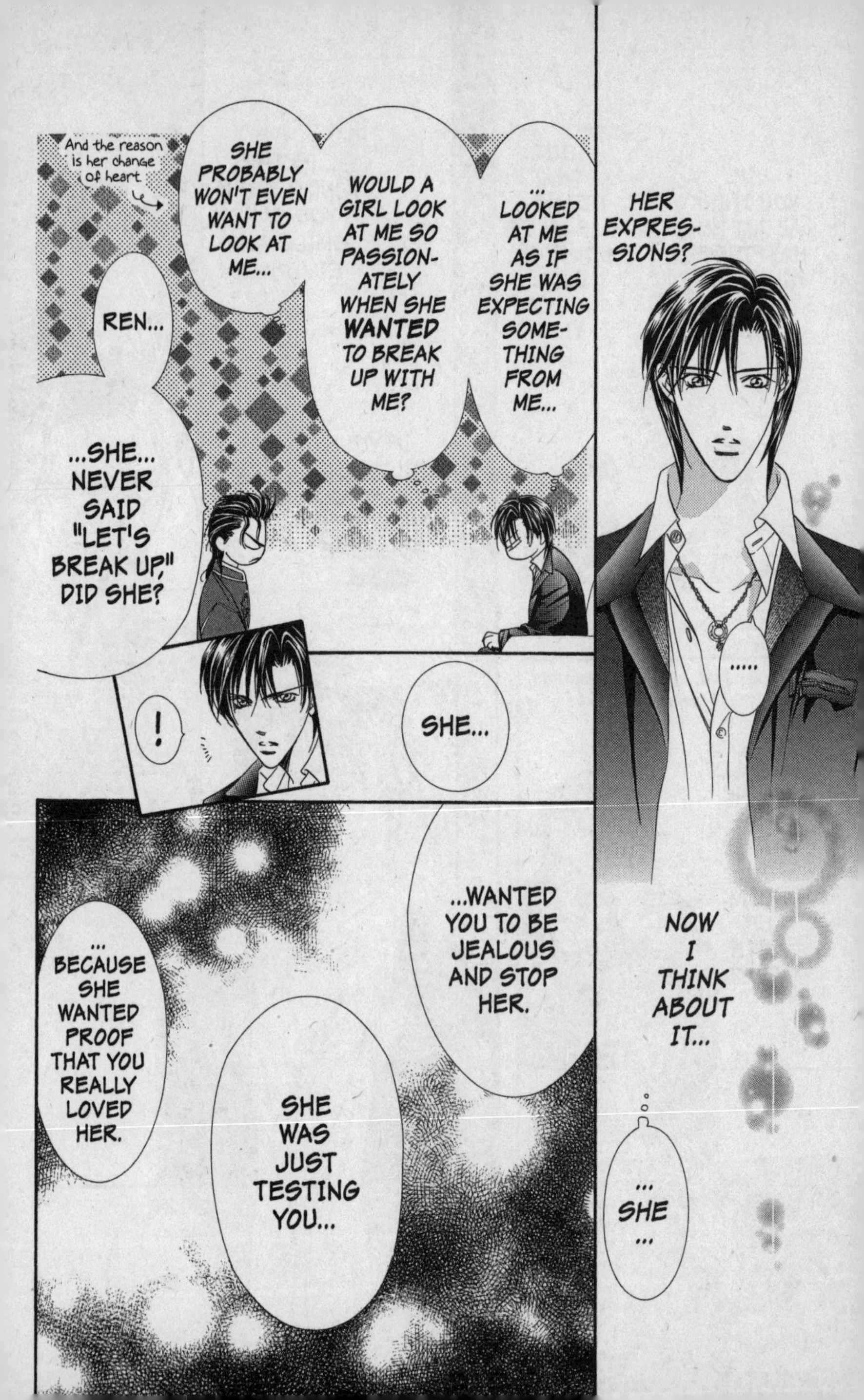
HER EXPRESSIONS?
.....
NOW I THINK ABOUT IT...
...SHE...
...LOOKED AT ME AS IF SHE WAS EXPECTING SOMETHING FROM ME...
WOULD A GIRL LOOK AT ME SO PASSIONATELY WHEN SHE WANTED TO BREAK UP WITH ME?
SHE PROBABLY WON'T EVEN WANT TO LOOK AT ME...
And the reason is her change of heart.
REN...
...SHE... NEVER SAID "LET'S BREAK UP," DID SHE?
SHE...
!
...WANTED YOU TO BE JEALOUS AND STOP HER.
SHE WAS JUST TESTING YOU...
...BECAUSE SHE WANTED PROOF THAT YOU REALLY LOVED HER.

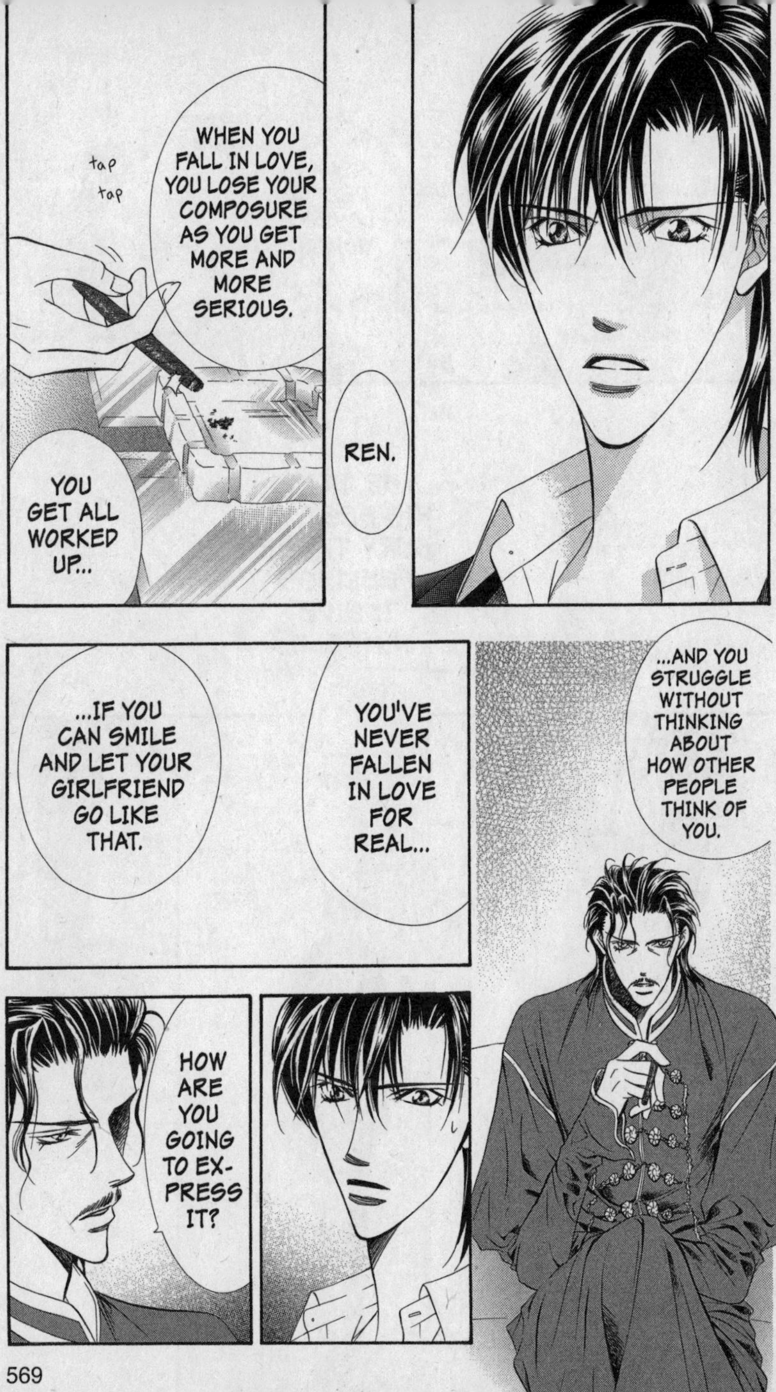
REN.
WHEN YOU FALL IN LOVE, YOU LOSE YOUR COMPOSURE AS YOU GET MORE AND MORE SERIOUS.
tap
tap
YOU GET ALL WORKED UP...
...AND YOU STRUGGLE WITHOUT THINKING ABOUT HOW OTHER PEOPLE THINK OF YOU.
YOU'VE NEVER FALLEN IN LOVE FOR REAL...
...IF YOU CAN SMILE AND LET YOUR GIRLFRIEND GO LIKE THAT.
HOW ARE YOU GOING TO EX-PRESS IT?

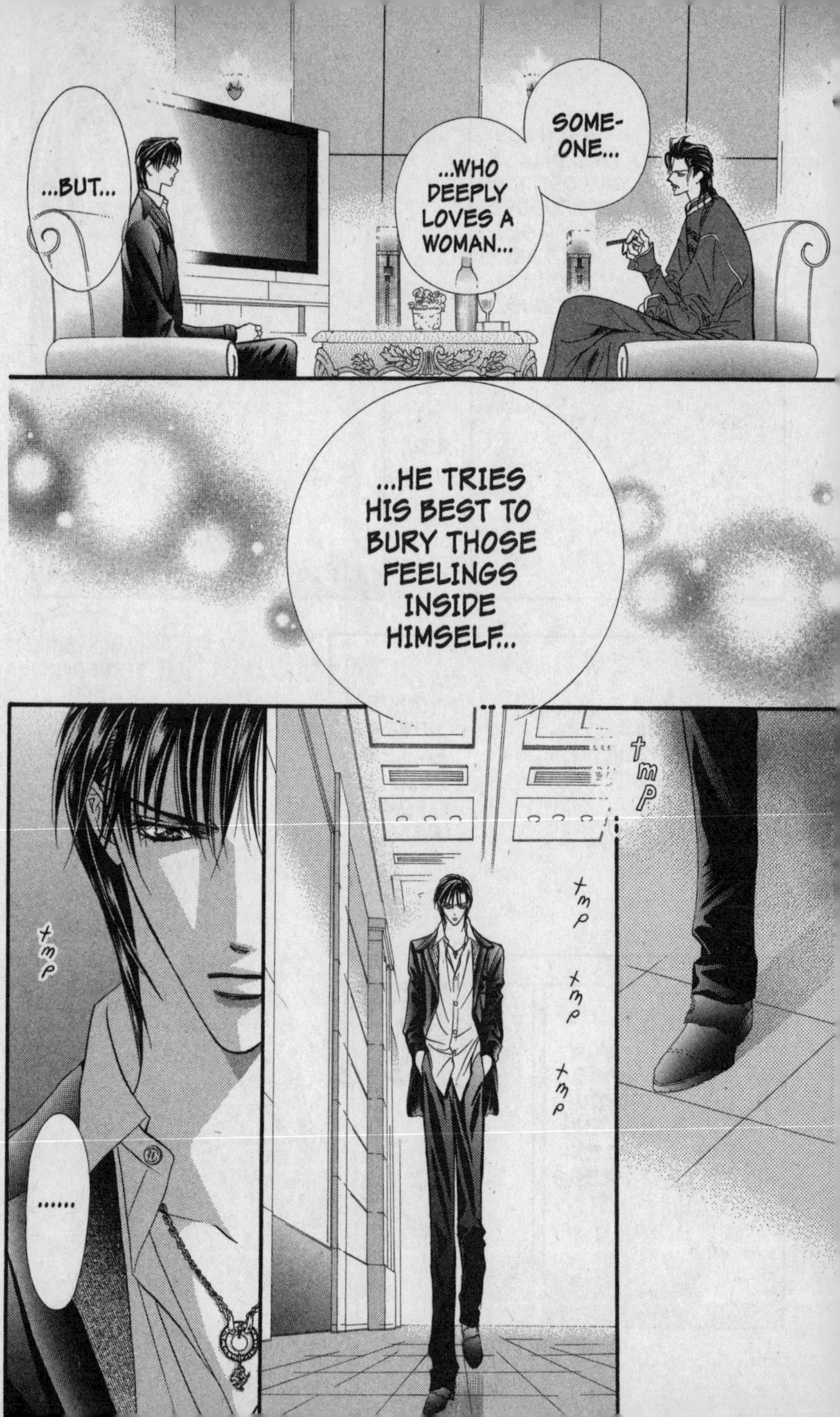
SOME-ONE...
...WHO DEEPLY LOVES A WOMAN...
...BUT...
...HE TRIES HIS BEST TO BURY THOSE FEELINGS INSIDE HIMSELF...
tmp
tmp
tmp
tmp
tmp
......

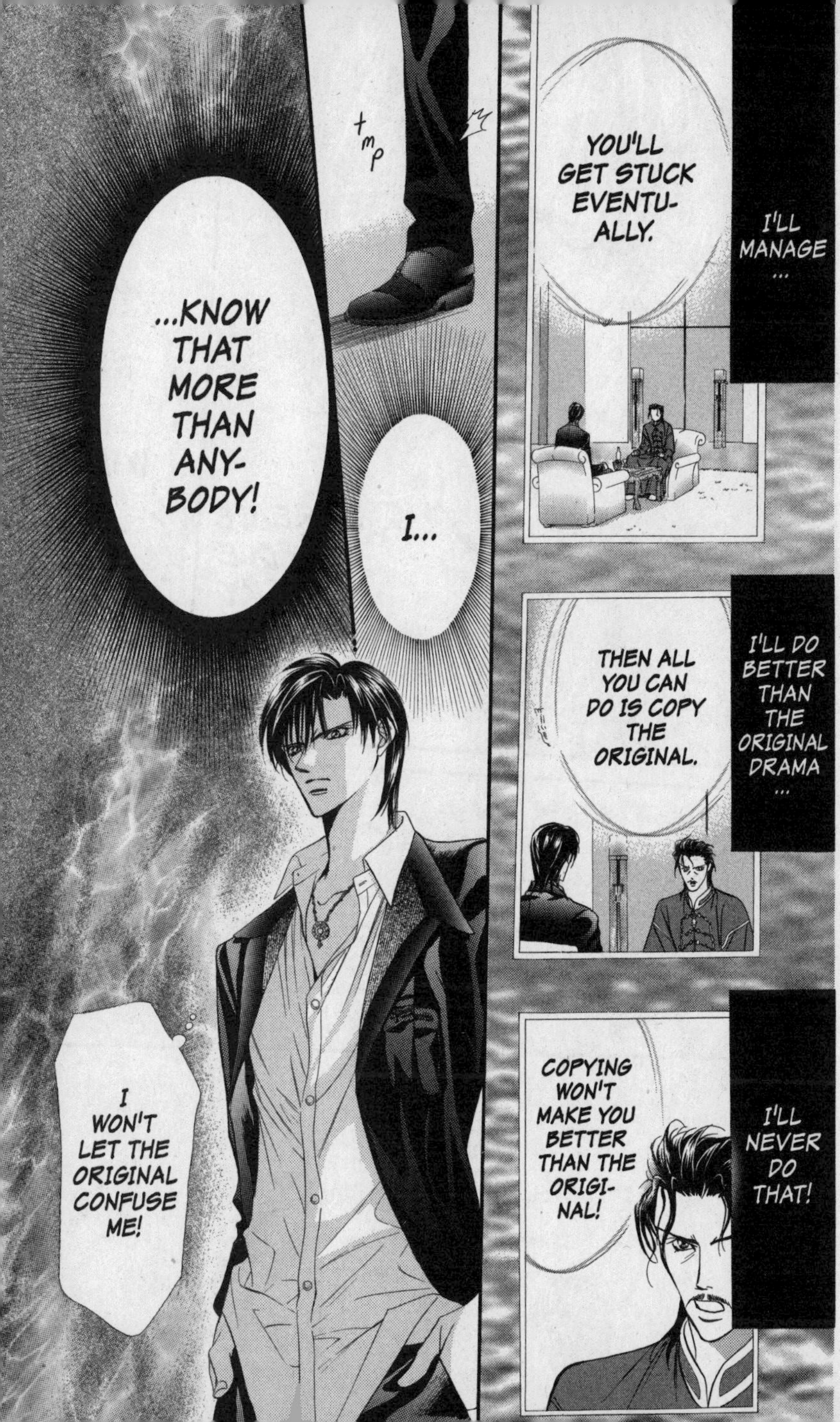
I'LL MANAGE ...
YOU'LL GET STUCK EVENTU-ALLY.
I'LL DO BETTER THAN THE ORIGINAL DRAMA ...
THEN ALL YOU CAN DO IS COPY THE ORIGINAL.
I'LL NEVER DO THAT!
COPYING WON'T MAKE YOU BETTER THAN THE ORIGI-NAL!
tmp
I...
...KNOW THAT MORE THAN ANY-BODY!
I WON'T LET THE ORIGINAL CONFUSE ME!

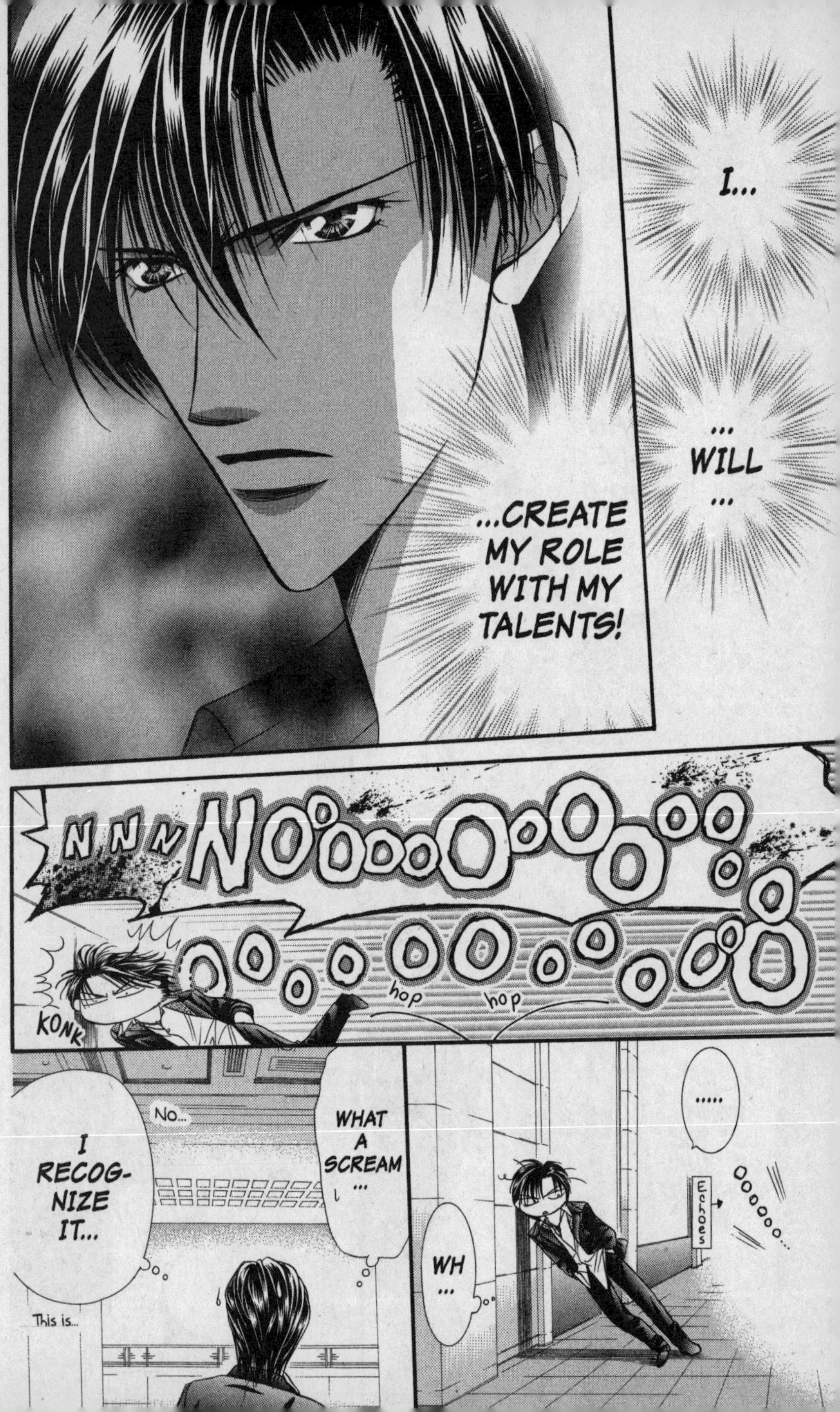
I...
... WILL ...
...CREATE MY ROLE WITH MY TALENTS!
NNNNOOOOOOOOOOOOOOOOOOOOOO
hop
hop
KONK
.....
OOOOOO...
Echoes
WH ...
WHAT A SCREAM ...
No...
I RECOGNIZE IT...
This is...

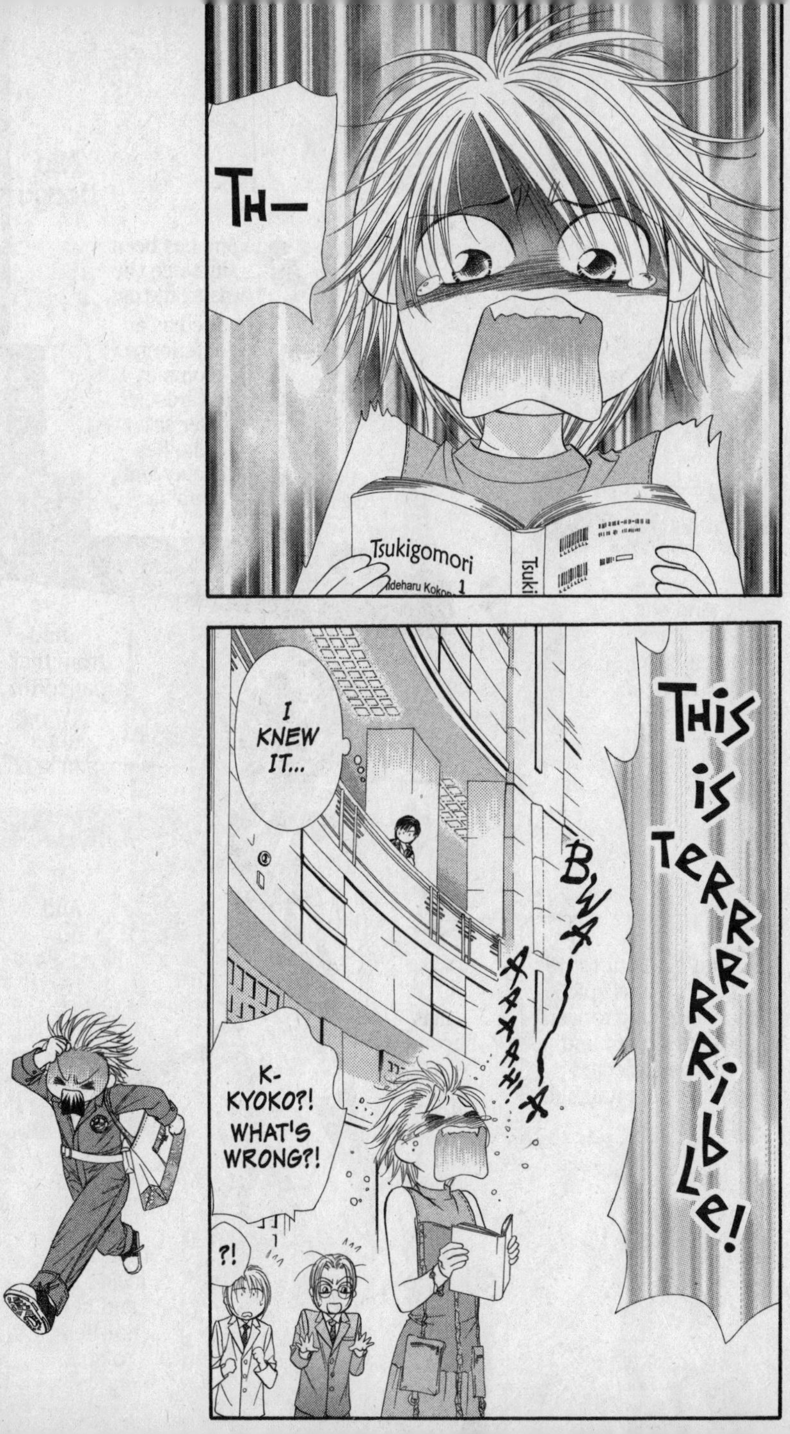
TH—
Tsukigomori
THIS IS TERRRRRIBLE!
BWA—AAAAAAH!
I KNEW IT...
K-KYOKO?! WHAT'S WRONG?!
?!

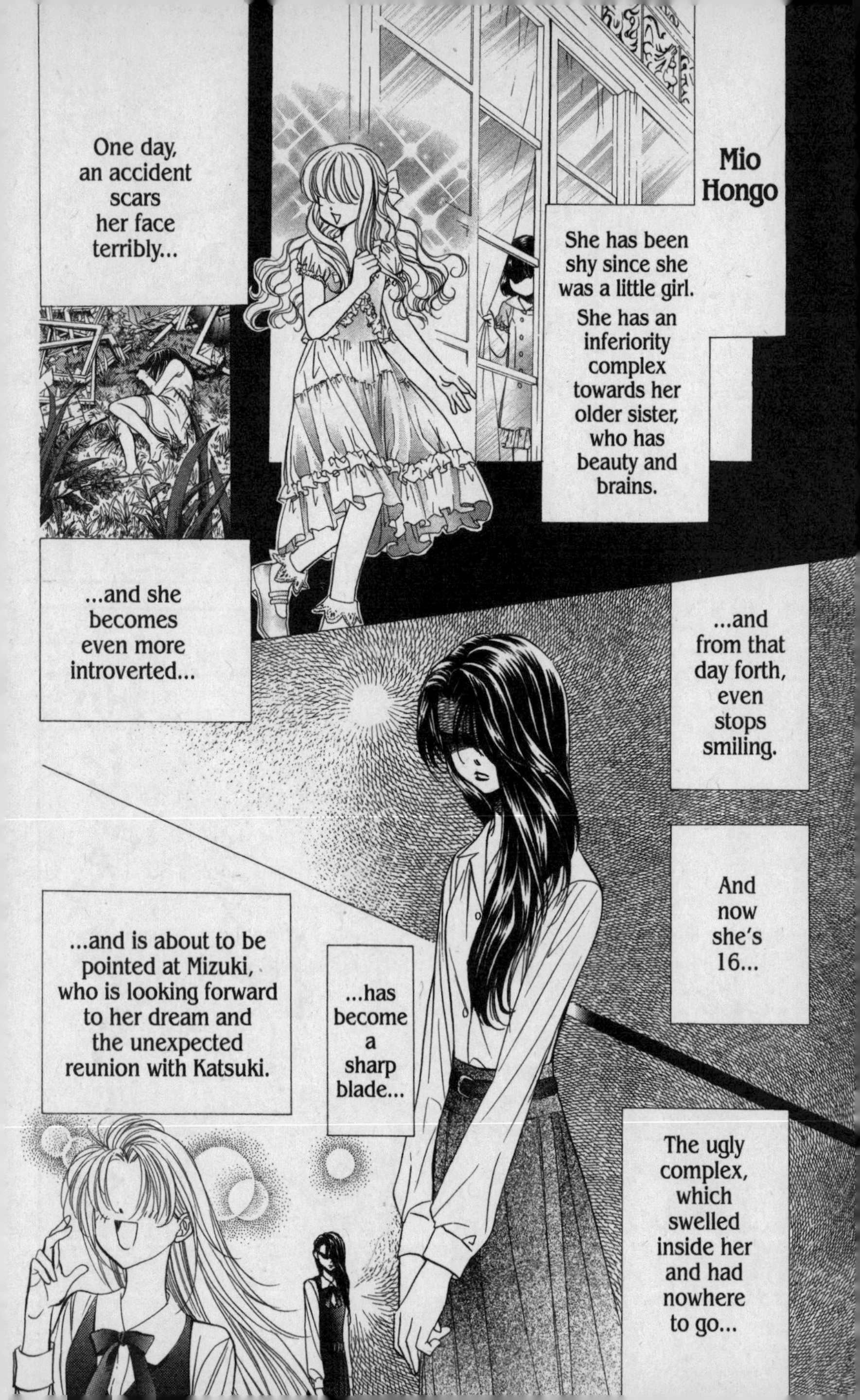
Mio Hongo
She has been shy since she was a little girl.
She has an inferiority complex towards her older sister, who has beauty and brains.
One day, an accident scars her face terribly...
...and she becomes even more introverted...
...and from that day forth, even stops smiling.
And now she's 16...
The ugly complex, which swelled inside her and had nowhere to go...
...has become a sharp blade...
...and is about to be pointed at Mizuki, who is looking forward to her dream and the unexpected reunion with Katsuki.

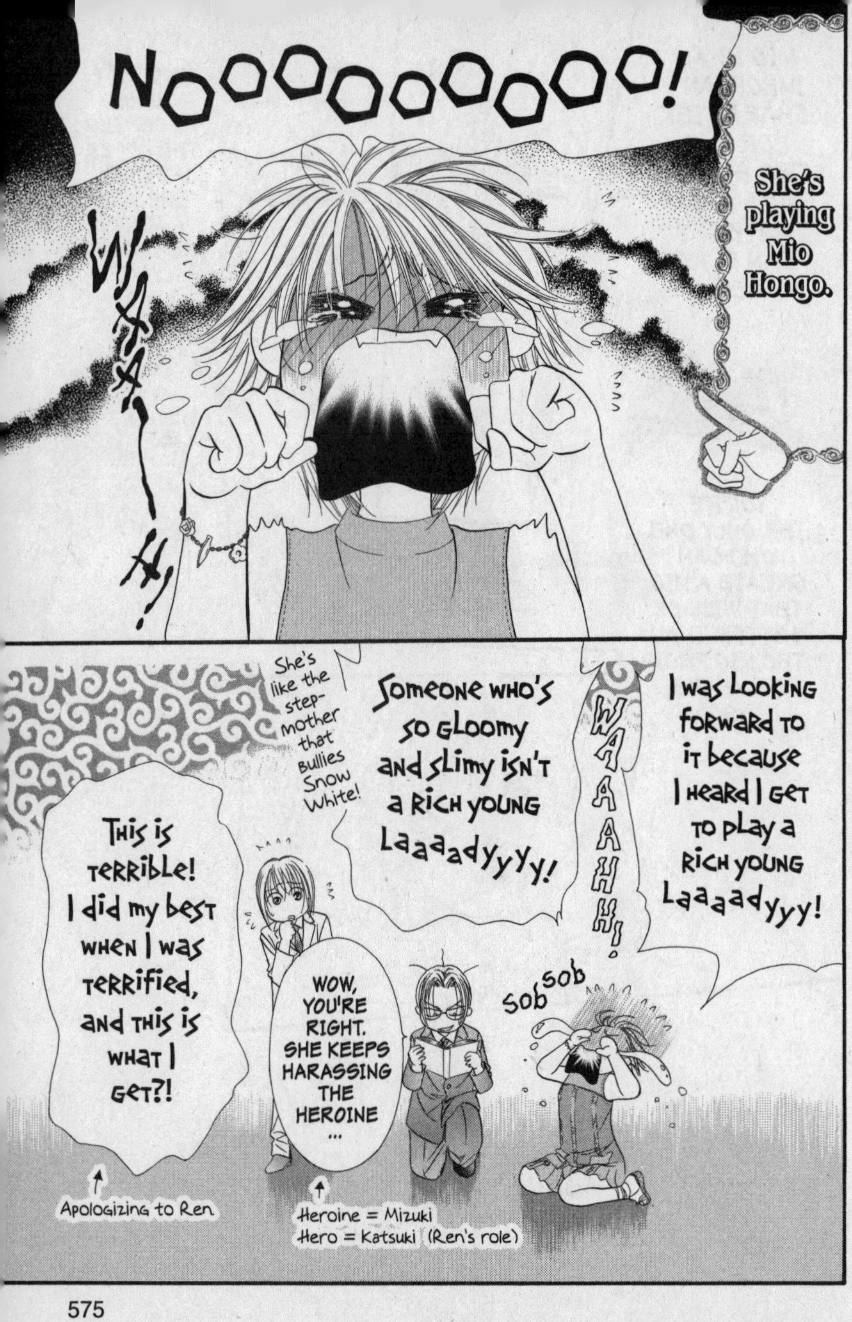
She's playing Mio Hongo.
NOOOOOOOOOO!
WAAA—AH!
I was looking forward to it because I heard I get to play a rich young Laaaadyyy!
WAAAAHH!
Someone who's so gloomy and slimy isn't a rich young Laaaadyyyy!
She's like the step-mother that bullies Snow White!
sob sob sob
WOW, YOU'RE RIGHT. SHE KEEPS HARASSING THE HEROINE ...
Heroine = Mizuki
Hero = Katsuki (Ren's role)
This is terrible! I did my best when I was terrified, and this is what I get?!
Apologizing to Ren.

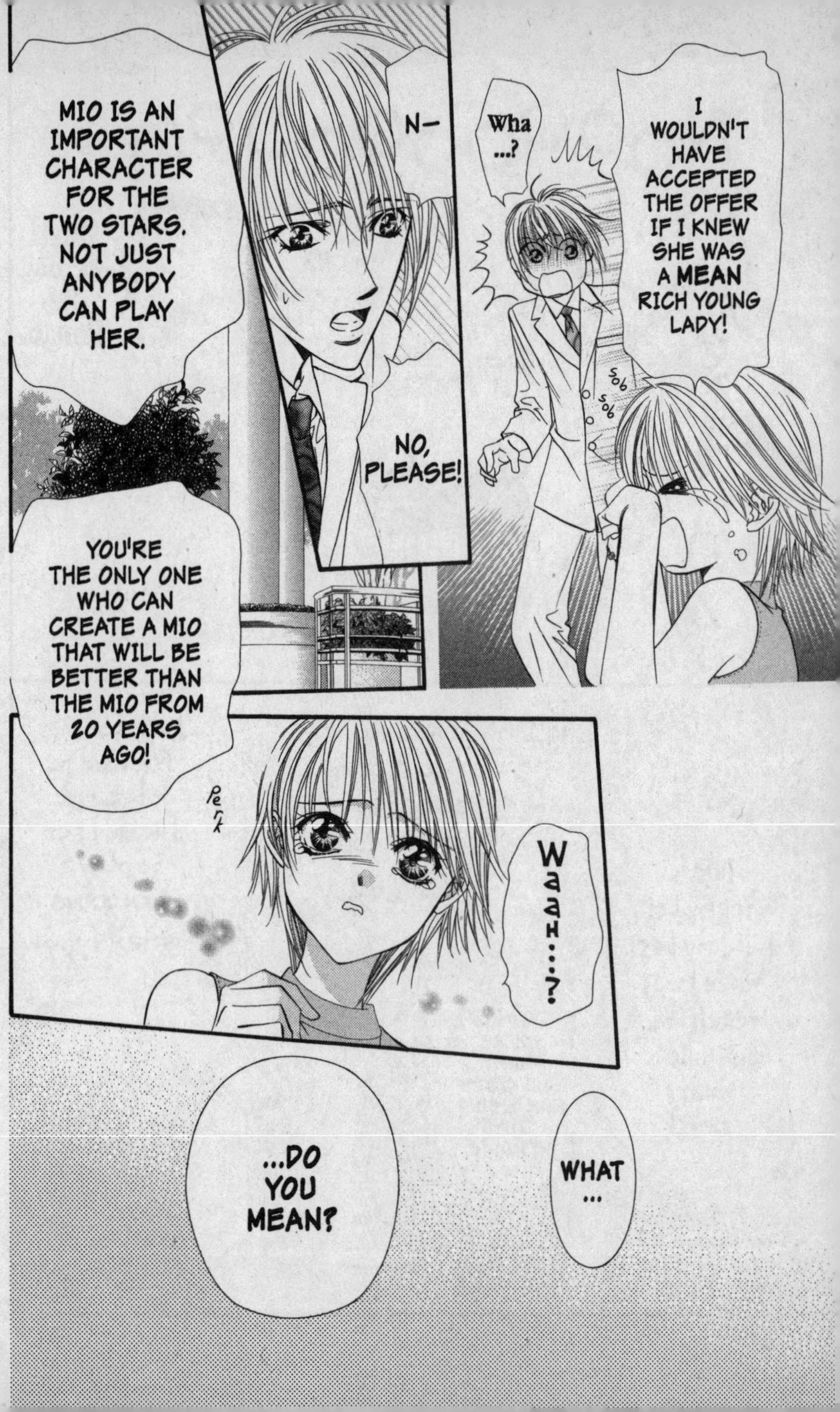
I WOULDN'T HAVE ACCEPTED THE OFFER IF I KNEW SHE WAS A MEAN RICH YOUNG LADY!
Wha ...?
sob sob
N—
NO, PLEASE!
MIO IS AN IMPORTANT CHARACTER FOR THE TWO STARS. NOT JUST ANYBODY CAN PLAY HER.
YOU'RE THE ONLY ONE WHO CAN CREATE A MIO THAT WILL BE BETTER THAN THE MIO FROM 20 YEARS AGO!
Perk
Waah...?
WHAT ...
...DO YOU MEAN?

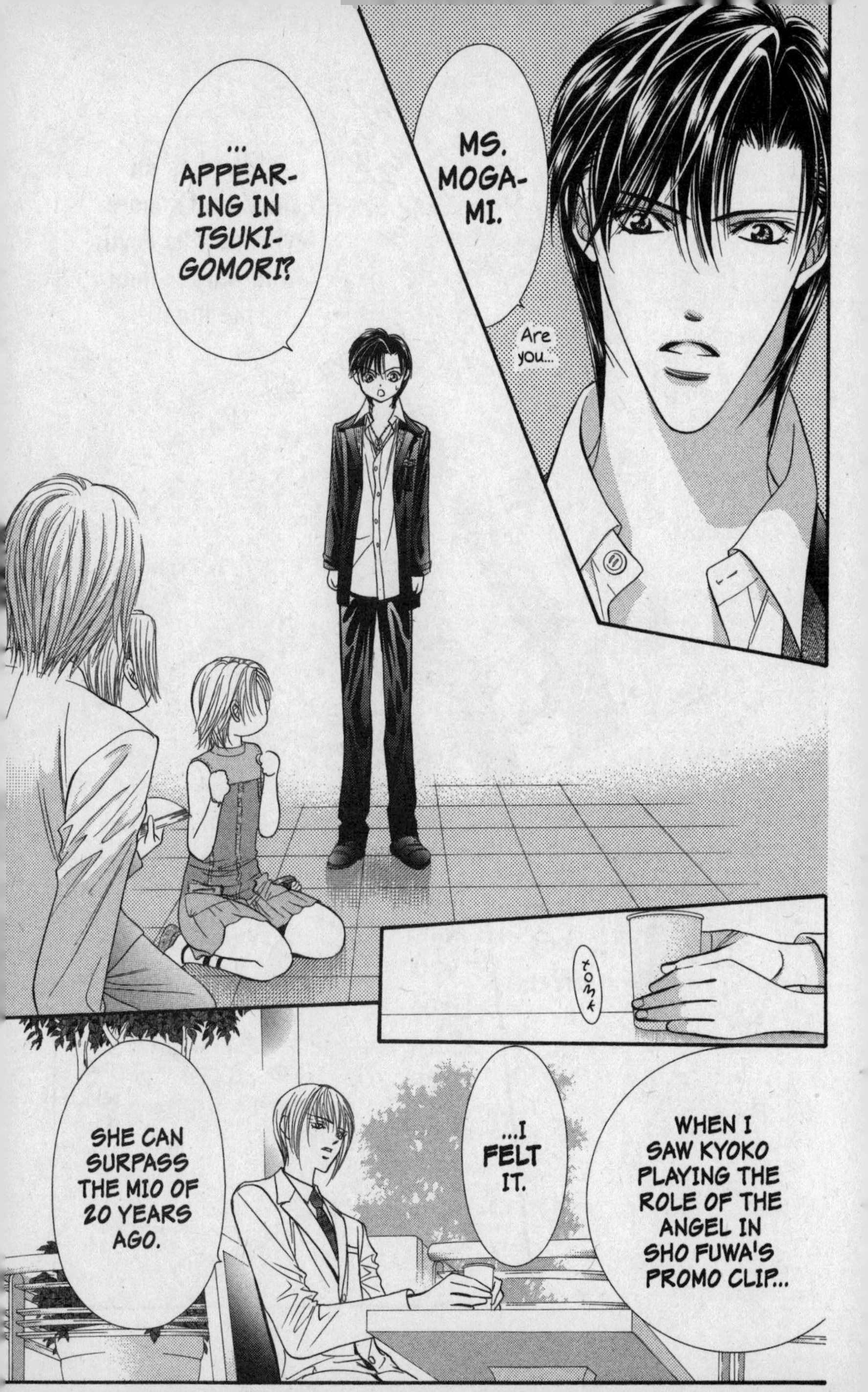

MS. MOGA-MI.
Are you...
...APPEAR-ING IN TSUKI-GOMORI!?
tonk
WHEN I SAW KYOKO PLAYING THE ROLE OF THE ANGEL IN SHO FUWA'S PROMO CLIP...
...I FELT IT.
SHE CAN SURPASS THE MIO OF 20 YEARS AGO.

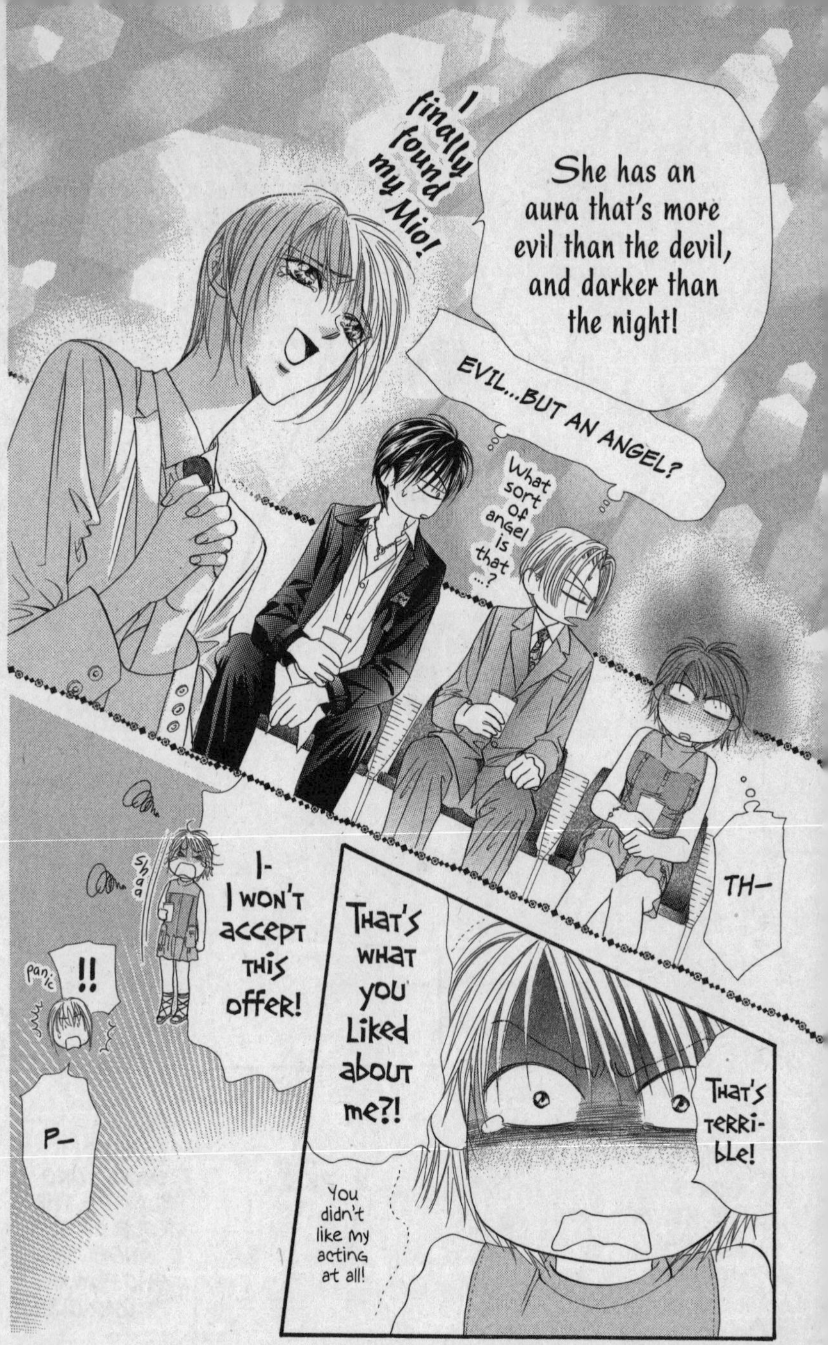
She has an aura that's more evil than the devil, and darker than the night!
I finally found my Mio!
EVIL...BUT AN ANGEL?
What sort of angel is that...?
TH-
That's terrible!
That's what you liked about me?!
You didn't like my acting at all!
I- I won't accept this offer!
Shaa
!!
panic
P-

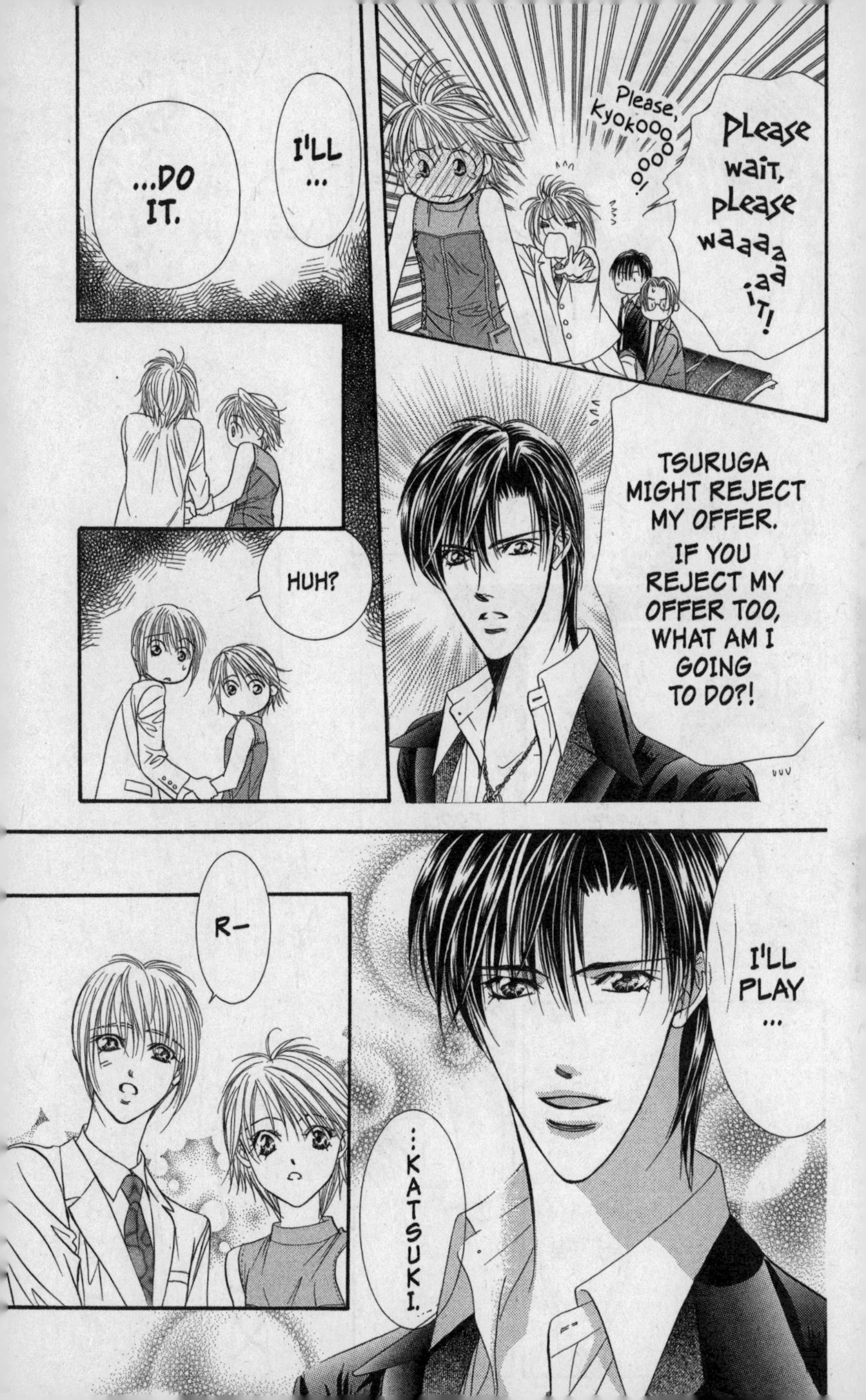
Please wait, please waaaaaait!
Please, Kyokooooooo!
I'LL ...
...DO IT.
TSURUGA MIGHT REJECT MY OFFER.
IF YOU REJECT MY OFFER TOO, WHAT AM I GOING TO DO?!
HUH?
I'LL PLAY ...
...KATSUKI.
R—

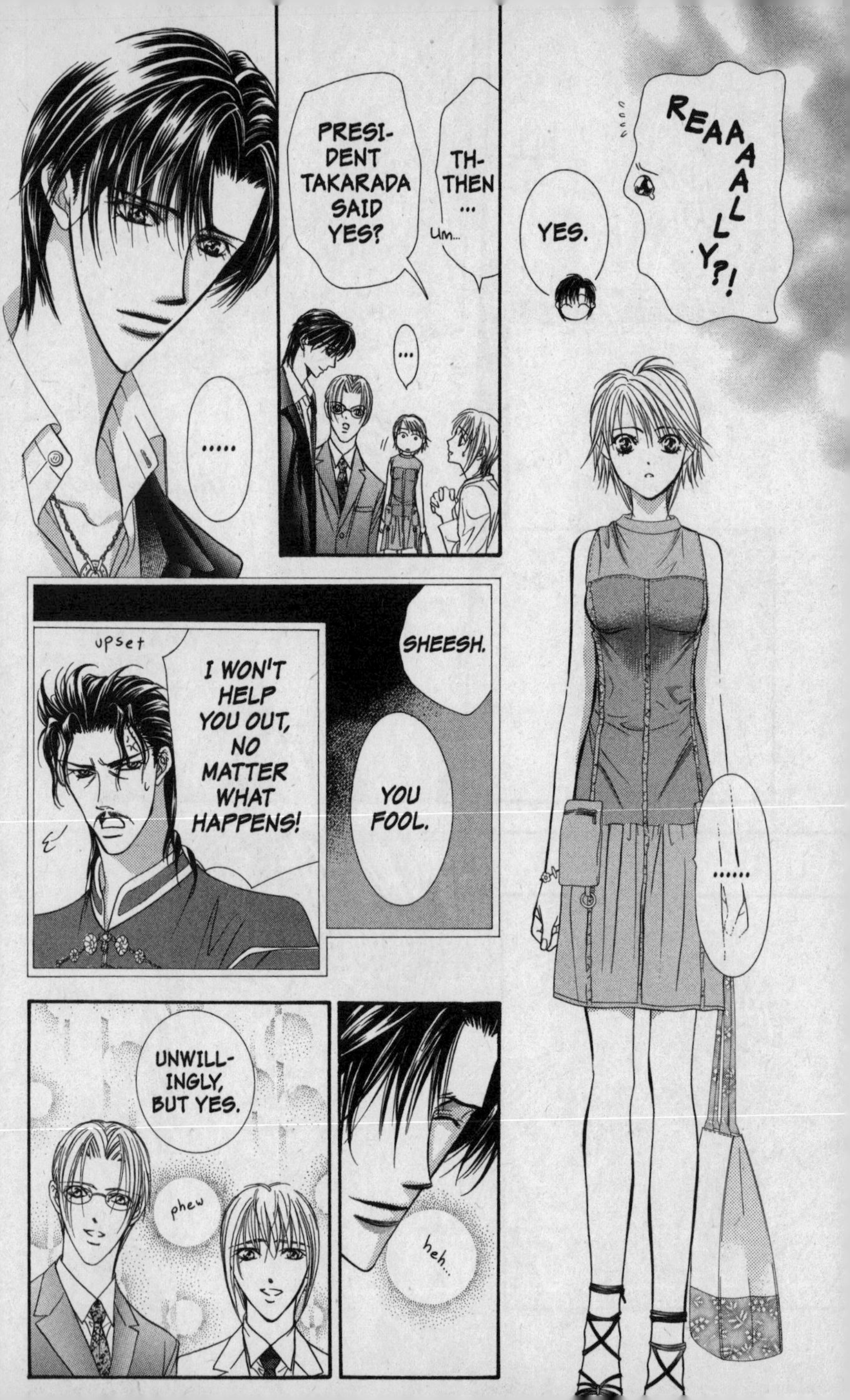
REAAAALLY?!
YES.
......
TH-THEN ...
PRESIDENT TAKARADA SAID YES?
Um...
...
.....
SHEESH.
YOU FOOL.
upset
I WON'T HELP YOU OUT, NO MATTER WHAT HAPPENS!
heh...
UNWILL-INGLY, BUT YES.
phew

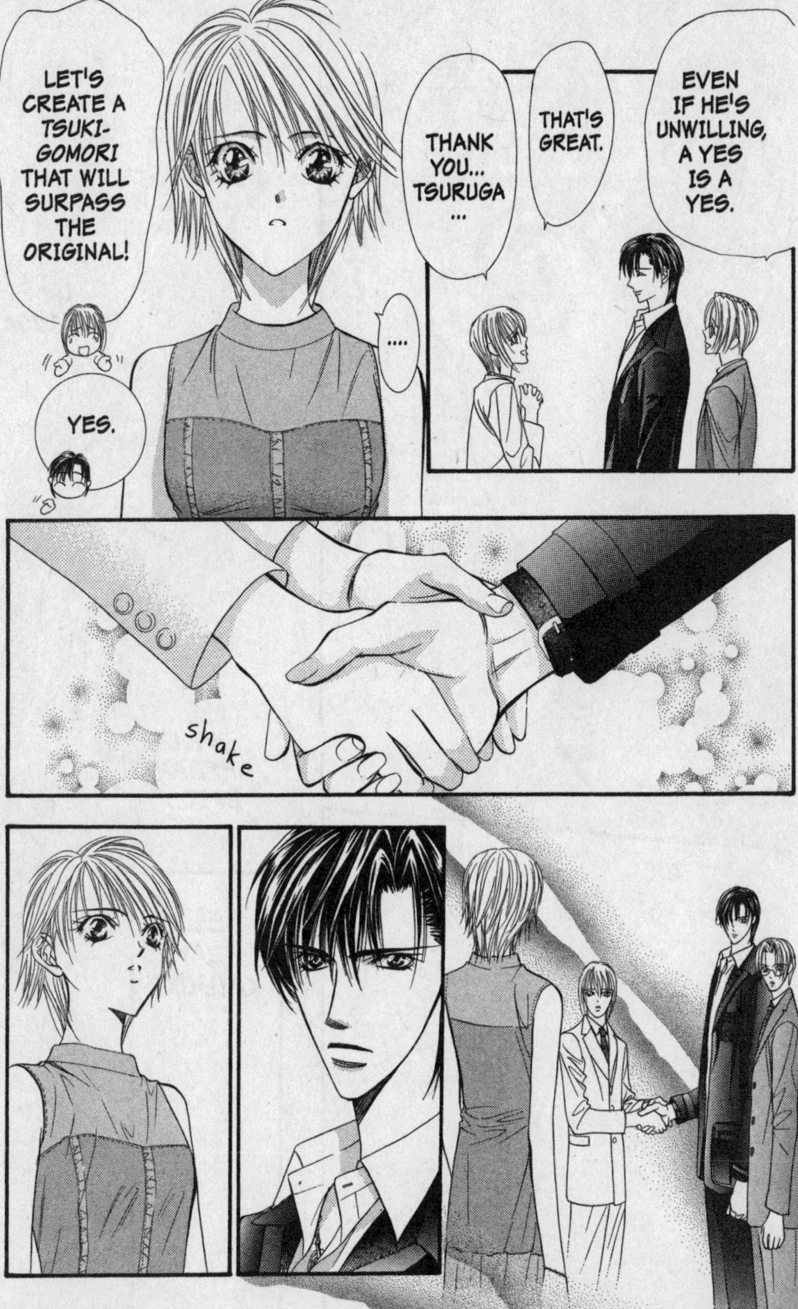
EVEN IF HE'S UNWILLING, A YES IS A YES.
THAT'S GREAT.
THANK YOU... TSURUGA ...
LET'S CREATE A TSUKI-GOMORI THAT WILL SURPASS THE ORIGINAL!
YES.
....
shake

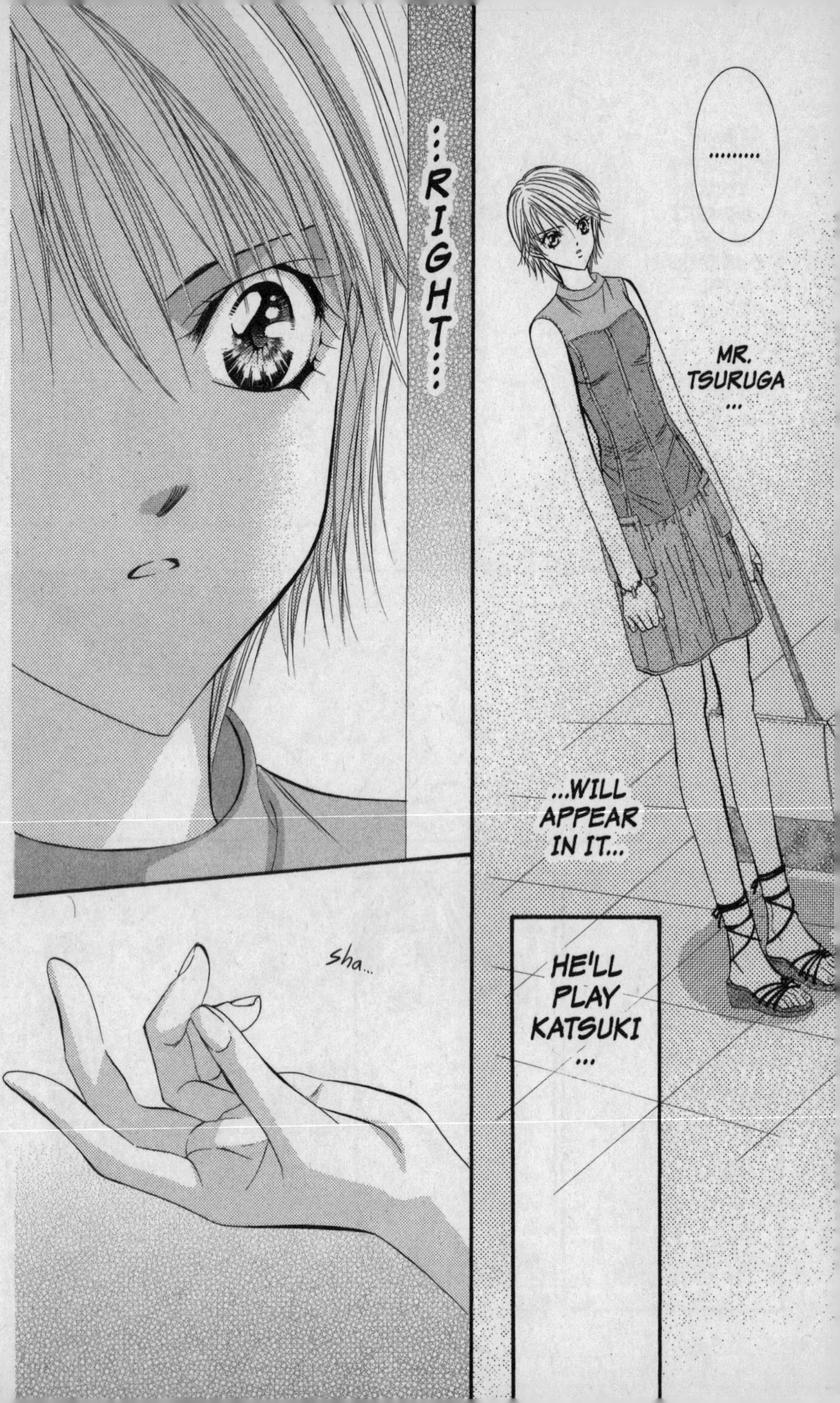
....
MR. TSURUGA ...
...WILL APPEAR IN IT...
HE'LL PLAY KATSUKI ...
...RIGHT...
sha...

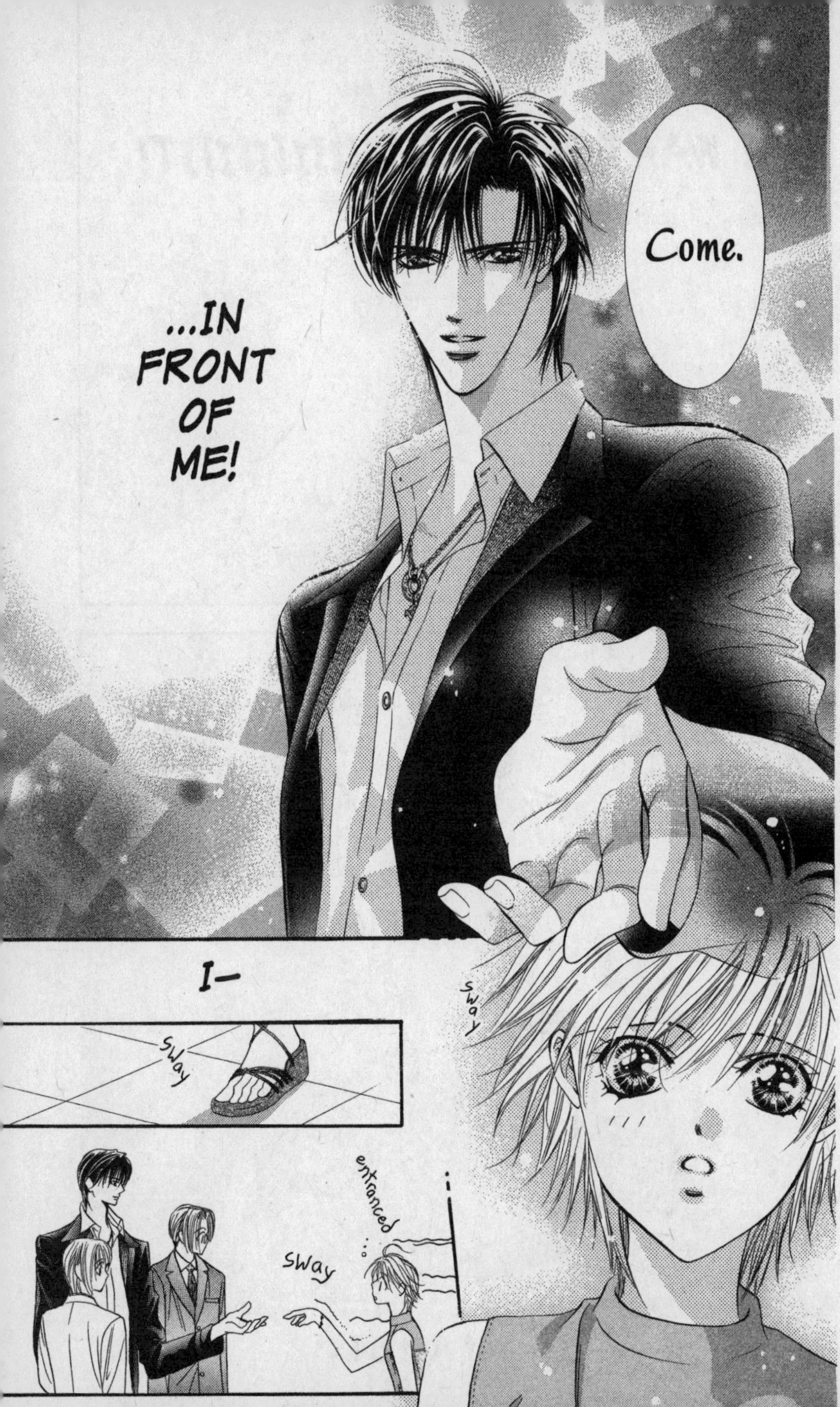
Come.
...IN FRONT OF ME!
sway
I—
sway
entranced...
sway
...

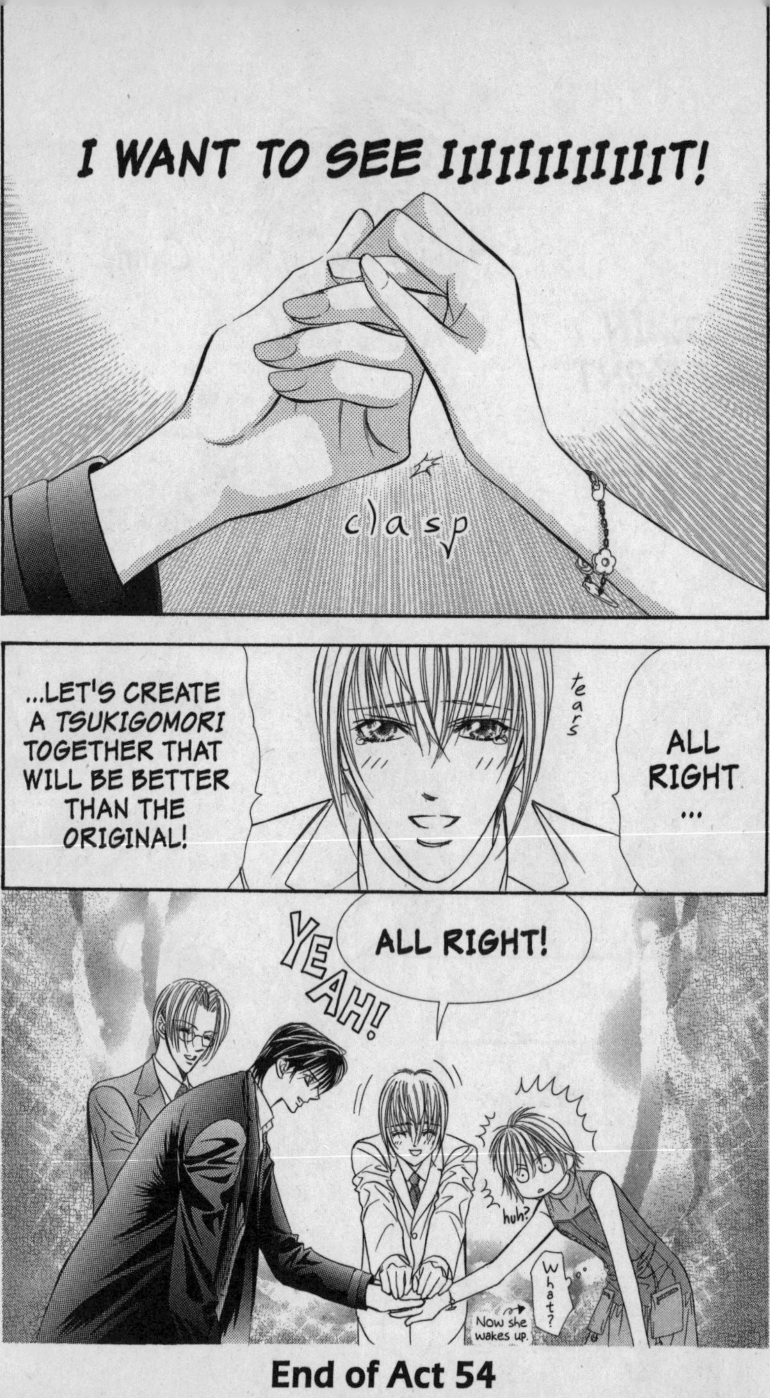
I WANT TO SEE IIIIIIIIIIIT!
clasp
ALL RIGHT ...
tears
...LET'S CREATE A TSUKIGOMORI TOGETHER THAT WILL BE BETTER THAN THE ORIGINAL!
ALL RIGHT!
YEAH!
huh?
What?
Now she wakes up.

End of Act 54

Skip-Beat! End Notes
Everyone knows how to be a fan, but sometimes cool things from other cultures need a little help crossing the language barrier.

Page 399, panel 1: Jidaigeki
Japanese period dramas such as the movies *Rashomon*, the *Zatoichi* series, *Azumi*, and *Ran*, and the TV dramas *Edo o Kiru*, *Tsukikage Ran*, and the annual taiga drama on NHK.

Page 422, panel 3: Moko
Hio thinks of the kanji for "ferocious tiger."

Page 434, panel 6: Makie
Kyoko uses the kanji for rolled-up paintings, but Moko is talking about "bait."

Page 472, panel 3: Tamagoyaki
Japanese rolled omelet. They come either sweet or salty, and can be filled with colorful ingredients.

Page 479, side bar: The hawk cowers at the chicken…
The kanji for *o* in Hio means "hawk" or "falcon," and the *hi* means "fly."

Page 504, panel 5: Sweet potatoes
This image refers to the Japanese saying "to tell things in sweet potato-vine fashion," meaning you have to confess to one thing after another, the way sweet potatoes are pulled from the ground.

Page 507, panel 5: Kanashibari
The Japanese term for a form of paralysis that occurs due to the presence of a ghost or evil spirit. Kyoko's evil spirits can cause it in sensitive people.

Page 517, panel 1: Karaoke Box
A private room with a TV and karaoke set up. These rooms are more private than the open karaoke bar, and are good for small parties and shy singers. Karaoke box establishments often sell food and drinks.

Page 542, panel 2: Dogeza
Bowing from a sitting position and pressing your head against the floor. The most contrite bow possible.

Yoshiki Nakamura is
originally from Tokushima Prefecture.
She started drawing manga in elementary
school, which eventually led to her 1993 debut of
Yume de Au yori Suteki (Better than Seeing in
a Dream) in *Hana to Yume* magazine. Her other
works include the basketball series *Saint Love*,
MVP wa Yuzurenai (Can't Give Up MVP),
Blue Wars, and *Tokyo Crazy Paradise*, a
series about a female bodyguard
in 2020 Tokyo.

SKIP·BEAT!
3-in-1 Edition
Vol. 3
A compilation of graphic novel volumes 7-9

STORY AND ART BY YOSHIKI NAKAMURA

English Translation & Adaptation/Tomo Kimura
Touch-up Art & Lettering/Sabrina Heep
Design/Yukiko Whitley
Editor/Pancha Diaz

Skip-Beat! by Yoshiki Nakamura © Yoshiki Nakamura 2003, 2004. All rights reserved.
First published in Japan in 2004, 2005 by HAKUSENSHA, Inc., Tokyo.
English language translation rights arranged with HAKUSENSHA, Inc., Tokyo.

Some art has been modified from the original Japanese edition.

The stories, characters and incidents mentioned in this publication are entirely fictional.

Printed in the U.S.A.

Published by VIZ Media, LLC
P.O. Box 77010
San Francisco, CA 94107

10 9 8 7 6
3-in-1 edition first printing, July 2012
Sixth printing, October 2019

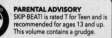

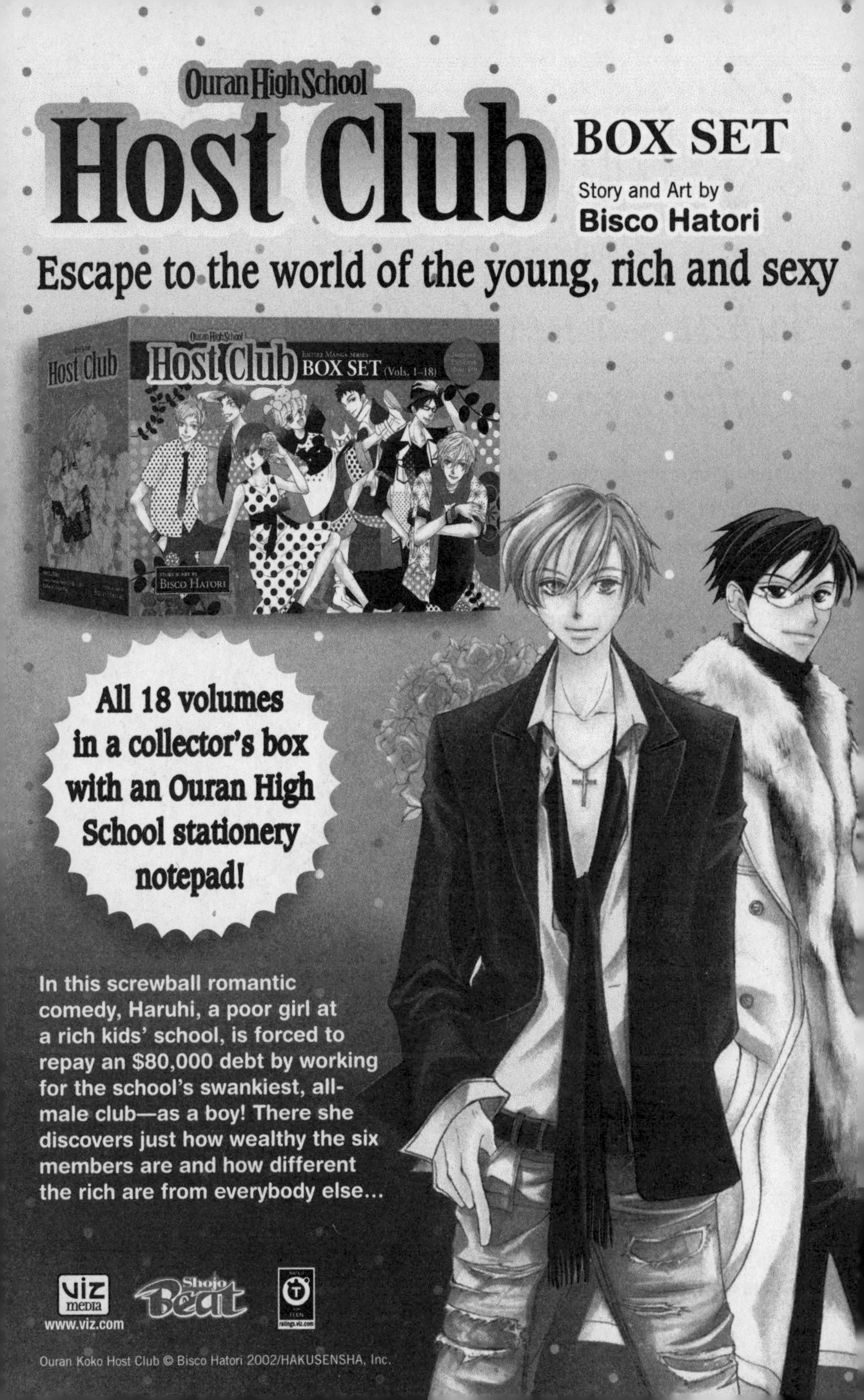
Ouran High School
Host Club
BOX SET
Story and Art by
Bisco Hatori
Escape to the world of the young, rich and sexy
Ouran High School
Host Club
BOX SET (Vols. 1–18)
Bisco Hatori
All 18 volumes in a collector's box with an Ouran High School stationery notepad!
In this screwball romantic comedy, Haruhi, a poor girl at a rich kids' school, is forced to repay an $80,000 debt by working for the school's swankiest, all-male club—as a boy! There she discovers just how wealthy the six members are and how different the rich are from everybody else...
viz media
www.viz.com
Shojo Beat
ratings.viz.com
Ouran Koko Host Club © Bisco Hatori 2002/HAKUSENSHA, Inc.

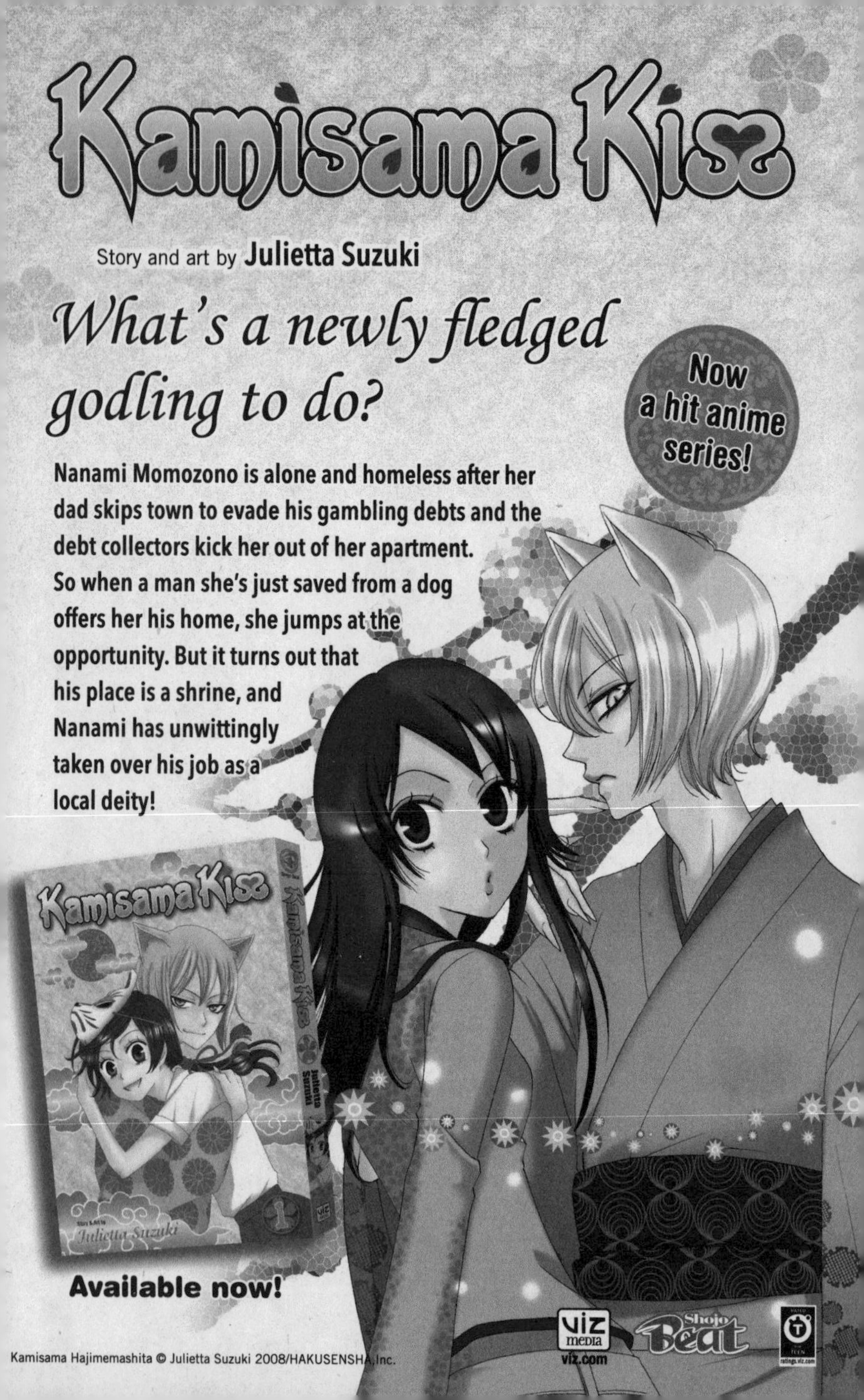
Kamisama Kiss
Story and art by Julietta Suzuki
What's a newly fledged godling to do?
Now a hit anime series!
Nanami Momozono is alone and homeless after her dad skips town to evade his gambling debts and the debt collectors kick her out of her apartment. So when a man she's just saved from a dog offers her his home, she jumps at the opportunity. But it turns out that his place is a shrine, and Nanami has unwittingly taken over his job as a local deity!
Kamisama Kiss
Julietta Suzuki
Available now!
viz media
viz.com
Shojo Beat
Kamisama Hajimemashita © Julietta Suzuki 2008/HAKUSENSHA, Inc.

Don't Hide What's *Inside*

by **AYA KANNO**

Despite his tough jock exterior, Asuka Masamune harbors a secret love for sewing, shojo manga, and all things girly. But when he finds himself drawn to his domestically inept classmate Ryo, his carefully crafted persona is put to the test. Can Asuka ever show his true self to anyone, much less to the girl he's falling for?

Find out in the *Otomen* manga—buy yours today!

SURPRISE!

You may be reading the wrong way!

It's true: In keeping with the original Japanese comic format, this book reads from right to left—so action, sound effects, and word balloons are completely reversed. This preserves the orientation of the original artwork—plus, it's fun! Check out the diagram shown here to get the hang of things, and then turn to the other side of the book to get started!

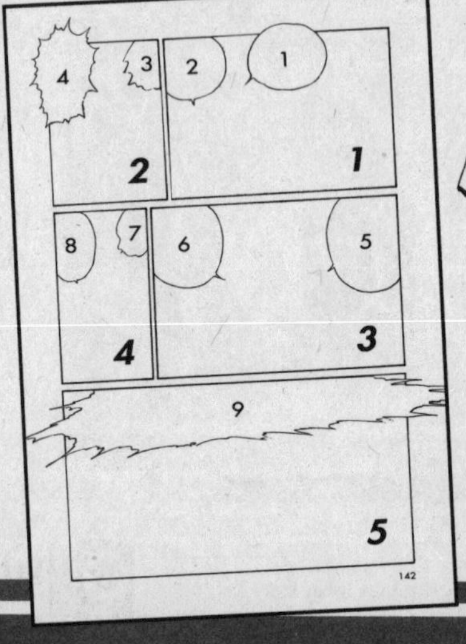
1
2
1
3
4
2
5
6
3
7
8
4
9
5
142

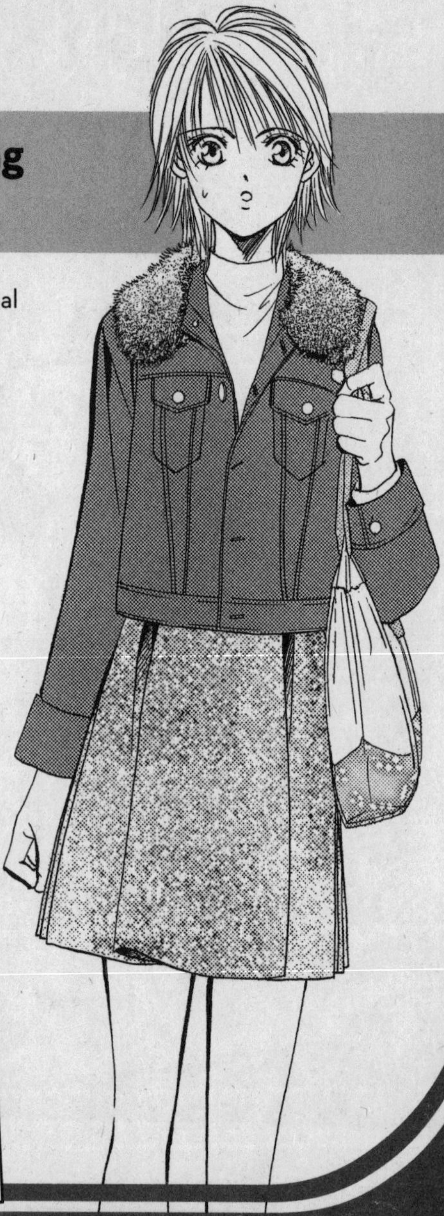